POWER PLAY SERIES
BOX SET

KENNEDY L. MITCHELL

ABOUT THE AUTHOR

Kennedy L. Mitchell lives outside Dallas with her husband, son and two very large goldendoodles. She began writing in 2016 after a fight with her husband (You can read the fight almost verbatim in Falling for the Chance) and has no plans of stopping.

She would love to hear from you via any of the platforms below or her website www.kennedylmitchell.com You can also stay up to date on future releases through her newsletter or by joining her Facebook readers group - Kennedy's Book Boyfriend Support Group.

Thank you for reading.

To those who strive to be more than who they are today.
You're someone's hero.
Never lose that fight.

POWER GAMES

POWER PLAY SERIES BOOK 1

INSPIRATION

"In politics if you want something said, ask a man.
*If you want something done, ask a **woman**."*
\- Margaret Thatcher

PROLOGUE
TREY

January

The big guy is overreacting, if you ask me.

The annoying clicking of keyboards, chattering government employees in the nearby cube farm, and the scent of burnt coffee surround us as we march side by side through the hall toward the director's office. We've been here enough times over the years that the desk jockey's stares don't linger when they glance up from their glowing computer screens. Some of the visits were scheduled, typically follow-ups, while the others weren't so mundane. I have the propensity to find my way into trouble if you ask our director.

My best friend and team lead grunts out another string of curse words under his breath. I can't help the smirk pulling up my lips in response to his pointed annoyance.

I feel great about the stellar life choices I've made up to this point and have nothing to regret. Tank, on the other hand, is on the verge of blowing a gasket if the fiery red tint beneath his dark complexion is any indication. Needless to say, he's still pissed at me, even though I did the right thing. The man can hold a grudge, that's for sure. The incident happened well over twenty–four hours ago, yet he's still pouting.

"If we get fired, I'll murder you with my bare hands, drive your dead-ass body down to Florida, and feed you to the gators. I cannot believe you pulled that fucking stunt."

Yikes, he's cussing. Never a good sign. After this meeting with the director, I should get him something special to make it up to him. I would say a double cheeseburger, but then his wife, Sarah—love her, though I'm scared of her—will ride my ass for feeding him the processed abomination.

I should pick up something for Rachel too. She was fuming yesterday when I told her what happened. No clue why, but damn, she was pissed. *Is* pissed. She wouldn't even talk to me this morning before I left. Whatever it is, we'll either figure it out or I'll apologize and buy her something pretty. That's always worked in the past.

"It'll all be fine like always. Just wait and see, buddy," I mutter under my breath as his thick knuckles pound against the dark wood door separating us from the director's office. "You worry too much."

"Worry?" He turns, facing me full-on. "You tackled the motherfucking vice president of the United States, you idiot."

I lift both hands, palms out, in surrender. "Listen, I don't mind you plotting my death and telling me about it in detail, but no name-calling. You know it hurts my feelings."

"Of course this is a joke to you. Everything is a damn joke."

On the other side of the door, a muffled female voice yells for us to come in.

Hand on the cool metal knob, I give the flimsy door a push and pause with one foot over the threshold. "If we're going to fight like a married a couple, the least you could do is cook every once in a while, or at least put out," I say over my shoulder with a smirk.

A muttered string of curse words flies at my back as I step deeper into the director's office and pause behind one of the two chairs. Damn, he's fun to rile up. You'd think I would be tired of it after all these years together, but nope, still fun as hell.

Hands tucked in the pockets of my slacks and wearing my signature smirk, I wait for the director to acknowledge our presence. My cocky smirk has gotten me out of more trouble than not, it's worth a shot to see if it can work its magic on her today.

"And what are you smirking about, Mr. Benson?" The director's pinched face peers up from the file flipped open on her desk. The tension in her tired eyes sobers me up a fraction. This could be more of a challenge than I initially expected. Still, not worried, it's me we're talking about here.

"Nothing, ma'am," I respond, still smiling. "You're looking lovely today. Did you do something to your hair?"

"No."

"Something is different. You look ten years—no, make that twenty years younger."

"Cut the shit." She grunts and rocks backward in her high-backed cheap leather chair. An ear-piercing squeak cuts through the otherwise quiet office. She winces as she adjusts, settling further into the leather cushions. "You know why you're here. Let's start with your side of the story, shall we?"

"Short or long version?" I slide my hands out of the silk-lined pockets to grip the mundane office chair's wooden frame in front of me.

"For fuck's sake." Tank stiffens, his back going ramrod straight beside me, shocked at his outburst. Never one to break the rules, that one. It's why we get along so well—I bend the rules to my liking, and he does everything he can to keep me or anyone else from dying. It's fun. "Sorry, ma'am," he apologizes with a slight dip of his head.

The director pulls her thick plastic-framed glasses from her nose and tosses them onto the desk in front of her. "Might as well tell the long version, Mr. Benson. No doubt this will be entertaining."

"Of course." I shift my attention to Tank. "Buddy, you should sit. You don't look so good." It's the truth. His large bald head gleams with beaded sweat, and the buttons of his dress shirt pull taut with each of his deep breaths.

The chair complains under his heavy weight as he sinks onto the stiff cushion. He looks like a cartoon, such a huge guy squished into a tiny chair. Tank's large size came in handy back in the day when he played college football and then went pro after those four years. Nowadays it's the perfect idiot deterrent when we're on the job. Anyone attempting to start shit takes one look at him and bolts in the opposite direction.

"Go on, Mr. Benson. I don't have all day."

"Right, sorry, ma'am." I clear my throat. "Yesterday we arrived at the VP's home, One Observatory Circle, for the start of our shift at eleven hundred hours. Nothing seemed out of place as we made our rounds outside. Inside we met with the beta team in the security office to cover the details of the previous shift: reviewing incident reports, any new threats, checking the VP's schedule for the day, things like that. Inside the security room, movement on one of the screens caught my attention. Zooming in, I recognized the room in question was the library, and inside was Vice President Nick and some woman. They seemed to be talking, but they were a little too close for my liking. Something didn't feel right about the situation, so I left Tank, my team lead, in the security room to see what was going on. When I arrived, I found the door locked, which raised even more suspicion. A loud noise and a muffled shout prompted me to kick the lock and barge in. Once inside the library, I scanned the room, made a quick assessment of the situation, and felt the vice president was in danger, so I handled the situation."

"You tackled a sixty–year–old man," the director says on an exhausted sigh. She seems to do this a lot with me. If she didn't like me so much, she would've canned my ass years ago. Having the Benson family name doesn't hurt either.

"Did Vice President Nick submit a report regarding my actions?" I ask before correcting myself and adding, "Ma'am."

Her pointed annoyed glare says everything I need to know. Of course that limp dick of a bastard didn't write a formal complaint regarding my actions yesterday. I caught him red-handed sexually harassing the woman when I barreled into the library. The director knows all this too. She hates Vice President Nick as much as, if not more than, our team does. Something tells me his hand, along with many other slimeballs' in this city, has found its way to her ass more than once.

Fuck, I cannot wait until the next election. Can't get this asshole out soon enough. Not that the next guy will be any better. At this stage in anyone's political career, they're all the same.

"He didn't, which you know, or you wouldn't be smirking like a kid who robbed a candy shop and got away with it. But dammit, Trey, we can't have our agents tackling dirty politicians any time they feel they're in the right." She lets out an incredulous huff. "There wouldn't be anyone left in DC." A small smile pulls at her lips before she purses them tight. "I've been directed to make an example out of you. Out of the entire team."

Tension tightens my shoulders. The cheap chair frame pops under my white-knuckle grip.

Well, fuck. Did *not* expect this. Accountability? What the hell.

"Gators," Tank grumbles, shooting me a death glare.

"Ma'am, it was my choice. Hell, the guys weren't even around to try and stop me." I jab my middle finger against my breastbone. "Punish me, not them." I may be an idiot at times, but my antics are my own. No way can I live with the team being canned because of my actions.

"You're a team." The chair squeaks again as she leans forward. "You're officially removed as alpha team for Vice President Nick." Her hand juts out, stopping my rebuttal. My lips snap shut, my jaw clenching tight to keep from speaking out of turn. "Beta team will shift into the alpha spot, and Charlie team will replace beta team."

The reality of the situation drops like a lead weight in my gut. I suck in a breath in an attempt to keep a level head. "Ma'am, you know why I did it," I grit out.

Her deep forehead wrinkles smooth a fraction, sympathy seeping into her clear blue eyes. "I do understand, but that doesn't change the impact of your actions. This isn't like your previous antics. You attacked the vice president, and something has to be done."

"Where does that leave my team, ma'am?" Tank asks, voice solemn. Elbows on his knees, hands clasped between them, he drops his head forward.

Double fuck.

"As punishment, your team is now beta team's backup. When the primary elections are finished and the nonincumbent candidates are selected, you will then move back to alpha team for one of the delegates. Dismissed."

The primary election? Nonincumbent delegates?

That's next fall, over a year from now.

I draw in a breath, ready to protest and ask for leniency, but Tank's tight grip on my bicep hauls me toward the door.

"Mr. Benson," the director calls before I'm out the door. Adjusting my suit jacket I turn back toward the office. "The woman, did she press charges?"

Hands fisted, I shove them deep into my pockets. A thick chunk of dark brown hair falls out of place, sliding across my forehead as I shake my head. "No, ma'am, just like the others. Tank tried to talk to her after, but she refused. Said she didn't want to risk her political career over a misunderstanding."

"Misunderstanding. Right." She sighs, her unfocused gaze landing on the wall behind me. "One day I'd love for someone to stand up to these pricks."

The longing in her voice urges me deeper into the office. "Why don't you? You know exactly what goes on behind closed doors." From harassment to bribes and dirty dealings, not to mention all the affairs going on amongst the small political circle, the director knows enough to take down half the men in this city. Then again, those secrets are how she landed this influential role in the first place.

Her perfectly cropped blonde hair swings along her jaw. "No, not me. I'm too deep in this city. I wouldn't survive. Maybe someday someone will come along who doesn't have as much on the table to lose."

Who knows? One day someone could move into this town who still has some morals left and is ready to wreak havoc. But considering I enjoy living, I won't hold my breath for that person to appear any time soon.

1

RANDI

April

No. Please no. Not today. I dip my head into the sink and look up into the still-dry spout.

I'm on *Candid Camera*, aren't I?

I glance around the trailer, waiting for someone to pop out and shout, "Gotcha."

Please tell me a friend is pulling a prank. Not that I have friends, but a girl can hope it's all a joke and her water isn't shut off the night before a court appearance. My one paying client needs me at her side tomorrow when the judge gives his final decision on the custody case I've worked on for months. Now I'll look like the low-rent attorney my fees depict me as being.

I twist both the hot and cold knobs, the chipped plastic digging into my palms until neither can turn any farther.

Nothing. Not a single drop.

"No, no, no, no," I groan as quietly as possible to not alert Taeler in the back of the trailer. Can't believe this is happening again. Yes, again. Because this is my reality, and it fucking sucks.

Giving up on the hope that magic water will suddenly pour from the rusted spout, I drop both elbows to the kitchen counter and hold my head between my hands.

Guess the check mix-up scam didn't work with the water company this month. I've pulled it enough times that it's no surprise they caught on to my creative bill paying—or not paying—tactics. I only need three more days. Three days until payday. But of course, some idiot set up a billing system that doesn't coordinate with standard pay cycles. I would file a complaint with the mayor, but said complaint would just end up on my desk.

Yep, the mayor of Boone, Texas, won't have a shower before work tomorrow. Unless I suck up my pride to walk a few trailers down and use Mom's. Chills rake down my spine at the thought. Who knows who her boyfriend is this week, though not a single one is someone I want hanging around while I'm naked, even with a locked door between us. Plus, her place is disgusting, a literal pigsty. As in she has a pig living with her. In the trailer. One of Mom's stupid-ass boyfriends gave her a miniature pig for a gift last year. Turned out it wasn't so miniature but actually a normal size pig, Big Patty, who Mom still refuses to give away.

Taking a small step back, I fall onto the couch. One benefit of a small single-wide is that everything is close. It's not the newest model—okay, it was born before me—but it's mine. Leaks and all.

For now.

Fuck, I don't want to think about that right now. I *can't* think about that right now. If I have to pay the fee to have the water turned back on, plus pay the electric bill on top of Taeler's monthly expenses, there might not be enough to make the full mortgage payment. Again.

My eyes burn with the welling tears. This is my shit show of a life. The life everyone in this small town knew I'd one day grow into. "Once trailer trash, always trailer trash" in most people's minds around here. I'll never amount to anything, and nothing I can do will change that. Well, on that front, yeah, I am proving them right. College and law school, yet I still ended up three trailers down from where I grew up. I like to pretend they aren't smiling behind my back because I'm proving them right each day I sink deeper into debt.

"Mom?"

The skin of my arm peels from my damp lashes as I slide it down. Blinking back the unshed tears, I raise both brows at Taeler.

"Good, you're still up. I wanted a chance to talk to you."

I focus past her shoulder on the dry sink. "Being clean is overrated, right?" I mutter more to myself than to Taeler.

"You are so strange, Mom," Taeler says with a huff, a small smile tugging at the corner of her lips.

"Heads up, the water's off. Something must have happened with a line somewhere. I'm sure we'll be all good tomorrow." Is it considered lying if you're attempting to hide your misfortunes from your kid? I'm going with no.

I groan in utter exhaustion from life and pull myself upright. Puffs of dust and who knows what else float into the air as I pat the other cushion. With all the dramatics of a teen, she flops down beside me. I start to ask what she wanted, but her eyes are glued on the phone in her hand before I can get a word out.

"Did you need something?" I nudge her shoulder with my own, fighting for attention.

Her blue eyes bounce between me and the screen before clicking it off and setting it aside. Once, twice, then a third time she swipes her long blonde hair behind her ear.

Oh no, that's her tell. We both have one. I bite my nails to the quick, and she fidgets nonstop with her hair.

"Mom...."

Shit. This is bad.

"You're pregnant," I blurt before covering my mouth with both hands. My pulse skyrockets with dread.

"What?" She groans. "No! I've told you a thousand times I'm still a virgin, and that's not going to change any time soon. I don't even have a boyfriend."

"Thank fuck," I mutter into my hands. The relief at her denial fades as a new worry seeps into my thoughts. "You're dying."

"Now you're ridiculous."

"What? You're acting more dramatic than usual. It's making me nervous."

"Well, then give me two seconds to explain what's going on."

"You need to speak faster! The suspense is killing me."

"Mom!" she squeaks, smacking a hand over her eyes. "Your first assumptions are pregnancy and death?"

I lift a shoulder in a noncommittal shrug, then circle my hands in the space between us, urging her to tell me what the hell is going on.

"After I graduate next month, I won't... I mean, I'm not—"

I hold up a hand, palm out. "Don't even say it. Not a chance."

"Mom," Taeler pleads, her voice taking on a high-pitched tone. "Just hear me out."

I shake my head and shove off the couch. Her eyes stay glued on me as I pace the narrow hallway. "You're going to school, and that's final."

"I can't afford it. *You* can't afford it."

I flinch, her words a knife to my tender heart.

"It's not your fault," she whispers. Her beautiful blue eyes dance between mine searching, pleading. She stands and grips my shoulders, stopping my pacing. "It is what it is. I'm not upset; I don't feel cheated. You've given me everything you can. I know that. Now, for me, after graduation, it's time to support myself. To be an adult."

"You're not an adult," I grumble. Lifting a hand, I slide my fingers through her blonde hair. We shuffle closer, her forehead finding my shoulder as she releases a long exhale.

"Per the state, yeah, I am. I know you want to change my mind, but you won't." Her words are muffled against my shirt. She's right; I won't change her mind. Taeler is as stubborn as an old mule—a trait she inherited from her father, obviously. "You think I don't pick up on all the stress you're under to pay those crazy student loans each month plus the other zillion bills? I don't want that for me. I'll go full time at the factory after graduation and save up. As I have money, I'll take courses at the junior college."

Lips to her hair, I smile. She's smart, wise even—a trait she received from me, obviously.

"Mom, I know you're behind on a lot of bills, including the trailer payment." Failure settles in my gut like a heavy rock. "I know you're on the verge of losing it, and then what will you do? Live at that crappy office the city lets you use? I'll figure this out on my own, promise. I can't sit back and watch you sink deeper in debt because of me. Please just let me do this, for you."

I tuck my nose into her hair and inhale deeply. "I want you to have so much, so much more than I ever had," I whisper past the knot of unshed tears lodged in my throat. "I'm sorry."

She deserves a better life than this, a mother who can provide more—be more. It's not for lack of trying, that's for fucking sure. I've worked my ass off, yet I'm still here scraping my way through life. I'm utterly exhausted.

Nothing I've done is enough to pull me out of the economic status I was born into. I've done what I can for a better life for myself and Taeler, but every time, despite my hard work, I keep failing. Some days I hope for that one chance, one opportunity to prove I'm more than this trailer park, more than an addict's daughter, more than this sleepy town. To ram my success down the throats of everyone who's judged, sneered, and laughed at my hope of breaking the cycle.

I've put in the work, put myself through undergrad and law school, yet the stupid poverty fate gods keep diverting me back to this path lined with bills I can't pay. One would think my résumé, University of Texas at Austin and then on to Harvard Law, would be enough to boost my status, to show everyone in town I'm more than who they judged me to be. But no, that would disrupt the tiny predestined box they want to fit me into.

I press my lips to Taeler's hair, murmuring a quick good-night. My heart sinks as she shuffles down the hall to the single bedroom.

Even with the odds stacked against me, I still have hope. Hope that one day I'll get a chance, that my luck will change for the better. Who knows, maybe the stars will align and I'll get that chance to prove to everyone I'm destined for so much more than this.

And maybe one day I'll have a unicorn as a pet and a genie as a best fucking friend too.

I JAM A RED, indented finger against the On/Off button again and again, each time more aggressively. "Come on, you lazy piece of shit," I curse under my breath. "Work. I'm freezing my tits off here." Still not even a flicker of heat. "I will toss your sorry ass into the closest dumpster if you don't turn on right now," I yell at the ancient space heater.

A click, then the smell of something burning, and finally the rusted metal heating elements flare to life.

Still bent over the contraption, I give it a condescending smirk and a hard pat. "That's what I thought."

"You're talking to the heater again," a female voice croons from the door. "I thought we talked about keeping your crazy under wraps."

Standing tall, I look over my shoulder and stick my tongue out. "Sometimes these things need a reminder of who's the boss around here."

"Right," Jennifer says with a chuckle. "I'm going out for a break. Want to come with?"

Peering through the dirty window of my mayoral office, I catch a tree's green-dotted branches bending in the hostile Texas wind. I walked out this morning without a warm jacket, and it turned out colder than I expected. A Texas April is a fickle time for weather. One day it's beautiful, the hint of spring making you whip out your flops, but then the next, it's bitter-ass cold like today.

"I do, but not outside. Forgot my coat." I glance to the window again and tilt my head toward it with raised brows. "I won't tell if you don't."

A sneaky grin spreads up her cheeks as she nods in agreement. "You're the boss. I can't say no, can I?"

Hands raised, fingers tapping, I let out my best impression of an evil chuckle. "I love all this power."

"Every day you're even stranger." Jennifer gives me a concerned once-over as I shove open the office window. We both visibly shiver as a blast of cold wind swirls into the tiny office. "Are you getting enough sleep? Maybe a lack of vitamin D is making you odd."

"I'm missing D, that's for sure," I say around the cigarette pressed between my front teeth. "I can't remember the last time I had sex."

"What about that guy you met a few months back? Brad... Brian... whatever his name was?"

I roll my eyes and blow a billowing cloud of smoke out the window. "Sorry, I retract the earlier statement from the record. What I meant was I haven't had good sex lately. That guy was a mistake." I shake my head at the memory. "He was super nice and paid for dinner, but he was too...."

"Sensitive?" Jennifer interjects as she leans toward the window, blowing a puff of smoke out into the cold.

"No."

"Hairy?"

"No, he was just—"

"Small in the one area that counts." She gives me a knowing grin. "I'm referring to his penis."

I let out an incredulous laugh. "I gathered that. And no to all that. He was too... handsy."

"Handsy," she deadpans.

"Yeah, too touchy." I shrug as I turn my focus to the glowing ember at the end of the almost-spent cigarette between my fingers.

"Um, Randi, not sure what kind of sex you've had, but I'm pretty sure good sex requires you to be touchy."

Again, my shoulders rise and fall. "He took his time too." My body shakes on a shudder. "Why can't it be good, no-touchy, fast sex? Is that too much to ask?"

"You sound like a guy."

"What? If it takes too long, then my mind wanders, and then I get antsy." I wave my hand dismissively. "So anyway, back to the date. I finished myself off at home that night, then never returned his calls."

"It's a miracle you've ever had an orgasm," she remarks with a snort. Her eyes widen at my one-shoulder shrug. "Randi, please tell me you've had an orgasm from sex."

"Technically?" I glance out the window and flick the now-extinguished cigarette butt into the bucket we keep below for break emergencies like this. "Yeah, I think so, but how do you—"

"Seriously?" a man's voice says, cutting me off. "Typical lazy-ass politician."

I cross both arms across my chest and lean a shoulder against the wall. "Ben." My baby daddy. My first love. My first heartbreak. My first everything. Tall with shaggy blond hair, crystal blue eyes, and solid muscle from working on his parents' farm—how could fifteen-year-old me not fall in love with him? Too bad his aversion to responsibility wasn't as glaring as his good looks.

"Randi," he says with a dip of his chin. "Jennifer. What are you two talking about?"

"Did you know Randi has never—"

Jennifer squeaks into my palm that's quickly suctioned over her mouth.

"Nothing. What are you doing here?" I cringe as a wet tongue laps over my palm. Nose scrunched in disgust, I yank my hand from her lips and wipe my palm down my jeans. Glaring at Jennifer, I shut the window tight. Her unconcerned giggle follows me as I take the two steps back to my chair and fall into it.

"Ah, that." Ben tugs off his ball cap and scratches the crown of his head. "I wanted to stop by, Taeler mentioned she spoke to you last night about her decision on college. Wanted to check in, see how you were doing with her news."

My hands ball into tight fists beneath the solid wood desk. "You knew, and you didn't tell me? How long have you known?"

"She asked me not to," he says, widening his stance and shoving his hands into the back pockets of his jeans.

"Fuck that, Ben," I grit out. Standing, I press both palms on the desk and lean forward. "Co-parenting means we talk about things. We don't keep stuff from each other. I was fucking blindsided. If you would've done the right thing and told me her decision before she talked to me, I would've had a counterargument prepared."

"It's only college, Rand." Ben twists the toe of his worn work boot into the thin carpet. "It's not like going to college did you any good."

True and false.

True, I'm in debt from the various student loans plus the few credit cards I maxed out to cover the daily expenses the loans, grants, and scholarships didn't cover. False that college didn't do me any good. The changes and growth that happen during those years are priceless. It was difficult, and I might have to file for bankruptcy soon, but priceless just the same.

"It's about getting out of here, seeing what the world has to offer outside of this small town." I focus on the peeling ceiling, searching for the right words. "It builds confidence, character—"

"Debt."

"Not everything's about money," I counter with a bit of annoyance in my tone.

"Right." He scoffs. "Look around you, Rand; everything is about money. It's all about who has it and who doesn't. If you haven't looked in the fucking mirror recently, you're in the group who doesn't fucking have it."

"Not yet, anyway."

All three of our heads jerk in the direction of the door, toward the deep, gravelly male voice.

My muscles seize, my lungs forgetting their one job as I lock eyes with the beautiful blue-eyed man. All words and coherent thoughts vanish into thin air. I open my mouth once, twice, but not a single sound makes it out.

Holy shit.

What in the hell is he doing here?

2

RANDI

"Miss Sawyer," the coldhearted asswipe, also known as Kyle Birmingham, says. His voice is just as icy and degrading as it was years ago.

My tongue sticks to the roof of my dry mouth. "What... what are you doing here?" I finally manage to squeak out.

Kyle fucking Birmingham.

In my office, of all places.

The last time I saw him, his middle finger was pointed to the sky as he glared at me from across the auditorium after graduation. We hate—nope, that's too soft of a word. We loathe each other. Opposites in every way. We clashed, fought, and debated constantly. This is the very man whose one mission in life those three years was to make my life miserable. There were only a handful of days that I went without breaking down from the constant bullying.

Kyle inspects his suit jacket, brushing off a piece of invisible lint. "I made an appointment."

My gaze darts from him to Jennifer, who's too busy drooling over Mr. Jackass to notice the beseeching look I'm throwing her way.

"Jenn?" I ask. Jenn's been my secretary for the past few years and knows I hate being unprepared, like now.

Her eyes reluctantly swing from him to meet mine, her face morphing into a cringe. "I told you. When you first came in, remember? Someone from his office called this morning demanding I make room on your schedule for someone from their office to meet with you. They never gave a name, just reserved the time slot."

"Oh yeah," I grumble more to myself than Jennifer. Mornings are spent at the small, and failing, family law practice I founded after law school, and afternoons are here acting as mayor for our small town.

"What do you want, Kyle?" Resting back in the rickety chair, I run a hand across my forehead, sealing my eyes shut in an attempt to get my bombarding thoughts together. The asshole is up to something, no doubt about that. If Kyle Birmingham flew from Washington, DC, to our small town, I need to be on high alert.

"You need some coffee or something?" Jennifer asks, her tone dripping in concern.

With a tight, pursed-lip smile, I nod. The silence in the room grows as Jennifer hurries out of the office for the small kitchenette just outside the door, catty-corner to her desk.

"We need to talk," Kyle says, answering my earlier question, cutting his eyes to a tense Ben. "Alone."

"I don't think so," Ben states, nostrils flaring. Have to hand it to Ben; it takes balls not to shrink under Kyle's direct scrutiny. I sure as hell never figured out how to stand up to him.

"It's fine, Ben. Thanks though." I force a fake smile to ease some of the building tension. "I'll hear Mr. Birmingham out, and then he'll be on his way. Right?" My hazel eyes slide back, locking with Kyle's ice-blue ones.

Jaw tight, he inclines his head in acceptance.

Eyes narrowed at the bastard, I blindly take the hot, disposable coffee cup from Jennifer's shaking hand. Still smiling, I motion for her and Ben to give us privacy. One more direct glare from Ben to Kyle, and then the door clicks closed. Kyle takes two steps deeper into the room. His expensive cologne fills the office, burning the inside of my nostrils. He always did put way too much of that shit on.

Lips against the rim of the cup, I take a slow sip of black coffee, peering over the edge to watch him survey the office.

His full upper lip curls. His scowl deepens when his attention falls back to where I sit behind the cluttered desk.

I frown at the minuscule shake of his head.

Not surprising that he finds me and the office lacking. With men like Kyle, nothing is good enough. The Birmingham name is a powerhouse in Washington, DC. Every member of the family is in some way involved in politics and wealthy beyond anything I can comprehend. He's never had to wonder if he would eat, only when and what. And of course, he's never worked a full day, something daddy dearest ensured by paying for his education plus a generous allowance.

How do I know this?

He constantly boasted of his good fortune, being born into the right family. It added to the various ways he bullied me back in Boston. The day he learned I was Harvard's 'good deed for the century' by allowing someone of my background and financial status to attend the prestigious school, he reminded me and everyone else of the broke scum I was.

His words, not mine.

"Let's get this started, Walmart. I need to get back to the jet before your condemned office falls apart with me in it."

I school my features to hide the blow to my fragile confidence, but the heat still builds beneath my cheeks. I'd almost forgotten the nickname he graced me with all those years ago. Fucking tool.

"Just get to the point of why you're here so I can tell you to go screw yourself and you can go."

Eyebrow raised, he tsks. The feeble chair wobbles as he settles into the seat. "Nice office."

"Nice face." Well hell. What am I twelve?

"You thought so before."

"I chalk that brief lapse of sound judgment up to a sporadic instance of psychosis. Plus, I thought that before I knew what a gigantic asshole you are."

His cocky smile falters, lips pressing into a hard line. "You and everyone else, it appears," he says with a huff.

"What in the hell are you talking about?"

"We'll get to that in a moment. First, I was surprised when an advisor of mine told me of your status as mayor in this shithole town. I didn't know you were interested in politics."

"Probably because you don't know a thing about me," I hiss, leaning over the desk. "I wanted to make a difference in my hometown." My main drive to come back to Boone was to be close to Taeler after missing so much of her life. A year after I moved home, the local elections came around, and the dumb fuck who'd won the previous cycles, yet done nothing to improve the town, was running uncontested—again. Knowing enough about the ins and outs of being a public servant, I decided to kill two birds with one stone. Be in a position where I could help and be in a position of power to change everyone's view of me.

Only one came to fruition. But hey, at least the few community projects I've spearheaded and after-school programs are successful.

His words finally sink in, smacking me in the face. I hold up a hand. "Why did your advisor even know about me being mayor? Are you keeping tabs on me?" My voice rises with each word.

"I wasn't until a recent development." He leans back in the chair, relaxed hands clasped on his lap. "It was brought to my attention because I need someone like you."

What? I collapse back in the chair, eyes sealing shut. Face to the ceiling, I blow out a tight breath. "I'm imagining all this, aren't I? I've officially sailed from the land of sanity, now floating aimlessly on the sea of lunacy."

"You always were a strange one." I peek one eye open, shooting him an annoyed glare. "It was one reason I hesitated at the mention of you for our plan, but here I am." His eyes flick around the office, disgust written across is perfect features. "You're my only option, or I wouldn't be here, believe me."

"Still not following," I mutter as I rub both thumbs against my temples. There isn't enough Tylenol in the world to hold off the headache this man's presence invokes.

A jostle, then footsteps draw my attention back across the desk. My horny side revels in the way his fit body folds out of the wobbling chair to stand. Long, lean fingers make quick work of his suit jacket's buttons, securing them once again. I chew on a nail as my eyes skim up and down his fancy suit. Damn. He really is beautiful. Silky jet-black hair cut and styled to perfection makes those piercing blue eyes shine, a clean-shaven jaw showing off spotless tan skin, straight nose, and dimpled chin create a Greek god come to life.

No guy should be this pretty. Evolution fucked up with him in so many ways. Why make a man with all that and a greedy black heart?

Yes, his behavior in law school was cruel, but his malicious nature goes deeper than name-calling. He's corrupt greed personified. It's in his arrogant looks, the emotionless aura surrounding him. There's no doubt he would take me out right here in this office if he heard it would benefit him mone-tarily or advance his career.

But that's a modern politician for you. Kyle Birmingham is one of thou-sands of corrupt bastards in DC. In that city, it's who can bribe or blackmail to get what you want done for yourself. It has nothing to do with doing right by the American people anymore. Their voice has been forgotten, thrown aside by the politicians assuming their superior mind knows what's best, when they haven't lived a day below the 1 percent—hell, below the upper middle class.

I shake my head to clear the random internal rant. Suspicion and curiosity grow as Kyle paces from one side of the office to the other.

He pauses, turning with his perfectly plucked brows pulled together. "I'm running for president in the next election."

My brows rise and my head tilts. "Congratulations, I guess? If you're here to gain my vote, you won't get it. I'd fill in Betty White as a write-in candidate before I check the box voting you for president of the United States."

"That's why I'm here. The fucking initial surveys say I'm an unfavorable candidate. Can you believe that? *Me*," he shouts. Pacing once again, he runs both hands through his black hair, disrupting the gelled style. "Apparently, the Birmingham name is associated with a dynasty in DC, like we're the damn Kennedys or something. Ignorant voters seem to think it's time for a change."

I raise my hand and nod in agreement. "Not ignorant, aware. I agree it's time for a change in that city."

"Why?" He stops behind the chair, both hands grasping the back as he tilts forward. I hold back from breathing deep as another strong waft of cologne infiltrates my nose.

"Nothing gets done anymore," I say with a held breath. "It's all pomp and circumstance. Nothing is being done to ease the burden on the lower class; instead we're taxed and taxed. All for the sake of more government programs that do shit because the money is mismanaged or whoever's running it doesn't understand the real plight of the American people." Palms down, I push off the desk's worn wooden top to stand. "We need someone who's been here, understands what it's like living below the poverty line and never, ever believing you'll break out of it. Someone who fights for our rights, our freedoms instead of handing them over to some jackass in Washington who thinks he knows better."

My chest heaves, eyes locked with his, tense silence growing with every second he doesn't respond. The wind howling outside the window and the clicking of nails as Jennifer types on the other side of the thin walls the only sounds.

"I one hundred percent disagree with you," he finally says. "But if I want to win the election, I need to embrace these fanatic beliefs. Which—" Kyle clears his throat. "—is why I'm here."

Hell. Either alcohol or nicotine is needed to process this shit and I only have one of those on me.

My legs wobble like a newborn calf as I move from behind the desk to the side window. I snag the pack of cigarettes Jennifer left and pop one between my lips. The window rattles open, a welcomed blast of cold, dry air cooling my heated skin. "You're here to ask me, Walmart, for my help?" Sparks fly from the flint as I flick the lighter twice, lighting the end of my cigarette. "To what, teach you how to have a fucking heart for the American people? To guide you on what it's like to be poor?"

"No." Kyle steps to my side, eyes narrowed at the cigarette. "That's a disgusting habit. And I don't need you to teach me, Walmart. I know who I am, and I know what I want. Adjusting to the voters' perception of me is simply a roadblock, one I already have a plan to overcome. You by my side."

Mid-inhale, I laugh, sending the cloud of smoke barreling down the wrong pipe. Tears well and my stomach tightens at the violent coughing attack it brings on.

"By your side?" I croak, throat raw. I bark a raspy laugh. "You can't be serious."

Right? He's crazier than me.

"I'm offering freedom, Walmart. Don't mock the hand that can save your poor ass."

I grind my teeth, jaw clenched tight.

"Nothing would convince me to help—"

"All your debt paid off, gone." Well, nothing except that. He smirks at my silence, knowing he has my full attention. "I'm talking about changing your life, the life of your kid. Pull your head out of your white trash ass and listen to what I'm willing to offer before saying you'd never partner with me."

As much as I don't want to hear what he has to say, I do. Talk about conflicting emotions. Do I want to stab him with any sharp object within reach, hell yes. Do I also want the chance of a debt-free life for Tae, fuck yeah. I'll give a kidney right here—hell, I'd even cut it out of my own body with a letter opener—to erase all the debt I've accrued over the years. Between student loans, which are currently in arrears, and the few maxed-out credit cards, I'm on the cliff of bankruptcy.

Add in being on the verge of homelessness and recently waterless....

That all sounds great, but at what cost? With men like Kyle Birmingham, everything has a cost. Every word, every move is a power play of some kind in their fucked-up game of life.

"I'm listening." I glare at his bleached-white, straight-toothed, victorious grin. "Begrudgingly, of course."

"Wouldn't expect anything less from you." His features harden as his eyes scroll over me from head to toe. A grimace deepens with each inch his dissecting gaze covers.

I squirm under his scrutiny. Here he is in a thousand-dollar suit—well, that's a wild guess, since I've never seen one before, but with the way said suit hugs his lean frame, there's no doubt it's expensive—and me, well, my dark-wash jeans lost their dark a hundred washes ago. My blazer, a recent Goodwill find, has seen better days, and let's not even get started on my hair. I freaked out at finding a gray hair two weeks ago and hightailed it to the Dollar General for a box of dark brown hair dye.

"What the hell did you do to your hair?"

My mood sours.

"I found a gray hair," I say like it explains everything, but by the look of his furrowed brows, it only explains things to a woman.

"It's the color of day-old dog shit."

"That's oddly specific," I retort, nervously leaning toward the desk as I gather the ugly strands. Grabbing a chewed pencil, I stab the pointy end through the messy bun I constructed and turn back to him.

"A complete makeover will be needed, obviously. Hell, maybe we could find someone to make you somewhat attractive." Those ice-blue eyes narrow as he scans down my frame. I wrap both arms around my waist at the click of his tongue. "Complete wardrobe plus a diet plan and workout regimen. You look like a fucking meth addict." He sighs and rubs the bridge of his nose between two fingers. A clear sheen reflects off his nails. Of course he gets manicures. "Fuck, I can't believe I'm doing this. Grasping at damn straws. Those assholes better be right about all this, or I'll kill them myself."

"You're wasting your breath—"

"All expenses paid by the Birmingham trust. Plus a monthly allowance."

"Allowance," I seethe. "I'll show you where you can shove your allowance, you asshat."

"Ten grand a month."

"Oh, well, uh," I stammer. Shit, that's a lot of money. But again, what's the cost? He's conveniently only covered the perks of the 'help' he needs. "For what, Birmingham? My soul?"

Kyle's chest rumbles, a deep chuckle vibrating through the office. "Basically. All this for your help during the campaign and after."

"After?" I hold a breath. I swear a suspenseful score plays somewhere in the background.

"While I'm president."

I swipe my tongue across my dry lower lip. "And I'm... I'm what? Your advisor on how not to be a conniving, greedy asshole? Not sure there's hope for accomplishing that."

My stomach sinks at the Cheshire grin spreading across his flawless face. Apprehension builds, but no matter what he says, I can't turn down what he's offering. It's a new life. A chance to get Taeler out of this town, to show everyone I can break the cycle.

"No, Walmart. My wife."

Well, except that.

"But I hate you," I respond, each word slow in case he somehow forgot our feud. "And you hate me. Hell, we can't be in the same room without plotting the other's slow death."

Or maybe that's just me. My imagination does tend to lean toward violence.

"Moot point." He shoves both hands into the pockets of his expensive slacks that accentuate his figure. "Most married couples hate each other, but it doesn't matter. I'm talking about you as my pawn, not someone I love." He snorts with one more condescending look up and down. "This offer will change your pathetic excuse for a life. Think about never having to worry about money again, about the opportunities that will be available after the four years. Don't think short term, think about your life, about your daughter's. You want her to grow up piss-ass poor with zero hope of ever rising above the lower middle class, just like her mom, because you're too self-righteous to accept a simple proposal?"

"You asshole," I manage through gritted teeth. Fuck, I hate him. "I know what's on the line. You don't need to remind me of my shitty-ass life." Breaking from his stare, I glance out the window. My chest expands, lungs filling with a deep calming breath to ease the resentment and anger clouding my thoughts.

"Your daughter applied to several colleges and was accepted to a few, yet she hasn't committed to one."

A sharp breath catches in my chest. "How do you know that?"

He waves a perfectly manicured hand in dismissal. "We'll pay for her college too, along with expenses and housing to ensure your... continued cooperation through the campaign and after if—no, *when* I win."

Hell, that's a lot of money in and of itself. Not to mention all the other perks.

"Why?" I blurt. "What can I do as your wife? What does that change for you in the campaign?"

"It eases my image. The people will see I understand their plight, have a voice in my ear from their perspective. With your background, people will eat up the rags-to-riches story you'll tell them. It'll be like saving an injured animal. People will fucking love me."

Oh hell.

He's serious.

But....

The biggest question is, can I do it? Be with him every day, playing pretend wife, all while I hope he dies of a heart attack with no one around to help him? And toss in lying to the American people about Kyle's true self daily, using my shitty history as a talking point in the campaign.

Can I live with being his pawn?

3

RANDI

"Jack on the rocks." Exhaustion slurs my words. I slide onto an empty barstool and hold up two fingers to the expecting bartender. "And keep them coming."

This bar is exactly what I need. The other patrons are clustered together in their own booths, leaving the bar entirely empty. It's a local place that used to be busy until the Chili's opened up down the road last year. Now most nights it's like this, a few customers and the lone bartender. It's not updated, but it has stools, booths, and alcohol—all the things a bar needs. Sure, the floors are constantly sticky, the lights are dim, and dust puffs up when you sit on a booth bench, but the happy hour is phenomenal.

I couldn't force myself to go home. Not with Kyle's offer consuming my every thought. I gnash my teeth at the text still on the screen from Taeler. She doesn't want to stay at the trailer tonight—I don't have water after all—deciding to stay with her grandparents instead. They already think I can't take care of my own daughter, and instances like this just prove them right.

Hell, I can barely take care of myself these days.

Maybe everyone is right. I'll never amount to anything. I should just toss in the towel.

I scratch a chewed-up fingernail along my scalp, raking my fingers through my dirty hair. A section of the slick brown strands falls in front of my eyes. I inspect it, holding it up to the light. Damn, Kyle was right. It looks like day-old dog poop. But the box of dye was five dollars, so... it is what it is.

But does it have to be?

I shake my head, swiping the locks behind my ear, and grip the chilled highball glass in front of me. I take a slow sip of the whiskey. The rows of liquor bottles behind the bar blur before me.

Debt free. Plus the monthly ten grand from now until he's out of the White House. All for me. After the 'wife' bomb, he spent the next hour detailing his expectations.

The contract.

I would stand by his side, allow my background to be used as a way to make him seem more human. Pretty much he needs Trailer Park Barbie next to him to show the voters he isn't the aristocratic douche they assume he is at the core. Which he is, so basically I'll lie, which isn't ideal, but no credit card debt and zero student loans to pay back, plus changing Taeler's life, make a convincing argument for hoodwinking the American people.

The last few drops of Jack slither down my throat, leaving a warm burn in their path. The slap of the glass on the smooth wood of the well-used bar signals the bartender for another.

A shadow creeps over, followed by the shuffle of feet to my right. "Celebrating or drowning your sorrows?"

Resting my chin on my shoulder, I flash Ben a tired smile. I should hate him, but I don't. He left me pregnant and scared, let his parents take Tae away from me. A piece of me might love him. Well, maybe not him but the memory of him, of the fun and love we shared before those two pink lines appeared. Maybe when the right man comes along, it'll make me realize my hang-up on Ben is simple infatuation and inability to let go of the past.

The right man. I huff and reach for the fresh glass of whiskey. *Like that will happen.*

In undergrad I was too busy studying and working to date, plus no one wanted to date the single mom. Then during law school, no one would touch me with a ten-foot pole because of the shit Kyle spread around about me. You would think those fancy-schmancy idiots would know poor choices and low economic status doesn't rub off with skin-to-skin contact.

"Both," I say after taking a quick sip as he slides on to the stool to my right.

"Budweiser." The bartender nods before turning to the cooler that holds the longneck bottles. "Do I need to kick that rich pussy's ass?" His smirk grows into a full-on mischievous smile. I love that smirk; it makes me forget to be overwhelmed. "I went to State in wrestling, remember?"

"Yeah, I remember." Mostly because he won't let anyone in a ten-mile radius forget.

"Those were the good old days, am I right?" His Adam's apple bobs with each long pull he takes of the beer.

"Maybe for you," I murmur. "I was pregnant and then had a baby to keep alive and fight to keep."

His shrug has sparks firing in my veins. Idiot. He really didn't get it then and still doesn't. He doesn't remember how difficult it was balancing school and taking care of an infant because he wasn't there. A slice of pain cuts through my heart at the memory of Ben breaking it off after I announced I was pregnant. He loved me but wasn't ready for that kind of *commitment*. Like love isn't.

"I'm sorry for not telling you about Taeler's decision. I really am." His short nails scrape at the bottle's label as he stares at the bar. "But it *is* her decision, and I can't blame her. I know you tried to make something of your-self, but look at you now. Was it worth it?"

All those years separated from Taeler plus the lifetime of debt I accumu-lated. Was it worth it?

"Yeah it was. Still is." I sigh into the glass at my lips before taking a sip of whiskey. The warmth blooms in my belly, adding to that first glass. For the first time today, I'm not chilled. "At least I know. At least I tried. That means everything. Sure, it's not what I expected, but I'm not giving up, and I feel like that's what she's doing. She's letting a little roadblock stop her from trying. What's the point of living if you don't risk everything for the dream of something better?"

"What did he want, anyway?"

I spin the base of the thin glass on the bar, the remaining slivers of ice swirling together. "A job offer of sorts." A little embellishment never hurt anything. "It could solve all my financial problems, but... I don't know. I hate the guy."

Ben's warm hand wraps around my wrist, stopping the glass. Turning on his stool, he leans forward, putting his face inches from mine. His long blond lashes flutter, drawing attention to his soft baby blue eyes.

"Is he asking you to do something illegal?"

"No." Unless you count lying about his character.

"Did he ask you for favors that involve your pussy?"

I cringe, sliding back on the stool. "So crass."

"Like you have room to talk. Answer me."

"No, he's not looking for sexual favors in return for money, also known as prostitution, which is illegal, which I covered with my 'no' answer to your first question."

"Smartass." The grip on my wrist tightens, sending a shot of excitement straight to my lady parts. What does it mean that a controlling grip gets me hot but a delicate one bores the shit out of me? Hmm, some hands-on research is needed. "I don't see the problem, then," Ben says, turning back to his beer.

My eyes are locked on my wrist, warmth still seeping into my skin from the earlier contact. "Exactly," I muse. "It could be fun research."

"What?" he says, the bottle hovering at his lips.

"What? Oh, sorry, wrong conversation."

"Hope you don't have to pass a psych exam for whatever job he's offering."

Hmm, didn't ask that. Probably should've.

"I'll ask, but this job isn't ideal. I'll lose my voice, my freedom. I'm not sure there's a large enough sum to convince me to give that up. Honestly, I'm not sure I even can."

Ben shakes his head as he angles the empty beer bottle to the bartender.

"I know you can't, baby girl. But I know you tackle anything you set your crazy-ass mind on. If you want more from this job he's offering, then ask for it. Demand it. You've never been shy about demanding what you wanted before. Why now?"

Hmm. Absentmindedly, I chew on a jagged nail. "You speak the truth, wise one."

"Fuck, you're getting weirder as you get older, you know that? You'll end up in a padded room by the time you're forty at this rate."

Five years from now... yeah, he's probably right.

"What's holding me back from telling him what I want?" I ask, more to myself than to Ben. "He told me what he expects and wants out of this deal. Now I need to come up with a counteroffer."

"Surprised you didn't earlier."

Nibbling on my pinky nail, I shake my head. "I was in shock. My nemesis in my office offering to shower me with money and gifts in exchange for my soul was a lot to take in at the time."

"No need to wonder where our daughter gets her dramatics," Ben mutters around the lip of the bottle before tipping it back. "But can I say something?"

I tilt the glass in my hand, indicating for him to continue.

"Why you? I mean, I'm not gay or nothing, but I saw that man, and he's way out of your league."

"Seriously, Ben!"

"What? He's good-lookin' and rich as hell, so what does he want with you? I mean, you're...."

"I'm what, Ben?" I glare into his eyes, wishing mine shot death rays. "You certainly liked the way I looked at one time."

"Yeah, but that was when you were, I don't know, happy? Full of life, maybe. Now you're just haggard."

My jaw drops, my hate-filled glare going with it. "Haggard?"

"Yeah, like life has beaten you down so far that you don't even care to try anymore. Have you looked in the mirror lately?"

I fight a cringe.

"If I were you, I'd have said yes before he had a chance to change his mind."

"I don't want to be someone's pawn."

"Then don't be," Ben huffs, clearly exasperated. "Fuck's sake, woman, isn't that the problem I just solved?"

Gazing into the final sips of whiskey swirling at the bottom of my glass, a poor man's crystal ball, I search for some kind of sign.

"I need to think. Be right back," I mumble over my shoulder as I slide off the wooden barstool. I step through the back exit and immediately wrap both arms around my body. *There goes all that delicious warmth the whiskey provided.* I look to the sky, searching the stars, and snag the pack of cigarettes from my pocket. Movement catches my eye, and I follow Kyle's business card as it flutters in the wind, landing on the gravel a couple steps away.

I snag the small, hard cardstock and flip it over to look at Kyle's hand-written cell number. He instructed me to call, soon, with my answer. But do I even have one?

It's an opportunity to make all my financial worries go away, but at the cost of my pride, my voice, my character. Is there a sum that's worth that?

Ben's right. I need to figure out a way to finagle what I want out of the offer so I'm not the pawn.

Find a way to be the queen in this political chess game *plus* everything he's offering.

But how?

He needs me to make him believable to the voters. What do I want in return? Deep down, it's always been the same—to prove everyone wrong. They think they know me, enjoy the addict's daughter stigma they keep shoving me into. I want to show Ben's parents that I am a good mother, that I can take care of Taeler. It might be a few years later than I wanted, but it still matters to me. Show my teachers, my professors that all the hard work wasn't for not.

A crazy—even for me, which tells you it's batshit—idea forms. One that would give us both what we want. I would come out ahead in my mind, but if it works, he'll be the president of the United States. Not a bad trade-off.

First, am I even qualified?

With a swipe of my thumb across the phone screen I tap the internet icon and type in my search.

Okay here we go.

Natural born U.S. citizen. *Check.*

At least thirty-five years old. *Unfortunately.*

Resident in U.S. for at least fourteen years. *Never even stepped foot in another country, so yeah.*

Nipping the cigarette between my front teeth, I hold out the business card and press the numbers into my phone. Depositing the card back into my pocket, I snag the dangling cigarette and wait for Señor Douchenozzle to pick up. Annoyance rises as it continues to ring. Of course he's not going to answer.

I swipe the screen with as much annoyance as I can channel into my thumb, hanging up on the generic automated voice mail. Just as I'm sliding it back into my pocket, it vibrates with an incoming call. I glance at the screen —Unknown Caller.

Being the one who calls, initiating the contact, is some kind of power play to him, I'm sure. As stupid as it sounds, if this is going to happen, I need to learn the rules of this power game. Fast.

"Walmart." Kyle's deep voice vibrates through the earpiece.

"Tool Bucket," I say on a gritty chuckle. "Get it? You're not just a tool, you're the whole tool bucket." I think I'm hilarious, even if the world doesn't always get my humor.

"Hilarious. What's your decision?"

Right. Decision time.

"Yes, but I want a few revisions to the agreement. I want a voice," I state, pushing as much conviction into my tone as possible. If I don't believe I can do this, there's no way he will either. I have to believe in myself, like I've done my whole life, even with the odds stacked against me.

I can do this. I have to do this. For me, for Taeler, for every person I can help.

"A voice?" Curiosity laces his tone. "Explain."

"I won't accept sitting on the sidelines, allowing you to use me as your poverty puppet to deceive the voters."

An irritated sigh crackles through his side of the line. "I expected nothing less from the only woman who can outdebate me. What does that mean, Walmart? A charity in your name? A fundraiser for the poor? Maybe a building?"

"More," I say, a cloud of smoke billowing out of my puckered lips. I watch it rise into the dark night sky before dissipating with a gust of wind as I wait for his response.

"What, then? What is it that you're asking for?"

Here I go. This is it. My chance to change the tide of... everything. My life and the lives of millions. Just the thought of being able to turn the tables for the working people of this country steels my spine. With my degrees and background, I can be the people's voice in Washington.

"Put me on the ticket. Make me your running mate. The VP." I pause, allowing my words to settle through the phone. "It'll make a bigger impact toward winning the White House. I can do it, I know I can. With me being mayor here plus my law degree, I'll figure it out. I meet the basic qualifications and okay yeah I don't have a lot of experience, but I swear I'll make it work. Hell, even a helmet-wearing monkey is more qualified than the idiot who's in the role currently. Anyone can do a better job than him, and that someone is me."

"You're fucking with me right now."

I shake my head. "No I'm not. I won't be Poverty Barbie who you can flounce around as your good deed. If you want the White House, if you want the most powerful position in the world, then list me as the vice president. I know it's a crazy idea but what do you have to lose? It's either this or nothing for me."

Nothing. His deep breaths huffing across the mouthpiece are the only indication he's still on the line. The silence is a good sign. It means he's considering it, not telling me to fuck off and ending the call. If he's not considering it, then I've fucked over my daughter's future. No pressure.

I rake a couple fingers through my nasty, dirty hair. A minute passes of deafening silence. I bob on the balls of my feet, attempting to get some feeling back in my toes.

"I'm inclined to tell you to fuck off and watch you fail miserably at life, but if I say yes to your proposal, then I'll have a front row seat to your failure here in DC."

"I won't fail." I flick the cigarette butt to the ground and grind it into the gray gravel with the toe of my shoe. No way. Not happening. This is my shot to get ahead, to prove to everyone, prove to myself, that I'm more than what I was born into.

His condescending laugh rattles through the phone, and my upper lip curls in a snarl. "Oh, but you will, Walmart. You think you can play with the most powerful people in the world and win with no experience? I'm questioning your intelligence. They will chew you up before you even start the campaign."

"Aw," I coo, faking surprise. "You do care about me."

"I care about winning. Tell you what. I'll pitch your ludicrous proposal to my advisors and campaign manager. I'll send for you when I know more. Just to make sure I understand this correctly, it's either the vice president position or nothing. Correct?"

"Correct." I swallow hard against the knot building in my throat.

"If I propose this, there's no going back. If we lose, there will be no ongoing funds since you won't be my legal wife. Understand?"

"Yes, yes, I understand everything, Kyle." Shit, didn't think about that side effect. If we do this, it means we have to win.

"Also know that the man who's currently slated as my running mate will not be happy if he's kicked off the ticket. If this does work, know you'll have a target on your back."

That's mysteriously ominous.

I open my mouth to ask what he means but snap it shut at the void on the other end of the phone. Peeling it from my ear, I scan the black screen and let out an incredulous snort. Of course the douche hung up on me.

Tapping the edge of the phone against my thigh, I again stare up into the dark night sky. My pulse races as the reality of the situation sinks deep.

I'm crazier than anyone gives me credit for. Vice president? For fuck's sake.

"Damn idiot," I mutter.

Now I wait and maybe run by Mom's to take a shower.

Hand wrapped around the cold metal handle, I give it a hard tug, swinging the exit door open. Laughter and old country music fill the hall as I make my way back to the bar. With every step, the same two questions repeat over and over in my mind.

What will I do if he says yes?

What will I do if he says no?

4

RANDI

The wheels of my rolling suitcase quietly whirl down the carpeted hall. Fancy chandeliers dot the long hallway's ceiling, making the suite of offices appear like a hotel rather than a place of business. Of course, I am in Washington, DC. Maybe people use this space for business and pleasure; the two go hand in hand in our nation's capital, after all.

Wait. I tilt my nose and inhale deep. *Is that vanilla?*

Midstep I halt, sniffing the air. Surely this building isn't piping a yummy scent into their hallways. I spin, eyes falling to the floral wallpaper. What if the wallpaper is scented and that's what I'm smelling? That would be opulent fancy. I cut my eyes both ways, making sure the coast is clear, and lean toward to the wall. The wallpaper brushes the tip of my nose, but the delectable scent isn't any stronger than when I was a few feet away.

Unless... it could be scratch and sniff—I saw that in a movie once. Forgetting my surroundings, my sole focus on the scent mystery, I scratch a mauve flower with the edge of my serrated nail. Nose pressed firmly to the same spot, I sniff.

"What the hell are you doing?"

Startled, I jolt back, my hand catching the extended handle of my rolling suitcase. It teeters before falling to the floor with an echoing thump.

I shift from one heel to the other, avoiding the man's pointed glare.

"Smelling the wall." I frown at my ragged bag on the pristine carpet.

"The scent in the hall... I thought it came from the wallpaper, so I sniffed it. I'm sure it happens all the time." My knees pop as I squat, righting the toppled suitcase.

"I can guarantee you it doesn't. Kyle mentioned you were a strange one." His near-black eyes flick to his watch, a frown forming.

Using the distraction, I take in the rude man. Dirty-blond hair, square jaw with high cheekbones, and a narrow upturned nose. Attractive if it weren't for the dark and foreboding aura pulsing around him. Every internal alarm sounds, the clenching in my gut telling me to get the hell out of here.

His eyes swing back to me, narrowing. "Hurry up. You're late."

I tighten my grip on the suitcase handle, the hard plastic slipping in my sweat-damp palm.

My steps are hesitant, the bag barely rolling behind me. "I'm at a disadvantage. Who are you?"

An unnaturally wide smile curls up his cheeks, and I retreat a step. He appeared dangerous before, but with this Joker-like smile, I'm sufficiently creeped out.

"Come on, Trailer." He shoves off the thick, dark wood door without a glance back, moving into the office suite.

"Asshat," I grumble under my breath. I grip the door's edge before it closes. Shoving it open, I lug the bag through, only for it to close sooner than I expect. Near my limit for the day, I hold back a scream of frustration. Backtracking, I give the heavy door another big shove, freeing my suitcase. Sweat beads beneath my arms and glistens on my forehead. Hopefully I don't look as discombobulated as I feel. The redeye flight out of DFW was rough in its own right. Add in the constant turbulence from there to DC, then the frantic scene at the taxi stand at Reagan and I'm whipped.

"Good to see you finally made it, Walmart." Kyle sneers as I cough at the assault of his overpowering cologne. "Come, we have items to discuss."

I swallow, fighting the panic that wants to seal off my airway as I follow him into the next room. Yesterday, Kyle called, informing me they'd come to a decision on my counteroffer and I was needed in DC as soon as possible. So here I am, sweating like a pig, nerves frayed.

What if they agree?

Oh hell, what if they don't? The prospect of zero debt, Taeler's college paid for by someone else, and proving to everyone I'm not worthless has filled my thoughts the last few days.

Now I'm here.

Shit, things just got real. This is happening.

The fancy décor and furniture in the large room Kyle leads me into match the opulence from the hallway. It resembles a posh living room rather than a boardroom, dotted with four large leather chairs and two dark fabric-covered couches centered around an imposing wooden table.

The four older men stand from where they sat as we enter the room. The lone woman remains seated as she types furiously on the cell phone inches from her scowling face. My eyes scan the room, falling on the mystery man from the hall. Pure hate fills his eyes from his perch against a sideboard, its top littered with decanters of various sizes and shapes, all filled to the brim with honey-colored liquid.

"My assistant and attorneys," Kyle states with a wave of his hand, not bothering with introducing everyone by name. "Sit." He points to the smaller couch. "We have significant information to discuss and little time to work with."

The delicious aroma of fresh-brewed coffee hits my nose, and a slow throb pulses in my head with the need for more caffeine. I dismiss Kyle, heading straight for the narrow buffet along the opposite wall. My mouth waters as the steaming dark brew streams from the thick metal carafe into my awaiting white mug. Wouldn't be shocked if the shit's china. Rich bastards. Even their mugs are fancier than me.

After one Splenda and a dash of cream—it's here, so why the hell not—I wrap both hands around the warm mug and turn to the group.

"Now I'm ready," I announce, sinking into the soft plush couch. The cushion molds around my ass and back like a fucking cloud.

Holy fuck, expensive furniture is soft.

Kyle sneers, gracefully sliding into the dark leather chair opposite me.

"After running the numbers and taking preliminary surveys, we found that, as far-fetched as it seems, you becoming running mate in next year's election will elevate the ticket higher in the polls." The white mug slips in my tight grip. "We need to switch the names on the paperwork as soon as possible. The convention is right around the corner, and all delegates must announce their candidacy by that time."

Little waves ripple along the surface of my coffee, my hands trembling in anticipation. I lift it to my lips, take a scalding sip, and then lean forward, setting it on the table.

Should I find a coaster or something?

I swipe both damp palms down my gray slacks. "Great, so what do you need from me? Birth certificate and proof of residency are two that come to mind that are required for eligibility."

An older, balding man slides a manila folder across the table. "We need several items to complete the submission process." I stop its path before it tips to the floor. "The list is in there, along with several forms that you must sign."

"Great." *Not great. So not great right now. Maybe it's not too late to back out. What the hell was I thinking! I can't do this, help run a fucking country. Maybe if I avoid eye contact and make a break for the exit, they'll forget I was ever here.*

"I asked my attorneys to draw up an agreement detailing everything we discussed. That is also in there," Kyle says, nodding to the folder in my hands.

My eyes flick to the door. If I back out now, what is there to go home to?

Just breathe, Randi. Deep inhale and slow exhale.

"Moving on to your cover story."

My brows draw together. "Cover story? I thought you wanted me *because* of my background, not despite it."

He nods, steepling two fingers beneath his dimpled chin. "With you switching from my wife to filling the vice president slot, we only need select portions of your background known, not everything."

"I don't understand." I shake my head and glance around the room, hoping someone will fill in the missing pieces.

"He means they need you poor, but not the poor white trash you are."

"Fuck you," I grit out to the man smirking against the sideboard. Knew he was an asshole the moment I laid eyes on him in the hallway. "Who the hell are you, anyway?"

"Shawn Whit," Kyle says with a tight smile. "Shawn's blunt but correct. We've decided to embellish your backstory so it's not so fucking depressing. No one would believe some low-rent trailer trash would be effective in the VP seat."

I relax, sinking farther into the seat. I'm not mad—I'm relieved. The thought of the whole world knowing everything added more pressure to the already crushing weight resting on my shoulders.

"I can see that angle. What are you suggesting we change?"

"We keep your loser mother out of the press. Instead we give the media a softer version of your story, a version we can spin to appeal to the voters."

"Sounds like a back-ass way of saying you want to lie to the voters."

No surprise that he ignores the accurate comment. "It will take a lot of maneuvering inducements—"

"Bribes. It's called a bribe, which is illegal," I interject.

"—but we'll make sure only the parts we want of your backstory make it to the press. If we feed them the information, they'll never bother digging to verify the facts."

"Now *that* I believe," I mutter. Leaning forward, I grasp the warm mug and take a long drink. I savor the warmth the liquid ignites down my throat, the smooth flavor unlike anything I've ever had. Bet it's laced with diamond dust or gold flecks. "I don't think it'll work, but you're the one in charge of this evil plot."

"I'll get the basic points of your improved background that you'll need to memorize before we hit the campaign trail. Also, to keep the media busy, the campaign will lead the press to believe we're romantically involved. Those idiots thrive on a good love story, a rags-to-riches sob story. Plus, it will give you a small foothold in the DC social scene if you're linked to me and my family name. If they think we're together maybe a few key circles will accept you, but it's a long shot. Now the next step, making you look the part."

I sink deep into the soft cushion, hoping it can swallow me whole. Every eye in the room zeros in, scanning me from head to toe, scrutinizing very inch.

"Hair, obviously," says the woman. For the first time since I entered the room, her attention focuses on me instead of the phone glued to her hands. "A few chemical peels can improve her skin tone." *Yikes. Didn't realize it was that bad.* "Botox around the forehead and eyes to make her appear less worn." I'd be pissed if I didn't agree with her assessment. "Lip injections, fast-track Invisalign, plus several whitening treatments."

Hell, maybe Ben is right. I am haggard. All that sounds not only expensive but painful. Not that they would have any sympathy to my plight.

"Is there enough time to make her believable?" Kyle asks. He leans back in the chair, blue eyes still assessing. "We only have two months until the convention."

The woman's blonde hair swishes along her collarbone. Everything about her is perfectly placed. Not a single wrinkle mars her crisp suit, and her makeup is dewy in all the right places, giving off a refreshed look.

Unease rolls in my gut. I shift my focus from her to the table, unable to take her disapproving scowl any longer.

"It won't be perfect, though a vast improvement from the distressed appearance she has now. We can continue the various treatments through the campaign as well. At that point the changes will be gradual. No one will take notice."

"Add in some etiquette classes." Shawn smirks. "I bet she eats with her fucking toes."

My nose and lips tug in a sneer. The earlier embarrassment vaporizes, red-hot anger blasting through my veins instead. "Fuck you." Palms pressed to the leather, I pitch forward, ready to tackle the asshole.

Shawn chuckles, glass clicking along the sideboard as he stands from his perch on the edge. "You've said that already. If you keep it up, I'll take you up on it. After the improvements, obviously."

"Great. So that settles it." Kyle's fingers dig into the cushioned arms of the chair. Standing, he straightens his navy pin-striped suit coat. "Shawn will be our advisor through the campaign." He gestures to the narcissist whose death I'm already mentally plotting. "What he says goes, just the same as me. You will do everything we tell you, or this contract will not only be voided, preventing any future payments from the Birmingham trust, but we will also pursue legal action against you, demanding repayment of every cent we've paid out to that point."

The blood drains from my face. "What?" I gasp.

"This guarantees your cooperation," Kyle says with a haughty chuckle. "We hold the cards, not you. Get used to it and maybe you'll survive this with minimal damage."

My mouth gapes, my coffee forgotten between my hands, as Kyle, the woman, and the four men file out of the room.

Nausea rolls as fear coils in my gut. Real fear. I've had tough times, had to get myself out of difficult situations, but this is different. I'm in over my head, *way* over my head, with no one on my side. These men are ruthless. I suspected this town is run by men like this, but when the evil and manipulation stare you in the eye, ripping through your soul, it's like a backhand to the face.

"Hey, Trailer." Slowly I lift my unfocused gaze to Shawn. Shoulder against the doorframe, dark eyes glinting in the overhead lights, the evil rolls off him, filling the room. "You're mine, puppet. Let the fun begin."

5

———

TREY

January

"It's open," I shout over my shoulder, eyes glued to the live debate on TV. Heavy footsteps thump closer as the person moves from the front door deeper into my condo. Tipping the near-empty beer bottle back, I flick my gaze to Tank as he falls into one of the five leather recliners stationed around the TV.

"Game's on," he grunts as he rearranges in an attempt to sink deeper into the soft leather. "Why are you watching this shit?"

Hitting the Mute button, I keep my eyes on the screen.

"Can you believe this?" I point the remote at the television, where a man and woman debate back and forth. "This candidate and the bullshit platform she's taking. No doubt she's lying through her perfect teeth, and the general public is fucking buying it. People are idiots if they believe someone like her is any different than the rest of the corrupt fucks running for office."

"Then turn it off." Tank's eyes slide shut. "When's the food getting here? I'm fucking starving."

"Second dinner?"

"Damn straight," he grunts. "That health crap Sarah forces us to eat isn't enough. Look at me." He waves up and down his massive body. "This tank don't run on fucking kale. I swear that woman's trying to kill me. I love my wife, but damn, give me the meats."

I smirk and shake my head. With a groan of my own, I shove from the recliner and amble to the kitchen. Head deep in the fridge, I shout, "That wife of yours is deadly in her own right; she doesn't need to kill you by starvation." The door rattles, beer bottles clanking together. I pinch my lips, letting out a short, high-pitched whistle. "You want a beer?"

A deep chuckle vibrates through the condo. "Hell no." He lifts his tight T-shirt up his chest, displaying the rippled six-pack he's so proud of. "With a body like this, I don't waste calories on beer."

I pop the cap on the bottle and toss it into the trash. I'm not worried about my figure. No one's warming my bed at night; no need to put in the hours at the gym to stay chiseled. The cold white marble digs into my side as I lean against it. "I know you're just saving those precious calories for your other addiction."

The man is the purest definition of a badass, yet he has a soft spot for one delicious treat.

Chocolate.

What can I say? My best friend has many strange quirks; that's just one of many. Not that I can judge, since I have plenty of my own. We balance each other. He's calm to my knee-jerk reactions. I'm the crazy offsetting his boring ass. At the academy we hated each other, mostly due to our equally fierce competitive spirits. We both strived to be first in everything, but in the end, we recognized we were more successful as a team rather than fighting each other. He's been my best friend ever since. The only real, honest man in this damn city.

I turn my attention back to the debate. My eyes narrow at the woman on the screen. She's beautiful, no doubt about that. Everything about her is perfect, from her dark, silky, full hair to the flawless makeup and St. John's suit. It's not her perfection I don't like, it's her type. The woman on the screen is the same as every other woman in this city. Beautiful, smart, the perfect arm candy for an up-and-coming politician. I know her kind—Mom. Fucked her kind—way too many to name. Fell for her kind—She Who Must Not Be Named. I'm over it. Over them, their agendas, the backstabbing and manipulating. Done.

This is my life, and I will live it the way I want, no matter the consequences.

"What's up your ass?" Tank questions. "You look like you have gas or something."

I loosen my lips softening the snarl and roll my shoulders to drop them from my ears.

"Her. I've known enough of her kind. No way in hell can I be around someone like that all day every day. What will we do if they win the primary and we're on her protection detail? Can you imagine the fucking drama that surrounds someone like her?"

"Our job doesn't change just because she's a woman. Makes it a little more challenging, but it's still a job nonetheless. It wouldn't be a problem if we were still on the VP's alpha team."

"That old fuckstick was asking for it and you know it." Of course he's still stuck on my fuckup from last year. I've gotten over it, somewhat. It's been a fun vacation, if you enjoy zero true responsibility and daily paper shuffling.

Who am I kidding? It's terrible. These past several months sitting idle have turned me bitter.

Didn't life used to be fun? Fun was before the demotion, before I realized Rachel was using me, before Mom and Dad threw down their ultimatum.

I point the lip of the bottle to the TV. "I'll bet you a hundred dollars that woman is a complete fraud, and this scheme she and Birmingham are spinning will fall apart."

"I'll take that bet. I doubt she's what you're thinking."

I scoff. Sliding onto the barstool, I lean back against the counter and stretch my arms along the top. "Look at her. No way that woman grew up the way she's saying. Lower middle class, my ass. For fuck's sake, she went to Harvard. I've never met anyone who wasn't a trust fund baby who went there."

"You're one to talk about trust fund babies," he grumbles under his breath.

"They haven't shown anything about this small town she says she's from. Nothing on her background, period. I'm telling you it's all made up to be some sob story. And don't get me going on her and that fucktard Birmingham. Of course they're a couple." My grip tightens, the sweaty bottle slipping in my palm. "Women like her are the same. Power-hungry users. All of them."

"Wow." Shoving from the chair, Tank lumbers over and leans a stocky hip against the counter. "You're one jaded son of a bitch, you know that? Not all women are like—"

"Don't even think about saying her name." It's bad enough I thought it. I shove the rising anger and regret back into the dark cavern where it belongs.

He raises both hands in surrender. "All I'm saying is you're being fucking judgmental right now. You don't know shit about that woman."

"I know enough," I say with a wave of my hand to the TV. "Every news channel is practically screaming that those two are a couple. And considering I've never heard of this Randi Sawyer until recently, I'm going with they're in it together. Just another power couple in the making."

"You can't be serious. Ever heard of the term 'fake news'?"

"This is different."

Tank chuckles. "Right." His back straightens, going on high alert at the shrill of my phone.

"That'll be the food." I swipe the screen and press a button, buzzing the kid up. "And listen, I'm not anti-women. I'm just... anti-that." I say with a nod to the screen. "Someone who will be whatever pawn they need to be to get ahead. And considering I've been up close and personal with women like that my whole life, I know what to look for. That woman is a fucking puppet if I've ever seen one. Look at her. No one looks that good unless they've grown up with money."

A knock on the door stops my rant. Grumbling under my breath I stride to the door and yank it open.

"Mr. Benson," the freckle-faced kid squeaks. "Your order from Uncle Wong's." Focusing on the receipt, he recites, "A number seven, number six with extra sauce, number three, two number tens, and an order of fried rice."

I nod, digging into the pocket of my black gym shorts. The kid's eyes widen at the hundred-dollar bill I slap in his extended hand. Generous, sure, but it's the smallest bill I have on me.

"Keep the change, kid." I slide the white plastic bags off his arm, tip my head in a silent goodbye, and let the door shut behind me.

A roaring crowd greets my ears over the rustle of plastic as I organize the various Styrofoam to-go containers along the bar. I swipe my tongue along my lower lip, eyeing the food to choose which to start with. I quickly snag the number three box. My muscles pull and ache as I stretch over the bar, dipping my hand low to reach into the drawer that holds my favorite set of porcelain chopsticks.

Positioning the two together, I shovel three pieces of sauce-covered chicken into my mouth before attempting to chew.

"I think you're wrong."

I raise my brows in Tank's direction. "Rarely. But what am I wrong about?"

"About that Randi woman. I think you're wrong. There's something about her, the way she carries herself. I think that's what you're seeing that you think is fake. It's not her background she's faking; it's the person she's trying to be for the DC dipshits."

I stare at my friend, lost for words. Maybe he's right. Doubt it, but maybe. Only time will tell, and it doesn't make any difference if she doesn't win.

"I'm surprised you don't love her for kicking that weasel Shawn Whit off Birmingham's ticket."

A barely chewed piece of chicken lodges in my throat. Coughing, I pound a fist against my chest to dislodge the bit of food. "What?" I croak out.

Tank's dark eyes glide from the TV to meet my own. "You didn't know that little tidbit? Rumor has it your favorite girlfriend stealer was the original choice for Birmingham's VP pick, not that Randi lady. Right before they had to file their registration, boom, it's her name instead of Shawn's. Interesting, right?"

"Very," I say after chugging half the beer to clear my throat. "Wonder what that's about."

Tank shrugs. "See, you don't know everything. Don't go tossing out judgments until you hear it from the source is all I'm saying."

Shawn is as manipulative and underhanded as they come in DC. I would know since we practically grew up together.

I shake off the shiver of apprehension that bolts down my spine. If that Randi Sawyer did knock Shawn off the ticket, she better watch her back. That man will be out for blood if they win. For her sake, I hope it's not true. I know firsthand the joy Shawn gains from watching other people suffer due to his actions. Borderline sociopath if you ask me.

I stare at the congealed sauce at the bottom of the container. Maybe Tank's right. Maybe I am jaded. I'm just over this city and the phonies in it. Everyone doing whatever they can to get ahead. Using, manipulating, lying —nothing is off the table.

After everything I've seen growing up in this fake-ass political circus, how could I not be jaded? This past year hasn't been a breeze either. Is this a good way to live, this bitter version of myself? No, but if I keep my guard up, no one will make me a fool again.

"Yeah," I mutter. Turning, I gaze out the wall of floor-to-ceiling windows, marveling at the soft glow of the Capitol Building. "Doubtful, but maybe. Let's just hope they don't win."

"I've heard she had a few run-ins with protesters. The campaign hired additional security for her."

"Wonder why?" I muse before shoving a warm dumpling into my open mouth.

Eyes glued to the game, Tank shrugs. "No idea. Maybe some people don't like the idea of a woman potentially being in the VP spot, or they don't like the idea of someone outside of the political powerhouse families in the election at all. All I'm saying is if they do get the nod for their party, it could get ugly early."

"Well, that could be fun. Change of pace."

"Fun for who?" He chuckles.

"Us, of course. Even before the demotion, the prior years were boring as shit. Why else do you think I stirred up so much trouble?"

"If I'd known that, I would've given you more to do," Tank mutters under his breath as he strides across the living room, eyes on the food.

"You love me and the entertainment I bring to the table."

He snatches the disposable set of chopsticks I launch at his head right before they smack his face. "Tell yourself whatever you need to make you feel loved."

"That hurts, man," I say with my lips around the top of the beer bottle. I tip it back only to get a few drops of backwash. Disgusting.

"The truth hurts. Speaking of your desperate longing for someone to love you, how are your parents?"

He should be glad I'm not carrying right now. Fucking prick.

"Still disappointed in my life choices and making sure I'm aware of that fact every time I see them. Last week my mom pulled me aside and asked me when I'm going to grow up and get a real job."

"Wow," Tank says around a mouthful of food. "Man, this is good."

I slide off the stool and make my way to the fridge. "Yep. They had the perfect plan for my life before I went and destroyed it. If I'd stayed true to their timeline, I'd be the one running for the president gig, not Birmingham." Swiping a bottle of water and another beer from the fridge, I kick it closed behind me. "His name being all over the news is making it worse. They can't stand that family, even though they're best friends. I know it's killing Mom and Dad both that Kyle is the political poster child, not me."

The stool wobbles on the tile as I sit back down, placing the bottle of water in front of Tank. Lifting the hem of my T-shirt, I wrap my hand in it and twist the cap off the beer.

"Knowing you all these years, I can't imagine you shoved into one of those political figure roles. You'd be like a bull in a china shop."

No doubt. It's why I went into the army after college. Damn, my parents were pissed when they learned I'd signed up without telling them. It pissed them off even more when not even their name—or their money—could change my enlistment. Best decision I ever made, breaking free from their perfect plan. There isn't a doubt in my mind that I would be as miserable as they are if I hadn't.

Not that the past year has been that great, but the others have. And the ones after this one will be. Change is coming; I can almost feel it. The past few weeks, I've been antsy, tense, like I'm waiting for something.

But *what* is the question.

6

RANDI

September

Holding in a shallow breath, I tug back the gold and green embellished curtain, peeking into the ballroom.

Wall-to-wall people dressed to the nines fill the room all laughing and mingling with a thrill of excitement in the air.

After various live debates and the hundreds of speaking engagements throughout the campaign, I'm used to all this. Well, except the pointed, hateful glares from those who deem me unworthy. No matter how many pep talks I give myself in the mirror, those crush the part of me that wants to be accepted.

They don't know me. They think they do because of what our campaign has told them, but they don't. No one out in the crowd knows the person they see in front of them night after night isn't the real Randi Sawyer. No, the real me was polished, waxed, highlighted, and sculpted away. Am I the perfect Politician Barbie? Yes. But not really me.

Not that I miss the five-dollar box dye job or the scratchy secondhand clothes, but I *do* miss having a choice in what I wear and say. For a chance at being more than the trailer park stigma, I gave up control of my life. Now here I am, about to walk on stage with Politician Ken to celebrate our primary win.

Now on to the general election.

I shake my head, dispelling the list that needs to be done and checked off for the next stage of the campaign trail. That prep can wait till tomorrow, because tonight I celebrate this win. In November, my name, Randi fucking Sawyer, will be listed as Kyle Birmingham's running mate on the presidential ballot for the United States of America.

Fucking hell.

Shit, hope I didn't say that out loud.

I cut my eyes left and then right just to be sure I'm alone in case another foul word slips. Per my etiquette teacher, cussing is trashy and unladylike. It was one of the first things they 'cured' me off. Like I had some kind of disease or something. But they can't control my inner thoughts—hell, I can't even control them. That's where I win in the long run. I'm the picture-perfect candidate for Kyle and Shawn, but inside, I'm holding tight to the pieces they're trying to erase. The pieces that make me, me.

I shift from one black stiletto to the other as I take one last look over the crowd. Over a thousand people wait to hear us, but not a single one I know. Taeler wasn't invited, by me, in a precise power move to keep her away from these leeches. The farther she is from this town, away from this corruption, the better.

I smirk.

Shit.

Fuck.

Damn.

Ha, they can't control me. In my head, I imagine raising a fist and shaking it in the air with my middle finger proudly extended. I glance over one shoulder, then the other, and my smile falters. The area surrounding me is vacant, signaling once again that I'm in this alone. Not even a single somewhat friend to laugh with about my crazy imagination.

I let out a slow, resigned sigh and release the curtain, the edge floating back into place.

"We're almost up, Walmart," Kyle says behind me.

I nod and turn back toward the stage to wait for the signal to walk out.

I gasp in a lungful of cologne filled air when something wraps around my waist. Before I can process what's happening, the heels of my stilettos teeter as I'm jerked backward, back slamming against Kyle's hard chest.

"We should properly celebrate after the party, together," he whispers against the shell of my ear.

I cough at the overwhelming smell of his cologne. *Damn, does he bathe in the shit?* "Not a chance," I grit out, shoving his arm down to release his hold on my waist. "Now let me go, you fucking bastard."

I grunt, a puff of air pushing past my lips as he adds pressure around my ribs. I gulp down tiny breaths, desperate for more than his tightening arm allows.

"All those etiquette classes and still that trash mouth of yours." Nose against the sensitive skin of my neck, he inhales. A shiver of disgust racks my shoulders. "You feel this between us. I know you do. We can be enemies and lovers too."

"You're delusional." Desperation shoots through my core, turning my movements frantic. I already dislike touch. Add in this scenario.... Tears, as well as panic, set in. "Let go, Kyle."

"Hmm, I don't think so." He chuckles into my hair. "Keep wiggling that fine ass of yours against my dick, Walmart, and I might not wait until after the party."

I still, the rapid rise and fall of my chest my body's only movement. My eyes dart around the dark backstage area, desperate to locate anyone who will stop this. Movement toward the back corner catches my attention. Locking eyes with the woman with a clipboard in her hands, I open my mouth to beg for help but snap it shut at the shake of her head. A single tear streaks down my cheek as I watch her walk away, leaving me alone with Kyle once again.

"You're acting like you have a choice in this, Walmart." The room spins, my brain barely able to keep up with the quick movement. The buttons of his dress shirt press against the exposed skin of my chest. "It's not a matter of if, but when." Hot breath brushes over my damp cheek. "You're a fool if you think you're anything more than a pawn in our game. I *own* you. I own you, your family, your whole fucking life. Every dollar I've paid wasn't a damn charity. It's a debt. One I will collect on one day soon."

Focusing the building fear into panicked strength, I press both palms against his chest and shove back as hard as I can. A demented smirk spreads across his face as he eases his hold. The unexpected release sends me staggering back, barely regaining my balance before I fall to the floor.

"Now, back to business. We've gotten this far, but we still have the main election to win. And believe me, Walmart, you don't want to find out what will happen if we lose." His cold eyes rake up and down my body, eyeing the curves my snug red dress accentuates. "Do whatever it takes to ensure a win in November. I don't care who you have to bribe, suck off, fuck, or kill. We have to win. It's not just your life depending on it."

My mouth gapes at the insinuation.

He wouldn't. Would he?

"Kyle." My head whips to the side as a suit-clad Shawn appears from the shadowed corner. The earlier light lunch churns in my belly at his evil smirk. "You're up."

"Right," Kyle acknowledges, shifting his hungry eyes from me with a long breath. "We're up. Let's go."

I scowl at Shawn as Kyle takes his sweet-ass time to adjust his suit jacket and smooth down his tie. A bright fake smile, one I've become very familiar with the last several months, spreads up Kyle's cheeks before he steps out onto the stage, waving.

"Why didn't you stop that?" I say, anger and confusion hardening my tone.

Shawn's smile falls. "I cannot believe someone as stupid as you took my spot on the ticket. You think I give a fuck what he does to you, Trailer? We own you from now until you lose or you're dead, and honestly, I fucking hope it's the latter. You don't deserve to be here, breathe the same air as us. I've worked my whole damn life for this shot, and you took it from me. You will pay."

The crowd behind the curtain roars in excitement at something Kyle said onstage. They're none the wiser about what's going on backstage—not that they would care or do anything to stop Shawn's threats.

My heart plummets, stomach rolling. I seal my hand over my mouth to hold back the bile rising in my throat. I shove around him and race to the bathroom. The door barely snickers shut before I vomit into the sink. My arms tremble under my weight, the white porcelain sink cool beneath my clammy palms. His words shouldn't rock me that much; the subtle threats are nothing new. The past few months he's done nothing but taunt and torture me with his words.

They know I'm trapped. *I* know I'm trapped, their caged plaything they enjoy tormenting. Everything I was promised, everything they've done to this point, adds to my gilded prison, locking me into doing their daily bidding. But tonight Kyle changed the game, stepped over the invisible line they've toed the past several months by touching me. Not that it changes anything. I'm still bound to them until this is done, and no one would care if I spoke up about their terrible treatment. Plus, it's not like my life didn't prepare me for this. At least now I'm beautifully dressed, have a sweet-ass condo, and more spending money than I can imagine in exchange for the daily torment; in the past, it came free to the bully.

I scan my reflection in the nearby mirror, carefully using the image to wipe away the smeared black mascara lines striping my cheek from the earlier tears. Shawn's threats, Kyle's advances. I have to see this through like I've done my whole life.

Prepare, plan, and push forward. This is my checklist, what will help me survive the next few months and next four years if we win. No, not if—*when* we win. I can't go back home now, a failure. No, I'll put up with their shit, and we will win.

I've accomplished everything I've set my mind to doing, and this is no different.

Graduating on time as a teen mom at the top of the class. Check.

Get into University of Texas. Check.

Score high on the LSAT for top law schools to take notice. Check.

Convince Harvard to offer me more grants and scholarships than anyone before. Check.

This is simply another hurdle in life. Win the election, no matter the cost, so Kyle doesn't kill me and hide the body, and don't let him touch me. Oh, and watch my back for when Shawn is there, eager to plunge a knife in when I'm not looking.

This would be easier if I had someone to confide in, someone to trust. But finding that someone in this town won't happen.

I'll tackle this like every other hurdle I've met in my life.

All on my own.

BEFORE THE BLACK limo's door shuts, I toe off one black Louboutin and then the other, the shoes clattering to the floorboard. An unladylike groan pushes past my lips as I wiggle my toes in their newfound freedom. Beautiful shoes, comfortable too, until hour four of standing in them. I didn't pick them out, or the beautiful dress I'm wearing. All my outfits and clothes are coordinated by my wardrobe consultants. Who knew that's a real job.

I don't glance back as the car smoothly pulls from the curb, easing into the constant traffic. I'll get an earful tomorrow from the campaign manager for leaving early, but I don't care. The cool, soft leather seeps through the back of my dress as I lean back, inhaling deeply for the first time all night. Pressing the heels of both hands to my cheeks, I massage the ache away. Holding that wide fake smile all night burned some serious calories. Head thumping back against the headrest, I allow my eyes to close.

The edges of my lips dip as I recall the night's events. My dress was gorgeous, shoes perfection, makeup and hair flawless—and still no one paid me any attention. Not that I wanted to fake chitchat with people I don't know, but feeling like you have the plague isn't the best way to spend an evening either.

Blowing out a slow breath, I relax my tense muscles. It's irrational that in this limo, alone, the suffocating weight of loneliness is less than earlier in a room filled to the brim with people.

The revving of a car engine draws my attention out the window. I gasp, hands slapping the seat for support. Glass shatters as metal against metal screeches through the night. I sail through the air, my head smacking the opposite window. The world spins, my thoughts fuzzy.

Blinking through the pain radiating through my scalp and shoulder, I open my mouth to shout for help.

I don't get the chance.

Another impact, this time from behind, rockets me forward. A scream scratches its way up my throat, but the screeching of rubber against asphalt gobbles up the sound.

Warm liquid trickles over my upper lip, building along the seam before seeping in between.

Demanding shouts call outside the destroyed limo, barely audible over the sharp ringing in my ears. I give my head a small shake, immediately regretting the movement as pain flares unbidden. My throbbing head gripped between my palms, I give it a hard press to prevent it from exploding from the building pressure.

More glass shatters, fragments scratching down my back.

The voices grow louder. Shock takes over all rational thought. Curling into the fetal position, I cover both ears to keep them from rupturing at the blaring sounds.

What the hell is going on?

Forcing my eyes open, I blink several times. Blocks of light from the streetlights seep through the shattered windows. Shadows shift outside, their inky figures skirting across the seat and floorboard.

I hiss through clenched teeth as I move across the floorboard toward the still-intact door. Everything pulses with sharp, breath-catching pain. Shards of glass slice at my knees and palms, but still I continue toward freedom.

The putrid scent of burning rubber wafts through the destroyed passenger compartment.

"Fuck," I wheeze. Lunging for the door, I grip the handle and shove.

It doesn't budge. A stronger waft of smoke fuels my frantic attempt at escape.

I will *not* burn to death in this fucking limo. Nope. Light breaks through the darkness, the grind of metal against metal piercing my sensitive ears.

A head pops through the now-open door. "Ma'am, we need to get you out of here."

Relief swells in my chest, calming my stroke-level pulse at the authoritative male voice.

I'm getting out of here. Today is not my death day. Whew.

"No shit." Okay, apparently near-death experiences shift the real Randi back into the driver seat of my mouth.

He dips farther through the door into the tattered interior, a hint of a smirk shining on his face. "Now," he commands.

I eagerly accept his extended hand. Calluses scrape along my palm as our hands slide together.

"So bossy," I grumble. I scoot across the leather, careful to not pierce my ass with the broken window bits. At the door, he snakes an arm around my waist and hoists me into the air.

My eyes dart around, taking in the flashing lights and utter chaos. A crowd with flashing cameras shouts from behind a line of suited men while another group on the other side of the street jerks handmade signs in the air, their faces contorted in anger.

"What... what the hell happened?" I ask, confusion filling my soft tone. He takes several long strides away from the limo with me still pressed tightly to his hard chest. "What are you're doing? I can walk."

"The glass, ma'am. You're not wearing shoes."

Okay, he has a point, but still, he could've asked.

I shift my focus from the crowds toward the direction he's headed. The bright lights of my condo building's overhang blare through the night across the block. At his back, lights continue to flash, red and blue beams like a colorful strobe light coming from the few police cars.

"Get her inside," says a deep, masculine voice. I peer over my hero's shoulder, and my eyes widen. The man is a fucking tank. The light reflects off his smooth bald head, shadows contouring to highlight his bulky frame. His dark eyes scan the area over and over again.

"Oh really," says the man holding me. "You don't say. Can't believe we let these fuckers slip through. We've gotten rusty sitting on the sidelines."

Despite the circumstances, a smile tugs at my lips.

"Not the time or place, Benson," the big guy says. "A doctor will be up in five."

"Where were those rent-a-cops she's had on her?"

"Not sure. Working on it." The big man presses two fingers to his ear. "On my way." His narrowed eyes meet mine before flicking to the man cradling me in his arms. "Just get her inside. We'll figure the rest out after we're secure."

Even with the man's quick steps, rushing us toward the glass doors of the condo lobby, his tight hold keeps me snug against his chest, preventing any jostling. Leaning back a bit to look over his shoulder, I sweep the area until I find the limo.

"What the...?" I whisper to myself as I scan the wreckage. The damage centers around the passenger compartment, the driver side unharmed except for where it nailed a light pole. "This is getting out of hand."

The man's annoyed huff pulls my gaze from the totaled limo to his face, and I take in every handsome detail. Light brown eyes rapidly scan our surroundings. Straight nose, nostrils flaring with each heavy breath. A full bottom lip presses tight against a thinner upper one, the soft pink color draining, leaving the inside edges white. Happy wrinkles crease his cheeks and the edges of his eyes from years of smiling. Naturally unblemished tan skin and silky, dark chocolate floppy hair accentuate his overall appeal. Attractive in a happy, mischievous way.

I lower my scrutinizing gaze to a dress shirt, tie, and suit jacket.

All the pieces snap together.

Of course they're Secret Service. I'm grateful for their presence tonight, but now that they're here, it means they're here to stay until the general election in November. Two whole months. I begged the previous security detail to keep their distance, allowing some semblance of privacy. There's no way I'll convince these guys of the same. They're hard core.

Those honey brown eyes pause their scan to meet mine.

I attempt a convincing smile, but a sharp pain slices through my head, turning it into a grimace.

"Knew you'd be full of drama," he mutters under his breath, which happens to be by my ear, as we step through an open door into the lobby. "You politicians will do anything for publicity."

Seriously? Him fucking too?

I'm so damn tired of people thinking they know me based on what they see. I thought being here, looking like this, changing my background would make people see me as an equal. But instead it's another set of judgments, different stigma for people to assume.

How do I change someone's perspective if they assume who I am instead of learning for themselves? If people continue to tell me who I am based on what they see, why should I keep fighting to prove them wrong?

7

RANDI

"I said I'm fine," I say with a sigh as the doctor sticks a metal contraption inside my ears. "My head hurts, my palms sting from the cuts, but that's it."

"You're not fine," the woman says again. The same words have been exchanged several times over the past hour. "Considering I'm the one with a medical degree in this room, we'll stick with *my* assessment over yours."

"Whatever," I grumble and lie back on the soft bedding, my legs dangling over the end. I nibble on the bright red-painted nail of my middle finger.

On the other side of the bedroom door, distorted male voices draw my attention. No one has mentioned anything regarding the wreck, which is fucking irritating. Add in my pounding head, which Miss 'I'm right because I have a medical degree' diagnosed as a mild concussion, and I'm on the sharp edge between holding it together and losing my ever-loving shit.

"Someone will need to wake you up every few hours tonight," the woman says more to the tablet in her hand than me. "Do you have someone?"

"No, it's just me."

Her gaze slowly rises from the screen, brow arched. "What about Mr. Birmingham? When will he be by?"

Fire ignites my blood, and I harden my features, narrowing my eyes into menacing glare. "He won't come by because he doesn't live here."

"Sorry, I just assumed...."

Of course that's what she assumed since the media has spewed tidbits about our fake relationship across every news channel. This is the part I hate the most about the lies we leaked to the press.

"Your assumption is wrong." Elbow digging into the duvet, I push myself up. I squint as the doctor splits, morphing into two people. "Doc, did you happen to clone yourself in the last two seconds?"

Both doctors frown. "Upgrading that concussion to severe."

When the two doctors mold back into one, I sit up straight on the bed. "When will someone update me on tonight?"

"As soon as we're done."

I flick my gaze to the closed door. "Then we're done. Leave a list of what I need to do tonight for the concussion, and I'll set my alarm."

"You really need someone to—"

"Well, lady," I say, pushing off the bed to stand. Tightening the sash of my long-sleeve terry cloth robe, I step toward the door. "I'm used to doing this thing called life on my own, so I'll figure it out." At the door, I turn the brass knob and pull it open. I wave a hand through the air, gesturing out the door with a smile. "Thank you for your help tonight. Contact my admin for payment." Because on top of the wardrobe coordinators, I also employ an admin to handle bills, flights, personal errands, and who knows what else.

With a huff, she storms out of the room. Without looking into the craziness of the living room, I slam the door shut behind the doctor and lean against it. A few bruises, cuts, and a concussion aren't too bad considering my end of the limo was crushed.

I chew on a manicured nail as I shuffle toward the en suite bathroom. For an additional layer of protection against... everyone, I lock the bathroom door behind me. The marble vanity digs against my lower belly as I lean closer to the mirror, inspecting the wounds for myself.

I tilt my head one way and then the other. The image follows. It's me— I'm not that crazy—but the woman staring back at me doesn't look like me.

The woman in the mirror strongly resembles a brunette Lindsay Lohan mug shot after an all-night bender.

Not good.

I tilt my chin down, hoping for a better angle.

Nope. Zero good angles.

I slide the multiple temporary extensions from my hair and lay them carefully on the sink. I stroke each piece, smoothing it out before pulling another free. With the final section out, I ruffle my real hair and sigh in relief. They make my hair full and beautiful but hurt after a full day of wearing so many.

Soap bubbles collect around the drain as I remove the grime from the wreck and a thousand handshakes from my hands. Pressing closer to the mirror, I widen one eye and then the other, removing the green-tinted contacts. It's nice not having to wear glasses, but the color enhancement to change my hazel to brilliant green is overboard if you ask me.

Not that anyone did.

Oh no, not once was I consulted on any of these 'enhancements.' Most days I don't recognize the beautiful woman staring back at me in the mirror. After several somewhat painful laser treatments, brown spots from years of sun damage and bad skin vanished. A little bit of lip plump here, some Botox there, a billion chemical peels, and months of Invisalign later, I'm this. Beautiful by some people's standards, a far cry from the haggard look I started with. The woman in the mirror would've been a part of the popular crowd in high school, not the weird one who ended up getting pregnant in the back seat of her boyfriend's parents' van.

Do I miss basic Randi 1.0? Yes and no. I enjoy feeling beautiful and the new attention from men, but with Randi 2.0 comes obligations and strings attached. All this and still it's not enough to be accepted in this city or back home, where people are waiting for me to fail.

Ugh. I rest my elbow on the vanity and cover my face with both hands to stop me from staring at my reflection. The condo, the makeover, the money —all for a chance to prove myself.

The intense throb in my head distracts me from the deep life thoughts I was falling into. I wince with each step to the shower. The large glass door whooshes open with a soft tug. Stretching, I twist the handle all the way right to steaming hot. Slow fingers release the sash knot and the robe parts, exposing me to the empty bathroom. I hiss through the soreness as I lift both shoulders, shrugging the soft material to pool on the heated tile floor. Initial pelts of steaming spray against the multitude of thin cuts cause bites of stinging pain along my battered skin.

I lean back, the cool tile sending a chill down my spine. A wave of homesickness barrels through me from the contradicting temperatures of the water and tile, the battle of the two similar to warm Texas spring days soaked in a cold rain shower.

Alone in the quiet, the steam wrapped around me like a security blanket, I replay the scene from earlier. Bile rises, pushing up my throat. My head screams as I pitch forward, palms slapping the opposite wall for support, and puke up the miniature hors d'oeuvres from the party.

Fuck, what will I do? Can I really expect to avoid being alone with Kyle for the next few months—or worse, four years if we win? There must be something to protect myself, but what? I'm weak. I'll own up to that. These narrow hips and soft arms didn't get their 'character' by hitting the gym, that's for sure.

I need a plan.

And mace.

Perhaps a stun gun too. Shooting those cords and electrifying Kyle's balls seems like a decent quid pro quo after his manhandling tonight. Eyes to the ceiling, I chant the words 'mace' and 'stun gun' three times to commit them to memory. This way I'll remember to add both to the Amazon cart after this glorious shower.

A sharp knock at the door sounds as I'm still weapons planning. With the pad of my thumb, I clear two small circles in the fogged glass door to clearly see through.

The door opens an inch or two, but no one steps through.

"Ma'am," a male voice calls out. "Everything okay in there?"

"Checking to make sure I cleaned behind the ears? Didn't realize that was in your job description," I mutter just loud enough for the guy on the other side of the door to hear.

"The doctor said we needed to check on you every hour."

I roll my eyes before sticking my hair under the water. "Okay, now she's just trying to piss me off. She told me every couple of hours." I attack my thick dark hair with ferocity, making layers and layers of cherry almond scented suds build along my scalp and cascade down my back. "But as you can see, or hear rather, I'm fine. Just trying to get the stench of almost-death off me."

"Ma'am?"

"What happened tonight?"

If we were in Texas, crickets would chirp in the blatant silence.

"Also, your daughter is on the phone, saying she won't hang up until she talks to you."

"What?" I growl and slam my palm against the faucet handle, cutting off the stream of water. "Why didn't you start with that?" Channeling all my anger into my movements, I snatch a towel off the nearby hook and scrub at the streams of water cascading down my body. Towel wrapped around my chest, I pause. "Wait, why did she call you?"

"She didn't, ma'am. She called your cell phone several times. By the twentieth or so missed call, we answered."

"That could've been China calling!" I yell. Okay, maybe I see how Ben believes Taeler inherited her dramatics from me.

The man on the other side of the cracked door clears his throat. "Her name was on the caller ID, and a picture of you two flashed on the screen as well, ma'am."

Hmm. Didn't think about that one.

"Good point. Still could've been China. They're sneaky little bastards. Or someone calling to tell me I was left a million dollars by a distant relative and I need to send them my social and bank account information." I chuckle to myself. I really am hilarious. Too bad either no one is around to hear me or doesn't get the brilliance of my jokes.

"I would advise against that, ma'am. Sounds fishy."

"No shit, Sherlock," I mumble under my breath as I press the length of my hair between a dry towel to remove excess water. Once again donned in the robe from earlier, I swipe my thick-frame glasses off the counter and yank the door open.

I eye the young man I've been talking to. His eyes flick from mine to the door leading to the living room and back again.

"Are you a super genius or something?" I ask, head cocked to the side as my eyes scan his baby face.

The boy's light blond brows furrow. "Ma'am?"

"How old are you? I'm guessing twenty. Did you just graduate from Secret Service school or something?" Not that I want these guys hanging around every second, but if I have to endure them, I'd prefer guys who are old enough to need a shave once a week.

Pops of crimson dot his cheeks as he shifts from one foot to the other, avoiding eye contact.

Well hell. I've embarrassed him. Sweet kid.

I hold out a hand, awkwardly patting his shoulder. "Sorry, that was rude. You're old enough, and cute." I leave off 'I could be your mom.'

"Now this I'm surprised about."

Junior and I turn to the voice on the other side of the room. I scowl at the man I recognize leaning against the far wall. He's the one who pulled me out of the town car and carried me inside. Damn, he's hot. Earlier, with my fuzzy vision and shock, I thought he was attractive, but here in my room? Attractive doesn't even count. On a scale of one to ten, he's a nine working his way to an eleven if he can grow a quick man bun. And old, thank goodness, unlike Junior here. Shit, not old. He's like my age.

"I'm not old, dammit," I mutter.

The two men exchange a quick look.

"Ma'am?" Junior asks.

I wave a hand through the air, dismissing him. "Sorry, wrong conversation."

"Did I miss something?" asks the hot, annoying one. I swear his light brown eyes fucking twinkle. *Twinkle.* Is he part unicorn or something?

"What are you surprised about?" I shoot back, relenting in our sudden stare-off.

He pushes off the wall to stalk closer. Why does he have to be such an asshole? In the baking of men, can the two ingredients hot and a nice guy not mix together or something? Even with the asshole factor, I'm drawn to him. Maybe the doc's diagnosis of a concussion is legit.

"That you'd be interested in a no one like Grem here."

My lips curve upward, matching his smirk, before my eyes track back to the Grem fellow.

"Grem, as in the Grim Reaper? You kill a lot of people or something?"

Grem chokes back a cough, whereas the hot one chuckles. "Grem, as in short for Gremlin. The kid hates the water."

"Funny. Can't wait to hear that story." I hold out my hand. "Now, give me my phone, please."

Gremlin drops the phone into my palm, avoiding skin-to-skin contact. His gaze darts from the hot guy back to me before he turns on his heels.

"Thanks," I mutter to his back as he fast-walks out of the bedroom. With a deep calming breath, I lift the cell phone to my ear. "Tae?"

"Mom! What the fuck happened to you?" I pull the phone from my ear with a cringe. The doctor did mention something about loud noises doing more damage. I think. Wasn't really listening, actually.

"Taeler Lynn, do not use that fucking language with me, dammit," I bite back. College has taught her the worst manners, I fucking swear.

Movement across the room catches my eye, reminding me I'm not alone. His lips curve in a sexy, mischievous smirk that flips my insides and warms the space between my thighs. Those brown eyes shine with amusement, his fine smile lines crinkling.

I wince at Taeler's continued high-pitched rampage on the other end. He takes a step forward, smirk gone.

"Wait," My shaky voice is barely loud enough for Taeler to hear. "Calm the hell down, Tae. My head is killing me, and your yelling is making it worse. Concussions are the worst. I wouldn't recommend ever getting one."

"Sorry, Mom, I'm just—wait, what the hell? Concussion?" A slight tremble resonates in her tone. For the second time tonight, tears build, but this time they're due to her worry instead of fear. "Mom, what happened? Tell me, please. I'm worried out of my mind over here. Do I need to fly up? I'm sure I can miss classes if you need me."

A magnetic pull draws my gaze back to the agent. "No, sweetheart, you don't need to fly up here. Everything is okay. It's being handled by the Secret Service as we speak." *Wait a second.* Careful to not make any sudden movements, I ease onto the edge of the bed and lie back. "Taeler, how did you even know something happened tonight?"

Her sigh sounds through the phone. At least she's calmed down a little. "You're all over the news. Whatever happened tonight is covered on every news channel. It's a big deal, Mom. You're a big deal now. Congratulations, by the way."

"Thanks," I mutter. "I still can't believe it." Securing the phone between my ear and shoulder, I roll to my side and swipe the remote off the side table. It clatters back onto the solid wood after I hit the Power button. No need to change the channel, since I monitored the big network news channels all morning as the votes were tallied. The large flat-screen TV snaps to life. Bright flashes from other cameras disorient the image, but the entrance to my condo building is unmistakable. Black Suburbans dot the area, along with several police cars and one fire truck. The woman on the screen waves a frantic hand behind her while talking to the camera.

"Watching now," I say more to myself than Taeler. On the other end of the line, Taeler talks a thousand words a second, demanding answers and threatening to fly up here, but all I can focus on is the footage on the screen. "Listen, Tae, I love you, but I don't know what to tell you. The Secret Service is here now and I'm safe, promise. I'll call you as soon as I know something. Love you." After a teary goodbye, the line goes dead.

Eyes still glued to the TV, I say, "Fill me in. Now."

"The investigation is ongoing. We don't know what happened," the hot agent says. You'd think his words would agitate me more, but the concern with a hint of frustration in his voice is soothing. "Not a well-thought-out plan, but still, whoever did this probably thought they could scare you out of continuing on to the general election."

"Up till this point, it's been protesters, a few things tossed on stage or toward me during a rally. Nothing violent. Whoever is behind this upped their game tonight." I tear my focus from the TV and attempt a smile. "Convenient that you and your friends were already here though. Thank you. I really didn't want to die tonight."

"Agents, not friends. And we were already here prepared to receive you after the party. I talked to the team lead while you were with the doc, and it seems there was some kind of communication breakdown. We were told the security team who's been with you up till this point would hand you off here at the condo. Instead, most were dismissed earlier today, and then the final few were told they were done after the party."

"Is my concussed brain confused or does that sound fishy? Do I have to keep you? The team, that is."

"Yes, ma'am. We're here to stay."

The room goes fuzzy as my eyes struggle to maintain focus. The daunting weight of the entire night's events settles on my shoulders. Exhaustion swoops in, draining the last bit of energy reserve I have left.

"I think I need a quick nap," I murmur. The bed dips under my hands and knees as I crawl up to the top but collapse before I can slide between the sheets.

"That's not a great decision."

"Just a few minutes, Trouble," I say on a yawn. Damn, I'm tired. The past few months—hell, few years—feel like they've finally caught up with me.

"Trouble?"

I smile into the pillow at the confusion in his voice. Maybe having these guys around won't be so bad after all.

"I can see it," I say and snuggle deeper into the soft bed. "You're trouble. I just know it. But don't worry. So am I."

He mutters something I can't make out, but I don't care. Just a few minutes of sleep; then I'll be good to go.

The last thought that slips through my mind before oblivion sinks in is the hope that he's still here when I wake up.

8

———————

TREY

A swirl of conflicting emotions and indecipherable thoughts floods through my mind. What in the hell happened during the last hour? My gaze wanders up and down her robed body, inspecting each inch, hoping to find the sign to help me understand her. To say I was floored when she stepped out of the bathroom earlier is an understatement. Curled on her side, the potential VP's breathing evens out, and her shoulders relax further into the mattress. During the primaries and televised debates, she seemed plastic, too perfect. But the woman lightly snoring on the bed is the definition of *real* perfection. The no makeup, wet hair, and glasses look is one most women wouldn't dare pull off even in the privacy of their own home.

But not this woman, this Randi lady.

I narrow my eyes on her relaxed face, skimming down to focus on her slightly parted plump lips.

"What in the hell do you think you're doing?" Tank whisper-yells from the doorway.

I jolt like I've been caught doing something inappropriate, and my gaze flicks to the floor. "Nothing. She fell asleep. Just monitoring her like that doc told us to."

I glance over to Tank, whose eyes are on sleeping beauty. She mutters something unintelligible and rolls to lie on her back. I look back to her, trying and failing not to notice the bare skin of her toned calves.

Tank clears his throat, dragging my attention back to him.

"You want me to take over?" he asks.

I wave a hand, declining his offer. "I'm good." Nodding to the soft armchair in the corner, I say, "I'll wake her up in an hour."

Tank's large bald head tilts to the side. Shit, I know that look.

"Odd, don't you think?" he muses. "Earlier tonight, you were complaining about this gig, and now here you are offering to watch while she sleeps."

My shoulders rise and fall in an exaggerated shrug. "Just doing my job, you nosy shit. Nothing else."

"Right." He drags out the word, making it clear he doesn't believe me. "We're in the next room piecing shit together. Let me know if you need me."

I track him until his back disappears through the door and it clicks shut behind him. Like a magnet drawn to metal, my eyes shift back to the woman on the bed. I startle when they meet her half-open hazel ones.

"You wouldn't happen to have any water on you, would you?" she whispers like every word hurts.

I nod and point to her side table. "Bottle is beside you, along with some meds the doctor approved you to take for the headache."

"Headache doesn't even begin to describe the death metal concert going on up there." A pained gasp pushes past her lips at her attempt to sit up. "Fucking hell." She groans before giving up on her water quest and lowering back to the bed. "It's like the worst hangover ever but without all the fun and poor decisions from the night before."

I open my mouth to say something sarcastic, but her wide eyes flick to mine just as a slight green tint washes over her face.

"Shit," I grumble. I race to the bathroom, my steps pounding against the soft carpet. I skid to a stop along the tile and grab the first trash can I lay my eyes on. Emerging from the bathroom, I lunge for the side of the bed just as she leans over and vomits.

"You should've left me in the damn car." Another wave of nausea causes her to curl into a tight ball as she dry heaves into the metal bin. Tears streak down her pale face, drawing attention to the light scattering of freckles that adorn the skin along her cheekbones.

All my smartass remarks—hell, even my annoyance at the woman, which has grown every day since she first appeared in DC—evaporate at her weak state. The metal of the bin digs into my fingers as I adjust my grip to hold it in one hand. With the other, I gather her long dark hair into a tight bundle at the nape of her neck to keep it away from her face.

After a few more heaves into the bin, she waves a weak hand and falls back into the pillows. Sweat glistens on her forehead, and a pain-laced grimace scrunches her features. I set the metal can beside the door to take out later and return to the bathroom to find a towel.

Her eyes are closed when I return but flutter open when I place the cool, wet washcloth along her forehead. For a minute, we stay in the cocoon of comfortable silence. Something in her eyes pounds at the thick walls I've built, telling me to reconsider my prejudgment of her. Before I fall further under her spell, I step back from the bed, snagging the bottle of water off the nightstand.

"Here." I crack the seal and hold it out over the bed.

"Thanks." The slight tremble in her hand as she reaches for the bottle doesn't go unnoticed.

What the hell am I doing? I roll my eyes at the concern and worry building in my chest, constricting my airway. She's fine, or she will be. Why the hell do I care anyway? She's the job, and she's with that fucktard Birmingham. She's just like them, all of them, and that's why I have to keep my distance. Even if she is beautiful. And somehow funny while in pain.

"Anything new about tonight?" she mumbles after a long, deep gulp from the bottle.

"Small sips or you'll get sick again. And try to sit up more." Her hazel eyes flick to mine, and a confused look lashes across her face. "No, I haven't heard anything new. I've been in here since you passed out on me."

Her dramatic eye roll looks painful. "I didn't pass out. I rested my eyes for a few minutes. It's been a long night okay."

"Nothing like almost getting killed to ruin an evening," I say dryly.

"Right," she groans in agreement. "Not that the party was any better. What a waste of money." Turning on her side, she tucks the edges of the robe together, covering almost every inch of her legs, and snuggles deeper into the pillow. "What's up with the small food at those things? Is it not okay to eat anymore?"

"What?"

"I mean, I had to eat like a hundred balls to—"

"Balls?" I raise my dark brows in question while attempting to hold back the laugh that wants to erupt. "You ate a hundred balls? Busy night." This time I don't mask my smirk.

Her eyes narrow before widening. "Didn't expect that."

I sink into the armchair opposite the bed. "Expect what, exactly?"

"You being funny. You seem more like a jackass with a chip on his shoulder." A sly smile tugs at the corner of her lips. She knows she's testing me, and for some reason, I'm enjoying it.

"And you seem more like a power-hungry political lackey who's willing to do anything, or anyone, to get what you want."

"I'm no one's lackey," she grits out, all humor fading into resentment.

Huh, that's the part she points out. Interesting. "Sure you aren't, puppet."

"We're done here. My head hurts," she deadpans, never dropping my gaze. Shit, if her gorgeous eyes could throw daggers, I'd be dead. "Leave. Now."

The soft fabric of the chair presses into my palms as I push against the armrests to stand. After fixing my suit jacket, I tuck both hands into my pants pockets and return her hate-filled stare.

"Don't think you can fool me, sweetheart. I see right through you."

"Might want to get your eyes checked, asshat." The edge of her left lip curls up in a snarl, but even still, she's a knockout. "But it's a good thing I don't give two shits what you or any of your little buddies out there think because—"

"Everything okay in here?" Tank's deep voice booms through the room, cutting the tight tension in the air.

Eyes still locked on mine, both of us vying for dominance, she hitches her chin. "Besides my pounding head, nausea worse than morning sickness, and this jackass pissing me off, yeah, it's just sunshine and unicorns in here."

I stifle a smirk as Tank covers his laugh with a fake cough.

"Right. Um, the nausea the doc said to expect that from the concussion, but you mentioned morning sickness. Any chance you're also...."

"Also what?"

I breathe a sigh of relief when her annoyed gaze slides to Tank. Shit, that woman can hold her own.

"Pregnant, ma'am."

An undignified snort echoes through the room. I chuckle with a shake of my head in disbelief. Who in the hell is this woman?

"No, absolutely not. You have to have sex for that to happen, if you believe my seventh-grade sex ed teacher."

My eyes meet Tank's, both of us clearly confused.

"Not that it did Mary any good, am I right?" she says with another snort. "Damn, I miss sex. Even boring, handsy sex would do at this point."

"Um... uh...," Tank stammers.

I bark out a quick loud laugh as his dark skin glows with a red tint.

"Not with you, Terminator. I see that ring on your finger. It's the first thing I noticed, that and your pretty shiny head and muscles." Her mouth stretches with a wide yawn. "And not Trouble either, unless he agrees to wear a ball gag."

"The fuck?" I say on a pushed breath.

"Night night, ladies," she mutters into her pillow as her eyes close. "I'm not good at this sleepover stuff, but next time I need wine and *Golden Girls*. 'Kay? 'Kay."

The second the last word is out, her body relaxes as she passes out cold.

I shake my head, completely dumbfounded, as Tank and I exit the room. We leave the door open a sliver to make sure we can hear her if she wakes up again.

"What in the ever-loving hell was that?" Tank asks, eyes wide in shock. "I couldn't keep up with the conversation, could you?"

"Barely. Did she call us ladies and say we were having a sleepover?" The wall shudders when my back slams against it. I pinch the bridge of my nose in an attempt to ease the pressure building behind my eyes. "How in the hell is she potentially our next VP?"

"She called me Terminator." A hint of awe clouds his tone, making me look across the room to where he's perched on a barstool.

The rest of the team ignores us as they type away on laptops and phones. I survey the room. Gremlin is nowhere to be found. Must be stationed in the hall.

"What was that about needing sex?" That gets the guys' attention. The low murmur and clicking of keys from earlier halt.

"Is there a signup sheet?" Champ offers from where he sits on the floor, laptop balanced on his knees. "I don't care if she is his sloppy seconds."

A collective growl vibrates through the room at the mention of him. No one except Shawn is more conniving, degrading, and overall a fucking bastard than Kyle Birmingham.

"No signup sheet," Tank barks. All humor melts from the room. "She hit her head, probably had no idea what in the hell she was saying. It's business as usual for us. We learn as much as we can about the attack tonight, and we do our job. You will respect her, you will protect her, and you will treat her like every other man that has come before her. Nothing changes. Got it?"

A resounding "Yes, sir" rumbles through the small room.

A drop of guilt settles in my gut. No way in hell is this business as usual. I will respect her, I will protect her, but treat her like every old fart who's been under our protection? Not a chance. First of all, I never had to deep breathe to stay focused on the job instead of their legs or had the urge to verbally spar with one just to hear what they'd say next.

No, this time it's different.

Hell, maybe I'm even different.

Maybe—

The door flies open, slamming against the wall and cutting off my thoughts. Tension consumes the room as Birmingham steps over the threshold. His cold eyes sweep across the team before settling on me. A condescending smirk rises up his prick face.

"Didn't see you with your parents tonight at the party."

I shrug, faking casualness when all I really want is to punch the slimy smirk off his Botoxed face. "Working."

"Ah, that's right. Sometimes I forget where you landed after you couldn't take the pressure of the game."

"Whatever you want to tell yourself, asshole."

The entire team snickers. I watch with pure joy and fascination as the tips of Kyle's ears redden.

"Show some respect, or I'll try you for treason after I win," he seethes. "Or maybe I'll torture you with the entertaining sex tapes Shawn and—"

Without thinking of the consequences, I lunge. Two anaconda arms wrap around my chest, hauling me backward before my swing can connect.

Rage burns through my veins, igniting my skin. With an arrogant laugh, he saunters to the bedroom door. Hand on the knob, he turns back to face me, his features hardening to stone.

"I've fucked that tight pussy so many times my dick is imprinted in her cunt. She's mine, so don't even think about touching my new favorite toy."

Fists at my side, I clench them tight and seal my lips to keep from responding.

"Good boy. And they say old dogs can't learn new tricks." He shoves the door open and steps into the bedroom.

Staring at the now closed door, I inhale a deep breath, mentally erasing every fucking emotion that woman conjured in me tonight. I erase the idea of thinking she's different than every woman I've ever met. A fucking liar. I should've known.

Turning, I yank open the front door. Gripping Gremlin's collar, I pull him into the condo and slam the door shut, leaving me alone in the hallway. Hands on my knees, I take several deep breaths, evening out my pulse and diminishing the boiling anger.

But hours later the bitter taste of disappointment hasn't faded.

9

RANDI

A cold, fear-laced shiver pulls me from a light sleep. Eyes closed, I wrap both arms around my chest to fend off the uneasy energy that's settled over my room. Something icy wraps around my ankle, slowly sliding my heel across the duvet, putting distance between it and the other. Behind my closed lids, my eyes twitch. The steady pulse in my head makes it impossible to gather enough energy to open my eyes.

"Get up, Walmart," a familiar deep voice says, cutting the ties the darkness had over me.

With a gasp, I bolt upright, eyes frantically searching the room before settling on Kyle at the end of the bed, one hand around my left ankle while he brushes his fingertips up and down my bare calf with the other. Another fear-filled shiver rattles through my body, shaking my shoulders and sending flairs of pain into my brain.

"Kyle," I rasp. Damn, my throat fucking hurts. Without taking my eyes off the pervert, I grapple for the bottle of water on the nightstand. My stiff fingers wrap around the thin plastic, the crackling sound piercing the heavy silence. "What are you doing here?"

"We seem to have a problem, you and I."

The room temperature water slides down my parched throat as I gulp the remnants in the bottle.

"The fact that someone tried to kill me tonight?"

His grip around the ankle tenses, signaling his annoyance. A creepy, sinister smile spreads across his lips. I press up to my elbows, putting my back against the headboard.

"That is unfortunate, but I did warn you this would be dangerous."

"I thought people would make fun of me for using the wrong fork or some shit like that, not try to kill me!"

"Well, now you know. Now, the issue I left my date tied to the bed for."

The soft skin of my palm smacks against my lips in a desperate attempt to keep my stomach contents down.

"TMI, Kyle," my fingers muffling the words.

"Just wait. You'll love it."

"You're sick," I spit back.

"And you're mine, bought and paid for, so it's a moot point. The issue is with your mother."

All annoyance and fear of the predator in the room vanish, leaving a weight of lead in my belly. "My mom? What's wrong with my mom?"

"I got an interesting call tonight from the chief of police in your shit-ass hometown."

The hand still at my mouth mutes my groan.

"Why did they call you? She's *my* mom, dammit. If something's wrong—"

"I pay a lot of hush money to that town to keep shit hidden we don't want public. You'd think you'd be more grateful." Right. Hell, he's so delusional. And this loon is about to be the president. Yay.... Sorry, America. "He didn't charge her. She's waiting in holding for you to come sort her shit out."

"What was it for?" I whisper in disbelief. Which is stupid of me. Of course she's fallen off the wagon even after I paid for those two weeks in rehab.

"Tested positive for meth plus possession, driving while intoxicated, and indecent exposure."

"Nice of her to wrap all that up in one arrest," I say on a fake laugh. "Meth? Never a dull day with that mom of mine."

"Go handle it. Tomorrow. Take the jet, but for fuck's sake, keep it out of the fucking press."

"Okay, go home, sort out Mom, come back. We need to solidify a plan for the next couple months." Mapping out the cities we want to hit in between the debates and other required appearances during the campaign is crucial to gain the votes we'll need to win.

Kyle's returning smirk sparks a warning as bright as a firework finale. "You do that, Walmart. Just handle your shit."

Wisely, I don't move an inch or even breathe too loud as he stands from the bed. After adjusting his jacket and buttoning the top button, he steps for the door. Not wanting to draw attention, I keep my unfocused gaze on the spot he vacated, ignoring his demanding stare. My skin crawls with the awareness of being watched.

"Maybe when you get back, you need a reminder of who's in power here. Because I can guaran—fucking—tee it isn't you, Walmart. Remember that, and maybe you'll survive the next four years."

TEXAS RANGERS BALL cap pulled low and chin tucked tight to my chest, I focus on my ratty Converses slapping on top of the black tarmac. Two sets of men's shoes match my steps on either side as we approach the jet. Thankfully the stairs are already down when we approach, allowing me to take the steps two at a time the moment we near the plane. Inside, I inhale deeply, scanning the partially filled cabin.

Laptop bag snug against my side, I shuffle down the aisle toward a grouping of empty seats. The seat belt clicks shut, and I tug the loose end to tighten it around my lap. Disregarding the final agents filing onboard, I adjust in the seat to stare out the window.

Outside a light fall wind blows through the trees' brightly covered leaves, loosening some with each pass and scattering them to the ground. I tug the edges of my lightweight jacket tighter. It's not cold outside by most northerner's standards, but for this Texas girl, if it's below eighty, a jacket and scarf are needed to survive.

Not that I'll need either where we're headed.

Movement draws my attention from the beautiful fall display. I take in the perfectly tailored pants lingering on the outline of thick thighs before scanning up a narrow waist, broad shoulders, tan neck—wait a second. Why in the hell am I focusing on his neck? Yes, it's kissable. Purely edible, actually.

No.

Stop it, Randi.

You will not lust after this asshole.

But I can't seem to stop myself no matter what asshole thing he does or says. Which is odd, and considering everyone else's odd is my normal, this is the oddest of oddities. Normally once I get a glimpse past the sexy exterior into the arrogant asshole that the man is at the core, I'm uninterested. Not simply turned off but revolted. But not with this agent. Oh no, that would be *way* too convenient.

The fact that I can't stop gravitating to him any time he's close should make me question his true self. Is he truly an asshat at heart or just bitter but has a good heart and soul beneath it all? Right now, with everything else going on around me, I can't dive into that theory. Later. Someday I'll work it out.

Plus, I'm his boss, right? Pretty sure an interoffice relationship is listed somewhere in the top things to avoid. Even though the mental image of us alone in a dark office, me sprawled on top of a disheveled desk with him between—

"Ma'am?"

Trouble's honey brown eyes brighten with humor, crinkling at the edges with a sunburst of lines. Whoops, I'm blatantly staring as I fantasize about an inappropriate work hookup. And I mean hookup, not relationship. Those things are way too touchy-feely for this emotionally unavailable, over-worked, 'too stressed to even remember to eat' girl.

"Sorry, still a little fuzzy, I guess." Clearing my throat, I distract myself by bending forward to rifle through my laptop bag in search of my iPad. "But that's not unusual for me." Fuck, I sound like an idiot.

I swear I'm smart and can rock the VP role if I'm elected. It might be wise to have that printed on a small business card to hand out after I've said something that displays my crazy.

A curse almost slips past my lips when the sexy Secret Service guy settles into the light leather seat across the tiny table that separates us. Not sure why he chose to sit close by, considering this morning he and the rest of the guys, minus Terminator, are acting frigid toward me. Why the mood from last night—tense but casual—shifted to all business, I have no idea. Maybe I said something strange in my sleep or to an agent when he woke me up per the doctor's instructions.

I part my lips and suck in a breath, ready to ask why the cold shoulder, but seal them shut when the captain's voice comes over the speakers, informing us we're cleared for takeoff.

The row shakes, jostling me in my chair, as the massive boulder of a man settles into the seat beside me. Instinct kicks in, pulling me away from Terminator until my right shoulder hits the thick plastic window. A flash of uncertainty crosses his face. Not wanting to hurt the big guy's feelings, I stretch my lips into a tight smile. It's not him I don't want touching me, it's most people. Casual or intimate, it doesn't matter; all of it sets off an internal timer, counting down how long I must endure the contact until I can pull way.

"How's the head?" he asks. His assessing gaze sweeps along my face like he can see through to my injured brain. Sweet man.

"Still hurts, but it's not pounding toward the edge of pulverizing my brain, so that's an improvement."

A corner of his lips tugs up. "That's good. We caught the driver of the truck that caused the accident last night."

That has my full attention. Brows raised, I lean back against the plane and rest my head on the window. "Oh yeah? Has he said anything?"

"Nothing, unfortunately. We've run his name though the various databases, but we can't connect him to any watch list groups."

The building hope deflates in my chest. Blowing out through tight lips, I roll my shoulders and shift my focus from Terminator to the table. Dammit, I can't stop the disappointment from dampening my mood.

"Hey, we'll figure it out." I nod, not glancing up. "I looked over the driver's background. No way was he working alone. Until then, you're safe with us."

A large hand rests on my forearm. As I return my attention back to him, I start my internal countdown till I can move out of his grasp without it offending him. Thankfully he pulls away before the ten-second timer buzzes.

"We're your primary or alpha team. Last night was a shi—" Terminator clears his throat. "Apologies, ma'am—"

I hold up a hand to halt his apology. "Stop. I want to be myself when you and the other agents are around, and I want the same from you. All of you. I'm not some sensitive, stuck-up Washington socialite. You don't have to pussyfoot around me unless we're in public."

The entire plane tenses, the air turning stiff and heavy.

"What?" I ask, letting a hint of annoyance seep into my tone. Terminator doesn't speak up, looking everywhere other than me. I scan the cabin, looking for someone who will explain. "Okay, what is going on?"

"We believe considering your relationship with Birmingham, it's best to keep everything professional, keep the lines clear." There's no mistaking the disdain in Trouble's voice.

What the hell?

I meet his flaring gaze. "My relationship."

"Oh, I'm sorry. Are you just his fuck toy?"

"Benson!" Terminator shouts.

"You know nothing about me," I grit out. Pressing my elbow to the table-top, I lean forward, shortening the distance between me and the judgy prick.

"I know enough."

Instead of launching across the table and wrapping my hands around his neck like I desperately want, I lean back into the seat and cross both arms across my chest. "Oh really? Go on, then, tell me a bit about myself."

His honey brown eyes darken with challenge. "You're nothing more than a pretty political pawn—"

"Aw, you think I'm pretty," I say, batting my eyelashes and pressing a hand to my heart before shooting him the bird. "And side note, I prefer Politician Barbie."

"You'll do anything that fuckstick Birmingham tells you—"

"Enough!" Terminator shouts and pushes up from his seat like he might take a swing at Trouble.

I hold out a hand to stop him. "No, let him get it out. Everyone can see he has a chip on his shoulder the size of Texas and has something to say." I swipe a hand across the table. "Well, here's your chance, Trouble. Get it out of your system now. But I will say we agree on one thing: him being a fuck-stick, not me being his puppet."

"Scheming puppet—"

"Judgmental asshole."

"Fuck, can I finish?" he grits out. Not sure how, considering his teeth and jaw are locked down tight.

"Oh, please continue. This is so interesting. I love learning new awful things about myself."

"You're nothing but a fraud."

Heavy tension settles inside the plane.

Swallowing back the lump lodged in my throat, I swing my gaze to the table, breaking from his hate-filled glare. If looks could kill, I'd be bleeding out all over this fancy plane. "There is a bit of truth in that statement," I whisper, "but not in the way you're thinking."

"Enough," Terminator says in a tight, quiet voice that's more terrifying than his yell. "Benson, you will keep your opinions to yourself and keep your fat-ass mouth shut. Ma'am, I apologize for—"

"I asked for it," I say quickly to stop him. No idea why I egged him on, but I won't play innocent in the argument. It's crazy, but somehow I know he doesn't believe those terrible things about me, not deep down. I know first-hand how people treat me who truly believe what they see is what they get, and Trouble isn't one of them. He's angry, yes, and from the outburst just now, I can tell it's because he was hurt by someone who is or was a political pawn. Maybe even more than one person. Something happened to cause the man sitting across from me to become this bitter shell of the fun, mischievous person I can tell he used to be. "We're good."

Trouble's eyes widen at my words. The minuscule dip of his chin signals to our spectators that the show is over. Once again the chatter increases, vibrating around the cabin, punctuated by the insistent clicking on laptops or their phones.

"What I was trying to do before you two got into your spat was introduce you to the team."

Oops, forgot I don't know anyone's real name. "Sorry, T." I give his rock-solid shoulder an awkward pat. "Go ahead with the introductions. Trouble and I won't cause any more... well, trouble."

Pointing across the table at Trouble, he says, "Benson." Then he shifts his finger to point to the next guy. "Jenkins, Hanks, Jones, Alejo, Walsh, Cole, and Banks. I'm Washington, the team lead."

I give a small wave and awkward smile. "Randi Sawyer. Are those last names or first names?"

"Last. Now, we're your primary team going forward. If you need anything, let me know. Beta team will meet us in Dallas before driving ahead to secure the area."

I snort. "Secure the area. You're hilarious, T-man. You know where we're going, right?"

"Boone, Texas."

"Well, there are around fifteen hundred people in the town, and I can guarantee you no one there will try to hurt me. And if some random snuck in to plot another hit on me, they'd be run out of town before they could settle into the only motel. I don't want a lot of attention drawn to us." Shifting in the seat, I fiddle with the iPad resting on my lap. "You know why we're going, right?"

Terminator shoots a quick look at Trouble.

You've got to be kidding me. "Seriously? No one told you what's going on?" My gaze bounces between the two men. So different physically and, from what I've seen so far, personality wise, but the two seem to gel. Trouble is the ying to T's yang.

"Birmingham told us he ordered you home and the jet would be ready, that was it. He said you'd fill us in."

"Motherfucker," I grumble and grip the iPad to keep from flinging it across the plane. "No wonder y'all think so little of me." Peering up through my lashes, I give Trouble a sad, tight-lipped smile. "He didn't order me to go home, but he did inform me of a situation that I need to handle." I huff a fake laugh. "You said I'm a fraud. Well, you're about to learn firsthand how right you are."

10

———————

TREY

My eyes slide across the back seat of the Suburban to Randi for the third time in the last thirty seconds. For forty minutes, we've been locked side by side with Tank—or Terminator, as she's deemed him—at the wheel. I focus back out the window to the acres and acres of open farm land. Terminator does fit him, and Trouble fits me with a capital *T*.

Not that I'll admit that to her.

The resentment and disappointment from last night fused in the early morning hours, turning to disdain. On the plane, I couldn't hold my anger back any longer, and it poured from me like water from an opened dam. Then she went and confused the hell out of me during the back-and-forth tirade. In that minute, everything I *thought* I knew about her changed. My disdain, the hate, and anger, it all receded, leaving confusion in its place.

Which is why I can't keep my eyes off her now. She's a puzzle, this Randi Sawyer, one I'm determined to solve.

Again my gaze finds its way to her side of the SUV. With her brows furrowed, her hazel eyes skim over the iPad screen, teeth chewing on her pinkie nail.

I shouldn't instigate another fight, but the last one was so entertaining. Plus I have to figure her out, and when she's pissed, her guard is down, providing a peek into the real Randi Sawyer.

"Facebook or Instagram?" I say, my tone bored.

She doesn't even glance from the screen. "How little you think of me is quite astounding. Really it is."

"Ah, you're on Twitter, catching up on the news."

I smile at the flare of her nostrils.

"No, you idiot." Sitting back in the seat, she adjusts her knees to angle to my side. Perfect. "Listen. I'm not sure what type of women you've surrounded yourself with, but based on your preconceived judgments of me, I'm guessing no one I'd be friends with. Stop trying to figure me out if you're unwilling to shove all your judgmental, idiotic, chauvinistic notions up your ass before you do. I deserve a clean fucking slate, cowboy, because I can guarantee you I'm unlike anyone you've ever met."

I smirk. "Cocky."

The tip of her ponytail swishes along her back as she shakes her head. Her pursed lips and loud sigh give off a disappointed feel.

My smile fades as lead sinks in my gut. "Then what?" I ask, desperate for the answer.

Randi sighs and nibbles on the corner of a thumbnail. "You'll figure it out soon enough." Adjusting her weight, she leans forward to point at something outside my window. "We're here." Craning my neck, I barely catch a worn sign announcing the town we're entering. "Let's see what you think of me by the end of the day."

My brows furrow at the uncertainty in her voice.

But that doesn't make sense.

Curiosity building, I shift in my seat, unable to sit still.

Tank's voice booms from the front. "Okay, ma'am—"

"I told you on the plane, T, only in public, okay? When it's just us, it's Randi. Or Rand. None of this 'ma'am' shit."

In the review mirror, his reflection smiles. An actual smile. It's unheard of for him to drop the professional mask when he's working. Tank says smiling comes off as unprofessional. It's a challenge I face daily, considering I find humor in just about everything. Well, I used to. The past few years have put me in the less humorous, more jaded category in life.

"Randi, where are we headed? You said you'd tell us when we made it to town." All traces of the earlier smile are gone, leaving his normal tense mask.

She pitches forward, our shoulders almost touching, her head between the front seats.

"What do you know about my past?"

Gremlin responds from the front passenger seat. "Grew up in Boone, Texas, pregnant at fifteen, daughter at sixteen, graduated top of your class—"

"The basics. Okay, well, if you can't tell by the current scenery, Boone isn't the wealthiest city or the biggest."

"So?" I say before I can stop myself. I need to get a fucking grip. I'm hanging on every word, desperate to learn more.

"What you've seen, who you think I am"—her hazel eyes slide to meet mine—"it's one layer, the tip of the iceberg. You're about to get a front row seat to who I've had to fight to *not* become."

For several minutes, the whirl of the tires along the asphalt fills the otherwise silent Suburban.

"I don't understand," I say, breaking the quiet.

"You will," she whispers, leaning back into the seat, her shoulders rounded and head lowered. "To answer your question, T, in two more lights, make a left and then take a right at the stop sign."

My focus shifts from her as Tank makes the various turns. Something antsy and desperate builds, begging me to grab her shoulder and pull her close.

What the actual fuck?

Comfort is not a top ten attribute of mine. Or twenty. Yet seeing her ashamed urges me to heal whatever pain is causing this strong woman to falter.

"Ma'am—" Tank clears his throat. "Randi, you sure you know where you're going?"

Her head bobs in a slight nod.

What the hell is going on?

Tearing my gaze from her side of the Suburban, I glance out the windshield and do a double take.

"The police station?"

Even with Tank's dark sunglasses, I can tell he's watching through the rearview mirror. I shrug and shake my head. No wonder she wasn't concerned with security. At least twenty cop cars and a few highway patrol SUVs fill the parking lot.

Tank eases the Suburban to the curb right outside the front door.

"I don't want to make a scene," Randi says to the window, staring at the glass doors of the station. "I'd prefer to go in alone." Tank starts to object, but she cuts him off. "But I know you won't let that happen. How about you guys stay out here, and I'll take Trouble in with me. It's safe in there, you know it is, and if anything shady happens outside, you can let Trouble know."

"I don't—"

"Please," she says on a heavy sigh. "I've done this before, unfortunately. We'll be in and out. Kyle said they didn't book her, so there shouldn't be any paperwork."

Her?

My already burning curiosity spikes. My eyes flick from Randi to the police station and back again.

"I've got her," I say, popping the door handle and shoving the heavy door open. "In and out, like she says. We're at a police station, for fuck's sake, Tank."

After slamming the door shut, I step to the driver side door and motion for him to lower the window.

"It's fine," I say reassuringly with two thumbs up and a smile.

"It's not, you fool," he growls. "You're putting her life in danger."

Gremlin shouts a curse. Both our heads whip to the other side of the SUV as two doors slam shut.

"Shit," I grumble and bolt around the hood. "Ma'am," I shout in warning just as Gremlin wraps his arms around her waist, halting her determined stride toward the doors.

"Let me go," she grunts, wiggling in his arms, unable to break free.

Gremlin's eyes lift up to mine, an unspoken question passing between us.

"Don't run off like that," I chastise, lifting the standard-issue dark sunglasses as I massage the bridge of my nose between two fingers. "It makes us look bad, and you could die. Neither is good."

Randi's fight against Gremlin's hold lessens.

I wave a hand for him to drop his restraint and hike a thumb over my shoulder. "I've got it from here. Take watch with Tank. Let me know if anything happens out here while we're inside."

With an annoyed glare directed at Gremlin's retreating back, Randi adjusts her jacket with frustrated tugs and pulls. I reach out and grip the metal door handle, pulling it open. A burst of dry heat singes up my nose and immediately dries out my throat. Fuck, it's hot in there. Just the thought of stepping into that makes me regret volunteering. September in Texas is fucking hot already; why do they have the damn heat on?

"After you," I say and sweep a hand between us. Sweat drips down my back from being sandwiched in the heat. She rolls her shoulders and shakes her hands like she's flicking out the tension, then walks through the door.

The linoleum floor squeaks with every step we take inside. I scan the waiting area; an older woman glances up from behind an aged, ragged desk. I match Randi's steps, staying inches from her back.

"Christy," Randi says, a full smile brightening her face.

The older woman, Christy apparently, smiles back. The white of her hair has a blue tint that matches the thick layer of eye shadow plastered across her eyelids. Deep wrinkles mark every inch of her face, giving her a kind, gentle look.

"Well, look who we have here. Randi Sawyer, look at you!" With a clap, the older woman slides off her stool and shuffles around the desk, both arms extended wide. Randi hesitates, muscles stiff before stepping into the woman's grasp, accepting the predestined hug.

What was that about? I step closer, curiously monitoring their interaction.

"Yeah, a bit of a change, right?" Randi gives Christy's shoulder an awkward pat and steps back, putting her at arm's length. "Somedays I don't even recognize myself." She shifts from one foot to the other, nibbling on the nail of her middle finger. "I'm somewhat pretty now."

"Randi," Christy admonishes. "You stop that right now. You've always been beautiful in the most important spot. Right here." She presses her right hand over her heart. "Now everyone can see what I've always known, sweet girl."

If I wasn't blatantly staring, I would've missed Randi's eyes flick to me before quickly going back to Christy.

"You know why I'm here?" Randi asks around the pinkie fingernail she's now nibbling on.

Christy's kind expression drops, the happy wrinkles falling and making her age instantly. "I do. Who's he?"

"Secret Service."

"Boyfriend too?"

"Christy!" Randi groans and shakes her head. "Stop it. That would be inappropriate."

"Why?" Christy blurts. I chuckle into the fist at my lips. "He has a sweet face."

"Thank you." I step forward, hand extended. "Trey Benson, Secret Service, ma'am. Pleased to meet you."

I barely grasp her frail hand, afraid even a gentle squeeze will break bones.

"My, my, aren't you a charmer. Trouble, that's what you are," she says with a wink.

"That's what I said," Randi grumbles beside me.

"Don't let this one push you around, you hear?" Christy says, nodding toward the huffing Randi. "She's got a good soul, a good heart. Best thing to come out of this town, if you ask me. She don't deserve the life she was handed."

I half turn to meet Randi's eyes, my brows raised in question, but they're too busy inspecting the blank, white wall to notice.

A puzzle indeed. All the pieces aren't adding up. Only way to solve this is to ask the right questions.

"Is that so?" I tuck both hands behind my back, my lips pulling up in a wide smile to Christy. Hopefully a little charm will open her up. "Seems like a pretty great life to me. UT, Harvard, on her way to being vice president."

Christy's eyes narrow. Shaking her head, she looks to Randi. "Cute but not that bright."

"Agreed."

"Hey now." What the hell? This is not going as planned. I glance between the two women. "Don't gang up on me. Just an observation."

"I'm worried for her safety if those are your observation skills, son."

Well hell. Did I just get smack-talked by an eighty-year-old lady?

"Leave him alone," Randi says, still smiling, clearly laughing at me. "You know why he doesn't know. It's why Mom's in holding instead of booked already."

The woman grunts in agreement.

"Wait," I state and turn to face Randi. "Your mom is *here*. In holding?"

She nods with a noncommittal shrug. "Not the first time either."

"Come on. I'll take you to her." The keys jingle as Christy's trembling hand slides the key into the lock and tugs the door open. Halfway down the narrow hall, she calls over her shoulder, "Everything else has been taken care of by that evil man of yours."

"She mean's Kyle," Randi says back to me.

"Take it you don't like him," I shout as we turn a corner, taking another short hall.

She shakes her head, her silver-blue hair bouncing with the movement. "Anyone can see through his charm. A wolf in sheep's clothing, if you ask me. If it weren't for Randi here, no way I'd want him in office."

"You and most Americans," Randi mutters, not bothering to turn to make sure I hear her.

"Here we are." Christy's hand pauses over the doorknob. With a resigned sigh, she turns to Randi, sympathy etched across her face. "I know you've tried to help her, but, Randi, some people just aren't ready for what we're so willing to give. You hear me? Your mother has made her own life choices, and you've made yours. She does not define you. Never has and never will. Now get your mama home and get your ass back to DC. Do something about those ridiculous damn taxes. I work hard for my money, don't want that government taking any more than they already are."

"Yes, ma'am." Rolling her shoulders, Randi stretches her neck to the right, then left. "Okay, I'm ready. Let's do this."

Why does it feel like we're about to go into battle?

"Do we need backup?" I question, though it feels stupid to suggest I can't handle her mom on my own.

Hazel eyes meet mine, flicking from one to the other, searching for... hell if I know.

"Maybe."

What the hell?

11

RANDI

Dammit, why did I ask him to walk me in here? Anyone but him. Internally I groan and turn back to the door Christy's unlocking. I'm not embarrassed about him seeing Mom; no that's something I got over a long time ago. It's everything Christy pointed out. Love that woman, but today I wish she'd keep her thoughts to herself. Trouble doesn't seem like the type of guy who needs his ego inflated any more than it already is.

The last thing I need right now is for him to think I find him attractive. The thin veil of anger keeping us apart needs to stay. Period. If he changes his attitude toward being kind and non-assy, I'll have a difficult time keeping my walls up. And those suckers are needed to survive the piranha-infested pond known as the DC political circle.

Relaxing both hands at my sides, I give them a quick shake, releasing the tension.

Christy pushes the door wide and steps aside, allowing me to walk in first. With a deep breath for courage, I step through. That same breath whooshes out at the sight of Mom passed out on the far side of the holding cell. All thoughts of Trouble at my back, wondering what he's thinking, vanish as I step closer and wrap my hands around the bars. The cold metal bites into my palms as I squeeze so tight my knuckles turn white.

Every time I see Mom, there is less and less of the woman I used to know left behind. The woman curled on her side on top of the lone metal bench is nothing but a shell of the charismatic woman she once was. Much thinner than the last time I saw her. Bones protrude, almost slicing through the thin skin covering her hips and shoulders. Deep lines mark her face, making her look ten years older.

The clanging of metal against metal draws my focus from Mom to Christy opening the holding cell door.

"Thank you," I whisper as I slip past. The overwhelming smell of urine, stale smoke, and decay halts my steps halfway into the cell. I raise an arm and bury my nose into the crook of my elbow before stepping closer.

"Mom," I say, muffled by the sleeve of my jacket. My chest expands as I take in a deep breath before pulling my arm away. "Mom."

Nothing.

Eyes focused on her chest, I squat low, watching for signs of life. A flash of relief settles and I release the held breath at the rapid rise and fall of her chest. At least she's alive. Forgetting about the stench wafting off Mom, I take a breath to call her name again. Nausea brews and I gag, instinctively shoving backward to move away from the stench. My ass hits the unforgiving cement floor.

Strong hands tuck under each armpit and haul me upright. The movement disrupts my already delicate equilibrium, and I sway once my feet meet the floor.

"What happened? Are you okay? Randi?"

I blink a couple times, attempting to make the room stop spinning. "Fine. I'm fine. I'm just... still a little dizzy from last night." Again, the room whirls in my vision, but this time it's due to Trouble flipping me around so we're chest to chest, his intense, assessing gaze scanning my face. "It's the smell. Really, I'm okay."

Still he doesn't release his hold. Heat floods from his warm body into my own. His hands slide from my shoulders to grip my waist, and my breath catches. Our eyes locked on one another's, everything else in the room fades. For a moment, I forget where we are and the fact that I'm comfortable in someone's hold. His honey eyes flash, opening up like a window into his soul. He's sucking me in, making me want to dive into his past to learn how he became the bitter man he is today.

"This isn't the first time, is it?" he whispers.

I shake my head. My gaze falls to his full lower lip, and I bite my own to keep from leaning forward and taking a nip.

With his chest pressed against mine, I feel the jolt of his breath catching. "Why didn't you say something?"

I furrow my brows. "Would it have changed anything?"

"Well, yeah. I didn't know... I thought...."

"You thought you had me all figured out." Reality snaps back to the forefront of my mind. Jerking out of his hold, I turn my back to him. The intensity of his stare burns the back of my neck. I rub at it, trying to ease the feel of being watched. "Now you'll move me from one stigma to another. Nothing changes. Nothing ever changes when it comes to people's beliefs on who I am."

"I'm sorry," he says. The sympathy dripping from those two words begs me to turn back around, to step back into that warm hold.

"I don't need your pity," I bite back. I lock gazes with Christy, who's still outside the cell watching. "Do you have any extra clothes?" I nod toward my passed-out mother. "I can't take her out in that. It smells too bad. I'll puke in the car before we even leave the parking lot."

My shoulders drop at the saddened shake of her head.

"Honey, my clothes will be a tent on your mama."

She's right, but it was worth a try. Sighing, I return my focus to Mom to keep from turning back to Trouble. Why, oh why, does the one person whose touch I'm not annoyed by have to be his? And why am I desperate to snuggle against his chest and stay there for eternity? Maybe I magically got high from the drug stench seeping off Mom.

That's totally a thing.

"Benson, can you run out and grab my bag? I'll use the spare set of clothes I brought in case we need to stay overnight."

"I'm not leaving you. Tank would shit a brick." I snort in response. His clipped directives echo off the bare cinder block walls as he talks to the agents outside. "Three minutes," he says to me once he's finished. "Christy, would you meet them at the door so they can get back here?"

I'm still staring at Mom when the door snickers shut, signaling Christy's departure. Neither Trouble nor I say a word as we wait. Breathing through my mouth, I approach the bench once again and squat, putting my face close to Mom's. Minutes pass of me stroking her stringy hair before a gentle hand rests on my shoulder. Turning on the balls of my feet, I find one of the agents from the plane now standing on the other side of the bars, eyes on Mom, holding a bag in one hand.

"I'll help," Trouble says beside me.

Cutting my eyes up, I shake my head. "No thanks. I can do it."

His grip on my shoulder tightens a fraction. "It wasn't a question. Walsh," he shouts. "Drop the bag and get out. I'll help Miss Sawyer and let you know when we're ready to move out."

The bag thumps to the floor, and Christy and Walsh exit the room. Alone again, Trouble snags the bag from across the room and hauls it deeper into the holding cell, dropping it at my feet. I unzip the top zipper and search through the duffel's contents. Selecting an older pair of Wranglers and a long-sleeve T–shirt, I pile them on top of the bag and push off the cold concrete to stand.

"I'll hold her and you undress, then redress her?" I suggest. I turned down his offer to help seconds ago, but I'm thankful he didn't give me the option. Doing this alone would take forever. A challenge I'm not up to taking on right now.

I shift angles a couple times, trying to figure out the best approach to help her sit up. With Trouble's assistance, we raise her to a somewhat sitting position, leaning against the wall, while I hold her shoulders so she doesn't slump forward.

"Do you want to talk about it?" he asks as he slowly peels Mom's tank top up her belly.

I cringe at the number of visible ribs beneath her pale thin skin as he pulls the ratty tank over her head. I give a half shrug in answer to his previous question. My head tilts up at Trouble's pointed cough. His cheeks are flushed pink, eyes a little wild. I follow his embarrassed gaze down to Mom's naked chest.

"Classy, Mom. Even if you don't have boobs, you still have to wear something." I shake my head and motion for him to hand me the sweater. "I can do it."

"It's fine, just didn't expect it. Hell, didn't expect any of the last thirty minutes, or twenty-four hours, honestly."

I scoff. "You've never had to bail a parent out or redress them after a drug-induced stupor?"

"That would be a definite 'never.'"

"That's a luxury I've never been afforded. It hasn't always been this bad, but it's never been good, that's for sure."

"Lay her back against the bench and make sure she doesn't roll off while I get her shorts off." His fingers pause at the button. "Uh, Randi?"

I glance up. I almost laugh at the uncomfortable cringe he's sporting. "What?"

"Just wanting to prepare myself here. Think the underwear situation is the same down here as it was up top?"

Now I can't help but laugh, then immediately gag. Shit, this place stinks. No. Mom reeks.

"It's fifty-fifty, honestly. You never know with this one." I stifle another giggle at his full-body shudder. "Come on. Let's get this over with and get her home."

THANK goodness it's not as cold here as it was in DC. This pleasant fall day at eighty–five degrees allows us to ride with the windows rolled down in the Suburban as we drive to Mom's. The change of clothes helped but not by much; the overpowering stench of stale smoke and body odor still wafts off her in waves.

The leather seat creaks as I lean forward to tap T on the shoulder. "It's your next right." Through the windshield, I watch the sign for Green Meadows come into view. The G is missing, and Meadows now says dows, but hey, it's home.

Was home.

T slows to make the turn but slides to a complete stop instead of turning into the run-down trailer park.

"Randi?"

"Yes, T. Here."

"Here?"

"Here."

"Randi, this is a—"

"Run-down trailer park. I know this. Believe me, I know exactly what it is. I'm the one who grew up here, after all."

"Here?"

"I thought we already covered that."

Trouble chuckles in the seat beside me, making me smile. At least someone gets my humor. Grumbling under his breath, T eases his foot off the brake and turns the SUV into the entrance.

"Okay, it's the third one on the left." I crane my neck to see out the window as we pass a turnoff, hoping for a glimpse of my old trailer.

"What's down there?" Trouble asks, leaning forward to look through my window too. "Old boyfriend's house?"

"Um, no."

"Then what? You were looking for something."

I lift my hand toward my mouth and nibble on the thumbnail. "Mine."

"Your what?"

"My trailer," I whisper, then cut my eyes at him to gauge his reaction.

A deep line creases between his neat brown brows as his eyes flick from me to the window and back again.

Before I can ask what he's thinking, we pull to a stop. A pained groan fills the back of the car. Everyone tenses but doesn't make a move. We're all probably thinking the same thing—maybe she'll pass back out.

No such luck.

Which shouldn't be a surprise. We are talking about my luck, after all. I thought my shitty luck changed when we won the damn primary, only to be painfully reminded the win locked me into an indebted contract with a dirty politician. Go me. Maybe if I wouldn't have been so focused on proving myself to my haters I would've realized the bear trap I was walking right into.

Another groan with unintelligible mumbled words fills the third row. I pull my knees into my seat and press a cool cheek against the headrest. Glassy, bloodshot eyes blink up but don't focus.

How long will it take for her come down from a meth high? She's always been an addict at worst, alcoholic at best, but she was a good mom. As good as she could be, I guess. Not great, but it could've been worse.

"Mom. You're okay. It's me, Randi. You're home."

A wet cackle rattles her chest, and I cringe back an inch. "Randi. I missed you, honey."

Right, and a Texas summer isn't hot.

"Let's get her inside." I turn to open the door but pause at Trouble's eyes focused on me. "What?"

He shakes his head and throws the door open like it pissed him off somehow. Before I can do the same, mine opens on its own with T just outside the door. I nod in thanks and slide out to access the back seat where Mom's laid out. Without a word, T reaches into the back and carefully slides Mom out, cradling her tiny frame in his arms.

Warm tears fill my lower lids as I stare at the two. His larger-than-life size dwarfing hers making her body look so tiny and frail.

My lips purse to keep the building emotions shoved down deep where they belong. Tonight I can break down. When I'm alone later, I can freak out and cry over the last twenty-four hours. Until then, I keep my shit together. No showing weakness.

"Okay, then," I croak, the rising emotions stealing my voice. *Dammit! Keep your shit together, Randi.*

Dead grass crunches beneath my Converses as I turn to my old home and march for the front door. My stomach lurches into my throat when the first step cracks beneath my weight. Moving slower, I gingerly step onto the next wooden stair, testing it before putting my full weight on the rotting wood. "Good to know the money I've sent you has gone to good use," I grumble.

I knew better then to send her money, but she's my mom, and I had it, so I sent her some when she was in a bad spot. I clearly remember those 'bad spot' days, or years for me; I couldn't turn her away empty-handed.

Stepping on the landing, I crack my neck and grasp the flimsy metal door handle. I pause, staring at the clouded window. What will the inside look like if the outside is the start of a horror film? The handle wiggles in my grasp. There's a screech of rusted metal bending, and then the door flies open. Adrenaline explodes from my belly, shooting scorching heat through my veins. I curse, jolting back to keep the door from giving me tetanus. Losing my footing, I stumble back a step. Arms flailing, I take another step back, only to meet air instead of more rotten wood.

Swinging my arms in large circles, I attempt to fight gravity from taking me down.

But like always, that bitch wins.

12

———

RANDI

The air whistles from my lungs, my neck snapping back against something solid.

"Fuck." A hot breath brushes through my hair, floating it across my face.

Heart in my throat, I take a breath and hold it to calm down before I stroke out. My entire body trembles, but I stay upright due to strong arms banded around my waist. A pleasant spicy scent hits my nose. *Hmm, that smells nice.* I take another deep whiff, my eyes rolling back in my head at the desire that sparks from the scent alone. To my credit, my odd behavior could be from aggravating last night's head trauma by cracking it again on... wait, what did I crack it on?

Following the mix of citrus and cinnamon, I sniff the air a few times, following it until my nose smacks into a solid, suit-covered chest.

"Seriously?" A deep chuckle vibrates Trouble's chest, tickling my own. "Did you just sniff me? Maybe we should get your head checked again."

"Probably wouldn't be a terrible idea," I mutter with my nose still buried in the soft fabric of his jacket. "Just one more sniff."

"Baby!"

The magical bubble his scent surrounded me in bursts. His arm tightens a fraction before helping me step out of his hold to stand on my own. I turn, a snarl pulling at my lips at the man standing on the landing.

"What in the hell are you doing here?" I demand. My fingers curl into tight fists at my side. "Mom, what is he doing here? Did you call him baby?" My gaze doesn't leave the piece-of-shit slimeball standing just outside Mom's trailer door. A sleazy smile spreads across his pockmarked cheeks, displaying what remains of his teeth—which isn't much.

"Well, I'll be fucking damned." A shiver runs down my spine as realization dawns. "Shoulda known she'd get your skinny ass out of jail."

"Ma'am?"

I reluctantly pull my attention from Jimmy, our small town's main drug dealer, to T. Mom wiggles in his arms, attempting to get away, eyes only for Jimmy.

"This can't be happening," I mutter. I gesture toward the ground for T to set her down. What other choice do I have? Make her come back to DC with me? Hell no. That town isn't ready for Mom's shit show life.

Her bare feet barely touch the ground before she wobbles toward the trailer, stumbling up the two steps only to fall face first on the landing. Jimmy chuckles as her frail arms give out under her light weight each time she tries to push up.

"Mom." She ignores me. "Mom!" I shout and step closer to the trailer. A tight grip on my bicep prevents me from moving closer. Whipping around, I scowl at Trouble. "I need to help her."

The shake of his head is barely noticeable. Eyes on the two addicts, he steps closer, putting his chest against my back. "Who is he?" The tension in his voice, the silent command, brings the whole situation into focus.

I glance around, looking at each of the agents. Everyone stands close, tension radiating off their stiff postures, hands at their hips in case they need their weapons quickly.

Shit, didn't think how this looks to them. To me it's a common scene. No doubt this is a first for them.

"Mom's new boyfriend, apparently. That's Jimmy Caster, criminal and drug dealer." A demanding throb pulses through my head. I tip my hat back and press both palms to my temples to ease the pain. It doesn't help.

"Damn, woman," Jimmy says, drawing my reluctant attention back to him. Bile rises up my throat at the sight of Mom hanging on his bony shoulders, rubbing herself against his side. "Look at ya." My back vibrates at Trouble's low growl. "Come on inside and I'll show ya what you been missin' out on." Mom giggles beside him. Fucking giggles. He tilts his head down to her. "If yer a good girl, maybe I won't tell everyone about your mama here."

My stomach lurches. This time there's no stopping it. Squatting to the grass, I vomit the water and bits of food from the light breakfast on the plane.

Shit, this is bad.

"Get her out of here," Trouble orders.

I don't fight it as I'm hauled up to a standing position and directed away from the trailer toward the Suburban. A blast of cold air at the open door has goose bumps pebbling my skin. A gentle hand presses against my lower back, urging me inside.

"I can't leave her like that," I tell Gremlin as realization dawns. "I can't leave her with him."

"We'll handle it, ma'am."

"This can't get out to the press. Kyle will kill me," I whisper.

"We'll handle it." A commotion draws my attention, but Gremlin stops me from looking around the door with a gentle hand to my cheek. "Sounds like Benson already is, ma'am. She'll be fine, but we need you safe, and that's inside here. Understand?"

I swallow down the lump clogging my throat. *Do not cry, Randi. Not here. Not yet.*

With a shaky nod, I climb inside the SUV and slide onto the soft leather seat. "Thank you." Meeting his light blue eyes, I attempt a grateful smile.

I expect to see pity written across his face and in his gaze, but instead all I find is something like compassion. With a quick nod, he shuts the door, enclosing me inside alone. An agent stands on either side of the passenger doors while the rest of the team forms a short line, shoulders touching, blocking my line of sight to the trailer. After a few minutes of gnawing on my thumbnail almost to the quick, the line finally breaks apart. T and Trouble wear similar grim expressions as they approach the SUV, Gremlin following, while the other agents march to the second Suburban and file in.

I keep silent, my frantic gaze flicking between the three men as they climb in. Unseeing gaze focused on my clasped hands, I clear my throat, trying to ease the tension-filled quiet. Everything feels heavy. I need one hour alone to process it all.

"I want to stay overnight in Dallas." My voice breaks from the lump of unshed tears in my throat. "We'll go home tomorrow."

"Ma'am, Mr. Birmingham said—"

Anger washes away the pity party I was starting at the mention of his name. Snapping my gaze up, I meet T's dark sunglasses in the rearview mirror. "I don't give a fuck what Kyle wants right now. I need one night away, an hour alone to deal with all this shit. Do you realize what happened last night?"

"Someone tried to off you."

I side-eye Trouble. "I was thinking about how I somehow won to potentially become the second most powerful person in the country, but yeah, toss me almost dying in there too. And this today." I shake my head and immediately regret it. I squeeze my head between my palms, attempting to alleviate the throbbing. "I can't go back tonight. Plus, I have to figure out how to fucking keep Jimmy quiet and what to do with Mom—"

"It's taken care of."

I shift in the seat, angling toward Trouble.

"What does that mean?"

"I made sure he understands the consequences if he speaks to the press." His shoulders rise and fall in a shrug, but his eyes won't meet mine.

"And that means what, exactly?"

"He beat the shit out of that fucker and told him worse would happen if he said anything about your mom." My eyes widen at Gremlin's words. "Oh, and told him to stay away from your mom."

"What the hell?" Too many conflicting emotions pour through me to decipher which one I actually feel. Happy, angry, sad, relieved.

Again, he shrugs.

"Look at me, dammit." I smack his shoulder to get his attention. "Seriously?"

Only the barest outline of his eyes is visible through his dark sunglasses, but I know he's watching me.

"He was a threat to you, so we handled the situation."

"Um, did anyone else throw a punch?"

He smirks and shakes his head.

"Then *you* handled the situation." Pinching pain fills my lower lip as I bite down. "What about Mom? She'll just go right back to him, and I'll be back down here next week hauling her out of holding. Again."

"Rehab."

I let out a sarcastic laugh. "Been there, done that. It doesn't stick."

"There are several good ones out in California. They have a higher success rate than others because of the long programs."

I purse my lips and raise both brows high on my forehead. "You seem to know a lot about it. Been recently?"

Silence.

Interesting. Interesting indeed.

"I've looked into those before, but if I remember right, they were way too expensive for what I could afford," I tell him.

"What about Birmingham?" All warmth from his features disappears at the mention of Kyle. "Won't he help you with your mom?"

I shake my head and turn to look out the window. "I don't want any more reason to be indebted to that asshole. I need to do this on my own."

It would make life a lot simpler if I asked Kyle for the money, but what would he demand in return? I'm already in too deep as it is with him and his corrupt family.

"I'll figure it out," I murmur to the glass. "I always do."

THE SUITE IS ridiculous in the best way possible. Every surface shines while light sparkles around the room. Sweet vanilla mixed with jasmine fills my nose as I step deeper into the living room. I shift on my feet, staring at the floral carpet while attempting to keep the tears I've held for hours at bay for a few more minutes as the guys secure the room.

Absurd if you ask me. It's not like this was a planned stop. Deciding to stay overnight at The Ritz in downtown Dallas before flying out tomorrow was too impromptu for someone to plan a master assassination attempt. The guys fought me in the car, saying it would be best if we went on home tonight, but using my award-winning debate skills I won the argument.

Hopefully Kyle won't ream them for going against his direct orders. He'll be furious with me, but I don't give two flying fucks. I need a hot bath, a Snickers bar, and no fewer than two boxes of tissue to get through the next hour. All these damn emotions need an outlet before I explode in a river of tears and a gooey mess of snot.

I never cry, but the previous twenty-four hours would get to anyone with a pulse.

"Clear," T's booming voice echoes through the room.

Almost like my tears know relief is coming soon, two escape, slowly rolling down my hot cheeks. Gaze lowered, I race to the master bedroom.

The fancy-ass door refuses to close quickly even as I shove on it, desperate for privacy. With only an inch to go, the sense of someone watching draws my attention. On the other side of the door, Trouble's worried face fills the remaining small gap. His lips part, but the door clicks shut before he can get out a single word.

The worry and confusion shining from his light brown eyes snap the thin restraint on my rolling emotions. Tossing the ball cap to the bed, I fall to the floor not caring that I'm falling apart in the middle of the room. My ass hits the soft carpet. Knees tucked to my chest, I press my forehead to my thighs and let the tears flow.

Seconds. Minutes. Hell, maybe hours pass, but I don't move.

Something taps my shoulder startling me out of my hysteria. Peeling my forehead away from my jeans at a gentle touch on my shoulder, uncomfortable dark brown eyes watch from where T is crouched beside me. It's stupid, and so unlike me, but instead of pulling away from his comforting grip, I lean in to it. Happy-filled tingles spark from his touch. It's nothing like the heat and desire that coursed through my veins from Trouble's, but still, the sense of support fills my heart with a friendly calm.

"You okay?" he asks.

Breaking his gaze, I rest my chin on my knees. A breath catches in my chest at the sight of Trouble, also in the room, perched on the edge of the large four poster bed.

"This won't be a thing, will it?" he asks, crossing his arms over his chest. The annoyed look on his face is almost believable if it weren't for the deep crease between his brows signaling the concern that lurks beneath the facade.

"And what would that be?" I sniffle and discreetly wipe my nose across my jeans in attempts to look somewhat presentable.

He waves in my direction with a pointed look to my tear smeared face. "The crying."

"For fuck's sake, Benson." Pure exasperation fills T's tone.

A genuine laugh tickles my chest, making the tears slow. "Fuck, I hope not. But if every day for the next couple months or worse four years is like the last twenty-four hours, I can't give you any promises." My teeth sink into the nail of my pinkie. "It won't be, right?"

Both men huff. "Sure as hell hope not. It's been a day of firsts for us too."

"Does that mean I win some kind of prize?"

"For what?" Trouble asks, his signature sexy smirk on full display.

"Being the biggest mess in the shortest amount of time." I flick my gaze between the two men. "Come on. I deserve something for adding some excitement to your mundane lives, right?"

T drops his head with a hint of a smile on his lips. "And what kind of prize were you thinking?"

"Candy, of course." Duh.

"Chocolate?" His voice rises, his eyes wide.

"Down, boy." Trouble laughs. "This is for her, not you."

"You like chocolate?" I can't help my growing smile. He looks like a guy who would snack on bullets or whole turkey legs, not chocolate. "We're going to be good friends, you and I."

"Friends?" His eyes narrow. "We're here to protect you, not be your friends."

Tears well again. Fuck, why does that hurt so bad?

"Idiot," Trouble mutters. His heavy footsteps pause in front of my Converse. "And you're the married one. Sometimes I feel sorry for Sarah." T grunts something in return I don't make out. "I'll take care of Hot Mess here. You go get her something to eat. It's been a while since breakfast."

T grumbles through his groans of pain as he stands and heads out of the room. The door softly clicks behind him.

"Come on." Trouble extends a hand down, wiggling his fingers in front of my face. "Get off the floor and I'll find you something better than chocolate."

I seal my lips to suppress my smile. The same lusty heat from earlier sweeps through my body when I slide my hand into his. One swift pull and I'm standing with one hand pressed against his chest, the other still wrapped in his. My heart pounds, pulse skyrocketing at our close proximity. Tipping my head up, I zero in on his soft, plump lower lip that begs to be nibbled on.

Holy hell, I'm in deep shit.

13

TREY

Maybe I'm the one with the concussion.

What the hell is wrong with me? This woman is everything I've written off in life. Well, that's not entirely true, now that I've seen the truth. Even if she's not like all the other backstabbing, opportunistic women I've known, she's still a fucking mess.

A cute mess, if I'm honest with myself.

Even now I should be turned off by her red-rimmed eyes, black streaks of mascara down her soft cheeks, and bright red nose. But I'm not. She's adorable, not revolting.

This is bad news. T will have a heart attack if he even gets a whiff that I'm attracted to this woman who we're to protect with our lives. Which I will, without a doubt. Me thinking she's hot and wanting to feel that skin hidden beneath all those layers...

Do not think about her naked.

Do not think about her naked.

"I need a shower to get mom's stench off me."

"Not helping," I grit out.

"Huh?" She shrugs out of my hold leaving the sense of an empty void in her place. Thank fuck she did though, I wasn't going to let her go on my own. Her hazel eyes scan the entirety of the room. Hooking her thumb in the direction of the bathroom she says, "I'll just go—"

"No." There's no way I can focus on her safety with her on the other side of the door, gloriously naked and waiting for me. Maybe not that last part, but that's where my dirty imagination will take me. I give my head a shake to pull it from the gutter. "Sit." I point to the small sitting area on the other side of the room. "Wait until Tank comes back with the food. Until then, I promised you something to take the edge off."

Arms crossed across her chest, she shuffles to the low buttercream-colored armchair and ungracefully plops into it. I hold back a laugh. This woman is proving the exact opposite of who I assumed she was. It puts me on uneven footing. All the women I've known are perfection personified. Graceful, manipulative, delicate, and vindictive —*that* I know how to defend against. But this? Her?

I pull one cabinet door open and then another before finding what I'm looking for. When I open the fridge, the cold air slides across my face feeling amazing against my heated skin. Earlier the boys turned down the air conditioning for Randi, we've all already picked up on her being cold natured, which means we're all roasting.

"White or red wine?" I call out over my shoulder loud enough for her to hear across the room.

"Tequila?"

"Damn," I mumble, a small smile pulling up the corners of my lips. Grabbing a small bottle of tequila, I slam the fridge door shut with a soft kick, then the cabinet. "You're a surprise at every turn, aren't you?"

"I'm taking that as a compliment." Our fingers graze as I hand off the tequila, shooting a bolt of want straight to my cock.

Fuuuuck.

A pop then crackle of the seal breaking sounds at my back as I move toward the bathroom. "You should. It's different for sure."

"Different how?" Her voice barely carrying over the running water wetting the cloth in my hand. After ringing it out, I step back into the bedroom and lean a shoulder against the doorframe.

"Here." I toss the wet rag across the room only for her to duck, a loud smack and squeak filling the room as it slides down the glass window behind her. "You were supposed to catch that."

"Right." Bending over the arm of the chair, she stretches to the floor, offering a great view of her round ass. I advert my gaze, pretending I wasn't staring when she pops back up, face flushed with the washcloth in hand. "What's this for?"

I maneuver a finger in the air circling in the direction of her face with a cringe. "You've got...."

A bright pink blush tints her cheeks as she dips her face to the washcloth and gives it a good scrub. "You didn't answer my question. Different how?"

Shifting my attention to the floor as she cleans up, I say, "I was wrong about who you are. I assumed you were like every other beautiful woman in DC."

"Beautiful," she says, her tone disbelieving. "And what's that?"

"You'll find out soon enough. Being different is a good thing, Randi. Don't lose it."

At her silence, I look up to find her now clean face tipped up with the small bottle pressed to her lips. A loud laugh slips past before I can stop it. Still chugging the golden liquid, her eyes cut over. The plump lips wrapped around the glass twitch upward.

"You know what? I don't think we have anything to worry about." I'm still laughing as I squat in front of the cabinet once again and retrieve another round, this time snagging a bottle of vodka for myself. Beta team took over an hour ago, so technically I'm off the clock.

"Catch it this time," I say holding up the bottle with a wink.

Her eyes narrow in concentration as she wiggles in the seat and extends both hands. "Ready."

"Wow." Never in my life have I been this entertained by a woman—with her clothes, on that is. "Here it comes. Nice and slow."

"That's not what she said." She chuckles to herself. "Not me, but any other she." Her eyes flick up to mine, and I smile while shaking my head in disbelief.

"You're kind of funny," I say, still smiling, the tequila still gripped between two fingers not wanting to make the move to hand it over. There's something special, bonding even, in this moment I don't want to interrupt.

"Really?" Hope and disbelief fill her voice. "Most people just think I'm crazy."

"Well, you're that too, but funny mostly. It's a clever funny, so I guess you have to be as smart as you to get your humor."

Her teeth sink into her lower lip. "I like that theory. I'll allow it."

"Thanks." I chuckle. "You'd rather it be hard and fast?"

"Sex or the bottle you're about to throw?"

"Sex." This is a terrible idea, but she started it. It's an excuse I can still use as an adult, right?

"Not that I remember that well," she mumbles. "But yeah, fast for sure. The quicker it's done the better."

My hand tightens around the bottle so it doesn't tumble to the floor. "I don't get that joke."

She tosses her head back with a laugh only to wince and grip her head between her hands. "Stop stalling and toss me that bottle. I need it." Her movements stiffen. "Wait, you wouldn't happen to have a cigarette on you, would you?"

"One of the guys might, but—"

"Bring the bottles." With a smile, she unfolds from the pretzel she'd scrunched into. Snatching her hat off the bad and tugging it down low, she heads to the door. "Hurry. I'm scared for my safety if this is as fast as you move."

Leaning against the living room door, I wait as I watch Randi shuffle around the room, asking each of the beta team agents for a smoke. A younger guy cautiously pulls a pack from his pocket and slides it into her hand. With her intentions clear, I tell one of the agents to go on ahead and secure the kitchen employee entrance. T shoots daggers from where he's sprawled out on the couch, no doubt needing a few minutes of sleep before room service arrives.

I slide both bottles into my pockets before raising my hands palms out. "She'll be fine. I'll go down with her."

"That doesn't make me feel better. I'm just as concerned about you two killing each other as an outside threat."

Randi snorts. "Wise man, but we're good. For now. But if he does kill me, I won't hold it against you, T."

"Yeah, because you'll be dead."

"Right, so I'll haunt him, obviously." I laugh at the sarcastic scrunch of her tiny nose. "Come on, Trouble."

Tank groans. "This is a terrible idea. I'm going with you."

"Now you're insulting me," I say, all humor gone. "Stay here, wait for the food. You know you ordered yourself something on the side. We're all starving."

"We skipped lunch," he snaps back. Yep, the man needs to eat. No one wants to be around this guy when he's hungry and tired. Terrible combo. He's my best friend and even I don't want to be near him when he's like this.

"Damn. That's my fault, isn't it?" Her eyes flick around the room, gauging the rest of the team. We all look worn the fuck out. It's obvious to her too, if the cringe she's sporting means anything. "When I'm stressed, I forget to eat. Old habits, I guess. How does this work? You guys eat when I eat or only when you're off?"

"We rotate while on shift usually, but today was a—"

"Complete mess," Randi cuts in.

"Anomaly." Tank's stress lines fade into a somewhat smile. Damn, what is it with this woman? How in the hell is she able to get to this softer side of him? "We'll figure it out, get into a routine. Now that we know you need a reminder of when to eat, that helps us. We didn't say anything today because we figured you didn't want to stop."

Randi shoves both hands to her hips. "Let's set up some rules. First, if you don't know something, ask. I don't like that you guys were starving today because you didn't ask. Second, no more of this ma'am bullshit from any of you, even in public. I swear I feel the gray hairs multiplying every time one of you says it, and I already spend way too much money on covering that shit as it is. Got it?"

Something flares in my chest at the stubborn and commanding tone in her voice. Maybe she can do the VP thing. If she can own Tank, how much harder can running the country be?

A random thought pushes through my thoughts. What if she's this commanding in bed? My lips tug down in a frown. Hopefully not. Watching her own the room is hot as hell, but alone, I want her begging for it.

The two of them continue the rules discussion as I walk to the door, discreetly adjusting myself to hide the semi I'm sporting. These next four years will be torture if I'm like this every time I'm near her. Good thing she's with Birmingham and the job or I'd pin her against a wall the first moment we were alone. Or even if we weren't. Hell, that would be hot, the risk of being caught. Past girlfriends worried about their reputation or someone seeing too much to be... adventurous.

"Ready?"

I cut my eyes to her at the touch of humor in the single word.

Shit, how long has she been there and I failed to notice? That's not good.

If I can't keep my focus, I can't keep her safe. Which is my motherfucking job. Shit.

I have to maintain distance whether my dick has other options or not. Her life depends on it.

Ignoring her pointed look I shift my attention on the hallway door and yank on the handle. The two agents outside the door stiffen, assuming full alert at her presence. Both flank us down the narrow hall and into the employee elevator, which is held, waiting, by another agent.

We stand stiff, as still as statues as the elevator descends while she shifts from one foot to the other. We're used to this. It's what we live for. Protection, constantly on high alert. The rush you get when out in public, needing your eyes on everyone and everywhere at once, provides the perfect high for an adrenaline junkie.

Like me.

Humid heat assaults me as we push the kitchen's swinging doors open, and my steps falter. Sweat builds along my forehead, a light trickle already dripping down my spine. Employees perk up from their stations as we move down the line, marching toward the back door. One glaring look and the curious glances shift away, focusing back on their work.

Good.

They should be afraid. We're all packing multiple weapons and are proficient in multiple types of hand-to-hand combat. Of course, I hope it doesn't come down to a fight, since my fists are tender from beating the shit out of that idiot earlier. I couldn't stop myself. The second his yellowed eyes raked down Randi, the leash I keep on my self-restraint snapped. Tank was beyond pissed but didn't stop it from happening, even though I broke a very fundamental rule.

One of the beta team agents files out the door first. Randi makes to follow, but with a hand to her waist, I tug her back to me.

"Wait until we get the all clear," I say into her hair. My eyes dart across the kitchen. Tension builds and my muscles tighten, readying for a fight. The agent beside me meets my gaze and nods. One hand pressed to her lower back, I push against the metal bar, releasing the latch keeping it closed.

A cool breeze swipes across my sweaty brow, instantly calming my frazzled nerves. I fucking hate being hot. After four deployments and various other missions in the Middle East, I can't shake the automatic tension that builds, ready to snap, in a hot room. I was one of the lucky ones who came back whole, but I can't untrain my mind and body to realize I'm not in a war zone when my body temperature spikes.

I scan the back of the building and our surroundings. Randi steps out of my reach, settling on a stack of plastic crates someone stacked together in a makeshift seat. The scratch of flint meets my ears in the otherwise silent alley. With it being dinnertime, all the employees must be inside hard at work, preparing various meals for the hotel guests. Hopefully she'll be done with this smoke break before a lull allows their own breaks. The fewer people out here the better.

"So." After one more scan up and down the alley, I turn my attention to her. "You bring those bottles or what?" she asks as a puff of gray smoke billows from her lips. Smoking really shouldn't be as sexy as she's making it.

Instead of answering, I take the few steps toward her. The silk lining of my pocket slides across my knuckles as I grasp the two bottles and pull them free. Careful to not make the same mistake again, I drop the bottle in her awaiting hand, preventing any accidental skin-to-skin contact.

I watch in fascination as she bites the end of the lit cigarette, allowing it to dangle from her mouth, to open the tequila bottle with both hands.

"Who are you?" I ask before I can think better of it. At every turn, she's shocking me off my feet, completely disrupting everything I thought I knew about her. Hell, about women in general.

"No one. Haven't you figured that out yet?" Anger and concern strangle my chest at the sadness in her voice. "Right place, right time. Lucky. Whore. Gold digger. Fraud." Hazel eyes stare into my own. "Right?"

Well, that solidifies one thing I've always thought was debatable.

I *am* a complete ass.

14

RANDI

The smoke burns in my lungs oh so good. Damn, I missed this. The gum and other shit I've tried isn't the same. Something about being outside, the smoke-filled inhales and exhales combined with the delicious burn stall my constant thoughts. This right here, these few minutes, I get to relax. It's few and far between on the campaign trail, and I cherish each second of calm I can steal.

"I'm an ass," Trouble finally says. Twisting my lips, I blow smoke out the side of my mouth to keep from sending it into his face. "I didn't... I thought I knew you."

"You didn't. You don't." The glass rim of the bottle, still warm from his body heat, slips between my lips as I take a sip. "It's okay though. I'm still trying to figure out who I am, so I can't expect anyone else to figure it out before I do, you know." I let the comfortable silence fill the calm space between us before I go on. "But I can guarantee what you see is what you get. I've always been me and have fought to accept who I am, hot mess and all." I smirk using his words to describe me. It really is a perfect description of this life I find myself living.

I look up at the clink of glass on glass.

"Cheers to you being a hot mess and me being an ass, then."

Trouble tilts the bottle back, sucking down the entire contents. His

Adam's apple bobs with each deep swallow. I stare transfixed at the way it slides up and down tempting me to lean closer and take a nip.

"So, now that you know I'm not who you thought I was... friends?" My pitch rises with each word. I should be embarrassed by how bad I want him to say yes, but I'm not. I'm desperate in more ways than one. If I can trust him, trust Terminator and the rest of the team, maybe I have a sliver of a hope of surviving the next few months until the general election. After... well, let's just take it one step at a time.

"I have a friend."

"Oh, okay." The slow sip of tequila slides down my throat. "But do you want another one?"

Trouble's assessing gaze swipes up and down the alley. "Depends."

"On?"

"You. What's your angle?"

I tilt my chin higher to get a better look at his face. Not a single emotion displays across his features.

"My angle?" Leaning forward, I rest both elbows on my thighs. "Whoever hurt you worked you over good. Believe me, I've seen it, been there. If you're still this raw over it, I'm guessing it was recent."

His lips purse, flattening into a thin line.

"Right, you don't want to talk about it. That's cool, I get it. But to answer your question, I don't have an angle. Well...." I sigh and straighten my spine. "That's not true. I do have an angle, but it's not a bad one."

"What is it?" If I'm not mistaken, a hint of curiosity lines his voice.

"I need a friend, okay? I don't have anyone in DC I can trust. It's fucking lonely."

Those light brown eyes stop scanning for threats to meet mine. His brows furrow, forming a deep line between them. "You think you can trust me?"

Tapping the crates with the back of my heels, I shrug. "Yeah, I do, even though you're an ass."

He smirks at my words. "Trust is dangerous in politics." Thumb between my teeth, I chew on the ragged nail, waiting for him to continue. "Friends. I can do that."

I release the breath I was holding in a whoosh.

"Thank fuck."

"But we're not braiding each other's hair—"

"Obviously. You don't look like you'd be good at it. No offense."

"And the second I think you're fucking me over, we're done." He extends a hand between us. "Trey Benson. Pleased to meet you, friend."

I slide my own hand against his callused one. "Randi Sawyer. Nice to meet you, friend."

"Tell me your story," he says, crossing his arms over his chest. The buttons of his light blue dress shirt pull under the pressure. "From trailer to vying for the vice president spot. Must be a good one."

I snort and take a sip of tequila. The earlier bottle already warms my belly and loosens my normal hindrances of talking about my past.

"You saw where I grew up, and until Taeler was born, I thought Mom's life was my predestined future. But when I found out I was pregnant, and even more so after she was born, I wanted more for her, more for me. At that point, everything was spiraling out of control. Mom didn't want a baby interrupting her and her boyfriend's alone time, so she kicked me out to the shed." Memories flood my mind of the makeshift room slash nursery I created in the old storage shed. An unstoppable shudder shakes my body. Which of course he notices with those all-seeing eyes. "That didn't last long though. Taeler's dad's family stepped in, and... well, that's a whole different story that I don't want to get into."

My eyes widen, brows rising in question when he snags the cigarette box from my lap and lights up.

"Don't look so surprised. I don't know a single person who left the military without some kind of nicotine addiction."

"You're a veteran?" Of course he is. Bet you he looks hot as hell in whatever uniform he used to wear. Wonder if he still has it stashed somewhere.

"I am."

"Which branch?"

"Army."

I nod and light another cigarette. "A lot of the guys from my high school went in after graduation. Not a lot of choices unless you got an academic or sports scholarship for college. I was proud of them. I could never be that brave."

"Most of the boys under my command were the same. So fucking young."

"Oh," I say with an exhale of smoke. "Of course you were an officer." So hot.

"What made you go to UT and then law school? And not just any law school but Harvard?"

I roll the butt of the cigarette along my lower lip as I debate my response. "Someone told me I'd never amount to anything. That I'd never be more than an addict's daughter and would live the rest of my life in that same run-down trailer park. I wanted so badly to show them all they were wrong."

"I'd say you did."

I shake my head and swing my legs back and forth, kicking my heels against the thick plastic crates. "Not at first. When I first came home from law school, I did end up right back in the same trailer park, still broke, and even worse, in serious debt. I could've taken a job in Dallas, but I wanted to be close to Taeler. I'd already missed so much of her life, and I didn't want to miss any more."

"What happened?" he asks, taking a step closer. My shoulder brushes against his arm. The heat radiating off him begs me to inch closer. Of course I forgot my jacket upstairs. A strong, crisp fall breeze rips through the alley, racking my shoulders with a deep chill. Sealing the lit cigarette between his lips, Trey shrugs out of his suit jacket and drapes it across my shoulders.

"Thanks." I tug the two sides together making a makeshift cocoon with his jacket. I inhale deep, relishing in the faint scent of him. "What do you mean, what happened?"

"From being back in that small town with a law degree to running for vice president with dipshit Birmingham."

"Ah, that." *Tell the truth or the story we spun for the campaign. I can trust him; we are best friends, after all.* "The short version is I ruined his plans for world domination. I'm in over my head though and not really sure of my next move."

I glance up, fully expecting him to have more questions about my relationship with Kyle, but find him frowning at something down the alley.

"Ruined his plan?" I smile when his warm hand slides into mine. With a sharp tug, he yanks me from the stack of crates, causing them to tumble backward. "I need the full version not the short. But first...." Only after lighting up and taking a deep inhale does he motion for me to start. "Now I'm ready."

"So that's where we are," I say before taking another large bite from the juiciest double cheeseburger I've ever had. Do I feel bad taking Tank's cheeseburger and making him eat the tiny salad he ordered me? Not one bit. Rule number one, like he and I already covered, if you don't know, ask. If he would've, then he wouldn't be frowning over a plate of rabbit food right now.

Outside, I covered the basics on how Kyle approached me to be his wife before Trey cut me off, saying it would be best to head back upstairs to eat and let T hear everything too. Now they're *both* caught up on everything from the cover story to Kyle's harassment and Shawn's less-than-subtle threats.

"So, you're not with Birmingham?" Trey asks, disbelief in his tone. He hasn't stopped pacing since we got back up to the room. There's an ease in the way he moves, one fluid motion. Bet he'd be good in bed, fast and to the point. He doesn't come off as the cuddling type—another check in the win column for Trouble.

My eyes drop low, sliding down his body, pausing on his crotch.

"Randi."

I jump, somehow holding back a squeak of surprise. My gaze falls to the carpet in guilt. There's a slim chance he didn't notice me focused on his package. Peering through my dark lashes, I catch Trey's signature sexy smirk and divert my gaze anywhere other than him.

Shit. Busted.

I clear my throat and raise the burger, bringing it close to my lips. "What was the question again?"

"Are you fucking him?"

"Wow, so blunt. And no. Ew. Not that he hasn't tried, the depraved prick." T and Trey exchange a look. "What?" I ask before sinking my teeth into the cheeseburger.

I moan as I chew. Delicious.

"Birmingham said something different," T says, stroking his bald head. "Last night when he came by your condo."

I sort through all the possible reasons he'd do that while I finish chewing the large bite. "He was peeing on me."

"The fuck?" Trey says with a disgusted flinch.

"Not like that. Gross! What kind of shit are you into if that's where your mind goes, hmm?" I waggle a finger in Trey's direction and tsk. "Dirty mind.

No, I mean he was marking his territory. But why? Why would Kyle want to keep you guys away from me?"

Trey clears his throat and pauses his pacing. Back against the far wall, he stuffs his large hands into the pockets of his suit. Two undone buttons of the crisp dress shirt pull with the movement, exposing a hint of chest. Why must he look like a mischievous male model? What stupid god did I piss off in life for them to dangle this untouchable hottie in my face?

It's mean. Wonder if there's a Secret Service suggestion box where I can file a 'please don't hire hotties' request so I'm not tempted on a second by second basis by a man I can't have. I should look into that.

"You with us, Randi?" T's deep voice pulls me out of my random thoughts.

"Yes. Of course I am. Well, maybe... actually, that's a hard no." I shrug and take another bite. I wink at T's glare as I chew. "It's really good. Thanks."

"You and my wife, taking my good food and replacing it with stuff fit for animals."

"I said," Trey interrupts, "before you got lost in your head—"

"It happens a lot. Get used to it."

"I grew up with Birmingham and Whit. Most of the fucksticks in DC, actually."

I nod, then shake my head. "Still though, why feel the need to pee on me?"

"Please stop saying that," Trey says on a sigh. I can't help but smile at his restrained annoyance. "Birmingham and I, plus Whit, have a rocky past."

"Ah, so it's less about me and more about you and Kyle." Mouth open, prepared to take another bite, I pause. "Wait. Oh hell, are you gay? Did y'all break up or something?"

"What the—"

"Now the bitter attitude makes sense. You were jealous, thinking I was sleeping with your ex–boyfriend."

Trey races closer, leaping over the coffee table. I shriek in excitement, the half-eaten burger falling forgotten to the plate. He grips the back of the couch on either side of my head, boxing me between his arms. In slow motion, he leans closer, and I sink deeper into the couch in retreat.

Deep, labored pants fan my face as he hovers inches from my face.

"Benson. Stop your shit. She didn't mean it," T calls out from somewhere in the distance, zero concern in his distracted tone.

"Take it back, or you'll regret it," Trey grunts, his almost smile taking the heat from his words.

"Are you a giver or a taker?" I say around a stifled giggle. Holy hell, it's hot in here. "I knew you were too pretty to be straight."

"There are twenty different ways I could kill you right now. I'm fucking badass, not pretty."

"Why does that turn me on?" His eyes widen at my breathy words. My chest rises and falls in quick succession, my pulse racing through my body, heating every inch. "There is something *seriously* wrong with me."

That damn sexy, mischievous smirk tugs at his edible lips. "Or very right." My breaths come in short pants. His lips brush against the shell of my ear, and I shiver at his raspy low voice. "I'm not gay, but I do love fucking a woman's nice round ass."

Who's wheezing? Shit. Am I wheezing? I'm wheezing.

What the hell? Sweat slicks my hands. At some point, my stomach slid up my throat and is now lodged there, preventing me from swallowing all the saliva building in my mouth.

"Get off her," T says, his words muffled like he's...

Tearing my lust-filled eyes from Trey's, I catch T as he shoves the last of the cheeseburger into his mouth.

"Hey." I pout. "That was mine." My hand vibrates with Trey's laugh as I shove against his chest to sit up.

T's broad shoulders rise and fall in an exaggerated shrug. "You dropped it, five second rule. Now back to business." The repetitive drumming of his fingers along the side table is the only sound in the quiet suite. Earlier Trey kicked the other agents out so I could tell the story without untrustworthy ears listening. "I'm guessing what happened last night with the accident somehow has to do with Shawn. I'll work on that angle once we get back to DC. It's good you told us; we can better protect you from inside threats now that we know to expect them."

"Great," I say with a yawn. A quick glance to the grandfather clock— because what hotel room doesn't have one of those—tells me it's just past ten. "As much fun as this has been, I have a shit ton of information to memorize before we head home tomorrow." The room spins a fraction as I stand. A hand dips beneath the suit coat I'm still wearing to slide around my waist, steadying me. I tip my head up. "Thank you."

"What are friends for?" A full, genuine smile spreads up Trey's cheeks.

For a second, I stay mesmerized by the change in his face. The smirk is sexy, yes, but this smile? Hot fucking damn. The lightness in his features, the happiness in those bunched cheeks, gives him a fun-loving, boyish look.

"You should smile more," I whisper, still staring. I want that happy. The carefree, self-assured rightness in my life.

Soon. Even though money isn't an issue anymore, the pressure to keep proving myself is still there. Too many people still doubt me, hoping I fail. Once I prove everyone how wrong they are, how wrong they've been my whole life, maybe then I can be truly happy.

"Nah." He tugs, drawing me closer. "Come on. I'll help you to your room."

Each step forces our bodies to brush, shock waves of awareness from my racing heart zapping me with each accidental touch. As subtle as I can, I dip my nose to the coat still cocooning me in its warmth. His unique spicy scent fills my nose. As I take another long sniff, the stress from the last few hours eases from my shoulders, allowing them to drop from their place at my ears.

We pause halfway into the room. The fingers wrapped around my waist tighten.

"Where do you want to sit? Bed or chair?"

"Chair," I say, pointing to the plush chair I sat in earlier. "Shoot, I need my laptop bag." I try to shrug out of his hold, but his grip tightens, preventing me.

"I'll get it. You go get comfortable."

My gaze follows him until he disappears into the living room.

I only make it a few steps toward the chair when Trouble marches back in, annoyance written across his tight features. "Your phone's vibrating." It lands on the fluffy duvet with a poof. Reaching over, I flip it to check who it is.

'Blocked Caller' flashes on the black screen.

Kyle.

I swipe to answer and press it to my ear.

"Where are you?" he demands, forgoing any niceties.

"Dallas." The mattress presses against my backside as I perch on the edge. Leaning back on an elbow, I let my head fall back. "Things are taken care of with my mom. I'm looking into some exclusive rehab centers that promise confidentiality."

"I don't give a fuck what you're doing with her. Get your ass back to DC now."

My elbow slides along the soft fabric as I fall back onto the bed. "A lot has happened in the last twenty-four hours. I need some time to—"

"This isn't about you, Walmart, or have you not fucking figured that out yet? This is about winning and doing whatever I need you to do to ensure that we do. Get back on that jet right now. I need you in New York City Friday night to meet with a campaign donor. He wants to meet you."

"Well, that's promising. Maybe he likes my platform for lower taxes on the working—"

"That's not what he likes, you idiot. Damn, you're ignorant. Get your ass back here now so we can go over what I need you to do when you meet with him."

'Kyle, I don't feel comfortable—" I peel the hot glass from my ear and frown at the dark screen. Staring at the ceiling, I hold the phone to my chest.

"What was that about?" Trey's concerned face peers over the bed, blocking my view of the ceiling.

I roll my head back and forth. "We need to pack up and get back to DC tonight."

A heavy hand rests on the crown of my head. "What don't you feel comfortable with, Randi? What did that dipshit tell you to do?"

"Does it matter?" I slide my gaze to focus on his shoulder.

"Hey, look at me. Friends, right?"

I nod and bite my lower lip to keep it from trembling.

"Then what? Tell me."

"He wants me in New York to meet with a campaign donor. I get the impression the guy has other things than discussing the campaign on the agenda."

Trouble curses. The bed dips, making me roll toward the middle, my side smooshing up against his thigh. Pressing my cheek against the duvet, I stare up at his profile. He's propped on the edge of the bed, his head tipped back, eyes focused on the ceiling.

"Don't do it." A hunk of dark hair slides across his forehead as pleading eyes meet mine. "I have zero right to tell you what to do, but don't do it."

"I don't have a choice," I whisper. The fear of returning home, once again unsuccessful in life, lodges in my throat. "I can't go home. Can't go back to living like that day after day."

"You always have a choice."

"Easy for you to say. You don't have as much to lose as I do."

"Don't I?" he grits out. "I have more on the table than you realize. Don't judge me when you get pissed that people do the exact same to you."

My lashes flutter closed. "You're right. But it doesn't change the situation or the outcome."

"Fight back. Be a fighter in this. Don't give in to his demands sitting down."

The determination in his voice, in the stern look on his face, urges me to listen. Digging my elbows into the duvet, I lean forward and knock his bicep with my shoulder. "Okay, Yoda. How do you propose I fight this when I have zero leverage?"

My heart thunders against my chest as one corner of his lip tugs up. "I have a few ideas."

Excitement and unease swirl in my belly like a group of butterflies all taking flight at the same time.

Maybe I am as crazy as people think I am, because I'm smiling right back.

15

RANDI

Rivers of rain stream down the town car's window, the stoplight above highlighting their path with a bright red backdrop. Elbow on the armrest of the door, I sigh, a patch of condensation appearing atop the dark glass from my breath.

New York City. I would be excited if it weren't for the crazy nerves hijacking my emotions.

A warm palm slides over my bare knee. I shift my observing eyes from the passing umbrellas lining the sidewalks to the contact.

Fine lines, some from age and some from injuries leaving faint white scars, mar Trey's tan hand. A simple swipe of his thumb along the inside of my knee sends a chill racing through my veins, having nothing to do with the cool temperature inside the car. I swallow back the building unease, my gaze shifting from his hand to the man himself.

"We'll be with you every step of the way," Trey says, his tone low, soothing. "If you want to cancel—"

I give him an adamant shake of my head. Peering through the darkness, I meet his concerned brown eyes. "No, I have to do this. You know I do. This is my chance to gain leverage on those assholes. It's a great plan."

"Some might even call it brilliant."

A snort tickles my nose. The expensive fabric of my cocktail dress slides along the soft leather of the seat as I adjust, angling my knees toward Trey, who sits inches away in the other passenger seat. "I'll call it brilliant if it works."

All humor leaves his face. His eyes shift, and I track the path of his gaze to where his hand still rests on my knee, that sneaky thumb still swiping along my bare skin.

He pulls his hand away, the heat that was building between my thighs following suit.

He clears his throat. "Sorry."

I bite the tip of my tongue to keep myself from begging him to move it back. His touch, the soft yet powerful way his skin feels against mine, is more than welcomed. Not sure what that means, but for the first time in my life, I want a comforting caress from someone besides Taeler. His comforting yet possessive hands holding me close.

In the back seat of the sleek black town car, I meet his intense stare as the passing streetlights filter in and out through the windows. It's only been a few days since we met, but there's something building between us. Something deeper than I've experienced even with people I've known for years. He sees me, the real me. And I see bits of the real Trey Benson. I see the slivers he doesn't intentionally show. The soft touches, considerate actions, and supportive words.

And I want more.

Want it all.

"Almost there," T says from the driver seat. I reluctantly pull my gaze from Trey's to glance out the windshield. The wipers swipe back and forth in slow repetitive arcs. "I still don't like it."

I bite back a smile. Of course the cautious and careful Terminator doesn't like this crazy plan. To be honest, I'm not a huge fan either, but it's the perfect scenario to kill three birds with one stone. If it works.

No, it will work.

My chest pitches forward as we slide to a stop in front of a dazzling hotel. The brilliant blue lights cast a strange hue over T and Gremlin.

I inhale deep, filling my lungs with the determination and strength to get through this night and finally, *finally* have the upper hand in life. The leather groans beneath my backside as I rotate toward the door, waiting for the approaching bellhop to pull it open.

"Randi?" I turn my chin, glancing over my shoulder to T. "If you feel this won't work, or if you're scared or... anything, get out. Give the code word and it's done whether we have the information we need or not. Got it?"

My dark hair slides forward across my shoulder at my tight nod.

"What's the code word again?" he demands.

"Pumpkin spice latte," I say with a grin. That was T's addition to the plan. I wanted 'sparkle the unicorn' as the code word, but neither him nor Trey thought I could find a way to work it into a normal sentence. Just proves they don't know me as well as they think they do.

A burst of cool, damp air brushes against my legs and floats a few sections of hair across my face. I face the familiar callused palm dangling midair, waiting for my own. With another deep breath, I slide my fingers between Trey's and wrap my fingers around his own. I fold out of the car, stepping cautiously onto the sidewalk in my heels. I glide both hands down the thick material of my black dress, repositioning the hem from where it rode up my thighs.

Tipping my chin, I take a step toward the enormous revolving doors. Sweat beads along my palms the closer we get. Rapid breaths steal the air from my lungs, making my head fuzzy.

"Calm down," Trey says. I flick an annoyed glance his way at the laughter in his tone. "You're fine."

A tight smile pulls at my lips for Gremlin, who holds the side door open for us, as we step into the hotel lobby.

All the building anxiety melts away as Trey presses his hand against the small of my back. Slowing my pace to increase the comforting pressure, I give my fingers a tiny shake. My heels click along the polished marble as we stride across the lobby toward the restaurant where I'm meeting the campaign donor.

The plan is simple: gain information we can use to blackmail him and get out. The information can be anything from bribery all the way to harassment. Whatever it ends up being, I hope it happens fast. The less time I have to spend with this guy the better. Being alone with him isn't on my top twenty things to do while in New York City.

"I wish I could see the city," I say to Trey, my attention staying on the approaching hostess stand. Mr. Hindle, the campaign donor, insisted we meet here. The fact that it's a restaurant inside this upscale hotel didn't pass my notice. "I've only been here for rallies or something else to do with the campaign. Never seen the city like a real tourist."

The pressure on my back changes as he guides me through the intimate tables of the restaurant. I scan the large area over the packed crowd for the man I'm meeting.

"Back booth. More secure," Trouble whispers into my ear. "Almost there. You good? Head in the game?"

No. "Yes."

We don't say another word. The restaurant darkens the farther back we go, the other patrons' murmurs growing quieter. An older man slides from a small intimate booth. I recognize him immediately based off the pictures and information Kyle had me review in DC. Early sixties, multimillionaire, wants world domination. Okay, that's not one hundred percent true. In exchange for funneling millions into our campaign fund, he wants a blind eye on his companies unfavorable working conditions if we win.

I shudder at the way his clouded eyes ogle my thin frame. Not as thin as it was last year before I met Kyle but still putting on weight in the right areas has been a challenge. The hand at my back tightens to a fist, the knuckles now digging into my lower spine. I chance a peek up to Trouble, but he doesn't notice. His intense stare is locked on the donor with a promise of a slow death behind those honey brown eyes. I love the humor and twinkle I normally see, the side he shows me, but this side of Trouble is just as sexy.

That intensity, the utter control the man exudes, zaps the final drop of worry clouding my thoughts. He's here. T's outside. Gremlin and the rest of the boys are waiting in the shadows.

I can do this. They're trusting me to have the balls to get through this, and I will not let them down.

They believe in me. It's time I did too.

"Miss Sawyer." Mr. Hindle leans forward, pressing a swift kiss to one cheek, then the other. "Thank you for meeting me."

"The pleasure is mine," I say, somehow suppressing my utter disdain from seeping through.

He raises his hand to the side, extending into the booth. I swallow hard and step out of Trouble's comforting touch. The dress's hem rides up my thighs as I slide along the supple leather semicircle booth. Settled on the opposite side, Mr. Hindle climbs in and keeps going, pausing when our knees touch but keeping a respectable distance between us for the world to see. Sneaky prick. I grip the hem of my dress beneath the crisp white table linen and give it a quick tug as I cross one leg over the other, sealing my thighs tightly together.

"You can leave."

My mouth pops open. Attention flying from the front of my dress to Mr. Hindle, I shift back against the tufted black leather of the booth at his pinched features. But his annoyance isn't directed to me. My gaze floats across the table in the direction of Mr. Hindle's glare. My own eyes widen in surprise.

Trey still stands at the booth opening. Stance wide, hands lightly folded in front, exuding refined power. Not money power like the filthy idiot beside me. No, real power. The kind of energy that radiates off someone who knows without a doubt he or she can handle whatever comes their way.

"My team is conducting one more sweep of the restaurant as we speak. I'll move as soon as I get the all clear."

If Mr. Hindle doesn't catch the unspoken 'asshole' at the end, I'll be shocked.

Several tense seconds tick by while the two men battle for dominance.

"All clear." Trouble's eyes flick to me. My breath catches knowing this means he's leaving me here alone. "Ma'am."

I watch as he turns and fades into the dark corners of the restaurant where no doubt the rest of the team is waiting.

My foot taps furiously in the air beneath the table.

I'm up.

Careful to keep my movements smooth, I slide my red clutch from where it rests on the seat to the table. It's not super close to Mr. Hindle, but T assures me the tiny listening device tucked in the pocket will pick up our conversation just fine as long as it's within reach. I tug it a bit closer just in case.

Hands fidgeting, nerves at an all-time high, I adjust and readjust the five forks and thirty spoons surrounding the single white plate to give my anxious fingers something to do while Mr. Hinkle smiles seeming to enjoy my uncomfortableness.

A stiff back waiter approaches with zero animation on his surly face. Without asking what I would like, Mr. Hindle immediately speaks up to order an expensive bottle of red wine and waves the waiter off with an arrogant flick of the wrist.

"How's DC treating you?" he asks after the waiter scurries away.

I roll my shoulders and adjust in the booth.

Game time.

"Different than Texas, that's for sure. Complex, fast paced, brilliant are a few words I'd use to describe what I've seen so far."

He chuckles and rests a wrinkled hand on top my own. He gives a pointed look to their constant movement. "First time doing this?"

"This?" Oh, please tell me he's going to say something sleazy so I can get the hell out of here sooner than later.

"Meeting with a campaign donor, of course." His easy chuckle rakes my frayed nerves. "Let's get some wine in us before we dive into the business side, shall we? I have to admit your background is intriguing to me."

"Oh?" I move my hand from under his, tucking it in my lap. "And why's that?"

"It's different. Most of the people in this town don't know what it's like to live below the 1 percent. Hearing your perspective through the campaign coverage so far has piqued my interest. Tell me a bit about yourself, Randi. Can I call you Randi?"

I force a stiff nod. "There isn't much to tell, but you're correct that my perspective is different. I know what it's like to scrape by, to have your hard-earned money be siphoned away before you even can cash your paycheck."

"And that's what you want to change. I like that. Tell me more."

The tight tension in my gut fades. My shoulders relax and my foot stops its midair thumping. Maybe Kyle was wrong about what this guy wants from me. He's pitched forward, elbows on the table, fully engaged in what I have to say. Embarrassed warmth sparks along my cheeks, no doubt turning them a bright pink. What if all this was for nothing and this guy is just a nice old man?

As the waiter holds out the bottle for Mr. Hindle's inspection, I detail out my thoughts and ideas on how to change the lives of those who fall beneath the middle-class financial status. By the time I wrap up my crazy ideas—Kyle's words, not mine—excitement flickers in my belly and hope flows through my veins, making my fingers twitch in anticipation. If I can get this man to see things from my point of view, maybe Kyle will change his tune and let me spearhead some of these projects.

A wide smile stretching across my face, I lean forward, reaching for my wineglass, only to find it empty. Huh, when did that happen?

"It's good, isn't it? At four hundred dollars a bottle, it should be." My fingers slip from the glass. I shift my gaze to his—still full. "I'll get you another bottle."

Another?

Frantic, I glance around the restaurant, but with the lights dimmed and zero windows, there's nothing to use to judge how much time as passed during my long-winded rant.

"Sorry, I-I got carried away," I stutter. Condensation slicks my palm and fingers as I grasp the water glass and lift it to my lips.

"No need to be embarrassed, Randi." The seat shifts my weight, angling me toward Mr. Hindle as he scoots an inch closer. My muscles tense at the brush of his suit pants along the skin of my bare thigh.

My breath hitches.

Kyle was right, I am an idiot. I played right into this fucker's hands.

At the first brush of his fingers along my knee, I jerk out of his reach.

"Come on now, Randi, don't be that way." This time his fingers clamp around my exposed thigh, preventing me from flinching away. "I can do so much for your cause."

"If...?" I ask, not having to add a tremble to my tone. It's already there.

"I think that's something we can discuss after dinner, don't you?"

No. I can't let it get that far. If I go up to his room, like I'm sure he'll suggest, I'm done for. He's twice my size; if he tries anything, there's no way I could fight him off. Plus, behind closed doors, I won't have Trey's hawk eyes monitoring the situation.

This needs to end now, even though he's not lying about the wine. That shit is yummy with a capital *Y*. I'd take a picture of the label to buy later, but even if I had enough money to wipe my ass with hundred-dollar bills, I couldn't justify spending that kind of cash on a single bottle of wine.

Case? Debatable. But bottle, no way. Do you know how many boxes of wine you could buy for four hundred dollars? A lot, that's how much.

His soft skin slides up toward the juncture of my legs that's securely sealed off by the closed thighs, pulling me back to the present.

"I know how much this means to you," he mutters. "Have you found a rehab center for your mother yet?"

The sip of water I just took sputters back into my glass. "What?" I say on a deep cough, trying to clear the rest of the water from my lungs and give me a moment to wrap my head around his words. "How did you—"

"Enough money in the right hands and you can find the truth in anything." I balk at his cold sneer. "You see, Randi, this is in your best interest. We can make a deal, you and I."

"And what deal is that?"

"Eager," he says, digging his fingers deeper into my flesh. I hide my wince of pain behind the water glass at my lips. "I like that."

"What do you want, Mr. Hindle?" I straighten my spine. I will not bow to this fucker. "I thought this was about your business and your donation to the campaign."

"Ah, that. Kyle and I already discussed the terms."

"What?" I gasp.

"You didn't know?" He releases my thigh. Immediately I move out of his reach, sliding to the other side of the booth. "Figures he wouldn't fill you in."

"In on what?" I grit out. Fuck Kyle and his power moves. Moving me around the country like his little pawn protecting the damn king.

"You sealing the deal, of course."

I slump forward, all fight draining from my muscles.

"Don't look so repulsed. I'm not that bad, am I?"

I school my features, keeping the hint of excitement from showing. *This is my opening.*

"Depends," I say in the meekest tone I can muster. "What... what do you want from me? I don't understand what you're referring to."

"You want me to spell it out for you, sweetheart?"

I fight a cringe.

Fluttering my lashes, I glance around the restaurant, pretending to ensure no one is around. I moisten my lower lip with a slow swipe of my tongue. "Yes."

His cold eyes fall to my wet lip as he licks his own in anticipation. I battle internally to not shudder in disgust. "Come to my room and I'll show you."

Well hell. Maybe a different angle?

"If I do this, if I come up to your room, you'll keep my mom out of this? You'll give the money to the campaign?"

"We can work out the terms upstairs, but yes, in a nutshell. Give me what I want, and I'll make sure the money is deposited tomorrow."

Rallying what bit of courage I have left, I scoot along the booth, our hips now touching. "So how does this work? A promise of a hundred grand for you to fuck my mouth? Five hundred for me to spread my legs?"

His eyes darken with lust, beads of sweat glistening across his creased brow.

This is where I want him. On the edge of reason, tipping over into the abyss of dark desire.

"And how much for my ass?" I whisper into his ear. Ugh, I'll need two scalding showers to remove the ick from my skin. "How much is my entire body worth to you?"

"Two million." His voice is coarse with the gallons of desire pumping through his veins. "Two million dollars to the campaign if you let me pound into your ass." His rapid, hot breaths brush over my face as he leans close. "Another million, and my promise to keep your family's finances out of the press, if you make that arrogant agent watch."

Fucking creeper.

I open my mouth to tell him just as much but gasp at the panic in Mr. Hindle's bulging eyes. The leather slips beneath my sweaty palms as I scramble down the booth.

Trey sits on the opposite side of Mr. Hindle, their shoulders close enough to touch.

"You want me to watch, do you?" Trey's arm beneath the table shifts, and Mr. Hindle gasps, face paling. The hate threatening behind Trey's light eyes disappears when his gaze shifts to me. "I think we got enough, don't you?"

Mr. Hindle's narrowed eyes flick between me and Trouble. "You set me up." Red clutch in hand, I raise it in the air. His clouded eyes search the bag like he's scanning the recording itself, replaying every word he said tonight. "Nothing will hold up in court. You've got nothing, you fucking conniving—" A sharp whistle of air cuts off his words as he sucks in a quick breath.

What in the hell is Trey doing under the table? I tilt my head in question, but he shakes his. Hmm, he'll tell me later, then.

I shift my focus back to the sweaty Mr. Hindle. The air of power and influence is gone, his older age showing as his skin pales.

"You're correct, nothing will hold up in court." His brows rise and a flush of life spreads back into his gaunt face. "But that wasn't what I was going for. You see, I've noticed that in today's social media society, justice doesn't mean anything. One slip of the voice recording leaked on the internet, one accusation, and poof, someone is guilty in everyone's opinion before the case ever sees a courtroom. Trial by Twitter. It's a thing." His shoulders round as the truth in my words sink in. "Do you care what the public thinks of you? What about that beautiful young wife of yours? Oh, and your five kids. What would they think if they heard daddy dearest demanding sexual favors in exchange for money?" I click my tongue and tilt my head. "And the watching part? That's dark."

"What do you want?" he bites out, holding as still as a statue.

Seriously, does Trey have this guy's balls in a vise or something? I fight the urge to dip under the table and see what the hell is going on under there.

"A few things, actually. First, I need you to tell Kyle everything went smoothly tonight and pay out whatever you agreed on." A blast of satisfaction fills every inch of my heart at the condemning look he shoots my way. Not sure why he's pissed at me; he's the old dirty bastard. "Second, you'll also tell him to keep his hands off me or you'll pull your donation."

"Why the fuck would I do that?"

I wave a hand in dismissal. "I don't know. Think of something. Maybe that you want me all to yourself or something. I don't care."

Seconds tick by, the murmuring of the other patrons, oblivious to what we're doing, filling the background. I lick my lower lip as I eye his still-full glass of wine. Would it be bad form to let that go to waste? I can't let down those poor grapes who lost their lives for this wine. Lifting one shoulder in agreement with my internal debate, I reach across the table and cradle the delicate glass in my palm.

"Seriously?" Trey admonishes.

I shrug and take a sip.

"For all this, you'll destroy the recording?"

I nod and pause, holding up a finger. "Also, no releasing my mom's information to the press. And if I ever hear you're attempting to extort sexual favors for political ones again, I'll release the recording and pay a visit to your wife personally to tell her everything that happened tonight. 'Kay? 'Kay."

I shouldn't wink. That would be an asshole move.

Eh.

I wink.

He begrudgingly grunts some form of acknowledgment. Good enough for me.

Another hasty sip. Yum, so good.

You know what? Fuck it. I slide my phone from the clutch and snap a picture of the bottle. Maybe it can be a special occasion bottle, like when the queen visits or I'm successful in securing world peace.

I scoot out of the booth to stand, skimming both palms down the black material, drying them and pushing the hem back down my thighs in one move. The dress is beautiful, classy yet sexy. Too bad I'll burn it after tonight. I don't care how much it cost; I could never wear it again without remembering this asshole's hands on me.

I'm held captivated with acute interest as Trey leans closer to Mr. Hindle, whispering something in his ear. I track Trey's movements as he shifts out of the booth and stands beside me. Our eyes meet, something dangerous and hot flaring between us.

I turn my attention back to the table, locking eyes with the slimy bastard.

"Nice doing business with you, Mr. Hindle. Thank you for the wine. It was delicious."

I spin from the table, more than ready to put this night behind me. My feet don't get a single step before a comforting hand presses against my lower back, guiding me through the restaurant once again.

I won this battle.

We won this battle.

One of many in this political warfare I've immersed myself in, I'm sure.

I glance over my shoulder to Trey, a smile spreading up my lips. At least I'm not alone.

16

TREY

Muscles tense, hands fisted, I fight the urge to turn and skewer that rat bastard's balls with the steak knife I left on the booth seat. The magic lessons as a kid come in handy at times; tonight was one of them. No one noticed the slight of hand as I swiped the seemingly unsuspecting knife from the table. No one except Mr. Hindle, who felt said knife slicing through his suit pants, readying to do the same to his sac if he so much as breathed too deep.

Tank set it up for the team to hear every word through the small listening device hidden in that tiny purse of hers. How I kept myself from tackling the fucker as he played Randi with the expensive wine and faking to be interested in the causes she holds close, I'll never know. I deserve a big fucking gold star next to my name.

The old fucker should be tortured and left for dead for even thinking it was okay to extort a woman like that. A snarl pulls at my face. I know from personal experience that he's just one of hundreds, if not thousands, in the corrupt political scene.

A forceful relieved exhale pushes from my chest as we exit the restaurant into the much cooler hotel lobby.

Instead of directing Randi toward the front doors where Tank and the other boys wait to whisk her back to the jet, I tug her close and divert us down a long hall.

"Um, Trouble, where—"

I press a finger to my lips, cutting her off. The clicking of her heels echoes down the empty hall, mine silent with each step. Searching right and then left, I grip her elbow and tug her toward a conference room door. I press an ear to the door and listen.

Nothing.

Perfect.

The door clicks open with ease, and I pull her through after me. Darkness engulfs the large ballroom except for the bright band of light cutting through its inky blackness from the hallway. I tip my face to meet hers, wide hazel eyes searching mine.

The door snaps closed, eliminating the last bit of light.

Darkness envelops us. A bolt of satisfaction shoots through my chest as her smaller body presses against my own. Without questioning the emotions spurring the moment, I wrap an arm around her shoulders, tucking her tighter against my chest. Here, she's safe. Away from the corrupt world that wants nothing more than to conquer and pillage her trusting soul. A growing part of me doesn't want her to win in the general election. She's too good for this town. I've seen what the political game does to women like her, seen the bitter shell left behind.

Through the earpiece, Tank demands our location.

"Tank, listen, man. Don't be mad." I wince at the explosion of curse words in my ear. "But we're going off-line for a little while. Don't worry, big guy, we'll be fine."

At that, I tug the earpiece from my ear and turn off the radio. Digging around my pants pocket, I pull out my phone and press the flashlight icon. Randi's sweet face pinches as she pulls back from the bright light assaulting her unprepared eyes.

"Do you or do you not want to see New York City while you're here?" Her eyes search mine before glancing to the closed door. "If you're ready to go back, then we walk out of here and head to the jet. I just thought after all that"—my muscles tighten, tugging her closer—"you'd want a night off. You didn't get one in Dallas. This is your chance."

"What about the team?" she asks. I tug on her hand for her to release the thumbnail she's chewing on. "Can we go out there alone?"

"Do you trust me?" I ask, seriousness filling my voice. If she doesn't, hell, that'll be a blow I'm not prepared to take.

An eternity seems to pass between the moment my question leaves my lips and her answer. I want her to rely on me. No, I'm *desperate* for her to rely on me, to see me as her protector. A man who will fight to keep her safe from the DC wolves and threats to her life.

"Yes," she says with a smile. "Yes, I trust you."

My lips curl, mirroring her own. "Good. Then let's go."

***

"Wow," she says on a pushed breath.

Standing close, I peer down, soaking in her palpable excitement. Around us, lights blink throughout glittering Times Square. Thousands of tourists shuffle, bumping against each other, moving bodies like human bumper cars. Horns blare over the music pouring from various stores. In the center of the exciting madness, the Naked Cowboy strums away on his guitar, eating up the attention.

With her excitement, it's like seeing it all for the first time, even though it could easily be my hundredth. I chuckle in amusement as she points at the nearly naked man, her brows waggling suggestively beneath the "I Love NYC" hat pulled low.

The hat and sweat suit, plus the flip-flops—all her idea, not mine—were a necessary purchase after we broke out of the hotel's back exit, hightailing it down various streets to escape a murderous Tank.

I offered to buy her something less... well, ugly. That's the best way to put it. But she refused, saying the New York Yankees sweatpants and sweatshirt were perfect. Paired with a pair of gaudy flip-flops from another vendor and she's a hilarious hot mess. Not that she seems to care one bit. Hell, she didn't even bat an eye at having to change in a dark alley or the hot dog stand I suggested for dinner.

This woman tosses everything I know about women out the window and has ruined me for the Political Barbies in DC forever. This is fun. Easy. The last time I was in New York, all I saw was the inside of high-end boutiques and department stores as Rachel lit my credit card on fire. Thank fuck I didn't give in to her pouting when I wouldn't go into Harry Winston with her. The media circus around our breakup would've been ten times worse if there was a broken engagement tossed into the shit show.

I stumble at the insistent tug on my elbow. A lock of hair falls along my forehead as I shake my head in amusement. Randi leads us through the swarm of people, talking a thousand words a second over her shoulder as she points up at the bright billboards with the hand not pulling me along.

Maybe I should send Shawn a thank-you card for helping me see that Rachel and I were a forced fit. It sucked at the time, yes, and hell, it still does at night when I fall asleep horny and alone. My poor dick hasn't felt anything other than my own hand in way too long.

My gaze falls to Randi's round ass accentuated by the draping material of the soft sweatpants. At my back, someone stumbles in to me, shoving me forward. Our feet tangle, her loud gasp barely audible above the other noise on the street. I wrap both arms around her waist, lifting her off the sidewalk and tucking her close to my chest. A couple intentional steps forward and I'm once again steady on my feet. But still I don't drop her. Instead, I tug her closer, the crease of her ass cradling my hardening cock.

Fuck, she feels fantastic, and this is with clothes on.

Her chest expands and shrinks in rapid succession beneath my forearms.

Around us the crowd shuffles, ignoring our tight embrace. Oblivious to my internal battle to not fuck her against the nearest wall. The need to take her, to make her scream my name, increases every day we're together, every second more torturous than the last. I shouldn't want her. Not because of her background or her lack of wealth but because she's the job. My job is to protect her, keep her safe, and here I am unable to think beyond the way my dick feels pressed against her.

This is a terrible idea, but I can't stop. I don't want to stop.

I want her, all of her, every inch and every breath begging for me.

"Trey?" Wiggling in my hold, she rotates to dip her head back, hazel eyes finding mine.

"Randi."

"Um, I can't really, you know, breathe here."

Shit.

"Sorry," I grumble and ease my hold, savoring the slide of her body against mine. "You ready to get out of here? Head back?"

The excitement and joy falls from her face.

"Do we have to?" she asks, looking to the sidewalk. I stare at her hat-covered head, not understanding what just happened to flip her mood. "If you're worried about the crowd, we can go somewhere else." Pushing to her tiptoes, she looks right, left, over her shoulder, and then over mine, looking back down the street. "Where's Central Park?"

Reaching out, I interlace our fingers and meet her hopeful gaze. "Come on, Mess. It's this way."

With the hustle of the crowd behind us, I flex my fingers to release her hand, but hers tighten, keeping my hand clasped.

Okay then.

Stepping over a line, but that's okay. She probably needs to feel safe as we navigate the streets of New York City, and holding my hand like a drowning victim does a life preserver offers that sense of safety. I should not read into the simple gesture. Which I'm not, except my semi isn't listening, and it's fucking chafing the hell out of the tip.

"You seem like you've been here before," Randi says beside me. Her head is on a swivel, taking in every building and storefront.

"I have—several times, in fact—but I'll tell you something, Mess. It's a different experience with you."

I smirk at her responding snort. "Mess? Is that what you're calling me now?"

I shrug and look away so she doesn't catch my smile.

"I should be offended, yet it fits. I'll allow it. And you know you use that word a lot when you describe me."

"Mess?"

"No, different."

"Ah." I tug her to a stop to keep from being run over by a speeding taxi. "It's the best way I can describe it. It's a good thing though, so you know. It's... vibrant."

"Vibrant."

I shake my head. "It's hard to explain. I've seen the world through a certain lens for thirty-eight years, and then you come along and turn things from versions of gray to full of color. Full of life. I've never known someone who sees the world for what it is and not what they can get from it."

I glance down to gauge her reaction only to find her head down, the bill of the hat blocking her face from view. A quiet sniffle meets my listening ears. Another has me tugging her to a stop, but still she keeps her face down. Bending my knees, I lower a few inches, putting me at her level. Two fingers beneath her chin, I tilt her face to meet mine.

Well, fuck me.

Wet streaks glisten along her full cheeks in the overhead streetlight. Unease at her red-rimmed eyes steals the air from my lungs.

Large tears roll down from the inside corner of both eyes. "That was the nicest... the nicest thing anyone has ev-ever said to me. About me. Thank you."

Talk about a knife to the heart. I ball my hands into tight fists as anger and resentment build, rolling together and growing larger and volatile. If that's the nicest thing anyone has ever said to her.... I shake my head. Nope, can't go there or I'll go on a killing streak, murdering everyone who's ever said an ill word toward her.

"You're breaking my heart here, Mess." I tug slightly on her hand until her chest is pressed against mine. Eyes to the sky, I mentally list the Redskins' roster, hoping to distract me from her squished tits rubbing against me.

I'm going through the 2018 lineup when she finally pulls back, wiping her nose with the sleeve of the sweatshirt.

"I'm okay, just didn't expect that, and after tonight with... you know. I'm just on edge. Then you go and say something nice, and here I am losing my shit on the streets of New York City." She takes another step back, fully pulling out of my embrace, and starts toward the park once again.

"Different circumstances, but I do know what it's like to not have support, or hell, even a positive word come out of your parent's mouth. How do you do it?" Hands in my pockets, I slow my steps to keep pace with hers. "Everything you've lived through, pushed through, yet you're still pushing forward, striving for more."

The tips of her fingers slide inside the sleeves of her sweatshirt before she tucks her arms around her chest. "Speaking of parents, thanks for the rehab referral. It's working out great so far. Costing me a kidney, but hopefully it makes a lasting impact this time."

"You're welcome. Glad I could help take some stress off."

"And to answer your question, I guess you can say me growing up the way I did made me positive instead of desolate. Everywhere around me I saw where giving up would get you, and I didn't want that. Not for me or for Taeler. So I stayed positive, kept that hope of a better life alive day after day, even when things were tight and I didn't want to stay strong. That's the thing about being a parent, you can't give up. You have someone looking up to you, counting on you to give them their best life. I couldn't give up because I couldn't give up on Taeler."

"You were fifteen when you felt that?"

She shrugs, dismissing the awe in my voice.

"Randi, most people don't realize that even when they become parents later in life. Our world is a selfish black hole that sucks your will to live—"

"You're kind of dramatic for a guy, you know that?"

A sense of relief floods through me at the smile in her voice. "All I'm saying is you're special. Don't ever forget that. Whether you win or lose in November, always remember there is no one like you out there in this world, and anyone who takes the time to get to know you, the real you, is lucky as hell."

17

RANDI

The night air turns crisp, any warmth from the day gone as we walk and talk through the nearly deserted park. Trey turned off our cell phones and the listening device before leaving the hotel to prevent T from tracking us, and the freedom from the stupid electric device is amazing. You don't realize the disservice the constant connection to the outside world is until its leash is severed and you're freed.

"I hope I get to meet her," Trey says. He hasn't wandered but a few inches from my side since we left the hotel. He stays close to keep me safe, but I can't help the building hope that it's more than protection keeping him there.

The desperate need to touch him, to feel his body against mine was merciless when we first met, but that was simple attraction. Now? Oh boy. Totally different ball game.

Not only is he attractive with his roguish good looks, but he's tough as nails when he needs to be, then comforting and sweet when he doesn't. And what he said earlier about me being bright and shit left my face and panties damp. I almost pulled the oversized sweatpants down right there on the sidewalk and bent over. I chose not to since, you know, I don't want to come off as desperate or anything.

Which I totally am.

"Not tonight. I didn't shave."

"Huh?" He stumbles midstep and turns with a confused look. "Mess, I don't even want to know what line of thinking made you respond with that."

I cringe. "Sorry, wrong conversation again."

"I was referring to Taeler."

Oh, right. "You might, I guess. Depending if we win or not. I'm trying to keep her as far away from all this as possible. The DC crowd as a whole, but mostly Kyle and Shawn. I wouldn't put it past them to leverage her in some way to use me."

"Smart. You should consider sending her to Oxford. It's farther, and not in America."

"Not a bad plan, Trouble, but so far UT is working out great." With a content sigh, I try to commit this moment to memory. "The fall is so beautiful here. At home, the leaves don't change to these bright colors, or if they do, it only lasts a week before the wind strips them bare." Bending forward, I swipe a wet yellow leaf from the walkway. Thank goodness the rain stopped sometime during the blackmail mission, leaving behind only crisp, damp air and sporadic puddles to avoid. "You've asked a lot of questions about my life but haven't really given me much about yours."

"Not much to tell," he says with a shrug. "I live in DC now, college on the West Coast, army. Nothing exciting."

I tilt backward, almost toppling over at his arm shooting out, pressing against my stomach and stopping me in my tracks. My heart rate ratchets higher as he scans a block of darkened path up ahead with intense scrutiny. Goose bumps spread along my forearms. The darkness of the night mixed with our isolation urges me closer to Trey's side. He wraps his arm around my shoulders, tucking me even closer. An engulfing sense of security warms my chilled body like a thick blanket.

"What's going on?" I whisper, my lips brushing the material of his suit jacket.

"You feel that?" Head on a swivel, he scans the area once, twice.

A sudden prickling spreads down my neck at the sense of being watched.

"Let's go back the way we came."

I'm still nodding when he whirls us around to retrace our steps. My breath catches as every muscle of his that's pressed against my right side tenses. The silhouette outside a streetlight's illumination pulls us to a hard stop.

Trey swears under his breath. The world spins as he rotates us back around only to find another person, this one in the middle of the path, not caring that the light gives us a clear visual of his features.

"Mess," Trey states as he looks from the man in front of us to the one at our back. "I need you to stay close, but know when to get out of the way if things get dirty. You understand me?"

My head bobs in rapid succession.

"Dammit, I really didn't think this through, did I?"

The regret in his voice tugs at my heart. "Hey, you didn't know. Don't blame yourself."

"It's Central Park at midnight."

"Who knows? Maybe these guys just need directions." I push as much humor into my shaky voice as possible.

As we talk, the two men move closer, boxing us in.

"Wallet, watch, jewelry," one guy orders, his voice gruff.

"So that's a no to the directions," I say on a giggle. Shit, why am I laughing? What is wrong with me? "This is not funny." Another burst of giggles erupts from my chest. I smack both hands over my mouth. "Sorry," I mumble.

"You don't want to do this," Trey says, his voice hard, all business. "I'm not your normal tourist."

Peering around Trey's shoulder, I shrink against his side. "That one's getting closer," I whisper.

"They both are, Mess. It's okay."

Is it? From where I'm standing, nothing is okay. My legs tremble with the urge to run.

"Money, now," the one in front of us demands, more grit in his voice this time.

"That's a hard pass," Trey says. His muscles bunch, the arm around my shoulders sliding to my lower back. "Duck and crawl to the edge of the path." His words barely register before he gives my back a hard shove. Gravity, that bitch, takes care of the first part of his directions. The cheap flip-flops skid a foot after hitting a large patch of wet leaves. My arms are whirling to stay upright as my feet sail into the air. I grunt in pain, my ass smacking to the asphalt.

Wetness soaks my backside as I blink up at the starless night sky.

The crack of skin against skin slices through the silence. Shouts from unfamiliar voices, too close. Pitching forward, I slap my hands on the pathway. On all fours, I crawl to the edge of the sidewalk to a spot dipped in shadows. I blink to reset my contacts, clearing my vision.

The scene in front of me still doesn't make sense.

One man stands above two others writhing on the ground at his feet. The man scans the area, searching. Honey brown eyes pause, locking with mine. Hair a mess, jacket ruffled, he gives a cocky smirk. I release my held breath with a whoosh.

With one more kick to each man's ribs, Trey marches toward me, his strides fast and sure.

"We need to move. Now." Hands tucked under my shoulders, he hauls me upright. "They won't stay down for long. Didn't want to add manslaughter to tonight's events."

I suck in a quick breath with a frantic nod. Right. Good plan.

We race down the path, my flip-flops sliding on the pavement. His grip on my elbow tightens to keep me from falling. After a few minutes of our fast pace, a stitch stabs at my side and my lungs burn. I wheeze, tugging against his hold to tell him to slow down, but he jerks us off the path. I slide along wet grass as I trail behind him, trying to keep up as he pulls us farther along.

A large bolder juts out of the ground up ahead, catching my eye. With a sharp tug, I divert us toward the rock, desperate for a break. The uneven surface pokes at my ass and back when I slump onto it in exhaustion.

I track Trey as he paces back and forth just in front of where I collapsed, never going more than one foot in either direction.

"That was intense," I say between breaths. Maybe I should move cardio up on the to-do list when we get back. "You pushed me."

Trey pauses, tipping his head back. "That's what you want to focus on right now?"

"Yeah. You should apologize." I'm kidding, but the tension radiating off him is freaking me out. I need something to distract him or he'll wear a rut into the soft earth beneath his pounding feet. "I fell on my ass. It hurts."

He slides his hands into the pockets of his slacks and steps forward to stand directly in front of me. Pushing up, I rest both elbows back and cock my head.

"I saved your life, and you want me to apologize for getting you out of the way?"

I nod. A new, sizzling tension pulses between us. The chill in the air evaporates. My skin heats, my pulse skyrocketing higher and tighter.

I hold a tight breath as he leans closer. His large hands rest against the rock on either side of my hips. Shifting closer, he pauses, our faces an inch apart.

"I'm not sorry." His warm breath brushes against my cheek, and my eyes flutter closed on a sigh. "Randi." My name is a desperate plea on his lips. I peel my eyes open, locking onto his. "What are you doing to me?"

"I don't know," I breathe. "But we shouldn't." I reach up, my damp, trembling fingers hovering just over his cheek. "But I can't stop either."

"It's dangerous." He tilts his head, pressing his hot cheek into my awaiting palm. Rough facial hair from his five-o'clock shadow prickles my fingertips as I brush them across his face. His brown eyes shutter closed. "This can't happen."

I ghost my fingers over his temple, across his forehead. Soft, silky dark strands of his hair glide past my hand as I rake it over his scalp down to the base of his neck.

"Fuck," he says on a forced breath. "You're killing me, Randi. Stop."

"I told you," I whisper. Sitting up a fraction, I shorten the distance between our lips. "I can't. I want this." A zap of blazing heat scorches through my core at the brush of my lips against his. "No, Trey, I *need* this."

A truer statement has never been said. I need him. Right here, right now.

His answering growl sends another bolt of excitement and want to the apex of my thighs.

"Anyone could walk up." I whimper at the thought. His answering chuckle is dark and seductive. I suck in a sharp inhale at his soft lips pressing against the sensitive skin of my neck. "You like that, don't you? Didn't expect that."

I give his hair a sharp tug in response to his tentative nip just below my ear.

"Trey," I beg.

He rips the hat off my head, fingers delving into my hair and gripping a section at the base. I gasp at the dominance in his hold. Soft lips brush against my own, teasing. I can't move; desperation ratchets higher and higher.

"This never happened," he growls, then seals his lips over mine. I groan into his mouth, pushing in a plea for more. His hand dips beneath my loose sweatshirt, his callused palm scraping along my stomach.

Pushing off the rock, I arch into his touch. Higher and higher his hand slides. Deft fingers dip inside my bra, yanking the cup low so my breast spills over.

My thoughts whirl. Normally this is when I'm ready for the guy to stick it in and get the show on the road. But now, here with Trey... I'm actually longing for each touch. Every kiss and swipe of his tongue along mine makes the throb between my thighs pulse with more need.

His lips curl against mine in a smile as he pinches my pebbled nipple between his thick fingers. I cry into his mouth as pain and pleasure mix. Panting, I tip my head back and shove my breast into his hand, begging for more.

Fuck, that was hot.

Another tight pinch, this time with a quick twist. I cry out, only for it to be smothered by his palm sealing to my lips. "Good girl," he praises.

I whimper into his palm at the loss of the hand from my breast. Not wasting any time, he dips a hand below the waistband of my sweatpants, sliding over the front of my satin thong.

"Yes," I mumble. The hand at my mouth disappears, replaced by his demanding mouth once again. I nip at his lower lip like I've fantasized.

With the heel of his hand, he presses against my clit, rotating in slow circles.

More. I need more.

The uneven rock snags the cotton sweatpants as I spread my legs wide, giving him access to do his worst.

Two fingers dip beneath my panties, sliding easily through the building slickness.

"Holy fuck." He rips his lips from mine before pressing them to my neck. "If we were somewhere safe.... I want to see all of you. See this soaked pussy, lick up every last drop."

Yes, please.

My elbow slips. Carefully he guides me back, releasing the hold on my hair and resting me against the cold stone.

Low gray clouds blow through the sky above me before my eyes shutter closed. I arch against the boulder as two thick fingers tease outside my slick entrance, plunging in an inch before slowly easing out.

"You're the most fascinating woman I've ever met, Randi Sawyer. And you smell—" He dips low, pressing his nose between my thighs and giving an exaggerated sniff, "—fucking delicious."

Accenting his dirty words, both fingers plunge deep.

I bite down on my forearm to keep from screaming out.

Reaching down, I grip his wrist as it jerks in pounding strokes. I rock forward, meeting the relentless push of his fingers.

Higher and higher I float above the world, every nerve, sensation, and thought focused on the ball of energy building deep in my core. Sweat drips along my hairline. Goose bumps spread over my stomach at exposure to the chilly night air.

I whimper, shaking my head against the rock.

"Come on, Mess. Give it up," Trey commands. The deep rumble of his demanding voice combined with a pinch and twist at my pebbled nipple sets off an explosion.

I sink my teeth into my arm, but still my scream of pleasure echoes around us. My thighs squeeze together, capturing his hand, but his fingers continue to pound deep, prolonging the mind-altering orgasm.

"Holy fuck," I pant, reality settling back in as I come down from my high.

Tipping my chin, I look down my body to where Trey's hand still rests inside my pants. I glance up to his face. His hooded eyes are focused on where his hand cups my mound.

"Trey?" I whisper.

"We need to go," he responds, eyes sliding up to meet mine.

I bite back a whimper as he withdraws his fingers, leaving me achingly empty. Embarrassment warms my cheeks, my movements jerky as I fix my bra and underwear. Trey backs up a step as I push off the rock to stand. I keep my eyes to the ground, attempting to conceal the self-conscious thoughts sprinting through my mind.

"Stop." I jerk my head up, brows raised. "Don't do that. Don't think anything negative. We have to leave because I can't focus on anything other than you, and that's dangerous for both of us. Anyone could've walked up just now and I wouldn't have detected them, too wrapped up in the feel of your pussy squeezing the fuck out of my fingers and imagining my...." My eyes dip to where he grips his crotch and adjusts himself. "Fuck. We need to go, or I'll fucking toss caution to the wind and take you right here."

"I'm okay with that," I say, a shy smile tugging at my lips.

"I'm not going to fuck you in the middle of the park on a damn rock. You deserve better than that, Randi." Debatable. "Plus, we need to get back before Tank calls in the national guard looking for us. We're already going to pay for being out this late. Don't want to push our luck too much in one night."

Leaning forward, he presses his lips against my forehead. I let my eyes flutter closed as a deep, relaxed exhale eases my racing mind. We both know this can't happen again, that *we* can't happen.

But knowing it can't happen doesn't mean it won't.

18

RANDI

October

Stuck with a dangerously hot man nearly around the clock is torture in itself. Add in the unforgettable memory of his hand between my thighs, the erotic pain shooting from my nipples dampening my center, and I'm a woman on the edge of sanity. For the third time in as many seconds, my attention flicks from the iPad in my hands to where Trey lies sprawled along the couch, eyes closed. His chest rises and falls with each deep, relaxed breath.

How is he not wound up too? Does he not feel the thick sexual tension that's only worsened these past few weeks? The easy smiles he's given me since that night, the sexy smirks and casual laughter, make me wonder if it's just me feeling it.

Surely not.

Surely.

Right?

"What, Mess?" Trey peeks an eye open. "Stop chewing your nails."

I drop the finger from my nibbling teeth. "Okay, Dad."

He closes his eye once again and smirks. Oh, how I want to smack—or kiss—that smirk right off his face.

Ugh, this man is driving me crazier then I already am.

I purse my lips and turn my focus back to the iPad. I've already memorized the possible questions for the debate tonight, but with a few hours to kill before I have to get ready, I might as well review them again. Being overly prepared is how I graduated with honors in undergrad and law school. For those seven years, I averaged three hours a sleep a night, but I did what I had to do. Unfortunately, that sleep cycle stayed with me after I graduated and moved back home. Nowadays, I get around four to five hours a night, but with the stress of the upcoming election, I've reverted back to the measly three.

I groan as the screen blurs once again and toss the iPad to the vacant chair beside me. Letting my head fall against the back of my chair, I close my eyes and press the heels of both hands against my lids.

"I'm so ready for this to be done," I mutter.

"Tonight's the last debate before the election, right?"

Eyes still squeezed shut, I nod. "Thank fuck. I enjoy a good debate, don't get me wrong, but I'm so tired of monitoring the polls, constantly being on edge."

"It won't stop if you win."

I roll my head along the soft cushion and open my eyes, smiling up at T.

"Yes and no. It will be exhausting in a different way. I'm just tired of this posturing, the constant need to be invited to sit at the cool kids' lunch table."

Trey laughs from his spot on the couch.

"We need to leave in four hours," T says, looking at his watch. "I'm meeting with the vice president's alpha team lead downstairs in five to go over the security plans for tonight." He shoots a glare at Trey before turning to me. "Can you two stay out of trouble while I'm gone?"

"Come on, big guy," Trey says, swinging his legs over the side of the couch to sit up. "It's been weeks since 'the incident.' We've been good ever since." I smile at the smirk and wink Trey tosses my way. "You go handle whatever you need. I promise we won't leave the condo." Three fingers in the air, he adds, "Scout's honor."

"You were never a Boy Scout," T grunts in an almost laugh. He runs a hand up and over his shiny bald head. "I don't have a choice, since the other guys are downstairs securing the building. I'll be back in an hour, two tops." At the door, he turns with a resigned look.

"For fuck's sake," Trey grumbles. "We'll be fine. You act like she died in New York."

I seal my lips together to hide my growing smile. We chose to keep the muggers and what happened after out of the story we gave T when we made it back to the jet that night. No need for him to worry when nothing bad happened.

"Keep him in line," T says, eyes on me.

I hold up three fingers. "Scout's honor."

He grumbles something about us being ridiculous and an accident waiting to happen. I'm still giggling when the door clicks shut behind him and the snap of the deadbolt sounds. Smiling, I turn to Trey, but my smile falters at what I find. I swallow past the stalled breath caught in my throat.

His eyes sparkle with restrained lust. Arms stretched out wide along the back of the couch, he widens his legs and arches a brow. "Two hours alone. What trouble can we get into all alone, Mess?"

My heart thunders against my chest. Holy hell, is this the first time we've been alone since New York?

Untucking my knees from where I'm curled in the chair, I stand on shaking legs. Toes pressed into the thick carpet, I tiptoe to the couch, pausing between his legs. A breath catches in my chest, my eyes closing as his wide hands grip my waist.

"Every day I've watched you knowing what you feel like, smell like. Fucking torture." He sits straight, pressing his face between my thighs into my thin cotton yoga pants. "I shouldn't be this wrapped up in you, Mess. But I can't stop wanting you." He tilts his face up, locking on my eyes. I stroke a hand through his hair, savoring the way it slides between my fingers.

"Then don't," I nearly plead. "I don't want you to hold back." There's so much I want to tell him. How his touch means so much more than any others. How I don't want to pull away but grow more desperate with each passing minute, each day he doesn't hold me close.

Gripping the hem of my long-sleeve T-shirt, he slides it up, exposing my stomach. Both hands slide into his hair, gripping chunks at the press of his wet lips just below my belly button. I suck in a breath and hold it as the tip of his tongue traces the skin just above my pants. Hooking his thumbs into the waistband, he tugs them an inch lower, repeating the same path with his tongue. Lower and lower my pants drop. My pulse races through my veins, and heat builds beneath my skin.

"I'll never get enough of your scent." His lips move against the sensitive skin above my mound. "It's even hotter knowing how wet I'll find you." Light brown eyes flick up, meeting mine. "And I've barely touched you. Tell me, Mess. Do you want me to lick it up?"

Oh fuck, that's dirty.

And oh, oh so hot.

"Yes," I whisper.

Eyes still locked with mine, he nips at my skin, grinning. "Say it."

"I... I...," I stammer. "I want you to... want you to lick it up. Fuck, please."

"Good—" His next word snaps off. I stumble back as he bolts from the couch. I blink, eyes wide, staring at the gun now in his hand. "Get behind me." I hastily duck behind him, my back to the wall, and tug my pants up. "Grab hold of my jacket and don't let go, you hear me?"

"What's going on?"

"Someone is at the door," he says over his shoulder as we move across the room. "They tried to get in, but the key didn't work."

I gasp. If T hadn't suggested I change my locks last week for increased security measures....

I shriek and jump backward, tugging Trey with me, at a pounding on the door.

Trey shoots an unamused glance over his shoulder and down to me.

"What? I didn't go to spy school. I'm nervous."

His brows tug together. "You do know the difference between the Secret Service and the CIA, right? You might not get my vote if you don't."

I give his jacket a sharp tug and glance to the door that's now shaking from the constant banging on the other side. "You're going to vote for me?"

He shrugs and turns to face the door, but I catch a hint of a smirk on his lips before he does. "Maybe. Now let's see who's knocking, shall we?"

Gun aimed at the door, Trey inches closer and rests his free hand on the deadbolt.

The fabric of his jacket bunches under my tightening fists.

With a quick flip of the lock and a tug on the doorknob, he swings around, blocking the opening with his body.

"What the hell are you doing here?" Trey bites out. His back muscles tense beneath my fists.

Still unable to see, I push to my tiptoes and peer over his shoulder.

"Seriously?" The building anticipation drains from my taut muscles, leaving them heavy and lethargic. Grumbling under my breath, I turn on my bare heels, shuffle back to the center of my condo's living room, and fall into a chair. "What do you want, Shawn?"

"Out of my way, rent-a-cop." Shawn shoulders past the fuming Trey and steps into the living room. In slow motion, Trey turns from the door, shoulders tense, his furious gaze following Shawn's every move.

"Watch it, Shawn," I bite out. It's one thing for them to make fun of me, but my friends? Hell no. "That man can smoosh that narcissistic, smug-ass look right off your ugly face. Not a smart move to piss him off."

Shawn's eyebrows rise a fraction, but the Botox in his forehead prevents them from climbing higher. "Is that so, Trailer?" The shock morphs into his signature smug sneer. "Been getting close to the help, have we?" Delicate fingers pop the button of his suit jacket as he folds onto the couch. "I'd say that's beneath you, but we both know there's not much in this world that is."

Trey's features darken as he takes a menacing step toward the asshole sitting on my couch. I hold up a hand, stopping his advancement.

"As lovely as this all is, what the fuck do you want, Shawn?"

He chuckles, smoothing out the front of his pristine blue dress shirt. "Make sure you're all set for tonight." His ice-blue eyes flick up to mine. "I am your trusted advisor, after all."

"Forced advisor, never trusted," I point out. "And yes, I'm ready. I was reviewing the potential questions one last time when you tried to get in." I narrow my eyes. "When did you get a key?"

"When did you change your locks?"

"Motherfucker," Trey hisses. "How the fuck did you get a key?"

Shawn simply smiles his Joker-like smile. "I have my sources." His attention shifts from Trey back to me. "Tell me, Trailer, is there something going on between you and the wash-up behind me?"

"Not that it matters, but no." Keeping my eyes on Shawn instead of flicking to Trey takes every last drop of resistance I have in my body. "Nothing is going on between us."

"I don't believe you."

Fuck. Not that I would care if people knew Trey and I are fooling around, but not Shawn. He'll find some way to use it against me, use it against Trey. I lose the internal fight and give Trey a pleading look. He doesn't notice, his attention solely on a patch of wall slightly above my head.

I swallow past the rising panic.

"It would be a shame, wouldn't it?" Shawn says, cutting through the uncomfortable silence. "For Benson to lose the job he so loves for a chance at a cunt that's already been passed around most of DC under Kyle's bidding." His eyes flash in victory. He doesn't know Trey knows the truth, everything. Even still, unease rolls my gut. What if Trey believes him? "Not to mention the media circus that would ensue at yet another disastrous relationship for him." He clicks his tongue. "His family name dragged through the media mud once again."

What?

When confusion furrows my dark brows, power lights in those evil eyes. "Ah, I see he hasn't told you everything. Well, it's a good thing I can fill you in—"

"Out," Trey bellows, stalking toward Shawn. Panic replaces the earlier victory in the asshole's wide eyes. "Get out now."

Not waiting for a reply, Trey wraps a hand around the back of Shawn's neck, hauling him off the couch.

"Get your hands off me," Shawn yells. "You'll regret this, Benson. I'll ruin you, ruin your family."

Trey's pounding feet don't falter as he flings the door open, slamming it against the wall. The crack of plaster sounds through the condo. With a final shove from Trey, Shawn stumbles out into the hallway. His face is beet red, nostrils flaring when he turns furious eyes on Trey.

"This isn't over." I blanch, shifting back in the chair when his focus turns on me. "You will pay for this, both of you."

The entire condo shakes at the slam of the door. I flinch at the sound.

Trey's shoulders rise and fall in quick succession, his palms sealed to the closed door, head hanging.

What the hell just happened?

I snap my attention back to Trey from where it'd fallen to the floor. Phone at his ear, he mumbles something, pauses with a silent nod, and then slides the phone from his face. He still hasn't turned.

Confusion morphs into hurt tinged with anger.

"What the hell was all that about?" My voice shakes with the swirl of emotions I can't get a handle on. "I know you said you two had a history, but what he said about another disastrous relationship? Media circus? What the hell, Trey?"

Time stands still. He releases a loud, resigned sigh.

"Look at me," I demand. I swallow back the unshed tears clogging my throat.

"Grem will be here shortly. Don't leave."

"Trey?" I can't keep the pain from seeping into my tone.

Why does my heart ache? He owes me nothing. I shouldn't care. But I do. Fuck, I do. Each heavy thud of my heart sends another aching pang through my chest.

"Good luck tonight," he mumbles in goodbye.

Anger at myself and rejection from his avoidance mix, needing an outlet. I furiously scan the room. Snatching the iPad from the other chair, I hurl it across the room with a banshee scream. The screen splinters against the wall before the device falls to the carpet with a deafening thump.

Chest heaving, I focus on the destroyed electronic.

At least now I'm not the only broken thing in this fucking room.

19

TREY

"What are you doing here?"

Ignoring the beta team member's question, I turn to close and lock the door. I wince at the dented, crumbling section of wall behind it. I need to remember to have that fixed. It was my fault, after all. Normally I keep a tight leash on my anger, keeping it from boiling over—unlike earlier. But Shawn fucking Whit shoved me headfirst over the threshold of my normal hold on that dangerous emotion.

What he said wasn't so much the issue; the disrespect toward Randi was what pushed me past my normal control. She might not have caught it, but I sure fucking did.

I give my head a small shake. Today was a disaster, which morphed into an even bigger disaster at the debate. It couldn't have gone worse for Randi. There's little doubt that the way I left things messed with her concentration.

I'm an idiot. An asshole and an idiot.

If she loses because of me....

"I need to talk to her," I say, turning back toward the living room. One guy sits on the couch, the rest of the team outside in the hall or downstairs at all the entry points.

"Not sure that's a good idea," the guy says with a laugh. "Birmingham just left. I heard every word. He ripped her a new one. If I were her, I'd be in there packing my bags with my damn tail between my legs."

I don't suppress my deep groan.

This apology will be expensive. Even something from Tiffany's might not make up for the last twelve hours.

Earlier, I retreated, not ready to admit why Shawn's words and insults to Randi hit deep. I needed a few hours to process it alone. Could I have told her all that so she didn't have to wonder all day? Yeah, but at the time, the rage clouded my vision; all I could see was my own pain.

"Tank asked me to come up and talk about tomorrow." Lie. "We need to go over a few things, so I might be a while." Truth. "Take a break. I've got this for a few hours."

He shrugs and lies back on the couch. "Don't have to tell me twice. Thanks, Benson."

Hand on the doorknob to the bedroom, I pause. Nervous energy builds, my chest tightening.

She has to forgive me.

I don't knock. With a quick twist of the knob and a push of the door, I step into her bedroom. Grief permeates the air, smacking me in the face. Each breath deepens the regret filling my chest.

"Randi." Not taking my eyes off where she's perched on the edge of the bed, I reach back, closing the door and flicking the lock. She doesn't acknowledge me, her eyes glued to the opposite wall. "Mess." Each step is tentative, careful, like I'm approaching a wounded animal. Technically I guess I am. Her, the most fascinating woman I've ever met, me, the one who hurt the insecure person she hides beneath the Political Barbie mask.

"What do you want, Benson?"

I cringe. Benson, not Trouble. Hell, not even Trey. Not a good sign.

Determination propels me forward, sitting me beside her. The bed dips, rocking her an inch closer.

"I wanted to check in on you." She huffs, her eyes rolling to the ceiling. "To apologize."

"Little late for that, don't you think?" She shoves her hands on the bed, pushing herself up. Slowly she turns to face me, meeting my pleading gaze for the first time since I entered the room. "You saw the debate?" Her shoulders slump. "I lost us the election tonight." Her eyes, brightened to a perfect green by the stupid contacts Kyle makes her wear, look to the ceiling. "I'm ruined. I'll have to go back home, failing again." Her gaze is still upturned as a single tear trickles down her cheek.

Pain like I've never experienced cuts through my chest, piercing my heart.

"It's too late. You left when all I needed was an explanation. You left me, confused, angry...." Her throat bobs. "Hurt. Fucking hell, Trey. You hurt me by not caring enough to stay and tell me what the hell all that between you and Shawn was. I didn't care—I don't care—what he says. I know every word out of his mouth has an agenda, some form of power play." Pain, anger, and, the worst, disappointment cloud her beautiful face when she finally looks back down. "You don't owe me anything. This, what we did in the park, the flirting back and forth, you don't owe me anything, but what hurt was that you didn't even stop to think I deserved an explanation. You just walked out, making me feel...." She stomps her foot against the carpet. "You made me feel as worthless as everyone else has my entire life."

I don't think, only react to the ripping, shredding of my heart.

Reaching out, I yank her into my arms, holding her close, squeezing her tight.

"I'm sorry," I plead into her hair. "Fuck, I'm sorry." Her shoulders shake. I tighten my hold. "Tell me what to do. Tell me what to say, what to buy. I'm so sorry, Mess. I fucked up. I couldn't... I didn't know how to.... It was me. All me. I was so angry at Shawn, I couldn't think past the need to beat the shit out of him."

Her soft dark hair slides beneath my palm as I stroke it over and over. With each breath, I apologize all over again. Time slows; nothing outside of the woman in my arms matters. Eventually her breaths even out, the shoulder-racking sobs ceasing.

So much needs to be said, needs to be explained, but the moment is still too raw for more words.

Her body molds into mine, folding between my arms as I lift her and walk across the room. Inside the bathroom, I carefully set her on the white marble counter, holding her shoulders to make sure she's steady before stepping toward the tub. Fingers beneath the heavy stream of water, I wait until it turns scorching hot and close the drain. Searching through the various bottles along the edge, I pluck a bottle of cherry vanilla bubble bath and dump a drop into the water. I frown at the small amount of bubbles that break the surface. Twisting off the cap, I tip the bottle over, emptying the entire contents into the water.

It takes a whole bottle per bath, right?

Fuck if I know.

I toss the empty bottle into the trash can across the room; it clatters against the metal sides as it descends to the bottom. I lift both hands into the air, pumping my fists in victory. Wearing a tentative smile, I chance a look to Mess. My heart leaps at the small smile she's desperately trying to not let me see.

"I'm going back to a life of destitution, and you're cheering over making an easy toss."

I look from her to the trash can and back again. "Easy? Like to see you do it." Her smile grows, bunching her adorable cheeks. "You're not going back. The election isn't over. We can figure it out, but first...." I point to the half-filled bathtub and overflowing bubbles. "Shit, maybe I put too much in."

"You think?" she says with a huffed laugh.

"Take a bath, relax. Then we'll talk." I pause at the door and look over my shoulder. "If you need anything, let me know. I'll be right outside the door."

At her nod, I step into the bedroom, closing the door behind me. The hinges give a tight rattle at the weight of my back slamming against the cool wood.

Now to come up with a plan to keep her in DC. If today taught me anything, it's that I'm not ready for her to be out of my life. Not yet. Hell, maybe not ever.

<hr>

"You look better," I say with a smile as she steps out of the bathroom. "How do you feel?"

"Better." The tension around her eyes still creases the edges, but the weight from earlier seems lifted for the moment. "Thanks for that." Her fingers fidget with the sash of her terry cloth robe. "Now what?" Her hopeful gaze meets mine.

Pinkie nail between her teeth, she shuffles across the room and plops down onto the bed, staring at me.

"First"—I turn, bringing a bent leg to the bed to face her straight on—"I need to explain today, what happened with Shawn." I clear my throat and grip the pant leg of my old jeans to keep from reaching for her. "I didn't know what to think when you stood up for me. Called him out for me."

A single shoulder rises and falls in a noncommittal shrug. The movement widens the gap of her robe a fraction, exposing more of the soft skin concealed beneath. "No one makes fun of my friends and gets away with it. I'm a bit protective, I guess."

I smirk. "Ditto, Mess. Which is why today blew the roof off the normal restraint I have on my anger. Hearing him call you... well, you were there. You know what he said." I tighten my right hand into a fist. "And I couldn't do a damn thing. I knew if I did, it would come back and hurt you. Hell, me being in the room already did some of that. He wouldn't have pressed you, pushed you, if I wasn't there. If I wasn't in the picture at all."

I huff out a deep breath and look to the ceiling.

"It's always been like this. Between Shawn, Kyle, and me, we've always been at each other's throats, vying for the upper hand. So what you saw today was all about me and Shawn, about our shit, not you, but I pulled you into it. That pissed me off."

"Not trying to be a dick here," she says with a shove to my shoulder, "but that's really arrogant of you."

I whip my gaze to where she leans back against the headboard.

"What?"

"Shawn already hated me. He might have found a new angle to push my buttons, but nothing about today started with you. It started the minute he caught me sniffing the wallpaper last year."

"Um, what?" I chuckle. *This woman.*

She swipes her hand through the air in dismissal. "All I'm saying is you're taking responsibility for something that isn't yours to take. I knew stepping into this spot, have known since I met Shawn, that he'll use anything and everything he can to bring me down." Her gaze turns unfocused. "Do you think he'd say something to the media about us? Try to sabotage the campaign even though Kyle's his friend?"

An incredulous chuckle rumbles in my chest. "One hundred percent hell yes. I think he already did."

Her mouth pops in shock, opening wide.

I can't help the dirty track my mind takes me down at the sight. I swipe my tongue along my lower lip. Oh, the things I want to do to those plump lips.

"You think he came over today with the intention of derailing my focus."

I nod.

"That motherfucking cuntcake."

"Always has been."

Her head thumps against the headboard, her eyes squeezing shut. "Well, he got what he wanted. Tonight was horrible."

"Well," I say as I lie back on the bed, tucking both hands beneath my head, "it wasn't great. But it doesn't mean it's all for not. On the way over here, the various anchors were saying it was a tie. You did good. Not great, but you didn't bomb it like you're thinking you did."

"That's not what Kyle thinks." She sighs.

"He's a fucking drama queen, has been his whole life. It's not as bad as you think." I cut my eyes to meet hers. "But nothing else can happen to derail your focus or shift the attention off your campaign points. You need to get back out there, hit the swing states hard. Remind them that you do know your shit, and you're the one who will have their backs. Remind them of your original platform. You're their voice in DC."

"Why aren't you my advisor?" she asks, arching both brows in question. "You seem to know a lot about all this."

"I was raised in this life. My parents wanted me to take a political path, but I didn't. Once I stepped away from it, I saw it for what it was, and I wanted no part of playing the political game the rest of my life. That's when I went into the army. It saved me from being a conniving, miserable fuckstick like everyone else in this town."

"What did Shawn mean by a media circus, a disastrous relationship?" Gripping the edges of her robe tighter, she slides down the bed, lying at my side, head propped up with an elbow digging into the mattress.

"Ah, that." I roll to face her, mirroring her pose. "The girl I was dating last year was the purest definition of a power-hungry political pawn."

"Ah, the person you thought I was at first." My gaze traces the curve of her lips as they move up her face in a sassy smile. "This mystery woman is the one I can thank for the incorrect judgments you spouted my way."

"Yep. Something happened, I did something last year that caused our team to be demoted. It was a rough patch, and during that time, she showed her true self. Later on, I learned my parents were in her ear, trying to get her to convince me to step back into the political scene. I was the idiot who went over a year not realizing she was playing me." Reaching out, I fiddle with the sash of her robe that lays in the small distance between us. "My family is one of the bigger names in politics. More behind the scenes, but they're the money to a lot that goes on in this city. That's what Rachel wanted. The power that comes with my name, the trust fund. Not me," I grumble and roll my eyes.

"So she left you because...."

"For Shawn fucking Whit." Randi's eyes widen to a comical size. "Yep. Apparently even my family name and millions in the bank couldn't cover the embarrassment she felt for being with a demoted Secret Service agent."

"I hate her." An evil smirk forms. "Wait. If she's with Shawn... oh, this will be fun."

Apprehension pulls me back an inch, scanning her face. "What?"

"Don't worry, Trouble."

"That's not reassuring." I give the terry cloth belt a hard tug. "What are you planning?"

Randi shrugs and flops back to the bed.

"Oh no you don't." The bed dips beneath my weight, and a shriek of surprise squeaks past her smiling lips. Hovering over her, I pull my face close, our noses a hairbreadth apart.

Her smile falls, her eyes slipping to focus on my lips. Her heaving chest presses her breasts tighter against me. A moan pushes past my lips, brushing across her face and fogging the lenses of her glasses. Pinching the frames between two fingers, I tug them free and toss them across the bed.

I rake the tips of my fingers through her dark hair, causing her eyes to shutter closed.

Each inch between us is the kind of torture that drives men insane. Her lips pucker, demanding more at the faint brush of my own. The softness of her lips ease the growing ache that's been building since Shawn interrupted us. I groan into her mouth at the shift of her hips, the spread of her legs beneath me.

"Randi," I whisper against her lips, then seal mine over hers, needing more. Tugging on her hair, I angle her head to deepen the kiss, taking control of the pace.

Her hands slide between us, gripping the hem of my black T-shirt. I lift up, helping her yank it over my head. Goose bumps spread across my back at her delicate strokes up and down my skin. I move my body against hers, eliciting a moan of pleasure from both our lips.

Sucking on her neck, I then nip beneath her ear. With a flex of my hips, I press my steel-hard cock against her core.

"Oh fuck," she whispers, squeezing her eyes shut.

The sweet scent of her arousal meets my nose, driving me lower. Gripping the inside edges of her robe, I slowly spread it apart, exposing the bare skin of her chest inch by inch. Her full breasts bounce with each of her sharp inhales. Eyes locked with hers, I lower my lips to a pebbled nipple, flicking the tip of my tongue against it before taking a quick, hard nip. Back arching off the bed, Randi threads her fingers through my hair, pushing her breast into my waiting mouth.

Her body writhes beneath me, each wiggle causing her to press against my cock.

The touch of her fingers at my waistband makes me pull back, dipping my chin to watch. The first few times, the button fails to pop at her demanding fingers, but eventually it gives, and the grind of the zipper lowering catches my breath. Her hand dips in, wrapping around my dick. I thrust into her palm, devouring the sensation of another's touch when I've gone so long without.

Knee to the bed, I press off and stand. Taking in every inch of her near-naked body sprawled across the bed, waiting for me, I toe off my tennis shoes and let my jeans puddle to the floor. I hiss in a breath, wrapping a hand around myself and squeezing tight.

"Condom?" she pants.

I nod and retrieve my wallet from my jeans, tugging the condom out and tossing the wallet to the floor. I rip the wrapper up and roll the thin rubber down my hard length.

"Is this what you want?" I ask, giving my cock another hard squeeze. Fuck, this isn't going to last long. It's been way too long, and the building fire between us is on the verge of an all-engulfing inferno.

A flush spreads across her fair cheeks, highlighting her freckles. Biting her lip, she responds with a shaky nod.

I start at her ankles, softly stroking the tips of my fingers up and down her skin, rising higher with each pass. The edges of the robe fall away, pooling at her side.

"This is dangerous," I mutter to myself. "This changes everything."

There's no coming back from this, from her.

Ask me if I fucking care.

20

RANDI

I can't breathe. No air will fill my lungs, even though I'm sucking in as much as I can with each short breath.

Holy hotness, the man is like the Italian statues I've seen in textbooks. He's strong but not bulky, lean and toned. Muscles bunch with every move he makes, snapping taut beneath his soft tan skin. A smatter of chest hair covers the space between his pecs, disappearing down his rippled stomach until reappearing just below his navel.

My gaze follows the well-named happy trail, pausing on his thick cock, mesmerized by each tug of his hand up and down his shaft. I lick my lips, desperate to lean forward for a taste. Up and down his hand moves, that damn smirk causing even more dampness to gather between my thighs.

So this is what handsy sex should've been like my whole life.

Or maybe handsy sex is only good with Trouble.

Hmm, need to think that through. Later.

His hands brush up my legs, shoving away the offending scraps of robe that still cover parts of my body. Over my waist, up my chest, lingering to pinch and twist both aching nipples, his hands finally dip beneath my shoulders, tugging the robe lower down my back.

"What the—" His mouth hangs open, eyes wide, focused on my right shoulder. I give it a little wiggle. "You have a tattoo. Tattoos."

I nod, reaching up and running my fingers across his chest. Touching him is a compulsion; I couldn't stop myself even if I drained every last drop of energy into trying.

He yanks the sleeve of the robe lower. "How far does it go?"

"My elbow." Reaching down, I wrap my hand around him. "Can we talk about this later?"

Hooded eyes meet mine as I stretch between us, squeezing him tight. Trouble's lids slam shut as his hips drive forward. The head skims between my folds, grazing my clit.

"Trey," I whine. I should be embarrassed, but I'm not—at all. This is fucking fantastic and terrible and wonderful all at the same time. The anticipation of what's to come, the feel of him inside me, is almost too much to contain.

He dips forward, his teeth latching onto a peeked nipple while his tongue flicks furiously, barely connecting and driving me crazy. I slide the rubber-covered tip up and down my slit, teasing myself while arching my chest against his torturous mouth.

He grips my wrist, tugging my hand away. My whimper morphs into a relieved moan as he pushes the first inch of his hard length inside me. He moves in slow, calculated strokes, pulling all the way out before plunging deeper than before.

Sweat beads along his forehead, gathering to drip down his temples.

I moan, but he quickly presses his lips over mine to quiet the sound. A soft, demanding tongue teases mine, caressing and plunging with expert strokes.

Heat crawls beneath my skin, sweat glistening over every inch and slicking the places where our bodies connect.

Taut energy coils in my gut, sending tremors through my legs. My toes curl, digging into the fluffy, suffocating duvet. Hips rocketing off the bed, I match his thrusts, pushing him deeper. With a lust-filled snarl, he grips both hips, lifting them higher, hitting my elusive G-spot.

"Fuck," I cry out. His palm seals against my lips effectively quieting my curses.

My nostrils flare with each erratic inhale.

"You have to be quiet, baby," Trey says, his voice rough with need. "Can you do that?"

The duvet slips beneath my hair at my urgent nod.

"Good girl." His fingers trace down my chin and along my neck before moving lower. The brush of his thumb against my clit shoots bursts of sparkling sensations to each nerve. My teeth sink into the tip of my tongue, the taste of blood filling my mouth.

Then I shatter, every cell exploding in insistent throbs. Forearm pressed against my parted lips, I scream against my skin. The outside world fades to white noise, my intense pleasure dangling me over an empty chasm where nothing but my orgasm exists.

Trouble grunts a curse, his hips thrusting fast and wild.

I huff a forced exhale at the unexpected weight of him falling above me, pressing my entire body into the mattress.

"I know I'm smothering you," he says into the geometric fabric of the duvet, "but I can't move. Sorry if you die."

My face splits into a wide smile, my cheeks bunching so tight they ache. I stroke up and down his back, slipping lower to brush across his tight ass.

Everything is perfect, calm.

Tomorrow, I'll fight to regain the traction I lost with the failed debate.

Tomorrow, I fight to win.

Because there's no way in hell I can go back now. Not after tonight. Not after him.

Maybe not ever.

Could a moment be any more perfect? I trace the outline of his pouty lower lip, brushing the pad of my finger back and forth. The softness of sleep eases the worry lines of his forehead, relaxing the normal intense focus. His neat brow shifts beneath my stroking.

Sunlight hasn't even begun to peek around the curtains it's so early, but this being the first night he's slept over, I can't find it in me to waste a minute of it sleeping. The past couple weeks of us finding time alone and keeping T's suspicions at bay have been a well-coordinated dance. But even then, moments like this are few and far between.

I trace the shell of his ear, shifting a lock of brown hair to tuck it back.

I've worked my ass off since the disastrous debate. Flying across the country, visiting state after state, trying to raise our poll numbers. And it's working. Our ranking, once steady, now rises with each preliminary poll. Which means we still have a shot to win.

T and Trey are at my side each step of the way, always encouraging and keeping me on point. The whole team has been, really. We've grown close, forming a familial bond since they saved my life two months ago. I'm not ready for that to stop.

I inhale a shaky breath and burrow deeper into the cloud-like pillow.

I'm not ready for any of this to end. It's exhausting, yes, and more work than I expected, but the relationships, the friendships I've built here, I'm not ready to give up. Not yet. It feels like we're all on the verge of something great, something bigger than all of us.

We have to win.

"What are you doing?" Trey mutters into the mattress.

Who sleeps without a pillow?

"Early voting starts today," I whisper into the darkness. Bits of light stream around the blackout curtains. "It's not that early. Look, the sun is starting to come out."

"Tell the sun to hit Snooze. It's my day off." Without opening his eyes, he shifts on the bed, turning his head from my ministrations. "This was not part of the deal of me staying over."

The bed shakes as I silently laugh. There was no deal. Last night, after he pinned me to the wall and had his way with me—three times—I asked him to stay, so he did.

"What time is it, anyway?" His grumbled voice is barely loud enough for me to hear.

I roll to my side and crane my neck back. "Would you believe me if I said close to five?"

The bed shifts as Trey rises up to his elbows, a pointed sleepy-eyed glare directed at me. "That's only four hours of sleep."

I purse my lips to keep from correcting him.

"Randi." His tone is frustrated. "Please tell me you've slept."

"An hour or two," I say with a shrug. "It's normal for me. I can't sleep when I'm stressed."

"You don't eat and you don't sleep." His hair falls across his forehead with the shake of his head. "Randi, that's not healthy or sustainable. When you're VP, you have to take better care of yourself." When, not if. I like that. "Tank and I try to help you manage it the best we can, but you have to put in some effort too. We can't make you sleep."

"I know, and I appreciate you and T for all that you do for me. I really do." Flipping to my stomach, I stare at the tufted headboard. "It's just that I've done this life stuff on my own for so long, you know. If we win, I'll get some help, I promise. Maybe a secretary or something; that way all the reminding and babysitting doesn't fall on the team."

"First of all, when you win, not if." I fight the smile trying to spread up my cheeks. "Second, you will need help. You won't be able to do it all on your own like you've done everything else. No one can handle that kind of pressure, understand?"

I roll my head, flopping it to the side to watch him.

"I understand." Reaching up, I trace the underside of his jaw, the morning stubble scraping my finger. "I'll figure it out. I always do." I bite my lip, nervous energy building beneath my skin, flashing heat through my body. "Trey?" I swallow and look over his shoulder, avoiding those knowing brown eyes. "What will happen, with us after the election?" The shake in my voice is proof of the emotions swirling around that single question.

He presses a callused palm to my cheek, swiping his thumb across my cheekbone, sending a shiver racing down my spine. I pull back to meet his gaze.

"I don't know, Randi. I really don't." My eyes fall to the expanse of white sheet between us. "Hey, stop that. Look at me." Scrolling up his bare chest, I meet his eyes once again. "I'm not saying I don't want us to keep doing this, but things will change if you're in the official VP spot. Expectations are higher, the scrutiny more intense—hell, you might not have more than thirty minutes alone until your four years are done. All I'm saying is I don't know what will happen next, but that doesn't take away from this, us, right now, does it?"

Thumbnail between my teeth. I shake my head. "No, no it doesn't. I just... I want to be prepared for what's coming. I feel out of control right now, and I hate it. I need one thing, one sure thing I can hold on to until the election, you know?"

The corners of his lips tug in a knowing smile. "I know, but the reality is anything can happen, and—"

A pounding on the door cuts Trey off, and we both jolt straight up. Trey hops off the bed, yanking his jeans up his thighs before I can blink. He scans the phone in one hand as he attempts to dress with the other.

The jerky movements slow, stopping completely with his T-shirt halfway on. Wide eyes meet mine, his nostrils flaring.

"What?" I breathe. "What happened?"

I ignore the pounding at the door, eyes searching Trey's. His face is paler than moments ago.

"Trey, talk to me." I blindly reach for the nightstand, hand slapping the surface in search of my phone. He races across the room, bare feet pounding against the carpet, snatching it away before I can grab it. "You're freaking me out," I shout.

"Open up," T's demanding, angry, and—if I'm not mistaken—a bit scared voice booms from the other side of the door.

I suck in a breath, eyes flicking to the door. Trey lets out a loud, slow exhale and walks to it, shoving his arms through the sleeves of his T-shirt. The sheets tangle around my legs as I kick them furiously until I'm free, then race to the bathroom. The door isn't all the way closed behind me when the bedroom door slams open.

Each move jerky, I bolt from one side of the bathroom to the other, searching for something to slip on. Once T finds Trouble in my room at this hour, it'll be obvious what he and I were doing, but that doesn't mean I want to confirm his suspicions by popping out there naked. Clothes sail behind me, floating to the tile floor, as I rummage through the dirty laundry.

The black yoga pants have some kind of food stain dotting the left thigh, but the sweatshirt I yank on appears somewhat decent. Whatever, it's just T and Trey. Quick stop for a hair tie and I ease toward the door. The tips of my hair flick and twirl beneath my hands as I wrap it in a makeshift bun.

T's voice vibrates through the painted wood at my face; I don't even have to try and eavesdrop to hear what's being said.

"You've crossed the line this time, Benson."

Oh snap, T is pissed.

"It's not what you think." Trey's tone is tight and low.

"Really? Seems to me you're fucking—"

"Watch it," Trey bites out. "I'm trying to tell you it's not what you think." A pregnant pause has me pressing my ear against the door, not wanting to miss a word. "I like her, okay? It's not just about the sex, but the fact that you think so little of me, that I'd use her like that, fucking hurts."

T mumbles something too low for me to understand.

Screw this.

Taking a big step back, I yank open the door. The two men stand inches apart, their hands curled into tight fists. Neither looks my way.

"Oh stop it, you two. Duke it out later, okay? Right now I need one of you to tell me why I can't check my phone and why T's here so early. What's. Going. On."

T's the first one to break the stare-off, his dark brown eyes finding mine.

"It's out."

"Not following. What's out, T?"

"Your mom. Your life. Plus some sources saying you're cheating on Birmingham with one of your Secret Service agents. It's being covered on every network. Hell, they already have people on location in Boone and camped outside that rehab facility you put your mom in."

I can't breathe. The room spins. All the blood drains from my face, and my hands tremble at my side. Eyes still locked with his, I shake my head, disbelieving his words.

"No, that's... no. It's impossible. Not now."

I stagger back, the wall stopping me from tumbling down. Both men rush across the room, Trey's arms reaching me first. I'm numb, barely registering the tight grip around my waist that keeps me from falling to the floor.

"Easy, Randi," Trey whispers into my hair.

My breaths come in short pants, desperate for small amounts of air.

"Randi, look at me." T's thick fingers wrap around my chin, tipping my gaze up to meet his. "Calm down. You can't solve anything passed the fuck out. Do you hear me?" His voice is stern, commanding. "Get it together. Now."

"Match my breaths, Mess. In." Trey's chest puffs out, pressing against my back. "And out." Wisps of my air float forward on his deep exhale. Over and over he urges me to mirror his deep breaths. After several rounds, the room stills, my vision clearing.

"I'm, okay. I'm... oh fuck." I gasp, clasping a hand around my neck. "This is bad. It's bad, isn't it?"

My eyes frantically search T's for answers.

"It's not good."

"Tell me." I ball my hands into small fists. "Give me my phone."

"Let's get you to sit down first," Trey says, already guiding me across the room. He sits me in the buttercream-colored chair but doesn't go far. Squatting between my legs, he gives a comforting squeeze above both knees.

"How bad is it?" I ask T again.

"The worst are calling you a fraud," he states, zero emotion in his tone, the stone-faced protector mask back in place. I groan, dropping my face into my awaiting palms. "The best are focusing on the cheating angle."

"This couldn't have come at a worse time. Now we have zero time to come up with a new strategy. Early voting starts today."

"The timing is... questionable." I drop my hands, blinking rapidly at T, his tone giving me pause. "I find it odd that right when you're making headway in the polls after that debate, this bomb drops. The timing of everything seems planned. Plotted."

My mouth pops open, gaping wide.

"Holy fuck," I whisper. "You think Shawn did this. You think Shawn's the one who leaked it all." I whip around to face Trey. "Before the debate, he suspected something was going on between us."

T huffs and crosses his trunk-like arms across his broad chest. "Anyone could tell there was something going on between you two if they saw you together." I cringe. "You're an idiot, playboy. I had no idea it was this"—his mitt of a hand waves between us—"deep."

"Whoa. Playboy?" I scoff.

"Can we focus on the issue at hand, please," Trey grumbles, running a hand through his hair. "Why didn't you say anything?" He turns on the balls of his bare feet to face T.

"I thought it was innocent flirting. If I'd known this?" He looks to me and shakes his head. "You both know you're playing with fire, don't you?"

"Is it that bad?" I ask.

"Yes." I shrink back into the chair. "It makes a weak link in the team, puts you at risk, not to mention how it would look to the public. It stops, now." T jabs a finger at Trey. "You know what happened the last time you bent the rules." I turn to Trey. His features are filled with remorse, guilt. "I will not let you sideline this team again. You two end today."

"Not that it matters." Emotions clog my throat. Tears well, stinging my eyes. "Nothing matters. It's over. How can I face the public again? They know I lied."

Trey leans a shoulder against the chair, focusing on the carpet.

"I am a fraud," I whisper, losing all restraint on the tears.

"But you're not," Trey mutters. "Everything is about perception. They only have the side Shawn gave them." He glances up from the floor, eyes locking with my questioning gaze.

"So?"

A smirk tugs at his lips.

Oh no. This could be brilliant or terrifying.

"So, we give them yours. I need something to write on," he says, shoving off the floor and striding away. At the door, he turns, excited energy pulsing off him. "Get dressed in your normal stuff, not the fancy dresses Kyle makes you wear in public. Minimal makeup." His gaze flicks to my unruly hair. "Might want to put a little work into that though. It's a mess, Mess."

"What are you going to do?" I ask, pushing up from the chair.

"Turn the tide."

Only a miracle sprinkled with unicorn blood could turn this clusterfuck around.

Which begs the question: What in the hell is he planning?

21

RANDI

I tug down the hem of my green V-neck sweater below the waistband only for it to pop right back up. Glancing out the glass doors to the mob of reporters, I swipe my sweaty palms down the sides of my dark-wash jeans. Like Trey instructed an hour ago, I'm normal Randi. Not the perfect Political Barbie Kyle always demands me to be in public. From the older sweater to my Wranglers and scuffed boots, I'm me. Still fancier then Randi 1.0 but not nearly the obnoxious sparkle of Randi 2.0.

So what does that make this version, Randi 1.5 or Randi 3.0?

Debatable for sure.

"You think this will work?" I ask over my shoulder to where T and Trey huddle with the rest of the team. Several came in on their day off to be here for me. Never in my life have I had this much support. It strengthens my resolve to get this right. My one shot to correct the damage Shawn did by leaking my background to the media. We don't know for certain it was him, of course, but I wouldn't put it past that conniving asshole

"It has to work, Mess."

I turn my attention back to the glass doors.

Due to the size of the University of Texas campus, Taeler is able to lie low until after the press conference, thank goodness. Still, T called in extra security to watch her until the story's initial sensation wears off.

Which it will, hopefully.

"Ready, guys?"

"Ready," the team announces in unison behind me.

I choke back the building tears. Without these men, one in particular, I couldn't get through this shit show.

A blast of bitter wind slashes against my cheeks, blowing my loose hair from one shoulder to the other. I suppress a shudder as I step deeper into the mass of reporters, all yelling my name and demanding answers while cameras snap.

I hold up a hand, hoping it's enough to quiet the crowd.

It's not.

Instead, several in the front lurch forward, propped up by the people behind them, closing the distance between me and them. Trey, T, and the rest of the agents rush forward, shoving the circling vultures back to their original distance.

A full-body tremble bolts down my spine, my hands twitching nervously at my side. This isn't my normal stage, the typical monitored debate. This is real, ugly, and terrifying.

"Everyone calm the hell down," T bellows.

The shouts quiet to murmurs. Seems no one can disobey a direct order from the big guy.

Locking his kind, dark eyes with mine, T nods. An indication for me to get this show on the road.

I clear my throat, widen my stance, and clasp both hands behind my back. Straightening my back, I smile into the crowd.

Here goes... everything.

"I know everyone has questions they want to ask regarding the details of my life which were released early this morning, but I won't be answering them." A chaotic shout of protests answers in response. "What I will do, however, is give you the true story. My story. The truth. All of it. But first I'd like to address the people whom I've misled these past several months." I pause, letting the crowd quiet down. Nostrils flaring, I inhale deeply and continue.

"To my fellow Americans, I'm sorry." I swallow thickly and wet my lips. "I'm not apologizing for the story you were led to believe early on but for being ashamed enough about my past that I felt the need to. I'm here to set the story straight, for you to see the real Randi Sawyer. The good, the bad, and the nitty gritty—and believe me, there's a lot of that. I was born to a teen mother who had no business raising a child but still did. She supported us through welfare and social security fraud and lived in a run-down trailer in the worst trailer park in town, where she went through a new boyfriend every other week.

"I knew early in my childhood that I didn't want her life for my own. I wanted to succeed, to be someone I could be proud of becoming. Most days after school were filled with my closest friends, Blanche, Sophia, Dorothy, and of course the hilarious Rose. There were days when she forgot to buy food, so I learned to depend on myself for everything. Homework, bathing, clothes—everything fell on me from about kindergarten on."

I tighten my hands into fists. Tears threaten as the memories flood through, a heart-shredding tidal wave of knives slamming into my chest.

"I was bullied, made fun of, teased, ignored, all of it. All because of whose daughter I am, of things I couldn't control at such a young age. I tell you this not to make you feel sorry for me or for you to pity my childhood. As neglectful as my mother was, I still had it better than some. I'm telling you this to explain why I did it. My entire life, I've been judged, overlooked, forgotten, and, worst of all, told repeatedly that I'm nothing, a loser, and that I will never, ever break the cycle my mother birthed me into.

"At fifteen, I proved everyone right. I got pregnant by my boyfriend in the back of his parents' van. I thought up to that point the harassment was bad, but oh no, it could get worse. It did get worse. I decided then, after my daughter was born, that I would do everything in my power to make sure my life didn't bleed over into hers. I wanted her to have it all, to be the pretty, popular girl in school that I had never been and would never be.

"Things got a little hairy after she was born. My mom kicked me out to the shed to raise my daughter, the schoolwork was piling on, and I was out of options. CPS was called in, and"—I swipe a lone tear dripping down my cold cheek—"I was devastated. Absolutely devastated. Only weeks old and I was already failing her. The justice system deemed me an unfit mother, giving my child—my daughter who I would've sacrificed my life for—to her biological father's parents. I had to fight to see her, and when I did, the hateful words, shaming, and disgust filled the house from the moment I stepped through the door until I left. It ripped me to shreds.

"Those following weeks changed me. My determination to change my life, to be more than a trailer trash teen mom, strengthened. The parts about me going to UT Austin and then on to Harvard are all true. You can ask any of my professors; I'm certain they haven't forgotten the student who asked for more work every class to stay one step ahead of everyone else."

My gaze floats up to the gray sky.

"How I got to this spot, well, that's another long story, but I'll keep it short. I knew Kyle Birmingham at Harvard, and we hated each other." An uncomfortable chuckle vibrates through the crowd. "After law school I went back to Boone, started my own family law practice to be the voice for the underprivileged, and became mayor to help implement some much-needed changes. One day last year, Kyle walked into my office declaring he wanted to run for office but wanted someone with a 'normal' life to help him see things from the people's perspective." Slight lie, but this is my spin on the truth. "He helped me pay off some of the student loans and other debt that hung around my neck like a boat anchor, got me to DC, and here I am. Here I am pleading for you to understand.

"It had nothing to do with you and everything to do with my fears. I was scared I wouldn't get a chance in this town, a chance to win your vote, if you knew the truth about my background. I've heard too many times the hateful words, the snap judgments people make when they know the truth, and I couldn't risk it.

"So, that's my story. That's the truth. All of it. And I'll tell you one more truth: I want this job. I want to represent you here in Washington. This town is full of people who don't understand the daily struggles of living paycheck to paycheck and the frustration when taxes go up again and less of your hard-earned money comes home. I will be your voice, the slap of reality to this town. If you'll have me."

Two seconds of shocked quiet pulses before the crowd erupts in shouts.

I smile, give a quick wave, and turn to head back into the safety of the lobby.

"What about the cheating rumors?" someone shouts above all the other voices. "A liar and a cheater. Sounds like the same old politician to me."

My steps pause. I suck in a breath and turn back to the cameras.

"Right, forgot about that one. First of all, let's get the thing cleared up about me and Kyle." I have to tread lightly here. The people might forgive me for being ashamed of my past, but admitting to lying about the relationship part might push them over the edge. "What's going on between us is our business. However, I can tell you we've decided we're best as political partners, nothing else. As far as a relationship with a certain agent, that's a load of fiction. I have made a few friends with the men who are at my side day in and day out the past few months. They've had my back and provided me with some great counsel, seeing as this whole political power game is new to me. I had no one to confide in until they arrived. Now I'm happy to say I have friends here—they just to happen to get paid to hang out with me."

I smile at the rumble of laughter.

"Early voting starts today. Go out to the polls, vote. Vote for me, vote for another candidate, but please, please vote. It's your voice, your chance to tell the people in DC who you want representing you. Change can happen, but it won't if you expect others to pull the load. Thank you."

Smiling, I wiggle two fingers in the air like a motherfucking idiot. Turning on my heels, I speed-walk back to the lobby doors, throwing them open and rushing inside, heat blazing across my face. I press the traitorous fingers to my cheeks, attempting to cool my flush.

"Was that a poor imitation of Nixon?"

I groan and throw my hands into the air in exasperation. "What the hell is wrong with me? I give the best speech of my life and then go do that shit."

"That was pretty bad, Mess." Trey chuckles, his signature smirk pulling at his lips. "Other than that though, I'd say you nailed it. Great job."

Our heavy footsteps echo through the otherwise silent lobby. Trey and T step into the elevator with me, the other guys staying down to secure the area.

"So now what?" I ask, flicking my gaze from Trey's reflection to T's.

T drapes a heavy arm across my shoulders. "Now we wait."

22

———————

TREY

She paces from one side of the condo to the other, rich brownie colored hair floating in her wake. Fingers steepled beneath my chin, I track each of her movements while monitoring the TV plus the two computer screens set up along the coffee table.

Election Day.

"I'm going to puke," Randi says for the tenth time in the last hour. "Can someone ask that doctor lady to prescribe me some Xanax?"

Tank chuckles from the nest he set up hours ago. Candy wrappers litter the floor around the chair. He's a nervous eater, what can I say? "Come on now, Randi. We have hours left of this. Sit down, relax."

"Relax?" she screeches. I cringe at the sharp sound cutting into my eardrums. "I think I'm having a heart attack. What are the signs again?"

"Do not WebMD it," I say over the TV. "You're fine, Mess. I agree with Tank, sit your ass down."

"You two are the worst friends ever. I'll go die alone in my bedroom so I don't interrupt whatever you're doing which makes you too busy to be concerned about my failing health."

Wow. I roll my eyes to the ceiling. Sure as hell hope Randi's daughter didn't get her dramatics.

The bedroom door slams shut. Tank looks to the closed door, then back at me.

"Give her some time. She's fine," I mutter. "When do we need to leave for that watch party she has to attend?"

"Few hours from now. It'd be nice if we knew before we left. Not sure the partygoers are ready for that." He jerks a thumb over his shoulder toward the bedroom. "She's living up to the name you gave her."

I smirk and turn back to the screens. As the California numbers scroll across the bottom, the hairs on the back of my neck stand, a tingling feeling of being watched itching up my spine. Peeling my gaze from the screen, I meet Tank's dark eyes.

"Creeper. What?"

"How's that going?" He tilts his head back. "Ending it with her."

"Motherfucking terrible," I grit out. "I don't blame you though, if that's what you're worried about."

"I'm not. I'm worried about my friend, actually." *Aw, big guy has a big heart.* "I know how hard the shit with Rachel affected you. That's why I didn't stop you two, the flirting. For the first time in a year, you were acting normal. Don't let this drag you back down."

I sigh, lean back against the couch, and scrub a hand over my face. He's right about the gloom cloud that hung over my head after Rachel left me for Shawn. Even more right about Randi being the one to snap me out of it.

"I won't," I say after a beat.

"Don't let it distract you either."

"I know."

"Do not give me a reason to fire your ass, Trey." I whip my head to the right. "You know I'd have to if you break the rules, even if you are my best friend. Don't put me in that situation, got it?"

My chin dips in a minuscule nod.

I have to be strong and keep my hands off her if she wins. No, *when* she wins. I can't risk the entire team's job, her safety, and my relationship with my best friend. Even if staying away from her hurts like a motherfucking kick to the balls with a steel toe.

Part of me hopes they don't win; that way, I won't have to be around the one woman I want but can't have day after day. I'm already dreading the torture those four years will turn into.

But the other part wants her to win. To smear her success in the faces of all those fuckers who doubted her, who made fun of her as a kid. Hearing the long, detailed version of her childhood that day ripped my heart out of my chest, her tears shattering my one resolve to never kill for pleasure.

"I'll be fine."

No more untrue words were ever spoken.

***

BOISTEROUS CHEERS POUR out of the ballroom into the hallway where Tank and I stand stationed at the door. I catch his eye and smile.

"That's a good sign," I mutter, going back to scanning the long, empty halls for perceived threats.

"I've never wanted to know the outcome of an election more," he says with an annoyed huff. "Fucking killing me."

"Easy, big guy. We'll know soon enough."

Almost on cue, the doors fling open, a teary Randi marching through.

"We did it," she breathes, clapping her hands in front of her chest with a hop of pure joy. "We won." Midhop, she turns to Tank. "We won!"

"Congratulations, ma'am." True happiness warms his tone, tugging his lips in an almost smile. "Looking forward to the next four years."

"Me too, T. Me too." She turns back to face me, and her smile falters. My brows rise up my forehead. "Can I talk to you, in private?" She shoots a worried glance over her shoulder to the now-frowning Tank.

"Fine," he says like a parent would to a needy child. "Make it quick; I can't make excuses for too long. The bathrooms are down that way. At least make it look like he's escorting you somewhere other than a dark corner."

Red flush spreads across her freckled cheeks. Ever since the press conference, she's dialed it back on the makeup and big hair, showing off more of her natural beauty.

I swing a hand out and bend at the waist in an exaggerated bow.

"Madam Vice President," I say with a smile.

Her lips spread wide. We walk side by side down the silent hall. "Wow, this is really happening," she says halfway to the bathroom sign. "Can you believe it?" Her shining eyes meet mine.

"I can. You deserve it, Mess. You and the people in this country deserve it. Someone like you has been a long time coming." I give my head a quick shake. "I can't wait to see what you do to this town. It might never be the same."

She snorts. "I sure the hell hope not. Now the real work starts, I guess." We pause outside the women's restroom. Her gaze flicks one way down the hall and then the other. "We haven't gotten a chance to talk... you know, about us and what's next."

The vulnerability in her voice shakes my soul, rattling the promise I made to Tank about staying away.

"That was then. You're the vice president elect of the United States of America. Things are different now. *You're* different."

Tears well in the corners of her eyes. Glancing up and down the hall, I grip her hand and tug her into a side door that leads to a large empty ballroom.

"Don't do that," I beg, my lips brushing against hers. "You're ripping me in two."

"I don't want it to end." Her voice catches. "Why can't we just keep sneaking around?"

"You deserve better than that, Mess. You know you do. And I need this solid line between us, both of us knowing that piece of us is tabled. Not over, just on hold." I tug her close, sealing her chest against my own. Lips in her hair, I kiss the top of her head. "Don't ask me to choose between you and this job, between you and Tank."

"I'm not. I swear I'm not. I'm just not ready for it to end. It's just started."

"I know, but it's not really over. I don't know if we ever could be."

Her shoulder shake, and I hold her tighter.

"Now what?" Lip trembling, eyes wet, she tilts her face up, eyes meeting mine.

The wet skin of her cheeks slides beneath my thumbs as I swipe away her tears. "Now... now we wait."

POWER TWIST

POWER PLAY SERIES BOOK 2

INSPIRATION

"I am in politics because of the conflict between good and evil, and I believe that in the end good will triumph."
- Margaret Thatcher

PROLOGUE
KYLE BIRMINGHAM

I flick the end of the half-smoked cigar, the ashes floating to the balcony floor before being swept away on a bitter winter wind. Even with the thick cashmere overcoat, a deep chill has seeped through to my bones. I tuck my free hand into the soft silk-lined pocket and ball it into a tight fist to warm my stiffly frozen fingers. Elbow against the stone railing, I stare out into the night, my focus zeroed in on the White House, my home in less than a month.

"Congratulations, motherfucker."

I shake my head. A small smile creeps up my wind-burned cheeks, stretching my dry lips. Lifting the Cuban, I take another long puff before turning to acknowledge the asshole standing just outside the balcony's double doors.

"No thanks to you, asshole. I should kick your ass for pulling that stunt with Walmart's background." I turn back to the spectacular view, dismissing Shawn and his cocky-ass smirk. "You had no way of knowing which way the poll would swing with her real background known."

The sharp click of dress shoes against the tiled balcony floor signals his approach. Cutting my eyes in his direction, I watch Shawn thumb through the box of cigars still open on the stone ledge. The fucker doesn't say a word as he snips off the tip and lights the end. After several puffs, the end glows red with the hot embers.

"We needed to know how she'd react under pressure," he finally says.

"That's bullshit and you know it," I bite out. The fucker was pissed I selected Randi as VP instead of him last year. I'm an opportunist at heart, so when Randi fucking Sawyer suggested the crazy-as-hell idea on how to win the White House, I went with it. Except that means I'm stuck with her—for now.

The dickhead simply shrugs like he didn't almost make me lose the goal I've been working toward my whole life.

"It all worked out. Don't get your thong in a wad." The cigar crumbles in my tightening fist. "You won. That's what matters. Move on. We have new shit to discuss."

I shift my focus back to the glowing White House in the distance. My future home. Two weeks from now, I, Kyle Birmingham, will be President of the United States of America. The most powerful man in the world.

Me.

I smile into the night, momentarily forgetting all the promises that were made to help me secure this seat and now need to be kept.

"I know what needs to be done," I say. "I have a plan."

"Does that plan involve taking Trailer out of the picture? She needs to be dealt with for me to claim my rightful seat as vice president. Her sideshow act is done. You got the sympathy votes needed to win. Now we get her the fuck out of our city."

I chuckle at Shawn's favorite nickname for Randi. I'm partial to Walmart, but Trailer is a great representation for the trailer trash she really is at the core. Once trash, always trash in my opinion.

"It does." Probably not the way he's hoping. He'd love to see her six feet under just because that's the way his evil mind works, whereas I have a less murderous plan. One that will drive her from this town and back to that dump she came from. I'm a conniving, deceitful bastard, but I'm no killer.

Not that I can say the same for Shawn.

I toss the ruined Cuban to the balcony floor and reach for the highball glass filled with my favorite scotch sitting on the metal side table beside me.

Shawn curses. "Details would be great right about now, fucker."

I laugh. "In two weeks, you'll be assigned your new role as secretary of interior. That's all you need to know right now. I have a different idea on how to handle our bleeding-heart VP to keep her off our tail."

"I'd love to make her bleed," Shawn says under his breath with a hint of hope in his voice.

"No," I state hopefully cutting off his mental planning of Randi's assassination. "I need you to be hands off. No more attacks, no more stunts." The cold stone digs into my hip as I shift to face Shawn. "I get you're pissed, but if something happens to her, there will be a fucking revolt. You releasing her background to the media only made the voters love her more. She's like their fucking Princess Diana now, you idiot."

He grumbles something before taking a puff from his cigar. "Sure, you're the boss."

An icy chill stiffens my spine. He's lying, no doubt about it. A slice of pity carves into my heart for Walmart. She has no idea the type of things he's capable of, that he enjoys.

"I won't lay a finger on her," he continues.

Like he ever would. No way in hell would he get his hands dirty like that. That's not his style. No, he prefers to stay back, to watch from a distance with his fucking cock in his hand. Creepy, sinister son of a bitch. If it weren't for our childhood, our family connections, I'd distance myself from him as quickly as I could. But it's too late for that. I'm stuck with the psycho from now until one of us is dead or I'm deemed no longer useful in his eyes.

"What's the motherfucking plan?" Shawn asks as he relaxes on the outdoor couch, his arms stretching wide along the back.

The plan.

"We have to make good on a few promises made through the campaign and before. That's where I need you. We have to put the main pieces in place day one, without Walmart catching wind of our plans."

"She could always disappear now, solve all our problems."

I curse under my breath. He's relentless. A dog with a bone, and that bone is Randi Sawyer.

"Just focus on the EPA regulations I tell you to and start a search for the best oil-rich federal land. We're on a deadline."

"*You're* on a deadline," he says, smiling around the cigar.

Damn bastard. Even though he's right. I'm the one who made foolish deals to win the White House and am now on a time crunch to keep them.

I shiver and tuck my chin into the collar of my coat. The people I'm now indebted to make Shawn seem kind. He's not the only man in this city with no qualms about taking a life for payback.

I shake my head to disperse the dark thoughts and weight of what needs to be done this first year.

"We get this shit done quick, day one. I distract Walmart while you shift the pieces in place to settle my debts."

"And what do I get in return?"

"The VP spot, the one she took from you." No harm in stoking his anger, considering it's a blazing forest fire already.

His lips peel back into a sinister smile.

Fuck.

Watch out, Walmart. You've made enemies even I can't protect you from.

1

RANDI

January

Maybe I smell and *that's* why no one will talk to me. Hell, even stand close to me.

With a quick glance left and then right, checking for the all clear, I inconspicuously dip my nose to my right shoulder to take a nonchalant whiff. Huh. Not stinky, just powder fresh like the deodorant label promised. Something else must be repelling these fancy-ass people; why else would I be bored in the corner still holding my first flute of champagne?

I glance around the packed room, a wide fake smile plastered across my face, desperate to make eye contact with someone in hopes to initiate a conversation. But no such luck. Like it's been all night. Well, let's be honest, it's happened since the day I stepped on the campaign trail. Only my do-or-die secret service team welcomed me in this town, and tonight is no different.

The White House sparkles like the strings of diamonds around every woman's neck and wrists in attendance. At least seventy-five couples fill the various rooms, all here to celebrate this morning's events.

Inauguration day.

Vice president of the United States, makeup perfect, killer dress with the coveted red-soled shoes, and still not a single person will talk to me. The women cut their eyes in my direction before turning up their noses and looking away, while the men get a calculating gleam before turning back to a 'worthier' partygoer.

"You look creepy."

The stretched fake smile turns into a genuine one. "I'm trying to look approachable," I say over my shoulder to T, also know as Davis Washington or Tank, alpha secret service team lead and my friend.

A massive shadow floats over me as he steps to my side. Glancing up, I take in my second-favorite agent. His bald head reflects the overhead lights while his massive frame encased in his usual black suit seems to soak it all in.

"You sniffed your pit and are now smiling like the freak from *Saw*. That does not make you approachable. It confirms their thoughts."

"I'm poor white trash made up to look like a DC socialite?"

I can't help but chuckle at his answering growl. "No, that you're not one of them."

"Thank fuck," I mutter, which earns me an almost smile. I'll take that win. Getting the tough guy to smile while on duty is a true feat. "Which one's Rachel?" Since no one is talking to me might as well search the crowd for Trey's ex-girlfriend. She left Trey for Shawn Whitt, the idiot, who was invited to the celebration tonight no doubt.

T blanches, his fingers flying to his ear and pulling the two-way communication device out a fraction.

"It seems Benson is adamant I don't answer your question," he says while readjusting the earpiece. "Not that I could, since I don't see her or Whit here."

Damn. That was the whole point of coming to this stupid thing tonight, plus the small fact that my presence was required. Actually, demanded and threatened is more like it. Kyle wasn't as accepting of my no RSVP last month as I hoped. I tried to explain that no one would care if I was there or not, but that didn't matter.

Speak of the devil.... An overpowering wave of his expensive cologne closes my throat as Kyle appears at my side.

"Not having fun, Walmart?" Tipping forward, he frowns at T. "We have things to discuss. Leave."

T's dark brown eyes meet mine before he dips his head and disappears into the shadows once again. Apprehension coils in my gut. Yes, we're in a room full of people, but being this close to Kyle still triggers every warning bell.

"Great party," I deadpan. "None of your asshole friends will talk to me—not that I'm complaining. But I would like to say, for the record, 'I told you so.'"

"Oh, Walmart, they're afraid they'll catch something that will require antibiotics." The corners of his eyes crinkle with the widening of his arrogant smile. "Or catch too deep of a whiff." To make his point, he leans forward to take an exaggerated sniff. "Nearly two years away from that shithole I pulled you out of and you still reek of trailer trash. How is that even possible?" Moving out of my personal space, he runs a slow gaze down my body. "At least you look the part."

"Fuck you, Kyle."

His ice blue eyes roll to the ceiling. "Everything except that mouth of yours. Now, as lovely as this is, I came over here for a reason."

"Then spit it out and leave me alone so I can people watch in peace."

"Tomorrow morning, eight o'clock, I need you in the Oval Office."

I bat my eyelashes. "Say please."

"You're an idiot."

I don't hold back my snicker. "I already have a meeting tomorrow morning. Call my secretary and she'll pencil you in sometime next year."

"Eight o'clock," he says, emphasizing each word. "I promise you won't want to miss it. There's an item or two on the agenda that I'm sure you'll be interested in learning about."

I tilt my head, my eyes searching his. "What are you playing at, Kyle? What's going on?" Dread sinks in my gut like lead. Kyle is not a nice man; no way in hell would he give me a heads-up unless there's an underlying agenda.

"Guess you'll have to show up to find out." His name being called draws his blue eyes away to scan the crowd. "See you tomorrow, Walmart. And hey, make sure you wear something sexy. First impressions and all."

Red-hot anger flashes through my veins, heating my skin. I take a heavy step in the direction he disappeared through the crowd only to be held back. I turn my attention to the football-size hand around my wrist and trail up the black sleeve to T's determined stare.

"Leave it," he mutters. "Nothing good would come from the VP kicking the president's ass in the middle of their first party."

"And last party. This one is boring as hell. They don't even have Jack Daniel's at the bar. Who does that?" I sigh and take a sip of the now-warm champagne. I don't care how much they say this stuff cost, it's awful—yet every woman here is downing it glass after glass. At least they're now at the point of intoxication where I no longer exist for them to glare at. "And side note, no way could I take Kyle. See these arms?" I hold up a bicep for T to inspect. "These muscles are only used for two things, lifting food to my mouth and carrying my laptop bag." I scan the crowd for Kyle and hoping for Shawn to appear too. "I'd love to learn though."

"What's that?" T presses two fingers to his ear. "No, I'm not saying that, you idiot. It's inappropriate."

"What did Trouble say to get him into, well, trouble?" I smile as I search the shadows for Trey.

"He can tell you later, even though he shouldn't. What were you saying you wanted to learn?"

I reach for a passing waiter's tray, gently setting my half-full champagne flute on top. "To fight, or at least defend myself. Maybe just the basics in case something happens when you guys aren't around. What time is it?"

"Ten, ma'am."

I shoot him a side-eyed glare. He knows how much I hate the 'ma'am' shit. Makes me feel older than I already am. Four years from forty, I don't need any more help feeling old.

"Great," I say as I gather the silky pink material of my dress and tug it up an inch. "Let's go to my new home. Where's the nearest exit?"

A sense of security washes over me, calming my jittery nerves the moment his hand presses against my lower back. There's no heat, no desire like there is with Trey; T's strong yet gentle touch is nothing more than protective and platonic. The fact that I'm not pulling away right now is crazy considering I've gone my whole life not being able to stand anyone touching me. It says something about T, about Trey. Maybe that I want their protection, want the sense of belonging their strong hands provide.

Eh, I'll think about that later.

We weave through the crowd, my wide smile falling the closer we get to the exit doors. T says something into his sleeve, and the double doors just ahead swing open.

A girl really could get used to this.

From trailer to vice president in less than two years was a big culture shock to say the least. Yes, the clothes are different, the food is better, and the 24-7 security is a nice perk, but it's the absence of financial worry that's the biggest change. Before, every minute of every day was spent worrying about money and how I needed more. A lot more.

My heels click on the concrete stairs as I descend toward the awaiting limo. A shiver of apprehension causes me to stumble forward, and I barely catch myself before toppling the final few steps. Tonight, the party plus the limo home is all too similar to the night someone attacked me last year. Even though the person was caught, we still don't know who was behind it all.

Our guess? Shawn Whit. There wasn't any evidence to support our claim, but me, my secret service team, we all know it was him.

I slide easily across the smooth black leather seat as I scoot toward the center. I tug the dress's train so it doesn't catch in the door when a head dips inside. Honey brown eyes meet mine in the shadows of the limo, a familiar sexy smirk pulling on lips I'm dying to taste again.

"See ya at home, Mess."

The door slams shut, locking me inside alone.

Home. At least for the next four years. Four years to make a difference in the world for the working class and those many Americans who fall below the poverty line. I promised them I'd be their voice if they voted for me. Now it's time to come through on those promises.

Leaning back, I close my eyes and sigh, letting the night's stressors fade.

Now the real work begins.

I WRAP the thick blanket tighter around my shoulders, warding off the damp late night air. Large puffs of frosty breath cloud with each exhale before floating down the wraparound porch and vanishing into the night. This porch is one of the many beautiful perks of my new home. One Observatory Circle isn't new by any means, but it is updated, and the character of the old Victorian is priceless in my eyes.

The white wicker chair creaks as I shift to tuck my knees against my chest. Wrapping the blanket around my shins, I stare out into the backyard, focusing on the brilliant crystal clear waters of the swimming pool. Yep, I have a swimming pool. A heated one at that. I shake my head and rest my cheek on top of my blanket-covered knee.

"Long night?"

My cheek slides against the blanket as I smile at the familiar voice but don't turn to look.

"My partner in crime was nowhere to be seen, so yeah, long night." I close my eyes and sigh. "Where were you anyway? I looked for you."

A suited waist steps into my line of vision, forcing me to tilt my head back to meet Trey's eyes.

"You know I can't be with the inside detail during those things." I nod in understanding when I really don't. "It's best if I stay hidden. It makes it easier on everyone."

"You mean you," I say with a shrug. "I missed you. I mean, I love T and all, but you're more fun."

Trey squats, putting us eye to eye. Two fingers slide along my forehead before tucking a rogue lock of dark hair behind my ear. A shiver zaps down my spine, heating my core at his touch.

"You looked beautiful," he mutters while his eyes scan every inch of my face. "It's why they hate you." I raise my brows in silent question. "All those women, they spend thousands trying to replicate what you have naturally."

Actually, it's not naturally. I shake my head and break his gaze to press my chin to my knee. The way I look now—the perfect skin, gorgeous healthy hair, weight in all the right places, zero wrinkles, and straight teeth—is due to the man I hate. Kyle Birmingham. Looking the VP role was part of the initial agreement. Now here I am, the perfect political Barbie.

At least I don't have to lie about my background anymore. Everyone knows my cringe-worthy upbringing and still voted for me. I say voted for *me* and not Kyle, since I'm the reason he won the White House. He said from the start most voters didn't want another pompous politician which is why he came to me in the first place. After my background was unexpectedly released to the media the polls swung in our favor proving without a doubt I'm the reason we're in these new roles not Kyle.

"You know all this is fake," I say, waving an edge of the blanket toward my face. "Kyle paid a lot of money to help me look this way."

"No." I side-eye him, watching his face scrunch in determination. "Maybe all that stuff helped enhance what was already there, but you, Randi Sawyer, are beautiful with or without that shit."

I give him a shy smile. "Thanks. I'll stick with believing the truth though. But you can keep believing that lie all you want." I laugh.

For a few seconds, neither of us says a word, building taut tension with each passing second. Like a magnet drawn to metal, an unseen force urges me closer to Trey until I'm almost toppling out of the chair right into him.

The past few months of staying apart, fighting this natural draw, have been hell. All I want is his calloused hands cupping my face and pulling me close. His lips sliding against my own while his fingers twist and pinch, creating the delicious torture I miss.

"Randi," Trey says reluctantly. His hot breath warms my cheek. I blink, pulling back an inch, surprised I'd gotten so close. "Please stop."

"Sorry," I mutter, righting myself back into the chair. I tuck my chin in the hope that Trey doesn't catch my embarrassed blush.

What the hell was I thinking? Burying my face deeper into the blanket, I shake my head. He said stop. My heart clenches as the word repeats in my mind. Maybe it isn't driving him crazy like it is me that we can't be together.

Per T, the lead of my Alpha secret service team, an agent 'mingling' with the VP is a big no-no. Though, I haven't found that particular rule documented in my research—yes, I've researched. Anyone would when it comes to the sexy-as-hell agent. Since T found us in bed together that morning, he's been adamant that the relationship Trey and I had started to form through the course of the campaign is over.

And it has been ever since that day.

Ugh, wallowing in this pitiful state does me no good. I need a distraction, to change topics, to choke on my own spit—anything to break the awkwardness surrounding us.

"Did you hear Kyle wants me at the White House tomorrow morning at eight?" I ask, my words muffled by the blanket. "He mentioned he has some topics I'll be interested in. Sounded fishy. When has Kyle ever helped me when he didn't have something to gain too?"

The chair tilts to the side and a groan of pain pierces the quiet as Trey shoves off the wicker to stand. Nose still tucked into the plaid blanket, I peer up to where Trey now leans with his back against a white decorative pole of the railing.

"What's he playing at?" he muses, his eyes fixed above my head, completely avoiding mine. "At least you don't have to wait long to know. Best to figure out his game plan and tackle it from there." He glances down at his watch. Lips pursed, he resituates his coat sleeve over his wrist. "I'm out of here in a few, and tomorrow's my day off. I won't be there—"

"It's okay," I say, attempting to put some strength into my voice. "I'll be fine. I can fill you and T in the next time I see you." I give him a dismissive wave beneath the thick blanket. "Go, have a good night." The tight, fake smile hurts my cheeks, my eyes burning with unshed tears.

Fuck, why does this hurt so much? Acting like his indifference, his rejection doesn't fucking slice me to the core. Because it does. Every step he moves away, the distance, every impersonal conversation wound my still-tender heart. The heart he softened with his sweet words and gentle touch all those scarce moments alone during the campaign.

"Randi—," he starts, empathy dripping in his soft tone, but cuts himself off with a muttered curse.

"Forget it," I bite out. Palms digging into the thin wooden rods, I shove out of the chair, the blanket pooling around my light gray Uggs. "See you when I see you," I toss over my shoulder as I hurry inside the house before the pooling tears can spill over.

You'd think after two months of this cold side of Trey, I'd be immune to it by now. But nope, it still hurts.

T shoots me a confused glance as I rush past him toward the stairs. His mouth opens, readying to say something, but I stop him with a hard look. I shouldn't be annoyed at him, but he's the cause of my current pain. He's the one who halted the one relationship I can't get enough of, keeping me away from the one man I crave.

I make it halfway up the stairs when a lone tear escapes to drip down my cheek. I hastily wipe it away with the back of my hand before it's visible on the security cameras for all the agents to see. The bedroom door bangs shut behind me as I storm toward the bathroom.

Hands gripping the marble vanity top, I hang my head. Every night, every day has been the same heartrending agony. Seeing him, wanting him, and not having him. Of his casual smiles, easy laughs, and cold touches. At least I only have to endure this cruel form of soul-crushing torture for 1,460 more days.

Fuck. Me.

2

RANDI

"Get me a coffee while you're up, sweetheart."

I grind my teeth to keep the building scream from letting loose. "I told you once, Dick"—his name isn't Richard—"I'm not your secretary or your wife. Get it yourself."

The Oval Office vibrates with the other men's resounding chuckles. The coffee carafe trembles in my white-knuckled grasp. Four damn hours of their shit. A drop of coffee sloshes over my mug, landing on the crazily ornate coffee cart. With a muttered curse, I swipe a napkin off the stack to wipe up the mess.

"Watch your mouth with the House minority leader." Kyle's hot breath brushes against my ear. I fight the urge to shrug him off, slamming my elbow back into his soft stomach and forcing him back an inch instead. "Careful, Randi," he practically growls. Gripping the offensive elbow, he gives it a too-tight squeeze. "Remember who holds your leash."

Anger churns in my gut. I want to defend myself, say I'm not his damn puppet, but I can't. I willingly signed the initial agreement to support him, to continue playing this game during the campaign and after, if we won, or I'll legally be liable to pay every dime back. The massive debt he paid off, the year he's paid for Taeler's school, the expensive wardrobe, the makeover—all of it. In summary, a shit ton of money which I do not have.

"Your part is next, Walmart."

The moment he walks away, I release the breath I was holding to keep from gagging on his overpowering cologne.

"Finally," I mutter into my coffee mug as I turn toward the center of the room.

Five men, plus Kyle, convene around the Oval Office, chatting and laughing like they've been best friends since the beginning of time. It's all fake, I know it is—deep down, they hate each other and would do anything for the upper hand—but it doesn't make the feeling of being left out any less hurtful. I stepped into a proverbial boys' club, and I'm the odd one out with my morals and a vagina.

At least Shawn isn't here.

I tilt my head as I list off the men's titles in the room. There's the secretary of state, House minority leader, Senate majority leader, plus two advisors, but no Shawn. This morning Kyle proposed to the group to select Shawn as Secretary of Interior, which caught me off guard. It's an odd move unless Kyle has a hidden agenda behind the choice.

Mental note: dig into that oddity at a later date.

"Let's transition to the voting bill," Kyle says, shooting a sly smile in my direction as he rests on the edge of the enormous dark wood desk.

Max Holster, House minority leader, leans forward, bracing his elbows on his thighs. His brown eyes meet mine before flicking to Kyle, who's still wearing a shit-eating grin.

"Your proposal is drastic, but it makes sense," Max says. He clears his throat and fiddles with the gold wedding band around his left ring finger.

Fucking hell, the suspense is killing me. I roll my eyes and mutter as much into my coffee mug. This meeting could've been over hours ago, but no, they like to make everything so fucking dramatic and gossip like high school girls. At least I know Brad's wife likes it in the ass, because that's information I really needed to be aware.

"We should have the votes in the House, but it will be close in the Senate."

I hold out a hand, stopping him from continuing. "Hold up there, Maximillian." Again, not his name. "Let's take a quick step back and go over the details of the voting bill one more time." Or the first time, since Kyle seems to think it's a fun game to keep me out of the loop. He always did enjoy seeing me floundering in uncertainty.

Max arches a perfectly plucked brow. *Seriously, does he get those threaded or something, because I might need to get his girl's number.*

"Revoking voting rights to anyone below a certain yearly income level."

I forget how to breathe. My gaze slides from Max to Kyle, whose shit-eating grin has turned into a full-on smile.

"Come again?" I say, hoping I heard him wrong. "Surely I didn't hear you correctly."

"Ah, but you did, Madam VP," Kyle grinds out, sounding like my title burns his fucking throat. "We've done a study that Americans below a certain income level don't have the intelligence—or mental capacity, rather —required for selecting candidates with the proper backgrounds and experiences to lead them. Present company included."

The building anger and frustrations from the past year and a half boil over. Red darkens my vision as I narrow my eyes on the man I truly loathe. My fingers tighten around the warm mug. I don't think just react to the sheer rage racing through my veins. I slam the full mug to the floor with as much power as I can muster. Shards of ceramic splinter around the room, coffee splattering over my pants and the pants of the others. Everyone shouts jumping to avoid the mess.

"What the fuck, Kyle?" I seethe as I shove off the couch. I lunge for the still-cowering president when strong arms band around my own, sealing them to my side and hauling me backward. I fight against the person's strong grasp. "Get off me," I yell, anger obliterating any hold I have on decorum.

"Everyone out." Kyle's sharp tone cuts through the chaos. I shiver when his ice blue eyes meet mine, rage flickering around the edges. "Now," he booms, slamming his fist on the desk. Eyes wide in fear and awe, the men shuffle out of the room. "You too." Kyle's eyes glare above my head.

"Sir—"

"I. Said. Out," he growls. His knuckles drain of color as he tightens his hold along the desk's edge.

I gasp in a deep breath when the overbearing hold loosens. Free to move, I turn just as a suited man steps out of the room, closing the door behind him with a soft click.

My fingers tremble with rage and fear. *Fucking shit, what did I just do? Showed my level of crazy, that's what.*

I swallow against a dry throat as I turn back to face Kyle only to stumble back a step. Anger radiates from where he still sits perched on the edge of the desk, his chest heaving.

"You will pay for that little display," he says. Releasing his death grip on the desk, he shakes out his hands and stands. For each of his steps forward, I take a cautious one back. A solid surface presses against my lower back, my head colliding with the wall.

"You can't do that." My voice cracks from the fear shaking my insides. "It's their constitutional right." Dread sinks in my gut. What have I done, helping this fucker get elected? "There's no way—"

My next words catch in my throat when thick fingers wrap around it. His grip tightens, sealing off my airway; only a sliver of air slides through with each desperate breath. My nails dig into the exposed skin of his wrist, clawing for freedom.

"There is always a way." He leans close. Cold lips sweep along my cheekbone. My knees give out, his hand on my neck the only thing keeping me upright.

"I'll stop you," I rasp out. Black dots sprinkle my vision.

He scans my face, pausing on my lips. "You think you can stop this from happening? Think you can gain enough supporters to side with your bleeding heart?"

I attempt a nod but whimper as the pain spikes down the back of my neck. The slick soles of my heels slide along the pristine carpet, desperate for traction.

"Challenge accepted, Walmart. We'll see who wins."

Slowly his fingers loosen their grip. I slump to the floor, gasping for air. Hands gently grasping my tender neck, I tuck into a tight ball. Traitorous tears slide down my cheeks. Eyes sealed shut, I attempt to block out the joy in his arrogant chuckle.

"Pathetic," he mutters somewhere in the distance. "Get up and get out. Countdown is on, Randi. I'm taking this to vote before the end of the year. Better use your time for gaining opposers to my bill instead of crying on the fucking floor."

I snap my eyes open at the sound of the door opening. Palms against the floor, I push up to lean back against the wall. The coolness seeps through my white dress shirt, calming my overheated skin. Anger, worry, and fear mix in my gut, scattering my thoughts and emotions.

"Shouldn't she be on her knees?" Shawn says with a condescending smirk. He tucks his hands into his suit pants and pauses beside Kyle. "Skirt next time, Trailer. If you're going to sit on the floor, at least make sure we get a good view of the cunt Benson's ensnared by."

Thank fuck that I opted for the fitted black pantsuit today. A 'power suit,' I thought when I picked out this outfit. Now look at me.

I give my head a small shake and angle my knees together, breaking Shawn's desire-filled stare.

"I'm assuming this means you enlightened Trailer about your brilliant bill proposal," Shawn says, half turning to Kyle. He moves around the room, taking in the various pictures of past presidents before pausing on a serene farming landscape. "And I'll take a shot in guessing she's not a fan." He cuts his near-black eyes to where I still sit on the floor.

"I will stop this," I rasp, my throat raw. Hands against the wall, I use it as support to stand. "You two are delusional if you think anyone will agree with you." I shoot daggers across the room at the two bastards. "I'll take it to the Supreme Court."

Kyle tilts his head and smiles. "If you weren't so dense, you might be pretty." He clicks his tongue and saunters around the desk before sliding into the sizeable leather chair. "I have the votes. I even own the superior minds of the Supreme Court. When you've been in this city long enough, you know everyone's secrets. And *that,* Walmart, is where true power lies." Steepling his fingers, he presses the point into the dimple of his chin. "And thanks to you, I'm now in a position to wield said power to get what I want. And what I want most of all is you gone."

"No." I shove off the wall, my trembling legs barely holding my weight as I advance toward Kyle. "I'll get the votes to stop this." The conviction in my strong voice surprises even me.

"Let's make it a deal, shall we?" He straightens the cuffs beneath his suit jacket, tugging on the glittering cufflinks. "*If* you get the votes—which, let's be honest, won't happen—not only will you stop the bill from passing into law, but I give you my promise to never bring it up again. Plus, I'll leave you alone the next four years, allowing you to focus on whatever you desire."

"And if I don't?" The words are like sand in my parched throat. I won't let the bill pass, but I need to know the terms I'm sealing my fate to.

"Ah, if you don't get the votes and the bill passes the House and Senate, then you'll be labeled the failure everyone knew you'd become. You'll tuck your tail and scurry back to that rat nest you call home."

All words leave my brain. I simply stare at him, mouth gaping like an idiot.

His white veneers shine as a smile splits his face. "Those are the terms. Yes or no?"

Still unable to form words, I nod in agreement. What choice do I have?

With a dismissive wave, he reaches for the phone. "Oh, and Walmart?" he says, the receiver now inches from his face. "Get with Todd. I need you with him the next few months at the various summits I'm unable to attend with him."

Why in the hell would he partner me with the Secretary of State? Unless... oh hell no. Of course, part of his evil plan is to take me out of the country so I can't be in DC rounding up the votes I'll need to ensure the bill doesn't pass. Deceitful brilliant prick.

For the first time since we won, a sense of unease sweeps in, making me question if I made the right choice all those months ago. I got what I wanted —debt free and a chance to prove to everyone back home that I'm not a failure, not just an addict's daughter. But at what cost?

"Don't look so surprised," Shawn says with a chuckle as he brushes some invisible lint off his suit jacket. "You know we fight dirty. Speaking of which, I'd be careful in your travels. It's a dangerous world out there. You never know who's watching."

<hr>

I STORM up the snow-cleared and salted walkway to the house. Beta team agents rush to keep up with my hurried strides. Grumbling a string of curse words, I march up the porch steps, causing the wood to rattle and groan. Eyes wild, anger rising, I shove open the front door. It pounds against the stopper before bouncing back, nearly hitting me in the side as I stomp into the house.

My heels skid to a stop on the polished cherry hardwood floor. My ragged breaths draw up in a quick surprised gasp as I take in the man standing in middle of the foyer. Dark jeans, black motorcycle boots, and leather jacket, he's the most delicious-looking bad boy I've ever laid eyes on.

"Bad day, Mess?" Trey's signature smirk falters as he scans me from head to toe, pausing on my raw neck. "What did that bastard do to you?"

I take a careful step backward at the menace in his tone only to slam into a solid chest of muscle. A hand encircles my bicep, holding me tight. I turn, looking up at the beta agent whose eyes are locked on Trey's.

"What are you doing here, Benson?" he grunts. The grip on my arm tightens. After this morning's encounter, my skittish heart races with panic. I yank my arm, desperate to be released from his hold.

"Step back, Roger." My head whips toward the library door at T's deep baritone voice. "We're here as friends today, not stepping on your toes." T's dark brown gaze zeroes in on where the Roger guy's hand grips my bicep. "Come on, Randi," he says with a wave into the library, his eyes softening when they meet mine. "Let's hear about this first day of yours."

All the anger and pent-up rage recedes from my tense muscles, leaving behind utter fatigue. I step closer to Trey as I loosen the sash of my soft gray cashmere coat. "You're here," I say, unbelieving. My gaze shifts between my two friends. "You're both here."

"Don't sound so surprised. Now come on, Mess, let's go have a more private chat."

Without waiting for a response, Trey spins on his heels and strides into the library. My attention falls to his firm ass as he walks away. He really shouldn't be allowed to wear jeans around me. Not that slacks are better, but then that would mean no pants at all, and that's an even worse idea.

I let out a tight breath and look to the ceiling.

Get your shit under control, Randi.

Once we're all inside the library, T quietly closes the newer-looking double glass doors behind him. Across the room, Trey leans against a window, focused on the winter wonderland that settled over DC last night. The snow is beautiful, making everything it touches glisten in the sun, but I'm not a fan of the stupid bitter-ass cold that accompanies it. I predict I'll never grow accustomed to the north's version of winter. At this rate, I might never be warm again.

Trey's honey brown eyes slide from the white scenery to meet mine. My breath catches and my stomach tenses with the intensity I find. Shrugging out of the coat, I break his stare to lay it over the back of a padded leather armchair. I have to stop letting my body react to his presence. We're friends now, nothing more. He's made that clear, being hands off and distant the past two months. There's a line in the sand—or snow, rather—now.

Friends.

Just friends.

No matter how much I hate it.

3

TREY

Muscles tense, rage at the boiling point, I stare out at the snow-doused lawn, hoping the serenity will calm me.

It doesn't do shit.

I shift my weight, fighting the urge to glance at the beauty only yards from where I stand. But I can't. If I see those distinct red marks around her neck again, there isn't anyone who will stop me from racing out of here to murder that fucker Kyle Birmingham. My fingers tighten into fists, my blunt nails digging into the skin of my palm. But I relish the prick of pain. It centers me, grounds me to the present, calming my heavy breaths. Keeping me from doing something I'll regret, like tugging her close to wrap my arms around her and never letting go.

That's a lie. I wouldn't regret it, but yet I would. I love this job, love working with my best friend and the other boys. But I also grieve her touch, her laugh and smile that only I can conjure. Every day since we ended, being near her but staying away, has been torture. Everything about her makes me weak, urges me to say fuck it all and devour her whole no matter the consequences.

I close my eyes and massage the bridge of my nose, hoping to alleviate the initial tingles of a headache. She needs me, and here I am reminiscing and brooding. *Get your fucking shit together, Benson.*

"What happened, Mess?" I ask, finally gaining the courage to look her way again. I curse at the glistening of her eyes. "Talk. Now." Yeah, I'm being rough, but what else is there to be? I can't hold her, can't comfort her. I'm fighting all the shit I want to do, which leaves me fighting a fucking never-ending battle inside my head.

I couldn't bring her into my family unaware of the shit show we are, couldn't do that to her career or mine. It's fine. We're fine. We can keep doing this 'we're just friends' dance for the next four years, then act. If she still wants me by then.

I wince and rub a fist against my chest right above my heart.

Fuck, this hurts.

Tank eases her into one of the chairs and drags the matching leather armchair directly in front of hers. My attention locks on where their knees touch. My skin flashing hot, I take a menacing step closer, ready to do what-ever it takes to break the contact.

"Stand down, Playboy," Tank grumbles, his dark eyes locked on me. He turns back to Randi, his features softening. "Go on, Randi. What happened? You're killing us here."

She nods, looking everywhere other than me. I swallow back the hurt her avoidance triggers.

"Kyle's proposing a change to the voting law. One that will prevent anyone below a certain yearly income level the *right* to vote. Taking away their fucking constitutional right to vote on who will lead this mother-fucking country because of their financial status." Her voice rises with every word, ending in a high-pitched panic tone. I turn from the window as she shoots from the chair. Using the backrest as support, she reaches down to yank off a black heel and chucks it across the room with a scream of rage. "That motherfucking cuntcake." She yells again, repeating the process with the other shoe. "He fucking used me!"

Randi steps toward the desk, Tank's fingers barely grazing her wrist in an attempt to stop her. She lays her forearms on the shiny dark wood, ready to demolish the stacks of folders and papers on top.

"Randi, stop."

She stands tall, her hazel eyes locked with mine. Her chest heaves at a rapid pace while a bright red flush stains her cheeks and chest.

"I did this," she whispers, never breaking my stare. She jams her finger into her breast. "I allowed this. I let my stupid wants get in the way. I should've seen it, should've seen his evil plan and stopped it then." My feet move on their own accord, stepping closer. Randi's head dips, her arms wrapping around herself. "I am his pawn like everyone knows I am. I let this happen. It's all my fault."

Before I can comfort her, Tank's there, standing between us. His massive hands rest on Randi's slim shoulders and give her a little shake, drawing her eyes up to meet his.

"If you believe that, then you *are* an idiot."

She blanches.

"Watch it, Tank," I nearly growl. I can't take him, but I'll fight to the death against the person who put that hurt look on her face.

He shrugs me off, keeping his focus solely on her. "What I'm saying is this isn't your fault. You had no idea this was the first thing that bastard Birmingham would attempt to push through."

"I should've seen it." She shakes her head.

"Doesn't matter," I say. Her wet eyes snap to mine and narrow. "What's done is done. Now we stop it." Something like hope flashes across her face, her dark brown brows rising a fraction. "He can't just write a law. He has to get it pushed through the House and the Senate." I smirk and reach over Tank to push her shoulder. "You're over the Senate, remember? You have sway there."

"But I don't. I don't know anyone in this town, and even if I did, I'm hated because of my background, because of where I come from. No one will side with me just because it'll make them look bad. He knows it too. The man practically begged me to try and stop this from happening. Probably just wants to sit back and watch me fail."

Her broken spirit shreds my soul. Turning on my heels, I pace the length of the office.

"What else did he say?"

"That this city is built on secrets and secrets are power, something like that," she grumbles.

With a small smile to Tank, she pats him on the shoulder and bends over to pick up her shoes. Her round ass presses against the dark fitted fabric of her dress pants, snagging my full attention.

"Benson." Tank snaps his fingers in my face. "Focus."

Dragging my hooded eyes from the ass I want to grab, I cock a dark brow at my best friend. "Oh I am," I say with a smirk.

"I swear," he grumbles and sits in the chair once again. Leaning forward, he clasps his hands between his legs and rests his elbows on his large thighs. "That means one of two things: bribery or blackmail. I'm going with blackmail. There's no way he'd pull enough votes for something like this without it."

"So where does that leave us?" Absentmindedly, she gently wraps her hand around her throat, caressing the marked skin. I want to know what happened—no, I need to know—but not now. Now we focus on the issue at hand; then I get the details of who laid their hands on my girl.

My girl.

Right.

Unfortunately, she's not my anything except the one I can't have.

"We get the votes we need to make sure it doesn't get through the Senate," I say, starting to pace again. "We'll meet with everyone if we have to—"

Her cackling laugh cuts me off. Brows raised, I look over my shoulder to her.

"Oh, wouldn't that be nice? But you see, that's another piece of his brilliant plan. He wants me with the secretary of state, and you know what that means."

Both Tank and I curse.

The man is brilliant, I'll give him that.

"You'll have to figure it out, Randi," I say, my tone harsh. "Find someone here who can talk to the various senators while you're traveling. You can't lose momentum once you gain it. It's crucial to make people get behind you when they think everyone else is."

"Or," she says, her tone hopeful, "would your parents be open to helping?"

I hold a breath and shake my head, preparing for her disappointment. "My parents would never use their pull to help sway a vote like this. They're too selfish to rock the political party yacht they've coasted on the past few decades."

Her shoulders round in defeat.

"We'll get the votes, Randi." If only I could hold her, whisper in her ear, bury my nose in her hair, I could tell her that it'll all be okay, that we'll figure it out.

She rubs a few fingers across her forehead. "Worst first day in the history of first days," she grumbles. A hint of a smile tugs at her lips, making an ounce of the heavy weight lift from my shoulders. "I told y'all I would keep this interesting."

Tank laughs and slaps the tops of his thighs before standing. "Yeah you did, Randi. But next time, how about less of the dramatics?"

A true smile forms, parting her pink lips. "Come on now, T, where's the fun in that?"

THE WOODEN DOOR thumps beneath the tap of my knuckle. Dropping my hand, I step back from the door and tuck both hands into the back pockets of my jeans as I wait. A bump from the other side and the soft padding of feet against the carpet grow closer before the door tugs open an inch.

I grin. Hair wrapped in some kind of towel turban, clean face, thick-framed glasses—this is my Randi. I've never seen anyone more beautiful and adorable. This version of her makes me want to cuddle her close while fucking her from behind. An odd mix of wanting to comfort and possess her all at the same time.

"Yeah?" she questions. Pulling the door open wider, she keeps her body tucked behind it.

Hmm, what is she hiding? I lick my lips and take a step forward, pushing the door open a little farther with the toe of my boot. Ever since she stepped out of the library two hours ago, I've died a little inside waiting to see her again, to ask her what really happened in the Oval Office earlier. I know she left chunks of the ordeal out when it was the three of us; hopefully she'll trust me enough to tell the truth, all of it, just her and me.

"We finished talking with the beta team, going over a few things for the upcoming change in travel schedule, and I wanted to say bye before I left." I shrug, acting like this isn't a big deal. She doesn't need to know the massive fight Tank and I got in just before I stormed up the stairs. Randi doesn't need that kind of pressure. It's not her fault I can't stay away.

I've stayed true to my word though and kept my hands off. Hands off *her*, that is. My hands have been all over my dick every night I'm forced to go home alone after being with her all day. How could I not? I know what those lips feel like on my skin, around my cock. Know what she sounds like when I hit her deep in just the right spot.

I grunt and adjust my stance to cover my stiffening dick.

"Okay," she says, drawing out the last syllable. "Bye, then. See you tomorrow."

"What really happened today, Randi?" I blurt. The door starts to close, but I tuck my foot farther between it and the doorjamb, keeping it open. "I just need to know. Please," I beg, staring at her neck. The faint red lines from earlier have turned a dark gray. "Tell me," I grit out.

With an exasperated sigh, she pulls the door open wide and gestures for me to come in.

"You're not going to like it," she chastises.

"Tell me anyway." Out of habit, I secure the room, checking every shadowed corner and closet before leaning back against the wall and crossing both arms over my chest. "Out with it, Mess."

"Fine." Cinching the belt of the terry cloth robe tighter, she rests on the edge of the bed and sighs. Like earlier, her hand comes up to her neck, two fingers tracing along the faint bruises. "When the voting law was brought up, I might have reacted... badly."

"There's nothing that would've ever warranted that," I say with a pointed nod toward her neck.

She shrinks back, her gaze slipping to the floor. "I threw a full mug of coffee at his feet with about five other people in the room and might have lunged at him intending violence while yelling several unfavorable words in there too."

The crack in her voice and softness in her tone break me. Before I know what I'm doing, I'm in front of her, fingers under her chin tilting that beautiful face up to meet mine.

"Nothing, and I mean *nothing* warrants violence toward a woman."

I see the wheels turning in her mind, her eyes searching mine just before her lips turn up. "What about Lorena Bobbitt? She cut a guy's dick off. Pretty sure he was pissed when that happened. I'm sure in every man's mind dick chopping warrants a violent response."

A rumbling chuckle vibrates my chest. Stepping back, I discreetly cover my cock and balls; just the mention of the loss of my boys makes all systems go into protection mode. "Pretty sure he was too busy trying to locate his chopped-off dick to fight back." I shake my head. "Nice diversion. Now spill it, Mess."

Knowing I caught her, she smiles and leans back on her elbows. The front of the robe parts, showing off more of the fair skin I'm dying to lick. She clears her throat, drawing my attention up to her smirking face.

"After I almost Bobbitted his head with the mug, he was pissed and tossed me against the wall," she says with a shrug like it's no big deal, but I see the tension in her shoulders, the tight lines around her eyes. "It's not like this is the first time he's touched me, just didn't expect it. Next time I'll do better."

"What did you do?" I grit out, my jaw clenched so tight I have no idea how I formed the words. I'm going to kill him. I'll start with cutting off the hand that held her against the wall, then go from there.

"Nothing, I didn't do anything." Her head falls forward, the tip of her chin now resting on her breastbone. "I couldn't do anything, Trey. I can hold my ground in verbal fights, but physical? Might as well have been a fight between a lion and a mouse."

I scan her thin arms and nod.

"We need to fix that."

"Exactly what I said last night to T," she grumbles and falls all the way back onto the bed with a moan. "What am I going to do?" She massages her temples. "Get the votes, then what? I feel like that's not enough. I need more. I need leverage or more power or something."

She's not wrong. I've been feeling the same thing since the conversation earlier but wasn't quite sure where to start. Plus, right now, all I can focus on is the slight opening of her robe, giving me a glimpse of her long lean legs.

I lick my lips, eager for a taste.

"Trouble?" Her breathy voice draws my hooded gaze from the apex of her thighs to her face. "What are we doing?"

What *are* we doing?

What the fuck am *I* doing?

I shake my head to clear the lust fog that had settled over my thoughts.

"We plan, we strike, and then we plan again. It's a never-ending battle here in DC, Mess. And in this role, it's a thousand times worse. People will come after you every second of every day trying to take you down and find faults. It's part of the job. *Your* job is to work in spite of them, not against them. Do what you promised your voters, and right now that's fighting for their rights to vote. Don't let them down, and if you can do that, then we move on to the next issue. I told you before and I'll say it again, you need help." I give her a pointed look and roll my eyes. "And I don't mean just that single admin you hired. You need someone who you can trust."

That bottom lip sticks out in an exaggerated pout. "But where in the hell do I find someone who I can trust *and is* willing to side with me? That's a tough find."

I dip my chin in agreeance. It will be a tough find, but we have to. There's no way she can be flying all around the globe, entertaining various country leaders, and get the votes needed.

A name, a familiar face, floats to the forefront of my mind. Groaning, I drop my head.

"What?" she questions.

"Not what, but who."

"Okay, who?"

"I might know someone who would be a good fit." I grab the back of my neck, massaging the tension out of the stiff muscles. Someone who can help us sway the votes Randi's way with a few well-placed suggestions if I asked her to.

"If you suggest Rachel, I swear I'll Bobbitt you."

"Is that a thing now? Bobbitting as a threat?"

"Is for me. Who is it, Trouble? I have a feeling I won't like this suggestion."

"You won't," I grumble.

Randi tilts her head. "Listen, I know we're doing the whole friends thing nowadays, but if you've slept with this person, I'll take a hard pass. Talk about awkward."

I shake my head, my signature smirk coming out for the first time in a long while. Fuck, I miss this woman. Not VP Randi but this Randi. The one who's relaxed, easy, simple yet challenging as fuck.

Suddenly, being in the small room with her is too much. My muscles twitch as I hold myself back from touching her. "No, I haven't slept with her. Hey, erm... listen, I gotta run. See you tomorrow for our shift." Before she can say anything, I bolt for the door. As soon as it's closed behind me, I fall forward, resting my forearms against the opposite wall.

I didn't lie. I've never slept with Jessica. Doesn't mean the woman hasn't tried on several occasions.

Having the Hawthorne family name, Jessica's been on Mother's top list of wife prospects for years. No doubt Jessica will jump at the idea of working with Randi just to be close to me on a consistent basis. As long as I make it out as a favor to me and my family, not Randi, Jessica should be on board. Shitty to bend the truth that way, yes, but if it works and we get the votes, who the hell cares?

This just keeps getting better and better. No touching Randi and now potentially having to deal with Jessica on a daily basis.

"Do you know what you're doing?"

With an annoyed groan, I fall forward even farther, smacking my forehead against the cool wall. Ouch. "And just what makes you think I don't know what I'm doing, Tank?"

"Honestly, man, I don't know. You've never acted like this before." The cool wall rolls along my forehead as I turn to my best friend and team lead. His head is dipped while his mitt of a hand swipes over his shiny bald head over and over. "I'm worried."

"I can keep it in my pants," I say, rolling my eyes to the ceiling. "Seriously, you think I don't know my limits?" I don't, but no need for him to know that.

"Not that, but since that's where your mind is going, maybe I should be worried about you keeping your hands off our job."

"She's not just the job and you know it."

A confirming grunt sounds down the hall. "She's safer when you're not distracted by what you two do in private. I know you hate it, and hell if my wife doesn't tell me I'm an idiot for it all the time, but it's what needs to be done. At least until she's established in her role, established in this damn town."

It makes sense, everything he's saying, but that doesn't mean I have to like it. Pushing against the wall, I lean a shoulder against it and cross both arms over my chest. "What are you worried about, then?" I stand straight with a quick glance back to the closed bedroom door. "Her?"

Hiking a thumb over his shoulder, Tank turns and tromps down the stairs. An uneasy feeling rolls in my gut as I follow, taking the stairs two at a time to catch up. Turning the corner, I nearly smack into his stone-like back at his abrupt stop.

"You. I'm worried about you." Tank turns only to take a quick step back while giving me the side-eye. "You need a hug or something?"

I smile and open my arms wide. "Always, buddy." I drop my arms at his sneer of disgust and chuckle. It fades as his words finally register. Tank's gut has never been wrong before; no reason for it to turn faulty now. "What do you mean, you're worried about me? Didn't we just establish I'm good, no need to worry about me going against your orders? I'm done with those antics, done with screwing around. That year sidelined nearly killed me—hell, it nearly killed all of us. I'm not screwing up and hurting the team again."

He steps around me, heading for the kitchen. With a sigh I turn to follow once again, the heels of my boots clomping on the pristine hardwood floor. In the kitchen, he heads straight for the pantry and steps inside.

"I'm worried you're going to do something stupider than that." Cheez-It box in hand, he steps out of the dark pantry and rips the top open, immediately diving into the cheesy goodness. I hold back a chuckle. Poor guy and his nervous eating habits. "You're protective of her, and she's already made some high-power enemies. I'm worried you're going to do something stupid like attack the president of the United States for manhandling your girl."

"That motherfucker shouldn't touch any woman like that," I growl, leaning over the counter to close the distance between us. "He deserves for someone to kick his ass."

His dark eyes meet mine, and the box drops to the granite counter. Pressing his palms to the white stone, he leans closer, pressing his stomach against the edge. "You mean like what you did to that tweaker in Texas?"

With an exaggerated eye roll, I shove my palms against the cold stone to stand straight.

"You did that before you even knew the girl. Now you're attached and volatile."

I slide my fingers through the soft strands of my dark hair as I pace from one side of the kitchen to the other. "Okay, I'll admit I took it a little too far—"

"You beat the shit out of him, then pressed the barrel of your gun to his temple."

My shoulders stiffen as tension radiates through them and down my spine. He's right. I did lose it that day. Looking back, I blame it on everything that past year had built up inside me. Still, no excuse. Thank goodness none of the boys or that idiot down in Boone reported it.

"I won't go after Birmingham," I grumble, admitting defeat.

"Or Whit."

I shoot him a glare. Of course this asshole is getting technical to make sure I don't find a loophole in his whole 'Save Trey from himself' plan.

"Or the sociopath Whit."

"Good. Now there's something else I've been thinking about, and those marks on Randi's neck solidified my decision. I want her to meet Sarah."

My eyes round with shock. "What?" He's never, not once, allowed his fierce wife to mix with his business. His take is our job makes it too easy for someone to notice and gain leverage over him, but I think it's because he doesn't want the whole team to know he's fucking whipped by that woman. Hell, I would be too if I were married to her.

"Last night, Randi mentioned wanting to learn to fight. At the stupid inauguration thing while you were outside playing the avoidance card."

"Touché."

"She needs to learn how to fight back. I'll crush her, you'll just end up fucking her, and if one of the guys touches her, you'll kill them, so that leaves the only other person I can trust."

I nod at the full truth in his statement. Damn, this is why this man is our team lead. He sees everything, processes it quickly, and does what needs to be done. I miss him in a way, miss the back-and-forth we used to have before Randi. I don't blame her for it, but my pull to her inadvertently changed my relationship with Tank. Not for the worse, just different. Hell, I'm different. There's more at stake now, less room for error.

"Then do it," I finally say. The pads of my fingers rap along the counter over and over as I process everything he's said. "Think it'll be enough?"

"Dunno." He shrugs while shoving another handful of processed carbs into his mouth. "She has us, but knowing how to defend herself is also a new priority. Who knows what this city has up its sleeve for that girl?"

"Fuck." I press my elbows onto the stone and run both hands through my thick dark hair. "We'll be ready, and so will she," I whisper, repeating it over and over in my mind like a mantra.

We have to be.

Nothing can happen to that amazing woman upstairs.

If something does, I'm not sure I'd survive it.

4

RANDI

I pace the length of the VP office, located just down the hall from Señor Douche's, where he's no doubt sitting back doing nothing except plotting more ways to ruin my life.

Huh. I slow my steps to search the ceiling as I run that line over in my head once more. Maybe people are right and I'm where Tae gets her dramatics. Eh, I'm not that bad. A single shoulder rises in indifference to my internal debate. Doesn't matter if I'm overreacting or not. The guy is a grade-A asshole and needs to be taken down.

"Being a massive arrogant prick should be listed as reasons for impeachment," I mutter around the ragged thumbnail between my teeth. "It would make my life easier right now."

"Aiming for the president's seat, are you?" I startle at Todd's voice, having completely forgotten he was in here.

I shake my head and pick up my pacing once again. "No, I don't want that kind of responsibility. Hell, I've barely survived a month into the VP role." My stomach twists with the simple reminder of all the shit I have on my plate. "That said, he still needs to go."

"Can't have both," Todd mutters and crosses his legs. My gaze falls to his crotch, and not in a good way. I never understood how men could sit like that. Doesn't it squish important man bits? Or maybe it's that his bits are too small for him to notice the squishing.

"Not that I want to find out," I say, pulling my attention from his lap to the large overstuffed bookshelf. Half are mine, and the other half I inherited with the office. I scan the rows and rows of hardbacks, a sense of comfort settling over me.

"What was that?" My loose dark hair swishes along my upper back as I shake my head, dismissing his question. It's not like I was talking to him anyway. "Anyway, as I was saying before you got lost in your head"—*whoops*—"we're leaving for the G7 summit in two days. Are you prepared for the various meetings?"

"Yep," I say, giving him two thumbs-up. No idea why I did that.

His eyes widen, and a hint of a smile pulls up the corners of his lips.

I like Todd. He's a nice guy, but that's where it stops. We've worked together side by side preparing for the upcoming summit for the past week, and he's been the perfect gentleman. Which is great since he's a hard no in my book. It's not that he's bad-looking, just not my kind of good-looking. His super-thin frame makes me think his pant size is smaller than mine, his delicate fingers have a slight tremble to them when he's nervous, and his petite nose and wide eyes are not what I find attractive.

What I do find attractive just walked into the office without knocking.

Damn, he's sexy. Tailored suit that fits his muscular frame, dark thick hair I'm dying to run my fingers through, honey brown eyes that somehow twinkle when they meet my own, and of course that smirk. That damn sexy, mischievous smirk that hooked me from the moment he pulled me out of the burning limo last year.

I narrow my eyes at Trey, which only makes his smirk grow into a full megawatt smile. The past few days, he's done this several times. Interrupting the meetings with Todd for lame reasons, most of which could've waited, almost like he's just checking up on me. But that's crazy, because we're just friends now, and he'd have no reason to be jealous of me spending time alone with Todd.

Right?

"The consultant I suggested is here to meet with you, ma'am."

My lips purse, making his split into a full-on smile. Bastard. He knows I hate that 'ma'am' shit.

"Thanks, we're almost done." I hold back from sticking my tongue out.

With a single nod, his eyes roam to Todd, who's too busy studying the papers in his lap to notice Trey's scrutiny. I raise both brows and tilt my head, flicking my gaze between the two men. A smug look washes over Trey's features as he tucks his hands behind his back, widening his stance like he'll be here a while.

Pushy bastard.

I shouldn't say that about him, considering said pushy bastard is saving my ass by introducing me to this consultant, Jessica Hawthorne. Hopefully, fingers and toes crossed, she can assist in getting things moving in DC while I'm flying around the globe meeting with various world leaders and trying not to use the wrong dinner fork.

"Do you want to have dinner tonight?" Todd asks, his words quick, voice tight.

"Sure," I mutter as I scavenge my desk for the list of items I created earlier this morning to cover with Miss Hawthorne. "Know any place good? I'm still learning where to go in this city." After pulling a slim manila folder from the stack, I thumb through the few pages tucked inside.

"I do. Pick you up at eight?"

I'm about to say "sure" when someone clears their throat, drawing my attention away from the task at hand. Trey stands beside Todd, his hands fisted at his sides while his face is a mask of stone.

"Send the information to her secretary and we'll get her there," he says, eyes boring holes into my own. Hints of flush dot his normally flawless cheeks, and the muscles of his jaw pulse like he's holding back from saying more.

"Whatever he says," I mutter to Todd while pointing the folder in my hand at Trey. "He's the boss. See you tonight, Todd."

Mindlessly, I maneuver around the desk and fold into the comfortable upholstered armchair. The cushion sinks down, molding around me as I adjust my weight trying to get comfortable. Behind me, the door clicks closed, signaling Todd's departure.

Focused on preparing for the next meeting, I don't notice anything amiss until a looming presence snags my attention. Slowly I slide my gaze up Trey's lean frame.

"Can I help you?" I raise both brows, not understanding the obvious frustration pulsing off his tense body.

"You said yes." The words were more of a hiss than syllables.

"Yeah, and?" Seriously, what is wrong with him today? It's dinner. Everyone eats, and honestly, I need to get out of that house. This past month has been nothing but worry and work and more work. I deserve a good dinner and a bottle or two of wine. Actually, the more I think about it, of course I said yes, I need a few hours of not feeling like the world is pressing on my shoulders.

"You actually like that beanstalk?"

A deep line forms between my brows. The muscle along his clean-shaven jaw twitches. "What's your problem? It's dinner. Do I not get a night where I don't have to worry about all the shit going on around me?"

"Not with him," he snaps.

"Then. With. Who?" I toss the file on the desk. It slides across the shiny surface before disappearing over the edge. "I have no friends in this town except you and T. All you two suggest is holing up in that damn house like I'm a prisoner. I need to get out for a few hours."

"Then you should've said something instead of agreeing to go on a date with that fuckstick." He rakes his hand through his shiny hair.

"Um, it's not a date. It's dinner," I correct. Seriously, a date? With Todd. I don't think so. It's dinner between two colleagues.

"It's a date."

"No it's not."

"Yes it is."

"It's fucking dinner."

"It's a fucking date."

"It isn't because I don't want to sleep with him."

"He does," he says as he steps closer. Shoving my chair back, he grips the armrests, boxing me in. Leaning forward, he pauses with his nose an inch from my own. "And now he thinks you do too because you said yes."

"To dinner, Trey." I fight the internal battle to reach up and cup his cheek, to draw it an inch closer and seal my lips to his. My thighs pinch together against the growing ache building at his closeness. Memories of us naked, wrapped in the other's arms, flood through me, making heat build beneath my skin. "I don't want him. I want you," I whisper.

A light knock sounds from the other side of the door, causing both our heads to snap that direction. The handle angles down, and then the door opens a foot.

"Trey? Madam VP?" a feminine voice calls out.

Trey shoves back, keeping his heated gaze locked with mine. Pulling at one sleeve and then the other, he adjusts his suit before striding across the room to open the door. "Come on in, Jessica. She's ready for you." With a pointed glare over his shoulder, he adds, "We're not done with this conversation, Mess."

Anticipation coils in my lower belly, building on the smoldering heat he already ignited between my thighs.

Should I be excited or worried?

Both?

Shrugging off the last two minutes of strangely hot angry verbal foreplay, I plaster on a fake smile, readying for the initial introductions. The smile immediately falls as the beautiful young woman strides through the door, looking confident in her thousand-dollar smile, full bouncing blonde hair, and perfect red wrap dress.

I hate her.

Okay, I don't hate her, but I want to, which just makes me hate myself for hating someone I don't know. Even my subconscious shakes its head, not understanding that line of thinking.

I swipe my clammy hands down the front of my navy slacks before I stand. Careful to not trip—that would be the epitome of embarrassing in front of this woman—I round the small coffee table with an extended hand.

"Jessica," I say as enthusiastically as I can. Instead I sound like one of the stupid mice from Cinderella. "Please come in, and it's Randi, please." Internally I high-five the shit out of myself for not stumbling over my words. Not that I'm attracted to her or anything, even though she does have great boobs.

Halfway across the room, I turn with an expectant look to Trey, but his focus is on the beautiful Jessica Hawthorne. Of course it is. My heart sinks in my chest.

A dainty hand slides into mine and gives it a hard squeeze.

"It's a pleasure to meet the first female vice president of the United States." She beams, still shaking my hand. Her aqua eyes are bright with excitement, highlighted by the fresh coat of red lipstick across her plump lips.

Bet they're fake.

Agh. I drop her hand and turn to the desk. *Stop comparing yourself, Randi. Don't be a bitch just because she's prettier than you. And richer no doubt. And looks like she would fit into this role better than you.*

"Everything okay?" she asks hesitantly behind me.

Glancing over my shoulder, I smile and nod. "Fine, just didn't expect this." I wave a limp hand toward her. "Sorry, I shouldn't say shit like that. Shit!" I whisper-yell. "I shouldn't say shit either. Fuck." Dammmmmmmmnit.

Both she and Trey bust out laughing.

"Mess, you are a mess, you know that?"

"Without question," I mumble as I flop into the chair behind the desk, groaning at my blubbering foul mouth. "I guess I just expected... hell, I don't know what I expected."

Jessica shrugs, tossing her long blonde hair over her shoulder as she folds into one of the two chairs opposite my desk. Of course she even sits pretty. Maybe I should've paid more attention during those etiquette classes Kyle forced me to take.

"I get it a lot," she says with an awkward laugh. "But I will say I'll take this reaction over the typical response from congressmen and senators."

I arch a brow. "And that would be?"

Jessica looks away and waves a hand in my direction. "I'm sure someone as pretty as you can guess."

I don't have to. I know firsthand.

Mentally, I give myself a hard 'wake the fuck up, you're on the same team' shake. Huffing a heavy breath, I shove out of the chair and stride back around the desk to pause in front of a wide-eyed Jessica.

"Let's do this again." My hand juts out between us. This time her grip is timid as those delicate fingers wrap around my own. "Hi, I'm Randi Sawyer, and I don't have a clue what I'm doing. I need your help whipping votes in the House and Senate to ensure the man I helped get elected into the presidential role doesn't take away the constitutional right to vote from a third of the American people."

A wide, true smile spreads across her face, making her look even more beautiful, but the honesty behind her eyes chases away any lingering animosity.

"Great," she says, dropping my hand. Tugging an iPad from her bag, she flips the cover open and rests it on top of her knees. "Then let's get started."

AFTER FOUR HOURS, two Starbucks runs, and too many handfuls of chocolate-covered almonds to count, we have a plan.

A great plan.

"This is a fantastic start," Jessica praises as she tucks the nearly dead iPad back into her bag. Standing, she rests both hands on her hips and arches back, twisting right and then left. "Where did Trey go?"

Glancing up from the piece of paper I've scribbled notes all over, I scan the room and shrug. "Dunno. Maybe he got tired of being our errand boy." I snort and go back to rereading my scribble. "He's around here somewhere."

"He's a good guy. You're lucky to have him on your protection team."

My ears perk at her new wistful tone. Peering up through my lashes, I catch her staring off into space with a sappy smile on her lips.

"How do you two know each other?" I ask, trying to keep the eagerness —and slight desperation—from my tone. "He didn't fill me in on y'all's history."

"Y'all's," she huffs. "I love your accent." *Um, I have an accent?* "It's warm, like you." *Me. Warm?* Maybe I should've drug tested her before agreeing to bring her on board to the 'save America' bandwagon. "Anyway, our parents are in the same social circles. We've been friends for, wow, a long time." Again, her eyes glaze over as a soft sigh pushes past her lips. "He was even my escort to my debutant ball."

"That's a real thing?" I ask before thinking better of it. I cringe and look back down at the paper. *Get your shit together, Randi. Don't go pissing off the first woman in this town who's been nice to you.*

Jessica shrugs off the comment with a soft laugh. Her thin fingers slide down her dress, straightening the bright red material. "Yeah, it's a big deal here. It marks you in the social circle. Everyone who's anyone has a blowout party trying to outdo the girl before them. It's all silly, but you know how it is."

"Not really," I grumble under my breath. She's either trying to be nice and not bring up my childhood or is ignorant to my past. I'll go with being nice. "Thanks again for your help in all this. With me going across the globe with Todd, I need a constant face here whipping votes our way."

"We'll get it done. 'Night." Before she can grab the door handle, it swings open. "Oh," she gasps, startling back a step. "Oh." This time it's breathier, less scared. "There you are. We were just wondering where you'd run off to. I was hoping to see more of you today."

"Were you?" he muses, those honey brown eyes finding mine from the doorway. I swallow back my reply as he turns his attention back to Jessica. "Glad you were available to help out here. I know this isn't your normal type of gig, but your connections in this city will be a huge help."

Even from here there's no mistaking the bright pink glow that brightens her cheekbones. "You know I'd do anything for you, just have to ask. It was great to see you, Trey. Looking forward to seeing you around."

"Looking forward to seeing you around," I mimic under my breath with a sneer. Jealousy has a funny way of making you forget the last four hours. I'm counting on this woman to help me, but I now want to punt her across the White House lawn.

Good thing there wasn't a maturity test to land this VP gig.

Or a psych eval.

"What was that?" Trey says, his voice light with humor.

"Nothing." I clear my throat and smack the edges of the papers against the desk to straighten the stack. Tapping the phone screen, I check the time. "I'm done for the day, plus I want some downtime before dinner tonight. Let's head out in five."

Trey scoffs. "You're still going?"

Rolling my eyes, I swipe my iPad and papers off the desk and shove them into my bag with more force than necessary. "Yes, I'm still going. I still need a break, and I still need real food. And wine, and a cigarette. Can we stop on the way home?"

"No, you're trying to quit, remember?"

Of course I fucking remember. Worst random life goal I've ever made, and I've made some pretty stupid ones. Let's be honest here—the likelihood of me quitting smoking for good is the same as me owning that magical unicorn I always promised myself I would have as a pet.

"Too bad unicorns aren't real."

"Sure they are," he says, and I bite back a smile. He and T both just go with the flow now when it comes to my ramblings. They both know I have a zillion random conversations going on up in my head at once, and some-times my response to those conversations becomes more vocal than imagi-nary. "Come on, Mess, let's get you home for your hot date."

"It's not a date," I bite out as I pass by him to exit the office. "He crosses his legs."

"What?" Trouble's laugh echoes down the bustling hall. Every set of eyes turns toward us before focusing back on their work.

"Nothing. Just know it's not a date, okay?" I tug my laptop bag higher up on my shoulder to keep it from slipping.

His fingers wrap around the leather strap, carefully pulling it from my shoulder and sliding it on to his own. "Whatever you say, Mess. Just know that tonight, when it does turn out to be a date, I'm going to love telling you I told you so."

Biting my lip, I shake my head and start down the hall.

Why does he have to be so adorable?

5

TREY

S he's too naive for her own good. Beautiful, hilarious, but naive on the extent of corruption and depravity in this city.

Of course it's a motherfucking date. And here I am stuck in the motherfucking shadows watching as my girl dines with a man I would kill to switch places with.

"You're glaring again," Tank says through the earpiece. "Do I need to put you outside?"

"I'm not a damn puppy," I say into the tiny mic hidden beneath my cuff.

"Then stop acting like a lovesick one."

Chuckles and razzing from the other guys sound through the connection.

"Ha, ha, ha, laugh it up, fuckers. I just don't like how close he's sitting to the VP."

"For reasons other than her safety," Tank retorts, and I grumble a curse to myself. "If you can't handle this, then I'm questioning your ability to keep her safe on the road."

My spine stiffens at the hidden threat.

"I'll be fine," I snap into the mic as nonchalantly as possible. "I just don't know this guy, and it has me on edge."

"Stop lying to yourself," Gremlin says over the line. "We know it. You know it. She knows it."

"Knows what?" I ask, curiosity lacing my words.

"That you're fucking pussy whipped." Gremlin cackles, and the entire team bursts out laughing.

"Shut it down." Tank's deep voice sobers the radio waves. "Stop being a distraction, Playboy, or you're off the team."

I fight the urge to throw my hands up in the air like a kid having a tantrum. "I'm not doing anything but my job. Ground the other kids, Dad, I'm innocent." Movement at their table snags my attention. "Focus, you assholes. She's on the move."

Before she's fully standing, I'm at her side, fingers wrapped around the back of her chair with a death grip as I tug it away from the table.

"It was fun," she says, her voice tight. I hold back a knowing smile. The tension in her shoulders and the fake smile plastered across her beautiful face signal that she's aware this was a date. Can't wait to tell her 'I told you so.' "No," she says in response to his request for another. "Thank you." Her hazel eyes flick to mine. "I need to get ready for the summit. I'll be busy until then."

My lips tug down in a frown. Why didn't she just tell him to fuck off and not ask her out again? Instead she gave the excuse of the summit, which means he'll try again there or after.

My mind works overtime as I scan the restaurant for threats. Gremlin tips his chin in a quick nod, signaling everything's clear from his vantage point.

"We need to move," I state to break up the long goodbye. We don't, but I need to get her away from this tool before she agrees to another date without realizing what she's doing.

Fingers pressed against her lower back I urge her to move toward Gremlin.

"Thank you again, Todd. Good night." The last part is said over her shoulder in a rush as I pressure her into a quick pace. "Is there something going on?" Randi asks. "Hey, Grem."

"Ma'am."

I smirk at her dramatic eye roll. "Not with that shit again."

"We're in public, ma'am. It's protocol."

"I'll show T where he can shove his protocol," she grumbles. In a flash, she grabs my wrist and yanks it up to her lips. "You hear that, T? You and I are going to have words at home."

A deep rumbling laugh, one I never hear on the job, vibrates down the line, tickling my ear.

"He's looking forward to it," I tell Randi as we pause at the doors, giving her time to slip her long wool coat on. And gloves. And scarf. "We're just walking to the Suburban." I chuckle as I take in her over-the-top winter attire.

"It's below thirty out there," she says while she focuses on fastening every single button of her coat. "Texans are not made for this kind of weather, okay? I have to be fully protected or I'll turn into a damn Randi popsicle out there."

Without thinking, I lean close and whisper, "That's a popsicle I'd love to lick. What flavor—" Tank's yelled promises of murder cut me short. Pulling back, I smirk down at her wide eyes. "Ready?"

Puddles of melted snow splash under my dress shoes as we exit the building, shuffling as quickly as possible to the waiting SUV. Pausing at the open door, Randi pats Tank on the shoulder and sighs. "Don't be too hard on him," she says, smiling back at me. "I am quite edible." Her sinister laugh follows her as she climbs into the back seat.

The door slams and Tank smacks his palm on the top, sending it barreling off into the night. An exact replica SUV follows close behind.

Once the taillights have faded into the distance, Tank turns, pinning me with his intense stare.

"What am I going to do with you?" he mutters.

"You love me." I slam a fist into his shoulder. "I keep you on your toes."

"Can you do your job?" he asks, his eyes searching mine for the truth. "I need to know right now, Trey. Can you do this job without being distracted by her? I can tell this goes deeper than a casual fuck, which is great for my friend, but for my partner, the one watching my back, I need to know where your head is."

Breaking his stare, I huff, the puff of breath clouding between us. I tuck my wrist behind my back to muffle my words from the rest of the team.

"I would rather die myself than allow anything to happen to her, or you, or the rest of the team. I can't stop being attracted to her, can't stop from wanting to be with her, but I know my limits, know when to work and when to play." I smirk, thinking about all the things I want to 'play' when it comes to Randi. "She changed me, man, and I can't go back to who I was before."

"Good. You were a fucking spoiled-ass adolescent."

My brows shoot up my forehead. "Tell me how you really feel."

A smile pulls at his lips. "Sarah agreed to training our girl—"

"Our?"

"Our. You think you're the only one who cares about her? She's going to make a difference here, Playboy. I can feel it." He looks down the street. "DC will never be the same after she's done with it."

———

THE PLAIN WHITE door stares back at me as I wait for it to open. This is a terrible idea, but I couldn't stop myself. Every step from my condo here, up the stairs, and now each second that ticks by as I wait, I know this will end badly. Or great, depending on which way you look at it. I see it as a good thing, but Tank might have other opinions on me coming up to Randi's room in the middle of the night when I should be home in my own bed.

Again though, I couldn't not come.

Seeing her with that dickstick on a date that I can't take her on messed with my head, brewed something dark deep inside me. That dark drove me here, urging me to lay claim to her, to make sure she knows she's mine even if we can't be together. It's crazy, idiotic, but it's there, still curling and brewing in my gut.

I knock again, this time with a little more force. Even though it's one in the morning, I know without a doubt she's still up. If I know her, she's probably going through the lineup of every congressman and senator, making a line chart of who she might be able to recruit to change their vote on the upcoming bill.

Inching closer to the door, I tilt my head, angling my ear closer. The soft padding of her feet against the carpet pushes me back a step, not wanting to be in her face the second she opens the door.

An inch gap appears between the door and the frame, a cautious hazel eye peering around only to relax the second it lands on me.

"Trouble," she says with a resigned sigh. "What the hell are you doing here? I thought you were someone here to kill me or something."

I arch a dark brow. "Would someone here to assassinate you knock?"

"Maybe. Could be their ploy to get me out of the security of my room."

I stifle a laugh but can't stop a full smile from crawling up my lips. "Let me in, Mess."

The door swings open, leaving just enough space for me to squeeze through. A single light gives the room a soft glow from the nightstand. As I suspected, the bed is still made, and her laptop and iPad are on the floor beside the chair in the far corner.

"Working late?" I ask over my shoulder as I move deeper into the bedroom.

"Always, you know that. Can't get anything done sleeping." I watch as she folds back into the chair, tosses a thick blanket over her bare legs, and leans against the high back, narrowing her eyes. "What are you doing here?"

"Honestly?" I sigh. "I don't know. All I know is I had to come over. I needed to see you after tonight."

"Don't you dare say that," she chides. "You don't have the right to say you needed to see me. You tabled us and any right you have of stopping by in the middle of the night."

"I know." I massage the bridge of my nose. Fuck, I'm tired. Worrying about her, staying away, pretending we're nothing more than friends has taken its toll these past few months. "Doesn't change the fact that I needed to see you. Everything is still there, Randi, you know that. It fucking kills me to keep my hands off you every time we're together." Her eyes widen. "I've done my best to seem impartial, but alone, like this, when it's just you and me and the night... I want...." Turning from her imploring gaze, I run a hand through my dark hair and tug the ends.

"You want what, Trey?"

"I want you," I whisper. "I can't stop wanting you." Turning to look over my shoulder, I say, "Wanting you to only be mine."

She shakes her head, biting back a smile. "I am yours. Have been since you ran me the most expensive bubble bath ever after the debate. I don't want anyone else. I'm not attracted to anyone else. Haven't you noticed what you do to me?"

This time it's me shaking my head.

"I want you, only you, touching me. It's your hands, your fingers I crave. No one else. Hell, I can barely stand to be touched for longer than ten seconds by anyone else."

"Who else has touched you?" I growl, swiveling around to face her straight on. Stalking across the room, I pause directly in front of the chair, my shins touching the soft cushion. "Tell me."

"No one," she whispers on a soft breath. "That's what I'm trying to tell you. You're different, Trey, in every way. And I only want you. I only crave you."

Forgetting the millions of reasons why we can't be together, I fall to my knees, putting us at eye level. My fingers delve into her thick brown hair and curl into a tight fist. Her breath hitches at the sharp tug pulling her lips an inch from mine.

"Say it again. Say that you're mine." The darkness from earlier spreads through my body, demanding I take her, reminding her of whose she is.

"I'm yours, Trouble."

With a desire-filled groan, I seal my lips to hers. She parts them, giving me access to tangle my tongue with hers. My fingers tighten, tilting her head and elongating her slim neck. Skimming along her soft jaw, I suck and nip at the skin beneath her ear.

"This cannot get out," I whisper against her skin.

"Won't T know you're here?" Her breathy voice, the soft moan at the end, urges me lower.

"We'll tell him. Fuck, I don't care right now." Releasing her hair, I tuck both hands beneath her arms. Standing, I take her with me. Immediately her legs wrap around my waist, the front of her terry cloth robe parting as her hands cup the back of my neck. The sweet scent of her wet center hits my nose, hardening my cock. Her hips flex, pressing her damp heat against my jeans and grinds.

A feral growl pushes past my lips. My fingers make quick work of the sash barely holding the robe together, allowing the white material to slide from her shoulders and fall to the floor. Leaning back, I take in her disheveled hair and bright eyes before trailing down to her perky breasts and lower to the teasing center that's sealed right over my dick, so desperate for release.

"I need a condom," I mutter, relaxing my fingers from where they're squeezing her round ass cheeks.

The shake of her head pulls my attention back up.

"I'm on birth control," she says, her focus on my lips. "I started last fall and didn't stop, you know, just in case...." A single shoulder lifts in a shrug. "I'm good if you are."

The wall trembles at the impact of her back slamming against it. Her quick gasp pulls me back, worry etching my features.

"More," she begs.

Mess likes it rough. I smirk down at the brunette vixen, mind spinning with all the things we can do.

"You want this?" I grunt as I flex my hips, pressing hard against her core. She cries out, but I smother the noise with my palm pressed to her lips. "Quiet, baby. Be a good girl and I'll give you what you want."

Fuck, this isn't going to last long.

Releasing my tight grip on her right ass cheek, I tap her thighs, signaling for her to loosen her strong hold around my waist.

Her soft body slides down mine. A finger on her shoulder, I press down, urging her to keep going until she's on her knees in front of me. Wide hazel eyes gaze up, her tongue sliding along her lower lip in anticipation.

"You want it?" I nod to my dick that's tenting the front of my dark jeans. Gripping myself through the thick denim, I give it a squeeze. "Then get it."

Immediately her fingers fly up to the waistband and fumble with the button. I hiss when the teeth of the zipper slide apart as the tease of a woman slowly pulls it down. I smack my palms against the wall, bracing myself at the slide of the pad of her thumb across the already slick head.

Warmth engulfs my length, sliding up and down as her mouth suctions from tip to base. Eyes closed, focusing on every sensation, I relax my neck and dangle my head between my shoulder blades.

Peeling my palm from the cool wall, I slide it around the back of her head, urging her deeper, faster.

My balls draw up tight. Fuck, I'm a pussy if I can't last thirty seconds of a damn blowjob.

I yank her head back by her hair, releasing my cock from her lips with a soft pop.

"Up," I command, shoving my jeans the rest of the way down my thighs while simultaneously toeing off my shoes. Ripping my dark long-sleeve T-shirt over my head, I toss it behind me before stepping out of my pooled jeans. The moment she's standing, I fall to my knees in front of her and bury my nose between her thighs, inhaling deep. My dick bounces in the air, eager for his turn. The wall rattles when she falls against it. Applying pressure on the insides of her ankles, I urge her legs farther apart. Fingers on her hip bones, I slide both thumbs between her swollen lips, spreading her wide.

"Fuck, I think I love you," I mutter as I lean forward, licking her dripping pussy.

"Me or my vagina?"

"Both." Sucking her little nub between my lips, I easily slide a finger inside her wet entrance. "Look at how wet you are for me, baby." Staring up at her, I flatten my tongue, licking her from my finger to her clit. Her eyes shutter closed as her fingers push into my hair, pressing my face harder to her center.

"Greedy." I chuckle, adding another finger.

"More," she gasps, tightening her hold on my head.

With one more lick, I tug both fingers out only to pop them into my awaiting open mouth. I stand, and she tips her head back to maintain the eye contact.

"Sweetest pussy I've ever tasted," I say around my fingers with a smile, then push them between her lips, urging her to take a taste. Eyelids fluttering closed, she sucks on them, drawing my fingers deeper into her mouth. My dick throbs, precum trickling down the sides.

Gripping underneath her right knee, I hook her leg around my waist and slam into her.

Teeth sink into my knuckles, breath hissing past her parted lips. I pull my fingers free to wrap the other leg around me.

"Harder," she urges, meeting my thrusts.

The soft flesh of her ass dimples between my fingers, no doubt leaving bruises behind.

Harsh inhales, the slapping of skin, and moans of pleasure fill the large bedroom as the scent of sex permeates the air. Her tight walls spasm just as she cries out, her head smacking the wall as her eyes slam shut. I watch in utter fascination as pleasure rolls through her body, her mouth gaping, breaths shallow and fast.

Tension builds in my sac. Gripping tight, I slam into her, swirling my hips to grind against her sensitive clit. Again, Randi cries out as her walls squeeze me mercilessly. With a curse I plunge deep, molding her back to the wall as I find my release. Sweat drips down my chest, slicking the places our bodies touch.

"You're mine, Randi Sawyer."

"Yours, Trey Benson. Only yours."

6

RANDI

April

I don't conceal my awe as I take in the scenery out the tinted window. Munich, Germany, is far more breathtaking than I could've imagined, and we've only been driving for five minutes. Twisting along the limo's seat, I grip the door handle and press my nose against the cold glass.

"Sit back, ma'am," Trey chastises from the opposite bench seat. "It's just the interstate."

"A foreign interstate," I say over my shoulder, still gazing at the strange landscape. "First time here in Germany, remember?" Sighing, I relax back against the seat, smile so wide a dull ache spreads. "I know I'm here for the summit and I have to do work—"

"You mean focus on climate change and how it will affect future generations."

I stick out my tongue and roll my eyes. "Exactly. Anyway, I still get to see a country I've never seen before. So don't judge me if I get a little excited about the things you seem to think are so mundane."

Cutting my eyes away from the rolling landscape, I see him give a stiff nod in return before shifting his intense focus back to Todd. My inspecting gaze trails from the huge gun strapped across Trey's chest down to the tactical pants and black military style boots. Sucks that we haven't had any time alone the past couple months. One night a month isn't cutting it for me, but traveling and fighting tooth and nail to convince every congressman and senator to stop the bill from passing hasn't left much time for us.

"What's with the outfit?" I ask, hoping to get some kind of reaction out of him. I get we're in a different country, but this is a bit extreme, in my opinion. It's not like I'm the president or anything.

I shift my gaze to Todd, who's sitting a little too close, a scowl on his face as he swipes across the screen of his iPad.

A hint of a smirk tugs at Trey's lips before he shuts it down. "There was some chatter surrounding the summit. We wanted the extra security inside the limo just in case."

"In case of what?" I ask, brows raised.

"Have you seen this?" Todd asks, sliding the iPad onto my lap. Trey's shoulders stiffen, his eyes flicking from mine to Todd's hand now resting on my knee. "The Russian President is requesting a meeting with you tonight."

I narrow my eyes at Trey's huffed heavy breath as he cracks his neck. What the hell is wrong with him?

Keeping a cautious eye on Trey, I grip the iPad between both hands and bring the screen a little closer. "What the hell?" I grumble.

"He's here."

I whip my head to face Todd. "He's here? As in Munich?"

He nods and points to the screen. "Yes. The Russian president wants a meeting. Tonight."

"A meeting."

"With you. Tonight. Keep up, Miss Sawyer."

"Watch it," Trey grunts, menace lacing his tone.

I hold out a hand, pausing their intense stare down. "I understood what you were saying, Todd. Why me though? Why now? Unless he's tried this with past VPs."

Todd shakes his head and slides the thin wire-frame glasses off his nose to rub both eyes. "It's unprecedented."

"Maybe it has something to do with me—my background in particular," I muse, shifting my focus back out the window.

"Likely," Todd says. "It would be a great time to use emotions to get him back in the US's good graces."

I hold a tight breath. Slowly, each inch a calculated shift, I face Todd straight on. "And why is that, Mr. Secretary?"

"Because you're a woman. The first woman vice president."

"So," I start, my tone even, hiding the rising fury building in my veins, "what you're insinuating is he believes I'll be kinder, more understanding because I'm a woman. That I'll let my emotions get the better of my sound judgment because I have a vagina instead of a fucking dick."

A bit of me rejoices at the slight tremor in his shoulders, at the bobbing of his Adam's apple as he swallows. "It's a theory."

"You're an idiot," I say with a huff. "For thinking that and voicing it. I highly doubt the Russian president is as ignorant as you as to how women work, thank fuck. He's playing at something else if he wants to meet with me." I lay my head back against the leather headrest. "And honestly, I think it's a bad idea to meet with him. If he wants to talk, then he should've requested a formal meeting before today. No, something else is going on."

"Agreed," Trey pipes up.

"Not your place, Agent," Todd snaps.

"Watch it," I snap right back. "He and this team have been with me since the primary. Do not talk to them like that. They are mine and know how I process shit. In fact"—I flick my angry eyes to Trey—"he needs his own transportation for the rest of the summit and on future travels."

Trey purses his lips.

"Randi—"

I hold out a hand to Todd. "We need to have our heads on straight at these things. We're about to meet with several of the most influential leaders in the world. I'm not wasting my time arguing with you."

"We don't have the manpower to split you two up all the time," Trey cuts in. "That would leave gaps in the security detail. Too risky."

I roll my eyes before pinning them on Todd. "Fine. But next trip I want my own fucking limo."

Trey's head dips, a hint of a smile playing at his lips as he messes with the big-ass gun. "Understood, ma'am."

"How do we respond to this request?" Todd asks like a pouting toddler.

"Tell him we'd love to meet; however, we're unavailable until after the summit."

"That's not very diplomatic."

"Neither was his last-minute meeting invite," I retort. "It must be some kind of power play. Trying to test me, see how far I'm willing to bend. If I don't put my foot down now, he'll think I'm just at his beck and call anytime he needs me. No, this is the right move. We tell him thanks but no thanks, and if he is serious about meeting, then he needs to make an appropriate meeting request for a future date."

Yep, this is the right move.

I hope.

THE MATTRESS MOLDS under my stomach and chest as I flop face-first onto the bed with an exhausted whimper. I thought yesterday was a long day with the flying and meetings, but man, was I wrong. A full day of listening to men bicker back and forth, not getting anything accomplished, and I'm thoroughly spent.

With the varying viewpoints on climate change and the effects everyone seems to be monitoring, with a wide range of results, the group fought on a solution. By the end of the summit tomorrow, I'm sure we'll be right back where we were before, all of us doing our own damn thing while blaming everyone else for pollution.

Ice clinks beside my ear, drawing my attention. Slowly I peel the down comforter from my face. My lips pull into a small, pursed-lipped smile at the sight of a dark liquid-filled highball glass dangling in front of my face.

"We need to talk."

My ears perk at the determination in Trey's tone. My arms tremble, barely strong enough to hold my weight as I push both palms against the bed. Flopping to my back, I gingerly take the sweaty glass from him and press up onto my elbows to take a sip.

The soft burn down my throat eases some of the tension from my shoulders and neck. Jack Daniel's. My favorite.

They love me.

"Did you guys pack me a bottle?" I ask around the crystal lip.

"We did." His features tighten with a grimace. Lifting his right shoulder, he brushes at his ear. "Grem would like the record to show it was his idea."

I nod in appreciation. The decorative material slides beneath my slacks as I scoot up the bed to rest against the modern-style metal headboard. "Thank you, Grem," I shout for him to either hear through the mic or on the other side of the bedroom wall. "It's exactly what I need. Except—"

"Don't even think about asking, Mess. I cannot sneak you out of here for a smoke."

My lower lip juts out in a dramatic pout. "Fine." After another couple sips, the effects of whiskey's magic elixir take hold, heat coursing through my veins before settling in my belly and warming my core. "What did you need to talk about?"

Peeking one eye open, I watch Trey as he tugs his earpiece out and does something with the cuff of his dress shirt. Today he's back in the normal secret service getup. I'm honestly not sure which I prefer more.

Yesterday he was all Rambo badass, looking like he could take down a freaking country if I were threatened. Today he looks no less badass, just a little smoother, like James Bond. Both are a great look on him, though no clothes at all is my ultimate favorite. His rippled abs and cut chest, those muscular thighs that flex as he pounds between mine....

I squeeze my eyes shut and tap the back of my head against the hard headboard. Fuck, why does my mind always go there? Every day at some point I picture the man butt naked. Sometimes on top of me, sometimes just watching from afar while he strokes himself.

Heat builds beneath my skin, warming my cheeks.

"I'd love to know what you're thinking about," Trouble says, his voice a deep rumble.

Peeling my eyes open, I flutter my lashes to clear my vision. Across the room, he leans a shoulder against a wall, brows furrowed, all focus on me.

"Go on, then," I say after clearing my throat.

"Keep that fucker's hands off you or I will."

"What?" I gasp.

His features harden as he takes a calculated step closer. "I can't take it, Randi. I can't sit back and watch him touch what's mine and do nothing about it. That idiot almost died yesterday."

"Todd?" I squeak. "Seriously, you're jealous of Todd?"

"Protective of my girl is not jealousy." Aw, his girl. I like the sound of that, even if we are a secret affair. "And next time, tell him to stay in his own damn seat."

I smirk behind the highball glass. He's not fooling me. He's jealous.

"And, pray tell, how did that weak man almost die yesterday?"

"Did you see my big gun?"

"I love your big gun," I say, waggling my eyebrows.

He shoots a cocky smirk. "Not that one, the one I almost aimed between his brows and pulled the trigger on."

"You being this obsessive and violent shouldn't turn me on, but fuck, does it." I swipe my tongue along my lower lip. "There is something seriously wrong with me."

"I'm—"

A high-pitched screech pierces through the room, overtaking his words. Drink forgotten, I let the glass fall to the bed, dark liquid spilling onto my clothes and bedding, in order to suction both palms over my ears to save them from bursting.

The door bursts open. A serious-faced T barrels through, shouting things I can't make out over the constant blaring noise. Both he and Trey lunge for me, gripping tight under my armpits and hauling me off the bed. My heels kick in the air, unable to touch the hotel room carpet as they carry me into the living room.

A nude heel slides off my foot and dangles from my toes before falling to the floor. I crane my neck backward, trying to see where it landed in order to grab it when we get back. Odd that the lone shoe is what I'm focused on in this moment, not the horde of men shouting and running frantically around the room.

I flinch, their tight grips finally registering, as we advance through the door and down the hall.

"What's going on?" I ask, my head on a swivel, but neither of them pays me any attention. Hell, they might not have even heard my shaky voice over the noise. The two shout, barking some kind of commands. T slams into the stairwell door, shoving it open. Gun drawn, he clears the space before nodding to Grem, who's positioned on the opposite wall, automatic rifle poised ready to fire.

My teeth rattle as we take the stairs, my toes barely scraping the cold concrete. We stop suddenly, my neck snapping forward as I'm jerked backward and shoved into a corner. T and Trey press their backs against the front of my body, officially boxing me in and cutting off my line of sight. The awkward stance of one heel on and one heel off throws off my balance. Leaning my weight against the wall, I trail a hand down my right leg, skimming my calf before flicking off the remaining shoe and allowing it to drop to the floor.

Pressing up to my tiptoes, I attempt to find an angle to see over the two men's shoulders.

"Get the hell down," T says, not taking his eyes off the stairs leading up, whereas Trey's focus is on the stairs going down.

Red lights flash, giving the whole stairwell an eerie feel. A slight tremor shakes my fingers as realization of the situation settles into place. Careful to not startle him, I dip a hand beneath Trey's suit jacket and grab a fistful of dress shirt. More men pour into the stairwell, all wearing huge guns strapped across their chests. Their voices mingle, not making sense as their yelling echoes in the concrete stairwell.

"Move," T shouts before reaching back and wrapping an arm around my waist. Hauling me close, he lifts me off the ground, practically carrying me like a football. Eyes wide, I try to take in the blips I get of the chaotic scene. Four men run ahead of us, guns at the ready, while T takes the stairs two at a time, flying down each floor faster than I ever could. Trey stays beside us, handgun drawn, face fierce.

My body bounces with every step T hops, my neck snapping up and down at the strange angle. When we finally reach the bottom, after what felt like a billion floors, everyone pulls to a stop. Arms swing in every direction, guns raised with their fingers close to the trigger.

I swallow against a dry throat, my breaths more wheezes due to my rapid pulse and T's tight grip. I open my mouth to ask what now when everything stops. The red flashing lights cease, leaving behind the normal glow of artificial light. The blaring alarm cuts off with one last low squawk. Yet everyone stays tense, their shoulders brushing their ears as they remain positioned for an attack.

"T," I whisper while trying to angle my neck up to look at him. "T." My voice trembles. Dark brown eyes pause their back-and-forth scan of the stairwell to lock with mine. "I. Can't. Breathe." In fact, talking just made it a hundred times worse. Black spots dance in the corners of my vision as the panic and lack of oxygen catch up to me.

A flick of a wince mars his face before he schools his features and slowly lowers me to the ground. The moment my bare toes press onto the cold concrete, a strong arm wraps around my waist, tugging me backward to lean against a broad chest. Trey's signature scent of citrus and spices fills my nose, calming me enough to catch a full breath. Seconds tick by turning into minutes, turning into hours. Okay, maybe not hours, but by the time T gives the all clear and everyone relaxes, my toes are frozen solid and shock has set in, making my entire body tremble.

"What... what happened?" I say between chattering teeth. Fuck, it's cold down here.

"Fire on one of the lower floors triggered the fire alarm." I raise both brows at T in a silent question. "It could've been a ploy to get you outside, exposed. We weren't taking any chances. We'll never take chances on something not being a threat when it comes to you."

Aw, T likes me and doesn't want me to die.

"You're my favorite agent," I say with a smile, knowing full well what will come next.

"Hey," all the other guys chirp in near unison.

"Yeah, Mess," Trey says at my back, his warm breath pushing through my loose hair. "Careful or you'll start an all-out war between us to try and win that favorite role."

I roll my eyes and wrap both arms around my waist. "Whatever, you all know you're all my favorites. Trying to pick my ultimate favorite would be like picking your favorite kid." I smirk, lips trembling and no doubt a blueish tint at this point. "It's Taeler. She's my favorite kid."

"Isn't she your only kid?" Grem pipes up.

"Yeah, that's why it's an easy choice." A full-body shiver racks my body. "Can we go upstairs now? It's fucking cold down here, and I can't feel my nose." To prove my point, I tap a finger to the rounded tip. "I hate being cold."

"Oh we know, Mess. We know. We sweat through our suits daily making sure you stay comfortable."

My mouth pops open in surprise. "Guys," I admonish. "You don't have to do that. I'm thankful that you do and would really like for it to continue being toasty in the house and hotel rooms, but we can turn it down... like half a degree or something."

The guys snicker, a few rumbling chuckles echoing through the concrete stairwell.

"Grem, Champ, you move ahead and clear the stairwell. Play, you get up to the room and clear it while the rest of us make our way up with Randi here," T orders.

"I still need to hear that story," I say, turning to look up at Trey. "Playboy, seriously?"

His arm slides from around my waist, leaving a patch of cold in its wake. "One day, Mess. One day."

With that, he whirls around and bolts up the stairs, taking them three at a time. Within seconds he's so far up his once thundering footsteps have turned to faint taps.

"Come on, Randi."

I follow as T leads everyone up to the stairs.

"Where's Todd?" I ask, suddenly remembering I'm not the only US representative here in the building. "Shouldn't he be down here with us?"

"Mr. Secretary was down at the lobby bar when the alarm went off. The agents assigned to him got him to a different secure location." Ah. "I wouldn't forget about him," T says with a smile. "I am good at my job."

"Yeah you are. Nice moves, by the way. Never been carried like a football down several flights of stairs before. Kind of fun even though I'll be sore tomorrow."

His deep chuckle vibrates along the bland cinder block walls. "It was easy, since you weigh nothing. Speaking of that, remember how you said you wanted to learn some defensive moves, know how to fight back?"

"Yeah," I say, eyes on the stairs. With my toes so cold, I've already stubbed the left big one twice not judging the steps height correctly.

"My wife, Sarah, she agreed to help—to coach you, I guess." My focus shifts from the stairs to T only to immediately whack the top of my right foot against the step's edge. I stumble forward, my fingers grazing the gray concrete before T hauls me back upright. Without asking for permission, he swings me around, draping my legs over one arm and tucking the other under my back.

"Thanks. I think I have frostbite on my toes. We might need to see a doctor to get them removed before gangrene sets in."

My lips tug upward at the way his whole body shakes with his laugh.

"I'll make a note to check your toes for any decay tomorrow, sound good?"

My chin dips in a nod. "So your wife, she's some kind of self-defense instructor?"

Pure pride radiates off T, his chest puffing out. "She's a marine, and a damn good one at that. All the men respect her, fear her a bit too." Watching the softness creep into his normally hard eyes, hearing the reverent tone he's using when talking about his wife, makes me love him even more.

"Could she kick your ass?" I question.

His head cocks to the side like he's thinking the question over. "Maybe, but just because I'd be too busy staring at her fine ass to notice anything else."

Men.

"So you're an ass guy."

T's full lips press together to keep from smiling. "That's a personal question, don't you think?"

Heat flames beneath my cheeks. "I wasn't asking if you... if y'all... hell, you know what I meant."

But he doesn't respond. The typical all-business mask slides into place as we approach the door to our floor. Gremlin and Champ are there, guns out but not raised.

"Benson needs help securing the room. Go," he orders. The two men immediately file out the door, leaving us and the other few agents waiting. Time slows as we stand outside the steel metal door.

"What the hell?" T mutters. His dark eyes flick down to me. "Seems you had a visitor."

"What the hell?"

"That's what I said." He nods to the door, and one of the other agents shoves it open. T marches us through and straight to Grem, who's holding the door to our suite open. "What's going on?"

"We took the flowers out, left the card for her to read. Sealed it in a baggie to get fingerprints and contain any contaminants that could be on the paper.

T lowers me to the ground. I sway on my numb feet for a second before finding my equilibrium.

"Let me see it," I demand, hand outstretched, palm up.

Motion from the other side of the room draws my attention. Trey stalks forward, forehead furrowed with a small plastic baggie dangling from his left fingers. "Don't have to guess who sent it. It's in Russian."

"Or someone could've used Russian to throw us off," T mutters, snatching the baggie from Trey before I can.

I frown up at him, but he ignores my death glare as he scans the note.

"Interesting. What does it say?"

My paper-thin patience snaps. Reaching out, I yank the baggie out of T's hand and flip it over to read the inscription. I scan over the words twice before peering up through my lashes at Trey.

He smirks, knowing full well I can't read Russian. "It says, 'watch your back.'"

Trey's features harden as he turns to T.

The two men step close, their words shifting to a low mumble. Exhaustion slams into me, nearly causing me to slump to the floor. My muscles ache, feet still freezing, and now I'm cut out of the discussion. Fine.

The soft carpet twists beneath my heel as I turn toward my bedroom.

"Mess?"

I don't stop or turn. "I need a bath," I mutter over my shoulder as I step over the threshold and close the door behind me with a quiet click.

I inhale deep and slump against the door.

The message should scare me, but right now I'm just too tired to care.

7

RANDI

The near scalding water stings my numb feet and toes as I slowly lower into the full bathtub. Only after lifting both feet out for a few seconds and dipping them back in several times does the pain subside, allowing me to settle back and enjoy the warmth and hot, humid air. If only I hadn't spilled the Jack earlier. Jutting my lower lip, I fake a pout with an exaggerated whimper. It was so tasty too. I'd kill to have its deep warmth swirling in my belly. One can never be too warm.

My pout fades into a frown. Except the guys don't have the same thoughts. Because of me, they're always hot, if I take Trey at his word from earlier. And that sucks for a lot of reasons. For the first time in my life, I'm not thinking about the cost of heating or cooling a house, but instead of enjoying it, I'm concerned about the needs of the other people living in the house with me. Well, kind of living in it. Hell, the boys *should* move in considering they spend most of their time at the house anyway.

So, what's the right call here? Be comfortable because I finally can, or think about the guys and their pit stains? You'd think it's an easy answer, but it's not. Everything in life has been an uphill battle with lots of falling down, and now that I have it 'easy,' I want to do what I want, no holding back. Does that mean poverty Randi was a selfish bitch but too poor to show it, or have the past two years in DC changed the real me into this inconsiderate person?

That's a terrifying thought.

I don't want to change. Don't want the power and money and 'easy life' to alter the core of who I am. But is there really a way to stop it from twisting my perspective?

Lost in thought, I raise one hand out of the tub, the steamy drips of water capturing my unfocused gaze. Just a year ago, I thanked every god I could imagine when I lowered into a hot bath, grateful for the luxury I'd never been afforded before. And now, here I am pouting because of the lack of a Jack Daniel's-filled highball glass in my hand too.

Fuck, I suck.

With an annoyed groan at my selfish ass, I drop my head back, resting it on the hard ceramic ledge, and shut my eyes. Not a second later, a faint knock sounds from the other side of the bathroom door. At the slight whoosh of it swinging open, I peek with one eye and roll my head toward the sound to see who's now in the bathroom with me.

"Just me, Mess."

Shutting my eye once again, I sigh and slink lower into the warm bath. His soft footsteps barely sound over the faint sloshing of water along the edges of the tub. "What are you doing in here?" I ask. "You'll get us in trouble, Trouble." The right corner of my lips twitches up. Not my best line, but hey, I'm funny.

"Nope. Tank's the one who sent me in here, actually."

My lids flick open at the closeness of his deep voice. He's standing just beside the tub, eyes roaming along my naked body beneath the crystal clear water, his eyes growing hooded with each inch.

"Oh?" I say, my voice tight with anticipation.

Attention on my bare breasts, he reveals the hand that was tucked behind his back. A new, very full crystal highball glass dangles above me. With a slight jostle, the ice clinks against the sides like a welcoming bell. Like Pavlov's dog, my mouth waters at the sound. Eager for a sip, I ease up to a sitting position and reach for it.

My fingertips barely brush the glass when Trey inches it higher, just out of my reach. I narrow my eyes at the mischievous glint in his. His free hand rubs along the dark scruff covering his strong jaw. "Again," he commands, lowering the glass.

The tips of my fingers barely swipe the bottom of the glass before he lifts it higher again. Confused, I follow his gaze to where my breasts now lie on top of the bathwater.

"Seriously?"

Still not looking away, he shrugs. "I'm a man. What can I say? Naked boobs absorb all my attention."

"Why are you here, Trouble?" I demand, covering my breasts so he'll focus on the conversation at hand.

Trey lets out a disappointed huff. "Tank wanted someone to check on you, make sure you're okay after everything that happened tonight." His gaze lowers to the apex of my thighs. The tip of his tongue swipes along his full lower lip. With a simple heated look from him, the water turns too hot, the earlier relaxing humidity clogging my throat. "And since you mentioned a bath, which meant you'd be naked and I'm the only one who's seen you naked, we assumed you wouldn't be opposed to me being the one to make sure you're okay. I told Tank I'd be in and out, hands off," he says more to himself then me, raking a hand through his dark hair and disrupting the gelled style. The disheveled look makes me smile. This is the Trey I like best: casual, funny, mischievous. "But with you like this, beautifully naked, how can I make myself leave?" He bites his lower lip.

Two can play his little teasing game. Ensuring his full concentration is on my center, I draw my knees up and rest them along the sides of the tub. His eyes widen. The tub shakes as Trey dares a step closer, slamming his shins against the edge.

"Why leave?" My pulse thunders in my ears.

His chest heaves, eyes still locked between my thighs.

"Touch yourself," Treys says, his voice so guttural I barely recognize it.

My skin heats to an uncomfortable level, sweat beading along my brow and upper lip. His hooded gaze meets mine. I suck in a quick breath at the desire behind his eyes.

"Now, baby."

I glance at the closed door. *Please let it be locked.* Self-conscious of my actions, I slowly glide a hand through the water, barely caressing my stomach before skimming lower.

"No," he chokes out. Just below my belly button, I pause, waiting for his instructions. "Your nipples first."

The building desire quivers low in my belly. As my hand glides up my own body, skimming across sensitive skin, his slides lower to grip his hard length over his black suit pants. Fascinated, I watch him stroke himself as my eager fingers brush both nipples, flicking the peaked tips.

"Rougher, Mess. Do it like I would."

I pinch both hardened nipples between my fingers. My back bows off the back of the tub, thrusting my breasts higher into the cooler air. The burst of desire shatters all inhibitions. "Trey," I moan, continuing to tease myself, no longer caring about anything but my release. "I want you doing this. Touch me," I begged.

"I promised him hands off," he spits like the words are acid on his tongue. "But we can make do, can't we, Mess?"

Biting my lip, I nod as another wave of lust washes to my core, slicking my already wet center further.

"Good girl. Now lower both hands."

"Benson," T's booming voice yells from the bedroom. My fingers still immediately. Widened in panic, my eyes flash up to Trey's. "I ordered you in and out. No funny business in there."

"Coming," Trey shouts back over his shoulder with a smirk. "She's working through the events of the night. Asking a shit ton of questions like always. Be out in a minute when she's good."

"Hands off, remember," T says, his voice causing the door to rattle on its hinges.

Trey motions for me to continue, but knowing T's on the other side of the door gives me pause. Trey raises both brows at my lack of response to his unspoken order and shoots a pointed look to my center.

"Yeah, I know. Hands off. I remember, big guy, don't worry," he calls out.

A rush of breath releases from my lungs at the sound of T's heavy footsteps retreating.

"Continue," Trey says, going back to stroking himself over his slacks. "We're getting to the good part now."

His enraptured focus plus his visible reaction to my ministrations encourage me to continue. The first brush of my fingers shoots an electric bolt to every nerve ending. This is a first for me—with an audience, that is—and it's fucking hot as hell. My lids flutter closed as my fingers slide deep into my core.

"That's it." His words are more a groan as I pick up the pace. "Imagine me, baby, my fingers, my tongue."

My breaths come in short pants, sweat trickling down my temples and between my breasts. I force my eyes open, and they widen at the sight of

Trey's zipper down, his heavy cock in his hand. His tight fist jerks with the same rhythm as my fingers.

"Trey," I moan, my hips arching off the bottom of the tub. Waves slosh against the sides, some spilling over the lip to the tile floor.

"Fuck," he grits out. "On your knees, Mess. Keep your hands where they are and face me."

Damn his words. The lust-filled tone nearly shoves me over the edge. I press my knees against the bottom of the tub, sliding forward an inch against the slick surface until they hit the side. Leaning down, Trey brushes his lips along my own in an almost kiss. The tip of his tongue traces my lower lip, slicking the surface before he stands upright once more.

Heated gaze locked with mine, he brushes the smooth head of his cock against my lips, parting them with a shallow thrust. A moan escapes as I open wider, allowing him to slide deeper.

"Faster," he pants, and I know he's not talking about my mouth. "I know you like it hard, baby. Give yourself what I can't tonight."

Bracing one hand along the ledge, I spread my knees wider, adding another finger. His thrusts increase, enticing my hand to do the same. I let out a frustrated groan, missing his hands in my hair urging me along. Trey curses and slides deeper down my throat. My nose brushes his taut stomach.

I angle my thumb over my clit and press down with every pump of my fingers. Ecstasy tingles my center, urging me faster and harder. With a muffled cry, I come hard, squeezing my fingers tight. The muscles in my thighs spasm and my grip on the tub's edge slips, forcing Trey to push even deeper. I gag as my hand slides along the ceramic edge, seeking traction. Trey grunts his own release, my name a barely there whisper as his thrusts turn erratic.

He steps back, slowly sliding from between my lips, and I slink back into the tub, utterly spent and happy. Eyes closed, I smile and stretch my tired jaw. "Well, that was new."

"Everything is new with you, Randi. Everything."

I peel open my heavy lids with a content sigh. After tucking himself back into his slacks and straightening his shirt, Trey leans forward, pressing his lips hard against my own. Taking the highball glass off the counter, he dangles it in front of my face.

The slick glass slides along my palm as I lower it to my lips to take a sip.

"I won't let anything happen to you, you know that, right?"

Looking over the rim of the crystal, I nod. "That's your job, right?" Not sure why I phrase it as a question. Maybe subconsciously I need to hear that I'm more than the job, more than a random fuck. I need to hear he's in as deep as I am with whatever is going on between us.

"Right," he says with a chuckle. My lips purse in annoyance, and Trey shakes his head. "Mess." He sighs, running a hand through his already disheveled dark hair. "Never once on this job have I considered the person I'm protecting's life more valuable than my own."

"And now?"

"And now." Turning on his heel, he retreats to the door. Hand on the handle, he says over his shoulder, "With you, I'd rather die than see you harmed. My life for yours, Randi. Because at this point, I wouldn't live if you didn't."

Minutes later, I'm still staring at the closed bathroom door, completely floored by his admission. Water drips from the corners of my eyes from being kept open so long. Blinking, I clear the dryness and take a deep sip. The whiskey slides past my lips, burning my throat on its way down.

"Don't you dare die for me, Trouble," I whisper to the empty bathroom. "Because I think I feel the same."

But I have no fucking clue where we go from here.

SHOULDER AGAINST THE WINDOW, I stare out at the craziest DC spring day. Snow swirls along the wraparound porch, the budding trees bending and whipping in the bitter forceful wind. The late snowstorm came unexpectedly, turning from the predicted couple inches of rain to snow and ice. How the weathermen missed it as badly as they did, I'll never know. Through the city and along the highways it's pandemonium. It might take days for the traffic to unwind itself. Thank goodness I chose to work from the One Observatory library today or I'd be out there in it too. But staring out into the bitter cold all I want to do is curl up in front of the old Victorian fireplace with a soft snuggly blanket, a glass of wine, and Trey at my side, forgoing any work. Why can't these people understand snow days should be appreciated not treated like a normal day?

Wait, maybe I should make adult snow days a thing. Or a holiday. That's not misusing power at all.

"It's not good," Jessica says with a resigned sigh behind me.

"Yeah, but it would be fun."

"What?"

I shift my eyes away from the window to where she sits, eyes closed and features tight. "What?"

"I'm talking about the votes we need to win the House."

"Oh." Focusing outside the cold glass once more, I monitor two bundled agents patrolling the property line. "They have to be freezing."

"It's their job. Don't worry about them. What you need to be worrying about is the fact that even with me working my tail off while you've been traveling, we're still several votes short."

Thumbnail between my teeth, I shuffle away from the window and flop into an armchair. "What do we do? What can we do?"

Jessica tosses a notepad onto the side table, its cardboard back slapping against the wood surface. The skin around her eyes tightens as she massages her temples. "Honestly, I don't know. I feel like I've tried all my contacts, used up most of the favors owed me, and still we're short."

"When's it going to the House?"

"Next month, if they stay on schedule. But they could move it up. You never know with them."

"Shit," I groan. "I can't let this happen. It goes against everything I promised through the campaign."

"I know," Jessica says, sympathy dipping her voice to a soft whisper. "But you're trying to stop it. Other than continuing to badger people, I don't know what else to do." Adjusting her watch, she swears. "I have a meeting with Congressman Trick in two hours across town. I better get going if I plan to make it on time in this weather."

She gathers her coat and scarf, draping both over her arm. At the door, she turns, dragging my attention from the unfocused stare I'd slipped into.

"We'll keep trying, Randi. I'm not giving up."

I give her a tight nod with a goodbye wave as she slides out the door.

The padding beneath my palms molds between my fingers as I push out of the armchair. My Uggs barely make a sound as I pace the length of the office, chewing on a fingernail while I debate my options.

What am I going to do? My first real test here in DC and I'm failing—miserably. A painful ache builds behind my breastbone as the discomfort grows in my chest.

This is it. I'm done. Done in this town. How could I not be? I really thought I'd last longer than this.

Chewing on the pinkie nail, racking my brain on additional *legal* options we might be overlooking, I fail to notice Trey stepping into the room. Spinning on the balls of my feet, I turn only to have my nose smack a solid chest.

"Ouch," I say more like a curse as I rub my throbbing nose. "You broke my nose."

"I didn't do anything. How'd the meeting with Jessica go?" he asks, pausing the hand still massaging my nose. Tipping my head up with two fingers beneath my chin, he inspects the area, eyes narrowed in concentration. "You're fine."

"Oh, you're a doctor now?"

Trey smirks. "Nope, just had enough broken noses to know what to look for."

"That many fights, huh?"

One shoulder rises in a half shrug. "It might shock you to know that not everyone finds me as adorable as you do."

I snort, and his brows shoot up his forehead in return.

"Adorable? I don't think I'd use that word."

"And what words would you use?" His voice lowers with each word as he steps closer, sealing our bodies together. "I can tell you what words I'd use for you." Chest to chest, he tilts forward. Two fingers brush the hair from around my face and tuck it behind my ear. Slick lips trail along my outer ear. "Delicious is the first word that comes to mind."

A shiver bolts down my spine, making my shoulders and legs quake. All the earlier worry and doubt fade to the background with me in his arms. With a content sigh, I relax further against his chest, savoring the feeling of comfort his arms offer.

Too quickly it ends. Hands on my shoulders, he inches us apart before stepping back, putting several feet between us. Lips pursed in what seems like annoyance, he shoves both hands into the pockets of his pinstriped suit. "Cameras." His honey brown eyes flick to a corner of the office before returning back to me. "You didn't answer my question. How did it go with Jessica?"

My hair shifts across my shoulders as I shake my head to help clear the lust fog his touch caused. "Not good. Terrible, actually. We don't have enough votes to kill it in the House and are several short in the Senate too."

Stepping around the massive desk, I relax into the high-back leather rolling chair. "What am I going to do, Trouble?"

His features soften, the thin worry lines along his forehead and between his brow deepening.

"I failed before I hit the six-month mark." Swallowing back the unshed tears clogging my throat, I turn my damp eyes away from his concerned stare. "I'm a failure, just like everyone knew I would be."

"Mess—"

I hold out a hand, cutting him off.

"How can I stay here?" The dam holding back my building tears breaks, sending streams trickling down my lightly freckled cheeks. Hastily I wipe them away with the back of my hand. "How can I show my face when the one thing I promised, their voice in DC, is literally being stripped away with one bill that I can't stop?" Leaning forward, I rest both elbows on the desk and cradle my wet cheeks between my hands. "I'm a fraud." The reality of the situation sets in, making me laugh. "Kyle's getting what he wanted from the start."

"What's that?" The pain in Trey's voice wrings a shuddering sob from my chest.

"Me gone. We made a deal, but even if we hadn't, I can't stay here if that gets passed. I'll have let every person who voted for me down." Deep in my gut, an unfamiliar feeling builds taking root, causing more tears to fall. What the hell? "I know this sounds stupid since I came here to get away from that stupid trailer park, but"—my damp palms fall to the desk, and I shift my gaze to meet Trey's straight on—"I just want to go home. Things might be hard as hell there, but at least the only person I'm letting down there is me. I can't take this, Trey. I'm not strong enough for this role like I thought. It's too much."

My heart and pride shred at the words I dared to say out loud. A soul-crushing sob rattles my chest, shaking my shoulders as the disappointment takes hold. Covering my face again, I sag against the desk.

A strong arm tries to wrap around my shoulders, tugging me toward his comforting hold, but I shrug out of it and shake my head.

"Just go, okay?" I cry, my voice breaking. "I need to be alone."

"Randi—"

Fury builds where pity and self-loathing had just resided. Spinning in the chair, I lunge out of it. Both palms slam against his chest, making him stagger back. Shock registers on his face just before hurt flashes behind his eyes.

"I said go," I grit out. "Get out, now."

"No." Gone is the hurt. His eyes narrow, funneling the steely look of determination straight through to me. "Are you serious with this right now?"

I flinch like he physically slapped me, and I swear a flash of pain tightens his features in return.

"It's done. There's nothing else we can do," I say, my voice as weak as I feel.

"So that's it. You're quitting. You're a quitter now."

My spine snaps straight, a bolt of annoyance rolling through my veins. "I'm sorry?" Surely I didn't hear him correctly. He's definitely not sitting here calling me out during my own fucking pity party.

"You heard me," he snarls. A slight tingle builds in my gut at the dominance in his tone and wide stance. "Are you a quitter, Randi Sawyer? Yes or no?"

"I... I—"

"It's a simple question, Randi," he says with a smirk as he takes a step closer, putting us dress shoe to Uggs. "You're the motherfucking vice president of the United States, so start acting like it."

I purse my lips to keep them from trembling, though from rage or agony, I don't know. Both twist in my chest, confusing the hell out of me.

"I'm not a quitter," I finally grit out through clenched teeth. "Fuck you, Trey Benson. I've fought like hell my whole life, scrapped by day after day and kept going when everything and everyone was against me. I'm no fucking quitter, and you damn well know it, you asshole."

"I do." My next snappy retort falls flat as my jaw pops open in surprise. "I needed to make sure you remembered who you are, Randi. This broken, sad, defeated person you're fading into is not you. Stop it with this crying and saying you're going home or that you're a fucking failure." He grips my chin and tilts my face up. "You're not going anywhere on my watch, you hear me? You're here until your term is up whether you like it or not."

I search his eyes, desperate to figure out what he's trying to say.

"You're mine, Mess." His calloused fingers slip from my chin as he steps away. "Now, tell me what Jessica's intel says, and then we'll strategize from there. We'll figure out a way to get the votes, together."

And just like that, another sliver of my heart melts for the mischievous, sexy-as-hell agent.

If I'm not careful, he'll have my whole heart in his capable hands before the year is over.

For the first time ever, I'm good with that. I don't know what the future holds, but if I can have this dedicated man by my side each step of the way, well then, it seems like a pretty great future to me.

8

TREY

I give a tentative knock and take a step back, not wanting to overwhelm Jessica the second she opens the condo door. It's late and this visit is unannounced, but I had to come tonight. The drive over was treacherous, but at least this is my last stop.

The snap of a deadbolt unlocking meets my ears. The door opens a foot, revealing a lingerie-clad, doe-eyed Jessica.

For a second I freeze, on the brink of ditching my plan and bolting down the hallway. This has to be the craziest idea I've ever had. It might work though. It has to work. Randi can't leave DC, and seeing her in agony felt like my heart was shredding right alongside hers. I'll do whatever I have to do to make sure those sad tears never happen again on my watch. Which is why I'm here. I'm doing whatever it takes, even if it means stepping back into the life I've tried like hell to run from.

"Not that I'm unhappy to see you, Trey, but what are you doing here?" Her blonde hair swishes as she turns to look into the condo. "It's almost midnight," she says, turning back, eyes wide. "What's going on? Are you okay?" She's opened the door wider, revealing all of her scantily clad body.

I swallow and stare into the condo behind her. If Randi ever gets wind of this, I'll be a eunuch for sure.

"Can I come in? We need to talk."

She motions me into the condo. I scan the modern living room and open kitchen. It's almost an exact replica to mine five floors up. Hers doesn't have the view of the Capitol, but not many do because of the cost factor involved for those select units.

"Wine?" she asks, making her way into the kitchen.

Fuck, why doesn't she put on a robe or something? Not that I'm fighting an emotional response based on her nearly naked body. Nope, my dick is as limp as an overcooked noodle. Randi did that. Somehow her crazy mixed with her natural beauty have formed some kind of shield, making attraction to other women nonexistent. And amped up my jealousy a thousand percent.

Stretching left and then right, I attempt to ease my stiff muscles. "No, thanks. Can you put something else on?"

"I thought you liked red?" The clink of glass against stone sounds through the living room. I don't turn from where I stand staring out the floor-to-ceiling windows.

Ignoring her question, I lean a shoulder against the cold glass, watching the remaining snowflakes whirl past on the strong wind.

"You have to have a guess as to why I'm here," I say with a sigh. "After the meeting with Randi—"

"Randi, is it?" she says, surprise in her tone. "A bit personal, don't you think? You're referring to the first female vice president this country has ever had. Are you intentionally trying to undermine her title by calling her by her first name?"

"What?" I'm shocked at the defensiveness Jessica is showing for my girl. "No, she asks us to call her that, just like you. No disrespect, promise."

"Good, because I like her. In way over her head, but I like her."

Interesting. Even the political ladder climber has fallen under Randi's spell. Not surprised. If you get to know her, the real Randi, it's impossible not to.

"She told me about the meeting earlier. I know we're behind on the votes we need in the House and Senate. I also know you're working to get more people on our side, but with Birmingham's connections and no doubt bribery and blackmail, this vote will go through unless we do something big."

"What do you have in mind?"

I glare at the shuffling sound behind me and immediately regret it. Sprawled back along a crimson chaise lounge, Jessica swirls the red wine, eyes locked on mine. Ugh, she's pulling out all the stops tonight, isn't she? Wonder if she'd be this forward if she knew Randi and I are together. Too bad she can't. No one can.

"Not what, but who."

Her brows shoot up her forehead. "You're joking," she says after a minute. "Our parents?" I tip my chin in acknowledgment. "There's no way they'd do anything without some kind of benefit for them. What are you willing to offer them, your soul?" She laughs and breaks our stare. "You know they probably created the insane bill with Kyle, right?"

I glide my fingers through the lengthy part of my hair, tugging at the ends. "I know. Fuck, I know. But we can't let this vote go through. It'll kill her."

"Why do you care so much?" Suspicion creeps into her voice. "What's in it for you?"

"Nothing's in it for me except supporting her cause. And to answer your earlier question, yeah, I know they'll want something in return."

"What are you thinking?"

"We give them what they both want."

Seconds tick by with her brows furrowed in concentration. "Oh," she gasps, finally realizing what I'm referencing. "You'd do that? Something you've fought against for years, all for Randi, for her cause?"

"For our country," I bite out. She can't know how much Randi means to me or that Randi's the sole reason I'm offering up myself like a sacrificial lamb.

My agitation and sliver of despair at what I'm about to do urge my need for a drink. I stomp to the wet bar and search through the various bottles of bourbon before settling on Blanton's. "Go put some damn clothes on, Jessica. We need to go over my plan. It'll be a long night for both of us."

THE PUDDLES of melted snow splash beneath my boots as I march up the walkway, the remaining bits of yesterday's storm disappearing thanks to the sweeping spring temperatures that followed like predicted. The warm sun, budding trees, and the crispness of a fresh start swirl in the sweet-smelling air. A fresh start for everyone but me. Hell, every breath feels like dark poison seeping into my lungs, crippling the ability to breathe normally.

I continue walking through the pain, knowing it's all for her. I can do this for Randi. Anything to shift that dark cloud that's hung over her head since the meeting with Jessica. Randi and I did come up with a solid plan to gain more votes, but it wasn't enough, so I stopped by Jessica's last night and made a deal with her, which leads me here today.

This town is all about who you know and your family name—and the money tied to it. If I don't do this, if I don't step in, she'll lose the vote, then lose her confidence. And then I'll lose her.

That can't happen.

Even if it costs me everything.

At the door, I pause and take a deep inhale through my nose, calming the growing agitation at just being on this property. After a quick knock, I dig my hands into the front pockets of my jeans as I wait for the butler to answer.

That's right, I knock at my parents' house. This is my childhood home—not that I was here much between boarding school and lavish family vacations—yet here I am knocking on the fucking door like a vacuum salesman.

Fuck, I hate my pompous parents. To think I could've grown up to be exactly like them. If it weren't for the last-minute decision to go to college on the West Coast, I would have. There, without their daily oversight and the impact of my family name, reality set in, making me realize how ludicrous our lifestyle and way of thinking really were. It was that clarity which caused me to dig my heels in, stopping their constant control over my life, and join the army.

College and the military. Those two decisions not only shifted me from an undeniably miserable life but also led me to the two people who would eventually make my life one worth living. Tank and Mess.

I won't let them down. A deep ache creeps into my heart just at the thought of either of them being disappointed in me. Tank jokes about my desperate need for approval and love, and maybe he's right. The loveless childhood I was raised in made me desperate for it. Maybe that's why I stayed with Rachel as long as I did. Even if it wasn't love, at least we pretended well together. Now though, after Randi, that's not enough. Fuck, it's not nearly enough.

I want—no, I deserve someone who's desperate for me. The real me, not the money or the name, but me, Trey. That's what Randi has shown me. That I am enough, for anyone. I might not deserve her or the trust and loyalty she easily hands over, but I for fucking sure will do whatever I can to never let her down.

The large solid dark oak door swings open on silent hinges. A familiar sour face scowls back at me from the other side.

"Ah, Gerard. Long time no see, man. How's life treating you?"

The old man purses his lips, fighting a smile. Gerard and his wife have been with my parents since I was a kid. Any kind word or encouragement was given by those two instead of my own parents. They were the type of parents I wish I would've had. Loving, considerate, grounded.

"Sir, welcome home."

Ugh, now I see why Randi hates the formal shit. I already feel older.

"It's Trey, and I'm not home." I pat the old man's thin shoulder as I step over the threshold. "Just stopping by to talk to the overlords."

Gerard covers his laugh with a fake cough, pressing a fist to his lips. He knows there's no love lost between me and my parents. Hell, he's not a fan of them either. But this job is steady, and from what he says, they pay well with great benefits, so he puts up with a lot.

"Your *parents* are waiting for you in the sunroom. Beth prepared coffee and tea for the meeting."

"And her cookies?" I ask, allowing a childlike hopeful tone to seep through.

Gerard smiles. "Of course." With a wave of his hand, he directs me toward the sunroom at the back of the mansion where my fate will be determined. "How's the new VP?" he asks as we walk along sparkling hardwood floors, going down one hallway and then another.

"Good. She's going to make a difference for the people who need it most."

He hums a response but doesn't say another word as we continue our trek. At the sunroom doors, he pauses with his hand on the knob. Facing me straight on, he narrows those gray eyes at me.

"I don't know why you're here, Trey, but if the look on your face is any indication, it's not good."

I swallow hard and clear my throat, fighting against the rising nerves that always come with being in this house. "It's not, but she needs my help. I'm out of options."

"Ah, it's always a woman, isn't it? The one who challenges us and pushes us to be better men. Whatever you need, if we can help, just ask. We're always here for you."

Agh, this man and the emotions he's stirring. My eyes sting, but I blink away the wetness before nodding.

"Thanks, Gerard. You and Beth, well, you're the only reason I survived long enough to get out of here. Now it's my time to do something great, to make a difference."

"You're a good boy," he says, gripping my bicep and giving it a tight squeeze. "Never forget that."

At that, he twists the knob and gently urges the door open. Sunlight pours through the wall of windows and pockets of glass ceiling. After the long walk through the darker house, I blink through the initial assault on my sensitive eyes. Squinting, I scan the room, pausing on my mother sitting on the white chaise, magazine in one hand and steaming teacup in the other. I search for my father but come up empty.

"Come in, darling," Mother coos. "Your father will join us when he can."

With one more look to Gerard, I tip my chin and stride into the proverbial lion's den.

A soft clink echoes around the otherwise quiet room as Mom sets her teacup back into its matching saucer and rests the thick magazine in her lap. Her eyes trail up and down my body, lips pursing, no doubt finding my attire lacking.

"Mother." I lean down to kiss her offered cheek. "You're looking well."

"Aren't I?" she says with a smile.

It's not a lie. She looks fantastic. No one would guess her real age of sixty-two. Her blonde hair, which used to be natural, is styled in long flowing waves cascading over her shoulder. Even though it appears she has minimal makeup on, I know it took her hours this morning to perfect the look and the real woman is buried under layers of product.

I really shouldn't poke the bear since I'm here asking for their help, but I can't help it. It's too easy. And fun.

"New filler?" I ask while pointing to her slightly overplump lips.

Her brow furrows—well, as much as it can with the billions of units of Botox in her face. Just the sight of her immobile features makes me chuckle, which pisses her off even more.

"Always a pleasure, my son." I barely hold back a shiver at that title coming from her fat lips. "You said you wanted to discuss something with your father and me, so I'd watch your comments if I were you."

With a one-shoulder shrug, I turn and make my way to the puke green love seat and flop onto the stiff cushions. Stretching my arms out wide, I relax back and smile.

"Where is my biological father?"

"Your only father," she snaps in a rare display of annoyance. Quickly she schools her features back into the appearance of pristine calm. "And as I said, he will be with us when he can. He had business to attend to."

"Right, well, this is pointless if he's not here, so I'll just grab a couple cookies and be off, then." I slap the tops of my thighs in a signal that the meeting is done, even though it never actually started, and lean forward to swipe a few chocolate chip cookies from the tray.

"Tell me why you're here. I can make decisions alone. We don't need your father here."

The still-warm cookie melts in my mouth. My eyes close as I chew, my only happy childhood memories flooding back at the familiar taste. I've been all over the world, eaten in almost every country, but these cookies right here are still the best things I've ever eaten.

Well, except Randi.

A smile quirks up the side of my lips at just the thought of her.

"Why are you here, Trey?" Father's bored voice booms at my back.

I fight the urge to sit up straighter and stand as a sign of respect, which was drilled into me since I could walk.

"Here to reconsider our terms we discussed so you don't have to give up your lavish lifestyle?" Mom pipes up. "I knew just the *thought* of living on a regular wage would set you straight."

"I have a proposition for you two," I mumble around another cookie. Mom's eyes narrow and I roll mine. "The H.R. 13 bill that's about to roll through the House and possibly the Senate, what do you know about it?"

Their eyes meet briefly in silent conversation.

"Enough. What about it?" Dad asks cautiously.

"It's wrong on too many levels to count, that's what. I want to stop it from passing."

Mom's high-pitched, obnoxious laugh grates on my already tense nerves. I clench my jaw to keep from saying something I'll regret. Whether I like it or not, I need their help.

"It makes sense, son," Dad says. He unbuttons his suit jacket and folds into the chair opposite of me. "The poor, they don't understand what goes into running the government or who would be best at the job. This is in their best interest, allowing the burden to fall on our shoulders instead of theirs. We're helping them, not hurting."

The muscles of my jaw twitch as I work it back and forth. They actually believe that load of shit.

"It's their constitutional right to vote, for everyone to vote."

Mom waves a dismissive hand. "That old document, is it even relevant anymore?"

Mouth gaping, I stare at my delusional mother. She must be high on prescription drugs or something. I hope that's the reason and not that she believes the Constitution that our country was founded on is just an old worthless document.

"Yes, it's relevant." I say each word slow to make sure she understands, then glance to Dad. "It's wrong to deny an American citizen the right to vote."

"Felons can't. How is this different?"

Holy fuck, am I glad I left my gun at home.

"Now you're just trying to piss me off," I grit out, glaring at him. His smirk—my smirk—tells me I hit the nail on the head. "Can you stop it?"

"Depends," Mom chirps. "What are you willing to offer in exchange?"

"What you want," I say with as much venom as I can muster. "After this presidential term, I'll jump back into politics. I'll...." I swallow and lean forward to grip the glass of water from the silver tray. After a quick sip, I rest both elbows on my knees, gripping the slick glass between both hands. "I'll leave the secret service."

Mom laughs and looks to Dad before turning back to me. "You think you can just waltz back onto the circuit and expect to go anywhere? You're a no one in our circles nowadays."

I nod, knowing that would come up. That's why Jessica was my first stop, to make sure she was on board for her role in my life.

"I've discussed a plan with Jessica Hawthorne." I pause, flicking my gaze between the two.

Mom leans forward, interest piqued. "What kind of plan?"

Shit, this is the part I'm looking forward to the least. I fight the urge to pace the room. There's no room for showing weakness here.

"I'll make the rounds at various fundraisers and events with Jessica, as a couple." I swallow back the bile rising in my throat. "A fake couple, mind you. She's well aware this is us using each other. There is no future for us together except politically. Jessica will reintroduce me to the right people to get my name back in the game, and I'll allow her to use our family name as backing when needed. It's a win-win for both of us."

The snakelike smile Mom gives in return drops a weight of dread in my stomach. I'm playing with fire while doused in gasoline here, but this is my only shot at helping Randi. At keeping her in DC. I have to take it.

"What's made you such the bleeding heart as of late?" Mother asks, her conniving smile growing.

"I'm no bleeding heart, you know that, but I also see how wrong this bill is for many Americans. I can't let it pass without doing whatever it takes to make it stop."

"Interesting. And it has nothing to do with the trash that's currently residing in One Observatory Circle?"

"Watch it, Mother," I say, just barely holding back the contempt from my tone. "That's your vice president you're talking about."

Mom huffs and crosses her arms. "Not my vice president. She doesn't deserve to be in that role, have that title." Tilting her head, she stares out the windows.

The room grows quiet as I give them time to think it all over. With them distracted, I sneak another cookie. Or two.

"End of the year," Mother says, breaking the silence. "I want you to leave the secret service by the end of the year."

"No." I shake my head for emphasis. "End of this term or no deal. I've committed myself, and I won't break the cohesive team we've built before then."

Sweat builds along my spine and dots my forehead. I raise the glass to my lips and drain the contents. The two stay silent as I roll the now-empty glass between my hands.

"The deal's off if you can't stop the bill from being passed," I state.

"Deal's off if you go back on anything you've promised," Mom retorts. "And if you do back out, then we officially cut you off from pulling your trust monthly and inheritance."

My breath stills in my lungs. Fuck, I didn't think she'd go that big. For the past few years, they've laid out an ultimatum of pulling access to my trust fund but never followed through. Something tells me this time they wouldn't hesitate. And fuck if I'm not worried. A lot worried, actually. Living on a normal salary, an agent salary… hell, that would suck. It's what I make now but all my extra expenses are paid by the Benson trust, the one Mother has threatened to take away on more than one occasion.

Would Randi even want to stay with me if that were the case?

I shake my head to clear the thought. Of course she would. She wanted me even before she knew about the money. Actually, she might not even really know the extent of the wealth at my disposal, so of course Randi wouldn't care if I lost it all. But I would. I love my bikes, my fancy-ass condo with the million-dollar view. Love the feel of a custom-made suit and the taste of a thousand-dollar bottle of bourbon. I'm not a pompous ass like my parents, but I sure as hell was raised with a platinum spoon and would prefer to keep that lifestyle.

But for Randi?

For us?

I'll give it all up. What they don't need to know is that my plan ends at the end of the term. No me moving into the political limelight like I'm promising. This is how you play this game, promising one thing and then delivering another. It's a constant trade of power, and right now I'm holding the cards.

Rolling my shoulders, I lean back against the couch. "Agreed. You get the votes and you get me in four years."

Mom claps her hands and leans forward. "This is wonderful news. Welcome back, son. Now let's discuss this," she says, twirling a finger in the direction of my face. "A fair amount of work needs to be done to get you ready."

Instead of responding, I snatch two more cookies off the tray and shove them into my mouth. And because I'm a little shit, I dust the crumbs off my fingers on the ugly-as-hell couch.

"Not a chance," I say around the mouthful of partially chewed-up cookie. "Jessica has the list of events we'll attend, so I'm all set to keep up my end of the bargain." At the door, I look over my shoulder and smirk. "Now you go do yours."

9

RANDI

May

I'm dying. Once again the floor rushes up close, my back slamming onto the cushioned surface. The hours have crawled by, yet here I am enduring this torture.

The heavy weight of exhaustion pulls at my arms; I'm barely able to lift them to defend myself from another attack. My ass throbs all over from how many times I've fallen on it, like now. Sweat drips down my temples, streaming to my chin. Fuck, I hope I remembered to put deodorant on this morning. If not, maybe I won't have to worry about defending myself against Sarah. She'll get a whiff and go running on her own.

I squeeze my eyes shut to keep the sweat from pouring into them.

"Get up," the strong female voice says above me.

I shake my head and tap the mat with as much force as I can muster. "I'm out. I can't do this."

"It's been thirty minutes." There's no mistaking the annoyance and exasperation in her voice. "Get up and try again."

"Why?" I nearly whine. "You're just going to knock me on my ass again. I'm tired of being on my back."

"Not what I heard," Sarah says. Squinting my eyes open, I find her standing over me, smiling. That smile drops as she looks across the room.

"Baby, I can't do this. She's weak. Plus I thought you said she wanted to learn." With the toe of her black tennis shoe, she nudges my sore ribs. "She's not even trying."

I grit my teeth to keep from responding only because I'm legit scared she'll kill me if I mouth off. T's wife is not only gorgeous but deadly. It's sexy in an 'I might die' kind of way, which apparently I'm into, considering my attraction to Trouble.

"Listen," I say with a grimace as I push off the blue mat to my elbows. "I've never done this before, okay?"

"Obviously." Her dark eyes narrow as they scan me from head to toe. "Have you ever even lifted a weight?"

"On purpose?" I ask, holding back my smile.

Sarah's lips twitch in a suppressed smirk. With a sigh, she reaches out her hand, which I grasp, allowing her to haul me upright. "Yes, on purpose." Again she looks across the room to the two men who are basically eating popcorn while they watch this mess of a training session. "You need to get her on some kind of workout routine before I can do anything. Cardio, weights, and core. She's weak."

"I would take that as an insult, but it's true," I say with a shrug, then wince at the pain that bolts through my shoulder at the movement. "I am slightly embarrassed. Last year was all about gaining weight, not really anything else. I had this special diet that Kyle put me on, which helped." My sweaty palms slide along my fuller waist and hips. "You should've seen me before."

Kyle said I looked like a meth addict, and he wasn't far off. Somehow during my lifetime, balancing between poverty and the lower class, food always took the back seat. Plus when I'm stressed, I can't eat—just the thought of it is revolting—so yeah, I was slightly underweight before Kyle's dietitian helped out. Now I'm full in all the right places. Padding around my hips, thin waist but not in the sickly way it was before, and somehow my ass has rounded to a perfect shape. I should write a quick thank-you note to the ass gods for that one.

"Now we add in adding muscle," Sarah says with a sharp slap to my ass. I yelp and hop out of her reach. "Keep up with the diet, but ask them to add in more protein. You'll need it."

"I'll get her a workout routine written up," Trey says behind me. I look over my shoulder to where he leans against the far wall. "Three days a week?"

"Four," Sarah quickly responds. "One of those days needs to be dedicated to core. If she can't protect herself, then all this is a waste. And honey," she says, pointing to Trey, "I ain't got time to waste."

His shoulders tighten and I swear he stands a bit straighter. "Yes, ma'am."

"Fuck, baby, you look good in those shorts." Eyes only on Sarah, T steps onto the mat and wraps both hands around her bare waist, then slides lower, palming her generous ass over her tight shorts. "My shift ends in two hours, and I can't wait—"

"La, la, la la," I yell, putting my fingers into my ears. "I don't want to hear that."

"Jealous?" Sarah says, leaning in and wrapping her arms around T's thick neck.

"Yes," I shout while stomping my foot. "He's the one who...." Hmm, how do I say this? "I can't have what I want because of him."

"What or who?" Sarah says with a knowing wink. "T's a gossip, Randi. I know all about you and the man child over there." She tilts her head toward Trey in the corner, her long dark braid swinging along her back with the motion. "Believe me, I'm on your side."

"Really?"

"Really."

"We've talked about this, baby," T says into her ear. "Don't get in the middle of my work and I won't get into the middle of yours."

With a single push, Sarah detaches from T. His eyes narrow, but an intense heat flares behind them. Sarah steps left. T steps right. The two circle the mat, eyes only on each other. T shrugs out of his jacket and tosses it on the ground before working his tie off and adding it to the pile.

A warm hand rests on my shoulder and tugs me backward.

"Best to stay out of their way. This is their foreplay," Trey whispers into my ear. "I shouldn't say anything, but fuck, you stink, Mess."

I relish the pain the quick movement causes me as my shoulder pops up into Trey's jaw.

"Oops."

"Oh, you'll pay for that later." His nose skims up my neck as he takes an exaggerated whiff. "After you shower, of course."

"Kick his ass, Sarah," I yell, trying to distract myself from Trey's presence behind me.

"Hey." T pouts without taking his eyes off his wife. "Don't gang up on me."

"You're the one who put the stupid hands-off rule in place," Sarah jumps in, defending me.

"Yeah!" I shout. A low chuckle sounds behind me.

"You know that man child wouldn't do anything stupid, yet you laid down a line in the sand because you need to control everything."

"Honey, stop while you're ahead," T grumbles.

Sarah's footsteps pause. Her body shifts, preparing to attack. In an instant she's on T. Every punch she throws, he defends, but he doesn't take his own shots. It's clear to see he's holding back. He's nearly double her size; even if she's trained by our military's best, she's no match for the Terminator.

"He won't hurt her," Trey mumbles behind me.

"This happens a lot, I'm guessing?"

Trey huffs. "Their living room is a gym with sparring pads spread throughout. So yeah, this happens every time I'm over." Resting my chin on my shoulder, I look back to find his eyes already on me. "I made them stop doing this shit at my place last year after they broke a fucking couch. Animals," he adds at the end with a smile that only has love behind it.

"You guys are together a lot, then, the three of you?"

A pang of jealousy settles into my stomach before rising up my chest. I glance back to the two still going at it on the mat. What would it be like to have that kind of friendship, have a makeshift family like these three have? Suddenly the feeling of being the outsider slinks through my veins.

Nervously I nibble on my thumbnail. "I'm going to take a shower," I mumble as I step toward the door.

"Hey," Trey says, following. "What just happened?"

At the door, I look back to where T now has Sarah pinned beneath him with her arms stretched above her head. I shake my head and continue out the door toward my room.

"Talk to me, Mess."

"I don't know. I'm just sad."

"About the bill?"

I shake my head, the tip of my ponytail swiping from one shoulder to the other. "No, that," I say, hooking a thumb backward toward the workout room. "You, those two, the friendship. I've never really had that, with anyone. I have Tae to talk to, but she's all I have." I stop suddenly at the bottom of the stairs. Trey's arms shoot out, gripping the banister and wall to keep from running into me. My tennis shoes squeak against the polished hardwood floor as I swivel around to face him. "I'm jealous, I guess, more than sad. Or sad because I've never had a chance to build a friendship like what you have with T. I want that. I want someone I can count on, that I can joke around with, have inside jokes with."

His head tilts, stray dark locks sliding across his forehead nearly swiping his eyebrows. "Isn't that what you have with me?"

"That doesn't count." I sigh. Leaning forward, I rest my forehead on his chest. "We're, well, you know."

"That doesn't mean we're not friends too. Do you have fun when we're together?"

I tilt my face up to meet his searching eyes. "You know I do."

"Listen, just because we have a physical side to our relationship doesn't mean we don't have a friendship too. Look at Tank and Sarah. They're best friends and married. Ask either of them. I'm the third wheel in their friendship, and I'm okay with that. I'm happy for my friends that they have what they have. Hell, I'm jealous most days. To be married to your best friend, to laugh more than you fight and to have the one person you're committed to for life be the one person you can't wait to see every day. What a life, right?"

Well shit.

Trey Benson, one billion.

Randi Sawyer's heart, zero.

Before I do something stupid like seal my lips against his and wrap my legs around his waist, I sit on the stairs and lean back.

"That would be amazing." My sweat-damp leggings slide against the wooden stair as I shift on my sore ass. "Never thought it was possible, really. Didn't have a great example growing up, you know."

Palm against my hip, he slides me across the wide step, pressing me to the wall and making room for him to sit down. "Me either. My parents are miserable and barely say a handful of words to each other, and those are all in public to keep up appearances. It wasn't until I saw Tank and Sarah together that I realized it is possible."

Silence fills the stairwell as we both sit deep in thought.

"Honestly, I never thought I'd find someone I'd enjoy being around who also put up with my version of crazy," I admit. Elbows on the step at my back, I relax my neck, allowing my head to dangle between my shoulders. "Or be touchy with."

"Touchy?" Humor and confusion mix in Trey's voice.

"Yeah, until you—and I'm getting more comfortable with T too—I've always had this... I don't know, a timer that starts the second anyone touches me. After ten seconds or so, it goes off and the person's touch just irks me."

"I don't understand."

"I don't either. I've been thinking a lot about it since meeting you though, wondering why you're so different. Even when you were a raging ass, I wasn't revolted by your touch."

"Guess we're meant to be." His shoulder nudges mine, a broad smile spreading across his handsome face.

Fuck, I could get lost in those sparkling eyes, could stare at that face forever and never grow bored.

Hold up.

Forever?

Who said anything about forever here? I don't even love the guy. It's just fun being sneaky, and the orgasms are mind-blowing. But love? No.

Right?

"Have you thought about why you're that way?" he asks. "Did something happen as a kid?"

"I think...." Huh. For the first time ever, my internal conversation's answer matches the external one. Must be a full moon thing or something. "I never had it as a kid. Never witnessed it either, so I don't know how to accept it."

"But you do from me."

"I do. I crave it, actually. And not just the sexy stuff. Even the simplest touches make me feel... I don't know, whole."

Trey's eyes widen. His mouth opens, but not a single sound comes out.

Great, I said something wrong. Now he's thinking I'm trying to rush him down the aisle or something. *Fuck. Backtrack, Randi.*

"I mean, it's nothing. Whatever," I say in a rush. "I'm cool. Who needs to be whole anyway?"

Fuck. I'm a lost cause. Just put me down. Send me out to pasture.

There's no recovering from this.

"When I touch you," Trey whispers, his voice barely audible in the quiet stairwell, "it's all that matters. You're life, Mess." Looking away, he groans and drops his head. His fingers massage the back of his neck. "Hey, listen, I need to tell you something. Fuck, I hope you don't Bobbitt me—"

Pounding footsteps cut off his words. Before I can blink, he's standing and ready to intercept the racing agent.

"Where is she?" Grem huffs.

Trey steps aside, allowing Grem a visual of where I sit on the stairs. Hand raised, I wiggle my fingers in an awkward-as-hell wave. *Seriously, what is wrong with me?*

"It's Taeler."

Time stands still as my mind processes his words. Above me, the two men talk, their voices rising with each passing second.

Suddenly a cell phone is shoved in my face. I blink at the screen before glancing up to Trey.

"She's on the phone. Take it, Randi. We'll listen in through another line." Grabbing the phone from Grem's extended hand, Trey yanks me off the step with a single pull. The world trembles as my legs revolt against holding my weight. Not wasting any time, Trey hauls me down the hall while pressing the phone to my ear.

"Tae?" I question. "What the hell is going on?"

"I don't know." My pulse spikes, dread sinking deep in my gut at her rushed, labored breaths. Panic flashes through my veins, reviving my expended energy.

"Talk to me, Taeler. What's going on? Why did you call?"

"I think someone... someone is following me. I don't know. I don't know, Mom," she cries. Car horns honking and the sounds of a busy street pour through the phone. "Something felt off. It still feels off. Fuck, I don't know where to go."

"Where is your security team?" I demand.

"Not with me."

Fury mixes with the growing panic. "You snuck out!"

"I'm downtown. I don't want to go back to the dorms where they are. Mom, I'm scared."

Those two words cut my heart. Pain like I've never experienced grips my soul, making my steps falter. A heavy arm wraps around my shoulders, but I shrug it off. I need to think, not be comforted while my baby is in danger.

Fucking think, Randi.

Pacing the length of the hall outside of the security office, I mentally flip through the options we have.

"Tiny," I say on a hushed breath. "Tiny. Go see Tiny. Tell him who you are and that you need help. He'll take care of you until the agents can get there. Until I get there."

"The guy you used to talk about?"

I nod even though she can't see me. "That one." I wince at the stinging pain radiating from my thumbnail. The coppery tang of blood hits the tip of my tongue. "Hoodwink Tattoos on Sixth Street. He'll be there. He's always there." Turning on my heels, I race back down the hall and up the stairs, taking them two by two. Panting, side pinching with lack of oxygen, I shove open my bedroom door and run to the closet.

"Keep talking to me, Tae," I wheeze as I slide my suitcase out. "I'm here." As she rambles, her voice quivering, I toss several types of clothes into the suitcase and the prepacked toiletries I keep on hand.

"I'm here." The light ding of an overhead door offers some relief. She made it. He'll take care of her until those dumbass agents can get to her. I'm going to kill them.

On the other end of the phone, she asks someone for Tiny, telling them she needs his help. Soon a familiar high-pitched voice pierces through the phone. "He's here," Taeler says. A long pause of the two talking, then more shuffling. "Okay, he's taking me to the back, said I'm safe until you get here."

I slump back against the wall, tears of relief welling in my eyes. "Great, I'll be there as soon as I can. I'm sure your protection team is already on its way to meet you, but don't leave, you hear me? I shouldn't be more than a few hours. Call me if anything happens. Love you, Tae."

Dropping the phone to the floor, I press both hands to my damp face and breathe in deep.

"We already called to get Air Force Two ready,'" Trey murmurs. I nod into my still trembling fingers. "It'll be okay, Mess. You got her somewhere safe and her agents—"

"They're fired," I hiss. "Idiots."

Guilt slams into my chest, making me almost double over at the building pressure. Yeah, they screwed up letting her out of their sight, but the only reason she's even *in* danger is because of me. My one reason for breathing is terrified right now because of my stupid ambitions and idiotic idea. I knew the risks taking this role, knew the dangers being indebted to men like Kyle and Shawn would bring. But I can't process this.

Discreetly, I wipe my snotty nose as I lower my hands. The moment our eyes lock, he offers a stiff nod of acceptance.

"Let's go." My gaze falls to his extended hand. Eager for the instant comfort his touch offers, I slide my fingers through his. With a small tug, I'm pressed against his chest, chin tilted up to see his handsome face. "And don't worry. You can shower on the plane."

I huff an unexpected laugh. Leave it to this man to make me laugh when the walls are crushing in all around me.

Rolling my shoulders, I stand straight and take a deep breath.

"Okay, Trouble. Let's get to Austin."

10

RANDI

Even the gentle hum of the plane's engines does nothing to calm me from the anxiety-riddled high. Two whiskeys and I'm still wired, worried as hell and nowhere to go. The two more hours to Austin might as well be ten with all the pent-up nervous energy coursing through my veins.

The ball of one foot bounces against the plane's belly while the other swings furiously back and forth in the air. Uncrossing my legs, I switch sides and recross them with a huff of impatience.

"You're driving us all crazy, Mess," Trey says through a yawn which he tries to hide behind a tight fist. "She's safe, and the agents are with her now. We can't do anything further until we get there, so calm the hell down, would you?" His eyes flick to Grem. "Get her another drink and some food." Looking back to me, those brown eyes narrow in concentration. "Have you eaten today?"

I shrug and go back to my fidgeting.

"This is bullshit," T grunts. "The other agents are there with her. We don't need to go. There isn't enough time to gather intelligence, plan a route, plan an alternate route. We need more time."

"I'll just tell that to the fucker who's following Tae," I snap. "We'll be fine, T. But we can't wait."

"We're running on empty as it is. Plus only a few of beta team's guys got to the tarmac before we took off. This is a bad idea, Randi."

"Fine, you stay on the plane with your graphs and shit while I go get Taeler." I plaster a sickly sweet smile on my face. "How's that for a plan?"

"Don't get sassy with me, Randi," T growls. "You're my responsibility—"

"And Taeler is mine!"

"We can't just go running—"

"She's in danger, T. What else is there to do but go after her?"

"Her agents are with her now. She's no longer in trouble."

I snort in annoyance, then cross my arms over my chest and shoot him a death glare.

Trey stands with a groan, his knees popping as he shakes out his legs. "Listen, kids, break it up. Tensions are high, and we all need sleep. You need food," he says, pointing to me. Turning to face T, he bends forward and rummages through his duffel bag. "You need a Snickers." Still bent over, Trey pulls something from the bag and tosses it to T, who catches it midair. "You're not yourself when you're hungry."

I huff, knowing full well that won't end this fight.

Wait, what?

My jaw slacks as I watch T devour the king-size candy bar in less than three bites. Did he even chew, or is he some form of chipmunk where he stores food in his jaw for later? I tilt my head, brows furrowed, trying to figure out what kind of twilight zone I've stepped into.

After licking his fingers, T nods to Trey and relaxes back into his seat, shuffling papers around the desk while murmuring to the few team members sitting nearby.

My seat jostles, snapping my attention from the now-subdued T to Trey as he situates in the seat beside me once again.

"Works every time," Trey whispers in my ear.

Still staring, I give my head a small shake. "Seriously? How many of those do you have in there?" I ask, hitching my chin toward his still-open duffel.

"I keep the bag stocked. Don't worry, I have enough to keep you two from killing each other." Leaning across the aisle, he thrusts a hand into his bag and pulls out another candy bar. "Here. You need one too if you won't eat real people food."

Gripping the edge of the brown wrapper, I split it open, revealing the delicious chocolate, peanut, and caramel creation. Normally at this point my mouth would be watering and a huge chunk would already be missing from the end, but even this is unappetizing. But if eating a few bites will get Trey off my ass, then this is the lesser of two evils. There's no way I could choke down real food right now, no matter how good it is on this plane.

Taking a quick nibble, I wrap it back up and set it on the side table. Trey's lips dip, his eyes following the mostly untouched candy bar.

"Thanks," I say, dusting off my hands. "Just not really hungry right now. Too worried. The fact that tonight is even happening...." Reaching over, I press the Home button on my phone, making sure I haven't missed a call or text from Taeler.

A large, rough hand wraps around my own, pulling it back to my lap. "She's safe, Randi. We can't do anything until we land, and once we do, it's our job to keep you safe and get you to her. Relax, think about something else."

I blow out a hard breath. "Like what?"

"I don't know." His gaze flicks around the plane before landing on the uneaten candy bar. "What's your favorite candy? Obviously not Snickers."

A small smile pulls at my lips. "I do love a good candy bar. I'm not sure you'd call that one my favorite, but it was one I bought a lot when we had the money."

"Why did you buy it, then, if it's not your favorite?"

Leaning back in the seat, I allow my eyes to flutter closed. The memories shift through of those rare times Mom was coherent and had some spending money. As a kid, I didn't think about where the extra money came from, but now I do. Maybe the revolving door of men in and out of our trailer weren't just boyfriends. My stomach churns at the thought.

"It might be hard for someone like you to understand, but when you get stuff like that from Dollar General, you want to make your money stretches. I learned quickly which candy was the biggest bang for your buck, and a Snickers was just that. Protein, caramel, chocolate. So I typically chose that one, though it was less out of it being my favorite and more out of need."

I peel my lids open, cutting my gaze to Trey at the long pause to monitor his reaction.

"Well, that's just fucking sad, Mess."

I can't hold back my obnoxious snort. Trey's eyes crinkle at the edges, displaying the laugh lines I like so much. The other men pause their whispered conversation to stare at me.

"Sorry," I mutter, still smiling. "Yeah, I guess it is, Trouble. I guess it is."

Chewing on my thumbnail, I think over his original question. "I don't know if I have a favorite though. Maybe hard candy, but I like chocolate too. Especially holiday chocolate."

"Like chocolate bunnies and Santas?"

I nod. "I don't know why it always tastes better when it's meant for something special, not just an everyday treat. Like those Reese's pumpkins around Halloween. Yum. And if you waited until the day after the holiday, you got the stuff on sale, so double bonus." I pick up the barely touched Snickers and take a small bite. "But not Peeps. That shit is disgusting."

"Agreed. If I wanted a marshmallow, I'd buy a big fucking marshmallow, not one that tastes stale."

"Right!" I agree with excitement. "Maybe I'll misuse my new power and ban those from the US. I can do that, right?" My cheeks begin to ache from the wide smile that seems to keep growing.

"Pretty sure people would question it, but sure, you could try. I'd back you."

"Benson," T calls out, drawing our attention. "I need your thoughts on something."

Trey's dark hair falls forward, brushing across his forehead as he nods. With a quick glance to me, he offers a smile and small wave. "Duty calls, Mess. Eat that, and then try to get some sleep. It will be a long night."

Watching him shift across the aisle to where T and the others sit, I admire his ass in those dark gray slacks. Wonder if I could convince him to sneak back into the bedroom with me for a quickie. I mean, I did shower, so there's that, and as hell-bent as he is on me relaxing, that's a surefire way to calm me down. It could even be one of those mostly clothed fuck sessions where only the needed areas are exposed.

Like he can feel my heated stare—or hell, maybe hear my thoughts—Trey peeks over his shoulder. I tear my gaze from his round ass as a knowing smirk pulls at his lips, his tongue sliding out to swipe along the full lower one. With an exaggerated wink, he turns back to the guys, jumping right back into the conversation.

Wetness pools between my legs and a throb beats with its own pulse between my thighs. I squeeze them together, hoping to quell the building ache. Fuck, this guy turns me on with a single wink. How does that even happen? I'm in such trouble with Trouble. No doubt about it.

I press a button, lowering the back of the chair nearly flat, and curl on my side.

The second my mind quiets, the magnitude of what Trey just did for me sets in.

Somehow, with my pulse raging, my mind a mess, and tension near the snapping point, that man calmed me down, took my mind off Taeler being in danger, and got me to eat all in the process of ten minutes. The leather groans as I shift to my other side to face the men. Tucking my hands beneath my cheeks, I relax my lids and attempt to sleep like he suggested.

Sleep doesn't come, but the erotic fantasies I conjure are just as distracting.

"BENSON, you're in the back with Randi," T shouts as we all stomp down the plane's stairs. Though I'm not sure why he's telling them *again*. I overheard them go over the lineup and plan more than a few times the last thirty minutes of the flight. "You three in the Suburban behind us, and you two in front." No idea who he's talking to, but echoes of "Yes, sir" make it over the low whirling of the plane's slowing engines.

A gentle hand presses against my lower back, directing me toward the middle Suburban of the three. Glancing up, I grimace in embarrassment. "Listen, T. I'm sorry about being snippy earlier. I—"

He holds up his free hand, halting my apology. "Not needed. We were both tense. I allowed the stress to get the better of me, and I shouldn't have said what I said. Friends?"

"Friends," I say with a big-ass smile. At one time T was adamant that we weren't friends, just business. Seems I'm growing on the big guy. "You know, even though I'm already sore as hell and got my ass kicked more times than I can count, I really liked Sarah."

T's stone-cold features break protocol with an almost smile pulling at the corners of his lips. "She's one amazing woman. We'll work on getting you strong when we get back, then pick the self-defense lessons back up after. I don't like you not knowing how to defend yourself."

"I haven't been able to, ever. Why does it bother you now?"

He shakes his head, the last bits of the fading sunset reflecting off his dark bald head. "I saw just how terrible you really are earlier." Reaching forward, he palms the door handle and yanks it open. "I didn't realize you were that bad."

"Eh, I have you guys now," I say, giving his shoulder a quick comforting pat as I crawl into the SUV. "Now stop stalling. Let's go get Tae."

Once I'm situated inside the dark interior, the door slams shut. Three other doors jerk open, the outside light pouring inside. Glancing over to the seat beside me, I offer Trey a tight smile as he adjusts the massive gun strapped to his chest.

"Is that really needed?"

"Yes," all three agents respond in unison.

I roll my eyes in exasperation and lean against the door to stare out the window at the glorious fading Texas sunset. Soon we're speeding from the small private airport headed toward downtown Austin, where Taeler is currently hiding out. The earlier nerves and anxiety inundate my thoughts once again.

What if we don't get there in time? What if whoever was following her is still around? How can I do this to Taeler? How can I be so selfish?

The twenty-minute drive flies by, and soon we're weaving through the downtown streets making our way toward Hoodwink. I track every building, each street, mesmerized by all that's changed in the past two decades and the few things that are still exactly the same as when I left this town. Ugh, fuck I'm old. How has it been that long since I was in undergrad?

"The fuck?"

T's confused tone pulls my attention from the window to where he sits tense in the driver seat. Grem is turned in the front passenger seat, his focus not on me but out the back window. Shifting, I ease the seat belt harness a little to follow his laser stare. My brows draw close, eyes narrow, attempting to see what they see.

But there's nothing.

I shrug and twist back around. Must be T being paranoid about something. Seconds tick by and still Grem doesn't turn, continuing to stare out the back window.

"There," he shouts, startling me. "I see it. Black Escalade. It cut between us and the follow Suburban. Seems to be taking every turn we do."

"Fuck," T and Trey say together. In the rearview, their eyes meet.

"What's going on, guys?" I say, trying to temper the nervous high pitch of my voice. But no one responds. The cab of the Suburban settles with an eerily tense silence.

T bellowing my name is the only warning before he slams on the brakes. The car skids along the dark asphalt, the screeching of tires bouncing off the nearby buildings. I lurch forward and my neck snaps as the seat belt catches, preventing my face from colliding with the back of the driver seat. The back end fishtails, tossing me one way and then the other.

Wide-eyed, I search for Trey through the madness. Now unbuckled, braced between the front passenger seat and his own, he's aiming the large gun out the back window.

"Hold on," T shouts.

I throw both hands out, grasping for anything to steady myself for whatever's about to come. T slams on the gas, jerking me backward at the force of the sudden acceleration. I sway as we weave in and out of the slower cars.

"Did we lose them?" T barks.

"No," both Trey and Grem respond.

"We have another visitor too," Trey shouts. His gaze flicks from the back windshield to me. "It's okay, Mess. We'll be all right. Trust me."

My head snaps up and down in a jerky nod. I do trust him, but that doesn't calm my heart from thundering against my chest.

"Get us out of downtown," Trey shouts to Grem.

"Trying," he growls in return as he flips through the Nav. "Here." Slamming a finger onto the screen, a new route appears. "This takes us to the local FBI office."

"FBI?" Trey and T shout, sounding annoyed rather than happy.

"Those fuckers won't do anything," T growls as he jerks the wheel right to avoid slamming into a slow older Ford truck.

I shoot out an arm, bracing it on the center console to keep from toppling onto Trey.

"I knew this was a bad fucking idea."

Why the hell T's words make me sad, I have no fucking clue. Hot tears well along my lower lids, threatening to spill over. "I'm sorry," I choke out around the burning of unshed tears now clogging my throat.

"Fucking hell, Randi. You get your shit together and don't fucking cry on me, you hear me?" T yells. "I didn't mean it like that and you know it. I'm just... fuck!"

For once my body doesn't respond to his direct command. In fact, it does the opposite. Warm tears stream down my cheeks, dripping from my chin onto my gray long-sleeve T–shirt.

"I can't help it, you ass," I yell, swiping away the traitorous tears with the back of both hands. "It just happens. I'm telling Sarah you yelled at me." Okay, not the best comeback, but it's all I can come up with at the moment.

"Wow, she's pulling out the big guns," Trey says, his serious tone completely lacking his normal happy-go-lucky pitch.

"Everyone hold on," T warns.

The soft leather digs beneath my nails as I tighten my grip and slam my eyes shut, preparing for the worst.

The squealing of tires rips through my ears. Reflexively, my shoulders shoot up in an attempt to protect my hearing from the piercing sound. T shouts something, sending the other two into a flurry of movement. The seat belt snaps against my chest, knocking the breath from my lungs and whipping my head forward, nailing the headrest of the driver seat.

"Tank," Trey shouts. The unease in his tone shoots my panic into overdrive. Strong hands unclick my seat belt and shove me to the floorboard. "Careful, you ass."

"Stay down," Grem yells above my head. "Fuck, this is bad. What the hell is going on?"

Using their bickering as a distraction, I press both palms to the coarse black floor mats to slowly rise up. Peering over the armrest, I glance right and then left, making sure no one is paying attention before popping up to look out the front windshield.

"Who's that?" I ask before a hand slaps me on the back of the head.

"He said stay down." Pursing my lips, I glare at Trey. "Sorry, but for real. This is serious, Mess. We're blocked in."

"By who?"

"We don't know."

"Where are the other guys?"

"Detained as well," T grumbles.

"Someone's getting out," Grem whispers like the guy can hear us.

"What is he doing?" I whisper back. "Wait, why are we whispering?"

"You do realize we're in a bad spot right now, right, Mess?" It's hard to tell, but I swear a hint of humor laces Trey's words.

"I do, but I can't see what's going on from down here, so you have to give me a play-by-play."

"He doesn't have a gun," Grem whispers.

"Seriously, why are we whispering?"

"Doesn't mean he doesn't have one. Here comes another," T says, confusion in his tone.

"Back here too," Trey adds, his intense gaze locked out the back window. "What the fuck is going on?"

"We could always just ask," I toss out. Makes sense to me. At the weight of all three sets of eyes zeroed in on me, I shrug. "Just a suggestion. Maybe they want an autograph or something." The gravity of the situation settles in my chest, causing an awkward chuckle to vibrate out. "Sorry, I'm not laughing." Another giggle bubbles out on its own accord. "Shit. Sorry, guys. I know this isn't—" I say through another giggle. "Funny." Clearing my throat, I swallow back the full belly laughs that want to burst out, but I can't stop my shoulders from shaking. "I did this when those muggers cornered me and Trouble. It's like some kind of—"

"Who did what?" T roars. I swear the SUV rattles with the force.

"Way to go, Mess," Trey mutters under his breath.

"We're having a serious talk when we get through this, Randi," T admonishes from the driver seat. He sighs and runs a hand over his shiny head. "But you have a point. Whoever it is isn't demonstrating the desire for violence." Tilting my chin, I catch T and Trey having an unspoken conversation through the rearview. "I'll go."

"No, I'll go," Trey grunts. "You have Sarah. If shit gets bad out there—"

"No," I shout, reaching out lightning fast to grab his slacks. "You can't go out there. What about me? You have me."

Trey's honey eyes soften with a sad smile. "It's my job, Mess. I'd rather it be me than you or Tank." His long fingers wrestle with my own, uncurling them from the fine material of his suit pants. A quick squeeze is all I get before he shoves open the side door and climbs out.

"Trey," I yell.

Shoving against the floorboard, I scramble up, attempting to dive out of the door before it closes behind him. An arm snakes around my waist, halting my advance before tugging me back several inches. Eyes wide, I watch in absolute horror as the side door closes in almost slow motion, officially cutting me off from the man I might love.

11

TREY

The thump of the Suburban's door slamming shut echoes down the dark alley. Careful to keep my hands where they can see them, I lift the shoulder strap over my head and carefully lower the assault rifle to the asphalt. The stench of rotten food and cat piss infiltrates my nose, forcing me to hold a shallow breath until I'm upright. My sole focus never leaves the lead man standing in front of the other four, hands carefully clasped in front of his large body. The hairs on the back of my neck stand on end at the weight of the stares from the other men at my back.

This has to be the worst situation I've ever been in, yet I'm not afraid. The only safe spot around holds the one person I'm willing to lay my life on the line for. No gun, no cover, at the mercy of the unknown, and yet I'm okay. There's a settled feeling about doing what's needed to protect the one you love.

Love.

Oh hell.

What a fucking time to figure that shit out. Not that I'd tell her. I haven't even told her about Jessica yet. The lie of 'there hasn't been the right time' only holds for so long. At this point it's obvious that I'm scared to tell her. What if she leaves, walks away because dealing with the plan I've made is too much to deal with? The woman has enough on her plate for me to toss this new kink into her life, even if it was all for her.

Palms out, I continue forward. Sweat drips down my temples and slips down my spine. Even with the cooler spring weather, it's fucking hot in Texas. How these people live here I'll never know.

A faint waft of gunpowder sweeps down the alley, bringing forth a buried memory. My nostrils flare with each deep inhale. My pulse races as I fight to keep the memories from those few deployments in the Middle East at bay.

Randi needs me. This is the mantra I hold onto to keep from slipping into war mode. She needs me here, not disoriented in my own mind. It's not often that a trigger is strong enough to pull my focus, but when they do, typically only a bottle of Blanton's can chase them away and bring me back to reality.

With each deep breath, I urge my body and mind to relax. The last thing I want is to react too fast, putting us all in danger.

I pause several feet away from the hood of the SUV, directly in the bright beams of the headlights, putting me about ten feet from the huge dude staring me down. Even with the draping shadows, there's no mistaking his type of build. Large bulky shoulders, thicker middle, tall as hell. The tattoo up his neck is a pretty dead giveaway too.

Seconds tick by, but neither of us says a word. What's the protocol here? Do they speak first or me? Leave it to Randi to put us all in new, unchartered situations.

You know what, fuck it.

"You guys lost?" I ask.

No response. Not even a blink.

Definitely Russian. They're the only ones immune to my humor. Any type of humor, really. As I wait in silence, something clicks.

"Were you the ones following her daughter?" My tone is more menacing than I meant for it to be.

The man tilts his head. "Da. She was alone. No protection. Not safe."

"And you followed to protect her." Right, and I have a ten-inch dick. "I'm not inclined to believe you, friend."

"I say so, means so."

"That doesn't really clear things up for me."

He cocks his head. "We no threat to girl." This makes him laugh. "Why we want girl?"

"You just happened to be here."

"We been here. Told to watch, protect. We watch, we protect."

"Well, that's just plain ominous." The man doesn't crack a hint of a smile. Fucking hate Russians and their stoic asses.

Shouting pulls my focus from him to our SUV. Narrowing my eyes, I try to see through the windshield.

"Let's just say I believe you. What's with all this, then?"

"We have message." Without turning, he holds out a hand. I flinch, readying to grab my sidearm from the holster under my suit jacket as another man steps forward and slaps a large manila envelope in his hand.

"For her," he says, jutting it out toward me.

This could be a trap, but hell, now I'm curious. What's that saying, curiosity killed the cat? Good thing I'm no pussy, because I'm curious as fuck.

Keeping my eyes on him but my attention everywhere, I take the remaining few steps between us and snag the envelope from his extended hand. But his hold only tightens.

"These are bad men your vice president is mixed with. Watch her back. He like her."

The memory of the note from Munich slams to the forefront of my mind just as he releases his tight hold.

"Who is he?" I demand. Kyle? Shawn? At his silence, I take a calculated step closer. "Who. Is. He?"

The concentrated malice behind the man's cold eyes sends a chill down my spine. The silence from his side makes it clear he's not willing to divulge the curious identity of the 'he.'

Glancing at the envelope in my hand, I lift it in the air. "It's not laced with anthrax or anything, right?" I say as a joke.

This gets a laugh. "No. We want you dead, we"—he makes a hand motion like a gun—"boom, you're dead."

"You have a way with words, man."

A banshee scream comes from inside the SUV at my back, making all of us turn.

"Sorry about that. She's worried, I guess." I give a pointed look to his hand still in the makeshift gun. "That's probably what's pissing her off. But don't worry. I've seen her fight. You can take her if all hell breaks loose." I look back to the SUV. "In fact, I have some news to share with her that I know she's not going to like. You guys available by the hour?"

When I look back, the four men are already sliding into their black Escalade. Shooting a glance over my shoulder, I find the SUV blocking us in from the other end of the alley is gone.

"Well, I'll be damned." The smacking of the envelope against my thigh is covered up by the roaring of the Russians' SUV vibrating down the alley. Almost as soon as the whole strange encounter started, it's done.

Turning on my heels, I trek back to the Suburban, the strange conversation replaying as I try to process his meaning. After picking up the discarded gun, I inhale deep, readying for Randi's fury.

The diffusing quip I prepared vanishes from my thoughts the moment I open the SUV door. It takes half a second to take in the scene before I'm flying into action. Lunging into the SUV, I grip the back of Grem's suit jacket and shirt collar, yanking him off Randi and out of the SUV. After a quick once-over, making sure she's unharmed, I turn to the panting agent leaning against the brick wall.

"She was trying to get out, Trey," Grem says, lifting his hands from his knees in surrender. "I wasn't hurting her."

His words should make sense, but all I hear is the roaring in my ears. My chest tightens as I fight the urge to knock him on his ass for touching what's mine. My common sense and anger clash, fighting an internal battle in my mind as I stare down my teammate and friend.

Cold fingers grip my hot neck, their touch seeming to sizzle against my skin. A sharp tug and I'm pulled down, soft wet lips sealing over my own. My body instantly reacts to her presence. Relaxing my tight fists, I wrap both arms around her waist, hauling her closer. Jagged nails scrape along my scalp before gripping the ends with a soft tug. I pour the intensity of the night into our kiss.

"For fuck's sake, you two."

Tank's rough voice breaks through the fog that settled over my brain, taking reality with it. With one last soft kiss to her forehead, I relax my hold but she doesn't step back, doesn't pull away. Palm to the back of her head, I tuck her face to my chest and rest my chin on the crown of her head.

I meet Tank's dark eyes, expecting to find anger but instead seeing understanding. A silent conversation passes between us until the screeching of tires at the end of the alley breaks our stare.

"It's the other guys," Tank mutters while rubbing his large palm over his head. "I can't stop this, can I?" I shake my head, causing him to expel a heavy breath. "Just keep it private, Benson. And don't let it affect your job." He points to me before swinging his finger to Grem. "He wasn't hurting her, simply protecting her idiot ass—"

"Hey," Randi grumbles against my blue dress shirt.

I smirk as I stroke two fingers up and down her spine.

"She wanted to jump out and save you."

Leaning back, I peel her face from my chest and arch both brows. "Save me, huh? With your mad fighting skills?"

A small chuckle vibrates in my chest as she purses her lips and avoids eye contact.

"What did they want?" Champ's voice carries down the alley from where he stands beside the other SUV.

Immediately I force my hands to drop as I put distance between me and Randi.

"Russians," I say, my eyes locked on hers.

"No shit," Tank huffs. "Tell us what we don't know, Playboy."

"I really need that story," Randi butts in. She wraps her arms around herself, rubbing her hands up and down her biceps.

I shrug out of my jacket and drape it over her shoulders. My chest swells with pride when she dips her nose to the lapel and takes a deep sniff with a soft sigh.

"They had something for her," I say, nodding to Randi while bending to retrieve the envelope off the ground where it fell in my commotion with Grem. "Here." I slice it through the air to Tank, who catches it easily. "They seemed...." I pause to crack my neck. Fuck, I'm tense. Even though my banter was relaxed with those guys, every muscle and nerve ending was on high alert the entire conversation. "I don't know the word for it, but I don't think they want to hurt Randi. It's more like they want a conversation or something. If you can believe what they said, they're the good guys. He said they were only following Taeler because she was left unprotected."

"Then why'd they leave?" she asks.

"Not sure. They handed me that envelope and bounced."

"Wonder what's in it," she mutters more to herself than to us as she steps toward Tank, eyes on the envelope. He lifts it high above his head when she tries to reach for it. "Hey, that's mine."

"Not until we run some scans on it. Ever heard of anthrax?" he chastises.

"They said no anthrax. If they wanted us dead, they'd shoot us."

Randi's dark brows rise up her forehead. "See, no anthrax. Give it to me."

"I'm not betting your life on the word of some Russian who blocked us into a dark alley just to talk."

"You really need to see the good in people, T."

"I will when they give me something to go on. Now if you don't mind, let's get back in the SUV where it's safe and get you to your daughter."

"Ah fuck," she exclaims. "Taeler. I... with all this and Trouble in trouble, it... come on, let's go. We can figure out the Russian's cryptic meaning later."

Storming to the SUV, she yanks the door open and climbs in, giving me a nice view of her jean-clad ass.

"Benson, a word." Rolling my eyes, I turn to face Tank. "Don't make me regret this, you asshole. Sarah's right, I can't stop you two, but I can ask—no, order you to keep it between us. She doesn't need the extra negative publicity if it gets out, and from what you told me the other night, neither do you." His focus shifts from me to over my shoulder. "She know about the deal you made?"

Chunks of hair slide across my forehead as I shake my head. "No, and she won't. I'll tell her about my deal with Jessica but nothing else."

Tank's large mitt of a hand slaps my shoulder and tightens. I fight a cringe at the pressure to my joints. "Hope you know what you're doing, man. This could get ugly quick if things go south between you two."

Glancing over my shoulder, I attempt to stare through the dark tint to the one woman I've ever needed.

"It'll work out, Tank. Stop your fussing."

With a huff, he gives my shoulder a shove, making me teeter slightly off balance, and strides to the driver side.

"It has to," I mutter to myself.

12

RANDI

Tiny's ostentatious squeal of laughter has every set of eyes in the restaurant trained on our table—again. He's not the only one drawing the attention though. Oh no, I've been responsible for some of the looks too. And not happy ones either. Each time I've made eye contact, only scowls with an occasional middle finger added in for emphasis have been shot back.

Strange. I'm in Texas, my home state, and yet everyone seems really pissed at my presence. We ended up here, much to T's displeasure, after the hour-long debrief and cry session at Hoodwink—the debrief between the guys and Taeler's agents, the crying all me and Tae. The shop hasn't changed a bit. The nostalgia of walking into my old employment, the sound of tattoo guns and smell of antiseptic, added to my rolling emotions.

"I'm just glad I got to see you again, Rand." Returning my focus back to the conversation, I smile at Tiny. "Never thought it'd happen."

"Yeah, well, me either." My gaze shifts around the restaurant. "It's strange being back in Austin. When I graduated, I didn't think I would ever be back. Nothing pulling me here, you know."

"Ouch." Tiny clasps both hands over his massive chest with a fake cringe. "You saying I'm nothing, doll?"

I shove his shoulder, which does nothing but hurt my palm. "You know what I mean. You knew I was just passing through."

"How did you end up working for him again, Mom?" Taeler interjects.

I shrug and take another bite of the mouthwatering brisket. My eyes flutter closed as the flavors explode across my tongue. Texans have perfected the BBQ-making technique. At least this place has.

I'd like to say the flavors and sounds bring back fond memories, but they don't. As good as the food in this place is, at the time it was way beyond my measly food budget. I could never justify spending a day's worth of allotted food money on a single meal.

The rough paper towel scrapes across my sauce-covered lips as I attempt to look less like a slob while I inhale the food in front of me.

"I needed a job so I could eat," I say with a shrug. "The student loans and scholarships only went so far. I applied to a bunch of different places but never heard back. One day I was walking past the shop, noticed his Help Wanted sign, and walked in."

"I thought she was fucking with me," Tiny breaks in. "This twig of a woman, arms loaded down with books, cracked glasses—"

"You make me sound pathetic," I grumble, shoving around the bits of creamed corn left on my plate with the plastic fork.

"You were. We made you badass." I incline my head, accepting his statement. "I took a chance on the poor girl, and it worked out for the both of us. Hardest worker I've ever had to date. On her breaks, you'd always find her with a cigarette in one hand and flash cards in the other."

I snort and push the near-empty tray across the rough wood table. "You and the other guys corrupted me in the best way." I don't stop my smirk as I glance over to Trey, who's scanning the restaurant with his head tilted toward the table, listening to every word. "Someday I'd like to come in and actually pay to have more work done."

"You for real?" he asks, uncertainty lingering in his questioning tone.

"Yeah. Why do you sound surprised?"

His wide shoulders rise and fall, and I swear the bench bounces with the movement. Tiny might be his name, but he's the exact opposite. The man makes T look small with his tall frame and bulk. Sure, he's not as in shape as my guys, but the man could still own any person in the restaurant if they so much as looked at him the wrong way. I'd like to call him a gentle giant, but he isn't unless you're in his inner circle. Which, thankfully, I weaseled my way into somehow.

"I watched you during the campaign and seen pictures since. You never show your tats. Figured you were ashamed of them or something now that you're big-time."

"First of all," I interject, "I'm not big-time. I'm just as small-time as I ever was, believe me. Second, it wasn't my choice to keep your pretty art covered. The campaign manager thought it would better if I kept them covered since it would already be an uphill battle getting the shitheads in DC to accept me."

"Did it help?"

"No," I grumble. Reaching out, I tug on Taeler's long blonde ponytail to draw her attention back to the conversation. Her eyes stay glued to something in the corner of the restaurant. Huh. Leaning forward, I look around Tiny and follow her line of sight.

My eyes narrow when I find what's snagged her undivided attention.

"Taeler Lynn, don't even think about it." I turn her face to meet mine, her eyes reluctantly following. "No."

"But he's cute," she practically whines as she bounces on the bench.

"No." One hundred percent no.

"Why?"

"You can't find one of my agents hot."

An interrupting cough sounds from somewhere close. I roll my eyes and wave Trey off.

"That doesn't make any sense. I'm just looking." Her eyes slide back to the corner where Grem stands, hands casually clasped. "How old is he anyway?"

"I don't—"

"Twenty-seven."

Eyes narrowed, I turn to glare at a smiling Trey. "Stay out of this, Trouble." For several seconds, I hold his stare in a standoff. "She doesn't need that kind of distraction."

"Oh, like you do?"

Shifting along the bench, I turn my annoyed glare to Tiny. "And what exactly does that mean?"

He laughs, smacking his palm on top of the table. The trays rattle and the roll of paper towels tumbles to the ground.

"Seriously, you think I'm blind or something? You two," he says, pointing between me and Trey. "There's something going on there."

"Tiny," I growl in warning.

"Mom! Wait, are you dating them both?"

"Shh," I hiss as I glance around, making sure no one's listening to our conversation. "No, I'm not dating them both."

"So you are dating one of them."

"Fuck me." Leaning forward, I rest my face in my palms. "Why are you ganging up on me?"

"Because it's fun," Taeler says on a laugh. "He's cute though."

Peering between my fingers, I catch her blatantly checking Trey out. "Taeler, watch it."

"Real cute." Leaning across the table, stretching out as long as she can, Taeler reaches out a hand to Trey. "Hi, I don't think we officially met earlier. I'm Taeler." With a tilt of her head, she nods to me. "Her amazing daughter who stupidly picked the wrong night to sneak out and get tailed by some random person. So tell me, are you dating my mom?"

With a smirk stretching his kissable lips, Trey grasps Taeler's hand and gives it a quick shake before resuming his 'high alert' stance.

"Nice to meet you, Taeler. I've heard a lot about you, all good things." My breath catches when his twinkling honey brown eyes meet mine. "And no, I'm not dating your mom, but I'd like to one day."

"Why not now?"

My gaze volleys between the two, a held breath burning in my lungs as I wait for his answer.

"Can't. Not yet at least." Something smolders beneath his gaze, a promise of some kind, before turning back to Taeler. "When I'm not responsible for keeping her safe, then I'll be able to properly date her."

"So you're not properly dating now?" Taeler says with a smirk of her own. "Does that mean you're just friends with benefits?"

"Okay." I hold up both hands in surrender. "We're done with this conversation."

"Why? It was just getting good, Mom."

"I am not talking about this with you."

"You mean sex?"

"Tiny!" I shout and immediately slouch lower to avoid the pointed glares from the other patrons. "Stop egging them on." Gripping my light windbreaker, I tug the edges closed. "Okay, I have to ask, what's with the glares people are giving me?" Part of me actually wants to know while the other part just wants to break up this slightly embarrassing and very personal conversation.

"Um, because they hate you," Taeler says with a huff. "Come on, Mom. Don't tell me you're so busy you're not watching the polls anymore."

"Umm," I draw out, trying to stall. Shit, when was the last time I checked our approval rating?

Taeler rolls her beautiful blue eyes. "Well, to catch you up, everyone blames you for living paycheck to paycheck."

"What? How? I'm doing what I can," I defend. My pulse races as I scan the restaurant again, finding even more glares focused my way. "I'm trying to stop it."

"How?"

"I'm trying to whip votes in the House and the Senate—"

"Mom, what the hell are you talking about?"

"The voting bill. What the hell are you talking about?"

"The stupid high gas prices." Looking left and then right, Taeler leans forward, pressing her elbows to the table. "Gas prices have jumped at least two dollars a gallon since you took office. Everyone's blaming you and Kyle. Something about tightening EPA standards on drilling. I don't know much. Do you really not know anything?"

My mouth gapes, but no words come out.

"I don't understand." Shaking my head, I lean back, resting against the metal wall. "I haven't been briefed on any of this."

"Haven't you noticed? Watched the news at all?" she questions.

Looking to Trey, I search his face for answers. "I don't drive anymore, so no, I haven't been to a gas station in forever. And honestly, I used to watch it every morning but lately I've been too busy stopping the ludicrous bill and focusing on other projects.

"Well, you need to look into it and figure that shit out." Tiny's hand presses on top of my own. "Rumors are it's only going to keep going up as the supply and demand continues to unbalance."

"What the hell is going on? Why would people think we are directly responsible for that?" I whisper to myself.

"That's what we want to know," Taeler says. Her phone chirps, drawing her worried gaze to the blinking screen. Immediately her eyes widen before flicking up to me. "Um, so Dad's here."

"What!" I shout and shoot off the bench. Only I don't have enough clearance to stand, and with Tiny's weight keeping the bench where it is, I bounce right back to the seat. "Why the fuck is he here?"

"I called him to let him know what was going on," she whines. "He must have gotten in the truck and headed south."

"What's going on?" T demands, palms on the table and leaning in close like we're about to discuss a top-secret mission.

"Taeler's dad, my ex, is here."

"Is he dangerous?" T asks, brows raised.

"No," I grumble, crossing both arms over my chest in a full-on pout. "Can this night get any worse?"

"I need fucking snacks for this shit show," Tiny says as he stands from the table. "Do not start the show before I get back. You want some banana pudding?"

Nodding, I flip him the bird. "I thought you were on my side."

"Doll, I am, but this is the most entertainment I've had in years. Don't blame me for enjoying it."

I watch as he ambles through the crowd, bumping against several guest's shoulders with his thick hips as he makes his way down the tight rows of benches and chairs.

"Should I be worried?" I startle at Trey's lips against my ear.

"No," I whisper. "It's... we're... it's history."

"Not very convincing, Mess."

Taeler pushes from the table and hooks a thumb toward the door. "You two talk, I'll go get dad. He's headed to the restaurant from Hoodwink."

"I'll go with you—"

A heavy hand shoves down on my shoulder, keeping me in my seat.

"Not a chance, Mess." Trey raises a hand and motions for Grem. "Go outside with Taeler. Make sure she's safe while she waits on her dad."

A sly smile spreads across Taeler's lips. "I like you already. Thanks, Trey."

The chatter of the restaurant filters in, providing the perfect background noise to keep our conversation private.

"He's a good guy," Trey says above me, his eyes tracking the entire restaurant. "Also he knows if anything happens, you'll have his balls for it, so she's safe on all fronts."

Not wanting to see another death glare, I keep my eyes on the rough wooden table. "What's with the gas price thing?"

His shoulders rise and fall. "Not sure. I've noticed it too but never thought you had something to do with it. No clue why they do, though maybe that's because I know what you do day in and day out. But it's not good. These people are not happy."

"Awesome. Just one more thing for me to fucking deal with." Pulling out my phone, I quickly type a reminder note to look into it once we're back in DC. "The bill, Russians, Taeler's hormones, and now rising gas prices I have no damn idea what to do about. Good thing none of those are major," I say with an incredulous laugh. "Fuck."

"You need more help, Mess. You need a team bigger than you, Jessica, and your admin."

"I know, but I don't have anyone else I can trust." Rolling my shoulders, I shake out my tight fingers. "It's fine. I can handle it."

"Mess—"

"It's fine. I have dozens of people working on other projects for me, so I do have help. I need to handle these things personally though. Especially the Taeler thing." Craning my neck, I try to see to the front door. "Think they're okay out there?"

"Pretty sure he already has her pants off," T deadpans.

I try to bolt off the bench, but two hands grip my shoulders, shoving me back into the seat with more force than necessary. "I'm kidding, Randi. They're fine. Grem just reported in. Your ex just pulled into the parking lot."

"I need a drink," I grumble.

"Not a great idea," T says, glancing around the small eating area. "In fact, can we do this reunion somewhere else?"

"Or avoid it altogether?" I say with a wince. "Ben's a great guy, it's just... awkward now. I haven't seen him since I left for the campaign trail, and that was what, two years ago?"

"Someone ask the manager if we can use his private office for a while." Relaxing his wrist from where it was positioned against his mouth, T purses his lips and looks around the restaurant. "Smells damn good in here."

I tug on his suit jacket, snagging his attention. "Once Ben's here and we're one big cozy family in the back office of this place, you and the guys rotate eating." His brows furrow as he shakes his head. "T, it'll be fine. Seriously, what else could happen tonight? China stopping by for a coffee?" I try to add as much humor into my voice as I can, but fuck, I'm exhausted.

"I'll think about it," he says with a sigh. "Only because as punishment for his going behind my back, Benson here will be stationed outside the door the entire time. I trust him to keep you safe."

"Me too." I smile up to the frowning Trey. "Sorry about earlier. Kind of forgot that we're not supposed to be a thing."

"It's fine," he grumbles. "But seriously, man, no BBQ? That's cruel on so many levels. Why you gotta be so mean?"

"Did you just quote a Taylor Swift song?"

"What?" he says, feigning shock. "I had no idea it was a song."

"Riiiight." I playfully shove his hip.

The feeling of being watched draws my gaze back to the front door. Ben's piercing blue eyes meet mine. Not sure what I expected, but the nothingness as our eyes remain connected wasn't one of them. I track his every move as he weaves through the crowded restaurant, Taeler several steps behind.

"Hey, Rand," Ben says, pausing on the other side of the table, both hands shoved deep in the back pockets of his Wranglers.

My lips part, ready to respond, when T presses a large palm between my shoulder blades, stopping me.

"The manager's office is clear. Let's get you off the floor."

"What?" All eyes turn to Tiny, whose tray is stacked with small Styrofoam cups. "I wanted to watch," he whines as he drops the tray to the table with a huff.

No one says another word as we shuffle through the kitchen's swinging door, down the dark hall, and then squish into the small office. Taeler asks Ben about his drive down, but I don't listen for his response as I turn to the still-open door.

"I'll be right outside," Trey says, looking at Ben instead of me. "You good?"

"Yeah." I glance over my shoulder. "This won't take long."

His lips purse, the edges turning white.

"It's fine. He won't hurt me."

"That's not what I'm worried about," he mutters under his breath as he closes the door. "Yell if you need me." With an exhausted sigh, I turn toward the middle of the office. "And Randi." Chin on my shoulder, I glance back to Trey with both brows raised. "You're mine. Don't forget it."

Wetness pools between my thighs as a quiver vibrates low in my gut at the intensity of his words and the blazing heat behind his eyes. Gawking at him, I hold a tight breath as the door closes, his face disappearing behind the thick door. I clear my throat, trying to regain some of the composure his claiming words stole. The edge of the desk presses into my backside as I sit facing Ben and Taeler. Once, twice, and a third time, I cross my legs and then cross them the other way, unable to get comfortable.

Fucking hell, why does his dominant possessiveness turn me on so much? If he were in here with me instead of these two, I'd win a gold medal for the fastest undressing ever.

I clear my throat and attempt to focus on their conversation, but the low throb between my thighs keeps drawing my thoughts back to Trey. I hope he's out there having to guard the door with a raging boner so he's as uncomfortable as me.

"What do you think, Rand?"

"Hmm?" I flick my eyes to the closed door. "Did you say something?"

"What's wrong with you? You're all fidgety."

Taeler bursts out laughing. I narrow my eyes at her and shake my head.

"Dad, seriously?" Taeler says, either not getting my 'shut it' hint or just plain not caring. "Have you never seen a woman turned on before? That's just sad."

"Taeler Lynn!" I yell and jump off the desk, ready to smack my hand over her lips to keep her quiet.

"Huh?"

I roll my eyes at Ben's typical guy response. "For fuck's sake."

"She and that agent guy. There's something—"

"Out," I screech as I throw a pointed finger toward the door like a spear. "Now."

"Fine by me," she says with a wink as she shoulders past me. "I'll just wait right outside with Chad."

"Chad? Who the fuck is Chad?" I blurt.

"The cute agent." She cocks her head to the side, her blonde hair swishing over her shoulder. "What do you call him?"

"Gremlin," I grumble. Turning to Ben, I give him my best pleading eyes. "Do something."

"So women fidget when they're turned on?"

"Oh, fucking hell. I seriously need a drink for this shit show. First the Russians and now my ex asking about the complexities of a woman's hormones."

"A simple yes or no would be just fine," Ben huffs, crossing his arms over his chest. The pearl snaps of his shirt pull at the movement, the sleeves tightening over his thick biceps. Before my world flipped upside down, that simple move was sexy, but now it's just a move.

"Everything okay in here?" Trey's voice cuts through the hot office air and the rising tension.

Sealing my eyes shut, I tilt my face to the ceiling. What gods did I piss off this time for this to be my day? First I got my ass beat, then my heart stopped when my daughter called scared, and now here I am with the man I'm sleeping with and my baby daddy all in one tiny office.

Hell, I don't need a drink, I need a fucking bottle.

"Taeler, leave. Trey, don't let her out of your sight. Ben, sit your ass down. We need to talk."

I swear a cricket chirps in the corner, which is concerning on so many levels.

Behind me, the door quietly clicks closed. Peeling my eyes back open, I take a deep breath.

"So you and that guy, huh?" Ben says, finally ending the awkward silence.

I nod and shrug, then shake my head. "Maybe. I don't know. I kind of have a lot going on right now."

With a chuckle, he falls into the rolling chair and leans back. "You look good, Rand."

The earlier anger drains at the sincerity in his voice.

"Thanks, Ben. I'm sorry I dragged Tae into this mess. I'll figure out a way to keep her safe."

Peering up through my lashes, I meet his stare.

"I know you will, Rand. You always find a way to make it work." The chair squeaks under his shifting weight as he leans back. "I was scared shitless when she called."

The desk gives a slight wobble as I hop up and lean back against the wall. "Same. At least you were in the same state. I felt so helpless. There was nothing I could do but get on a plane." The backs of my black wedge booties tap the thin metal file cabinet under the desk as I swing my legs back and forth. "Thanks for coming down though. It makes it easier knowing you're just a few hours away."

"She is my daughter too, Rand," he says, his tone defensive.

I want to retort with all the times he hasn't acted like the standup father he is now but swallow the words down. We've had that fight before, many times; no need to beat a dead horse.

"You know," he says, "I kind of thought we'd figure it out one day."

A corner of my lips tugs upward. "Yeah, before all this, me too. But I don't think either of us would've been happy."

"No, you wouldn't have." It takes a few seconds for his words to sink in, but by the time they do, he's at the door, hand on the knob. "Keep me updated on the security you're gonna get for Tae. If those assclown agents let her sneak out once, it'll happen again." A blast of cool air sweeps into the overheated office as he pulls open the door. "And Randi?" I look over at him. "Should I try?"

"Try what?" Okay, did I miss a conversation or something?

"Try to win you back. Make this, us, work."

My lips pop open, each breath shallow and quick as I try to come up with an answer. I run my tongue across my lower lip, stalling.

"Just think about it. Bye, Rand."

The door shuts behind him, leaving me alone in the office. At first it's just a tickle, then a quiet giggle. Soon tears are rolling down my cheeks and my arms are crossed over my flexing stomach as I laugh harder than I have in ages.

Let this day go down in the history books as the day Randi Sawyer finally lost her ever-loving shit.

THE CLAMMY SKIN of my palms sticks as I rub them together, attempting to bring some heat back into my chilled fingers. It's a beautiful night here in Austin but the nerves flowing through my system have left me chilled to the bone which is why I asked T to turn the heat on while we wait in the Suburban outside Taeler's dorms.

"You sure they'll be okay?" I ask for the third time since we parked our convoy ten minutes ago. "I don't trust these guys at all. They let her get out once; who knows who can get in? I get I can't fire them right now or that would leave her completely unprotected, but maybe you should go up too, T. You know to check on things, and it's been a while. What are they doing up there anyway?"

"They're fine, promise." For emphasis, he taps his ear. "I can hear what's going on, remember?"

Nibbling on my pinkie nail, I turn to look out the dark window once again, waiting for the rest of our team to emerge and let me know Taeler's room is clear. I didn't trust those other fools enough to do it alone.

Comfortable quiet falls, allowing me to retreat into my own mind and zone out completely until Trey shatters the calm with a statement I wasn't expecting.

"I heard him when he left."

Well, hell. I was so wrapped up in my own mess that I didn't even think about Trey and what he thought of it all. Not that it matters, but it kind of does. This is why I shouldn't get involved with him; it makes everything more complicated than it already is. Today was terrible, but adding in the terror of watching Trey confront the Russians alone, plus having to manage his emotions in response to Ben's presence, I can see why T thought our relationship was a bad idea.

"Can we talk about it later?" I ask. "I don't have the energy for that conversation right now."

"Fine."

My stomach drops at the annoyance in his voice, but movement down the sidewalk distracts me. T and Trey file out of the SUV, the latter slamming the door a little harder than necessary. Leaning back against the soft black leather, I roll my head against the headrest to watch the group of men deep in discussion. Their figures blur as my eyelids grow heavier with each blink.

A sharp blast of cool spring air snaps me from the light sleep I slid into. Peeling my eyes open, I blink back the dryness and rub at the corners.

"We have a problem," Grem says, leaning against the door to keep it propped open. T and Trey circle around him, blocking anyone from seeing inside the SUV.

Of course we do, because this wouldn't be my mess of a life if we didn't.

13

RANDI

I'm going to kill him. Punch him in the nuts, cut off his dick, and carve out his heart with a rusty spoon. I had the whole flight back from Austin and the morning to plan his slow death, and I intend to act on it as soon as the bastard gets out of his damn meeting.

Why would he do this?

Is it connected to the person who was following Tae who the random Russian said they took care of?

Why was there a random Russian even in Austin watching Taeler?

Pacing up and down the hall in front of the Oval Office I clench and unclench my fists as the unanswered questions keep coming. One of Kyle's secret service agents eyes me as I furiously stomp, my black heels nearly piercing through the ornate carpet. Whirling around for the hundredth time, my loose dark hair swirling in a circle around me, I march back to the office door and raise my hand to knock, but a quick hand juts out, wrapping around my wrist.

"No," the agent snarls. "I told you that ten minutes ago when you tried the same thing."

"Let her go, Kent," Trey says behind me, his voice deep and menacing.

Reluctantly, the warm palm slides from my wrist. My knuckles arch back, readying to knock, when movement on the other side causes me to pause and take a step back just before it swings open. Four men file out of the Oval Office, three whom I don't recognize and one who I most certainly do.

"Trailer," Shawn says with his Joker-like smile plastered across his plastic face. "How was Austin? *Sounded* like it was an interesting trip."

My heart stutters. I suck in a deep inhale.

Somehow his smile grows more sinister. A fear-laced chill creeps down my spine.

"I look forward to continuing this game, Trailer. All's fair in this power war you started between us." Leaning forward, he whispers, "I'll get what's mine in the end, but the road to your demise is proving to be quite a fun ride. Your move, Trailer."

Bile rises in my throat. I clamp a hand around my neck in an attempt to keep last night's BBQ down. I don't say another word as Shawn saunters down the hall, glancing back once with a wink before disappearing around a corner. The fingers around my neck twitch, and my knees buckle. Palm out, I smack the wall to stay upright and bend forward to stop the room from spinning.

"Ma'am," Trey says at my side. Fuck, when did he get here? "You need to sit down?"

I shake my head, my dark hair falling forward in a makeshift curtain. Licking my lips, I force myself to stand tall and take a deep breath.

"Did you hear him?" I ask as I glance back down the hall, fully expecting Shawn to be there enjoying my mini breakdown.

"You've got five minutes," Kyle bites out, clearly in a foul mood.

He wraps his fingers around my bicep and tugs me into the room. Before Trey can get a word out, the door slams closed.

"Talk." Releasing me, he marches over to the side bar and pours two fingers of a dark liquid into a crystal highball glass.

My earlier fury smothered by Shawn's comments, I mindlessly shuffle to the couch and fall onto the soft cushions. Staring unseeing at the far wall, I shake my head in disbelief. "It wasn't you."

"Four minutes, Walmart," Kyle barks from behind me.

"We found bugs, listening devices in my daughter's dorm, and I thought... I just knew it was you."

In my periphery, he folds into a chair and messes with his suit jacket. "Why in the hell would I want to spy on your daughter? What would I gain from it?"

"I couldn't think of anyone else until... just now Shawn said something that makes me think it was him. But you're right. What would he have to gain from it?"

"Probably was him." My gaze slides from the wall to Kyle. Head back, his eyes are closed, stress lines marking his normally flawless face. "And as to why, you never know with Shawn. Maybe he did it to mess with your mind or to learn information that he could hold over your head one day."

I shudder at the thought. Again I take in his unusual rumpled appearance. "You look terrible," I say before I can stop myself.

"He has it out for you, Walmart." Ice blue eyes meet mine. "Don't think you can ask me to control him. No one can. I tried to pull him back, but it seems he chose not to listen." A high-pitched squeak sounds through the office as he tightens his grip around the slick crystal. "Not the first time or the last. Just watch your fucking back."

Why does it seem like everyone is spouting that warning at me lately?

"Aw, you care about me." My voice is fake and cheery. Suspicion creeps up my neck, making the tiny hairs stand on end. "Wait, why are you being nice to me?"

"Two minutes Walmart."

"What do I do?"

"Resign and let him take his rightful spot."

"Not going to happen," I grit out and slam a fist into the cushion. "Not that it'll matter if I can't get the votes to stop the bill."

"Good to know even white trash sticks to the losing end of a bargain."

"Fuck you."

"No thanks, I'm too tired." With his free hand, he massages the bridge of his nose. "Fuck, I'm tired, and it's only been five months."

"Yeah." I relax back into the couch. "No one gets it. They try, but it's hard to explain when the weight of the country falls on your shoulders. Did you know it would be this consuming?"

"No fucking clue." A shimmer of humor laces his words but in a sad way.

"Same." Behind my closed lids, my eyes flick back and forth, my mind working overtime. "Hey, so last night in Austin, someone mentioned gas prices are skyrocketing and they think we're to blame. Something about the EPA tightening regulations?" Peeking an eye open, I catch Kyle's intense stare zeroed on me. I swallow against a dry throat and push up, sitting ramrod straight. "You know anything about that?"

"Time's up, Walmart." Lips against the rim, he tips the crystal back, taking down the remaining liquor in one swallow. "Don't worry about the gas issue. I'm already on it. Also, cancel your trip to the OPEC summit next week. Too many protests and chatter about potential attacks."

"Fine by me." Standing, I retuck my crisp white dress shirt into my slim black suit pants. "More time for me to win the House before the vote."

"Yeah, good luck with that. Oh, and Randi?" My steps falter as I turn to gawk. *What the hell is he up to using my actual name?* "I'm not kidding with Shawn. He's a dangerous motherfucker."

"Then why are you two friends?"

A sad kind of resigned smile pulls at his lips. New wrinkles form along the edges of his eyes, making him seem even older than he did moments ago.

"Because I'm dangerous too."

A SERIES OF ANNOYING, high-pitched beeps resounds in the small gym as the treadmill gears up to torture me for the next fifteen minutes. With a small jolt, the belt beneath my feet slowly rolls, dragging me backward with it.

"This is where you pick up your feet and don't let the machine win," Trey says with a chuckle. "Damn, Mess. You're a mess."

"Don't I know it." Pressing the up arrow button, I increase the speed to just above a turtle pace. "Should we monitor my heart rate or something while I'm doing this? Maybe have one of those cardiac zappers around just in case I collapse?"

"Wow." Reaching across the complex dash, he presses the button a few more times, increasing my speed. "You're not going to die. But if you want to pass out, I'd gladly give you mouth-to-mouth." He offers me an exaggerated wink and climbs onto his own treadmill. A million sharp beeps later and he's practically sprinting, the heavy thuds of his steps shaking the machine.

"I'm sure you would." With my own smirk tugging at the corners of my lips, I shake my head and press the speed button one more time, setting me at a brisk walk. "Maybe this is what I need after the meeting with Kyle yesterday and all that Shawn mess."

"Speaking of—"

"Speaking of Austin, have we learned anything more about the message the Russians left in that envelope?"

"Nope, only the cryptic message of wanting to meet."

Chewing on my middle finger's nail, I mull over his words. It was cryptic, but not. After several tests, they cleared the envelope and the contents late yesterday, allowing us to finally see what was inside. A single white sheet of paper with a date, time, and coordinates typed across the top. The paper, ink, and envelope are so ordinary there's no way to trace them. The coordinates are for a swanky hotel in Chile where the OPEC summit is to be held, and the dates coordinate to the summit as well.

But why is the main question. Then also *who.*

"If you're not breathing hard," Trey puffs, "then kick that speed up. We need your heart rate up for at least fifteen minutes before we stretch and then move to weights."

"Joy," I say sarcastically while obeying and inching up my speed. "I think it's the Russian president."

"Agreed."

"Wonder what he wants."

"Same."

"I think I should go."

His steps falter, causing him to wrap his hands around the side bar to keep from falling forward. "What?"

"I want to get to the bottom of the gas price thing at the summit. If there's any place to gain clues to what's going on it's there. Plus Kyle was super evasive yesterday. Shady almost."

"That's Birmingham."

"Agreed, but this was different. Usually he taunts me, but this he outright avoided. I'm going to the OPEC summit and think I should meet with the Russian while I'm there. Clearly he has something he wants to tell me."

"Or kidnap you and use you for ransom."

"We don't negotiate with terrorists, remember? Everyone knows that."

"The fuck? Did you hear that in a movie or something?"

"Maybe," I grumble between heavy breaths. "It's true though, right?"

"Sometimes I'm afraid for our country." Grabbing my water bottle I chuck it at his head. Catching it midair, Trey twists the top off, takes a sip, and sets it in his cup holder. "Meeting with the Russians is a bad idea. Not only because of the press you'd get but also the danger involved. It's a hard no."

"Pretty sure it's a solid yes."

"Pretty fucking sure it's a fuck no."

"Guess I'll just have to go alone, then," I snap. Jamming my finger against the speed button, I push myself into a jog. "You can't tell me what to do, Trouble." At his silence, I look over, finding his features hard, nostrils flaring. "I know you mean well, but something tells me I need to do this."

"I thought Birmingham told you to cancel the trip." Not missing a step, he grips the hem of his black dry-fit T–shirt and rips it over his head before tossing it to the floor. Sweat gathers between his defined pecs and beads along the soft tan skin down his back. Back and forth his arms pump, moving him faster and faster along the treadmill. His chest rises and falls in rapid succession, keeping me transfixed on the demigod beside me. "Mess?"

"Hum?" Not looking away, I sigh at the beautiful man. "You're so pretty."

"I'm a hard-ass," he fake growls while flexing his biceps. "Do you need a reminder, baby?"

"Fuck yes." Now my sharp breaths stem from something other than my forced cardio.

"Later, promise."

Lower lip forced outward, I huff and turn back to the machine.

He chuckles. "Needy little thing. Now, back to OPEC. Birmingham said to cancel that trip."

"I'll just happen to forget to cancel it and end up going." With the hem of my gray tank, I swipe the building sweat along my upper lip and forehead.

"It'll piss him off, that's for sure." His face breaks out in a wide smile. Eyes meeting mine, he nods. "Let's do it."

"I have another great idea." Brilliant actually, and I'm pretty sure he'll agree.

"Hit me."

"How about we stop this boring cardio and opt for a more... group cardio session up in my room?" The last word is barely out of my mouth when his palm smacks the emergency stop button, halting the treadmill's spinning belt in an instant. "Guess that's a yes?" I say with a giggle.

Instead of responding, Trey hits my own emergency stop and hauls me off the treadmill with an arm around my waist. We're nose to nose, our heaving chests meet with each deep breath.

"That's a hell yes, Mess." His sweat-slick fingers slide through my hair, catching in the thick locks. "Like I could ever say no to you."

"You do," I say with a pointed look. "All the time."

"When I'm working, yeah, but today is my day off and I can do whatever I want."

"Whatever?" I ask, anticipation lacing my breathy one-word question.

A mischievous smirk pulls at the right corner of his lips as his eyes blaze with desire. "Come on."

Eagerly I pad behind him, our fingers interlaced as he tugs me along, ready to get my version of a perfect cardio session started.

The moment the door closes and the lock snaps in place, Trey's lips are on mine. Hands cradling my cheeks, he deepens the kiss, pouring intensity and passion into it with each slide of his tongue along my own. Already my heart races, my breaths shortened.

I hook my thumbs inside the elastic band of my running shorts and hastily tug them and my underwear to the floor, blindly stepping out of them before toeing off my tennis shoes.

Trey's lips vibrate against the soft skin of my neck with a laugh. "Eager?"

"Very. It's been too long."

"Agreed, baby. Now let's finish what you started." Gripping the hem of my tank top, he quickly lifts it over my head and tosses it over his shoulder. My snug sports bra proves to be more of a challenge, but with a frustrated grunt, he maneuvers it carefully over my breasts and drops it to the floor.

"Damn, you're beautiful," he says as he scans my naked body. Instead of shying away from his close inspection, I brush my fingers down the slopes of my breasts, along the curve of my waist, and across my hips. "And a tease."

I bite my lower lip and nod. Reaching forward, I loop my fingers into the waistband of his athletic shorts and tug them down to the floor, freeing his already-hard cock. Forgetting about the rest of his clothes, I wrap a hand around his thick shaft and give it a squeeze.

Trey hisses and grips my waist, tugging me to him. The slight scattering of chest hair tickles my sensitive pebbled nipples, sending a shiver down my spine. He bands an arm around my back, pressing me tighter and lifting, allowing only my toes to dance over the carpet. Quickly he toes off his own shoes and kicks out of the shorts pooled at his feet.

The soft duvet conforms around my back like a soft cloud. The cool thin material chills the heated skin of my back, causing goose bumps to sprout along my arms. I roll slightly as the bed dips to the left, the mattress shifting under the weight of Trey's supporting hand.

He licks his lips, eyes only on my breasts. Using his free hand, he twists a pebbled nipple tight while pinching the tip to the point of pain. His brown eyes sparkle, locked with my own at my gasp. A smile pulls at his lips as he lowers. With another twist, he nips at the opposite breast. My back arches off the bed, though desperate for more or to run away I don't know.

Slickness builds between my thighs as the earlier slow throb turns demanding. Standing straight, Trey brushes the tip of an index finger down the middle of my stomach and dips lower. A sharp inhale tightens my chest as his finger slides between my folds. Up and down he traces, pausing just outside my entrance before sliding back up to tease my tiny bundle of nerves.

I whimper in frustration as I shoot a pleading glance at the grinning man. "And you call me the tease." The last word is more of a hiss as he pushes three fingers inside all the way to the last knuckle.

"Shhh, baby. I'll take care of you. I'll always take care of you." Kneeling at the edge of the bed, he keeps his eyes locked with mine as he lowers his lips to my center. My eyes roll, the lids flickering closed at the flick of his tongue against the tip of my clit just as he curls his fingers.

It doesn't take long before I'm crying out his name, falling into the abyss of ecstasy my orgasm induces. My chest is still heaving when he tugs behind my knees, urging me off the bed. My legs wobble, barely supporting my weight. The room whirls as Trey spins me around to face the bed. With a light shove, I fall face-first to the mattress, my nose buried in the fluffy duvet.

"Don't move."

My heart ratchets against my chest. His soft footsteps signal his departure only to return seconds later. I shiver as he trails a finger down my spine. "All you have to say is stop, understand?"

Oh hell.

"Baby, say you understand."

"Yes" is all I can manage.

"Give me your hands."

Awkwardly I maneuver along the bed to reach behind my back. His calloused palms scrape along the skin of my wrists. Something soft wraps around both wrists before tightening, holding them close together. I give my arms a tug, trying to free my hands, but whatever's wrapped around them won't budge. A bolt of panic shoots through me, making me fight the restraint again.

A sharp smack stings across my bare ass, halting my movement. I pant into the covers around my face. Craning my neck, I try to see over my shoulder but can't. Hot hands grip both hips, lifting them higher into the air.

The position is awkward, straining my muscles, but the feel of his hot body behind mine makes the discomfort disappear. I tense at the feel of him at my entrance, not knowing what to expect. Inch by inch he slides deeper, the hands holding me up tightening their grip. His pelvis presses against my ass, the heat from his skin sizzling against my own.

Pulling out an inch, he shoves back in. Again and again he keeps going with the shallow thrusts. My sensitive nipples scrape along the bed, adding to the soft torture. Suddenly he pulls out all the way, leaving my body empty and wanting.

My groan of displeasure cuts into a gasp of surprise as he flips me on the bed, pinning my bound wrists behind my back. A shiver of anticipation quivers in my lower belly at the look of pure desire in his eyes. Without a word he pushes my thighs wider, making room for him to move between them.

Unlike minutes ago, this time he doesn't ease in. With one rough thrust, he slams into me. My hands knead awkwardly into my back, making it arch higher to ease the discomfort. Teeth digging into his lower lip, Trey continues to go as deep as he can before withdrawing to the tip and pushing back inside until we're sealed together once again.

My pleasure builds, growing low in my belly with each of his demanding thrusts. Hand beneath my knee, he hikes my leg higher, allowing him a different angle. I cry out as my orgasm crests, pleasure bursts sending tingling sparks through my body. Trey growls through his release at the same time, elongating the ripples of pleasure.

Our heavy breaths mirror one another's. A smirk pulls at my lips, causing one to form along his.

"See?" I say through my panting. "Isn't my version of cardio more fun?"

I relish his deep laugh. His eyes flick to the bedside table. When they meet mine, a mischievous glint sparkles behind them

"And look at that. We still have two minutes."

My snappy retort melts on my tongue as his fingers slide to my center and flick against my too-sensitive clit.

Best. Workout. Ever.

14

RANDI

Kyle's furious screech echoes inside the limo. Oh, he's pissed. Like so pissed he might just fly down here and take me out himself. I sigh and slouch deeper into the seat.

"Yeah, I heard you the first time," I say. "Listen, it is what it is. I need to be here for several reasons. I'm already in Chile and—"

"Fly the fuck home, right now," he grits out. I'm surprised I can't hear his teeth grinding through the phone.

"Not going to happen, asshole. I'll see you back in DC in four days. Until then—"

"You do not want to defy me like this, Walmart."

"Or what?" I snort. "You'll send the marines after me? I don't require your permission on my travel and daily schedule."

"You'll regret this."

"Pretty sure I won't." The line goes dead before the last word can leave my lips. "Fucker," I yell, shaking the phone before chucking it onto the seat. "Fuck!" I slam my fist against the leather armrest.

Okay, maybe going against the president's direct order *was* a dumb idea. Based on that conversation, I have now added him to my list of formidable, dangerous enemies. Not that he wasn't penciled in before this, but based on the murderous rage in his tone just now, my choice to ignore his order tipped Kyle over the edge from angry little politician to violent, rabid killer.

But what was I supposed to do? Just let the oil issue slide? Sure Taeler said she thought it was due to EPA regulations, but what if it's something else. Here I can get answers, uncover new information. Plus I had to come, I couldn't miss my chance to meet with the Russians to figure out what the hell they want to tell me so badly they've reached out several times.

I need to be here, even if the decision has put me in Kyle's crosshairs more than ever before. My guys will keep me safe, and Taeler's new secret service team lead will ensure her safety too. I'll miss Grem a lot, but when he offered to stay behind to kick those idiot agents into shape, I couldn't say no.

The unease of those two together on a daily basis is still there in the back of my mind, but who am I to say it's wrong if they do get together? They're both consenting adults just like me and Trey. All I asked of Grem was for him to keep her safe above everything and use protection.

I'd never seen a man blush like that before. It was adorable.

Shifting against the leather, I attempt to ease the soreness in my tight leg muscles. Stupid T and Trey and their workout routines are killing me slowly. There hasn't been an ache-free day since they put me on the stupid plan. Running a hand down my slim black trousers, I massage along the tight muscles. Already there's a difference in the muscle tone, which is kind of nice—not that I'll admit that to them. That would only encourage more running and weights.

Outside the window, the passing of buildings slows as we approach the convention center. Arriving late to the summit isn't exactly the impression I want to make, but better late than never. As we approach, a massive crowd comes into view. Hundreds of people congregate along the sidewalk behind a row of SWAT-like officers. Their shouted words are muffled through the thick glass of the limo's windows, but the fury etched on their yelling faces, the anger rolling off the crowd, speaks for itself.

The leather groans as I shift forward, snagging a bottle of water before twisting off the cap to take a quick sip. The cool water slides down my dry throat, relieving a portion of the rising nerves.

What if Kyle was right about the protests and potential attacks and I shouldn't be here?

The limo rocks slightly at the slamming of the front doors. I slide trembling fingers down the front of my silk blouse before checking the back to make sure it remained tucked in place. Too soon the door swings open, a burst of warm humid air brushing across my face.

The moment the heel of my black Louboutins hits the pavement, an arm locks with my own, urging me forward. The crowd continues to roar their displeasure as I'm rushed down the narrowly cleared path. The pointed toe of my right shoe catches on a deep crack in the concrete. I suck in a breath at the sense of falling, but T's strong arm tightens, gripping the crook of my elbow between his and keeping me upright as he continues moving us toward the front doors.

Inside, the blasting air conditioning sends a chill down my spine as it brushes against my clammy skin.

"What is that all about?" I ask, turning to face the rest of the team as they file inside.

"Environmentalists," Trey explains. "With all the fracking and deep sea drilling, they're here every year. Don't worry, Mess, it's not just you they're pissed at."

Okay, that does make me feel a *little* better.

A man in a tailored gray suit approaches, a grim smile on his leathered face. Sunspots dot his forehead, extending back onto the top of his bald head. Clearing his throat first, like he wanted to make the agents aware of his approach, the mystery man steps closer.

"Welcome, Madam VP." Internally, I roll my eyes. "Come, the summit began this morning. I'll show you to your assigned seat."

When the man turns, starting back in the direction he came, I look to Trey, then T.

"We're here, Mess," Trey whispers as we march step for step following the man. "You focus on your job and we'll do ours. You're safe, promise."

I should tell them about the conversation with Kyle, make them aware of the new foe I've stirred up in case it turns into a real threat. But before I can get a word out, the man turns, lips pursed and waving a hand, urging us to hurry.

Right.

Swallowing back the words, I shake out my hands just before he tugs a wide metal door open, rushing us inside.

Later. I'll tell them later. It's not like anything will happen before I have a chance.

I hope.

WHAT DOES one wear when attending a secret meeting potentially with the dictator of a human rights-violating country? Dress or pants? Tough decision.

"I suggest wearing something that you can run in easily."

Looking over my shoulder, I stick my tongue out at Trey before turning back to my two choices.

"So that's a no on the dress, then, because the only shoes that match are four-inch heels. But," I say, picking up the stilettos and inspecting the spiked heel, "these could be used as a weapon in a pinch."

"Let's hope it doesn't come to us needing to use your shoes as a weapon tonight. If we're at that point, I'd venture to say we're fucked."

That leaves the black leather leggings, black booties, and black off-the-shoulder sweater. Still facing the clothes, I smirk and let the long soft robe slide off my shoulders to puddle around my feet.

"You're cruel," Trey practically growls behind me.

"What?" I respond innocently as I slide the sweater over my head. The hem falls just below the crease where my ass and thighs meet, the perfect length for leggings *and* to tease.

Turning on my heels, I face Trey. Both his hands grip the doorframe as he leans into the walk-in closet, blocking the only exit. My skin heats beneath his stare. Starting at my toes, he scans up my legs, pausing at the junction between my thighs and licking his lips. The air heats in the closet, making the light sweater suddenly too warm, too itchy against my sensitive skin.

"Tease," he says with no bite behind it. "Now stop trying to distract me." The heat behind his eyes simmers, leaving behind cold determination. "We leave in fifteen." The wooden doorframe cracks at the force of his arms shoving off. "Oh, and Mess? Do me a favor tonight."

A single dark brow arches up my forehead in question.

"Don't do anything stupid."

I huff a scoff. "Who, me?"

With a shake of his head, he turns and walks away, leaving me alone in the closet once again. Without his distractions, I make quick work of tugging on the leggings, then the boots. After a hasty once-over in the mirror, I head out to meet the guys in the living room.

I pull up short at the entry, brows furrowed as I scan the quiet room where each of the agents stands strategically at the exits and windows.

"Something wrong?" I ask. Worry gnaws in my gut at their severe behavior. "You guys seem so serious."

"This is."

"I didn't mean it like that, T. It's just—"

"Let's move," he orders, cutting me off midsentence. Three agents file out into the hall with me, Trey and T hot on their heels while another four agents follow behind.

Five of us step into the waiting elevator before the door closes, leaving the other five on the presidential suite's floor. Tension pulses in the small space. Heat from so many bodies builds, making me light-headed. The tips of my fingers graze down Trey's suit jacket before gripping the cuff for stability. His concerned eyes flick down to me.

I shake my head in response. Damn, when was the last time I ate? Just as the thought crosses my mind, Trey's eyes narrow and his lips purse like he heard.

"I'll be fine," I murmur, attempting to keep my weakness between us two. "You don't happen to have a Snickers on you, do you?"

Something dark flashes behind his eyes as he shakes his head.

"We need to reschedule," Trey states loudly, his gaze never leaving mine.

"No," I retort, letting go of the soft material of his jacket to cross both arms over my chest. "I'm fine. This needs to happen tonight. The suspense is killing me." My joke falls flat as every set of eyes turns to me. Swallowing, I look down to the decorative tile beneath our feat. "Poor choice of words?"

"Yes," the four men say in unison.

"Sorry," I mutter.

A sharp ding echoes in the elevator just before the doors slide open. The loud sounds of the busy lobby filter in, shattering the building awkwardness. Three agents wait for us, one holding the door open as we file out. Again they surround me, offering protection from every angle as we march through the lobby and out the front doors. The moment I step outside, an agent tugs the limo's door open, waiting for me to climb in.

The limo door shuts behind, Trey sealing us inside. My knees bob up and down as I chew on a pinkie nail. I'm not so crazy to have thought this wouldn't be scary, but hell if I knew it would be this intense. The seriousness of what we're doing, where we're going, and who we're meeting with settles like a weight in my empty stomach. I press the heel of my palm against my lower abs, hoping to quell the gnawing of my insides.

Too soon the limo slows before pulling to a complete stop. Angling my head, I look out the window, trying to see into the darkness. Three quick pounds on the roof startle me, causing me to jump out of the seat. T purses his lips but doesn't say a word. The door handle clicks. Not a single street-light brightens my path as I'm led through the darkened alley toward a nondescript door. My palms turn clammy as we near the point of no return.

What's crazy—okay, maybe not for me—is I'm really not scared. I have faith that these men will keep me safe. It's the unknown, the anticipation of why this important man wants to meet with me in private, that's causing my frayed nerves and spiking anxiety. I need a plan, always, and I hate being underprepared, so this meeting is everything I hate. But what was I supposed to do, call up the Russian president and ask him for a meeting agenda? Pretty sure he'd nuke me just for calling.

Shit, do they have nukes?

As the door swings open, I flip through everything I studied on the plane about Russia, our tense relations, and the various countries they're allied with—which, crazy enough, is a lot. Ever since their new president took office two years ago, various countries have pledged their support of the underdeveloped Russia, which makes me assume I'm not the first secret meeting that's been conducted. That could be good or bad. Good that he probably just wants to win me over to mend our strained relationship, but bad that he's done this before, putting his protection detail at an advantage, whereas my agents are going in blind.

Shouting voices, the clang of pots and pans, and rich smells of cooking meats barrel into the alley as the door swings open with a groan of metal against metal. I hesitate, flicking my eyes up to search Trey's stone face.

"We're good," he barely whispers over the noise. "We knew."

A sliver of worry eases from my shoulders. Okay, so this part is a shock for me but not them. Good. Well, not great, because it sucks walking in blind, but at least I'm safe.

With T leading the way and Trey at my back, we snake down the various kitchen lines toward a side door. T's wide fist pounds on the door, practically shaking the wall. Glancing over my shoulder, I scan the kitchen. Not a single worker looks up from their station, their eyes trained only on their work. The one other time we've done this, snuck through the kitchen, you would've thought I was a celebrity or something the way people stared, but not here. Interesting yet concerning.

The squeal of metal draws my attention forward. On the other side of the now-open door stands the physical perfection one imagines when you mention Russians. I crane my neck to look up at the strangely tall man and smile. His gray eyes seem to stare blankly at me, his features completely void of emotion. He takes a step back, allowing us to move past him deeper into the well-lit dining room.

Careful to keep my movements small, I slowly swipe my sweaty palms down my leather leggings, which are already suctioned to my legs with the humidity and heat. I better be careful going to the bathroom or I might never get these things back up again.

Igor the Giant motions us toward the center of the room where a single table sits. The top is adorned with several silver dome lids, candelabras of various heights with tall glowing candles flicking at the wicks, and matching place settings—without the fourteen rows of forks and spoons I'm now accustomed to seeing in formal settings.

And of course, two chairs accompany the table.

One empty.

One not.

15

RANDI

The guys stick to my side as I cautiously approach the table. Under the bright chandeliers, the man already sitting appears young and exactly who I expected. The pictures of the Russian president haven't done him justice or maybe the warm Chilean sun has helped add some color to his normally stark-white complexion.

Staying seated, he motions for me to sit in the unoccupied chair across from him.

"Sit, please."

Another surprise—no accent.

With a nod, I reach to pull the chair out, but Igor the Giant is there in a flash, pulling it out for me like a proper gentleman. Careful not to flop, I ease into the plush high-back but keep my back ramrod straight instead of relaxing back. "Thank you," I say, tilting my face way up to smile at the not-so-jolly giant. Again those gray eyes stare blankly back. Geez, Russians are uptight. Trey mentioned they were a little stiff, but this is more like rigor mortis.

"Thank you for meeting with me, Madam Vice President." Not trusting my voice, I dip my chin in acknowledgment. "I'm sure you and your men are wondering why you're here, why I was... vigilant in gaining an audience with you."

"If you mean slightly stalkerish, yeah, we can go with vigilant," I say with a huff and then immediately cringe. "Sorry," I mutter. *Shit, Randi, not the time for your smartass mouth.* Digging my ragged nails into my thighs, I take a deep breath. "What is this all about?"

"Ah," he says, his dark eyes lighting up with excitement. "That will come later. First we chat, become friends, eat."

"Become... friends?" Surely I didn't hear him right.

He scrapes a palm along his thick dark beard. "Yes, you and I have a lot in common, no?"

"No? Yes? I don't know much about you." Breaking our stare, I scan the table, looking for something to nibble on in hopes it will quell my queasy stomach. A plate with a large loaf of thick white bread and several dollops of butter calls my name. Without thinking of repercussions, or anything to do with politics for that matter, I stretch across the table toward him, eager to get a slice of bread in my belly as quickly as possible.

Shouts ring out and a hand grips my shoulder, yanking me hard against the back of the chair. My head snaps with the force and I gasp. A pain-laced groan pushes past my lips.

"Stop," the Russian president bellows as he slams his palms on the table, making the dome lids and glasses rattle. "She reach for bread not knife," he shouts again, but this time a bit of a Russian accent slips through. "She is friend, not prey."

"Not sure if that makes me feel better," I mutter under my breath, but the hand at my shoulder tightens to the point of pain. I hiss, glancing from the hand up to Trey's face. My eyes widen at the anger and hate written across his scowling features as he scans the room.

"She is safe," the president says with a nod to me. "No harm."

Several tense seconds tick by with the men in some kind of stare-off.

"I'm fine. Please let me go," I say, attempting to shrug out of Trey's protective hold. Turning back to the president, I attempt an easy smile that comes off more like a grimace. "You guys take table manners to the extreme, you know that?"

Wrinkles form along his brow before vanishing with a growing wide smile. "You are funny."

"Thanks?" Again I shrug off Trey's lingering fingers this time to lean forward, placing my elbows on the table. "Can you pass the bread, please? I'm starving."

With a nod, he passes the butcher block, setting it on the table beside my water glass. The second it's on the table, I tear into the loaf, dipping a piece into the butter before taking a bite. The outside layer flakes off in my mouth while the moist inside melts like the butter.

"We are the same, you and I," he says, leaning back in his chair and resting both hands atop of the arm rests where everyone can see them. Smart man. "Same poor background, same struggles."

After wiping my fingers on the crisp white napkin, I grab the ice water glass and take a hasty sip. "You watched the campaign, then?"

He shrugs.

"It's either that or you pulled information on me, which would be concerning."

"The campaign, then," he says with a smirk.

"Right," I say slowly. "But in regards to our backgrounds, if you say they were similar, I assume with you being in Russia that you had it harder than me. I hear it gets a bit colder there than Texas."

"Hungry is hungry, poor is poor, no matter the continent you are on."

"Touché." I wave a hunk of bread, emphasizing my point. "Look at where we are now."

"Yes, but I am president and you are vice, the second."

"That's right." Not sure if he meant that as a jab or not. Hard to tell with these guys.

"I wish to change that."

A chunk of half-chewed bread lodges in my throat at my gasp of surprise. Bits of it launch into my hand as I cough uncontrollably to save myself from choking. "What?" I rasp.

"I wish to help you to be first, president."

I take a sip of water, easing the scratch and burn of my throat. "You want to kill the president? Pretty sure that's treason talk."

"I not say kill."

I arch a brow, peering over the rim of the water glass as I continue to nurse the soothing elixir.

"Americans," he huffs, falling back against the chair.

"Don't 'Americans' me," I say through another cough. "You set a room on fire in Munich to deliver me flowers—"

"You declined my meeting."

"Then you had your guys corner me and mine in a dark alley after you stalked my daughter—"

"Yes and no."

"Sorry if I don't believe you here, Mr. President—"

"Call me Vlad."

"Vlad, you're the president of a country that's made questionable human rights decisions in the past. You've harbored terrorists, tried to take over innocent countries, and are now threatening the man running our free country. Forgive me if I don't believe a damn word you're saying."

I slam the now-empty glass on the table and lean forward.

"I'm trying to change our ways, but I cannot change our past," he grits out. Leaning toward me, his knuckles go white on the armrests. "Would you want people to blame you for your past when you had nothing to do with it?"

A bit of the rising indignation falters. Okay, maybe my reasoning isn't sound, but still, how am I to trust him?

"I don't trust you," I state, holding his gaze.

"We will build. To start." Raising a hand, he flicks two fingers in the air in a summoning gesture. Igor the Giant steps forward and places a manila envelope in Vlad's awaiting hand. *What's with them and envelopes? Haven't they heard of email?* Vlad stands, straightens his suit jacket, and steps around the table to stand in front of me. In my periphery, two bodies shift closer, their movement rigid.

Vlad's dark eyes meet mine. Slowly he extends the envelope toward me and nods, indicating for me to take it. The smooth, thick paper slides over my fingertips as I carefully tug it from his hand.

"That will have the information you want on the man who follows your daughter."

"Follows?" I gasp.

His bushy dark brows furrow. "Yes, follows."

"How do you know this?" My fingers itch to rip open the seal and scour the information inside. Instead I hold the envelope close to my chest, protecting it with my life.

"I'm Russian," he responds like I'm an idiot. "We know." His gaze softens. "This builds trust, yes?"

"Yes," I whisper.

With a nod, he gives a few shouted commands in Russian. Four men appear at his side within seconds.

"Madam Vice President, it was a pleasure. When you are ready to know truth, you come to me. I have it all."

With a nod of respect, he turns on his heels, the four guards following step for step.

"Why do you hate him? Kyle—I mean the president. Why do you want me in that role instead of him?"

Now at the edge of the room, Vlad turns back, cloaked in shadows. "He is not a good man."

"And you think I am, or a good woman, I mean? You don't know anything about me. I'm not that great."

He takes a menacing step forward; the shadows pull away from his face, revealing the hate sketched across his features.

"He prey on the weak. Takes advantage because he can. Uses his power and money for those he favors. You know this." I'm about to say I do but seal my lips when I realize he's not talking to me. Following his hard gaze to Trey, I bolt up from the chair. "I know his plans. He must be stopped. War will come unless we stop it now."

"What if I don't want it?" I whisper, voicing the growing fear pricking the back of my mind.

"We do what we have to do to protect those we love," he says, a nostalgic tone in his voice. "We, you and I, know there are those who cannot protect themselves, who are kept behind by those who wish to rule without push-back. It will not be easy, but nothing has been, correct?"

"No." My eyes search his, desperate for more reasons than the shitty ominous one he just laid out.

"Neither this. Come to me when you need the proof. I'll be waiting."

Loud bangs and excited shouts pour from the kitchen, filling the private room as Vlad and his protection detail quickly file out. Only once the door clicks closed do I take a deep breath.

Turning to the guys, I search their rigid faces.

"What the actual fuck was that about?"

"I'll take that," T says, tugging at the envelope clutched tightly between my hands. I tighten my grip, holding it firm. "Randi."

I shake my head, unwilling to let the information go.

"What did he mean by follows?" I ask, my eyes searching his dark ones. "We knew about the listening devices in her dorm, but someone following her? Is that why he had his own guys out there making sure she was safe? I don't understand his angle in all this."

"Do you trust me?" T asks. I dip my chin in a small nod. "As you should. You know I'll take care of it, whatever is revealed inside this envelope."

"And tell me," I whisper, still not letting go.

"And keep you in the loop. Let me handle this for you, for Taeler." Reluctantly, I let the envelope slip through my fingers. "Come on," T whispers barely loud enough for me to hear. "Let's get you back."

I nod and don't put up a fight. Hell, I barely even notice my own feet moving in sync with theirs as they shuffle me out the door, back into the dark alley and then into the waiting limo. I stare unfocused at the floorboard as we drive through the city. A warm hand wraps around my cold one, fingers interlacing with a quick squeeze.

"You're okay, Mess. It'll be okay."

I don't have the energy to tell him somehow I know for a fact that it won't. Whatever happened tonight was the catalyst of something big. But what that is, only time would tell.

———

THE COLD CONCRETE bar top sends a shiver from where my elbows press against it all the way to my toes. Even with the humidity and heat, I can't stop my teeth from chattering. The glass shakes in my trembling hand as I lift it to my lips, but even the slow burn of the cheap whiskey does nothing to warm me.

There have been times that I've felt the world was falling apart around me, but this, today and last night with Vlad, made all those other times feel like a fucking vacation—if I knew what one of those felt like.

Squeezing my eyes shut, I take a deep inhale. Behind me the other hotel patrons mill about, having no clue the fucking shit show I'm dealing with —alone.

Being yelled at for the past ten hours, everyone and their neighboring countries blaming me for the oil crisis on our hands. One would think the spike in oil would make these money-hungry assholes happy, but oh no, they're pissed because they think I, the Americans, are doing it to somehow overthrow the OPEC alliance and out produce them, making us the leading supplier of the liquid gold in the world.

If only I knew what the ever-loving fuckity fuck they were talking about, maybe I wouldn't feel so... lost.

But I don't. No matter how many times I explained our situation, that we are not the cause, only hate and anger were spewed right back. Apparently we were never a fan favorite of the alliance anyway, and this just tipped their hands to pure loathing for my beloved country.

Top off this fantastic fucking day with getting a text from Jessica that the House decided to vote on the bill early. That's right, for the first time in our government's history, they did something early. Just my horrible luck.

Of course it passed. Not sure why I'm so sad to learn that what I knew would happen is now a fact, but I am. Super sad. And the only thing that's going to make today right is another drink. Then another. Then another.

A voice in the back of my mind screams at me to stop drinking, that this is no way to handle my problems like the second most powerful person in the world would. But you know what I tell that voice? Fuck. Off. Sure, this is a dangerous ledge to lean over considering I'm the daughter of an alcoholic and addict. But I'll worry about that tomorrow.

Maybe.

A gentle grasp around my elbow snags my wandering attention. Slowly peeling my dry eyes open, I blink several times to clear my vision. Across the bar, a row of mirrors lines the wall. A familiar set of honey brown eyes meets mine in the reflection. His normally styled dark hair is disheveled, like he's run his fingers through the thick locks over and over the past few hours. There's no mischievousness in his eyes, no humor in his pinched features as he stares down at me. Guess it's been a long day for everyone.

"Let's get you upstairs," he mumbles while reaching for the highball glass clutched between my hands.

"Go away. Can't you see I'm drowning my sorrows?"

"Yeah, everyone can, which is why it's time for you to go up to your room."

"No." I give my head a shake for emphasis, causing the room to sway. Focusing on a stationary object, I inhale deep through my nose. "One more."

"That's what you said three rounds ago, which was already two too many."

Rolling my eyes, I yank my elbow from his grasp, causing a few precious drops of whiskey to sprinkle to the bar. "Never had a dad and don't need one now," I state.

Wait, why am I mad at him? Am I mad at him?

I tilt my head and narrow my eyes, hoping that will help me concentrate.

Oh yeah, that's right. I'm pissed at the world, not Trey. But he's the one trying to cut me off, so....

"I'm not your fucking daddy," he hisses into my ear. I lift a shoulder to relieve the tickle caused by his hot breath. "You're drunk. If I don't get you upstairs now, I'll have to carry you up. Look the hell around you, Randi. Do you want me to carry you out of this bar with all these people watching?"

"Get the hell off me."

"I thought you wanted to break the cycle, not repeat it."

The air catches in my lungs, and the heavy highball glass slips from my hand. Trey snatches it midair, keeping it from shattering on the bar.

"How dare you," I seethe. Doesn't matter that I just had that same thought. He can't say that shit. "I've had a bad fucking day, okay?"

"Yeah, I know, Mess. I know. But this isn't how you handle it. Getting piss-ass drunk and making a fool out of yourself is not going to help anything."

"Then what is?" Tilting my face to ceiling, I blink rapidly, attempting to keep the building tears at bay.

"Honestly, I don't know, but not this. Come on, let's get you upstairs. You're better than this, Randi. I know it's hard right now, but you're stronger than you realize. You'll get through."

"How are you so sure?" I whisper.

"Because even though you hit like a girl—" Pursing my lips, I shoot him a glare, causing him to chuckle and a bit of the normal brightness to shine through his eyes. "—you're pretty badass."

"I am."

"I know. That's what I just said. Anyone who's done what you've done in your life, all that you've accomplished on your own, has to be. Remember who you are, Randi. Remember what you've been through to get here."

Sliding my gaze back to the mirror behind the bar, I focus on my own reflection. He's right. Why the hell am I sitting here having a damn pity party—and alone at that. I've made it this far in life, accomplished so much with very little; why do I think this is the one thing that will take me down?

The reflection tilts its head as I do. My slightly frizzy dark hair swooshes along my back. Fuck, I look like hell.

"Why does it feel like we're always having this conversation?" Palms to the bar, I use it for balance as I slide off the stool, giving myself a second to steady my footing. "It must be exhausting always having to pull my shit together."

"That's where you're wrong. I know you're new at this friends thing, but I'm not. I can't tell you how many times Tank's pulled my head out of my own ass or slapped me straight. That's what friends do for each other. They're there when we fall."

"So which are we? Friends or more?"

Peering down, Trey smiles. "Why do you think they're mutually exclusive?" His eyes leave mine to scan the room. "Elevator's waiting. Come on, Mess."

The guys form a tight grouping around me as we march to the elevator. Between the four bodies, I bounce around like a damn pinball, but somehow they keep me upright. The moment we step inside the elevator, the doors close and we zoom upward. "Oh, hey, and one more thing."

"What's that?"

"Don't mention to Sarah how I said you hit like girl. She'll beat me up for sure."

I snort, then slam my hand over my nose and mouth to keep the sound from happening again. Tears from laughter prick the corners of my eyes, dripping down my cheeks as I tilt my face to see his.

"You think I'm kidding," he groans.

The elevator slides to a halt, the movement throwing off my equilibrium and making me sway into Trey's hard chest. Thin smile lines spread from the corners of his eyes with his smile. "If you wanted a ride, all you had to do was ask."

Before I can respond, my feet leave the ground and his firm chest is pressed against my shoulder as he carries me out of the elevator bride style. Tucking my chin, I keep my face hidden from him so he doesn't see me smiling. In a few short steps, we're maneuvering through the door.

"Here," Trey says like he's out of breath as he slowly lowers me to the ground. The moment our eyes lock, the rest of the team fades to the background. Maybe it's the alcohol or not giving a shit anymore about what any of them think, but something fuels me to press up to my tiptoes. Slowly he lowers, his lips a hairbreadth from mine.

"Knock it off, you two," T says, sounding completely exasperated.

Trey clears his throat and straightens. With a huff, I whirl around, ready to tell T off, but the room keeps going.

Fuck.

"Get her in the shower, Benson." Around me, the team snickers. "Alone," T bellows. "We need to sober her up."

"Where's the fun in that?" I giggle. Shit, I'm drunk. Clearing my throat, I shake out my hands, attempting to regain some composure. "Can someone please order me a cheeseburger with fries? And a Coke. Oh, and a cake. A big fucking cake that says 'worst day ever.'"

Before I attempt a step on my own, I slide one foot out of a pump and then the other, leaving the thousand-dollar shoes abandoned in the middle of the suite's living room.

"You stay there," I say to the shoes, pointing at them like they're a dog.

"Seriously? Fuck, you're shithoused." A snarl pulls at my lips at the laughter in his voice.

Instead of responding, I flip Trey the bird over my shoulder as I march to the bedroom door—which keeps moving. Closing one eye, I focus on one door and aim for it. Unfortunately for me, I chose the wrong one. My face smacks into something hard, followed by a big toe. Stumbling back, I lose my footing. A quick free fall and then my ass slams to the floor. Giving up on life, I lie back on the suite's hard floor, pressing a palm to my throbbing cheek.

"I thought you wanted to break the cycle."

With my free hand, I jam a middle finger high into the air, hoping it's directed at T.

"I hate you both," I mumble.

"We didn't do this to you. We're just reminding you of what's on the line."

"And what's that, sensei?"

"Everything you've fought for."

"Oh, fuck," I grumble. Rolling to my stomach, I push up to all fours. "Seriously? It's just a few drinks. Can you two just relax for one night?"

"No."

Indignation grows into anger until it's boiling in my veins. My breaths shorten as heat builds beneath my skin, causing my stomach to roll and sweat to bead along my upper lip.

"Get off your fucking high horse," I grit out through clenched teeth. "You think you're better than—"

The breath whooshes from my lungs as I'm hauled into the air by an arm around my waist. Kicking and thrashing, I fight T's strong hold as he marches into the bedroom. We bypass the bed, heading straight to the bathroom.

"Put me down, you bastard!" I screech. My eyes widen when his intention becomes clear. "No, no, no!" I beg.

He doesn't listen.

The shower door nearly shatters at the force of it being yanked open. With little care, he deposits me on the hard tile. I smack my palms on the floor, struggling for traction. Every curse word I can think of, plus some made-up ones, spew from my lips as a cold spray of the water assaults my face.

"You listen to me, Randi Sawyer. I will not let you do this to yourself. You got yourself into this mess, and I'm going to make sure you get out of it fucking alive, you hear me?"

"Fuck, Tank," Trey's concerned voice pours over the pounding of the water.

"This little pansy ass behind me is too wrapped around your little finger to give you the tough love you need right now, so I'm gonna do it. I know this is more than you expected. Fuck, I can't imagine the kind of pressure you're under, and honestly, I don't want to. But I will not let you give up or give in. You're better than that, you hear me?"

A hot hand presses against my cheek, turning my face up. T's dark eyes search mine with a kindness, maybe even worry, that I've never seen before.

"You hear me?"

Swallowing, I nod. "I hear you."

"Good, because you're the only woman besides Sarah I've ever taken to, and I won't let you destroy yourself."

With a not-so-gentle pat, his hand pulls from my cheek. I follow his movement as he stands and shakes off water from his soaked jacket sleeve. Behind him, Trey's lips are pressed into a thin line, his forehead wrinkled. Embarrassment washes over me like the water still pouring over my head. Turning my face, I bite my lower lip to keep it from trembling.

"We'll be outside the door if you need us."

The glass walls rattle when the door closes. Through my drenched hair, I glance out only to find both men gone.

A sob bubbles up my throat. Leaning back against the white tile, I tuck both knees to my chest and press my forehead to my thighs. T's words replay in my mind, making me sob harder than I ever have because of the truth and conviction behind them.

A little thought in the back of my mind pulses, niggling its way to the forefront.

What if they're wrong?

16

TREY

The ugly-ass fancy carpet silences my heavy pacing steps just outside the bathroom door.

"You're babying her," Tank snarls from where he's lounging on one of the two sitting chairs across the room.

"And you're being an ass," I snap back, curling both hands into tight fists.

His eyes follow the movement, and a smirk tugs at his lips.

"You wanna fight?"

"No. Yes." Leaning back against the wall, a quiet thump sounds when my head hits the drywall. The door to the bathroom whooshes open, a billow of hot, wet air pouring through. I cautiously watch as Randi steps into the bedroom, fingers fidgeting with the sash of the thick, oversized white robe.

Her throat bobs. Red-rimmed eyes meet mine before sliding to Tank.

"I'm sorry for my behavior," she says. Rolling her shoulders, she straightens her spine. "You're right, both of you."

"You need to let others help you, Randi," Tank says. "All this wouldn't be too much if you let other people help you every once in a while."

With a sigh she moves toward the bed and perches on the edge.

"It's tough, you know. It feels like everything would be easier just to do it on my own, to make sure everything gets done."

"Never said it would be easy, but you have to keep trying." Tank sighs and rubs a hand over his bald head. "Now come on. Your food's in the living room, and we need to talk about the information in that envelope from last night."

Her brows shoot up in interest. When she takes a step toward the door, following Tank, I reach out, snagging her wrist and tugging her to a stop. Hazel eyes meet mine, a small, sad smile pulling at her lips. She tucks a few wet locks of hair behind her ear and clears her throat.

"It'll be okay, Mess."

"I know," she says. "Or I hope, I guess. Come on, I'm starving."

Her forced fake smile pierces my heart with the uncertainty and sadness behind it. I allow her to tug me along, and we walk into the living room. Releasing her wrist, I position myself in the corner where I can see every angle of the room. The savory smells intensify after she yanks the silver lids off the room service cart.

She takes the plate with the cheeseburger and fries and sets it on the low coffee table in the middle in the room before sitting on the floor in front of it. Two huge bites and a few fries later, Randi finally looks up.

"I'm sorry, guys," she says with a sigh, meeting the eyes of every man in the room. "I—"

"I looked over the information in that envelope."

Randi's head whips toward Tank, her eyes the size of saucers.

"From what I can tell, it's all legit. Someone was, or is, following Taeler under orders. That's what the Russians were doing there, why they've been there. My guess is they saw her sneak out, and since they were ordered to keep her safe, they followed to make sure the other person didn't take the opening and snag Taeler off the street."

Nibbling on a fry, she says, "I need to thank Vlad next time I see him. No doubt it was his orders that had those guys there offering the extra protection. Probably to get on my good side if I had to guess, but hey, it worked." After a quick sip of her bottle of Coke, she asks, "Do we know who's behind it?"

"Who do you think would stoop so low to have your daughter followed to gain leverage on you?" I ask.

"Fuck," she shouts, throwing a half-eaten fry across the room. "Which one?" Shoving up from the floor, she stumbles forward, catching herself on the arm of the couch. "Which of those fuckers hired someone to follow my daughter?"

"Based on the evidence—" Tank starts.

"What evidence?" she asks, sinking onto the couch, her unfocused gaze on the opposite wall.

"Various correspondence through the dark web and cryptic phone calls were all documented in that file. I have no damn idea how they got the information."

"Let's be honest, it's Russia," she says with a huff. "They probably started the dark web just so they could monitor it."

"There's something else, Randi." Every head in the room turns to Tank at the seriousness in his voice. Even mine. What the hell is he about to say?

She gives an exhausted sigh. "That's ominous. I'm not sure I can take any new shocking news. Do I need to know?"

Tank's eyes narrow. "No."

Chewing on her thumbnail, she flicks her gaze to me. "Is this one of those things I need to let go, let someone else handle?"

"Yep," I respond immediately. I have no idea what Tank's referring to, but if it has anything to do with her safety, then hell yes she should leave that up to us. There's no need for her to worry about things like that when it's our job to keep her safe.

She releases a heavy breath and nods. "Okay." Smacking her thighs, she rolls her shoulders and stretches out her neck. "I trust you, T. You handle whatever *that* is you're not telling me about plus continuing to handle the security aspects for Taeler in Austin. In my mind, I'm taking both off my worry list." She arches a brow at Tank. "Happy?"

A broad smile spreads across his face, one I rarely see and never on shift. "Very."

"But what *can* we do about whoever's following Tae?" she asks, the worry back in her voice. "I'm not naïve enough to think I can stop them from trying to hurt me directly or through Taeler. But I also can't just ignore that there's some guy following my daughter around for fuck knows what reason."

Tank's dark eyes meet mine from across the room. In the few seconds we hold each other's stare, a silent conversation passes between us.

"We have to be careful," I say, drawing her hazel eyes to me once more. "Whether it be Whit or Birmingham, both are dangerous and have unlimited funds, and now we know they have friends in shady places. Once we know the why and we have more proof, then we act, but until then, it's just your word plus some files we shouldn't even have as evidence." I massage the bridge of my nose and seal my eyes shut to calm the dryness. Fuck, I'm tired. We all are. "We wait, get more information, and then act. Knowledge is power in these fucked up games."

Randi nods and slides from the couch back to the floor in front of her food. At the obvious conclusion of the meeting the other guys move about the room, murmuring to each other as they prepare to switch the on-duty shift to beta team.

Tank gives his head a slight tilt snagging my attention. I shove off the wall to follow him into another room, where he tells the agents inside to clear out. Once everyone is cleared out, he shuts the door with a quiet click but doesn't turn around.

"The information inside that file proves it's Whit playing his fucked up mind games by having Taeler followed. Various emails back and forth between the two parties confirm it. It's not much but enough fucking verification for me. But, now there's more. Not only is Whit having Taeler's *and* Randi's movements tracked, but it seems the damn president joined in the game too recently."

"What?" I growl between my clenched teeth, the muscles along my jaw twitching.

"Seems Whit has gathered information on her, having her followed from afar since... well, since she started the campaign, but Birmingham's reconnaissance started recently." Turning from the door, I can't help but notice how tired my best friend looks. Puffy dark bags weigh under his eyes, and his normal steely expression appears more exhausted than mean. "As in since we landed here three days ago. She mentioned he didn't want her coming to the OPEC summit, but I just thought it was because he told her no and she went and did the opposite. But now?" He shakes his head and moves deeper into the room. Falling into the plush upholstered chair, he leans forward, balancing his elbows on his thighs, his head hanging. "Now I think it's more than that. He's trying to keep her from something, and he's willing to put a hit out on her to do it."

"The fuck?" I whisper-yell. "Did I hear you right?"

Tank nods. "The new information the Russians had is different than Whit's. Trey, that fucker wants her dead sooner than later."

MY CLENCHED FIST slams against the thick imported Italian wood door, demanding it to open. It swings forward, permitting a small gap for me to squeeze through with a bit of force. The childhood part of me feels guilty about bypassing Gerard without our usual happy greeting, but the rest of me doesn't give a flying fuck. Storming through the ostentatious foyer, I march deeper into the house and pause.

"Where is she?" I demand, not turning to look at the old man, afraid of the disappointment I might find behind his caring eyes at my rude behavior.

"Entertaining," he mumbles behind me. "Upstairs, master bedroom."

Of course she is. When he says *entertaining*, I know for a fact that he isn't referring to my father.

Gerard calls out my name, but it's lost to the pounding of my boots atop the polished cherry wood steps. Chest heaving from the mounting anger, I pause at the top of the stairs on the third floor, my focus narrowing on Mother's bedroom door. Slowly I move down the hall, the sounds of shuffling and hushed voices slipping beneath the closed door. Forgoing any politeness, I shove my shoulder against the door as I push the lever down.

A sharp female gasp sounds through the massive room. Sheets clutched to her bare chest, Mother stares in horror while the man frantic to not be caught hurries to get one leg into his suit pants.

"Trey Carl Benson," Mother screeches. "What are you doing?"

"We need to talk. Now," I bellow. After a look of pure disgust at the man who just fucked my mother, I turn on my heels and march out of the room.

Oh hell. Maybe some of Randi's dramatics are rubbing off on me. What the hell did I just do?

I shudder at the image of Mother partially naked and the sleepy old guy standing terrified in his tighty-whities. No man should ever be exposed to that kind of horror. I'll probably be scarred for life—more than I already am, that is.

Gerard is nowhere to be seen when I hurry back down the stairs. The earlier guilt rises again, but I shove it down as I make my way through the maze of hallways to the sunroom. Pacing the row of floor-to-ceiling windows, I glance to the door every few seconds, anticipating Mother's arrival so I can get answers and leave this hellhole. Being in this house does something to me, darkens my mood and maybe even my outlook on my future. With Randi, her positive nature—well, usually positive nature—the way she keeps fighting and striving for more bleeds over to me, making me feel the same. But all the anger, all the hate, the years of lies and deceit soak back into my soul with every second I'm here.

It really is a miracle I didn't end up the way both my parents wanted. If I hadn't gone across the country, released their claws from my life, who knows who I'd be today.

Cracking my neck, I try to ease the tightness in my shoulders that hasn't relaxed since Tank revealed that Randi has a price on her head.

Thirty minutes pass, my annoyance and temper rising with each passing minute, before a soft creak comes from the direction of the door.

"It passed the House" is all I say as she enters the room.

A soft scoff meets my ears, cranking up the heat building in my veins. "Of course it did."

Turning, I narrow my gaze on her, allowing all the menace and hate to pour through. "We have a deal."

"Ah, the deal," she says, ignoring my death glare. "Funny thing about that deal is you haven't seemed to keep up your end of the bargain either."

"What?" Stalking across the room, I pause in front of Mother.

"I seem to recall you saying you'd ease your way back into the social circles needed to uplift your political career, yet," she says with a sigh and condescending pat to my shoulder, "I haven't seen you at any functions recently. Seems I'm not the only one not following through."

"Fine," I grit out, knowing she's right. "Name the next gala or charity shit I need to go to with Jessica and I'll be there."

Locking her honey brown eyes with mine, a sinister smile pulls at her lips. "Oh, Trey. Trey, Trey, Trey. You've been out of this game too long. Do you think you have the upper hand in this? It's too late for that."

Grinding my teeth, I force myself to stay quiet. Behind me the door's hinges creak.

"Ah, there you are," my mother says, her tone bright. "Thank you for coming so quickly."

I crane my neck to see who's interrupting our wonderful family reunion and my eyes widen.

"The fuck are you doing here, Jessica?"

"Language," Mother spits out. "We need to get you away from that trailer trash of a woman soon."

"Watch it," I snap, turning back to her.

Her smile widens and she glances behind me to Jessica. "We'll have to cure him of this little crush he has for her. That's your first order of busi-ness." Sliding her gaze back to me, my mother gives me a once-over. "Sad, really. You have so much potential." She motions for Jessica to join us. "I've been doing a little digging of my own, and it seems you have more of a vested interest in this bill not passing than you originally led me to believe."

My nostrils flair, lips pursing into a thin line, but still I say nothing. I need to know what they know first before I open my fat mouth and give them more information to use against me.

"I've heard you and this woman"—disdain drips from her lips as she says the word—"have a relationship of sorts. Which will be a problem if you're with the lovely Miss Hawthorne."

"What?" Jessica gasps. Her eyes dart from me to Mother. "I didn't... Trey, you didn't... I thought it was just flirting and—"

"I never agreed to be with Jessica. I said we would go to the functions together so she could help introduce me to key players, nothing more."

Mother looks to Jessica. "See, now that I know what's on the line for you, well... that's just not enough."

My throat goes dry, and dread twists in my gut. Jessica's face turns pale, a greenish tint marking her usually bright features.

"We had a deal," I snarl, taking a menacing step toward Jessica.

"I didn't know." She takes a step back. "She didn't tell me. I wouldn't have...."

"What did you do?" I seethe. "What did you do, Jessica?"

A soft cry bubbles up from her chest, which she covers with a delicate hand to her pale lips.

"She made a better agreement with me," my mother responds with a sigh as she motions between her and Jessica. "Here's the new plan in place that you will follow. I will seal the votes needed to stop the bill from passing in the Senate for that pathetic excuse of a vice president. In exchange, you will announce your *engagement* at the celebration ball we will host after the bill fails, and you will keep your promise to enter the political scene, but sooner."

I turn from the two women to pace the length of the opposite wall to keep from punching either of them.

Shit, this is bad. Think, Trey.

Engagement? Fuck.

Sweat builds along my forehead and slicks my palms. Every scenario of how to get out of this whips through my mind, but nothing makes sense. Nothing would work. What I'd planned before—walking away after the four years, because then their influence in this town wouldn't matter when I screwed them over—won't work now. It's like they knew I planned to back out only when it wouldn't affect Randi's term negatively. But the only person who knew that plan was....

I lock eyes with Jessica. "You sold me out. You told them my original plan."

She nods, tears glistening along her lower lids. "Do you love her?"

"For how long?" I grit out. Sliding my clammy palms into the front pockets of my black jeans, I dig my stubby nails into my thighs. "How long will we have to play the engagement? What are the terms?"

"One year," Mother says, inspecting her perfect nails. "This isn't something you can just step away from like I know you were planning to do before. A deal is a deal, son. I get you the votes and you stick to the engagement and the marriage next year. After the wedding, you'll leave the secret service for good."

I shake my head. "Not going to happen. I'll play the charade, but I will not marry her," I shout, jutting a finger in Jessica's direction, "or leave before the end of the term."

"Of course you will, sweetie. This is an alliance," Mom says with a laugh. "Not marriage in the technical term. You need me, and you need this."

Turning my gaze to the window, I stare out onto the lush estate, still budding with the last effects of spring. I could always get the votes needed and back out; it's not like they would send the bill back to vote. But what about the backlash I was worried about before? If I back out after the bill fails, my family will ensure Randi is ruined. So which would be worse, Randi's political ruin or me marrying Jessica?

I could always go along with their plans—the engagement, the marriage —then end it after Randi's term. But will I really leave the secret service? Leave Randi unprotected for the remaining two years of her term? Or I could agree to everything right now, then back out of the resignation piece once it comes time.

"Oh, and son."

I slide my annoyed gaze to Mother, who's now lounging along her favorite chaise while Jessica silently sobs in the corner. Crying over hurting Randi or knowing I'll never love her because my heart belongs to another?

She really didn't know. A part of me feels bad for her. She made this new deal with Mother not knowing all the pieces, and she was played just like me. This will kill Randi. She thought she had a friend in Jessica. Maybe she does still. Jessica wouldn't be this visibly upset if she knew she was screwing Randi over.

"Don't even think about double-crossing me. I've done my research. You see, I've played this power game longer than you, honey, and I can spot loopholes in any deal. If you back out of any part of our new deal after you've gotten your end of the bargain, well then, I might be forced to release some less-than-positive information about you to the press." Her lips dip in a fake frown.

"And what's that?" I ask. Tugging my hands from my pockets, I cross both arms over my chest and widen my stance, readying for a fight I'm not sure I'll be able to win. How's that for a slap to the balls.

"Oh, let me see here. How about assault with a deadly weapon? What is that nowadays? Ten, maybe fifteen years in federal prison? Maybe more since you're an officer of the law."

I feel every last ounce of blood drain from my face. "How...?"

"Come on now, dear, don't think so little of me. It was easy when you know where to look."

Realization smacks me in the face like a sack of bricks. "Who told you?"

"Ah, ah, ah," she says while wiggling her finger back and forth. "I don't reveal my sources. So, son, what will it be? Jessica and your whore of a girlfriend, or no Jessica and no VP? Easy choice if you ask me."

Right, like I have a choice at all. And knowing Mother, this is only the beginning. From here on out, new items will be added on, new expectations. This new deal is just a baseline for my future torment.

The real question is, can I live with myself with Randi gone or with her here and hating me for doing this behind her back? Sorrow wells in my chest, pushing a tightness in my throat.

Neither outcome ends with me with the woman I love.

17

RANDI

June

My cheeks pulse with a low ache from holding my broad smile for so long. After a quick professional goodbye, I unseal the phone screen from my ear and rest it on the desk. I scribble the location and confirmed time into the planner, underlining it several times for emphasis. This is my fourth meeting to get on the books with an influential senator since the OPEC summit three weeks ago. Two of the senators I met with last week said they would consider my counterpoints to the bill while the one yesterday flat out said no, but hey, can't win them all. Hopefully the one I just scheduled for Thursday night swings my way.

With an excited groan, I pitch the pen onto the desk and lean back in the large leather-back chair. Closing my eyes, I relish the few seconds of peace this moment offers. Since the cold shower intervention, I've worked diligently to hand some responsibilities off to those who are capable. With the various committees and obligations taken care of by others, I've had time to focus on stopping the bill and delegating the other things as they've come through. I hate to admit it, but T was right. The suffocating pressure and stress I was carrying would've drowned me.

Thank goodness for friends who are willing to give the tough love needed to save you from yourself.

Pressing the tips of my heels to the rug, I swivel left and then right, smiling with my eyes still closed. T and Trey—all the guys, really—are amazing. Even though Trey's been acting funny the last couple of weeks. More closed off than usual, sad almost. We haven't had a chance to talk alone, but hopefully we can soon so I can stop the nagging feeling that something's wrong. Surely he would've told me if there was, right?

Shaking my head, I lean forward and reach for the pen to jot down a few more notes when the phone vibrates against the polished dark wood. My brows furrow as I read the bright screen: Unknown Caller. Swiping my thumb against the smooth glass, I press it against my ear.

"This is Randi," I say. Pinching the pen between two fingers, I spin it along the desk.

"Madam Vice President, this is Senator Johnson." Johnson. Johnson. Johnson. Which fucking one? I open my mouth to ask which state he represents, but he continues on before I can. "I've heard you're wanting to stop the voting bill that was recently passed by the House."

"I am."

"I'd like to help you."

Excitement buzzes in my belly. Sitting up straighter, I twirl the pen again, the whirling of the metal against the wood offering the only sound in the office.

"I would love that. How—"

"There are a few others I think you need to talk to, help them understand exactly what this bill entails. The wording is put in a way that most aren't sure exactly what they're voting for."

"Right," I say, feeling vindicated. "The president wants that. He wants this bill to go through without any pushback."

"When can you meet the others?"

Hastily I flip through my calendar, looking for an opening. "Let me—"

"How about Thursday evening?"

I bite my lip and stare at the appointment I just made with the other senator. "I already have a meeting that evening."

"What about after?"

A sense of foreboding pricks in my gut.

"What's the rush?"

A heavy sigh comes from the other side of the phone. "I'm sure you're aware, Madam VP, that you're not the only one trying to solidify votes in their corner. The president is making his rounds, and he has... formidable pull. If you want to win this, you need to get these men to your side before he does."

I nod, gripping the phone tighter. "Thursday night. It'll have to be late."

"Aren't most deals in this city made in the shadows of the night?"

I release an uneasy laugh. "I guess. Let's say eleven o'clock. That'll give me plenty of time with the other senator. Where should we meet?"

"Charlie Palmer's Steakhouse."

I wince at the stinging pain coming from my lip just as the sharp tang of blood slides across my tongue. "They close at ten, do they not?"

"I'm a very, very loyal patron, Madam VP. They'll stay open for us. I look forward to meeting you in person."

"You too," I say, somewhat in disbelief.

"Good day, Madam Vice President. Until then."

Pulling the silent phone from my ear, I stare at the blank screen. So odd. But also not. In this town, with all its pomp and circumstance, everything is laced with an edge of drama and suspense. Good thing I am too.

At the knock on the door, my head shoots up from where I'm detailing out my new meeting on the calendar. Trey's somber face peeks through the crack, eyes scanning the room before landing on me.

"Hey," he says.

"Hey, back." I toss the pen onto the desk and swivel in the chair. "You need something?"

His dark floppy hair slides along his brow with the shake of his head. "No, just wanted to say bye before I head off. Shift's over."

"Oh," I say, not hiding my disappointment. "You coming back by later?"

Again he shakes his head. "I can't. Family obligations. I just needed to see you before I go."

"What's going on, Trouble? You seem... troubled." I smile at my own joke, but it falls when he doesn't return it. "Something's wrong. Tell me."

"I can't. Not yet, Mess."

"Did I do something?" I whisper with a glance up to the security cameras hidden in the corners of the office.

"Of course not," he bites out with more conviction than I've heard from him in weeks. "Don't ever think that, you hear me?" Stepping deeper into the room, he quietly closes the door behind him and leans against it.

"I miss you." My words are barely audible, but the way he closes his eyes, wincing like he's in pain, there's no doubt he heard them.

"I know. Fuck, I know. But I just can't right now. I'll tell you more soon, I swear. Just don't... don't give up on me." With that he turns, pulls the door open, and slides out without a goodbye.

Pressing against my chest, I attempt to ease the ache radiating from my heart.

Something is wrong, very wrong, but what can I do if he won't tell me?

***

NEEDING to release some of the pent-up anger on the verge of bubbling over, I grip the SUV's door and slam it shut behind me, almost severing my foot at the ankle in the process. Flipping my loose wavy hair over my shoulder, I sink low in the seat before reaching back for my seat belt.

"Guessing that went well," Trey says from the front passenger seat.

"Waste of my damn time," I huff. Reaching down, I tug at the hem of my skirt. "Why do these people even agree to meet with me if they know their bigoted little black hearts won't hear a word I say?"

Both men upfront remain silent. My annoyance grows. Smacking T's headrest, I lean as far forward as my seat belt will allow, placing my face between their shoulders.

"You're both awfully quiet. Surely you have some ideas."

Trey chuckles and adjusts in his seat, allowing him to look back at me. For the first time in weeks, his eyes are light with humor. Too bad this time it's him laughing at me.

"You're hot, Mess."

My mouth pops open. "He's married," I say, pointing back to the restaurant we just left. "And old."

"That didn't stop Hindle, did it?" I grumble a few curse words under my breath. "All I'm saying is you're beautiful, smart, and the hot new thing on the DC scene. Plus, you're powerful. Of course they're all going to say yes when you call them up to schedule a meeting. They're hoping your version of meeting means sans clothes."

"I just threw up a little in my mouth," I say, fake gagging. "Old saggy balls. No thank you." With a resigned sigh, I relax back into my seat and look out the window. "Well, if what you say is true, then hopefully this next meeting will be better since *I* didn't schedule it."

T slams on the brakes, shooting me forward until my seat belt catches. The air whooshes from my lungs as the tight material cinches across my chest.

"What the hell, T?" I rasp, inhaling deep to regain some composure. "Did you almost hit someone?"

The leather groans as he twists around. Trey mirrors his move.

"Who made this meeting if you didn't?" T demands.

"Senator Johnson. He called me—"

"Which one?" they say in unison.

Well, fuck. Bouncing my gaze between their stern ones, I lift my shoulders with a grimace. "Not sure."

"Randi fucking Sawyer," T yells. "Which one?"

"I don't know, okay?" I shout back, but not with nearly as much... wait, is that fear? "What's wrong?"

The two men share a glance. "It sounds suspicious is all," Trey says after clearing his throat. "Tell us about the call."

Horns blare all around us. Glancing out the window, I realize we've stopped in the middle of an intersection. With a huff of annoyance, T slowly eases back into traffic while I detail out the specifics of the call as best I can remember.

"Sounds shady as hell," Trey says to T with a glance back at me. "Is there any way for us to trace the call?"

I shake my head. "It was an unknown caller, but that's not strange. Most calls are blocked."

T yanks the wheel a little harder than necessary. I smack both palms against the window to keep my head from doing the same. "Easy there, big guy," I say. "Don't blame the messenger back here."

"Sorry," he grumbles. "It's just that you don't know everything that's going on."

I toss both hands in the air in utter defeat. "Because you told me not to worry about all that shit. Remember the cold shower incident?"

"I know," he grits out, slamming a fist into the dash.

"What do you want to do?" Trey asks, looking at T.

"Abort."

"Whoa." Grasping both men's shoulders, I give them a quick shake. "Let's go check the place out first. If there are other cars in the parking lot, some activity at least, then we go in. If not, then we leave. I really need this, guys."

"Do you?" T says with an incredulous tone.

"Um, yeah, I do." Looking to Trey, I roll my eyes.

Trey sighs and runs a hand through his hair. "Mess...."

"For fuck's sake, just tell her," T barks. "We're almost there."

I peer out the windshield. At this time of night, the traffic is still so heavy that we have a few minutes of traffic lights and waiting before we reach the restaurant, even though the building is within sight.

"Tell me what?" I ask, confusion clear in my voice. When he doesn't respond, I shove his shoulder. "Tell me what, Trey? You're freaking me out back here."

"He bought the motherfucking votes you need," T grits out.

I tilt my head, eyes searching Trey's, probing for the truth. "What does he mean?"

Trey's Adam's apple bobs as he swallows. "I went to my parents. They've promised me the Senate."

I slam my back against the seat. The pulsing energy from seconds ago drains from my veins. "What?"

Trey unclicks his seat belt and climbs over the center console into the back seat. A few awkward moves later, he slides into the other captain chair and closes his eyes. "I knew you didn't have the votes, so I went to my parents and asked for their assistance." His eyes flutter open and find mine. "They have a lot of pull in this town. I just wanted to help." His chest balloons up with his heavy breath as he stares down at it. "I can't imagine you leaving."

I suck in a harsh breath, suddenly remembering I need to breathe to survive. My eyes search his, but I know I won't find any deceit behind them. His heart was in the right place, sure, but he still went behind my back. These past few weeks of fighting to schedule meetings, the highs and lows of wondering if I'll secure the Senate, was it all for nothing?

"Say something, Mess," Trey pleads.

"I don't know what to say." It's the truth. I'm not mad, yet I'm not happy. So what does that leave? Empty?

"We're here."

Glancing out the window, I see several cars in the parking lot plus the lights still on inside. I swallow and look back to Trey, whose honey brown eyes are burning a hole straight through me. The need to breathe grips my lungs, but his presence, the closeness, prevents me from taking a deep breath.

"I need some air," I rasp before yanking on the handle and shoving the door open. T and Trey both shout behind me, but I'm already halfway out of the car. The moment both feet are on the black asphalt, I shut the door and lean back against it. Beside me, the driver door surges open with T barreling out at the same time. The agents in the other two SUVs file out, assuming the normal formations.

The back of my head smacks the window. Staring up into the cloudless, starless dark sky, I take a deep breath and hold it.

"He means well," T mumbles. Peeling my eyes open, I find him standing in front of me, gun between his hands. "Can we just get back in the damn SUV, please?"

"If he meant well, why didn't he tell me to begin with? Was he going to let me think all this was done on my own?" Sighing, I pitch forward, placing my hands on my bare knees. "I don't know how to feel."

"Can you sort through your feelings in the safety of the—" He cuts himself off but immediately recovers with a shouted "Cover!"

Before his bellow has stopped ringing through the parking lot, another sound bursts through the night. The distinct bang of a gun shoots panic through my system, forcing me to my knees. The asphalt bites into the skin of my knees and palms as a heavy weight presses on top of me, nearly folding me in two. The glass above my head shatters, showering the ground with tiny shards of glass.

"Get her out of here," T barks near my ear. Another set of arms slides along my back, hooking around my waist and hauling me upright.

A second shot booms through the night, eliciting a scream from deep in my throat. The person holding me grunts, his body slamming into me. My hip and shoulder collide with the unforgiving metal of the SUV. I cry out as pain sparks at each point of contact. Still the agent continues forward, practically dragging me to the other side of the SUV. Two more shots ring out, one splintering the side of the SUV inches from my face. Eyes wide, I glance from the bullet hole to across the street, where it seemed to have come from.

Another agent grips my arm. My eyes fly up to Trey's profile.

"Move your feet, Randi," he barks, yanking me behind him. The metal

digs into my back as he presses his full weight against my chest. "Get to—"
He grunts before sliding to his knees, leaving me exposed.

"Trey!" I yell, falling to the asphalt with him. Hands roaming his chest, I
search for where he was hit when another set of hands grab under my arms,
hauling me into the air. I scream for whoever is holding me to let me go.
Legs and arms flailing, I try to break the person's hold to get back to where
Trey lies still on the ground, his eyes locked with mine. Before I can escape,
I'm thrown into the back of the third SUV, my head smacking a hard-plastic
cup holder.

The SUV accelerates immediately. I roll backward, almost sliding into
the next row before my ragged nails gain traction on the soft leather, halting
my fall. Left and then right I roll as the SUV takes turns down various
streets, bolting from the ambush.

Arms trembling, it takes two attempts to push upright into the seat and
another few to fasten my seat belt.

"We're secure, ma'am," says a voice up front.

Too dazed by shock, I fail to place the voice of the driver, but looking to
the passenger seat, Champ's good-looking profile affirms I'm in good hands.
I slide my slick palm through my hair, over my blouse, and down my skirt,
making sure everything is where it should be and there aren't any gaping
holes I've somehow failed to notice up to this point.

"Trey?" I rasp. "The others?"

Champ swallows deeply. Gaze fixed out the window, gun at the ready, he
shakes his head. "Let's get you home."

Not the response I was looking for.

18

RANDI

Thumbnail between my teeth, I watch the closed bedroom door, begging for it to open. My feet bounce along the soft carpet, making the entire bed frame shake beneath me. What the hell is taking them so long? Sighing, I switch nails, hoping maybe the middle one will ease the panic building in my gut.

Two hours ago, I was rushed inside the house and up to my 'secure' room. Which it is, I guess, but secure doesn't mean shit when I have no clue what's going on.

I'm not crazy enough to not realize what happened tonight, but everything still seems fuzzy. I was set up, that's clear, but by whom and why? What would've happened if I had gone inside as planned? Would I even be here right now? My safety is the last thing on my mind, coincidently. More than anything I need to know all my guys are safe, especially one mischievous man I can't get enough of, even though he's on my shit list for keeping stuff from me.

Seriously, how many times were we together the past few weeks where he could've told me what was going on behind the scenes?

I shake my head, causing the makeshift towel turban to loosen and tumble to the bed. Gripping the damp towel, I shuffle into the bathroom and toss it into the hamper.

Instead of retreating to keep my vigil from the bed, I pause in front of the mirror. My dark, damp hair hangs in disarray around my face, cascading over my shoulders. I slide my fingers into the terry cloth robe, brushing along my collarbone and pulling the soft material away as I go. Lifting it, I inspect the already deep purple and blue bruise that's forming.

Carefully I trace along the edges, feeling the swollen muscle beneath. It could've been worse. A lot worse. Like the guys. Damn, where are they?

My eyes flick to the bathroom door, hoping Trey will materialize and tell me everything's okay. But the doorway remains empty, the bedroom just beyond quiet.

I tug at the ends of the robe's sash, allowing the two sides to part. Skimming my fingertips down my belly, I move the right side of the robe and pop my hip to see the bruise in the mirror. From hip bone to midthigh, another dark bruise has already formed. I'd be sore as hell if it weren't for the pain meds the annoying doctor made me take before she left an hour or so ago.

I close the robe and cinch the sash tight before turning from my disheveled reflection. Worry clenches my lower belly for my guys. Where the hell are they? A wide, open-mouth yawn escapes as I trudge to the soft bed. The fluffy duvet rustles as I pull it and the top sheet back. Snuggling into the covers, I fluff the pillow and angle it so I can lie down *and* have a good view of the door.

Resting my cheek on the pillow, I tuck my arms beneath it and draw my knees up close to my chest. Soon my eyes grow heavy, my slow blinks turning into minutes of darkness behind closed lids. Each time, I fight to reopen them, determined to keep my vigil for when he'll bust through the door and explain everything.

After several attempts at fighting the inevitable, I lose the battle, slipping into a dreamless sleep.

"MESS."

The familiar voice urges me awake, pulling me from the darkness. I peel my eyes open, blinking several times to allow them to adjust to the soft glow of the bedside lamp. Searching for the owner of the voice that woke me, I scan the shadowed room, halting on the figure at the end of the bed.

"What time is it?" I rasp, my throat dry with sleep.

"Almost five," Trey responds, his voice low.

"Is everyone okay?" Palms against the mattress, I push up to a sitting position, leaning back against the headboard.

"They will be. No fatalities, but there were a few injuries." He opens his mouth to say something more but snaps it shut.

"What?" I ask anxiously. When he doesn't respond, I crawl along the bed toward him. Hand against his prickly cheek, I turn his face to meet mine. "Tell me."

His eyes slide low, locking on my lips. "I'm sorry I didn't tell you. I know I should've, but I won't apologize for what I did. I'm not letting you go home, Randi, no matter what I have to give up."

"What do you have to give up?" I question, swallowing thickly.

"I need you, Randi."

Not giving me a second to respond, Trey shifts forward, closing the few inches that separate us. Cupping the back of my head, he threads his fingers through my still-damp hair. Tightening his grip, he shifts the angle, deepening the kiss. The tip of his tongue slides along the seam of my lips, begging me to open. The pent-up worry seeps from my body as I part my lips, eager to let him chase away the remaining fear.

With clumsy fingers, I work down the buttons of his dress shirt. Shoving the material off his shoulders, I brush two fingers down his sculpted chest, following the small trail of chest hair over his abs before pausing just above his belt. Tracing the top of his suit pants, I seal my lips harder against his, pouring all my want and desire into him. With a growl, Trey yanks the loose sash of the robe, exposing me fully.

My knees dig into the mattress as I kneel and shrug off the robe, allowing it to puddle to the floor beside the bed. Keeping one knee planted, I slide the other across his lap, securing it to the bed on the other side of his hips. Trey breaks the kiss, nipping at my lower lip. My eyes flutter closed as he kisses along my jaw, scraping his along the column of my neck as he makes his way to my chest. Wetness pools between my spread thighs, an aching throb pulsing, demanding some kind of relief. Sinking against his lap, I rub my slick center along his hard cock still trapped inside his suit pants. I moan at the friction, and a wicked smile tugs at his lips just before he bucks his hips off the bed, slamming against my sensitive center.

I cry out as his teeth nip at my pebbled nipple before sucking it between his lips, flicking the tip with his tongue. Palming the other, he teases me mercilessly, the twisting and tugging bordering on the edge of pain. Again and again I rock against him, seeking some kind of relief, my body desperate for his.

The earlier emotions of the night come seeping through, causing a deep ache to build inside my chest. "I was so worried," I whisper against his ear, tugging him close. His lips brush along my neck, his nose delving into my hair to take a deep inhale. "I was afraid I'd lost you." The words pour out of me, cracking open my heart and allowing the swelling emotions to pour out. Chest to chest, I squeeze him tighter.

"Thank God for Kevlar or you would have."

My heart stutters. Palms against his shoulders, I push back to search his face. "What?"

His knuckles skim along the curves of my breasts. His chest rises as a pinch of pain scrunches his features. "I was hit in the chest, but my vest saved my life."

"Damnit," I shout. "I'm sorry! And here I am crawling all over you." I shift to move off his lap, but his hands clamp around my hips, holding me in place. With a scowl, I attempt to roll my weight. Before I register the absence of his right hand against my skin, a loud smack sounds in the room and a hot stinging pain radiates from my backside.

Eyes wide, I search his. "Did you just spank me?"

The corners of his lips tug upward. Biting his lower lip, he nods. "Try again." His voice is deep, full of need.

With little conviction, I wiggle like I'm trying to slide off his lap. This time I'm prepared for it. The sharp slap from his palm causes my breath to hitch but not in pain. The coarse calluses along his palm scrape my now sensitive backside, soothing the sting.

Eyes locked with his, I lift off his lap, my fingers delving between us to fumble with his belt. The ripples of his abs flex as I tug on the leather and unfasten his pants, dipping inside. A sharp hiss pushes through his clenched teeth as I wrap my hand around him and slide up and down, my thumb smearing the beading moisture along the soft head. My grip still around his hard shaft, Trey rolls us, pinning my back to the mattress.

His brown eyes scan every inch of my body, pausing to stare between my thighs. Two fingers tap my wrist, urging me to release him. Sliding off the bed, Trey shoves his suit pants to the floor and toes off his shoes. Climbing back onto the bed, palms pressing into the mattress beside my head, he stares down at me.

The soft pad of his index finger trails along my forehead, grazing along my cheekbone, down my nose, and across my lips like he's memorizing every inch of my face.

"You've changed me, Randi Sawyer. I'm a better man because of you. For the first time in my life, I have someone I'm willing—no, I want to give it all for. No matter what happens in the future, I want you to know that I don't regret anything. The only thing I could ever regret between us is for you not to know how much you mean to me. I love you, Randi."

A single tear drips from my eye. Tracking the drop, he leans forward, kissing it from my skin.

Lips against my ear, he whispers, "I'll never not love you, Mess."

Gripping my hip, he thrusts forward, easily sliding inside and causing my words to vanish on a gasp. His eyes shut as he pushes deeper, sealing our lower half tightly together. The soft skin of his back molds beneath my tight fingers. A hand slides down the outside of my thigh, hiking my leg higher, my knee nearly touching my shoulder. He thrusts hard, and I cry out as pleasure swells deep in my belly. Arching up, I nip at his lower lip, begging for his mouth to connect with mine.

Our tongues dance as his hips pound against mine. Our harsh breaths and the distinct slapping of skin are the only sounds in the quiet bedroom. When he pushes deep, I groan, my head digging deeper against the mattress as he circles his hips.

"I love your sounds," he mutters against my lips before sucking along my neck. As if for emphasis, he circles his hips again, his lower half somehow pressing hard against my clit and eliciting another pleasure-filled gasp from me. "That's it, baby."

I pop my hips off the bed, matching his demanding thrusts. His grunts and whispered curses drive me higher, inching closer toward the peak of pleasure. His bruising grip on my thigh slides lower, dipping between our bodies. He pinches my swollen nub at the same time as he thrusts in as deep as he can go.

My scream is swallowed up by his lips sealing against mine. I writhe beneath his heavy weight, soaking up every second of body-pulsing pleasure as his own orgasm ripples through his body. Beneath my fingers, his sweat-slicked back muscles quiver.

All the stress from earlier melts away, leaving my muscles relaxed and my entire body placid beneath his.

With a groan, his supporting arm gives out, causing his full weight to press me into the mattress. His hot, quick breaths brush against my ear, producing a sensual shiver that snakes down my spine. Unable to breathe, I press a palm against his chest. The pain-filled curse that passes his lips has me jerking my hand away like I've touched scorching hot metal.

"What?" I ask, trying to wiggle out from under him. "What did I do?"

He groans and rolls off me but immediately slides off the bed and heads for the bathroom instead of answering.

"Trey," I say, my tone like a schoolteacher.

A minute later, I watch him saunter back from the bathroom gloriously naked. A smile pulls at my lips at the undiluted confidence radiating off him. Squatting at the edge of the bed, he wraps a hand around my ankle and yanks me toward him. With a reverent touch, he swipes a warm, damp washcloth between my legs. His gaze flicks up to me with a shy smile before gazing back between my legs.

A couple more swipes and he tosses the dirty rag to the floor, then pushes off the mattress with a groan to stand. I suck in a sharp breath when the low lamplight hits the right angle of his chest, highlighting the hand-print-size bruise between his pecs. My fingers pause, hovering just above the darkening skin.

"I...." Tonight could've gone a different direction. The moment I just shared with the man who loves me, the real me, would've never happened if it weren't for his vest. Biting my upper lip, I let my hand drop. "You could've died," I whisper around the ball of unshed tears lodged in my throat.

A warm calloused palm presses against my cheek, tilting my face up to meet his. "But I didn't. Now come on," he says, brushing a thumb along my cheekbone. "Get dressed and come downstairs."

"Huh?"

Trey smiles, his hand sliding from my face as he steps away from the bed. I watch, mesmerized, as he dresses, loving the way his body moves. While buttoning up his shirt, he flicks his gaze to mine, catching my stare. "You look like you want to eat me."

"And what if I do?" I murmur while ogling his long, lean body. "What's so important that we have to put clothes on?"

"Don't say shit like that, Mess." His hands delve into his pants, tucking the tails of the light blue dress shirt inside before fastening his button and belt. "You know I'd rather stay up here with you, but I also know you'll want to hear the details of tonight."

I pop up from the bed, the earlier lusty haze gone.

He smiles while shaking his head. "See? Get dressed and meet me downstairs. T and the guys are waiting."

He chuckles as my eyes widen. A warm flush builds beneath my cheeks at the implication. If they've been waiting for Trey to bring me down and it's been… a while, they'll have put two and two together. With a curse, I lean over, intending to bury my face in the pillow, but my shoulder lands on the mattress at the wrong angle. Throbbing pain bolts down my shoulder, and I hiss as I smack the bed before rolling to take some of the pressure off my shoulder.

Trey's at my side, eyes and hands roaming my body, searching for injury. His gaze pauses on my shoulder, his face hardening with restrained fury. He brushes a thumb across the purpling skin so softly I barely even feel it.

"This happened tonight," he says more like a battle cry than a question. I swallow and nod, not really sure what to say. I've never seen him this intense before. It's almost like I can see the plans working in his head on how to kill the person who did this very slowly. "When we find out who caused this, I will make them pay for hurting you."

"I know you will." For several seconds, we sit in silence, his furious stare never leaving the bruise. Reaching out, I rub up and down his bicep. "I need to get dressed." When he still doesn't release me, I give his shoulder a hard shove. "Trouble, snap out of it. It's a bruise. I got hurt. You almost died. It's been a tough night for everyone. Now let me up so I can change and we can both find out what the hell is going on."

Those long dark lashes flutter open and closed several times before he finally pulls away. Running a hand through his dark hair, he shakes his head and moves toward the door.

An earlier conversation pops into my mind just as he reaches it. "And, Trouble?" He turns, brows raised in anticipation. "You are in trouble for not telling me everything. I'm not mad, but I will be if you don't come clean on everything. Understand?"

His features fall. Dread drops in my gut like a bowling ball into water.

"And I fully expect you to make it up to me, the omitting information part," I say while brushing the tips of two fingers up and down my inner thigh, his gaze tracking every inch.

His lips tug up in his signature smirk. "Now that's something to look forward to."

After the door clicks shut, I take a deep breath and roll off the bed, heading for the closet. Apprehension swirls in my lower belly as I yank a random pair of yoga pants from a drawer and slide a T-shirt off a hanger. Between Trey's revelation about buying the votes and the shooting, I'm not sure which one I'm more anxious to learn the truth about.

19

TREY

Back against the wall, I monitor the empty stairwell as the picture of ease, but inside I'm a fucking mess. Not only do we have to tell her there's a price on her head, but I also have to reveal the shit show my personal life has turned into these past few weeks. Who knows how she'll react.

With a soft groan, I relax my head back against the wall.

"It's your own damn fault, you pussy."

I eye my best friend. "Come again?"

"You heard me. It wouldn't be that big of a deal if you would've told her your plan from the start instead of doing it all behind her back."

"She would've said no," I say with a deep exhale. Shit, I need a cigarette. And a drink. Several, in fact. "I did this for her. She'll see that."

Tank barks out a laugh, garnering the other agents' attention. He waves them off and turns to me, still chuckling. "Keep telling yourself that."

He's wrong. Everything I did was for her. She didn't want to go back to Texas a failure. She's the one who was so upset that the vote might pass. Yes, there was a part of me that couldn't stand the thought of her leaving, stepping out of my life. But that's a small portion of the reason. I'm selfless, damnit.

Right?

I shake my head, the ends of my floppy hair sliding across my eyebrows.

"You need a damn haircut," Tank tosses out.

"You need to mind your own damn business. I'm doing it for her."

A wide, all-teeth smile spreads up his cheeks. "Ah, did I hit a nerve?"

"No."

He attempts to suppress his smile and fails. "Right. All I'm saying is be careful how you approach this with her."

Reluctantly, I close my eyes and motion for him to keep talking. "I'm listening."

Tank twists one way and then the other, stretching out his back. "First off, search her for weapons." Lightning fast, I reach out and smack the back of his bald head. "You think I'm kidding," he says on a laugh. "That girl is amazing, but she has a different level of crazy in her. All I'm saying is check her for anything sharp. I'm thinking of your balls here, Playboy."

Just the thought of her attacking my boys makes me cringe. I cup myself, giving them a reassuring squeeze.

"Thanks."

Tank nods and glances to the stairwell. "Make sure you don't—"

A soft creak sounds just as her feet appear, taking the steps hesitantly one at a time. Tank looks to me and shrugs.

The fuck.

"Don't do what?" I hiss, gripping his shoulder and pulling him back to me. "Don't do what?"

A look of pity flashes across his face, pulling a snarl from mine. "Lie. Be honest with her, lay it all out on the table. Hold nothing back. If I've learned one thing from marriage, it's that women can sniff that shit out. One small detail you purposefully withhold will come back to bite you on the ass one day." I arch a brow with an unbelieving look. "You think it'll be worth it, saving some of the pieces to ease the blow now, but when she finds out you held information back when she thought you were being honest with her, it'll be like a fucking atomic bomb—parts of your relationship destroyed, never able to recover. Trust me, Trey. Tell her *everything*."

I wince. Hopefully that doesn't count for friendships too. I've conveniently withheld the part Mother is using as leverage to ensure I do her bidding instead of the other way around. That snippet of information I'm keeping to myself until I know more.

Did that weasel back in Boone say something, or was it one of the team members, mine or beta team? Somehow she knows about me beating that fucker within an inch of his life. Hell, if Tank hadn't pulled me off him, I probably wouldn't have stopped there. Yes, I was pissed at that loser for how he spoke and looked at Randi, but it was more of a last straw kind of thing. So much had built up over that past year, and that idiot was just the match to ignite the inferno inside me. Either way, Mother knows, and now not only do I have to figure out how and who, but also how to get out of the shit I've stepped into with both feet.

Releasing his shoulder, I step back and turn to the stairwell. Hazel eyes meet mine. Swallowing back the guilt and nerves, I turn for the door and yank it open.

"I need some air."

Well, that solidifies it.

I'm a chickenshit.

I'm running from the woman I love so I don't have to tell her how I've screwed everything up. There has to be a way to spin it all to make her see my side. Make her see I just didn't want her to hurt, didn't want her to leave.

Silky strands of my dark hair slide through my fingers. Tugging on the ends, I use the sharp bite of pain to ground me to the present.

I'm in such deep shit, and not only with Randi. Just being at the estate causes the cold, malicious feelings to surface; how will I survive diving back into that world full time? Randi saved me once from the jaded, bitter cavern I'd settled into, and she's the only one who can keep me from sinking back. The question is, after I tell her everything, lay it all on the line, will she want to?

The wooden railing presses into my palms, supporting my heavy weight as I lean against it, head drooped forward. Digging my nails into the wood, I tighten my grip, the muscles of my arms and back flexing. Pain radiates from the center of my chest, causing my breath to catch.

Behind me the back door opens, the door's hinges whining. Two sets of distinct footsteps parade out onto the wraparound porch, one soft, barely audible, while the other is heavy, purposeful. Not moving, I take a deep breath and wince at the blooming ache. Hell, being shot sucks. Even with the vest it fucking hurts. Without the vest, I'd be dead, so I can't really complain, but still, hurting with every breath isn't my idea of something to celebrate.

To my right, the wicker rocking chair creaks with the weight of someone settling into it. Neither has said a word, waiting for me to collect my thoughts, I suppose. But where do I start? Everything seems fuzzy with the exhaustion and the handful of Advil I took before heading up to Randi's room.

"What do you want to know first?" I ask, still staring at the wooden planks of the porch.

The wicker creaks, the legs rocking backward and then forward once again. At their lack of response, I glance over my shoulder, making sure they're still there. Tank leans against the house just behind where Randi sits, rocking. Neither is looking at me; both have their gazes locked on the vast backyard. I scan the area, searching for whatever they see but coming up empty.

"Tonight," Randi eventually says in a tone that tells of her own exhaustion.

Guilt eats at my gut, forcing my attention off her and back to the decking.

"Part of what you didn't want to know back in Chile is why tonight happened," Tank answers for me. A sliver of the tension eases from my shoulders as he takes the lead. "Based on the information inside, we believe Whit is the one responsible for the tracking of Taeler and you. However, along with that information, there were new details that were specifically about you. And not with the sole intent of gathering intel but for a deadlier outcome."

The slow rocking stills. Again the thin wooden rods creak as she shifts her weight.

"It's Birmingham. He wants you dead," I say, making what T so carefully beat around the bush blatantly obvious. She needs to know she's in danger. Her role comes with it, but never has a VP had to also be on their guard against internal threats as well.

"Oh."

At her simple response, I push off the railing and lean back against a supporting wooden post. Knees against her chest, chin on her knees, she looks young, innocent, vulnerable. Every muscle twitches, eager to wrap her up in my arms, to ease the thoughts racing through her head.

"I'm not surprised," she says moments later.

I shoot a concerned look at Tank. "What do you mean, you're not surprised?"

The soft skin of her cheek molds around her knee as she tilts her head to focus on me.

"He was really pissed I went to Chile, to the OPEC summit, when he specifically told me not to. He said I'd regret it, but I have to admit, wanting me dead is a little extreme even for Kyle." She huffs and presses her forehead against her thighs. "Is there anyone in this town who doesn't want me gone or dead?" Deafening silence fills the porch. "That's not a rhetorical question," she adds.

"We don't," Tank says, stepping forward. Wrapping his big hands around the top of the rocker, he gives it a small shake, causing her head to snap up. "Tonight you were set up."

She snorts. "No shit, Sherlock."

Tank glares down at her. "Smartass. You were the only target. The only other injuries on the team were minor, except Benson's, which would've been fatal if he didn't have his vest on. And his was due to him blocking the bullet that was intended for you."

Her head whips around. I hold her intense stare, allowing her time to process Tank's words.

"I'd do it again, Mess," I say, not looking away from her wide eyes.

"Those bastards could've taken us all out, but they didn't. We were fish in a barrel out there."

All the blood drains from her face. Trembling fingers wrap around her neck before sliding down to press against her chest. She sways in the chair. Lunging forward, I grip her shoulder, keeping her upright. I hiss in pain at the quick movement pulling my aching chest muscles. Tank tugs her feet from the seat and straightens them out, allowing the blood to flow easily in an attempt to keep her from passing out on us.

"Randi," I demand. Tank's words from weeks ago filter in. "Stop."

Hardening my gaze, I give her shoulder a quick shake. I will not be her downfall. I will not baby her and make her weak. She's stronger than this, stronger than I give her credit for, and it's time I remember that. If I love her, I'll stop being the person who coddles her, who weakens her inner strength. No, I'll be the one who pushes her, makes her stronger, reminds her of how strong she really is.

"Tonight happened, and we'll be better prepared next time." I flick my gaze up to Tank. With a nod, I step back. Sliding my hands off her takes more effort than ever before.

"And to be prepared," he says, his voice hard, "we need to know everything. Every strange phone call, every battle with Birmingham or Whit. Everything, you hear me?"

Pinkie nail between her teeth, she nods. "Okay, I just didn't realize...." She shakes her head. "That fucker. I hope he dies a slow death." She purses her lips, a determined look flashing across her features. "I will not let him win. Trying to off me because I didn't follow one of his requests is utter bullshit. Who does he think he is?"

"I'm not sure he's really thinking." Shoulder against the post, I stare out into the backyard. "I'll admit Birmingham is a manipulative, power-hungry fuckstick who thinks everyone is beneath him, but this?" I shake my head and turn back to face them. "It seems desperate. Over the top for him, for anyone—well, anyone except Whit. Whit keeping track of you and those important to you doesn't surprise me at all. He's probably hoping for some kind of leverage to use against you or dangle like a cat and mouse game." I roll my upper back against the rounded post, attempting to massage a knot from my muscles. "You said Birmingham was pissed on that call?"

Her head bobs up and down. "Now that you mention it, there was something different about the whole thing. Yeah, I've pissed him off plenty of times, but that call, his voice... there was something more than rage in it. Maybe a hint of panic?"

"But why?" Tank adds in. "What could he be hiding that he'd risk hiring a contract killer to take her out? What's worth that?"

"Ah, remember, I'm not worth anything to him anymore," Randi says with a bite to her tone. "I served my purpose, got him into the White House. Now I'm disposable in his eyes." Her eyes seem to glaze over, a far-off look settling into an unfocused stare. "In law school, he enjoyed pushing me to the brink, testing how far he could go before I would break, but you're right, this seems like more. Then it was all fun and games to him, but now, if what y'all say is true, then something changed. Almost like... almost like I'm a liability."

Half of me wants to cradle her in my arms, protecting her from that dipshit, while the other half is eager to race straight for the White House to put an end to all this now. But neither is possible or helpful. What good would I be in protecting her if I'm in federal prison?

"Also, while we're on the subject, Grem has decided to stay down in Austin leading Taeler's protection detail permanently."

"Of course he did," she says. "At least I know someone capable is watching out for her. That's a small concession to knowing it won't take long before they're all over each other." She smirks and flicks a quick look at me. "Not that I can say anything. I just want her to be careful, you know. She's all I have—well, besides my mom."

"How's she doing, by the way?" I ask. Perching along the railing, I stretch my legs out and cross my ankles.

Randi nods several times before speaking up. "Good, I guess. She's still out at the rehab facility, but more in their recovery program side. It's expensive, her living there and trying to adjust to normal life, but it's better than her going back to Texas and relapsing. She can't stay there forever, but for now it's the best place for her. Even if it costs me a kidney." Leaning back in the rocker, she rests her head and closes her eyes. "It's crazy. How much I'm paying a month for that place used to be what I made in four. Now it's still a big expense but not out of the question. It's been over two years since Kyle walked into my office and changed my life. Now here I am." Her eyes flutter open and scan the porch, then the backyard. "I'm in this amazing house, have no financial worries, have friends," she says with a smile, "and a price on my head."

"Would you say it was worth it?" Tank asks, coming to sit beside me. The railing shakes under his weight. I shoot him a look and stand before the wood splinters beneath us.

A cool spring breeze whispers through the night, brushing along my exposed forearms and cooling the sweat beading along my neck and brow. Randi shivers and wraps her arms tight around her torso. Without a second thought, I head inside and snag a blanket from the nearest coat closet. Back outside, I unfold the thick material and gently wrap it around the shivering Randi.

"Thank you," she whispers.

"You're welcome."

A pointed, annoyed cough interrupts the small moment we slipped into. Eyes on hers, I step back, putting space between us.

"Was it worth it, or is it worth it?" she says, repeating Tank's question after clearing her throat. Sliding her gaze over to him, she shrugs. "Yes and no. Right now, with tonight and the upcoming vote, knowing I'm the one who put that dipshit in office, I'm going with a no. But then I see the good I'm doing with the other committees and projects I have going on all around the country, plus you two, and I know I'd do it all over again just for that."

Do not kiss her.

Do not kiss her.

Do not kiss her.

Even with the mantra running over and over in my mind, I can't stop my feet from taking a step and then another toward her. This pull, her smell, her voice—everything about her calls to me. The back of the wicker chair digs into my bare forearm as I support my weight to lean low, putting my head level with hers.

I take in every beautiful inch of her face before meeting her confused gaze.

Here it goes. Now's the time to tell her. Everything.

"Before I tell you about the bill, I need to know something, Mess."

A quick breath whistles through her teeth. "And what's that, Trouble?"

"Do you have anything sharp on you?"

20

RANDI

"The hell?" I ask, pushing his shoulder, needing a few inches between us to breathe normally. Ugh, it's so hard to think straight with him close. His intoxicating cologne, that smirk, his knowing eyes, the love pouring off him. And then he goes and says that? "Seriously, Trey. What the fuck?"

The heaviness of our conversation and the gloomy mood whip away with the breeze, leaving behind a lot of confusion on my part and humor on his.

"Smooth, Playboy. Real smooth." Tank's voice lightens with laughter, even though it's clear he's trying to suppress it.

"So you're in on this together?" I ask, shifting in the wicker seat to glare at T. "What's he talking about? Sharp things?"

"We thought it would be best to make sure you weren't armed before Benson here came clean on his... side agreements."

All the fight leaves my body, my muscles turning useless. "Is it that bad?"

Trey shakes his head, his hair brushing onto his forehead. My fingers itch to reach up and push it out of his eyes. I love his hair, especially the way it feels sliding between my fingers. The stubble along his jaw twitches in time with the tight muscle beneath, signaling the tension below the forced humor.

"I don't know where to start," he says, breathing out a slow, controlled breath. Pushing off the chair, he stands to pace along the length of the porch. T and I monitor each of his movements as he strides away and then back again.

Trey pauses at the farthest point away, keeping his back turned to us.

"It started that day in your office after Jessica left. She'd just told you that the vote would probably pass the House and you were close in the Senate." Tipping his chin toward his shoulder, he keeps his back to us but says, "Do you remember that? When you were so upset about going home, about having to leave DC?"

I swallow hard, hoping it'll help keep my voice from quivering. "I do."

"After that, I looked at the numbers Jessica had pulled together and I saw it, I saw why you were so upset. Unless something big happened, the bill would pass the House and Senate with ease." Turning on his heels, he faces our way but doesn't take a step closer. "I'll admit I thought I was doing this all for you, but tonight, Tank made me realize that I did it for me. I couldn't let you leave, not when...." Pausing, he runs a hand through his hair as he collects his thoughts. "Not when I wasn't ready to let you go. Seeing you so upset broke me, and I knew right then that I'd do anything, give up anything and everything, to make sure you got what you wanted. And me too.

"I know what people say about you in this town, knew you'd never get the votes even with Jessica's help. She whipped a lot of votes your way but not enough, and I knew someone who could get us the right people, enough people, to side with you."

Staying on the other end of the porch, he leans against the railing, gripping it while he stares out at the rising dawn. Pinks and blue burst across the sky, signaling another beautiful spring day ahead. But I can't appreciate its beauty, can't look at anything other than the man in obvious inner turmoil, all because of me.

"I went to my parents."

"You already said that in the SUV earlier. What's so bad about that?" So he asked his parents for something, big deal. I'm a little jealous that he has someone he can go to and ask for help when it's always been the opposite relationship between me and mom.

It's a great idea, one I....

Hold on.

"I suggested going to them at the beginning of all this shit, that day in the library. And you were all 'no, they're sailing on the easy boat down the sea of tranquility' or something stupid like that."

"It wasn't an option then."

"But it is now?"

"Well, yeah."

I scoff. "Because now it's your decision and not mine? Now you get to play the brilliant save-the-day idea."

"Seriously?" he bites out. "You know I wouldn't do that."

"Then what?" I nearly shout. "What made the timing different?"

"Mess," he says, his nervous tone and sad eyes smothering my rising frustration. "My parents aren't the best people. They're fucking awful human beings actually. Everything comes with a cost, even for me."

The soft flannel fabric of the blanket slips between my fingers as I tighten my grip, waiting for the bomb to drop. "Oh, so what you mean by timing is really bargaining chips. What did you give them?"

Shoving off the banister, Trey picks up his pacing once again. I track each of his steps, anxiety and worry rising higher with each second he doesn't respond.

"Trey, talk to me."

"Me."

I shake my head, not understanding. "I don't—"

"It was only going to be for show. I was going to walk away, despite the consequences, but now I'm fucked." Turning his focus to T, he gives him a hard look. "I should've told you this before tonight, I get that, but... I think we have a rat on our team."

An animal-type growl rumbles from T's chest. I shrink back at the look of pure vehemence on his normally emotionless face. "What the hell are you talking about, Trey?"

Trey holds up his index finger, putting a pause on that part of the conversation. "In exchange for the votes, I promised my mother I'd step back into the political scene—"

I lift the blanket to cover my open mouth. "But you hate it. You've said many times how glad you are that you didn't take that track for your life. Why would you do that?"

He nods. "It was all I had for a bargaining chip. My parents are desperate to get me back in that scene, so I used it against them. They were for the bill, Randi, I didn't have any other choice."

"Okay, well, we can figure it out. That's not so bad. I mean—"

"There's more."

I snap my lips shut and press the blanket against them to keep from interrupting again.

"I had to bring Jessica into this mess. I knew they would want me to ease back into the scene, so I asked her to help. She was more than willing, considering she knew how much stopping the bill meant to you and she sees you as a friend."

Jealousy heats my core. I fist the blanket tighter, my nails digging into the flannel cloth.

"I told them it would be a fake couple-type thing, just her on my arm at charity functions and galas and shit like that. My parents have wanted us to join our two families, the Bensons and Hawthornes, and this was a way for me to make sure they couldn't say no. My plan was after the four years—"

"Four years!" I exclaim, nearly jumping out of my seat.

He shoots me an incredulous look. "I wanted to wait until you were done with your term before backing out on my end of the bargain so the backlash wouldn't affect you. My parents are vindictive assholes. If I showed even a hint of not following through, they would've turned every last person in DC against you."

I let out an annoyed huff and situate the blanket back around my shoulders. "Everyone is already against me. Not sure how anyone could make it worse."

"If anyone could, it's my parents."

With a heavy sigh I press the blanket against my closed eyelids. "What do you have to do at the end of the four years?"

"I was to truly enter the political scene, run for office, whatever my parents deemed me fit for. Wouldn't surprise me if they had hopes of me running for president or vice." He rolls his shoulders and stretches out his neck.

"What's with the snitch you mentioned?" T interjects.

"It's why I can't back out like I planned. This was all for show, even with their promises of cutting off my inheritance and trust if I backed out. I never intended for it to go further than Jessica and me attending a few parties. And why—" I watch his Adam's apple bob as he swallows hard. Shit, this is bad. "Why I couldn't say no when they altered my original plan in their favor. Instead of using Jessica as *my* pawn, I'm now theirs. After we win the Senate, after the bill fails, my mother will host a party where she will announce my engagement to Jessica."

"Engaged. Like an arranged marriage type of thing," I deadpan. "You're joking. Did I time warp into eighteenth-century England where parents can do that legally? What the hell, Trey?"

He shakes his head, those shiny dark locks glinting in the rising sun. "I suspect Jessica told them of my plans to give everything up, to not follow through once I got what I wanted, which is why they changed the plan. There was still a loophole, one I saw immediately. I could still walk away, maybe losing a little face with the media, but I could still do it. That's when my mother dropped the fucking bomb on me, saying if I didn't follow through, she'd make sure I was charged for assault with a deadly weapon."

The two men share a hard look. T curses and storms to Trey's side, shoving his shoulder hard. "Why in the hell didn't you tell me sooner?" he roars right in Trey's face.

"I didn't know if it was one of our guys or that fucker in Boone. I still don't know."

"Jimmy," I whisper to myself. "That's what she's holding over your head?"

Trey glances over T's shoulder and nods, his eyes dark with guilt and sorrow.

"So all this is because of me. All of it." Emptiness swallows up my earlier surging emotions, leaving me cold from the inside out. "Why? Why did you do it, any of it?" Nothing makes sense. Why would someone like him put so much effort, so much care into me, us? He had the perfect life before I walked into it, and now it's fucked because of my sheer presence.

A shadow drapes over me, forcing my eyes up. Trey's honey brown eyes search mine, the laugh lines I love so much now creased with visible concern.

"You know why," he whispers. Bracing one hand on the back of the rocker and one on the armrest, he leans forward, brushing his nose against my own. I inhale deeply, soaking in his scent and the warmth radiating off him.

"I feel... I feel guilty," I admit. I search his eyes, looking for any signs that he also blames me. "None of this would've happened without me here."

"I also wouldn't have had a reason to fight, to want to give my all for someone. I love you, Randi Sawyer, and there isn't anything I wouldn't do for you." Inching closer, he closes the distance between our lips, brushing his softly over mine. "Don't feel guilty, please. I did this, and I'll get out of it. Somehow."

"Damn," Tank grunts, breaking our tender moment. Trey shoots him a glare, his eyes softening when they meet mine again. The wicker groans as Trey pushes off to stand straight. "That mother of yours is one cruel piece."

A grunt of agreement from Trey has a small smile pulling at my lips.

"That she is. Threatening to send your son to federal prison isn't really something that's listed on the top ten things a decent mother does."

Flicking the blanket off my hands, I reach forward and interlace my fingers with Trey's, giving them a squeeze of reassurance. "I'll admit my mom is a lot of things, and I've cleaned up after her a lot, a lot a lot, but even her shit show is nothing compared to what your mother sounds like. I didn't think it would be possible for me to feel sorry for you, Trouble, but I do."

"Any idea who the fucker is who told her about that incident?" T asks.

Trey shakes his head. "No clue. The past couple weeks, I've been trying to feel the guys out, but hell, it could've even been one of the beta team members. A couple were there too, remember? Or one of our guys could've mentioned it to someone on another team and somehow my mother caught wind of it. Or that fucker I beat the shit out of said something."

T lets out an annoyed grunt.

Footsteps and then the opening of the back door draw our attention. My secretary, looking a little disheveled like she'd been snatched out of bed, pauses when she finds three sets of eyes on her. Chewing on her lip, she tucks a chunk of hair behind her ear and shuffles her weight from foot to foot.

"Madam VP?"

I roll my eyes and push up from the chair, casually snaking my hand from Trey's to tuck it back under the blanket. "It's Randi. How many times do we have to cover that?"

She nods fast like a bobblehead doll. "The president's secretary called, said the president demanded I find you."

"Of course he did." I look from Trey to T and back to my secretary. The fucker probably wants to ask how I'm still alive. If the boys' pursed lips and tight eyes say anything, it's that the two men agree.

"He wants you in the Oval Office as soon as possible," she says, her voice trembling.

"Okay, thanks." The woman doesn't move an inch. My paper-thin patience from the long night and too-heavy morning conversation snaps. "I got it, okay? You're good to go back home. I'll see you later."

With a relieved exhale, she flashes a quick, uneasy smile and darts back into the house.

"I'm going home," T announces, sounding tired. I take in the deep bags under his eyes and the slump of his normally straight shoulders. Fuck, how could I forget these guys have been up for nearly twenty-four hours? Plus the stress of the night would wear even the toughest man down. "I'll let beta team know you're heading out and to not leave your side."

Not giving it a second thought, I stride across the porch and wrap my arms around his thick waist. The buttons of his dress shirt press into my cheek as I squeeze him tight.

"Thank you for everything, T. I'm so glad you're okay."

"It'd take a lot more than last night to take me away from my Sarah." Pressure against my shoulder urges me back a step, putting a gap between us. "But I do need to know you heard me earlier. To make sure this doesn't happen again, we need to know *everything*. Every conversation, every strange call, every weird feeling. You have a big part in keeping you and us safe. Do you understand?"

I nod and bite my lip to keep it from trembling. "I do. I'll be better, promise. Now that I know what's going on," I say, giving him a glare with zero fight behind it, "I'll be sure to keep you guys in the loop. But you have to do the same with me. I know I carry too much on my own shoulders, and I know I let the stress weigh me down, but I need to know all this stuff. I'll relax when I'm dead." I give him a weary smile, which he returns with a soft chuckle.

"Not on my watch, Randi." With a wave to Trey, T marches into the house, leaving Trey and I alone on the now-glowing porch.

"What are you thinking, Mess?" The stress and exhaustion in his tone pulls at my heart.

"Do you like her?" I ask before I even process my own words. They just slip out like my heart is talking instead of my head.

"Jessica?"

"Yes." I roll my eyes. "Jessica. Are you not too disappointed about the relationship aspect of the agreement?"

Trey's nose scrunches, his whole face pinching. "Fuck no. Listen, my parents and her parents have wanted this for a long time. That's all this is. I don't like her. Hell, I can barely stand being around her. I love you, Randi. You're the one I want to be with."

I wince and press the heel of my palm against my breastbone.

What do I feel? I search my heart, dig through my thoughts, trying to figure out what to tell him. I'd love to put him at ease, let him know what he did was okay, but I can't. Not until I know what I'm thinking, what I'm feeling about it all. A lot has happened in the last twelve hours, and I need time to process everything.

"I need time," I say, looking away before his sad puppy dog look breaks me. "I don't know how I feel about last night, about what you said, what you did. Part of me is grateful that you'd give up so much for me, that you'd even think about doing something like that for me. I've never had someone who gave up everything. That was always my role—giving and giving and never getting anything back. So it's new, and I don't know how to process it, because then there's the fact that you've known about this for months and didn't tell me. Did you think I would be mad? Did you want to let me think I did this all on my own once the bill failed?" I shake my head. "When did you know about this forced relationship with Jessica?"

His silence speaks volumes.

"See?" I toss my hands up and immediately regret it when a burst of cool morning air slides along my toasty body. "You've known and kept it from me. I know your heart was in the right place but still I feel," I massage a fist against the ache growing in my chest. "I hurt because of it all. I need to separate it, understand why I feel the way I do before I can move on from this."

His expression falls, his head dropping forward as he nods in agreement.

"Okay," he croaks. "Space, time. I hear you. I don't like it, but I hear you."

The distance between us feels like miles as I stare at his broken posture from across the porch. Every muscle screams to run to him, to wrap my arms around his neck and ease the pain he's clearly going through. But I can't. I won't. I deserve the time to process it all. He's had months to work through it, to come to terms with his actions. I've had fifteen minutes.

"Just don't tell me we're over," he whispers, the words barely audible over the birds' cheery morning songs.

"Of course not," I say with force so he knows that's not even a consideration. "I just need a second to think this over. I know you meant well, Trey, and I know you did it for both of us, but I still need time to process it all, you know?"

His shoulders slump, rounding further. I swallow back the building tears and take a step toward the back door. Once inside, I shut the door behind me and lean against it, tugging the blanket tighter around my shoulders and resting my chin on my fists. For the first time in my life, my mind is silent, no internal conversations to decipher through.

Around me, the beta team scuffles about, their loud voices and heavy footsteps barely registering as more than distant background noise.

I almost died.

Trey almost died.

Trey's engaged.

Raising my shoulders, I take shelter in the thick blanket as I move toward the stairs to get ready for my meeting with Kyle.

First I'll handle Kyle, and then I'll process this morning's conversation.

One thing at a time.

21

RANDI

I take a deep inhale of the stale warm air. I'd actually prefer it to be colder than this stuffy, germ-breeding hotness. Careful to keep my movements inconspicuous, I slide two fingers beneath my stiff collar and give a slight tug away from my sweaty skin. Maybe it's not that warm in here to everyone else, but to me, with my body on high alert, I'm not sure an ice bath would be enough to cool me down. My pulse races beneath my skin, making my core temperature soar even higher.

My tongue sticks to the roof of my dry mouth as my palms dampen with a slick sheen of sweat.

The thick mahogany door stands before me. With a quick glance right and then left, I rap my knuckles against the solid surface. I smooth my palms down my jacket and ensure the bright blue dress shirt remains tucked in on the sides of my black tailored pantsuit. I have a love for good suits, but this one is my favorite by far. The tailor cut it to accentuate the curves I have while hiding the areas that still need 'filling out.' Even with the muscle-building workouts Trey planned out and the self-defense lessons with Sarah, I've only gained ten pounds and have several more to go. Even at five foot seven, my frame is still too thin. Where most see a woman dedicated to her appearance, I see a woman still clinging to her past life. Strange how those two contradict each other in this world. They see someone thick and beautiful where the reality is the person is only eating just enough to stay alive.

Two years ago, when Kyle pulled me from the desolate spot I was in, I hated the idea of the woman I am now. But now that I'm here, I want more, think I deserve more than I was given. A good thing or a bad thing? Who knows.

I knock again, this time putting a little annoyance into my three sharp taps. Before my hand can fall back to my side, the door whooshes open. I take a hesitant step back at the wild look in Kyle's bloodshot eyes. His suit is wrinkled, tie askew, and hair disheveled like he's run his fingers through it too many times.

It's not even 8:00 a.m.

Not the typical perfectly styled Kyle I'm used to.

"What's wrong?" I ask.

Squaring my shoulders, I step into the Oval Office, barely squeezing between Kyle and the doorframe without touching either. My steps falter when I find Shawn lounging completely relaxed along one of the love seats. I give him a quick once-over but find nothing amiss, unlike Kyle.

Shawn's gaze cuts to Kyle, his smirk growing to a full grin.

"Yeah, man, what's wrong?" he asks innocently, but the hint of a taunt laces his words.

"Get out, Shawn. Go do your fucking job," Kyle barks.

The two men engage in a stare-off as Shawn meanders to the door. Before he steps out, he glances back to where I still stand, unmoving, in the middle of the room.

"Good to see you in one piece, Trailer." That sinister smile of his pulls his lips up. I suppress a terrified shudder. "Maybe next time you won't be so lucky."

I suck in a quick breath and hold it.

His chuckle continues as he marches down the hall until Kyle slams the heavy wooden door shut, cutting off any noise.

"I heard about last night," Kyle grumbles as he brushes past me to sit behind the most important desk in history. "How'd you make it out alive?"

Interesting way to phrase that question.

"My secret service team. They got me out and home safely."

"No fatalities?"

I shake my head. Forcing my feet to move, I walk toward the grouping of couches and lower to sit on the edge of the one Shawn just vacated. "A few injuries but nothing serious."

Head down, he doesn't look up from the stack of papers he's thumbing through. "That's surprising."

"How come I don't hear any empathy or shock in your voice?"

His ice blue eyes peer up through dark lashes. "If you're looking for emotional support with me, you're the idiot I always knew you were."

I flip him the bird. "Then why'd you call me here if not to make sure I'm okay?"

"Couple things. First, are you already packing your bags to head to that shithole you call home?"

I tilt my head, not understanding his question.

"Don't play dumb with me, Walmart. My bill won the House, and we have the Senate locked in. Next month you'll be turning in your resignation to me and getting your ass out of my city. This is the push you need to realize you don't belong here. You're no one, and no one will miss you when you're gone. Hell, someone might even throw me a fucking party."

Pursing my lips, I hold back the need to tell this fucker it's not won yet. But something tells me it's best to keep Trey's parents help to myself. If Kyle knew they were swaying to my side because of their selfless son's love for me, he might put pressure on the few key senators to keep them voting no.

Glancing to my suit pants, I pick at an imaginary piece of lint to avoid showing my hand.

"The OPEC summit—the one I specifically told you not to go to." His brows raise a fraction, but his Botoxed forehead stays smooth, keeping them from rising higher. Speaking of that.... I graze the pads of two fingers along my own brow, feeling for any wrinkles. "What happened?"

"Why do you care? If you didn't—"

The lamp and bottle of water on top of the desk rattle at his tight fist slamming against the shiny surface. "Just answer me, damnit!" he bellows. A red flush spreads along his cheeks, his nostrils flaring with each heavy breath. "Tell me what happened, every detail."

Something about the look in his eyes, the 'on the edge of reason' appearance, shifts me into self-preservation mode. So I tell him everything, from the moment I arrived until Air Force Two touched down back in DC. Well, everything minus the random meeting with my new Russian friend. If I've learned anything these past few months, it's good to have secrets up your sleeve, and having the Russian president offering me inside details on things he shouldn't know is definitely a secret I want to keep to myself.

"That's it?" he asks, visibly relaxing into his chair.

A soft knock sounds at the door leading to his admin and secretary's area, drawing our attention.

I nearly snort at the beautiful brunette cautiously stepping into the office. From her perfect pencil skirt suit to her flawless makeup, this is exactly who I expect Kyle to have as a secretary.

"Mr. President, Sam with the Department of Justice is holding for you. Again."

The earlier relief disappears in an instant. Face contorted in anger, Kyle's face flushes scarlet.

"Tell them I'll get to them when I can. Again," he grits out. The pen in his hand nearly breaks at the pressure of bending at both ends between his hands. "I'm in the middle of a fucking meeting."

The young woman clears her throat and shuffles from one high heel to the other. "He says he'll hold."

The small twitch of his head causes my brows to furrow. The way he's avoiding eye contact and the nervous way he fiddles with the pen are a dead giveaway for the reluctance he has with talking to this Sam guy.

"Then let him wait," he says on a heavy sigh. He runs his fingers through his hair and swivels around to face the large bay windows.

At his obvious rude dismissal, the secretary gives me a sympathetic smile and leaves us alone once again.

Minutes pass after her departure, but still Kyle doesn't say a word, doesn't turn to face me.

My foot bobs against the oriental rug as I gnaw on my thumbnail. After another minute of silence, I toss my hands in the air. "Guess we're done, then?" Palms against the couch cushion, I make to stand and leave.

"One more thing." His overstuffed leather office chair is silent as he swivels back around to face me. "Next time I say no, it means fucking no. Don't pull that shit again, or next time you won't be so lucky."

A tremble starts in my fingers before racking my entire body. It's one thing for the guys to tell me what they suspect or know, but it's a totally different feel when it's confirmed from the horse's mouth. Or ass's mouth, in this case.

"That's attempted murder, you psycho," I spit out before I can think better of it.

Anger and a bit of fear boil in my gut at his nonchalant chuckle.

"Only if you can prove it, Walmart. Don't you remember that from law school? A conviction only holds if you have evidentiary support. Which I can guarantee you don't have."

I open my mouth, ready to blast the fool with the fact that I do, but snap it shut at the last second. I need to keep that tidbit to myself for now.

Balling my fingers into a tight fist, I swallow back the words and march for the door. Just as my fingers graze the doorknob, Kyle's words take root, snapping a light bulb on in my mind.

"Proof," I whisper. A genuine smile pulls at my lips as I turn to face the man sitting behind the desk once more. "You're right, Kyle. No matter who you are, you have to have proof."

His lips dip in a frown. "That's what I fucking said. Get out. I have shit to do."

Eagerly I give him a two-finger salute—*What the fuck is wrong with me and hand signals?*—and yank the door open before speed-walking down the hall. The two beta team agents flank me as we march through the White House. Practically running down the stairs, I dive into the waiting SUV and immediately search through my laptop bag.

Pulling out my iPad, I open a blank document. Fingers flying across the flat screen, I have ten bullet points down on how we can oppose Trey's mother's blackmail when I pause. I stare at my list. It's a great list, if I do say so myself. It's the few cases I remember from law school and others I've randomly followed in the past. This is what I need to show Trey, that the case against him would never make it to court, and if it did, he would win. But there's something holding me back.

Fuckity fuck.

Biting my lip, I pitch the iPad aside and lean back against the leather seat to stare blankly out the side window. Outside, the buildings race by, pedestrians stare at the procession, and cars honk, annoyed that we're inconveniencing them with traffic. A thick ray of sun cuts through the dark tint, warming my cheek. Closing my eyes, I take a deep breath and hold it to ease the growing ball of dread in my gut.

I have the knowledge. I know the loophole to get Trey out of the mess he's gotten himself into—all for me.

Now the question is do I use it and make a formidable enemy?

Or do I play the political power game where knowledge is power and hold this information close to my chest for now, leaving Trey in the trenches of this political battle he brought on himself?

My heart begs me in one direction while my mind, focused on my political career, tugs me another.

Which one do I listen to?

22

RANDI

July

The celebration is in full swing by the time I arrive. Limos and town cars idle along the tree-lined drive, waiting to drop off their passengers. Careful to not snag the soft silk of my dress, I tug at the tight midsection, hoping to give me an extra inch to take a deep breath for the first time since I slid the beautiful thing on. White is not my normal choice in dress color, but my wardrobe assistant told me it was perfect for this celebratory party.

A single strap cuts across my chest, leaving both shoulders bare. I suggested we leave my tattoos uncovered as an additional slap to Kyle tonight, but I was overruled by, well, everyone. Apparently there are still some parts of me, parts of my past, that people don't want to know about. So after layers of careful tattoo-specific cover-up, both shoulders now appear classy—their words, not mine.

I finger an earlobe, fiddling with the diamond chandelier earrings just to make sure they're still there. No way would I spend the kind of money needed to buy these suckers, but the jewelry shop was more than happy to lend them to me for the night.

The SUV inches forward, drawing us closer to the entrance. Swiping the black clutch from the other seat, I snap it open and pull out my phone. A bolt of anticipation shoots to my gut as I press the Home button with the hopes of seeing a text from Trey. The anticipation evaporates, leaving behind disappointment at the blank screen.

Today was a whirlwind for him too, preparing for the party and keeping his mother placated. It's no surprise he hasn't reached out in the twenty minutes it took for us to drive over here. We've texted all day, mostly him making sure I'm okay and not planning to bail on tonight. It was a valid concern to have; all day my stomach has twisted with nerves.

After tonight, when his mom introduces Trey and Jessica to everyone as a new up-and-coming power couple, it'll be hard to turn back. But this is what needs to happen. This has to go forward if I want anything to go smoothly over the next three years I'm in office.

After leaving the White House that day, I realized making enemies with his mom, all for a man, was putting my eggs in one basket, so to speak. A man who I like a lot, but love?

What is love anyway?

I thought I loved Ben way back in the day, but look how that turned out.

My love for Mom is so dysfunctional that it would take years of therapy to untwist that relationship.

I do love Tae, with all my heart, but that's a different type of love. That love is incomparable to any other.

I think.

Pursing my lips, I slide them back and forth along the layers of red lipstick.

Maybe after the life I've had, I'm incapable of real connection. I didn't have anyone to lean on, no one to really trust and depend on. But now there's Trey. But is great sex and dependability love? I'd rather be around him than anyone else. I trust him wholeheartedly. I'd do anything for him and know he feels the same. My heart races when he's around, but that could also be because he's smoking hot and always looks damn edible in his tailored suits and sexy smirks.

Where's the line between lust and love? And how do you know which side you're on?

I pitch forward slightly as the SUV comes to a slow stop. With a deep breath, I turn, angling my knees toward the door, preparing to step out once it opens. Warm summer air breezes through the SUV as the door swings outward. A dark mitt of a hand extends into the SUV. With a small smile on my perfectly painted lips, I grasp T's hand and step out onto the path.

"No seat belt?" he grumbles as he flicks his gaze from me to the back seat.

I shake my head, the soft waves of my dark hair gliding along my exposed back. "It would wrinkle the dress."

"Wrinkles or potential death by being thrown through glass. Yeah, I can see how wrinkles won out."

My red-tipped fingers pat his wide shoulder. "It's okay, T. I'm here and safe. No more worrying. We won, remember?" My smile grows wider as I take in the beautiful estate in front of me. "We fucking won."

"That you did, Randi." A hint of adoration seeps into his softly spoken words. "Now everyone in DC knows you're someone to reckon with."

"So, smooth sailing the next few years?" I ask facetiously. Of course, thinking that would be as dumb of me as believing I'll ever have my pet unicorn. No matter how much I wish it, that doesn't mean it'll come true. Seriously though, how awesome would it be to have a pet that could impale people? It could be my secret assassin. "That would be so cool. Death by unicorn."

"I don't even want to know." T chuckles.

The thick summer air feels heavy on my exposed skin as I walk toward the front door, which swings open the moment I'm close. Candles flicker inside, creating a warm feel to the space while the glittering chandeliers sparkle and dazzle with their brilliance. Most conversations stop as I move through the crowd. The weight of a thousand eyes tugs at my shoulders, but I continue forward, my gaze set on the most beautiful thing in this room.

The bar.

I order a bourbon on the rocks and take the cool highball glass from the bartender's extended hand. Turning, I survey the room. Most of the faces I know, and most I don't like, but hey, it's politics—no one likes each other. My searching gaze lands on one sneering face. Lifting my glass, I tip it toward Mr. Hindle. Why the fuck he's here, who knows. Not my party.

A calloused hand caresses my shoulder. I smile behind the thin glass at my lips.

"Careful, Paul went to a lot of trouble to cover up my tattoos. He'll be pissy if you mess up his work."

"And Tiny will be pissed when he learns you covered up his art."

"Touché."

Finally I slide my gaze to Trey, and my stomach flips. Fuck, he's gorgeous. The dark navy suit fits him perfectly, showing off his long muscular legs and trim waist. The crisp cream dress shirt brightens his honey eyes, which are just as greedily taking in every inch of me as I am him.

"You look stunning," he says, leaning close and ghosting a kiss to my left cheek.

"Same, handsome," I reply with a wide smile. Taking another sip, I allow the smooth burn down my throat to ground me. I can't jump him in a roomful of people. "How's the *happy couple* doing this evening?"

"Ecstatic, if anyone else is asking," Jessica says, coming out of nowhere. Sliding her thin pale hand over Trey's shoulder, she shoots me a sympathetic smile. "I'm sorry, Randi. I know... I mean, I didn't... it's not personal, I swear." She turns her worried gaze to Trey. "I know who his heart belongs to, but... you wouldn't understand."

Jealousy blurs my thoughts as I glare at her hand on him. This is the first time we've been together since Trey revealed everything, and it's just as awkward as I knew it would be between us.

"Try me," I deadpan. My grip tightens around the now-slick glass, threatening to shatter it into a million pieces. How can she say it isn't personal?

Dropping her hand from his shoulder, she holds it out to me. "Let's go somewhere a little more private."

Ignoring her offered hand, I shoulder past her and Trey toward a more secluded area of the crowded room. Taking a left down a dim hall, I pause after a few steps and turn.

"Explain, then," I say with a swipe of my hand, indicating Jessica has the floor so to speak.

She wraps her arms around her middle, her eyes flicking from me to the floor and back again.

"First of all, I didn't know you two were so involved when I conspired with his mother on the new agreement. I had no idea that he... that Trey loves you." I arch a brow and take a sip of bourbon while holding her imploring gaze over the rim of the glass. "He told me after, but honestly, it wouldn't have changed anything. I'm nothing, no one without being tied to someone like him. Sure, I have some pull, but with Trey, with the Hawthorne and Benson families tied together like this, I'll finally be someone in this town."

I feel my lips tug downward. "You're saying you're nothing without a man to stand behind?"

Her slim shoulders rise and fall in a small shrug. "We can't all be like you, Randi." Her voice is low, but the bite in each word snags my attention.

"Sure you can." Not sure what the hell possesses me to do so, but I reach out and gently squeeze her thin arm. "Who says you can't?"

She shakes her head. When her gaze finally lifts from the floor, there are tears dampening her lower lids. "Everyone but you," she chokes out. "I've used my looks and my family name to get where I am today, but that will only last for so long. I need him to survive in this town, Randi. I'm not saying I'll ever compete with you for his love. You already have it. All I'm asking is to borrow him in a way."

Maybe this is my role in this city. To show all these ass-backward medieval-thinking asshats that we don't need a man to stand behind to be seen. Fuck that.

Maybe that's why I love Trey like I do. He's never asked me to stand behind him, never made me feel like—

What the what?

Maybe that's why I *love* Trey?

This isn't the first time the phrase has flitted through my mind, but it *is* the first time I've said it and had my heart swell with the word.

Good thing it's not bad timing or anything.

"I don't want to hurt you, Randi," Jessica says, drawing my attention back to the conversation. "I like you. You're amazing, and I want to continue working with you and helping you get a foothold here in DC. I have your back, I swear. I just need him too. It's a long history between our two families. His mother wasn't the only one pushing this coupling."

"Agh," I growl. "Coupling. It sounds so ancient. Did y'all's parents just read *Pride and Prejudice* or something? I swear this is a play created by the evil aunt from that book."

Jessica smiles. "If you knew the inner workings of this town, the deals and bargains made, you'd realize this is all a tragedy, not a romance."

Well, shit. Her words constrict my heart in a vice grip.

Why didn't I just stop all this when I had the chance? Guilt rolls in my gut, turning the bourbon sour.

"I really don't have a choice, do I?" I say on a heavy sigh. "Let's agree on one thing. I won't stop this, but it won't last forever." Her smile falls. "But in the meantime, we work on you and this town. Let everyone see I'm not the only strong woman in this city, that you don't need a man to prove your importance."

"Madam Vice President."

Jessica whips around to find the owner of the voice just down the hall.

"Todd," I say. "Haven't seen you around in a while. What's shakin'?" *Seriously? What the hell is wrong with me?*

"I'll leave you two alone," Jessica murmurs. Turning back to me, she searches my eyes. "Thank you, Randi. For everything." With that, she ducks her head and slips past Todd to head back in to the celebration.

"We need to talk," he says, following Jessica out with his eyes on her ass.

I snap my fingers, drawing his attention back to me. "Then talk."

"I know about your meeting in Chile with the Russian president," he says too loudly for my liking.

"Shh," I scold. "That's on a need-to-know basis."

He steps closer, bordering on entering my personal space.

"Do you know what that means?"

"I get a discount on vodka?"

His brows furrow in a scowl. "This isn't funny, Miss Sawyer." He says my name like a curse. "That country has been tied in years past to espionage, collusion on cyberattacks, and much, much more. What the hell do you think you're doing?"

Pursing my lips, I force a tight smile. "Pretty sure I don't answer to you, Mr. Secretary. I don't have to explain anything to you. Now get out of my way. I need another drink."

Todd steps in my path, pressing the heels of his palms to my shoulders. "This could ruin you, Randi. I don't want to see you get mixed up with the wrong people." Wrapping his fingers around my arms, he rubs his soft hands up and down in a comforting gesture. "The attorney general and Department of Justice, they're circling, looking for who knows what."

The hairs on the back of my neck stand on end. My breaths quicken as I fight the urge to yank free of his grasp. Between it being him and my avoidance to touch, I'm a hairbreadth from screaming.

Sarah's latest training session snaps to the forefront of my mind. With my free hand, I snake my arm around his and grip his shoulder before using the angle to twist him around, slamming his chest to the wall.

"Don't you ever touch a woman without her consent, do you hear me,

Todd?" Relaxing my grip, I step back and smooth out my dress in case the scuffle caused the material to ruffle. "Now, I'm going to get my drink, and you're going to keep your mouth shut on what you know. It's not what you think. I can trust them. More than I can you, actually. So don't you act all chivalrous in trying to manage my friends list. I'll see you next month for the G-20 summit."

Without looking back, I stride down the hall. Cutting the corner into the lively party, I nearly smack into Trey.

"Hey," I huff and make to skirt around him toward the bar, only for him to match my steps, preventing me from passing by.

"Nicely handled, Madam Vice President. Sarah will be proud."

I pause my attempt to sneak around him. Tilting my chin, I get lost in his beautiful brown eyes that are staring down into mine adoringly.

"Thanks," I say with a small smile playing at my lips.

"What did you and Jessica talk about?" he asks as he takes a step closer, putting us nearly chest to chest as a waiter passes by with a tray full of tiny hors d'oeuvres. Seriously, why do they think this fancy food is impressive? Why not have a full tray of fried cheese sticks or potato skins? Now that kind of appetizer I can get behind. These fancy caterers need to take a hint from Applebee's and adjust their menus.

"You, me, you two as a couple." Saying the words leaves an ache in my chest.

"Please tell me you didn't tell her the plan."

"Of course I didn't," I snap. Tipping the highball glass back, I knock an ice cube into my mouth. "Trey," I say hesitantly, "there's something I need to tell you."

Almost like he can read me, knows the words I want to say, his facial features soften with a shy smile.

"Not here, Mess. Later, when it's just you and me."

Swallowing back my rising emotions, I clear my throat and force a smile. "Okay, yeah, that sounds good. So, are you coming—"

"There you are, honey."

My shoulders tense at the fakeness in the voice, and the earlier love and adoration shining through Trey's face shutters closed, leaving behind a blank expression. Looking over my shoulder, I keep my features neutral.

She's beautiful, no doubt. Perfection personified. Plump lips pressed into a tight-lipped smile, thin delicate nose that no one is born with, and just enough filler to make her years younger. It's when I catch her eyes, the same beautiful honey brown of Trey's, that I put two and two together.

Ah. The evil mother.

"And you must be Randi," she says with a fake smile.

"It's Madam Vice President, actually," I correct her as I spin on my heels to face Trey's mother. "And the pleasure is mine, Mrs. Benson. I believe I have you to thank for the bill's failure in the Senate."

Her gaze quickly flicks to Trey. "I'd do anything for my only son."

"Tonight, Mess. Wait up for me," Trey mutters before slipping through the crowd and leaving us alone.

"Love your dress," she says just before taking a sip of champagne. The judgy look on her face tells me she's lying through her veneers.

"Let's cut the bullshit, shall we?" I laugh and smile in case anyone is monitoring our conversation.

His mother does the same, tilting her glass to me in a mock cheers. "Let's."

"He told me what he did for your help, how you turned the tables and upped the ante." To keep my hands from trembling, I grasp the empty glass in both hands. "Brilliant. It really was, the whole thing. But there's a loophole," I whisper conspiratorially.

For a blink, that fake-ass smile falters before recovering. "Oh, do tell."

"You see, it doesn't matter how you gained the information you believe is true on Trey and that man in Boone. There is no proof. You'll have zero leverage when I tell Trey of the dozens of cases which were found not guilty or outright dismissed based on little to no proof."

"I have eyewitnesses—"

I hold out a hand, stopping her. "Ah, see, that's another flaw in your plan. I was there too. Two eyewitnesses contradicting each other is never looked upon well by a jury."

Like a cat backed into a corner, her face contorts, ready to fight her way out of this conversation. "Randi, you poor thing. You don't know how this town works yet. All it takes is the mention of wrongdoing and he's finished."

"And so are you. Pretty sure you two share the same last name, if I'm not mistaken."

Her eyes, Trey's eyes, flick around the room as she laughs nervously.

"But I'm here to make a deal with you, Mrs. Benson." The fingers flittering over her delicate neck settle as her attention falls to me. "I know you're formidable in this town; you proved that helping the bill fail. All I'm asking in return for keeping this little bit of information to myself, is your continued support."

"You'd do that?" she questions, and rightfully so. "I've heard you two are... intimate."

I nod and conjure up my best sly smile. "That we were, but that doesn't mean anything when considering an alliance such as this one. I'd rather have your support than him in my bed."

A true, easy laugh pushes past her plumped lips. "You know, I might actually end up liking you. All you want is my support in return for keeping this information to yourself?"

I nod. Fuck, I should've gotten a drink before I started this. It would've made the lies and deceit go down easier. "You get him on track for his political career, Jessica gets him, and I get your help in this town. It's a win for everyone."

Except Trey.

"Agreed. But I will tell you that if you plan to go back on this agreement, double-cross me in any way, I will find out. I keep my loyal listening ears eager to pass on any information." Okay, well, if that doesn't confirm we have a snitch on the team, and that she's fucking them, I don't know what does. "And I will do everything in my power to ruin you in this town, your entire life, if you do."

"Is that a threat?" I bite out, taking a menacing step toward her.

A flash of hesitation blinks across her features before she schools them back into the perfect hostess mask. "No. It's a promise."

The air between us crackles with animosity. Only when her name is called does she end the stare-down. Without another word, she tips her champagne flute in a goodbye salute and glides around me, her arms opening in greeting to the worthy guest behind me.

Around me, the party continues. Laughter bounces off the walls, and servers weave in and around the tipsy crowd, keeping their bellies full and alcohol flowing. In the right corner of the room, Jessica stands partially draped over Trey's shoulder as they laugh in unison at something another couple has said or done. His hand snakes around her thin waist, tugging her closer to his side.

I suck in a quick breath, unable to look away from the happy couple. Alone in the middle of the celebration, the need to escape strangles my throat, making it difficult to breathe deep. Gut wrenching pain strangles up my throat as I watch the happy couple. As I watch the man I might love in the arms of someone else. Desperation itches beneath my skin, I twist toward the exit but don't move. I can't. Glancing to my feet, I half expect the hardwood to have grown around my heels, keeping them sealed to the floor.

A high-pitched laugh seems to slice through my ears. The closeness of the bodies packed into the room causes my skin to itch. The sense of the room shrinking, pushing the people closer, envelops me.

Frantically I scan the area for a friend. T's dark eyes meet mine. With every ounce of energy I have left I pour out my desperation for an escape through my eyes into his. Immediately he's in action, shoving his way through the crowd toward me. His hot hand presses around my waist, tugging me against his side. With his help, I put one foot in front of the other, shouldering through the crowd.

At the front door, he mumbles something into the sleeve of his dress shirt. Before stepping over the threshold, I dare a glance over my shoulder. Our eyes lock across the room. Trey's happy expression falls, a look of concern washing over his features just before I'm tugged outside, snapping him from my field of vision.

What have I done?

Dread sets in my stomach. What if what we've put in motion can't be undone? What if he'll never be mine again?

"Did you do what needs to be done?" T asks as he tugs me down the front walk.

I nod, unable to speak with the fear choking my words. I didn't expect the weight of what we set in motion to be so... overwhelming. I just locked my future, and Trey's, into this political shit storm for the next three years, and for what? Power, money, control?

T slows his steps before pausing, his head tilting like he's listening to something in his ear. Out of the shadows, a man steps from behind one of the awaiting cars. T tenses but doesn't shove me to the ground or haul me away. As the unknown man steps into the lighted path, I can't help but hold a breath.

Where Trey is handsome in his mischievously good looks, this man is breathtakingly beautiful in a dark, intense way. Much like Trey, his suit is expensive and tailored to his fit frame. Cropped jet-black hair seems to soak up the night, whereas his light green eyes reflect every ray of light, giving them a shimmering brilliance.

Too soon, the man is in front of us. T's hand slips from mine to step back, giving us space. I shoot a worried glance over my shoulder. He nods and motions to the man.

I turn back, a hint of familiarity hitting me. I filter through the thousands of faces I should know in this city, trying to figure out who he is before he speaks.

"Madam Vice President." His voice is low and gravelly.

Not wanting to miss a word, I step closer. Shadows dance around his face, making it hard to place him.

"Sam Pierce. Department of Justice." He reaches out a hand, which I take and give a tight squeeze. "You need to come with me."

POWER SWITCH

POWER PLAY SERIES BOOK 3

INSPIRATION

"You may have to fight a battle more than once to win it."

Margret Thatcher

PROLOGUE
JESSICA

It's a strange concept, this notion of a morally sound conscience. Never once in my thirty years have I considered myself to have one at all—moral or not—until tonight. Yet here I stand in the middle of this political win/engagement announcement party with my stomach in knots because of said conscience telling me I'm doing something wrong. I should be happy, overjoyed that a life goal I've had since grade school is now being realized.

Trey Benson is mine.

Well, most of him.

I'm careful to hide the cringe of pain from the cramping of my lower gut behind my nearly empty crystal champagne flute. Trey's deep rumbling laugh pulls my attention from the inner turmoil I have going on. With a lovesick sigh, I watch as he charms Senator Torres and take another sip of the remaining crisp liquid. The delicious tiny bubbles explode along my tongue, helping calm the earlier unease. Maybe if I keep drinking I won't care too much about the lack of joy behind his light eyes.

Pressing the cool glass against my overheated cheek, I smile.

He really is perfect. The handsome prince charming starring in all my childhood daydreams, and most of my adult steamy night ones too. Now here he is, with me. Half of my heart doesn't mind that he's not *wholly* mine—yet.

Tonight he wears a custom-tailored black suit that draws attention to his fit physique, emphasizing his backside that every woman in this room can't keep their eyes off of. His dark hair, a bit longer than normal, is styled back away from his eyes. The dusting of dark facial hair along his sculpted jaw draws attention to a full lower lip, or maybe it's because I'm standing here fantasizing about it pressed against my own. With the perfectly proportioned straight nose and naturally tan skin, he could give any model a run for their money.

Those honey brown eyes cut to me, brows furrowing. Something I can't make out flashes behind his usual political mask before he turns back to the still-rambling senator.

A smidge of my building hope drains, leaving sadness in the new fissures in my heart. Filling my lungs with a full, determined breath, I remind myself that just because he sees this as an alliance and not true love doesn't mean I have to. Do I hate that he thinks he's in love with someone else? Sure, but I've never let a little hurdle like that stop me from getting what I want before, so why start now? Of course, it's even worse than that—he's in love with a woman I respect, one I hate doing this to, but what's done is done. This wasn't all my doing. Trey made a deal of his own; I just capitalized on the opportunity. There's nothing wrong with that.

Trey Benson has always been mine. I sat back and watched him waste years with Rachel, waiting for my chance to be with him. Then Randi moved to DC, stealing my moment. I've waited, pined, sulked for long enough. This is my time, my chance to win him. Who does Randi think she is anyway? But then again, she *is* amazing in many ways—in all the ways needed to make a change in this city. To transform mindsets, correct their moral compass.

Maybe even mine.

Again, Randi's face flashes in the forefront of my mind, instigating the earlier internal conflict once again.

No. I shake my head, blonde tresses sliding along my bare back. Trey is mine. Randi needs to come to terms with that. I will support her, support her cause, but Trey will be at my side instead of hers. Maybe once she realizes this is true love on my part, she'll step aside, allowing him to fall out of love with her and in love with me. He loved Rachel those few years and now loves Randi; surely his heart can change its course once more.

"There's the happy couple."

Smile widening, I turn toward Celia Benson's voice. Trey's shoulder stiffens beneath my hand.

"Wonderful party," I say, tipping the empty flute in her direction, acknowledging that all this was her doing. "As always."

With a smile that doesn't reach her eyes, she loops an arm through my own and rests five red-tipped fingers along my forearm. "Come," she encourages with a small tug. "We have numerous things to discuss." Tilting forward to see past me to Trey, her smile grows. "Don't worry, honey. I won't borrow your beautiful fiancée for too long. Don't go anywhere."

The senator continues chatting, completely oblivious to the direct command from Celia to Trey. But the flush blooming across Trey's high cheekbones signals he didn't miss the superior tone in his mother's words.

I swallow hard at the tension between the two. Searching for a distraction, I lift the flute to take another sip of champagne only to remember it's empty.

With a quick commanding snap of Celia's thin fingers, three servers appear out of nowhere, carrying silver trays weighted with fresh flutes filled to the brim with bubbling liquid. The slight tremor in my fingers gives away my growing nerves. Careful to not knock off the ten other delicate flutes, I rest the empty glass atop a tray and take a full one in return. With both our glasses refreshed, we nod to Trey and the senator before shifting away from the men. Weaving through the partygoers, Celia smiles at several, quickly dismissing their attempts to engage her in conversation as we continue our short journey across the bursting room.

"Is he behaving?" she asks, head dipped to keep the words between us. We pause at a secluded spot along the far wall where we can talk freely and watch the room.

"Of course. Trey knows how to work the crowd in situations like this. Were you concerned he wouldn't?" I ask cautiously.

Not a single hair in her fancy updo shifts as Celia shakes her head. With the movement, her diamond chandelier earrings catch the light, the bursting sparkles snagging my envious attention. The Hawthornes are rich, but the Bensons are richer. No doubt those earrings are worth over a million and aren't her only pair.

"I'm afraid he might act foolish. He truly believes he's in love with that wretched woman," she says on a disappointed sigh. With her free hand, she presses two fingers to her left temple and massages the sensitive area. "I'm concerned about him, about our family."

Closing the gap between us, I clasp her elbow. "Why? What's going on that has you concerned?"

"She's not the right woman for him, for us. That woman is selfish and deceiving. I'm almost certain she's manipulated his feelings for her own safety. Were you aware he almost died for her recently?"

A gasp escapes. To cover my shock, I hold two fingers in front of my lips. "He did what?"

"My son is blinded by what he believes is love. I can't—" Celia stops to clear her throat of the building emotions. "I can't lose him. He's my only son. Which is why I did what I did, why we made our agreement. I know he considers what I did to be deceiving, but I'm only trying to save him. Save his life. That woman is not only a threat to his budding political career but also his safety."

"I—" I stop, unsure of what I want to say in response. My thoughts jumble between knowing Randi isn't the type of person to manipulate someone for her own gain and wanting to believe Celia. I shake my head to clear the conflicting thoughts, but the several glasses of champagne are making my judgments and emotions unclear on where I stand. One thing is clear: Trey's safety is as important as my own. "What can I do?"

An almost smile lifts her sullen face. "I knew I could count on you, Jessica. Your love for him is clear." Celia gives a reassuring squeeze to the fingers still wrapped around her elbow. "I need you to show him that it's simple attraction, not love, with that Randi woman. Make him see that you're the right choice for him, to come back to his family, his destiny. Bring my son back to me and his father. Please." The glowing overhead lights shimmer off Celia's damp dark lashes.

"How can *I* accomplish that?" Even with the champagne coursing through my system, I'm aware what she's asking is a near impossible feat. Trey has run from this life for years. He lives for his role with the secret service. Only recently did he begrudgingly accept to come back into the spotlight—all for Randi. How can I convince him that he not only doesn't love her but needs to come back into the political fold for himself, not her?

"My son is a good man, one who is driven to protect no matter the odds. This is where you need to draw his focus. Pull it away from protecting that woman to protecting *you.*"

"I don't understand." My head swirls. *How many glasses have I had?*

Her honey brown eyes narrow in frustration. "If he's busy worrying about you, protecting you from some unknown threat, he'll forget all about this Randi woman. Use his weakness for our benefit."

I sway slightly as the implication of her words slams home. "You want me to create a threat against myself so he'll feel the need to protect me? How will that convince him to love me and not her?"

Celia's tone turns menacing. "If you're unconvinced you'll be able to pull off what needs to be done, I can always arrange for the threat to be real."

"And if I don't? If I can't convince him?"

"Then I'll make sure all your secrets are shared, and all the work you've put in to be someone in this town will be wasted. Your personal life, career, family, everything turned against you."

I swallow against the champagne that's fighting to surge back up my throat.

"Now," she says, giving my hand a condescending pat, "earlier I overheard my son make plans to meet up with that woman later this evening. Your first role as his fiancée is to make sure he's unable to keep that commitment."

I nod, still unable speak.

"I know you love him, as do I. This is for his benefit. We're just having to get creative on how to save him from himself. This is the life for him. This is his destiny."

"And me?" Does she consider me as a part of that destiny?

"You'll have what you've always wanted. Him. If we play this right, this time next year, you'll be happily married, and Randi Sawyer will just be a distant ugly memory."

Taking a slow sip from my glass, I process Celia's words.

Married.

Happy.

Mine.

All those words are exactly what I want out of my future. Now's my chance to make it happen.

"I'll do it." Celia smiles, and we click the edges of our flutes together. "Now if you'll excuse me. I'll grab Trey a bourbon from the bar. He's been drinking beer all night, and if I can convince him to mix, there's no way he'll be able to see Randi tonight. That man's never been able to mix a day in his life."

Her smile widens, and if I'm not mistaken, a pulse of pride shines through her bright gaze.

"You'll make an excellent daughter-in-law, Jessica."

But for some reason, the praise falls flat. With a forced smile, I shift my way back through the crowd and head for the open bar, one thought swirling through my mind with each step.

What the hell have I sealed my future to?

1

RANDI

I waited.

Waited until the sun's first morning rays warmed the fading dark sky. Waited in the wicker rocker on the back porch, watching the pool's sparkling water, anxious to see the man I love and finally say those words out loud.

But he never came over like he promised.

With each minute that ticked by, disappointment constricted my heart, making it ache like never before.

As I slip off the pair of black yoga pants and crawl into bed, I attempt to convince myself everything is okay. It's one night, one promise.

At the ridiculous fake engagement party/celebration for defeating Kyle's bill to strip low-income Americans of their voting rights, I didn't expect the influx of emotions that bombarded me when confronted with Jessica on his arm. It was then—actually, maybe even before today, but I wasn't willing to admit it—that I realized I love him. Granted, this is me we're talking about, so it might not be normal love, but I'm not normal, so I guess its par for the course. With my childhood, I don't know if I'm even capable of whole-hearted love, but I do love Trey in my own unique way.

But here I am going to bed alone with those three words still on the tip of my tongue, unable to speak them out loud to the man I feel them for.

Because he didn't come.

Leaning over, I stretch to flip off the bedside lamp, dousing the room in darkness, the morning sun's bright rays kept hidden by the thick blackout curtains. The sheets rustle as I wiggle to get comfortable while tugging the comforter up to my chin.

I've just closed my eyes, ready to get an hour or so of sleep before I start my day, when a bright light flashes, causing my lids to slide open once again. Not moving from my warm spot in the sheets, I scrutinize the glowing phone screen, debating if I should check it or not.

Part of me knows I can't handle any more disappointment tonight if it's not Trey with an explanation. Yet the other half of me thinks if it is him, I'm not ready for an excuse. Maybe it would be better to shut my eyes once more and let this fucking terrible day finally end. Let myself get the couple hours of sleep I need to be somewhat functional for today's meeting with the Associate Attorney General, Sam Pierce. I have no idea what he wants to talk to me about but if someone from the DOJ wants to meet with me it can't be good.

Not having the energy left to continue fighting the internal battle I glide a hand out from under the mountain of covers and pick the now dark phone off the nightstand.

Deep breath in, I tap the screen to bring it back to life.

A single text stares back at me.

Trouble: I'm sorry.

I frown at the screen, unsure how to feel with those two words. Am I sad? Jealous? Mad? What is he even sorry for? Not coming over or something worse, something involving him and Jessica?

Exhaustion from the day and my racing thoughts heighten every swirling emotion, making everything too much. With more force than necessary, I shove the annoying phone with its stupid message under the pillow and close my eyes, forcing myself not to acknowledge the dampness along my lashes. All I needed was a phone call, a text earlier in the night just explaining he wasn't coming over. Anything that would calm my crazy thoughts and visions of him and Jessica together. But apparently I wasn't on his mind until five in the morning, my worry and time never crossing his damn mind.

Does that mean he was with her until now?

What could they have been doing?

Curling on my side, I try to picture dancing unicorns to get the visuals of Trey and Jessica together out of my mind.

It's fine. I'm fine. We're fine.

As I relax into the mattress, a small seed of doubt plants itself in the conflicting thoughts, keeping sleep at bay.

What if... what if this is the beginning of the end of us?

2

TREY

*F**uck it to hell.*

A pain-laced groan rumbles in my chest before pushing past my dry lips. Back flat to the bed, I glower at the ceiling like it's the reason for my pain. A headache throbs a slow beat in the back of my skull like a resounding warrior's march. I should've just fucking stuck with beer and said no to the bourbon. Amateur move. I know better.

Groaning again, this time with a bit of a whine to it, I press the heels of both palms against my closed eyelids and press hard, hoping the pressure will make the painful world I've woken up to somehow disappear around me.

If it was only my throbbing head and sour stomach, I might not be hating life as much as I am in this moment. But it's not just the physical aches from the hangover that are haunting me. One is of the heart, something that isn't as easily fixed with Tylenol and caffeine. Last night, I didn't show up when I promised I would, and I'm not sure if there's anything to make *that* better. Recalling the melancholy look she shot over her shoulder as she left the party has the twisting of my stomach worsening.

What's left of the bourbon and beer mixes in my gut, making me consider throwing up just to have some relief. I have no valid excuses for not making it to her place last night when I promised I would. I got drunk, and by the end of the night, when I could finally leave without Mother or Jessica making a scene, it was late and I was done.

But as much as I want to blame Jessica for starting the bourbon trend halfway through the night, she wasn't the one who kept going back to the bar. No, they weren't the ones who tried to dull their misery with one more sip, one more glass.

That was all me.

Now I understand how Randi suffered that night in Chile just wanting to get so drunk that the world and all its troubles faded away. That's what I wanted last night, what I needed to survive the entire party without strangling those bottom-feeding asshat aristocrats.

Years have passed since I've been on this scene, yet nothing has changed. Everyone wants something, and no one thinks about anything other than their own ambitions. Every breath, every laugh and word were a struggle knowing this is the life I've sealed myself to for the unseen future. All for Randi. And even though last night was a beating—more like an MMA fight—I don't regret any of it.

I strain to swallow down the rising emotions, but my cotton mouth prevents it. Fuck, I love her. I miss her desperately, like she's the air I need to survive, and it's only been twelve hours since I last laid eyes on her.

I shouldn't have let last night get that far. Should've turned Jessica down when she offered me my favorite bourbon. But I didn't, and now here I am alone, hungover and pining for the only woman I've ever truly loved.

Scrubbing a hand down my face, I slap my cheek a couple times to get my head in the game. Going into the party last night, we both knew what this arrangement would require. Our plan to keep Mother on Randi's side while I played along with the engagement shit made sense at the time. But now I'm not so sure. Everyone is getting what they want except me. Because all I want is Randi. Us together. Never apart, from now until the end of either of us.

But I can't. She can't. This is a delicate power game we're playing with Mother and half of the city. And Randi ending up in a smear campaign because of me isn't an option. So maybe not showing up on her doorstep at four in the morning was a better idea than I'm giving myself credit for. Unlike during the campaign, so much more is on the table now, so much to lose if anyone finds out about us and our grand plan to make it through the next three years and then be together.

A thump at the front door drags me out of my depressing thoughts. Pulling the hand away from my face, I squint a single eye at the open bedroom door, wishing I had X-ray vision to see who's waking me up at... shit, what time is it?

With another cranky groan, I smack the bed blindly, searching for the phone I know I pitched haphazardly onto the comforter after texting Randi the two words that shredded my heart.

Fuck, am I catching her dramatics?

Squinting at the phone in my hand, I scan the time, then drop it back to the rumpled sheets. Who the hell is pounding on my door at nine in the morning on my day off? Someone who wants a good Bobbiting, that's who.

Yep, Randi is 100 percent rubbing off on me. For the first time this morning, I manage a smile.

The beating against the front door turns into an impatient jackhammering.

Grumbling a string of undecipherable curse words, I stretch my tight arms high above my head, letting the stiffness slowly ease from my shoulders. Bare feet on the floor, I arch my back, making it pop in several places and creak in others, ignoring the person now using what sounds like a battering ram against my condo door. Not bothering with clothes, I shuffle through the living room, my annoyance and the throbbing in my head increasing with every step.

Face pressed against the cool metal door, I peer through the peephole, blinking a few times to clear my foggy vision. Annoyed dark eyes stare back at me like he can see through the door right into me.

"Motherfucker," I grumble as I snap the deadbolt free and yank the door open, not caring if there's anyone in the hallway who could see me in my birthday suit. "What the ever-loving hell do you want, Tank?" Tank—real name David Washington—is my best friend and team lead, and Randi's only other friend in this town. He leads the alpha secret service team assigned to protect Madam VP ever since the campaign trail.

"Put that thing away," he grunts, avoiding looking at my naked junk. Ignoring my smirk and enticing swivel of my hips, he shoves the door open enough for him to step past without touching me and slips into the condo. After securing the door, I follow as he marches through the living room and turns into the kitchen.

"Good morning to you too," I mutter. "I feel like shit, man, so tell me what you're doing here and get out. I need my beauty sleep."

"You're already pretty, Playboy. All the girls tell you that. But you do look a little worse for the wear this morning."

"Tank," I whine.

His upper lip twitches in a sneer at my pouting. "You really have no clue?"

"For my endless supply of bacon the housekeeper keeps on hand just for you?"

"You're tossing around jokes while your girl's on the lip of a boiling fucking pot?" Tank lets out an incredulous huff. "Knew you didn't deserve her."

In two steps, I'm in his personal space, our faces inches apart. "What the hell are you talking about?"

"Unless you want me to whip mine out to fucking compare, get that limp-ass dick away from me." He steps back with a snarl. "Go get some fucking pants on, Playboy. Shit happened last night while you were playing the perfect politician."

"What—"

"Clothes," he thunders. "I don't want to see that shit." A smirk pulls at his lips. "Makes me feel bad for Randi knowing that's what she's settling for."

Middle finger in the air, I spin and stride to the bedroom. The dresser shakes at the force of me opening one drawer after another in search of a clean pair of workout shorts. Not wanting to waste a second, I tug the Dryfit shorts on as I walk back into the living room, pausing at the edge of the kitchen. Tank's head is buried in the fridge, searching for the bacon, no doubt.

"Bottom drawer."

The clatter of the plastic drawers opening and closing fills the kitchen. Knowing this conversation won't start until the bacon is cooking, I search under a cabinet and snag the first frying pan my fingers touch. I toss it onto the stove, the banging metal making me instantly regret that choice.

"Start talking. What the hell could she have gotten herself into in the past twelve hours?" Stretching above the microwave, I snag a bottle of aspirin from the cabinet and pop four of the small white pills into my mouth. Dipping my head beneath the kitchen faucet, I suck several mouthfuls of cold tap water down, soothing my dry mouth and throat while swallowing the much-needed medicine.

"You know as well as I do that girl attracts the trouble," he says, cutting his dark eyes to me. "Present company included."

"Ha ha," I mock. Instead of watching him destroy the sealed bacon package with his bare hands, sending the uncooked meat flying around the kitchen, I lean over the counter, pull open a drawer, and feel around for a spare buck knife. "Here," I mumble, getting his attention before tossing it to him. "You've got jokes for someone who's eating forbidden food in front of the man who has your wife's number on speed dial."

Tank's shoulders stiffen. I can't hold back a chuckle at his clear fear of his wife. Not that I blame him. That woman is a badass. Anyone smart would be more than a little terrified of her.

"You wouldn't," he says, voice tight.

"Then talk, big guy, and my lips are sealed."

When he shoots me a glare over the sizzling pan, I motion like I'm zipping my lips, then toss the imaginary key over my shoulder for emphasis.

He just shakes his head before turning his full attention to the cooking bacon. "I have no idea what that woman sees in you."

I waggle both brows and point to my crotch. "You did earlier."

"Poor girl."

"Fuck off. Stop stalling. Tell me what's going on." I massage my temples, thinking good thoughts that the medicine will kick in soon. The savory aroma of the cooking bacon churns my already sour stomach while also smelling fucking delicious. "I want to puke and eat at the same time. I'm getting too old for this shit."

"Did you mix or something?"

"Yeah."

"Amateur."

"Don't I know it." With a less-than-dignified groan, I press my forehead against the cold marble counter. "Are you *ever* going to fill me in on what happened last night?"

Just to be an ass, he waits a few more beats before saying, "Did you know the Department of Justice is snooping around?"

My neck almost pops with whiplash as I bolt straight up. "What?"

He nods while nudging the bacon around the popping grease with a spatula. "I don't know what they want. All I know is the associate attorney general blindsided us while leaving last night. And I don't think Randi has a clue as to what he wants to talk about, because she looked just as shocked as I did."

His dark eyes flick to mine, a grimace pinching his features. I know that look. He's holding something back.

"What are you not telling me?"

"Listen, I'm not gay or anything, but... Playboy, that man, the AAG, is one sexy-ass motherfucker."

"What?" I shout, immediately regretting it. I slam my hands against both sides of my head to keep it from exploding.

His massive shoulders rise and fall in a shrug. "All I'm saying is her shock might not be from his title. Just a feeling I got."

"Shit," I exclaim, leaning forward and pressing my elbows to the counter.

Silence falls between us as I process everything he's dumped on me. One part bothers me the most.

"Sexier than me?" I question. I know I should be worried about why the AAG is snooping around more than his looks, but I'm not.

Spatula in the air, he leans against the corner of the counter and motions for me to stand. No idea why, but I do without question.

He twirls the spatula. I follow the movement, holding on to the counter for support as the room spins with me.

"Neither of you is my type, but I'd say you have a run for your money with the AAG. Add in the fact that he's an attorney, like her, and he has a few more points on his side."

"But she loves me," I state. "I think." My jaw drops as a scene from last night flashes through my still somewhat fuzzy memory. "Shit." I sink back onto the stool and stare at the white marble. "She wanted to tell me something last night. That's why I said I'd come over."

"You didn't go over last night," Tank states.

"I know. I didn't want to go over that late and drunk. I forgot she had something to tell me." With a curse, I shove off the stool to pace the expansive kitchen. "Fuck, this is worse than I thought when I first woke up. I thought I'd just disappointed her by not showing up when I said I would, but now she probably thinks I'm avoiding her or didn't want to hear what she had to say. Or—"

"Get your head out of your ass, Benson. This is bigger than that. Did you hear me? The associate attorney general demanded a meeting with her.

Today. Something big is about to drop, and we have no fucking clue what that entails."

"Her meeting with the Russians?"

"Maybe."

"Maybe it has something to do with Birmingham."

"Possible. But why approach her if that's the case?"

"Shit."

"My thoughts exactly, which is why I'm here so damn early on our day off getting ready to eat through my stress with two pounds of bacon."

I arch a brow. "There's another pound in the freezer."

"Fine, three pounds of bacon."

"When's the meeting?" Pausing in front of the Nespresso machine, I pop a pod into the dispenser with one hand while swiping a mug off the exposed shelf with the other. After hitting the brew button, I turn to face Tank, who's busy placing several crispy slices of cooked bacon on a plate. "You said today."

"This afternoon. He's coming by the house around three."

"We need to be there for her." And I want a good look at this guy.

"It's our day off," Tank states like I could've forgotten as he shoves three pieces of hot blackened bacon into his mouth. "What excuse would we have for showing up and sitting in on her meeting? We're her friends, yes, but not everyone is good with the notion that she tells us everything. We know we'd never use it against her, but others don't."

The gurgle of the bubbling water pulls my attention to the brewing coffee. Focused on the dark streaming liquid, I shuffle through the options. I hate to admit it, but he's right. We don't need to draw attention to our friendship with Randi. Who knows? The fuckers might take us off her protection detail just to be assholes.

But I can't *not* be there.

"Call in a favor to the beta team lead, Chaz. He owes you, I'm sure." Before the last drip reaches the foam, I pull the mug up to my lips and take a scalding sip of the steaming liquid. Hopefully this will help clear my head. "Tell him we want to sub in for two of his agents for a few hours today. That way we'll have a legit excuse to be there, nothing suspicious."

Excuse or not, I'll be at that meeting.

I cringe behind the coffee mug.

Even if Randi might be pissed as hell and not want *me there.*

THE WOODEN FRONT porch step creaks under my dress shoe as I travel up the short set of stairs toward the front door. The unknown of the next few hours rakes at my nerves. A thin sheen of sweat dampens my palms and shines across my forehead. It's hot as a sauna in hades today. I hate these humid summer days where Mother Nature attempts to smother you with the heat.

I pause at the closed door, half ready to get inside to the AC while the other part of me doesn't want to face her. I hate disappointing the people I love. That's due to those childhood years I spent doing whatever it took to make my parents proud of me, working for the parental love that should've come easily only to be rejected at every opportunity.

Instead of knocking, I twist the knob and push the heavy door open. Inside, a beta team agent perks his head up, eyes scrolling across my face and then down my chest before turning back to his phone. Quiet day, I guess. Wonder if anyone else knows about the upcoming meeting with the associate attorney general, Sam.

Sam.

What kind of name is that anyway? Three letters do not make a name. That's like Bud or Rob, neither of which are strong names, which means this Sam character will be weak as fuck. Just like his name.

No, I'm not jealous.

Keeping my steps silent, I move around the house, searching each room for Randi. My ears perk up at the sound of a voice I know and hate.

At the edge of the living room, I pause just out of sight, giving myself a second to observe her. Dressed in dark jeans and a lightweight long-sleeve T-shirt, she's curled on the lush sofa, iPad forgotten on her lap, attention riveted on whatever is on TV. Again, Birmingham's voice pours through the house.

I shift my attention from the beauty I love to the idiot on the screen, my brows furrowing in confusion at what I see at the bottom of the screen.

Special Briefing with President Birmingham.

Birmingham stands behind the podium in the White House press briefing room, face flushed as he points to someone in the row of chairs in front of him and leans forward. The reporter's words are mumbled, but he must hear her clearly. With a nod, he leans back and clasps his hands on top of the podium.

"Yes, this is a last resort. Leading this country into a war that, in the past, has proven to be unwinnable is not ideal. However, we cannot allow these countries to continue extorting us. The price of oil continues to rise, and something must be done."

A hand shoots into the air. The prick of a president points to the woman, who stands. After straightening her skirt, she locks eyes with Birmingham and raises her chin. "There's talk that the DOJ is seeking responsibility for the spike in gas prices closer to home. Is this true?"

"No," Birmingham brushes her off. He scans the room, looking for another question to answer, when the woman speaks up once again.

"Why would the leaders in the Middle East do this now? What are you saying has changed to make them drive the cost higher only for Americans?"

Absorbed in the press conference, I step through the door, pausing at the end of the couch. Randi's eyes flick to me before turning back to the TV. Shuffling on the couch, she leans closer to the screen.

"We don't know the why. But as the leader of this great nation, I cannot sit back and do nothing while the hardworking Americans bring home less and less due to the cost of getting to work. We will stay strong. We will push back. Thank you."

With that, he walks off the stage, but not before shooting that one female reporter a death glare.

The moment he's out the door, the screen flips to a beautiful blonde sitting behind a newsroom desk. Her fast words lull to background noise as I turn to face Randi.

"Did you hear that?" she asks, lost in thought. Nibbling on her pinkie nail, she stands and moves to the other side of the room. "Vlad said something like that," she whispers. "Said if we didn't stop Kyle, there would be war."

"Maybe you should call the Russian president and ask him."

She shakes her head, her loose dark hair falling over her shoulders and hiding her face before she tucks the rogue locks behind her ear. "No, I don't want to draw attention to my... friendship? Relationship? Whatever Vlad and I have with the DOJ looking around. The tension between our two countries is still tense, and Kyle still isn't aware that I've been in contact with Vlad. The meeting he and I had in Chile wasn't illegal, per se, but it could add clout to an investigation if the AAG is trying to find dirt on me. I mean,

Vlad did openly say he wanted to help me get into the president role. That's borderline treason talk."

"True. Didn't think about how the AAG would view that relationship. Those fuckers are always snooping around, trying to find anything that'll stick. Fucking lawyers."

She blinks. Not a single emotion shifts across her blank face as she stares me down.

"Okay, no lawyer jokes. Noted," I say, daring a step closer to where she stares out a window at the backyard. "Randi... fuck, I'm sorry about last night."

"Yeah, that's what your text said." My gut clenches at the annoyance in her tone. "Sorry for what exactly?"

"I didn't—"

"Actually, stop," she says with a huff before turning to me. "I can't process all this right now. I'm mad, hurt, and a whole bunch of other emotions I can't filter through, but honestly, I don't have the capacity to deal with it. I'm the vice president of the United States, and our idiot of a president is about to lead us straight into a war which he said himself is unwinnable. In less than an hour, I have a meeting with the AAG, and I have no fucking clue what he wants to discuss. I'm tired, hungry, and on the verge of losing it because I'm so unprepared for what this day will bring me. So I just can't right now." Motioning between us, she purses her lips and shakes her head. "In the last twenty-four hours, this has gone from complicated to a weight I'm not sure I can bear at this point. I know that was my doing, asking you to play the part with Jessica until we figured out things with your mother and stopped her from sabotaging my political career. Guess I wasn't prepared for the suspicious thoughts and doubts that seeing you together created. It doesn't change how I feel about you, and it doesn't change us, but right now, I'm not ready to hear your explanation."

"I understand," I rasp. Heat builds beneath my skin, making my stiff clothes unbearable. Shrugging out of my jacket, I lay it across the back of the couch and perch on the armrest. I lean forward, resting both elbows on the tops of my thighs and clasp my hands together. Looking up through my lashes, I wait until she's focused on me. "Just let me say one thing."

Her eyes roll to the ceiling in annoyance, but a hint of a smile tugs at one corner of her lips. "*One* thing."

"I screwed up not calling or coming over. I can see my actions, or lack thereof, hurt you. Seeing you upset because of me is the kind of torture that would break the strongest of men. I handled the situation badly and have no excuse besides saying I'm an idiot and I'm sorry."

The bright overhead light reflects off the wetness building along her lower lids. "It was the not knowing. The wondering if.... Trouble, were you with her? Tell me now. Were you sorry because of something you did with her?"

Jolting up from the couch, I stride the few steps toward her before pausing. Two fingers beneath her chin, I tip her gaze up to meet my own.

"No, baby. Fuck no. There's no one else for me. I was drunk and didn't want to come over like that." I search her face, wishing to every god that I could ease the hurt I caused.

"With Jessica in the picture now—" She blows out a breath. "I'm not sure where I stand, and when you didn't come over, I just assumed, which was stupid."

"Like I said, I have no excuse. I was drunk and it was late, that's it. But I hope you'll forgive me for not following through on something I said I would do, and the thousands of other times I'll act like an idiot in our future. It will happen again, but I can promise causing you pain, hurting you, will never be intentional. It's just a piss-poor side effect of me being a guy."

A full smile lifts her cheeks. "Well played, Trouble. Well played."

"Does that mean I'm forgiven?" I ask, not hiding the hope in my voice. "Tell me what I need to do, Mess. I'll do anything to ease the hurt I caused."

My heart falls a little at the shake of her head.

"Not forgiven yet." With a quick glance at her watch, she interlaces our fingers and tugs me toward the door. "But I'll give you thirty minutes to convince me."

"Thirty minutes, huh?" I say to her back as I follow her up the stairs toward her bedroom.

At the landing, she pauses and turns.

"Not up for the challenge, Trouble?"

With a near growl, I tighten my grip around her thin fingers and shoulder past, practically dragging her behind me into the master bedroom.

3

RANDI

Oh hell, I don't have time for this, or the energy, but him between my thighs might be just what I need to survive this day. My chest aches with the growing ball of stress building behind my breastbone. I wasn't exaggerating downstairs. I can't add any additional complications to this day. But even though Trey is one of those complications adding to my strain, the second he walked into the room, everything felt easier. Almost like his presence alone offered the reassurance of an extra shoulder to help carry the weight piled on my own. How he does it, I don't know.

Tricky Trouble. That's his new name. Because somehow with his simple yet sincere rambling speech, him not showing up last night no longer feels like an attempt to keep a shady secret involving Jessica away from me. It cleared the growing suspicion and doused my self-doubt.

And what a speech it was. He really would make a great politician if his heart was in it. Addressing the fact that our miscommunications, disappointments, and unintentional hurt will happen again was like gaining a "get out of jail free" card for future use. And curiously enough, I'm okay with it. Because in all honesty, I'm terrible at this relationship stuff. The only serious relationship I had was when I was fifteen, and I ended up alone and pregnant—not really a high bar to set for future relationships. But what makes Trey special is I'd rather be with him, knowing pain and headache will happen, than never experience the highs, laughter, and smiles that come with being with him.

Maybe that's the simplest sign of true love. When the hard work, the fighting for each other is worth it because you have each other in the end.

A hard shove against my shoulder sends me tumbling back to the bed, a wide smile splitting my face as I sink into the cloudlike down comforter.

"Thirty minutes, you say," he muses while rubbing along his clean-shaven jaw. He sinks his teeth into his full lower lip, his heated gaze slowly scanning down my body. "First, these need to go." With deft fingers, he makes quick work of the top button of my skinny jeans and the zipper quickly follows. With an impatient tug, they pool around my feet. Watching him, my breaths turn to short, needy pants as he stares fixated at the apex of my thighs, sliding the tip of his tongue along the edge of his straight white teeth.

After discarding the jeans, he pulls the long sleeve T-shirt over my head. I cringe internally as he unclasps the plain nude bra I'd chosen this morning, not thinking anyone would see it today. The self-conscious thought vanishes as the tips of his finger trail down my bare arms when he slides the straps from my shoulders. With a flick of his wrist, it flutters to the floor, adding to the growing pile.

Every article of clothing is gone—except one.

"Aren't you forgetting something?" I ask with a pointed glance to my sailing unicorn-printed boy shorts. Okay, not the sexiest things to be wearing, but to my defense, I figured I'd be the only one to see these. At least I shaved my legs yesterday for the party. Thank unicorns for small miracles.

Trey shakes his head with his signature mischievous smirk tugging at his lips.

"You and unicorns."

"They're the best of all the mythical creatures. They have a weapon on their heads." Duh.

Without another word, he turns, sliding his leather harness off his shoulders as he walks toward the bathroom. The harness and two sidearms clunk to the top of the dresser before Trey disappears through the door. When he reappears, his smirk has grown to a full grin. Displaying his prize in his raised hands, he stretches the long white tie from my robe and yanks it tight, twisting the ends around his fists.

I seal my thighs together, hoping to quell the pulling need between them. With a deep shuddering breath, knowing magical things are to come, I relax against the bed and wait.

The mattress dips by my feet.

"Arms above your head, baby. Wrists together."

Maybe a little too eagerly, I slide my arms up the smooth fabric of the duvet, stretching them high above my head. Trey makes quick work of binding both wrists together before testing the tie once to ensure it's not too tight. The bed shifts again as he hops off to round the footboard, coming to stand on the other side. Tipping my head back, chin to the ceiling, I try to figure out what he's up to. The binding tightens and tugs, stretching my arms even higher as he secures it to something I can't see.

Trey's handsome face fills my vision as he leans over the bed, hands on either side of my head. Deliberately slow, he lowers his face to mine. His fuller lower lip presses between the seam of my own, sucking mine between his lips in an erotic upside-down kiss. Dotting light kisses along my cheek and sucking down my neck, he caresses his calloused palms over my shoulders before skimming down to cup both breasts. I don't hold my low moan of need back.

I gasp, eyes sealing shut at the bite of pain as Trey pinches both pebbled nipples and twists. There's no dignity in my whimper, not that I care in this moment. The curve of his lips along my shoulder tells me he's smiling through the delicious torment. Too soon his lips lift from my overly sensitive skin and his hands pull away from my aching nipples with one last torturous pinch.

"Trey," I beg. Opening my eyes, I lift my head as high as I can with my hands tied, searching the room. "Where are you?"

"I think you've seen enough." He chuckles behind me before sliding something soft over my eyes. I blink frantically behind the material. It allows light to pass through the cloth but prevents me from seeing anything. A few strands of hair tighten painfully as whatever is around my eyes is secured behind my head. "Now, be a good girl and stay quiet. I'll be back."

"No," I gasp. Panic sets in. Yanking at my arms, I fight the hold while rotating my head back and forth along the bed, attempting to dislodge the material covering my eyes. "Trey, get your ass back here," I hiss quietly. Surrounded by agents trained to protect me, yelling out in my current naked and tied state seems very, very unwise.

No response.

Fuck. He really did leave me.

My heart thunders against my chest with fear while my body betrays me below, dampening with heavy arousal. I clench my thighs together, hoping to hide the slick evidence of how much I love this despite my reservations. Giving up on breaking free—because let's be honest, I don't want to—I relax as much as I can to listen for his return.

A soft click comes from the direction of the door. Near-silent footsteps draw closer to the bed.

I hold a shallow breath.

"Trey?" I whisper.

No answer.

The press of something cold and wet against my inner right thigh startles a gasp from my lungs. Slowly the freezing sensation slides up, leaving a trail of cool liquid in its wake. The ice-cold tip then traces along the line of my boy shorts, barely peeking beneath the tight elastic band before disappearing completely. Ice clinks against glass, my ears perking at the sound. Another icy tip circles along the inside of my other thigh, slowly climbing higher. Edging along the elastic band, the ice slides over the thin cotton to press against my burning folds.

I groan in frustration, need, annoyance. My hips jut off the bed of their own accord, seeking more of the delicious cold sensation against my center. Short, sharp breaths brush past dry lips.

Up and down he glides the bit of ice along my panty-covered slit, pausing at my swollen bundle of nerves. The biting cold presses hard before swirling in fast, tight circles. Unable to stifle my groans, I struggle to swallow each moan of pleasure that wants to rattle the walls.

Water drips down my center, some from the melting ice, the rest from my own slickness.

He swirls the nub of ice faster against my clit, pressing harder and eliciting sharp gasps.

Cold fingers slide along the top band of my panties before tugging them down to my ankles and ripping them off, displaying his urgency.

My thigh muscles stretch wide at the insistent press of his palms against the insides. Hot breath brushes along my center, dissolving the earlier chill. At the feel of his warm tongue as it slides up and down my slick center, I whimper and arch my hips off the bed, searching for more.

A heavy palm smacks against the side of my ass, the loud sound of skin-to-skin contact making me tense.

Trey's mouth pulls back, leaving me desperate and wanting.

"Please—"

The press of an ice chip directly to my hot, sensitive clit cuts my words off with a short scream.

"Shh, baby, or I'll have to gag you too." More slickness trickles out at his words. Something is definitely wrong with me. "Oh, you like that idea, don't you?" He chuckles. The resulting vibrations tickle my center, causing me to moan. "Next time, Mess. Next time I'll bind you and gag you and fuck you until you're hoarse."

Oh hell. I shudder on the comforter.

"Until then." The melting ice cube returns along with the heat of his mouth, almost like it's held between his teeth or pressed between his lips, and descends lower toward my entrance. Little by little, his ice-cold tongue dives inside, pushing a bit of the ice in with each thrust.

I fight the restraints. A frustrated grunt comes out at being so out of control.

Up and down he licks, flicking the ice against the tip of my nub.

"Do you forgive me, Mess?" He sucks me hard into his mouth. Again I scream. "Is that a yes."

"Yes," I groan. "Fuck yes, Trey. Finish it. I can't take this anymore." My tone is desperate, and almost whiny.

"Thank fuck." Two cold fingers slide in deep, curling to hit my most sensitive spot at the same time he nips at my clit.

The world ceases to exist. Every nerve ending, every muscle tenses and freezes in rapid succession as the building orgasm explodes through my veins. A silent scream makes its way out of my gaping mouth as I suck in deep breaths.

Slowly peeling my thighs from around his ears, I let my legs fall to the bed, too exhausted to hold them up on my own. Smiling like a fool, I close my eyes behind the blindfold.

After several seconds pass, my breathing slows to a normal pace as my mind clears.

"Mess," Trey says beside my ear. The tension holding my arms high loosens, followed by the bind around my wrists. "Mess," he calls like he's trying to bring me out of a dream. Hell, maybe he is. Maybe I never woke up this morning and this is all one amazing wet dream. "You have five minutes before the AAG meeting."

My eyes pop open, my lashes brushing along the cloth still covering my eyes. With a curse, I bolt up. Halfway off the bed, I yank the material off my eyes and look down to see what's now slung around my neck. My eyes narrow at my T-shirt.

"Seriously? You used the one I was wearing?"

"I'm resourceful," he says with a shrug as he adjusts his massive erection beneath his dark suit pants.

I wince at the clear discomfort he's in. Pointing at his crotch, I waggle my finger back and forth. "What about your situation?"

"It's my penance."

I snort and swipe my bra off the floor before sliding the straps up my arms. With the unicorns officially drowned, I slide on a fresh pair of underwear before searching for my other discarded clothes. As I get dressed, Trey grabs his holster off the dresser.

The holster, suit, styled hair.... Wait a second.

"Are you working today? Yesterday you said today was your day off."

Only once both guns are situated and secured does he answer. "It is, technically."

"Okay," I say slowly. Shoving my arms through the sleeves of my shirt, I push it over my head. "Then why are you here, armed? You never carry unless you're working."

His sigh increases my nerves.

"Is there some kind of threat? Am I in danger?"

Trey reaches up to rake his fingers through his hair, then pauses like he just remembered it was fixed and shouldn't mess it up. "No. Well, I guess technically you always are, but nothing specific as to why I'm here."

"Then why?"

"I wanted to be here for your meeting with the AAG. Tank stopped by this morning and brought up what happened last night with the Sam guy. We didn't want to raise any red flags by coming by as your friends, so we switched places with a couple of the beta team agents." He shrugs like the gesture isn't a big deal. With a tug on one sleeve and then the other, he peers up through his dark lashes. "Is that okay?"

It only takes two running steps to reach him. His eyes go wide, understanding my intentions just before I jump, latching onto his shoulders and wrapping my thighs around his waist. Once we're nose to nose, my large smile causes a low ache to build along my cheeks.

"Yes, it's okay. It's more than okay. I can't believe you'd do that."

He tilts his head to the side. "I love you, Randi. There's nothing I wouldn't do for you."

"Oh, you mean like selling your soul to the dark side and pretending to be engaged to a woman you can't stand?"

"Something like that," he says with a chuckle.

With a quick peck to the tip of his nose, I release my hold and slowly slide down his chest. Toes against the floor, I wrap my arms around his waist and tighten my hold. Cheek flush to his chest, I take a deep inhale of his unique spicy cologne.

"Hey, Mess?"

I hum a response, savoring the feel of his strong arms wrapped around me.

"Last night, you wanted to tell me something. What was it?"

My tight breath pushes back against my cheeks. "Later, Trouble. Okay?"

The way his muscles tense tells me he's not okay with that response, but he doesn't say a word about it.

"We'll get through this, right? Jessica, your mom, Kyle, your job, my job, everything and everyone that's standing between us." Dread builds in my gut as I wait for his answer.

Two fingers beneath my chin, he tilts my face up. "I won't allow any other outcome. You're mine, now and forever, Randi. I'm not saying it'll be easy, but we'll figure it out one day at a time."

"And the whole Kyle wanting me dead stuff? Because there's that, and Shawn, who's an evil psychopath who's probably plotting my slow death as we speak."

His features harden, lips pressed into a thin white line. "Don't worry about Kyle, or Shawn. We're all here to protect you."

Nodding, I lean forward and rest my forehead against his hard chest.

We can do this. Fake it until you make it, right?

Three years really isn't that long.

If you're an immortal magical fucking unicorn.

THE SHARP RAP of knuckles against the library door kicks my anxiety into overdrive. Swallowing down the ball of nerves in my throat, I slide my hands down my T-shirt and jeans, making sure everything is on straight. Shit, I hope my shirt isn't on backward. Surely Trey would've said something if it were.

My hammering heart tightens in my chest as Sam strides in, gaze immediately locking with mine. Reaching up, I wrap my fingers around my throat to keep the erratic pulse from beating out of my neck.

To say I'm nervous is an understatement. I loathe being unprepared like right now. It makes me edgy, frantic almost, not knowing what to expect or preparing my responses.

"Madam Vice President," he says in that sexy-as-hell gravelly voice. His gaze settles on my jeans and ballet flats.

Shit, maybe I should've dressed up, worn a suit like I normally do. But with everything else going on in the past twenty-four hours, I just couldn't muster the energy to put something fancier on.

Not that he's dressed to the nines, but he's still more business casual than going to the grocery store like my look. Instead of a suit, he's in a pair of dark gray slacks with a stark white dress shirt, sleeves rolled to his elbows exposing thick, corded forearms. My gaze latches on to the bit of ink peeping under both tight cuffs.

Well hell.

Deep breaths, Randi. Deep, calming breaths. Who knew I was a forearm type of girl? Or maybe it's just Sam's forearms I find sexy, along with the teasing ink I want to see more of.

"Sam," I say, my voice trembling. His lips twitch upward before sealing back into an almost frown. "Please, it's Randi."

Sam dips his chin in acknowledgment and casts a quick glance around the room. With an inquisitive expression, he angles his head toward the grouping of leather chairs in front of my massive desk. That's one thing I didn't expect when arriving in DC. The men here must equate their dick size to how large their desks are, because every single one of them could double as an unbreakable barricade. I gesture toward the chairs. Sam steps to the grouping and folds into the plush leather, resting one foot over the other knee.

"What I need to discuss requires them to leave," he says, picking at an invisible piece of lint from the bottom part of his slacks. I hold back my surprise that he noticed Trey and T's presence. "I know they can't leave you alone technically, but they need to station themselves just outside the door for now."

"They can hear whatever you have to say," I respond, my tone flippant. The last thing I need Sam to know is how I tell Trey and T everything, how they're my only friends in this town.

"Actually, they can't, Randi. It's a matter of their level of security clearance compared to ours." For the first time since he entered the room, he levels a look to T. "And cut the audio part of the security feed. I don't mind you keeping a visual on the room, but this conversation is between the VP and myself, no one else."

Oh hell. What is this about?

With a quick questioning look between the two men, I sigh and nod. It would've been nice to have them with me, but he's right. If this is something to do with national security, neither Trey nor T has security clearance as high as I do, or the AAG apparently. If it's nothing that will jeopardize the safety of the American people, then I'll fill them in later. Easy peasy.

Irritation radiates off both men as they shuffle through the door. Only once it shuts behind them do I let out the breath I was holding. With less pulsing testosterone in the air, the office seems lighter.

Angling toward Sam, I press my shoulder against the paneled wall and level my best no-nonsense look his way.

"Okay, they're gone. Now tell me what the hell is going on so I can get back to the thousands of other things I need to get done today."

"Straight to the point, no bullshit. Nice," he says, leaning back in the chair and sliding around the stiff seat cushion to get comfortable. "Have you noticed how meetings in this town drag on for hours with idiots talking about things that don't matter before finally getting to the issues the meeting was called for?"

I snort and then dip my chin in embarrassment at the slip. Kyle tried to train my snorting, nail biting, cursing, man walking—okay, most of my mannerisms out of me during the campaign in hopes I'd turn into a more presentable VP.

Obviously it didn't work.

"How could I not notice that most of the meetings around here run over their scheduled time and still don't get anything done?" His earlier wording replays in my mind, piquing my curiosity. "You said 'in this town.' Are you not from here?"

Sam's lips spread in an almost sneer. "No, thank goodness. Not that I care. Honestly, with what I've seen out of the men in this town, I'll take it as a compliment."

"As you should." The overhead soft lighting does amazing things to his already deviously handsome face. Something familiar tickles in the back of my mind as I really look at Sam. "Do I know you?" Now that he's not cloaked in darkness like last night, there's something familiar about him. Then there's the fact that he seems fairly comfortable for a first meeting—almost too comfortable, like there's an air of familiarity between us. Daring a step toward the circle of chairs, I squint to scan his features, this time not focused on his beautiful face but searching for any hint to tell me who this man is. "You seem—"

"Familiar?" He tugs the cuff of his pants toward his ankle. "I wondered if you'd recognize me."

"Should I?" Hell, I've met so many people over the past couple years, there's no telling how I know him.

"It's been a while, so no. If the roles were switched, I'm not sure I would've recognized you, especially looking like this."

So he knew me before Kyle's required transformation. Before the extensive overhaul from Randi 1.0 to Randi 2.0, I was... well, as my ex put it long ago, haggard. Growing up near the poverty line and clawing your way through life will do that to you.

"Had to look the part," I finally say. "Not that I'm complaining."

"I was a TA your first year at Harvard. Constitutional law. You weren't in the class at the time since you were a freshman, but everyone knew who you were."

The charity case. Trailer trash who didn't deserve a spot at the prestigious Harvard. Yep, that's me. White trash Randi. And with Kyle's help, those bastard students never let me forget it.

I push down the rising despair thinking about those lonely days and nights during law school evokes. Clearing my throat of the lump lodged in it, I offer a tight-lipped smile. "I'm sorry, I don't remember you specifically, but you do seem familiar." Unease curls in my belly. What does he think of me based on the rumors, the taunts, and hate dished out because of my background? Searching his green eyes for the answer, I find nothing but steely resolution.

He waves my comment away. "On to the topic I wanted to discuss with you. What details do you know regarding the rising price of oil?"

My shoulders tense, hiking up close to my ears before I roll them back. Straightening my spine, I turn to stare out the window as I debate my reply.

"The truth, as hard as it is to believe, is I don't know a damn thing," I finally say, hating the words. I'm the fucking VP, yet I have no clue what's going on in my own country because the president wants it that way. He's been keeping me running around the globe, attending summit after summit with Todd, so when was I supposed to catch wind of it all? "I watched Kyle's press conference this morning, but that's all I know about the overseas angle. But honestly?" Leaning harder against the wall, I press the side of my head against the cool dark wood paneling. "I don't believe it's an overseas issue. Something else is going on." After a moment lost in thought, I shift my weight to turn toward Sam. "Why?"

"We're investigating the cause."

"Why you?" I ask. My nose scrunches as I rack my brain trying to remember exactly what his role is responsible for over at the DOJ. With so many job titles and so many jurisdictions, it's hard to keep them all straight.

"Our office oversees the Environmental and Natural Resources Division, among others. That's how this falls under my jurisdiction."

I nod. "Right. But this seems like a stretch for you to investigate, right? Why would you focus resources on an issue that's so... commercial? Why is this attracting federal attention?" Sure, it's attracted mine too, but only after my college-age daughter, Taeler, pointed it out months ago while in Austin. The fact that I didn't notice before her insight still rubs me the wrong way. I'm turning into one of "them" the longer I'm in this city. Too caught up in what's going on in front of my face to see what the day-to-day life issues are in this country. I need a reality check to pull my focus back to my main goals.

"We have our reasons," Sam states, giving nothing away.

With a huff, I push off the wall and walk to the grouping of chairs. Choosing the one directly across the hand-carved wooden coffee table from him, I sit and lean back, rubbing my temples. "That's an evasive answer."

"Don't you remember from law school? Don't ever give details, incriminating or not. Anything can be used against you at a later date. This is me protecting myself."

"From me?" I snort. "And why would you need to do that? I'm just me."

"Maybe that was a plausible response for the Randi from law school, but this Randi Sawyer looks just like one of them."

"The fuck?" I snap. I've never been so insulted in my life.

"Classy." His tone comes off as chiding, but the smile he's fighting back speaks volumes. "I need to evaluate if you're in on the circumstances we believe are the cause for the oil spike."

Again with his wordy answer that doesn't actually say anything. "Circumstances?" I question with annoyance. "Care to elaborate, Sam?"

"Let's see here." Leaning forward, he braces his elbows on his knees. "It's a surprisingly long list. Abuse of power, fraud, bribery, extortion, corruption." He ticks off each with a finger, his hard stare never shifting from my shocked one.

"What the hell?" I demand, my spine going ramrod straight. "That's a... I mean... what are you even talking about?"

"I'll break it down for you. Abuse of power and fraud by using your role to misuse federal land, allowing drilling in protected oil rich areas. Corruption, bribery, and extortion due to only approving companies with offshore accounts so there's zero way for us to track where the money is going. Driving the price of gas so high because the other companies can't compete, causing production in Texas and Alaska to drop so far that the tables of supply and demand flip." With each word, he's inched closer until he's practically leaning over the coffee table.

Holy fuck, that's a lot of accusations. Detailed ones. Where in the hell does he think all that's coming from?

"I don't know... I didn't... who the hell would do that?" My words are rushed and panicked.

"The president."

Ah, well, that makes sense. I'll give him that much.

4

RANDI

All I can do is gape at the fuming man sitting across from me. No words come to mind. Once, twice, I open my mouth, but when the right words don't form, I close it tight once again. Fingers digging into the worn leather armrests, I push to a standing position and maneuver around Sam, careful not to get too close. I pause in front of the massive desk and tilt forward, grasping the edge for support. For several moments, I stare unseeing at the polished wood, processing his accusation and planning my next move.

"I don't know. Didn't know." Long dark locks of hair fall over my shoulders, creating a curtain around my face. "Why are you here, Sam? To pin this on me?"

"We're investigating the president's involvement and several of his major campaign supporters. I needed to know, needed to ask you the hard questions personally and gauge your reactions to know if you're involved too."

I shake my head. "I wouldn't do that."

"You have to admit it's farfetched that you haven't noticed, or aren't involved. You're his VP, up at the White House almost daily to meet with him and other members of your party. Hell, you're even the one who went to the OPEC summit, not Birmingham."

Indignation slams through me. Whirling around, I take a step toward Sam, my index finger raised at his chest. Hands in the pockets of his slacks, he doesn't retreat. Hell, he doesn't even look bothered by my sudden burst of anger.

"Do you have any clue what I've been focused on the last seven months? Do you?" Sam shakes his head. "Trying to make sure that prick of a president doesn't whisk away voter rights with a fucking bill that he knew would pass." I jam my finger into his hard chest. "And if you *must* know, that fucker doesn't let me in on anything. He used me to get the president spot and has shut me out ever since. I don't know what he's doing behind closed doors or who he's meeting with. And yeah, I did go to the OPEC summit, but it was to try and understand what's happening."

The only sound in the room is my heavy breathing.

Reluctantly, I pull my finger from his chest and retreat a couple steps to sit on the edge of the desk. Embarrassment fills my thoughts as the anger ebbs away.

"That Birmingham always was a prick."

I huff and hang my head in defeat.

"Hey," he says, the earlier accusatory tone gone replaced with hesitation. With an impatient groan, he cuts himself off before he can say any more. The tips of his black dress shoes, which are nice but not nearly as expensive as Trey's or most of the other men I've met in DC, stop just in front of my ballet slippers. "I believe you."

"That I'm a fool, or that I didn't know about the president's illegal activities he was conducting behind my back?"

"Both."

I roll my eyes. "Ass." But his response does what it intended, breaking the growing self-accusing black hole I was slipping into.

Giving my head a slight shake, I grasp my thick hair in a makeshift ponytail. With a few twists and a random ballpoint pen I find along the desk top, I secure the mess on top of my head.

"Okay." I slap my hands on my thighs and stand. Walking around the desk, I fold into my oversized leather chair. "Now what? Was that all you came for? To make sure I'm not a part of it so you can keep zeroing in on the people who are?"

Hip against the desk, he crosses both arms over his chest, causing the sleeves to ride a little higher up his forearms. More colorful tattoos peek through, drawing my gaze.

"Nice ink," I comment.

His gaze flicks from mine to his arms. When he looks back up, a small smirk pulls at his lips. "Thanks. You're not the only one in this town who doesn't truly belong."

"Is that so?"

He dips his chin in acknowledgment. "The investigation is at a standstill. We have assumptions of illegal activity but can't prove it. Either Birmingham is innocent and someone else is doing all this behind the scenes, or he's very good at covering his tracks."

Thumbnail between my teeth, I tuck a knee to my chest and rest my chin on top. "Could be both." A million different angles slip through my head. A hint of something I should remember flares in the back of my mind but disappears before I can grasp hold.

I sigh. "I can't help you. Not only do I have zero connections in this town, but I don't know anything that's going on in the White House unless it's directly connected to me or my team." I take a deep inhale and release it slowly to quell my racing mind. "I wouldn't put it past him though. Any of it. I say keep digging. You'll find something, but I guarantee it won't be with me. I know less than you do."

He arches a single dark brow and leans forward across the desk.

What is up with the guy in wanting to get all up in my personal space? Not that I mind. His bad-boy hotness isn't at all offensive.

A faint waft of crisp, cool cologne hits my nose. The scent tightens the awareness of how alone we are. I scan his harsh features that somehow work for him, the main focus being his piercing green eyes that seem to suck you in with the intensity behind them.

"What if I asked for your help?" Sam asks, placing a palm in the middle of the desk to support his upper body as he leans closer.

Ah shit. Averting my gaze, I switch to chewing on the middle fingernail. That's a hard no, even though I'd love to—for more reasons than one. What Sam isn't privy to is that stupid agreement I signed to support Kyle during the campaign and after. No doubt aiding in gaining information needed for impeachment goes against said agreement, which states if I breach the contract, then I have to pay every cent he spent on me back to the Birmingham estate. There's no way I can do that considering they paid off my massive credit card debt, student loans from undergrad and law school, the makeovers, clothes, travel, campaign, and Tae's school. Sure, I make decent money now, but that's a shit ton of money I 100 percent don't have waiting in the wings.

Knowing Kyle and his awful family, if I fail to pay every cent back, there's no doubt some kind of indentured servant clause in the fine print that I missed, and I'll be his unwilling slave for the rest of my life.

"Not cleaning toilets," I mutter, ignoring Sam's confused head tilt.

Okay, surely after UT Austin and Harvard, I would've caught something that drastic. But all those months were a blur. All I heard was "out of debt" and didn't consider the long-term effects of signing on with the Birmingham family.

Now I do. I'd like to say I regret it, but I'm the vice president of the United States, so... I don't. Sure, earlier this year when Kyle was trying to take away the voting rights for the lower class, I regretted my decision to be his running mate, which in turn aided in him winning the White House. But now that we stopped that bill, I'm glad to be in this role. On a daily basis, my team and I help thousands across the states.

Currently we're fighting for a different way to support low-income families who fall just above the food stamp cutoff. What these fuckers in DC haven't wrapped their brains around is that they're punishing people who are trying to make a better life for themselves and their families. The second they get a job and push out of the poverty status, thousands of dollars in benefits are ripped away from them, making it impossible to take care of their family and work. Where's the incentive? Why try to find a job, to work hard, if nothing will be better?

And don't even get me started on low-income housing and what happens if someone gets a bonus or higher-paying job.

This is why I'm here. This is why I was voted in. To be their voice. To show these asshats the right way to take care of *all* the citizens.

"Randi?"

"Asshats," I grumble.

"Excuse me?" he says with a chuckle.

I wave a hand, dismissing him. "Sorry, wrong conversation." Damn, I forgot what it's like to be around someone who doesn't understand my level of crazy. Ugh, if he's going to stick around, I'll have to train him in all the "Randi-isms." Which could be fun. Teacher, student... plaid skirts—on me, not him. Lots of possibilities.

I bolt out of the chair, slamming the tops of my thighs under the desk.

Fuck, what is wrong with me? I love Trey. Trey loves me. *Stop thinking dirty thoughts about the attractive-as-sin lawyer who keeps getting too close, Randi.*

Just because he's sexy. And smells good. And is smart as hell. And has this arrogant authority thing going on. Oh, and don't forget the tattoos I want to investigate further....

Shit.

Shit.

Shit.

I'm in deep shit.

"You okay? You're all flushed." I swear there's a hint of humor in his tone. The bastard knows I'm flustered.

Crap, what if he knows I was thinking about him naked?

Wait, was I thinking about him naked?

Well, hell, now I am.

Ugh, I'm a lost cause.

"Fine, just hot flashes."

Fucking hell, Randi. Now this guy thinks you have the uterus of a fifty-year-old.

"Right." Glancing over, he straightens from the desk and slides both hands into the front pockets of his slacks. "We need help, inside help, to gain proof that this is all going on. We need to know who his partners are inside, who he's funneling money to."

I shake my head.

"You heard what that idiot said this morning. If we don't prove that the cost of rising gas prices is due to his dealings, not others', we'll go to war. A war where men and women will lose their lives on a lie. Is that what you want, Madam VP?"

I swallow the bile rising up my throat. Choosing me is selfish. But still, I can't risk it. I can't risk everything I've built, who I've become, for his wild-goose chase.

Old Randi, sure. She would've jumped in the ring without a second thought.

But new Randi, well, she's a little more cautious. More is riding on each decision. I have to look at the big picture nowadays. New Randi has more to lose.

"I'm sorry, but I can't help you," I whisper, not daring to look him in the eyes. Walking to the bookshelf, I pretended to scan the spines. "I have another meeting I need to prepare for. I think it's time for you to leave."

The soft click of his dress shoes echoes around the library. Out of my periphery, I see him pause at the door.

"I know I didn't know you back then, but I sure as fuck expected more out of you than this. You're no better than the rest of them."

With that, he throws open the door and storms out.

I slump forward, pressing my forehead against the hard spine of a massive book. My stomach cramps at the frustration and disappointment in his voice. The sexy gravelly tone he has going on didn't do anything to soften the blow of his words.

Movement by the door snags my attention. The soft leather rolls along my forehead as I shift to see who's entered the library.

T and Trey stand at attention, hands lightly clasped. Blowing out a heavy breath, I stare at the book spines.

"That seemed to go well," Trey says, zero humor in his voice.

I huff. The skin of my forehead peels from the spine as I stand straight. "I need a drink."

"No," T says.

"Fine, a cigarette."

"Negative."

"Killjoy," I retort.

"Been called worse." T shoots a mock salute my way.

A corner of my lips turns upward. "Same." Hanging my head back, I let out a loud unladylike groan. "Fuck," I say, drawing it out into multiple syllables.

"Tell us," Trey demands. "We can help."

I shake my head and turn to my two best friends. "I wish I could. You have no idea. But what he told me is real shit. Beyond Kyle creating that stupid bill to take away voting rights. If I disclose what Sam and I discussed, I could be prosecuted, and I won't do that to you or to me."

A ball of nausea rolls in my gut. Sweat dots along my forehead and dampens beneath my arms. I make quick work of shoving my sleeves up to my elbows before toeing off one shoe, then the other. The cold hardwood quickly soaks into the bottoms of my bare feet, instantly cooling the sudden hot flash.

I swallow and glance around the library, hoping the answer lies somewhere in this room.

"But I want to tell you," I admit.

T and Trey share a quick look, an unspoken conversation happening in that split second.

"I think you need to get out of this house," T says.

"Okay," I agree, uncertain of his change in topics but whatever. "But remember, the president wants me dead, which is why I've been held captive in this house." They've kept me locked in the house since that night we were ambushed. Going out for the party last night was a rare taste of freedom. No matter how many times I told them, "All work and no play make Randi a dull girl," they were relentless about keeping me safe in this house.

Both men nod.

"My apartment is secure." My mouth gapes at Trey. "We can keep her away from the windows."

"We'll sweep it for bugs—"

"The hell?" Trey groans. "You're an overprotective busy bee."

"Busy bee?" I say on a giggle, rewarding me with an almost smirk from Trey.

"This is national security we're talking about. Mix that with the two fucktwats, Birmingham and Whit, I'm not taking any chances. We go to your place, scan it for bugs, then... eat lunch." The exaggerated wink T shoots my way causes a snort to escape. I slap a palm across my nose just as another slips out. "Have Jessica order the food. That way no one knows it's for Randi."

My gaze snaps to Trey's. "I'm sorry, what? Is she fucking living with you now?" I take a deadly step toward the two men, my eyes no doubt blazing with jealousy and giving them a peek into the violent side of my crazy.

"Calm down there, Carrie." Trey gives T a worried glimpse. "Jessica isn't living with me. That will never happen. She lives in her own condo, several floors below mine." Keeping his attention on me like I'm about to strike, he says to T out of the corner of his mouth, "Negative on Jessica. I repeat, negative on Jessica."

All the anger and tension seep from my tight muscles, leaving them heavy. "Oh. Okay. Whew, you almost died."

Wait, can I get jealous when I was just imagining hottie Sam and me playing "spank the student"?

"Wow," T says on a whistle.

"Yeah, I was a little scared, and I've seen her hit."

I let out a sarcastic laugh at the two with narrowed eyes. "Hey, I'm getting better. Look at these guns." Lifting my twig-like arms, I flex, allowing the small hill to bulge along my bicep.

"You are improving," T agrees. "Sarah says you've come a long way."

Pride radiates in my chest. Sarah, his wife, is one tough cookie, so impressing her is like winning the lottery—it never happens. "Really? She said I was getting better?"

With a smile, he nods. "Still a long way to go, mind you." I roll my eyes to the ceiling. "But better than the worthless duck-and-roll strategy you started the training sessions with."

"That's what they taught me in elementary school," I say, hiding my laughter. Trey is right, T is so fun to rile up.

"That's tuck and roll," T says, throwing his large hands in the air in clear exasperation. "That's when you're on fire, not when you're getting your ass—"

I lose control over my giggles, cutting him off.

Eyes narrowed, he squints from me to the chuckling Trey. "Funny."

"You're not laughing," Trey points out.

"I don't laugh."

I nod, causing the earlier makeshift messy bun to come unraveled. "Sure you do. I've seen you do it a lot around me." The pen falls to the floor, and my hair tumbles the rest of the way down my back.

"That's me laughing *at* you, not with you."

I grasp my chest and lean back against the bookshelf, faking pain. "You cut me deep. Real deep, T."

With a roll of his dark eyes, he marches to the library doors and gives an impatient wave out into the hall. "Let's go, you two. I'm fucking starving."

$$5$$

5

TREY

*W*hy the hell am I nervous?

Keys in hand, I slide around Randi and the rest of the alpha team to open the condo door. The moment the deadbolt clicks, four of the guys, plus Tank, push past me, shoving the door open. Tank adds a little more shoulder into his push than necessary, making me stumble to keep from falling backward.

Randi moves around me to follow the five. Snaking an arm around her waist as she passes by, I haul her backward, sealing her back to my chest.

"Not until they clear the room," I chastise. "It's like you've never done this before."

She shrugs. "It's your place. No one knew we were coming. What's the big deal?"

"You. You're the big deal, Randi. Not sure if you've realized it yet, but you're the vice president, and with that comes constant threats. Not everyone agrees with what you're trying to change in this city, plus the less local threats."

"I know," she grumbles. Relaxing a bit against my chest, she takes a deep breath. "Which floor does Jessica live on?"

"She's five floors down." I tug her closer, relishing the feel of her ass molding around my growing cock. "But she doesn't have the view I do. I pay top dollar to be on this floor and this side."

"Oh," she says mockingly. "So I should be impressed."

"Yes." I press my lips against her ear.

The feel of her in my arms, each breath calms the unease in my chest that's taken residence since I woke up this morning. I got a good up close and personal view of the Sam guy, and I hate to admit it, but I agree with Tank—the fucker is sexy. Hell, I kind of want to be him when I grow up. That's a fucking paper cut to the dick too. I don't want him hanging around her; anyone would be susceptible to someone like him. Hell, I'm straight and I got a little turned on. Nope, not turned on. A man crush. Yeah, that's the cool term. I have a man crush on the guy, and I don't even know him.

"Clear," one of the guys calls out from inside the apartment.

Slowly, I ease my arm from around her, allowing her a bit of room to wiggle out of my grasp. Inside the apartment, she stops suddenly, causing me to crash into her back.

"Wow," she says. "Okay, this is amazing. I'll give you that." She turns fast, her long dark hair fanning around her with the motion. Eyes searching my own, she wraps an arm around my waist. "You'd give this up for me?"

I nod, unable to express that I'd live in a cardboard box if that made her happy and gave me her. Nothing matters anymore but her. She's my future, my everything. My parents' money, them threatening to take it all away, doesn't register as a concern anymore.

Three years. I just have to get through these three years. Then we can be together, openly, with everyone knowing I'm the luckiest guy in the world because she's by my side. I get Randi's earlier concern, wondering if we can do it, if we can make it through the shit show we've created with Mother and Jessica. But there isn't another option. There is no room for failure when it comes to us.

The repetitive beeps of the sensing wands sound through the living room and toward the bedroom, indicating the team is still conducting the bug sweep. Holding her close, I rest my chin on the crown of her head. Several more minutes pass before they're finished. Once the rest of the guys move to their stations outside the door and around the perimeter of the building, I reluctantly leave Randi to lower the blackout blinds over the floor-to-ceiling windows.

The motors whirl until the last bits of sun disappear behind the blinds. A low grumble has me turning to where she stands, arms wrapped around her waist.

"What's for lunch?" she asks.

"I thought I'd cook."

"This should be interesting," Tank grumbles. Elbow to her bicep, he nudges her, which almost sends her toppling over. "He's the worst cook."

"Hey, I can cook," I say defensively. He scoffs. "Okay, fine. I can cook *one* thing. How about my famous grilled cheese sandwich?" Shrugging out of my jacket, I place it, my holster, and my guns on a side table. Unbuttoning the cuff of one sleeve, I fold it up three times before doing the same with the other.

Randi's hazel eyes sparkle, locked on my exposed forearms. "Sounds great."

"Sounds great," Tank mocks. "Fuck, you're so cock whipped."

Randi and I exchange a glance before busting out laughing. A single happy tear streaks down her cheek. Together we walk into the kitchen. I head for the refrigerator while Tank and Randi slide onto two stools at the bar.

"You've seen it. Wouldn't you be?" she says, her smile broad and happy.

Tank snarls and covers his ears.

"I put bacon, gouda, cheddar, spinach, and tomato on it, cool?" I pull all the ingredients out of the fridge and line them up along the counter. The knife hisses as I slide it from the block. Setting the cheese on a cutting board, I begin slicing.

Palms against the marble, she stands and ambles around the counter. At my back, I hear the fridge open.

"Do you have any avocado?"

I turn to look over my shoulder, pointing to the lowest drawer with the tip of the knife. "If I do, they'd be in there. I think Martha keeps a few on hand."

"Martha?" she questions as she rifles through the drawer before pulling out an avocado.

"Yeah, Martha. My housekeeper and cook."

"Wow," she says, but not in a positive way. My hackles rise at her tone.

"You act surprised. You saw where I grew up, saw the wealth. Don't be shocked by me having all this," I say with a little too much annoyance.

"Um, what?"

I turn from the eight slices of bread I was buttering and lean back against the counter. "Last night, my parents' house. My childhood home."

"Your childhood home," Randi says unbelievingly. "Yeah, you said the party was to be held at an estate. Not *your* estate."

"Well, it's not mine."

"Technically it is."

"No it's not. I hate that fucking place."

Silence falls around the kitchen.

"So, what did the AAG have to say?" Tank asks, clearly doing his best to ease the awkwardness that's settled between Randi and me. "You're free to talk here. No bugs, no cameras. Just us."

Nibbling on the corner of her thumbnail—how the woman has any nails left, I'll never know—she steps to the knife block and grabs her own. Her shoulder pressing against my bicep helps ease a bit of the indignation she'd somehow riled up with her words.

Slicing the avocado in half, she remains silent for several moments.

"They're investigating Kyle," Randi finally says. The slow thump of the knife meeting the cutting board echoes through the kitchen. "And I'm a fool. That's a good way to summarize it."

Setting a slice of bread in the hot pan, butter side down, I begin layering the cheeses and toppings. With a spatula, I shift it around, though it's more to have something to keep me busy than the fact that it needs any attention.

"It would seem all the anger from the OPEC summit was warranted," she adds. Moving to the sink, she rinses the knife and rests it in the strainer. Turning so she can face Tank and me, she hops up on the counter, her grasp on the edge white-knuckled. She hangs her head, her dark hair cascading down and creating a barrier. "I was so focused on the bill, stopping that and going to the summits, I didn't see the signs."

"Probably his doing," I say, flipping the sandwich. The butter sizzles, crackling and popping in the pan.

"What do you mean?" Tank asks.

"I mean I bet that was his plan from the start. I would even bet my left nut that the bill was just a distraction, something to keep her focus—hell, maybe everyone's—away from what he's doing behind the scenes."

"Please don't bet your nuts," Randi says with a huff. "They're lovely nuts."

"Thanks," I reply with a wide smile. "I've always thought so."

"Can we stop talking about Trey's balls, please?" Tank groans. "What do you mean about the OPEC summit, Randi?"

"The DOJ believes Kyle is the cause of this oil issue. They suspect he's utilizing federal land for drilling for his own gain. Not only that but selecting companies which are tied to large campaign supporters while putting tighter restrictions on other private drilling companies."

"How in the hell...?" I say, trailing off as I slide the first sandwich on to a plate. Slicing it in half with the warm spatula, I slide it down the counter to Randi. "Order up."

A slight tilt of her head parts her curtain of hair, allowing our eyes to meet. "Thanks, Trouble."

I nod and start the second sandwich. If I know Tank, he's teetering between the line of happy and hangry.

"That's what they want to know." A crunch of crispy bread draws my attention from the pan to where Randi is taking her first bite. Slowly, her eyes close, and my heart splits open with joy.

"You're a keeper," she says, locking eyes with me.

"It's all I know," I say, trying to keep it light even though I want to fall on my knees and propose to her right here in the kitchen. But fucking hell, I can't because I'm already engaged.

Fuck my life.

"It's all I need," she replies with a wide smile before she raises her hand to take another bite. "And they don't know how, just suspect," she continues around a mouthful of sandwich. "He asked me for help."

Is there any sexier sight than the woman you love devouring the food you cooked for her? I think not. Well, unless she was naked. And spread-eagle on the marble. With me feeding her the food with one hand while the other played between her legs.

"Help?" I cringe at the huskiness in my voice, giving away the lust riding through my veins. "In convicting Birmingham? As in teaming up with DOJ?"

She shakes her head. "No not as an attorney but in gaining evidence." Attention on me, she says, "Proof. No matter if you're the president or a sexy-ass secret service agent, anyone needs proof for a case to even be considered to be taken to court."

"Um, have you seen the last few years in DC?" Tank says with a laugh. "Pretty sure fast allegations get blasted across every news channel and social media daily. Proof isn't needed in today's trial by Twitter."

"I agree, but the public opinion of guilt is different than actual guilt. To have both the House and Senate agree to proceed with impeachment, there has to be substantial evidence or they're risking their own careers. Kyle has material on them, don't forget. So they'll have to know 100 percent that there will be a guilty verdict to even consider moving forward."

Nodding to an unheard beat, I flip the bread as I process her words. "He needs inside help."

"That's exactly what Sam wants." A light flare of pink highlights her cheeks. "I think I can trust him." I school my features to keep my emotions from showing. "Not that it matters."

"Order up," I grumble with less enthusiasm than earlier.

"I agree that we can trust him, but why doesn't it matter?" Tank asks as he leans across the counter with plate in hand, waiting to accept the hot sandwich. I slide it onto his plate and turn back to the stove to prepare the next one.

"You both know what I signed with Kyle," she explains. "I can't risk being in breach of contract. I'd have to pay everything back, and even with the salary I make, it wouldn't be a drop in the bucket to what I'd owe." She shoves the last piece of toasted bread into her mouth and shakes her head. "I won't risk it. I have to think long-term."

Neither Tank nor I say a word. Butter sizzles in the hot pan, filling the otherwise silent kitchen. I chance a look at Tank, whose dark eyes are already on me. He nods, knowing exactly what I'm thinking, and goes back to his sandwich, confirming we're on the same page.

Part of me wants to push her to help the DOJ, even if it means her working closely with Sam. Randi came to DC to make a difference, to stop the political leeches from taking advantage of the people they were elected to fight for. The Randi I met on the campaign trail would be furious at her current desire to stay out of this fight, and for what? Money? Status? Randi's current mindset is selfish, which isn't her.

But it *is* the safe option.

That's where the other half wants me to plant my flag, to side with her. Randi already has a target on her back between Birmingham, Whit, and the rest of the aristocratic dipshits who don't want to change. Assisting on this investigation will put her safety in more jeopardy. Plus it'll put her working side by side with the man she no doubt finds attractive.

So which do I vocalize?

The smell of burnt bread draws my focus from the white subway tile I'd mindlessly focused on to the pan.

"Shit," I hiss. Flipping the sandwich, I curse again at the blackened bread. Out of nowhere, my patience snaps. The knob nearly snaps as I twist off the gas flame. Grabbing the sizzling pan with the ruined sandwich, I toss it into the sink with more force than necessary and storm out of the kitchen.

The soft leather recliner molds around my ass and back as I fall into it. Closing my eyes, I take several deep breaths in an attempt to calm my rising anger as heat fills my veins. I shift in the chair, grumbling to myself as I try to get comfortable but fail miserably.

With an annoyed sigh, I reach up and massage my forehead where a blooming headache has started. Even with the soft groan of the leather as I attempt to settle deeper into the chair, her soft footsteps meet my ears. An intoxicating cherry vanilla scent fills my nose, easing the building stress behind my chest. I peek one eye open and watch as she removes one small shoe and then the other.

Slowly, she crawls into the recliner, settling in the small open space between me and the armrest. I exhale long and hard through my nose, pushing out the earlier annoyance. Fingers in her hair, I tuck her head against my chest, then rake them through the soft strands. With each stroke, my earlier anger at the world disintegrates.

"It'll be okay, Mess," I whisper. Her head lifts, lips parted, but I capture her mouth with my own before she can get a word out. "Let's just relax, hang out. Let everything else wait. I need this, just us acting like there's nothing else going on, even if it's just for a few minutes. Let's pretend to be a normal couple for just a little while," I say against her lips, my eyes searching her wide hazel ones.

"Okay, Trouble." With another quick peck, she lowers her head and snuggles deeper into the chair, moving me out of the way until she's comfortable. "Wanna watch a movie?"

Unable to resist, I press my lips to the top of her head and smile. "Sure, baby." Stretching to the side table, I swipe the remote off the metal top and press a few buttons. The massive TV comes alive with *SportsCenter* as their voices boom from the surround sound. "What do you want to watch?"

No response comes. Tucking my chin, I search her face and smile when I find her eyes closed. Leaning back, I press the button that extends the leg portion of the recliner and leans the backrest backward. She grumbles as the chair moves but doesn't wake.

With another soft kiss to the crown of her head, I rest my head back and close my eyes, savoring the moment. I know it won't last long, but I wish with all that I have that it would.

6

RANDI

A loud noise interrupts the peaceful sleep I'd slipped into. Blinking a few times, I keep my cheek nestled against Trey's chest as I fight the lingering drowsiness that always comes after taking too long of a nap. Trey's arm tightens around my waist, preventing me from wiggling out of his snug hold.

Lifting my head, I search the room. T sits on the couch, eyes glued to the baseball game playing on the massive screen. His attention swings to me before focusing back on the game.

"How long was I out?" I whisper to not wake Trey.

"Nearly two hours," he says, a hint of a smile tugging at his lips. "Playboy there fell asleep almost immediately after you. I'd say you both needed a break."

I let out a deep breath and lay my head back on Trey's chest. "Two hours," I say in disbelief as the realization shatters the peaceful calm. My mind races with all the things I need to do. Adrenaline pumps through my veins, dispersing the lingering effects of the nap. "I need to go."

T shakes his head. "You're right where you need to be." His eyes leave the screen to meet mine. "You both have a lot on your plate. You need times like this to make it through it all." I swallow back the emotions his words evoke and nod in agreement. "It won't be easy, but the stuff worth fighting for never is. But you have to realize he's under just as much pressure as you are.

Different pressure, but it's there. Add in this new challenge with the DOJ, and our boy here's near the snapping point."

"What about the DOJ?" I whisper, stealing a quick look up to make sure Trey's still asleep.

Tank shakes his head. "Sam might be someone we can trust with whatever shit Birmingham's stirring up, but can you trust yourself around him?"

Heat flashes beneath my cheeks. "What's that supposed to mean?"

Tank shoots me a knowing look. "We're not blind, Randi. He's a good-looking man who will probably be around a lot over the next few months. Add in the fact that you two connect on a different level than you and Benson here because of the law school stuff, and it's a concern for him. It's one more thing on his mind, something else for him to worry about when it comes to you. Not only is he worried about your safety—even more so now that Birmingham has a target on your back—but now he has to worry about some other man encroaching on what he considers his."

"Yeah, I mean, he's attractive and all, but he's not Trey."

"You say that now," T says on a groan as he stands and stretches his thick arms above his head. "But what about when you're spending hours on end together as you piece together the evidence needed to impeach Birmingham?"

"I already said I wouldn't," I state, but even I don't believe it.

T winks. "We all know you will. Just go easy on my boy here is all I'm asking. And fight for him. He needs to know you're all in too."

The soft leather gives beneath my elbow as I push up to a half-sitting position. Trey's eyes remain closed, his lips slightly parted. Reaching up, I stroke a fingertip along his hairline and down his strong jaw. With his features soft in sleep, I realize how stressed he's been lately. The faint lines along his forehead are gone, the tick of his jaw not there. He looks younger, softer. Still sexy as fuck, but without the stress of the world resting on his shoulders.

"How long do we have before we need to head back?" I whisper to T without taking my eyes off the sleeping Trey.

"You're the boss. You tell us."

"Give us thirty more minutes." I flick my gaze to T and nod to the door. "Alone."

Lips pursed to suppress his smile, T nods and turns to leave.

Once he's out of the condo, I turn my full focus back to Trey. The silky strands of his dark hair slide through my fingers. Guilt eats at my gut. I should've been more understanding of the stress he's under instead of focusing on my own issues. Plus he wouldn't even have all this extra stress if it weren't for me coming in and interrupting his perfect life.

Leaning close, I press a soft kiss to his full lower lip. Kissing along his jawline, I slide a hand down his hard chest, along his trim waist, and lower to his muscular thighs. A soft groan pushes past his lips as I trail my fingers up and down his inner thigh, my knuckles purposefully skimming against his crotch with each pass. His eyes blink open, those honey brown orbs meeting mine instantly.

"Mess," he says, voice gritty from sleep.

I don't respond, just continue stroking. A sharp hiss pushes through his teeth when I latch my own onto an earlobe, nibbling before sucking it between my lips.

"Where's Tank?" he asks as he grips my waist like a lifeline.

Cupping his straining erection over the thin material of his slacks, I give him a tight squeeze. Lips against his ear, I whisper, "Outside. It's just you and me, Trouble. We have thirty more minutes as a normal couple. Enough talking."

He grumbles a curse before tugging me across his lap until my hips straddle his own. Hands on his shoulders, I stare down at him as I grind my core against him. My eyes flicker closed at the contact. He dips a hand beneath my T-shirt, his calloused palm scraping up my stomach before wrapping around a breast and squeezing almost to the point of pain. I hiss in pure pleasure at the feel of his fingers dipping into the bra cups.

Releasing his shoulders, I snag the hem of my long-sleeve T-shirt and tug it over my head. A small whimper passes my lips at the loss of his warmth as he unclasps my bra. A quick tug at the middle slides the straps down my arms.

A hot hand presses between my shoulder blades, urging me lower. The cushions beside his head give as both my elbows sink into the chair. His teeth nip at a pebbled nipple. Digging my fingers into his hair, I press my hips lower, desperate for friction as I rock against his straining cock. The seam of my jeans adds to the fabulous resistance. Again Trey presses, this time against my lower back, urging me to grind harder against him.

"Fuck, baby," he says, kissing the valley between my breasts. "Get your jeans off."

On trembling arms, I push off the chair to stand. Hooded eyes watch each move as I undo the top button of my jeans and slide the zipper lower. Wetness pools between my thighs as he strokes himself over his pants.

"You're still dressed," I say, my voice husky with desire.

With a mischievous smirk, he stands and begins to unbutton his dress shirt. Shrugging out of the sleeves, he tosses it to the floor before working his belt free. My mouth waters, heat soaring through my veins as his pants and underwear drop to the floor.

"You're too slow," he says as he steps out of his pants and toes off his socks.

I swallow hard as I take in his naked body. Lean muscles twitch and flex beneath his naturally tan skin, showing off the strength beneath.

Trey takes a step, closing the distance between us. My lids flutter closed as his warm palms wrap around both cheeks, delicately cradling my face. Heat trails in their wake as he slides his hands lower, down my neck and over my shoulders. A whimper escapes when he pinches both peaked nipples simultaneously.

My heart thunders in anticipation. Back and forth, Trey trails a finger along the top of my jeans, dipping low where the button and zipper are already unfastened. I gasp, my hands shooting up to grip his bare shoulders, when he dips his hand deeper and plunges a finger inside my slick core without warning. My lip sinks beneath my teeth as I attempt to keep my noises to a minimum—who knows how thin these walls are.

I rock my hips against his hand, sending zaps of pleasure sparking through me each time my swollen bundle of nerves hits the heel of his palm. A cool waft of air brushes against my heated skin when he withdraws.

"Trey—" I gasp, my next words forgotten as I'm scooped up in his arms. My arms around his neck, he strides across the living room. His soft lips crash against my own, which immediately part at the insistence of his tongue as he consumes me whole.

The hold beneath my ass eases as I'm lowered to the floor, my toes barely touching a rug before my jeans are ripped down my legs. He lightly shoves my shoulder, and I fall backward, landing with a gasp on top of a bed. Breathless, I take in the room as he tugs my jeans the rest of the way off before climbing up the bed.

Trey hovers above me, eyes intense as he stares down.

Fuck, I love him. I should tell him. But not now, not right before sex. After. Yeah, after is when people do that shit in movies.

My hands come up to grip his shoulders. His brows furrow, not understanding, until I give him a hard shove, urging him onto the bed faceup. A small smirk spreads across his lips as he gives in to my request.

Lying back, he grips my hips and hauls me over his own, positioning my wet center above him.

Hands on his chest, I lower, pressing his hard-on between my slick folds.

"Ah hell, Mess. You're cruel."

Back and forth I rock my hips, causing me to slide along his length though never letting him enter me. The head of his dick skims across my clit, forcing a squeak to push past my lips. Unable to wait any longer, I grasp his hard cock while lifting my hips and position him directly outside my entrance.

I lock my gaze with his as I lower, pushing him deeper inch by inch until my ass hits his thighs. We both let out a relieved groan as I rock forward, allowing him to sink in even deeper.

"That's it, baby," he grunts out. The hands on my hips tighten as I rise and lower to a quick rhythm. One hand slides forward and delves between my slick folds. I cry out, my pace faltering at the first hard flick against my sensitive clit.

Stars explode behind my eyes and my thighs quiver. I struggle to keep moving as an orgasm slithers through every inch of my mind and body. Trey shouts a curse, both hands holding my hips as he slams his own against me, driving himself in to the hilt over and over, riding out his own release.

The second he relaxes his hold, I slump forward until my forehead hits his sternum.

"I like you on top," Trey mumbles. Reaching up, he runs a hand over my head and down my neck. With a tug, he brings my face parallel to his own and captures a chaste kiss.

"I...." *Just fucking say it, Randi.* "I love...." *Oh hell, I'm an idiot.* "I love it too."

Trey's dark brows rise up his forehead in confusion.

You and me both, buddy. No idea why I can't get my shit together and just tell you what I already know.

I love you.

See, easy in my head, but not so much getting that thought past my lips without sounding like a complete moron. You'd think, "Hey, the first woman vice president of the United States has her shit together." Well, you'd be wrong. Because I 100 percent have a ton of shit, but none of it is together.

The only thing to sway in my favor these days is Mom sticking with rehab and starting to act like a real mom who calls and cares and shit.

Speaking of that, I need to call Taeler.

"We still have a few minutes before we go back to reality," Trey mumbles as he plants soft kisses on my shoulder. "Since I'm responsible for getting you dirty, I feel obligated to help you get clean."

The corners of my lips twitch upward.

"What a gentleman you are, Mr. Benson." Leaning forward, I nip at the soft skin beneath his ear. "If I wasn't bound to a bed earlier by you, I'd actually believe it."

"You loved it," he says with a growl. Calloused hands swipe down my back before grabbing handfuls of my ass.

"Um, yeah I did."

"I love your ass."

"Thanks." I giggle.

"And your pussy."

"Figured that one."

"And your tits are perfect."

"Really? I kind of want a boob job."

He shakes his head. Dark thick locks fall along his forehead, covering part of his right eye. "They're perfect. But do you know what I love most of all, Mess?"

"What?" I whisper. The sudden heaviness of the moment tightens my throat with clogged emotions.

Why the hell is he better at this emotional stuff than I am? I'm the girl, damnit!

"You. Your brilliant mind, quick wit, and giving heart. You think of others before yourself. It's why you're here. It's why you sold your life to Birmingham. You had a chance to make a difference, and you took it no matter the consequences."

"I was an idiot," I grumble.

"Maybe a little," he says with a chuckle.

Shifting my weight, I attempt to roll off him with an annoyed huff. Still laughing, he rolls with me until we're face-to-face lying on our sides. He tucks a rogue lock of dark hair behind my ear. All humor leaves his features, a deep line forming between his brows as he trails his fingertips up and down my bare arm. "You know you have to do it."

There's no need to question what he's referencing. I knew the second I made the decision not to help the DOJ that it was the wrong choice. I never back away from the fight to help others, and that's exactly what I'd be doing if I chose to hide my head in the sand.

"I know," I whisper. "But maybe, just for a bit, I wanted to pretend I could walk away, that I didn't have to add this to my already full plate. Sometimes I wish I didn't give a fuck about anyone other than myself."

"But that's not you. It's never been you."

I nod with a resigned sigh. "Maybe I should take pointers on how to be more selfish from your mom." I don't hide my smirk as I search his eyes, hoping he finds me as funny as I find myself.

"A mom joke, seriously?" Reaching around, he smacks my ass, earning a yelp. "And no way in hell would I want you to be around her more than needed to keep up this charade we have going on. I can't believe I have to pretend to be engaged to Jessica." He groans and rolls to his back, tucking me against his side as he moves. With two fingers, he pinches the bridge of his nose. "I don't think we thought this through well enough."

Yes and no. We didn't have many options, and this was the lesser of two evils. Do I hate the idea of him parading around town, getting all handsome and scrumptious for various events and galas with her on his arm? Well, yeah. But we were in a damn corner. His mother upped the ante by creating the engagement angle and holding assault with a deadly weapon charge over his head to make him do it. We both knew there was an out, that he could walk away without those charges ever sticking, but that would've left my political career in shambles, his mother going on the warpath and turning everyone against me—even more so than they already are. So we did what we had to do.

We're playing the player, who happens to be his own mother. Trying to, at least.

"I know," I say as I stroke two fingertips down his sternum and back up again. "But now we have time to get my footing here in DC, find out who your snitch is on the team, and be together. It's not ideal, but nothing has been since Kyle stepped into my run-down office over two years ago. We'll make it through it all."

"Where does that DOJ guy fit in all this?" he asks, his voice guarded.

"Trey." I groan and seal my forehead against his bicep. "Don't do that."

"Do what?"

"Be that guy, the jealous type. I have to work with him. We just established there's no way I can refuse to help them gather evidence on Kyle. To do that, I'll have to work alongside Sam."

His silence tightens my gut with dread.

"Okay," he says finally. "I don't like it though, Mess."

"You don't trust him?" The mattress gives as I push up to my elbows to stare down at his handsome face. Stretching, I swipe the hair out of his eyes. "You need a haircut."

Trey rolls his eyes and shakes his head, dislodging the remaining dark locks from his forehead. "I don't trust him with you."

"But you have to trust me," I plead. "Don't make this a big deal. Don't make it awkward or tense for me. Trust me. Can you do that?"

His honey brown eyes connect with my own. A sad smile tugs at the corners of his lips.

"Okay, Randi. I'll keep it reined in. But if I think he's crossing a line, pushing outside the professional boundary, I'll say something."

"Oh, you mean like *you* did during the campaign?" I say with a smirk, trying to lighten the mood.

"Exactly my point," he grits out through clenched teeth.

Well, shit. That backfired.

7

RANDI

Steam billows out of the shower as I push the heavy glass door open. I tug a plush warm towel off the warming rack and wrap it around my flushed chest. The soft bathmat pushes between my damp toes as I step out of the shower and grab another towel for my legs. My hands pause, at the sound of hushed voices on the other side of the door, streams of water continuing to cascade down my thighs and over my knees.

Careful to keep my steps silent, I tiptoe across Trey's bathroom and lean close to the closed door, hoping for a hint to who's on the other side. Trey's annoyed grumble causes my lips to curl, but a soft female voice, in his bedroom with me on the other side of the door, drops them to a pursed-lip frown.

What the hell?

Ear to the door, I strain to get a better idea of who the voice belongs to, even though I have a sneaking suspicion I already know.

"We didn't agree to this," says the familiar female voice.

"We didn't agree to anything."

"We're engaged," the female voice blurts. "How does this look? I will not be made a fool, Trey."

Ah. Jessica.

Instead of hiding behind the door, spying on their conversation, I take a quick step back and tug it open. A flash of satisfaction passes through me at Jessica's shocked features as I move to Trey's side. Her wide eyes trail down my nearly naked body and back up again. Lips pursed, she shakes her head.

"You both know how bad this looks right?"

"And what does it look like, Jessica?" I sneer.

"That he's cheating on me with you. The vice president who he's tasked to protect."

Trey wraps an arm around my shoulders, sealing me against his side. "I never agreed to stop seeing Randi. I'm not sure what promises my mother made to you, but ending this between Randi and me was never in the agreement."

Jessica's cheeks flame pink.

"You know how he feels about me," I add. *What happened to the "I want to be friends" conversation from last night?* "What did you expect? Last night, you were all 'You have his heart. Let me borrow him.'"

"Borrow me?" Trey questions with an amused smirk. "Am I the man equivalent of Tupperware now?"

I snort and shake my head. "No way. You're more like a casserole dish. I'd never lend out good Tupperware."

Jessica huffs and opens her mouth to cut us off, but Trey beats her to it.

"Am I at least a fancy casserole dish?"

"Of course," I say with a smile.

"You two are not taking this seriously," Jessica barks. Trey shoots me a wink before turning his attention back to her. "There's a lot at stake."

"For you or for me?" I ask. Stepping out of Trey's hold, I move to grab my jeans off the floor.

"Both. You need her support, and I need his. I told you this last night. I thought you were on my side."

"Your side?" I sneer. Forgoing underwear, I tug the tight dark jeans up under the towel. "I think we both walked away from that conversation with different views of the context. I thought you saw my side of me trying to help you stand on your own as a strong, independent woman, not cowering in the shadow of some man."

"Hey," Trey calls out behind me as I stride into the living room.

After snatching my bra and long-sleeve T-shirt off the floor, I turn on my heels and march back into the bedroom.

"Don't get me wrong, Trouble. It's a great shadow," I say with a wink. Slipping inside the bathroom, I drop the towel but keep talking. "But it's still a shadow. Jessica here seems to think she needs a man to stand beside for her to be anyone in this town, and I wanted to help her realize she does not actually need anyone or anything except for morals and brains." The soft cotton of the T-shirt slides over my face as I tug it over my head. "Guess we need to work on both if we're having this conversation. Again."

"I take offense to that," Jessica snaps.

"Okay."

When I move around the open door to the bedroom, I find Jessica's cheeks flaming red.

"Take it back."

"Um, no?" I say, shooting a confused look to Trey. "Is she serious?"

Instead of responding, Trey covers up his amused grin with a fist to his lips.

"Anyway," I say, moving on from the sidetracked conversation, "I get where you're coming from, and I agree. Trey and I do need to be ultra-cautious now that the whole charade is public."

Jessica's eyes go wide. "Please don't tell me you still think you can get out of this. Your mother will castrate you and ruin me." Taking a step closer, she wraps her thin fingers around his bare bicep.

I fight against the annoyed grumble building in my chest at the sight of her touching him. Fucking hell, why didn't he put a shirt on while I was in the shower?

But she does have a point.

"I'll do what I have to do," Trey says before I can. He meets my gaze. "But like Randi said, you know where my heart lies, and it's not with you, Jessica."

I wish I was the type of person who can feel victorious in the crestfallen look that takes over Jessica's face, but I'm not. Even though she's trying to finagle my sexy agent into her grasp, I still can't rejoice in her obvious sadness.

"I need to go," I mutter. Digging into the back pocket of my jeans, I find a hair tie and quickly whip my hair up into a messy bun. I take a quick glance at my watch and cringe at the time. "Guess you'll be by in a couple hours for your shift?"

Trey nods. "Wouldn't miss it."

Jessica pouts. "I don't like how much time you two spend together. I'm not getting a fair chance."

"Who are you, and what have you done with the real Jessica?" I narrow my eyes and move to stand directly in front of her, poking a finger into her bony shoulder. "It seems real."

"I am real," she blurts. "And stop touching me."

"What happened last night after I left?" I scan her from head to toe, attempting to find the answer. I thought Jessica was still my friend through all this mess, but now I'm not so sure.

"Nothing," Jessica says quickly and averts her gaze. "I just realized he's what I want for my forever, and I'm willing to fight for that."

"Even though your engagement is based on his lying-ass mother and a backhanded deal you made with her? Great way to start a budding relationship." I fail to keep the snark out of my tone, because let's be honest, this is dumb. What does she actually think she'll accomplish? Trey is mine. Period.

"I'm willing to fight for him, for our future," Jessica states, gripping Trey's arm tighter and squaring her shoulders.

A grimace mars Trey's handsome face as he glances between us.

I need a drink for this crazy show.

"Good luck to you, then, because so am I." The coarse rug digs into my bare heels as I turn to face Trey. The rough scruff scratches my palms as I cup his cheeks and bring his lips down to meet my own for a deep goodbye kiss.

Petty?

Sure.

Warranted?

Hell. Fucking. Yes.

If Jessica wants to play. I'll play.

"This is ridiculous," Champ mutters under his breath as he stretches his arms high over his head. The edge of his Dryfit T-shirt inches higher, exposing the pale, hairy stomach underneath. Quickly I look away and try to find anything else to focus on. Shouldn't be difficult since the core of my alpha team surrounds me all decked out in running gear.

I do agree with Champ, however. This is a bit ridiculous. Last week when

I reached out to Sam telling him I'd reconsidered the situation and decided to help the DOJ investigate Kyle, he suggested we get together somewhere private to discuss our options.

This is private all right.

Since he's training for some marathon, he asked to meet at a large park so he could get his run in and talk without anyone knowing about our meeting. However, Trey and T were adamantly against running somewhere too public. So we're meeting in the middle of nowhere, at the head of a several-mile training trail somewhere near the Quantico marine base.

Having a small army close eased Trey and T's stress enough that they agreed to only have half the alpha team trail after Sam and me. The others, plus more agents, are stationed along the trail and deep in the woods.

Bending my leg, I grip the top of my tennis shoe and pull it back, stretching my tight thigh. The workouts with Trey and training sessions with Sarah have paid off more than I'd like to admit. Now not only can I somewhat defend myself without a weapon, but my endurance is high enough that I won't completely embarrass myself today in front of Sam.

Hopefully.

With the back of my hand, I swipe at the beads of sweat already building along my forehead. I'm usually the cold-natured one, but a DC August day with zero breeze is stifling to say the least. I glance around at the guys, who are already sweating profusely. I swipe the water bottle I'd grabbed from the SUV from the bench beside me and take several long gulps of the somewhat warm water.

"How is it this hot so early?" I complain.

Trey gives an annoyed huff. "Don't look at us. We're not the ones who suggested this little outing."

I roll my eyes and turn my back to him. He's been testy the past week knowing this day was coming. To say he's not a fan of Sam and me working together is an understatement. The same as me not liking how much Jessica has been hanging around his place. It is what it fucking is.

Nothing is ideal right now. Of course, my life has never been ideal, so I'm used to rolling with the punches. Seems Trey is not. He's like a spoiled man child getting pissy that some other guy is playing with his toy.

Wait, bad analogy. I am not a toy, and Sam is definitely not playing with me.

The crunch of gravel snaps the five men to attention, their heads swiveling in the direction Sam approaches from. My jaw drops as he swaggers closer in nothing but a pair of running shorts and tennis shoes. I can't help it. No woman could.

A low growl comes from beside me, but I can't tear my eyes off his sexy tatted chest and arms.

"Holy fuck," I mutter under my breath. Absentmindedly, I bring the water bottle to my lips, downing what's left. It feels heavy in my empty stomach. Skipping breakfast, and maybe dinner last night, wasn't my brightest idea, but I have to maximize every second nowadays with the work that's piling up.

"You're gawking," T chides behind me.

"Just admiring the art," I say unconvincingly.

"Madam VP," Sam says in greeting as he moves closer.

Trey steps between us, cutting off his approach.

Champ comes up behind Sam and pats down his shorts before crouching low to check his socks and shoes. Then he stands and nods, giving the all clear.

"He's clean."

"Seriously?" I say, glancing over my shoulder at T. "Is that necessary?"

"Considering everything going on with you and the trouble that seems to follow you, yeah, it's necessary."

"I told you from the start that I'd keep your lives interesting," I say with a smile and a soft pat on his shoulder.

A shiver pulses down my spine when Sam moves close. It takes everything in me to not glance down to his toned chest now that I have an up-close view of his colorful tattoos.

"Ready?" I ask, swallowing back the rising nerves. "It's already hot as hades out here."

It takes a few minutes for us to find a slow rhythm that works for the entire group.

"So," Sam says, breaking the silence, "what made you change your mind?"

I shrug a single shoulder. "It's the right thing to do. I can't just stand back knowing I could help when it affects the people who voted me into this role in the first place."

"Why are you in long sleeves?" he asks, not even breathing hard.

"I wasn't sure who all would be out here, and I like to keep my tattoos covered."

"I don't remember you having visible tattoos."

I hop over an exposed root and smile. "Because those classrooms were the same temperature as a meat locker. I was always in long sleeves and a jacket, so you never had a chance to see them."

"How do I know you're not working a different angle?"

I furrow my brows. "Why would I work an angle about my tattoos?"

From the corner of my eye, I catch him smiling. "About the president and the investigation."

"Oh." I cringe at my ignorant response, though who knows? Maybe that was what he was going for, to see how I'd react. A guilty person would already have a response prepared and immediately follow his line of questioning. Smart, actually. "I see what you're doing." That smile of his widens. "And I guess you just have to take my word for it."

"About the tattoos or the genuine reason why you decided to help?"

"Both," I say, shooting him a grin. "Why did you want to meet all the way out here? Couldn't we have found somewhere closer and safe?"

My breaths come faster as we head up a steady incline. Shaking my hands, I struggle to get my muscles to relax to make the pace less strenuous. It's either the hot man running beside me or the brooding hottie at my back who's making me tense. Who knows? Maybe both.

"I don't want the president to know you're working with us. It'll be easier for you to gather inside information if he's unaware. That's why I chose this area. Plus these trails are challenging and a great workout."

"Two birds, one stone. Nice." I roll my shoulders, trying to get them to drop from my ears.

"You seem tense."

I nod. "Comes with the job. What do you expect from me in all this?"

"Just listen, be aware of who he's meeting with behind closed doors. Try to get in on meetings, gain more of his trust so hopefully he'll confide in you."

I snort. "Not likely."

"All we need is direction. We think we know how he's doing it and who he's manipulating to get his way, but the asshole has covered his tracks so well that it all appears legal. We have to get him on something that he's hiding."

"Like what?" I huff. A sharp pain cuts through my chest. I suck in a quick breath, and my stride falters.

"Randi," Trey's deep voice calls out behind me. "You okay?"

Instead of responding—not that I could if I wanted to—I nod and keep running.

"The EPA regulations he's putting into place and the drilling on federal land are all somewhat legal. His secretary of interior is brilliant in that regard."

"Shawn," I wheeze.

Okay, something's wrong. We've gone less than a mile and I'm barely able to breathe.

"Whit, yes. The funding and who he's selecting for the companies allowed to drill are where we need to catch him. We have to find proof that the companies he's chosen did not follow the normal bidding process and were selected based on who gave to your campaign. As I said before, that's where we lose the trail. We can't prove any of it."

Warm liquid tickles beneath my nose. My hand seems to weigh several pounds too much as I reach up to my face and swipe above my lip. Again my footing stumbles at the streak of red now coating my fingers.

"Trey," I call out, frantic, but my voice breaks as another pinch of pain steals the breath from my lungs.

Sam curses as I stumble forward. A tattooed arm shoots out, wrapping around my stomach to keep me from falling face-first onto the dirt path. More shouts echo above me. The trees whirl in my vision as I'm rolled to my back, completely helpless to stop what's happening.

I blink as I stare up at the cloudless blue sky, fighting to take a deep inhale.

"Randi." Trey's face hovers over mine, blocking the pretty view. "What hurts?"

"Everything," I gasp. "My chest. I can't breathe." Tears trickle down my temples, soaking into my sweat-slick hair.

"Poison," someone says beside me.

"Champ, fucking run," T shouts, a hardness in his tone I've rarely heard. The unforgiving earth rolls beneath my head as I turn to the voice. T's dark eyes scan my face, his own pinched with worry.

"It's okay, Mess. I got you." The callus on Trey's hand scrapes down my cheek. "Fuck," he roars too close to my face. I flinch, my eyes sealing shut.

A sweaty palm presses against my cheek, rolling my head for me to face the other way. Sam's bright green eyes scan over my face, his brows furrowed. Something presses against the top of my eyebrow and lifts my eyelids.

"Roll her over." When nothing happens, he shifts his focus up. "For fuck's sake, roll her over. We need to get her to vomit up whatever she ingested."

Before I can fully process his words, I'm on my side and something's being jammed down my throat. I gag and my stomach heaves, pushing out the bottle of water.

"Again," Trey says more like a curse.

I lose count of how many times they jam their fingers down my throat, causing my gag reflex to spasm and shove out what little remained in my stomach. The muscle along my jaw tightens in an effort to keep my teeth from chattering.

A new shadow draws my attention as Champ squats low and grabs my arm. Vision blurry, I watch as he tightens something around my bicep. Panic sets in. My fight-or-flight kicks in, sending a burst of energy to my limbs. Squirming against the ground, I try to move away as Champ bites the cap off a syringe and lowers the needle.

"Easy there, lady. It's a multipurpose antidote," he mutters around the cap still between his teeth. "You know we wouldn't hurt you."

Desperate for comfort, I search the few faces hovering over me until I find Trey's.

"You're okay, baby. Trust us."

Our gazes locked, I nod. I barely feel the needle prick my vein. Coolness flows from the injection point and spreads up my arm, through my shoulder, and into my chest. A wonderful lightness settles over my muscles. With a raspy sigh, I sink into the soft dirt, relishing the glorious relaxed state the medicine washes over me. I lie like that for what feels like hours, watching the sun's bright rays sparkle through the trees.

"I feel like a soft rainbow. All glittery and beautiful and wonderful."

"What the hell is in that stuff?" someone asks beside my head.

My limp body is hauled into the air. My head dangles back, my muscles unable to hold it upright.

"There's a medical facility on the base."

"Someone support her head. We need to run back."

"If we had a unicorn, we could ride it," I say with a giggle. "Am I dying?"

"No, Mess. You're just fucking high."

I hum a noncommittal response. Something slips beneath my head, hoisting it higher, offering the support my neck can't.

"Let's move."

8

TREY

I failed.

The one thing I've promised her from the beginning of our time together, and I couldn't follow through with. How can I promise her anything at this point? How would she ever trust me again if I do? I swore with every breath that she was safe. Yet today, she wasn't. Isn't.

Poison. What the fuck?

Who? How? The two questions that consume my thoughts as I stare down at the love of my life sleeping. Sleeping in a hospital bed, recovering from fucking rat poison.

Exhaustion pulls at my thoughts, turning them sluggish and more self-deprecating. The rough scruff along my jaw scrapes against my sweat-slick palm as I scrub a hand over my face.

"It's not your fault," Tank says beside me without looking up from his phone. He's been glued to the thing since we arrived at the military hospital, keeping everyone updated on the situation. Thankfully, the medical center had more of the multiuse antidote available to administer as soon as we carried her through the doors. The entire compound is on lockdown, soldiers stationed at every entrance keeping the media's nosy eyes and ears far away from where Randi lies recovering.

"Feels like my fault. I promised her we'd keep her safe. Does she look fucking safe to you?" I growl.

"We don't even know how she ingested it. We'll backtrack her steps the past twenty-four hours once she wakes up and isn't talking about damn unicorns. Start there. Don't lose focus."

"I'm not," I hiss, narrowing my eyes at my best friend.

"You are. You're making it personal."

"It is fucking personal."

"Exactly," he grits out, his jaw clenched so tight the muscle along his cheek twitches. "This is why I said to stay the fuck away from her. You're too focused on blaming yourself, not looking at the bigger picture, just wallowing in self-pity. Pull your head out of your ass, Benson. We have a job to do, and you can't do it if you're too busy feeling sorry for yourself and hoping she'll forgive you."

"I wouldn't," I admit. "I failed her."

Slowly, his dark eyes shift from the screen to meet mine. I flinch at the intensity and annoyance behind his challenging stare.

"Then you're off the team," he states. My breathing falters. "You're no good to me like this. And you're no good to her."

"No. Davis, please."

The tightness around his eyes eases. He shakes his head, breaking the standoff.

"What do I do with you, Trey? You're thinking like her boyfriend rather than her protector. You want to stay on the team?"

I dip my chin, eyes pleading. I can't get kicked off the alpha team. This is my life. The team, the job, her. I can't lose this.

"Then move on," Tank continues. "It happened. Now we find out the who, the why, and the how."

"And kick the coward's ass."

A small smirk pulls at his lips. "Now you're thinking like an agent."

The wall trembles at my back as I slam against it and cross my arms across my chest. Closing my eyes, I center my focus. Images of her lying on the dirt trail, blood trickling from her nose, keep trying to divert my attention, but I shove them to the back of my mind to process later.

"Isn't poison a woman thing?" I ask absentmindedly. "I feel like I read that somewhere or heard it on a crime show."

"A woman or a coward. And we know two who have reason to hurt Randi."

My upper lip curls in a snarl. "But neither has had access to her food, her water."

"Doesn't mean they couldn't pay someone. Hell, Birmingham already hired someone once to take her out. Maybe this is his backup plan."

Reaching out, I pop the knuckles of my right hand before moving on to the left. "Maybe he already knew about Sam meeting with her. That first meeting when she initially turned him down. Birmingham wouldn't have known she said no; maybe he assumed she was already working with him." Focusing on the stark white wall across the small medical room, I work my way through all the possibilities. "Maybe the fact that they used rat poison was symbolic almost."

"I thought that too."

"You did not," I say, shooting him a condescending look.

"Did too, while you've been brooding over in the corner for the last hour."

Eyes to the ceiling, I turn my thoughts back to the issue at hand.

"The doc said she had to have eaten or drank the poison recently. So the last twenty-four hours. We were with her this morning. Did you notice anyone, see anything out of the ordinary?"

Tank shakes his head. "I've been texting with Chaz. He doesn't remember anything from the prior shift, but he's calling all his guys to ask them personally. The one thing he does remember is she was locked in her office all night. She skipped dinner, again."

I groan. That woman, I swear. "We need to talk to her about that. Again," I mumble. Glancing at my watch, I flick my gaze back to the beauty on the plain white sheets. "She should be waking up soon."

A light rapping against the thin wooden door sends Tank shooting up from the chair. Shoving off the wall, I reach for my ankle holster, grabbing the small 9mm and pointing the barrel at the slowly opening door.

"Down, boy," Sam says as he pushes the door open just wide enough for him to slip through. Shutting it, he leans against it, his hands tucked behind his back. "I have to head back into the city for a meeting but wanted to say bye to her first."

Every muscle itches to throw him to the hard linoleum floor as he approaches her bed.

"Did you notice anything strange this morning?" I ask instead of resorting to jealousy-induced violence.

"Besides her almost dying?" he quips, eyes still on the sleeping Randi. "Was she complaining about not feeling well?"

Tank and I both shake our heads.

"So it had to have happened just before you left, then. I overheard the doctor say she had high levels of the poison in her system. If she'd ingested it yesterday, she would've reacted sooner."

"Is that your official medical opinion?" I toss out with a condescending smirk. "Leave the investigation to us. You focus on taking down that bastard Birmingham."

"No love lost there, I see," he says with a chuckle. "And what makes you think I'm after the president?"

"Uh," I say, trying to come up with something to cover my tracks. Tank relaxes in his chair, pulling out his phone once again and leaving me to handle my own slipup. "We believe he's targeting the VP."

"Why?" His hands tighten around the railing along the side of her bed.

"It's a rocky relationship. Plus she went against his direct order to not attend the OPEC summit."

"Why did she do that?"

I huff out a laugh. Stretching my arms high above my head, I groan as the tightness seeps out of my shoulders. "Because that's the VP. And she'd heard the rumbling about the gas prices while on a trip to Austin. She wanted to get to the bottom of it. For some reason, Birmingham didn't want her to go."

"Interesting."

"After that, there was an attempt on her life. It was a setup. We walked into a trap."

Sam's eyes widen a fraction. "I didn't hear anything about that."

I nod and relax back against the wall, gun still in hand. You know just in case the idiot decides to do something sketchy like touch her.

"We kept it out of the media," Tank responds, not bothering to look up from his phone as his thumbs fly across the screen.

Sam nods. "Smart. So you think this, today's incident, has to do with a past disagreement."

"Sure." The fool knows why today happened. Looks like we can't depend on him to be straightforward during this process. Sneaky-ass attorneys.

A soft moan snaps our attention to the waking Randi. Her eyes slowly flutter open. After a few long blinks, like she's attempting to refocus her vision, she scans the room. Confusion registers on her face, her brows pulled and lips pursed.

"Where am I?"

"The Quantico marine base. Do you remember what happened?" I ask. Guilt eats at my gut as I stare at her pale face.

She nods. "Yeah, I almost died. I think I remember someone saying something about poison?" she asks. Again her gaze searches the room. "Am I okay?"

"The general antidote Champ gave you on the trail gave us enough time to get you here before there was any permanent damage done. I'm sure the doc will be back in shortly to give you a rundown. We'll also need to have you checked out by your personal physician when we get back to DC."

Her hazel eyes roll to the ceiling. "Can't wait." Her left arm rises a fraction before halting midair when the IV line snags on the railing. Sighing, she lays her head back. "What happened though? How did it happen, I guess is the right question. Poison? That seems so... antiquated."

"That's what we're hoping you can help us with." Tank slides his phone into the pocket of his shorts and leans forward, resting his elbows on his knees, hands clasped. "What all have you eaten in the last twenty-four hours?"

Attention on the corner of the blanket, twisting it between her fingers, she shakes her head. "Hell, I don't know. Water, coffee at the house." Her shoulders rise and fall. "I didn't take any food from a stranger if that's what you're asking."

Tank huffs. "This is serious, Randi."

"I know it is, T." An exhausted sigh pushes past her lips. "It's just that nothing seemed strange." She pauses. "You say the last twenty-four hours?"

Tank nods, eyes locked on hers.

"Okay, so...." She closes her eyes. "Yesterday was breakfast with Senator Bradley. We ate at the yummy little diner around the corner from the house, remember?" I nod, even though she can't see me with her eyes sealed shut in concentration. "I actually ordered something different than my usual, so I wouldn't think someone could've prepared for that."

Tank pulls his phone out again and begins typing. "I'll have someone stop by the diner and check it out just in case. What else?"

Brows furrowed, she crinkles her nose. "Shit, I forgot to eat the rest of the day." Peeking one eye open, she looks to me. "Oops."

"Madam VP." I groan and run a hand over my face. "You keep forgetting to eat."

"Guessing this is a normal occurrence," Sam pipes up with a questioning glance between the two of us.

I grunt a response.

"That's very unhealthy," he adds, narrowing his eyes on Randi.

"Thanks, Doc," she huffs. I don't stop the smile from pulling up my cheeks.

"Okay, so you didn't eat anything else yesterday afternoon or night. What about drinks? You mentioned coffee this morning. What about food?"

She nods. "Water yesterday, maybe a Coke or two." Again she lifts her arm but winces when the IV line snags. "Can someone get this fucking thing out of my fucking arm," she shouts.

Tank raises a bushy brow, flicking his gaze up to meet mine. "The doctor did say she might be more irritable than normal."

"I'll show you fucking irritable," she practically growls. "Get the damn doctor in here."

"The coffee, Randi. Where did you get it? What did you eat for breakfast?"

"The kitchen where I always get my coffee. Which is protected, all the time, by you guys. My chef, the cleaning staff, everyone is background checked. And not only that, they like me. They wouldn't have done that. And food?" She shrugs. "Oops again."

"*That* as in poisoning you. *That* as in attempted murder, tacking on treason." Sam leans closer with each word. What's his deal with creeping into her personal space?

"Yes," she grumbles at him. Focusing on the closed door, she sighs. "Birmingham or Whit is my guess."

"Either, maybe both," I say, stepping closer to her bed. I slide a finger down her bare arm, desperate for any connection, not caring about Sam seeing. The need to comfort her, touch her outweighs the consequences of him knowing about us.

She follows the movement. "When can I go home?"

A shuffle sounds behind me before Tank appears at my side.

"I'll go get the doc. Once he releases you to be under the care of your personal physician, we can fly you out of here."

"Is that necessary?" She groans. "I don't want the media to get wind of this."

Tank, Sam, and I exchange looks.

She tips her head back against the bed. "Let me guess. Too late."

We all nod.

"Awesome. Has Tae called?" she asks me directly.

"The guys are fielding her calls and a few from your ex," Tank responds. "Playboy and I were on protection duty while you were knocked out."

"Right," she says with a tight smile. "In case someone else tried to kill me. Nice."

"You can call her when you get back and settled. The doc mentioned you'd need several days' rest to allow your body to recover. There wasn't permanent damage, but it could turn that way if you don't take it easy." Hopefully if I say it enough times, she'll actually do it. But knowing her, it wouldn't matter if we chained her to the bed. She'd find a way to work.

"You still on board for helping us, Randi?" Sam asks.

His poor timing for the inconsiderate question snaps the hold I've been fighting on my anger. Forgetting everything, I lunge forward, aiming to wrap my hand around his neck. Shock registers on his face before he quickly steps back just as my fingertips slide along his throat.

"Trey!" Randi shouts. The heart monitor picks up, sending frantic beeps blaring through the room.

"Benson," Tank yells, yanking on my shoulder.

All I see is red. Again I lunge over the bed, desperate to get my hands on the fucker.

"She almost died, you fucking cunt."

"Not because of me," he bites back.

"It was fucking rat poison," I shout. A massive arm wraps around my stomach, hauling me backward. The wall rattles, pain bursting along my spine as Tank slams my back against the drywall. "Why do you think that is?"

The door slams open, and three men in suits storm through the door. Another set of hands pins me to the wall, but still I struggle. All the pent-up rage and all-consuming guilt fuels my every move.

"Get it together," Tank grits out in my ear with another hard shove to my right shoulder. "We don't know, remember?"

I cringe at the bite of pain piercing my shoulder.

"Everyone, out," Randi calmly says over the chaos I've created. "Let him go. He won't hurt me." Over the one marine's shoulders, I see her turn to Sam. "But he might kill you."

"He could try," Sam says, glaring at me.

"Just stop," she snaps. "Yes, I'm still going to help. But not if you don't leave right now." He doesn't make a single move toward the door. "Out!" she yells. "Everyone."

The hands restraining me loosen. When the men step back, I inhale a deep, calming breath. The cool air burns down my dry throat. The three marines file out, the last one shooting a daring glare over his shoulder before disappearing through the doorway. Sam grumbles something I can't make out as he strides out seconds behind the uniformed men.

Randi looks to Tank and arches a brow. "You too, T. I need to talk to Trey, alone."

"That's not protocol. I can't leave you, not when this just happened, with only one agent—one psycho agent, at that—to protect you."

Her hospital gown-covered chest rises with a deep inhale. "Fine. Go stand in the corner and don't listen to our conversation."

He smiles. "I'll sit right here and play Candy Crush."

"How about you look up lasting effects of rat poisoning on a late-thirties female."

"Not nearly as fun."

"But useful," she says with a smile. "The doctors talk gibberish. Tell me what WebMD says I should do."

Still smiling, he shakes his head. "Glad you're okay, Randi."

Tank's features harden when he looks to me. "You're a fucking idiot."

"I know," I admit. "But you love me."

A heavy sigh sounds through the small room. "No clue why. You're a pain in my ass."

"And mine." Randi reaches out to me, palm up. "Come here, Trouble." Soothing calm washes through my veins as I interlace my fingers with hers, silencing the worry and halting my rising anger at the whole damn situation. "What am I going to do with you?"

My knees pop as I crouch low, putting us nearly eye to eye. Careful of the tubes and wires, I slide her hand to my lips and press a hard kiss to the inside of her palm.

"You know it's not all his doing," she continues. "Kyle's had it out for me before Sam walked into our lives. It might make things a little worse if Kyle finds out, but none of this is because of Sam. We don't even know if it was Kyle. I'm on a lot of people's shit list, you know."

I nod. She's right. But I still want to blame someone right now. Anyone. I need a direction to turn my anger and frustration toward. A goal. A face. An enemy. Someone other than myself.

"I almost lost you, again." My voice is raspy as I fight through the battling emotions.

What the hell is wrong with me? I'm stronger than this.

It's her. She's a piece of my soul now, a part of me I don't ever want to lose.

It's fear. This unknown feeling churning in my gut is fear of losing the one person I want to live for.

My heart wrenches in pain when she slides her fingers from my own, only to have it thump with pure joy at the feel of her palm against my cheek. I lean into it, closing my eyes and savoring the sensation of her comforting touch.

"But you didn't lose me. Look, I'm right here, still being a pain in the ass. Whoever's idea it was to keep an emergency antidote injection in our medical bag was brilliant. I need to thank them." Her strained smile does nothing to ease a new wave of guilt.

"It shouldn't have been needed. This shouldn't have happened at all, Randi. Don't you see that? You're in danger. And now they know they can get to you without us knowing. What good am I to you? I can't even protect you when you need it the most."

The side of her thumb strokes across my brow.

Then she says two words, ripping my soul in two.

"You're right."

9

RANDI

Hurt and agony cover his features at my words. Leaning back, he attempts to draw away from my hand.

"You don't understand," I say quickly, hoping to dash the sadness in his lowered eyes. "What I meant was I agree with you. I shouldn't need things like an antidote on hand. But this role I'm in calls for it. I'm guessing that stocked medical pack wasn't special ordered for me. Every VP before me has been targeted in some way. But unlike the others, I know who wants me dead."

Trey nods but doesn't relax against my awaiting palm.

"Hey, look at me." I wait until his gaze locks with mine. "None of this is your fault. I'm in a targeted role. I get that. I'm not mad, not disappointed. Well," I huff. "Not at you. More me."

"Why the hell would you be disappointed in yourself?"

The corner of my lip twitches up in an almost smile.

"Because I've allowed this. I should've stopped Shawn and Kyle's bullying, the harassment and violence the second it started. I wouldn't be here in this bed, poisoned for fuck's sake, if I would've confronted them head-on months ago. But I didn't. I made them think they can push me around without any repercussions. I made myself look weak in their eyes." Anger at the man responsible for my pain swirls within me, heating my core. "This has to stop. They've crossed a line, and I'm done."

"I don't like the sound of this," T says from where he sits, phone forgotten. "Plus, we don't know for certain *who* poisoned you, remember?"

"I told you not to listen," I say, not dropping Trey's searching gaze. "And in this one case, I'm okay with finding guilt without the evidence. We know who was behind this. Besides, it's not up to you, T, and it's not up to Trey." Sighing, I find the ceiling and focus on making all this make sense. "I'm stronger than them, stronger than their attempts to knock me down. I was a teen mom who scratched and clawed her way through a crappy life in hopes of a better one. And now I'm here, in a stressful-as-hell but amazingly rewarding job, and they're trying to take that from me? Hell to the no. I will not sit back and let two asshats continue to play their version of cat and mouse with me as the prey."

Taking a deep breath, I glance back and forth between the two men, who stare back wide-eyed.

"I assume you have a plan," Trey asks, a mischievous twinkle in his eye. I knew he would like the idea of fighting back.

I shake my head with a laugh. "Not yet, but I will."

"I don't doubt it." Standing with a groan, Trey strokes a hand over the top of my head. "But before we start planning their demise, you need to get out of here."

A slight buzzing draws my attention to his shorts. After pulling the phone from the side pocket, he cringes at the screen.

"What?" What else could happen today?

"I have to get back for this event tonight with Jessica."

I snarl and roll my eyes.

"Don't give me that," he responds with a chuckle. "Just playing my part in your world domination plan."

"Still don't like it," I pout. Yeah, he's doing it for me, but I don't have to be happy that another woman gets him for the night. Especially Jessica, who's pulled a complete 360, going from friend to foe overnight. Something tells me I don't know the whole story behind that, and I should dig deeper to find the reasons behind her about face. But when? I've just made a declaration of war against the two most powerful men in DC, one who's already after my head and the other who'd probably get off watching my murder.

Sickos.

I really need to make a list. A kill list, sans the kill part.

What would that make it?

"Think your mom will help us find dirt on Kyle?" I ask absentmindedly.

I can't call it my "to do" list. That makes it sound sexual, and the last men on Earth I'd "do" are number one and two on that list.

"Probably not. It's one thing to help us stop the bill, but this is...."

"My level of crazy but not hers," I say with a genuine smile. It's cool. I know it sounds a little off thinking I can take the two on. But one of them just tried to kill me—again—so all sanity has left the building. If it ever resided there in the first place, that is.

"Exactly." Leaning forward, he brushes a barely there kiss along my lips. "I'm going to get the doctor."

I watch as he crosses the small room, checking out his muscular calves, flexing thighs, and round ass. Biting my lip, I stare at that ass until the door closes behind him.

"Down, girl," T says, humor in his light tone. "So, we're going after Birmingham and Whit."

I nod. "I think Kyle first since the DOJ already wants him gone as well, and then we focus on Shawn. The easiest out would be to get the information needed to impeach Kyle, even though gaining said information wouldn't be the easiest."

"We don't know if it was one of them who planted the poison. You're jumping to conclusions."

I shrug. "Even if Kyle wasn't directly responsible for today's incident, we know from the Russian intelligence we were given that he's contacted people to harm me. I have to do this, T."

"You realize if you do take these men on, your political career and your life will be at risk even more than they are currently."

"I don't care about the first. The second, well, that's what you and the guys are for, right?" I shoot him a hopeful grin.

His cheeks bunch with a wide smile. "Hell, woman. You weren't kidding about keeping things interesting." He chuckles. "Do what you need to do. We've got your back."

The door swings open, and a doctor walks through with Trey hot on his heels. As the doc goes through the motions of his release checklist, readying me to get the hell out of here, I zone out.

Kyle will get what's coming to him. Then I'll tackle the Shawn issue. Not much of a plan, but I'm done sitting back and being on the defensive.

It's time to take control of the game.

No matter what it takes.

<hr>

TWO WEEKS of taking it easy. Two weeks of being waited on hand and foot and meetings coming to me. Two whole weeks of plotting Kyle's demise, and still I have zero clue as to how. Sam is still optimistic that I'll somehow gain information on the oil scam he has going on, but I'm not so sure. If the poison was planted by Kyle, or someone he paid off, then he already knows I'm working with the DOJ and will keep things even closer to his chest than ever before.

No, the original way to help Sam is scrapped. It has to be something else. Or another way for me to gain the information we need without involving Kyle at all.

I do have another way, but... do I really want to involve the Russians with Sam around? That relationship is controversial at best, but do I really have another choice?

This is what I've debated back and forth while lounging around the house, hating the easy life. Outside of this beautiful prison, life has continued. My various community projects are performing well under those I've selected to lead them. Small positive impacts for those living below the poverty line are dotting up all over the map. Which is good since my mind is elsewhere.

Trey's annoyed voice reaches my ears where I sit in the living room. Unpretzeling my legs, I quietly press my toes to the vintage rug beneath the couch. Tiptoeing across the floor, I let my ear lead me, hoping to catch bits and pieces of his conversation as I creep toward the open french doors.

"You know I can't," he says, voice tight. "Don't ask me that again." I hold my breath so he doesn't hear me through a long pause in the private conversation. Taking a step closer, I stay hidden behind the wall and angle my ear closer to the door. "Stay at your place until I can get there, then." My heart drops. "I gotta go. Yeah, bye."

Sucking in a sharp breath, I seal my back against the wall as his footsteps draw closer. He searches the room as he steps across the threshold, gaze darting until he finds me.

I wave.

Wave.

I'm the vice president of the United States, and I just gave a spirit finger wave. Go me. I'm so winning this day.

"Mess."

"Trouble."

"Questions?"

I fake confusion. "What are you talking about?"

He laughs into his fist. "You'd make a terrible spy."

"No doubt. Okay, fine, you caught me. What was that call all about, hmm?"

Trey drags a hand down his face. "Jessica. She's getting fucking clingy. Calling all the time, asking me to come over. And now she thinks someone is following her and keeps trying to get me to come over and protect her."

My forehead wrinkles as I raise both brows. "Really? That's scary. Think it has something to do with Shawn? I mean, he went after Rachel, so he might do the same with Jessica since he thinks you two are a real couple."

Anger flashes in his eyes. "Maybe. Doubtful though. Plus, I think she's making it all up."

"Why would she do that?"

He offers me a pointed look before rolling his neck. Reaching back, he massages the muscles there. "Who knows? All I know is I'm damn exhausted."

A tingle of guilt eats at me. He's only in this exhausting situation with Jessica because of me. How can I be so selfish, asking him to keep this up?

"If you want to back out—"

He shakes his head. "It's not that. It's all of it combined. And we're still trying to figure out who my mother's inside guy is on the team. It's nonstop."

Shit, here I've been relaxing and taking it easy while the guys are running ragged. I'd forgotten about the inside man we have somewhere on the team. Trey's mother didn't give a single clue as to who's been feeding her information, just that she has someone. Based on the information she had on the altercation in Texas between Trey and my mother's slimy boyfriend, we believe her. But they still don't know who it could be.

"We need a vacation," I say in jest.

His head pops up, offering me his full attention. "You do."

"Not just me. All of us."

"I will in three and a half years," he says with a smile. "But until then, you deserve one. You get several weeks off a year during your term. Take a week off, go somewhere you can relax."

Chewing on my thumbnail, I debate the suggestion. "Maybe Taeler could come with me. Somewhere for Christmas would be fun, and she'll be out of school for the long break. Somewhere warm maybe."

His smile widens, displaying his straight white teeth. "That's a great idea. Past presidents have visited Hawaii, which means there's housing with the level of security we would need."

My head bobs as the idea takes root. "Let's do it. I'll talk to my secretary about the arrangements, and T can work out the security details with her. Four months' planning should be enough, right?"

Trey nods.

"Planning for what?"

I gasp in surprise as Trey reaches for the gun nestled beneath his suit jacket while turning toward the door. Kyle steps through the parted french doors, broad smile stretched across his arrogant face. His gaze flicks between Trey and me as he pauses behind a red velvet wingback chair.

"Benson. Walmart," he says in way of greeting. Rounding the Victorian-looking chair, he unbuttons his suit jacket and folds down into the stiff cushions, the picture of ease.

Trey looks to me. "Were you expecting him?"

I shake my head.

"What are you doing here, Kyle?" I snarl. My hands shake with nerves and fear races through my veins just at the sight of him. Rolling my shoulders, I push off the wall, marching across the room toward him when every cell in my body screams at me to run in the opposite direction.

"Came by to see how you were doing. I heard about the... incident." He smirks.

"Incident," I say with a snort.

"You look well enough. Must not have been as bad as the media was making it out to be."

"We had it under control," Trey says close behind me.

A tense pause pulses through the room.

"That's reassuring," Kyle finally says. Brushing off a fleck of white lint from his otherwise pristine black suit pants, he raises his blue eyes to mine. "Seems your protection team is always in the right place at the right time"

I nod and shrug. "It's their job, isn't it?"

His hard gaze shifts over my shoulder. "It is. And here I thought you were nothing more than a rent-a-cop, Benson. Looks like you're useful after all."

A low growl vibrates against my back.

"I came to warn you, Walmart." Kyle sneers.

"Seriously?" I choke out. "You. Warn me. Against... what?"

"Not what. Who. I hear you've made some unsavory friends."

Well, hell, that doesn't really narrow it down.

Russians?

DOJ?

Trey's mom?

It's a growing list.

"And if I did, why would that be any of your concern?" I ask. The plush cushions give under my weight as I drop to the couch and lean back like I'm not the tense ball of nerves that I am.

Something cold flashes behind his eyes. "Have you not learned your lesson? This city is not some damn hick town in Texas. These people play for blood and money, and you sure as hell can't pay with cash. Take my advice, Randi. Not only are you in the wrong league here, you're in the wrong fucking game."

"But the game is so fun," I tease.

"You're a damn fool." Pursing his lips, he slides them back and forth, almost like he's debating telling me more. "Just stay the hell out of my business, or it won't matter who you've fucked to keep you safe. No one will be able to protect you."

"Is that a threat?" Trey's deep voice promises pain as he takes a challenging step toward Kyle.

"Take it how you want, but know this. If you don't keep her trailer trash ass out of my affairs, there will be no more warnings."

"This trailer trash ass isn't stupid." Both men shift their laser focus to me. Stretching my arms back along the couch, I give Kyle my best conniving smile. "You're doing something behind my back that's... unsavory at best, illegal at worst. However, I specifically remember signing an agreement stating I'd support you through the campaign and after. If I break said contract, I owe you a shit ton of money, which, as you know, I don't have."

Kyle's eyes narrow. "Surely you don't expect me to believe that."

I lift a shoulder. "Believe what you want. I stopped the bill." I smirk. "Now all I want to do is focus on my other projects. Yes, the DOJ came to me asking for my help investigating something to do with you, which I'm assuming is what you're referring to in the 'unsavory friends' category. But I shut it down."

Kyle steeples his fingers, pressing the tips into the dimple of his chin. "Interesting story. Keep going."

"That's it," I admit with a laugh. "You're getting all stabby about something that hasn't happened. I know they're after something, yes, but that's it. I've learned that to get anything done in this town, you have to play the game. I've said before that I refuse to be your pawn, and I refused to be theirs as well. I'm in this for me. What I can do for the American citizens. Nothing else matters. You promised to leave me alone if I defeated your bill, which I did. Now you need to uphold your end of the bargain."

Sweat slicks my palms and the back of my neck, but I refuse to drop his probing stare, refuse to show him any weakness. This is how I'll eventually beat him, by winning his trust. Shoving as many truth-laced lies as possible down his vile throat until he believes me.

"I'm inclined to disbelieve you."

I lift my brows in a silent question.

"If you turned them down, as you say you did, then why has AAG Pierce been stopping by? Why was he on that random outing of yours out in the middle of nowhere, where it seemed you didn't want to be seen together?"

Dread seizes my lungs, cutting off my breath.

Well, fuck. I walked into that one.

Think, Randi, and think damn quick.

A story forms, a bad one, but still a story I can spin.

Sorry, Trey.

"Have you seen him?" I ask, forcing my brow to arch when everything else seems frozen in panic.

"I don't follow." Kyle tilts his head, studying me like I'm some kind of freak show. Who knows? To him, maybe I am.

"He's hot as hell, Kyle." I try to ignore the stiffening of Trey's shoulders. "And I'm not one to pass up someone like him when it was so freely offered."

"You're fucking him." A hint of belief lightens his tone.

"I don't kiss and tell." I laugh with a wink. "But yeah. Did you know he has tattoos?" I close my eyes like I'm imagining them and sigh in pleasure.

"And you're okay with this?" I peek one eye open, knowing full well he's not talking to me.

"I got what I needed out of that relationship." I hate the vile words coming from my mouth. Even if Trey does know they're all lies, it hurts saying them. I can't imagine what it's like to hear them.

"So I heard. Nice move, by the way, using him to get to the real power in the family. Did not expect that level of play from someone like you." If I'm not mistaken, a hint of approval lingers in Kyle's voice. "Maybe you're cut out for this city after all. However, I'm no idiot. I don't believe you."

"How do you suggest I prove it?" There's no need to fake the exhaustion in my voice. Fingers to my temples, I slowly massage in small circles. "Not that I need your approval for any of this, but I would love to not die a slow death. If I can find a way for you to call off the target on my back, I'll do it."

Tipping his head back, Kyle's loud, full laugh shudders around the room. "I take back what I said. You're a damn fool. As far as making me trust you, I'll think on that, Walmart. I'm sure I can come up with a way for you to prove your... loyalty to this office."

A shiver of dread slides down my sweaty spine.

"You do that and let me know."

We push out of our seats at the same time. With a nod, Kyle adjusts his jacket and strolls out of the room just as quietly as he appeared.

I keep my gaze focused on the hallway wall just outside the doors, afraid to turn and face Trey.

"Trouble—"

"I know, Randi. Fuck, I know."

I swallow against a parched throat and slowly turn to him. Panic sets in when he won't meet my pleading stare.

His hands tighten into fists at his side. "Doesn't mean I have to like it."

With that, he storms to the door, leaving me gaping at his back, struggling to find the words to call him back and ease his frustration.

But the right words don't come.

10

RANDI

The coppery taste of blood slithers across the tip of my tongue as I glide it along my lips. Frowning at my thumbnail, I tug a tissue from the box on the side table to dab at the crimson liquid seeping down to my nail bed. I wince at the initial sting of the rough tissue against the raw section where my nail used to be.

I shouldn't be this nervous. This meeting with Sam is nothing new, except for the conversation I'll unload on him. That's the part I'm dreading. What if he laughs or outright refuses to be my pretend boy toy? Or what if he already has a girlfriend?

Or a boyfriend?

Groaning, I wrap the tissue around my thumb in a makeshift bandage and press the heels of both palms to my forehead. I really didn't think it through last week when Kyle stopped by unannounced. He threw me off my game. Well, he would've if I had any. Let's be honest, I've winged everything since the day we stepped on the campaign trail.

Maybe it's a good thing he stopped by. It pushed me into action. Sure, the direction I chose isn't the best route, but at least I'm doing something now instead of sitting on my ass trying to come up with the perfect plan.

Even if I have zero clue where I'll go from here, where I am now is better than where I was last week. Kyle's somewhat off my back, which means the attempts on my life will stop—hopefully. Now all I have to do is figure out what's next in my master plan to take down Kyle.

But that's what's adding to my nerves.

If we gain the information to impeach Kyle, if I help dethrone the asshole, then that will leave the president spot available.

For me to fulfill.

A wave of nausea churns my stomach and heat builds in my veins, making my skin hot. I can't run a country. Hell, I'm barely doing my part as the second-in-command. To be the main person, the head honcho? That's a hard pass.

No.

Just no.

But I've kind of backed myself into a corner with my whole "Kyle and Shawn need to go down" plan. Because if Kyle steps down, then I have zero choice in the matter. I'll be sworn in as Randi Sawyer, President of the United States of America.

Shit.

I swallow down the light lunch I ate earlier with a senator across town that's trying to make a reappearance. Shaking my head, I lean back and take a deep breath, hoping the nausea spell will pass.

"You're feeling sick again," Trey states somewhere behind me.

Eyes closed, I inhale through my nose and nod, not daring to respond.

"I'll call the doctor."

I shake my head and squeeze my eyes tighter to fight the wave of dizziness.

"It's been three weeks, Randi." This time, it's T who's voicing his concern from across the room. "She didn't say anything about the side effects lasting this long."

"I'm fine," I rasp. "Can one of you get me some water?"

Within seconds, a cool plastic bottle is pressed against my hot cheek. Forcing a tight smile, I grab the bottle with a shaky hand.

"Thanks," I say around the lip as I take a small sip. The cool water soothes the unease churning in my stomach, dispelling the urgent need to puke. "I don't think it's from that."

"You're pregnant," T says as a joke.

"Not funny," Trey snaps.

"Not funny at all." After another few sips, I set the bottle down on the polished wooden side table. "No, not pregnant. The doctors at Quantico verified that. I'm just nervous, I guess. All of this is taking its toll."

Peeking my eyes open, I find the two staring at each other, a nonverbal conversation going on from across the room.

"Randi," T says in a tone that makes me brace myself for something I know I won't like. "What if you put aside the idea of helping the DOJ, buried your plan to stand up to Birmingham and Whit? Your health is priority, not them."

"I disagree."

"We don't."

I shift in the seat to look over my shoulder where Trey leans against the built-in bookshelf. He's been standoffish since Kyle left that day. Since I randomly made up the cover story that Sam and I are a couple.

"I'll be fine," I mumble.

"Damnit, woman," Trey growls. "Stop being so damn stubborn."

"So you both think I should tuck my tail and hide, is that it?" They're right, but it's not like it's even a choice at this point. What's done is done. I have to move forward, have to keep going. Even if I do step back, the attacks, the bullying, the attempts on my life won't stop. So would I really be safer doing nothing?

"Yes," they say in unison.

I shake my head. "I wish it were that easy. But it's not. You both know it's not." Tense silence fills the library. "I don't want to be president," I admit in an almost silent whisper. "I want Kyle and Shawn to pay for everything they've done to me, what they're doing to the American citizens, but...."

"Mess," Trey says with an exhaustion-laced sigh. "That's part of it. If you want to continue down this path, if you want to help the DOJ, that will be the end result."

"I know. Doesn't mean I have to like it." Resting my hands in my lap, I fidget with the tissue still wrapped around my thumb. "I'll do what I have to do. I always have, always will. Just because I'm nervous as hell doesn't mean I shouldn't keep going. If I thought that way, I'd be stuck in my hometown following in Mom's staggering footsteps. Just because something is challenging and overwhelming at first doesn't mean it should stop you from trying."

"Then suck it up and accept it," T adds. Shifting my gaze to where he sits by the door, I watch as he scrubs a hand over his bald head. "You can't keep living like this."

"Tied up in knots?" I say with a forced laugh. "I need a plan. I know what I want, but how do I get there? I've bought us a little time with the lie about Sam, but now what? Maybe once I know how to meet my goal, I'll relax. I just need a plan."

Maybe if I say it one more time, *I'll* believe it.

A hard knock against the closed library doors beats through the large room. Hands on his knees, T pushes to a standing position with a groan. His broad shoulders rise and fall as he circles them forward and backward like he's trying to ease the stress tightening the muscles. Massive hand on the doorknob, he pulls it open wide and waves the other hand toward me.

"Washington," Sam murmurs as he passes T. His bright eyes scan the room. "Benson," he grumbles with a hint of annoyance.

"Pierce." There's no mistaking the tension clipping the single word.

Finally, Sam's piercing green eyes slide to me. "Randi." Silence fills the room as he waits by the door. "You wanted to see me?"

I nod.

"You okay?" he asks, taking a tentative step deeper into the room. "You look...."

"Like I was poisoned three weeks ago?" I force a smile to lighten the weight of my words. "Yeah, I know. Come on in. We need to talk."

Lips pursed, Sam attempts to suppress a smile. "Never a good sign when a woman says those words. From my experience, that is." The clicking of his dress shoes against the hardwood floor goes silent as he steps onto the area rug. I motion to the chair beside me, requesting him to take a seat. His features harden, closing me off from reading his emotions as he folds down into the chair and leans forward, closing the distance between us.

"You're backing out," he grits out as a statement, not a question. The muscle along his square jaw twitches like he's grinding his teeth. "Listen, I don't blame you after—"

I hold up a hand, cutting him off. "The opposite, actually." Relief sinks in at the steadiness of my hand as I reach for the water bottle, proving the earlier panic attack is easing. Yep, panic attack, because I'm not going to dwell on the thought it could be something more sinister. Taking a deep breath, I hold it until it burns before letting it out slowly. "Kyle stopped by last week."

Both brows climb up Sam's forehead. Sweeping my gaze over his cropped black hair down to his clean-shaven jaw, I take in his hard features. Handsome yet stern. The overall look, bad boy in a nice suit, works for him. A little too well. The humor dancing behind his eyes hints that he knows exactly what I was doing.

Clearing my throat, I swing my focus to my hands clasped in my lap, thumb still wrapped in the blood-dotted tissue.

"And?" he asks, encouraging me to continue. I decide to overlook the smile in his tone.

"He knew you and I met more than once." Sneaking a peek through my lashes, I find Sam studying me, the earlier bit of humor gone.

"How?" he demands. Inching forward, he perches on the edge of his seat. I seal my back against the chair, trying to maintain my personal space.

"There's an unknown individual on the protection team who's leaking details of her comings and goings, and other details as well. We thought the informant was just working with... well, someone else, but this person could also be giving the information to Birmingham," Trey says.

A chill slides down my sticky neck at the closeness of his voice. Everything in me twitches to turn and tug him close. I'm near desperate for his comforting touch that's been lacking the past week.

"We're handing it," I say, cutting Sam off when he opens his mouth, frustration clearly written across his features. "I didn't ask you here to discuss that issue."

"Then what?" he practically snaps.

"Watch your tone," Trey bites back.

Sam lets out an exaggerated laugh. "You and your fucked-up team have now jeopardized the entire case, and you want me to watch my tone?"

"She's still the VP. Talk to her with the respect she deserves."

"Trey," I groan.

Sam looks from me to the man hovering over my shoulder and back again. "Oh, hell. You two are...." His green gaze slices through me. I shrink back deeper into the chair. "Forget it, Randi." Fingers gripped around the armrest, Sam pushes out of the chair so hard it tips on its back legs from the force. "I'm not getting into the middle of this. I've worked my damn ass off to get this AAG spot, and I sure as hell won't let the shit storm you two are creating take me down with you. I'll get the information I need on my own."

"Sam," I beg. Before he can step away, I lunge forward and wrap my fingers around his wrist. "It's too late for that."

"What?" he growls as he turns back to me, every muscle taut like he's ready for a fight. "What the hell did you do?"

"I panicked."

"What the fuck did you do?" he shouts.

I wince. "Can you please sit back down and I'll explain. This is not going as planned."

"How else did you think I'd react to you fucking me over?" he roars, tossing his arms out to the side.

Trey maneuvers between us, placing his tight ass right at my eye level.

Sam's words finally click. I tilt around Trey's shoulders and look up at the now fuming Sam. "What are you talking about?"

"You sold me out. You told that fucker what we're—"

"Whoa there, cowboy." I push out of the chair and step around Trey, who moves with me, cutting off my path to Sam. "I didn't sell you out. I was forced to concoct an excuse—on the fly, mind you—for why you've been coming around so much and why we nearly traveled to a different state for a damn run."

"And what did you come up with, Randi?" Chest heaving, Sam steps around the coffee table, putting him in Trey's personal space. The three of us stand crowded in the tight four-foot area.

Terrible idea, Sam.

"Trey, please move," I say on a slow exhale while rubbing my temples. "You know he won't hurt me. Just let us talk without you acting as a wall."

Trey doesn't shift even a centimeter.

I press a reassuring hand between his shoulder blades. "He and I have to talk this through, and we can't with you standing here."

A jagged fracture bolts through my heart as Trey shrugs off my touch and steps around the chairs. Without another word, he positions himself along the bookshelf once again, his eyes never meeting mine.

"What did you tell him, Randi?" Sam says behind me. "Worry about your personal life later. Tell me what the hell is going on."

"I told him we're together." My shoulders rise in a half shrug, half cringe. "That's the excuse for why you've been coming over. I reassured Kyle that I wasn't helping you in the investigation, that I wasn't that dumb to go against him, and you and I are... well, intimate."

"And he believed it."

Exhaustion swoops in, draining the minuscule amount of energy I had left. Falling into the chair, I rest my head back and close my eyes. "No, not at first, and not really by the time he left. But I think I bought us time. Plus, he said he'd think of some way for me to prove my loyalty of sorts."

"That doesn't sound good."

I chuckle a fake laugh. "No joke. But at least it got him off my ass for a while and out the door. I was in shock when he showed up unannounced, and then he knew everything about you coming over, the run, the additional meetings. Listen, I'm sorry I said it without consulting with you first, but I had no choice. I don't even know if you have a girlfriend. Or boyfriend for that matter." The last few words come at as more a grumble.

"Girlfriend."

"Oh," I say, unsure why I'm so disappointed.

"No, you misunderstood. I'm not saying I have one at the moment. I'm saying it would be the girlfriend, not the boyfriend. I'm not gay."

I open one eye, relief setting in at the smile he's trying to fight.

"Oh, okay. That's good, I guess."

"If we're supposed to be together, then yeah, it's a good thing. So what's the plan now that Birmingham thinks we're together?"

My hand lifts halfway to my mouth before I think better of it and tuck both hands beneath my thighs. "I haven't actually gotten that far. I was hoping you could help with that."

"Seriously?"

"Unfortunately."

Sam groans and crosses his arms over his chest. "Well, at least you bought us some time with him. Maybe if we go through with the charade, make him believe we're together, then you can still work your angle on gaining inside information for the investigation. This could work." Stepping around the chair, he moves to perch on the edge of the desk. Fingers wrapped around the dark wood, he flicks a glance to Trey. "And how do you feel about this? Anyone can see there's something going on between you two."

The soft material of my black slacks slides along the worn leather cushion of the chair as I turn to gauge Trey's response. Hands shoved into the pockets of his navy pants, shoulders against the hard spines of the endless hardback books, Trey keeps his focus on the opposite wall.

"It's fine."

"Wait." Sam leans back, eyeing him. "Didn't I read something about you being engaged?"

Trey dips his chin in a clipped nod.

"Oh fuck, Randi. What have you pulled me into? You made me out to be your fake boyfriend while you're screwing around with some other woman's fiancé? Hell no, I will not be made to look like a fool. I'll find some other way to get the information we need."

I remain silent. What is there to say back?

There are too many balls in the air, too many lies I'm juggling, and here I go adding Sam into the mix. I'd probably be pissed at me too.

"We're over." Trey's words, the uncaring tone with which he says them, are like a knife to my soul. I hold in the whimpering gasp, my shock and hurt. Still, Trey doesn't look my way. "Nothing to worry about, if you want to keep Randi in on whatever you need her help with."

"A little overprotective for it being over between you, don't you think?"

I feel Sam's gaze burning the back of my neck, but I don't look away from Trey.

"It's my job. It's all it's ever been, just with side benefits." Trey's unfeeling gaze slides over me before meeting Sam's. "Have you seen my fiancée?" He smirks. "Why would I want to mess that up?"

T coughs from the corner of the room. "Benson, a word."

Without another glance, Trey stands straight without removing either hand from his front pockets and strides across the room. T whispers something to Trey, who nods and then leaves.

"Is it really over, Randi?" Sam asks.

Tearing my wet eyes from the empty door, I wipe the corners with the back of my hand.

"It's complicated, let's say that. But it's fine. I'm fine."

"Say it one more time and I might believe you."

"Trey's one piece in this damn game I'm forced to play for this role. Honestly, I can't tell if I'm winning or losing any more." My voice cracks with the lump of emotion clogging my throat.

"You won't know until the end of the game."

"And when's that?"

"When Birmingham is impeached and you're sworn in as president."

"It won't stop there." I know it won't. This is only the beginning. The storm before the tornado. I hope I survive the damage once it's all done.

Damp lashes flutter as I try to keep the remaining unshed tears at bay. "So what can we do now with this new kink in the plan? I need something to focus on. A plan of action that I can follow. It needs to be more than me trying to overhear conversations, because that won't happen. Kyle's a manipulating prick, but he's smart. Too smart."

Sam leans back on the desk, supporting himself by hanging on to the hard edge with a tight grip. "So you're my girlfriend now, huh?" A devious smile spreads across his face. Something about it urges me to smile back. "Not a hardship to endure, I'll give you that. But I won't be made a fool, Randi. If we're going to pretend to do this, then I need you to keep your distance with that agent and anyone else. It doesn't seem like you're too concerned with your reputation in this town, but I am. I won't look like the idiot who doesn't know his girlfriend is sneaking around behind his back again."

"Again?" The word's out into the world before I can stop it. I snap my mouth shut hoping he didn't hear me. But I am curious.

"I've been burned in the past. Let's leave it at that. Getting to my role as AAG took a lot of long hours. Hours away from home. Hours your wife is filling with one of your old business partners while everyone else knows but has too much pity to tell you to your face."

"Wow," I breathe. "That's... she sounds terrible."

Sam laughs. Inhaling deep, he leans forward and drops his head. "You being with that agent is a bad idea, Randi, for a lot of reasons. If that gets out, your political career could be over. Think about what the media will spin. Making it seem like you're doing nothing in your role here except sleeping around with the entire team."

"It's just—"

"That's not what they'll spin. I'm not here to tell you how to live your life or what you should or shouldn't do. But if we figure out a plan, a plan that keeps me as your boyfriend, then I'm asking you to lie low. You have someone in your group who can out us fast if they see you with someone other than me. I can't go through that kind of humiliation again."

I nibble on my pinkie nail, debating what to tell him. What good would come from telling him the truth about everything? From Trey and Jessica's fake engagement, which she seems to now think is real, to me partnering with his mom. Oh, and being besties with the Russian president. None of that matters right now, which means none of it would keep me from being hands-off with Trey. At least until this whole mess is done.

"Things aren't what they seem," I say around my finger. *Let's see how Sam likes the ambiguous lawyer talk.* "I might have a way to get the information we need, but it's not the most legal of strategies."

Sam tilts his head, his gaze slowly assessing. "I don't like the sound of that. Would it hold up in court?"

I laugh and swipe my hand down my thighs. "Absolutely not."

"Then we figure out a more legal avenue first. If worse comes to worst, we'll use whatever connections you have, but until then, I want something we can present to the attorney general." The light reflects off his dark shiny hair as he stretches his neck. Reaching up, he massages the tight muscles while he stares at the floor. "I think we can use the couple story to our advantage."

"And how will we do that?"

"You're invited to all the galas and parties in this town because of your title."

"And because they know I won't go."

"We're changing that. With you, I have an invitation to the functions I've never been able to infiltrate before."

"You don't get invited?" I ask, surprised. With the way he looks, I figured everyone would be lining up to have him as eye candy at their party.

"I don't come from the type of family people want to associate with. Plus, no one likes attorneys, remember? This could be my way to listen in on conversations, pick up on connections and relationships. Maybe all I need is to find a few key members, connect them, and the rest will become clear."

"I hate getting dressed up," I whine, crossing my arms over my chest. The snug dress shirt tightens around my shoulders and elbows, restricting some of my movement. Shifting in the seat to get comfortable, I roll my shoulders, trying to loosen the tight material.

"You're either one of them or no one. Haven't you learned that yet?"

I lift a single shoulder in a noncommittal shrug. "Yeah, but I don't want to be one of them. That's the point of not going."

A groan passes his lips, drawing my attention to them. "It's just like this fake relationship you've created. Create a fake Randi. I hate them too, but I'm willing to go if it means we gain information on the oil scheme Birmingham has going on. You don't have to like it, but to get anything done in this town, you have to pretend everyone is your friend."

I huff in acknowledgment. Little does he know I already have fake Randi down pat. Between dealing with Kyle and Trey's mom, I've gotten pretty good at playing the game. At being the woman I've never wanted to become.

"Next week."

"Huh?" I respond, still lost in my own thoughts.

"There's a function next week at the White House. Some type of party welcoming several of the Middle East leaders as they converge to discuss the oil issue." Sam's green eyes narrow. "I need you to make sure you get an invite."

"Are you sure—"

"He's taking all this too far. Birmingham knows he's the cause of this mess, yet he's purposefully dragging other countries into this shit to cover his own ass. We need information, any information to add to the case we're building, before it's too late."

"Fine," I grumble, letting him hear the disdain in my voice.

"You wanted a plan. First step in this plan is to do something. And that something is attending these functions and galas as a couple, giving me access to a world I wouldn't even be able to sniff at without your name tied to mine." With a flick of his wrist, he checks his watch and slides off the desk. "Sorry, but I have another meeting I need to get to. Let me know when you get us on the list and what others you can score for the next month or so."

Sam pauses in front of my chair, the toes of his dress shoes touching the points of my pumps. "See you later, honey."

His light chuckle follows him through the library and out the doors.

"He's not going to like this, Randi."

I startle, shifting quickly in the chair to face the deep voice. Hand scrubbing the top of his shiny bald head, T stares at the floor.

"We don't have a choice," I say a bit defensively.

"Sure you do, but for some reason, you and that idiot Benson keep making the wrong ones. The lies are stacking up, Randi. What will you do when one card slips and the whole damn house comes falling down?"

I don't respond. There's really nothing to say back to that.

"I'll go get, Benson."

For several moments, I wait in the silence, gathering my thoughts and courage, dreading what needs to happen next.

Trey will understand that we need to keep our distance while I play the fake girlfriend, attending every fancy-ass party this city has to offer with Sam on my arm, right?

Well, when I put it like that....

11

TREY

Do *not shoot him.*
    Do not shoot him.
Do not shoot him.

I don't pause the calming mantra until the dickwad is out the door and his pounding steps down the front porch stairs are no longer audible. Still, I allow a few additional seconds before sliding my tight fists from the silk-lined pockets of my custom-tailored slacks.

The tendons and muscles in my fingers protest as I flex them wide, stretching out the tightness from holding a knuckle-cracking fist for too long. It was the only way I could hold the involuntary reflexes at bay to reach out and strangle the man encroaching on my girl.

My girl.

Hanging my head, I massage the back of my neck, hoping to ease the building tension making it stiff and sore.

We're in the middle of a shit circus caused by our own doing with no way out. We'd both love to shed the fake lives we've crafted to survive in this political power game, but that won't happen anytime soon. The one bright spot in my day, the one part of this craziness I look forward to, is our time here at One Observatory. Our alone time, the stolen moments when I'm on shift or the hours together when I'm not, are what's driving me to see this through.

If I didn't have those stolen moments with her, the daily reminder of what I'm fighting for, this game we're playing against the world would break me. Break the resolve we made to do whatever it takes to get through the next three years with her political career and life intact.

"She wants to talk to you," Tank says with a sigh. "I told you two this would end badly. Now I'm forced to play damn mediator."

I furrow my brows in confusion. End? Maybe he's referring to the less-than-pleasant remark I made in the library about Jessica or how Randi I were done. But that was me playing my part for the dipshit AAG, keeping up the façade we've carefully constructed to appease my mother and make sure Sam keeps Randi on the inside of the investigation. Randi knows none of what I said was true. No doubt the words stung like hell; hers did that day with Birmingham in the living room. I thought I've felt pain before, but nothing compares to hearing the woman who holds your heart talking about how attractive another man is to her.

Holding Tank's unforgiving stare, I squeeze between the small space he's left between his broad shoulders and the doorframe.

"Do not make a scene," he mutters under his breath as I move past. "Your actions reflect on the team, and I will not have us sidelined again because of your hot head."

I send him a wink over my shoulder. "Ten-four, buddy. Don't worry though, we're good. It's all just part of the game we're forced to play. You know that."

A flash of what appears to be fear passes across his dark gaze before he breaks the connection to focus on the hardwood floor. With a few muttered curses, Tank steps out of the room and shuts the french doors with a hard pull, leaving me alone with Randi.

Pondering Tank's strange warning and behavior, I approach the middle of the room with caution. You never know when crazy Randi might come out to play, and I sure as hell don't want to be caught off guard when she does. But Randi doesn't even glance in my direction as I approach the grouping of chairs where she sits. Even when I'm standing directly in front of her, she doesn't acknowledge my presence.

"Sam's good with what I told Kyle," she mumbles around the nail between her teeth.

Grasping her hand, I tug until she drops it from her mouth to the chair. My knees give an audible crackle as I squat low, putting us eye to eye—if she would look at me, that is. Gripping her trembling chin, I tilt her face until those hazel eyes lock with mine. The sadness and pain swirling in them fuel my earlier anger.

"What did that fucker do?" I demand, my grip tightening a fraction.

"Trey." She groans. "He didn't do anything."

"Then what's wrong, Mess?" Wetness pools in her lower lids, eyelashes damp from previous tears. Dropping her chin, I run my hand through my hair and tug at the long ends. "Are you upset about what I said earlier about Jessica? You know—"

"I love you, Trey." Large tears slip down both cheeks that are bunched with her sad smile. "I love you so much that sometimes it physically hurts, and I shouldn't ask you to keep doing this, but I am."

For one beat, my heart is so full it could burst. How long have I wanted to hear those words from her, to know she's in as deep as I am? Only to have fear seize the next beat at the heartache dripping from her tone and choice of words, both sounding more like the ending rather than the beginning.

"Keep doing what, Mess?" I say cautiously. Pulling back an inch, I force myself to give her space to breathe. Unlike Sam, the personal space invader.

"Sam is okay with the fake couple angle and even has some ideas on how it could work in our favor of gathering information for the case against Kyle. But he has one request."

Pleading hazel eyes flick between mine and the floor.

Unease tightens my gut. Nerves have me shifting on the balls of my feet with eagerness. "And what did he request, Randi?"

"He doesn't want to look like a fool if we're caught together when he and I are supposedly a couple."

"Okay," I say, not understanding.

"That means giving up what time we have alone for a while. With the mole we have on the team, it wouldn't be smart for us to even be together in this house. So we have to put a pause on... on us."

I stand before she can finish. The oriental rug slides under the heel of my dress shoes as I turn to put some much-needed space between her and me. Hurt blends with anger merging with heartache as I pace from one side of the library to the other. The back of my neck burns as she tracks my movements.

"You say you love me, then agree to putting us on hold, all so people don't think you're cheating on him? It's a fake relationship, Randi. That doesn't make any damn sense." The knuckles of my fingers pop as I curl them into tight fists at my side.

"He's been hurt before and doesn't want it to happen again. Trey, please understand, I'm doing my best with what I've been handed. You think I want to do this? You think I want to keep you at arm's length until this charade with Sam is done? You know I don't. But I have to."

"You don't *have* to do anything," I snarl at the book spines. I can't turn to face her. The pain of betrayal aches too much. I'm not really angry at her, more so the situation we're in. This fucked-up game we're playing that seems to get more complicated by the day.

"You know I do. You know what I'm up against and what has to be done."

"Everything I've done to this point was—is—for you. Going to my parents, agreeing to be with Jessica, attending all the lame-ass parties this city loves to hold, and yet you want me to give up the one piece of us that's fucking holding me together?" Unable to stop, I slam a tight fist into the row of hardback spines that seems to be mocking me.

"Trey," Randi yells. There's a quick clicking of heels against the hardwood floor, and then she's on me, holding me tight, her front against my back. A sliver of the anger melts away with her touch. How does she expect me to give this up even for a day? "Please stop and let me explain."

I turn so quick that she teeters back on her heels, eyes wide as she tips backward. Before she can fall, I grab hold of her shoulders. Without over-thinking my actions, I haul her close and seal my lips over hers. A faint whimper pours from her mouth as I empty the overpowering emotions from my own body into hers with the devouring kiss. Her fingers wrap around the lapel of my jacket, pulling our bodies tighter together.

"Don't ask me to give this up. I can't," I say against her lips before nipping at her lower one and sinking my teeth into the tender flesh. "Don't you see how much I need you, Mess? I can't give you up, not even for one fucking day."

With all the unstable aspects of me that have settled since she's stepped into my life, I'm a little worried that without her, the unbalance will tip the scales once again. I don't want to go back to being that person, the man without a purpose.

"I'm not asking you to give me up, Trouble. But like after the campaign, we need to stay at arm's length for a little while, that's it. We've done it before and survived, and we can do it again. I have to do this. You know I do. Every day, the stakes in this game are rising, and I want you... no, I *need* you by my side while I figure this out. Please don't give up on me."

"What if I say no, Randi? What if this is my line in the sand?"

"You won't," she says softly. Hot breath brushes along the skin of my neck as she nuzzles me like she can't get close enough.

"Oh? And what makes you so sure, Mess?" She's right, but I'd love to hear her reasoning.

"Because you know if I don't do this, don't play along with the lie I've already created, then I'm back in the crosshairs with Kyle. This gives me a few months to figure things out without his threats. If he believes I'm truly not working with the DOJ, then maybe I'll have a couple months of no one trying to kill me."

I grumble into her hair knowing she's right.

"What are you more worried about? The distance part or me playing fake girlfriend with Sam?"

"Fucking both," I admit. Resting my chin on the crown of her head, I wrap both arms around her, closing any space between us. "He gets to play the part I've never had with you. I've never been able to take you out on a date, hold your hand in public, touch you when others are looking. He'll get that with you."

"I guess I get that, but what you and I have had this past year is more than any public date can offer. Our stolen moments, the time we get to spend together, I cherish all of it. You know it will all be fake between Sam and me. He knows it's not real."

"You sure about that?"

Pulling back, she searches my face. "Yeah, he knows. It's just about someone else finding out. That's why he's asking me to be so cautious."

"Right, that's it," I say with an incredulous huff. "You're smart, beautiful, and fun to be around. What guy wouldn't jump on the opportunity to make the moves on you? He will, I know he will, and that's also what I'm dreading. That and the no sex part." I smirk, trying to hide the nerves drowning me inside. "The AAG prick thinks we were just a fling. At least with Jessica, she knows who has my heart. She knows about you."

"Not that that's stopping her," she grumbles.

I purse my lips to keep from saying something I might regret.

"It'll be fine. You'll see, Trey." Stepping close once again, she wraps her arms around my waist, resting her cheek on my chest.

Eyes closed, I take a deep, relaxing breath in. "And what's worse is I'll have a front row seat to it all. You're lucky you don't have to see me and Jessica together since you never go to those parties Mother forces me to attend to bolster my political future."

Her back muscles tense beneath my palms, putting me on alert.

"Randi?"

"Sam wants us to attend as many of those parties as possible. To solidify us as a couple to Kyle but also to give him an inside eye and ear. He hopes he can make connections or see something that will aid in the investigation."

"Great."

"Trouble?" The shake in her voice slips through the wall of anger, breaking down my defenses. "Please don't be mad."

I'm not mad with her, not upset that she took this avenue. I'm fucking pissed we're even at this point. And maybe a little worried that this isn't the last of the hurdles we'll have to face together.

How much more will we have to endure before it becomes too much?

Will we hold on?

Will we stay true to the end goal—us together, no games, no Kyle, Jessica, Shawn, or Sam?

Only one thing is certain at this point.

Letting go would be the easy route, even if just the thought rips my heart in two.

"Bud Light," I grumble over the wooden bar to the older man behind it as I slide onto the creaky stool directly beside Tank. "Fuck, what a day."

A single grunt of agreement is his only response, his attention still riveted on the large-screen TV above the row of liquor bottles showing the final World Series game.

"What do you have to complain about?" I nod my thanks to the bartender and accept the outstretched longneck in his hand. The cold glass chills my sweaty palm from the muggy temperatures outside. How it's still hot as balls when it should be fall is beyond me.

After a long pull of the ice-cold beverage, I wipe the few remaining drops from my lip with a swipe of my thumb.

"What do I have to complain about?" T says with an incredulous tone. "What do *I* have to complain about?"

"That's what I said," I say, giving him the side eye. What the hell is his problem? I'm the one with women issues, not him. He has Sarah. Amazing, no complications, a bit crazy and scary Sarah. I have a bit crazy and scary Randi who I miss like hell, even though we're together most days, and also a lot crazy—and way too clingy—Jessica, who I can't stand to be around longer than a few seconds when we're forced to interact.

Faster than I can react, his palm smacks across the back of my head. With a harsh curse, I press a couple fingers against my skull.

"What was that for?" I snap. Frowning, I tip the bottle back and drain the contents.

"For being obtuse."

"Me? Obtuse?"

"Yes. You act surprised," Tank huffs, finally turning his attention to me. Not breaking his expecting stare, he takes a sip of his drink, the tiny fuchsia-and-teal umbrella brushing against the tip of his nose.

"You're so damn embarrassing," I say, giving a pointed glance to the decorative addition to his drink.

"*I'm* embarrassing?"

"Fucking hell," I groan. "Stop taking everything and turning it around like a question, like I'm some dumbass who's not catching on to what's going on around him."

"You *are* that dumbass. These past few weeks have been hell for all of us, Playboy."

My eyes widen in surprise. "What? Why?"

"The tension between you and Randi is extreme. We're walking on eggshells around her, and you're no better. I'd say you both need to get laid to stop this madness, but that won't help since you can't be together, and if either of you slept with someone else, it would be like dropping a damn atom bomb on our lives."

"Has she mentioned wanting to sleep with someone else?"

His dark eyes roll to the ceiling, and he shakes his head and takes another sip of his Long Island iced tea. Most bars don't add the umbrella. Oh no, my best friend asks for it specifically. If you ask me, it's his signal that he's looking for a reason to fight. Just waiting for some smartass to make fun of him.

"That umbrella match your panties?" I ask with a knowing grin.

Yep, I'm that smartass who's also looking for a fight.

He's not wrong about the tension around the house. It's palpable. And I'm at the center of it every single day. I need something to help me let off some steam since I haven't been able to get to the club lately to row. Taking Mess to Central Park at midnight is the worst idea I've had in a really long time, but asking for a beating from a cousin of the Hulk is a close second.

"I know what you're doing," he replies. "Get your rocks off with someone else."

"I'm not asking to backdoor you."

"Fucking hell, Benson," Tank chastises with a chuckle. "You're a damn moron. Me kicking your ass won't make things better. She'll still be keeping her distance, and you'll still have that constant hard-on at work."

"Why can't she wear more clothes around the house?" I grumble. Lifting the empty longneck in the air, I wait until I make eye contact with the bartender and lower it back to the bar with a thunk.

"Because it's hot outside."

"She's always cold. Why this week did she decide that shorts and tank tops were acceptable after work? And do her suits have to fit her ass so well? I mean, fuck, it's like a little taunt every time she moves."

"You're a terrible human being." Tank laughs, smiling into his drink. "Have you not noticed anything besides her ass and legs this week?"

The bartender slides another cold one down the bar. The second it's in my hand, I take a quick sip flipping through my memories of the week.

"I'm sure I did, but you have to admit her ass is distracting."

"Only to you."

"Did you have a point besides making me think about her butt?" With my free hand, I adjust my hardening dick. I can't help that every move, every breath of hers turns me on. It'd be one thing if it was just her body I was attracted to. *That* I could turn off easily. But oh no, not Randi Sawyer. No, that woman has enraptured me heart and soul with her wit, quick mind, and slight crazy.

His attention flicks down to where I'm adjusting myself. "Maybe I *should* kick your ass, take the edge off."

"Can't believe I'm saying this, but yes, please."

Tank's loud rumbling laugh draws a few other patrons' attention. "When you have a black eye for your fancy-ass dinner tomorrow night, don't blame me." He nods to his drink and pushes the bar stool back. "You're buying. Meet me out back. And, Benson, if you poke me with that thing, I'm breaking it."

At his words, my cock softens and practically scurries up into my belly.

Huh, now I know what works better than a cold shower. I just need a voice memo of Tank threatening to crack my dick off to ease the constant boner I have at work nowadays.

A few quick swallows later, I skim the empty bottle a few inches along the bar. After tossing a couple twenties on the wet bar top, I slide off the hard stool and make my way through the growing crowd.

The humid, suffocating air smacks my face the moment I open the door. I suck in a quick breath and hold it, hoping it'll help fight off the rising panic swelling in my gut. I'm teetering on the edge if I'm this close to snapping to memories of past deployments with just a flash of heat. The past few years I've done better at managing the instant tightness in my muscles, the dread and nerves the heat causes. But with my nerves at a constant high lately, it's no wonder my buried emotions are on a hair trigger.

"You okay?" Tank asks, sensing my unease.

"Yeah. Let's do this."

"Not if you're not in the right mental space. You with me, Benson?"

I shrug off my suit jacket and nod. "Fine."

"You're not fine." The streetlights engulf his face in a dull yellow glow. "Talk to me."

"It's just the same as always. I'm fine."

"It's getting worse?"

"Not worse, just... closer to the surface."

"That's worse."

"This will help." I roll up my cuffs and shove them over my elbows while he shrugs out of his own jacket. "I have to get some of this... whatever it is out."

"I think it's called feelings. And normal people go to therapy or work out, just so you know."

"I haven't made time to get to the club between Randi, Jessica, and my mother's constant need for me to come by the estate. And really I know I just need Randi," I mutter, not happy that it's the truth. "No amount of exercise or talking to some stranger will fix that. It's only been a year, and somehow that woman is the one thing I need to stay sane. How is that?"

Instead of waiting for his answer, I take two quick steps and throw a hard right hook, knowing full well he'll block it. His forearm slams against my own, keeping my fist inches from his face. With a quick push, he shoves me back three steps.

"She's just as miserable as you," he says, holding his own fists up, preparing for another attack.

My raised hands drop an inch. "What?"

"That's why I asked if you've noticed anything besides her ass this week. Have you seen her face? She's miserable. The desperate glances she sends your way are enough to break my own heart, you son of a bitch."

I duck in time to miss his fist slamming into my skull.

"Really?"

"I swear you're a fool and don't deserve her. Yes, she's just as miserable without you as you are without her. Pull your head out of your ass, Trey. Look at her. *Really* look at her."

My elbow ricochets off his thick bicep just as his slams into my ribs. All the air explodes from my lungs as pain shoots through my side. Not giving in to the desire to fold over and nurse my bruised ribs, I take a step back to catch a breath.

"Don't you think I know that?" I wheeze. Fuck, he might have broken a bone. "I think you punctured a lung."

"Told you this was a bad idea. Better yet?"

A snarl pulls at my upper lip. "Not even close."

Shadows dip across his face as he leans forward. "Then what are you waiting for, pussy? Fight."

I start forward only to pause. "Wait. Are we talking about this fight or a metaphorical fight for my relationship with Randi?"

"You really aren't as smart as you think you are."

I hold up a hand, palm out. "Is that a yes? Wait, which is it?" Leaning back against the building's crumbling brick, I scrub a calloused palm across my face. "I need a damn road map for this conversation."

"Both. Neither. Which is worth fighting for?"

The noises of the city filter down the dark alley. Glaring at the concerning oily puddle at my feet, I search the nasty asphalt for the right answer.

"Both." My tone is firm with the knowledge that my best friend is a brilliant man. The brick scrapes across both palms as I push off it, standing tall once again. "Now, where were we?"

A sinister smirk pulls at his lips, showing off his brilliant white teeth.

I swallow hard as I step closer, fists up.

I really am an idiot.

Fuck, this is going to hurt.

12

RANDI

November

The glass of champagne between my pinched fingers has long since warmed, and the last of the dying bubbles pop to the top. My fake smile hasn't faltered once since we arrived as I nod, laugh when appropriate, and offer phony words of agreement.

At least the party was an excuse to buy a new pair of shoes.

Flicking my gaze down to the floor, I smile at the nude high-heel sandals. Sure, they cost a fortune, but they make me happy. And goodness knows I need some happy in my life right now since I can't be with Trey.

Just the thought makes the practiced smile falter. Scanning the room, I press the balls of my toes harder to the floor as I stretch high in hopes of catching a glimpse of Trey.

Disappointment washes through me, making the sadness from the past couple weeks come rushing back. The past three weeks have been miserable. The worst three weeks of my adult life so far.

Okay, that's a bit dramatic. Being poisoned was obviously the worst week of my adult life.

But the past three weeks are in the top ten, for sure, with having to see him dressed up with Jessica smiling on his arm instead of me at all the functions we've attended. Watching them is torture, yet I can't stop.

I miss him, desperately. Sure, I see him when he's on shift, which is just about every day, but I miss us. The easy laughter, the conversations, the friendship. Things have been awkward, making me wonder if we'll ever get back to the ease of things.

"I need to get laid," I grumble.

Sam and the senator shoot a confused look my way but keep talking. Whatever.

"You're frowning, honey," Sam says into my ear.

I fight the urge to rub my shoulder against the ear his breath tickled. "Sorry," I mutter. Turning my face up, I offer my biggest, fakest smile. "Better?" I say through clenched teeth.

"A lot worse, actually." He laughs, then flicks his gaze to the champagne glass. "Why do you always grab a glass if you won't drink it?"

"That's exactly why I grab it." Slowly, I ease the overzealous smile to relieve the ache in my cheeks. "If I don't like it, then I don't have to worry about drinking too much and doing something stupid."

"Like what?"

Biting my lip, I scan the crowd. "Oh, you know, like walking up to Kyle over there and punching him in the throat."

I startle at Sam's sudden laugh.

"Seriously?"

I lift a bare shoulder in a half shrug. "I've always had to hold myself back from physical violence with him. One time I even launched a coffee mug at his head—in the Oval Office, mind you. Holding back was easier before though."

"And why's that?" he says, humor in his voice.

"Sa—" T's threats of ever mentioning his wife flash across my mind. "I mean, my trainer taught me self-defense, so now I know how to hit, where to make it hurt. So now that makes holding back that much more difficult. Before, it was just all a fun fantasy. Now I can actually do it."

"Your fantasies are strangely violent."

"You have no idea. I also have several involving utilizing unicorns as weapons of mass destruction."

Curious gazes shift our way at Sam's full, real laugh rumbling through the politely quiet conversations going on around us.

"Now that I'd like to see."

"Same." I shift my weight from one foot to the other. "How much longer do you need to stay here?"

Sam's gaze scans the room before settling on me. "A while. There are several campaign supporters here tonight who I haven't spoken to before. Ready to leave so soon?"

"Hell yes. This thing is killing me slowly. I'm pretty sure my lungs are only functioning at 5 percent."

"Your dress?" His brows rise up his forehead as he lowers his gaze to my midsection, pausing briefly at the small amount of cleavage on display.

"Yes, I swear it has a built in girdle meant to squish all my organs. I'm dying slowly here." His gaze remains low. Snapping my fingers at my belly button, I draw his attention back up to my face. "Eyes up here, boyfriend."

"Okay, girlfriend." Humor dances in his green eyes. For a moment, I relish the ease of the conversation, the simple back-and-forth. I miss doing this with Trey, but since he seems unable to play nice right now, I guess I'll have to get my friendship fix from Sam.

"What are you doing for Thanksgiving?" I ask, once again looking out amongst the crowd in hopes of a glimpse at Trey. The last time I saw him and Jessica, they were entertaining a group of old fat guys, also known as several of our key senators and congressmen.

They were holding hands.

Holding hands!

I feel like that's breach of contract or something. Maybe when I suggested this whole "on hold" scenario, we should've hashed out the parameters. As in no physical contact with the people we're pretending to date/be engaged to.

Just as I think that, Sam rests his hand on my shoulder. I stare at his thick knuckles and wide fingers for half a second, enjoying the touch, before carefully stepping away.

Awareness at being watched prickles at my neck. Searching over my shoulder, my gaze locks with a pair of furious honey brown ones.

Back and forth, his gaze bounces between the shoulder Sam touched and my eyes. With a slight tilt of his head, he whispers something to Jessica and then moves through the crowd in the direction he'd just indicated, leaving her behind.

My heart races. The glass between my fingers trembles. Careful to not spill a drop, I secure my palm over the top of flute.

"I'll be right back," I say to Sam. I take a step only for my next to be halted. Turning, I look between his hand around my elbow and his face.

"Do not leave without me, Randi." Lips pursed, he shakes his head. "It worried me the last time you did that and I couldn't find you."

Whoops. Okay, yeah, he does have reason to be concerned. Last week I bounced from a party without telling him because I just couldn't take it anymore. One more minute faking it and I was going to crack and show everyone just how crazy I really am.

Which is scary because I don't even know the extent of my crazy. It seems to get deeper with each passing year. Probably something I should work on containing, but, meh, next year. Maybe when I'm forty, things will even out and I'll be just as normal as normal can be.

Or maybe fifty. It can be a stretch goal.

"Sixty seems like a good age."

"What are you talking about, Randi?"

I smile to Sam. "Nothing, and noted that I'm not to leave unless I send you a text."

"Not. At. All." His eyes narrow like he's trying to make a point.

"You know, you give off this bad guy vibe with your dark hair, tattoos, and emotionless face, but I see through you."

"Oh?" he asks, clearly amused.

"Yep."

"Go, Randi," he says with a confused smile. "I'll be doing our espionage job alone while you're gone."

Two fingers to my brow, I give him a mock salute.

What the fuck is wrong with me and my damn hands? Do they plot to embarrass me?

Grumbling my annoyance at myself, I shift through the crowd. Halfway through the crowded room, a hand wraps around my bicep, tugging me backward.

"Trailer," Shawn says behind me. "We need to talk."

Like Sarah trained me, I use my weight to yank the arm from his grasp. Surprise flairs behind his evil eyes before vanishing as quickly as it came.

"No we don't." A few guests flick nervous glances between us. Remembering my role, I try for my best smile, knowing it's more of a grimace at this point. "If you'll excuse me, I need to go piss." Fuck. A few women gasp, their

French-tipped fingers lightly pressed to their painted lips. "Sorry. I need to find the toilet." Oh hell.

Not wanting to say anything else that will lower their already devastatingly low opinions of me, I turn quickly and move toward the door Trey walked through what feels like hours ago. Before exiting the room, I rest the full glass of champagne on a side table. Nerves riding high, I swipe both hands down the front of my red dress and step into the hallway, inspecting to the left, then the right. Both directions are empty. The hope of seeing Trey deflates, leaving only the aching pain of my kidneys being pushed to the front of my body by the torture contraption strangling my waist.

"Turn right," T says behind me.

After having him at my side for so long, sometimes I forget he's even there. Not turning, I smile at the opposite wall. "Thanks, T."

The stiletto heels make zero sound as I make my way down the dimly lit hall, anticipation rising with each step. The overhead chandeliers—because who doesn't have chandeliers in their hallway?—give off a soft glow, casting shadows in every corner and disappearing altogether into the few empty ballrooms. I pass one darkened room only to pause at the sight of movement. I cast an apprehensive glance into the darkness.

Out of the shadows, Trey materializes. He extends a single hand, palm up. With zero doubts, I smile and take it. As he guides me deeper into the darkness, I mirror his smile. With a small tug, I'm against his chest and being lifted in his arms as he kicks the door shut behind us with the heel of his dress shoe.

"What are you—" The rest of the thought vanishes with the heat of his lips pressing against mine. I forget everything. All the worry, anger, frustration, and disappointment from the past three weeks vaporize with one simple kiss.

His hands skim up my bare back, down my arms, and back again. Mine do the same, enjoying the dips of his strong, lean muscles beneath his tux. I gasp into his mouth as the cold wall presses against my back.

"This has to be quick," Trey mutters against my lips. Pulling back an inch, I can barely see his face, but somehow I know he's waiting for permission. That this isn't just him needing this reminder, this connection.

"Yes," I groan as his hand cups my breast, pinching the hard nipple over the dress. "Fuck yes."

Terrible idea, but hell yes.

My hair whips around my shoulders as I'm spun in place. The wall now presses against my warm cheek. Each panting breath pushes back against my face. A knock against my ankles urges me to widen my stance. Anticipation builds, dampening my center, readying me for whatever he has in mind.

The danger and possibility of getting caught hype up my desire. Warm fingers trail up the inside of both legs, bunching the satin material around my waist. Not wasting any time, he slides a hand forward, dipping underneath my already wet lace thong. My gasp turns into a pleasure-filled groan as he slides two fingers inside, slowly pumping in and out.

With less finesse, he rips my underwear down my thighs. The clink of his belt followed by the slow sigh of his zipper lowering has me pushing my hips back toward him, eager for him to take what he knows we both need.

The flesh of my hips molds beneath his tight grasp as he pushes in deep with one thrust. Our groans mirror one another's. Palms against the wall, I push back, desperate for him to move, to give me what I've been denied the past three weeks.

The smacking of flesh and slick sounds of our bodies connecting echo in the darkness, only interrupted by cries stifled by his palm sealed to my lips. Pleasure tightens low in my belly. Chasing the building orgasm, I quicken my pace, thrusting hard back into him.

Heat engulfs my back. Wet lips press to the shell of my ear, sending a desire-induced shudder down my spine.

"You're mine, Mess," Trey breathes into my ear. "We're not on hold. We're not over. This is just the beginning of us, and I will not lose you."

I cry out, biting his palm to quiet the sound. Grunting into my ear, Trey slams into me over and over, drawing out my orgasm as he curses, finding his own release. Panting, his uneven breaths brush against my shoulder.

I smile into the dark. Stupidest, most glorious thing I've ever done.

If only we had time to do it again.

The sense of loss fills my belly as he pulls out. Something soft presses against my center as Trey gently wipes up the evidence of our sexcapade.

"Thanks," I mutter, trying to find my normal voice. "Do I say thank you?" Just saying it out loud causes a giggle to bubble from my chest.

"I miss that sound," Trey says, lips against my neck. "I miss you. I miss us."

"Me too," I admit. "But this was...."

"Fucking hot as hell."

A full laugh bursts past my lips. Both hands seal over my mouth to keep the noise to a minimum. "That, and stupid. What if we get caught? We both know what's on the line."

"We just have to be careful, Mess. It's not just the sex I miss, it's you. The real you, not the one you allow everyone else to see."

"This will all be over soon, and then—"

"Then it will be something else, then something else. I'm fighting for us, Randi, how I can. I need you to fight for us too. Don't close me out. Don't keep your distance anymore. I can't take it. It's breaking me every day I don't get you." His wet lips press hard against my shoulder. "I love you."

After assisting in situating my thong back to its rightful place, he smooths down the skirt of the designer dress. Without another word, he tugs the door open. The bright light of the hallway blinds me. I hold a hand over my closed eyelids to dampen the visual assault.

When I find the nerve to move my hand away, I blink at the person holding the door.

"Where'd he go?" I ask T.

"Back where he should be." His words hit me like a sucker punch to the gut. I suck in a quick breath, and his eyes flare with realization. "Tonight. Where he should be tonight, right now. He's a fool sneaking you away, but I also know he couldn't hold back any more."

Stepping into the bright hallway, I smooth down my hair and run a finger along the edge of my lips to wipe away any smudges.

"I noticed," I say with a satisfied smile. For the first time in weeks, I take a deep breath. "I needed it as much as him."

"Damn, you two have it bad."

Slowly, we make our way back down the hall toward the craziness I've sold my life to.

"Lust?" I say, hating the word because of the cheapness it offers.

"It's more than that and you know it."

With the high fading, the realization of what we just did, what could've happened, sinks in. "Sam...." I don't know what to say other than just his name.

"Don't worry. We knew to keep this discreet. Since we still don't know who the leak is, I sent the other guys to the perimeter except them." I sneak a peek over my shoulder. Champ and Walsh match our steps, their attention scanning the hallway for threats. "I trust these two. It's why they're here and no one else."

Turning back, I slow my steps, giving us time to finish the conversation before I reenter the ballroom.

"We'll find the guy," T assures me.

"It's odd though, right?" I raise a hand to my lips to nibble at the already too short pinkie nail. "You'd think we'd have felt something... off with someone by now. Or at least had some kind of hint. Maybe it is someone on the beta team, and that's why we don't have a good read on them because we're not around them every day."

"Could be. I'm having their team lead look into each agent. Listen." He rests his large hands on my shoulders. I smile at the comfort it offers when just a year ago, I would've shied away from his touch. "Don't worry about it. You keep working with Sam, do what you can to keep my best friend from jumping off the deep, and I'll focus on the leak. Deal?"

"Deal." The AC brushes against my hot skin the moment he removes his somewhat sweaty palms. I shoot a nervous glance into the packed ballroom. Immediately my gaze falls on Trey, who has his arm wrapped around Jessica's waist. She's laughing, smiling up at him as he animatedly gestures between himself and another couple.

"He can't stand her."

"I know," I whisper. "Doesn't make the jealousy go away. We've never even had a date, you know."

T remains silent.

"One day I'd love to be able to show him off, to go out like this with me on his arm." I fill my lungs with a steadying breath. "You think we can do it? Get the information we need to impeach Kyle?"

"Honestly," T says, making me rest my chin on my shoulder to face him, "I think you can pretty much do anything you put your mind to. You're not alone in this town, Randi. Lean on your friends, on the alliances you've already formed. Everything else will fall into place."

Turning back to face the room, I step across the threshold. The clinking of glass, the growing chatter, and haughty laughter fill my ears as I shoulder through the crowd in search of Sam.

"Walmart."

I freeze in my tracks. Kyle's soft chest brushes against my shoulder and arm as he moves around, stopping in front of me.

"Kyle," I murmur in greeting while fighting to keep the hate from bleeding into my dry tone.

"You're here again, with Pierce."

"I am. That's what couples do, isn't it?"

"And Benson is here with his new... fiancée." I fight the instinct to curl my fingers into tight fists. Instead, I clear my throat and plaster the practiced smile across my face. "Does your boyfriend still suspect me of wrongdoing?"

"Wouldn't know. You really don't come up during sex."

Amusement flashes across his face. "Too bad. I might enjoy that."

"You're a disgusting pig."

"Maybe we could all have some fun together."

"Together?" That sounds like a terrible idea. "I'm not really into that kind of thing."

"Thanksgiving, you and Pierce come to Camp David with me and Cindy and a few others." He tips his chin toward a voluptuous blonde. "I must insist."

"Must you?"

"It's not a request, Walmart."

I swallow past a dry mouth and throat. "We're not at that point yet. You know, the whole weekend getaway." I give a nervous laugh, searching the room for Sam, anyone who will help me. "That's a big step in a relationship."

"Again, Walmart, not a request. You want to uphold your contract," he hisses close so no one else can hear his words, "then you bring that fucker to Camp David. There you'll show him just how much you support and trust me."

"Like group trust exercises or something?"

"Something like that. Plan to be there for lunch and staying the night."

I narrow my eyes. "I am not, I repeat, *not* tossing my keys into a fishbowl to prove my loyalty."

His condescending chuckle rakes on my already frayed nerves. Heat builds beneath my skin, making the tight dress even more suffocating than it already was. I sense beads of sweat building along my hairline.

"Oh, Walmart. You're hilarious. We don't use either." Ice blue eyes narrow at me, allowing a window into the narcissist that lies within. "We take what we want. Not that you should be worried about that. You're still just as much trailer trash today as you were back then, and people know it. Besides, I have another surprise in mind."

"Kyle, I don't—" I call after him as he walks off, disappearing into the crowd.

"Fuck, fuck, fuck. I need to get out of here," I say over my shoulder, knowing T is there. "Can someone please let Sam know I have to get out of here? Now."

The crowd doesn't budge as I try to squeeze through. Two familiar faces slide up close.

"What's going on?" Trey's signature citrus and spice scent envelops my senses, though it's a bit duller than usual.

"Are you okay, Randi?" Jessica asks, her tone light, no genuine concern filtering through.

"I need to get out of here." I take another step, trying to break through the crowd, when the room sways. Both hands jut outward, desperate to hold on to anything, anyone to keep me on my feet. "T, I need some air."

His heavy arm wraps around my waist, holding me close to his side. The crowd parts for us—mostly T's wide frame as he barrels through—allowing us to make it across the full room in half the time. Outside, I savor the brush of the cool night air as it soothes the uncomfortable heat building beneath my flushed cheeks.

Leaning into T, I relax against him, knowing I'm safe with him close.

"What the fuck was that all about?" I whisper just loud enough for him to hear. "Kyle wanting me and Sam at Camp David? What is he up to?"

"Not sure, but nothing good, that's for certain."

"He's planning something. Let's just hope it's not poisoning the entire turkey to get to me." I snort at the audacity, but T doesn't laugh. "It was a joke. He wouldn't dare risk that kind of exposure."

"Wouldn't he? Just to be on the safe side, I'll have your cook prepare a few meals, and we'll bring enough bottled water—"

"And whiskey. That's a must." I nod vigorously.

"Fine, and whiskey—"

"Well, while you're being so accommodating, how about a pack of cigarettes too? I've been good. I deserve a reward."

"No. Food, water, and whiskey. That's it."

"Killjoy."

"When we get back, I'll let the other teams know of the change of plans. We'll plan accordingly, knowing we can't let our guard down even though we're at one of the most protected locations on Earth."

In the distance, the dome of the Capitol Building stands out against the other monuments and buildings. The late-night traffic honks and roars around us as we wait for Sam.

I sigh. "Hopefully that'll be enough to prepare for whatever Kyle has planned."

13

RANDI

Outside the tinted window, the nearly naked trees speed past in a blur. Miles and miles of nothing but trees. Complete isolation. Which is why Camp David is where it is, I guess.

I press my palm to my chest in an attempt to calm my racing heart and building sense of foreboding. Coming out here is a terrible idea. Isolated with only my protection team, and maybe Sam, with their thoughts on my safety. Being out here on his turf is making us all anxious.

A nagging unease keeps pestering at the back of my mind, urging me to have my team turn the SUV around, to head home and ignore Kyle's demanding invitation to spend Thanksgiving with him. But I can't, can I? Last time I ignored a direct order from him, he put a price on my head, and the alpha team and I were ambushed. Maybe that overreaction on his part was because I defied his direct order, messing with his narcissistic ego, or the fact that it was the OPEC summit and I had the potential to gain insight into his dirty oil dealings.

Whichever it was, I'm not that crazy to test my luck again.

Twice I've lived when he wanted me dead.

I'm not a kitty with nine lives. This is the real world, and at some point, the hazards around me will succeed in removing me from office. Dead or alive. An unsettling thought, sure, but at least I have the men in this SUV and the ones in front of us and behind. Their presence is what helps me sleep at night.

Well, that and the sleeping pill the doctor prescribed. That shit is legit. Not that it's helping with the stress while I'm awake, but the much-needed sleep makes everything during the day more manageable. Between the normal sleeping patterns and basically being force-fed several times a day, I'm living a healthier life since the poisoning.

Go me.

"How much longer?" I ask, fighting with the thick material of the seat belt tightly secured across my lap. Freaking T. I swear, if he could put me in a five-point harness like a five-year-old he would.

"Ten minutes," Champ says from the front seat.

"Nervous?"

Elbow on the window's edge, I rest my head in my hand and turn in the leather seat to face Sam. Today, he's ditched the normal suit attire he's always wearing, instead going for a more casual look with trendy jeans that hug his thick thighs nicely and taper at the cuff. The black sweater is tight along his defined chest, showing off the curves of the pecs I know he's hiding under the thick clothing. The sleeves are shoved up his forearms, allowing a hint of his colorful artwork to peek out near his elbows.

It's a good look for him.

When I finally meet his intense gaze, a small knowing smirk is tugging at his lips. Damn, he's handsome. His dark hair, tan skin, and piercing green eyes perfectly encompass the brooding look he's no doubt going for. I'm sure all the women fall at his feet, offering themselves for just a date with him.

"Why don't you have a girlfriend?" I ask instead of answering his question. This one is more pressing. "How long ago was your divorce?"

I swear a hint of blush flushes his cheeks before he turns to focus out the windshield.

"Seven years ago. And as to why I don't date, work mostly. It's hard to treat a woman right when you're working eighty-plus hours a week."

"Did you always know you wanted to go into the justice department?"

He nods as his Adam's apple works, sliding up and down his throat. "I always wanted to make a difference."

"Oh?" I lean forward, pressing my elbow onto the center console. "Why's that?"

Sam flicks a quick look my way before leaning back into the leather seat.

He slides his hand down the thighs I was just admiring, widening his stance on the floorboard and shifting in the seat.

"My parents."

I wait for more. And wait. And wait.

"Good story," I say with an incredulous snort.

With a shake of his head, he begins to systematically pop the knuckles on his left hand, then right.

"We were wealthy growing up, but then it was all taken away. Bad investments with a guy running a Ponzi scheme. One day we had it all; the next we were nothing. Our friends turned their backs on us, we lost the house, the staff, everything. I was fine with it, wasn't that big of a deal. I was about to graduate high school, already had college locked up with scholarships."

"Academic or sports?" I cut in.

The corners of his lips twitch up. "Both."

"Which sport? You seem like you'd play...." Finger to my lips, I tap against the soft surface as I give him a pointed full-body scan. "Chess."

The men in the car chuckle while Sam's lips split in a full smile.

"Rowing."

"Oh. Didn't even know that was a sport."

"Really? That's surprising." He narrows his brows, causing a deep line to form between them.

"And why's that?"

He shoots a concerned look up front, his eyes meeting T's in the rearview mirror for half a second.

"I just assumed... since you and Benson were whatever you were...."

"What about Trey?"

"He rows. I didn't know who he was until I met him that first time, but I started to notice him at the club."

"The club?" I whisper.

"The Potomac Boat Blub. We've crossed paths a few times since then."

"Oh, right. That club," I say with a nervous laugh. Embarrassment at not knowing this side of Trey's life creeps up my neck, heating my cheeks. Sliding along the leather, I adjust in the seat to lean my forehead against the cool, dark-tinted window. "We digress. Your family. The Ponzi scheme."

"Like I said, I wasn't devastated." The heaviness in his tone has me rolling my forehead along the glass to see across the SUV. Gaze locked on the headrest in front of him, he slides his palms up and down his dark jeans. "But my dad was. Hated that we lost everything because of him."

"Sam, I didn't—"

"I was the one who found him." The pain in his voice cuts through my earlier embarrassment. Again he adjusts uncomfortably in his seat. "Nothing was the same after that." His longing-filled sigh envelops the silent SUV. Even the guys up front stay quiet, their normal banter dropped for the moment. "It was then that I knew I wanted to be in a role to take down people like the man who took my family from me. With the DOJ, I get to uncover the filth of America who think they're above the law." The thin muscle along his jaw twitches. "I don't want anyone else to go through what I did."

I swallow hard before taking a sip from my water bottle to soothe my dry throat. "Did they ever convict the guy?"

Sadness settles in the SUV like a heavy blanket. Sam shakes his head, his shoulders rounding slightly. "They had enough, but someone leaked the information before they could arrest him. He's been in the wind ever since. Every now and then, I try to track him down using my connections from work, but every time I get close, he vanishes."

"I'm sorry," I say, meaning it from the bottom of my heart. I reach across the center console and grip his hand with my own. "Truly. I can't imagine any of that. It makes sense why you're so insistent on making sure Kyle pays for his crimes, what he's trying to hide from everyone."

"It's an abuse of power on his part," Sam grits out, the fingers beneath mine tightening into a fist. I hold back a cringe of pain. "That's what we can get him on. He's using his role as president to manipulate laws, to allow federal land access, not doing due diligence in contracting drilling companies. He has to be stopped. No one, and I mean no one, should have that kind of power."

I nod in agreement, because I do agree 100 percent, but it won't be easy. Maybe he's too focused on tracking the information to see the other hurdles we'll have to get through. Getting the House and Senate to agree on moving forward with the impeachment trial is the biggest one. It's one thing to have the evidence, but for them to agree on anything will be a damn miracle.

Sweat builds beneath my palm where our hands are still connected. Clearing my throat, I slide my hand from his, pulling past the bit of resistance he gives by holding on tight.

"You realize the evidence is a small portion of what needs to happen for impeachment, right?" Careful to not attract attention, I drag the sweaty hand down my thigh to rid myself of the evidence of the touch. Thank goodness Trey rode in the lead SUV today or he'd have pitched Sam out of the moving vehicle by this point.

"One step at a time," Sam mumbles.

"I don't think that's the smartest plan, Sam. We need to start working on congressmen and senators. Planting the seed of what we're planning and getting them on board now."

"And what if they tell Birmingham?"

"He already knows you're looking into him. If anything, it'll confirm what he already thinks, that I'm an idiot and can't see that you're using me for my connections. We'll have a better idea of what he suspects after this fun getaway, you know."

He shoots a side glance my way. "I suppose."

Sighing, I press my fingers against my throbbing temples. The headaches aren't nearly as bad as they were days after the poisoning, but when they do come, it's unexpected and nearly debilitating.

I feel his stare even with my eyes sealed shut. Damn, this headache came on faster than the others. "Just think about it." The throbbing in my head intensifies, making each thought more painful than the last. "Let's talk about this later. T?"

"Two minutes."

Leaning back against the seat, I inhale deeply, focusing on the cool air filling my lungs and trying to get my muscles to relax.

"Have they run any more tests since the incident?" Sam asks, concern in his voice.

"No," T practically growls from the front seat. "She's as stubborn as a damn mule."

Good to know the guys are comfortable around Sam now, dropping the "ma'am" shit and back to talking to me like they always did when we were alone.

"But way prettier," I whisper. "If I have an opinion on the matter."

"No doubt, but it doesn't change that you're acting like an ass."

Even with the pain, his words make me smile.

"What if they're still poisoning her?" This time Sam's voice is closer, no doubt encroaching on my personal space once again. I urge my eyelids to open but can't find the energy to fight through the pain. "Ever thought of that, Randi?"

"We're monitoring everything she's eating, everything she's drinking. There's no way." The resolve in Champ's voice fades with each word, making the last one sound more like a question.

The men continue talking, but I tune them out, trying to keep their loud voices from splitting my sensitive ears. Maybe Sam is right and I should let the doctor run more tests. More because this is becoming a nuisance than anything. But it could also simply be the stress of this job taking its toll in a more physical way. At least that's what WebMD said. It's either the stress or I'm dying and should seek immediate medical attention.

Eh, those websites are always a bit dramatic, probably written by someone like me. It could be the common cold or Ebola.

Yet I search the stupid site time and time again, thinking their prediction will make more sense or at the very least offer a smaller lethal gap in diagnosis.

"Death would really suck," I whisper.

At some point while I'm preoccupied with simply surviving this migraine, we arrive at our destination. The SUV pulls to a slow stop, the seat belt tugging slightly to keep me from falling forward. Crips fall air brushes my hair across my face as the door swings open. Slowly opening my eyes despite the pain, I focus on the dark mass now blocking out the sun.

"Another headache?" Trey's familiar deep voice soothes the anxiety of being helpless these headaches invoke.

T answers for me. "Yeah. This one seemed to come on quicker than the others."

"What the hell is going on with you, Mess?" he whispers as he dips into the cab, no doubt readying to scoop me into his arms and carry me into the cabin.

Nope, not going to happen.

"Stop. I can walk," I grit out as another burst of pain flares behind my eyes. "I can't let you carry me in there. Kyle cannot see me weak or he'll take full advantage."

Grinding my back teeth, I scoot to the edge of the seat and grip the door handle with a white-knuckled grip. Even with the overcast day, the peeking sun's brightness assaults my eyes. Instinctively I squint to minimize the damage. Trey grumbles something as I step out onto the smooth concrete.

Hard plastic slides along my temples before settling along the bridge of my nose, casting darkness over my vision. I let out a sigh of relief and adjust the sunglasses to keep the heavy frames from slipping down the bridge of my nose.

"Thank you." I tilt my head left and then right, looking at all the different angles through the expensive sunglasses the agents are required to wear as part of their uniform. "Wow. No wonder they seem attached to your face at all times. Can we order me a pair?"

With a grunt of what seems to be agreement, Trey places a hand against my lower back, guiding me toward the massive set of wooden doors with ornate iron work decorating the front.

Did I say cabin? I retract the earlier statement and now would like to add to the record that we've arrived at the estate. I should've known *the* Camp David would be a massive compound.

Both doors swing open. Welcoming smells and the murmur of happy chatter greet us as we step over the threshold into the gilded cage. At my side, Sam slips his hand into mine, giving my cold fingers a slight squeeze for reassurance.

The murmuring silences as my entourage and I stride into the large living room. A few women openly roll their eyes my way and then turn back to their conversation partners, dismissing me outright.

Palpable anger attracts my attention to the roaring fireplace. My stomach tightens at the pure hate seeping through Mr. Hindle's hard stare. Beside him, a lovely woman, who I recognize from the research I did last year on his family, holds his bicep, struggling to draw his notice back to her. Of course he's here.

Wait a minute.

If he was a big campaign donor, then maybe....

I make a mental note to think harder on that when my brain doesn't feel like an ice pick is piercing through it with every thought.

A man stands from the overstuffed couch and turns to face me. Todd's smile is strained as he approaches. His weak hand extends between us, slightly shaking. Which is fine because mine is too, considering all my energy is channeled into my knees not buckling under my weight.

Revulsion slides down my spine, churning my stomach as his moist palm slides into my own and gives it a squeeze that wouldn't even crack an egg.

Ugh. Weak handshake. Who chose this guy for our secretary of state again?

Kyle moves into view, pausing beside Todd, whose face is overly tight like his Botox is just now kicking in full force. His lower lip appears slightly poutier too.

"Good to have you here, Madam VP," Kyle says. "Pierce, welcome to Camp David."

"We didn't really have a choice, now did we, Mr. President," I say just as lackluster as his greeting was. We both know this is all for show. There are more hate-filled forced encounters between us than pleasantries at this point. "Todd, good to see you. Haven't seen you since that night at the Benson estate. You know, the one where we celebrated that horrible bill failing in the Senate."

"Take those damn glasses off," Kyle hisses as he reaches out and swipes them off my face. I blanch at the bright overhead lights but hold back from showing any other reaction. "Of course you're hungover." *Sure, we'll go with that, not dying from the inside out.* "The apple isn't falling far from the white trash tree, is it?"

Sam grumbles something of discontent as Trey tightens the hand still at my back into a fist. Todd just tucks his chin to his chest, avoiding the confrontation altogether. I open my mouth, readying to tell him to fuck off and starting to believe my failing health is his doing, when a familiar face catches my attention.

My jaw drops, the pain in my head forgotten, overtaken by pure disbelief.

I tilt my head one way and then the other, my hair shifting from side to side as I try different angles. Confusion sets in as those innocent blue eyes continue to stare right back into mine from across the room.

"Taeler?"

14

TREY

Whether from the headache or the startling bombshell of seeing her only daughter here surrounded by her enemies, Randi's first step toward the giddy Taeler falters, almost taking her to the floor.

Sam forces his hand between mine and her back, taking over the role of supporting boyfriend. The role I should be playing, not him. Anger hardens my resolve to get his hands off her, completely forgetting our surroundings. Nothing else matters, just removing that hairy fucking hand pressing against the small of her delicate back, way too close to the curve of her ass.

"Secure the room," T says loudly beside me, almost like he's yelling directly in my ear. Who knows, maybe he can see the murderous glint in my eyes as I plot Sam's demise. "Playboy." I don't break my focus from the two moving across the room with Todd and Birmingham close on their heels. "Do not let them get too close. Stay glued to her fucking side. Watch what she eats, what she drinks. Hell, watch the air she breathes."

I nod, already moving forward.

"Mom," Taeler exclaims, clapping her hands together, having no idea the egregious amount of stress she's added by being here in the grasps of those who want her mother to fail. "You're finally here. I was beginning to wonder when you'd show up. Who's this?" Her light brows furrow at their joined hands, confusion written over her tiny features, which are nearly identical to her mother's. Tilting her chin up, she searches the room. Her gaze slides over me only to halt and zero in. "Hey, Trouble."

"What are you doing here, Taeler?" Fear, pain, and anger bleed through Randi's quivering voice. She rubs a hand down her daughter's arm in long, comforting strokes.

Once again, confusion takes over Taeler's innocent face.

Fuck, she doesn't need to be anywhere near here.

I stiffen as movement behind Taeler catches my attention.

Gremlin.

A portion of the nearly debilitating tension lessens from my shoulders. At least her protection team is here and has her security covered.

"He said you'd be surprised."

Randi's mouth opens and shuts twice before she shakes her head and shoots a death glare at Kyle, who simply smiles wider—well, as wide as his plastic face will allow him nowadays—and folds his arms across his chest

"I thought you'd like getting to spend the holiday with your beautiful daughter, Randi. It's a shame this is the first time we're *all* getting to meet her. Isn't that right, Shawn?"

On cue, Whit materializes next to Birmingham, sporting a creepy, sinister tight-lipped smile.

Without responding, Randi grips Taeler's wrist, pulling her close as she steps between her daughter and the two men. Not liking the small distance between Randi and Birmingham, I step closer, bumping the fool, Todd, slightly out of the way to place me within arm's length of the two women.

One of the guys chirps through the earbud hidden inside my right ear. *"Hallway to your right, Benson. Second door on your left."*

Forgoing any niceties, I shoulder past Kyle, making him knock into Shawn. Both men grumble their displeasure, not that I care.

"This way," I say under my breath as I spread both arms wide, herding Randi and Taeler toward the hallway indicated by my teammate. At the second door on the left, I pause, turn the knob, and step inside for a quick sweep. Walsh nods as we enter, immediately leaving once the two women are secure inside with me as the sole agent in the room.

The door clicks closed. Turning on my heel, I scan each corner of the formal entertaining room for video surveillance and listening devices.

"What are you doing here?" The fear in Randi's voice slices into my heart. I wince like her pain is my own. "What the actual fuck are you doing here, Taeler?"

"Don't yell at me," Taeler shouts back. "It was supposed to be a fun surprise since I haven't seen you in months, Mom. *Months.*" Her young voice trembles. Out of the corner of my eye, I watch her wrap both arms around her waist in a defensive move.

Not that Randi notices. Oh no, she's too busy scowling at her daughter to realize she's being insensitive to the situation. No doubt her normal sensors to Taeler's emotions have been overwhelmed by the fear for her only daughter.

"Randi," I mutter and nod to Taeler, widening my eyes.

"Stay out of this, Trouble," she snaps. Gripping her head, she pushes both palms against either side. "Can someone get me an Excedrin?"

"On it," I respond and mutter her request into the sleeve of my jacket.

"Okay, let me ask this a different way. *Who* said it would be a surprise? Who invited you here?" Randi asks, just as tense as before but with less of the fury.

"President Birmingham."

"What! Taeler, I've told you what a twatwaffle he is!" Raising her hands in the air, Randi then drops both to the top of her head and takes a deep breath. "How did he even reach out to you to extend the invite?"

With an exaggerated groan, Taeler falls into one of the ten stiff leather armchairs scattered around the room. "Someone stopped by the dorm to tell me."

"What?" Randi and I both shout.

Taeler rolls her eyes, a move I've seen time and time again from her mother. "It was fine. Chad and the guys checked out his story and credentials. They even called someone to verify everything was legit. He was some kind of aide for the president, I guess. Anyways," she draws out the last syllable like the child she is, "the guy said the president wanted to surprise you. Said you've been working too hard lately and having me up here for Thanksgiving would ease some of your worry. And he's not as bad as you've made him out to be, Mom. He's been great since I arrived, even planned out the whole trip for me and the guys."

"What was his name?" I demand, moving amongst the chairs until I'm hovering over the one she's sunk down into.

Taeler shrugs, another of her mom's favorite moves.

"Fine. What did he look like, Taeler?" I try and fail to keep the frustration from my tone.

"I don't remember. Ask Chad."

"Who?" Randi snarls. "Who is this person you keep talking about?"

"Grem. Damn, Mom."

"Why did you say yes, Taeler? Ever heard the term 'stranger danger,' or did I totally fuck up that part of my parental responsibilities in teaching you not to talk to strange men? Especially ones who invite you to cabins in the woods. Have you ever seen a horror movie? The blondes die first."

Taeler flicks an annoyed look my way. "Still dramatic as ever, I see." I'd laugh if the situation weren't what it is. "And I said yes because I wanted to see you, and Mom, it's fucking—"

"Don't fucking cuss, damnit."

Taeler's eyes roll to the ceiling. This time I can't stop my smile at the familiar move. "*Anyway*, it's Camp David. I wasn't going to miss this opportunity. Plus, Chad checked the guy out. So here I am with you yelling at me for trying to do something nice for you."

"Taeler." Randi groans. "You have no idea what you've stepped into." Massaging her temples, she sways a little on her feet, catching herself before she topples over.

For the first time since we arrived, Taeler seems to take in her mom. Really see her. The annoyance drains from her features, leaving her blue eyes tight with worry. "You okay, Mom?"

Over the earpiece, someone states they're coming in just as a light knock sounds, halting Randi from responding. Champ strides in, scanning the room as he moves toward Randi.

With a smile of relief, she takes the pill from his outstretched hand and the glass of water from the other. She wastes no time downing the medicine and the entire contents of the full pint glass.

"Are you sick?" The leather groans as Taeler pushes to a standing position. Her steps are hesitant as she closes the distance between her and her mother. "You look terrible, Mom."

"Thanks," Randi rasps. "I love that I get to see you, Tae. I really am so, *so* happy to see you." With that, she reaches out and pulls Taeler in for a tight hug. Through her daughter's blonde hair, Randi's focus falls on me, and she mouths, "Sorry."

"You smell funny," I hear Taeler say into her mom's hair.

Randi chuckles, the laugh sounding forced. "So I look like crap and I smell. Thanks, Taeler. So glad you could come. Now it's time for you to go back to Austin."

"I'm not leaving." Hands on her mom's shoulders, she pulls back at arm's length. "Something's going on with you that I need to know about, and I miss you. So there are two great reasons for me to stay through the weekend as planned."

"The weekend?" Randi and I both say at the same time. We share a concerned glance.

Randi shakes her head. "These people are terrible human beings, Tae. I don't want you anywhere near them. Hell, Texas might not be far enough away from their games. It's why I've never invited you to visit me in DC. You're my main priority. I need you safe. And now you're here, brought here by my manipulative asshat of a boss, and I'm pretty sure he did it to use it against me in some way."

Realization of the situation seems to settle over Taeler. Swiping the hair behind her ear over and over, almost like a nervous twitch, she shifts on her feet. "How would he be able to do that?"

"To prove that he can get to you without her, or us, knowing." The two women turn to face me, worry etched across both their faces almost identically. "He wants to prove he can hurt Randi without laying a hand directly on her. He's tried twice—" Randi slicing her hand across her throat freezes the next words in my throat. "He's a brilliant motherfucker, I'll give him that."

"I need to get back out there and schmooze those jackasses. I can't let them know how much their plan affected me." Randi groans, her concerned gaze flipping between me and Taeler. "Trey, would you stay with her?"

"I don't need a fucking babysitter."

"Watch your fucking language, Tae." With an eye roll that makes my head hurt, she turns back to me. "Please. I need to know someone is with her at all times."

"She has her own team, Randi. You need someone with *you* at all times too." Lifting the cuff of my sleeve to my lips, I order Grem into the room. After several tense moments, the heavy wooden door swings open, allowing Grem to march through. Neither Randi nor I miss the way Taeler's face lights up when she sees him.

I hide my knowing smirk behind the fist at my mouth covering a fake cough.

"We need at least two men with Taeler at all times while she's here," I order. Grem responds with a firm nod, lifting his own sleeve to his lips.

"And keep that asshole Shawn and cuntcake Kyle away from my daughter," Randi adds. "If they so much as get within five feet of her, I want you to pick her up and physically remove her from the room. Hell, from the damn state."

"Understood."

Something irks in the back of my mind as I take in our old team member. It hasn't been that long since he volunteered to stay in Austin and lead Taeler's security team, so this awkwardness shouldn't be between us, or him and Randi. There's no lightness in his presence like there used to be. His back is ramrod straight, and not once has he looked at Taeler or Randi since he entered the room.

An uncomfortable silence settles around the room, inching up my awareness to the fact that something is off with him. Sliding my phone from the pocket of my slacks, I type out a quick text to Tank before slipping it back inside.

"Okay, well, I have to go out there and play nice," Randi says, drawing out each word while she regards Taeler and Grem.

"I'm right behind you."

Randi pulls Taeler close, whispering something that makes the girl groan. At the door, I motion for her to step through first, conscious of the other agent stationed on the other side. Halfway back down the hallway, the sounds of the gathered politicians and spouses reaching my ears, Randi slows her steps.

"I think you're right about Kyle, about why he brought Taeler here. And if that's the case, he's crossed a line. He and Shawn and all the other pompous pricks in DC can mess with me all they want, but do not mess with my daughter." A blazing fire flares behind her eyes. "Those two will regret the day they forced my hand."

Something resembling pride swells in my chest at the conviction in her words. A bit mixed with fear for the havoc she's about to rain down, yes, but pride nonetheless. Last time she had this conviction, she was recovering in that hospital bed, and it was about how they've treated her and pushed her around. Now that they've fucked up and messed with her daughter, a new type of resolve has chimed through her tone. This time, without a doubt in my mind, she *will* find a way to make those two pay.

And honestly, I can't fucking wait to see it. Yes, it'll put her life in more danger, and that alone nearly scares me enough to ask her to pull back, but she's changing, and I don't want to stop the woman who's evolving right before my eyes. She's tougher than she was even a couple months ago. She's always been resilient, but now she's... edgy. Sharp as a knife and becoming deadly in her own right.

Which—and this might make me a demented freak—is sexy as hell.

Not that I needed another reason to be turned on by her at every turn. At this rate, my perpetual boner might be the reason for my death. Blood loss due to it all being funneled to my dick is a thing, right?

An exhausted groan rattles in the back of my throat as I sink down into the ugly-ass green armchair across from Tank. Beer in hand, I put it to my lips as I lean back, desperate to get comfortable as quickly as possible. I'm past exhausted. We all are. Even Tank, whose eyes are peacefully closed, hands folded neatly in front of him. But my best friend isn't fooling me. He's awake and alert to everything going on around him, even if he appears asleep.

With a mischievous smirk, I reach behind me, gripping the coarse pillow stuffed between the couch cushions and my back. With a hard tug, I pull it loose and launch it across the coffee table straight at my friend's face. It whirls through the air, its trajectory exactly where I aimed.

Half a second before the stuffed square can whack into his relaxed face, he snatches it midair. He tosses it a few times, like he's judging the weight, before launching it back across the room with twice as much force behind it.

"Hey," I complain while dodging the projectile meant to decapitate me. "Mine was thrown with love."

Tank huffs out a laugh, his chest rising and falling with a deep inhale. "Little shit." Reaching back, I snatch the pillow off the floor and secure it behind my lower back once again. "Sarah and I don't need kids. We have you."

My laugh reverberates inside the longneck bottle at my lips. After a long pull, I rest the glass bottom on top of my knee, spinning it as I focus on the sweating brown bottle.

"We didn't talk about my text earlier," I mutter under my breath so no one else in the house can hear.

A loud sound comes from the direction of the kitchen, the guys' laughter filling the small living room. I have to hand it to whoever planned this portion of Camp David. Having a separate house for the off-duty agents was brilliant and very much needed. Here we get to relax and let loose a little from the stress of the day while the other team works their protection shift. The few hallways are lined with rooms filled with the basics: single bed, nightstand, gun safes, and a few hangers in the closet for our suits. It's no Ritz, but it's perfect for working getaways.

The only thing this place is missing is a hot tub to ease my aching muscles and seep the stress from my neck and shoulders.

Tank peeks one lid open. "We didn't."

"Just saying it was off. Not sure what that means, but just... off."

He runs a palm across the thick scruff that's sprouted along his cheek since this morning. "Could it be the girl? That relationship?"

I roll the empty bottle between my hands, my gaze unfocused as I replay every movement, every word from earlier.

"No, I don't think so."

"You'd know what to look for, I guess."

I nod, smirking. "Sure would. I, out of anyone, would know the signs. No, it was something else. He wouldn't even look at Randi. Hell, he barely glanced at me." I hush my tone and lean forward. Tank mimics the movement, resting his elbows on his tree trunk like thighs. "Before he left, we were solid, joking around with her, so he *knows* she's not someone we have to be on guard around. I don't know, Tank. I don't like it."

For several seconds, he just stares at the coffee table, foot restlessly bouncing against the carpet. "He was there when you beat the hell out of that piece of shit in Boone."

I nod.

"But he's not on Randi's security team anymore." He shakes his head like he's trying to clear the fog. "Why would he offer up going to Austin if he was your mom's informant?"

That's the part I can't figure out either. I've racked my brain since the strange encounter earlier today and still none of the pieces fit together.

"Unless that wasn't part of the original plan and he did it in spite of being my mother's eyes and ears on the team. But that wouldn't explain how

Randi's comings and goings with Sam early on were reported back to Kyle. None of this makes sense."

"Agreed. At this point, I'm wondering if your mom was just being a dick and there isn't an inside person, she just found out about the Texas incident by asking around."

"Wouldn't put it past her."

"I'm done, Playboy. This day has maxed me the hell out." His knees protest, cracking and popping as he stands. A pain-filled grimace pulls across his face. Those few years playing professional football still haunt his body. I'm not sure there's a day he isn't in pain. It would be manageable if he could get some relief, but with the drug tests and tight medication requirements for the secret service, he can't take anything that helps. Maybe once Randi is president, we can convince her to approve medical pot to be on our permitted drug list—though not while on duty, of course. Then he could get a full night's sleep without waking up in pain.

"Same. I'm beat," I say on a yawn while stretching my arms high overhead.

I follow behind Tank as we make our way down the hall toward our rooms.

"Hey, Benson?"

My hand rests on the doorknob. "Yeah."

"Keep it in your pants while we're here, for fuck's sake."

I bark out a laugh and shove the door open. "Where's the fun in that, big buddy?"

The door swings closed behind me. Heel to the stained wood, I kick it the rest of the way, cutting off Tank's muttered curses. I smile to myself as I work the knot of my tie loose.

Sometimes riling him up like old times is just what I need.

15

RANDI

I'm a creeper.

It is not normal for a mid-thirties—okay, late thirties—mother to stare at her older daughter while she sleeps. But I can't help it. First of all, she's beautiful, a trait she got from me—obviously. And second, she's actually here, with me, when I least expected it but needed her the most. With the stress of the job, I haven't had a chance to sit and think, to realize how badly I miss having Taeler close. Sure, I was terrified when I caught her bright blue eyes from across the room when we first arrived. But now that I know she's safe and securely tucked in bed beside me, I'm thankful she's here.

There are a few different reasons why I'm happy she's here, but the most prominent is that she's the one lying beside me in this plush king-size bed, not Sam. I'll admit the thought of sleeping arrangements for this overnight stay at Camp David never crossed my mind. But with Tae here, I was able to ask Sam to swap rooms with her, the one right next door to this one, without it being awkward.

I'm sure the change in plans pissed Kyle off. Why he's so eager to push me and Sam together, I haven't figured out yet. A nagging thought in the back of my mind tells me it has to do with his longtime running beef with Trey and nothing to do with me and Sam. Everyone can see it kills Trey when Sam and I are together, which makes Kyle want it to happen as often as possible. That's the most likely scenario I've come up with, at least.

What T and Trey think, who knows. Since the poisoning, they've kept their cards close to their chests. Which is fine, since I've got my own issues to handle at this point in my term. Eleven months in and I'm barely keeping my nose above water. But I haven't drowned yet. Nor will I.

I'll make it through all this if it takes everything I have.

"Mom, you're being weird... again," Taeler mumbles, licking her dry lips without opening her eyes.

With a content sigh, I rake my fingers through her blonde hair, relishing in the way it slides against my skin and how it automatically calms my racing thoughts.

"I've missed you."

"We covered that in detail two hours ago around several bowls of ice cream, remember?"

I snort and roll to rest my head back on the feather-stuffed pillow, focusing on the ceiling. "Yes, I remember hearing way too many details about you and Gremlin."

"His name is Chad, Mom. But now that you mention it, you know what we didn't cover?"

The cream satin pillowcase slides beneath my hair as I roll my head to face her heavy-lidded open eyes.

"What's that?"

"The new guy, Sam. You two were acting like a couple earlier, but the past month or so, you've only mentioned him as a work colleague, never, like, a boyfriend."

"I don't remember telling you anything about him," I say, searching her face, trying to recall our phone conversations.

Taeler smiles. "Mom, you tell me everything, which is why when I heard you introducing Sam as your boyfriend to those old guys who are here with us, I was surprised."

"But I didn't mention why, right?" *Please tell me I haven't spilled national security secrets to my daughter.* Maybe the lasting effects of the poisoning are affecting me more than I realized.

"Nope, just that you two were working together. So tell me, why is this Sam guy in the picture and Trouble out?" I open my mouth to explain but snap it shut when she continues talking. "I saw the way you and Trouble acted in Austin. It wasn't just a fling. Why are you ignoring what you have with him for this new guy?" Black-tipped fingers slide under her cheek, propping her head up slightly. "Don't get me wrong, he's all kinds of hot, but...."

"But what?" I encourage. Now I'm curious what she sees. I agree with her, of course, but he's no Trey.

"He's not your match. Hot is hot, but compatibility beyond the attraction? I don't see it. I don't see you... happy."

"That could be a side effect of almost dying several weeks ago."

"I still can't believe you didn't let me come visit after that. When Trouble called to tell me what was going on, I flipped. I still don't know how he talked me out of flying to DC." I smile knowing Trey has that way about him, able to talk his way into or out of anything. "I still have no idea how you kept the real cause out of the media. Whoever believes you were just sick on that jogging trail is an idiot for trusting something just because it's on the news."

"Yeah, my media team is fantastic. I have no idea how they do it, but they've kept all the close calls out of the news. Thank goodness. And yes, I understand you were scared, kind of like me being scared shitless when I first saw you today. You don't belong here, Tae. These men are ruthless. I want you as far off their radar as possible. They're dangerous, and as much as I'd like to think I can protect you from everything, I can't from these men. They're power personified, and it messes with their morals, if they had any to start with. You're not safe."

"Come on, Mom," she grumbles into the pillow. "Chad is here, and the other guys on my security detail. You're here. You're whole first and second team of agents are here. What could happen?"

Faster than a west Texas rattlesnake, I snap my palm over her lips. "Don't say that," I cry. "That's exactly how every horror movie or thriller starts, with someone thinking they can't be touched. Then *bam*, they're dead." I widen my eyes and scan the room. "What if they're listening?"

"You're a freak of nature sometimes, Mom," she mumbles as she pulls her face away from my palm. "Stop avoiding my question. What's with this Sam guy?"

The wafting cool air from the overhead fan brushes over the skin of my exposed arm, causing goose bumps. I slide it back under the covers, tucking cold fingers between my flannel-covered thighs to warm them up.

"He's more than a friend." *Shit, how do I explain this without letting all my secrets out of the bag?* "It started as a work thing, and then we just hit it off, I guess."

"Which is why you begged him to switch sleeping spots with me." The sheets inch toward Taeler as she rolls onto her back, stealing most of the covers. "I don't buy it. Something else is going on that you're not telling me."

"He's a good guy," I say a bit defensively. Not sure why. "He was at Harvard around the same time as me, did I mention that?"

"Is he one of the assholes who made your life miserable?"

"Nope," I grumble. "That was just Kyle and his merry little entourage of dickheads."

A quiet giggle bubbles from her chest, making the bed tremble.

"Does he make you happy?" Her tone is thoughtful as she rotates her face to search my own. "It doesn't seem like it. You look stressed, Mom. And sick. I'm not sure what's going on, but are you sure all this is worth it?"

"All what exactly?"

"This role. Look at what it's doing to you. Doing to us. I haven't seen you more than a couple times since the campaign started. You're sick, you're exhausted, and now you're hooking up with a guy just because he can somehow help your political career."

"I never said that," I chastise.

"You didn't have to," she says just as disapprovingly. "I see it, Mom, and if I do, then you better believe *everyone* else does too. There's no passion between you, no chemistry. No one can fake the real deal. It's 100 percent obvious that you two aren't a real couple. Hell, it's clear you two haven't even had sex."

"Taeler Lynn!" I whisper-shout while laughing. "How would you know?"

"How would you not?" Taeler asks, shaking her head. "Your touches are stiff, planned almost. There's no comfort or ease between you two. And you're lacking that fire that's palpable to everyone around you when you're together. *That* is unmistakably missing with you and hottie Sam."

"It's foolish, that's what it is." Thumbnail between my teeth, I think over her words. "That's just the honeymoon phase anyway. Everyone grows out of that eventually."

"Maybe? I don't know, not a whole lot of experience. Let me ask you this, Mom, without you getting mad at me."

"Not off to a great start, but go ahead."

"Are you subconsciously pushing Trouble away because you don't want him to get too close?"

Her words smack me like a palm to the cheek. Stunned into silence, all I can do is lie here, my mouth opening and closing like a gulping fish. The thin chain of the ceiling fan tinks against the glass fixture, offering the only noise in the uncomfortable silence.

"I'm only saying that because you two seemed to have it. And the way you talked about him those nights when we could actually catch up... it was more than your words. It was in the lightness of your voice, the happiness that seeped from you all the way to me in Austin."

"Why would I push him away?" I ask the ceiling.

"Because anyone you've ever depended on let you down."

Huh.

"Because you've always done things on your own, and you don't want to owe anyone anything."

That's true. I went against my better judgment with Kyle, and look where that landed me. I thought turning the tables on him and making him choose me as his running mate would put us on equal footing, that I wouldn't owe him anything. What a cluster that's turned out to be. Maybe that's also why I'm hesitant to trust Vlad, the Russian president.

"All I'm saying is trust him, Mom."

She doesn't know the real reason I'm pushing Trey away. But could what she's saying somehow be festering in the back of my subconscious, altering my decisions and choosing my path for me, and that's why I keep taking the option that pushes us apart rather than together?

Growing up near the poverty line was difficult. So yeah, I've done a lot on my own because, well, someone had to. I've fought for everything I've had and always been one step behind. Maybe this whole time, I've just been waiting for Trey to disappoint me or leave or just say he's done because that's my life.

"When did you become so smart?" I mumble with a smile, rolling my head along the soft pillowcase to face her.

"Always have been. Got it from Dad, obviously."

That's it.

Reaching across the bed, I dig my fingers into her ribs, searching for her ticklish spot. Taeler lets out a shriek as she attempts to wiggle away from my prodding fingers.

"Get off me," she screams while sucking in air between laughing fits.

"Never," I say in a deep, evil voice.

She shrieks again, swatting at my arms and tangling herself tighter in the quilts and sheets.

A whoosh of chilled air bursts through the room as the door swings open. One of the beta team agents rushes inside, gun in hand, eyes furiously scanning the room.

Taeler and I both pause, eyes blinking at the unexpected visitor.

"Can I help you?" I ask, trying like hell to remember the guy's name.

"What's going on in here?" Finally his intense gaze lands on me as he slowly holsters his gun. "I heard a scream."

"Just a tickle fight. We're cool." I shoot him a thumbs-up. When that doesn't ease the concern from his harsh features, I drag the other hand out of the covers to make it a double.

Yep, I'm a moron. It's cool. I'm actually starting to embrace it.

What's the phrase? If you can't beat the weirdness, just go with it?

I swear I saw that cross-stitched on a pillow, or maybe it was in the window at Hot Topic years ago. Either way, the phrase rings true.

Another body steps into the room behind the agent. Taeler sits upright beside me, quilts held close to her chest as Sam steps around the agent, moving closer to the bed.

Of course he's shirtless.

Not that I'm complaining. At all.

Low-rise gray sweatpants hang on his hips in that seductive way that begs you to tug them down to discover the bulge beneath. Because yes, there is a bulge. A significant one.

Trailing my gaze up from the spot my attention should not be on, I follow the happy trail north over a muscular stomach and defined chest. A smirk plays at his full lips.

"Randi. Taeler."

"Sam," Taeler says with a bite to her tone I've never heard before.

His features tighten, leaving little doubt that he didn't pick up on it too. What the hell is her problem? Earlier she was acting just fine around him; now he's getting the cold shoulder.

"Welcome to the party," I say, gesturing to Taeler and the uncomfortable-looking agent still standing by the door. "Did you bring snacks?"

Sam shakes his head and smiles. "No, sorry. I heard a commotion and thought I'd come check on you."

"Without a shirt," Taeler asks, crossing her arms over her chest.

"It's how I sleep," Sam responds, not breaking the sudden stare-off the two started.

"We're fine, just goofing around. You can leave now."

"Taeler," I chastise with a grimace. "Stop being so damn rude."

Sam holds up both hands in surrender. "Don't worry about it, Randi. I'm leaving. Glad it was nothing." Halfway out the door, he pauses and turns. His piercing green eyes dart from me to Taeler and back again. "Let's talk in the morning, Randi, go over strategy."

"Strategy. Yeah, right," Taeler says under her breath. With a dismissive wave, she snuggles back into the covers, her back to me.

"Okay, yeah," I say more like a whisper, focusing on Taeler's back. "Kyle wants to meet with me at some point too, so best we meet before that."

"Night."

I mutter a similar goodbye, still staring at Taeler. After the door clicks closed behind the retreating agent, I give her shoulder a hard shove to gain her attention.

"What was that about?" I hiss.

The bed doesn't jolt, doesn't wiggle as she stays facing the wall. "I've chosen my side."

"What the hell does that even mean?" The entire bedframe shakes as I flop onto my back and begin to massage my temples.

"It means I'm Team Trouble."

"Seriously?"

"Seriously. That man wants you, Mom." Finally the bed shifts under her weight as she rolls to face me. "What guy walks into a woman's room looking like that if he didn't?" I open my mouth to defend him when she holds up a hand, stopping me. "Now I'm going to bed."

"Team Trouble," I grumble over the rustling of the sheets and quilts as I snuggle deeper. The thick duvet between my curled fingers, I draw it up close to my chin and stare at the slightly outdated wallpaper. "There are no teams," I whisper against the soft fabric.

"Oh, there are teams, Mom." *How the hell did she hear that?* "And if you haven't chosen a side, then shit's about to get real messy."

"Language," I hiss over my shoulder. "And it's not like that."

"Okay," she replies, her tone letting me know she clearly thinks I'm an idiot.

"It's not. It's business, not personal."

"Sometimes I worry about you," she says with an annoyed sigh. "Good night, Mom."

I pat her tiny heinie under the mountain of covers and close my eyes ready to beg sleep to come.

As the long "to do" list, "not to do" list, and "holy hell, why haven't you done this yet" list flip through my overactive mind I can't help but wonder if Taeler is right.

If I had to choose right here, right now, whose team would I be on?

It's the easiest answer I've ever had to give.

Trey. One hundred percent Trey.

So if that's my answer, then why aren't I with him? Why am I letting this stupid fake game with Kyle ruin the one good part of my overworked life?

Or did I leave one "team" out of the equation?

Maybe I'm not Team Trouble or Team Sam.

Maybe I'm Team Randi.

And you know what? For the first time in my life, I'm okay with that.

16

RANDI

The black SUV speeds down the drive, growing smaller and smaller with each passing second until it vanishes below the horizon. Fingers against my lips, I huff hot, humid air into my frozen hands, desperate to keep frostbite at bay. Even though the SUV is long gone, here I stand in the early morning frigid air, wishing I could've had one more day with Taeler.

"You okay?"

I turn toward the deep voice, my hair whipping across my face. Reaching up, I tuck the few dark locks behind my ear and hold on to the strands to keep them in place.

I quickly scan Sam, who stands just inside the large double doors, hands tucked into the pockets of his slacks. He looks good again. Of course he does. That's him. But do I feel that pull, the fire Taeler spoke of last night? Yes, I'd love to see him naked, but do I want to be naked with him?

Is that an odd question to ask?

"Not sure," I say honestly, somehow answering both my internal ramblings and Sam's actual question. Does that mean I get a triple-point score like in Scrabble? "I didn't want her to leave, but I was desperate for her to go."

"Conflicting," he says with a small smile.

"Very."

"Seems to be your life these days."

I meet his knowing gaze and dip my chin in acknowledgment. "You have no idea."

"You wear your emotions on your sleeve, Randi. It's not that hard to figure out."

"Not the first time or the last, I suppose."

"No wonder you never went the corporate or defense attorney route after school."

I snort. "That among other things."

"Yet you went the political path. Strange, if you ask me."

The few agents and Sam follow me as I move through the front doors. Inside the house, dry warm air warps around my chilled body, slowly thawing my fingers and toes.

"We all do what we have to do," I say with a shrug. "I've always wanted to help people, and what better way to do that than at a large scale. I have billions at my disposal, yet you say this role is a strange path."

He trails me to the roaring gas fireplace. The heat stings my cold hands, but that's easier to ignore than his pulsing heat as he stands too close, also gazing into the flickering flames.

"Most people think what they see is what they get with me," I say, not glancing away, allowing the dancing orange and red to pull me into a near hypnotic state. "In some ways, I guess that's true, but they don't know what drives me, what made me do all this. What makes me put up with all this."

"And what's that?" he asks. The weight of his stare urges me to turn. Instead, I turn my cold ass to the fire.

"Her," I say with a nod toward the front doors. "Them. Everyone who's been forgotten by the people in this town. I'm their voice, and I won't let anyone take that from me, from them, now that I'm here. You said you wanted to strategize." A glance around shows us alone in the grand living room. "Let's do it."

"Not here," Sam says, bending down to whisper into my hair. "Walk with me."

I shoot him an incredulous look before waving a hand down my black leggings, Uggs, and sweatshirt. "I'm not prepared for a hike."

"I said a walk."

"In the fucking cold? I don't think so."

"It'll be fun," he says with a chuckle, amusement glittering in his green eyes.

"For snowmen and Eskimos maybe, but not this girl."

"It's fifty degrees," he says, now all-out laughing at me.

"Exactly. It could start snowing any minute."

"You're ridiculous." He steps closer, wrapping an arm around my waist and tugging me close. "What is it with you?" he mutters. "Why can't I stay away?"

Lowering my shoulder, I wiggle out of his embrace, putting some distance between us.

Ah, hell, was Taeler right? Does Sam want more than a business relationship?

"I'm Team Randi," I say like he should know what the hell that means.

One dark brow rises up his forehead while he shakes his head. "You're a strange one, Randi Sawyer."

"Not the first or last to make that observation, my friend," I grumble. Wrapping my arms around my waist, I look out the floor-to-ceiling windows. The sun sparkles through the glass, making the day seem beautiful and warm out. "I'll go get my jacket. Then we talk. There's a lot we need to cover."

I don't wait for his response. As quickly as my rubber soles can carry me, I hustle out of the room. At the corner, I dip out of sight and lean against the hall wall.

"Give me a second," I beg to the agent hovering too close for me to think straight. He doesn't move. "Please. I won't move from this spot."

With a reluctant grunt, he steps around the corner, giving me some semblance of privacy.

A deep breath fills my lungs, tightening my chest. I hold it for three seconds before slowly letting it loose through my nose.

When did my life become one big game of political Twister?

Hand on fixing the bill.

Foot on setting up your love with another woman for political gain.

Head on creating a fake relationship with a guy you're physically attracted to, all while trying to not be attracted to him because you're in love with someone else.

Other hand on treason and trying to take down the president because he's a narcissistic twit.

Ass on the fucking ground because you're out.

I cringe and scan the long hall. If I'm out, that could be detrimental not only to the part of life I enjoy the most—living—but the American people as well. Without me, Shawn would step up to the plate as the VP. That could trigger the end of the world.

Dramatic, yes, but that doesn't make it any less of a possibility.

The wall pops behind my back as I push off with my shoulder to stand tall. Nope, this clusterfuck is one I've created and one I'll see through.

"Team Randi," I whisper to myself and raise my fist high.

"Trailer."

Ah, fuck.

Maybe if I don't acknowledge his presence, he won't notice me. Acting like the gleaming hardwood floor is the most intriguing thing I've ever seen, I shuffle down the hall, desperate to get away from evil personified. The last thing I need on my plate is to be dead. That would really hinder my "save the world" plans.

A viselike grip wraps around my upper arm and yanks me to a halt. Every muscle contracts and icy fear races through my veins, causing my heart to thunder in my chest.

"What do you want, Shawn?" I somehow manage to get out even though my tongue feels too thick and my mouth too dry.

"We need to talk."

"Contact my secretary and get on my calendar," I snap. Indignation surges at his hold cutting off the blood supply to the lower half of my arm, shooting a rush of confidence to my system. Gathering leverage, I step back, trying to yank my arm out of his grip. I wince as his fingers dig deeper, trying to keep his hold, but in the end I win, slipping out of his grasp.

Stumbling backward, I retreat two steps, putting me out of his reach.

"I know what you need."

For the first time in this short confrontation, I snap my gaze to meet his. Dark eyes seem to absorb the bright sunlight pouring from the windows and overhead lights. I suppress a shudder at the malevolence lurking behind them. It's vast, unending darkness, like a blaring warning to run and never look back.

"I can give it to you," he continues. "For a price."

Hell no. No amount of money in the world would make me consider partnering with him.

"I don't know what you're talking about," I rasp. Reaching up, I wrap a palm around my throat.

He dips his chin an inch, angling a knowing look my way.

"Step the fuck away from her."

The wave of relief at the angry, gravelly voice weakens my knees. I shoot an arm out, palm smacking the wall to keep me upright.

"Benson." Somehow the hate pours off him in larger waves as his gaze shifts over my shoulder. "How's your fiancée?" Shawn asks, an edge to his voice.

Trey moves fast, situating his body between me and Shawn.

"Not sure. How's Rachel?"

I wince at the mention of his ex.

"Tied up at home, just how I like them."

There's a cruelty to Trey's responding laugh. "Only way you can get them to stick around."

"You can't protect her," Shawn chides. At the laughter in his tone, I step around Trey, putting me at his side. Shawn's gaze slides to me with a smirk. "It's hilarious that you think you ever could from me."

With that, Shawn gives us a knowing malicious smile, then turns, marching down the hall and disappearing into a side room.

The fight drains from Trey's muscles where my hands grip his bicep. With a heavy breath, he hangs his head, eyes closed.

"You okay?" he asks.

"Fine," I say with a shrug. "Are you?"

Brows raised, he angles that handsome face my way. I suck in a quick breath at the emotions swirling behind his honey brown eyes. The pull is undeniable. I give an inch, resting my head against his hard shoulder, then sigh, letting the simple connection help seep the stress from my strung-out mind.

"Am I okay? Doubting if I can take care of myself, Mess?"

"Never," I say with fake shock. "The mention of Rachel.... I don't know. Just asking."

Something passes over his features. "Yeah, that's not pleasant." He chuckles. "But she doesn't matter. You do." He cups my face. "Only you."

"Team Randi," I say more to myself to hold my focus on the end objective.

His signature smirk pulls at his lips, showing off the boyish charm I've wholeheartedly fallen for. "Is there any other?"

In a quick move, he tugs me close, our lower bodies pressing together.

"Some people might say there are others," I whisper, face tilted up toward his. I fight against sighing in the comfort and safety of his arms. A faint whiff of his unique expensive cologne wafts off his jacket. Losing the battle, I lean my nose closer, hoping for a stronger hit of the scent that drives me wild. My muscles quiver with need. Need for him. For his touch, for his lips and tongue sliding along my skin.

"Well, then, they're idiots." *Wait, what were we talking about? I feel like it was important.* "It's your world, Mess. We're just revolving around it."

"I think that's just you," I say into his chest. A vibration tickles my lips at his chuckle.

Thick fingers press under my chin, tipping my face up.

"It is to anyone who matters," he murmurs, his eyes searching my own. "I miss you, Mess."

"I know," I say around the growing lump in my throat. "I think I—"

"I thought you were going to get your coat." The resentment in Sam's clipped words is clear.

Panic seizes my thoughts and my muscles. The slight twitch of Trey's muscular arms around my waist tells me he's not thrilled about the interruption or Sam's tone. Quite frankly, neither am I.

"She was accosted in the hallway on her way." If premeditated death had a tone, it would be the one dripping from Trey's words. He turns his fury to the agent who I'd begged to give me space. "And where the hell were you?"

"I'll be right back," I grumble as I maneuver out of Trey's embrace. With zero desire to stick around for this pissing contest, I scurry down the hall, eager to get my coat so I can get out of this suffocating house and away from the infuriating men inside it.

Just to be on the safe side, I slip on a pair of fleece-lined leggings, then snag a scarf and a toboggan from the room too. The bedroom door clicks closed behind me, my attention on finding the back to my soft hat and not on the lurking danger.

"Walmart."

I startle with a curse. Narrowing my eyes down the long dark hall, I find Kyle leaning against a doorframe several feet away.

"The hell, Kyle?" I snap, tightening my grip on the knit cap.

"I told you we needed to meet. Don't act surprised."

I take a nervous glance over my shoulder at the beta team agent who's standing a couple feet away, attention on the wall like a good agent, not seeming affected at all by Kyle's presence.

"I was just about to go on a walk," I say, putting some power into my voice that I don't exactly feel in the moment. I'm a strong, independent woman, yet every time this asshat is around, all my confidence flees. Maybe it's from those few years of his daily torment during law school. "And I need coffee."

Lots of coffee to put up with your twatwaffle ass.

"That can wait." His voice is hard and determined. "You," he says, pointing to my agent. "Stay out here. My guys will cover her inside." Without waiting to see if I follow, probably knowing full well that I will, he shrugs off the wall and disappears into a room.

I cast one more pleading look down the hallway at my back, hoping Sam or Trey will pop around the corner and save me from going into this alone.

But they don't.

I straighten my spine and head to my fate.

No protection. No friends. No support.

Just me meeting this head-on. Like it's always been.

17

RANDI

The dark green walls seem to absorb the light and heat from the room. To my left, a roaring wood fire crackles inside the stone fireplace. Several deep leather armchairs scatter the floor, all in groups of three or more around low dark wood tables. Across the expansive room, an antique-looking pool table sits with the balls perfectly lined up, ready to be broken and played.

Studying the pool cues along the side wall, Kyle absentmindedly rolls up one sleeve, tugging it above his elbow, then does the same with the other. Uneasily, I step deeper into the room, scanning the dark corners for Shawn but come up empty. That's one small blessing.

"Give us a few minutes to talk," he says, not addressing the three agents directly. "Watch from the security feed, no audio, and have two men stationed outside all the doors to make sure Benson or any of the others don't get in before the meeting is over."

I swallow as the three agents nod like this isn't the first time they've been asked to leave the room for a secretive meeting. I watch them file out, my gaze still stuck on the closed door minutes after they've left.

"Choose," Kyle commands, never looking up from the end of the pool cue he's holding. The light blue dust flakes into a small cloud as he chalks the end.

I roll my eyes. "You can always say please."

"Not to you."

"Your personality needs work."

I swear a near smile tweaks at his lips before he schools his features. My defenses slip a fraction at his ease. It seems today isn't one of those days when we're at each other's throats.

Eyeing the rack, I toss my coat onto a random chair and slowly unwind the scarf around my neck, adding it to the small pile along with the hat I never managed to tug on.

"I'm not terrible," I say over my shoulder as I pull a cue off the wall and lift it to eye level, ensuring it's straight. "Just a fair warning."

"Would you like to break, then?"

I nod and take a step toward the head of the pool table.

Smiling, he leans forward and draws his cue back. The booming crack of the balls bursting apart startles me even though I knew it was coming.

"You're an ass." I chuckle. Two stripes and one solid fall into various pockets. "Choose a side."

He nods, his smile falling. "Coincidentally, that's what I wanted to talk about."

A soft snort leaves my nose. "I've never known you to talk about anything. You demand, Kyle. So go on, tell me what this is all about."

He stalks around the table, eyeing the balls still dotting the top. Those ice blue eyes narrow on a complicated shot just before he leans forward, inspecting the various ways to address the ball. Today he's more casual in dark jeans, loafers, and a light blue button-up that makes his eyes seem more blue than clear. The dimple of his chin seems to twitch as he raises the cue to strike.

Of course he sinks it.

I groan and lean my forehead against the narrow part of the cue in my hand.

"I'm aware of everything you're doing to cover your tracks. From you and Benson to the idiotic farce you're playing with Pierce. Which means you're still moving forward with helping the DOJ. I wanted to explain my side and let you see there's more going on than you realize, Walmart." Straightening, he eyes the table, searching for his next target. "You think you know what I'm doing and why, but you don't."

"Then explain." Putting a bit of weight on the cue, I lean forward, meeting his surprised eyes. "I'm not going to sit here and spill everything I know hoping you'll do the same. You want to set the record straight, then go ahead." His head dips in acknowledgment. "Spill it."

Maybe if I can get him talking....

"You wouldn't understand the pressure I'm under," he says under his breath.

"Pretty sure things aren't just rainbows and unicorns in my role either. We're both under a lot of pressure. That doesn't mean you can—"

"It doesn't matter the why," he grits out as he draws his cue back. The ball goes wide by half an inch, missing the hole. "Damnit."

I don't stop the slow smile from spreading up my cheeks.

Finally.

Leaning over the pool table, I search for the shot I want.

"I need you to make Pierce drop his case, stop looking into it."

I peer up through my lashes before focusing back on the cue ball.

"Even if I wanted to, which I don't, I don't have that kind of pull over him."

"You do and you will."

The three ball smacks the back of the pocket before dropping inside.

"And why would I do that?" I ask, lining up my next shot. "You act like we're friends, or that I owe you." Point aimed at the cue ball, I flick a look up at Kyle. "We're not and I don't. And your *assuming* I'm working with the DOJ isn't enough for me to be within breach of our contract, so you can't hold that over my head."

The solid ball lands softly into the pocket exactly where I aimed it. Who knew those nights playing while in Austin would help me defeat the president in his own game room one day? Tiny loves to play pool and had a beat-up table in the back of the shop to help with his "creativity." It was a way to shoot the shit while the shop was empty, usually early afternoons when the drunk college kids were still recovering from the night before, too hungover to get out of bed and venture back downtown.

"Randi."

My attention flicks from the white ball the split second before the cue tip connects, making the shot go right, missing the seven ball completely. Still bent over the table, I don't move. I shiver at the real fear lurking behind his eyes, something I've never seen. It's disturbing as hell. With a slow blink, he shakes his head, and the vulnerability that was there for a half a second vanishes.

"I'm not asking. This is bigger than you, bigger than me. You have to stop Pierce. Make him realize too much is on the line for him to keep at the investigation."

"What's on the line?" I ask hesitantly.

"My life. Yours. His maybe."

I swallow and stand, leaning a hip against the dark wood. "What's going on, Kyle?" I search for another spark of that fear he let slip, but his normal arrogant mask keeps it covered. "You're the president, for fuck's sake. You have the power to do or stop whatever you want, which is how you're in the position now." I shake my head. This is crazy. He's just trying to get me to feel sorry for him. "What you're doing is wrong, and they will figure out a way to stop you."

His malicious chuckle has the hair on the back of my neck standing on end. Pool cue still in hand, he maneuvers around the table, putting himself on the same side as me. Warning alarms ring in my head, demanding I match his forward steps with ones in retreat, but I don't. Instead, like a confident fool, I stand my ground, our gazes locked in a battle of wills.

Only once has he dropped the gentleman façade and lowered himself to physical violence. Then I thought it was in direct retaliation to my own, but now I know the truth. It had nothing to do with me.

Fast as lighting, his hand lashes out, fingers diving deep into my hair at the scalp and curling into a tight fist. A whimper passes my lips as he tightens his hold with a sharp tug. I tip my head back, exposing my neck to keep him from pulling my hair out by the root. Tears prick at the corners of my eyes.

"You think this is just about the fucking oil?" he hisses in my face. Bits of spit spray across my cheek. I cry out at the sharp pain when I try to turn away. "This is so much more. I will not let you or that weak-ass fucker Pierce ruin me." His eyes sparkle with hate and arrogance. "You have no idea what I did to win the election, to get in this fucking seat. You were just part of it. A small fucking part. I had to—" He cuts himself off with a huff. "You have no idea who we're in bed with now. This isn't just about money. It's power they want." Something like regret flashes across his face. "What I've put in motion can't be stopped now."

Fear races straight to my heart. It thumps erratically against my chest, nearly pounding out of my body. Where is his security team? Can't they see this on the video feed? Where's mine, for that matter?

"Then tell me," I rasp through the pain. "Tell me what's going on. Maybe I can help—"

Kyle tips his head back with a haughty laugh. I grimace as the shake of his hand yanks a few strands from my scalp. When he straightens, a different kind of arrogance fills his eyes.

My stomach dips. I've seen this look before. Not on him but other men. The look of knowing you're at their mercy. A lustful, predatory gleam.

"Maybe you *can* help," he says, the corners of his lips ticking up. "I need a bit of stress relief, Walmart. Get on your fucking knees."

Forgetting the pain, I shake my head. Without thinking of the repercussions, I drop the pool cue, lean back into his tight fist, putting some distance between our faces, and slam my knuckles against his cheekbone.

A loud crack resounds through the room. The hold on my hair loosens. I use the moment of distraction to my advantage, slipping farther away from the cursing Kyle. When he finally looks up, hand on his swelling cheek, there's shock written across his features.

"You hit me," he says in awe.

The door swings open and several men pour in only for Kyle to jam a finger toward the hallway. "Out," he bellows.

Immediately they follow his order.

"You told me to get on my knees," I hiss. The green felt scrapes under my ragged nails as I grasp for the pool cue on the table. Squeezing it tight, I lift it between us, pointing the end toward his chest. "Stay the fuck away from me."

"You're a fucking fool." Still staring, he bursts out laughing. My resolve wavers as confusion sinks in. "I bring your daughter here to prove I can get to anyone and everyone you love, and you go and hit me." This time his laugh has an edge of hysteria to it.

Anger festers. Lunging forward, I poke his chest with the blue felt tip of the cue. We both stare at the blue dot now marking his dress shirt.

"Stay the hell away from my daughter," I grit out.

"I see you started without me."

Losing focus on Kyle, I swing around to face Shawn. He sits relaxed in one of the deep leather armchairs by the fire.

What the hell? Those were empty earlier. Right? My brows furrow in confusion.

"This is Camp David, Trailer. Every room has multiple entrances and exits. A safety precaution, yes, but also great for sneaking in unnoticed." Leaning forward, he rests his elbows on his knees and steeples his fingers, his chin on the high point. "I like where it was going before. Get on your knees like a good girl, Trailer, and no one you love will get hurt."

"Fuck you both," I hiss. The wooden rod trembles in my shaking hands, giving away my mounting terror. Shit, this is bad.

Movement in my periphery snaps my attention toward the encroaching Kyle. I move around the pool table, putting it between me and the two men.

"I call the ass," Shawn pipes up. I scowl. "It'll be fun tearing you apart from the inside out." A shiver of revulsion rakes across my shoulders. I fight the urge to vomit all over the clean floor. "Not that I'm not already." Again the fog of confusion overtakes me. It must read on my face that I have no idea what he's referring to. "You haven't figured it out yet?" A sinister smile spreads across his face, making his features tighten.

I glance at Kyle, who's staring at Shawn with just as much confusion on his features. Then something clicks in place, and his features shift from a frown to annoyance.

"You fucker." Kyle shakes his head. "I told you to back off after the first time."

"I remember." Shawn raises a shoulder and leans back, getting comfortable. "And I did, just not completely. She's too fun to fuck with. Plus... well, this way I'll get the VP spot one way or another."

"You're so fucked up," Kyle says, exhaustion in his tone. He swipes a palm down his face before leaning forward to grip the edge of the pool table, head dangling between his shoulders. A pang of sympathy hits me in the chest. Yes, he's mean and manipulative and an arrogant ass, but he's still a man. A man who seems to be in over his head.

If only we could work together, give each other a high five and figure this shit out that he's gotten himself into. But that will never happen. He's too arrogant to listen to me. Hell, I've heard he doesn't even listen to his press secretary or advisors. Why in the hell would he listen to me if he doesn't even value their opinions?

"One way or another?" I ask, the only question I can form that makes sense.

Shawn just continues to smile.

"Drop the investigation. The inquiries. Fuck, drop even the thought of getting me out of office," Kyle says softly, palming the cheek I hit.

"You know I can't do that," I reply with a shake of my head for emphasis. "It's abuse of power, Kyle. I can't sit back and let this mess you've gotten our country into unfold when I know I could've done something."

Well, there it is. Gone is the illusion of Sam being the one working the investigation. If Kyle is smart, he'll realize I just admitted to helping the DOJ and am now in direct conflict of my agreement with him and the Birmingham estate.

"Told you Miss Self Righteous wouldn't drop it." I narrow my eyes at Shawn. "You should've just let me take her out like I suggested." Carefully unfolding himself, he stands and dusts off some invisible lint from the sleeve of his dark blue dress shirt. "I still can."

I follow his questioning look across the room to Kyle, who shakes his head.

"You're talking about killing me," I say, astounded. "Right in front of me? For real?"

Kyle sighs and leans against the edge of the pool table. "Just stop looking for the answers, Walmart. Don't push me on this. Don't make me be the person who takes it too far."

Like Shawn.

"Didn't you already?" I ask, poking the pool cue in his direction. "You put a hit out on me!" I shriek. "You tried to poison me!"

"How the fuck do you know about that?"

I open my mouth only to snap it shut again. Well, shit. Can't really tell him I'm BFFs with the Russian president. Pretty sure he'd skewer me right here if he knew I had access to that kind of information.

"Don't give him all the credit," Shawn says behind me, now too close for comfort. I swing the pool cue around, ready to defend myself.

A commotion outside the room draws our attention.

"Seems your fuck buddy has had enough of waiting." Shawn sneers.

"Randi." I whip my head toward Kyle. Again the exhaustion and fear shine through his posture and tired eyes. "I will take everything you love. Remember that when your morals get in the way of doing the smart thing."

My knees go weak. "Okay," I whisper. "You have my word. I'll talk Sam out of the investigation." I suck in a deep breath. "Please don't hurt her." My voice trembles.

"What a waste," Shawn bites out. "I should just finish this now."

"Shawn," Kyle growls. "I cannot add her murder investigation to my plate right now."

"Wow," I snap. "Sorry if me dying would be an inconvenience to you."

"Not enough time in the day," Kyle muses. "Follow through with Sam, Walmart, and Taeler stays safe. And you." He levels a hard stare at Shawn, who appears unaffected by the ire in Kyle's glare. "Stop it with the assassination talk. Someone will hear you. And while we're at it, stop whatever else you're doing."

Shawn stuffs his hands into the front pockets of his tailored suit pants. "I don't know what you're talking about."

"I told you to fucking stop after the first time, and now I'm telling you again. Stop it with that shit. It's a cunt thing to do."

"Oh, like putting a hit out on her and changing your mind at the last minute to only scaring her?" Shawn scoffs. "Weak-ass pussy." Rolling his shoulders, he angles his head left and then right. "No wonder those fuckers pulled one over on you. Weak."

Agitation rolls off Kyle. He stands tall, puffing his chest out in a dominating move. Eyes wide, I take a step back, not wanting to be anywhere between these two. It seems not all is hunky-dory in their odd friendship.

"Know your place, Secretary." Shawn's title comes out as more of a hiss than a word.

I take several more steps backward until my back hits a wall.

"For now. What's fucking funny," he says with a chuckle, looking as relaxed as a tiger after a full meal, "is you truly believed I'd stop with her."

My mouth pops open. A quick look to Kyle shows his mouth gaping as well.

"And with all that I know," he continues with a confident, sinister smirk, "it's too much to risk getting out for you to do anything about it. So no, Mr. President, I won't back off, and as soon as I have her out of the way, you're fucking next."

At that moment, the door I entered the room through sails open, banging against the wall as four agents pour in. The three I don't know scan the room and march to Kyle's side, putting themselves within arm's reach.

Trey's narrowed honey brown eyes soften a fraction after I'm looked over head to toe and found whole. He takes in the pool cue and my back at the wall and immediately goes back on guard. Three steps and he's beside me, arm wrapped around my waist, tugging me closer.

"You okay?" he asks, not looking down but keeping his focus on Kyle and Shawn.

Physically, sure, besides my heart pounding out of my chest and zero oxygen getting to my brain. But mentally? Hell no.

What the hell just happened? I search the billiards room in a daze, hoping something will help piece together the last half hour.

"Yeah, um, I'm good," I stammer. "Just get me out of here, okay?"

With a crisp nod, we're on the move. Out in the hall, another five agents stand ready for anything. Champ stares me down like I've done something wrong while T looks ready to blow a gasket. I swear steam is coming right off his shiny bald head.

Trey starts to lead me toward the room I stayed in last night, but I balk at the doorway.

"No." I swallow, trying to get my thoughts and emotions in control. "I want to go home."

T nods and mutters orders into the cuff of his sleeve.

We pass Sam in the living room, his face scrunched with concern. "You're with us," I say, pausing even though Trey attempts to tug me past. "I need to talk to you three. Alone."

No one seems happy about the request, but I don't care.

I put up no resistance as I'm ushered into the dark SUV. My feet bounce against the floorboard as I wait for the rest of the team and Sam to load.

Now the hard part. I have an hour and a half to convince Sam to drop the case, figure out what the hell Shawn's up to, and make a plan to get Taeler somewhere safe.

Because one thing is for certain: I might have sworn I'd make Sam drop the investigation, but I didn't say *I* would.

18

TREY

Fuck protocol.

Instead of directing Sam to the back seat with Randi, I shove him up front, mumbling something about safety and any other bullshit I can think of as an excuse for me to be in the back with her instead of him. "He got her on the way here" wasn't an excuse Tank was willing to hear when I first called dibs. But, me being me, I went rogue and now here I am, happy as a fucking clam in the back seat with Randi while Tank glares at me through the rearview mirror.

I raise my chin and smile when our eyes connect again. I don't stop my soft chuckle when he grumbles a few curses and tightens his white-knuckled grip on the steering wheel. He loves me. I just push the envelope sometimes. But let's be honest, Sam sitting up front isn't putting her or us in danger. Now if I would've been forced to sit up front while he sat inches from the one woman I want the most but can't have... well, then *his* life would've been in danger.

Adjusting in the seat, I shrug out of my jacket and toss it into the back. Randi's gaze stays out the window, seemingly deep in concentration as I attempt to get comfortable. Whatever happened in that room shook her. When I burst in with the other agents, she looked downright terrified. But of what? I'm guessing that's what she wants to discuss now.

"First of all, I feel like we need to get everything out in the open." Randi doesn't turn from the window. Her hot breath fogs the thick glass where she's leaning so close her forehead is nearly touching it. "Kyle knows the front that Sam and I are a couple is fake. He didn't say how, but hell, even my daughter knew we weren't really a couple, so it wasn't a shock that he didn't believe it either. I never admitted to helping you, Sam, but I did confirm the DOJ is looking into some aspects of his decisions." She sighs and presses her forehead against the glass.

Desperate to take a bit of the stress weighing on her shoulders, I slide my hand across the center seat and lace my fingers around her own. At my gentle squeeze of encouragement, her forehead rolls along the window until her hazel eyes meet mine.

"Earlier this year, Kyle put a bill in front of the house that would've stripped many Americans' right to vote. It was worded in a way that no one noticed. Hell, I might not have even put it all together until it was too late if Kyle hadn't brought it to my attention that first day in office." Her attention focuses on our connected hands. "Trey here knew we wouldn't be able to stop it in the House or Senate without help. Which is why he's now in a forced relationship with Jessica Hawthorne." A rustle in the front seat draws my attention to where Sam has now turned around, leaning against the center console staring at Randi. "I lied to you before, and for that I'm sorry, Sam. Trey and I aren't done, and honestly?" She clears her throat. "I don't think we ever will be."

"Why keep up pretenses, then?" Sam asks, glancing between us.

I nod. "There are some things keeping me tied to Jessica for the moment," I clarify. "I have to tread carefully because—"

"Because of me," Randi cuts in. "If he goes back on some promises, ones he made to help us defeat the bill in the Senate, then he's sunk and I am too. I don't have a lot of support in this town, and right now I need all I can get, which means partnering with people and using others as leverage."

Silence fills the SUV, the whirling of the tires zooming down the highway the only background noise as we wait for Sam to process every-thing we've known for months.

He sighs. Disappointment seems to waft off him, and I can't say I blame him. If I thought I had a chance with Randi, had hopes of her being mine, and then those were dashed, plus finding out it would've never happened to begin with? Fuck yeah, I'd be disappointed too.

"I can't say I'm surprised," he says.

"I'm sorry." Randi's shoulders round further.

"What's all this about?" I interject in an attempt to pull her out of whatever self-deprecating thoughts are running through her head. "Why are you bringing this up?"

"What happened in that room?" Tank's deep voice resounds through the cab.

Randi takes a deep breath and leans back against the headrest, slowly letting the breath out through pursed lips. Her fingers tighten around mine.

"I'm fucked."

Well, that's one way to stop my heart.

BY THE TIME we get back at One Observatory Circle, unload, and have her safe inside, my rage is just below erupting. Randi heads upstairs for a quick shower and to get caught up on emails, leaving T, Sam, and me standing speechless in the foyer.

"It goes against everything I believe in to just give this up when I'm so close to taking that fucker down," Sam seethes. Stretching, he laces his fingers behind his head. "Plus, I don't like her doing this on her own."

"She won't be," I snap. Closing my eyes, I massage the bridge of my nose while taking three deep breaths. "But for her safety and Taeler's, we need you to step back. Give off the impression that you're dropping the case. We'll... we'll figure out how to get the information without Birmingham or Whit knowing." I shoot a quick look at Tank.

Sam also looks at Tank, then me. "What am I missing?"

"She has some friends," Tank admits reluctantly. "Friends who can help us get the information and who won't leak the fact that we're still looking into his illegal dealings."

"Then why didn't she go to these 'friends' in the first place?" Sam's eyes narrow. Smart man. He knows something's up.

"She mentioned it before to you. It's not the most legal of avenues and might not hold up in court." I sigh. Fuck, I'm tired. My focus goes to the stairs, following the path Randi took minutes ago. "But it might be enough for that not to matter."

"Of course it'll matter," Sam counters. "If we take the evidence to the House, it has to—"

"What if we don't?" I muse. Thoughts swirl, pieces fitting into place. "What if we gather enough to intimidate him?"

Sam's brows rise up his forehead.

Fuck, I have to give it to the guy. At least he's not like the rest of the men in this town, all Botoxed out. "He told Randi it's too late to go back, that things are set in motion. What if it's worse than what we're thinking? We already know he's pulling several Middle East countries into this as a front to what he's causing. Maybe that's what he was referencing, or maybe it's worse."

Sam nods absentmindedly as he focuses on the floor, his fingers swiping across the dark stubble on his chin. "It would have to be completely heinous for him to step down without a true impeachment."

"Knowing that fucker and Whit, I'm sure it is."

"We already have proof he put a hit on Randi," Tank adds.

"This way we don't have to worry about getting enough votes in the House and Senate for the impeachment," Sam says, seeming lost in his own thoughts.

"Exactly. It could be the only way to make it work."

"What about Whit, then?" Tank asks. "He made it sound like he's still hurting her somehow, and I'm willing to bet it has something to do with those headaches she's been getting since the initial poisoning."

"Agreed," I say, beginning to pace the small area. My fingers tremble with excess energy.

"If what she shared on the way here is exactly as it happened, it sounds like Birmingham wasn't the one who plotted the initial poisoning anyway." We all stand in silence until Sam speaks up again. "And if all this works out, she'll move up to the president role, which means she'll have an even bigger target on her back. Are you two prepared for that when you can't even figure out how he's hurting her now?"

I take a menacing step toward the fucker, but Tank's arm lashes out, smacking across my heaving chest.

"Yes, she'll be safe. And we'll figure out how he's still poisoning her." He shoots a concerned look at me.

"I'm doing this for her," Sam says, looking straight into my eyes. I bristle at the challenge behind the stare. "I'll back off the case—for now. But don't expect me to stay away, not when she's in danger because of what I've dragged her into. If you need anything from the DOJ office, just let me know." With that, he nods to Tank and turns to the front door.

Only once the door is shut behind him and it's just me and Tank do I let the worry and fear for Randi sink in.

"What are we going to do?" I ask, pacing the small foyer once again. I feel like a caged animal. So much needs to be done, to be handled, but instead I'm standing here doing nothing.

The phone in my pocket vibrates for what feels like the hundredth time in the last few hours. I slide it out and glance at the screen, already knowing who it'll be.

"She's getting clingy," Tank remarks with a tilt of his head toward the phone in my hand.

I grunt in acknowledgment. "She keeps telling me she feels like someone is following her. That she's scared."

He arches a brow. "Not like you to just ignore something like that."

I shake my head. "Normally I wouldn't. You know that. But this feels fishy. It just all of a sudden happened out of the blue. My gut is telling me she's making it up and using it as a way to get me to come around more."

"Well, she is your fiancée," he says with a chuckle.

"Shut your damn mouth," I say with a smirk. "Not too much longer."

"Yeah, if your mother has any say in it, she'll be your wife by the end of the year."

I shudder. "That will not happen."

"Even if she can help us?"

"Jessica?"

"No, you clown. Your mother. We know she has inside eyes and ears on the team. Maybe we should use it to our advantage instead of trying to eradicate the rat."

My brows dip as I think through all the different ways what he's suggesting could go wrong. But am I willing to sink deeper into metaphorical debt with my conniving family?

Yes.

Fuck yes.

Every day, yes.

19

RANDI

December

Waves crash somewhere in the distance. Taeler screeches in excitement nearby before a loud splash meets my ears. A lazy smile tugs at my lips. Behind my borrowed sunglasses, I keep my eyes closed, knowing there are at least ten agents protecting me in the distance, plus the few standing close. A relaxed sigh passes my lips. Beneath me, the heat from the pool deck seeps up through the lounge chair, keeping me warm even though I'm in a bathing suit and the soft breeze is crisp.

"This is the life," I say to no one in particular.

Peeking one eye open, I search for my hunky agent. Dressed in shorts, a snug Dryfit shirt that leaves nothing to the imagination, and armed to the teeth, he's sexy as hell.

Feeling the weight of my lusty stare, his gaze flicks to me.

"Aren't you glad we made you put the iPad down?"

Okay, yes, there was a little skirmish inside earlier when T and Trey tried to get me to come outside and relax. We've been here three days, and this is the first time I've allowed myself to enjoy the beautiful tropical island. Who could blame me though? I had nothing to compare it to. This is my first vacation... ever. I'm not one to relax anyway, and with everything else going on, it took them basically ripping the iPad out of my hands and pushing me outside to realize what I was missing.

"Maybe," I grumble, not wanting to admit that they were right in making me leave the house.

Another screech from Taeler has me leaning up on my elbows to peer down to the beach. The sun glistens off the rolling waves. A beat of panic thumps in my chest until her head pops above the water, her wide smile clear from here.

"My view isn't so bad either."

Dipping my chin, I give my head a shake while Trey grumbles something in exasperation.

"Thanks for the glasses." I tap a finger against the steel frames.

He shrugs and goes back to scanning the area, giving me another moment to check him out without him noticing. Damn, he's hot. I love his suits, the way they fit him to perfection each and every day, but the shorts showing off his thick calf muscles and strong thighs are a very close second. I lick my lips and bite down on the lower one as I imagine the rest of the goods hidden beneath his clothes.

"My eyes are up here," Trey says with a deep chuckle.

"Like you care that I'm checking you out." To prove a point, I lean forward to get a better view of his tight ass.

He shifts, giving me a better angle.

"You two are ridiculous," T complains.

"You'd be this way too if it'd been weeks since you got to squeeze that hot ass," I whine. Falling back, I groan and wiggle against the towel. Weeks. Hell, it feels like years. But with everything going on, all the planning and secret meetings, there hasn't been enough time or energy for the fun stuff.

But now that we're here....

"Never been tempted, so I wouldn't feel your pain," T says like he ate something sour.

"Sarah says you can't get enough of hers," I whisper so only us three can hear.

"Have you seen her fine ass?" He whistles low. "Edible."

"Ew." I scrunch my nose in disgust.

"Don't knock it until you've tried it," T says with a wistful tone.

"No thanks."

"Can we talk about something else?" Trey grumbles, adjusting his hardening dick in the loose shorts. "Not much I can do to hide this."

"We could always use it," I offer.

"Fuck," they both grumble, one more of disgust and the other of pleasure.

"Sweetie, have you had your daily honey and almond milk?"

Now it's my turn to groan.

Pushing up to my elbows, I dip my chin to peer over the rim of the sunglasses at my mom. Yep, I'm the idiot who thought pulling her mom out of the long-term addiction recovery care center for a family Christmas in Hawaii was a brilliant idea. Don't get me wrong. Things are going great. She's clean. As in vegan clean. Okay, not that clean, but it feels that way considering she used to think an RC and a Twinkie constituted a healthy dinner for a nine-year-old.

Now she's the mother I always wanted but never had. But at thirty-eight.

Doting, comforting, hospitable—hell, she even tried to sing me to sleep last night.

Sing. Me. To. Sleep.

"No, Mom." I sigh, wiggling to stop the slow throb between my thighs that the sight of Trey's hard cock caused. "I'm good though."

"Oh no, honey, you're too stressed to skip the honey and milk. I'll go make it and be right back. How about a pomegranate paste to chase it with?"

I nearly throw up the tofu she made me eat last night.

"I'm good," I rasp, trying to keep the non-food food down. "Just the milk and honey will be great."

I mirror her wide smile. Yes, she's annoying with the hovering, but seeing her like this, clean and happy, my heart is so full I almost think it could burst.

Until...

"Have you considered your womanly health?"

"Huh?" This is not happening.

"At the center, they've taught us to take care of every inch of our bodies. Including sexual health."

"Mom, not the time."

She shakes her head, her limp, mousy hair swishing from one shoulder to the other.

"No, the director says we must treat our bodies as a temple. We've abused our bodies—"

I hold up a hand, stopping her. "We?"

Her eyes scan the area like she's searching for answers. It dawns on me then that she doesn't mean anything by it; she's just a little confused.

"Mom." I sit up, wrapping my forearms around my shins. The two guys make some lame excuse to step out of hearing distance. I make a mental note to hug them for that later. I pat the end of the lounge chair, urging Mom to sit. "I didn't get to this role by sleeping my way to the top."

A blank stare is her only response. Okay, different angle, then.

"You know I went to law school, right? You remember that part."

She nods.

"You know the president, Kyle Birmingham?"

She shakes her head.

"Okay, well, he's the president, and I went to school with him. It's how I'm the VP now. Nothing shady or illegal going on for me to be in this role."

"Ma'am." I turn my attention to Champ, who's walking with a purpose from the massive house we rented out. "The call you've been waiting on is on hold."

Normally my admin or secretary or someone else would let me know about phone calls, not an agent, but these days security is tight. We can't let anyone outside of the people we trust know what I'm doing behind the scenes. So only me, T, Trey and Champ. Not even Taeler knows what's really going on. Her only focus is that I've finagled it for her to study in Oxford this next semester instead of being on the *why* I went to so much effort to get her accepted with zero notice. Hopefully the fruit basket I sent the prime minister was enough of a thank you.

"Oh, and Mom." Her light eyes turn up to mine. "If you ever see the president, Kyle Birmingham, or if anyone comes to the rehab facility looking for you who's not me or one of these guys standing around me... I want you to run. Slip away and run as fast as you can."

With a confused look, she nods, nibbling on her lower lip. "Thanks." I pat her still too thin thigh and stand with a groan.

"If your muscles ache, I can get some essential oils..."

I stride away before she's done explaining the concoction of pricy oils she'll make me slather on later. I shiver. As long as she doesn't try to rub it on herself. Now, Trey on the other hand....

I sneak a glance over my shoulder and smile.

"Do I even want to know?" Trey asks.

I shake my head.

"At least we know your mom talking about sexual health is one quick way to make a hard-on vanish."

A snort escapes as I snag the phone from Champ's outstretched hand and hold it to my ear. "This is Randi."

"Madam VP."

Vlad's monotone voice snaps me into work mode. This is the call I've been waiting for the last twenty-four hours. Everything is in place; now we just need the Russian president's help in securing the needed information to follow through with the plan. Okay, the semi-plan. Eh, more of a rough sketch of future events we hope will fall into place.

So really, no plan.

"Is this line secure?"

"As secure as it can be," I respond, knowing full well the team has taken the necessary precautions for this important call.

"Tomorrow we talk."

I nod even though he can't see me.

He rattles off an address that I quickly jot down on a nearby notepad. Without a goodbye or "see you soon," the line goes dead. The smooth screen peels from my cheek, sticky with sweat from the humid island weather. The tip of the pen taps against the notepad as I flick it up and down, staring at the address.

"It's a park," T says behind me. A quick look up shows him scowling at his phone. "If we hadn't already met this guy, I'd say hell no, too many vulnerable points."

"But we have, and we're going," I say, my focus on the mosaic tile decorating the outdoor bar stool top.

A calloused hand rubs against the exposed skin of my lower back, dragging my deep thoughts from the millions of possibilities that could come up in the meeting to the breathtaking man beside me. A happy smile pulls at my lips. "He'll have access to the information we need, right?"

Trey nods, his eyes searching. No doubt he's taking in the tight features of my face which give away the layers of stress building beneath my skin and stuffing every corner of my mind.

"I'm sure he will. In Chile, he said you should come to him when we wanted the truth." A deep line forms between his brows. "It's almost like he knew this would happen."

"No," I say in dismay. "There's no way he knew all this would come to a head like it has." Doubt sinks in even though my words ring true. "Right?"

The slick fabric of his shirt presses against my sweaty back as he steps closer. Leaning forward, he slides his lips across the shell of my ear, causing a delicious shiver to zap down my spine.

"I have something planned for tonight," he whispers. I close my eyes, focusing on the building heat low in my belly. This is the fire Taeler was talking about last month. His close proximity can set my hormones ablaze.

"What is it?" I ask, my breathless words giving away the heat pulsing through my core.

"Dinner."

My eyes pop open. Angling my head back, I search his intense gaze. "Dinner? You're still fake engaged, remember?"

He slowly nods. "Which is why what I have planned will happen here, just us." His gaze cuts away as he chews on his plump lower lip. This sudden shift from confident Trey to vulnerable catches me by surprise.

"What's wrong?"

"Fuck," he mutters, dragging a hand through his long dark hair. My attention follows the motion.

"You need a haircut."

"Will you go on a date?"

I raise my brows. "A date."

Trey clears his throat. "With me. Tonight."

I chuckle at his stammering. "Trouble," I whisper, shaking my head. "I think we're past that part of this"—I motion between us—"don't you?"

He shakes his head, determination now steeling his features. "Never. I never want to take what we have for granted, Mess. Plus, this would count as our first date."

Chewing on my thumbnail, I think back. "New York?"

"If you think a street vendor hot dog and almost getting mugged constitutes a date, then I need to raise your expectations. Tonight, Mess." Again he leans close. This time his dark stubble scrapes across my cheek as he slides a kiss to the corner of my lips.

Before I can deepen the chaste kiss, he pulls back with a cocky-ass smirk.

"Tease," I mutter. "Any particular time?"

"Eight. And wear something you don't mind getting sandy."

Excitement bursts through, chasing away the earlier longing. "What are you planning?"

His eyes trail down my nearly naked body and back up again. And just like that, with one look, the excitement is blasted away with a burst of desire so strong I have to squeeze my thighs together to quell the throbbing between them.

"A gentleman never divulges his secrets. But I will tell you one delicacy that's on the menu."

"What?"

"You."

"Cut it out, you two," T barks. Trey steps back, allowing the cool ocean breeze to flow between us, freshening my heated skin. "Benson, go secure the package that just arrived."

I watch his fine ass as he marches away.

"You've got it bad," T says, humor lining his tone.

"One day we'll get to be that normal couple, right?"

Silence.

I cut a glare to where he stands leaning against the wall.

T lets out a heavy sigh, the movement pushing the tight T-shirt he's wearing to the max.

"Randi, you're both in a tough position. He has the mess with Jessica and his mom, which might get worse before it gets better. Then you... well, if what needs to happen happens, you'll be the president of the United States."

"What do you mean, it might get worse before it gets better?" Shuffling, I slide onto a bar stool and lean my elbows back on to the cool tile. Apprehension flashes across T's features. "Tell me, T. I'm not letting that man get himself deeper into this shit for me." He still doesn't utter a word. "You really want your best friend married to that awful woman? You want him tied to his family more than he already is?"

"Low blow," he huffs.

I shrug. "I'm learning you have to take the junk shots in politics or you'll never get what you need."

"Ruthless." His smile turns predatory. "I knew you had it in you."

"You're stalling."

"We need to know what Whit is up to. We have zero clue how he's getting past us, if he even is. But based on the fact that you haven't had any headaches or been sick since we arrived here, I'm betting he wasn't lying in the game room that day."

I nod, the nail of my pinkie finger sliding between my teeth at the sharp movement.

"What does that have to do with Trey and his evil mother?"

The knowing look he gives me should mean something, but I come up blank.

"She has someone on the inside, remember?" I dip my chin and motion for him to keep going. "We're hoping we can use that person's knowledge to our advantage. Hopefully they know how Whit is still getting to you."

The hand at my mouth falls to my lap with a smack. "You're kidding me."

Those boulder-like shoulders shrug.

"And you're okay with this?"

This time his shrug is less convincing.

"I won't let that happen." Movement inside the house catches my attention, alerting me to Trey's impending return. "When?" I ask quickly.

"He's meeting with her after the new year."

"Let me know when and where. I'd rather die than have him ensnared by that woman any more than he already is. This has to end."

A sad look crosses his face, but he nods.

Turning to face the approaching Trey, I plaster a fake smile across my face.

No way in hell will I let him give any more of himself for me.

Been there, done that, and ended up with my boyfriend with a fake fiancée.

Nope. All this with his mother, Jessica, and Trey ends as soon as we get back.

Ends for good, no matter the effect on my career.

20

RANDI

"You're wearing that?"

I stick my tongue out at Taeler's reflection in the full-length mirror before running an assessing eye over my outfit choice for what seems like the hundredth time.

"He said we'd get sandy," I say more to myself than her. "I'm not so far gone in this new life that I can justify ruining a nice outfit. Not that I packed any." That's one part of this life I'm not sure I'll ever get used to. Packing multiple outfits for one day just because you can and not knowing what you'd feel like wearing that particular day. Me? We're here five days, so I packed five basic outfits, one swimsuit, and a set of pajamas.

Her tiny button nose scrunches in this adorable way that makes her look like a bunny. "But cutoff jean shorts and a sweatshirt?"

My reflection twists left and then right as I do. "It's off the shoulder. It's cute." Turning back straight, I slide my hands down the soft cotton and slip them into the front pockets of my favorite jean shorts. "He knows you," I whisper to my reflection, giving her a pep talk. "He won't expect anything fancy." But the longer I stare, the more doubt slips into my confident words.

I give my head a quick shake, dislodging the growing unease. This is me, and it is what it is. It's not like I have much else to choose from in my small bag.

At one minute till eight, I tiptoe across the room, hoping Taeler won't look up from her phone and make this awkward.

"Have fun on your date," she calls out as I tug open the door. "Don't do anything I wouldn't do."

I whip around with an expectant expression. "Which is what exactly?"

She snorts and rolls her eyes. "Go have fun. You deserve it, Mom. You both do."

A single hand glides down the smooth banister as I descend the stairs of the rental. I inhale a deep fortifying breath. Tae's right. I do deserve this one night of carefree thoughts. Of love and passion and feeling normal after so many days of constant pressure. So does he. We've both had unending distractions and things pulling us apart since we met.

Not tonight. Tonight, it's just us.

A heavy floral aroma causes my foot to waver as I lower from the final step. The lush scent fills my lungs as I take a deep breath and force my bare feet forward, padding along the stained concrete as I follow the smell through the darkened house toward a flickering light.

A soft gasp slips past my parted lips as my feet pull to a stop of their own accord.

Hundreds of roses fill the living room, vases upon vases of crimson long-stemmed roses in every nook and cranny. Candles flicker on each flat surface, making the living room seem to move with the shifting flames.

I startle at movement in the corner until Trey's handsome face comes into the light.

"Trey," I breathe and scan the room once again, taking in even more detail than I did with the first glance. "How...? When...?"

A nervous smile pulls at his lips. He dips his head and looks up through his dark lashes.

"I'm sorry it's taken me this long to do this." He shakes his head like he's fighting some kind of war in his own mind. "You deserve this kind of wow every day, every second."

I shake my head as I move toward him, a smile spreading up my cheeks and happy tears prickling in the corners of my eyes. "No one has ever done anything like this for me," I admit. "It's beautiful." I cringe, remembering what I'm wearing and my bare feet. "I should go change."

I don't get one step away before I'm tugged against his chest and held tight.

"Don't you dare. I've had wet dreams about these shorts for months, and tonight"—his nose slides into my hair as he takes a deep inhale—"if you let me, I'll get to turn those dreams into reality."

Well, when he puts it that way....

I bite my lip as I grin up at his answering one.

His attention flicks to something over my shoulder. I follow his gaze toward the kitchen. With a hard press of his lips to my forehead, he steps back, tugging me to follow him.

"Since we still don't know how Whit is getting to you, I didn't want to risk ordering in or having someone we don't know cook, so...." He waves a hand toward the spread of bread, cheeses, and other various toppings.

"It just so happens that grilled cheese is my new favorite food." Butterflies erupt in my gut at his soft grin.

"Good," he says, tugging me deeper into the kitchen. Hands on my waist, he lifts me onto the counter and steps between my legs, which I widen to accommodate his larger frame. "Because it was either that or bacon." His grin widens at my laugh. "Do you know how lucky I am?" His tone makes it clear it's a rhetorical question. "Of all the women I've dated, your easygoing nature, the joy you find in small gestures, is... refreshing."

I hook a thumb over my shoulder. "That's not a small gesture. It's like the Disney World of romantic gestures."

He just shakes his head. "That right there proves my point."

"You're looking at it from a dollar sign, not the effort that went into it. All for me. Just me. It's not like we're home and you could call up your favorite florist. I can't imagine the research and planning that went into securing all this, plus the searching and scans that went into every flower." Turning, I take in the beautiful display. My heart wobbles at the love each and every single rose represents.

"I'd walk through Hell for you, Mess. Haven't you figured that out by now?"

I nod, keeping my focus on the flowers, not wanting to see the emotions on his face that are clearly in those words. "But why?" I ask. "I'm no one. I'm a flash in the pan. This will all be over in three years. Why give so much of yourself?"

Palm to my cheek, he turns my face. Honey brown eyes seem to smile down into my own.

"Because you're not asking me to."

I shake my head, not understanding. His calluses scrape my cheek as that hand slides up, his fingers delving into my loose dark hair.

"My whole life, people have expected things from me. Money, prestige, power when dating me, or hell, even being my friend. But you, Randi Sawyer, love me for me."

"I do," I whisper through the tears clogging my throat. "Because you do."

"And that's why I'd give my life for yours, because it's not a life I want to live without you in it."

"Don't say that," I cry. Reaching out, I grab a fistful of his black T-shirt. "Not when it's a reality every day I'm in office."

"Mess, this kind of pure love, this devotion, can't just be turned off. You're everything to me. When I'm not with you, I'm thinking of you. I worry about you every second of every fucking day. I want you happy for the rest of your life. You're the end of my story. There's no coming back from this, from you."

Tears streak down my cheeks. "I should fire you," I say. Resting my forehead on his muscular chest, I take a deep breath of his unique scent. "Problem solved."

"Nah, you like the eye candy too much." His fingers wiggle through mine, loosening the grip I still have on his shirt. "Come on, Mess. Help me make dinner?"

"I can't believe you never told me." I wipe the remaining butter off my fingers with the rough paper towel before swiping my mouth one last time. I toss it to my empty plate resting on top of the coffee table and lean back against the couch, my backside sliding forward a bit on the rug. "I mean, how has your hobby never come up in conversation? I see you almost every day."

Shoving a handful of Cheetos into his mouth, Trey shrugs where he lounges beside me, head lying on top of my thighs.

"I always wondered what you did to make your hands so rough," I say absentmindedly.

He lifts the hand that's intertwined with my own, examining the palm with a concentrated expression.

Leaning low, I whisper just above his lips, "I love it." Before he can pull me in for a kiss, I sit back and rest my head on the couch cushion. Around us, the candles continue to burn through the dark, the flames a bit longer and brighter. The overpowering aroma of the roses mixes with the savory scent of burnt butter and melted cheese. It's intoxicating, really. Or maybe it's the man I don't deserve resting on my lap who's causing the almost out-of-body feeling to rush through my head.

"It's just something I've always done."

I run a hand down his strong shoulders and over his pecs, savoring the hard muscles beneath my fingers. "Do you enjoy it?"

"I do. It's the best workout, and it helps me process everything. It's a few hours of silence, just me and the river."

I scratch at his nipple over his shirt. He hisses and smacks my hand away.

"Would you ever take me with you?"

I immediately miss the weight of his head when he leans up onto his elbows and turns his chest toward me. "You'd want to come out with me?"

"I mean, I'd just sit there, you can do all the work, but yeah. I think it would be fun to see what you enjoy. Rowing really isn't something that's big in Texas, or at least not that I'm aware of, so I don't understand it."

"It's a date." Leaning close, he brushes his lips over mine.

"We're not done with our first one. What makes you so cocky to think you'll get another one?

He pulls back and waggles his eyebrows, exuding boyish charm. I miss this Trey. The one who flirts, fights, and laughs. A part of me hates that I've changed him.

"Do you think I've changed you?" I blurt.

"Yes," he says quickly, not understanding the strain in my voice. "In a good way. Why?"

"When we first met, you were... I don't know, more mischievous maybe. Freer, not as stressed. And now you sometimes look like you have the weight of the world on your shoulders. Do you blame me for that?"

He shakes his head, his dark hair swiping across his eyes before he flicks it back with a toss of his head. Something like humor shines in his eyes. With a grunt of pain, Trey pushes off the floor to stand, stretching his arms to the ceiling. A few cracks pop from his back through the quiet living room.

"I wouldn't use the word 'blame,' Mess." I eye his outstretched hand with caution before lacing my fingers through his. With a quick tug, I'm on my feet and tucked to his side. "Next time you see Tank, ask him how I've changed. I'd say I've grown up more than changed."

Not given a choice in the matter, I match his long strides toward the back door. Outside, the earlier cool breeze has shifted colder. Snuggling against his side, I turn my face into his ribs.

"There's some things that come into your life that make you have a purpose. Before being assigned to your detail, I was lost, I guess. Nothing mattered. Well, Tank and the team mattered, but other than that, I was a selfish SOB."

A grunt in the dark as we follow the path to the beach makes me smile.

"Pipe down out there," Trey shouts with no heat to it. "As I was saying, I'm a better version of myself with you in my life. Do you not agree?"

The squishy, cold sand slides between my bare toes, shooting a chill up my spine. Scanning the beach, I squint at the faint outline of a tent-like structure closer to the water. Anticipation boils in my belly, sending excitement rushing through my veins.

"Yeah, I guess, but I never really saw that side of you. I only saw the asshole who softened. But I do kind of miss that mischievousness we used to have. Now things are so... heavy, if that's the right word to use. It's like every breath, every word in every day has some kind of weight to it that's tied to something that's life-threatening." I smile at the white canvas popping in the quick breeze. "What's this?"

"You didn't think me cooking was the best surprise of the night, did you?"

That and the hundred—hell, maybe thousands—of dollars of flowers.

Releasing his hold around my waist, he grips my hand and tugs me into the makeshift enclosure. Once inside, the wind ceases instantly, making me warmer without its cold breath brushing against my bare legs. I grin at the blanket spread along the sand highlighted by the few glowing lanterns dangling from above.

"When did you have time to do all this?" I ask in awe.

"I might have had some help." He tugs me toward the blanket, forcing me to follow him as he lowers onto it. "When I told Tank about my plans, he didn't want the whole team to see us, so we came up with a way for you and me to have some privacy while getting out of the house and being secure."

"It's perfect." Lying back, I track the slow sway of a lantern. "High hopes of getting lucky?"

"You could say that." His voice is deeper, huskier than just moments before.

The sand shifts beneath my head as I roll it to look over to where he leans on his side, head propped up on his hand with his elbow dug into the blanket.

"As much as I hate that idiot Birmingham, I'll always be grateful for his hand in bringing you into my life."

Love swells in my chest and my heart thunders, each beat making me fall deeper in love with this man before me.

"I love you, Trey." His eyes close like he's savoring my words. "I didn't know what living was before you." The honest words, words I've never spoken out loud, bring tears to my eyes. "I knew deep love because of Tae, but this, what we have... it's different. It's... soul-consuming because I chose this. You chose this. This, what we have, is on purpose. I didn't know—"

Thankfully he interrupts my lovestruck rambling with a searing kiss. With a content sigh, I lift higher, sealing my lips harder against his. Sliding a hand beneath my head, he supports me as he pours his deep emotions into me with a single kiss. Warmth quickly races through my veins, heating my skin and causing sweat to dot along my forehead and temples.

Following me down to the blanket, he shifts to his side. A single hand dips beneath my sweatshirt, swiping lazy strokes along my stomach and circling my belly button. High and higher his fingers travel. I gasp against his lips at the brush of his knuckle against the underside of my breast.

His movements stop.

"No bra, Mess?" he mumbles against my lips. "I approve."

My happy giggle turns into a groan as he cups one breast, the sharp edge of his nail skimming over my pebbled nipple. Back and forth he glides the pad of his thumb, sending small shock waves of rolling pleasure pulsing to my core.

I skim a hand over his shoulders and down his spine, gripping the hem of his shirt before tugging it up his back. With some assistance, I pull it over his head and toss it to the sand. Using the brief moment, Trey drags my sweatshirt over my head, kissing along the exposed skin as he works his way toward my jean shorts.

I sigh in complete bliss as he undoes the button, kissing the bit of skin he exposed beneath. Lost in the sensations of the cool night air, heated skin, and slick lips kissing every inch of my inner thighs I fail to notice him removing my shorts or his own until he's hovering above me. I smile. A happy, completely lost in love smile. Lost in him. And what's even better is the one shining back down at me. It's in his eyes, the pure devotion and adoration. I soak it in, savoring the feel of his bare chest, the beat of his heart in sync with my own, and the weight of him settling between my thighs.

He doesn't break eye contact as he pushes himself in deep, and the almost purr of pleasure rumbling from his chest doesn't go unnoticed. Trey slides his fingers through my hair, cradling both my cheeks with his palms as he kisses along each cheekbone.

"I love your freckles, did you know that? I love your natural beauty because it's what's inside that shines through. I love your crazy, your strange obsession with unicorns, and the man you make me want to be. I'll never deserve you, Randi, but I promise every day I'll do my best to make you happy."

I try to respond, but his lips press against mine, cutting off the words. Our tongues dance in an unhurried, sensual way we haven't had before now. Tonight, we're untouched, uncensored or rushed. Just us and the beach and the ocean. The waves crash along the sandy shore, the only other sound along the beach except our sweat-slick skin moving as one and our moans of pure ecstasy.

I like it rough, but this, this I love.

Digging the back of my head into the sand, I squeeze my eyes shut. Flexing off the blanket, I urge him faster, chasing the orgasm I'm teetering on the edge of.

Taking my cue, he presses onto his elbows and shifts his angle and pace, immediately sending me into a spiral of erotic pleasure.

The world goes black, everything around me fuzzy. Somewhere around me, Trey grunts a curse, and a heavy weight crushes to my chest. Peeling my lids open, I smile up at the swinging lanterns and wrap my arms around his back. Stroking my fingertips up and down his spine, I relish our one moment alone.

Tomorrow, things will change, but tonight, we have only each other.

21

TREY

Not sure why I'm so shocked that Vlad chose *this* location or the time of day, but I am. Just because they're Russian doesn't mean they only come out at night and meet in dark alleys. I'm sure they won't melt in the sun. Like I am this very moment.

I scan the small, empty park again, searching for any threats in the lush trees and bushes. The agency-issued sunglasses keep the brilliant overhead sun from attacking my vision, but nothing can stop the sweat from building beneath my T-shirt and sliding down my spine. At least we're not in our typical suit uniform today. I'd be a puddle of sweat and curses if we were.

Out of the corner of my eye, Randi's alternating bouncing knees draw my attention. She sits atop a stone picnic table, feet bobbing on the bench seat, middle fingernail between her nibbling teeth. I fight a grin as I sweep the area again, noting the other agents dotted around the perimeter of the park. Only Tank and I stand close to Randi, per her request. Tank wanted more, but with the sensitivity of the conversation to come, he settled for it being us and about ten guns hidden along our bodies, plus many, many more on the other guys keeping an eagle eye on the park.

I blow a slow breath through pinched lips, hoping that'll help ease my growing agitation from the heat. In typical Randi fashion, she's decked out in leggings, Uggs, and a lightweight sweater when the rest of us are teetering on the edge of heat exhaustion. A few weeks ago, I made the mistake of calling her cold-blooded instead of cold-natured. I shake my head at the memory. I'll never do that again. That slip of the tongue earned me the cold shoulder for several hours.

She knew what I meant. I think.

After last night though, none of that seems to matter. The past distance, the times apart, and the longing seem like a trial we had to get through to be where we are now. Making love on the beach with the cool breeze coming off the crashing waves and her beautiful body beneath mine made our connection deeper. It wasn't the first time we've had sex, but it was the first time it was slow and sensual. Not a quickie in her room before Tank could catch us or in a darkened ballroom. No, last night was what intertwines souls. It molded us together, made us become one.

Love.

Soul-clenching, mind-numbing, breath-stealing love.

It's scary as hell. All love is, of course, but we have higher stakes. So many people are against us, as a couple and individually. It won't be easy, not that it ever has been, but somehow last night sealed our fate.

Together.

Forever.

No matter the cost.

The roaring of a revving engine snaps my thoughts back to the potential danger we're about to be surrounded with. In my earpiece one of the guys lets us know three black SUVs are approaching via the only road with access to this area. Seconds later, the three Suburbans appear over the crest of the hill the park is situated on. One after another they park. Several large fuckers step out of the SUVs wearing...

"What the hell?" I whisper at the same time Tank's shocked chuckle rumbles through the picnic area.

"Don't you dare make fun of them," Randi says, though a lightness to her tone signals she's holding back her own laughter. "I think it's cute."

I shoot her a quick glare.

"Don't get your holster in a twist. They're not nearly as cute as you, Trouble."

Satisfied by her response, I swing my attention back to the eight men all wearing stiff khaki shorts and varying bright Hawaiian shirts. I cringe at the bright glare bouncing off their white legs that somehow cuts through my state-of-the-art sunglasses.

Dressed in his own horrible ensemble, Vlad strides toward Randi, no smile on his harsh features. The bright and loud outfits are a complete contrast to the men wearing them. There are too many quips I could make about... well, everything encompassing the approaching men's attire, but I somehow manage to keep them to myself.

"Madam VP," Vlad says as soon as he's close.

"It's Randi, Vlad. You know that. This is our second secret meeting after all. I think we can drop the formalities."

He dips his chin before saying a few words in Russian that disperses his men to various points around the small picnic area. Tank and I tense, muscles at the ready for anything, as Vlad climbs up the picnic table and sits beside Randi.

"Festive outfit," she says, biting into her lower lip to hold back her smile.

Vlad tips his head back and laughs. "We wanted to blend in during our time on the island. But we might have taken it to the extreme. "

Randi nods, still trying not to smile. "Maybe just a little. How long are you here for?"

He shrugs, the large floral print seeming to reflect the sun's rays. "Not sure. When you reached out to schedule this meetup, I had my team book the arrival flight but leave the return one open-ended. I needed the break."

"Same," she says with a sigh. Leaning back on her palms, she keeps her focus straight forward. "Thanks for coming, Vlad. I'm in a pickle."

"In a pickle?"

She smiles. "It's a figure of speech. It means I'm in a bind, or in a touchy spot."

"Ah. And anytime, all you have to do is ask." He pauses. "Your call came at an interesting time, I have to admit. Did you know another person from your office requested a meeting as well for after the new year?"

Randi's smile falls, her eyes narrowing on the man beside her. She looks so tiny beside him; all it would take is one move and he'd crush her.

"The president, I'm assuming."

Vlad shakes his head. Placing his hands back along the stone surface next to hers, he leans back, mirroring her. Tank monitors the movement of his hands as I watch his face, trying to decipher his next move.

"No, your secretary of state."

Shock morphs across her features. "Todd." The scrunch of her nose as she says the name tells Vlad exactly how she feels about the man.

Vlad nods. "Says he wants to meet but has not disclosed as to why. I am not getting the impression his intent is honorable, however."

Randi snorts, causing Vlad's bushy eyebrows to rise a fraction.

"He's an opportunist, I guess." Randi scans the park like the bushes and trees hold the answer she's searching for. "He knows about our meeting in Chile somehow. Maybe he's trying to capitalize on our... whatever we are to use to his advantage." Leaning forward, she braces her elbows on her still bouncing knees. "It would be huge in the Americans' eyes if he claimed to settle the rocky relations between our two countries."

"Agreed."

Tense silence passes between the two leaders.

"I am assuming you need the proof I offered at our last meeting."

Randi nods, her dark hair shifting over her shoulders to form a dark curtain, keeping me from seeing her beautiful face. "I need evidence but can't get it on my own." Her backside shifts against the stone table as she turns to face Vlad. "I need your help, Vlad. You offered proof, offered friendship in our last meeting, and I'm taking you up on that offer now. I know what Kyle's doing, but I can't prove it."

"Your American courts will not accept any information you obtain from someone like me."

I hold a breath at the tense pause from Randi. She knows what she's asking for isn't exactly legal, but what option do we have at this point?

"Can you help me?" she grits out. "I don't care how you get it, but I need something strong enough that will cause Kyle to step down immediately, on his own, not daring to risk the details being released to the public."

"What information do you need?"

The way he says it, his apprehensive tone speaks volumes. It seems there's various dirty dealings Kyle is a part of, and Vlad is asking which one Randi wants him and his team to target.

"He's abusing power. Allowing certain companies to drill on federal land. We need proof that those companies can be tied directly to campaign supporters. Some kind of money trail proving he's offering kickbacks. And there's something else." She takes a deep breath and releases it slowly. Tucking a lock of hair behind her ear, she flicks a quick look at me. "Give us a minute, Trey."

Unease and anger battle inside me, each fighting for the dominant emotion to direct my words and actions.

"No" is all I can get out between my clenched teeth.

"Trey, please." When that doesn't work, she switches tactics. "Step back, Benson," she says, her eyes bearing down into my own. "That's an order."

Pursing my lips, I glance at Tank, who nods. Hurt slashes through the other emotions raging in my chest. Taking three steps back, I stare back at Randi, proving this is as far as I'm willing to go.

With a resigned sigh, she leans in close to Vlad, their low voices a gentle murmur not clear enough for me to catch a single word.

Vlad nods and stands.

"I will see what we can dig up." Large hands slide down the hideous shirt, smoothing out the nonexistent wrinkles. "I will warn you, friend. What your president has already set in motion cannot be undone. But if he is out of office soon, maybe you can smooth relationships over before war can happen."

"That's the second time you've mentioned that," I interrupt, stepping back to Randi's side. I release a tense breath when she doesn't push me away.

Vlad nods, his gray eyes sliding to me. "The situation has escalated. The true reasons behind closed door meetings and secret alliances are coming to light."

"What does that even mean?" Randi asks. "Stop talking in riddles, would you?"

Vlad smiles. Well, I think it's a smile. His lips twitch, at any rate. "Your president is an idiot."

"Tell me something I don't know," Randi mutters.

"He made promises, deals with certain players who were playing him the entire time. Birmingham was greedy, his sights only on one thing, and he was willing to do anything to get it."

"The White House."

"Yes. He did not see their true desires."

"Money, right?" Randi questions.

"Yes."

"That's what I'm asking about. The oil—"

Vlad laughs. "That is small money compared to what they are planning. You will have your work cut out for you, but I will help as much as I can."

Randi's head falls forward. "What am I walking into, Vlad? Just tell me. If I'm successful in getting Kyle to step down, what's ahead of me?"

"There is great money during war. Panic causes prices to rise, demand to spike. That is just in commercial goods. Think about the companies who supply the metal, the gunpowder, the technology to your military. Do you not think they would benefit off the threat?"

"You're saying what Kyle thought he was doing was like a small fish in the big pond. He actually set in motion something much bigger than he ever expected."

Vlad nods, his brows furrowing. "It will take some time to get the information you need. I hope you can end him before it—"

"Whoa there, friend." Randi tosses her hands out in surrender. "I never said anything about ending him. Just presenting him with the information you'll give me, threatening to release it, and proving what a son of a bitch he is to everyone, then praying he resigns on his own."

"That is a terrible plan."

"So is 'ending' someone."

"If they are dead, they cannot retaliate. Which your president will if you follow through with your plan. He will not take defeat like a man."

"I know. I'm sending my daughter away. I'll add more protection to Mom's rehab center too. Those are the only ways he can really get back at me." Nibbling on her thumbnail, she shakes her head like she's debating Vlad's words. "No, this is the best way. I can't take him out just because he might escalate things. This is the most legal option." Her lips twitch upward. "My law professors would high-five me for the thick gray line I seem to like dancing on. They always said I saw things too black and white."

"We agree to disagree, then." Raising a hand, he motions for his team to gather close. "Give me some time to find the evidence you need. It is one thing to know what is going on and another having the information available to prove it."

"Cool, yeah. Whenever you can would be great. No rush." She tilts her head. "Nope, wait, there is a rush considering everything you've just exposed. If I can get this done before the idiot can shove us into a war that's all for money, that would be awesome." Both her thumbs flick up before she tucks them under her thighs. A bright flush spreads across her cheeks.

I hold back my laugh. Fuck, she's so damn random. But I'd be lying if I said I didn't love it.

Vlad smiles—legit smiles—and nods.

"We will be in touch." He starts to turn but pauses. "What should I do about the secretary of state?"

"Don't kill him!" Randi blurts.

This time a full-body laugh rumbles from Vlad, catching everyone off guard. I swear his security team thinks he's having a stroke by the way they rush to grab him. He simply shrugs their concern off.

"I meant should I meet with him or not. Which would you prefer?" He strokes a hand over his dark beard. "But if you want me to end—"

"No, please no. Um, the meeting? I don't know. I don't see the harm in it. I really don't care what people think about Todd or if they think he's the one fixing the tension between our countries."

"But it is not him, it is you."

She shrugs and pushes off the table. Standing on the bench seat, she stretches her arms up high. "Yeah, but I don't care if he gets the credit. I know we're the close ones." With a quick hop, she lands on the soft dirt below. "How long are we thinking? For the information."

Vlad raises a single shoulder. "Not sure, I will get someone on it today. What you are needing is specific, something that is indisputable, not just vague emails or conversations. You will need pictures, recordings, proof he now knows what he has stepped into and how it all started."

"Yeah, it's a lot." Walking toward Vlad, she extends her hand. After a quick shake, she steps back. "Thank you. For everything. I appreciate your help."

The Russian's facial expression morphs to more contemplative as he looks Randi over. "It is an honor, Madam VP. One day soon you will return the favor, I am sure."

With that, he turns and strides toward the SUVs they evacuated less than thirty minutes ago.

"I love the way they handle meetings," I say, stepping to Randi's side. She angles her face up to mine with a questioning look. "In and out. Get what you need done, say what needs to be said, and bounce. If all politicians did that, maybe they'd get more done."

She smirks and nods. Turning her attention to the retreating SUVs, she blows out a slow breath.

"I think that went well."

"Agreed. Now, why did you ask me to step away?"

Instead of responding, Randi takes a cautious step to the side and starts to walk away. I follow close behind, having nothing to do with safety and everything to do with getting answers.

For a few steps, she says nothing, eyes to the ground watching the grass bend beneath her Uggs.

"If we're going to do this, you and me, us, we need to be honest with each other." Reaching out, she takes my hand in hers, lacing our fingers together and giving a quick squeeze. "No more surprises, no more committing to things that affect this relationship without the other one's consent." Hazel eyes slide to meet mine. "Okay?"

I nod, not understanding what she's getting at. Okay, yeah, I made a bad decision not telling her about the agreement I made with my parents for her to win the Senate and defeat the bill, but I thought we were past that misstep.

"Is there anything you want to tell me, Trey?"

I search her face, trying to figure out what she's referring to.

"Um, I guess Jessica's been more of a handful lately." Randi's dark brows bolt up her forehead. "I'm not sure what's gotten into her, but it's fine. Nothing I can't handle and keep pushing back on." I think back through the past few months. "My mother is pushing me to set a date for a true engagement party, one that will be thrown by her and Jessica's mother." I feel the deep line form between my brows. "I snuck a cigarette last week." Raising my shoulders, I press my lips together and give her my best "not sure what you're looking for" look.

A quick breeze sends her dark hair floating across her face. After tucking it behind her ear, she turns and starts walking again.

"Good to know about Jessica and your mom. Hopefully we can get all this wrapped up before you have to commit to a date for the engagement party." Those last two words are said with bitterness engulfing her tone. "And the cigarette, fine, that means I get to sneak one too. What else, Trouble?"

"Just tell me what you're looking for, Mess, and I'll tell you, but I honestly have no idea what you're wanting me to say."

"T told me about your plan."

"My plan to... what? Need to be more specific here. I have a lot of crazy plans that I toss out to him but never come to fruition."

"About going back to that evil woman who birthed you and digging yourself deeper into her fucked-up plot to take over the world all to learn how Shawn is still getting to me." Her tone is angry, and a dash of hurt bleeds through with each word.

I pull to a stop, tugging on her hand for her to pause too. With another sharp tug, I tuck her against my chest and rest my chin on top of her head. I love holding her like this. Feeling her small frame wrapped in mine. Protecting her from anything that would cause her harm. But doesn't she see that's exactly what I'm trying to do with going back to Mother for answers? Everything is for her.

"Ah, that plan," I try to joke as I take a deep inhale of her cherry-and-vanilla-scented hair.

"Yeah, that one," she grumbles into my chest, tickling the skin beneath my Dryfit T-shirt.

I relax my hold enough to stroke two fingers up and down her spine. Staring off into the thick cluster of trees, I try to pretend everyone can't hear our conversation from their close proximity.

"You're right," I admit. "I should've talked to you considering how badly the last agreement with her went." I cringe at the reminder of what Mother pulled. I've always known she's a manipulating opportunist, but holding aggravated assault charges over your son's head just for him to do your bidding is over the top. We still don't know how she knew about the altercation with that bastard in Boone, Texas, Randi's hometown, but she does, and she sure as hell jumped on the opportunity to use it to her advantage.

"If we're going to make this work, then we have to be honest with each other."

I nod, my chin popping lightly against the crown of her head.

"I asked Vlad for information on her, your mother. And Jessica if he can find it."

Shock halts any response I could've come up with. Wrapping my fingers around her slim shoulder, I push us apart an inch. Looking down, I wait until she focuses up on me.

"And you didn't think that was something we should discuss together?"

Now it's her turn to look confused.

"Mess." I sigh. My fingers slide through the longer portion of my hair as I try to gather my thoughts. Damn, she's so innocent. "You know every favor comes with strings."

The line between her brows deepens. "I'm already asking for help with obtaining the information on Kyle. What's one more favor when so many are stacking up anyway?"

Reaching up, she grips my T-shirt and curls her fingers into tight fists.

"I'm done with you being the only one sacrificing bits of yourself, Trey Benson. What's done is done—"

The vibrating of my phone in my pocket stops her from continuing. As soon as it stops, it starts back up again.

"Need to get that?"

I sigh, knowing full well who it'll be. Reaching inside my shorts pocket, I slide the thin device out and hold the screen up so Randi can see.

Her eyes widen. "That's the fourth call you've missed." Once again, the phone shakes in my hand as Jessica tries calling for a fifth time. "Answer it and put it on speakerphone."

I groan but do it anyway. I glance across the small clearing to where Tank stands and send him a helpless look. My best friend just holds up his hands palms out and shakes his head, smiling.

Fucker.

I mouth just as much his way as I slide my thumb across the glass screen and hit the speakerphone button.

"What do you want, Jessica?" I say, letting the exhaustion from the last hour seep into my weary voice.

"Why didn't you pick up?"

I stifle a laugh at Randi's annoyed eye roll.

"Working."

"Listen, you've been gone for a while. Why don't you just come home and we can work on the party plans—"

"I've got to go, Jessica."

"Wait." Her voice turns panicky. "I don't feel safe on my own anymore."

Randi's questioning gaze flicks to me. I shake my head, letting her know I'm not buying the bullshit Jessica is selling.

"Jessica, we've talked about this. I know what you're doing, and it's not going to work."

"I'm telling the truth," she says on a sad whisper. "Why won't you protect me like you do her?"

Randi's upper lip tugs upward in a snarl. Somehow, I hold back my amused chuckle—barely.

"For lots of reasons. You know that, Jessica. Listen, you're the one who went behind my back to make this fake engagement part of the deal I had with my mother to stop the bill. Don't act like I'm the one to blame for this mess."

Silence is her response for several seconds before she drops a bomb on me that leaves me stunned.

"I'm done being second, Trey. I've already cleared it with the management office and your mother. I'm moving in."

With that, she hangs up.

I stare at the blank screen, a little too nervous to glance up and get a front row seat to Randi's reaction to this. Love her, but she's a tad crazy. Who knows what elaborate plan she's thinking through to get back at Jessica.

After a few moments, it becomes obvious that I'm avoiding the inevitable. Taking a deep breath in for strength, I stand tall and slide the phone back into the mesh pocket of my shorts.

The smile on Randi's face is the last thing I expect.

"Looks like T and Sarah just got themselves a new roomie," she states, her words and tone leaving no room for discussion. The grumbled string of curses from across the clearing makes her laugh and glance over her shoulder. "Don't worry, it won't be for long. I have a feeling it won't take long for my little Russian friend to dig up usable dirt on Trouble's mom. We'll all be back to normal in no time."

I groan and close my eyes, tipping my face to the bright sun.

Why do I get the feeling she's really, *really* wrong in that assessment?

22

RANDI

June

Six long months.

Six.

Six months of waiting for a phone call from Vlad saying he has the information we need to corner Kyle.

Six months of waiting for Vlad to slide the incriminating evidence I need to get Jessica and Trey's mother out of our lives.

Six months of that little tart living in Trey's condo, acting like it's hers, and bringing it up whenever we happen to run into one another. Even though he's not living there, it still stings every time it's mentioned in passing.

Him living with T and Sarah lasted all of one week, three days, and part of one shift. Apparently they weren't discreet in their intimate times, and Trey is a spoiled man-child who expects someone to cook and clean for him.

To save their friendship, Trey moved out of their two-bedroom apartment. Since he was obviously not moving back into his condo with her and happens to have unlimited funds, he ponied up the cash for a small furnished efficiency close to my place. Jessica and his mother think he's still bunking with Tank. Not sure how he's pulling that off, but so far, he's skated under their radar.

Since that day we left Camp David, Sam has been true to his word. He talked the attorney general into believing there was no reason to continue the investigation, claiming there was no substantial evidence there and it should be tabled for the time being. He bought it and moved Sam to a different case. Of course, just because Sam isn't investigating for the DOJ's case doesn't mean he's dropped it during his private time. He's getting nowhere, which frustrates him daily, but that's what you get when you're forced to use your own resources. He calls at least twice a week asking if my illegal source has anything for us. And each week I have to tell him no.

I hate it.

I hate it for the American people, I hate it for me, for Sam, for everyone who knows that Kyle is getting away with... hell, borderline treason at this point. He's in too deep with whoever is running the show. Each meeting he appears more exhausted than the last. The dark heavy bags under his eyes, the deepening wrinkles. He's aging drastically from week to week. Already his previously thick black hair is grayer than ever before and appears to be thinning near the temples.

But there's nothing I can do but wait.

And wait.

Until today.

It started out like every other day since that afternoon in Hawaii, waking up and talking to Taeler before I even roll out of bed. With her using the summer to travel around Europe, I have to catch her at the same time every day so she's available and expecting my call. I'm slightly jealous of my daughter, if I'm honest with myself. She's having the time of her life visiting various countries with a new best friend she's made while abroad —and of course her security detail. It's taken some finagling to make sure the guys have clearance for each of the countries they enter, but the director over the secret service has been more than helpful at every hurdle.

Apparently she loves me, because one, I stand up for myself against these so-called men in this city, and two, I've helped calm Trey down from all his "shenanigan ways"—her words, not mine.

Back to this morning. Everything was normal until it wasn't.

One unexpected guest showed up bearing a sizable, stuffed-to-the-brim manila envelope. *Seriously what's with the Russians and envelopes?*

"Maybe the Dollar Store was running a sale?" I mumble to myself.

The stranger's nearly black buzzed hair, thick black beard, and cold eyes were the first indication that Vlad had finally come through.

"Manila envelopes, makes you so hipster am I right?"

Nothing. When my joke about their abundance of manila envelopes falls flat, it confirmed my assumption.

Russian.

Without a word, or even a raised brow at my lame joke, he stretched the thick envelope out toward me only to be intercepted by Trey. Instead of getting bent out of shape, I just sighed and folded my hands in front of me, the perfect picture of patience.

"What's in here?" Trey demands while taking a challenging step closer to the very tall man.

Geez, what do they feed those guys?

Our mystery man just arches a brow and looks down at Trey, remaining silent.

"You know what's in there. Stop causing trouble, Trouble." I smirk at my words. "Go run whatever tests so we can look through it. We've waited long enough, and my patience is nearly spent when it comes to that idiot sitting in the Oval Office."

Trey gives me an annoyed glance over his shoulder. Before I can think better of it, I stick my tongue out at him only to suddenly remember we're not alone. Tongue still stuck out, I peek at the stoic man. My apprehension slides away to relief at the small twitch of his lips at my expense.

"Thank you," I say, straightening my blouse and smoothing my hands down my cropped black slacks. "Any insight or warnings, or should we just wing it as we go through the papers?"

"Everything inside."

Right. A man of many words.

With a dip of his head, he turns on his black boot-looking shoes and strides out the door T yanks open for him. A hot breeze blasts through the opened door, warming the air-conditioned entryway before T can slam it shut.

Trey holds the envelope up to the light, squinting at it like he might've somehow developed X-ray vision in the last few minutes.

"Give me that." T grunts and yanks the envelope out of Trey's hand. Seems I'm not the only one who's out of patience.

"We can't let anyone outside of us know what's in there, T," I say, stepping up beside the two men. "I say we toss caution and protocol to the wind and open it. Fingers crossed for no dying."

Two sets of accusing scowls land on me.

"You know I'm right," I grumble. The way T's tight, fierce expression falters slightly confirms my claim. "It is what it is. We know Vlad and know he wouldn't do anything to harm me or our budding relationship. Come on, you two, let's do this in the office."

Now here I sit shocked beyond belief, staring at information anyone in this city would kill to obtain. Hundreds of pictures, several audio files with transcripts, and thousands of incriminating emails. It's been almost an hour since the information was dropped in our laps, and even with the three of us reviewing each document, we're only halfway through. But it's already enough to make Kyle step down.

Which should make me beyond ecstatic, right? This is what I've been waiting for, what I've worked toward for many, many months. But now that it's here, and the evidence is literally in my hands, my emotions are the complete opposite of happy.

I'm fucking terrified. As in my knees are knocking under the massive desk I'm cowering behind at the moment. Palms-sweating, heart-racing, gut-churning fear.

"This is so bad," I whisper, my rising terror and horror cracking my hushed voice. "Guys...."

Maybe if I run right now. Maybe if I hide under the desk, take the way of the ostrich, I can avoid what's coming my way. Not the best solution to this problem, but it's way better than the alternative—me compiling the information into a more organized and concise format, marching over to the White House, and giving Kyle the option of stepping down on his own or me going through with the true impeachment.

Either option leaves me as president.

President of the United States of America.

Holy fuckballs.

I press the heel of my hand to my sternum in an attempt to keep my heart from beating out of my chest. Up and down my hand falls with each rapid breath.

"I can't do this," I state to myself, but the way the two men's heads snap to attention, focus going from the papers in their hands to me, tells me they heard it. "I'm not fit to be the president. Hell, I'm not fit to be the vice president." My voice shakes, giving away my rising panic. "I put my underwear on backward this morning. *Backward*," I shout to no one in particular. "And didn't realize it until way later. Yesterday, I thought someone was talking about a certain type of coffee, but nope, they were referring to a country. I thought a country was a fucking brew they serve at Starbucks. I can't do this."

Not waiting for a reply to my very random rant, even for me, I push off the desk, my sweaty palms sliding forward on the shiny surface as I stand. Before I can take a single step, T moves to one side of the desk and Trey to the other, officially blocking me in. Feeling like a cornered wild animal, I crane my neck behind me, searching for another exit.

There isn't one.

"Randi, you've known the whole time this would be the result."

Fuck T and his solid reasoning. I don't want reasoning. I want to leave and never look back. Maybe Switzerland will let me stay for a bit.

"Mess, calm down. Take a deep breath—"

I point a ragged nail at Trey's chest. "I know I'm freaking out, okay? Stop it with the reasoning and deep-breathing calming treatments. Just let me freak the fuck out for a second!" The soft leather of the chair molds under my tightening fingers as I lean forward, gripping the top while the other hand rubs circles along my breastbone. "It's not you two who will be asked to lead a country. To lead the most powerful country in the world. It's me. Not saying Kyle is any better, but do you two really think I should have the authority to nuke a country?" I arch a brow at them. Shaking my head, I close my eyes and tilt my face to the ceiling. "Tell me there's another option."

Silence meets my question, confirming what I already knew.

"Mess, look at me." A hand wraps around mine, tugging it around a lean waist. The comforting heat and the faint spicy and citrus scent wrap around my frazzled mind, soothing the panic. Forcing my lids open, I tilt my head back to find his worried gaze scanning my face. "I know you're scared. But you can do this. You see what Birmingham has brought on our country in just a year and a half in the role. Imagine what will happen over the next two and a half. I'm not saying it'll be easy, but you can do it. And we'll be there with you every step of the way."

"He's right, Randi," T says somewhere behind me, tightness in his words proving his worry for me, or hell, maybe America. "We won't leave your side. I don't know shit about running the country either, but we'll figure it out."

"I'm a nobody, remember?" Needing to steal a bit of Trey's strength, I wrap the other arm around his waist and squeeze. "Why in the hell would anyone follow me? Other leaders will know I'm just a poor man's excuse for a president."

"You listen to me, Randi Sawyer. You're no poor man's anything. You think money makes a person more capable of running this country? Just look at Kyle, at my parents, at this whole city. They're selfish pricks who only focus on one thing—themselves. You're a better fit for this role than anyone I know because for the first time in a very, very long time, the American people will have someone who's looking out for them. Who knows their struggles and actually cares. Don't you ever think you're less than these fucking pricks again."

A part of me wants to believe him, but the realistic side knows he's just saying it because he has to. Like he'd tell his girlfriend that she's in over her head.

The comforting strokes up and down my spine relax me further.

"We'll get through this together, Mess."

"What's this?"

The rough starched material of Trey's dress shirt slides along my cheek as I shift to see what T is referring to. Brows furrowed, he stares at a small flash drive between two of his massive fingers. Flicking it this way and that, he inspects every inch before looking to Trey.

"It looks different than the others that held the pictures and voice recordings."

I take a step out of Trey's tight embrace. "I didn't open that one yet. It wasn't labeled."

"Could be malware of some kind."

I shake my head at T's guess. "No. He wouldn't go through all this just to plant some kind of listening software on my computer."

"It's Russia." Trey's tone is cautious.

"It's Vlad," I respond. Reaching out, I pluck it from T's pinched fingers and pull it close, inspecting the small flash drive. "Only one way to find out."

"You still logged off the Wi-Fi and servers?"

I nod at T. I might put my underwear on backward, but I'm not that much of an idiot to load this while logged on to the government intranet.

The small metal device clicks into place easily. A slight whirring sound comes from my government-issued, state-of-the-art laptop before the external drive pops up on the screen. I steal a quick look at both men before clicking on the little icon.

I hold a shallow breath as it opens.

A small blue folder is all it contains.

The label of that folder causes my eyes to widen. I hover a finger over the mouse, not clicking on it just yet.

"The favor," I breathe out. A heavy weight seems to settle in the office. Once again, pressure builds behind my chest. Warmth seeps over my shoulder just before Trey's face aligns next to mine.

I swallow, waiting for him to give me the go-ahead to open it. Not because I'm worried that Vlad put some kind of malicious software in there but because whatever's inside this folder could change Trey's life. Forever. This folder could condemn his parents and/or Jessica.

Once we see what's inside, there's no going back.

"Open it," Trey says, his breath brushing against my cheek. I hesitate. Without looking away from the screen, he covers my hand with his own and clicks the mouse for me. "Let's take a look at what my parents have been hiding."

Sometimes the truth hurts.

And what pops up on the screen confirms that theory.

23

TREY

The vibrations between my thighs and the rumbling of my idling bike cut off with a flick of my thumb. Not ready to view the home I was raised in just yet, I lock my gaze on the glossy black paint of my bike. It's strange the number of warring emotions that churn inside me. Agony, anger, sadness, hate. There isn't one that outweighs the other, each taking a few seconds to wrap around my heart and soul before shuttering to the next. It's fucking exhausting. I'd ask Randi if this is how women feel most of the time, their emotions all over the place, except I don't want to die, so I'll keep the thought to myself.

I wish there was only hate and anger to deal with since there isn't any love lost between me and my parents. But yet they are still my parents. Even with Mother's manipulating behavior, a small part of me always wanted just a portion of her love, for her to love me. I shake that thought out of my head and tug the tight helmet off. Immediately the sweat that was trapped beneath slides down my neck and jaw.

Being raised privileged came with high costs, and not being loved was one of them. I did have Gerard and his wife filling in some of the gaps, but the hole left behind by an absent and cruel parent is nearly impossible to fill. Maybe that's why I fell so hard for Randi. I saw that she gave that love willingly and without strings, even giving up a piece of her soul for the millions of Americans she'll never know personally.

Fuck, do I have mommy issues?

A few chunks of damp dark hair shift into my line of vision. Maybe I should see a shrink after all this. If I can afford one, that is.

My gut bottoms out at the thought of my cushy lifestyle going away. Swallowing, I look to the massive estate. If I go through with confronting them, all this will be gone. My trust fund, the safety net, everything. If I truly thought this day would come to fruition, I would've invested the monthly income from the trust. Done something smart with it instead of spending it on... well, everything but saving.

I'll have to figure out that part of this fucked-up situation later.

At my back, an engine cuts off, settling a heavy silence around the quiet estate.

With a groan, I hike my leg over the bike and rest the helmet on the seat I just vacated as I turn to the two approaching men. Both wear the standard-issue black suit and typical grim face of a federal employee. The one on the right nods, indicating they're ready.

"Wait here a minute," I say, glancing back to the house. The front door opens, Gerard stepping out, his weathered face full of worry. "I want a word alone with them first."

Both nod and retreat to their dark SUV, no doubt ready to get out of the heat. I wait until they're back in the Suburban before I move toward the house.

"Gerard," I say, unable to keep the sadness from my voice. "Where are they?"

"In the sunroom, as you requested." I move past, not meeting his eyes, only to have him grip my bicep, bony fingers digging into the exposed skin. "What's going on, Trey?"

I close my eyes and fight the grief pounding through my veins. I'm not only about to alter my life forever but his too. Who knows what will happen to my parents once all this gets out? At least they didn't skip town after I called yesterday to schedule this meeting. That alone confirms they have zero clue as to why I'm here.

After reading through the files in the "Favor" folder yesterday, I was ready to storm over here and beat my dad to a pulp. Randi and Tank held me back long enough to calm my rage and form a plan. A plan of action, really.

First, I confront my parents, and then we tackle confronting Birmingham later this evening. One fucker at a time.

"Please tell me you didn't know." My voice cracks. Turning, I search his confused face. My heart breaks a little more. "Tell me you didn't know about my dad, about what he does outside the house."

His bushy white brows draw together. "I don't understand."

A bit of the tension releases from my chest. I knew deep down Gerard didn't know, but still I had to ask to know for sure. Reaching out, I grip his thin shoulder and give a gentle squeeze, not wanting to break the man in two. The scratchy material of his uniform scrapes against my palm as I pull away.

Only the heavy thump of my boots sounds down the long dark hallway. Normally when I'm in this house, a type of darkness encases me. Maybe it's from all those years of this being an estate, never a home; it made every inch cold and in turn froze me for nearly two decades. But today is different. Today I hold all the cards, and I know who they really are. I no longer want their approval or their love.

The closer I get to the sunroom, the more anger trumps the other emotions. Who cares what happens to me? Fuck their money that they've held over my head. I'll land on my feet. But my father... that's a different story. Today he'll be exposed and held accountable.

I swear steam sizzles off my palm as I tug the gold metal lever down to release the door latch and push it open. My steps falter at the normalcy I'm about to explode into chaos. Everything looks as it should, as it always has. Sparkling clean, sun pouring through the thick windows. The AC on full blast so the room remains cool unlike the hot summer temperatures outside.

"Trey, darling." Mother reclines on her favorite chaise, a glass of champagne in her hand. Jessica sits at her feet, a full glass of bubbling liquid between her fingers as well. Mother tilts her head, catching my scrutiny of their drink of choice at ten in the morning. "We're celebrating, of course."

"Celebrating."

She nods as that snakelike smile I've loathed my entire life, a little plumper nowadays, spreads across her wrinkle-free face.

"Yes, it's why you called us all here. To finally accept your role in this family, leading the Benson name into political fame, and to set a date for the formal engagement announcement with the lovely Jessica and her family.

And hopefully narrow down dates for the wedding too while we're all here."
Reaching out, she clinks her glass against Jessica's.

I ignore her and glance around the room. "Where's Dad?"

"Behind you, son."

His voice triggers the building agony and rage to let loose. I don't think about my actions, only react to my exploding emotions with a bellow as I twist around, putting all my strength behind the sailing knuckles. His eyes widen in pure shock before cringing shut as my fist slams against the side of his face. He stumbles to the side, arm out in a desperate move to catch his balance before his knees buckle under the pain and he falls to the floor. A high-pitched scream pierces the room from behind me, either Mother or Jessica, I don't give a rat's ass.

"You sick motherfucker," I spit. His face pales, no doubt seeing I'm on the verge of killing him with my bare hands. Palms smacking the hardwood floor, he scurries back, hands and feet slipping beneath his weight as he retreats like the damn coward he is. "You perverted son of a mother-fucking bitch."

Someone grips my arm, urging me back, but I fling it off. Pausing over my cowering father, I funnel all my disgust, hate, and pain into my hard stare. My fingers tighten into fists at my side. Everything in me tells me to strike again, but I hold myself back knowing if he's dead, then he can't pay for his crimes.

"I know about that fucking place, The Boardroom." Somehow, his face pales even further, understanding dawning on the reasons for my actions. The bones of my fingers groan under my tight fists. "They were just girls."

Close by, someone sucks in a harsh breath, confirming what I had already known. Jessica had no idea the fuckery she was desperate to marry into. Hell, I'm already a part of this fucked-up family and I didn't know until yesterday.

"Get out." Tilting my head, I level an emotionless glare to where Mother now stands, champagne glass discarded on the side table. "You have no right—"

"Oh, that's where you're wrong, Mother. I have every right. Not only do I have every right to stand here and beat the shit out of my own father for fucking underage girls, I have the damn proof." The sheer disgust in my tone echoes off the floor-to-ceiling windows. I suck in deep breath after deep breath. "And you knew." My voice cracks, giving away the pain I feel. "You knew the whole time what was going on, and you did nothing to stop it. Just kept fucking your own way through senator after senator, leaching off each person for more secrets and power."

My chest heaves as I turn back to my father where he sits against the wall, one hand cradling his swelling cheek while the other supports him from falling over.

"It's the way this city works, son." I blanch at his words, which he notices. Thinking he has some footing, thinking his excuse is valid, he straightens and stands, wobbling in place as he does. "You have no idea the deals that are made, the power and secrets that are exchanged there."

"I do not care. Those girls were held there, and you knew. You knew it was a hub for sex trafficking and did nothing except condone it by going back over and over and over again."

"I had to do it to stay at the top of this city. It was nothing, just sex. I didn't know their age."

"It's illegal and wrong," I somehow grit out with my jaw clenched tight.

"It's politics."

Another wave of disgust rushes through me. Blood pounds in my ears, distracting me to the point that I don't catch the door opening. I'm still transfixed by the perversion in his words when a cold hand rests on my shoulder. I go to shrug it off when it slides to my bare neck, sending a shiver down my spine. Immediately my swirling, out-of-control emotions settle. Confusion sets in briefly until Randi steps into my periphery.

"You didn't think I'd let you face this alone, did you?" The softness in her tone is a complete contradiction to the vileness coating the room. She gives the back of my neck another squeeze before sliding her hand down my arm to take my own and interlace our fingers. Shifting her attention to my father, the warmth in her features drains away. "Now, Mr. Benson, I walked in on the tail end of this conversation, so why don't you catch me up to speed."

"No."

My muscles bunch, readying to launch another punch at his sneering face, when Randi tugs on my arm.

"Okay, that's fine. I'll talk, then." Two sets of stomping feet enter the room, signaling the agents from outside have decided I've had enough one-on-one family time. "You're under arrest for statutory rape, enabling in sex trafficking, and the bribing of federal employees." A smidge of pride blooms in my chest at her calm tone, the firmness in her words. "I tried to have them tack on being a fucking lousy-ass father as well, but apparently CPS won't investigate since said child is nearly forty." Her brows shoot up like a light-bulb goes off. "Wait, do you turn forty this year?" she asks me.

"Can we talk about this later?"

"Right, sorry." Turning back to my father, she again settles that cold mask over her face. "As I was saying—"

"Don't you say another word to him," Mother screeches. The tips of her heels clip against the pale wood floors, her hate-filled eyes locked on Randi. Unfazed by the outburst, Randi turns to meet Mother, who looks ready to strangle the woman I love. With a growl, I tuck Randi behind me, putting my body between the two women. "What are you doing, Trey? What has she done? She's turned you against us."

"No." The hand wrapped around Randi's thin waist tightens, reassuring me that she's secure at my back. "She showed me how screwed up this family really is. I've always known we were dysfunctional, but this...." I shake my head. I can't even look Mother in the eyes knowing what I do now about her too.

"What he's referring to is we not only have proof of your perverted husband's kinks, but yours too." A bit of the ire fades from Mother's snarling face. "And I have to admit, I'm not straitlaced by any means, but you are one kinky lady." She blanches at the laughter in Randi's tone. "You like toes *where*, exactly?"

A panicked cry bursts from Mother's lips as she lunges around me toward Randi. Releasing Randi, I wrap an arm around Mother's waist, hauling her away before she can make contact. Still she swings, claws out, trying to scratch the humor from Randi's face.

"So here's what's going to happen." Randi pauses and looks to me. "I kind of took over. Do you want to tell them?" Smirking, I shake my head. "Great, okay. So, Jessica." She turns on her Uggs to face the nearly translucent Jessica. "There will be no wedding. The engagement is off."

"No shit."

A laugh bubbles from my chest.

"Exactly. Now, after all this is through, you'll have your stuff removed from Trey's condo and release a statement stating you two have called off the engagement due to family differences. Soon, the arrest of Mr. Benson will be public. I suggest getting ahead of the media swarm and letting them know you had no idea what you were about to marry into."

"Done. And Randi?" Jessica's hand flutters to her neck, her fingers tugging on a thin gold chain. "She threatened me."

"You lying whore," Mother yells, now lunging toward Jessica. I slam her back against me with a quiet grunt.

"She said I needed to make sure he chose me and not you. That I needed to do whatever it took. Including making up that someone was harassing me."

"I knew it." The validation does little for my disappointment in both women.

"And if I didn't, she'd ruin me and my family."

Randi sighs and relaxes her shoulders. "I figured something was up with the drastic change from the celebration party. Doesn't excuse your actions. You could've always come to me or told Trey what was really going on." Jessica's sad gaze slides to her shoes. "But I'm assuming you were still hoping for him in the end, so you didn't." Jessica's blonde hair swings with her nod. "I get it. He's pretty amazing, But that's still not an excuse. You're free to go."

Not missing her chance, Jessica pretty much races from the room, tears flooding her eyes with a final glance back at me before she disappears through the door.

"There's no way you have proof," Dad says, inching toward Randi's back.

"Ah, well, I do, and it's enough for these two gentlemen to arrest you on the charges I explained earlier."

"Nothing will stick," he says proudly. "I know every judge in this city."

Randi just shrugs. "Well, that could be the case." Turning, she faces my dad straight on. "But you see, someone is raiding The Boardroom right now." At the horror in his face, Randi nods. "Yep. Think about all the physical evidence you've left behind, and then there will be the testimony of the girls. Plus, even if charges don't stick, we've at least helped those girls involved and ruined your family name. I highly doubt the snobs of this town will play nice with that kind of charge hanging over your head."

It happens too fast. I watch in shock as dad's face turns into a hate-filled sneer. The tight grip I have on Mother's shoulders slackens as I attempt to maneuver around her, knowing exactly what's about to happen.

Before I can take a step, which Mother blocks with a step of her own in the same direction, Dad's hands are reaching for Randi.

Then it's over.

Once again, Dad is laid out on the floor, groaning.

I look between him and Randi, who's cradling her right hand in utter dismay.

"You punched him."

A grimace marks her face. "Sorry, not sorry?"

Shoving Mother behind me, I stride toward Randi and pull her into my arms. Not caring who sees, I seal my lips over hers and squeeze her tighter, molding her chest to my own.

"I love you," I whisper against her lips. "Thank you for being here."

"Always, Trouble. I'll always be here for you."

A loud interrupting cough snaps me out of our bubble. Heavy footsteps draw closer. Dad groans in pain as he's hauled to his feet. Hands on each arm, the agents haul him from the room.

A wave of sadness and regret rushes through me as I watch them disappear around the corner.

"You did the right thing," Randi whispers. "I'm proud of you."

"What have you done?" Mother shrieks from the middle of the room. "We're ruined. You!" She jabs a finger toward Randi. "You're the one to blame. You'll pay for this. And you." That trembling finger swings to me. "You're cut off from this family."

"Um, one more thing," Randi says, raising her hand like she needs to be called on to speak. "With the kinky shit we know you're into—" I grimace, and she stops. "Sorry, sweetie, but I have to bring it up. With the kinky toe-fucking shit you're into, I suggest you hold off on the whole revenge part of your plan. You wouldn't want that to get out to your fancy friends too, now would you?"

"Get. Out," Mother says before screaming the same words over and over again.

Her screams fade as Randi and I walk hand in hand down the hall. With her at my side and the confrontation behind me, the darkness of the house no longer pushes at the corners of my mind. For the first time ever, I feel free from the burdens of a joyless and loveless childhood.

At the front door, Tank and a few of the other guys wait, his concerned gaze locked on me.

"I'm fine," I say to my best friend with a pat on his shoulder.

"Can't say I'm surprised," Tank says as we step out into the sweltering June heat. "Still sucks. And to think I thought my parents were bad."

"Ditto," Randi chimes in. "Who knew cleaning up your mother after a bender would be better than that fancy shit show."

"Wow, you two don't hold back on my account," I grumble. Running a hand through my hair, I tug on the ends.

In unison, our heads turn at the belligerent shouting pouring from the inside of the first SUV. I fight a smile at the annoyed scowls of the two agents assigned to take him away. No doubt Dad will be out on bail by the end of the night, but the charges are there, and that's what matters.

"Not anymore," I mutter.

"Hmm?" Randi asks, tilting her face up, a hand coming up to shield her eyes.

"Inside, Dad said it's how deals were made in this town, at places like The Boardroom. And I'm just saying not anymore. Not with you."

"By making a few waves, and even more enemies."

"But you're doing the right thing. Tank was right all those months ago."

"About what?"

"You're the change this town needs. After you're done with this place, DC will never be the same."

She presses her forehead against my bicep. I stroke the back of her head, threading my fingers through the silky, dark locks.

"Ready to take on the next asshole tonight?" I toss out, changing the subject from one heavy topic to another.

"Not really," she grumbles.

"What if I let you ride back home with me instead of him?" I hook a thumb in Tank's direction.

Her head pops off my arm, a wide smile splitting her face.

"Really?"

"No," Tank barks. "Not going to happen. Randi is getting in this SUV and we're going straight home to plan for tonight."

I smirk ignoring my friend. "Sure, baby. I'd love to feel you behind me."

"I said no."

Randi and I exchange a quick look, both knowing what the other is thinking, and take off in a sprint toward my bike, Tank's demanding shouts trailing behind us.

24

RANDI

I'm going to vomit.

Again.

Yep, I said again, because I've thrown up consistently for the last hour as I waited at home, nerves going haywire, for this moment. Now the time is here. Outside the Suburban's dark windows, the city zooms past as we glide through the downtown DC streets, getting us to our end destination faster than I'd like. If we never got there, I might be okay with that too. Not that I want us to die in a crash, but maybe slightly injured where they have to wire my jaw shut?

I shake my head and swallow past the anxiety lumped in my throat making it difficult to even breathe normally. Reaching down, I snag the spare bottle of water always stored in my side door and pull it free, the crinkle of the thin plastic breaking the tense silence.

Trey shifts in the passenger seat but doesn't turn. He's been quiet since this morning, not that I blame him. We did accuse his father of sleeping with underage girls and his mom for some pretty random kinks. Jessica, the smart woman, has already released a statement on social media that she and Trey are done. She also sent text earlier saying she was sorry for everything and was leaving for a few weeks to escape the media storm in Switzerland.

I wish I could forgive her, especially knowing that Trey's mom was behind some of the cattiness Jessica showed, but I can't. Not yet. I'll give it a few days and revisit it then. It would be nice to have my friend back, someone to talk to besides Taeler and Trey. But once trust is broken, it's difficult to reestablish.

Only time will tell.

The plastic teeth of the bottle crack as I twist the cap. It's almost to my lips when Trey turns.

"You okay?"

Lowering the bottle, I twist the cap back on and set it in the cup holder.

"Yes. No. Maybe. Can anyone be okay with what's about to go down? Knowing they're about to alter a country's future?"

Understanding settles over his features. "Right." A quiet pause settles over us. "Sam still pissed?"

I snort. Yeah, he's still pissed. When I told him I needed to do this alone —well, alone with T and Trey and the fifteen other agents at my side in case Kyle goes all violent on me—Sam was less than pleased. But he really didn't have a choice in the matter. We don't need the DOJ present tonight. We're not filing for impeachment unless we have to. It's still in the best interest of everyone to get Kyle out of the president seat sooner rather than later, before more damage can be done. Tonight we tell Kyle to either step down effective immediately, or we'll present the evidence to the attorney general, who will then file for impeachment.

At this point, honestly, I'm not sure which way Kyle will go.

On one hand, he doesn't seem to be the type who will take being cornered without a fight, but then again, if we go through with the impeachment filing, everyone will know what he's done. Which will he choose, pride or the public's perception? I don't care what excuse Kyle gives for him needing to step down immediately, just that he does, by eight tomorrow morning.

There are a lot of unknowns, which is why my stomach churns again, readying to push whatever I have left inside it up my throat. I hate this. We have a plan, but it could go sideways at any second.

Not ideal. We did plan ahead and request extra security put on Taeler. Even though the possibility of Kyle even knowing where she is over in Europe is slim, I didn't want to take any chances.

"Can I have some of that?" Turning from the window, I catch Trey hitching his chin toward the water bottle.

"Yeah, sure. Haven't even taken a sip yet. I'm a little afraid it'll just come right back up. The last thing we need is me puking on Kyle and ruining his political career all at the same time."

"He deserves it."

With a comforting smile, he takes the bottle from my outstretched hand and twists back around to face the windshield. Needing a distraction, I slide my thumb across the phone screen, causing it to brighten the dark back seat.

It was my idea to hold the meeting in a more public area. The Oval Office doesn't have cameras or anything that would protect us if Kyle goes postal. Instead, I turned this into an informal—or so Kyle thinks—dinner meeting at an overpriced trendy new restaurant close to the Capitol. Even though we have a private room reserved, it's still more visible than anything inside the White House.

"Why does this smell weird?"

I ignore Trey as I scroll through the few news sites, searching for anything new. Ever since I found out about the oil issue through Taeler instead of someone on my team, I've dedicated myself to looking through the news at least twice a day to make sure nothing slips through the cracks again.

"Where did you get this, Mess?" The tightness of his voice draws a bit of my attention from the phone. Without looking up, I give him a questioning "Hmm?" not understanding what he's referring to and not really caring. "Randi."

"Yep." I click on an interesting article about the upcoming July 4th holiday and the ten best dips to bring to a picnic. "I want a picnic."

"Randi, focus."

"I am focused," I say. I shut the phone off and slide it back between my jean-clad legs. "I'm just distracting myself...." I cock my head to the side, not understanding the panic flaring in his honey brown eyes. "What?"

"Where did you get this water?"

I hook a thumb to the door. "Down there, where I always have water waiting. Why? If you want more, I'm sure there's another bottle in the other door." I glance across the SUV, tilting forward slightly to look into the other door's side pocket.

"Randi, baby, we don't leave water for you in the SUV. Too many ways for it to be tampered with. So where did you get it?"

"Right here." I point down with more emphasis. "And yes you do. I've always had a bottle in here. Well, since... since recently, I guess. Huh. I just assumed it was just a new service you were offering." Shrugging, I lean back against the cool leather, letting the AC seats help keep the stress sweats at bay. "I broke the seal myself. I heard it. So what's the big deal? It was sealed, so no harm, no foul."

"There *is* harm, because there are other ways to tamper with the contents without breaking the seal."

The hair along my arms prickles, standing on end as I put two and two together. Mouth gaping, I shift my unfocused, shocked gaze out the front windshield.

That's not right though... right? It can't be something as simple as tampering with the water in the SUV.

"Benson, stop," T says his voice tight. "Let's not freak her out before we know."

"Too late," I squeak.

The bottle in question dangles from Trey's fingers as he holds it up to the light.

"Tank's right. We don't know for sure, but it's suspicious."

"Besides the fact that it's not supposed to be in here, what else is suspicious about it? It looks perfectly normal to me."

"The smell." Settling his hand around the top, Trey twists the hard plastic top off and holds the open bottle back to me. "Smell it." I give it a quick whiff to appease him before leaning back, putting as much distance as I can between me and the bottle. "Smells off, right?"

I nod, then shake my head. In defeat, I raise both shoulders in a dramatic shrug. "I don't smell anything."

I shiver under his assessing once-over. "Could be the long-term effect of the poisoning from last year. The doc said your taste and smell might be off for a while, and since you've continually gotten small doses, it would never return to normal. It smells like almonds. It's a sign of cyanide being present. But like Tank said, we don't know for sure. I could be way off base and over-reacting."

"But you don't think you are." I wrap my arms around my chest and rub my hands up and down my thin sweater.

"No, I don't. The biggest indicator is that the bottle is in here, in the seat you always choose."

"I don't always choose this seat," I say absentmindedly.

"Sure you do. It gives you a better visual of me." His cocky smirk looks forced, but he's doing his best to lighten the mood, so I'll take it. "Which means whoever planned it knew your usual routine." His jaw tightens, the muscle twitching beneath the passing streetlights. With one last hard look, Trey turns in the passenger seat. "What are the odds both my mother *and* Shawn have eyes on the inside?"

"You're thinking it's one and the same?" T responds. He flicks the blinker, the yellow flashing and clicking seeming too normal for their conversation.

I stare out the window once again, watching the cars drive by, unaware of what's about to happen. At the stoplight, I watch a couple holding hands, laughing as they stroll down the somewhat busy sidewalk. Everything is as it should be for a Friday night in our nation's capital.

And here I am like some kind of atomic bomb circling, readying to slam to Earth, altering everyone's lives. Some for the better, others for the worse. I won't go easy on those in this town who think they're better just because of money or a title. My DC will be different. I'll put the focus back on the American people, on their core issues and needs.

"Shawn did say he'd be vice president one way or another," I mutter, sealing my forehead against the cool glass. "What a sicko."

Both men grunt, their anger and tension now almost palpable in the confines of the SUV.

"We're here."

The black Suburban lurches forward as T pulls to a stop outside the restaurant entrance. Tense silence fills the cab as I inspect the entrance to the restaurant, desperately wishing it would somehow get sucked into a black hole, saving me from what has to happen.

The weight of their stares shifts my attention to the two men.

"You can do this, Mess."

"We're right there with you, Randi. That bastard won't lay a hand on you."

"And what he said," Trey says, hooking a thumb toward T.

I bite back a smile and shake my head, my hair sliding over my shoulder. Taking a deep inhale to steady my nerves and dispel the worry about the water bottle, I sit up straighter in the seat and roll my shoulders back.

"Let's do this."

SEVEN AGENTS DOT the edges of the room, my two and five of Kyle's; the others are standing guard outside the doors and the perimeter. I fight the urge to chew on my nails at the intensity beneath their concentrated focus. I guess I can see why they're zeroed in on me. In this room, I'm the wild card from their point of view. Which, based on my unexpected and slightly violent actions in the Oval Office that first day we were in office, makes their analyzing stares warranted. But what they don't know is this time it won't be me who'll be caught off guard with a shocking revelation.

"Walmart." The smug bastard doesn't even get up from where he sits.

"It's proper to stand when a lady enters the room," I say sugary sweet while batting my lashes his direction. I force my feet forward, making my way toward the empty chair situated across the small intimate table intended for two from where he sits watching my every move.

"I will when I see one."

"Burn," I mock.

Trey slides the wooden chair out and helps me glide it back into place after I've sat.

A nearly empty highball tumbler twirls beneath Kyle's twisting fingers, the slivers of ice left swirling with the action.

"Started without me?" I say with a pointed glance to the glass in his hand.

Lifting the glass, he drains the contents and lifts it up, those ice blue eyes never leaving mine. An agent approaches and replaces the empty glass with a fresh one.

"You're not my first meeting tonight. This place is a bit boring, if you ask me. I would've suggested another, but"—Kyle's icy gaze skims over my shoulder—"I hear it was raided earlier today based on a tip." I shiver when Kyle returns his full focus to me. "Breaking up families is a good way to make powerful enemies in this town, Walmart. You have enough, don't you think?" After a long sip, he rests the amber-filled glass on the table. "Where you learned about the dark corners of this town is what I'd like to know. Who's been sharing our secrets?"

Needing to do something with my hands, I swipe the knotted black cloth napkin off my empty plate and pull it to my lap. My fingers fidget beneath the tablecloth as I pour all my nerves into anxiously twirling the corners around one finger and then the next.

"Worried those slipped secrets also involve you?" My bravado is all fake.

Hopefully he can't hear the thunderous pounding of my heart. The tip of my index finger begins to throb as the circulation slows due to the napkin twisted and knotted around it.

"I have nothing to hide." For emphasis, he spreads his arms out wide like he's giving me free reign to look for any misdealing. But the flash of apprehension in his tired eyes is a sign of the worry he's hiding beneath his own brave mask.

Taking a moment, I observe the man sitting across from me without the usual fear and my normal loathing seeping through, clouding my reflections. Similar to the past few months, there are dark circles beneath his eyes, signaling his continued exhaustion. A few wrinkles crease his normally pristine dress shirt, displaying the telltale signs of yet another long day. Then there's the drinking. I eye him as he tips his glass back, emptying it of its contents, and holds it up for a second time.

"Why are you looking at me that way?" he asks, apprehension in his tone.

"I have no damn clue why, but for some odd reason, I'm worried about you." I huff at the ridiculousness of my statement and rest back in my chair.

Genuine surprise blooms across his face before he schools his features back into the smug smile he loves to wear.

"Now why would you do that, Walmart? You're the one with Shawn nipping at her heels."

"Not for long if he was serious at Camp David that day."

The condescending smirk falters. "I'll worry about him when I have to."

"But to answer your question, you look tired. Exhausted even."

"I'll let my plastic surgeon know," he grumbles. In an uncharacteristic show of weakness, he traces the few fine lines marring the delicate skin around his right eye.

"Kyle...." I don't know what to say next. How do you even start this kind of conversation? When I thought he poisoned me, I wanted revenge. Then when he dragged Taeler into our fight, there was only pure rage fueling my focus to take him down. However, now that the fury has ebbed and months have gone by, apprehension has taken over, repressing the condemning words from leaving my mouth.

"You can say it, Walmart. I already know you find me oddly attractive and want to suck my fat cock."

Sensing Trey's movement in my periphery, I whip out an arm, stopping him from doing something we would all regret.

"No, you disgusting pig. I have proof of it all," I snap.

"Of my fat cock? Of course you do. I've fucked half this city."

"Of the drilling on federal land that you sanctioned for personal gain, the illegal selection of which companies to hire, the offshore bank accounts of those companies which are linked to other companies who supply most of the metal, machinery, and arms to our military . Oh, and let's not forget a few terrorists groups that are also utilizing those funds to attack our allies, forcing us into a battle that we caused. And that's just page fucking one of the shit you've gotten us into!"

All humor slides from his face, leaving a cold menacing glimmer in his calculating eyes.

"I see."

"Do you?" I snap. Reaching up, I fling the twisted napkin onto the table and pinch the bridge of my nose. "I can't believe you did this. It's over, Kyle. I know, and there's nothing you can do to stop this from moving forward. You've made your bed, and now you have to lie in it." I take a slow breath to steady my shaking voice. "You have two options here, Kyle. Step down from the president role effective immediately—you can make up whatever bull-shit reason you want—or I *officially* file this detailed evidence with the Department of Justice, who will kick off the impeachment process."

His scoff is forced. "It wouldn't get past the House."

I cock my head and meet his gaze straight on. "Kyle, when this information is released, impeachment will be the least of your worries. Powerful leaders here in DC would be swept up in the case, their names all over the media. Not only would you have them to worry about, but the American people will know what you've been doing. That their hardships for the past year were all due to your greed. So yeah, you might be right about the House, but it won't matter at that point. You'd be ruined, if not dead."

I swear the silence in the room has a pulse. My muscles tremble and twitch with anticipation of his response. I swallow past a dry throat and shoot a worried glance at Trey.

As casually as if I'd never said anything at all, Kyle huffs out a laugh. Lips against the rim of a newly filled highball glass, he smiles. "Do you really want to do this, Walmart?" His words are muffled by the glass. "Play with the big boys?"

"You know where I stand with things like this, Kyle. My world is black and white. I wasn't raised in the moralless haze of gray like you. We're on the verge of war because of the sequence of events you started. Do you really think I'd sit back and just let that happen without a fight?"

"This goes against the contract you signed, if you remember. You will have to pay every last cent back that we spent to help you land this role."

"I understand." The sudden urge to pee slams through me. I seal my thighs together to make sure a few nervous drops don't slip out. Because the truth is yes, I'm aware I'll be forced to pay it all back, but how? Well, that's something I haven't quite figured out.

"And where is this alleged evidence you have against me?" The calm in his voice is scarier than the snakelike grin.

The flash drive I'd asked Trey to hold on to appears next to me. Without looking, I snag it from his extended fingers and place it on the table. Slowly I inch it across the table toward Kyle, the tension tightening with each little push.

Disdain drips from the snarling look Kyle gives the flash drive now resting beside his glass.

"You don't expect me to give you an answer tonight, do you? To step down from the most powerful position in the world based on this supposed evidence?"

I nod. We assumed he'd balk at the presentation of evidence that he hasn't reviewed.

"I require a decision from you by eight o'clock tomorrow morning. If I don't have your resignation letter in hand at that time, I'll send that very large file of incriminating evidence to Sam. I don't think I have to tell you how quickly he'll act."

"I see."

"Do you?" I question. "You're taking this in stride right now, which is kind of freaking me out."

"Ah, Walmart. It's easy to be calm when you still hold all the cards."

"What?" The word is more a pushed breath. I'm still attempting to understand the meaning behind his words when he stands from his seat, towering over the small table. Taking his time buttoning his suit jacket, he straightens his shirt sleeves and gives me a mocking bow.

"Until tomorrow."

"Eight o'clock, Kyle. I mean it."

"Or sooner." I swear he's stifling a haughty laugh.

Two of his agents stride to the door and step through, followed by Kyle and the other three agents right behind them.

"That was cryptic." I fail to add the lightness to my tone I was going for, the creeping dread from his words keeping the relief I hoped to have after this meeting was done at bay. "What do you think he meant by him holding all the cards?"

The plates rattle against the white tablecloth as I use the table as leverage to scoot the chair back a few inches. Slacks sliding along the smooth wood of the seat, I twist toward the guys. Trey's typing furiously on his phone while T has his sealed to his ear, both their faces fierce with concentration.

"Hello? Guys?"

"It wasn't cryptic, Mess." A new wave of panic slams into my chest, stealing my breath when Trey looks up from his phone, fingers still moving across the screen. "It was a damn message."

Well, fuck.

25

RANDI

The thin wooden rods of the wicker rocker press into the exposed skin of my thighs as I tilt back and forth, hoping the relaxing rocking motion will soothe me. An hour ago, we arrived back at One Observatory Circle. An hour and a half has passed since I presented Kyle with the evidence and he responded with his cryptic message.

To my right, Sam stomps up and down the short flight of steps leading to the backyard, his dark brows furrowed in concentration and worry. At my back, Trey and T murmur to each other, their voices too low for me to make out a single word.

And here I am, in this frozen state of panic and worry. Several times over the past hour, I've caught myself not breathing at all, having completely forgotten that one necessary function needed to live. I changed out of my earlier suit like a zombie, my mind in a fog of what-ifs. It's unnerving not knowing what Kyle has planned, because that much was clear earlier. He has one more card to play in this game, and we all have a feeling it's the trump card none of us can stop.

Before the meeting, we had added to Taeler's security detail, thinking that would be enough, but now we've taken it ten steps further with her and others. In a flurry of phone calls and texts, we've done everything we can possibly do at this point to warn those who we love. Sam's family is secure,

Mom's rehab facility is on lockdown, and I've even had them reach out to the police in Boone to make sure Ben stays safe.

The security around the house is unreal. An agent armed to the teeth stands on guard almost every two feet. There's no ease in the house, no laughter, everyone knowing to stay hypervigilant.

The final piece we're waiting on now is Taeler, to confirm they made it to the US embassy in Paris safely.

The all safe call should come through any minute now, but I've yet to hear either man's phone ring or beep with an incoming text. My phone sits eerily quiet atop my lap, all focus absorbed on its blank screen.

"They'll get there, Randi." I welcome the comforting warmth that seeps from Trey's hand into my tight shoulder and the strengthening squeeze. "She's surrounded by trained agents, and they were only an hour outside Paris when we called."

Those details should offer comfort, but until she's safe in that embassy surrounded by deadly marines protecting her, I can't stop freaking out.

No one has said it out loud, but without a doubt we're all thinking the same thing: Kyle had a contingency plan in place in case Sam didn't drop the investigation against him.

The bushes farther down the wraparound porch rustle. Everyone tenses, Trey's hand tightening in a protective grip, ready to toss me to safety if needed. Tearing my focus from the phone, I scan the darkened backyard, peering through the shadows for the perceived threat. A shadow shifts as a man steps into the porch light.

Trey's grip loosens as the agent continues his patrol along the border of the property.

Geez, we're all strung tight.

Nine more hours of this breath stealing worry. Nine hours until the deadline I presented Kyle expires. If we can keep our loved ones safe over these next several hours we will be in the clear. There's not a single doubt in my mind that my guys will keep me safe, and the protection we've put in place for everyone else will hold against any threat.

Just one final piece needs to fall into place. The most valuable and vulnerable piece of them all.

Taeler.

Time slinks by, the minutes like hours and the hours feeling like years as we wait.

And wait.

And wait.

The call that changes everything comes through around one in the morning. Call it motherly instinct, but the moment T's phone rings, I know deep in my gut it isn't the news we've been hoping for. The fact that I remain calm is a testament to the way the VP role has molded me into a somewhat leader. The wicker creaks as I stand, continuing to rock as I step around it to face T. Phone to his ear, his features fall, his dark eyes refusing to meet mine.

Too wrapped up in trying to hear what's being said on the other side of T's conversation, I fail to feel the vibrations from my own ringing phone, my body too numb to notice.

"You need to get that," Trey says, his voice tight.

Fog coats my brain, jumbling his words. Eyes wide, I just blink as a visual sign of my confusion. His lips purse as he searches my face. Careful fingers loosen my grip on the thin metal, peeling it from my hand. After swiping the screen, he presses it to my ear and nods.

Closing my eyes, I focus on Kyle's voice slithering through the speaker. "You thought you would outplay me. I've been a step ahead in this game, and now you're in a fucking corner. Erase all the evidence, *you* step down from the VP seat, and your daughter goes free. If you don't, well, what happens next is on you. Checkmate, Walmart."

The line goes dead.

The sliver of strength I've clung to the past few hours wastes away. My knees buckle, the stained slats of the porch quickly approaching as I fall until I'm caught midair. Legs dangling over one arm, the other secured against my back, Trey holds me close against his heaving chest.

My vision blurs as my eyes dry out from not blinking. Shapes move. My body bounces with each of Trey's steps, the breeze from the movement brushing along my clammy cheek.

With an almost reverent touch, I'm lowered to the couch. I try to move, but the orders from my brain don't seem to make it to my limbs. A burst of cold settles over my legs and chest before slow warmth cuddles around me. I gaze down at the flannel blanket that was laid over me, hoping it will have the answers I need.

"Did you hear what he wanted?" I hear T ask.

"Her to forget this whole thing happened and step down. Fucking hell, Davis. What have we done?"

Maybe if I just ignore everything and everyone around me, everything will go back to the way it was this morning. If I just close my eyes, I'll wake up and find all this was a dream.

My eyes burn as my lids scrape down, fluttering before opening wide once again.

Nope. Not a dream.

The couch cushion dips under Trey's weight as he perches on the edge by my hip.

"They were minutes from the embassy when they were attacked."

My neck creaks in protest as I shake my head, silently begging him to stop.

"So far there are four casualties." This time the shake of my head shifts the long strands of hair resting over my shoulder. "Five injuries, and one missing."

I lock eyes with Trey. The pain and concern on his normally happy features somehow makes all this real.

"No," I rasp. "I don't believe you."

"Mess," he chokes out. An arm snakes around my back and hauls me close. Lips press against the crown of my head. "We'll find her. I swear on my life that we will find her unharmed."

"How? She's my baby. I can't lose her," I croak, the words burning my throat. Guilt slams into my chest, stealing my breath. "I'm doing it, everything he asked. That's how we get her back. That's what he said. He said she would be safe if I just did what he asked."

"I can't let you do that." The fine material of Trey's suit jacket sticks to my forehead as I peel back to find Sam standing in the corner. "You know I can't."

"Get out," Trey grits out. "Now!" he bellows.

Sam doesn't move. "I file no matter what at eight. I'm sorry, Randi, I really am, but you're thinking as a mother, not as the VP. I'm making the call for you."

I track his movements until he's out of the room.

"I just killed my daughter," I whisper. I slide my pleading gaze to Trey. He blanches and shoots a worried glance to T, who paces the room.

"We need you to call the French president," T says as he storms from one side of the room to the other in quick clips. "We need to get as many agents on the ground in Paris to search for her as we can. I doubt they'll take her far."

The words filter through with a vague recognition that he needs me to do something.

T's mouth opens, ready to continue with his plan, when shock registers on his face and his steps slow before stopping altogether. He holds his wrist up to his lips. "Who the hell did you say is here?" T's face flashes red. Trey bolts off the couch, the quick movement rocking me into the thick cushions.

I open my mouth to ask what's going on, but they're already across the room, creating a human wall between me and the only exit.

"What are you doing here?" The anger and hate dripping from Trey's words perks my attention. Sitting up a little straighter, I lean one way and then the other to see who the hell they're talking to. Hope blooms in my chest. If it's Kyle, maybe he's here to tell us where Taeler is. My jagged nails scrape the soft leather as I struggle to sit up, the blanket wrapping around my legs.

My knees wobble with each step I take toward the arguing men.

Gripping Trey's jacket, I use him for support as I step to his side. The building hope dies, leaving a desolate emptiness in my heart at finding Shawn's near black eyes focused on me instead of Kyle's ice blue ones.

"Trailer."

"Get. Out." Trey wraps an arm around my waist, hauling me back until I'm safely behind the two men once again.

"Ah, ah, ah," Shawn tsks. "I think she'll want to hear what I have to say. Considering it's her daughter's life on the line."

I stumble around Trey, nearly falling into Shawn's chest until Trey steadies me.

"What did you just say?" I wheeze. Desperate, I latch on to his starched shirt and fist the crisp white fabric.

Disgust floods his normally evil sneer. I wince as he peels my fingers from his clothing and shoves me back into Trey's awaiting arms.

"Do not touch me again," he hisses. Something deeper than hate flares in his eyes. Shivering, I sink deeper into Trey's hold. "I need a drink, Trailer. Where's the liquor?"

"Get the fuck out." Trey's body trembles with restrained violence. These two hate each other on a good day. Add in the extra intensity of the day, especially the last few hours, and the tension between the men can be cut with a dull butter knife.

"I might have information, *exact* information, on where to find the girl."

"Tell me," I plead, lunging for Shawn again only to have him sidestep my outstretched hands. "Please, Shawn. I'll do anything."

"I know you will."

His patronizing tone stutters my thundering heart. Trey's chest rumbles at my back with a warning growl.

"Liquor. Now."

The command snaps me from the zoned-out state I'd slipped into. I fight my way out of Trey's unrelenting hold. As soon as I'm unrestricted, I rush to the liquor cart tucked in the corner and gather as many of the bottles as I can in my arms before turning and heading back to the middle of the room. Depositing all the bottles along the table, I purse my lips to keep the tears at bay.

"Glass."

"Get it yourself, fucker."

Ignoring Trey's outburst, I grab a glass. I get why he's pissed, I really do, but right now all that matters is getting the information Shawn has on Taeler. I'll deal with the repercussions of my weak actions later.

Shawn is settled into the deep leather couch when I return with the crystal highball glass. The leather groans as he leans forward, lifting the bottle of Blanton's from the coffee table.

My teeth sink into what's left of my ring fingernail as I watch his purposefully slow movements. I hold back a pitiful squeak as he takes a savoring sip of the bourbon he just poured. The asshole knows exactly what he's doing.

"Do you really know where she is?" I ask after he's relaxed back into the couch, looking like we're about to discuss anything other than my daughter's life.

"You doubt me?" He arches a brow, those dark eyes never leaving mine as he takes another sip. "How do you think he knew where to find her in the first place?"

I choke back a sob. Sealing my palm over my lips, I curl forward, trying to ease the ache in my lower belly.

"What is it you want in return for this information, Whit?" T asks. "We all know you won't give it up out of the goodness of your heart."

Shawn dips his chin. "Most would tell you I don't have one at all."

"I'd be inclined to agree." T's smile turns sharp, all his teeth showing. "Tell us what you know, or I'll skin you myself."

A bitter chill settles over the room.

"You know what I want in return," Shawn says to me, ignoring Tank's threat. "I give you the girl's location, and when you're sworn in as president, you select me as vice."

Something about his words or maybe his tone breaks through the remaining fog coating my brain, clearing my head enough for the pieces of the night and what he's saying to seep in.

"You knew this would happen. From the very beginning, you knew."

"I'd be a fool if I didn't." His tone and pointed look tell me I'm the fool. "I hedged my bets two ways to ensure I'd be in my rightful role by the end of the year."

"Meaning keeping tabs on where my most vulnerable weakness was at all time and trying to kill me with poison." They're my words, I said them, but I still don't believe it. Shaking my head, hoping that will make everything clearer, I seal my chin to my chest. "You bastard." Rage obliterates the guilt and shock. "You rat fucking bastard. She's a kid!" I scream.

"She's a pawn. Just like her mother." The crystal thunks to the top of the side table. "Birmingham used you to win the White House. Don't think this move is all me. He's a shit player in these games, which is why I knew he'd need... leverage over you in some way. This didn't have to happen, you know." He gives me his Joker-esque smile. "You could've taken the easy way out and just died."

My mouth gapes. What am I supposed to say back to that?

"But you didn't, so here we are."

"What about Kyle?" I blurt. "There's no way he's aware that you're here right now, offering to help."

Shawn huffs into the glass now at his lips. "He's a fool too. Didn't even think twice as to why I was offering up her location without any strings attached to the favor. He's panicking, which is deadly to everyone around him. You cornered a wounded animal, Trailer. What the fuck did you think would happen?"

"Why are you helping me?"

"Like I said, I hedged my bets, and right now you're the winning dog in this race. What will it be, Trailer Trash? Your daughter's location for a small nomination, or sticking to your guns and hoping that pussy is bluffing?"

Sweat dots my brow and upper lip even though I'm shivering. I gnaw on a bit of ragged nail. Trey's intense stare burns into me, but I don't look to him for guidance because this isn't about him. It's only about saving Taeler.

"I'll do it. Now where's my daughter?" I put as much strength into the words as possible, but it costs me. Slumping back, I steady myself against a built-in bookshelf to stay upright.

"If only it were that easy. I'll need a written agreement before sending the coordinates and details to your rent-a-cop boyfriend."

My ears and lawyer brain perk up at the mention of a written agreement.

"Seriously? You want a paper trail or an electronic trail of what you're agreeing to? It's blackmail, Shawn. Now who's the fool?"

A high-pitched squeak from his grip tightening along the sweating glass pierces the room.

"They won't be traceable."

I force a snort—first time for everything. "You can't believe that. Did you see the information I have on Kyle? The videos, the voice recordings, pictures, emails. Everything is traceable, Shawn. *Everything*."

He leans forward, holding the delicate glass between both hands.

"How *did* you get that information, Trailer?"

My smile is edged with near hysteria and a shit ton of loathing for the bastard sitting on my couch. "Not a chance in hell am I giving up my source."

I can almost see the wheels turning in his brilliant yet evil brain. "Fine. No agreement. But if you go back on this, Trailer, you *will* pay. With your life or someone's you love, there will be retribution."

Swallowing hard, I dip my chin in agreement. Whatever. I'll worry about all this later. Right now all I need are those damn coordinates.

"Fine. Now where the hell is my daughter?"

26

TREY

Strain pulses through the Suburban with a throbbing beat as our caravan of SUVs speed through the empty streets of Washington DC. Our destination? The White House. Our goal? Kill the motherfucking president.

Okay, that's not the *actual* goal, but I desperately wish it were.

Instead, our less lethal objective is to bitch-slap the bastard until he resigns from the presidency. Behind me, Sam fidgets to the point of annoyance, and to his left, Randi stares, uncommonly calm, at the back of Tank's shiny head.

Glancing over my shoulder, I check on her again. She's been in this strange catatonic-type state for a while, only breaking out of it the few minutes after we got word that Taeler was rescued and safe. It took the team in Paris just a couple of hours to get her to the embassy after receiving the exact coordinates from Shawn.

I tighten my grip around the hard handle. It had to happen. I know it did; we wouldn't have gotten Taeler back if Randi hadn't said yes to Whit's demands. But holy hell, we might be in worse trouble with him as VP than Birmingham as president.

"Is your head in the right space for what's about to go down?" Tank murmurs. Stealing a quick glance my way, he sighs. "You know things can go from zero to shit storm in less than a second."

"I'm aware. Don't worry about me. I'll be fine."

He huffs. "I'm more worried that you'll see Birmingham and kill him on sight before we even get a chance to confront him."

My fingers tighten around the "oh shit" bar of the SUV. "That's a warranted concern, I suppose. But I'll keep my cool. If I shoot him, then his guys will shoot me, no matter how much they like me—"

"Which they don't."

I chuckle, a bit of the building tightness in my muscles and the single-minded drive to hurt Birmingham dissipating. "You're kidding me, right? Everyone loves me. I'm the fun one."

"And that makes me what?"

"The dad. Plus, they like me because I always pay when we go out." My smile drops. "Guess that won't be happening again."

"Why do you say that?" Tank keeps his gaze forward as we approach the White House. "Get your IDs ready."

I toss mine to the dash and reach back for Sam's. "Because I'm not rich anymore. I have to live like...."

"The rest of us?" Tank laughs as he hands all the security badges to the gate guard, who inspects each one carefully before looking into the back seat.

"Madam Vice President," he says with a dip of his chin. "Is the president expecting you?"

"I have no doubt that he is," she says, her tone even, void of any emotion.

The SUV inches forward, nearly hitting the rear bumper of the one in front of us as the gate opens wide, allowing our caravan access.

"I'm assuming he'll be in the residence side," Randi says. "Go through the side entrance."

Tank nods and presses on the gas once we're clear of the gate.

"And you know you're wrong, right?" Randi says.

"About what?" I ask. I lean forward to get the full view of the iconic building as it grows larger through the windshield. Examining the property, I identify the extensive security presence on the grounds and on the roof, massive guns at their sides.

"Just because your mother said you were out of the family doesn't mean that it actually happened. Do you remember who set up the original trust?"

"My grandfather, I think."

"Well, there you go. She actually has no rights over your trust unless he made her some kind of advisor or trustee. Plus, there is a crap ton of paper-work involved that has to be signed and filed to remove someone's access."

"No shit," I mutter to myself. "You mean this whole time I didn't have anything to worry about?"

"All you had to do was google it, Trouble."

"Live and learn, I guess."

"Can you two discuss this later?" I want to snap back at Sam for interrupting, but he's right. There's a time and place to talk about my inheritance, and that sure as hell isn't now. "We need all our heads in the game. Who knows what else Birmingham has up his sleeve?"

Nodding in agreement, I reach for the door handle and push it open as Tank shoves the gearshift into Park. The early morning breeze offers little relief from the heavy humid heat. Even at five in the morning, it's still fucking hot. Immediately I sense sweat beading along the nape of my neck and along my temples.

The other two SUVs have already parked, and the teams inside have unloaded, ready to escort Randi and keep her safe. They don't know the full extent of what's happened in the last twenty-four hours, only that a threat was sensed and security was heightened.

Leaving Sam to open his own damn door, I stride around the Suburban and tug Randi's open. I wait, keeping the door held open wide for her to exit, but she doesn't move.

"Randi?"

"She's safe now," she says to no one in particular. "But what's to say it won't happen again? What if she's taken again and Shawn isn't there to give us the location?"

"It's part of the job, Randi," Sam says somewhere behind me. "But after today, once Birmingham steps down, the threat to her lessens significantly. Once he steps down, he loses all standing, any leverage he had with those with power here in DC. I wouldn't be surprised if they turn their focus to silencing him, to be honest."

"Will it be enough?" Finally acknowledging my presence, she turns in the seat, allowing her legs to dangle outside the door. "I don't know if I can go through with this."

"You don't have a choice."

Closing my eyes, I take a deep calming breath in before turning to face the DOJ jackass. "Listen here, you—"

"I have a choice of turning in my resignation too."

Sam's eyes widen at her words, as do my own.

"You can't mean that," he says, taking a step closer. Hand to his chest, I shove him backward.

"If that's what she wants, then that's her call, not yours." Turning back to Randi, I step between her legs and hold her face between my hands. "Mess, baby, I know it's a lot to take in. I get that 100 percent. Your daughter was in trouble, she was taken, but she's fine. The marines have her. She's safe. But you can't let that fear drive you, drive your decisions from here on out. You took this job to make a difference. Do you think you've accomplished everything you wanted to?"

Her dark hair sways with the shake of her head.

"You have so much more to offer, so much more to change in this city. Don't give up because of tonight. Don't be afraid to continue forward. I'll be here, and so will Tank. We'll move Taeler into the White House if that's what you want. There's no place safer."

The soft delicate skin of her cheeks slides beneath my brushing thumbs as we all give her a few moments to consider my words, consider what she really wants. If she wants to bounce out of this town, give up and walk away, I'll support her. But as much as she considers herself drowning in the VP role, she's killing it. I've never seen a VP work so hard and get so much accomplished in a short amount of time. If she leaves, the inky darkness that has begun to recede from this city will swallow it whole once again.

But as much as I don't want that, as much as I want her to stay and fight, I won't make her.

"Okay," she says with a tight breath.

"Okay what?"

I roll my eyes at Sam, all for Randi's benefit, rewarding me with a small smile.

"You're exactly what I imagine as an attorney," Tank grumbles to my left.

"And what's that?" Sam says, just as annoyed.

"Annoying as hell and can't take a fucking hint."

And just like that, the world rights itself with her growing smile. I return the look and move back, allowing her to step down. Skimming her small hands over the black tailored pants and retucking her pale pink dress shirt into the back, she stares up at the White House.

"Let's do this."

Tank seals himself to her left side and me to her right. Stride for stride, we march toward the door currently being held open by an agent. The rest of the guys flank around us, creating several layers of human armor with her in the middle.

"Madam VP," the agent says in greeting. "Washington, Benson." Tank and I dip our chin in acknowledgment but continue forward, keeping pace with Randi. "He's in his personal office waiting for you."

"Joy." Randi sighs.

With her fast pace, it takes less time than normal to reach the president's personal office in the residential wing.

"You're with me, right?" she asks under her breath before turning the doorknob.

"Always," I say at the same time Tank gives her a "Hell yes."

The door opens noiselessly. Inside, the four of us pause, giving Tank and me a moment to assess the room.

Three agents linger along the wall, two on the left side and one on the right, and I can sense at least two more at my back. The large space has a single sitting area with four leather chairs surrounding a low coffee table. The mahogany desk similar to the one in the Oval Office sits near the back of the room but is clearly the center of attention. American flags dot the two front corners along with a single lamp and other papers and knickknacks scattered over the top.

Kyle sits behind the desk, his dimpled chin resting on the point of two fingers with his elbow anchored to the desk. A heavy scent of alcohol wafts through the room. Upon a deeper inspection of Birmingham, I notice his bloodshot eyes, pale skin, and nearly white lips, as if all the color has leaked from his face.

Tank and I notice his drunken state at the same time, seconds after entering the office. As one, we step in front of Randi, creating a human wall between her and Birmingham.

"Everyone out," Birmingham barks, and if I'm not mistaken, there's a slight tremble in his words. "Except her."

"Not a chance," I say back as composed as I can. Drunk, this clown is a loose cannon. Even I know not to poke him in this state.

This is a terrible idea. We need to get her out. Now.

It only takes a single glance from him to the two behind us before arms wrap around mine, sealing them to my sides. With grunts of exertion, the agents haul us back, edging us toward the door. Well, me. They're edging me. The other agent has yet to make Tank budge.

"Stop," Randi shouts, her voice firm and commanding. All movement ceases. "Everyone stays in this room, Kyle. It's over." The buttons of her shirt strain with each of her heavy breaths. "You have no more cards to play."

"How did you do it?" he asks. Grabbing the empty glass, he strangles a nearly empty decanter and pours four fingers of the dark liquid over the melting ice. I don't miss the tremble of his hand or the bits of liquid that splash out.

"You really don't know?" Her steps are hesitant as she approaches the back of one of the leather chairs. Leaning forward, she rests her forearms along the back. Everything in me tenses the closer she puts herself to that ticking time bomb.

"Whit," Birmingham snarls.

Randi gives a slow nod.

"That bastard," he mumbles. Taking a few swallows of his drink, he slams the glass to the desk, splashing liquor over the top and several nearby papers. A single dribble slides down his chin.

"It's over, Kyle. You'll find a prewritten resignation letter in your email." With a glance over her shoulder, she nods at Sam, who has his phone in his hands. "It's in your email now. This is what you'll sign, and the other attachment is what you'll read on camera."

"You really think you can do this role?" Leaning back, he tucks both hands beneath the desk. Tank and I share an apprehensive look. "The country is on a downward spiral. It's fucked. There's nothing we can do about it except exploit it where we can. I did nothing wrong," he yells. "And you." The hairs on the back of my neck stand on end at the pure loathing in those two words. "You don't deserve this seat, this position. I pulled you out of that ass-backward town and gave you everything. This is how you repay me, you fucking cunt? You're nothing but trailer trash and never will be anything more."

I jerk against the arms still holding mine down. I'm going to kill him. Tear him limb from limb and bathe in his fucking blood.

"That might be the case, but here I am. I've struggled my whole life, fought for every single thing I've earned. Did you think I'd just step aside now because it's going to be difficult? This country, its people, are worth me fighting for. I might not be the best option out of everyone in the city, but I sure as hell am the best option between the two of us. Now sign the fucking resignation papers."

"I underestimated you, I'll give you that. But so have you with me. Desperation makes for desperate actions." He stands, the office chair he was sitting in rolling back a foot. In slow motion, he raises a small-caliber gun from beneath the desk, the shaking barrel pointing at Randi's chest.

Seven other guns slide from their holsters.

Five are pointed at me and Tank, two at the current president.

"Everyone, stop," Randi says, voice shaking. Raising her hands, she takes a step backward. "Kyle, what are you doing?"

"I will not be ruined, Walmart, especially not by someone like you. You're nothing. No one. I'm the fucking president of the United States." I catch the uneasy exchanges between the agents at the hysteria in Birmingham's high-pitched voice. "I am not stepping down."

A somewhat insane laugh bubbles out of Randi. Another strangled chuckle bounces off the walls. Leaning forward, she presses her hands to the top of her thighs as the strange laughter continues.

"I'm sorry," she says between breaths. "This isn't funny. I just can't—" A loud snort booms through the office. The other agents' eyes slide to me for guidance. "Shit, this is bad."

"Birmingham, this is it." Against my better judgment, I lower my sidearm and slide it back into the holster at my ribs. "Let me talk him down," I say out of the corner of my mouth to his personal agents. "What do you think you'll get by shooting her?" I ask him.

"Her not in office."

Well, there's that. Maybe another question is better.

"You know if you shoot her, you're not walking out of here." I tilt my head to where Tank stands, his gun trained between Birmingham's brows. "So yeah, you might hurt Randi—because let's be honest, there's no way you're a good shot under pressure—but you'll be dead. Whether you step down or are six feet under, it doesn't matter, because she'll still be in the president seat, not you. You hear me? Now lower your fucking gun."

"It got out of hand. It wasn't supposed to get to this point. Fuck." Still holding the gun, he presses both hands to the side of his head.

"He's cracking," Sam says behind me.

"No shit," I growl. Kyle takes a step right before turning and moving to the left in a strange one-step pacing motion. "Do you mind pointing those somewhere else?" I hiss, not letting my focus leave the unraveling president while directing my words to the other agents in the room.

They don't.

"No." Everyone in the office holds a collective breath. Even Randi stops her hysterical laughing at the single word. Kyle stares at the gun in his hand. "I'm not stepping down."

It's written across his sullen features, the desperation and darkness giving away his intentions. I know that look, have seen that look. When someone thinks they're out of options.

I can't make myself move. Nothing will compute as the man I've hated most of my life slowly raises the gun. Unsure of what to do in the situation, his agents stand, jaws slack, guns slowly lowering from their ready positions.

"Fuck," I groan. "Cover me," I say over my shoulder.

Thank goodness the motherfucker is drunk, making his movements sluggish and uncoordinated. I'm halfway to his desk when he realizes my intentions. Rotating his wrist, he aims the gun barrel right at my chest as I continue racing forward to prevent him from taking his own life.

A knowing gleam flickers in his eyes just as his finger twitches on the trigger.

Pain stabs into my shoulder. Randi screams. Tank bellows in rage, shaking the walls.

Another shot booms through the white-paneled room just as another punch of pain slams into the center of my chest. I stumble, inches from the desk. With a determined roar, I lunge over it, my thighs slamming against the edge but not before I wrap my arms around Birmingham. In a tangle of limbs, we crash into the desk, his weight slamming me onto it. Wrestling for control, I fight back the pain-filled tears leaking from my eyes to locate the gun.

As quickly as it happened my arms are suddenly empty. Kyle's heavy weight is gone, leaving me heaving atop the desk alone. Shouts echo around me, but I can't focus on anything other than the pain. Somewhere in the room, Randi cries my name, the desperation and fear in her trembling voice urging me to find her.

Grunting, panting to keep from crying out, I press the palm of my unin-jured arm to the desk. I lift a couple inches before I fall back to the hard wood.

Tears, or maybe sweat, drip into my eyes, blurring my vision, but still I'm able to make out the shit-for-brains Birmingham wrapped up in Tank's anaconda arms across the room.

"Trey." Peeling my cheek from the paper it was stuck to, I turn my head toward the soft voice before it thunks back to the desk. "Trouble." Tears stream down her face, leaving black lines dividing each cheek. "Please. Please be okay." Her rapid breaths breeze over my damp cheek. Those edible lips I love so much brush along my cheekbone. "What the hell were you thinking trying to stop him?"

I open my mouth to tell her that I have zero idea, but a spike of pain shoots from my chest, stealing my breath. Slamming my eyes shut, I grunt in pain, my back arching off the desk.

"No," she cries. "Trey. No, please, stay with me. You're okay."

My heart thumps against my ribs as warm liquid slides along my skin beneath my dress shirt, leaving a chill in its wake.

"Mess."

Giving in to the darkness, I welcome the peace it offers.

"I THINK HE'S COMING TO." Something soft and cold presses against my cheek, helping me fight through the grogginess that still has a hold over me. A quiet beeping sounds somewhere around me while the crisp scent of ammonia permeates my nose. "Trouble, wakey wakey. You've taken a long enough nap."

"Madam President, we need to leave right now."

My senses flicker to life at the sound of that unfamiliar male voice. A florescent overhead light assaults my eyes when they finally deem to respond to my demands to open.

"Fuck," I grunt. I go to cover my eyes to save them from being blinded, but something at my wrist prevents me from raising my hand. I tug again a little harder this time—same result. Blindly, I jerk at the restraints holding my wrists down, the desperate need to be free overriding everything else. The beeping sound picks up, turning frantic, matching the beats of my pounding heart.

"Trey, you're safe. You're in the hospital." Randi's voice cuts through the panic, but it's not enough to stop yanking at whatever the hell is restraining me.

"Off," I hiss, the single word scratching my dry throat.

Warm, humid breath brushes against the shell of my ear. "So you like to restrain but don't like being restrained. How interesting."

I'd laugh at her comment if I weren't freaking the hell out. What seems like hours later, the restraints restricting my movement loosen from my wrists. The relief is short-lived, however. Just as I lift both arms to relish in the newfound freedom, massive palms seal around my wrists, holding them to my side.

"You'll rip out your IV again, you idiot." Tank's deep rumbling voice quells the desperation building in my chest. "It's why we had to have these on you in the first place. I'll let you go, Playboy, if you promise to stop acting like a damn kid."

Peeking one eye open, I attempt an easy smile. "Got it." More snappy comments filter through, but I can't muster the energy to say them. Relaxing against the stiff mattress, I close my eyes again. "What's going on?"

"Madam President, it's time."

"Who's the new guy?" I demand, cringing through the discomfort each word causes.

"Here's some water, Trouble."

I blink open both eyes. Randi hovers over me, her smile wide and fake while fear flickers in her hazel eyes. I wrap my lips around the thin plastic straw and take several pulls of the room-temperature water. A grunt of displeasure rumbles from me when she pulls back before I've had my fill. "Doctor said to drink it slow. How much do you remember?"

Allowing my lids to slide shut once again, I search my memories.

Birmingham, gun, pain.

"That asshole shot me."

"Once in the shoulder and once in the chest. Thank goodness you had your vest on or you would've been.... Kyle would've—"

Sensing her own pain, I slowly reach up, careful to not snag my IV, and cup a palm around her anguished face.

"Shh, baby. I'm okay."

"They had to do surgery to repair an artery the bullet nicked. You've been out for almost six hours," Tank says from his post against the wall behind Randi. As angry as his tone makes him sound, there's only relief written across his face.

"Birmingham?" I question. Searching the room, I note two of the agents from inside the president's office hanging back along the wall, their focus on Randi. "Why are they here?"

With a hand to my jaw, she turns my attention from the agents back to her. "Kyle is being detained somewhere." I catch the annoyed glance she shoots the two newcomers. "We had to wait a few hours for him to sober up and sign the resignation papers, but he refused to meet with the media."

"Madam President." That unfamiliar voice from earlier speaks up again.

Her dark hair slides over her shoulder as she shifts to address the person. "Five minutes."

Turning back, she tucks the rogue locks of hair behind her ear. Only now do I notice the layers of makeup on her normally natural face. The outfit she's wearing is different than the one from earlier too.

"Mess?"

"I was sworn in while you were in surgery," she whispers. She scans my face as she rakes two fingers through my hair, lulling me into a near hypnotic state. "I wanted to wait, wait for you to be there, but the moment Kyle announced he was stepping down and made it official, they... well, it had to be done."

"And now?" I ask. Obviously they're trying to pull her away for something important.

She sighs and looks to Tank. "I'm addressing the nation as soon as I get back to the White House. I didn't... I couldn't do it without knowing if you were awake yet. I've held them off as long as I could, Trouble."

Rubbing the side of my thumb along her cheek, I nod. "I'm going with you."

I smile at her snort. "You just woke up from surgery. There's no way the doctors will release you, and even if they did, I wouldn't let you."

"Fuck," I grunt. As much as I don't want to admit to this weakness, she's right. There's no way the doctors will let me leave. Hell, I don't know if I could if I tried. My entire body feels heavy, like it's somehow molding deeper into the mattress. Plus, a nap sounds damn amazing. "Go. Go make the announcement." Inclining my head to the flat-screen mounted to the wall across the room, I say, "I'll watch from here. Go do what you need to do, Madam President."

The fake smile fades, leaving behind the one I fucking live for.

"I'll be back as soon as I'm done." The bed creaks, the side rails rattling as she leans forward, pressing a single kiss to my cheek. "There's a lot to talk about."

The needle imbedded in my left hand tugs when I capture her chin, holding her beautiful face close. Ignoring the pain each move causes, I lean forward and seal my lips over hers.

"Now you can go."

"You're bossy when you're shot," she remarks with zero heat in her words.

"I'm bossy when I'm not," I retort, fighting the wince as I lower back to the mattress.

"It's one of the things I love." She smiles. "I'll be back."

The bed moves, shifting my body as she stands. Gaining Tank's attention, I nod toward Randi. "You go with her. I'll be fine."

"No shit," he grunts. "We'll be back." Before he steps out the door, Tank turns. "If you ever pull that stupid shit again, I'll shoot you myself and then let Sarah kick your wounded ass, you hear me, Benson?"

"I love you too, big guy." Holding up both arms, I motion for him to come closer. "Do you need a hug?"

"You're impossible." His words say he's annoyed, but the relief on his face tells me what he won't put into words. "Those two are staying here with you to protect you. Be back when we can."

Resting back onto the flat pillow, I don't fight the smile that wants to split my face. Closing my eyes, I take a deep breath, immediately regretting the motion.

Holy hell, being shot sucks.

"Wake me up when it's time."

27

RANDI

"Have you heard from the hospital?" I ask as the makeup artist dusts my face once again with oil-absorbing power. "Any changes with Trouble?"

Tank runs a hand over his shiny bald head. "We left twenty minutes ago, Randi. He's fine. Get your head in the right space. You're about to address the country as the president of the United States."

I nod and turn my attention back to the slips of paper in my hand. Again I scan over the words, though I already memorized them while we waited for Trey during surgery. After Taeler being taken and held hostage, and then Trey getting shot, I've no doubt aged years overnight. I still can't believe he did that, stepping in so Kyle wouldn't harm himself.

Movement in the mirror catches my attention. Sam's reflection nods. I nod back, both of us on the same page about what's to come.

"They're ready for you, Madam President."

Closing my eyes, I inhale deeply and hold it until it burns in my lungs before slowly releasing all the negative nerves and self-doubt. I can do this. Not that I have much choice. Sure, I have the option of stepping down too, but that's an escape, one I don't intend to take.

Standing from the makeup chair, I toss the few pages of notes onto the table in front of me and meet Tank's eyes. We nod to each other in unison.

Show time.

The chatter of the reporters silences the moment I walk through the press room door. I clear my throat and focus on each footstep to ensure I don't stumble on live TV.

Live.

Behind the podium, I grip the sides and stare directly into the fifty or so cameras, their lenses all trained on me.

Here goes nothing.

"Thank you all for being here today. A lot has transpired over the last twelve hours here in the White House, as many of you have heard through various sources. As of 9:15 a.m., President Kyle Birmingham has stepped down from his position effective immediately." I pause, letting the gasps and murmurs settle before going on. "With the role abdicated, I was sworn in as president of the United States as of 9:17 a.m."

The chatter level rises, and a few reporters shout out questions. I shake my head and hold up a hand.

"I know everyone has questions, but please let me get through this before there are any interruptions. I do not know the specifics behind Kyle's sudden departure"—slight lie, but it's not like I can tell everyone the truth—"only that he has officially stepped down, and I was tasked to fill the role. Everyone knows my story, my background, and I have zero doubts that many of you are questioning my ability to lead this country with only a year and a half of politics under my belt. I'll admit that two years ago, I would've agreed with your assessment. However, now I 100 percent disagree. Some people see my common upbringing as a weakness, and I believe they're wrong. It's a strength, an insight into the core of the country. An insight I intend to filter through every aspect of the White House, my advisors, and my cabinet. It will be beyond difficult to fill the shoes of the many strong men who have come before me, but I am up for that task. No longer will titles, money, and power be the decision-makers of this town. With me as president, I'm bringing the people back into the picture, their lives and their families the center of our focus. I'll make mistakes, there's no doubt about that." I give a weak smile. "All I'm asking is for you to trust me. I know that's asking a lot coming from a politician." The crowd of reporters laughs. "But at the core, I'm not. I'm Randi Sawyer, daughter of an addict, a teen mother, and a proud American. That's who I'm asking you to believe in. Believe in me."

Crickets.

I breathe deeply and slowly peel my fingers off the podium, their joints stiff from the white-knuckled grip I had on the shiny wood.

Suddenly the room explodes in a flurry of questions, shouts, waving hands, and a few cheers. I search the room, my attention falling on a familiar reporter, the one who asked the tough questions during the briefing I saw Kyle host months ago. I point to her and smile.

"What are your plans regarding the oil crisis and our allies demanding our help overseas?"

My smile widens. "Tossing out the tough questions first. I like it." The reporters around her elbow her and pat her shoulder. "Honestly, I don't know. There was a lot of insight and data I wasn't privy to in the VP role that I will be now. I don't want to give an answer without knowing the facts and looking at the options we have. The last thing I want is to go into a fight if we don't have to. Those men and women of our amazing military count on me to send them into a battle that we can win and is the absolutely only choice for success. I won't let them down by skimping on the details and sending them over to fight when we don't have to."

"So you're pro military?" a man shouts.

I level a glare his way that makes him shrink back into his seat. "I'm pro any American man or woman who gives a piece of their lives to serve this country. It's a sacrifice that is priceless in my eyes." I turn to look over my shoulder. "Dumbass," I whisper before turning back to the crowd with a fake smile.

"With you as president, that means your previous role as VP is open. Have you decided who will fill it?"

I try to swallow back the bile climbing up my throat. This is the part of the night I've dreaded the most. Shawn demanded I make him vice president after I was sworn in, stating very clearly that if I went back on my word, then someone I love would pay the price. I can't let that happen. Having Taeler in the arms of the enemy for just a couple hours was a horror I never want to repeat.

I clear my throat and grip the podium once again, using its strength to ground me as I make the stupidest, most selfish choice I've ever made in my life.

"You're correct, sir. With me shifting to the president seat, it has left a gap in the vice president role. After careful consideration, I've made my decision on who will not only best serve in that role for the people of this country but also be a strong partner for me." I inhale deeply, my knees knocking behind the podium. "Please join me in congratulating our newest vice president of the United States." I wave to the man standing off to the side of the room. "Mr. Samuel James Pierce."

POWER SURGE

POWER PLAY SERIES BOOK 4

INSPIRATION

"Don't follow the crowd, let the crowd follow you."
   - Margret Thatcher

PROLOGUE

UNKNOWN

The arrogant bastard strides from one end of the opulent living room to the other, his face wrinkled and bunched as badly as his expensive suit. The cell phone pressed hard against his right ear has stayed suctioned there for hours now. Bits and pieces of the one-sided discussion are negotiating terms, but most of the high-pitched words passing his lips are him begging and pleading with whoever is on the other end.

An honorable man would slide from the shadows, reveal himself now to relieve this man of his insistent begging. Too bad for him, I'm nowhere near honorable. Maybe I once was, ages ago, but now there's no hope for me ever returning to a redeemable man. It's the thrill, the power I hold watching my prey and knowing their life is in my hands to take whenever I damn well feel like it that hooked me. Watching and waiting for the right moment is my favorite part of the job.

Does that make me a bit of a voyeur? Maybe. It would be a lie if I said I wasn't semi-hard right now from the anticipation coursing through my icy veins as I watch this man's final few minutes of life. The growing erection has nothing to do with his gender, but the power I currently hold with him none the wiser. Tonight, when I'm done with the job and home in my multi-million-dollar brownstone in the heart of DC, washing away any evidence of this evening's hit, I won't be whacking off in the shower because he's a man but because of the fear that emanates in his last breath.

That's my second favorite part about my livelihood. The pure, soul-shaking fear that rolls off them in waves as I extinguish their miserable lives.

Women tend to beg for their lives and, more times than not, offer their bodies for me to do anything with in hopes of me sparing them. Once or twice, a woman was tempting enough to consider the offer, but I'm not a damn rookie stupid enough to leave DNA evidence behind—and disposing of a whole body is a pain in the ass and not worth the quick lay no matter how attractive the mark.

Men are the worst of the two genders when it comes to death staring them in the face. They melt into blubbering messes, pissing themselves and crying because they know. The men know the moment they see me emerge from the dark their life is over, and the fear turns to mourning for the future they've lost. They're scared of the pain too, which, coincidently, has never been voiced as a concern by a woman. Guess that makes them the stronger gender, even though the women are foolish enough to hold on to a glimmer of hope until the last second.

I feed off the tantalizing, invigorating, desperate fear they all produce during our... *encounter*. But the most delicious and erotic fear comes in that very last moment. Those few fleeting seconds before their life is snuffed out forever. I've tried to recreate it. Kill them, resuscitate them, then kill them again. But the second, third, and fourth time the light leaves their eyes and their soul dies, it loses something. So now, unless requested by whoever hires me, I stop at the first final breath, savoring that memory for when I get home and can wrap a fist around my thick dick, then stroke myself until I splatter cum all over the shower wall again and again as I replay the scene like a short horror trailer.

And sometimes, like tonight, I record those last seconds. It's reckless, of course, and the agency who trained me would be highly disappointed by me keeping a kill memento, but since I can't stand the touch of another human being except in violence, a man has to do what he has to do to take care of his needs.

Tonight's recording isn't only for my sick pleasures, however.

I don't ask for details on why a client wants a certain person dead. It's a simple call, all clients vetted through a referral system, relaying the who and any specifics they'd like to add on to the hit. Each specific detail, anything veering off the normal hit menu, costs extra. Which is fine by me. I don't do this just for the fear high alone. Leaving government work and freelancing has made me a very wealthy man. The way I see it, I'm one of the lucky ones. I do what I love and get paid a shit ton of money for it. I relish the lavish lifestyle I live with zero desire to go back to the basic life I had before.

A noise draws my wandering focus back to the room just beyond the balcony door hiding me from view. The ex-president halts his pacing, launching his phone against the stone fireplace a few feet from where he stands panting. The small device shatters into a million pieces against the stone hearth, the breaking glass piercing the otherwise quiet room. Two suit-covered men bust through the doors, guns at the ready, scanning the room for the cause of the noise.

Careful to keep each movement smooth, I slip deeper around the balcony's edge, allowing the dark shadows to conceal me from sight.

A shiver runs down my spine despite the humid July heat. This is a new challenge. One I'm fucking greedy for after a few months of simple kill jobs. Never have there been so many erratic complications to work around to complete the job. The two federal agents—secret service or FBI is my guess based off their cheap-ass suits—will present a challenge, but I'll take it on like no one else can. That's why the men hired me specifically. I'm the best. No one will ever suspect I was here tonight. Not even when I leave a dead body in my wake.

Sure, people will question why the recently dethroned president of the United States would kill himself, but that's not my problem. Once I walk out of here, the job is done, and those bastards who hired me will deal with the media storm that will come after the body is discovered.

Clearing my thoughts, I close my eyes and focus every cell on listening to the quiet conversation inside.

"Are you okay, sir?" says one of the agents, annoyance in his clipped words.

"Get the fuck out."

"Sir, we're tasked to—"

"I said get out. And unless my damn lawyers show up with my deal in hand, *do not* open these doors again."

The quiet click of the doors is faint but sends excitement pulsing through my chest. A small smile tugs at the corners of my lips. I should thank him for clearing the room for the rest of the evening.

Peeking through the glass pane, I move until a crack in the thick curtains crowded at the edges of the door allows me a visual inside the room once again. My mark slumps his shoulders, rounding in what looks like exhaustion or defeat, using a few fingers to massage tiny circles along both temples. Based on images from his time in office, he looks like a completely different person.

The man elected president two and a half years ago was polished, smooth skinned, and had a confident aura about him that somehow slithered through the television screen. The defeated man in the room appears to be a shell of that man. Not a single drop of sympathy tightens my gut at the sight, however. He mixed himself up in whatever shit placed him in this position, putting him in my crosshairs. He should've known the type of men he was entangled with, and since he didn't, he'll die a fool.

I'm not aware of the full extent of the why and frankly don't care. A job is a job. No emotions, no judgment. Stalk, kill, leave. This is the job. It's *always* been the job.

My calculating gaze flicks from the room to the moon slipping in and out of the clouds overhead. Rain is rolling in at some point tonight, at least that's what the weather man predicted. It's the reason I chose tonight for the kill despite it being a full moon. As long as it doesn't—

Before I can finish the thought, the clouds to the west illuminate with flickers of lightning.

I mouth a curse as I shift back to my target. Thanks to the weather, tonight's hit now has to be hastier than I originally planned, which fucking sucks hairy balls. My anger grows as another violent display of lightning flashes in the building thunderheads. The need to off those inaccurate motherfuckers on the Weather Channel builds. How did they fucking miss the fact that tonight's simple rainstorm would include a freaking lightning show?

Calming my raging pulse, I start to move, edging along the brick wall quieter than a slithering snake. My entire focus is on the man just beyond the balcony doors, Kyle Birmingham. Former president, current target, soon-to-be dead body.

I open the glass-paned door with ease, having picked and adjusted the locking system two days ago. Careful to not make a single sound, I step into the massive home before slipping behind the curtains. At my side, my fingers twitch as excited energy zips and zings through my veins, making my breaths short.

The idiot doesn't turn from the flameless fireplace as I creep up behind him, each step soft and calculated. Holding a tight breath, I slip a gloved hand over his mouth and yank, sending him careening backward. The moment his back slams against my chest, he struggles, fighting my hold with the blind panic of being caught unaware. Like I've done so many times before, I pop the lid off the plastic syringe with my thumb before stabbing the needle into his thick neck and shoving the plunger down, shooting the drugs into his veins.

The effects of the tranquilizer happen within seconds. His tight muscles, flexing as he fights me, immediately relax, his hands falling limp by his side. Ten seconds after I administer the drugs, his knees give out. I grunt at the large man's full dead weight in my bear hold. Careful to keep quiet, I drag him to a single leather chair and fold the body down into the soft cushions.

Wonder if he knows this is the exact spot where he'll die.

Grabbing several ugly-ass throw pillows, I cram one on either side of his legs to keep him from slipping around on the leather. Squatting, I push against his chest, sealing his back to the chair, and hold him there. I smile at his blank face. It will only take a moment before the initial effects wear off, allowing him the ability to blink and eventually speak. With the lightning storm outside threatening the darkness I need for an invisible escape, I'm eager to get this show on the road, but unfortunately for me I can't. A special —and costly—request of tonight's job is to ask Mr. Birmingham a few questions before I take his life.

Which means instead of wrapping the tie I brought around his neck and getting this over with now, I'm forced to wait.

A corner of his lips twitches, followed by a sluggish blink.

Perfect. Both are the signs I need to get this show started, but not without some reassurances that he'll stay quiet with some of his faculties returning. I shift to slip the 9mm from the leg holster around my left thigh and withdraw the silencer from a compartment of my cargo pants. With practiced ease, I screw the silencer to the barrel of the gun, my gaze never leaving his.

His hazy blue eyes widen, attention fully on my actions. The faint scratch of metal against metal is the only sound in the gloomily silent room. I pause, twisting on the balls of my feet at the muffled male voices carrying from beneath the door, reminding me of the high risk of being caught red-handed. I smile as a shiver of thrill zips down my spine.

"I'll make this quick," I murmur, my lips barely moving.

His lips part, his chest puffing out with a deep inhale. The twitch of his right eye tells me exactly what he plans to do next. With a bored expression, I thrust the end of the silencer into his slacks, right against his ball sack, and pull the hammer back. Arching a single brow, I give a shake of my head in disappointment.

"The only sound you'll make is when whispering the answers to my questions. If you comply, then I won't blow off your balls one by one. Understand?"

A single tear streaks down his pallid cheek. Scanning his face, I don't hold back my sneer of disgust. Sweat dots his brow, more tears build in those lower lids and if I'm not mistaken, the faint scent of piss wafts up from where my silencer is still lodged deep in his balls.

Fuck, now I have to scrub the silencer with bleach.

He's fucking pathetic. Women really are the stronger gender.

I situate the tiny video camera onto the front pocket of my long-sleeve shirt and hit the Record button on the app. Bone popping against bone sounds as I crack my neck, bringing my thoughts to focus on the next several minutes. "First question, what do your lawyers know?"

His gaze drops. "Nothing." The word is garbled and wet as saliva builds in his mouth, unable to swallow it down. "Yet."

"Second. What does she know?"

I have zero idea what they're wondering she knows, or who "she" even is, but it's critical enough to tack on an additional quarter million to the contract to gain the truth to these two questions.

The man blinks once, twice before sealing his lips shut and shaking his head as much as he can with the drugs still coursing through his veins.

"I don't believe you," I murmur, my words barely audible.

Sweat glides down from his forehead to his temples before combining with the stream of tears streaking his cheeks.

"Doesn't know," he finally rasps. He tries to swallow a few times before he's successful. "Idiot."

I let out an inaudible huff. Adjusting my slight weight from the ball of one foot to the other, I debate his response while taking in his nonverbals. He's lying, but why? Is it the nature of what this woman knows, which would potentially put her in my crosshairs down the road, or is he only protecting this mysterious female?

"You will die tonight." A stifled wail rattles from his throat. "Might as well tell me the truth."

The blood seeps from his already pale lips as he seals them firmer together.

"Who is she?" I ask, curiosity getting the better of me.

His head ticks to the side. Internally I curse at myself for letting the question slip.

"Why are you protecting her?" Fuck, what's wrong with me tonight?

His eyes flick to the closed door. "I did this," he rasps, his voice like sandpaper against course wood. "Me. Don't let them drag her into this."

"I'd love to help if I gave a flying fuck."

"She's just a pawn. A no one."

"Your lover?"

A haughty laugh tries to escape his trembling throat. "No."

"If she's no one and not involved, why is she so special you're willing to risk your right nut being splattered all over this chair?"

His Adam's apple bobs. Fuck, the tranquilizer is wearing off more than I'd like. This needs to end soon. I could take him, but if I leave any mark on the body, they'll know it wasn't a suicide.

I tug the ugly-ass tie I stole from his closet last week from the clear plastic baggie in my cargo pant pocket and dangle it across my thigh.

"Tell me," I demand a little louder than I should.

"Do it." Calm settles over his ragged features. This stage always happens, the mark thinking they've come to terms with death. And some have until death is a hairbreadth away. That undiluted terror will roar back the moment I slip this silk around his neck.

A minuscule amount of respect pulses through my veins for the man in front of me. With his death imminent, he continues to protect this mystery woman.

"Just tell me one thing." Vacant eyes stare back into my own. "Why are you protecting her?"

Something like sadness leaks through his ice blue eyes. Confusion sets in. I purse my lips in pure annoyance. If I wasn't required to make this look like a suicide, I'd make him talk.

Without another word spoken between us, I slip the tie around his neck, double-checking the slip knot so it'll tighten with a simple tug. Scanning the side table, my gaze rests on a medium-sized iron sculpture. It's hideous. Rich people and their shitty art. Blue eyes track each of my movements as I secure the opposite end of the tie to the sculpture. I cradle the sculpture in one hand, pressing the other against the top of the chair beside his head, allowing me to hover over him.

"Any last words?" I never ask that; this fucking night is messing with my mind. A part of me wants to allow him one more opportunity to identify this mystery woman and explain why in the hell he's willing to let the secret die with him.

This curiosity, it's a new, uncomfortable emotion.

"This ends with me. I hold the evidence. I'm the proof."

The weight slips from my fingers, the knot tightening as the sculpture lowers to the floor. Soft gasps fill the room as I watch the light leave his eyes, making memories of each second, each ragged breath for later.

It's not until I'm on the balcony ready to shimmy back down the wall that his last words resonate. Turning back to the glass doors, I track the iron sculpture swaying back and forth along the back of the chair. From this vantage point, I'm unable to see where the body of a once powerful man lies still and nonbreathing, but I know it's there.

"I hold the evidence. I'm the proof."

To anyone else, it would sound like a confession, a last testimonial. But I know better.

It's a diversion.

QUIETLY CLOSING THE BACK DOOR, I don't bother to flick the dead bolt. I'm the scariest thing on this block; only an idiot would try to break in here. The dark hardwood floors creak under each footstep as I stalk through the townhouse. The soft glow of light from the streetlamps slices through the slats of the plantation shutters covering each of the windows in the formal living room. The stairs pop and crack under my weight with each step toward the master bedroom. At the landing, I tug the black long-sleeve T-shirt over my head, tossing it to the floor as I continue on my route to the shower. With my pants hanging open, my cock resting against the teeth of the zipper, I pull my phone free from the back pocket and dial the number directed in the initial instructions for tonight's contract.

"Is it done?" says the weak voice on the other end of the line. I've never seen a single client face-to-face, but this person's voice is unforgettable, one I've heard a few times before. Gotta love returning customers.

"Yes." I eye the shower and gently stroke my cock, readying it for the fun we're about to have.

"And the answers to the questions."

"He said the lawyers don't know anything yet and that she didn't know." I pinch the head of my dick, focusing on the pain to keep me from asking who the fuck "she" is and why everyone's so interested in this cunt.

"Did you believe him?"

I sigh as I release my hold, the earlier bite of pain morphing into delicious pleasure.

"Yes to the lawyer portion. His answer was quick. No to the part about the woman." I stroke myself, impatience rising as the silence stretches. "Unless you want to create another contract for this mystery woman, we're done here. Wire me the final amount tonight as promised. I've got shit to do."

"It's not just some woman. She's untouchable."

My interest piques. The fucker knows exactly what he's doing using those words. It's a challenge, something I never back away from.

"You're aware I'm the best," I grit out. Not sure why I'm fighting to take on this contract—jobs come to me, not the other way around. Not to mention I have another contract in the wing, one that will take months of recon to ensure its success and me not being hung as a traitor. But there's something about this mystery and the fucking curiosity that hasn't waned since I left that corpse in his fancy-ass estate.

"They cannot allow loose ends." The long pause on the other end of the line signals he's debating his next steps. "We will get you close. Close enough to funnel information on her whereabouts and vulnerabilities. But you would not be the one hired to take her out. It would be too obvious and lead every agency back to us as the responsible party."

I huff and shove my cargo pants the rest of the way down my legs before stepping out, leaving them in a puddle of thick fabric in the middle of the room.

"Don't doubt my restraint. You only want information, I'll only gather information."

A quiet curse comes from the other end of the line. "This has to happen even with the risks. She has to know more about the group and their goal than he let on or he wouldn't have stepped down." A long quiet pause in the conversation eats at my nerves. "We will get you close and form a plan from there with others to eliminate her as a threat."

More silence, this time from my end as I deliberate if this contract is even worth the hassle. Intelligence gathering then allowing someone else to take the hit isn't something I've done before. Sounds like I'd do all the leg work and get cut out of the fun part.

"We will pay triple your normal rate."

My hand hovers over the chrome shower handle. Fuck, that's a shit ton of money.

"Who the fuck is this woman?" I say, allowing some of the intrigue to flow through my gritty voice.

"Randi Sawyer, the president of the United States."

"Interesting." My thoughts swirl. "Agreed with one exception. I know someone who will take the final hit. I won't trust anyone else with the kill other than him."

I smile as I twist the handle all the way to the right and maneuver around the initial cold spray. Tossing the phone onto the tower of towels, I brace an arm against the shower door.

This is a first.

Two contracts, shit ton of money, same mark.

Randi Sawyer is a dead woman.

1

RANDI

July

The adorned black casket drops an inch at a time into the grave. It disappears until merely the deep crimson petals of the few single stem roses atop, one of which I placed, are visible. Within seconds they too fade beneath the saturated ground.

All that's left to take in are the trails of rain and mud sliding down the earth walls, yet still I don't move or alter my focus from the grave just a few feet in front of me. The heavy weight of the empty space threatens to cut off my already shallow breaths. The other mourners, friends and family, left long ago. T and the team left with Sam after the service held at the church just down the road, and Trey disappeared through the crowd at some point here at the gravesite.

If I'm honest, it's the shame that weighs so heavily. The shame of not really knowing this man, yet he gave his life to protect my daughter.

The jagged edges of Taeler's bitten-down nails cut through my light-weight black suit jacket, no doubt leaving half-moon indentions in my bicep. The heavy rain that began late last night pounds against the umbrella, muting the outside world with its thundering. Streams of rainwater run off the black dome hovering over my head, cutting through my line of vision and puddling beneath my black pumps. Goosebumps sprout along my stocking-covered legs as a cool breeze whips through the graveyard. My hold on Taeler tightens as I fight to suppress a shiver.

I can't appear the slightest bit weak or frail. Not here—not anywhere since I was sworn into the presidential role. Even something as simple as a shiver could trigger a negative media swarm, one I certainly do not want or need. Three weeks have passed since the day I gave a portion of my life to serve my country as president, and the media vultures swarmed in moments after the official announcement and haven't retreated in the slightest. I'm told this is to be my new normal. Those previous incidents when I was VP which were carefully covered up by my PR and media relations team are now a thing of the past. According to the American people, my life is to be on full display at all times no matter if it's personal or business. Business being running this amazing country.

Through the pounding of the rain above us, Taeler's muffled cries somehow reach my ears. Turning to my only daughter, I wrap a hand around her thin shoulder and pull her closer to my side. Trembling arms wrap around my waist, clenching tight. Her chest heaves with each sob as she grieves for the only man she's ever loved. Strands of her loose hair, damp from the rain's spray, adhere to my jaw following a strong burst of wind.

No one informed us he was one of the fatalities that night in Paris. It wasn't until days after the kidnapping, when Taeler was safe by my side, that the director of the Secret Service stepped into the Oval Office and informed me of Grem's death.

It was a shock, but more so to Taeler since they'd been avoiding giving any real answers on his whereabouts since the incident. Those first few days she was angry, in denial about his death. Of course, I understood the protocol they were forced to follow. Identifying the body and informing his family came first; me being president and his girlfriend the president's daughter didn't change anything. I admire the respect shown to his family by allowing his mother and father to be the first to know of his death.

My gaze shifts from the mud to Chad's parents, who, like Taeler and me, still linger with their focus on the sole grave. Thankfully there was little awkwardness between us at the service when we met face-to-face for the first time just hours ago. Grief does that to strangers, connects individuals on a deep, soul-felt level. If their grief is equal, deep, and heartrending, an almost familial bond snaps into place.

With a white handkerchief pressed to her red lips, Chad's mother weeps while desperately clinging to her husband. His father, dressed in his naval uniform, silently cries while holding tight to his wife, offering her the strength she needs to not fall face-first into the saturated ground.

Sad, red-rimmed eyes meet mine from across the massive hole in the ground now containing their only son. The utter agony behind his eyes causes a breath to catch in my chest. I wait for the accusing glare I expect at any moment, but it doesn't come, even as the time ticks on with our stare never faltering.

Finally he breaks eye contact to lean close to his wife, pressing his lips near her ear. The wife's head bobs, agreeing to whatever he whispered. Moving like two stone statues, they start around the open grave toward where Taeler, the swarm of Secret Service men, and I stand. When they near, an agent steps into the couple's path, cutting off their access to me. Outrage bubbles in my chest as I clench both fists at my sides at the audacity of the fool.

The agent supporting the umbrella over my head steps with me as I stride through the multiple puddles. After maneuvering around the idiot standing between me and the parents of the man in the grave, I pause, waiting for whatever they need to say.

"We don't blame you or your daughter," Chad's father shouts over the hammering rain. "Our son—" His voice catches. "Our son knew what could happen in the line of work he chose."

Taeler doesn't reply, just simply presses her forehead against my shoulder, the rattling sobs starting once again. I gaze at the crown of her blonde head. If I'm honest with myself, I envy her ability to show emotion. Standing here, stone faced without a single tear shed, I must look like a fucking bitch. Inside I'm suffocating on guilt and grief. A young, vibrant kid is no longer here because of me. I take full responsibility for Grem's death, even if his parents don't place the blame on my head.

Grem's mother directs her attention to us, her gaze flicking from me and my entourage before settling on Taeler. A sad, watery smile ticks up the corners of her smeared red lips.

"He talked about you to us, often. Did you know that?" Taeler stifles a cry beside me at the mother's confession. I rub a hand up and down Taeler's bare bicep, offering what little comfort I can out in public. "I know he did what he had to do to protect the woman he loved."

The crack in my already wounded heart deepens at her words.

Tense silence passes between us as we wait for Taeler's response. The rainfall continues to pound against the umbrella as the wind whips through the graveyard, dusting my face with a fine mist.

A low mumble comes from my side, the words lost due to the loud background noise surrounding us. The three of us lean closer together, our attention on Taeler as we strain to hear whatever she's trying to say.

With her beautiful face directed toward the soggy ground, she whispers once again.

"Taeler, we can't hear you over this rain." The urge to shake her permeates every cell in an effort to pull her out of the zombie-like daze she's been in since this morning.

"I'm pregnant," Taeler says loud enough for us to hear.

My eyes widen to the size of saucers. Those two words out of her mouth are like a punch to the face.

"Come again?" My voice is tense as I hold on to a sliver of my composure.

"I'm pregnant," she says again, this time looking up from the mud. Her blue eyes, her father's blue eyes, lift to meet Grem's mother's searching ones. "I loved him. I still love him, and he'll never—" Her words are cut off by a gulping breath as a renewed set of sobs commences.

Breath stagnant in my chest, I glance between Grem's parents, who seem as shocked as I am based on their wide eyes and slack jaws. Hand to my stomach, I fist the pristine shirt beneath my jacket, right above my belly button. Shutting my eyes, I inhale deep, forcing control over my storming emotions.

Not here. Not in public.

No, I have to get somewhere private. The desperate need for Trey's arms around me nearly breaks what's left of my composure.

I blink, hating what I have to do next, only to find Grem's parents now smiling with happy tears glistening in their eyes.

Well, fuck. I'm an evil witch for what has to happen now.

"You can't mention a word of this to anyone," I state, my voice cold and emotionless, a complete contradiction to what's eating at my insides. "You'll both need to sign a nondisclosure agreement regarding this news to protect Taeler, the baby—" I swallow hard at that word passing my lips. "—and me. This cannot get out to the media."

Horror-stricken faces turn to me. Yep, I sound like a bitch. No, actually I sound like the fucking president of the United States who just found out her daughter is pregnant with zero warning. I have to contain this for her safety, both from my enemies and the harassing media storm that will commence if this gets out before we're ready.

Tugging on Taeler's arm, I angle us toward the waiting motorcade.

"Someone will be in touch with developments," I say over my shoulder.

Not waiting for a response, I hurry us across the graveyard.

"Mom, stop. I—"

"Not here." I offer a stiff nod to the unfamiliar agents as we pass. My heart pounds against my ribs, threatening to crack them wide open. Stars dance in my vision as we march through the grass with the implications those two words have on her, on me.

My feet slow as a familiar woman waiting beside a town car comes into view.

Celia Benson smiles when our gazes meet. Without an indication from me, she starts toward us. Standing beside the limo, I forget any sense of decorum and shove Taeler into the dry passenger compartment, then slam the door shut, sealing her away from the approaching evil.

Dread sinks into my gut at even the sight of her. I'd hoped that day in their sunroom when I punched her husband and effectively ruined their lives was the last time I'd ever see her. Guess I'm not that lucky.

What the hell is she even doing here?

A few paces behind me, Grem's parents' squelching footsteps grow closer.

"Let her through," I shout to the agent blocking Celia's path. Immediately I regret those words. I loathe this woman. Loathe as in I wish I could punch her in the boob and tell everyone about her kinky ass. But I can't. Why? Because I'm the president of the United States, and apparently there is no boob punching in this role.

Or so says my chief of staff. It might have come up in a conversation or two recently.

"What are you doing here, Celia?" I demand, keeping my voice bored.

"Here supporting my friends," she says while waving a hand toward Grem's parents. "What a tragedy losing such a promising young man for something so fleeting."

I grit my teeth, my back molars nearly cracking under the pressure. "How do you know them?" I grit out.

"We met Celia and her husband at a fundraiser years ago," Grem's father, now standing at my side, says. "When we found out her son worked in the Secret Service here in DC, we asked her to keep an eye on Chad while we were stationed in California for a few years."

Oh. Fucking. Hell.

Bile rises up my throat. Reaching up, I wrap my fingers around my throat and squeeze to keep from puking.

Great. Just fucking great. It seems my daughter's dead lover—and baby daddy—was my current lover's mother's spy.

Someone should call Jerry Springer.

The massive amount of varying emotions this day has conjured barrels into me, suddenly becoming too much to bare in front of others.

Flicking my gaze between the two grieving parents, I purse my lips. "I'll be in touch."

Three fingers graze the wet door handle of the idling limo just as it's pulled open for me.

"Madam President," the agent mutters. "Please, allow me."

I use my last scrap of energy to *not* roll my eyes at the man. Every day since shifting into this role, I've missed my old alpha team, but today it's almost painful. With a parting smile to Grem's parents, I duck inside the limo. The dry, warm air of the interior brushes against my damp arms, and goosebumps cover my legs and the back of my neck. I rub my arms despite the July heat as I settle back into the black leather seat.

Taeler's pleading expression urges me to talk this through now, to comfort her somehow, but I don't.

"When did you find out?" We both know what I'm referring to; no need to mention the P-word again.

"This morning," she rasps, tucking her damp blonde hair behind her ear. She repeats the move over and over as she stares at the floorboard. "Are you mad?"

I sink my lower teeth into my upper lip to keep the string of profanities from slipping out. She needs my support, but all I can do is focus on not falling apart right here in this damn limo.

"You're staying with me, at the White House. How in the hell did you get a damn pregnancy test, Taeler?"

She wraps her arms around her chest, a wounded expression passes her face. "One of my agents ran out and grabbed it for me." Her breath catches. "Mom—"

"Great, another NDA we need to have signed. Fuck." The smooth material of my black skirt slides against my palms as I rub them up and down my thighs. "Fuck," I shout again, letting my rising frustration echo in the word.

"Why the hell are you mad?" Taeler yells back. "I'm the one who's pregnant, not you."

"I told you—" I cut myself off to take a deep, calming breath. Screaming at her will accomplish nothing. "I can't have this conversation with you right now, Taeler. You just told me you're pregnant in front of two strangers, in public, at a funeral."

I slide my phone from the inside pocket of my tailored suit jacket. After swiping the screen open, I press the number for my new chief of staff, Blake Jansen. The moment he picks up, I dive in. "We need an NDA sent to the fallen agent's parents right now. We need them to sign it immediately and get it back to us." Taking a deep breath, I hold it in until it burns in my lungs. "I need a meeting with you and the press secretary the moment I get to the White House, ETA thirty minutes." Hanging up, I toss the phone to the seat, then lean forward and massage my temples with my thumbs.

"I'll get a doctor to come to the White House. You'll need to get on prenatal vitamins immediately." Tears clog in my throat. "And I'm not mad, Taeler. I'm confused and really, really disappointed in you and this situation."

"Mom." Her voice breaks. "You're embarrassed?"

Dropping my hands, I turn in the seat to face her straight on. "No, I'm not embarrassed. This has nothing to do with me being president. It has to do with you and me, Taeler Lynn. I told you time and time again to use protection. I've told you to be smart so many times I've lost track. You know how hard being a single mom was for me and that I didn't want that life, that struggle, for you."

"I didn't mean for this to happen," she says she silently cries. "It was just once or twice. I didn't expect—"

"I can't do this right now, Taeler." I press the palm of one hand to my chest, trying to quell the building ache. Outside the dark-tinted window, the trees rush by as we drive back to the White House. Through the streams of water, I focus on the iconic building that grows larger in the window. My new home. A home I didn't anticipate and sure as hell don't deserve.

My breathing turns erratic.

The moment we're through the gates, I snatch my phone off the neighboring seat and type out a quick text to Trey.

Me: Your presence is needed ASAP in the Oval Office.

A response comes back almost immediately.

Trey: You okay?

Me: No.

Trey: Randi, you can't say shit like that. Are you safe?

Me: Physically, yes. Emotionally, I'm about to detonate.

Trey: Be there in thirty.

I REST the phone on top of my lap and stare at the blank screen.

Thirty minutes. I can hold it together for thirty more minutes.

I think.

2

———————

RANDI

"We have options."

I monitor my press secretary as I wait for her to continue. Well, not *my* press secretary. She was Kyle's before he was forced to step down. When the change in command happened, she offered to stay on until I figured out whom else to hire for the role. Crazy enough, most of the staff had the same mindset. Which was fucking amazing, because I wasn't in a place where I could restaff the whole damn White House. Hell, it's weeks later and I'm still not. With my lack of connections in this town, I might never be ready to staff.

She skirts her nervous gaze from me to Blake, who's perched on the edge of one of the two love seats in the Oval Office.

"Just say it," I urge on an exhausted sigh, peeking at the clock on the massive desk phone—the phone that could launch a nuclear war against the world with just a simple call—to gauge how much longer I have to put up with this bullshit before Trey arrives.

"We could have it discreetly taken care of—"

"No," I say immediately. "That will *not* be our call. What are the other options?"

"We keep her here, locked inside the White House until she delivers, then send the baby to a relative," Blake replies.

I snort and swivel in the high-backed leather chair to look out the massive glass windows. Rain continues to pound against the panes, the streets below resembling flowing rivers rather than asphalt lanes.

"No, she won't be my prisoner," I say over my shoulder.

"We announce—"

Three sharp raps at the door stop her cold. My new secretary's ball of frizzy red hair pops through the door. "Madam President, Agent Benson is here to see you. He said you requested a meeting."

I nod, offering a weak smile, letting her know she was right to interrupt the meeting. When I hired her last week—the one I had as VP lasted all of two days in the new higher stress role—I laid out a few ground rules. Trey and Taeler always being priority no matter what I was doing or who I was meeting with was the most important rule for her to remember.

Curling my fingers, I motion for her to let him in. Mumbles of discontent come from Blake and the press secretary at my decision to allow an agent into our meeting. Not that I give a rat's ass.

"Agent Benson, perfect timing." I swivel to face the middle of the room. Palms to the edge of the desk, I give a hard push, shooting the chair's rolling wheels backward a foot. My stiff joints protest as I stand from the ass-conforming seat. Light-headedness sparkles in the back of my mind for the second time today, making the room sway. Fingertips pressed to the polished surface, I lean my weight onto them to center me and keep from tipping over. The episode doesn't last long, but even that blip doesn't slip past Trey, who narrows his honey brown eyes my way.

I take him in as he strides across the room before coming to a stop beside the mahogany desk. Dark gray slacks drape over his lean hips and muscular thighs, highlighting the strength hidden beneath with each of his steps. The plain baby blue dress shirt is unbuttoned at the top, offering a glimpse of naturally smooth tan skin beneath.

Every cell, every muscle, demands I collapse into his strong, comforting arms. But I can't. Not yet.

"Continue," I say after swallowing down the building emotions. "What do we announce?" Shifting my focus back to the press secretary, I raise both brows expectantly.

"We announce the pregnancy." Trey's shoulders tense, and a painful grimace mars his handsome face. The faint laugh lines I love so much are now hidden behind deep stress-filled wrinkles. "That way we can get ahead of the media before it's escalated. We give them the story we want them to run with. If we don't, who knows what they'll create on their own."

"Madam President?" Trey hisses like the two words cause him physical pain. The muscle along his narrow jaw twitches. "Who's pregnant?" Hurt and anger swirl behind his searching eyes.

Well, shit. Way to go, Randi. Didn't even think he'd assume I was the one pregnant. Well, us pregnant.

Oh hell.

I'm a moron. And president of the United States.

Fucking hell. This will not end well for anyone.

"Taeler," I blurt. My right hand slides across the desk, inching its way toward him. "That's who's pregnant, with Grem's baby. I found out today, about an hour ago."

"What?" Shock registers across his face while his entire body relaxes, releasing the shoulders that were stationed by his ears.

A pang of hurt pulses through me, eradicating the other swirling emotions. Not sure why the idea of him being relieved that I'm not the one pregnant hurts so badly, but it does. I'll have to figure that out later. One issue at a time, or I'll end up being a multi-episode on Jerry Springer.

"The media will have a field day with this information if we don't guide them," Blake says, drawing my attention back to the issue at hand. "They'll drag her through the mud, both of you. We already have a difficult time getting the media and voters to see you as presidential. And now your daughter, who's living in the White House is unwed and pregnant. Fuck, they'll just assume she plans to park a double-wide on the front fucking lawn." He twirls a pen between his fingers. "They'll call her a trailer trash whore just like her mom. It won't be good."

An angry grunt rumbles from where Trey stands with a straight back, hands fisted at his side.

Leaning forward, I press all my weight onto the desk and drop my head. "Noted. What about the NDAs? Did you get those out like I requested?"

Blake huffs like it's a ridiculous question. "Yes, an agent hand delivered them moments ago. I requested he wait until both were signed before heading back to the White House."

My head bobs at the somewhat good news. Then a conversation from the limo comes to mind. "Taeler had an agent run out and purchase the pregnancy test. Will that be an issue?"

At his silence, I raise my head. Blake rubs a pale hand along his square jaw, the scratch of his palm against his stubble audible from several feet away.

"All agents sign NDAs when hired," Trey adds.

"Right, but that doesn't mean he wasn't caught on camera, or the cashier didn't notice his suit and guns and drew conclusions. That's not even factoring in the other customers in the store at the time of the purchase," Blake states. Leaning back against the couch, he groans. "I'll send someone to clean up *that* mess too."

Tears pool in the corners of my eyes, threatening to fall and expose the emotional mess I'm holding inside. Twisting fast, I perch on the rounded edge of the presidential desk to hide my face by putting my back to the room.

"Great." I clear the lump of tears clogging my throat to make the words audible. "I'll let you know what plan of action I decide on later. As of now, we're done here. You two can go. Agent Benson, you stay. We have more to discuss."

There's a shuffling noise behind me as soft footsteps grow closer. A single hot tear escapes. I fight the urge to wipe it away until I know the room is clear.

Trey steps in front of me in his expensive custom suit, blocking out the back lawn I was so focused on. "They're gone," he murmurs as he swipes the lone tear away with the pad of his thumb.

That's the breaking point. The softness in his touch, the concern in his voice. Pitching forward, I press my forehead to his sternum and release the firm clamp I had been holding on my sorrow and grief.

Muscular arms immediately swallow me up, wrapping around my trembling shoulders and cocooning me in unrelenting support and comfort.

"Shh, baby," he whispers into my hair. A hiccup escapes between sobs. "Come on, please. Please don't cry. You're killing me." The long calming strokes of his fingers up and down my curved spine have the opposite effect of his words as fresh tears stream down my cheeks and drip off my jaw and chin. Fisting the front of his shirt, I tug him closer.

This festering buildup of emotions and smothering stress began collecting the moment my hand rested on that Bible and I repeated the vows to serve this country. Since that moment, every flicker of anger, every blip of sadness or unease, and the mounting pressure have been shoved into a deep chasm somewhere in my chest.

Until today. Because he's here. Holding me. Protecting me. Letting me grieve openly and supporting me through it all.

Knowing Grem—the man whose name I could never remember—died protecting my daughter was the tipping of the scales that pushed me over into the madness my pent-up emotions have brewed. Add in the fact that he died also protecting their unborn child makes the guilt unbearable.

The tears burn as they pour from my eyes. My breathing turns ragged as the backlog of unshed tears fight to escape.

Pregnant.

Taeler's pregnant.

I should be happy about a grandchild, but I'm not, not at all. And I can't help the way I feel about the situation—the churning anger, fear, and disappointment. I wish I was excited, but too many negative memories surround those two words: the way her father reacted to them, the backlash from the community and his parents, and then, of course, the struggle I fought against every fucking day to keep from repeating the cycle I was destined to fall into by being a single teen mother.

It will be different for her, yes, but I know all too well the struggle that all single mothers face. A part of me resents her recklessness of not using protection. And a much larger portion hates me for resenting her.

For what seems like hours, Trey holds me close, whispering calming and supportive words as I cleanse out that emotional chasm, clearing it of the backlog in the presence of the one person I trust enough to break in front of.

Trey won't judge me, won't see this as a weakness. Which is another reason I've missed him the past few weeks. Sure, I've missed his sexy body, mischievous smirk, and arrogant personality, but I've also missed my friend. The phone calls and texts can't offer the same connection as him being here, standing in front of me, holding me tight.

"You're upset about the pregnancy," he says when the tears slow and my breathing normalizes.

The cotton material of his dress shirt moves with my forehead as I nod.

"That's okay, Randi. Today you said goodbye to Grem, and now this news was tossed into the mess. It's okay to be at emotional capacity. But know this, Mess. Are you listening?"

Again I nod.

"How you feel right now is okay." I swallow back my disagreeing response. "What you went through all those years ago as a teen mother left a scar that no one understands but you. I can't even imagine the types of emotions this news brings to the surface, but it won't be like that for Tae. Know why?"

I shake my head.

"Come on, baby, look at me."

This time I shake my head in more of a panic than disagreement. No way in hell am I letting his perfect face see me like this. Drips of snot flow from the tip of my nose. No doubt my eyes are red and swollen. Oh, and can't forget the black streak marks lining my cheeks from the running mascara and eyeliner. Like hell I'll let him see me like this. I might be the president, but I'm still a woman who doesn't want her hot boyfriend to see her looking like shit.

Except he doesn't give me a choice. At his retreating step, I whimper, hating him a little and missing the way his hold blocked out reality just for a little while. Desperate to hide my face, I tuck the tip of my chin to my chest. *Fine. Asshole.* Blindly I stretch a hand behind me, smacking against the desk in search of the tissue box I know I've seen. A stiff cardboard box taps my pinkie. Tracing the box upward, I yank several soft tissues free. Only when I'm fairly certain snot and tears are gone do I dare a peek at the still waiting Trey.

"Um, yeah, so you were saying?" I say, ignoring the fact that I spent five minutes attempting to make myself presentable for him.

His fuller lower lip slides from where it's snagged between his teeth as his signature smirk tugs at the corners. The same mischievous smirk that won me over during the campaign. The smirk that gets him into and out of anything and everything. It's confident, mischievous. It's wholly Trey Benson.

A pulse of relief eases through me at the sight of him standing in front of me, finally, after way too many days, weeks apart.

"I asked, do you know why pregnancy and being a single mom will be different for Taeler?"

"Because she's not fifteen with the only life skill in her arsenal being how to stock shelves at Food Lion?"

His mouth pops open and then shuts. Head slightly tilted, he considers me for a second before speaking. "Your first job was stocking shelves at a grocery store?"

I lift a single slim shoulder. "Yeah. It was the only business that would hire a minor and wasn't shady as hell. The store owner paid me in cash until I was legal and could be processed through payroll." Sticking to this diverting topic, I hitch my chin in his direction. "Everyone's first job was awful as hell. It's character building. What was yours?"

Pink flush sprouts along his cheekbones. After running a hand through his long dark hair, he shoves both hands into the pockets of his slacks and avoids my questioning stare.

"Oh, right," I say on a soft laugh. "You never had the typical first job hell, did you?"

"I worked," he says, half pouting, half defensive.

"Oh really, Mr. Richie Rich? Then do tell. I'm all ears here."

"My job was to get good grades and focus on sports," Trey says with a sheepish shrug.

"That's what all rich kids say." I snort. But the mention of his childhood reminds me of seeing Celia this afternoon and the evidence I now have identifying Grem as the mole who's evaded us. "Oh, and speaking of your childhood—"

A light knock at the door cuts me off. Swiveling on the desk, I watch the door, waiting for it to swing open, but it never does. Glancing over my shoulder, I shoot Trey a questioning look.

"Mess." He chuckles, raising a fist to his mouth, hiding his smile. "You have to tell her it's okay to come in."

"Oh, right. I forget that part." Shifting to face the door, I remember our earlier conversation and swivel back around to face Trey once again. "Did you make your point from earlier?"

"What point?"

"You said it will be different with Tae because...."

"Because, Mess, she has *you*."

I sink my teeth into my lower lip to keep the trembling to a minimum. *Why the hell does he have to go and say sweet shit like that?*

"But I don't know how to support her like she'll need and do this." I sweep both hands out, indicating the historic office. "And what if I'm bad at being a grandparent? What if she's bad at being a mom? And most importantly—" I inhale deep to quell the nerves churning my stomach. "—what if this ends badly? What if this is what Shawn uses against me?"

Both our heads turn at the next knock on the door, this one more forceful.

Trey steps close, placing his hips between my spread knees. The hem of my black pencil skirt slides higher up my thighs, drawing Trey's gaze.

That's another thing I've missed since I was sworn in.

Zero, and I mean *zero*—not even hand stuff—sex time. Between his recovery, him handling his parents' shit show, and not having any excuse to come to the White House, we haven't had a single moment alone together until now.

Smooth palms brush along my jaw as he cups my cheeks, his thumbs beneath my jaw, holding me still and putting me completely at his mercy. Honey brown eyes search mine as a smile plays at the corner of his lips.

"We'll figure it out, Randi. We always do. You focus on running this country and taking care of your daughter. She needs you now more than ever. Let me and your new alpha team handle all your protection, including that fuckface Whit. Let us take that stress from you, okay?"

"But—"

Soft lips slam against my own, cutting off my next words—hell, my next thought. I slide a tentative hand up his chest, clasping the back of his neck. The strain of the day seeps away with the way he consumes me, with every demanding swipe of his tongue against my own. Within the passing of a few seconds, nothing matters except him and me.

I whimper in disappointment at the pounding against the office door that forces him to end our moment. Hands gripping my lean waist, he helps me off the desk and doesn't let go until I'm steady on my heels.

"Tonight," I blurt. "I need to see you tonight. I miss you. I need us, Trouble." It takes every ounce of courage to expel those words. I don't want to be this needy and desperate for him, but at some point in our relationship, I've come to depend on his strength and unwavering support. I've felt lost without his daily presence the past several weeks.

Trey's confident smile goes shy. After clearing his throat, he shakes his head. "You know I would, but it's too risky. We both know what the media would say, what the people would say if they found out I was sneaking into the White House to sleep with the president."

"Figure out a way." I hang my head. "I'm drowning in this stress pool, and you're my unicorn float."

He tips his head back and lets out a full, boisterous laugh. The sadness that had begun to seep in with his certain departure lifts, and a smile spreads across my dry lips.

"You and your damn unicorns. The obsession is getting worse, Mess. What's next? Federal funding for genetic testing and DNA mutation in hopes of building a unicorn army?"

"Not a bad idea, Trouble. I'll look into it."

He smirks. "I'm sure the citizens of this country will love to know what their tax dollars are going toward."

Smiling, I straighten my shirt and swipe under my eyes once more. "Maybe I'll give everyone a Lisa Frank unicorn eraser or something as a thank you."

"What is this, a third grade Valentine's Day party?"

"You'd be surprised at all the shit I want to buy now that I can." Pausing on my way to the door, I glance over my shoulder. "Do you think they still sell Trapper Keepers? I always wanted one of those."

"What time, Mess?" he says on a resigned laugh.

Facing the closed white door, I give him a victorious smile. "I should be done around ten."

"I'll make it eleven, then."

Confused, I turn, my brows dipped.

Trey runs a hand down the front of his dress shirt, smoothing out the wrinkles I caused. "You and Taeler need to talk before I stop by. You two will be fine once you have a chance to discuss what this means to both of you and hash out a plan. Do you even know what she wants?"

My long dark hair swipes along my back as I shake my head. No, I haven't a clue, because I was too wrapped up in my own emotions earlier to ask.

Great, I already suck at this supportive grandparent thing.

The door rattles with another demanding knock. Twisting around, I fist the doorknob and yank it open, frustration clearly written across my face.

"What?" I snap before I register Sam's blazing green eyes staring back at me.

He blinks, completely unfazed by my outburst. His attention shifts over my shoulder, where Trey now stands based off the tension radiating at my back.

"We need to talk," Sam states, sliding his narrowed eyes back to me. "There's been an incident."

The sharp edge of the door digs into my forehead as I press it against the wood. "You can't be serious. What else can go wrong today?"

"Birmingham is dead."

3

TREY

The hard plastic bubble indents a fraction as I stab a finger into the button indicating the floor to the condo. Shoulder against the metal wall, I stabilize myself for the jostle that will come as the elevator starts its ascent. The mechanics whir to life, shooting me upward.

Exhaustion grips me, making my legs feel loose and unstable. The venture out into the real world for the service and to see Randi took nearly every reserve of energy I had. Even though I'm bored as hell on medical leave, I can't imagine getting through a twelve-hour shift like this. Not that I'm anywhere close to being in any shape to return to duty.

The elevator slows its ascent before coming to a smooth halt. Listing forward, I force myself into motion as the doors open with a silent whoosh. Taking a right, I fumble for my keys as my heavy footsteps pound down the empty hall.

Damnit to hell, I fucking hate this. My weakness is pathetic. I shake my head, a few thick locks of hair sliding in front of my eyes. Even with the agency-issued physical training, the recovery is slower than I expected. It was a simple through-and-through shoulder wound, but somehow I know it's not the physical wound that's keeping my healing stagnant. Other aspects of those chaotic twelve hours have stuck with me, things I just can't seem to move past.

What those are, hell if I know. Not that I'm telling my appointed therapist the agency requires me to see weekly. But there's something in there, something that's building, making me moody, angry, despondent, and fucking tired. But today, seeing Randi and holding her in my arms, lifted a layer of that heaviness that's slowly suffocating me.

At the door, I slip my key into the deadbolt and twist, but it doesn't move. Confused, I narrow my eyes at the deadbolt before shifting my annoyance to the gold number hanging in the middle of the door.

"Fuck," I grumble and drop my hand, taking the nonworking key with it.

This isn't my condo anymore. It was, up until about a week ago when I sold it to Jessica Hawthorne.

Careful to not make a noise and attract Jessica to the front door, I turn and retreat the few steps back down the hallway toward the elevator.

Damnit, I really need to snap out of it. Get over this anger and resentment festering deep in my wounded soul. From challenging my parents on their perverted hobbies, to Taeler going missing, then confronting a drunken Birmingham before getting shot by the fucker, then Randi being sworn in while I was in surgery.

It's a lot to let go of when you're not really sure where to start. Top it off that my stronghold, the key to helping me work through it all, is locked up tight in that white prison. Earlier I couldn't even stick around while they talked about Birmingham's death. Like a useless accessory, I was shoved out of the room the moment details were discussed.

Now here I am back home—well, almost. I hit the button for the third floor and cringe as the elevator begins its decent.

Randi doesn't know about all this yet, and I'll keep it that way until I can figure out how to unfreeze the money stored in my trust. Mother might not have been able to cut me off from the money herself, but the FBI can. One mention of those funds being secured by my father at the Boardroom, where the trafficking of young girls was taking place, was enough evidence for a judge to freeze all assets.

So now on top of figuring out this emotional turmoil shit and healing, I'm fucking broke. Good thing I found roommates willing to help out with this new, much cheaper mortgage.

At the third floor, I exit the elevator. Door after door is crammed along the long hall, a visual display of how tiny these condos are on this level compared to the ones on the higher floors. Before I insert the key into the deadbolt, the door swings open, familiar bushy gray eyebrows and tired eyes greeting me.

"Master Trey," Gerard says as he opens the door wider, waving me into the tiny condo.

A huff brushes past my lips as I step around him. "I've told you over and over to stop it with that shit. Especially here, now." Rubbing my forehead, I sigh deeply and continue the couple steps to the living room. "That was one of the conditions for you and Beth staying here, remember? Well, that and her cookies."

That and I need the minimal amount they've offered to help me pay for the condo. There's also the guilt factor. It eats at my gut knowing I'm the reason they lost their jobs, that I'm the reason my family estate is now empty and for sale.

"Right, sorry. Old habits. How was the service and burial for your friend?"

"What you'd expect, I guess." Yep, not allowing those emotions an outlet either. No, that grief will stay stuffed deep down like all my other issues. "I would've been back sooner, but I was summoned to the White House."

An almost smile tweaks at the corners of his wrinkled lips. "And how is the president?"

"Randi," I correct. An almost insecure feeling churns my gut at the simple mention of her title. It's not that I'm jealous, that I'm sure of. It's that I'm... lost, not really knowing where I stand with her now and where our relationship falls in the hierarchy of her priorities. Fuck, I sound like a pining girl. "She's okay. Today was difficult for her."

"For all of you. He was a part of your team too at one point," Gerard says as he dangles a highball glass with two fingers of dark liquid between us.

My mouth waters at the sight. This right here is the new normal, the new and less improved Trey Benson. Drinking too much to deflect and hide the pain, not sleeping enough because of the drinking and self-wallowing, over-analyzing everything, and—bonus—random bouts of pure rage.

"Yeah, he was a good kid" is all I say before taking a deep swallow of the burning liquid to chase back the lump of emotions clogging my throat. "Do you know why my mother would've been there? I swore I saw her tucked and injected face in the crowd."

"Probably did see her," Gerard says at my back. "From what I under-stand, they were friends."

I jerk to a halt to spin around. "What?" I ask, utterly shocked. "Why didn't I know about this?"

The wrinkles marking his forehead deepen as he furrows his brow. "I don't know much about the how or why, but Mrs. Benson was acquainted with the young man's parents somehow. They stopped by the estate once or twice several years back."

At the sight of my deep leather recliner, one of the pieces of furniture I couldn't part with despite it crowding the entire living room, I yank the ends of my dress shirt from my belt with my free hand before toeing off one Ferragamo, then the other.

Somewhat more comfortable, I drop down into the cushions. Immediately the soft leather molds around my ass and back. A distant memory of my girl curled in my arms, the two of us acting like we didn't have a worry in the world, assaults me, taking me back to that moment. I can almost smell her cherry vanilla shampoo and feel the chill of her always cold hand seeping through my dress shirt. That day there were no stressors, no obligations or worries. It only lasted all of a few hours before the world came crashing back down around us, but those few hours I cherish even more now. Little did we know what lay ahead for her and how much of an impact it would have on us.

Swirling the ice and liquid around the thin glass sides, I observe the small waves. I should text Tank, tell him about my suspicions regarding the ongoing mole investigation. With my concerns at Camp David last fall and now the new information brought to light today, there's no doubt Grem was Mother's inside man.

Why? Guess we'll never know.

Tipping the glass up, I finish the drink in a single swallow.

But if I text Tank, that will open up the flood of questions I know will follow. I'm not ready to confront him. I don't have it in me to convince him I'm not slipping down a very dangerous path.

Without a doubt, Randi will take notice of my issues too when she's not consumed with grief and confusion. Which makes tonight a precarious situation I'll need to carefully navigate through. If I can even get past the side gate entrance unnoticed. Sure, I could always go through the front gates like a normal visitor, get the pass waiting at the guard tower like I did today, but being there at night is a different scenario entirely. No, going through the front gate isn't an option; it'll raise too many questions. And attract the media, which neither she nor I need right now. The reporters waiting outside the building and the constant calls asking for a statement about my father's arrest have finally died down, and I want to keep it that way. I have to figure out a plan to get inside the gates without drawing attention.

"You need to talk to someone," Gerard says from where he hovers.

Peeking one eye open, I take in the concern written across his face.

"Like who? That shrink I'm assigned to is a damn fool." Shutting my eyelid once again, I shift in the seat to find a more comfortable position. "Plus, I am. Tonight. Things will be better once I see her."

"You saw her today, yet here you are drinking and sleeping the day away, again."

"That was different," I protest.

"You need to get better, Trey. To get past this."

"I know, and I will." I sigh. "I just need to see her for longer than ten minutes without her upset about something I can't fucking fix." I curl my fingers into a tight fist. Heat washes along my skin, making a warm flush build beneath my undershirt. "I just need to get back to work."

"You'll end up shooting someone."

"If they deserve it, that's what guns are for."

"I'm more worried about you hurting someone who doesn't."

"I wouldn't do that. I wouldn't hurt an innocent person."

"You are right now."

A deep line forms between my brows as I give up on my nap and open both eyes. "I don't understand what you're implying."

"You, Trey. You can't continue to beat yourself up about things that were out of your control. Your parents made their own choices and are now facing those consequences. Those were their own actions, not yours. You were shot protecting the vice president, doing your job. Then come to find out one of the fatalities in Paris was a young man who you knew, who you trained. You have to let all this go and move on. None of it was your fault."

"Whatever," I grumble. Not the most mature response, but he's digging deeper than I want to dive at the moment—or ever. "I'm taking a nap."

After setting an alarm, I toss the phone to the side table and press the button on the inside armrest to raise the leg rest. "Everything will work out just fine. I'll see her tonight, talk things through, and be back to normal in no time. No need to worry," I mumble, already halfway asleep.

"Thanks for picking me up, man," I say while focused on the phone in my hand to avoid eye contact with Tank. Since the moment I woke up a couple hours ago, I've used the time to catch up on current affairs in case Randi wants to discuss anything. In my major news website searching, there wasn't one mention of Birmingham's death. Either the media doesn't know yet or someone slapped every news channel and paper with an injunction to keep the information from being released.

"It's fine," Tank says from the driver's seat.

The government-issued jet-black Suburban coasts down the empty streets. For the first time in our friendship, the silence is tense with unspoken words. The awkwardness eats at my resolve to not talk to him, knowing I'm the cause. But still here I sit, not offering any explanation to my absence in his life since I was released from the hospital or why I'm strung tighter than a damn hair trigger.

At the White House's fortified wrought iron gate, Tank rolls down the window as a marine approaches, readying to offer both our IDs.

The young kid takes the IDs while casting a suspicious scan inside the SUV. "Are you both expected?"

Tank hooks a thumb in my direction. "He is. The president wants to talk with him about the incident." We all know what incident he's talking about. Everyone does. My chest tightens, making it hard to inhale deep.

Fuck, what the hell is wrong with me?

The guard hands the IDs back and motions us forward. Again the silence in the cab feels heavy as we wait the eternity it takes for the gates to swing open wide enough for the Suburban to slip through unscathed.

Without any indication from me, Tank turns the wheel, taking us toward the residence side of the White House with the side entrance that's less visible.

Flexing my fingers, I attempt to loosen my tense muscles when the SUV comes to an abrupt halt. I snap forward. The seat belt engages, catching me before my nose collides with the dash.

"What the hell?" I grunt. Groaning, I sit back while rubbing at my chest. A new ache throbs from the still healing wound in my shoulder. "What the fuck is wrong with you, man?"

"Exactly, you idiot." Knowing full well where this conversation is headed,

I reach for the door handle readying for a swift exodus. "Oh hell no," Tank yells as he lunges across the SUV, smacking my hand away with one of his large mitt-like hands. "You're not going anywhere, Playboy."

"Fuck," I grunt as he bats my hand away at my second escape attempt. "Damnit, Tank. Let me out of this damn thing, now."

"Not on your life," he states. "Tell me what the fuck is going on with you."

"Nothing's 'going on with me,'" I mock, using air quotes. His eyes narrow as steam seems to billow from his ears. "What the fuck is going on with you?"

Still radiating with tension, Tank props his back against the driver side door, keeping a watchful gaze in my direction in case I try a third jailbreak.

"Talk. To. Me. I haven't seen you since the hospital, and then the first text in weeks, after all of mine have gone unread, is for a damn ride to help you sneak in to see your girlfriend?" He shakes his head. Averting his eyes, he looks out the front windshield. Rubbing a hand over his bald head, he exhales. "Whatever's going on, we'll figure it out. You can talk to me, Trey."

"Can I?" I say on a huffed breath. Sure, I'm being a dick, but you know what? So is he. Tank's sitting there completely unaware of what he's wanting me to share. Asking me to shed the multiple layers of grief, fear, and other emotions even I haven't been able to identify that I've carried the past few weeks. Right, like I'm just going to open up and spill my pussy-ass guts right here in the SUV moments before I visit my girlfriend—who, bonus, is now the leader of the free country. Yeah, he's the one being the dick, not me.

"You've been busy," I say, no doubt adding insult to injury based on Tank's pain-laced expression like I just backhanded him.

"True, I'll give you that," he grits out. "Pierce's international travel has been significant while you've been out on medical, but shit's hit the fan over in the Middle East. He goes where she sends him, and as team lead of his alpha protection team, I had to go too. It's my damn job, your job too once you come back. So don't fucking deflect that shit back on me. You haven't responded to a single call or text, so even if I was stateside, it wouldn't have mattered."

"Yeah, I know, man," I reluctantly grumble. "That was a dick shot."

He dips his chin in acknowledgment, immediately accepting my apology. Because he's the best damn friend a guy could ask for, and I'm an asshole.

"So tell me what's going on. The same as before?"

Before meaning the way heat and close quarters could trigger a panic attack stemming from my multiple deployments in the Middle East with the army.

"Different," I rasp. Clearing my throat, I swipe my clammy palms down my dark-wash jeans. "I just... can't. Not yet, Davis."

At his silence, I dare a glance at my friend only to find him carefully considering me. "Fine, I get that. Don't like it, but I get it. You have to be ready, which is why I'm guessing the agency shrink hasn't cleared you yet." He dips his head with a knowing expression. "But soon. And I want to see you at the club tomorrow morning. Your ass is out of shape."

My brows jump up my forehead. "How do you know I haven't been going?" The depth of care and devotion this man has for our friendship—for me—is incredible.

"I'm on the VP's detail, remember? He goes every morning we're stateside, and I haven't seen you there once. He'll be there tomorrow around five o'clock, and I expect to see you there too. You hear me, Benson? You've got to get back to life. Your medical leave ends next month, and I need you 100 percent."

Scrubbing a hand down my face, I offer a reluctant nod. "Yeah, sure. Tomorrow." Without glancing across the center console, I yank the chrome handle, opening the door without his interference. "It'll take me time, but I'll get back to normal soon."

At least that's what I'm telling myself.

"Trey, we don't have the luxury of time."

I pause and turn to cast a cautious glance over my shoulder. "What do you mean? What's going on that you're not telling me?" For the first time in weeks, intrigue slips in, pulling all my attention back to Tank.

"Sucks, don't it?"

I narrow my brows with a "don't fuck with me" expression.

"War, Benson. Like that Russian warned us in Hawaii, war is approaching, and it's up to our girl to prevent it from going down. To prevent thousands of our boys and girls from putting their lives on the fucking line for a conflict that's based off the greed and lies of others."

"Shit. Fucking Birmingham."

"Exactly."

With that heavy-loaded conversation in the forefront of my mind, I wave a goodbye and slam the door behind me. Taking a moment to process the information Tank revealed, I regard the brightly lit building in front of me. Dread drops like a ten-ton lead weight in my gut while the mounting anticipation at seeing her makes me jittery. It takes a minute to wrangle all the erratic emotions and shove them down deep, leaving me deceptively calm.

Inhaling a deep calming breath, I slowly release it through pursed lips and start toward the four agents guarding the entrance to the White House.

4

RANDI

"I mean, what the actual hell," I mumble under my breath as I tread down a long hall that will take me to the residence side of the White House. The perk of working and residing in the same location lost its glamor after day three of living here. Besides the funeral, I can't remember the last time I left this fancy prison. It's partly because I don't have to leave the grounds for a commute to the office, and the other part is the more intense security now that I'm president. Protecting me is the number one concern for everyone nowadays—which is a good thing, it really is, but it's not my guys, my trusted team, following me around. No, they had to stay with the VP, my friend Sam Pierce.

Lucky bastard.

There has to be a way to influence the director of the Secret Service to switch the teams out. And I will find a way... soon.

But right now that's the least of my concerns. Because holy fuck, Kyle is dead.

Really dead. With suicide as the cause of death.

Everyone else is taking the coroner's report at face value, just accepting that Kyle would take his own life, but to me, something feels *off* about that. Though the evidence collected was all conclusive to him strangling himself with a priceless piece of art—even the tie that was used as the noose was one of his apparently. Yet something nags in the back of my mind, something that keeps tickling every so often, making me question the validity of that conclusion.

Okay, sure, Kyle deliberated putting a bullet in his head that awful morning when I forced him to step down from the presidency, but he was drunk and cornered then. He was different after he resigned. He had hope because he knew he had options, since he held the information we need to end the corrupt scandal he left behind. Up until yesterday he held all the cards. A power he was exploiting, demanding amnesty in exchange for the names needed to stop whatever those men have set in motion.

I would ask Sam where they were in meeting his demands—maybe they denied Kyle and that's why he killed himself—but I've learned the hard way not to mention Kyle in front of Sam. It was a fucking horse pill for Sam to swallow when his boss, the attorney general, considered Kyle's demands, stating it was the lesser of the two evils. It's true, but the thought of him getting off scot-free for all his transgressions prickled at me too. But justice isn't always black and white, and if Kyle's information could help me stop the rising conflicts in the Middle East—conflicts that his scandal created— I'd take it no matter what he asked me to give up.

But now what will we do? What options do I have in finding the names and identities of the guilty?

It's a mess. All of it. The entire country and our Middle East relations. Most of the country is in an uproar at the still high gas prices while the others are furious that a woman is leading the country. Sure, they were okay with a woman in the secondary role, but the primary? Oh hell no. The news channels debate daily if I'll drive our country deeper into trouble or just not do anything at all.

Good to know they have such little faith in me.

Not that I have much more than they do. About every other minute, I wonder if I should've taken the out when I had it and stepped down when Kyle did. But there's no doubt in my mind that Shawn Whit, the sociopath best friend of the recently departed Kyle Birmingham, would've figured out a way to swoop in and fill one of the vacant roles. I might be unprepared and uneducated in most things politics, but at least I'm not a sociopath.

Hey, looky there, that's one positive I can focus on.

"Not driven to murder for fun. Go me."

The stoic agent beside me shoots me the side-eye.

Shrugging, I hold my hands out to my side. "What? I see it as a positive."

He turns his laser focus back down the hallway, completely dismissing my ramblings.

Damn, I miss T and Trey. Hell, all the guys. Soon I'll get them back. I just needed these few weeks to get my feet under me and understand what power I hold over urging the director to change my alpha team.

Right now, I have to fix what I fractured earlier in my callousness.

Pausing in front of Taeler's room, I rap two knuckles against the solid wood door and swallow down the uncertainty rolling in my gut. A million thoughts cross my mind as I wait for the door to open.

It cracks an inch, revealing puffy red eyes staring blankly into mine. Leaning against the door's edge, Taeler widens the gap and tilts her head inside the room. She turns to stalk toward the unmade bed without waiting to see if I follow.

I cast a worried glance at the agent to my left, then to the one stationed on my right. "Wish me luck?" No answer. "Rough crowd tonight," I grumble.

Mental note: getting my old alpha team back has officially moved up to number one priority for tomorrow. If I'm going to make it through the next two and a half years without cracking under the unrelenting pressure, I need the agents with personality who understand my quirky humor.

Once inside the room, I quietly shut the door behind me and lean against it, keeping my fidgeting fingers tucked behind my back.

Lungs filled with a deep encouraging breath, I launch into my planned apology.

"I know I didn't handle your news well." Taeler snorts, her back to me as she crawls into the king-size bed. "And I'm sorry," I continue. "I won't make excuses because none of them make this"—I shift a hand between the two of us—"any better."

"Yeah, you were kind of a bitch," Taeler says, her face downturned as she picks at a loose string on the embroidered cream duvet cover that came with the house.

"I'll take that," I reply, sucking in a breath. Daring a step, then another, I slowly approach the bed. "I should've put you first instead of thinking about the perception it will give, but that was just one reason, one of the many reasons why... why this is a difficult announcement for me."

"And you think it's easy for me?" Taeler seethes. She fists the thick fabric covering the bed and narrows an emotional glare up through her lashes. "I'm fucking pregnant, Mom. I'm still in college, Grem is... gone, and bonus, my mom now sees me as a problem instead of simply the beloved daughter I was just yesterday. I think this is all just as difficult for me to process, don't you?"

I swallow hard. "You're right. It is, and all I was thinking about earlier was myself. I'm terrified my enemies, who are numerous nowadays, will use this news to their advantage. I'm worried about how the media will react for *your* sake, not mine. They're vicious in their efforts to make us look like the white trash they believe we are, and believe me, with my past, I've given them a lot of ammunition to pick through. And I'm scared you'll live the life I did, always struggling and a step behind everyone else despite the effort you're putting into life."

The struggling ancient air conditioning vibrates in the vents as it pumps cold circulated air into the bedroom. The low hum is the only noise as the tense silence stretches.

"I'm scared," she finally admits. Her shoulders round, and her head droops.

"I know. Believe me, if anyone can say they understand, it's me." Stretching across the duvet, I take her hand and interlace our fingers. "But we'll get through this, together, just like everything else." My throat dries, making each word hurt. "Now, Taeler, I have to ask you something, and it's a decision you get to make and you only." I clear my throat, fighting with the way to word this next question.

"Yes, Mom. I want to keep it. I want to keep this baby. His baby."

A heavy exhale whips through my pursed lips. "Okay. Decision one down. Now on to next steps. I thought about it earlier, and I don't want you leaving the White House for the initial checkup. Call it paranoia or straight-up helicopter parenting, but I don't feel it's safe just yet. I'll have someone schedule an ob-gyn to come here tomorrow to check on you." I pause, the hard acrylic tip they've started to make me wear chipping beneath my gnawing teeth. "I have a full day tomorrow and the next—well, for the fore-seeable future, actually." I offer her a small smile. "But I'll make time for the appointment. Promise."

"Mom—" Her voice cracks. "I'm sorry I disappointed you. I didn't—"

"No, sweetie. Come here." A soft tug on her hand and she's in my arms. My fingers interlaced behind her back, I rest a cheek on the crown of her head. "I shouldn't have said that. I know for a fact Chad's parents are excited to have a piece of their son preserved in the form of a baby who's half him. We have to stick together like we always have. We're survivors, you and me. We get through shit no matter how tough the road looks. Right?"

My head moves up and down as she nods beneath me. Pulling from my tight grasp, Taeler wipes at her weeping eyes and reaches toward the tissue box on the nightstand.

"You get some sleep, Tae. Today was a lot to process for anyone. Tomorrow we'll tackle the next steps." A tentative smile pulls at her trembling lips. Tilting forward, I press my lips to her forehead. The bed dips as I push off the mattress. At the door, I look back over my shoulder. "Good night, Taeler. Everything will be fine. Don't worry about a thing."

The wide grin she sprouts brings about one of my own. But once I'm outside the door, it immediately falls as the full force of what's on my plate comes slamming back to mind.

"I need a cigarette." Both agents shake their heads. "Does that mean you don't have any or that I can't?"

"Both," the agent on the right says. "It's not safe to leave the confines of the White House, ma'am. Especially for a smoke break." His disdain and condescending tone rake at my nerves.

Asshat.

"The latter," says the other.

I whip my head to the left and smile at the somewhat familiar agent.

"Good thing I wasn't planning to pitch a plastic lawn chair on the front lawn and light up. Do you have a pack on you?" He glances to the surly agent instead of responding. "Hey, it's a simple question: Do you, or do you not?"

He grimaces and nods.

"Great. Follow me."

"Thanks, boys."

Beneath the rumbling exhaust vent, Trey's deep voice is barely audible. After another deep inhale of the cancerous smoke, I twist my lips upward, sending the gray cloud up the vent hood.

"Don't even start," I say when Trey stops at my side. Smiling, I focus on the burning ember of cigarette number two. "It's been a day." I snort. "Hell, it's been a life." Shifting to press my hip against the stove's edge, I angle my body toward him.

"It's been a life." His hand dives into the front pocket of his jeans before withdrawing a pack of Ultralights. "Figured we both could use this small escape, but it seems you beat me to it. How'd you manage that?" He hitches his chin to the lit cigarette between my fingers.

"Ted had a pack."

"Tom," says a voice somewhere from the other side of the refrigerator.

"Right, Tom, sorry." I shrug and take another inhale as Trey pulls his own from the pack and lights the end with my lighter that was resting atop the counter. "Side note, I apologized to Taeler." The soft filter rolls along the outer seam of my lower lip as I stare unfocused at the industrial-size iron grill top. "I told her everything would be okay, that we'd figure it out and get through it."

"Good."

The undercurrent of annoyance doesn't slip by me. "Is it?" I shake my head in an attempt to pull my volleying thoughts together. "I'm not sure it will. I'm not sure about anything anymore."

For several minutes, we burn one after another in silence, both of us seeming to be lost in thought. The instant I finish one, I light another, now tugging cigarettes from Trey's pack instead of bumming off Ted.

The rough wheel of the lighter indents into the pad of my thumb as I roll the flint to spark the flame needed to light my next casualty.

"So, Birmingham's dead," he says, letting the heavy words hang between us.

"I know. It's crazy. And I don't.... Actually"—I press my thumb and forefinger to my forehead—"can we just... *not* right now? I need a break from all that."

Trey nods, continuing to stare into the shadows, only lifting and lowering his hand to take a drag.

With a sigh, I consider the man standing beside me.

His typically styled and sculpted dark hair is disheveled, like he needs a haircut and is too distracted to care about his appearance. Dark stubble sprinkles along his jaw and down his neck. Purple circles and paler than normal skin signal the exhaustion he's attempting to hide.

Lips sealed tightly together, I bump his shoulder to gain his attention. "What's going on with you, Trouble?"

"Nothing." With a soft shake of his head, displacing a few loose locks of his lengthy dark hair, he offers a strained smile. "All good. Smart thinking, by the way, to use the vent hood for an indoor smoke break."

I narrow my eyes at the clear deviation from my original probing question. "Yeah, thanks. I had to get creative since it's apparently not very presidential to sneak out back for a smoke like a rebellious teenager." I force a smile, desperate to lighten the strange mood between us. I nod to the opened pack he brought, now lying on the stove. "That was half gone."

He coughs, covering his mouth with a tightly fisted hand. "Off the wagon again. What can I say? It's been a stressful few weeks."

"Tell me about it," I say as I blow a lungful of smoke up the vent.

Again that fake, forced smile pulls at his lips.

Tossing my hands in the air, I release an exaggerated sigh. "Okay, what the actual fuck, Trey."

He startles, almost dropping the cigarette dangling from his fingers to the white tile floor. "What?"

"Exactly," I hiss.

Trey's dark brows dive between his eyes, making a deep line form between them. "I'm confused."

"Same."

"Mess, you can't just agree with what I'm saying," he states, his tight voice revealing the underlying frustration that's desperate for an outlet.

"Yes." Pushing his buttons is fun and simple when he's obviously already sitting at the eruption point.

"Damnit, Randi, I said stop it," he grits out. The muscle along his jaw twitches as he keeps it tightly clamped together.

"Randi, is it?" I snap. I shove his shoulder a bit harder than he's expecting, causing him to step back. "Talk to me, Trouble. What's going on with you? Something is obviously wrong."

"I'm fine." Right, and unicorns aren't the coolest magical creature. "Let's talk about you." He shifts the hand holding the cigarette in my direction.

Now it's my turn to be confused. "Um, okay. But what about me are we talking about?"

"You're as stressed as I am, for fuck's sake."

"Um, yeah, because I have a fucking stressful job as president, Trey." I spread my arms out wide, indicating the expansive kitchen we're standing in as a reminder of my current job.

"Thanks, but I don't need a reminder," he hisses under his breath.

Stunned, I stagger back a step, bringing my hand to my chest. "What did you just say?"

"Nothing."

"Oh hell no. This"—I flick my index finger between us—"is not nothing, you asshole." There's a high-pitched hiss as I drop the spent cigarette into the bowl of water we've been utilizing as a makeshift ashtray. This time I slam both hands against his muscular shoulders with each word for emphasis. "Talk. To. Me. Damnit."

His own cigarette falls into the water, extinguishing on impact. Rotating, he places his back to me, shielding me from the array of emotions I swear just flashed across his tense face.

Once, twice, he rakes his fingers through his hair as his shoulders rise and fall at a rapid pace with deep breaths.

After a moment, he clears his throat but still doesn't turn to face me. "I should go. Now seems like a bad time for both of us."

Desperation, dread, and anger battle for dominance inside me. Before he takes a single step, I clasp one shoulder to halt his retreat.

"Hell no, you're not walking away from me. From us. What the actual fuck is wrong with you, Trouble?" My voice cracks. He can't go. I've waited three weeks to see him in private, to feel somewhat normal again, and he's acting like an ass and about to leave.

This isn't my Trey. Whatever is going on with him runs deep, deeper than T or I realized.

"Let me go." The warning in his voice is palpable. Sensing the threat, three agents step from their invisible posts along the wall, their focus solely on Trey.

"Everyone out." My words are soft with the worry clogging my throat. No one reacts. Trey stands taller, readying for a fight as one agent advances another step. "For fuck's sake," I shout, stomping my bare foot on the tile. "I said get out!"

Shock registers on the approaching agent's face before he glances to his team members. One by one, they reluctantly file out of the kitchen. The final agent narrows a glare at Trey before trailing the others.

"Fuck you, Trey Benson," I mutter before slamming the heel of my hand against the center of his back.

5

RANDI

Trey whirls, strands of hair lifting with the fast move. His fury is palpable. Face flushed, chest rising and falling at a rapid pace with each short breath, he looks terrifying, menacing—deadly. To anyone but me. I don't flinch, don't shrink away even though he has the power to kill me in a single blow. No, I don't move because in my heart, deep within my soul that's been imprinted on by this man, I know Trey would *never* hurt me. The thought would never even cross his mind.

"Back off, Randi. I'm begging you. Back the fuck off." His words are strained. The vein along his neck throbs at a quick beat.

"No," I nearly hiss as I dare an inch closer, shrinking the distance between me and the man I love. The same man who is clearly fighting an internal war over things he won't allow me to understand. "I'm not backing off. And you know why, jackass?"

His jaw works back and forth, but he doesn't respond.

"Fine, I'll tell you anyway. Because I love you, you jerk!" I shove my arms out wide, fingers splayed. "I love you, and I'm dying inside right now not having any clue what you're dealing with, what you won't let me see. I want to. Fuck, I want to know, and I want to help, desperately. Don't you see that?" My last word is barely a whisper.

With both our cigarettes extinguished, I flick the vent hood off. The loud hum immediately dies, leaving the kitchen depressingly quiet.

"I wish it were that simple, but it's not," he states, his focus slipping to just over my shoulder.

"Yes it is. I'll show you, how's that? I'll start with this impromptu amateur hour counseling session." He arches a brow with a condescending tilt of his head. "Fuck me," I groan. Massaging my temples, I lean fully against the counter. "You're a dick for pushing me away, you know that?"

"I'm not... I'm not pushing you away, Mess. Don't take it so personal. I'm simply processing, that's all."

"For the past three weeks?"

"I was fucking shot, damnit!" he roars. "Cut me some damn slack, woman."

"Slack? You want me to cut you some slack because you're 'processing'?" I add a sneer to the end of the air quotes in hopes of pissing him off. "You know what I'm processing? The fact that I'm carrying the legit weight of the free world on my shoulders *without* my boyfriend to support me." This gets his attention. Those light eyes focus back on me, searching my own. "And I don't know why you resent me for that, since you're the one who convinced *me* to take the damn job."

"I don't resent you, Randi. It's just—"

"I've needed you every day, Trey." Looking to the ceiling, I fight the tears that want to fall. "It's not that I can't do all this alone. I know I can. I've been through a shit of a life and fought for every single step forward I've taken. But I don't *want* to do this alone. I don't want to be in this role, in this city, without you near me, with me."

"Mess," he whispers. Shaking his head, he runs a hand through his hair and tugs at the ends. "We've talked, texted. I am here."

"No you're not." Ignoring the warning bells, I jam my pointer finger to his sternum with each word.

He reacts lightning fast, grabbing my wrist to keep me from poking him again.

My heart sprints at the feel of his tight grasp holding me firm. And because there is something really wrong with me, the area between my thighs slicks with desire. I wet my upper lip, and his eyes track the small movement. Desire floods into his darkening stare while the restrained anger that was evident the moment he walked in the door still radiates off him.

Neither of us moves. Heat and passion spark between us.

I know what he needs. What we both need.

"Do it," I breathe.

Without warning, his lips crash against my own, our teeth connecting amid the searing kiss. I scrape my fake nails along his scalp before gripping a shaggy section of his hair. This isn't sweet or tender. It's angry and devouring, using all our pent-up stress and aggression to fuel the raging passion between us. Back and forth, we struggle for control with each tangle of our tongues and nip of our lips. A cool wall of metal meets my back, the air in my lungs leaving in a violent whoosh.

With an animalistic growl, he relaxes his hold on my waist only for rushed fingers to slip between the small gaps between the buttons of my dress shirt. I gasp, the shock quickly morphing into blinding desire as he rips the shirt open. Buttons fly around the kitchen, pinging on the tile floor and counter.

Chest heaving, I arch my back, head pressed to the unrelenting freezer door, effectively thrusting my breasts into his face, demanding attention from his talented lips and teeth. He gives a harsh tug on the soft lace demi cup, and my breast pops free, exposing my already hardened nipple. Gripping his hair, I attempt to urge him faster as he licks a thin line down the pounding vein along my neck with the tip of his slick tongue.

My hips jolt forward, seeking connection at the scrape of his teeth against my hard nipple. Adjusting his stance over me, Trey slips a muscular thigh between my legs. His knee dips beneath the hem of my pencil skirt, shoving it north to bunch around my hips.

Weight forward, his hard thigh seals between my own, applying agonizing pressure to my hot, slick core. Dignity gone, I grind down on his thigh, providing the friction I'm desperate for. His cool palm sizzles against the overheated skin of my stomach as he skims a hand around my ribs and down my back. Without missing a beat, he unfastens my skirt and works the zipper down.

A whimper escapes at the loss of his lips on my breast and his leg between my thighs. With a swift yank, the Gucci pencil skirt drops to the floor, pooling around my bare feet. I say a quick prayer of thanks to the unicorn gods that I ditched the heels and hose earlier beneath the presidential desk.

Shutting my eyes, I focus every nerve ending on his demanding grip around both hips. His thumbs draw tight circles just above my thong before hooking the elastic band. The near painful scrape of his nails down the inside of my ultrasensitive thighs as he drags the thong toward the floor hurls a breath-catching shiver through my body and soul.

The moment he stands from his low crouch, I fumble at the front of his jeans with desperate fingers, eager to pop the top button and work the zipper down. Just as I connect, he swats my hands away. Half confused, half pouting I peek up through my dark lashes.

There's a deviousness in his half smile, one that sets my pulse racing even faster with anticipation. Without a word, he gathers both my wrists in one constricting grip and guides them high up over my head. The cold metal of the fridge is a stark contrast to my overheated skin along the back of my arms and wrists where they now connect with the smooth surface.

I watch in fascination as the hand not restraining me works to pop the button of his dark-wash jeans. Frustratingly slowly, he drags the zipper down, his hard cock bursting free immediately without the confines of boxers *or* briefs.

Allowing the jeans to sag halfway down his hips, Trey grasps his dick, giving it a tight-fisted pump followed by another as he focuses at the apex of my thighs. The wetness dribbling down my inner thighs is no doubt visible under his scrutiny.

A bead of precum wets the head of his swollen cock. After a swipe of his thumb, he lifts the smear to my dry lips and shoves it deep into my mouth. My tongue swirls around the digit, licking every last drop, the salty taste of him driving me even deeper into a lusty haze. Without warning, he pops his thumb loose, leaving me whimpering for more until his lips slam against mine once again as he slips a hand beneath my left knee, hiking it high over his hip.

I moan against his mouth as I feel him slide between my folds. Up and down he travels, never dropping low enough to breach my entrance. I squirm, lifting to my tiptoes. The grip on my thigh and wrists constricts, a silent command to stop struggling for control.

Without warning, he raises me higher and slams through my core, thrusting deep. The tips of my right toes scrape the tile as he pins me back with his steel-hard cock, my thigh hooked around his waist. Panting, Trey presses his forehead to my own.

He still hasn't moved inside me, driving me nearly to the brink of insanity. I yank against his grip, eager to clutch his firm, round ass and urge him even deeper, but his hold doesn't budge.

My entire core aches as he withdraws to the tip only to thrust deep. My pleasure-filled cry is cut short as his teeth sink into my lower lip and tug it into a pitiful whimper.

His cadence quickens, thrusting hard. Every nerve tingles; my thoughts and concerns vanish. All I can do is give myself over to his control.

Each time he sinks deep, he swirls his hips, driving pressure to my clit. Breathing shallow, eyes closed, I lose all grasp on reality as I tumble into a mind-clearing orgasm. Tremors rack down my spine as aftershocks pulse with his determined thrusts. I fall limp, only staying upright with his support. He presses his lips against the shell of my ear, a harsh grunt pushing past as he finds his release, shoving himself as deep inside me as possible.

His panting breaths fan through my hair where his forehead presses to the freezer beside me.

The hold on my wrists loosens, and he carefully helps lower them to hold behind his neck. Tingles erupt as blood rushes to my fingertips. A soft caress along my outer hip before he eases my leg from around his waist.

My muscles twitch at the sudden exertion, but I couldn't care less. "Damn, I needed that," I mumble into his hair. With a deep inhale, I savor the unique spicy scent that is all Trey Benson.

"I don't resent you." The confession is a mere whisper.

I shake my head. Dipping both hands beneath the collar of his T–shirt, I scratch my jagged nails along his upper back.

"Let's not do this here, not now. Let's go to my room where we can talk freely. I think we both have a lot to get off our chests."

The loss of him from between my thighs leaves a void in my heart and core. Trey assists me back into my damp panties and skirt before tucking himself into his jeans.

"Commando, huh?" I question, biting my upper lip as I work to piece my shirt back together. With a huff, I give up. Gripping the two ends, I secure the sides together in a tight eighties-style knot. The upper portion still gapes if I don't hold it together, but at least now I'm not flashing who's left in the White House at this late hour. "Shit. They'll know what we were doing when I walk out looking like this."

His honey brown eyes eat up every inch of me, devouring me with his still hungry gaze. "Pretty sure your scream already gave them a hint. But don't worry, I know those guys. They won't say anything."

Peering up, I smile, feeling a little better about the unconventional situation I've found myself in. Shirt situated enough to be decent, I grip his hand and interlace our fingers. Without a shred of embarrassment or shame, we walk out of the kitchen, my chin held high. The Secret Service agents don't give a second look to my haphazard appearance, simply fall in step behind us. I wince as the evidence of our sexcapade slips past my panties and begins to lazily trickle down my inner thighs. Quickening the pace, I accelerate my barefooted steps down the carpeted hall.

Inside the master bedroom, I don't pause, continuing my beeline to the attached bathroom. The ripped shirt goes first, then my bra, stripping as I move. By the time I step through the glass shower door, I'm completely naked. The immediate steady flow from the rainfall showerhead drenches me in cold water for half a second before changing to scalding.

I breathe out as I step farther under the spray while a leering presence looms nearby, lingering in the middle of the bathroom.

"Sorry," I mumble, my words more bubbles than actual words. "I was sticky."

At his nonresponse, I turn, putting the pounding water to my back to face Trey.

His hands are shoved deep into his front pockets, his thick hair hanging in front of his downcast face.

"Okay," I state, putting force behind the word, hoping to gain his attention. "Out with it. Tell me. What's going on, Trouble?"

"I don't know," he admits, the words muffled by the water pounding around me.

I release an exasperated sigh. "Trey, really? Don't—"

"I'm telling you the truth, Randi. I don't *know* what the hell is wrong with me. I'm a fucking mess inside." Lifting his head, he meets my searching gaze. "So much changed in a short period of time, and I... I'm...."

"Lost?" I offer.

He nods and shrugs in the same move. Him uncertain, almost broken slices deep into my heart. Making quick work with the fragrant body wash, I clean myself. Pressing the faucet handle down, I turn off the downpour of water, only a few trickles escaping the chrome shower head. Water streams down my bare legs and chest as I step from the steam-filled shower. Normally the sight would urge him into action no matter if we'd just made love or not, but now Trey just stands there unmoving, his focus on the marble tile floor.

Using the fresh towel that magically appeared in place of the one I used this morning, I dry off and then wrap it around my chest, securing it by tucking it into itself.

"Trey," I say while attempting to tame my thick damp hair into a messy bun. "I'm not a mind reader here. I have zero idea what's going on inside that head of yours. Remember that conversation in Hawaii? That we need to tell each other everything?" I pause until he answers my question with a reluctant nod. "Well, this is one of those times. You tell me what's bothering you. Don't be embarrassed or afraid if it all seems... heavy. You confronted your parents on some shady and quite troubling shit and got shot all in the same twenty-four-hour period. It was a lot. But I need you to talk to me, tell me. Don't push me away by saying it's nothing."

The last of the water trickles down the shower drain while the overhead fan hums, absorbing some of the humidity from the thick air.

"I can't tell you what's wrong when I don't know myself," he says, hesitantly pulling his stare from the floor to me. "I don't even know where to start."

I sigh and nod, completely understanding where he's coming from.

I remember those periods when everything seemed too much to understand, much less explain to someone. How many times did I lose myself in my studies because those emotions were overflowing? How many times did I avoid people in general to keep from being forced to acknowledge what was going on inside? Understanding through trauma, which is exactly what he went through with the shooting and his parents, is difficult for anyone to process, but especially him. Someone who's never really known true devastation. He's lived a cushy life up until this point, always knowing if he failed, his family would catch him.

Sure, he's a little depressed and confused. Who wouldn't be?

Maybe that's what he needs to hear. That he's not alone.

"You remember when you helped me clean up my mom in that jail cell?" Taking a deep breath, I close the distance between us. "That was the first time anyone had ever helped me, and it was awful," I say with a forced chuckle. "I detested you seeing that side of me. The ugly, trashy side of my life. The real Randi Sawyer. I mean, if you thought my mom was a mess, would you think the same about me? And then she wasn't wearing a bra." This time my laugh is genuine. "And your shocked face. But you kept with it, stayed with me. You helped me even though you knew it was a fucked-up situation. What I'm trying to say is"—reaching forward, I link our pinkie fingers and hold my focus there—"I know what it's like to be entangled in your emotions, to not know which way is up or how to even see through it all to the light. I know what it's like to deal with it on your own, to not have a single person there to talk to. It divides you between the person you know you should be on the outside and the twisted, miserable thing living inside you. Don't be that person. You don't have to be. You have me. You have T and Sarah. Don't separate yourself from us. Don't divide who you are to be half what we see and half what's really going on." I draw in a deep inhale, trying to catch my breath from the rambling speech.

One finger and then another wrap around mine until all our fingers are interlaced. A soft tug and I'm blissfully encased in a strong embrace. Ear pressed to his chest, I relish the steady beat of his heart and calming warmth enclosing me.

"I'm here, Mess. And I promise to talk to you, to talk to T, when I'm ready. I can't lose you, lose us, on top of everything else I've lost recently."

"Lost?"

"My parents, my job for a while, my mon—" Catching himself, he seals his lips together. "A lot has changed."

Tilting my head, I settle my chin on the hard bone of his sternum.

"When you're ready, I'm here. I'll always be here, Trey. Win or lose, we have each other. Good or bad, we're in this *together*. Never think you're battling all this alone. You'll alienate yourself that way. I won't push you to talk about it now, but know that even if I'm negotiating world peace, I'll drop everything to listen. This job is a job, not a life. You're my life, Trouble. Before as a measly candidate, today as the president of the United States, and in the future as a forgotten has-been."

Relaxing a cheek against his chest once again, I inhale a deep breath. It won't be easy getting him through whatever this is, but nothing that's worth fighting for ever is.

And one thing I'm certain of is *we're* worth fighting for.

He might have to hurry along the path of healing, however, not that I'm bringing that up now. This lack of communication is a minor hurdle compared to the months to come. With Kyle gone and the vital information we need having died with him, we're up shit creek.

War is coming, and it will take everything I have to stop it.

6

TREY

With one last peck to Randi's forehead, I turn, leaving her to wrap up work in the massive king-size bed. I check my watch as I stride toward the door. Two in the morning. Perfect time to slip out of the White House, if I can get one of my fellow agents to give me a lift back to the condo.

I scrub a hand down my face, the feeling of a headache coming on making my thoughts sluggish. Randi and I spent the last few hours talking over her three weeks in the presidential spot and the news that released today about Birmingham's death. It's a shit show, that's for sure, but in true Mess fashion, she's handled each incident like a damn pro, even though she feels as if she's failing the people counting on her most.

Just over the threshold, I glance into the bedroom. As if she can feel my gaze, she peers up from her iPad, a wide smile spreading along that gorgeous face. My heart constricts at the sheer happiness radiating off her—because of me and me alone. Not thousands of dollars of roses, or jewelry, or a fancy dinner. Just me and her, talking, laughing, and holding each other, conjured that grin. Returning the smile, I swing the door closed, sealing her safely inside.

I wave to the agents, not meeting their knowing hard looks. I know what they're thinking. Hell, I've thought it before when stationed outside past VPs' bedroom doors. But it's a little different now. This is the president, and

I'm an agent. We're not supposed to be together; it's unprofessional and puts me as the butt of every inappropriate joke and innuendo.

One agent I recognize from previous encounters opens his mouth, readying to say something shitty no doubt, but the don't-fuck-with-me glare I send his way makes him seal his lips shut, his Adam's apple bobbing with a hard swallow. I have to get out of here before someone insinuates anything or I might pummel them, unable to stop before committing murder. Gerard was right—I'm nearing a snapping point.

Both hands shoved into the front pockets of my jeans, I travel down the short hall but divert at the last second, taking a left instead of a right, where the main control room is located. My feet and heart have a mind of their own, knowing there's one more person I need to see before I leave here tonight.

My chest tightens as I stand in front of the closed bedroom door. Sensing watchful eyes, I nod to the agent farther down the hall, glaring. The door rattles under my fist. Hopefully she's like her mother and is still awake at this early morning hour.

A new round of nerves tenses my gut as the door swings open. But the sight of Taeler's smiling face loosens the growing knot in my stomach.

"What the hell, Trouble? Is everything okay?" The smile disappears as a worry line forms between her light eyebrows. Her soft blue eyes dart up, searching over my shoulder. "Is my mom all right?" She takes a step, hand at my side as if she's readying to shove me aside and race down the hall.

I smirk at her courage to forget her own safety when she believes someone she loves is in danger. Just like her mother.

Hand to her shoulder, I hold her back from slipping past me. "She's fine. I actually wanted to talk to you about... well, nothing to do with your mother."

"Me."

"You." I steal a side-eye glance at the agent who seems to be listening to the conversation. "Can we talk about this inside?" I ask, motioning inside her bedroom.

"I'm intrigued. Come on in." Taeler moves aside, opening the door wider.

Inside I scan the room in search of a seat that's not the pillow-filled bed in the center of the room. A desk and chair in the far corner catch my eye. After folding into the small chair, I lean forward, my clasped hands dangling between my spread legs.

"I wanted to stop by and tell you I'm sorry about Grem," I say, my voice gritty as it pushes past the emotions I'm fighting to keep locked down. "We.... He was a part of our team for years. He and I were friends along with being teammates. I know he meant a lot to you—"

A surprised grunt escapes my chest as a small force slams into me, shoving me back against the chair. It takes a moment to register the trembling shoulders and thin arms wrapped around my neck as Taeler, not an attack. Shoving my attack mode reflexes down, I clear my throat and give her back a tentative pat. But she doesn't let go, just continues to hang on me like one of those spider monkeys I've seen on the Discovery Channel. Not sure what else to do, I attempt the back pat again, this time with a little more force.

"Stop trying to fucking burp me. Hug me," Taeler says softly against my chest.

I look to the ceiling with a grimace as I prudently drape an arm across her back, careful to keep the contact to a minimum. My love for Randi's daughter is purely platonic, and Taeler feels the same way, but that doesn't mean I'm comfortable hugging a young woman in her bedroom at two o'clock in the fucking morning, even if it is innocent.

My brain screams to abort mission.

"She told me about the pregnancy," I say tentatively, in case the words do more harm to my already complicated situation than good. "How you doing with the news?"

Tilting away, she unravels herself from the tight hold and moves to the bed, perching on the edge. With plenty of space between us, I inhale deeply.

"You know, I'm okay, actually. I should be afraid, but I'm not. That might change tomorrow when I see the doctor or when I have to tell people, but right now, I kind of love it. Maybe because today we buried him, and in that same day I found out I'm carrying a piece of him inside me. He...." She swallows and glances to the ceiling, but that doesn't prevent the steady line of fresh tears from trickling out the edges of her eyes. "He was a good man. You'd be proud of him." A watery smile pulls at her lips before she sinks her teeth into her bottom lip. "He spoke about you and the rest of the guys a lot, told me all kinds of stories. Sounded like you got him into trouble quite often."

I laugh, a memory of one of our rogue nights in Argentina filling my thoughts and putting a wide smile across my face. "He was an active participant." I chuckle. "He's.... He was a good kid though." I swipe two sweaty palms down my thighs. "How are you doing with the whole kidnapping piece? Randi mentioned you're seeing a therapist?"

She nods, her blonde hair slipping over her shoulders with the motion. "Yeah, he comes here daily. And it's good, I guess, better than if I didn't talk to anyone at all. Loud noises are still a struggle, and the constant fear-laced worry that I'll be taken again, but talking it through and being honest has helped." The tremble of her hand as she reaches up to tuck a chunk of hair behind her ear doesn't go unnoticed. "I don't know why though. He asks me to relive that night almost every session. The first time, I could barely get a single word out. It took an hour to get to the part about the initial attack. But yesterday, it only took twenty minutes to get through the entire ordeal. It's almost like saying it out loud, to someone else, takes the fear out of it, gives me the control back. If I let that fear rule me, then, even though I was saved, they still win." Her delicate fingers fist the ancient white duvet cover. "They took hours of my life... the man I loved. I won't give them anything more."

I nod, pretending I understand even though I have no fucking clue what she means. How could talking about it make it better when it hurts to even say the words? Not only that, how can you talk about something when you don't even know what you're feeling yourself? It's all a crock of shit, which is why I haven't opened up to my appointed therapist.

Comfortable silence fills the room, both of us lost in our own thoughts.

"I'm a fucking mess." Raking a hand through my hair, I shake my head. "I don't deserve her," I mutter as a wave of self-loathing fights its way into my thoughts.

"My mom?"

I dip my chin.

"Are you serious?" One corner of her lips tugs up in a wiry smile.

"Maybe at one time I did." A slight tremble starts in my fingers. "But now look at me." A harsh laugh rattles from my chest.

"Trey." Her soft voice pulls my focus away from my swirling fears.

I open my mouth, but she starts again before I can get a single word out.

"My mom would never think that about you, you know that, right?" I swallow hard. "And whatever is going on between you two will work itself out. Listen." Taeler slides off the bed to stand in front of where I sit. "I don't know what's going on in that head of yours, but let me tell you something about my mom that might ease some of your worries. Are you ready?"

The wooden frame of the chair creaks as I lean back, crossing both arms over my chest.

"She's used to people disappointing her. She used to doing everything on her own, not depending on a single soul because, well, people are shitty. But she's opening up to you, so don't mess that up. And it's been hard for her, because you're you and she's her."

"Oh, you mean the president and a now nameless, no family agent who follows her dutifully wherever she goes, no questions asked?" I seal my eyes shut, focusing on calming my ragged breaths. *Fuck, why did I just say that?*

"Is that what you think?"

"Guess so." I didn't even think that until the words were spilling off my tongue.

"You're a fool, then. If you don't see what we all see, then that's your fault."

Confusion muddles my thoughts, making everything that used to make sense seem sketchy and messy.

"I should go. You need to sleep," I mumble. "I just wanted to stop by and tell you I'm sorry about Grem. He was a good kid, and I'm going to miss him."

"Thanks, Trouble." Minding boundaries this time, she leans in for a quick side hug. "And like I said earlier, talking to someone is helping me. You should try it, even though you don't seem too good at it." Her wide smile eases the sting her sarcastic words leave behind.

Just as I reach the door, she calls out my name. Both brows raised in question, I glance over my shoulder to where she still stands in the middle of the room, an arm wrapped around one of the bed posts extending high into the air.

"I have this feeling you both feel the same way. Just think about that as you work through whatever it is you're not wanting to admit to yourself."

A smirk tugs at my lips. "And how do you think we both feel?" This kid, so much like her mother in looks and personality.

Nibbling on her lower lip, she tucks a stray wisp of hair behind her ear over and over again.

"Undeserving."

The single word smacks across my face, leaving me stunned. I force myself not to flinch. Without another word, I step out into the hall and storm toward the control room.

Bits of the tangled web of my fucked-up mind loosen, offering a moment of clarity before jumbling back to the damn mess it's been for weeks again. At least the conversation with Taeler confirmed one thing I was afraid of: that young woman who was abducted for several hours on foreign soil and who lost the man she loves is doing a hell of a lot better than me.

Maybe there's some validity to talking to someone.

Taeler's parting word shadows me as I work through the maze of connecting halls.

Undeserving.

It's never been a word I've used, but that Trey Benson is hidden deep. That Trey lived a lie shielded behind a solid family name, knew where he stood with his girlfriends because the relationship was superficial and common. Pre-shooting Trey didn't comprehend the true heartrending fear of leaving this world with the woman you love left behind unprotected without you there by her side. Today's Trey fears the media won't look down on him for dating Randi, because of her poverty background, but will destroy her for loving a simple agent, the son of a sick bastard whose dirty laundry is plastered across the papers daily.

Undeserving.

Never a better word could be used to describe the paralyzing doubt and gut-wrenching uncertainty that's now my daily companion.

Undeserving.

And there's nothing I can do to change the outcome. That day warped me, warped us. I just hope we can somehow find our way through the wake of uncertainty. And that she'll give me the time to free my old self from the confines of my own doubts and fears.

THE NEXT MORNING, I don't wake up early to meet up at the rowing club like I promised Tank, or the next. His calls and texts go unanswered, just as they did before the confrontation in the SUV. The days and nights flow together, making all concept of time a vague memory. It's only after a lonely text from Randi that I realize two weeks have passed since I saw her that night in the White House, two weeks since I've seen my best friend.

What can I say? Avoiding my mounting problems by drinking too much and being lazy as hell is a time suck.

With a scratchy throat groan, I stretch my stiff muscles along the cool satin sheets and crack an eye open. Late morning light filters through the edges of the blackout curtains, casting a single line of sunlight on the nearly empty bottle of Four Roses on the nightstand and knocked-over tumbler. An annoying ding of an alarm chirps happily from my phone. Smacking the top of the quilt blindly, I search for the device that woke me so rudely, ruining my plans of sleeping until noon.

The thin metal shell of the phone connects with my pinkie finger. Sliding it from where it burrowed itself beneath the blanket, I hold it above my face and squint at the screen.

An event reminder blinks back at me. A reminder I set weeks ago. Exactly one week from today, I'm eligible for active duty.

My stomach, still sour from last night's bourbon binge, rolls as a chill skates across my clammy skin.

Instead of dealing with the information like a healthy bastard, I toss the phone back to the bed and roll over. Deep breath in and out, I fight back the growing nausea—from the hangover or the alert, I don't know. Hell, maybe both.

An unfamiliar sound from beyond the bedroom door sidetracks me mid-inhale. I hold the half breath, letting it burn in my lungs as I wait. The wind rushes out of me as I heave my lethargic legs over the side of the bed. The movement makes my fuzzy head swim, but I push off the mattress only to stagger forward, colliding with the dresser against the wall. A booming voice I know all too well rattles the thin walls. Cursing, I yank the bottom drawer open and fish out a pair of running shorts.

I tug the soft Dri-Fit material over my ass, feeling a bit more snug since the last time I wore these, just as the bedroom door erupts inward. The bastard doesn't even offer the decency of knocking. The door crashes against the opposite wall, adding to the many dents put there by me and the previous owners. Tank stands in the middle of the doorframe, arms crossed over his broad chest, blocking my only exit.

"I put pants on for you," I say, forcing a fake smug smile while waving toward my black Under Armour shorts. "You should work on your stealth mode a little more. I had all the time in the world before you barged into my room."

His dark eyes narrow. A bolt of apprehension races through my sluggish veins at his obvious ire directed solely on me.

"Get a damn shirt and running shoes on, you lazy ass."

"Can't," I say with a smirk. "I have brunch plans."

My eyes widen, the faux cocky prick attitude falling as Tank rushes toward me. My back slams into the edge of the dresser as I retreat deeper into the bedroom.

"Two minutes or you're running like you're dressed."

Lips pursed to keep my retorts to myself, I nod. I know he won't let this idea of a run drop no matter how many snappy comments I toss his way. Hell, it might make him tack on more miles.

The man scowling at me doesn't joke around when comes to fitness. It seems he feels I've been out of the workout game too long and need his help in restarting a routine. Which he might have a point about. The high-end workout gear stuffed in various drawers hasn't been used for anything other than lying around this small-ass apartment, besides the few less than vigorous physical therapy appointments, since I was shot.

"You going to watch?" I jest as I extract a white T–shirt from the dresser.

"I'm not going to enjoy the sight of your pale bourbon gut, if that's what you're hoping for. But apparently you can't be trusted to follow through with what you say you're going to do anymore, so yeah, I'm staying right the fuck here until you're ready to go."

I grumble a response as the soft fabric slides over my hair and along my face. Far sooner than I'm physically and mentally ready, I've laced up both tennis shoes and am following Tank's massive back out the door. Gerard and his wife, Beth, are nowhere to be seen as I'm escorted to my death.

"Nice of you to tell me you moved, fuckface," Tank mumbles ahead of me.

"Been busy," I snap. "How'd you figure out the new condo anyway? Should I be concerned you're stalking me? You know I don't swing that way, man."

"Jessica."

"I think Sarah would be pissed if you swung that way."

"You and your damn mouth," he says, a hint of laughter in his voice. "I went to your old place. Jessica opened the door and told me you sold her the condo. She gave me your new number." We pause at the elevator; the down button nearly cracks beneath his slamming knuckles. "She seemed good."

"Yeah." I run a hand through my hair as I stare at my reflection in the metal doors, trying to tame my bedhead. "She just got back from Switzerland. Said she needed a few weeks after everything to avoid the media and all. I didn't even have to see her when selling the condo since she was gone. Everything was done via her estate broker."

"Why'd you sell?"

The sharp ding of the arriving elevator stops me from responding until we're inside the metal box.

"Money. A lot has gone down since I confronted my parents."

"Such as?"

I choose not to respond, instead focusing on stretching my arms overhead. He rolls his eyes as I moan and groan through a few short stretches, utilizing his shoulder to help keep my balance on a few.

Inside his pristine black Escalade, the icy air conditioning kicks on immediately, cooling my already sweaty forehead and upper lip. During the short drive to our normal running spot, the Anacostia Riverwalk, we remain quiet, the smooth jazz music coming through the speakers helping ease my anxiety of what's to come. With Tank, this could be an easygoing run or a reenactment of boot camp's hell week. I guess I'll find out which here shortly.

After circling the parking lot twice, he backs into the perfect parking spot far away from all the other cars and kills the engine. Without the blasting AC, the inside instantly warms from the scorching sun blasting through the windshield.

Fuck, I'm over this heat. At least the summer should be winding down now that it's August. Wait, is it August? Yeah, has to be if the alert earlier said I'm to report back to work next week. Internally, I curse my lazy ass. What have I done the past five weeks besides dwelling on my current string of shit luck and drinking myself into the initial stages of cirrhosis? The only workout I've had during the five-week medical leave was pinning Randi to the fridge that night in the White House kitchen—the best kind of workout, in my opinion—and the few physical therapy appointments. No surprise the elastic waistband on these normally loose shorts is digging into my skin more than usual.

Tank exits the SUV with a tilt of his head, indicating I should follow him. The car door slams behind me. Utilizing the passenger side door for balance, I kick one foot behind me, grasping my shoe to stretch my underused thigh.

The sense of falling makes my breath catch as I topple forward when

Tank smacks my hand off the shiny black paint. Using the hem of his tight shirt, he rubs away the palm smudge I'd left behind.

"Ungrateful ass," he grumbles with a side-eye glare.

"Ungrateful? I didn't ask to be here."

"You're practically screaming it, Playboy." Without another word, he ends his meticulous polishing with a satisfied nod and storms out of the parking lot, headed for the trail. I'm already panting from the brisk walk to catch up with him. "We'll go slow today since you're so out of shape. But from here on out, we'll increase the pace daily, working toward our normal." His accusing glare slides to me as I speed up to match his slow jog. "The pace that's required by the damn agency to remain on the vice president's alpha team."

I'm dying. I know it. Dying a slow, suffocating death. Already my breaths are labored and we've gone less than a quarter of a mile. But even with the burning in my lungs, legs, arms... hell, my entire body there is one positive: running means no talking.

Just like old times, we stay shoulder to shoulder, our strides matching the other's. And like normal, the steady pound of our feet against the concrete and the drag of my repetitive ragged breaths in and out of my nose shut out the outside world. Only today, I don't want to get lost in my own thoughts. I've been stuck there for weeks without a way out.

Hell, this is going to be a long fucking day.

7

RANDI

August

Several sets of curious eyes peer above rows of the standard beige office cubicles. Ignoring them the best I can, I continue through the office space, my eyes forward, surrounded by the president's alpha team. I don't smile or wave, ignoring the urge to finally show off the princess wave I've been practicing at night in the mirror, like old Randi would have. But once again the coldness of this role—being presidential, as I've been told—prevents me from being... well, me. At first it was just my fiery anger and sailor mouth they wanted me to alter, but unfortunately it's now *every* emotion—good or bad. They seem to think the American people will lose faith in me if I remind them I'm a real live oxygen-breathing person.

Somedays I want to just run out on the back lawn, shoes off with my arms stretched out wide, allowing all the backed-up feelings a means to escape. What would the people think of me then? What if they saw me smile, or grieve, or, God forbid, laugh?

I've been on my own my entire life, always fighting for the next foothold, yet I've never felt more secluded and alone than now.

"Being the president sucks," I grumble under my breath as we round a corner.

But I'm also well aware I'm not in a position to challenge their annoying rules, seeing as I'm a little over seven weeks into this gig and am barely surviving. The workload increased significantly, and with a thousand times more pressure, that fateful day. My days now consist of twenty-hour work-days seven days a week, and it's still not enough to keep up with everything going on across the globe. Even without the scandal and mess Kyle left behind, I'd be buried in urgent issues and updates. Add in the Kyle mess I'm tasked with cleaning up before it escalates and I'm suffocating under the pressure.

Or maybe this all feels worse because for the first time, I don't have my friends surrounding me. Which is why I'm in this late-eighties-style office building today. Trey returned to active duty last week and has adjusted well, per T. With the team whole, it's time for me to present my case to the direc-tor, to fight for my team.

There isn't a single miniscule doubt in my rambling mind that they can protect me as well as, or maybe better than, any one of the men on my current alpha team. The current team is great at their job, but I miss the relationships, the laughter and sense of ease the other guys bring with them. They were with me for two and a half years; I need that stability back in my daily life.

The director turned me down previously when I requested the switch, but that attempt was over the phone. Now I'm here and not leaving without a time frame of when the shift will occur. Actually, scratch all that shit talk about me *asking* her for my friends back. Today I'm here abusing my presi-dential power and *demanding* she order the change.

I can do that right?

Surely I can do that.

Eh, can't hurt to try.

Murmured voices vibrate through the director's office door. A booming rumble from the other side signals Tank is already here and getting an early start on the meeting.

Knuckles to the fake wood door, I give it a hard rap and step back, swal-lowed whole by the swarm of suited men. Even after the order to enter, I stay back like I've been trained. I shift from one red Manolo Blahnik to the other, briefly distracted by how the patent leather shines under the florescent lights.

Tom—or maybe it's Ted?—dips his chin, indicating the all clear. I roll my eyes at the stupidity of the situation—it's the director's office, for fuck's sake, not a terrorist cell meeting—knowing full well no one besides the agent glaring at me can witness the small rebellion. A corner of my lips twitches, wanting desperately to smirk. They can take the girl out of the trailer park, but they can't take the "fuck it" attitude out of the girl.

We move as one into the room. Inside, T stands from the ancient wood and leather office chair. I hold in a giggle as the small chair hugs his hips and thighs, staying with him as he stands before dropping back to the floor. Ignoring the rude chair, T straightens his jacket and locks those dark, knowing eyes on mine.

At the imperceptible shake of his head, my earlier bravado falters. Seems the director is primed to disregard our request.

A sudden urge strikes me to crack my knuckles one by one and stretch out my neck from one side to the other like they do in the movies when they're preparing for a fight.

"Madam President," the attractive older woman says from where she stands behind a solid dark mahogany desk.

"Director," I respond with a curt nod. An eerie feeling of being watched creeps up the back of my neck. Spinning on the balls of my feet, I scan the room for the cause. In the back of the room, Trey leans against the far wall, arms crossed, his features a cold blank slate. It shouldn't affect me—T told me they both had to play the personal relationship between us three carefully—but still, not even a flicker of warmth in his honey brown eyes pours salt in the wound from him not coming by the past few weeks.

"Let's make this quick. I only have a few minutes before I'm due somewhere else," I state.

The director motions to the rickety-looking chair beside T. The stiff bun at the nape of my neck that I twisted my hair into this morning doesn't shift with the quick shake of my head due to the amount of product I applied to make it sleek and sophisticated. And ugly. Very, very ugly. "I'll stand. This won't take long. There are no more requests about the alpha team change. Today I'm here to tell you my previous alpha team *will* be placed into the current alpha team slot beginning next week."

Her fine-lined lips pop open, but I raise a hand, the shiny fake red nails shimmering in the light pouring through the large window at her back.

"I understand your concerns and your reason for previously denying the request. But Agent Washington's team is now fully intact"—I tilt my head back, indicating Trey—"and from what I've been told, Agent Benson has made a full recovery and is ready for this new challenge."

Her eyes narrow. I stifle the urge to bite at my nails under her intense stare. *Yikes, no wonder she's the director. She's deadly with a simple glare.*

Truth be told, I haven't the slightest clue if I can make her do what I'm asking her to do. But she can't go around a directive from the president. Technically I'm her boss' boss. Right?

"I need an organizational chart," I mumble. The director's penciled brows furrow. Tank covers a smile with a fake cough, and Trey shakes his head, the cold demeanor slipping a fraction.

"This is unprecedented," she states with an exasperated sigh. Seems I have that affect on a lot of people in this city.

"So is a woman president," I retort.

Her blonde bob slides along her petite jaw as she nods. "Is there anything I can do to change your mind, Madam President?"

Searching the room, I meet the eyes of every man in the office. I hitch my chin toward the door. "Give us a minute, please."

They all file out, except two. Trey and Tank. With only these three as witness to the tiny rebellion against the cold woman I'm being molded into, I roll my eyes to the ceiling and point to the door. "And you two. Shoo."

"Come on now, we're not pu—cats howling at the back door," Trey declares as he shoves off the wall. Our eyes lock across the short distance between us. Regret and desire cramp my stomach. We've talked daily, texted nonstop, but nothing face-to-face since that night weeks ago.

"No, Agent Benson, you're more like a curious raccoon," I say with a grin.

T grumbles under his breath, too low for me to hear, but Trey's face lights up, shooting his friend a mischievous smile. Without another protest, T stands from the tight chair and grasps on to Trey's arm, tugging him along on his way toward the door, and they both stride out without a single glance back.

With the office empty except me and the director, I allow another facet of the bravado to slip. Folding into the chair T vacated, I lean back and rest both arms on the armrests.

"How are you doing? If I'm allowed to be ask." The director's intuitive gaze skims my face.

"Honestly?" I blow out a long breath. "I'd be up shit creek if it weren't for good concealer," I say with a quick gesture to the dark circles that have been ever present since that day Kyle walked into my run-down mayor office in my hometown of Boone, Texas.

A tiny grin curls her lips, breaking the resigned act she dutifully played while the male agents were present. I tilt my head, really taking in her appearance for the first time since I entered the office. She's beautiful, a bit taciturn, but maybe that's what's expected of her in this role, or possibly who she's had to become being a high-ranking woman commanding hundreds of dominant men.

Like me.

"Does it ever get easier?" In a moment of weakness, I raise a finger to my teeth and attempt to gnaw on the fake acrylic nail.

The director relaxes into her office chair, causing a high-pitched squeak to cut through the quiet. She cringes as I find joy in the sheer normalcy of the situation. It's a wonderful reprieve to not feel the strain to be polished political Barbie.

"I'd like to tell you that it does get easier with time, but no, it doesn't."

"Honesty," I huff. "That's refreshing."

"Madam President, I—"

"Please, call me Randi. I'm less than two months in and I'm already sick of the title."

A frown shifts her features. "I'm sorry, that I cannot do."

"That's what everyone else says," I grumble like a pouting five-year-old girl.

"Back to the reason you're here, Madam President. The Secret Service teams assigned to the presidential protection detail are required to complete more situational training than any other team. You're requesting an unqualified team for the level of security needed to protect you. I advise against that."

"I understand your concerns, but you aren't seeing things from my perspective. Those men know my routine, know what to expect from me even sometimes before I do. They know my strengths and weaknesses. They can protect me *better* than anyone else because of our history. Sure, other agents tested higher or have been through more challenging simulations, but that doesn't mean they are the better fit for *me*." Leaning forward, I widen my knees—another no-no—and press both elbows into my thighs. "I need some semblance of comfort back, and they offer that."

"Comfort will get you killed."

"They'd never allow it." I shake my head. "You have to trust me that I'm making the right decision here."

"Not that I have much of a choice. When the president makes a direct order, I have to obey it." Her thin lips purse in obvious disapproval.

"Great." I release a measured breath at the simplicity of this meeting. The continuous meetings revolving in and out of the Oval Office are mostly crisis control, meaning every word I choose, every decision, means life or death for someone. Too many choices over the past several weeks had the potential to impact millions; this here today just impacts me.

And the guys too, I guess. But they're all on board with the change and additional responsibility. At least that's what T says.

"I presumed today would come to this." Her gaze flicks to the desk almost in avoidance. "Which is why I came prepared too." Middle finger to a button on the phone, she leans in close to the speaker. "Pamela, please send in Agent Smith." At the mention of the unfamiliar agent joining us, I straighten in the chair, sliding my polished presidential facade back into place.

A rush of cool air breezes along the back of my bare neck, the clatter of the office space increasing before ceasing once again.

My skin pebbles down my arms as a sense of vulnerability blankets me. I resist the impulse to twist around and see the stranger at my back. Steady footsteps approach, increasing my anticipation before a man clad in a gray suit appears at my left side.

"Madam President," the director says, still avoiding eye contact. "This is Agent Smith. He will be the new team lead for your alpha team."

"No," I retort. "Not happening."

She exhales. "Agent Smith will make up for the lack of experience on your alpha team."

"They aren't inexperienced," I snap. "Those men have kept me safe from a hell of a lot the past couple of years." I struggle to keep my cool. "How about a compromise?" I arch a brow. "Agent Smith can join the team but not as team lead. Those agents follow Team Lead Washington because he has *earned* their trust and respect. I won't leave my team vulnerable while you try to make another agent fit into a role that is already filled."

"Noted."

The worn fabric of the chair's seat catches the fine material of my Chanel suit pants as I twist to look at my team's new agent.

Taller than me by a few inches, from what I can tell still sitting, with dirty-blond hair and smooth fair skin. Stormy gray eyes slide to me, and the emptiness behind them draws me back an inch. With his average haircut, standard charcoal gray suit, and nondescript facial features, he's someone I could forget the moment he's out of sight. Almost like he's trying to look as plain and blendable as possible. Maybe he was trained to do so.

Interesting.

"CIA." Agent Smith doesn't even acknowledge I said anything. "NSA?" Nothing. "Homeland Security?" The loose-fitting jacket shifts with his deep inhale. Seems I'm either annoying or boring to Mr. Spy. "MI6, Mossad, Russian intelligence?"

Even though I know he's not a part of the latter because the Russian president and I are besties, and he would've given me a heads-up about this.

The director speaks up, halting my interrogation. "With several years of service to this country in a different capacity, Agent Smith was recently reassigned to the Secret Service Division."

I shoot her a suspicious side-eye perusal. "Reassigned, you say." I chew on my lower lip, something I've been doing more since my attempt to stop anxiously chewing on my nails. "Here's what you need to know about my expectations of the team. If you're an arrogant bastard, it's fine, you'll fit in well, but I won't put up with sexist or male chauvinist shit." I wince at the curse slip. "Chauvinist crap." There. That's *slightly* better. "And Agent Washington will be the one to make the final call on all decisions."

The director's chin dips in acceptance, but Agent Smith doesn't make any attempt to acknowledge I spoke.

"I'll ensure Agent Washington understands the situation and consequences of not utilizing Agent Smith's unique skill set for the team," the director states.

I debate this kink in the plan to gain my previous team back. Rolling my shoulders, I stiffen my spine. In negotiations, you always get out when you're ahead, which I did today, even if it comes with a small burden.

"Sounds like I don't have an option if I want my team back." I steal a quick glance at my watch. "Hell, I'm already running behind and it's only nine." Rubbing at my temples, I sigh. "I'll leave you to figure out the logistics of the team switch. I'll need to meet with Agent Washington before the official change to inform him of my upcoming travel schedule and additional adjustments that have changed since I stepped into the role."

The wooden frame creaks as I push off the thin arms of the chair to stand. The new agent shifts, his light gray eyes meeting mine when I pause in front of him.

"You have a first name, Agent Smith?" I ask as I straighten out my jacket and grab my handbag from the floor.

"Yes."

I pause, waiting for more before realizing he's said all he's going to say on that subject. "Fine." I roll my eyes in sheer annoyance at him and this already off-schedule day. His widen a fraction before flashing back to general boredom. "Don't worry, I'll get it out of you at some point over the next couple of years. I'm Randi Sawyer, by the way. Nice to meet you." My extended hand dangles in the small space separating us, waiting for him to reciprocate in my common courtesy handshake.

After a few tense moments, his hand engulfs mine. The contact lasts less than a second before he returns his hand to his side. I gape at my now empty hand, deliberating if I imagined the brief encounter entirely.

"This will be interesting," I mutter under my breath as I brush past him. At the door, I school my features and pull it open.

Ten sets of intense stares greet me, but I only focus on Trey.

"Walk with me," I order while motioning between Trey and Tank. The two fall into step beside me as we march back through the office building. "She agreed with one condition." Hooking a thumb over my shoulder, I gesture to the near-mute Agent Smith. "He's joining the team effective immediately."

Tank grunts a curse. I refrain from wincing. I know this isn't ideal for him.

"I had to give somewhere, T. We need to discuss a few things that have changed since I left the VP role, go through my routine in the White House, upcoming travel, and I'd also like for you to meet with the team lead of the current alpha team to discuss active threats against me and your plans for protection detail. Can both of you come by one day this week?"

"Yes," T says, responding for them both. "What day works best for you?"

Our quick pace slows as we approach the bank of elevators. Trey hits the Down indicator before moving back to my right side.

"My schedule is crazy these days. I'll ask my secretary to give you a call to find a time that works for all of us."

A rude, sarcastic snort to my right snags my attention. Rotating, I arch a questioning brow at Trey. "Is there a problem?"

"Not at all, *Madam President.*"

Irritation flares through my veins, building heat beneath my skin. The sharp ding of the arriving elevator doesn't deflect the tense stare down he and I are having. Tank steps into the awaiting elevator first, followed by another agent.

"Out," I say, snapping my fingers.

"Ma'am," the agent replies, sounding conflicted.

"They're both agents. I'll be fine. I know you have at least ten guys on the bottom floor waiting anyway." Not waiting for his answer, I step into the elevator and not so gently shove him forward while signaling for Trey to take the agent's vacated place. The doors glide together, cutting off the furious agent's face from my view.

The metal cage gives a soft jolt before descending. Tank, appearing to want to stay out of the little conversation Trey and I are about to have, positions himself in front of the doors, giving us some semblance of privacy.

"Cameras," Tank mutters over his shoulder while keeping his dark eyes forward.

"Right." I sigh. Squaring my shoulders, I face the elevator doors. "What the hell was that comment about?" I snap at Trey, whose shoulder almost touches mine, while also glaring at the reflective metal.

"You know as well as I do how we have to address you in public."

"It was your tone," I hiss.

"My tone?"

"Yeah, like...." I wave a hand in front of me as I try to find the right words.

"You were trying to make a point."

I point to T. "Thank you, T, exactly."

Out of the corner of my eye, I watch Trey scrub a hand down his face. "I didn't mean it any way. I'm just tired, okay?"

"Can you come over tonight?" I whisper while turning my face down so the cameras can't see my lips moving.

"We're on shift tonight."

"Oh, right." Disappointment drops my stomach, the earlier anger morphing into acute loneliness. "Okay, yeah. I'll see you soon though, right?" There's no masking the hope in my wistful tone.

"Mess," he says on a sigh. There's a long pause before he speaks up again. "You have enough on your plate besides trying to plan around me."

Forgetting all presidential decorum, I spin on my heels and face him straight on.

"Don't use my job as a damn excuse, Trey Benson. If you don't want to see me, then just say it. I'm a big girl. I can take it." That's a bald-faced lie. Him saying those words would break me. "Are you done with us?" Somehow I continue to breathe past the mounting panic in my chest. The elevator seems to heat. Sweat slicks my palms, and my head swims as I teeter on my heels.

The elevator glides to a halt.

Pursed lips mixed with Trey's annoyed glare offer me zero indication on how this monumental conversion will end.

When the doors slide open, those ten agents I knew would be down here securing the lobby stand waiting, their attention everywhere, searching for threats. But I don't move toward the open doors; instead, I glower right back at the frustrated asshat I love.

"That's not.... What are you talking about? You're blowing this way out of proportion," he whisper-yells. "Calm the hell down."

"Excuse me?" My tone, those two words like a cracking whip, triggers every man in the vicinity to hold their breath.

"Damn idiot," I catch T grumble. Turning to face us both, he levels Trey with a hard look.

"Can you shoot him for me?" I question, pointing to the man I can't even look at right now without wanting to wrap my fingers around his throat.

"Just listen to me," Trey grates, the words more of a low hiss than actual syllables.

"Fucking hell." T grunts. "We're out. You have her," he declares over his shoulder to the awaiting agents. "Now get your stupid ass out of the damn elevator."

Trey winces at the viselike grip T slams on his shoulder to drag his best friend out of the elevator.

Their hushed exchange fades as they stride toward the glass doors. Filling my lungs with a deep inhale, I settle my stoic features back into place before striding out of the elevator.

Even though my stomach churns with worry and anxiety, I have to shut it down. Now. I cannot let what happened affect me, not anymore. I no longer have the luxury of dwelling. Old Randi, sure, she'd probably go have a few shots of expensive booze she couldn't afford and list his number on Craigslist in the M/M personal section.

New Randi can't even blink too long or everyone will know I'm dying on the inside.

Of course, that's not what he meant earlier, and sure, he was slightly right about me blowing things out of proportion. But it's been too long since I've seen him, since he's wrapped me in his protective hold and held me together in a way only he can. I need him near as my balance. The calm to my sometimes dramatic thoughts and fears.

Since the night he walked out of my room, I've felt adrift. Those few hours we shared reminded me of how amazing it feels to have someone near who actually cares about you, not the role you currently fill.

A burst of repetitive vibrations against my side shifts my thoughts back to the present. After clearing my throat, I continue to move with the mass of men toward the limo while reaching inside the bag hooked over my shoulder. My fingers shift through the contents until I locate the vibrating phone.

"Blake," I say in non-greeting. I learned the first day that no one wastes time on pleasantries.

"We have a problem."

Clenching my teeth, I shut down the urge to scream and heave the phone at the hot cement sidewalk.

"Of course we do. Be back in ten."

Bending at the waist, I fold into the limo and wait for the agent to shut the door before chunking the annoying device as hard as I can against the leather seat.

I fucking hate my job.

8

TREY

"Take your giant fucking mitt of a hand off me," I complain as I stumble behind Tank, who's still dragging me like I'm a disobedient toddler. At the door to the SUV, he chucks me forward. Reacting fast, I catch myself on the hard metal before my face can collide with the dark-tinted window. A sudden pressure between my shoulder blades keeps me against the hot metal.

"I just saved your damn life, you motherfucking fool." If Tank presses any closer, the bystanders will think he's about to Mike Tyson my ear. And he's cussing. This is bad. He's hot about something, and that something seems to be me. "You do not, under any circumstances, tell a woman to calm down during a fight." With a firm shove, he removes his hand from my back. Not wasting the newfound freedom, I flip around, pressing my ass to the door to bend forward, hands on my knees, listening as he continues his lecture. "And you do not ever, *ever*, say they're blowing something out of proportion. That's asking to be smothered in your damn sleep. How in the hell are you still alive is what I'd like to know."

I gesture over my face. "Money, good looks, and a fat dick." My lips tilt south as my new reality reminds me that's no longer true nowadays. "At least I still have the last two." Randi still doesn't know, nor will she if I can keep it from her. Unease tenses my gut, making my chest constrict.

"You're a lost cause."

"She loves it," I say, forcing the same fake smile I've worn for weeks now. "Not currently."

The frown on my lips deepens. "You don't think she loves me anymore?"

"Get in the damn truck."

"SUV," I correct.

"Get. In," he bellows while thrusting a finger against my breastbone. "I'm done pussyfooting around your pansy ass. We're dealing with your shit right now."

"Now?" I ask, hesitating over the door handle, the scorching chrome heating my already sweaty palm.

He ignores my question as he rounds the hood, making his way to the driver side. I consider the busy sidewalk in search of a rapid departure. The mention of working through my fucked-up head ignites my fight-or-flight instinct, insisting I run from my friend.

"Don't even think about it." I choose not to turn toward Tank's deep voice. "I know where you work and live. I will find you, and I will make you deal with this. It's time, Benson. She needs you, and you're too messed up in the motherfucking head to see that. Pull your head out of your ass for one minute and stop being a spoiled, selfish bastard."

I huff, my lips parting to disagree, but he slams the door after sliding inside the car, preventing me from defending myself unless I climb into the SUV too. Groaning combined with a fragment of whining, I yank the door open and fold myself inside. The arctic AC immediately greets me, chilling my heated cheeks and sweat-dotted forehead.

"Where are we going?" I cross both arms over my chest and slouch in the seat like a pouting teenager.

Not deeming me worthy of a response, Tank ignores me as he presses a button on the steering wheel. The speakers crackle to life, and the distinct ring of an outgoing call pours through the small space.

"Hey, baby," says the one voice that can be loving and terrifying as fuck in the same breath.

I sit up straight and uncross my arms. "Why are you calling her?" I hiss.

"Man Child?" Sarah says over the speakers.

"We're headed your way. I need your help getting through to him."

"Finally," she grumbles, annoyance clear in her voice. "I'm done with you moping around the apartment because you're worried about him."

"Aw." I shift in the leather seat to face T, placing my elbows on the center console and resting my chin on my fists as I bat my lashes at him. "You were worried about me."

"We're twenty minutes out. Be there soon." The background static cuts off as he ends the call.

"You love me," I say, reaching over and laying a hand over his thigh. Surprisingly, keeping a straight face is more difficult than keeping my shit together the past few weeks.

"I will break every finger on that hand, Playboy." I snatch it back to my side, a genuine smile fighting its way through for the first time in weeks. "And yes, if you must know, I've been worried about you."

Dropping the act, I rest my head back against the headrest and close my eyes. "I just need time."

"You're out of time. We all are. We're stepping up to the presidential alpha security team. I need you on fucking point, and I need my friend."

"I've told you I'm fine."

"You think you're the only one who thinks he failed that kid?" Peeking an eye open, I watch my friend's fingers as they tighten, his knuckles going white around the steering wheel. "I was his team lead. I allowed him to lead that team in Austin. I knew he wasn't ready for that kind of responsibility, but it was what he wanted, and I knew he'd do a good job. I put him in the role that got him killed."

Suddenly the selfishness comment he shouted earlier takes root, supporting his claim. I am a selfish bastard. Here I am dwelling on all my issues when my best friend is drowning in guilt. I'm a damn asshole.

"Davis." I scrub a hand over my face before running my fingers through my hair. "He was ready for that role. How would any of us have known something like that would happen to the VP's daughter? We had extra protection that night even. It could've been any one of us."

"Is that what's eating you?"

I mull over his question, not really sure of the honest response. "Maybe. It's a damn punch to the balls when the reality of what could happen to any one of us actually happens." The cold air fills my lungs as I inhale deep. "Being shot didn't help either. I was almost a casualty to this job too."

"Yeah you were."

Shifting in the seat, I rest my elbow on the door and press two fingertips to the cloth-covered roof. "A lot changed that day." My uncomfortable cough diverts his attention from the windshield for half a second. "I think that's what's wrong."

"Do you regret confronting your parents?"

"Fuck no," I say with strength behind it. "My father is a perverted asshole who is currently getting what he deserves. Same with my mother. She's finally being exposed for who she truly is. No, I don't regret it, but that doesn't change the fact that the core of who I am shifted that day. Then the shooting, surgery, waking up and finding out Randi was sworn in." The hand on my thigh tightens into a fist. "What do I have to offer her now?"

"I don't follow." Switching hands on the wheel, he leans an elbow against the door, mirroring me. "You're still the same idiot you were before you were shot. She knows all about your parents and knows it had nothing to do with you."

"Am I? Am I the same person now? I don't feel the same."

"Describe it."

The tendons of my fingers ache as I stretch them out to rub a sweaty palm along my thigh. "I can't."

"One thing."

I huff a laugh. "One thing." Gazing out the window, I try to pinpoint just one of the messed-up thoughts that have been on a continuous loop the past several weeks. "It hurt," I say after a few minutes of comfortable silence. "The pain was worse than I expected, but that's not what's playing on repeat. I can't shake the fear."

"That's normal, man."

I shake my head. "No, not fear of dying." Sliding my gaze to his side, I wait until we're through a yellow light before continuing. "Fear of leaving her behind." Turning, I sigh and stare at the buildings flashing past my window. "For the first time in my pathetic existence, the thought of not being there for someone, for her, was terrifying. I can't describe it any other way, but that's what keeps me up at night. The look in her eyes when she thought I was leaving her and the absolute pain that it caused knowing I failed her."

"Yet you're doing it now on purpose."

I shoot him a look. "That's different."

"How in the hell is that different? You say you were afraid of leaving her behind, yet you've seen her once, twice since you got out of the hospital?"

"It is different," I demand. "I'm messed up in the head. I'm doing her a favor keeping her out of this."

"Her a favor, right."

"She's got enough to deal with."

"Yet all she wants is to help you."

"She's the president of the free world," I grit out. Again those fingers ball into a tight fist as anger at my current situation flows through my veins.

"Yet all she wants is to be with you."

"Stop saying that," I shout. My chest heaves. "I'm not the same person I was. One day I had a strong family name, I had money, status, her. Then the next I'm forgotten in a hospital bed while she makes a fucking decision that puts a target not only on her back but on her damn forehead without talking to me about it."

I suck in a breath and slide my wide eyes to Tank.

"Holy fuck," I say, slowly letting my held breath out.

"Now we're getting somewhere."

"She thought I was too weak to tell me before she left for the press conference."

"I'd go with it more being about the element of surprise, but that's my take."

I nod. He has a point.

"What else?"

Now my quick breaths stem from excitement. For the first time in weeks, the weight sitting on my chest eases. "I loathe the fact that I have nothing to offer her now."

"Did you ever?"

I shoot him another "fuck you" glare. "Not helping."

"Benson, you're the same fucking idiot today as you were the day you met. Nothing has changed."

"Everything has," I say, my voice tight.

"Not the things that matter. Sure, her job has changed, she has a new title, but that hasn't changed who she is. She's still just as crazy, just as honest and good-hearted as she was when we dragged her out of that smashed-up limo years ago. And if you believe your family name, your money, hell, anything other than the unwavering support you offer her meant a damn thing to her, then you don't deserve her."

"I'm afraid she'll see that now." A sliver of the tension coiled around my constricted chest eases with the admission. "What can I offer her now that I'm this and she's that?"

The seat belt catches against my chest at Tank slamming on the brakes a little too hard after whipping into a parking space. The gear shift slams forward into Park, his palm engulfing the entire thing.

He rips the agency-issued sunglasses off his face and narrows his dark eyes. "You listen and you listen good, Trey Benson. You are not any less of a person, of a friend, or of a man to that woman because your parents are fucked in the head. Your money only mattered to you and those people who didn't matter at all. Me, Randi, Sarah, we all, for some unknown reason, love your scrawny ass without all that shit. Take away your last name, take away your money, your old life, and you're left with the man who wins people over just by being his own damn annoying self."

I'm not crying, you're crying.

"And you know what else?" he adds on while pointing between my brows. "Yes, I love you, and these few weeks seeing you sinking has gutted me worse than knowing I set that kid up for failure. You're my best friend, and I will not let you lose that woman, the best thing that's happened to you since me, all because you're worked up about something that does not matter. She loves you, Benson, really loves you. The way Sarah loves me. Faults and all, those women love us to our core. I have no idea why or how it happened, but I thank the good Lord every night that she does. Stop thinking you're in this alone and have to figure it out by secluding yourself."

I can't look away from my best friend. Thank fuck he chooses to not point out the unshed tears dampening my lower lids that he can no doubt see.

Clearing my throat, I shift in the seat. "Well, hell. Should we make out now?"

Lips twitching, he suppresses a smile. "We good?"

"We're good."

"Good," he responds as he shoves the heels of his palms to his lids. "Damn dust in my eyes."

"I was going with pollen."

Movement in front of the windshield snatches my attention. My heart stops before kick-starting again at a rapid pace. Sarah, Tank's frightful wife, now stands at the hood of the SUV with a coiled rope dangling from her left hand. Not taking my focus off her, I nudge Tank with my elbow. "What the fuck were you two planning to do to me?"

A loud, rumbling laugh belts from his chest when he sees what I'm seeing. "That woman."

"Is violent as hell?"

"Perfection." I swear he lets out a love-filled sigh. Shaking his head, he flicks a look to my side. "She'll be disappointed that she doesn't need to follow through with whatever crazy-ass plan she concocted to make you open up."

I flinch as Sarah narrows her eyes and rests both hands on her hips. "Get out of the car, Man Child," she yells through the windshield.

I'm armed and outweigh the woman, but somehow, I'm still a bit terrified. "Protect me," I beg.

"You're on your own, man." The car door slams shut behind him. I watch as he strides to his wife and engulfs her in a bear hug. A hint of a smile breaks through her tough exterior. An exterior she has to wear on a daily basis commanding several hundred marines.

Grumbling to myself about how unfair my life has turned out to be, I climb out of the SUV. "What exactly were you planning to do to me?"

Sarah sighs and leans against Tank's wide chest. "Tie you to a chair and come up with creative ways to make you talk." She rests her head back on Tank's shoulder as she gazes up at him. "But it seems all my planning will go to waste." The loving concern behind her wide eyes as they meet mine is crystal clear. "Seems you two started the conversation without my help, which is good."

"So I don't end up tortured to talk through my feelings?"

"Because you have bigger issues to deal with," she says, watching my reaction.

"What's going on?" Tank demands, shifting into full protective mode. Gripping her shoulder, he steps back, putting a foot between them. This is another reason why I'm terrified of Sarah. If you as much as look at her the wrong way, not only do you have to deal with her, who's a badass in her own right, but protective papa bear will rip off your arms and legs after she's through with you.

They're perfect for each other.

"It's all over the news. Saudi Arabia, our ally, is taking live fire as we speak. Sources over there are begging for a response from the US, for any kind of help. Which means your girl's under fire, Man Child."

"What?" I snap, my own protective instinct kicking in knowing Randi is not only in the middle of this shit storm but is dealing with it alone.

A million thoughts and questions flash through my mind. Taking a quick stride forward, I grip Tank's arm. "Call Pierce, tell him to get to the White House and we'll meet him there."

"It'll be a war zone. No way will they let us through the front gate."

A sharp tug on his bicep puts us nose to nose. "Then we'll break it the fuck down. She needs me, Davis. I'm not letting her go through this alone."

9

RANDI

Chaos mounts behind me as I stare out wide windows onto the back lawn. Reporters line the fence, the lenses of their cameras reflecting in the afternoon light. Through the shouting behind me, a particularly loud voice booms above the others, demanding attention, but no one heeds his words.

What the hell am I supposed to do?

I'm *so* not prepared for this. Call me naïve, but I assumed I had... I don't know, more time, maybe, before the preverbal shit hit the fan, all stemming from the fool who was in this role prior. Sure, there have been a few attacks between the volatile countries, but we were handling it. Sam and Todd were working on it. Doing a decent job at it, I thought. Not great but holding down the fort while I figured out how to stop everything from here.

"Quiet," I say loud enough to be heard over the other voices. Turning from the window, I take in my advisors and commanders from each military branch. Six weathered faces focus on me, their skin wrinkled with the massive amount of stress that comes with being the president's military advisors.

Todd, the weaselly secretary of state I don't trust as far as I can throw him, leans forward from his position on the couch, tension radiating off him in waves as he wipes his palms up and down the length of his thighs. Blake paces the back of the room along with the defense secretary, both mumbling to themselves. A few other advisors are scattered around the room, their worry palpable.

"General Carpenter, I want your insight first," I say to the man with more service bars and medals than I knew even existed secured to the front of his army green uniform. "You have the floor."

The intimidating man rises from the ornate stuffed winged-back chair. Hands clasped in front of his hips, he widens his stance and centers his heavy focus on me.

"I've read the initial reports coming out of Saudi Arabia. Several small attacks have erupted along the borders. No one has claimed responsibility, but the pressure is mounting, and it seems more attacks are expected. The king is asking for our assistance in defending their borders and protecting their civilians from the continuous attack. It's not a well-organized army, more like several small cells attacking in sequence."

"Do we know who ordered the attacks, or do they seem like random acts of violence?" I ask. My gut clenches with trepidation. Small attacks like these have sprouted up all through the Middle East, causing unrest between our allies and enemies. The turmoil is bubbling over, threatening to send that part of the world into war, attacking anyone they assume is behind the attacks.

And I know the reason why.

"Based on my meetings with the various leaders over the previous few weeks, I suspect Russia," Todd chirps in.

I shoot him a condemning expression, nearly mirroring the scowl the general now wears, which seems to agree with my silent "shut the fuck up" hint to my idiot secretary of state.

Folding my arms across my chest, I lean a hip against the edge of the desk, looking down my nose at the man. What the hell is Todd thinking, tossing out Russia? He's up to something. He requested a meeting with Vlad before the New Year, but I never heard if it actually happened.

I shove the nagging feeling away, needing to focus on the issue at hand.

"Highly unlikely that it's Russia," the general says. "We suspect Yemen or Syria based on the initial intel. I suggest sending in a small force to take out the groups targeting our ally and secure the area to ensure there aren't any additional flare-ups. We can gain information while on the ground. In and out in under twelve months."

"Twelve months?" I grit out. "That's your version of in and out?"

"If we do not secure the area, more militants will come in and do the exact same thing. This is a part of the world that is in constant turmoil. The fact that they've been in relative peace for the past few years is unheard of."

No doubt that's why whoever was manipulating Kyle wanted all this to happen.

"What are our other options?" I ask, masking the hopeful tilt of my voice with a fake sigh.

The room swells with a pregnant pause. The general exchanges a sharp look with Blake. "Minimum casualties on both sides and we help an ally. This is the option."

"You're telling me with all the intelligence we have, everything we know about this situation, that military force is the only course of action?" I scoff and move around the desk to stand behind it once again. Fingertips pressed to the hard surface, I lean forward, putting most of my weight on the desk. "No."

The room erupts with disagreeing shouts. I lift a hand, urging them to let me finish.

"First of all, this is not our fight." Well, technically it is, but as far as they know, it's not. They have no idea we might be the ones who actually funded this fight. Hell, I didn't even know until I received the evidence Vlad furnished. I still don't know the major players; even Vlad wasn't able to obtain those details, which says a lot. The file was crystal clear on one aspect of the scheme. The drilling, rising gas prices, and funneling the profits to offshore accounts was a drop in the bucket to the overall plan. All that money was then channeled out to various for-hire militant groups to force that part of the world into war.

Dozens of times, I've listed the pros and cons of informing my military advisors of what was put into action by Kyle, but it always comes down to the same answer: I can't. If the information gets out, if our allies knew what American dollars had funded, we'd be friendless in less than a week and the target of their ire, followed by attacks.

No, this stays with those few who know the truth: me, Sam, Trey, and T. Plus Shawn, I guess, who's been creepily absent since I announced Sam as VP. Every day I don't hear from him, the little voice in the back of my mind warns me there's a reason and I should prepare for the worst.

I shift my focus to the small American flag standing proudly at the corner of the desk. I can't justify leading our men and women in uniform into this fight, putting their lives on the line, for a lie. Those countries think their neighboring enemies are responsible for the attacks and are ready to respond with more might and harshness This has to end soon before things get out of hand, but not with military action. Not yet.

"Second, we don't have enough solid intel to justify deploying several thousand troops." I shake my head and shove off the desk. Walking around to the front, I lean back against the edge and cross my arms. Hopefully this pose looks intimidating. "No, we will go about this in a different way."

"Madam President, I disagree with—"

My sharp look cuts Blake off.

"I understand most of you are not a fan of my decision. I'm well aware of that." A sharp knock at the side door triggers me to pause. Sam stalks through half a second later, quickly shutting the door behind him. A swift nod in greeting and he relaxes back along the wall, those green eyes taking in the grumbling group crowding the Oval Office. "No military action. Todd, get the king on the phone. He and I can talk about next steps and how we can help without sending troops."

Todd's already pale face loses more color. "I'm not sure that's a great idea. He's mentioned a few times in the past that I'm not his favorite person in this office. Maybe the vice—"

"Man the fuck up," I snap. How has Sam not killed him over the past few weeks as they traveled together? "Get over the king not liking you and get him on the damn phone. We will figure this out. Today. I need to know who he suspects ordered the attacks, and then we go from there. Next I want to have a conversation with whoever the hell is running Yemen, Syria, Oman, and Iraq these days. We figure out what the actual fuck is going on over there today, gentlemen."

Done with the conversation, I flick my wrist toward the door, waving them off, and push off the desk.

Disgruntled grumbles resound through the room as the men exit. Only once everyone except Sam is gone do I allow myself to sink into the massive desk chair.

"I don't know which is worse," I say, my eyes closed as I massage both temples. "My military advisors knowing what I know or continuing to keep them in the dark, making them assume I'm an idiot for not heeding their sage advice."

"Both." Sam's deep gravelly voice carries though the now still office. "But you know as well as I do that they *can't* know. You and I agreed on that weeks ago, Randi. Even with Birmingham removed from this office, we *cannot* risk the repercussions if the countries who have sustained casualties and damage find out the United States are the ones funding—"

"Funded, not funding," I correct. "I shut all that shit down and cut ties with everyone we could tie the scandal to the night I was sworn in."

"Fine," he acknowledges. The wall groans as he shoves off to move toward the center of the room. "But funding or funded, it's all the same. The money these militant groups are using to buy guns, supplies, and intel came from *us*. If this attack on Saudi Arabia is the militia group funded by whoever constructed the shit Birmingham dragged us into—which, like you, I suspect is true—this is their first major attack. I'll be honest with you, Randi, I don't think it's the last. If we don't do something about this now, things will get worse fast."

"I agree, which is why I want to bring the higher-ups in the CIA into the fold." Peeking my eyes open, I slide my gaze to the closed door he came through. It's wishful thinking that Trey is just on the other side. Not after the morning we had, not with his avoidance the past few weeks. I'm desperate to know what's bothering him, but being locked in this gilded cage has me limited on how to get to him. "We have to identify and stop the ones responsible now. With Kyle gone, we need to get the names another way, which will take time. While I'm working to keep the peace over there, the CIA can be behind the scenes, working on identifying who's behind all this. Once we figure that out, we take them out and we're in the clear."

"Correct, resolving the unrest those bastards are stirring up is priority, keeping this from escalating further than it already has. Todd and my visits over the past few weeks have done minimal damage control, but we need more. We've let the other countries who've sustained smaller attacks know we're willing to assist in searching for the ones responsible while keeping it vague. We need to identify and locate them and hold them accountable."

"And the one lead we had, the one person who knew all the players, is dead." I gnaw on the red acrylic tip of my pinkie finger. "Speaking of Kyle, any news on that front?"

"What do you mean?" He undoes the two buttons of his suit jacket before reclining on the stiff couch, stretching his arms along the back. "The traitorous bastard did us a favor, even if it did leave a gaping hole in the investigation."

"That's just it," I muse. The chair swivels as I dig a stiletto heel into the carpet, twisting left, then right and back again. "It all seems convenient, doesn't it? He demands a plea deal to keep him out of federal prison, offering the names of those he knew were involved on a silver platter. Then he ends up dead? It doesn't make sense."

"You've been watching too many crime shows, Madam President." I whirl the chair around and stick my tongue out at his smiling face. "Birmingham simply realized no matter what information he gave the attorney general, he would see jail time."

"I just think it's fishy is all. And not like him. He was an arrogant son of a bitch, narcissistic at times. Hanging himself like that... hell, having the balls to do that...." I swivel the chair an inch right, then left as I process what I want to say. "I think someone else did it to shut him up."

Sam's bright green eyes light with humor. "Oh really? And you think someone just snuck onto his estate while he was under federal house arrest and hanged him? All without leaving a trace of evidence behind? Come on, Randi, look at the evidence. It's clear he took the easy way out. There weren't any defensive wounds, no sign of someone else being in that room the night it happened."

Again my attention finds its way to the closed door that leads to the admin area. Something on the other side calls to me, urging me to swing it open and see what's waiting.

"They're the ones who called me." He inclines his head toward the door I can't drag my attention away from. "I would like to add that I was already on my way over."

"Who?"

Giving in to the temptation, I grip the armrests and push myself out of the chair. My heels dig into the carpet as I stride to the door and pull it open. The clacking of keys, low murmuring voices, and high-pitched ringing of desk phones greet me. My secretary stands, hands fumbling at her side. With a forced tight-lip smile, I search the room, stopping when I find Trey and T lingering on the opposite side. Careful to keep my excitement and relief hidden, I motion for them to join me in the Oval Office.

Butterflies take flight in my stomach at the smirk Trey shoots my way as I stride across the small office. Yes, I have a potential war to resolve, but I can't help the giddy feeling of seeing him here. He came. Even after this morning, with the turmoil between us, Trey came.

For me.

"Feels like old times, meeting like this," Trey says the moment the door shuts behind T. His honey eyes search mine, uncertainty pouring through them. I offer a hesitant smile, letting him know we're good—for now. "I'm sure you're aware, but those assholes who just left were visibly pissed about whatever happened in here. And that secretary of state of yours looked about to pee his cheap-ass slacks."

An obnoxious snort escapes me. I slap a hand over my nose and mouth to make sure another doesn't sneak out. The mischievous twinkle and smirk Trey sports as he crosses the room tells me my laugh was what he was striving for.

With a groan, I stretch both arms out wide before interlacing two fingers above my head, attempting to ease the ache building in my shoulders. "Yeah, they want military action and I said no. Which you're both aware of the why behind that decision."

"Yes and no. It's been several weeks since we've all been a part of detailed discussions," T interrupts. "Catch us up."

A grimace curls my lips as I slide one throbbing foot from its high heel jail, the other following immediately after. The soft carpet brushes the tips of my toes as I curl them, relishing in the freedom from captivity.

"Right, of course, T. I guess it has been awhile. As you both know, the money from Kyle's drilling and oil scheme was being deposited into offshore accounts, then funneled to other groups and banks around the world. We don't know who that money was going to, but we do know the why. The money Kyle made by drilling on federal land is now funding—" I catch Sam's arched brow. "Sorry, funded. The money funded several small insurgent groups of sorts, which are now wreaking havoc across the Middle East, making each country look to their neighboring enemies to blame. The best Sam and I can gather is their main goal is to stir shit up. Today's attack wasn't the first, but it is at this scale. My military advisors want to move straight into military action, sending in troops to squash the threat."

"Sounds like a solid plan," T says as he sits on the rounded armrest of the couch opposite of Sam. "Guessing you don't like that plan or you have another in mind."

I shake my head, my loose dark locks falling forward over both shoulders. I twirl a section between my fingers. "No, I don't like the military angle, and I don't have another plan. None of my military advisors know what you know, and I don't want them to. If word gets out on what the US has inadvertently started, all hell will break loose. I will not let our country be blamed and attacked because of Kyle's actions. No, I will work with the leaders over in the Middle East to settle tempers a bit, at least give the CIA some time to work their magic. Once we have the names of the men running it all, we can stop all this at the source. Sending in the military will be a Band-Aid, not taking care of the actual problem."

"You're saying *you* want to *talk* to them," Trey says, both brows raised in question. "I get you don't want to involve the military at this point in the game, but do you think talking to them will actually resolve anything?"

"They'll think you're weak." I shoot T a glare, and he shrugs. "I'm just voicing what we heard when those men left the Oval Office earlier. And they're right, Randi. Are you prepared for the world to see you as soft? They already assume you're not fit for the role because you won't make the hard choices. Now you're wanting to decline military action to help out an ally and instead just *talk* it out?"

I soak in his question, debating the right response. He's right, but so am I.

"Of course I don't want to appear weak. They already think that because I'm a woman. Asshats. But I also won't approve of our first steps being troops on the ground. This, my plan, is the right first step. I asked Todd to get a call scheduled between me and the king of Saudi Arabia. Then we go from there. I'll have the CIA identify the main players in this shit show, we'll take them out when they do, and then we're good to go. Easy."

At least that's what I'm telling myself. This would be so much easier with unicorn assassins as an option.

"And what are you going to tell the king exactly?" Sam cuts in. "You know he'll ask for military action. Hell, he already has, and now the media has caught wind of it. If you don't offer aid or show him you're serious about finding out what the hell is going on over there, then he'll question your loyalty."

I stare unfocused at Sam, processing his words. "You're right. He needs to see that I'm taking the attack on their soil seriously." Fingernail between my teeth, I pace from one end of the desk to the other. "I'll go," I blurt. A collective breath reverberates through the room as the three men ready themselves to insistently disagree. "No, wait, hear me out. I don't have it all figured out just yet, but I will. I'm thinking if I can go over there, show the king I'm serious about our support, I can convince him to wait on a direct response against those he believes are responsible. We can settle this with minimum bloodshed by me meeting with him face-to-face."

"Why not ask Vlad?" Trey asks.

"Can't believe you're friends with the Russian president," Sam grumbles. "Todd mentioned it to me, by the way. He wondered if I knew."

I furrow my brows. "What in the hell is Todd up to with the Russian angle? And what can I say? Vlad is a nice guy. Terrible fashion sense, but he comes through when I need him." Trey fights a smile, the corners of his lips twitching upward. "But even he couldn't get the names we need."

"What if we can't find who's funding them?" Sam asks, lost in deep thought as he stares at the imitation fruit piled in an ornate bowl on top of the coffee table.

"Funded, remember? And we will. One way or another, we will." Dipping my chin, I take a deep breath. "This situation isn't ideal, but if we don't do anything, then those countries will turn on each other thinking the other is responsible for the attacks, and then we'll be pulled into it to help our allies. If we tell them what's going on, then we risk their vengeance for inadvertently funding a terrorist cell that's currently attacking them. Anyone else have a better idea?"

At their silence, I nod. Standing tall, I fix my dress shirt, tucking it back into my black slacks.

"So there we have it. I'll reach out to the director of the CIA and get him up to speed. Then I'll talk to the Saudi king, telling him to not retaliate but defend himself until we can figure out what's going on."

"And when we do? When we find these bastards, what's next?" T asks.

"We take them out. I think the SEALs are speed dial four." I attempt a nonchalant smile, but it falls flat. "The bigger threat is the men moving the money around, forcing us into a war all for their monetary reasons. This is a solid-ish plan. I like it." Their shared look tells me they don't think it's as solid as I think it is. "I'll try to calm the king down, and any other surrounding countries if I have to, all while the CIA finds out who's behind all this and then we take them out. Problems solved, and I'll have officially granted every Miss America contestant's wish for world peace." I raise both hands, sporting peace signs for emphasis.

I'm officially a lost cause. Let's just hope I can refrain from doing anything stupid with my hands when I meet the king.

"Just one small hurdle in all this," Trey says, his tone low and serious.

"I see no holes," I state, completely bluffing. This plan is like crumbling swiss cheese.

"There is no way in hell we will let you enter a country that is currently under attack."

I shoot a side-eye glare at Trey. "Doesn't everyone have to do what I say? Isn't that perk number one of being president?"

"You're not the queen," Sam interjects, humor lacing his tone as he watches Trey and me. "But yeah, you have—"

"Let me rephrase that, then. *I* won't let you step foot in a country that is being fucking bombed."

My jaw pops open, my mouth gaping at Trey in astonishment. I should be furious at him not "letting me," but the bolt of fiery desire that shot to my core at his authoritative tone and words keeps the anger at bay.

"Excuse me?" I breathe.

"Tank, Pierce, give us a minute." Trey's hard stare never leaves mine. "I need a moment alone with the president."

The room shrinks even more as the other two file out, shutting the door behind them. My fingers tighten along the edge of the desk at the building anticipation. Each step is calculated as Trey stalks from where he leaned against the far wall to where I rest on the edge of the desk. He doesn't pause until we're toe to toe. My back bows as I'm forced to lean back to see his face when he places both hands on my hips and dips closer.

"I'm fucking done with you making decisions on your own that risk your life. You hear me, Mess? I don't care what your title is or who you've sworn to protect and uphold above yourself. You're mine, and I'm hell-bent on protecting you from *yourself* from now on."

10

———

RANDI

"I should be pissed at your sexist claiming, but—" I don't stop my visible shiver. "—I'm too fucking turned on by it to be mad."

Then it happens. The flicker of confidence mixed with the cocky, caring asshole who's been missing for weeks lights behind his eyes. The fine lines at the corners spider outward with his signature smirk.

"Something happened," I say in awe as I place a hand against his cheek. "Something good."

"Yeah, something happened. I'm figuring things out, slowly." Leaning close, he brushes his slick lips along the shell of my ear. My lids flutter closed. I press both thighs tightly together to relieve the painful throb building at the apex. "And you forget how well I know your kinks, Mess. You've always loved when I take control in the bedroom. I'm not shocked my demand made you wet for me. It did, didn't it, baby? Tell me. Tell me how you'll be a good girl and listen to me."

With a sexually frustrated groan, I pitch forward, pressing my forehead against the soft fabric of his dress shirt. Forcing each breath in and out of my nose, I attempt to slow my heavy breaths.

"What do you expect me to do?" I ask, trying to get this conversation back on track before I give in to the urge to lean back on the desk and beg him to take me right here in the Oval Office. "Sam's tried to settle the leaders. Then there's the fact that they hate my secretary of state—"

"Because he's fucking weak and a conniving fool who's trying desperately to prove his worth right now and failing miserably."

"Wow, tell me how you really feel," I say with a grin tugging on my lips. "But that leaves me to work my magic, to see what I can accomplish by meeting with the leaders over there while the CIA finds out who's behind all this."

Every nerve ending flashes red hot as two of his fingers trail up the inside of both thighs. Even with the thin fabric of my slacks blocking his touch from brushing bare skin, tingles erupt in their wake.

"I understand that, Mess. I'm not demanding you step away from the responsibilities of this role. What I'm telling you is you're done making rash decisions that you think impact only you. Stop committing to trips or plans without consulting the security team, without talking to *me* first. You've preached that we need honesty and open communication to make this work. That's all I'm demanding in return."

"Demanding," I whisper. My lids flutter closed as those fingers stroke along the center seam of my pants, pressing right against my core. "I really like your demanding."

A soft chuckle brushes along the sensitive skin of my neck. "It's not just your life on the line anymore. Mine is tied to yours from now until the end of me. If something happens to you, then they might as well dig two holes in the ground because I'll be right beside you."

"That's drastic." My voice trembles at the gravity of his statement.

"That's love."

Filling my lungs with a full breath, I lean back to gaze up at his handsome face once again. Dark hair brushes against the naturally tan skin of his forehead. His strong jaw is lightly dusted with facial hair, indicating he wasn't on duty today or it would be as smooth as a baby's bottom. Long dark lashes flutter as he watches me taking him in almost like it's the first time.

And it kind of feels like it is. It's been so long since I've gotten this side of Trey, my Trey, all to myself. My heart swells with the flood of love I have for this man.

"I've missed this Trey." I bite back my nervous grin.

"Me too," he admits with his own look of uncertainty. "I won't lie to you and say everything is solid. I'm not 100 percent, but I will be. Thanks to you, thanks to Tank and his crazy wife."

I snort. "You got to see Sarah? I'm jealous. I miss that woman."

"And I miss your tasty pussy."

Before his words register, he drops to a crouch, putting his face eye level with the apex of my thighs where I sit perched on the desk. He pushes a hand against the inside of each knee, spreading my legs wide enough for his shoulders to wiggle between. My stomach clenches, my breaths quick pants. Eyes wide, I dart my focus from the closed door to his face as he presses close. Those dark lashes flutter as the tip of his nose brushes along the same path his fingers trekked moments before.

A desire-laced groan rumbles through the office as he inhales deeply. "I'm fucking starving for you, baby. Say yes. Let me eat my fill of you."

"Not here. I can't," I plead, even though every inch of my panting soul wants to ignore the world-changing concerns that linger just outside those doors, waiting to weigh me down again, and let him do whatever the hell he wants with my more-than-willing body.

"Why not?" he says, his voice muffled from his lips pressed against my damp slacks.

I swallow back the yelp that snaps from my throat at the feel of his teeth nipping and tugging at the fabric covering my core.

"Um...." *Wait. Was there a reason I said no? There's a good reason, right?* I feel like there's a big legit reason why he shouldn't, but I can't think straight with his face between my legs.

"See, it's a great idea." My eyes pop open wide at the sudden release of my snug waistband. Trey's light eyes twinkle with amusement as his deft fingers tug the zipper down. "Come here." Gripping the front of my slacks and a fistful of panties, he tugs me to a standing position. Not breaking eye contact, he guides me toward the bank of windows and urges me forward. I stumble as he whips me around, putting my back to his chest. "Palms on the window, baby."

"There are people out there." My voice is weak, the words barely a rasp with the need constricting my lungs and throat.

"They can't see inside, Mess. Now, palms on the fucking window, and spread those pretty little legs of yours. You need this. I need this."

All reason vanishes at the first swipe of his finger between my swollen lips. Eagerly I obey his orders. The warm glass suctions to my sweaty palms. I dig my bare toes into the carpet, fighting to remain upright as his hand slides along my slick skin.

My head lolls forward. Eyes hooded, I stare at his forearm as his hand moves beneath my gaping black slacks and hot pink lace panties. He positions a solid steel rod between my ass cheeks with a hard thrust. Arching my back, I grind my ass against his hard cock.

"Fuck." The word is more of a hiss, his lips hot against my ear. "If I can't lick you, at least I can sink some part of me *into* what's mine." A sharp gasp passes my dry lips before morphing into an unladylike moan as three fingers plunge inside. I whimper, giving myself completely to the elation coursing through my veins. Those deft fingers set a fast, demanding pace, taking me closer to the edge. Without breaking the pounding rhythm, he rotates his wrist to flick my swollen bundle of nerves with his thumb.

Ignoring how I should act, my powerful title, and *where* we are, I ride his hand, grinding down hard, desperately wishing it was the hard cock currently bruising my ass.

"That's it, baby," he murmurs into my hair. "Fuck my fingers. Give yourself to me."

I groan and lean forward. The hot glass heats my forehead. A palm slips on the windowpane as I press against it, needing help supporting my weight as my knees wobble. Wet lips crush against the column of my neck. Blunt teeth skim along the tight tendons and my throbbing pulse. I squeeze around his thick fingers, thighs flexing as my short breaths stutter. Sealing my lips to hold back my cry, I shatter around his hand.

My knees buckle. I sink a few inches before I'm saved from falling to the floor in orgasmic bliss by a strong arm snaking around my waist.

Still attempting to catch my breath, I'm twirled around until the window presses against my back. Heavy lids fight to stay open, only to widen at Trey's lips sealed around those three glorious fingers.

"Now," he states after sucking every last drop of me off those long digits. "Go negotiate world peace. But you will not commit to anything without talking to me and Tank first. Understand?"

Unable to speak, I respond with a simple nod.

"Good."

I'm still blissed out as Trey makes quick work of tucking my dress shirt back into my trousers and refastening the zipper and clasp. After a retreating step, he gives me an approving nod at his work and lifts his gaze to meet mine. "I'm on shift tonight, but how about we pick this back up tomorrow night?"

Again all I can do is nod. I have something tomorrow night, a dinner with a foreign dignitary or a fundraiser of some kind, but it doesn't matter. Nothing matters but seeing him again. I have to find balance in this role or it will eat me alive.

And the only thing I want eating me is Trey fucking Benson.

"I'LL ASSIGN our top analysts to this issue as soon as I get back to Langley."

The CIA directors' cold hand slips from mine as I step back with a confident smile. "Thank you, Director. I cannot emphasize enough that the sooner we find those responsible, the better. Time is ticking, and it is not on our side. Keep me updated on your findings."

With a quick nod, he makes for the door.

"Oh, by the way," I say, making him pause. "I have a new agent assigned to my alpha Secret Service team. They mentioned he came from the CIA." Okay, that's a tiny lie. No one confirmed my suspicion on Agent Smith, but the director doesn't need to know that. Hell, who knows, he might smell the lie itself. Wonder if the CIA chemically alters their agents to detect lies to make them smell a certain way. If a lie did have a smell, I'm sure it would 100 percent smell like black licorice. "Nasty stuff."

"Excuse me?" The director narrows his brows my direction.

"Sorry, I meant to say his name is Agent Smith. Heard of him?"

Something was off about Agent Smith that day in the Secret Service director's office three days ago that still nags at me. Or maybe it was her, the way she already had his file and him there ready to infiltrate my team. Even her body language changed after the mention of the new agent.

Or maybe I'm paranoid. Let's face it, I've kind of had a rough go the last year with Shawn trying to poison me and Kyle abducting Taeler. Add in Kyle's mysterious suicide and being very aware that Shawn is out there somewhere plotting to take me down by harming someone—or hell, knowing him, everyone—I love, I think being paranoid is warranted. We've done what we could to keep everyone safe. We relocated Mom to a different recovery center with better security that's off the grid. And of course I moved Taeler into the White House for her safety.

Ben refused the small protection detail I offered him on the slim chance Shawn would go after him. He's a damn fool, not understanding how awful Shawn is at the core, but I can't force protection on him; it was his choice to decline help. Tiny, my old boss in Austin, laughed at the idea of having bodyguards. In the end, he said if someone wanted to hurt me through him, it was their funeral.

Is it bad to hope Shawn does target Tiny so he could make good on his threat and take out the sociopath? I could get Tiny out of jail, pardon him or something if he got caught. Or even use the angle of Tiny doing a public service in getting rid of Shawn Whit.

"We have over three hundred Agent Smiths, Madam President." His forced smile is cold and calculating, resembling the one Shawn always wore when he thought he had the upper hand. I force myself not to flinch away. "Not that I would confirm or deny that anyone was once an agent."

"Right, of course. I just wanted to vet him before he starts in a few days."

A look of confusion flashes across his features, breaking the emotionless mask, before he turns. Hand on the doorknob, he pauses to glance over his shoulder, brows furrowed. For the past hour, he's been unreadable, not once balking at the information I offered about Kyle and the situation we're now in because of him. The potential of war didn't affect him, yet right now, something like worry or concern seems to radiate off him. "I will say this, Madam President. It would be the first time ever in my long career that we willingly transferred someone from our exclusive agency. If I were in your position, I'd ask why."

I'm still staring at the door long after he's gone. Still staring when it swings open minutes later and Blake strides through, head down, eyes focused on the iPad in his hands. He doesn't look up when he stops beside me behind the desk.

"We have a problem," he states.

I massage both temples to ease the impending headache before running a hand through my loose hair. "Why do I feel like that phrase is your signature opening line?"

"Because it is. Look at this." Spinning the device, he shoves it forward, thrusting it inches from my nose. I shoot him a glare before leaning back to see the screen. It takes a few blinks to moisten my eyes, shifting the soft contacts around to see the small print.

See it but can't read the words. Hell, what does he think I am, an elephant?

Or wait, is it rabbits with good eyesight and elephants with good hearing?

"Memory, maybe?" I mumble.

Blake lets out an exasperated sigh and shoves the screen close once again, determined to make me read the fine print.

Giving up on reading, I shove the iPad away until the screen presses against the vest of his three-piece suit.

"Just tell me what it says, Blake. It's been a long damn day."

"It's noon."

"Fuck," I groan, drawing out each letter in agony.

"Back to the topic at hand, Madam President. Some reporter put two and two together about the ob-gyn making frequent visits to the White House. This article is listed on a small website now, but a larger site—hell, maybe a network—will pick it up. Soon."

"What are you getting at, Blake?" I tap the spacebar to wake my sleeping laptop.

"They suspect that you, the president, are pregnant, not your daughter. This is bad. We knew it would get out, and now we're behind the media on this."

My breath catches, my fingers hovering over the keyboard as a million different outcomes of this mess filter through. None of them good, for me or for Taeler. I'm already known as the trailer trash president in this city, things printed about me in the papers personal and vicious. What will they do to Taeler? I swallow hard and start typing, trying to push the worst-case scenarios from my thoughts.

"Let them assume what they want. Even if I were pregnant—which you know I'm not—it would be my business, not theirs. When did this role mean the president's private life was fair game for attacks?"

"Your business is their business, Madam President. It's part of the job. It always has been and always will be. You're the leader of this country, and how you and your family members conduct yourselves reflects directly on the American people."

The rounded edge of the wooden desk digs into my forearms as I flex, balling my hands into tight fists. My knuckles protest under the strain, the skin of my palms pinched under long nails indenting crescent moon shapes.

"It's fine. We have bigger things to worry about." Slowly I relax my fingers one by one, the blood flowing freely back to the tips. "Anything else? I've got real problems to solve before my next meeting."

The weight of his glare doesn't go unnoticed. "You can't push this issue under the rug for long. The story won't go away and will only get bigger if we do nothing. We need to address it *now*."

"What would you suggest I do? Tell them it's not me who's pregnant but my daughter? My daughter who's still reeling with emotions from the death of her boyfriend and father of her unborn baby? Let her shoulder all the negative and fucking vicious media attention, all the taunts and name-calling and shaming that I've kept her from since I stepped into this city? You think I want that for my only daughter?" Elbows on the armrests of the chair, I cover my face with both hands.

"It's too late for avoidance. If we come out about her pregnancy now, we can control the message and—"

"I said *no*, Blake." Heat sweeps beneath my skin as my temper rises. "I understand where you're coming from, I do, but you're not looking at it from a mother's perspective. My job above any other is to protect her and now my grandbaby. Taeler is still in the early stages of pregnancy, and I will not have her upset, jeopardizing either of their health. My answer is no. Ignore the post. I sure as hell will."

A knock at the door prevents him from continuing the argument. The side office door swings open, my secretary's hand still on the door handle as she shuffles to the side, allowing Trey, T, and—

I narrow my eyes at the ice storm of a man who's right on their heels.

Blake grumbles his discontent about... well, probably everything to do with me, then exits the Oval Office, slamming the door behind him.

"Agent Smith," I grit out. "I wasn't aware you were joining us for this meeting today." I swing an accusing glare at T.

The annoying new agent doesn't say a word as he takes a position along the back wall, where he no doubt has a perfect view of every square inch of this room, and interlaces his fingers in front of his hips. It's concerning the way he blends in with the wall despite the fact that it's some awful yellow color, which I'm told is soothing, and he's wearing a dark gray suit.

"Our director made it clear that he's now our third wheel." If T's looks could kill, Agent Smith would be a pile of ashes right about now.

"Fourth," I say, drawing T's attention back to me. A line forms between his dark bushy brows. "You, me, Trouble, and now Agent Smith." Again my attention swings to the unassuming man with his back against the wall. "We need a nickname for him if he's going to be part of the squad."

"Squad?" The laughter in Trey's voice makes a corner of my lips turn upward even with the shitty day I've had.

"Tribe?" I retort.

"How about protection detail?"

"Always so serious, T." Pushing up from the desk, I arch my feet to stand on my tiptoes and stretch both arms high above my head. "In other news, a small blog caught wind of the type of doctor who's been frequenting the White House. It's not that big of a deal now, but it might be. I want extra security on Taeler if she ventures outside the gates. Her next appointment is next week, but I'll make sure the doctor continues to come here." T's thumbs fly across his phone screen, I assume taking notes. "Also I met with the director of the CIA this morning." Keeping my head tilted toward T, I monitor Agent Smith's reaction in my periphery. "He understands what I need done and will keep me updated while we're overseas."

Trey clears his throat with an attention-seeking cough. "Which is why Tank and I needed to meet with you today. There are a few details on the logistics of next week's trip we need to cover. We also need to discuss any changes in your behaviors or routine since you were at One Observatory Circle."

I look to the ceiling like I'm concentrating. "Let's see, I've picked up smoking again, which Trouble is aware of." I shoot Trey a wink. "I work a little more and sleep a lot less."

"Not sure that's even possible," T grumbles.

"And I've pretty much given up on eating an actual meal at a dinner table outside of diplomatic dinner parties."

"So the same, then," Trey says with a smirk. "Just a little extra now."

"Sounds about right."

Our eyes stay locked as Tank rattles off a list of preparations for the upcoming trip to Saudi Arabia. The weight of Agent Smith's gaze burns the skin along the back of my neck as I creep toward Trey, who's posted up alongside the desk, hip digging into the edge. "Hi," I whisper once I'm close.

"Mess."

"What do we do about him?" I incline my head toward Agent Smith. "Can we act normal?"

"You mean can we make out in front of him?" He lifts a shoulder in a half shrug. "Only one way to find out." A quick twist and I'm pinned between him and the desk, Trey's mouth sealed to my own. His lips thin, spreading into a smile as he flicks his humor-filled gaze from me to the back of the room. My wide eyes follow.

Agent Smith blinks, the only sign he's not dead or a robot, before shifting his attention to the empty center of the room once again.

"See, he doesn't mind," Trey says, pressing one last peck to the corner of my lips.

I frown, my brows furrowing and forming a deep line between them. "You're okay with that?" I question Agent Smith while wagging a finger between my chest and Trey's.

"Sure," he responds.

"Really?" I rest both hands on my hips and angle my chest toward him. "You're okay with me being romantically involved with an agent?"

"Are you?" he questions.

"Well, yeah."

He lifts a single brow.

"You're not going to lecture me on how this is a terrible idea or how I'm putting myself in danger or whatever?"

"Why would I do that?"

"Because you're tasked with protecting me."

He tilts his head as if he's considering me. "I'm tasked with protecting you from external threats, not from yourself."

"Harsh," I huff. "But okay, noted. Just so you know, whatever you see or hear is not to be disclosed to anyone outside of the people in this room. The director seems to want you around me at all times like these two, so that means you'll be privy to my personal life and... quirks."

"She mean's varying levels of crazy, an obsession for unicorns, and some-times responding out loud to conversations that she creates in her head." Humor laces Trey's voice.

"Thanks?" Smiling, I shake my head and fold both arms across my chest. The silk material of my shirt slides beneath my forearms. "I'd like to disagree, but... Trey's assessment is pretty accurate." Pitching forward, I smack my palms to my thighs and stand. "Now that the gang is back together, let's go save the world."

Trey clears his throat with a pointed look.

I roll my eyes. "Sorry. Once you guys approve my every breath and step while on this world peace adventure, of course. Then we save the world."

T's and Trey's chuckles fill the room.

I stare at Agent Smith, hoping it will give me insight into his nonexistent personality. He really needs a nickname. "Are you as controlling as these two?" I ask while hooking a thumb in the direction of the two other men in the room.

A hint of a smile lifts the corner of his lips. "Worse."

Awesome.

11

TREY

Every muscle twitches on a hair trigger, ready for action. Energy-fueled blood thrums through my veins, heightening every instinct honed by the agency's training and hours of self-practice. It's not just me either. Our entire team is like a live wire twitching along the floor, our instincts heightened, knowing what's at stake tonight and where we are.

Not only is Randi's life in peril in this foreign country but the safety and peace of our country as well. If something were to happen to her while we're here, all hell would break loose, probably resulting in nuclear war.

This is why we're ultravigilant tonight. Why I haven't taken my eyes off her since she stepped from her suite all dolled up for tonight's banquet with her as the honored guest. It was on the agenda, so we knew to plan for this, but knowing and actually being here are two very different feelings.

Possessiveness rears its ugly head the farther down the hall we walk. I can't let my emotions and feelings for her warp my attention. With an internal punch to the balls, I shove those personal feelings aside and focus on treating her like any other politician. It's a fucking losing battle though when her ass looks like that. After scanning the area, my gaze lands on her delectable ass. That fucking gown leaves nothing to the imagination.

A low angry animalistic growl rumbles through the earpiece in my right ear. Reluctantly, I tear my gaze off her for the thousandth time in the last fifteen minutes. Tank curses, and a smile ticks at my lips before I shut it down. Around me, other guys of the alpha team scan the room, one seeming more on edge than the rest of us.

Agent Smith. There's no doubt he's good at watching for threats. Randi is in good hands with him around. Now, safe *from* him, that's a different question. Tank and I agree there's something off about him, something that keeps me on alert any time he's around.

An agent murmurs one word, and acknowledgments of the potential threat echo in my earpiece as Randi moves about the large ballroom, greeting the various minsters and advisors of the king. The king himself stands at the end of the receiving line several people down, the last for her to thank for the opulent banquet tonight. The purpose for this trip has been successful so far. The call last week between the king and Randi, and now her being here showing her support, has eased his twitching finger off the rocket launchers. Somehow she's convinced him the US is already looking into the attacks and will hold the people guilty of the bombings accountable.

Which we will.

We are.

As long as our time doesn't run out before it's too late. These countries are balanced on the tip of a sharp knife; one skirmish, one more conflict, can cause all hell to break loose.

But if anyone can stop it all from happening, it's her. Beautiful, caring, crazy, and lovable Randi Sawyer. I was a fool to let those several weeks slip by without being at her side. Not anymore. No, I'm here now, and I'm fucking here to stay.

Her high-pitched fake laugh pierces through my distracting thoughts. Scanning the room, I sweep the crowd with a calculating gaze, monitoring their proximity to the president before focusing back on the woman now conversing with the king.

At his beckoning, the two make for the obnoxiously large dining hall. Sweet scents of roasted meats, crisp wines, and other delicacies float through as two white-gloved servants swing the doors open. A low grumble releases from my stomach. Fuck, of course I forgot to eat before leaving the suite. Randi's eating habits are rubbing off on me, it seems.

Shit, that means she didn't eat either.

Not that any of us have had time to today. Air Force One touched down before the sun was up this morning. Immediately we raced to the king's palace, where Randi was ushered into several grueling hours of closed-door meetings. Hell, Randi barely had time to change into that red Carolina Herrera gown before rushing through the long stone hallways to not be late for her own welcoming banquet.

At least our stay is a short one. For optimum security, Tank decided the visit would be in and out, leaving less time here for something to happen.

Too bad, really. I'd love to check out the pool.

Inside the banquet room, everyone finds a seat in one of the twenty chairs lining the long table. Servers rush through the service doors, each balancing platters of varying foods or trays holding long-stemmed glasses with bubbling liquid. Around the room, the king's security line the walls with US agents scattered throughout.

I don't search for T or any of the other guys. I already know where each are stationed and what their main focus is from the detailed rundown Tank made us cover four times on the flight here.

The clatter of silverware echoes around the open room while soft murmuring and boisterous laughter carry through, bouncing off the gilded walls. The device at my wrist vibrates, signaling the half hour mark.

Only four more hours before we can tuck her safely back into her suite.

Fuck, this will be a long damn night.

I wince as the leather harness slides over my shoulders, the muscles protesting the small movement from being tense for the past five hours. After securing both of my sidearms in the provided safe, I perch on the end of the bed to toe off one shoe and then the other. The clatter of the second shoe hitting the stone floor is muffled by a pounding knock. Before I can call out to whoever is on the other side, Tank shoulders through the door and steps inside the small room.

"I need you to do something for me," he says, exhaustion and worry evident on his tight face and tired eyes. We all are. Even though Saudi Arabia is our ally, we're still in the middle of a potential war zone. Even without that threat, there are several insurgent groups excited for a chance to harm Randi, which would send the US into a tailspin. Plus, we still haven't identified Whit's plan to follow through on his threats since Randi didn't choose him as VP. That's a whole other shit pile we're trudging through each day.

"I'm not rubbing your feet," I respond, attempting my normal humor. "Go haze Smith and tell him he has to since he's the new guy."

"I don't like her being in that room alone."

"Agreed." Even with two agents stationed outside her suite's door, I don't like it. There's more than one way to get into that room, even if the other is a good three-story climb to her balcony. "What are you suggesting?"

"You, in there with her, tonight."

The skin along my forehead creases as both my brows rise. "That will look a little suspicious, won't it?"

Tank reaches up to run a hand over his shaved head. "It will, but I'd rather people talk, not having any evidence of foul play, than her be in there alone and vulnerable. Without a female on our team, we're up shit creek in situations like this."

Weak, tired, and fucking cranky as hell from the near twenty-four-hour shift, I gaze back at my bed longingly.

"I'm not asking you to stand guard all night," Tank clarifies, no doubt seeing that I'm just as exhausted as he is. "I'm only asking you to stay in the room with her overnight and get the hell out before anyone wakes up tomorrow morning."

I huff and shake my head, a few dark locks falling across my forehead. I swipe them out of my eyes and focus on the floor. "I'm fucking sick of sneaking around." Annoyance at the whole situation and why we have to still hide our relationship simmers in my gut. "Why does her personal life matter? Why would anyone care if she was caught screwing an agent?" I yank a sock off my foot and hurl it into the corner.

"You know why, Playboy. Especially now, with your family name plastered all over every paper in this city, you two together would be damn near Christmas Day for the media. Those bloodsuckers are looking for anything to help with their smear campaign against our girl. And before, when she was VP, your relationship with her was frowned upon, but now she's under a damn microscope. Don't go adding that stress to her plate because *you're* tired of the secrets. Don't ask her to make your relationship public because that's what *you* want."

Without any better comeback, I throw my other dirty sock at his face, aiming right between his eyes. The bastard bats it away. With a grumble, I press off the bed. The cold stone floor seeps through my bare feet, calming some of the ache my shoes caused.

"Can I at least walk through the bedroom door, or do I need to sneak through the window?"

"I stationed Smith and Champ outside her door, since they both know about you two after that dumbass stunt you pulled in the Oval Office the other day in front of Smith. I asked both to hang around until you came by, and then I'll switch them out with two beta team members."

Lifting my arms up high, I stretch until the edges of my dress shirt slip out from the confines of my pants. "He seemed on point tonight."

Tank follows me as I move into the bathroom. "There's something about him that's off, but he's damn good at keeping her safe, and that's all we can ask for."

"You think there's a hidden agenda to why the director put him on our team?" I ask around the toothbrush in my mouth.

A slow nod is my only answer, leaving more questions in its wake.

"I'm still trying to figure that part out." Shoulder digging into the door-frame, he remains silent until I'm done brushing my teeth. "Sleep with one eye open tonight. If you sleep at all, that is."

Hand towel pressed to my face, I finish wiping the remaining toothpaste off my lips. "You think they're planning something?" Nerves take flight in my gut, hastening my steps as I slip on a fresh pair of socks and a new pair of shoes.

"Just a gut feeling, nothing confirmed. Hell, there isn't even any chatter."

Lips pressed into a thin line, I walk behind him to the door. Halfway down the hall, I cover a wide yawn with a fist to my lips. "As much as that woman turns me on, the thought of sleep is more appealing than anything else. Is it just me, because of my relationship with her, or is this ten times more stressful than our old gig protecting the VP?"

"Twenty times from my perspective. So much more goes into each step she takes and the various angles and supplies and transportation. If it weren't for her, I'd say screw this and step back to our old detail. But it is her, and I'd be more stressed wondering if she's protected and safe if I weren't the one in charge."

I grunt in acknowledgment.

At a door matching my own room's, Tank pauses and grips the handle. "Radio me if you need me."

"Sleep with some damn clothes on." I slap his back and continue down the hall. "No one needs to see your fat naked ass racing through the halls if something does happen."

"Yeah, best keep my weapon concealed unless we need me to club someone with it."

My low chuckle rumbles down the hall. Looking over my shoulder, I smile back at my tired friend, who's yet to enter his room. "Hostile takedown by massive dick. That would be a new one."

"One for the books. Keep her safe, Playboy."

Hand in the air, I offer a goodbye wave and start my trek to her suite once again. The halls are silent as I make my way through the maze of walkways and rooms. A few of the king's guards watch me, their gazes monitoring each move I make. I tap two fingers to my brow in a small salute and take a right at a corner, continuing toward my destination.

A cold breeze rushes through an opened window, the sheer curtains framing it floating along, dancing in the shifting air. I walk past only to pause and turn back to the window.

Odd.

Head whipping every direction, I search the empty hallway for the king's ever present guards but can't find a soul. Unease churns my stomach at the randomness of the only open window being along this deserted hall. My shoes clip the stone floor as I pick up my pace to a quick jog.

As her suite door comes into view, I let loose a tight breath at the sight of Smith and Champ outside. Smith's unfaltering gaze zeroes in on me as I continue my hasty approach. After a quick glance over my shoulder, he shoots me a questioning look.

"Open window, seemed odd," I say, pointing behind me.

Something like recognition flashes across his gray eyes. Before I can get another word out, he's shoving open Randi's suite door without warning. I follow hot on his heels, Champ staying outside guarding the hall, and step around his slim frame to take in the entire room.

Eyes wide, Randi bolts up from the low lounge chair in the far corner of the room, blindly setting her laptop aside before it plummets to the floor.

"What's going on?" she asks. Gripping the edges of her thin silk robe, she tugs them together, closing the gap exposing her chest and legs. Possession blazes through my veins, triggering my temper at the hint of what Smith caught a glimpse of. Even though the tight tank top and soft cotton shorts covered most of her even without the robe, the hard peaks of her nipples standing at attention from the chill in the room are for my eyes only, even hidden beneath a layer of clothing.

I motion to Smith, letting him explain, but he seals his lips shut.

After mentally punching him in the balls, I turn back to Randi. "It's nothing, Mess."

"What are you doing here, Trouble? What's going on?"

Slipping both hands into the pockets of my slacks, I hitch my chin in the direction of the room I left behind for this one. "Tank asked me to do him a favor."

"And what was that favor? To race into my room and scare the shit out of me?" A single dark brow lifts higher on her forehead.

"Nope. To stay the night, with you, in this room."

"Together?"

"Together."

Her sharp snort fills the room. I can't help but smile even though I'm dead on my feet. Randi's loose dark hair shifts along the silk robe with the shake her head. "I'm not buying it, Trouble. Like T would allow you to stay in here with so many curious eyes around us."

Hitching my chin toward the door, I point an elbow in the same direction. "I've got it from here. You're good to go, Smith. Radio Tank and let him know I'm in place and to send the beta team agents to relieve you."

"I don't like it," he states, his eyes scanning every corner of the room.

I glide my fingers through the soft strands of my hair. "Don't like what?" I don't cover the exhaustion in my gritty tone.

"What you said with the open window. It doesn't make any sense why it would be when all the others in the place are sealed tight." Randi and I share a surprised look. Smith said a whole sentence. Two, in fact, back to back. That's the most he's spoken since he was forced on the team.

"Maybe one of the guards got hot," Randi suggests. She wraps her arms across her chest and chafes her hands up and down her biceps.

"No, those guards wouldn't leave their king or our president vulnerable by leaving such a gaping hole in our defenses. An open window offers anyone waiting a way inside undetected."

"And how would you know what to look for?" Randi asks, pitching forward an inch, completely engrossed in Smith's words. Hell, I am too.

He shoots a condescending expression across the room at her before going back to examining the area with his laser focus.

"Let's secure the room," I offer, ready to get it cleared and myself in the massive bed that looks like absolute heaven. It's not that I don't buy his assessment, but we have too many agents and twice as many guards protecting Randi and the king. Unless someone knew our weaknesses or plans, there's no way someone would get close enough to do either harm. "Then you go get some rest. You're no good to her or us exhausted. That publicity breakfast first thing in the morning is a security nightmare with all the press that's invited, so we need everyone on their A game."

An expression I can't read flashes across his face. Eyes narrowed, I take in the agent beside me, trying like hell to figure him out.

"Are you concerned?" Randi asks. She looks to the balcony doors and takes a cautious step toward me.

If I weren't studying him, I would've missed his minuscule nod.

"Because an open window is what you'd look for if you were trying to find a way inside," I say as a statement. "What are you thinking, Smith? Spit it the fuck out. We don't have time for bullshit." His file was so redacted we have no idea which agency he came from, but my gut tells me CIA. Which means we should heed whatever concerns he has.

"It means one of two things. Either it's a signal for something or an access point for someone to gain entrance into the palace. Either option says someone inside this damn place is working with someone on the outside."

My protective instincts flare. In two strides, I'm beside her, gripping Randi's thin waist and locking her to my side. "Secure the fucking room, then radio Tank and tell him we need more agents stationed outside her room than we planned."

Randi's entire body trembles beneath my tight hold as Smith combs the room, checking every nook and cranny with his gun drawn. Taking a knee, he shines a light under the bed for several moments to check the shadows beneath.

"I thought monsters under the bed were a myth," Randi says, her voice high.

Smith stands and shifts across the room to check the reading area she was in when we first arrived. "The monsters I know don't live in the shadows, and they sure as hell don't need you to believe in them to exist. They wait, they watch, and then they strike without you ever aware they were there."

Randi's throat works, her breaths quickening. "The ones I know stalk you out in the open, making you feel trapped, surrounded." She sneaks a glance to the open hall door. "Hopeless."

Smith pauses his examination of the room to focus on her before sliding his hard stare to me.

I let out a sigh. The returning callouses on my palm scrape down my face. "The previous president, Birmingham, associated himself with more than a few sketchy characters." His attention hones in, listening to my every word while he continues checking the room. "There was—*is*—one worse than the rest. One who's more sociopath than conniving. Shawn Whit, the previous director of interior. He's always had it out for Randi, going as far as poisoning her even." My grip tightens around her waist. "A few months ago, he propositioned Randi with something she wanted to force her hand—"

"Not something," she hisses, maneuvering out of my tight hold. Swiveling on her bare feet, Randi turns her full focus to Smith, who's checking behind the curtains and thick tapestries draped along the windows and patio doors. "The location of my daughter, Taeler." Smith's hands pause, his attention now solely on her. "She was abducted while in France, and the bastard knew where she was and who was holding her."

Stretching between us, I lace my fingers with hers and lift her hand to kiss the inside of her palm. "For the location of her daughter in Paris, Randi was forced to agree to Shawn's demand. Then when it came time to follow through on that promise, she went another direction."

Those thin, burdened shoulders round. "I couldn't put a man like him in the vice president seat. I know what I did—or didn't do, rather—put a larger target on me, but I couldn't do that to the American people. He's a fucking sociopath, not an arrogant asshat like every other politician in DC. I stand by my decision. There's no doubt he'll get his payback one way or another, but when, who the hell knows. The waiting for him to strike has all of us on edge even more than normal."

"Why not kill him first?"

Both Randi and I snap our heads to Smith, who's paused his search, placing his full focus on us.

"Um, because that would be wrong," Randi says with a shaky laugh around the nail between her teeth. "I can't cross that line. I couldn't want someone killed because I didn't like them or because they want to harm me. No, we wait and catch him in the act and let the justice system handle it, like we did with Kyle. Not that it worked. He was still killed, just not by me."

"Randi," I groan, the exhaustion morphing into irritation. Fuck, I need some sleep. "Why do you refuse to believe Birmingham killed himself? Let it go—everyone else has. You have other things to worry about."

"Why do you think he was murdered and not a suicide?" Smith asks.

Randi shrugs, the soft material of her robe swaying with the move. "I knew Kyle. Hated him, but there were some redeemable qualities about the man. One of which was attempting to protect me from Shawn's devious plans, and the second, he wanted me to stay far away from the scandal he'd caught himself in. He warned me to stay out of it time and time again. Not that it did any good, but still he tried, and I'd like to say it was for my sake, not his. Kyle was a narcissist and craved power. There's no way he would've taken an out when he held all the cards."

"What cards?" he asks.

Randi seals her lips shut. Her eyes cut to me.

"Right." Releasing her hand, I seal a quick kiss to her forehead. "I'll clear the bathroom. You check the balcony and finish up in the room, Smith. Let's get this done. I'm fucking exhausted."

12

RANDI

One-handed typing is for the birds. It's taken a whole minute of my life to type out a single sentence. Only a few hundred more before this email is finished and ready to be proofread by my admin. It's miserable. My elbow hurts from the strange angle and awkward movement, as well as my wrist and back, and the pain in my neck is causing a low throb to radiate at the base of my skull.

It would be simple to ease my pain, to adjust in the bed to get my work done quicker.

But no way in hell will I.

Tearing my eyes from the glowing laptop screen, I cast a soft look at the man snuggled beside me, his arm wrapped protectively around my waist and my fingers entangled deep in his thick hair. I scrape the acrylic tips across his scalp, ensuring he stays asleep as I finish up work.

A content smile spreads across my lips as I take him in. Asleep, he looks like the boy he acts like most of the time. The fine wrinkles along his eyes are nowhere to be seen, the constant concentrated furrow of his brow relaxed.

Sliding my fingers through the locks one more time, I trace the arc of one dark brow, then the other. My touch lighter than a feather, I brush a fingertip along his scruff-covered jaw and chin. The sharp edges snag the pads of my fingers as I memorize each inch. His lips parted in a peaceful sleep, I fight the urge to close the distance between us and press my own to his.

Those long dark lashes flutter, nearly fanning across his unblemished cheeks. Sleepy honey brown eyes slowly wake. They meet mine only to blink closed once again.

"Mess," he groans, his voice thick with sleep. "What are you doing?"

I huff in full pout mode when he rolls, dragging his radiating body heat with him. Stretching out a long toned arm, he grips his phone from where he left it on the opposite side of the king-size bed and activates the screen. I wince when the time flashes across. He curses and tosses the device back to the bed. "It's four in the damn morning," he complains while scrubbing at his face.

I bite my lip to suppress a growing grin. This isn't the first time we've slept all night together, but I'll never get tired of seeing him like this. Hair rumpled, lids heavy, and lips pouty, he's 100 percent adorable.

"I have one more email to get out, but the progress is slower than normal." I lose the fight with the growing smile. "You're so cute."

"I'm a badass," he grumbles with a fake pout, making his already fuller lower lip stick out even farther.

"A cute badass."

A high-pitched squeak erupts as he attacks. The laptop slides to the side, his ninja-like reflexes catching it before it can crash to the ground. Nose to nose, our matching smirks bloom into wide smiles.

"Your cute badass," he whispers while ghosting a kiss across my lips.

Searching his eyes, I debate asking the question that's been nagging at me since Agent Smith left the room hours ago, then decide to just go for it.

"Do you trust the new guy?"

"What happened?" Trey demands, going from cute and sleepy to protective boyfriend in a flash.

I take the laptop from his outstretched hand and rest it on the floor. Wiggling low, I snuggle down the bed and turn to lie on my side. Tucking both hands between my cheek and the pillow, I wait while he does the same. Head propped in his hand with his elbow pressed into the mattress, Trey gazes down with an expectant expression.

"Nothing happened. He's just hard to read. I can't.... I don't understand him."

Trey's focus shifts over my shoulder like he's processing through my words. "I trust him. He has an edge to him that no one else on this team has. It's a positive addition, especially now that you're president and have three times more enemies and threats than you had as VP." He inhales deeply, swiping his tongue along his lower lip. "But that edge comes with... something. I can't pinpoint it either. Yes, he's closed off, but not in a way where I think it's personal. If that makes sense. It's almost like he's closed off in the way a tiger is caged. It's for the safety of others that it's behind bars."

"He's a tiger?"

"On our team I'm the one with the looks and charm." I snort and shove his shoulder, resulting in his signature cocky smirk pulling at the corner of his lips. Fuck, I love it. I love him. "Tank's the one with the leadership and size. That man could stop a speeding car with his shoulder. The other guys are great at following orders and observation. Smith... he adds a violence to the team. That's what I mean with the caged tiger analogy. I have no doubt if you asked him to take someone out, he'd do it without question, or if you're in danger, the threat would not only be eliminated but they'd never find the body."

I swallow, shifting my gaze from Trey's face to his bare chest. Reaching forward, I trace his collarbone. "Is he unstable?"

"I think we all are. His comment about monsters earlier was curious though. But that kind of statement makes me think he knows what lurks just under his skin. As long as he's in control of it, well, then I'm good with him."

"The CIA director said they would never transfer someone out of the agency willingly. I think what he wasn't saying was no one leaves the CIA still breathing."

Trey smiles. "Not everything you see in the movies is real, Mess."

"I know that," I say, even though my comment was based on the Jason Bourne movies as my reference.

"Right, well, the CIA, especially at that level, they're all dicks. They'd never admit someone wasn't cut out to be an agent and they had to transfer them out. But I don't think Smith flunked out of the CIA, if he even was CIA. He could've been NSA or Homeland Security."

"He seems strung tight," I say as I allow my fingers to slide along the naturally tan skin of his hard abs.

"I wouldn't let him be around you if I thought you were in danger. I don't get that vibe from him."

"He doesn't laugh at my jokes."

Trey's breath hitches, a small groan pushing past his parted lips at the scrape of my fingertips down his happy trail.

"Give him time, Mess. He'll be in love with you in no time, just like the rest of us."

"That doesn't bother you?" I ask, halting my pursuit as I anticipate his answer.

His gaze burns with intensity. "If I thought he was a threat to us, he wouldn't be breathing. What I meant was anyone who spends time with you falls under your spell. Mine just happens to induce lust and vivid pictures of me fucking you every which way."

Tingles erupt in my lower gut. I suck in a shaky breath.

A hot palm wraps around my wrist and tugs it lower down his abdomen. Our gazes stay locked as I trail my nails down his skin until my knuckles graze his hard cock. It twitches in my grasp when I wrap my fingers around him and squeeze. Trey's dark lashes flutter, his eyes barely open as he gazes down at where I'm slowly pumping my hand up and down the silky smooth skin.

His breath hitches; beneath the covers, his hips flex, thrusting himself harder into my hand. Desire blooms through my veins, scattering any thoughts of the email I never finished or the nagging questions I still have about Agent Smith. The soft sheets glide beneath my hip and shoulder as I wiggle down the bed to dip beneath the layers of covers. Darkness envelops me. My desire surges at the heavy scent of Trey's spicy aroma mixed with both our arousals.

A groan rumbles in my throat, matching his as I wrap my lips around the soft head. Flicking my tongue along his slit, I lap up the few drops of desire. Long fingers slip through my loose hair, tightening into a fist. Following his urges, I glide up and down, my lips suctioning around his throbbing cock. The bed shifts and his hips lift, diving deeper down my throat. The grip in my hair holds me steady as he thrusts in and out. Muffled curses make their way down through the blankets, but I don't pay them any attention, too engrossed in my ministrations and the feel of him coming apart because of me.

Suddenly the light of the bedside lamp assaults my eyes, and cold air fans along the bare skin of my legs and arms, causing goosebumps to erupt. The hand at the back of my head releases its hold before hooking beneath my arm and hauling me upward. I glide up the sheets with ease. The room rotates with a single urgent shove to my hips. My nose buries into the pillow as my hips and legs jerk with hard tugs on my sleep pants and panties until they're fully removed.

Rising up, I dig both elbows into the soft mattress and glance over my shoulder. Trey kneels on the bed, stroking his cock, which is still glistening with my saliva, his focus solely on my ass. The tip of my tongue glides along my lower lip, licking up the last tastes of him. He swipes the fingertips of his free hand along my spine. Fevered chills sprout in their wake, and I shudder in response. The bed shakes as I press up to my knees. My spine arches as he trails lower, gliding between my cheeks. A finger hesitates over my tight hole. Instinctively I feel a hot flush spread across my cheeks. Unsure, I shy away from his touch.

"Not tonight," Trey says, his voice a deep rumble through the room. "But one day soon, baby." Every muscle relaxes as he continues the path south before diving deep into my wet center.

My head relaxes forward, the feather pillow a cushion for my forehead. For half a second, I'm empty, the sense of loss like a stone sinking in my gut, before I feel the bed shift beneath his weight and a different pressure against my entrance. I brace myself for him to thrust forward, giving me exactly what I need.

But he doesn't.

My entire body trembles in desperation. I shift back, urging him to hurry the hell up, but am met with a resistance that's not his cock. The soft pillow-case shifts along my forehead as I turn my head. Mouth open, ready to scream at him, I look over my shoulder. The words evaporate in my throat; I still, not daring to even breathe. The desire-driven, sexy-as-hell Trey is long gone. Instead kneeling behind me is concentrating, tense Agent Benson with his full focus directed at the balcony doors.

As graceful as a born predator, he shifts off the bed, his hard gaze never faltering.

"What—" I snap my lips shut at his raised hand. Trepidation takes over, smothering the earlier need. The edge of the sheet folds between my fingers as I tug it upward, covering my naked lower half.

On silent feet, Trey rounds the bed. I track the quick movements, each breath tighter than the previous. Still gloriously naked, Trey yanks one foot and then the other through the legs of his suit pants from where he draped them over the chair before climbing into bed hours ago. Leaving the top clasp dancing open, he swipes the radio and earpiece from the side table.

Time stands still as he fiddles with various knobs and switches. His lips move with a silent curse. The radio is launched through the air, landing on the bed with enough force that I feel the impact. Running a hand through his hair, Trey locks his intense gaze on me.

"Do you have a gun?"

I yank the sheet higher, savoring the false sense of security the thin material offers. "Why would I have a gun?" I whisper back.

"You need a gun."

"I don't know how to use a gun," I whimper.

Even in the faint light, the deep dip of his brows is visible. "You're from Texas. Everyone there knows how to use a gun."

A hysterical giggle bubbles past my lips. I slap a hand to my face. "No gun. No radio. Now what?"

The color drains from his lips as he seals them tightly together and casts a look to the door leading to the hallway.

"Something doesn't feel right," he mumbles more to himself than to me. In a flash, he's on the bed, a hand pressed to the mattress to lean close enough for me to hear his quiet whispers. "I heard something outside. It could be nothing, but I'm not taking any chances. The radio is fucking dead, and I left my guns locked back in my room." His harsh tone and annoyance are no doubt at himself rather than me. "Be as quiet as possible. Grab your phone, and lock yourself in the bathroom."

I snatch his wrist to keep him near before he can stand. "What are you going to do?"

"Go, Randi." With a fast flick of his wrist, he dislodges my hand and steps back to the chair. "Put this on while you're at it." The bulletproof vest that was slung over the chair's armrest sails through the air, landing on the bed beside me.

"What are you going to wear?" My voice rises with my panic.

A loud thump reverberates from the other side of the hall door, followed by another. Trey's expression turns grim. "Fucking go, Randi. I can't handle this without knowing you're somewhere safe."

Okay, yeah, that makes sense. Total sense. Except one minor issue.

I can't fucking move. Nothing wants to obey my desperate pleas to scramble off the bed and race to the safety of the bathroom.

"I said fucking go. Now."

It's not the words or command that sets me into action. It's the fear laced into his harsh rasp. A fear for me and my safety, not his own. Sweat slicks his forehead and shoulders, glistening in the low lamplight. Forcing my arms into action, I snatch the vest and tug it over my tank top before securing the sides. Inch by inch, I work my way off the bed. Cold stone greets my bare feet, biting into my toes as I tiptoe toward the bathroom.

That's when I hear it.

It's barely audible over my thundering heart and pulse pounding in my ears, but it's there. My steps falter, and I suck in a tight breath as I stand frozen halfway between the bed and bathroom.

Trey pauses in the middle of the room, his head on a swivel, turning from the balcony to the hall door and back again. Dread cramps my stomach. I blindly attempt a step back toward the bathroom, but something snags my heel, wrapping around my ankle. I free-fall, the sheet I stupidly caught my foot in floating down with me. A rattling boom shakes the room as my flailing hand smacks the bathroom door, which slams it against the wall with the force of my body weight.

My ass smacks the floor, my lower back and tailbone nearly breaking with the impact. The white sheet settles around me along the floor, covering my bare legs but leaving the rest of my naked lower half exposed. Ignoring the radiating pain coming from my ass and back, I snap my gaze forward in search of Trey.

Shrouded in the shadows cast by the billowing curtains, he lingers at the edge of the balcony door, worry etched across his features as he stares at my awkward position on the floor.

In a classic Randi move, I raise both hands and shoot him two thumbs up.

A small bit of the worry fades from his pinched features as he shakes his head and turns back to the balcony door.

The balcony door that's now slowly easing open.

Trey retreats a step, sealing his back to the wall. Partially covered by the sweeping tapestries, he keeps his focus trained on the shadow of a man moving into my suite.

I gasp, both hands grappling with the sheet, trying to untangle it from my legs in a desperate attempt to cover myself. Even with the darkened room, the man's unnerving smile is crystal clear. With another step, he moves deeper into the suite. He slides something from around his neck, tugging it over his mouth as the glow of the side table light highlights his features.

A gun dangles from his right hand. Each step brings him closer, yet I can't move, can only stare wide-eyed, fully entranced by the damn gun. A full-body tremor rattles my shoulders as a sinister chill settles into my bones.

Sarah's training vanishes, wiped clear by the undiluted fear coursing through my veins.

Black gloves cover the intruder's hands, with dark clothing hiding the rest of his body. Not a single patch of skin shows. A black scarf encases his lower jaw, covering everything from his neck up to his eyes before wrapping around his head, concealing that too.

A subtle movement behind him reminds me I'm not alone. Trey is here, and nothing and no one will harm me while he's on watch.

"What do you want?" I ask, forcing every ounce of strength I can muster into my voice to keep it from shaking.

The man hesitates, tilting his head like he's considering me. "You."

"Why?" My voice trembles. A million thoughts pepper through, but one snags. His response was one word, but even with that simple word, one thing is clear—American.

"You know why."

Hope bubbles as the silence stretches. If he'll talk, maybe I can gain some information before Trey attacks. Fuck knows we need any help we can get, even if it's off this fucker. Who sent him, for starters. The list is growing on who I could guess, with Shawn Whit at the very top.

The hand holding the gun twitches. Slowly it rises in the air, the barrel aimed at my forehead. All hope drains, leaving devastating emptiness.

The shadow in the corner moves. A silent scream lodges in my throat. Forgetting about my white-knuckled grip on the sheet and why I'm holding on to it, I slap both hands over my gaping mouth as Trey lunges form the shadows, hands outstretched for the gun. The explosion of the gun rattles in my eardrums. Terror taking over, I curl into a small ball, the vest poking me in the ribs as I try to make myself as small as possible.

The corners of my vision darken with the lack of oxygen even though my chest heaves in desperate attempts to fill my lungs.

Eyes wide, I peer through the strands of hair strewn across my face as

Trey struggles with the intruder, attempting to overpower him. The men fight over the gun, holding it high over their heads as both grapple for control. The floor rattles under them as they fight, punching and snarling as they stomp around the room.

Trey hooks a leg around the other man's, sending them both tumbling to the floor. I watch unmoving as the gun clatters to the floor and slides across the stone tile before pausing just a few feet in front of me. With the weapon forgotten, the two men wrestle along the ground, their bodies flipping and rolling trying to gain the upper hand.

The suction of my hands against my ears pops as I move them down to my cheeks. Dampness coats my palms as I place one to the floor and then the other, heaving myself up to all fours. Bare ass in the air, I shift forward an inch on trembling arms. Almost there, my right elbow gives out, sending me face-first to the unforgiving ground. Pain radiates from the cheekbone that takes the brunt of the fall.

Where the hell are the agents stationed outside my door?

As soon as the thought slides through my mind, dread and fear grip me all over again. Those thumps earlier, the noise I couldn't identify.... Bile rises up my throat, burning as I swallow to keep from gagging.

A sharp agony-filled cry rips through the room.

My head snaps toward the center, searching for the fight. The sight of Trey's arm wrapped around the man's neck should ease some of my worry, but it doesn't in the slightest.

My eyes widen at the man's face. The white, American-looking face now uncovered from the struggle. Shock settles in, making me almost numb. He was here to kill me. To kill *me.*

"Why?" I whisper. "Why?" The second time the word is more of a shriek. "Why would you do this?"

The man seals his lips tightly together, his features masked, cutting off all emotion.

"Randi."

My gaze locks with the man's cold eyes. A determination lingers there, even as his face reddens from Trey's arm cutting off his much-needed oxygen.

"Randi."

Slowly I trail my gaze to the sound of that voice. A million different emotions seem to swirl behind Trey's eyes. A wince tightens his features as the man he's restraining bucks beneath his hold.

"Get in the bathroom." Trey's light eyes flick down, no doubt noticing I'm mostly naked. "Pants first."

I know he said words. Important words. Commanding words. Yet I can't get my muscles to respond. I shift my gaze back to my attacker. The long black gun lying innocently on the floor. I've seen enough movies to know it's some kind of handgun with a silencer on the end.

Movement on the other side of the room catches my eye. I tilt to the left to see around Trey and nearly fall to the floor, catching myself at the last second at the new shadow creeping in, this time from the direction of the hall door. With Trey's back to the new intruder, he's completely unaware of the threat.

Another shadow shifts along the balcony doors.

Shit. Two more?

My dry lips part to scream a warning, but no words come out, only a short high-pitched squeak. The gun lying on the floor is my only hope.

I know what I have to do.

Acrylic nails dig into the hard floor as I lunge the remaining distance. My teeth rattle as my chest slams onto the floor, my hand fumbling with the gun instead of softening my fall. Not nearly as smooth as in the movies, I flop to my side, the gun unsteady in my sweaty palm, and point the barrel toward the looming figure.

Shock and understanding wash over Trey's features. Acting faster than any human should, he drops to the floor.

Sealing my eyes shut, I aim in the direction of the intruder striding from the balcony and tug on the trigger. With one breath, the world stills. Everything is silent, and then there's chaos. The gun clutched between my trembling hands fires with a simple flick of a finger against the trigger. The force of the kickback is so unexpected and strong it pops from my clammy hands. I can't track the movement as the gun launches into the air. Somehow midair, another round fires. And another before dropping to the stone floor.

I gape at the weapon, unable to look away. Muffled male voices followed by shouts drag my unfocused gaze to the middle of the room.

Trey pushes up from his crouch as fast as a whip, turning to face the other two men now coming closer to where he stands over a body.

A body with a river of deep red flowing from beneath him, tracing its way through the thin grout lines of the floor.

Holy fuck.

I shot a gun. I shot *someone.*

And I'm pretty sure he's dead.

13

RANDI

A flurry of movement ensues all around the room, but I stay frozen in place on the floor, gaping at the man I murdered. A light and silky cover drapes over my still exposed lap before gravity vanishes and I'm hoisted into the air. Every muscle seems at the verge of snapping, the tension locking them in place making them stiff as boards. I stay rigid in the bridal-style hold, unable to relax into the strong arms carrying me.

Soft, comforting whispers are muttered into my disheveled hair as we make our way the few feet to the bathroom, the room that was supposed to be my sanctuary all along. The double doors slam closed, and then we're moving again. I barely take notice when I'm lowered and sat on the edge of the large sunken tub. The arm around my waist flexes, holding me in place as a bare chest leans over me. The scent of jasmine and honey wafts through the room as the pounding of water fills the tub behind me.

With two hands on my hips, he crouches down, meeting my gaze. Concern swirls behind Trey's light brown eyes as he scans my face.

"You're all right, Mess." One hand slides up my bare arm, fingertips skimming along my neck before a palm cradles my cheek. His usual warmth seeps into my skin, his scent filling my lungs, slowly loosening the hold shock has on my body. "I've got you. No one will hurt you. Not now, not ever."

"I shot him," I whisper, terrified to admit those words.

What does this even mean? Will I go on trial? Would they put the president in jail for murder? It was in self-defense. They were attacking me and Trey in my suite....

Oh hell. I'm 100 percent fucked. I'm in another damn country, not in the US. I have zero rights here. I could be put in a Saudi prison. Forced into slave labor to pay off my crimes.

Each scenario is worse than the previous until my heart nearly races out of my chest. My fingers wrap around Trey's muscular shoulders and tighten, digging my chipped and jagged nails into his perfect skin.

"I don't want to be a part of a chain gang," I squeak, my eyes searching his.

Fine laugh lines crinkle around the corners of his eyes as they alight with humor. His lips fight the smirk desperate to make an appearance.

"I could be imprisoned, you ass. This isn't funny." My voice's high pitch gives away my increasing panic.

"Mess, baby," he says on a snicker. A fucking snicker. I'm about to wear orange for ten to twelve years and he fucking snickers. "You didn't shoot anyone."

Oh hell. Poor guy. He must have hit his head.

"Trouble, baby, that man out there is dead because of me." I scan his forehead as I weave my fingers through his thick, sweaty hair, searching for the laceration or bump. "Did that guy hit you in the head? I think you need a doctor. You're not remembering things."

Now that I really take in his overall appearance, he actually might need medical attention for other issues besides the hit to the noggin. A dried trickle of blood lines his chin and continues to seep from a split lip. Splotches of bright red dot his right cheekbone, the surrounding area swelling and puffing around his eye.

Trey teeters on the balls of his feet to lean in close. I feel his smile as he presses a chaste kiss to my temple.

"You did shoot *something*, but not that guy, or the other one, thank the fuck." While he talks, the tearing of dislodging Velcro assaults my ears. With a quick tug, he pulls the vest over my head, followed by my damp tank top that seems to have adhered to my sweat-slick skin.

"Trey," I complain, giving his shoulders a small shake. "You were there. You saw it all happen."

He just shakes his head, a few damp locks of hair falling across his forehead and sticking to his temple. Carefully he helps me stand, allowing the sheet that was draped around my naked lower half to puddle to the floor. The corded muscles of his biceps flex, his pecs tensing as he hauls me high into the air like I weigh nothing.

I latch on to his forearms, my fingers barely able to wrap around the flexing muscles. Hot water engulfs the tips of my toes as he slowly lowers me into the tub filled with steaming water. Submerged up to my neck, I lean back into the milky water, his hand on my back guiding me until I'm comfortable with my head resting on the edge.

"Why are you so calm?" I ask. The water's warmth and whatever product he added works voodoo magic, relaxing the tension from my shoulders and back. "Someone broke into my suite." My brows furrow as the gravity of what happened—or what would've happened—tonight hits. I sit up straight, water lapping along the edges, some escaping over the rim. Streams of bathwater glide over my shoulders and down my back. "If you wouldn't have been.... If I'd been alone...." I can't get the next words out; they stay lodged in my throat.

"Hush, baby." Sheer agony drips from those two words.

"They would've killed me." Tears leak from the corners of my eyes. "Why would they...?"

With a frustrated growl, he shoves off the tub to stand, stripping out of his still partially undone pants as he does. Even the sight of his naked body as he steps into the tub can't pull my internal thoughts from the morning's events. Water laps around me as Trey slides his long lean body into the water, tucking himself behind me.

Both arms circle my stomach, sealing my back to his front. "Just relax, baby." His lips and breath brush along the delicate skin of my neck. "I've got you."

"But don't you—"

"They'll take care of it. I'm here to take care of you." As soon as the words are out of his mouth, a pounding knock vibrates the bathroom door. A very angry T bellows from the other side. Trey's chest rises and falls with a heavy sigh. "If you come in, keep your eyes closed," he shouts.

An uncomfortable laugh bubbles from my chest as T storms into the room, a hand sealed over his eyes in a childlike way. He turns, slamming the door shut with both hands.

"Are you okay?" T asks, still facing the door, his voice tight.

"We both are—" Trey starts, but I cut him off, knowing he won't admit to his injuries.

"Trouble is a little banged up. I think he hit his head," I add.

The arm around my waist tightens.

"Do you need a doctor?" Yep, that's worry lacing that deep rumble.

"No, I'm fine. She's good too. In shock but no injuries."

"Why the hell did you bring her in here?" T's shoulders twitch like he's desperate to turn and face us. "There's a dead fucker out there, and they—"

"She was in shock, Davis." *Oh, pulling out the first name. This is serious.* "There are a dozen agents in that room right now, along with the king's security. I had to get her away from it all. Don't fucking judge me on how I'm taking care of my girlfriend."

"Not your girlfriend right now, you idiot. The motherfucking president." I jerk in the water, curling tighter into Trey's arms at the crunch of wood beneath T's fist. A wide fissure opens in the door.

"Fucking cut it out, Tank. You're scaring her," Trey hisses. "There is no fucking protocol for any of this," he yells. "I'm doing the best I can." Water trickles as he raises a hand from the water and glides it from the crown of my head to the wet tips of my hair. "I'm not doing so great either."

"I can't do this, can't talk to a damn door. Both of you get the hell out of that damn tub and get a robe on her now," Tank bellows. "I'm turning around in twenty seconds no matter what. It's up to you if I see you both butt-ass naked. Your choice."

With an annoyed grunt, Trey slips from behind me and exits the tub. After grabbing two towels off the shelf where several others are neatly stacked, he dives both hands beneath the water and scoops me out. My reaching fingers are ignored; instead, he stretches out the towel and wraps it around my chest himself, securing the end between my breasts.

With a satisfied nod, he flicks a glare to his friend's back. "She's covered," Trey snaps.

Worry eats at me. I've never heard them talk like this to one another.

Tank whirls around and steps to the middle of the large bathroom. His gaze scans me first, then Trey as he finishes drying off. Only once he's given us the once-over, several times, do his shoulders relax. He scrubs a hand over his exhausted-looking face.

"Tell me what happened. Every detail."

Trey dives in, recounting the past hour, even down to the detail of what we were doing when he first heard the noise. I feel my skin heat with embarrassment. With my muscles weak as noodles, I perch on the edge of the tub to keep from falling over. That's just what I need right now, another smack to the face. Remembering the earlier fall, I brush the pads of two fingers over my right cheekbone and wince.

"She's hurt," Tank bites out.

"I fell on my face," I say on a hysterical laugh. I cover my mouth as another chuckle bubbles up. "When I was reaching for the gun." I cackle. "Me, with a gun. Bang, bang."

Oh hell, there is something really wrong with me.

"Why did you give her a gun?" Tank chastises.

"I didn't. I was getting to that part before Mess here fell over the edge of sanity. I fought that bastard for the gun. It got loose. I'd like to point out, again, that I instructed her to get to the bathroom and seal herself in, but she didn't."

All humor dies as T sweeps his angry gaze toward me.

"I didn't do it on purpose. I fell, my feet tangled in the sheet, and then I couldn't move. Sorry, this was my first assassination attempt. I'll do better next time."

Both men growl their discontent.

"I had him in a choke hold. He was subdued. That's when Barney Fife here grabbed the gun and aimed it toward us."

"There was another man coming through the balcony doors," I cry, jabbing a finger in the direction of the bedroom. "I was protecting you, and I saved your life, you ungrateful ass."

Trey holds up both hands palms out. "Baby, you almost shot another agent."

Everything silences. The stomping of heavy feet, loud masculine voices, and arguing shouts pour through the cracks in the door.

"Huh?" It's not the smartest thing to say next, but well, after tonight, I'm truly at a loss for words.

Trey relaxes a bit, lowering his hands to hook both thumbs on the edge of the towel secured around his hips.

"Somehow one of the beta agents got around to the balcony. That's who you saw and who you tried to shoot."

"There was another—"

"Another agent came in after hearing the commotion in the suite." He chews on his lip like he's debating telling me more.

"But that first guy, the one who you fought with. I killed—"

"One of the agents shot him after I'd dropped to the ground. The only thing you shot, Mess, was your bed."

Relief and embarrassment wash over me, relaxing some of the tightness in my chest.

"The bed was—"

"Nowhere near either of us, yeah, I know. It's safe to say we need to work on your aim."

"The agents outside her door—" T starts.

Trey launches a folded towel at his friend cutting him off, causing the towel to loosen a bit and slide lower, showing off more of that sexy V of muscles. "Not now." His gaze searches the tile like it holds all the answers for tonight's shit show before snapping to T. "Those balcony doors were locked. Smith checked them. That means—"

"Either he made a mistake or..." T trails off.

"He had a key," we all say in unison.

DON'T GET ME WRONG. Air Force Two was great—way better than flying commercial—but Air Force One is immeasurable to any other experience I've ever had. Everything has a use, yet it's comfortable and classy as hell.

For some reason, things are more relaxed here. Like now, the office door is wide open, allowing me to watch the agents and other personnel as they walk by. It's nice. Maybe it's the fact that we're high above all the issues plaguing our country and threats against me that make everyone seem more relaxed. Whatever the difference is in this small flying city, I wish I had this more casual feel at the White House too.

Across the small office, my two boys nap side by side on the leather couch. Trey's head rests on T's wide shoulder, and T's head is tipped all the way back, mouth open slightly, snoring. It's too adorable of a moment to not capture and maybe use as blackmail at a later date. Snagging my cell from the desk, I swipe open the screen and take several shots. Grinning at the set of pictures, I pull up Sarah's number and forward them all to her with a heart emoji.

I miss that woman desperately. Yes, the workouts were great, but it was nice having a female friend I could count on, someone I trusted with my secrets and knew she'd go to the grave with them.

As I type out my "I miss you" text to Sarah, the weight of someone's stare draws my attention from the screen to the doorway now filled with Agent Smith.

"Monster?" I say, my tone questioning as I test the nickname. "How about that as a nickname going forward?"

His nose scrunches in an uncharacteristic response from the normally bland man.

"Agreed, not good. Okay, I'll keep brainstorming." Careful to not wake my two friends, I drop the phone to my lap and lean back in the chair. Swiveling an inch one way and then the other, I purse my lips and hike both brows high in an expectant expression. "Did you need something, Agent Smith, or just wanted to chitchat?"

There's half a second of hesitation before he nods and steps deeper into the room. Hands clasped behind his back, he widens his stance. I give him a calculating once-over, taking in his "at ease" type stance.

"SEALs," I state. One of these times I'll be right, damnit.

"The door was locked." I shift in the chair to see around him to the door at his back. "The balcony doors, ma'am," he clarifies.

"Oh, right." I knew that. Clearing my throat, I twist the pen on the desk until it spins on its own. "I'm inclined to believe you, Cold One." He shakes his head in what seems like exasperation at my nickname game. "You're right, that one doesn't work either. You're a tough one."

"The doors, ma'am."

"Please drop the 'ma'am' bit."

"No."

"Fine, Monster it is, then."

His lip arches in a snarl as a growl rumbles through his chest. "Fine."

I beam at the small victory. "As I said, I believe you." The unspoken "but" hangs between us.

"I was unavailable."

Therein lies the reason for the suspicion now shadowing the agent. It wasn't until hours after the incident that they were able to locate Agent Smith. Not a trace of where he was during the altercation, and he still hasn't presented T with an explanation for his disappearing act.

"I was off duty, ma—" I cut a no-nonsense glare his way. "Randi." The word rasps from his throat like it was painful to speak. "I was preoccupied and unaware of the situation."

"You're defending yourself like a guilty man," I muse, going back to twisting in the chair as I consider him.

"I am not." He stops himself from saying more and inhales deep. A quick flash of pain breaks his normally stone features with a grimace before he settles his face back to looking bored with the conversation.

"Are you okay?" Both palms seal to the top of the desk as I make to stand.

"Fine." Narrowing my eyes, I scan his chest, searching for what could be ailing him enough for him to wince like that with a simple breath. "Randi," he snaps, breaking my attention from my visual inspection.

The two on the couch jolt awake at Agent Smith's loud voice. Trey sits up and blinks several times as he squints from me to Agent Smith and back again.

"What's going on?" Tank asks, sleep clogging his throat and making the words more of a croak. They have to be exhausted. All the guys, for that matter. It was a long night for everyone. Hell, I haven't even slept yet.

As if the thought triggers the reminder of my lack of sleep to my body, I yawn wide, my jaw popping as it stretches to its max behind my palm.

Three sets of eyes narrow at the action.

"You need to sleep." Trey grunts, standing and approaching the desk like he intends to take me to the bed whether I'm willing or not. "Have you even eaten?"

"Yes," I snip.

"A donut."

I shoot a glare at Agent Smith for his less than helpful detail on said breakfast.

"And orange juice," I add like it made the sugary breakfast a bit healthier. "I thought about eating more, so there's that."

"Thinking about it and doing it are very different things," Tank admonishes.

"Will you three busy bees just get out of my office?" Falling into the chair, I yank my glasses off and toss them to the desk to massage my nose where the plastic was digging in. I've gotten so used to contacts that wearing glasses is a pain in the ass—or head, if you want to get literal.

The contacts were a requirement of Kyle's when we first hit the campaign trail, and now they're just easier.

Kyle.

Those years at Harvard and the more recent ones with us despising each other, all the hateful words and actions between us, causes guilt to build within me. Pressing a hand to my belly, I attempt to ease the gnawing sensation those memories conjure.

"What's wrong?"

Hold the phone. Is that concern in Agent Smith's tone. Surely not. I must be hearing things.

"I'll never get to apologize," I say, closing my eyes. "To Kyle. Yes, he was awful, terrible to me more times than not, but still there's something about that door being closed."

"What door?" Trey asks.

"Resolution. Closure on that destructive relationship."

"You need protein."

My lashes stick together as I fight to open my lids. Blinking away the blur, I gape at Agent Smith. And I'm not the only one. Trey and T both wear dumbfounded expressions.

"Um, okay?" I say, not really knowing what other words to use.

"It's scientifically proven that a proper diet, filled with lean proteins and healthy vegetables, helps regulate moods." My confusion shifts to annoyance. "Not moods in the way you're thinking. Moods as in guilt, depression, anxiety, and overall despondent thoughts. It helps fuel the body physically and mentally."

"Isn't that what Jack Daniel's is for?" I smirk. Okay, I can't be frustrated at the guy now that he explained himself. He didn't mean to offend me by hinting that I'm in a piss-poor mood. Even though he's right. "I'll think about it."

"Seriously?" Trey complains. I swivel my chair an inch to the right so I can face him. "That's exactly what I just said. You need to eat."

"This isn't a competition, Trouble." Trey rolls his eyes and sits back on the couch while running a hand through his hair. "Plus, he's not just bossing me around—"

"You like me bossy." A playful smirk pulls at his lips, a sexy gleam shining in his eyes as he looks up through dark lashes.

"Do not start that, you two," Tank groans.

"He gave scientific proof." I shrug and sit up enough to tuck a foot beneath my backside. At least I was able to change into different clothes the minute we stepped onto the plane. Nothing beats a baggy set of sweatpants and oversized T-shirt for comfort. "You can't doubt science."

"There are so many flaws in that statement." Tank shakes his head, but the barely covered laughter in his voice warms a piece of my heart.

"But I will concede to the fact that I need to sleep." Stretching my arms high above my head, I work out the tightness from my shoulders. "Being almost assassinated takes a lot out of a girl. That reminds me, I need to thank and apologize to that agent. Who was he? The one I almost shot?"

"Wright, I think. I'd like to know how he got on that balcony," Trey says, arms stretched out along the back of the couch, looking sexy as hell. And if his growing smile means anything, he knows I'm totally checking him out. Which who wouldn't? He's sexy as hell no matter what he's wearing or doing, and we kind of left each other hanging earlier. If a woman could have blue balls, I'd definitely have them.

"Blue ovaries?" I muse.

"I don't even want to fucking know." Tank barks out a laugh.

"What's blue?" Agent Smith questions, casting a curious look between the three of us.

I attempt to chew on one of my broken acrylic tips, my lips spreading wide as I smile around the nail.

"Is he new? I guess they're all new to me since the previous beta team didn't move with you guys."

"We've known most of them for a while, all good guys. There are a few new ones on the team, however." Tank clears his throat like he's just stopped himself short of saying more.

"What," I say. Not a question.

"A few didn't want to stay on the beta team when the presidential seat shifted to you."

I lift my chin in defiance. "Because of my background, or because I don't have a dick?"

Agent Smith coughs into the fist against his lips.

"Does it matter?" Tank responds.

"No, I guess not. Good riddance, then. Their loss, if you ask me. I'm fucking fun." Twirling in the chair, I watch the room slowly spin. "Minus almost shooting one of them. I'll apologize later. Right now I just need a nap." The edge of the desk digs into my palm as I stop my turning. Flipping through the files spread across the top, I stack them and push the pile forward a few inches. "I'm nowhere near caught up, but I'm at a place where I can take a twenty-minute break."

As long as nothing else happens.

Just as I think it, those words barely through my overactive mind, my cell phone vibrates on the desk.

All our eyes fall on the moving phone. A whimpering groan passes my lips as I bang my forehead against the top of the desk. Keeping my forehead sealed to the hard wood, I blindly reach for the still ringing cell phone and pull it to my ear.

"What, Blake?"

"We have a problem."

I lightly pound my forehead against the desk again. "We really have to stop meeting like this." I let out a dry chuckle at my joke, which sourpuss Blake doesn't return. "If this is about the pregnancy thing, it will have to wait—"

"Worse."

"Natural disaster?"

"No—"

"Taeler's sick."

"Madam—"

"I'm dying!" I gasp. "I have had these strange dreams—"

"Randi," he shouts, stopping my rambling. "Fucking hell. It's none of that."

"Why didn't you say so?"

"I'm getting too old for this," Blake grumbles. "It's your ex, Taeler's father."

"What about Ben?" Leaning back, I meet Trey's intense stare.

"He's here."

"He's here," I say on a pushed breath. Fire blasts behind Trey's stare. His hands tighten their grip on the armrest. "As in, in DC sightseeing?" I grimace. It's a false hope, but it's worth a shot.

"No, Randi, he's *here*. In the White House. Waiting for you."

14

———

TREY

A fiery burn scorches through my bare shoulders and back as they stretch and flex with each pull of the oars through the still water. Sweat slicks along both temples, dripping down my jaw before splattering to the boat. The push and pull of the heavy oars over and over provides a soothing cadence as I glide along the water.

Out here, everything makes sense. Nothing matters except for you, the boat, and the water. The oars go in, you pull back, and the boat glides. Every single fucking time. The guaranteed repetitive outcome so unlike my everyday life.

Up ahead, the docks come into view again.

Just like the few other times I've glided past the docks, Tank, Pierce, and several beta agents are all watching. Probably wondering if I'll venture in this time.

Maybe.

It would be a good idea to head in before I cramp up and become stranded out here. But the chaos that will greet me, the issues I'll have to face, prevent me from stopping, offering my body the rest it desperately needs. The moment my foot connects with the worn boards on that dock, every issue I'm able to avoid out here will return like a damn sucker punch to the balls.

With a grunt, I throw my weight into the oars, rowing faster in hopes it'll keep reality away for a few more minutes. But even the trembling muscles and heaving lungs can't keep it at bay for long. Between the even strokes, slivers of the thoughts weighing on my mind slip through.

Dad's upcoming plea hearing.

Near assassination of my girlfriend.

An agent missing during the entire incident.

A world on the edge of war with her as the one to keep the balance.

And, of course, the icing on the shit cake, that motherfucker Ben Hopkins.

My lungs burn, each breath like sharp glass gouging my dry throat. A grunt of pain slips past my cracked lips as both thighs, weaker than normal after sitting on my ass for weeks, spasm in exhaustion. The left oar skims off the top, jerking from my hand and nearly taking me over into the water.

I bellow at the top of my lungs, letting loose the frustration and stress as I slam both oars to the scull, tucking them out of the water. A breeze of my own making whips along my neck and back, cooling not only my skin but my boiling temper too. A slow current drags against the scull, reducing the momentum until slowing to a halt several feet from the dock I've been avoiding.

"You are a dumbass," Tank shouts from the dock.

A genuine smile spreads up my cheeks despite my ragged breathing. Shifting in the custom-fitted seat, I press the side of one hand to my forehead, blocking the rising sun's blinding rays. Pierce stretches along the dock, talking to someone I don't recognize, while Tank leans against a support post, eyes only on me. Large drops of sweat drip over my eyebrows and eyelids, preventing me from making out the other people strolling along the wood planks.

Fighting through the pain, I grip the oars once again to pull toward the dock. A deckhand holds the boat for me to stand the moment I pull alongside. I wince at the tightness already stiffening my muscles. Almost the same time I realize there's no way I'm getting out of this thing without help, a large dark hand dangles in front of my face. Without thinking twice, I smack my hand into his and grip. Tank hauls me up and out with ease.

"Solve all the world's problems out there?" Tank asks once I'm somewhat steady on my feet.

Snagging a club-provided clean towel from the stack closest to us, I swipe it across my sweat-slick face and dripping hair. "Hardly. Who's that?" I ask, nodding toward Pierce and the man he's talking to.

"Hell if I know or care. Not my problem anymore. You went twenty minutes longer out there today and cut several seconds off your time. Want to tell me why?"

"I regret ever suggesting you be the one to help me get back in shape." Unable to continue supporting my own weight, I collapse onto a wooden bench and lean forward. The white terrycloth twists between my rotating hands. "Damn, I'm glad we don't work until tomorrow. I'll be worthless in a few."

"Tell me what's going through that head of yours. This is part of the deal, Playboy. I agreed to help you physically and mentally. Talking this through is part of the latter."

The soft threads of the towel push against my closed lids as I rest my head in my hands.

"It's nothing. It's everything. Hell, I don't know." Something cold presses to my thigh. I peek over the towel to see a glistening water bottle offered by one of the helpers. Nodding in thanks, I twist the cap and chug half the bottle before tightening it back on. "I hesitated." Now my heart thundering against my ribs is for a whole different reason than exertion. I zero my focus on the head of a rusty nail securing a plank to avoid Tank's penetrating scrutiny. "I almost let my relationship with her overpower my training."

"You were shot. It's natural to hesitate after—"

I shake my head, droplets of sweat raining down around the dry wooden bench and over the bare skin of my shoulders. "You don't understand what I'm saying."

"Then speak clearly, dumbass."

My chest rattles with a soft chuckle. "I almost killed him," I whisper, daring a glance at my best friend. "He threatened her, my girl. She was fucking terrified because of him. My arm was around his neck, securing him." I let my vision unfocus as I stare out over the water. "All it would've taken was one twist, one flex, and the man responsible would be dead. A part of me knew I shouldn't because he would be worth more to us alive than dead, and still I wanted to murder the motherfucker. I wanted him to die slowly at my hand."

A board creaks, signaling someone's approach. Shaking out of the memory-filled daze, I lean forward to see the length of the dock. The man

Pierce had been talking to passes without a single glance, his dress shoes clicking as he vanishes down another walkway.

"But you didn't," Tank mutters under his breath. "You knew what needed to be done and fought it."

"Is it bad to admit I want to punch that fucker Ponder for taking my kill?"

Tank's dark eyes meet mine. "I've been meaning to ask you about that. I read your official report on the incident and his." He shifts, crossing both arms over his chest. "It didn't seem like you or the president were in mortal harm, so why did he? Why did he shoot?"

"That's your job to figure out, not mine. What did his report say?"

"That night, he was stationed outside her door along with three other agents. He thought he heard something and went to investigate with another agent. When he got back, the two agents stationed outside her suite were dead, one shot to the head each. Hell, those guys didn't even have time to draw their weapons. He was checking them when he heard Randi and went inside to investigate. The other agent who'd broken off from Ponder investigated the room next door to the president's. That's when he noticed that balcony door ajar. He put two and two together and scaled the wall to gain access to her balcony—"

"Scaled? That was a three-story drop and at least ten feet between the two balconies."

Tank nods, sunlight reflecting off his bald head. "Seems Wright does some shit called bouldering in his off time. That's when he entered, saw you struggling with the guy. Back to Ponder's report. He thought you were injured because you dropped to the floor, heard a gunshot, and that's why he fired."

"Little did he know it was Randi who I was hiding from, and who fired the first shot." The rough scruff along my jaw scrapes my sensitive palms. "We need to teach her how to shoot. Not arm her, obviously, but how to aim at the very least so she can protect herself if necessary."

"Let's hope it's not necessary ever again."

The plastic bottle crinkles in my hand, drawing my attention and triggering a memory of another time her life was in danger. "Not that it would've done much good when she was being poisoned by that fucker Whit." I press the hard edge against my lips and drain the last of the water. "What happened with tying Whit to that dumbass in the motorcade service department? Last I heard, they were trying to find a money trail, but of course, fucking Whit was too damn smart to leave evidence."

"The case went cold, and the fucker is looking at years in prison. He wanted to take a deal but didn't know enough about who hired him to be of any use, so the AG threw the book at him."

I twist the towel around my raw hands until it's almost cutting off circulation to my fingertips.

"You think it was Whit who sent the guy in Saudi Arabia? I've had my suspicions, but then again, Whit would want it to be more personal than an assassin. Unless they were hired to take her and deliver her to them." My stomach knots tighter than the towel around my hand.

"Not sure. Either way, it was a real threat, and many more where that came from. On top of those she's accumulated on her own, there are many who hate this country and would love to kill off the first female president. Hell, any president would do, but she seems like an easy target to them."

"What's your take on Smith?" I launch the empty bottle through the air; it sinks into the recycle bin with a quiet whoosh as it slides down the plastic bag. One of the deckhands notices my raised hand and tosses another. Damn, I love this place. Hopefully the feds unfreeze my accounts by the time the dues are required so I don't have to give it up. "The vanishing act he pulled is concerning, even if he was off duty. You were, the other agents were too, but they sure as hell were there."

Tank scrubs at his bald head and leans back against the wooden railing. It complains under his heavy weight. He glares at the length of wood like it personally offended him. His ire slides to me when I don't restrain my barking laugh.

"Your skinny ass wouldn't know what it's like," he grumbles.

"Um, fucker, I'm lean. Not skinny. Just because people don't mistake me for a fully armored tank doesn't mean I'm skinny." I huff into the water bottle at his returning grin. I've missed this. The back-and-forth, the ease of conversation with my best friend. I was too far gone during my "depression episode," as Tank likes to call it, to realize how badly I need him in my life. I need him and Randi as much as I need air for survival.

"And I don't know what to think about Smith, honestly. He could've been off fucking one of the women hanging around the palace for all we know. I'm more concerned with the fact that either he screwed up or someone had a key to the president's suite."

"Or they could've picked it," I muse. "That initial noise I heard could've been him picking the lock. We didn't test it like the hall door since there was no way inside, or so we thought."

"No more assuming. This is the president of the United fucking States."

"I see what you're doing," I say with a side-eye scowl. "Don't think I don't."

"What?" Zero innocence laces his tone.

"That you keep referring to her as the president so I'll keep the two separated."

"If I don't, then you'll be boyfriend protective, which means volatile and emotional."

A mischievous grin tugs at my cheeks. "You say that like it would be a bad thing."

"If someone came after my Sarah, I'd burn the city down looking for the motherfucker and make him pay. So no, not a bad thing, Playboy. But not something we need to add to our plate of issues right now."

"It kills me that people don't know," I admit. "That no one knows she's mine. Even that jackass squatting in the White House."

"Ah. So there's the rub that's eating at you today. That's where all the extra energy came from. The ex is back in the picture."

"He's *not* back in anything," I say through gritted teeth. "He's exploiting the situation with Taeler, using that as his in to freeload off Randi."

"Hmm."

"Hmm," I mock. "What?"

"Does she feel this way? About Ben freeloading, or does she see it as him being a caring father?"

A dribble of water slips past my lips. Wiping it with the towel, I toss the nasty thing to the laundry bucket. "She never said he was a bad father, just left her when she needed him most. Then let his parents railroad her." My anger simmers. She did everything she could with what she had, and no one gave her a chance. It's why she's doing things right by the people of this country now.

Greed isn't in her vocabulary. Power isn't something she wants. Hell, I wouldn't even say acceptance or likability is something she strives for. Justice, state rights, and helping those who need it most are what drive Randi. And what makes her sexy as hell in my eyes.

"It's been three days since he showed up and posted up next to your girl, and here you are doing shit about it."

"I'm not doing shit about it," I snap. "She asked for some time to handle the media storm that came after the incident in Saudi Arabia and to deal with that fucker, so I'm giving it to her."

"Really?"

"Really what?"

"When have you ever in your life done what you're told to do?"

My lips part, ready to spew another round of comebacks, but nothing comes. Slumping back against the wooden bench, I rub a hand through my hair.

"Never."

15

RANDI

"I understand your words, Brad, I just don't agree with you," I snap into the receiver at my lips. Thank fuck he can't see the look of absolute disgust and hate on my face right now. Not that I care too much about being diplomatic with this asshat, but I have to play nice or I'll never get this bill pushed through the House.

"The housing bill you're proposing doesn't make sense. Why would we spend half a billion dollars renovating housing that isn't turning a profit?"

The hard plastic slips in my sweaty palm at my tightening grip.

"Those people living in government-provided housing deserve these renovations. Those houses and apartment buildings I listed for renovations are *years* behind in basic code compliance. They're unsafe, and it's time to do something about it."

"It's a drain on society," he shoots back.

Allowing my lids to flutter closed, I inhale deeply to keep from calling in a presidential favor to the CIA and ordering a hit on the moron I'm speaking with. How this asshat weaseled his way into the House majority seat, I'll never know.

"Get it through the House, Brad," I grit out, "or our next conversation will be very different."

Slamming the phone into the cradle, I shove the rolling chair away from the desk and stand to pace along the bay window.

That call was one of many this morning. Every politician in this city wants to make a deal; nothing is cut and dry. They offer support, but only if it will benefit them in the long run. Who knew being president was simply a high-paying sales job with the added stress of running the country.

A faint knock taps on the door.

Without turning, I call out over my shoulder for the person to enter. Even as the door pushes open, I don't turn to see who it is. I already know.

Ben.

Again.

His constant, pestering presence is part of the stress overload problem I'm drowning in. Not that I mind him being here for Taeler or that I'm struggling with feelings toward him. Since he's arrived, Ben has pressed the subject of us every chance he's had me alone. For me, the chance of us getting back together closed in my mind, and heart, a very long time ago. At first it was annoying how he's using Taeler's pregnancy as a reason to be here, but now I'm fed up with the sideshow and ready for him to leave. Which he shows no signs of doing any time soon.

I'm in desperate need of silence. Peace. Even if for a measly three minutes. Three minutes of nothing, and maybe a cigarette. And Trey, if he can keep his mouth shut. Or busy. Smiling into the bright August sun pouring through the windows, I imagine all the ways I could keep his mouth busy. His lips gliding up my inner thigh, my back pinned to the wall—

"Hey, Rand," Ben calls out behind me, stopping my dirty little daydream.

"What do you need, Ben?" I grumble over my shoulder but keep my focus on the tourists lining the fence along the back lawn. At his silence, I twist at the waist, searching the room for where he meandered. He's standing on the seal in the middle of the room, his blue eyes latching on to mine.

"When did our conversations have to have a purpose?" Dimples dot his cheeks as he offers an impish smile.

"When you showed up unannounced and keep interrupting my workday to talk about the good old days." The phone resting atop the desk shrills. "Listen, I have a call—"

"Yeah, I know you have another important call to make or take. Listen, I stopped by to see if you wanted to have dinner with me tonight."

I freeze. "Dinner."

"Yeah, you do remember what that is, don't you? Two people, real plates, and actual food at a table that's meant for dining on."

A corner of my lips twitches. "Smartass." I don't have anything tonight, but I was also looking forward to doing just that—nothing. "I can't."

"Tomorrow, then?" My lips part, the rejection speech ready, but he cuts me off before a single word can slip out. "Just to talk, about Taeler. We need to have a real conversation about what we're going to do here. It's my grandbaby too in her belly, and I'm not walking away from that."

Red flashes across my vision as heat blasts through my veins with the rolling anger. "Really, Ben, really? You walked away from her when I was pregnant, so why the fuck can't you do that now?"

He tosses both his hands in the air before lacing them behind his head. Features tight, he groans in frustration. "Hell, Rand, that was years ago. I'm a different person now. I helped raise her. My parents stepped in—"

"Don't you dare bring up your parents." My hands tighten into fists. "Not after what they did."

"Did?" He scoffs. "Did as in taking care of the baby you couldn't?"

His honest words cut along the jagged scar etched in my heart, opening the old wound. The familiar agony leaks from the wound, infecting my entire being with self-loathing and inadequacy.

"Did as in railroaded me, took my baby, and treated me like shit for even living." Each word is difficult as war rages in my mind.

"Fuck you're dramatic," he mumbles, but the words carry, making each one crystal clear. "Why can't we have a damn civilized conversation like we used to?"

"Tomorrow night," I relent. "I'll tell Tae to be there too because it's her baby. We won't make any decisions without her. And—"

A quick knock at the door stops my next anger-filled rant. It's swinging open before I can stop the person from entering.

My breath whooshes from my lungs as a tense Blake strides through the room with purpose before stopping in front of the desk.

"If you say we have a problem, I might toss myself onto the letter opener hidden in my desk drawer," I say, my words signaling how weary I am.

Blake seals his lips together and clears his throat. "There was an earthquake in Southern California moments ago."

My spine straightens as a shot of renewed energy flashes through me. "How bad?"

"Bad."

It takes two long strides to reach my desk and slide into the chair. Snagging a pen, I jot down notes as he continues to detail the destruction.

"One hundred casualties is the preliminary number," he says, now beside me, eyes on the iPad glued to his hands. "The governor is calling in—"

"The governor is on line one," my secretary calls from her desk outside the still open door.

"Thank you," I yell back while watching the red blinking light on the massive multiline phone.

"He'll issue a state of emergency momentarily and will seek federal funds." His fingers fly over the screen. "I've asked several analysts and experts to email you initial estimates for the cost of recovery and rebuilding. You can't make the decision alone with how much federal funding they'll be offered. Listen to him, get their inside details, but do not promise anything until we know what we can get approved."

"Listen," I whisper to myself. "No promises. Got it."

"Be empathetic but not sympathetic. No emotions, just obtain numbers and the details of his plan going forward to help those affected."

"No emotion." Nodding, I angle my head toward the door. "Ben, we'll talk tomorrow night. Blake, give me the room and please ask Janet to cancel my meeting with the deputy director of defense. Tell him I'll reschedule for tomorrow." I grimace. "Well I'll try to fit him in anywhere I can."

Both men exit the room, leaving me alone with the still ringing phone. Stealing my spine, I sit up straight and roll my shoulders back.

Time to get to work.

"BEETHOVEN," I plead the moment the office door slams shut behind me. "Please tell me someone here has a cigarette I can bum."

A few stifled amused coughs from the agents surrounding me pulse down the hall from where we stand outside the Oval Office. The desks in the neighboring offices and bullpens are empty, lights off except a soft yellow glow from the two desks stationed in the small adjoining room. Normally everyone stays until I'm done for the day, but today was hell for us all, so I sent them home a few hours ago.

"It's Braxton," the agent says.

Ah, that's right. Knew it was something unique.

An agent shifts in my periphery, one I somewhat recognize. Coarse, thin carpet grinds beneath the balls of my bare feet as I twist to face the approaching man.

"Agent Wright," I greet as I accept the cigarette tucked between the two fingers of his extended hand. "I've been meaning to talk to you, but things have been...."

"It's okay, ma'am. You're the President." Our fingers graze, and his hand snaps back to his side, a flash of annoyance clouding his features.

"It's no excuse." Waving the unlit cigarette, I motion for everyone to follow me. "There isn't an easy way to say this, so I'll just say it. I'm sorry for almost shooting you." I grimace as we take a sharp corner, heading for the stairs.

"I saw your aim. I was in no danger of being shot." I silently mouth his words, mocking him, highly annoyed that everyone now knows I can't shoot worth shit. "But apology accepted."

We continue to march in unison down hallway after hallway toward the kitchen. At least they know I won't try to trash up the place by lighting up on the front lawn. My nude Prada heels dangle from one hand as I fiddle the cancer stick between two fingers of the other.

"Can I ask something?" an agent from the very back of the entourage asks.

"Ponder," Bert says. *Wait, it is Bert, right?* "I said no."

"He can ask. We're all friends here, right?"

The stark silence is the answer to that question. Fine. I didn't want them as friends anyway. I have enough friends—said no one ever.

"What's your question, Ponder?"

"Why was he in your room that night?"

At the kitchen door, I slow my steps before pausing and turn to face him.

Head tilted to the side, I narrow my gaze at Agent Ponder. "How the hell would I know why he was in my room? You think I invited him to, what, play fucking Scrabble?"

The four agents wear the same confused expression before snapping back to attention, their only focus on something, or someone, behind me. Shoulders tense, hands at the ready, but none of the four make a move for the guns at their sides.

A spicy citrus scent envelops my senses. Wearing a wide smile, I spin to face Trey. Kitchen door open, he leans against the doorframe, having appeared out of nowhere.

"I think Ponder means me, Madam President," Trey says. All warmth falls from his features as he shifts to survey the agents at my back. "To answer your question, Agent Ponder, it's none of your fucking business. What the president here does in her private life should not be questioned by an agent. Your responsibility as an agent is to keep her safe, not gossip like a fucking teenage girl about shit you see. Do you understand?"

At Ponder's lack of response, I shift to glance over my shoulder. Instead of pleading for forgiveness and peeing himself, like I would if Trey's fierce anger and direct reprimand were targeted at me, Ponder's eyes are narrowed, his pale cheeks flushed in what appears to be more restrained fury than embarrassment.

Trey moves quickly, stepping around me and stopping directly in front of Agent Ponder's face.

"I said do you understand, Agent Ponder? You're 100 percent disposable. I'll have you ripped from the beta team to protecting the first fucking dog if you don't mind your own damn business from here on out."

"Um, Trey... I mean Agent Benson," I whisper with a light tap to his back. "I don't have a dog, so there isn't a first dog for him to protect."

"It's a damn metaphor, Randi," he snarls in Agent Ponder's face.

"Oh, right. Good one. Continue. But just so you know"—I hook a thumb over my shoulder—"while you two measure those manly bits, I'm stepping inside the kitchen to have a quick smoke and possibly two whole minutes alone without knowing if the world is falling apart. Cool? Cool." I shoot both thumbs up in the air and disappear through the door.

Trey's voice booms through the gap as it slowly closes behind me. The cool plaster is solid against my back as I lean against the wall. It gives a small rattle at the back of my head smacking against it. The clatter of my over-priced shoes hitting the floor when I release them echoes through the other-wise peaceful quiet of the empty kitchen. Silk glides effortlessly against my back, slipping from the confines of my cropped black suit pants as I shimmy down the wall. Cold hard tile greets my tailbone.

Forearms wrapped around bent knees, I attempt to shut out the world. Eyes squeezed shut, I struggle to clear my mind, to prevent the issues of the day from stealing these few moments of serenity. To my right comes a soft squeak of hinges combined with a waft of cool air brushing a few wayward strands of dark hair across my face. Tucking them behind an ear, I peel my lids open to find a sexy-as-hell agent hovering close, concern lining his pinched features.

The door shudders with the impact of his shoulder. Shoving both hands into his jeans, he crosses one ankle over the other. Like this, in dark jeans, a tight dark gray T-shirt, tousled hair, and a bit of scruff lining his strong jaw, he looks more like a model than a badass agent.

"Long day?" he questions, sincerity softening his tone.

"The longest so far, I think." Unfolding one arm, I give the tile to my left a soft pat. "Sit with me?"

Trey swings his gaze from me to the stove. "Didn't you come down here for a smoke?"

"How'd you—" I follow his pointed stare to the unlit cigarette still clutched between my fingers. "Right."

"Come on, up you go." Trey drops to a low squat, sliding one arm behind my shoulders and the other beneath my bent knees. A restrained grunt escapes as he stands with me clutched to his hard chest. The rubber soles of his tennis shoes squeak against the ceramic with each long stride toward our designated smoking area. With more tenderness than needed, he sets me atop the smooth stainless steel counter.

"Got a light?" I ask. His answering smirk and nod warm a part of me that's been bleak since the last time we had a minute alone. Just his presence, the support and love he freely offers, awakens part of my soul in a way no one before him ever has.

At the grind of the flint and metal of the cheap blue plastic lighter, my hand instinctively draws up, inserting the filter of the cigarette between my parted lips. Only when the end glows orange do I lean back, a hand resting along the cold metal keeping me propped up.

"Do you want to talk about it?" he asks with his own cigarette snagged between front teeth.

"Not really. It was just a day from hell that never let up. Everything terrible and evil and catastrophic in the world finds its way across my desk. And somehow everyone expects me to know how to fix it all. Like the US somehow has a cure-all in its back pocket for dictators, bombings, and natural disasters." A quick drag fills my lungs with the awful smoke; it seeps out through my slightly parted lips as I debate my next words. "The role isn't more work than I expected. I knew it would require more of me and my time than anything I've ever done. It's the *type* of work, I guess, that surprises me, daily sometimes. Everything I do, every word and approval or denial affects millions of people's lives, and I make those kinds of decisions every hour. In the VP role, there was this—" I wave a hand in front of me as I search for the right word. "—failsafe, I guess. I know that doesn't make sense because I was still responsible for a lot, but in this role, it's all me. I'm the final word, *the* opinion." I kick my legs back and forth, knocking my bare heels against the cabinet beneath me. "And honestly I don't want to know the evil in our world. How there's a typhoon in Asia while our own country is crumbling along the West Coast. But you know what?" I meet his honey brown eyes. "Even with all the stress and headaches, I'd rather it be me than anyone else. Sure, I'm overwhelmed all time, and there's always something for me to stress over and issues to solve, but it's my call. That's so empowering considering most of my life, I felt powerless." He remains quiet, tracking my hand as I lift it to take another hit. "I'm meant to be here, in this role. I don't know why, but I can feel it in my bones."

"I agree, Mess. I know this is hard on you. Those around you every day see the toll it's taking, but there is no doubt in any of our minds that you can do this job better than anyone else." Hip against the counter edge, he slides a palm over my thigh and squeezes. "What are you doing hiding out down here tonight?"

The tiny circles his thumb traces along the inside of my thigh send waves of chills along my skin. "After the shit show in Saudi Arabia, coming back and having Ben here, dealing with Taeler's pregnancy and doctors' visits... things have been nonstop since we landed. I just needed five minutes to myself, five minutes of... normal."

"Normal?"

"Yeah. To give me a few minutes away from that office upstairs. Some time to remind myself of *who* I am despite my job. My title is president of the United States, but at the same time, I'm still Randi Sawyer. Teen mother, foul-mouthed, and a bit crazy Randi. I don't know why, but today more than ever, I needed to remind myself who I am. If I'm not careful, the shadiness of this town will engulf me and make me forget between right and wrong. My morals, who I am at the core is why people voted for me in the first place, why they trust me. It would be so easy to get lost in the power I now have. So here, right now, I'm taking my five-minute time-out to remember who I am, why I'm here, and who I'm fighting for."

A devious smile pulls at his lips, a sparkle shining in those light brown eyes.

"What?" I ask drawing back a few inches. "What are you planning?"

"You want normal?"

"Desperately," I breathe.

Extinguishing the cigarette butt in the sink, he grabs mine and does the same.

"Do you trust me, Mess?"

There's zero hesitation in my honest answer. "Always, Trouble."

Sheer joy washes over his face, softening his previously tight features. "Good. Now come on. We need to get you changed."

16

RANDI

A giggle tickles in my chest as I press my forehead harder against Trey's flexing back. Fingers curling into tight fists, I grasp his T-shirt as we maneuver our way down the dark alley and through the back door of his condo building. With the hoodie of my zip-up sweatshirt tugged low, covering my face, I'm forced to monitor the back of Trey's gray tennis shoes to keep from stepping on the backs—again.

"Quiet back there," Trey admonishes with zero heat. "We're almost to the lobby."

The soft fabric of his T-shirt slips beneath my forehead as I nod in acknowledgment.

A gaggle of agents shuffles ahead while a few hover close. We told them to act as casual as possible, but that was wishful thinking on our part. There's no mistaking the dozen or so suit-clad men all wearing shoulder harnesses beneath their jackets and serious-as-hell expressions. At least we escaped without taking the whole damn motorcade. That little bit of freedom made me happy beyond belief. Two cars, the most nondescript SUV we own, and a small army on standby two blocks down was the least amount of force I negotiated out of the lead beta team agent, Bass.

It's Bass, right?

"Elevator hundred paces to the left," Trey says under his breath to the closest agent. "Going to the third floor."

Erm, what? I raise my head off his back and cast a quizzical look at the back of his neck. "Third floor? You live on the top floor."

Trey doesn't respond, just keeps us moving at a fast pace toward the bank of elevators. Up ahead, an agent holds the elevator open, his searching gaze taking in the expanse of the lobby. Trey rushes us into the small box, and three other agents file in behind us. Shoulder to shoulder, the heat magnifies in the small space making the long sleeves and hoodie almost unbearable. Peering around Trey's bicep, I watch as he presses the glowing button for the third floor.

Butterflies erupt in my empty stomach as the elevator shoots upward, settling as we slow to a stop at the third floor. The doors slide open with a near silent whoosh. In a herd of black and gray, we shuffle down the hallway, coming to a stop at the second door. Confusion and curiosity mix, making me forget that I'm hiding from the public eye. Releasing my tight hold on Trey's shirt, I shift to take in the hall. Every few feet, a different door faces the hallway, the sheer amount of condos on this level vastly different than the one I've visited before.

"Trouble, what's going on?" I ask as he shoves a key into the door and twists. The deadbolt releases with an ominous click.

Worry lines along his forehead deepen as he rests his chin on his shoulder. At a hard shove with the heel of his palm, the door swings open. Several of the waiting agents brush past him to secure the inside.

Frustrated, I arch a questioning brow at Trey.

"Right, well, there've been a few changes that I haven't told you about. I didn't know how. Fuck, this is a cluster."

I swallow back the worry tightening my throat. "Trey Benson, if Jessica Hawthorne is in that apartment, I will commit murder tonight."

The agent beside me shuffles on his feet. Guess hearing the president openly talking about killing someone isn't a normal thing. They'll learn soon enough that it is with this crazy-ass president the longer they're around me.

A shy smile spreads across his lips before he sinks his teeth into the lower one, fighting the growing grin. Not sure why he finds my growing anger funny, but he won't for long, that's for fucking sure.

One of the previous agents who slipped inside to clear the condo moves into view and gives us the all clear. Reaching behind him, Trey grabs my hand and laces his fingers with my own. A hard tug and I'm sealed to his back once again as he steps over the threshold into the strange condo.

It's the smell that hits me first. The powdery sweet scent of fresh baking and thick aroma of seasoning from cooking. The underlying smell of lavender and mint mixes the earlier scents, confusing me further. With only two steps from the door, we're in the living room area. A short window dots the wall while two chairs—one recliner I recognize—are all that fill the cramped space, along with the familiar massive flat-screen from his old apartment attached to the wall. To the left, the room opens up to a dated kitchen complete with a breakfast nook, and to the right is a darkened hallway.

An overwhelming sense of home envelops me, like a warm blanket fresh from the dryer. The soothing smells combined with the cozy space and something else that lingers in the air offer all the comforts a loving home should offer. For the first time in weeks, I relax, feeling comfortable in my own skin and my surroundings.

I shake my fingers free from his tight hold. Moving around him, I carefully inspect the living room in search of personal touches or knickknacks. With nothing to snag my curious attention, I rotate to make my way toward the kitchen.

Unease twists my stomach as I run a finger along the worn countertop. Yet another direct contrast to his previous condo. It's not the outdated appliances and decor that have caught me off guard, no, it's the fact that this kitchen looks used. *Currently* used. Clean baking pans and an assortment of pots rest on the drying rack beside the sink with several cups and plates stacked neatly alongside. My heart hammers, and a short breath catches in my chest. Trey doesn't know how to cook *or* clean up after himself.

I grip the damp dishcloth hanging over the side of the sink and tighten my grip around the coarse material.

"Trouble, I need you to start talking. Now." My entire body quivers with tension as I turn on my heels, my worn Converses squeaking against the linoleum floor. Twisting the damp rag, just one piece of evidence that someone else was here recently, I wait as he plops into a chair near the small breakfast table. The quaint nook is barely big enough for the round table and three wooden chairs.

A repetitive grinding sounds from the table where he passes the salt shaker along the wooden surface from one hand to the other.

"Things fell apart after I was released from the hospital." His Adam's apple bobs as he takes a hard swallow. "You were right, my mother had no right or the ability to cut off my trust fund, but the feds do. It's all frozen except for a small sum that was already in my bank account from the last deposit."

I scan the small apartment, considering it in a new light with that revelation.

"I sold the condo upstairs to Jessica." He releases a shaky laugh. "She could afford it and wanted it. They haven't given any indication to how long the trust will remain frozen, which means I didn't know how long I could continue affording the large mortgage payment. So I sold it, used the money to buy this one, and stashed the remaining funds in an account in case the trial against my father drags on."

"Trey," I say on a breath. "Why didn't you tell me?" The stack of clean dishes pulls me away from the beautifully broken man in front of me. "And what's all this?" I wave a hand to the drying rack. "You have roommates now too?"

"Kind of." The chair legs scrape along the floor as he shoves away from the table. "I'm not doing a good job of explaining all this." Reaching up, he runs a hand through his already disheveled hair. "I thought coming here would be relaxing for you. I'm sorry, Mess. We can leave if you want—"

"No," I say quickly, cutting him off. "I'm a little disappointed you didn't tell me about all this before now, but I like being here." Taking in the cozy condo, I smile at Trey, who's monitoring my every reaction. "It's cozy, homey almost." Lifting my nose in the air, I take an exaggerated sniff. "Are those cookies I smell?"

Trey grins. "I'm glad you like it. It's small, but it honestly hasn't been as terrible as I thought it would be. It needs a remodel, but I'm not at a point where I want to waste the cash when I need to conserve."

"Why did they freeze your trust?"

An incredulous huff pushes past his lips. He inches closer to lean a hip on the edge of the counter. Slowly he unravels the towel from my hands and tosses it to the counter. "My mother mentioned funds from my father's dirty dealings and exchanges from the Boardroom were funneled into my trust."

"That's not solid enough evidence for them to freeze the funds. Have they provided you with documentation?"

He shakes his head. Several thick sections of his long hair fall across his eyes.

I sweep two fingers across his forehead, pushing it to the side. "I'm guessing haircuts aren't on the new improved budget."

That smile of his widens. "I've been a little busy."

Chewing on a hard fake nail, I nod and allow those fingers to trail down his face. "Tell me about these roommates of yours. Are they cute?" I waggle both brows suggestively to lessen the heavy cloud that's hanging in the room.

Trey's hands lash out, gripping my hips with enough force that I wonder if I'll bruise, and yanks me forward. A sharp breath escapes as our lower halves slam together. Desire quivers low in my gut as warm tingles erupt through my chest, heating my normally cool skin.

"Watch your mouth, Madam President. You're mine and mine only." A shiver races down my spine at his deep, commanding tone. "My mother dismissed the entire house staff after we confronted them that day in the sunroom. Part of me wonders if she couldn't afford their salaries with their funds frozen or if she knew how much it would upset me since I was the cause of them losing their jobs."

"Trouble, none of what happened that day was your fault. You stopped your father, that's it." I mold a palm against his scruffy cheek, brushing a thumb along his cheekbone.

"There were two people, a couple. I just couldn't.... So I asked them to move in with me." He shrugs, acting like the genuine act of kindness isn't as big of a deal as I believe it to be. "They were there when my parents weren't. I consider them surrogate parents at this point. I couldn't let them be homeless because my mother is a fucking bitch. It's worked out well so far. They're looking for new positions in and around the city, but there aren't many jobs out there for a live-in butler and cook."

"Where are they?" I ask as I step backward, putting several inches between us. If I'm to meet these people who mean so much to Trey, I sure as hell don't want our pelvises touching. Call me old-school.

"They're out for now. I wanted to tell you all this alone before you met them. It's a lot to take in."

His teeth nibble at that fuller lower lip, allowing a bit of insight to his apprehension.

Sucking in a breath, I let it out slowly. "Yeah it is. I'm just confused on why you didn't tell me sooner. Why didn't you at least tell me about the frozen accounts?" I give his shoulder a playful shove. Palms pressed to the counter, I hop up and hook my feet around his narrow hips. A gentle tug is all it takes for him to seal himself between my spread knees.

"So much changed those few days. I had a tough time processing it all myself."

"Is that why you were so despondent those few weeks?"

He nods with a grimace. "Amongst other things."

"You know the money means nothing to me, right?" I ask, searching his face.

"I do know that. I honestly do. Deep down I know that even if I lost everything, nothing would change between us. But that wealth and the status that comes with it has been a part of my identity for my whole life. Having that part of my identity, the safety net money like I have, or had, ripped away left me foundering. Add in being shot, you announcing Pierce instead of that fuckface Whit as your VP, and me finding out at the same time as the rest of the world?" His chest heaves with a deep breath as he runs a hand through his hair. "I didn't know how to process it all."

"You know the reason I chose Sam over Shawn. It was the lesser of two evils. If I selected Shawn as the VP, I'd have a larger target on my back than I do now. He would've manipulated and snaked his way into the president spot—"

"I know, Mess. I know." Calloused hands cup my cheeks. "I agreed with your decision wholeheartedly and understand your rationale on why you made that choice. It was the timing of it all. It left me feeling helpless."

Wrapping my arms around his lean waist, I tug him closer. The soft material of his T-shirt imprints on my chin as I press it against his breastbone and stare up.

"I've believed many different things about you since we first met on the campaign trail. Asshole, spoiled, twatwaffle, rich brat, idiot—"

"Are you going somewhere with this?"

My lips part, spreading into a genuine grin. "I'm getting there. 'Helpless' has never been a word I would or have used to describe you. And I know without a doubt I never will."

Along the wall, a basic chrome and white-face clock ticks, marking the seconds turning into minutes as we hold each other in comfortable silence.

"All right, enough of the heavy shit. What do you want to do next, Mess?

We have a half hour or so before your surprise gets here." Pulling back, he plants a hard kiss on my forehead.

"Surprise?"

Undiluted joy radiates from his wide smile, those fine laugh lines crinkling along the corners of his eyes turning my heart to pure jelly.

"Honestly?" I respond with a loose breath. Straightening my spine, I attempt to search over his shoulder into the living room. "I have an idea. Where's your room?"

Trey inclines his head toward the darkened hallway. Twisting until his back is between my knees, he rests his chin on his shoulder to gaze back at me. "Hop on, I'll give you a ride."

Giggling for the second time tonight, I wrap both arms around his neck and tighten the hold around his waist with my thighs as he hooks both hands beneath my knees.

"Not so tight," he wheezes.

"Sorry," I mutter, my lips pressed against the shell of his ear.

The agents stationed around the condo track our movements, offering confused looks. My gaze connects with Agent Wright's—huh, almost killing someone imprints the correct name in my brain, though it's probably not a good tactic to test to learn the others' names—his demeanor and focus stiff as he tracks our every move. We round the corner when I find Agent Ponder also watching us closely. No, not us. Trey. Intense fury blazes in his eyes, completely focused on Trey like a predator watches its prey.

My muscles protest as I crane my neck, attempting a glimpse inside the first room he storms past. A made bed and a dresser topped with knick-knacks is all I can view before we continue down the hall.

Trey opens the next door and steps inside.

The massive bed is familiar, along with all the other furniture from his previous condo which all seems crammed into this tiny room. There's hardly any space for someone to walk without maneuvering around something. Along the far wall, two racks of suits jut out, making movement on that side of the room impossible.

A high-pitched shriek escapes as I free-fall to the bed. I bounce off the mattress as Trey falls backward, landing beside me on his back.

"Now what?" His light eyes twinkle. I've never met someone whose eyes legit twinkle, but Trey's do. Always when he's up to no good, scheming to get his way or covering some mischievous shit he's already done.

I love it. Love him. Fuck, do I love him.

Forgoing words, I crawl up the large bed. The feather pillow fluffs under my soft pats before I lie down, curling on my side. Extending a hand back, I pat the area directly behind me.

"Cuddling, that's what I want to do. You're the big spoon." Eyes closed, I feel every jostle of the bed as he moves up it to lie beside me. Warmth radiates off him, seeping into my back as he snuggles close. A heavy arms drapes over my hip, situating our lower halves until I'm tucked as tight against him as possible. "Thank you," I whisper, the smooth sheets brushing along my lips with the two words. "I just need a few minutes, okay?"

"I'm here as long as you need me, Mess."

Several moments pass without another word. The issues of the day fall away, leaving my mind gloriously empty except for the thoughts surrounding the man behind me.

"Trouble?" I whisper, careful to not shatter the perfectly normal moment.

"Mess."

"Tell me something good."

"This. Right here, right now with you."

My cheek glides along the pillowcase as I smile. "What else?"

"I've seen countless pieces of art in my life in museums all around the world, owned a few even. But for the first time in my life, because of you, I'm truly able to comprehend the meaning of something being priceless. That's you, Mess. One of a kind. Priceless."

I flip over, putting us nose to nose. I press my trembling lips to his. "Thank you," I whisper.

"For what?" A deep line forms between his brows.

"For reminding me of my value when I can't see it myself."

"Every day for the rest of my life, Randi, I'll remind you, because it would be a fucking sin for you to ever believe you're anything less."

A lone tear slips from the corner of my left eye and trickles down my cheek until it's absorbed by the pillowcase. I scrape the pads of my fingers over the scruff along his jawline before delving into his silky hair.

"I love you," I croak. A lump of restrained emotion makes the words raspy and quiet. "Today, tomorrow, the next day, and the day after that. Don't ever leave me." His lids droop, long dark lashes fluttering closed. "I wouldn't survive it."

Honey brown eyes search my own. Excitement and energy roll off him in pulsing waves as he shoves an elbow into the mattress and hovers just over me. Swooping low, he steals a pulse-racing kiss before pulling back.

"Marry me."

"What?" I somehow manage around the astounded shock freezing every cell in my body.

"Marry me." Interlacing our fingers, he brings the hand to his mouth and presses his soft lips to each knuckle. "We're stronger together, and then everyone will know you're mine. No more hiding, no sneaking around like we're doing something wrong."

My heart thunders against my ribs, threatening to crack bone as he anxiously waits for my answer.

"I, um...." Too many thoughts and what-ifs barrel through. "Trouble... Trey," I start, not knowing how to explain what I'm feeling.

The joy drains from his face, leaving a sad, forlorn expression in its place.

I suck in a breath, readying to defend myself and help him understand. "No, stop," I command as he retreats back to the mattress, avoiding my attempts to snag his attention. His bicep slips from my grasp. Flopping to his back, Trey glowers at the ceiling. "Of course I want to marry you." His eyes shifting in a side-eye stare to where I lie is the only acknowledgment that he's listening. "But now? We've never even talked about that step. And—" I bite my lip and lock my focus on the bedside lamp as I figure out a way to word this. "—you didn't really ask me."

"Sure I did," he defends.

Shaking my head, I release a heavy sigh. "It was more of a demand than an ask."

"I thought you liked it when I was demanding."

I grimace. "Yeah I do, but this is different. And maybe I'm a traditional girl and want the whole proposal... I don't know, planned?"

"Don't worry about it. Forget I ever said anything," Trey grumbles, clearly upset by my lack of enthusiasm on the subject.

"Trey, don't be that way." Picking at a loose string on the duvet, I avoid his eyes. "And the way you put it made it sound like you were trying to stake your claim, not confessing your undying devotion to the one you want to spend your life with."

"You know how I feel about you," he snaps.

Sighing, I fall to my back and rest both palms on my stomach. "We've been through a lot the past few months, wouldn't you agree?" His grunt causes an exaggerated eye roll I know he can see. "I do want to marry you. I want to spend the rest of my life with you, but now? It's not the right time, and I think you know that. Deep down you know we should wait."

"How long, Randi?" The heaviness of his gaze weighs on me as he props back up onto his elbow, resting his head in his flattened palm. "How long do I have to wait to make you mine, for everyone to know? How long do we have to wait until we can be together forever?"

"When I'm out of office?" An acrylic tip cracks beneath the pressure of my nibbling teeth. "Did you even stop to think about your job? How you'd have to quit to become the first husband? Then *you'd* have agents following you around to protect you at all times, not the other way around."

I squeak. The room rotates as a firm grip twists me until I'm lying on top of a solid, hot body. A tentative smile plays at his lips, the earlier disappointment fading.

"I don't give a fuck about that job. Once, it was all I had. Those boys were my family. But now there's you, and that's all that matters. I'll wait for you, Randi Sawyer. I'll wait until you're ready, until it's the right time, as long as you can look me in the eye right here, right now, and tell me that you will marry me one day. That one day in the near future you'll allow me the honor of being your husband."

"Yes." A half laugh, half sob strangles from my chest.

A deep booming voice reverberates down the hall and echoes in Trey's small overstuffed room, breaking the moment.

"T?" I rasp, still trying to wrangle my emotions.

"You wanted something normal tonight. There's nothing more normal than hanging out with your friends, right? I texted Tank and Sarah on our way here." Shoving off the bed, he digs both elbows into the mattress, closing the distance between our faces. His nose brushes against my own. "Come on, Mess. Shove aside the shit day and the marriage conversation I threw on you and come have a beer with me."

Tears leak, dripping over my bunched cheeks.

Smiling while crying. This is a new development.

"You know I'm a whiskey girl," I say after clearing my throat.

"I might have a small stash of whiskey you can sip on if you play your cards right." Shifting, he wraps his arms around my back, sealing our chests together. "Tonight it's just us and our friends, okay? Normal."

I mouth the word.

It's not the one I'd use for this moment, for the effort he put in all for me.

No, the word I choose is...

Perfection.

17

RANDI

"Thank you," I say with a small smile to the woman as she places the edible art on the table in front of where I sit. A low grumble vibrates in my stomach at the savory smells now wafting through the large dining room. Adorning the plate is a colorful display of the most enticing array of beef, vegetables, and a type of fancy rice. "Smells delicious."

"Sure does." I fight to ignore Ben's words—mostly his overall presence—so I don't lose my eager appetite.

"Excuse me," Taeler whispers, her face pale, nostrils flaring as she shoves from the long table and bolts from the room with a hand over her mouth.

Ben frowned. "I thought that stuff ended early in pregnancy."

"For most, yes, but for a few unlucky ones like Tae and me when I was pregnant with her, it could last the entire pregnancy." I struggle to keep the annoyance from my tone. Tonight was a bad night to do this. I should've canceled. After a long day of fixing the world's problems—or, in some cases, adding to them—I'm in no mood to play nice with my ex. My ex who has this strange delusion that we'll get back together at some point.

Even now he tosses another one of those longing looks from where he sits across the ten-seat dining room table. Not once or twice but three times now, his foot has rubbed mine in a lame attempt to play footsie. To make matters worse, the alpha team is on shift tonight.

Yep. Trey, current boyfriend and lover, has a front row seat to this shit show, and if the smoke coming from his ears is any indication to his thoughts, Ben better hope he's still breathing by the time dessert is served.

"Did you really? Get sick that much?"

"Yep." I pop the *p* and slice into my steak.

"Guess I was too busy with wrestling. You remember how good I was, right? Fuck, I could've gone all the way."

"Gone all the way to where?" I question. Okay, that was a low blow, but fuck, if I have to hear this story one more time in my life, I'll hand myself over to Whit with a damn bow tied around my neck.

"College, Olympics, I don't know. Somewhere," he grumbles. "I do feel bad about all that, you know I do. But hell, we were just kids. I wasn't ready to be a parent."

"And I was?" Movement in my periphery urges me to glance up from the plate, but I keep eating instead. Acknowledging Trey will only make matters worse for everyone in this room.

"Yeah, well, women are predisposed to be ready."

"Please, stop while you're ahead, Ben," I groan. The fork clatters to the plate, and I wince at the reverberating sound. "You wanted to discuss Tae and the baby. Let's focus on that and not the past."

Ben grumbles something under his breath before shoving a hunk of steak into his mouth. "I think I should move in."

Wine sprays out of my nose. Wide-eyed, I suck in a miniscule amount of air as I cough and hack up the alcohol that made its way into my lungs. Ben jumps from his seat and rushes to my side of the table.

"Do not touch her." Water pouring from my eyes, lungs burning, I look from Trey on my right to Ben on my left. Trey's features soften, worry etching around his tight lips. "Here, drink some water." A cold, sweating glass goblet is shoved into my trembling hand. "Little sips."

With a few more hard coughs and several sips of the ice-cold water, I settle back against the chair.

"Thanks, Agent Benson." But he's not focused on me anymore. Oh no, Trey's hate-filled stare is focused over my head on my ex "Ben, go sit back down. I'm fine."

"I want to be a part of this, Rand. Don't shove me away."

"A part of what?" I take another gulp of water. "Of me being president and living in the White House or a part of your grandchild's life?"

"The kid's life!" he shouts. Throwing his hands in the air, he interlaces his fingers behind his head. "What, you think this about you? Damn, you always were the self-centered one."

My hands tighten into fists beneath the table. It's official—he's a jackass, and now I need to figure out how to get him out of this house and back to Texas.

He says it's about Tae and the baby. We'll see about that.

"What's Taeler having?" I ask.

"What?" The indignant mask falls from his face, shifting to confusion.

"The baby. If you care so much about Taeler and her baby, what's the gender?"

"A girl of course." Ben scoffs.

"A girl?" Sliding against the cushioned seat, I angle myself to face Ben with Trey now at my back.

"Sorry, a boy."

"Hmm, a boy?"

"Hell if I know. That shit doesn't matter. It's not even here yet."

"Ben." The glasses and plates rattle at the slam of my elbow on the table before I rest my head in my hand. The long fake nails glide through my freshly washed hair. I can't believe I wasted a hair wash day on this tool. "We're not finding out. Taeler wants to be surprised, and you would've known that if you'd asked her anything about the baby."

"You fucking tricked me to prove your point," Ben growls with a menacing step back around the table toward me.

"Watch your fucking language, you ignorant bastard. You're talking to the president of the United States."

Fire flames in Ben's eyes as he glares at Trey. "What's it to you?"

"You need to leave." My voice wavers with the building tension between the two men. "Ben, you need to leave. Not just this room but the White House. You're not staying here."

"Rand, baby—"

"She said out," Trey growls. A comforting hand rests on my shoulder in support.

Ben tracks the gesture, and a snarl pulls at his lips. "Is this the one you're fucking?"

"Ben!" I gasp. "Stop."

The fool doesn't know he's seconds from a very slow, grueling death at Trey's hand.

An arrogant snarl curls Ben's upper lip as he sizes Trey up. "You're just pissed I hit that before you. Wasn't that great—"

One second Ben's standing being all kinds of douchey. The next he's against the wall with T's thick forearm pressed to his throat. The hand on my shoulder tightens before slipping away.

Trey stalks toward the other two men, menace and fury fueling each calculated step.

"Benson, you stay the hell away from him," T shouts over his shoulder, having zero effect.

"I'm not scared of that pretty boy." Ben wheezes, his face beet red and eyes starting to bulge. "I'm staying."

"You damn fool," T shouts, a spray of spit dotting Ben's grimacing face. "Trey, I said back the fuck up."

"Come on, man, I only want to kill him."

"I know, but I don't have time or the energy for burying a body tonight. That shit's for the kids. We're too old to be dragging around dead weight."

"Get Smith to carry the body. It'll be part of his hazing."

A wave of fear passes over Ben's features. His wild eyes connect with mine.

"Rand, do you hear this? Stop them."

"And why in the hell would I do that?" I ask on a laugh. Trey won't really kill him. I think. Maybe. Eh, who knows? There are so many metaphorical bodies buried in this building; might as well add in a real one. I saw a great place by the rosebushes on one of my walks the other day.

"Probably not a good time to bring that up," I mutter under my breath. Twisting back to face the table, I take another bite of the steak and wash it down with the best cabernet I've had since that night in New York with that asshole Hinkle. The reminder of that night and his roaming hands turns the juicy bite in my mouth to ash.

Ben whines, the sound like nails on a chalkboard, followed by two murderous rumbling chuckles. They continue to whisper—conspiring on Ben's murder, no doubt—when a low hum along the table redirects my intrigue. The cell phone vibrates, shifting against the unused salad fork—or is that the dessert fork? With the tips of two fingers, I flip the device over to view the screen.

"What the hell?" I mutter. Snatching the napkin from my lap, I toss it to the table.

The earlier commotion behind me is now silenced with the weight of listening ears.

I slide the side of my thumb against the screen, stopping the annoying vibrating and answering my Russian friend's call.

"Vlad," I breathe into the mouthpiece now pressed beside my lips. "This is an unexpected call."

"Madam President." His thick voice sends a bolt of excitement and dread through my system. "I have need of your assistance."

"My assistance." Two looming shadows appear over my shoulder. "Care to be a little more detailed?"

"No."

"Right." I press the pad of my index finger against my right temple to soothe the low throb this night has already caused. "Okay, what do you need my help with?"

At this, Trey and T both shift, resting their asses on the table to face me. Trey shakes his head, his face pinched with concern, while T pitches forward, listening to my every word.

"Not on the phone. This needs to be handled in person. You come to Russia. It will be fun."

"Russia?" I scoff. "You want me to pick up and fly to Russia to help you with some mysterious issue?"

"Yes."

"No."

"Madam President, you owe me a favor, and I am calling that in now. I need you in Moscow as soon as possible. It is a matter of life and death."

The top of my head burns with the scalding stares from both men. They wave their hands in front of my face, grip my chin, anything to get me to look up.

I've promised Trey I wouldn't make any rash decisions, not when it put my life in the crosshairs and others' too, but this is different. This is Vlad, and he's right, I do owe him a favor. When I asked him to look into Trey's family, I sealed myself to this agreement between us. And now it's time to pay up.

"Okay." The two men shout curses as they leap off the table to pace the room. "Moscow. It'll be hard as hell convincing everyone that this trip needs to happen, but I do owe you." I dare a peek through my lashes and immediately regret it. Trey's fury-laced glare might burn me alive right here in this dining room chair. "I'll let you know when to expect me."

"Thank you. And Randi?"

"Yeah?"

"Don't forget your coat."

"COAT?" I grumble as I bury my face deeper into the thick scarf tucked into the collar of my navy peacoat. "Fucking Vlad. I need a damn parka."

"That's your penance for agreeing to this trip before consulting with us," Trey says out of the corner of his mouth as we continue toward Vlad's home —or should I say estate—in Moscow. Surrounded by agents, our strides mirror the others to not cause another to stumble. It was difficult to keep the cadence at first, but now after so many outings being engulfed in an agent cocoon, I've finally gotten it down.

The agent in front of me grunts as the sharp point of my pump stabs into his Achilles' heel.

Okay, maybe I'm still working on it.

The ten-foot double doors swing open in greeting as we approach. Several armed men pour out of them. Trey, T, and the other guys tense at the sudden swarm, the show of force. The agents stop short. My nose nails the back of Agent Smith at the sudden halt.

Tensions rise as my agents and half of the Russian military standoff, each waiting for the other to make the first move.

A voice I recognize bellows in Russian from inside the estate. A corner of my lips tugs upward as Vlad appears, still shouting, no doubt chastising these men for the rude welcome.

"Madam President," he states at the top of the stairs, looking down to where we stand two steps below. "Come, we have much to discuss."

The end of my red nail digs into Smith's back, urging him into action. But his feet stay planted. Hell, his upper body doesn't even shift with my insistent single finger shove.

"I think your welcoming party made my team a little anxious," I shout over Smith's shoulder. A low grumble resounds from my right, but I ignore Trey's obvious displeasure. "Care to call them back so maybe we can have that discussion inside where it's hopefully warmer?"

"Warmer?" Vlad laughs. "It is a beautiful day."

The cold gray October skies and whipping wind beg to differ, but to each their own, I guess.

With a sigh, Vlad turns, putting his back to us to face his men. With a few sharp words, the men fall back inside the house without a single glance back.

A collective breath releases from the agents surrounding me. Smith's shoulders drop three inches, but his hands twitch at his side like he's a hairbreadth away from drawing his gun.

"Okay, guys, let's get inside before I freeze to death."

This time Smith advances with my less than gentle shove.

At the top of the stairs, Vlad greets me with a kiss to each cheek.

"So I'm here. What's the favor?" I'll be honest, my curiosity hasn't stopped since we hung up last week. "I'll go ahead and put this out there: no, you cannot borrow a submarine or a carrier. I know we're friends, but we're not at that level yet."

Vlad smiles, deep crescent-shaped lines forming around his spread lips. "And what level of friends are we, Madam President?"

"The kind where I don't shoot you, you don't shoot me, and we occasionally do supersecret favors for the other."

"I like this friendship," he says, gesturing inside the opulent home. "Come, we will talk inside."

"Me too, Vlad. Me too. I have to say it *is* strange that the one politician I feel like I can trust is the Russian president. What does that say about the men and women I'm surrounded by every day in DC?"

"You should off them." The words are monotone, his features relaxed.

I stumble. "That's mass murder."

Bushy dark brows furrow. We're halfway through the entryway when he laughs. "Wrong English word. Not off as in kill, off as in fire."

"Whew, I was beginning to wonder if my best politician friend was a bit crazy." I take in his profile. "You're not, right?"

A chandelier hangs above our heads, its circumference nearly three of me, the setting sun's final rays glinting and glittering off its crystals. The wallpaper covering the walls looks dated and exactly the unique style I expected here. Thick, dark wooden planks cover the floor from room to room.

Vlad leads us into a sizeable room with couches in evergreen fabric and deep leather chairs scattered throughout. Beside each of the ten windows lining the back wall, men and women stand, ARs strapped to their chests and their weighted stares all on my agents.

Vlad helps me into a chair, the leather groaning as I slide back and shift to get comfortable. He settles into the chair opposite of me, resting an ankle across his other knee. A woman enters, her uniform a pair of loose dark pants and matching black button-up dress shirt, and pauses beside our host.

"Drink?"

"Got any whiskey?" I ask, kind of as a joke yet hoping they have some Jack stashed around here somewhere. The increasing nerves fluttering in my belly tell me I might need a whole bottle by the time we're done here in Russia.

He nods and shifts to speak softly to the woman.

"You're in so much trouble." Trey's warm breath and harsh tone send a shiver down my spine.

"Oh?" I say more of a gasp than a word.

"Stick to the damn security plan, Randi. We're here to keep you safe."

I turn, resting my chin on my shoulder and putting us nose to nose. The world stills as we battle an unspoken war. Yes, I get what he's saying, but at the same time, I can't live a life where every move is planned out, every interaction on a schedule. That's not me, and it never will be me.

Minty breath brushes along my warming cheeks. I lick my lower lips before sliding the tip of my tongue along the edge of the upper. Brows creeping up his forehead, Trey tracks the movement. The shuffle of feet drags his gaze away. Ever so slowly, he stands and adjusts his suit jacket.

Smooth, expensive fabric rubs beneath my sweaty palms as I swipe them up and down each thigh. I'm about to follow through on an owed favor to a Russian. That's where my head should be, not on my hot-as-hell boyfriend who I can't even look at without my breath catching.

Focus, Randi, focus.

Think with your head, not your heart.

Okay, fine, I shouldn't think with my demanding lady bits. What can I say? Any time Trey's around, they shift into overdrive, making every thought and action revolve around us naked.

No. Stop it. Bad Randi.

Russian. Favor. President to president.

Our drinks arrive on a silver tray, the woman bending at the waist to put it at eye level. I grab the tumbler she indicates and slowly bring it down to rest on my knee. After Vlad has his glass engulfed in one meaty hand, he lifts it across the small distance between us. The clink of the thick crystal tumblers resounds in my chest at the weight of this moment.

I huff a laugh, my breath pushing against the ice and dark liquor as I take a short sip.

"What?" Vlad asks, relaxing back.

"Who knew, right?" The cold glass rolls between my palms, centering me somehow. "Where we came from to this. So much has changed in the few years I've been in politics." The ice clinks against the edge as I raise the glass to my lips once again. "And now I'm here. I've seen the world since Kyle and I won, and now I'm here having drinks with the Russian president—"

"Your friend, remember?"

I smile, balancing the glass on the worn leather armrest. "Now I'm here having drinks with my friend the Russian president. It's surreal, you know. Did you ever expect this life?" I wave my free hand around the room. "Did you ever even dream of something like this?"

"Of the position or wealth?"

"Both. Or... I don't know, did you ever dream you'd be someone who could have so much impact? That you would one day be the savior to some and Satan to others?"

The clear liquid in his tumbler swishes around the edges as he twirls the glass hanging between two fingers. Vlad drums his fingers along the other armrest, gazing at the unlit floor-to-ceiling fireplace.

"No, never expected it, but I could not deny the want to be the change one day. You and I are unique in the way we were not taught to fight for more, to fight for someone other than ourselves, yet we did. We do every day. That spark was in us from the beginning and grew with our daily challenges. So maybe I did know I would have impact, because for me, there was not another option."

A beat of silence settles around the room.

Exhaling a deep breath, I raise my glass to my friend. "That was fucking deep."

Vlad grins. "Thank you."

"Now, what's this favor?"

That earlier grin dies and his features harden, not with anger but with almost sadness. Moving to the edge of his seat, he dangles the tumbler between his spread knees. The room expands with anticipation as he inhales deeply and shoots the remaining liquid before resting the glass on a side table.

"It is my girlfriend."

I gasp. "Is she missing? You need the CIA to look into it?"

"No." He scoffs. "Your CIA is nothing compared to what I have access to. She's—"

"Did you kill her?"

"Do not be ridiculous."

"Does she know she's your girlfriend?" I say with a cringe. Shit, I hope he doesn't shoot me.

"Yes, but that is where the trouble is."

"Vlad—"

"She will not talk to me. Very angry."

My jaw slacks, leaving me gaping at the clearly distraught man sitting beside me. Heartache is painted across his harsh features. Eyes still wide, I lean between us and rest my nearly full tumbler in his open palm.

He sends a weary smile my way before downing the contents.

"Vlad... friend Vlad. Please, please tell me you didn't ask me to fly around the globe for us to discuss your relationship problems."

A knowing grin bunches his cheeks. "Is that not what friends for?"

18

RANDI

Side by side, we march down a long hall, the walls decorated with ornate picture frames filled with pictures of stoic, cold men frozen in time. I arch a questioning brow at the suit of armor we pass.

"It came with the house," he says with a laugh.

"I know how that goes." We take a right, then a left, and go down a set of stairs, seeming to move deeper and deeper into the massive house. "Vlad, I have to tell you, friend. If you've locked her in the dungeon, there's nothing I can do or say that will fix your issues."

"Not in the dungeon." His shoulders rise with a cringe.

"Vlad... where *do* you have her locked?" Trey chuckles beside me, knowing full well I'm at my limit for patience. "You do understand that if she's held against her will, I will help her escape and then kick your ass." I take in the bulging man beside me and rethink that statement. "Okay, maybe I'll have someone else beat you up. But the ass kicking will happen—"

"She is in our room. Not locked or held or bound. I am very concerned at the lack of humanity you think I possess."

"Eh, well, your predecessors didn't have much, so I just go based on history."

"I could say the same, Madam President."

I nod in concession. "Okay, so what started the fight?"

"I told her she could not leave the estate grounds," he says matter-of-factly.

"Right, so you're holding her against her will?" I question, making sure he understands what he's saying. "Didn't you just deny holding her against her will ten seconds ago?"

"It is for her own good. There are threats—"

Lips pursed to hold back a smile, I peer over my shoulder to Trey. "This sounds oddly familiar, doesn't it, Agent Benson?"

"I cannot see her hurt," Vlad continues, ignoring my side conversation with Trey.

"Yep, you and I've had this conversation before, I'm sure of it." Trey shakes his head, keeping his intense focus forward.

"She will not listen," Vlad says on a sigh.

"That does sound oddly familiar," Trey whispers out of the side of his mouth.

"This is why I called you. You know. You two know." Vlad gestures between Trey and me. I gape at his swinging finger. "What, you think I did not notice in Hawaii? To stay alive in my role, you have to know all, see all, and observe all. Please talk to her, let her know I only mean to keep her safe."

We pause in front of a twelve-foot-tall dark wood door. Vlad rests his hand on the round brass knob and shoots a pleading—well, as pleading as a Russian can look—glance at me.

Groaning in frustration, I tip my chin to the ceiling and close my eyes.

"Fine. I'll talk with her, but just know it might not turn out the way you're hoping."

THE HAPPY COUPLE—THANKS to me and my power of persuasion—laughs as they clink their glasses together in cheers. I gaze longingly at the empty chair beside me. The chair that would be occupied if my boyfriend weren't on duty.

A glow seems to surround the two at the head of the table, somehow making this cold room warm with the love they clearly have for one another. I'll go to my grave saying I was the catalyst for them to solve their issues, but really it was all them. I just helped start the conversation that needed to be had.

Having a few years of experience and practice under my belt because of the past fights Trey and I have had helped me speed the resolution along. She needed to see things from his point of view, and he needed to listen and respect hers. That's all it came down to. It's all it ever comes down to.

Mutual respect, listening, and love.

"Randi Sawyer: president by day, love whisperer by night," I say to myself with a smile.

Vlad and his girlfriend don't notice my random thought, too wrapped up in each other. Even though I hate to break up the happy reunion, there are some things I need to discuss with Vlad since I'm here. Might as well make this visit multipurpose.

He must feel the weight of my gaze as I attempt to figure out how to get him alone, because across the table, his gray eyes meet mine. Vlad dips his chin at whatever he finds written across my face and leans over to whisper in the woman's ear. With a goodbye kiss, she excuses herself from the table, leaving Vlad and me alone. Well, as alone as I ever am these days. Several of his men and my agents still accompany us in the gilded dining room.

"What is it you wish to speak about?"

Leaning back against the chair, I swirl the red wine around the glass. "What you told me about Kyle was true, and the information you provided helped me convince him to step down. But now with him gone, I'm.... I don't know what to do. We don't have the names of the people behind it all. The CIA can't find anything." I narrow my eyes at his huffed chuckle. "You don't think very highly of our CIA, do you?"

"I do not."

"Care to share why?"

"I do not."

I glare at my friend over the rim of the wineglass as I take a patience-fortifying sip. "I don't know what to do."

Vlad sips at the clear liquid in a short shot glass, his fingers drumming along the table. "What do your advisors say?"

"I... uh...." *Well, shit. Did not expect that question from him.*

"Have you not spoken to your military advisors, informed them of what you know, and work together on how to stop war from coming to the Middle East and dragging your country into the conflict?"

"Kind of?" I squeak. "That's what I asked the CIA to dig up, the names—"

"The names of those responsible are only part of the problem. The attacks are hurting civilians, taking away homes and loved ones, yet you are doing nothing about it?"

"I am. I'm working with the leaders of the countries affected and calming their—"

"Do you know what I keep hearing?" I shake my head. Edging to the edge of the chair, I hold my breath. "You've said 'I' several times."

I purse my lips. "Well, I *am* president."

With an air of disappointment, Vlad sighs and shakes his head. "Your role, my role, cannot be done alone. You are trying to manage a situation on your own, which is impossible. It is why we have advisors, why we put people in place who we trust to help guide us. We cannot know everything there is to know about military strategy, or economic growth, or foreign relations. Being president is a group effort."

"You don't understand. I'm trying to protect everyone. This isn't me just trying to be the hero. No, what I'm doing is keeping this to those who know what's going on and protecting my country. The less people who know, the better."

"You are wrong."

I slam the wineglass to the table. The plates rattle with the force. "I'm doing the best I can."

"More people will get hurt if you continue to think so narrow-mindedly, my friend. This will escalate, continue to escalate. You cannot handle this situation alone. It proves those who believe you cannot handle the president role correct."

"Excuse me?"

Glass to his lips, Vlad gulps the remaining liquid from his glass and sets it on the table. "I do not mean to insult you, but you are not acting like a president in this matter."

"All I need is the names," I say through gritted teeth.

"You need to learn to lean on other expertise or you will fail."

Fail. The word rattles in my head. Failing at this level would be... world altering. I've never failed, and I sure as hell don't plan to start now.

"I'm tired. If you'll excuse me." Shoving from the table, I stand and make to leave. "I'll do this on my own, Vlad, and you'll see you were wrong. I can do this."

Halfway to the door, he calls my name, pausing my retreat.

"When depending on only yourself fails, know it is not a reflection on you. You have worked alone for so long that it is nature to think single-mindedly. Before you go, I need to warn you about that man."

"Kyle's dead."

"Your secretary of state. He serves the highest bidder, not you or your country."

Not surprising. Maybe that's why the Saudi king hates him so much. Hell, why most of the world doesn't like him. They see it, and if I'm honest with myself, I see it too. But who would I replace him with? I know no one in DC, no one with the qualifications to take on that role. So instead of agreeing with Vlad and admitting to the weakness in my administration, I simply cross both arms over my chest. "Noted."

"You are taking this too personally, friend. I only offer to help."

A comforting hand presses to my lower back. I lean into the touch.

"Maybe, Vlad. Maybe I am, but it is a little personal when you say I'm setting myself up for failure. That's not really something anyone wants to hear over dessert."

"I tell you because no one else will. I tell you because we work together for the better of those we serve. Your success is mine. We are a team, yes?"

"I'm doing the right thing, Vlad. The more this is contained, the better. I appreciate you trying to help, but I'm respectfully declining your opinion."

His chin dips. "That is your choice. Good night, my friend. Rest well knowing you are safe here in my house."

I take in my strange friend. Really look at him. There's an aura of power around him. I've seen it before, but it's magnified here, in his home country. I want that. Want people to see me as a true president, not some worthless pawn or self-serving prick like the assholes before me.

So what if I want to do this on my own?

I can.

I will.

I will not fail.

19

TREY

March

The seat jostles with my sinking weight, shaking the short row and waking the sleeping giant I've plopped beside. Peeking one eye open, Tank inserts as much annoyance as possible into his side glare.

"What's on your mind now, Benson?" Tank mumbles, the vibrations from his deep voice making their way to the back of my seat. He shuffles, sinking lower for a more comfortable position to finish his nap. The seats on Air Force One are as comfortable as any I've ever sat my rich ass in, but it's still an airplane seat; real comfort only goes so far.

"There are holes in the plan." My foot bobs at a rapid pace, Tank tracking the up-and-down movement. "I don't like it."

Glancing across the aisle, I meet Smith's gaze. With a dip of my chin in acknowledgment, I shift my attention back to Tank, who's now clearly given up on sleep. Stretching both hands high above his head, he practically scrapes the ceiling of the plane even in a sitting position.

"What exactly don't you like about it?" Joints snap and pop along his spine as he twists one way and then the other.

"There are holes—"

"Which is why we have a plan B and a plan C."

I shake my head and run a hand through my recently trimmed hair. "Yeah, I know we do, but I still don't like it. There are too many opportunities for an attack. We're too exposed."

Tank groans as he pitches forward to rest both elbows on his tree trunk thighs.

"You're thinking like a boyfriend again," he admonishes. "We've been over this, Benson. Too many damn times over the past several months. The plan is solid. The security impenetrable. What you really want is her in a damn bubble, a bullet- and bomb-proof bubble."

"Or the popemobile," I mumble. "I knew I should've hijacked that little car while we were in Italy last month."

"Didn't you say that about the royal guards too during our visit with the queen of England in December?"

Ignoring his comment, I adjust in the seat, angling my upper body toward him.

"You know this trip isn't comparable to any of those. Egypt is unstable, and I don't need to remind you that the United States isn't on their top ten list of allies right now." Worry eats at my gut, making me push harder on my best friend than I normally would. I trust his plans, trust his decisions, but something feels off about this trip.

Sources say the Egyptian president is under the impression that the US is behind all the unrest still plaguing the Middle East. They're not wrong—not that we'll tell them that—but none of this is Randi's doing. The outbreaks of attacks have spiked since we first visited the area last year, making those of us in the know wonder if whoever's in charge of the entire operation knows we're attempting to keep the peace until we can identify the key players.

Then there's the Russian president's advice, which Randi is still not open to taking. I've tried reasoning with her these past few months, but she doesn't want to involve anyone who doesn't already know. Which means no military action against those insurgents on the ground causing the small-scale attacks.

Tank nods, his gaze searching the blue and gold carpet. "Okay, Benson, okay. Tell me where you see the weakest point."

The eerie sensation of being watched has me searching the surrounding area. Smith leans forward, completely absorbed in my conversation with

Tank. Around us, the other alpha team members and a few beta team agents are either playing on their phones or are asleep like Tank was before I disturbed him.

"Where it always is," I say on a sigh. Some days I feel like a broken record, but our weakest point is always the same. The cushioned seat forms around my tender back muscles, sore from yet another intense rowing workout yesterday morning. The soft material of my Armani slacks bunches beneath my massaging fingers, attempting to ease some of the tightness gathered there.

"To and from the Beast," Tank replies.

"Exactly. Once she's in the limo, she's protected until she gets out again. Those few minutes out in the open, anything can happen."

"Agreed, but she has to get out of the limo at some point. We can't ask for all meetings to be held inside the Beast." Tank rubs a hand over his head and heaves a heavy sigh. "I can double the snipers at the airport and at the first stop. The embassy there in Cairo has the three dotted along rooflines for the arrival as planned." He scans the few beta team agents. "I'll talk to their team lead and ask them to offer double protection from the plane to the Beast."

"I like that." I grimace as I prod at a particular sore spot just above my knee.

"You pushed it too hard yesterday," Tank says in an "I told you so" tone.

"You're the one who keeps pointing out that this detail is tougher than the previous years with the VPs. I agree and decided to train like it. I'm no good to her fucking weak like I was. Plus"—I grin—"I'm trying to keep up with your fit ass."

"Keep dreaming, Playboy. Keep dreaming."

Soft footsteps approach and pause to my right, a set of long thin legs nearly brushing my own. "Two hours until we land," says the tall blonde. "Do you need anything, Trey?"

"I'm sitting right here," Tank grumbles. "Along with the rest of the team."

I shoot a smirk to Tank. "No, thank you. I'm good." Hooking a thumb over my left shoulder, I smile at the woman I can't seem to remember. "But I'm sure Agent Smith could use something?" A faint curse sounds behind me, causing my smile to widen. "I'll be back in a bit. Going to check on the president."

Careful not to make any physical contact, I maneuver around the sweet girl and stride down the hall, Smith's emotionless voice demanding he's good chasing me with every step.

Outside her office, I lean against the doorframe, taking in the sight of my girl hard at work. Nail between her teeth, she scribbles something on a yellow legal pad, then violently scratches it out. Twice she does this before whispering a string of very creative curses and tossing the pad of paper to the desk.

"Make sure you don't include that bit about fucking a duck in your speech."

Her cheeks round, a wide grin forming even before she shifts her attention to where I hover just outside the door. When she does, those hazel eyes lock with mine. Even the smile she's wearing can't hide the turmoil and stress weighing behind her gaze.

"But it's a good line," she retorts. Leaning back, she tosses her tortoise-shell glasses to the desk and massages a temple. "I'm excited to share this new bill with the country, but it has to be just right. This plan will offer the needed support for those lost between the lines of poverty and lower middle class and will change the lives of millions. But only if it passes the House and Senate, and I have zero clue how to make that happen."

The soles of my black shoes slide over the well-worn carpet. No doubt many presidents have paced the small office of Air Force One. Wonder what else has been done in here.

On the opposite side of the desk, I lean forward, knuckles pressed to the hard flat surface, closing the distance between us.

"You're doing a good job, Mess. You'll find a way to convince those assholes in DC what's best for the American people."

"Without selling my soul?" she jokes on a huff.

"One can hope."

Long silky brown hair slips over her slender shoulders as she shakes her head. "I want to do so much more with my time in office, be the president who actually accomplished something. Who knew this job would be more like herding donkeys than actually getting shit done."

"Isn't the phrase 'herding cats'?" I push off the desk to retreat to the still open door.

"Have you *met* the politicians sitting in the House and Senate? Herding jackasses is the more appropriate description."

"I don't know, herding pussies is also a good metaphor for those spineless shitheads who can't make a decision without worrying about offending a monetary supporter."

Chuckling at her chastising huff for the crass word, I search the empty hallway. Hand wrapped around the knob, I tug the door closed and flick the lock.

The earlier curiosity at what has and hasn't been done in this room has bloomed to a full-on fantasy. Fantasies of her on that desk spread-eagle while I lick her dry. Of her face plastered to the polished surface while I fuck her from behind. And my personal favorite of me on the couch, head tossed back in beautiful bliss with her on her knees, taking all of me between her lips and down her swallowing throat.

The vivid fantasies ramp up the anticipation flowing through my veins, heading straight to my stiffening cock. It eagerly twitches inside my boxer briefs.

I lean back against the closed doors and take her in. The stress and tension I noticed the moment I walked in are nowhere to be seen as she nibbles her lower lip. Her lids droop, turning heavy with desire as her gaze tracks the hand now gripping my stiff dick over my slacks.

"You seem stressed." A shiver of pure joy bolts down my spine at the flush spreading across her cheeks and neck.

"A little, you could say. Running the country and all leaves a girl tense."

"Get on the desk, Mess." My eyes flare, my cock somehow getting harder at her immediate response to the order. The chair shoves back, almost toppling over in her haste to stand.

Hell yes. Two hours until touchdown, which means I have a full hour to play dirty with my girl. Plenty of time to help her relax.

Several times.

THE TENSION PERMEATING the air is so thick I can almost taste it as the first set of agents disappears through the open plane door. Beside me, Randi fidgets with a loose button on her blazer with a red-tipped fake nail cracking between her front teeth. Tank scans the line of agents waiting to exit again and again, seeming to check off some mental list.

"You're next, Madam President," Champ says, standing beside the open door, keeping one eye on her, the other examining the tarmac for hostiles.

"They're more scared of me than I am of them." Randi's words are a soft whisper, barely loud enough to be heard over the murmuring voices of the agents crowded around her. "A unicorn is exactly what I need. Nothing says power like a horse with a weapon on its head."

A minuscule smirk tugs at my lips before I shut it down. Clearing my head, I focus every cell, each breath, on the task at hand.

We step as one toward the door. As planned, I exit first. The soft morning glow of the sun barely cresting the surrounding buildings greets me. We calculated the timing perfectly; anyone looking to do her harm would be forced to stare straight into the rising sun, whereas we have the perfect vantage point with the sun at our back. The metal stairs shake beneath my weight as I carefully take each step down, scanning the entire area and the group of Egyptian delegates.

A stilted round of claps rings out in the quiet morning, signaling to me that Randi and Tank have exited the plane. At the bottom of the stairwell, I stop, waiting until my girl is at my side before shifting to the next step of the plan.

A rhythmic clink grows closer as she descends the stairs one step at a time in her stilettos.

Movement toward the end of the receiving line snags my attention. A man, one of the Egyptians, shifts anxiously from foot to foot. Even from here, the sweat dotting his brow and his shallow breaths are evident. My unease from earlier spikes. Wrist pressed close to my lips, I order a beta team agent to keep an eye on him. Agent Wright confirms visual, indicating he'll handle the situation.

A breeze kicks up, wafting the aroma of sand, spices, and cherry vanilla my way as Randi pauses beside me.

With some gentle prodding, we help Randi make it through the receiving line within the fifteen-minute window we'd scheduled for her. One hand holding hers, the other cupping the back of her head, I help ease her into the limo and follow immediately after with Tank right behind me.

We all situate in our various seats. Tank beside Randi, me across but only a few seats away. Thankfully the Beast has been running and the air inside is crisp and cold, unlike the already steamy temperatures outside.

Desperate for the arctic blast, I angle several vents toward my clammy face and inhale deeply.

"You with me, Benson?" Tank questions from where he sits, his thumbs bouncing over the phone screen.

"Yeah, I'm good."

"Why wouldn't he be?" Randi asks, not diverting her eyes from the iPad in her hand. An index finger slides up the screen over and over as she reviews the agenda for the day for the thousandth time and reminds herself of the names of the people she'll be meeting with at the award ceremony at the embassy.

"It's nothing. Tank is just a hovering mother hen." I adjust against the leather seat to scan the scenery as we zoom toward the embassy. "Think you can convince the Egyptian president all the uproar isn't the US's fault?"

"I have to, don't I?" Her shoulders round from the weight of the world—literally—resting there. "Kyle left us in a fucking mess. I spoke to the CIA director two days ago. He said the names, locations—hell, any information—has been more evasive than he expected. They're still working on identifying the men Kyle was in bed with, which means we need to keep this part of the world from warring against each other until they can. Until we have those names, I have to do everything I can to keep the peace."

"What about what the Russian said, that you should consider military force? Get your military advisors' advice."

She shakes her head. "No, this is the best course of action. We continue to keep this as a need-to-know, and no military. Vlad meant well, but he doesn't understand where I'm coming from."

"Exactly. He's used to military force and when to use it. I think—"

"We've been over this too many times, Trouble. I've made up my mind, and that's how we're going to handle it. We stopped the attempt on my life in Saudi Arabia, so they know I'm well protected. I'm safe." I steal a worried glance at Tank. "Now stop diverting. Why wouldn't you be good?" With more force than necessary, she presses the power button and tosses the now dark iPad to the seat beside her.

"It's nothing, like I said. Sometimes the heat and smells, occasionally tight spaces remind me of a few unpleasant deployments. I'm fine."

"Are you okay to be here? Should you go back to the plane—"

"I'm not fucking weak," I bite out through a clenched jaw. "I said I'm fine, so I'm fucking fine."

"Okay," she says slowly, shifting her attention to Tank, who shrugs. "I know you're not weak, Trouble. And that's great that you're fine, but I was asking to learn more about this side of you. You keep those years of your life hidden from me. if you haven't noticed."

"Can we talk about something else?" I point out the dark-tinted window. "ETA ten minutes."

The pointed once-over she gives me says we'll finish this discussion later whether I want to or not. A relieved breath brushes past my lips as she breaks our stare-off and reaches for the iPad once again.

The remaining ten minutes to the embassy are uneventful. Too quiet, in fact. I curl both hands into tight fists as guilt eats at my gut for disregarding her concern.

The Beast decelerates, slowly coming to a stop directly in front of the embassy's steps. Several marines stand at attention at the doors and scattered down the stone stairs. An alert scan of the surrounding area locates two of our snipers by the sun's rays gleaming off their scopes.

"Let's do this," Tank says as he tucks his phone away and reaches for the door handle.

Randi nibbles on a nail, her face scrunched with worry.

I grip her hand and give it a hard, reassuring squeeze. "We've got you, Mess. Focus on what needs to be done and let us worry about the rest."

The buttons down her black blazer pull as she inhales a deep breath. "Will this ever get easier?" she asks.

"No," Tank and I say in unison.

Tank's deep voice clips through our earpieces, signaling our ready to exit. An acknowledgment is returned, and the door swings open. Randi accepts the offered hand and slides out of the limo into the brightening morning. Tank follows, with me hot on his heels. Hands at the ready, I match her step for step as we ascend the stairs, skimming a searching scan over the crowd. Bright light flashes from the multitude of cameras, holding my focus for half a second before shifting past to assess the countless faces once again.

We almost make it without incident.

We're halfway to the embassy doors and the protection they offer when the false sense of safety shatters.

A single shot of a high-powered rifle booms through the peaceful morning. Three steps ahead comes a shout of pain, the marine's face contorting as he stumbles forward before slipping on the edge of the stair and falling. The clatter of metal from his assault rifle hitting the concrete stairs muffles the second shot and following screams.

"Sniper," Tank and I bellow in unison, mine as a warning to the marines within hearing distance, Tank's a command to our guys on the roof through our connected coms.

The years of training in the army and Secret Service slam into place, washing a calming wave over my panicking thoughts. Wrapping her in a bear hug, I send us into a controlled fall and cover her body with my own. Through the madness, agents bark their visuals as everyone works to identify the location of the shooter.

I squeeze my lids shut and hug her tighter, preparing for impact of another round of shots. Through the coms, an agent yells to get her inside the building. The concrete at our feet takes the full impact of a round; bits of rock break apart, slicing through the thin material covering my legs and imbedding in my calf and thigh.

Too close.

Again a shout comes through the coms, ordering me to get her inside. My protective instincts kick into hyperdrive, and I hesitate moving her out from under me. First, that wasn't Tank's deep voice issuing that order to move her inside, it was someone else—someone whose voice I can't identify with all the chaos around me. Second, my gut fights against the idea that we'll be safer inside.

I have to make a choice. Lying here on the steps, we're sitting ducks.

Follow the sane choice and rush her inside those doors, or listen to my gut that's kept me alive this long?

Decision made.

Scooping her off the ground, I race to take cover between two large supporting columns. Their wide circumference offers protection from the direction of the gunfire.

"What the fuck?" Randi's voice is quivering as badly as her shaking body.

I palm the gun in my hand, adjusting the grip. With a slow exhale, I shift to look around the massive column and take in the full scene. A half-second glance is all I get before a round nicks the stone inches above my head. I whip back around to safety, panting at the close call.

"Why didn't they take you out first?" I mumble into her ear, though it's more to myself, attempting to make sense of it all. Voices shout and snap through the earpiece. I sort through them all, piecing together what's going on out in the open. The cuff of my sleeve scrapes across my lower lip as I shout into the mouthpiece. "Tank, where are our fucking snipers?"

The returning silence has dread sinking in my gut.

"Tank?" I say again, louder this time.

"Little fucking busy here," his deep voice says over noises in my ear. "The three original fucking snipers are unresponsive."

I curse. Whoever this is knew the original plan right down to the placement of our snipers. Hell, they knew when we were fucking arriving.

"What? What's going on?" Randi begs beneath me. "Is T okay? Please tell me T is okay. This is my fault. This is all my fault." The words are barely over a whisper. I wonder if she even knows she's saying them out loud.

"He responded. Tank's okay," I say into her hair. For now, I leave off the end. Who the hell knows where he is in all this. It's not like I can peek back around to make sure he's somewhere safe. "We have to get you out of this shit." But the not knowing who leaked the day's security plan, whether it was someone on our team or those who knew from the embassy, makes me hesitant to seek shelter inside.

"Our sniper is on the move," Tank says. My heart races at the lack of chatter in the background. Tank must have switched to our one-on-one channel. He knows something is off just like I do.

The cool, smooth stone meets my forehead as I lean forward. "If we go inside, then we're trapped, forced on the defensive."

"Where else is safer than the embassy?" Randi questions. "Should we call the president?"

I shake my head. "What if they're the ones behind this? No, we can't trust anyone but our team." And maybe not even that. But I leave that part off for her sake. "Tank," I say into my mic, using our private channel, "we need to get her out of here, back to Air Force One. Cover me while I get her to The Beast."

I switch back to the main channel. Hysteria floods through, with that same unidentified voice hollering above it all, demanding we get her inside the embassy.

"Covered," Tank clips.

"Baby, on the count of three, we're moving. Just follow me, and I'll get you out of this. Do you trust me?"

"Yes."

"One." I thread my free hand in her hair and yank her head back. My lips slam against hers in a demanding kiss. "Two." Releasing her hair, I wrap an arm around her waist and lift her slightly off the ground.

"Three."

Forcing my feet into motion, I slip around the column, placing us right back into the line of fire.

Fuck, I hope I know what I'm doing.

20

RANDI

Stomach acid rises up my throat, threatening to spill from my parted lips. Marines, agents, and streams of crimson scatter the once pristine embassy steps—the same steps I ascended moments earlier, unaware of the life-altering attack about to commence. Pain-laced moans and desperate calls for anyone's help filter through other screams and shouts.

Guilt cuts my heart like a dull rusted spoon.

A stiletto snags an edge of the concrete. Lurching forward, I free-fall for half a second before Trey's strong arm wraps around my waist and tucks me close to his side once again. The pointed toes of my pumps scrape as I'm dragged down the remaining steps. A few agents stay hunkered down behind the limo while Tank stands tall, a gun in each hand, the barrels pointed toward the chaos ensuing in the streets.

A scream rips from my throat as I'm pushed from behind, forcing me to stumble the last step. Hands outstretched, I prepare for impact when an agent catches me before I hit the ground. A familiar face peers down at mine.

"I've got you," Champ says, his face pale and pinched in pain. Without another word, he shoves me into the now open door. A dark-suited body barrels over me, diving deep into the limo, followed by two others. A screech of rubber against asphalt assaults my ears, the smell burning my nostrils. The limo lurches forward, tossing me back, my head nailing the headrest.

Tank shouts commands and directions into his coms. Trey's deceptively calm voice doesn't fool me, and probably not the person he's on the phone with, detailing instructions to the crew on Air Force One. While Champ....

Fuck. Champ.

He slouches, an elbow pressed against the leather seat, cursing like a sailor as he peels his jacket off. Red, and lots of it, stains his previously pristine white dress shirt.

My arms shake, nearly as useless as overcooked noodles, as I ease my ass to the floorboard and crawl toward my injured agent.

Buttons ricochet around the limo, the tiny bits of plastic hitting the windows and leather seats. Carefully, I help him strip out of the soggy shirt. The ripping of Velcro sounds around us as I remove his vest straps and tug it over his head. A hole at the curve of his waist weeps blood, trickling little streams to the seat beneath him.

Staring at the wound, I shrug out of my blazer and press it tentatively against Champ's side.

"Harder," Trey's voice rumbles behind me. Checking over my shoulder to make sure he's talking to me, I see he has the mouthpiece pulled away from his lips. Hitching his chin toward Champ, he sends a pointed expression to the jacket bunched beneath my hands. "More pressure, Mess."

I wince and dare a peek at Champ, scared of what I'll find. Skin a bit paler, sweat dots his forehead and upper lip, but he doesn't pay me any attention as he types one-thumbed on his cell phone. "It's just a graze," he says on a hiss as I press the jacket against his side once again. "Still hurts like a dirty motherfucker."

"Air Force One is ready for departure. We can take off as soon as we arrive. Any remaining agents and personnel can catch a flight with one of the cargo planes." The coarse carpet of the floorboard digs into my palms and knees as I twist to face Trey, waiting for more information.

In unison, the three agents bark unique curses. I stumble back, my heart racing as the limo takes a hard right.

Phone forgotten, Trey stretches toward me, hauls me off the floor, and manhandles me into a bucket seat before strapping me in tight. My shallow breaths are more like wheezes with the near suffocating constriction of the seat belt and lung-seizing fear creeping its way back into my veins. I observe in awe as the three secure their lap belts while keeping their guns and intense focus trained out the window.

"What—" I start when a sudden lurch of the limo cuts me off. Like a rag doll in a dryer, my arms and legs sail through the air while my core remains safely strapped into the seat. The seat belt digs through my dress shirt as I'm shifted right, then left. Tears threaten at the overwhelming terror for not only my safety but those in the limo with me. I swallow hard, shoving them down, and concentrate on stabilizing my neck to prevent my head from snapping off with every sharp turn.

The nerve-racking strain and chase last several minutes before Tank relaxes and gives an all clear. Out the window, the city of Cairo fades and the airport we flew into just hours ago comes into view. Just like in the movies, the limo speeds down the runway, skidding to a halt directly in front of the stairs. US mixed with Egyptian military surround the jet, their massive guns pointed every direction.

With a resounding click, Trey unsnaps my seatbelt and urges me out of the limo into T's awaiting hands. Right before we ascend the stairs, my heel slips, twisting my ankle in an unnatural way. Agonizing pain screams from the tendons and ligaments from below the knee down to my toes.

I lean heavily on T, his hand nearly swallowing my slim waist. Supporting most of my weight, he assists me up the stairs at a rapid pace until we're safely inside my second home.

Doctors charge toward me, ripping me from T's hold and hauling me toward the back of the plane. Questions about injuries are tossed one after another, so fast I can't respond quickly enough. Stumbling, I strain to see over my shoulder, desperate to make sure Trey makes it onto the plane all right.

Our eyes meet the moment he steps through the open door. My lips part, ready to call out to him. I need him, his arms, his whispers of comfort. I can't breathe... and I can't do any of this without him.

No doubt seeing the panic in my eyes, Trey advances toward me but is stopped by T, who shakes his head and points toward a section of seats where other ragged and torn agents sit.

For the first time since the whole ordeal began, I allow a single tear to slip free.

Men died today keeping me safe. Others are injured and bleeding, all for a fight we didn't start.

And one... one of those men, I can't fathom losing.

Once again, I was too close to losing Trey. Today I almost lost my future.

That single thought transforms the panic and uncertainty dictating my every breath and emotion to anger so hot I'm tempted to burn the world to the ground to punish those responsible.

Someone almost took away my forever today.

That someone better be fucking petrified.

Because I'm done playing their games. Those fuckers just messed with the wrong woman.

Up to this point, I've held back the full force of what's at my disposal. Now?

Now they'll feel the wrath of a pissed-off Texas woman.

May God have mercy on their damned souls.

"IT'S FINE," I grumble under my breath. What is it about personal physicians and being so damn hovering? I never had a doctor so observant until I moved into politics. "I've been through worse and just shook it off. Slap a Band-Aid on it and I'll be perfectly fine."

The two male doctors share a confused look before directing their overly attentive focus back on me.

These two remind me of someone—but who?

"It's a sprain, Madam President. A Band-Aid wouldn't fix the issue at hand."

I roll my eyes and shift, allowing my legs to dangle off the table that's worked as my doctors' makeshift workstation for the past hour. "Yeah, I know. I'm not that ignorant. It was a joke. Listen." I huff and tuck a lock of hair behind my ear. "You've wrapped the ankle all nice and tight. I have my little baggie of ice." Grasping the massive ice pack from beside me, I shake the goo-filled bag for emphasis. "And now I need to get back to work. Because I'm pretty certain someone tried to assassinate me—again—and they hurt several Americans in the process. I'd really like to discuss the details with my intelligence team and agents to find out who the hell that was so I can punish them severely."

The two blink in unison. Turn in unison. Part their lips in unison.

I got it! Bert and Ernie! That's who these two morons remind me of.

Hell if I know why though, since neither actually has a similar appearance to the loveable Sesame Street puppets. Maybe it's how they do every-thing in unison and act like they both have a hand shoved up their ass.

"I appreciate you fixing my ankle, but I've got shit to do." I ready myself to stand when the set of crutches they've demanded I use to keep weight off the sprained ankle is shoved against my chest. "Fine," I nearly growl. "I'll take your crutches, but we don't need no stinking crutches." My loud and a bit obnoxious snort vibrates the tip of my nose. The two doctors blink, not finding my joke nearly has humorous as I do. "Seriously, it's a quote from a movie, but I switched out the word badges for crutches." Raising both brows, I consider one doctor, then the other. "It's supposed to be funny."

"What movie, ma'am?" Bert says.

I lift both shoulders in a dramatic shrug. "No clue, but I know I've heard it somewhere. Or maybe it was a poster?" Eager to check on my agents, I plant the pads atop the crutches under my armpits and pitch forward, making for the exit. "Ask Alexa. She'll know."

Managing the door with the crutches and distracting throbbing pain radiating from my ankle proves to be as difficult as getting the House and Senate to agree on anything, but I manage to tug it open. I shuffle down the narrow paths, making my way toward the front of the plane where I last saw T and Trey. The sharp scent of gunpowder, blood, and stale sweat guides me toward my friends and agents.

I round a corner to a small conference room, the door wide open, allowing me to see the devastation inside. My knees buckle at the sight, the crutches I was against the only thing keeping me from collapsing to the floor.

"We're okay, Mess." Trey's words filter through one ear and out the other as I take in the agents coated with sweat and dirt; a few have crimson staining their clothes. "Only a few fatalities. Those in here are wounded but nothing fatal."

My observing gaze pauses on Champ. I saw that wound. There's no way it didn't need to be treated the minute he stepped on the plane.

"Where is the doctor?" I don't recognize my own voice. Cold, focused... determined. The sinking feeling in my gut fans the guilt already flaming inside me.

Not a single agent responds. A few share worried expressions. They must see the edge I'm teetering on.

The crutches creak beneath my weight as I pivot to face Trey.

"Nothing was life-threatening. We've patched up what we can, cleaned the wounds. We'll get detailed medical attention once we land." I try to shove down the ire rising in my chest at hearing they have to wait when medical attention was so readily available to me for a fucking sprained ankle, but it still pours into my narrow-eyed glare. Wisely, Trey retreats a step, his hands raised in surrender. "Don't kill the messenger, Madam President. It wasn't my decision."

"Bert! Ernie!" I bark over my shoulder, directing my voice back the way I'd just come. When the sound of hurried footfalls doesn't immediately come, I mumble a string of curses and hobble out of the room, heading for the small medical office where I last saw the two puppets.

"Hey," I shout once I'm close enough to see inside. Their heads snap up from whatever they were studying. "Get your asses down there and patch them up."

"Ma'am—"

"They are my responsibility. I don't give a rat's fat ass what their roles are, their titles, or their damn income bracket. You get your asses over there now and take care of my guys," I grit out, thrusting my pointer finger in the direction of the injured agents. "You will give them the same obsessive attention you gave me. Every medicine, every bandage is available to them. What's mine is theirs, do you understand?"

Their heads bob up and down, but they still don't move.

"This is not a request. Go. *Now.*"

Their chairs clatter together as they shove to attention. Eyes downcast, they sidle past me and rush down the hall.

Satisfied they'll do exactly as I ordered and the agents who made it back to Air Force One before we took off will be taken care of, I wobble back down the hall toward my office.

Tank and Trey stand waiting just outside the doors, heads together, whispering conspiringly. I failed to notice earlier how both are freshly showered and in clean suits. I take in my own disheveled appearance and wince. I'd love to get out of this pant suit that reeks of sweat and is dotted with Champ's blood.

But no rest for the weary in this job.

"You two, my office." Not waiting, I ignore their shocked expressions and hobble inside the office. Holding back a cringe, I ease myself into the unforgiving desk chair. Try as I might to conceal the pain, a slight wince stretches my features as I relax back.

Trey's laser focus from across the room takes notice of the quick pain-laced expression. The corners of his lips dip in a deep frown. Hands balled into fists, he strides to my side. A bit alarmed at the irritation somehow directed toward me, I shy away, sealing my back against the hard leather. He drops to a low squat, balancing on the balls of his feet. Like my injured ankle is made of glass, he gently lifts until it's level with the desk's polished surface.

"Pillow," he commands over his shoulder. A split second later, a decorative throw pillow from the couch zooms through the air. Trey catches it before it can smack me across the face. The rough material snags the bandages as he slips the pillow beneath my foot and gently rests my ankle on top. I hiss at the instant freezing sensation as Trey drapes a gooey ice pack directly over the injury. "It needs to stay iced and elevated or it won't heal." A sadness lurks behind his eyes as he says, "Give us a second, Tank."

T silently slips through the closed doors and seals them shut behind him.

Reaching across the small distance between us, Trey cradles my face between his calloused palms, the rough skin scraping along my cheeks. For a perfectly silent moment, he searches the entirety of my face, studying every detail before pitching forward to press his soft lips to mine.

One simple kiss from the man who owns my heart and all the overwhelming, terrifying, conflicting emotions from this awful day vanish. I'm lost. Lost in him with zero desire to ever be found.

The kiss turns desperate as we attempt to merge our souls into one with our lips. Too much happened today; this is the way for us to drain the emotions to see clearly later on.

Trey's talented tongue controls my own, lapping me into submission. Seeking hands delve into my hair, fisting at the base and taking a chunk between his fingers. I sigh against his lips at the dominance in the hold. Him taking my control is exactly what I need to feel centered and capable to take on what needs to happen next. A harsh tug snaps my neck back, our lips breaking apart. Our chests heave as we attempt to calm the raging desire he conjured with a single kiss.

Without a word, his grip loosens. With a groan, he stands to full height and retreats a single step, then another, adding unwanted distance between us.

"I don't know how many more instances of your life being in immediate danger I can take, Mess." His raised hand trembles before it glides through his disheveled hair.

"I know, Trey, and I... I know this, what happened today, is partially my fault. I didn't listen to Vlad's advice before, but today... today that changes. Grab T, will you? He needs to hear this too."

With a furrowed brow, Trey turns and moves the few feet to the door. Even with the world literally falling apart around me, I can't help but take notice and admire the way his ass looks in those slacks. Somehow the draping material accentuates the flex of his delectable backside with every step.

A large shadow snaps my ogling from Trey's ass to T, whose intense face appears over Trey's shoulder as he joins us in the office.

"I'm sorry, first off. I know today wasn't my fault, but it feels like it was," I say through a deep breath. Their lips part, chests expanding, but I hold up a hand, stopping their rebuttals. "I should've listened to Vlad when he told me to listen to my advisors, but I didn't, and now we're here. Men lost their lives today, others hurt because someone out there thinks I'll run scared or am an easy target. Well, guess what? Fuck them."

With the excitement of my speech, my foot had slipped off the pillow. I finagle it back on top, hoping for a more comfortable position.

The two share a confused glance.

"What do you mean?" T asks as he paces the small office.

"I mean I'm done with these jackasses calling the shots, putting me and my men in danger. I'm fucking done. Let's go over what happened today and put together an actionable plan that I can present to my military advisors when we return to DC. As soon as we land, I'll fill them in—on everything. I need their advice. I need their help. At first I thought that made me weak, or maybe incapable of performing at this level, but now I know I'm more a fool for ever thinking I could do this without them."

"You sure today's attack and the one in Saudi Arabia were spearheaded by those involved in the Birmingham scandal and not Whit?" Trey asks as his unfocused gaze zeroes in on the wall just over my shoulder.

"You know, I really do. Shawn is a calculating, smart-as-hell evil psychopath, not... sloppy. If that explanation makes sense. The past two attempts have failed because of you guys. I think Shawn would manipulate a sinister plot, not a simple assassination."

Chin to his shoulder, Trey casts a look I can't identify at T. A silent conversation flows between them as the seconds tick by.

"What?" I question, suspicion in my tone. "You two think I'm wrong about Shawn having nothing to do with this?"

"Honestly, I'm not sure. But you're right, this doesn't feel like Whit. But... how much do you want to know about today?" T asks as he scrubs at his bald head over and over.

"All of it," I respond with zero hesitation. "Tell me what you know."

Crouching to the floor beside my chair, Trey rocks back, falling to his ass with a groan. He leans back until he's prone along the floor beside me. Interlacing his fingers behind his head, he smirks up at my raised brow.

"We had a solid plan in place prior to boarding the plan for Cairo. A plan that was thought through, every detail hashed out with not just us but both military personnel and other Secret Service teams. Somehow, those bastards who attacked today knew exactly where our *original* snipers were located, as if they had been warned of their exact position."

"Suspicious," I mumble. The phone rings on the desk. Three sets of eyes follow the sound, focusing on the blinking red light. "Probably the Egyptian president. He called while I was with the doctors demanding an explanation to what happened, but I said I'd call back when I had more details. Impatient man." Ignoring the call, I return my attention to Trey, whose honey brown eyes are already on mine.

"I don't like seeing you hurt," he says, a mix of concern and restrained anger softening his tone.

"I'm safe because of you, remember? And it's only a sprained ankle." Shooting him a tentative smile, I wiggle down the chair, trying to get comfortable with my foot propped up. "Now out with it. What aren't you two telling me?"

"Your boyfriend here has been an overprotective pain in my ass lately, but today I think he saved all our lives with his insistent need to wrap you in a bulletproof protective bubble. He identified two areas where we could potentially need more coverage. At first I didn't agree with him, thought the plan was solid, but something told me to listen to his whining today. To make Benson here happy, we decided to add a few more snipers at the airport and around the embassy." T breaks our stare-off to study the floor.

"Okay, I don't get where this is going. What am I missing?"

"We made that specific change on the plane, Mess. Yet somehow those fuckers today knew about the extra coverage and took out the original snipers *and* the additional ones—well, all except one. Now, how would they have known about the new addition to the plan?"

My stomach clenches with a mix of disappointment and dread as the pieces fall into place.

"You've got to be kidding me," I snap. "You cannot be suggesting there is yet *another* mole on our team. That's absurd."

"We know the men running this shit show have money, and money talks, Randi. They very well could be paying someone off to get close to you, to learn our plans and—"

"Oh good, it gets better." My words drip with sarcasm.

"Today, they could've taken you out with a single shot. Our snipers were down, so why didn't they? Why did they just take out those around you?" Trey says from the floor, now propped up on his elbows.

"My brain hurts. Just tell me."

"It was like they wanted to force us to take refuge in the embassy."

"So?" I question.

"Where we would've been trapped with no way out," T finishes.

A crack reverberates against my teeth as yet another nail snaps beneath my nervous gnawing. "Okay, okay, I see what you're saying. You think their goal was to trap us and go from there? That doesn't make any sense. We would've been hunkered down in the safe room with the Egyptian army as backup."

"Just like in Saudi Arabia, these plans are not well thought out. It's almost as if someone is feeding them the intel, but there are some details lost in translation."

"All but one of our snipers were incapacitated the moment we arrived. They had people waiting, but I shifted one of the added snipers to a different location for a better angle at the last second. I made that move in the limo on the way." T's normally booming voice sounds weary.

I nod like I'm actually tracking with what they're saying. Which I guess I am, but a heavy fog has spread over my thoughts, making connecting the pieces more difficult than usual. "Was the sniper the only shooter?" I ask.

"No, we believe there were additional hostiles in the crowd, but they were more to create chaos than harm the civilians."

"A chaotic scene out front would play into your conspiracy that they needed us stuck inside the embassy instead of escaping. Why?"

"To take you alive," T states matter-of-factly.

"Damn, T, tell me how you really feel." His bulky shoulders rise and fall in an "I don't give a fuck" shrug. "It would make sense if they took me alive. Then they could use me as a bargaining chip, I guess? Or hold me and place the blame on various countries to make the US engage with military force? It's not much of a plan if it is one though."

"Agreed. We never said they were military minded, just sneaky as hell. The fact that the CIA hasn't located them yet says a lot about the money at their disposal and their ability to hide under the radar."

"Let's say you're right," I muse. "And the bastards orchestrating all this did hire someone. Who would it be? You two know everyone, right? Especially everyone on the alpha team."

"Mess, you're forgetting one person." A pinch of pain pulses from my ankle as I swivel to peer down at Trey. His light blue dress shirt stretches across his lean chest, the top two buttons undone, showing off the tan skin beneath and diverting my thoughts from the conversation. "Mess?" A bit of humor laces his voice, like he's trying not to laugh. "Focus, baby."

"Right." I offer a wiry smile. "What did you say again? The pain meds Bert and Ernie gave me are starting to kick in, I think."

"Bert and Ernie?" This time Trey's chuckle goes unchecked.

"The doctors."

A corner of Trey's lips twitches. "I don't even want to know, do I?" Shaking his head, the almost smirk falls. "And I said you're forgetting one person. Smith is new to the team and basically attached to our hips by order of the director. I'm not saying it is him, but the timing is right."

Tiny pinpricks sting the tips of my toes, fingers, and nose, slowly spreading, leaving a warm numb sensation in their place.

"I think it's time for my nap." The words slur with my heavy lips. "Those fuckers drugged me."

As graceful as a cat, Trey stands and carefully scoops me in his arms. "We'll finish this later, Mess."

T swings the door wide and offers my head a little "night night" pat as we pass.

Several curious eyes pretend they're not watching every step Trey takes toward my room with me in his arms.

"They're all looking," I say out of the corner of my mouth. The hand not gripped behind Trey's neck gives the more obvious stares a little wave.

"You're hurt."

"To your knowledge, has a president *ever* been carried back to their bedroom bridal style because they were injured?"

His gaze flicks to me before focusing back on our destination. "I think you've shattered the ceiling on what's precedent for this role."

An agent stationed outside my room pulls the bedroom door open for Trey. With a quick dip of his chin in thanks, we slip through. It clicks closed almost immediately behind us.

"I'm taking that as a compliment," I muse. Numbness weighs down the muscles in my arms and legs. Maybe it was a good idea for Trey to carry me, even if it'll be discussed at every water cooler in the White House starting tomorrow.

Trey smiles and rests me softly on the edge of the bed. One hand helps me lower to the soft mattress as he moves in front of my knees. A quick flick and tug, and the tight waistband gapes open. Features scrunched in pure concentration, he urges the fabric down my thighs, paying extra attention past my knees to make sure the injured ankle remains untouched.

With a forearm behind my neck, he helps me sit up, holding me there as he works the buttons of my shirt free, sliding each tiny slice of plastic through its respective hole with efficiency. Brows furrowed, I watch closely, confused by his careful actions.

"You're about to pass out on me, Mess. Yes, I'd rather rip this shirt off you and give in to every dirty thought, but I'm holding back because you're hurt and drugged."

At that exact moment, the muscles supporting my back soften completely with the influx of pain meds. Before I can crumple to the bed, Trey steadies me and eases me back. The comforter slips beneath me before folding back over my mostly naked body, cocooning me in its warmth. Several solid tucks along one side of my body, then the other, and I'm offi-cially a stuffed and drugged Randi burrito.

Giving up the exhausting fight, I allow my lids to flutter closed, dousing me in a peaceful darkness.

"Trouble," I slur.

"Mess."

His voice is distant, too far from where I lie completely vulnerable.

Anxious thoughts bloom in my gut. Forcing my eyes open, I frantically search the room. I find him at the door, hand on the knob.

"Don't go," I beg. "Lie with me for a little while." Swallowing hard, I fight to stay awake. "I... I don't want to be alone."

"They'll talk, Randi. More than they already are."

"I don't care," I think I mutter, but the numbness in my lips make it hard to tell if I said any words at all. The need for him to hold me grows urgent. Shifting along the cool sheets, I attempt to sit up, but a heavy hand presses on my shoulder, keeping me in place.

"Okay, Mess, you win."

Relief washes through me. With a content sigh, I allow my heavy lids to fall closed once again. The bed dips just before a comforting heat snuggles beside me. His heavy arm drapes across my upper chest, securing me closer. "Now, go to sleep. And when you wake up, I'm force-feeding you."

I snort—at least I think I do.

"Trouble, I love you," I mumble as I continue to slip into the blissful darkness.

"That word doesn't begin to cover how I feel for you, Randi Sawyer."

With one last deep breath, inhaling this moment filled with peace and his unfaltering love, I give in to oblivion.

21

RANDI

"I can't believe this. You've known this entire time what was going on, and you kept it to yourself?" the general, my top military advisor, says, his body trembling with restrained anger. Would he have already blown a gasket if I were a male president instead of a female? If that's the case and my gender is helping him control his temper, this is the one and only time I'll be good with him treating me differently than a male. No way could I maintain this calm facade if he were to leave his emotions unchecked.

Tilting my head ever so slightly, I study him from behind the desk, taking in the full chest plate of medals and stripes.

I get *why* he's this pissed off at me. I've kept all my military advisors in the dark with the situation Kyle unknowingly trapped our country in. Vlad was right all those weeks ago. I was a fool for thinking I could accomplish anything on my own. This role cannot be done by one person alone, but with one person surrounded by those they can trust and depend on. That's the wisdom I lacked. Until now.

"It was need-to-know," I state, arching a brow. Heard that line once in a movie, and it's saved my ass more times than I can count since moving to DC. Once someone hears it, there are zero comebacks.

"That's utter bullshit and you know it," he retorts. The earlier pink tainting his cheeks is now a fiery red.

"Bullshit or not, it was need-to-know at the time, and you weren't one of them." Standing from the desk, I tilt forward, pressing my knuckles to the polished surface in an effort to keep weight off my injured ankle. Sure, the insistent throbbing is annoying as hell, but what other choice do I have? It's not like I can meet with this group of badass men with my foot up on my desk, or even worse, lying on the couch in order to keep it elevated. "The CIA is working on obtaining information on the men who run the group, but I've decided we will move now on military force, taking out the insurgents who've attempted to kill me and continue to spread chaos and uncertainty in the Middle East. However, I'm aware this is your area of expertise, which is why you're here today. I need to know our best course of action, one that will require the fewest troops and little to no casualties." I motion for them to begin.

For over an hour, they debate the best plan, me adding my two cents or asking questions every so often. Two believe a full-on deployment of several thousands of troops is needed to end what we've started. The other one, the quiet one who has the full attention of the room when he speaks, suggests a small special operations team to take those responsible out quietly.

While they resume the arguing, I swivel in the chair, placing my back to the center of the room. A quick peek finds my ankle twice the size it was earlier this morning. The radiating pain is now so intense that sweat collects along my palms and my hairline.

With a grimace, I gradually turn back to the men, my stoic mask back in place before I make the full turn.

"I like the special forces plan," I say. I need to wrap this up and get my ankle elevated before Trey comes by. He'll be pissed seeing it on the floor instead of on the desk. "SEALs?"

The general shakes his head. "Delta Force. They're already on the ground in that area of the world, which means little to no adjustment period. We get a team the intelligence they need to locate the insurgents and it'll be handled. Simple as that."

I swallow. Beneath the desk, my hands begin to tremble. Shit just got real. Our Delta Force is the most elusive subset of our military—hell, any military. Most people don't even believe they exist. But they are still men, men with lives outside the military. What I'll ask them to do will put their lives in danger. Yes, they're in danger all the time, being in the military, but this is different. They need to know what they're fighting for, what they'll be stopping.

And they need to hear it from me. Their president. I need to show some fucking backbone while holding on to some semblance of empathy.

"One caveat to your plan." The general tilts his head in question. "Before they head out on the mission, I will meet with them to discuss the importance of what I'm asking them to do." The room falls silent. If they were to listen closely, I swear all three could hear the throbbing of my ankle.

"No," one of the other advisors says.

"Incorrect answer," I snap. A single drop of sweat trickles between my breast as more forms along the back of my neck. "Get the intelligence you need to put a plan in place for Delta Force, but I will talk to them before they go out on the mission, is that clear?" No one responds. "I said, is that clear, gentlemen," I nearly growl.

One after another, they all slowly dip their chins in acknowledgment.

"Great, this meeting is over. Keep me updated."

Two grumbling men file out. Glancing up from the iPad I can't even focus on, I find the general hovering in front of the desk. There's something about his presence that offers a comforting, protective feel that drains a bit of the tension that's been at a constant high since we landed yesterday afternoon.

"It's dangerous."

"I understand. But I have to do this."

"Why?" Chewing on my lip, I hold back from gasping as I shift in the seat, the bit of movement jarring enough to shoot a bolt of pain straight up my leg. "You should elevate that, you know."

My eyes widen in surprise. His answering smirk produces a light chuckle in my chest.

"Who told you?" I laugh as I carefully lift the injured ankle to the desk and gently rest it on the edge so it hangs over the other side.

"Everyone. Why do you want to meet with the men?"

Sighing, I rub the bridge of my nose. "Because this is different than me asking them to do the job they signed up for."

"Which is?"

"Serving our country, protecting us against the bad guys. In this case, *we* are the bad guys. We're the ones who allowed this to happen, maybe not directly but indirectly for sure. We aren't the ones pulling the trigger, but we fucking gave the insurgents the guns. I just want our men to know what they're stopping, what they're risking their lives for. I owe that to them."

Comfortable silence settles between us as he stares me down.

"I'll make sure it happens, but know it will have to be in and out, and only a few can know. A small team of agents and you. You can't fly Air Force One onto the base. You'd get every man on the entire base killed."

I nod as he speaks. "I only need two agents if we're going in undercover. Maybe I should get a wig, go incognito."

A deep rumbling laugh fills the office. I smile at the rare one now adorning the general's face.

"I didn't know how it would be advising you, Madam President, but I must say it's an honor. What you're doing for our country with the various programs for those trapped in the lower class is exactly what this country needs. No one like you, with your understanding, has sat in the chair you occupy now. Those people have been left alone with no voice for far too long."

I arch a brow. "You sound like you know their plight all too well."

A soft smile causes deep lines to crease his leathery cheeks. "Our ranks are filled with kids with similar backgrounds to your own. Poverty, no way out, terrible home life. I served with many and have trained many more. I've heard the stories, I've listened, and now I'm honored to be advising someone who is focused on a group that most want to forget. Recent intelligence withholding aside."

A lump forms in my throat. "Thank you for your service."

"Likewise, Madam President."

He strides out of the office at the same moment Trey and a very pregnant Taeler shuffle around him to enter.

"How's my grandbaby doing today?" I smile at her rounded belly. We kept the secret as long as we could, but once she started showing, we had to announce it to the media. At first, everyone was disappointed it wasn't me; guess there aren't as many ratings in the first daughter being pregnant as there would've been if I were. The announcement held the public's attention for less than a week before they moved on to something else.

We kept the details of the first assassination attempt in Saudi Arabia out of the media, but with all the cell phones at the Cairo incident, there was no way my media team could keep it under wraps. Now the media sharks are back camped outside; they haven't left since Air Force One landed on American soil. Each reporter and news station wants an interview, details on what happened and how I plan to respond. Most of the news anchors want us to react with the full force of the American military. Not sure if they feel that angry at the thought of me being hurt or if it's sheer bloodlust for higher ratings. Nothing says more viewers like the threat of war.

"The baby is kicking my fucking spleen like it's a plush soccer ball," Taeler says, easing herself onto the couch with Trey's help.

A love-saturated sigh fills my chest. Swoon. Can he get any cuter?

"Language," I grumble at my foulmouthed daughter. I should kick her father's ass for teaching her such fucking language.

"*I'm* okay, by the way. Thanks for asking how your only daughter is doing."

Rolling my eyes, I shoot a pleading look at Trey, who raises his hands in surrender and backs away until his back seals to the far wall. The building smile on his lips falters when he notices my swollen ankle. His narrowed glare burns through me.

"How's your father doing?" I rush out to avoid the verbal lashing I know is sure to come from Trey. "He should be here in the next couple of weeks, right?"

"Dad's fine. Still pouting about how you made him leave."

We both roll our eyes, making us giggle.

"It was your decision too, remember?" I say with a pointed look. "I told him he couldn't move in, but you're the one who sent him packing the next day."

"Yeah, just because—" She cuts herself short and busies herself with tucking a rogue lock of hair behind her ear over and over again. "Anyways. It was best for everyone."

"What do you mean?" Trey asks.

Groaning, she reclines her head, resting it on the back of the couch. "Mom, Dad is great, but... you know."

I frown at her. "No, not at all. What the hell are you talking about?"

"Listen, he's great—"

"You said that already, even though I highly disagree."

"Can you let me—"

"From a partner standpoint, at least. And the sex? Meh."

"Mom," she screeches as she suctions her palms over her ears. I shoot Trey a sly smile before swinging my attention back to Taeler. "I don't want to hear about that. Now, can I fucking finish?"

"Even though you're carrying my grandbaby, I will ground you, Taeler Lynn. Watch your damn language and act like a fucking lady."

"Pot, meet kettle," Trey pipes up, then shrinks back when both Tae and I shift our irritation to him. Fist to his lips, he clears his throat. "Right, sorry. You were saying, Taeler?"

"All he did was talk about you and compare himself to Trouble!"

My mouth gapes. A glance at Trey shows him beaming with pride.

Men.

"He knew something was going on between you two, and I think he was a little insecure about it. That's the only thing I can think of, at least. Why else would he care what was going on?"

"Why else indeed?" I mutter. "Why didn't you tell me when he was here?"

She shrugs. "I liked having him here. You're gone a lot, Mom, which I get considering you're running the country and all, but it gets lonely when you're not around. When he was here, I had someone to talk to, someone who wanted to be around me instead of being paid to babysit me."

A pounding on the door draws all our attention. Trey stretches toward the door and pulls it open.

"We have a problem," Blake states before he's fully over the threshold, with Todd hot on his heels.

"Now I think you just don't know how to start off a conversation without your opening line." Sighing, I direct my attention to Taeler. "Thanks for stopping by, but my five-minute break is officially over." With a sad smile, I watch her waddle out. Trey shuts the door behind her, remaining inside the office.

Blake shoots him a reproachful glance.

"The president is injured. I'm not leaving her alone with you two." His tone leaves zero room for negotiating.

"You first, Todd," I say with a small flick of my wrist.

"The Egyptian president is demanding more answers from you after yesterday's mishap—"

"Mishap," Trey cuts in, the word as sharp as a machete. "It was an assassination attempt on his soil."

"He claims to have no prior knowledge of the attack, and with their casualties, it looks bad. I think we need a show of force—"

"For the final time, no, Todd. I am not sending in our military to retaliate," I seethe. No way will I reveal the plans about Delta Force. The fewer people who know about those plans, the better. It's the best way to ensure the mission goes as planned and the insurgents are caught unaware. "I told the president every detail of the attack once we landed. We were there to visit them, to calm their fears and answer questions. Which we would have, except we were attacked at the first damn stop. Our own embassy at that. Us planning it—" I stop short. Todd's words replay in my mind, snagging on one bit of information. "What do you mean, *their* casualties?"

"Three bodies were found amongst the crowd after we were already in the air." I flick a quick look at Trey in an attempt to confirm or deny Todd's statement. "They were all shot once in the head execution style."

Clenching my fists, I fight the nausea rolling in my gut. "And they think it was us."

"We know it was us," Trey says. Gone is my lovable, mischievous Trey; now standing at full attention is Agent Benson. Which I have to admit is fucking hot as hell. "Smith took the rogue Egyptians out. He states they were part of the attack, firing into the crowd and assisting in creating chaos, yet the Egyptians report there were no guns found on their bodies."

I mull over his words as I point to Blake. "Your turn."

"The media is demanding a press conference. They want to know exactly what happened in Egypt and how we'll retaliate." A calculating gleam sparks his gaze when it lands on my oversized ankle. "The fact that you were injured will make our responding attack justifiable in others' eyes."

The chair groans as it tips back, and I rest my head on the stiff cushion. Eyes closed, I weigh my options while processing the information Todd revealed. "Set up another call for the Egyptian president and me. I will do a press conference, but from behind this desk, not standing behind the podium in the briefing room. There will be zero mention of my injury, and I will highlight that three of the insurgents are already dead and no further military actions will be taken at this time."

"At this time" is my loophole. Hey, I *am* an attorney by trade, after all. What can I say? Once a lawyer, always a lawyer.

The two men bicker between themselves as they file out of the office, Todd visibly upset at my lack of military action. Once they're both gone and the door is sealed shut once again, I roll my head along the chair until I meet Trey's concerned gaze from across the room.

"Tell me your thoughts on what Smith did," I whisper, though I'm not sure why. It's almost like my voice knows my body is running low on energy and needs to conserve.

"I don't know what to think. The surveillance footage we can find doesn't show anything conclusive. In Smith's initial statement, he said the men had ARs and were firing them at random into the air, increasing the confusion and fear around the embassy. But now... now he's clammed up, won't say another word to me, Tank, or those on the review board."

"Maybe I should try. We have a rapport of sorts, I think."

Trey's features turn contemplative. "Couldn't hurt for you try. There is something off about all this that I can't figure out. Maybe if you get him talking, pieces of this damn puzzle will fall into place." Sleeve to his lips, he whispers something about Smith before lowering the arm to his side once again. "We'll figure out a time for you to meet with Smith before the end of the shift. Now, what the fuck did you do to your ankle? Run a marathon since this morning?" With a few quick, determined steps, he's at the desk, fingers carefully prodding the bandage nearly cutting off the circulation to my toes. "What am I going to do with you, Mess?"

"I can think of a lot of things, Trouble."

His lips twitch. "How did the meeting with the military advisors go earlier?"

"Good. The general suggested Delta Force." Rubbing a jagged nail along the edge of the iPad, I avoid looking up as I continue. "I agreed, and then I told them I want to talk with them before the mission. In person."

The gentle swipe of his fingertips along my shin pauses. After a few moments, I relent on the avoidance and turn to gauge his reaction.

Face flushed, brows furrowed, lips pursed.

Not good.

"No," he barks.

"Yes?" I say, tilting my head. "Pretty sure it's my call."

"Damn sure it's not, Randi. I told you no more making life-threatening decisions without discussing it with me, with your protection team, first, and you go and do this shit?"

"I have to talk to them," I hiss. Shifting my foot off the desk, I carefully lower it to the floor. "They need to know what they're fighting for."

"Call them! Hell, send them a secure text or email. But you are *not* going where those men are stationed."

"And why the hell not?" I yell.

"Because I know where they station those men. You are not putting yourself in that kind of unnecessary danger. The answer is no."

"The answer is yes."

"Randi." Stepping back, he runs a hand through his hair. "Stop fighting me on this. Let me do my job. Let me protect you. I've told you I can't keep seeing you in harm's way. Do you not give a damn about that?"

"I have to do this," I say, a bit of the venom from earlier gone from my tone.

"No you don't, and it makes me fucking miserable knowing that you don't even give a damn about anyone else but yourself. You know I'm not trying to control you, yet that's how you're taking it. Stop being so damn selfish, Randi, and see what your actions do to me, to Tank. Hell, the whole team. This country. It's not just you anymore. If something were to happen to you, the *world* would be impacted."

"Anything could happen to me at any moment," I say, trying to keep my cool.

"Exactly, so why increase the odds by going into an area known as a terrorist hotbed? To a base camp where attacks happen daily and survival is only for those who can take the pressure of being under constant threat? Listen to me, please, Randi. I'm begging you. Do this for me. Don't push this. Don't go."

The urgency in his forceful words, the plea behind his searching eyes, catches me off guard like a punch to the chest. To the heart, to be exact.

Could he be right? Am I being selfish not considering the impact of my every move and decision? Am I really willing to put the agents and the men and women at the base in harm's way just so I can slough some of this guilt at what's been done off my shoulders? This, and a million other reasons, is why I'm the shittiest president ever to occupy the White House. And the exact reason someone more deserving, tenured, should be in this role. Someone like Trey. He sees the big picture, the thousand-foot view. Whereas mine is the two-foot leap from the trailer park door to the cinder block makeshift stair below.

"You're right," I finally say. Shaking my head, I lean forward, resting my face in my awaiting palms. "I wasn't thinking."

"Yeah you were, Mess. Just with your heart instead of your head. And that's okay. It's one of the things I love about you."

Inhaling a deep calming breath, I blow it out slowly before leaning back and meeting his smirk.

"You gotta remember," he says. "Men are better at using their heads because we have two."

A loud, obnoxious snort tickles my chest and nose. A tentative smile tugs at my lips, matching his growing one.

"And I can honestly say, Trouble, I'm not quite sure which of your two heads I like the most." Thin smile lines appear at the corners of his eyes as his cheeks bunch. "Thanks, Trey. What would I do without you?"

I hook a finger through a belt loop and tug him closer. His fingers delve deep into my hair. Closing the distance between us, he brushes an almost kiss over my lips.

"You'll never have to wonder, Mess. I'm not going anywhere."

The desk phone screams with a shrilling ring, breaking the intimate moment. Two red lights blink along the front, indicating multiple calls coming through. Without a warning knock, the side door swings open, causing both our heads to snap to attention. My secretary steps into the Oval Office, her eyes purposefully downcast.

Trey's fingers loosen their hold before sliding free.

"Your noon meeting is here, Madam President. Also the press secretary is waiting for approval on the documents I emailed you. And Vice President Pierce has called multiple times requesting a meeting this afternoon."

"Who's on line one?" I ask with a resigned sigh. *Damn. Playtime is over.*

"The French president."

"And line two?"

"Your ex, ma'am." Her eyes snap up at Trey's predatory growl. "Sorry, Mr. Ben Hopkins. He says it's urgent."

Groaning, I bang my forehead on the desk before stealing my spine and rolling both shoulders.

Back to work.

22

TREY

Arms folded across my chest, I monitor every blink, every breath Smith takes as Randi asks about Cairo. Every word, the explanation and details, are the same as in his report. I glance at Tank, and he breaks his focus on Smith. A whole conversation passes between us without a single word spoken.

We're both in agreement.

Something doesn't add up.

Which seems to be a common occurrence when Smith is involved. That time in Saudi Arabia when we couldn't find him wasn't the only one. A few times, Tank or I've looked for him off shift and been unable to reach him. Sure, I used to do the same thing, vanish when my shift was over for some local fun, but I was a mischievous dumbass, not... suspicious.

Everything about him is suspicious: his redacted file, the coldness in his demeanor. Add in his constant disappearing act and how could we not think he's the one leaking the information on Randi's whereabouts?

"And you're telling me the truth?" Randi asks. She flicks a quick questioning look my way before focusing back on Smith.

Fuck, she's beautiful. How I got so damn lucky, I'll never know. Now to convince her to marry me. I was serious that night in my small-as-fuck bedroom. She wasn't ready then, but I'll never stop waiting for her to be.

"Madam—" Her hard glare cuts him short with a throat-clearing cough. "I know what I saw. I did what needed to be done."

"What do you do for fun?" she asks.

For the first time since I've known the guy, sheer surprise registers across his face before he slams the impassive mask back in place.

"When will the official review be complete, ma'am?" he asks instead of responding to her question.

"Did I mention I've been eating more protein?"

"No, ma'am. Is it helping?"

Her smile widens, and a shallow breath escapes me at the sight. Even after a full day of work, she still manages to find a reason to smile. If I do find a way to get her to say yes, I'll do everything I can every day to make sure those beautiful smiles never stop.

"Eh," she says with a shrug. "I'm kidding. Yes. Do you believe unicorns are real?"

"Excuse me?"

"Unicorns. The magical horned horse that is beautiful and could double as a badass secret weapon."

"Is she serious?" he asks, turning to me.

I just shrug, a smile fighting to escape. Damn, I love this woman. This has to be the most random interrogation tactic I've ever seen, but it's all Randi. Hell, she might not even know what she's doing—she's just being her.

"No, I lost the hope of mystical creatures and heroes a long time ago."

"Well, that's sad." Disappointment laces her words.

"That's the reality of this world."

"Even you?"

"Even me what?"

"You're not a hero?"

His nostrils flare. "I'm no one."

"I know how that feels." Picking at a button string, she turns her attention to her lap. "Doesn't make it true." Looking up through her dark lashes, she flashes me a smile. "Someday, someone will come along and show you how untrue that statement is."

"I thought we just covered the fact that I don't believe in mystical creatures."

A tremor shakes her shoulders. Chafing her hands up and down her arms, she turns her full focus back to Smith. "Just wait. It'll happen, and I'll get to tell you 'I told you so.' So why would you kill those guys anyway?"

"It's my job to keep you safe, is it not?" Three shallow lines form along his scrunched brow.

"It is, but why shoot them? Why not arrest them?"

"I don't follow." The lost expression on his face makes me want to believe him.

"She wants to know why shooting them in the head was your first reaction," I say to help clarify.

"It's efficient."

"Efficient," she says, shaking her head. "Now I'm the one who doesn't understand."

"If I shoot them in the head, then I know they're down for good and can't recover to come back and shoot me or you."

"Logical," she muses. "I suppose I'll never understand the first reaction being to kill someone or be killed. Where did you learn to be so... efficient?"

I drop my arms to my sides. Leaning closer, I wait eagerly to hear his answer. All the guys on the team have their own suspicions. Most assume he was a Ranger or SEAL before flunking out of Homeland Security or NSA. But the quietness about him, the hidden darkness that he keeps tucked deep inside, makes me think CIA.

He makes to shift on the couch, and if I weren't watching like a hungry hawk, I would've missed the hint of a wince at the small movement. I scan his starched white dress shirt, wishing for the first time since I was six years old that I had X-ray vision.

"A little bit of everywhere." His cold gaze slides to me, then to Tank. "You don't seem the type to beat around the bush, Randi. If there's something you want to ask me, ask me."

"Did you inform the insurgents of the change of plans in Cairo?"

I'll give it to my girl, her voice stays steady and strong as she holds his gaze.

"Are you accusing me of treason?"

"I'm asking a question, Agent Smith." Randi shifts on the couch, causing the pillow supporting her ankle to slip. Before I can even think about helping, Smith has the rogue pillow back in place and, if I'm honest with myself, at a better position than I had it originally. "Thank you. Boy Scout?"

"No."

"Mr. Prepared?" she challenges, her voice lighter than just moments ago.

"Absolutely not." Squinting, I barely make out the hint of a smile fighting to the surface of his blank face.

"Bond?" Dark locks float over her shoulder as she shakes her head. "No, too cliché. Guess it's back to the drawing board. It would help if you, I don't know, opened up a little more. Gave me a little insight to your personality."

"Personality." A single light brow ticks up his forehead. "You seem to think I have one."

"You do." Smiling, she glances to the phone vibrating on the table. "And we'll find it, promise."

"Don't try to save me, Randi."

"Who said anything about saving?"

Leaning forward, he presses his elbows on top of his knees and clasps his hands. "I know what you're doing. Building rapport, trying to find a baseline of trust, hoping I'll tell you what I know. It won't happen, and I can guarantee you there's nothing you can do to alter what I am."

"What are you?" she asks. Again the cell phone rattles on the coffee table.

"Unsalvageable." A quick glance to the phone screen and he pushes off the couch opposite of Randi. "I'm sure you need to take that." At the door, he turns and looks me straight in the eye. "I'm a lot of things, but a traitor to his country and the person running it is one thing I will never be. I agree, there is a leak, but you're looking in the wrong direction."

"Think you can find out who it is?" I ask quietly.

With a dip of his chin, he slips out the door, all without a sound.

Randi's quiet voice filters through one ear and out the other without me processing her words as she speaks to the person on the other end of the phone.

"Did you get what you needed?" I ask Tank at the feel of a large presence at my back.

"He's hiding something, but hell if I know what."

"Agreed. I can't shake the feeling that there's something we're missing." I shake my head as I run a few fingers through my hair, disturbing the gel holding it in place. "Nothing can happen to her." A commotion snaps both our heads toward the couch, where Randi struggles to stand on her own. "Fuck me."

"That's her job," Tank retorts with a laugh as we stride to the middle of the room to offer aid.

"Seriously?" she hisses, the mouthpiece pulled away from her mouth. "On the phone here."

The silk blouse beneath her jacket slides as I wrap an arm around her waist to support her weight as she hobbles around the room, acting as her human crutch. The voice on the other end continues talking, but the words are too muffled to catch a full sentence. Her soft curves mold under my hand as I wrap my fingers around her thin waist. That simple touch, over clothes, and my cock twitches to life.

Twisting as we walk, I attempt to adjust myself without drawing attention to the situation growing in my pants.

"Really?" Tank chastises.

Busted.

"What?" I say, waving a hand down the front of Randi. "How could I not?"

"We discussed this already, Ben." Her light weight leans harder against me. Eyes closed, she presses her forehead to my shoulder. "That's not going to happen. I don't—"

That fucker. What the hell does he want now? If only there was a way to distract her from the call, or hell, better yet, make her want to hang up on the asshole. Pressing the side button of my phone, I check the time. Eleven. Which means our shift ended an hour ago.

A smirk plays at my lips. The muffled voice of that dipshit ex of hers continues to sound through the phone as I guide her across the Oval Office floor and out the door. Halfway to the residence side, she holds the cell away from her lips and tilts her face up to mine.

"Where are we going?"

I arch a brow in response and continue helping her down the hall. By the time we make it to her room, she's nearly limp in my arms. Once inside, I help her to the bed before unwinding my arm from her waist.

"That doesn't help anything, Ben. It's more stress on Tae." Those hazel eyes roll to the ceiling and stay there.

A quick snap of my fingers gains her full attention. I motion down the line of buttons. "Off," I mutter. A single tug on my tight tie loosens it, allowing the silky material to hang haphazardly from my neck. The jacket slides from my shoulders as I shrug out of it and place it, my shoulder harness, and sidearms on a stuffed chair in the corner of the room.

Phone tucked between her ear and shoulder, Randi never shifts her curious gaze as she pops one button after another until the soft material hangs open. A small gap shows off a strip of bare chest and a glimpse of black lace.

"Ben, listen, I understand you're upset— No, what happened in Egypt has nothing to do with— You will not." I hold her rapt attention as I work one cufflink and then the other before peeling my own dress shirt off. The vest and then the undershirt are next, carefully deposited to the small pile of discarded clothes and firearms. Metal clinks as I tug on my belt.

She nibbles on her lower lip, her lids lowering as she watches the thin strip of leather slide from one belt loop and then another until it too ends up on the floor.

"Ben, I need to go." I shake my head and press a single finger to my pursed lips. Randi's dark brows furrow, a thin line forming between them. "Um, actually... hold on." The phone peels from her ear. Pressing the screen face to the bed, she tilts her head, eyes searching mine. "What are you doing?"

"Having a little fun, Mess. Now be a good girl and keep him talking." The phone stays on the bed. "Now, baby. I won't ask nicely a second time."

A red flush spreads across her cheekbones and down her neck. I watch each inch that phone rises, my cock hardening with each passing second at the thought of what's to come.

"Sorry, someone needed something," she says to Ben as she shrugs out of her jacket. "What were you saying?"

Her cherry vanilla scent envelops me as I step closer to the bed. With a soft caress along her shoulders, I slide the silk blouse off one and then the other. Trailing two fingers down her spine, I flick the clasp causing the black lace bra to loosen.

The moron on the other end of the call keeps talking, completely unaware of my devious plan.

With both palms on either side of her knees, I urge them apart until I'm able to kneel between.

A deep sigh pushes past her lips at the first soft kiss I press to her collarbone. Her normally cool skin is now hot to the touch. Sucking and nibbling, I bite at the soft flesh between her shoulder and neck.

She gasps before remembering she's on the phone and covers it with a fake cough.

"What?" she says into the phone. "Oh, nothing. Stubbed my toe?"

I chuckle against her skin. Cupping one breast, I circle the pebbled nipple, drawing closer and closer to the tip with each pass. A full-body tremble rakes through her as the edge of my nail slides across the tip. Pulling away, I watch with utter fascination as her head falls back, the ends of her dark hair brushing the white duvet. Pinching the hard tip between two fingers, I suck the other between my lips, flicking my tongue rapidly over the sensitive nub.

Heat builds beneath my skin, a raging inferno urging me to hurry this the fuck along and rip her damn pants off. My dick throbs, pressing hard against the zipper of my slacks. I groan against her nipple, taking more between my lips at the threading of her fingers into my hair and not-so-subtle urge for more.

Careful to not injure her ankle any more than it already is, I work her soft gray trousers and black lace thong over her hips and down the thighs I desperately want wrapped around my waist. Once she's completely naked, I assist her in lying back on the bed.

With a cocky smile, she complies, that cell phone still glued to her ear.

Admiring the unobstructed view of the treasure I'm desperate to lick, I slide both palms up and down the soft skin of her inner thighs. With every teasing stroke, I pause at her center before massaging back down to her knees and making my way back up again. The sweet scent of her wet center shoves me over the edge of patience into instant fucking gratification. Without warning, I spread her slick lips apart with both thumbs and suck her clit between my lips.

A high-pitched moan passes her lips, followed by a mumbled apology, but I'm too lost in devouring her delicious center to fucking care what she's saying to that dumbass.

In fact...

It's time for my fun little game to be over.

My palm sinks into the mattress as I lean up, the heat pouring off her wet pussy now pressing against my upper abs. Eyes wide, she shakes her head as I reach for the phone, but I ignore her pleading. Snatching the damn thing from her hand, I give my lips one more long lick, savoring the flavor of her before hitting the speaker button.

The sound of that dumbass's voice almost kills the mood, but her writhing beneath me, sliding her wetness across my bare skin, wins.

"Your time's done, fucker," I say, my gaze locked on Randi's as I shift enough to slide two fingers deep inside her. Those hazel eyes roll to the back of her head. "Stop using your daughter to win Randi back. It won't happen, and you know how I know that won't happen?"

"Who the fuck is this?" His voice shakes through the line, no doubt with barely controlled rage at my voice.

"You know who it is." A squeak cuts through the room as I add another finger. Randi's hips lift from the bed. Sliding a hand up her stomach, I tweak one nipple, then the other. A pleasure-filled groan passes her lips.

"What the fuck are you doing to her?"

I shake my head. Dumb bastard. A part of me will always hate him for having Randi first, but at least now I know for certain she didn't know pleasure with him.

"I'm about to fuck her so hard she forgets who she is. Stop fucking calling. Stop trying to take what's mine."

Releasing the nipple between my fingers, I tap the screen, cutting off his responding tirade.

"Trey," she pants.

"Shh, baby, I know." Dipping low, I seal my lips over hers. Our teeth clash at the force of her hands gripping my hair, yanking me closer. I twist my wrist, placing the heel of my palm against her swollen clit. She cries against my lips with each curl of my fingers and circle of my hand.

Randi's chest heaves against my own. Our tongues flick and slide, dueling against the other's.

"You," she whimpers against my lips. "I want you."

Fuck yes.

One-handed, I undo my slacks, allowing them to pool at my feet.

Dark hair fanned against the white duvet, cheeks flushed, eyes hooded, she looks like a sex-starved angel. My breath catches as I grip and stroke my aching cock, taking in all of her laid out like a damn present.

Her whimpers at the loss of my fingers fill the room. The wetness coating my digits smears along her skin as I slide my hand beneath her backside, lifting her hips to the perfect angle. Knee to the bed, I slide just the tip of my swollen head inside.

"Fuck," I hiss. Every cell in my damn body screams to shove in deep and take what's fucking mine. My muscles tremble with restraint as I ease inside her, careful to not jostle her too much.

Our gazes lock. I skim the fingertips of the hand not holding her hips along her injured leg, stopping at the knee. Cupping it at the bend, I raise her leg until it's hooked over my shoulder.

"Really? You're multitasking?" She chuckles.

"Hmm, I remember you wanting to be gagged." Her eyes widen to the size of golf balls. Thumb to her lips, I breach the edge and push past her teeth. "Suck."

My hips jerk at the feel of her lips engulfing my thumb, her tongue dancing across the pad. The soft suction of her lips breaks the thin grasp I've held on my restraint. I slam deep, and she bites down on my knuckle as her harsh breaths pant against my skin.

Skin slapping against skin turns the erotic scene beneath me even hotter.

My thumb pops from her mouth as her head thrashes along the bed, her moans and whimpers the most beautiful fucking music I've ever heard. With a sharp cry, her lids slam shut, her whole body tenses as release shocks through her system.

Skin slick, my grip slips on her hips. The soft muscle molds beneath my fingers, and I hold on for dear life as her pussy clamps around me, shooting me over the edge. All the pent-up anger, uncertainty, and every other damn emotion she invokes barrel out of me with a string of muttered curses as my hips jerk in an unsteady cadence.

Trails of sweat slide down my bare chest, droplets gathering at the edge of my hairline as my shaking arms hold my weight above her. A relaxed, happy smile splits across her face with a content sigh.

"That was exactly what I needed," she says, those hazel eyes scanning my face.

I huff, the small movement making my softening dick twitch inside her, readying for round two.

Her eyes widen.

"What makes you think we're done, baby?"

The responding gasp urges me lower until we're nose to nose.

"I promised I would fuck you till you forgot your name. And I always keep my promises."

A light vibration has me arching a brow.

"My phone," she says, still smiling from her postorgasmic high. Blindly, she pats the bed, searching for the discarded phone. It's still vibrating with an incoming call when she slips it between us to read the screen. A thin line forms between her brows. "I need to get this." With a bit of work, she maneuvers her arm around my own. "Hello?"

Confusion and then surprise registers on her beautiful face. Palm pressed to my chest, she gives me a soft push, urging me off her. With a frustrated groan, I slide out of her and carefully lower her leg back to the bed. The bed jostles, making her naked breasts shake with the movement as I drop to the bed beside her.

An attention-grabbing cough pulls my attention from her chest. Annoyance laced with humor covers her features as she rolls her eyes, telling me she full-on caught me ogling her tits. What can I say? She's beautiful with clothes on and without. And I'm a guy, and she's naked, so yeah, of course I'm fucking distracted.

"Are you sure?" she says into the phone. "When?" Rising to her elbows, she shoves off the bed to sit up. "I have other things in play that need to happen at the same time as what you're suggesting. I'll have more information tomorrow on a timeline. Let's book a meeting with you, me, and one of my military advisors first thing."

The phone slips from her hand, falling to the bed. Concern shoves the last drops of need from my mind. I push up to sit beside her, putting us shoulder to shoulder.

"Mess?" I say, wanting to pull her unfocused gaze from the floor to me. Worry eats at my gut when she doesn't respond. "Randi, come on, talk to me. What was the call about?"

"It's over," she says. A single tear glides down her still flushed cheek. She turns to face me, a wide smile bunching her cheeks. Additional tears stream down her face; she doesn't bother to wipe them away before they drip off her jaw. "That was the director of the CIA. They've located everyone. They identified the group running it all and can take them out at my call. There are seven men and one woman, located around the globe. They found them... all of them, Trey." The bed bounces beneath us as she hops, clapping her hands in childlike excitement. I'm completely unprepared when she lets out a squeak and launches herself on me, wrapping both arms around my neck.

"And?" I ask.

"At my word, once the Delta Force is in place, they'll be brought into custody or... well, you know. It's over, Trouble. In a few days, it'll all be over.

Everything Kyle put into place, everything he dragged us into, will finally be fucking over."

Another high-pitched squeal echoes around the room as I flip us, putting her beneath me once again.

Her happy tears wet my lips as I kiss each one away on my way down to her neck.

"Well, then, we should celebrate."

Hope fills every cell. Happiness races through my veins, making my own happy tears build.

The shit Kyle left behind for her, for our country, is over.

Now we can focus on our future.

Together.

23

RANDI

June

The stillness of the night offers a soothing caress to the constant anxiety and worry that have been my relentless companions the past few months. Next to me in his large bed, Trey sleeps soundly, his soft breaths deep and even against my bare shoulder. A thin strip of light beams under the bedroom door from the illuminated hallway where I know two beta team agents wait. The darkness surrounding us is a comfort, but only because of the man beside me. For a while, the dark was something I feared because of the unknowns and enemies lying in wait there. But now it provides the peace and serenity I don't have with my overwhelming responsibilities as president.

With the scandal Kyle left behind over, the men and woman responsible in custody or dead, I can breathe a bit easier. Delta Force lived up to their notorious name and took out the few insurgent strongholds with zero casualties on our end and left enough survivors for us to gain information on other terrorist cells. The only regret I have regarding the military force is that I didn't do it sooner. Vlad and I have spoken, on several occasions, to help me identify other areas where I'm weakest and need additional advisor support. The CIA came through as they said they would. At the end of it all, three of the masterminds were detained, AKA still breathing, and have spilled their knowledge on the scandal helping us ensure we detained/killed everyone involved.

But even with that handled there are more issues and incidences and policies to manage in a day than I have energy to handle.

Add in being a doting grandmother and wanting to spend every moment with that little cuddle bug and there is *never* enough time in the day. I'm overwhelmed, overworked, and in desperate need of a full night's sleep. But these nights, the few a week I sneak to Trey's condo for a few blissful hours, have kept me sane—well, sane-ish. It is still me, after all.

On top of everything else, next year is an election year, which means I have a decision to make: to run again or endorse someone else for my party. The deadline for my decision ticks closer with each passing day, but I can't decide.

I have no clue what I want.

The moon peeks from behind the clouds. The few soft rays filter through the thin blinds, highlighting Trey's handsome face.

He's why I haven't made the decision yet.

I hate the job, but I'm doing well, which makes me want to run for another term.

But I also want him. All to myself. Every minute, every second, us together without any worries or interruptions. If I decide to run again and get elected, then the crazy schedule I keep now will continue another four years, leaving little time or energy for him.

Sighing, I relax back against the pillow and shut my eyes.

The sneaking around would change if we went public with our relationship. Which we could, but at what cost to his life? If we announce our relationship, it either needs to be all or nothing. I can't imagine me introducing him to the country as my boyfriend and then having to come back here at the end of every shift. The media swarm would engulf him daily.

No. If we decide to do this, I have to be all in.

Which I am. Who knows why I'm holding back from saying yes to the question he didn't really ask so many months ago. There's no doubt in my mind he's waiting for an answer. Waiting for me to be ready. Trey hasn't brought it up since that night. Which makes me love him more. He's offering me time, even when he's the one paying the price for my indecisiveness.

The sneaking around, watching me from the sidelines, it's getting to him.

I want to say yes.

Every piece of my untrusting heart begs me to scream yes.

So why haven't I?

"I can feel you thinking." Trey's soft lips move along my tattooed skin before pressing a quick kiss to my bicep. "What time is it?"

"Almost three," I say on a sigh. "Which means it's time for me to get going."

The mention of me leaving shifts the comforting silence to something weighted with dread.

"You know what I hate the most about all this?" he says, tucking his hands behind his head.

"What?" I whisper. The long strands of his dark hair glide through my fingers. What I wouldn't give to do this every night.

"When you're here, I can't fully enjoy our time together because I know it'll end. You'll leave, and I'll wake up here alone."

"I know. Trey, I've been thinking—"

A sharp knock at the bedroom door cuts me off. Trey leaps from the bed, gloriously naked, and takes the two steps to the door.

It opens an inch, pouring more bright light into the dark room. "We need to leave, Madam President," a muffled voice says through the small crack in the door.

Trey smacks the heel of his hand against the wood, slamming it shut in the other agent's face.

"Stay," he says without turning. "Just tonight, stay."

Pursing my lips, I shuffle along the sheets and reach to the floor for the clothes Trey ripped off me a couple hours ago. The heavy silence stretches, making the distance between us feel farther than the few feet. Whipping my dark hair out from the collar of the gray T-shirt, I twist it up into a makeshift bun, securing it with a rubber band I discovered in the back pocket of my jean shorts.

After sliding my flip-flops on, I shuffle to the door where Trey still stands, his forehead pressed to the wood.

Both arms secure around his waist, squeezing tightly, I squish my chest to his bare back. Nose pressed to his spine, I infuse my lungs with the scent that's all him.

"It wouldn't be any easier," I whisper against his skin. "There isn't a good choice in this."

"Yes there is, you're just too scared to make it. I don't know what's holding you back, Randi, but I wish you'd stop fighting it."

"I love you, Trey," I say, tightening my arms in an attempt to mold us into one.

"That's never been the issue, Randi." Turning, he wraps his arms around my shoulders. For several moments, we hold on to each other like a lifeline. "I love you, Randi. I will always love you. And I'll wait until my last breath for you to be ready. Just know when you're done doubting, done debating the options, I'll be here."

"Ma'am," says a deep voice from the other side of the door. "We need to leave now."

With one last squeeze, he releases me and reaches behind him to open the door. I blink past the bright light that spills through the room.

"Trouble," I say, my voice quivering. Each time I leave, it's been harder to say goodbye. Tonight is the worst yet because for the first time, he's asked me to stay.

"Go, Randi. I'll see you tomorrow. We're good." With a quick peck to my lips, he urges me out the door with a hand to my lower back.

What am I doing? Why do I think I have to choose? Men have been married, had relationships for years as president, so why can't I? Why do I feel this strange sense of needing to prove I'm capable on my own because I'm a woman?

Yes, I can do this on my own. I've done this thing called life, living and working, all on my own. I put myself through undergrad, I worked my ass off through Harvard, and I passed the bar in Texas.

And I'm so tired. Exhausted from proving to everyone that I can do this on my own.

But behind me is a man. A man desperately trying to show me I don't have to. That he won't control me, won't hold me back but instead challenge me and encourage me.

I don't have to do this alone.

I slow my steps until I'm standing still in the hallway. The thin rubber of my flip-flops twists beneath my toes as I turn and race back to his room. Throwing the door open wide, I leap onto his retreating back, wrapping my legs around his waist and my arms around his shoulders.

"Ask me again," I beg out of breath. "Ask me again, Trey. Right here, right now, ask me again."

Chin to his shoulder, he attempts to face me. Leaning forward, I press my cheek to his.

"Ask me," I whisper.

"Marry me," he murmurs. "Fucking marry me, Mess."

"Yes," I say on a choked sob. "Yes, I'll fucking marry you."

My squeal bounces off the walls as he somehow untangles my legs and arms and swings me around. Our lips clash, tongues dancing like we're suffocating and the other is the life-sustaining air we need. His hands roam up and down my back, my own scraping along his scalp.

A throat clearing breaks the spell we fell into.

"Tomorrow." My swollen lips slide against his. "I'll call a press conference to announce us, plus my decision for running next year, and then I want you to move into the White House with me." My breaths come fast with the excitement racing through my veins. "I never want to fall asleep or wake up without you again."

"Tomorrow." He presses his hot forehead against mine. "I'm coming with you tonight."

I shake my head, our foreheads rolling. "I want to tell Taeler alone, and I need to work on what exactly I need to say. But know this, Trouble: tomorrow starts our beginning."

"No, baby, we began that night in Central Park. This is just the next chapter."

"The best chapter."

"The chapter filled with me fucking you every night. With me waking up to you every morning. To us never being apart again."

With the hood of Trey's black zip-up hoodie pulled low, I smile like a damn fool as the asphalt crunches beneath my feet. A hand between my shoulder blades guides me through the dark alley toward the awaiting town car. A deep glorious ache throbs in my cheeks from holding the face-splitting grin since we walked out of Trey's condo minutes ago.

The flip-flops pop against my heels with each step, mirroring the click of the agents' dress shoe heels. A few feet ahead, the door to the town car is swung open, an agent holding it for me as he scans the empty streets for threats. Adrenaline pumps through my veins, adding a small bounce to my steps.

"You seem happy tonight." I tilt my head just enough to keep my face covered but also to see who spoke. Agent Ponder's profile slides in and out of the shadows cast by the low streetlamp, his hand still on the open door.

"You could say that," I say, barely able to contain my excitement.

"And why's that?"

"Ponder, what are you doing here?"

Turning, I look to the agent at my back. Agent Wright frowns as he takes in Agent Ponder's hand now gripping my bicep before shifting his gaze to the agent himself.

Forgetting about the need for concealment, I tilt my face up for a better view of Agent Ponder.

"I called the boss. He ordered me to meet up here before you escorted her back."

I furrow my brows, looking from Agent Ponder to Agent Wright. Neither looks very happy about the other being here. Which doesn't make sense.

"For fuck's sake, call him if you need to, but we have to get her secure, not lingering on the damn streets." He grumbles a string of curse words under his breath as he turns us toward the car. He urges me into the back of the vehicle and slams the door shut.

Unease weighs in my gut. Nail between my teeth, I lean closer to the tinted window to see out. Whatever tension was building between the two men disappears as they slap each other's backs. The agent who had been waiting in the front passenger seat relaxes back, his shoulders lowering as Agent Wright slides behind the wheel. The remaining agents pile into the lead and follow SUVs. When everyone is situated and I'm buckled in, we zoom off through the early morning darkness.

I exhale deeply to ease the ball of dread restricting my breath. Whatever that was between the two agents was nothing. Agent Wright and Agent Ponder are freaking Secret Service, not bad guys. Everything is fine. I'll get back to the White House, take care of a few emails, and work on the speech for tomorrow.

Tomorrow.

My ass vibrates with a text or call. Pitching forward, I pull it from the back pocket of my faded jean shorts and check the screen.

Trouble: I love you. Can't wait to celebrate.

Trouble: Ass play?

I snort, distracting the agent up front from the low conversation he and Agent Wright were having. I wave him off and swipe the screen open to respond to my idiot boyfriend.

No. Idiot fiancé.

Smiling, I move my thumbs across the screen.

"Watch out!"

My head snaps up just in time to see the front of our car smashing into the lead SUV's red brake lights.

24

TREY

"Hello," I croak, my voice raspy with sleep. The bed frame rattles as I flop to my back. Squinting one eye open, I glance at the window, expecting the morning sun pouring through but finding darkness instead.

A knowing dread scatters goosebumps along my arms and the back of my neck.

Something's wrong.

Bolting up to a sitting position, I scrub a hand over my face to help me wake up faster. "What happened?" My voice is deep and edgy with determination and fear.

"I don't have all the details," Tank shouts through labored breaths.

I leap from the bed and begin pulling on clothes, not even checking to see if they're on correctly.

"What do you know?" I demand. Hopping on one foot, I shove the other through a pair of jeans before switching. Leaving the front dangling open, I yank a discarded T–shirt over my head.

"There was a wreck, an ambush. They're all dead, Trey. They're all fucking dead," he bellows into the phone. The roar of an engine rumbles through from his side of the call, followed by the high-pitched squeal of tires peeling out.

"Randi.... Davis," I plead. "Where is she? Is she—"

Please, no.

My heart aches with a pain so intense I fall to my knees.

"We don't know, Trey. She's... the president is missing."

The world stops. My lungs burn from the lack of oxygen, but I've forgotten how to fucking breathe.

"Benson! Get your head in the fucking game right now, you hear me?" The steady, calm, commanding voice of the alpha team lead yanks me from the black hole I've fallen into. "She needs you now more than ever. Get your shit together and meet me at the damn crash site."

I suck in a breath and nod. "Where?" I croak.

"Four blocks east of your condo."

The line goes dead. I loosen my hold, allowing the phone to crash to the ground. Bile slithers up my throat.

"Trey?" Light bursts into the room when the bedroom door swings open. "Trey, what's wrong?" Gerard's shadow hovers over me as I continue to pant through another wave of fear-driven nausea.

"She's gone. Someone...." I can't bring myself to utter the words.

"Is she dead?" he whispers.

I cry out like his words are a knife to my heart. "We don't know," I finally manage. My knees wobble as I force myself to stand. Shoulders rounded, I suck in deep gulps of air to keep from passing out.

A set of old, fragile hands grips my shoulders with surprising strength.

"Then pull yourself together and go do whatever needs to be done to get her back."

I meet his narrowed eyes and nod.

Rolling my shoulders, I scan the room with new purpose and race from one side to the other, piling a small arsenal of guns on the bed as I go. After concealing three, I secure the shoulder harness with the other two guns and rush out the door. Forgoing the elevator, I race down the stairs, the pounding of my boots against the concrete steps echoing in the still stairwell.

Determination and life-taking rage course through my body, driving me faster and faster. I burst through the back door, which slams against the brick before swinging closed. My nostrils flare with each deep breath as I pause to take in the alley. This is the way they would've left just an hour ago. Maybe if I'm lucky, there's evidence of someone waiting, watching from the shadows for the perfect moment to attack.

At the end of the alley, I glance both ways before turning left and bolting toward the shrill sirens and the glow of flashing lights cutting through the night just a few blocks over.

I will find her.

She will be alive.

And then I'll kill the motherfucking bastard who dared to mess with my girl.

POWER TERM

POWER PLAY BOOK 5

"Defeat? I do not recognize the meaning of the word."
- Margret Thatcher

PROLOGUE

RANDI

A sharp, high-pitched screeching in my ears threatens to rupture my eardrums and liquefy my brain. Combine that with the pounding in my skull that's nearly as brutal as the ringing, and my thoughts scatter as I try to decipher what the hell is going on and why I can't move.

Something happened to me.

What happened to me?

Fucking focus, Randi. Get your shit together.

But I can't. Nothing makes sense through the all-consuming pain keeping me from processing what the hell is going on. A memory flashes through my mind like lightning, there and gone quickly but enough for me to remember one thing.

A car wreck. I was in a car wreck, and now... now I can't move.

Panic races through my veins, skyrocketing my pulse to race faster than humanly possible as heat swells beneath my skin. Anxiety festers, generating fears of paralysis and dangling severed limbs to be the only logical reason for my immobility. Willing all my focus to one simple move, I slowly lift my chin from where it rests along my collarbone.

The simple movement rips a gasp from me as agonizing pain blazes down my neck to my lower spine, like hundreds of tiny knives stabbing those sensitive nerves repeatedly. Every movement is worse than the last, but a nagging sense of foreboding urges me to keep going.

Finally my head meets the back of the seat. I gasp a full breath as hot tears drip down my cheeks. Teeth clamped hard, I swallow a cry of agony and seal my lips to keep from calling out. Chest heaving from the exertion of that simple movement, I take a moment to let the pain ease to a manageable level.

The ringing in my ears and throbbing in my head continue, but it's a fraction less with the new position. I could easily give up in this moment, stop refusing the intense need to drift asleep. Abandon this mad idea of consciousness. But I won't.

I don't know how, but I know one thing is for certain.

I'm in danger, and I need to stay awake to fight.

Digging my teeth into my lower lip, I fight my lids to open. Slow at first, my lashes flutter as I blink past the haze clouding my vision. A sticky glaze makes each slow blink more difficult than usual to peel my lids apart once again.

As my vision sharpens, I observe my surroundings without moving. The back of a black leather seat is unmistakable directly in front of me, and just beyond that is a shattered, splintered windshield with something sticking through it from the outside.

Yells and gunshots sound in the distance while long shadows flutter outside the smashed tinted window on my right. Sucking in a breath for courage to take stock of the damage to my lower half, I slide my gaze lower. Yellowed light filters through the fissures of the town car's various broken windows, offering enough illumination from the streetlamps above to highlight the awkward angle of my legs and torso. But it's what I *don't* see that causes a swift wash of relief. No dismembered legs or arms, no gaping holes in my torso, no rushing blood. Besides my throbbing head, which probably caused the spiderweb-looking crack in the window, I'm unharmed.

The ringing in my ear seems to swell, cutting off what minimal outside noise I could hear before. Pressure builds in my skull, causing my stomach to roll with nausea. Surrendering to the demanding fight to close my eyes, I rest my lids, dousing myself in darkness once again.

Focus, Randi. I'm a sitting duck wherever we are. I have to move, have to fight to find Trey.

A renewed sense of urgency blooms at the thought of Trey. I have to get to him, or get somewhere safe so he can find me.

But to do that, I have to move.

Fuck, this is going to hurt.

A pitiful whimper breezes past my dry lips as my fingers shift along the seat. The smooth baby-soft leather brushes beneath the tips, the texture a complete contrast to everything else in this moment.

With every move, pain infiltrates each cell and nerve, but I push through the agony. The leather sticks to my slick palm as I seal it to the seat and slowly rotate my upper body to align with my lower half. I sink my teeth into my upper lip to stifle the cry of pain that wants to escape.

I slowly peel my skin away from the leather, each square inch sticking from blood or sweat—I'm too chicken to glance down and find out which. The muscles of my right arm burn in protest as I reach out to grope along the door, fingers desperate in their search for the handle. The tremble in my arm turns into a quake before my muscles give out, slapping my hand back to the seat.

A low groan fills the air.

A groan that was not my own.

Forcing my eyes back open, I scan the inside of the town car once more, slower this time to pick up any movements. Nothing. I didn't imagine that sound, did I? Or maybe it was my own and the hit on my head has caused temporary hallucinations.

My nostrils flare as I inhale deeply; the heated air burns down my windpipe and scrapes through my raw lungs. I release it slowly through pursed lips as I rotate to face the window. Bones creak, tendons along my neck and upper back tightening and stinging with the movement. Tears well, making the cracked window swim before I can blink them away.

All of a sudden, the entire car shifts. I slide to the left with the movement, almost as if someone's rocking the wreckage.

Movement in the front snaps my attention from the window. The previously unconscious agent in the passenger seat rolls his head along the headrest with a guttural curse. Over and over the mangled car rocks, shifting me one direction and then the other. My eyes widen, a squeak of surprise lodged in my throat when his door wrenches open with a squeal of metal against metal. I blink past the sudden flood of light that only lasts a moment before a tall shadow shifts into the rays, offering a momentary reprieve from the blinding light on my overly sensitive eyes.

The relief is short-lived.

A long gun barrel points into the front seat. Brightness flares, and a splatter of warm liquid covering my face and neck is the only indication a shot was fired. In slow motion, the once barely alive agent slumps forward, his body position matching the one behind the steering wheel digging into his chest.

A scream works its way up my throat, and my lips part, readying to release a plea for help, only nothing happens. I work my jaw, move my lips, but still my cries and screams stay locked in my tight throat. Even my whimper is silent as I mentally rail on myself for allowing the shock to freeze my basic functions and inhibit me from calling out.

The shadow dousing the front seat and dead agent moves, allowing light to pour back into the car. Half a second later, the strange rocking movement from earlier shakes the car again, this time more pronounced.

Metal crunches and squeals as the door opens an inch and then another before it swings all the way out with a resistant groan. I blink past the assaulting overhead light. The snug seat belt digging into my shoulder and chest keeps me in place even as I struggle to shift away from the swallowing shadow that engulfs the back seat.

A man stands between the seat and hanging mangled door. With his face shadowed, I take in what I can see.

No tie or jacket. A simple oversized black T-shirt covers his chest and slightly protruding belly.

Realization hits me like a physical slap to the face. I attempt to shift away from the open door and the man blocking the only exit who is clearly *not* one of my agents.

I blink, unable to move with the seat belt still tight against my chest as he leans into the back seat. The leather dips beneath his weight beside my shoulder as he uses the seat as leverage to bend around me. A sharp yank tightens the seat belt, hampering my breathing only for it to release almost immediately, the restricting hold now gone from my hips and upper body. When his hands slip under my legs and around my back, I have no option but to allow him to move me like a limp doll. It takes little effort for the man to slide me along the seat toward the open door and then haul me out into the open early morning air.

I try. I really fucking try to move, to fight his hold, but nothing will work. Maybe it's from shock, or who knows, maybe my spinal cord is now severed, but whatever the cause, I can't fucking move at all, leaving me fully exposed and vulnerable. The world spins, what once was up now down and back again. His hard shoulder slams into my gut, shoving bile and air up my throat. I bob up and down as he jogs along the black asphalt and leaps to the sidewalk.

Regaining some mobility, I press both hands to his waist, my arm muscles trembling with the exertion, to lift my head.

Even with the constant movement, there's no mistaking the utter destruction that was once my security convoy. My heart stutters. For several seconds, even the need to breathe vanishes as I visually piece the mangled mess together. The lead SUV is a crumpled pile of metal, the front end gone, almost like it was blown off by a blast of some kind. It's back end isn't much better, securely lodged into the windshield of what must have been my town car. The two other SUVs have minimal damage, but all the doors are swung open, a few limp-suited bodies slumped half in, half out.

An ambush. We were ambushed. This was a smash and grab—for me.

With the pressure digging into my stomach and the gore surrounding me, mixed with the overload of fear pulsing through me, I can't stop my stomach from clenching, my abs flexing and sending anything I've eaten in the last few hours up and out. My arms give out, dislodging the needed support to keep my head up, as liquid splatters to the sidewalk. Strings of saliva, bile, and probably blood drip from my trembling lower lip as I'm carried farther from the wreckage.

Surprised shouts break through the ringing in my ears. Pops of rapid gunfire sound close—too close.

The man abducting me slows as another set of shoes enters my line of sight along the dark asphalt. Muffled words are exchanged between the two. The chest of the man who holds me vibrates against the front of my thighs where they're clamped tight with an arm around them, securing me to his body.

Then we're running again, faster this time, as if someone is now chasing us. Hope blooms in my numb chest at the thought.

Someone is coming... for me.

Trash and debris litter the grimy-looking ground as he dashes through one alley before darting toward another in a random pattern. Every step causes excruciating pain to blast down my curved spine. Every attempt to support myself, to help ease the jarring movements, is unsuccessful due to my weak arms and his quick pace.

The thought-scattering confusion that immediately followed the attack has lifted enough for one truth to solidify: I have to fight back, or I'm as good as dead.

Gathering what little strength I have—and a hell of a lot of courage—I wait for my moment. It only takes a few seconds for my opportunity. We take a tight right around a brick building, putting me close enough to grab the corner if I reached out.

This is going to hurt.

Without a second thought to the pain or what the hell I'll do next, I reach for the building. I cry out as the rough edges of the brick scrape down the length of my forearm. Curling my fingers, I grapple to hold on to the building's edge. The man carrying me loses his grip with my sudden jerk of a stop against his forward momentum.

I free-fall for a second, releasing my grip on the building and leaving bits of my skin, blood, and nails imbedded into the shallow rough grooves. The asphalt slams into my knees, bits of rock slicing through my bare skin and embedding themselves, adding to my laundry list of injuries.

A low curse sounds behind me, but it's the shouting from the direction we came that I focus on. Muscles quivering, knees and palms bleeding, I push to all fours to crawl toward those searching for me.

Hopefulness burns in my chest as my shaking arms support my weight and I make a single forward movement. Then a handful of my hair is gripped tight behind me. Knowing what's coming, I dig my nails into the sticky asphalt, desperate to hold my ground. A screech rips from my lungs as I'm yanked backward, my scalp burning where several strands have ripped free. Once again my own body is manipulated against my will as I'm thrown over someone's shoulder.

Whoever this is doesn't waste any time racing away from my would-be saviors.

With my head dangling, my forehead sliding along a sweat-damp T-shirt, my tears of frustration and desperation leak from my eyes, slipping through my dark eyebrows and gliding along my forehead to disappear into my hairline.

The shouts grow distant before vanishing altogether as we slip through a rusted metal door into an abandoned concrete structure. The man's boots echo around us, spraying a few droplets of water along my dangling arms and hands as he tromps uncaring through the various puddles of rainwater. At least I hope it's rainwater and not rat pee.

I eye the puddle we've just passed through. It would have to be a big rat to make that size puddle.

Another door opens and closes behind us. The structure is more of a cement maze than a parking garage. Fresh air breezes over my damp cheeks for only a moment before we slip into another building.

At the third or fourth building, the man's steps slow, as do the other set that's been keeping pace since we ran from the wreckage.

"Fucking finally," the man holding me grumbles as his long strides take us across the dusty floor.

"Toss her in," another voice says from somewhere behind me.

Before I can register his words, the one who's been hauling me around DC like a sack of potatoes grips my waist and lifts me off his shoulder. Dangling me in midair, his grip loosens before releasing completely. A silent cry burns in my raw throat as I plummet to the ground. My ass hits first, sending a shooting burst of pain along my tailbone up my lower spine as it takes the brunt of the fall, but the side of my head still collides with the ground with a... hollow thud?

Not the ground.

I furiously flick my gaze around, absorbing what I can of my surroundings.

No, not the ground. Worse.

A fucking trunk. I'm in the trunk of a car to be taken only the unicorn gods know where. I part my lips, inhaling deeply and readying to scream for help while praying this time my voice actually cooperates, only for a hot, sweaty palm to slap over my nose and mouth, stifling my attempt to call out.

I thrash my head left and right to dislodge the meaty hand only for it to tighten. A ski mask-covered face looms over my own. The malice in the beady eyes zeroed in on me kicks my unconscious fight-or-flight drive awake. With desperation and terror as my fuel, I kick against the carpeted trunk, my bare feet sliding along the coarse material, trying to gain traction. Skin rips beneath my nails as I claw at the arm holding me down.

Another shadow appears, the person looming just outside my field of vision. One of the two mutters something about holding me still. A prick, almost like a gnat bite, pierces the delicate skin of my upper neck.

I don't even have time to register what happened before my muscles tingle, their revived strength vanishing. I slump against the trunk's interior, the cheap mat fibers tickling my palms and cheek. My erratic breaths slow to a calm cadence as a warm rush washes over me, relaxing me deeper and deeper as the drugs move through my veins.

"No." The word is more of a slur with my numb lips.

A dark laugh rumbles through the trunk. Revulsion churns my already sour stomach as hot breath brushes against my ear.

"He doesn't like to play with his toys, but don't worry, Madam President. I do."

I scream and scream, but the trunk remains silent; I'm only able to call out for help in my mind.

"Stop fucking with the mark. We leave now to stick with the timeline." Even with the distance and hollowness of the trunk, I hear the annoyance in the clipped tone.

The tip of a slick tongue slides down the exposed column of my neck. "Soon."

A hand presses over my eyes and slips down, closing my lids with the movement.

For what feels like the hundredth time tonight, my body is moved against my will. First my legs are bent and maneuvered, something tight bites into my skin securing them together, and then the same with my hands before the trunk shuts with a deafening bang above me. The coarse floorboard rattles at the roar of an engine starting. With every bump I'm bounced and jostled, and at the turns I roll to and fro, unable to steady myself.

Panic sends my pulse racing. The roar of the engine and honking of other horns are all I can hear, leaving me alone with my darkening thoughts. Tied, drugged, and suffocating in the intense heat and no air, claustrophobia grips me, stifling my already short, raspy breaths.

Before I succumb to the panic attack, a pleading prayer blasts through my thoughts and images of the death that awaits me.

Find me, Trey. Find me.

1

TREY

The unmistakable stench of death fills my nose as I run along the sidewalk, my boots pounding the pavement, untied laces flying in my wake. There's a heaviness weighing in the early morning air, thickening as I grow closer to the chaotic scene. I could find my way by the scents filling the air alone—scorched rubber, burning fuel, and the sharp coppery tang of spilled blood—but there's no need. No, I only need to follow the bright search lights of the low-circling military helicopters, flashing red and blue of local police units, and, of course, the growing crowd.

I pause at the edge of the onlookers, men and women alike who've poured out onto the streets in their nightclothes and robes from the neighboring apartment and condo buildings. I inhale more to steady my nerves than being out of breath from the quick sprint from the dark alley behind my own building to here.

Forgoing pleasantries and gentle prodding, I shove a shoulder through the outer layer of people and make my way to the center of the crowd, where I'm needed and my answers await.

Almost to ground zero, the crash site, I slam into an immobile human wall. A wall wearing fatigues, a massive assault rifle held between two hands secured across his chest, and a clear "don't fuck with me" expression on his serious face.

"Step back, sir," says the kid who's about to be on the wrong end of the fury-laced panic that's thrumming through my veins, making me slightly unhinged.

"Secret Service," I state impatiently.

The flickering camera flashes and overhead streetlamps highlight his unimpressed gaze as he slowly gives me a once-over. Lips pursed, he shakes his head and goes back to scanning the area for threats and keeping the excited crowd at bay.

Huh. Never had that kind of reaction before.

I glance down at my own appearance to see why he so quickly dismissed me as a real agent.

Well, hell. Okay, now I get it. Dry-Fit T-shirt inside out and backward—I was wondering what was tickling my neck on my run over here—wrinkled-as-hell jeans with the zipper half up and button unfastened to the point that I don't know how they even stayed up this long, and untied military-style boots. No wonder this kid thinks I'm a fake and probably in need of medication.

I search through every available pocket for my credentials to prove to this asshole that I am in fact a legit agent, but I come up empty. Pursing my lips in annoyance, I inhale deep, my nostrils flaring at the foul smells that assault my nose.

"I left my shit at home, but I'm telling you the truth. I'm Trey Benson with the fucking Secret Service. Now let me the fuck through." Nose to nose, I'm screaming in his face. He doesn't know why I'm so on edge, why the accident behind him is extremely personal to me, but I don't care in this moment. All I want is for him to fucking move so I can find out what the hell is going on and find my fiancée.

"No one gets through," he hisses through gritted teeth as he widens his stance, readying for a fight.

Already on a hair trigger, my rising annoyance mixes with the desperation to get past this fucker, shoving me over the edge of reason. Lips pulled back in a snarl, I reach for one of the guns strapped to my body, 100 percent okay with shooting my way through if I have to.

Just as my fingers brush the grooved grip of my nine millimeter, familiar broad shoulders and a bald head rising over the soldier's catch my attention. On the far side, several feet from where I stand, Tank stalks along the inside circle of the soldier wall, peering over their heads like he's searching for someone in the crowd.

Both hands cupped around my mouth for maximum volume, I let out a sharp attention-grabbing whistle, one I used during widespread canvassing assignments in the army, then bellow his name over the thumping of the helicopter blades and excited crowd. I debate shoving my way toward him when he pauses and turns my direction.

His intense gaze locks on me. Immediately he sets across the closed-off street, his focus never wavering as he weaves through the FBI agents inspecting the evidence.

My trepidation rises with each step Tank takes as he draws closer. I'm eager to get around this fucker who's holding me back from entering the scene, yet at the same time I know the moment I walk into the protected circle, all this becomes true. Right now I straddle a fine line. On this side, I have the knowledge of what happened but not the proof or the details. If I don't see it, it didn't happen, right? If I don't step over the invisible line, thus changing me from outsider looking in to acting agent, none of this is real. It's crazy to think this way, sure, but compartmentalizing this shit might be the only way I keep my emotions in check until we find her.

Tank's mitt of a hand encases the soldier's shoulder and yanks him backward. He struggles to stay upright, opening a small gap just wide enough for me to slip through.

"He's with me." Tank dangles his credentials in front of the kid's face, and I take the opportunity and move to stand beside my friend.

Not wasting time, Tank turns on his heels and strides from the sidewalk, stepping down onto the street where the destruction waits.

A couple feet from the town car—*her* town car—I pause, taking in the mangle of metal. My heart squeezes like someone has it in a vise grip as I stare at the open back passenger door and the empty back seat.

Tank's heavy footsteps pause, his comforting presence welcome as I inhale a shaky breath, doing what I can to keep the fear of what's happening to her in this very moment from shutting me down. I can't break, not when she needs me.

"We'll find her. We'll get her back."

I nod, not daring to speak past the lump lodged in my throat. My fingers tremble as I rake them through my hair, relishing the sharp bites of pain as a few tangled strands yank and pull at my scalp.

"Get it together, Benson. Randi is out there waiting for you to piece this together and find her. She's counting on you finding her before it's too late."

Again I dip my chin in agreement, but this time with conviction. Rising determination shifts my focus into overdrive, shoving aside all the other swirling emotions keeping me from thinking straight.

Wrangling the varying emotions that radiate from the happy memories we made only hours ago in my condo when she said yes to the paralyzing agony of the unknown, I shove them down with a deep fortifying breath.

Tank's right, like always.

She needs me more than ever. I can't fail her. I *won't* fail her. Not when our happy ever after was within our grasp. Whoever did this will pay, but first I have to find her.

"What do we know so far?" I ask, my voice void of any feeling.

"Did you know your shirt's wrong?" Tank asks. Normally we'd joke, have a good laugh at my haphazard state, but not tonight.

Stripping off the shirt, I flip it right side out, sink my arms back through the sleeves, and tug it over my head. Then I button my fly, tie the damn boots, and fix the jean cuffs to look somewhat more professional than the disheveled mess I was moments ago.

A puff of air explodes from my lungs at Tank's palm connecting between my shoulders for a comforting pat on the back. With a firm grip on my shoulder, he guides us around the town car to the hood, where the lead SUV is practically sitting on the dashboard. His grip tightens as we take it all in from this new angle.

"I don't know much, got here a minute before you. Plus I want our take on it all before I listen to their bullshit investigation."

"Why?" I ask as I crouch low, pressing the tips of four fingers to the road for stability, and inspect the SUV's undercarriage. Loose pebbles of asphalt crunch under my boots as I swivel in varying directions for different viewpoints.

"We know the standard routine when she visits you, but no one else does. We're aware of how many cars, agents, the route, backup... that gives us different insight. Not better but different. Now tell me what you see."

Damn, the man is smarter than most people give him credit for. With his large size, people think he's all bulk and no brains. But he's not in charge because of his size and past NFL record. It's because of this, the way he processes things and sees different angles. On top of that, he's observant and insightful, two of the main reasons he's the alpha team lead and we all follow him with our full trust.

A few chunks of dark hair slide across my sticky forehead as I lean closer to the still warm blacktop. I'm no mechanic—I don't even drive my own car to get serviced, it just magically happens—but the twisted metal beneath the lead SUV looks wrong.

"Did something explode from the ground?" I ask. Knee to the blacktop, I lean closer and inhale. "Smells like explosives, but hell if I know what kind." Tank's hulking figure settles beside me to see where I point under the front portion of the undercarriage. "Just there, it's blackened and twisted." I stand and step away from the two entangled vehicles to see the picture as a whole with this new slice of information.

"The blast point could be covered up by the debris," Tank muses through a grunt as he shoves off his thick thighs to stand.

Rock fragments and other questionable material sprinkle from my dirty palm as I rake a hand through my hair.

"This was well thought out, meticulously planned, unlike the prior attempts." Rounding the SUV, I pause on the other side. Blood drips from the gaps in the metal where the front passenger seat should've been. Grief grips my stomach like a tightening fist. I force my gaze away. There's no need to know who was riding shotgun, or driving, or in the other SUVs. Only one thing matters now, and that's finding the clues to locate Randi. Then murder the devil behind the abduction.

A vaguely familiar agent approaches, his wide eyes taking in the mess before him. "The FBI director will be here shortly, and ours is back at head-quarters reviewing the information as it comes in." At my side, he takes a deep breath and rests both hands on his hips. "Every single agent was shot in the head point-blank. A few appear postmortem. Whoever did this covered their tracks to make sure no one could identify them."

"What about the new video surveillance we had installed?" Tank asks, his head on a swivel as he searches the lampposts for our cameras. He requested several to be secured along this route once we realized her visits to my condo would be a weekly routine.

"Nothing."

"Nothing?" I snap, clenching my jaw so tight the muscles ache. "What do you mean? There can't be nothing."

"Whatever stopped the lead SUV also disrupted the video feed. All signals are down in a two-block radius." Tapping a pen against his palm, the agent takes in the surroundings. "What in the hell was the president doing in this area so early?"

Tank and I exchange a quick look. Neither of us is answering that loaded question.

Clearing my throat, I bring the topic back to the surveillance issue. "I'm no expert, but a sizeable explosion to halt a small motorcade coupled with an EMP of some kind isn't normal." I shake my head, trying to get the pieces of information we know to fit together somehow. "That is fucking sophisticated. Who are these assholes?"

I say assholes knowing full well this couldn't have been done by one man. No, this was a team, a highly qualified and funded team with one objective: Randi, President of the United States. And now they have her. For what—

No, I can't let my mind go down that dark path. I have to stay here in this moment if I want to help find her.

I swallow hard, my feet moving of their own accord before stopping in front of the open passenger door of the town car. Her flip-flops lie discarded on the floorboard, shimmering drops of crimson dotting the leather. Fear rakes like talons into my chest, stifling my breathing at all the blood. Leaning deeper into the interior, I examine the spray pattern. A spray of tiny droplets and chunks of something coat the back windshield and seat. It's all covered in sprinkles of red except a small void where she would've been sitting.

I shift, turning to the front seat, where it seems most of the blood exploded from. A shouted curse slips as I'm met with a gaping, oozing skull cavity pointing at me from the front passenger seat.

Seeing the dead agent with the back of his head missing shouldn't fill me with relief, but it does. Because the blood splatter isn't hers.

It's not her blood.

I make it a mantra to keep my focus from slipping as I examine the back seat again, hoping to find anything useful. A blinking light from the floorboard on the other side of the car snags my attention.

"Gloves," I grumble over my shoulder and blindly stretch an open hand behind me.

The soft thin latex glove slapped into my awaiting palm is a complete contrast to the brutality of the incident I'm investigating. It slides easily over my fingers, catching on my sweaty palm. Reaching to the other side, I stretch as far as I can without disturbing the other evidence. With the tips of two fingers, I slide the phone closer until it's within reach and duck back out of the town car with it carefully cradled in my hand.

With a press of the Home button, the screen flares to life, displaying the red battery in the right-hand corner, several unread texts, and ten missed calls from Taeler. The sliver of optimism that she'd somehow managed to keep the phone and the tracking device within on her through the wreck and abduction dissolves, feeding the worry about how in the hell we're going to find her in time.

"It's hers," I say, dropping it into Tank's large latex-covered hand.

Arms crossed over my chest, I stare into the dark car. There has to be something we can use; no one's that good to not leave anything behind.

Diving back into the wreckage, I scour every square inch of the area void of blood splatter, looking for something, anything that will help us find her. If she was fighting, there could be hair, skin, clothing left behind. Unless she was unconscious from the impact of the SUV or drugged.

I shake that thought before it can fester and distract me from the task at hand.

Fuck, I have to find her.

The tips of my fingers tremble as I run them along the smooth thick polyester seat belt down to the metal clasp and back up again in case I missed something lodged in the chest strap.

I pause their journey halfway up as a thought hits. Going back to the metal clasp, I pull it out for further inspection. I glide two gloved fingers along the shoulder strap and lap belt again to double-check I haven't missed a cut or slice. But I haven't. The entire belt is still intact.

Gripping the outside frame, I haul myself out of the town car and turn, pointing back inside. "We need someone to dust for prints on the seat belt release. There aren't any lacerations on the strap, which means they released her or she did."

Something deep in my gut tells me she didn't willingly release her safety belt. If she did, there would be evidence of her attempting to scramble away to the other side of the seat or blood on the door handle where she tried to escape.

Tank bellows the order for an FBI agent, sending several jogging our way.

"Tank, Playboy. Over here."

Tank and I turn our attention to the far side of the secured perimeter. Champ squats at the very edge, his back nearly leaning against a soldier's legs, pointing at a glistening puddle on the ground.

I arch a questioning brow Tank's way as we stride toward our fellow alpha team agent.

"I reached out to them all after I spoke with you," he says in response to my silent question, pursing his lips at the end like he's holding himself back from saying more.

"Looks like vomit. Already had someone bag a swab and sample for testing. If it's from Randi, we'll know if there were any drugs in her system." Champ's determined gaze meets mine. "Don't worry. We'll find her." The resolve in his hard tone and clipped words offers the boost I need to push past the idea of her possibly being drugged and unable to fight back against whatever is happening to her.

Hands tightened into white-knuckled fists at my side, I slowly turn, taking in the entire scene from this new vantage point.

"We know there had to be more than one attacker," I state more to myself than to the other two waiting as I talk through the details we know. "But there isn't any sign of *how* they got away before the backup units arrived. What do we know about the timeline? From the moment the possible explosion went off in the street to when the standby convoy arrived?"

"When other agents arrived and realized she was gone, there was zero sign of her or the attackers. There were only dead agents and the wreckage. I spoke with one of the backup agents when I arrived on scene. He stated several canvassed the surrounding area while other secured the scene. Every alley was checked, but they didn't find any evidence indicating which way they'd gone or how they got away."

I nod absentmindedly at Champ, letting him know I heard him even though my unfocused gaze is on the surrounding crowd. There were only two options for escaping before the backup arrived just moments after the crash: by foot or by vehicle.

I have to think like them. How would I get the most protected woman on the planet away from the wreckage before the cavalry arrived? Based on the details so far, these fuckers knew the route, the number of men, hell, even the new surveillance we installed recently. They had to know additional backup would arrive within minutes of the wreck.

I glance back to the town car, this time looking at it from their perspective.

It would need to be quick and undetectable.

The blacktop pounds under my boots as I stride to the open back passenger door of her town car. Mimicking what would've been done to remove her, I go through the motions like I'm unstrapping Randi and tugging her out into the early morning air. She doesn't weight much, so even if she was drugged, her limp body wouldn't be too much for an average-size man to carry easily.

I count out ten medium-length strides from the car to what we believe is her vomit, which could either be from drugs administered to keep her compliant or from a concussion. Based on the town car's impact with the lead SUV, I suspect the nausea was from a concussion.

"Twenty seconds to remove the president and carry her here," I state to Tank and Champ. "Now where would I go if I didn't want to risk a getaway vehicle being spotted and pursued by the coming backup convoy or a man being seen carrying a limp body down the street?"

A beat of silence falls between us as the repetitive thump of helicopter blades pulses above us. Spotlights illuminate the area, eliminating every shadow while Secret Service and FBI agents alike shout to each other about evidence collection or needing more body bags.

"We need to move, search, do fucking something." I rake my fingers through the longer strands of my hair, tugging at the ends to help keep me focused. "We split up. Each take a different alley. That's the only way to escape this shit show with the president without being seen."

Assuming they're on board, I scan along the length of the street. I count three alley openings close enough for an optimal escape route. "Tank, you take the one there." I point to the farthest from where we stand, then to the next closest. "Champ, you take that one, and I'll take the last one."

I shoulder through the wall of soldiers and shove through the spectators. A pulse of anger sizzles through me at their ogling. This is a fascination for them, a bit of drama for their boring everyday lives. But for me, it's my life. They're staring, whispering at the visual representation of what remains of my heart and soul with Randi missing.

Wrecked.

Burning.
Destroyed.
I have to get her back.
My life depends on it.
Hold on, Randi. I'll find you. Hold on for me.

2

RANDI

A chest-rattling bang from somewhere close by jolts me awake. My brain batters against my skull with its own thundering pulse, making me loathe this day before I've even opened my eyes. The intensity of the headache feels like a migraine, but I haven't had one of those in years.

Fuck, I wish I could stay in bed, or even have the luxury of hitting Snooze. But the country's problems won't wait. There's no lazy morning for the woman running the United States.

I toss my head to shift the hair that's fallen across my nose, the small movement sending a stabbing pain along my neck all the way down to my toes.

Another noise, something I've never heard while snuggly tucked in bed within the safety of the White House, drags my attention from the new odd pain.

What the hell is going on out in the hall?

I shift to sit up and find out what the racket is about, but I can't. I try again but fail to move even an inch. Confusion clouds my already slow thoughts as I jerk at my hands to move the infuriating tickling hairs strewn across my face. More strange pain radiates from my wrists.

My heart races, slamming against my chest. Blinking through the stickiness coating my lashes and dry, scratchy eyes, I will my lids to stay open. My blurry vision clears, revealing an unfamiliar exposed industrial-looking ceiling above me.

Instead of smooth white plaster, rusted metal beams crisscross with bundles of exposed thick black wires and silver-coated ventilation ducts of some kind. Struggling through the sheer agony of the simple movement, I twist to look toward the only natural light shining in the run-down warehouse. It takes a moment of zero movement and deep inhales and exhales through my nose for the discomfort to diminish to a non-excruciating level and my vision to focus. Across the expansive abandoned room, along the far wall, a row of filthy cracked and broken windows allows slivers of warm sunlight to filter through. The soft rays that make it through the grime and gaps highlight the dust floating in the stagnant air.

The oblivious bliss that my confusion offers only lasts a few seconds before the swarm of images and memories assaults my already struggling brain. I squeeze my eyes shut.

Shit. Shit. Shit. I'm so fucked.

Dread settles in my gut like lead weighing me down from the inside at the last thing I remember before the trunk shut over my unresponsive, drugged body. Of what that one dick for brains whispered about playing with his toys. A shiver of revulsion shakes my shoulders.

I need to get out of here. Now. No matter what I have to do or endure.

Whatever they have me tied up with digs into the bare flesh of my wrists and ankles, but I fight through the slicing of my skin and protesting muscles. Panting, I give up after a minute of attempting to escape with brute force, which is obviously getting me nowhere. Resting back on the hard surface, I grit my teeth as the adrenaline fades and the damage I caused shifts into a fire-hot burn along my wrists and ankles.

"Think, Randi." My cracked voice is barely a whisper. What do I know? What do I have that could help me get the hell out of here without ripping my hands and feet off?

First things first, I need to take inventory of what's broken, bruised, and okay on my own body.

I lick my dry lips, preparing for the worst—the pain and knowledge that even if I do get out of these restraints, my legs could be broken, or something else that could hinder my escape. I start with my toes, wiggling one and then adding another in. Besides the raw sensation along the tips of my toes and feet, I'm good there. Slowly I work my way up my shins, past my knees. And because avoidance is the healthiest option at this point, I skip over the apex of my thighs, too scared that will break me mentally if I discover I was abused while drugged.

Swallowing the tears that are lodged in my otherwise dry throat, I take a deep fortifying inhale.

Terrible idea.

Horrible, awful, delusional idea.

Immediately my lungs revolt as if I'd swallowed burning coals. A violent cough shoves all that air back up my dry throat with a hacking cough. To force whatever is lodged in my lungs up and out, my abs tighten and flex while my back presses hard into the solid surface beneath me in an attempt to gain some leverage, doing whatever needed to not choke to death on my own phlegm.

That is *not* an option for tomorrow's headline.

President found dead. Choked on own spit.

She should've swallowed.

A delirious snort tickles my nose between violent coughs at my slightly disturbing and gross humor. A cool smooth surface slides along my cheek as I force up whatever is lodged in my chest. A tangy, metallic taste fills my mouth as I ready to spit whatever was in my lungs as far as I can.

Which, of course, doesn't even go half a centimeter. Spit and what I now suspect is mucus and coagulated blood oozes along my warm cheek before slowly dripping away.

Awesome. Tied up and covered in my own spit—and from the skull-splitting pain in my brain, probably a concussion too boot.

Oh, and bonus, no fucking clue where I am or who the hell took me. Or why.

Let's be honest: there could be a lot of answers for the "why" question. I've made some formidable enemies since appearing on the DC scene. One who's already tried to poison me once and another group who've sent multiple assassins to kill me.

But with those assholes who attempted to drive the world into war for monetary gains dead, or worse, at some nondescript CIA black site location, there's only one asshole whose loathing exceeds all others.

Shawn fucking Whit.

Shawn is who I'd place my bet on setting this all up. There's no way he could've pulled this off on his own though. Which doesn't surprise me in the slightest considering he isn't the type of sociopath who gets his hands dirty. Watch someone destroy me and get off while doing it, sure, that's Shawn. But not actually executing the kidnapping of the president and murder of over a dozen agents.

I choke on a sob.

Those men, my agents, are dead. All of them.

Warm tears escape from the corners of both eyes, descending over my temples and trailing along my jawline. Despair grips what little hope I've held on to this far, suffocating it until all that's left in its place is a desolate chasm where it used to live.

Seconds turn to minutes. Minutes turn into what feels like hours of lying there despondently, staring unseeing at the ceiling. Eventually the leaking tears dry even though the grief continues to strangle my heart.

The bright glaring sun through the windows and the increasing sweltering heat are both signals I've been here for a good while. Yet no one has checked on my well-being or explained their demands. I'm not sure which is worse: lying here alone with only my increasingly dark and rampant day dreams as company or meeting the men who took me and them clearly detailing out what they have planned for me.

I could die here today. More than likely I *will* die right here in this abandoned warehouse alone and in quite a bit of pain.

Stealing my spine, I drum up any semblance of courage I can, preparing myself for the inevitable.

It's okay if I die. Everyone will move on. The world will still turn and live their lives.

Then a happy memory of a smirking, honey brown-eyed man flashes before my eyes. The look of sheer happiness and relief when I said yes sticks to the forefront of my mind, reminding me of what I have to live for and blasting through the despair I unconsciously slipped into for self-preservation.

A new wave of agony takes hold as more faces, more memories, emerge, reminding me of what I would leave behind if I just gave up now.

Taeler and that sweet baby. I'd never get to see my only daughter become the fantastic mother I know she'll be. Or get to see my grandbaby grow up to be just as crazy and dramatic as her mother and grandmother.

Tank and Sarah. I wouldn't ever get to thank them for being the friends

I've always wanted but never had and for showing me what true love and respect in a relationship looks like.

Mom. A bit of an odd cookie now, sure, but I'm so proud of her, even if she thinks everything can be cured by honey or an oil.

Vlad. Okay, that one is a stretch.

This is my inner fighter, the badass I've always wanted to be, pushing me to not give up but to wage the same war on them that they've done to me. I'm not some helpless victim who takes things lying down. That's never been me. I've always fought, struggled, and worked to get anywhere in life. Sure, escaping all this alive might be a bit trickier than undergrad and Harvard, but I have to at least try.

The emotionless chill that settled into my blood is driven out by their love for me and mine for them.

I can't give up.

What the ever-loving fuck was I thinking?

Yes, I'm miserable, yes, I'm frightened, and hell yes, my chest and soul ache with the deep, urgent need for Trey, but I can't let that hold me back from fighting.

It's me and me alone until Trey finds me. Until he and Tank swoop in and save the day. Which, deep in my gut, I know they will. Before it's too late, well, I'm not sure about that one, but I know they will come. I just have to hold on, not give up until they do.

Which means I have to fight.

Fight for my life and for the lives that will be affected if I die here.

Today is not the day I take my last breath.

Neither is tomorrow.

Trey and I will have our happily ever after. I won't let anyone take that away from me, not now, not when I've finally found my source of happiness.

No. I'm not giving up.

Whatever happens next, whatever they want from me, I'll hold on and wait for Trey.

I can do this. I'm the motherfucking president of the United States of America, and I will not bow down. I will not give up or give in.

These fuckers think they've already won no doubt.

Too bad for them, they don't know how damn scrappy a girl from the trailer park can be.

I picture myself bursting out of these restraints and going all assassin on the assholes the moment they bust through the door. Like all those heroines do in the movies. I just need to channel my inner Beatrix and go all *Kill Bill*.

If only I had a sword like hers in the movie. Oh, or a black mamba in my pocket. Maybe I should commission one and a secure traveling case for future abduction attempts. Hell, what a time for a unicorn army. All I'd have to yell is the code word "Impale," and everyone trying to hurt me or those I love would die by unicorn stabbing.

"Fuck yeah," I whisper to myself. "Impale. Impalement for them all."

A heavy scraping sound echoes through the empty room, putting a pause on my vindictive thoughts and daydreams of becoming a killing machine. I survey what I can see of the room but come up empty. Straining to see what's behind me, I jolt, the restraints holding my jerking body in place, at the bang of what sounds like a heavy door slamming shut.

A soft squelch, like rubber shoes against a slick surface, causes the hair to rise along the back of my neck and down both arms. My chest shakes with the ramming pound of my heart. Fear clogs my throat and steals the breath from my lungs.

Closer and closer the even steps grow until they stop, still out of my line of sight. An eerie sense of being watched crawls across my skin. Jerking against the restraints, I attempt to angle my body to the side and for a better angle to see who's lurking behind me, but I can't.

Frustrated, I flop back prone on the table. "What do you want?" I growl like a wild animal as I test the restraints once again. Now would be a grand time for the plastic ties to somehow weaken on their own, allowing me to break free and play out the massacre I plotted moments ago.

My question receives no response. Blood rushes in my ears, making it difficult to hear anything, but still I strain to listen, not wanting to be snuck up on. Something moves directly behind me, casting a long shadow across my face and chest.

Chin in the air, I strain my neck, arching as far as I can to look behind me.

Ice licks down my spine as an unfamiliar set of uncaring eyes locks with my own.

"Please," I beg. "What do you want? Let me go."

A harsh chuckle escapes his lips as he reaches closer to fist a thick handful of my dark hair, his short jagged nails scraping across my scalp. I cry out, my hands fighting to be free and help alleviate the pressure. With a painful yank, he jerks my face forward, my chin slamming into my collarbone, severing my visual of the man. A pitiful whimper escapes as cool, rough fingers firmly trace along the edges of my trembling upper lip before moving to the lower. The scents of dried blood, gunpowder, and onion infiltrate my nostrils, evoking my gag reflex. Not wanting him to see how much his proximity and touch terrify me, I restrain the sob that's desperate to escape.

Those same two fingers shove between my lips, forcing them apart and invading my mouth. I thrash my head, attempting to dislodge them as he thrusts them deeper. I gag, revolting against the intrusion, but the hold on my hair tightens, keeping me at his mercy. Something hard presses against the crown of my skull. Up and down it rubs against my hair as his fingers mimic the movement inside my mouth.

My attempt to scream is choked back as he forces another finger into my already full mouth. Jaw straining, tears flow as saliva drips from the corners of my mouth and down my neck.

"Just prepping your fuckable mouth for my big cock to shove down it. I want to feel you choke on my dick until you can't breathe."

Revulsion sends a shudder down my spine, but there's nothing I can do to make him stop.

Then it does.

The fingers are ripped from my mouth, and his unimpressive dick stops humping my head. I scream in pain as chunks of hair rip from my scalp as the hand still gripping it is jerked backward.

Heaving for breath, weeping, and trembling all over, I almost miss the hushed words said somewhere behind me.

"I told you the rules," someone, a male, states.

"Fuck you. We're not partners. This is a onetime deal between us. You can't tell me what to do. I risked my life helping you get that woman, and now I'm going to reap my rewards."

"I paid you plenty."

"Well, unlike you I always play with my toys before I destroy them. We're not all fucked in the head like you, you damn freak."

I hold my breath, waiting for the other man's response.

"I wanted to wait until later to do this, but you've pushed my hand." A soft pop of air has me stiffening at the distinct sound of a gun fired with a silencer. "Fucking hell, I hate carrying dead bodies. This is why I wanted to wait." The distinct click of a man's dress shoes draws closer. "That is now two of my so-called acquaintances you owe me for." I jerk at the voice, its somewhat familiar low, rough tone. "Maybe I should make you carry him instead."

"Why am I here?" My voice shakes, giving away the utter terror engulfing my every thought and cell.

A shadow creeps closer and looms over my face. I blink at the change in light to refocus my vision. The image clears, but all I can make out is the end of a blue tie, a white dress shirt, and barely a hint of a smoothly shaven chin.

"You were my toughest challenge to date, you know that? Twice, you avoided what the other client had planned for you. That was their fault though, not involving me in the execution of the plan and only using me for information." Shifting against the table, I try for a new angle to see the man's face. It's someone I've met before—the voice is too familiar—but the drugs or maybe the concussion keep his identity deep in the recesses of my mind. "Not that it matters now. They failed and I still got paid by them, and now I'll collect the remaining funds of this second contract as soon as you're... handled."

"Second," I rush out. What is he saying? "Two people wanted me?"

Okay, yeah, not sure why that should surprise me, but it does. I mean, do people hate me that much for what I'm trying to accomplish? I'm more than just the president. I'm fucking fun, and happy, and witty. Why in the hell would people want me dead when I can bring all that to the table?

"Ah, you are listening. Good." The shadow shifts as he raises an arm, a hand dangling midair above my face. I flinch, sealing my eyes shut, preparing for the hit I know will come next.

Only the blow never comes.

A soft *tsk* has me peeking one eye open. "You don't have to worry. I won't touch you, at least not until he arrives. That's when you should be afraid." The inkling in my stomach tells me I know exactly who he's referring to. "As much fun as this is," he continues, though his exasperated tone says he's having the opposite of fun, "there are a few loose ends I need to remove before the client arrives and starts your final party." He sighs. "And now I have to clean up this mess. Fucking hate burying bodies. Such a time suck." A palm smacks against the table, and I jolt against the restraints in surprise, expecting the next hit to be directed at me.

Light blares down on me once again, the looming presence gone.

"Wait." I arch my neck, desperate to catch a glimpse of my captor before he leaves me alone again. "Just let me go, please."

"Not a chance, Madam President."

"What do you want? Why are you doing this?" My words come out stronger with my growing frustration and disdain for his man and my situation.

"You. It was always about you. I'm not sure how you managed to piss off so many, but you did, and now I'm here. Don't take it personal. It's business."

"This isn't business. Kidnapping the president is a fucking felony, you traitor," I snap. "I'm a good fucking person and don't deserve any of this." My voice echoes through the large space.

After a moment with no response, I catch an exasperated sigh and a mumbled "I don't care."

The annoyance in his tone stops me from uttering another word.

"I'll be back soon, and then the fun will start. Oh, I almost forgot." The outline of a black rectangular shape hovers over my face. A click and flash of a picture being taken, and then he's gone again. Eyes wide I stare at the ceiling as grunted curses and the brush of something heavy being dragged fill the area.

"Oh, and, Randi, don't bother hoping that motherfucker Benson will find you. I'm the best at what I do. There's no way for him to track you. No one will find you. No one is coming to save you."

The dragging sound grows distant. A squeak of metal against metal cuts through the air, making me wince. With a few more distant curses, all noise is cut off with a bang, the vibrations from the force reverberating along my spine.

It's the following quiet that terrifies me. Now I wait. Wait for whatever he and his demented client have planned. Darkness encroaches on my vision as I struggle to suck in enough gulps of air to keep me conscious.

Inhaling deep through my nose until my ribs protest, I let the breath out slow through pursed lips.

I use deep breathing to relax my racing pulse. I have to calm down. I'll be useless passed out. That fucker said no one would find me, but what if someone hears me?

A spark of hope bursts in my chest, making my heart race all over again, this time with excitement instead of dread. Drawing in a lungful of air, I scream for help at the top of my lungs, my voice straining into silence at the end. Over and over again I yell. Some of my screams are calls for help, others attempting to shatter the remaining intact windowpanes with my shrill.

I call out for what feels like hours, attempting to draw attention to my location. I'd take any help that comes my way. Hell, maybe my screams will attract a wild animal and they'll come nibble through the restraints setting me free. Oh, or a bird. No, not just any bird—a pigeon, one that delivers messages. Shit, that won't work. I don't have a pen to write an SOS note to Trey.

For far longer than would be considered "sane thoughts," I debate which of the many wild animals I'd choose to come rescue me.

In the end of the too long mental debate, the masked bandit raccoon wins out. Their opposable thumbs would come in handy with the restraints. Plus, they're curious little guys and have sharp teeth in case they can't figure out how to unsnap a zip tie.

Wait. Do I even know how to unsnap a zip tie?

"What is wrong with me?" I whisper. A wobbly smile tugs at my dry, cracked lips, and a delirious giggle bubbles in my chest, coming out as a rasp. Once it starts, I can't stop. Harsh chuckles fill the room, cutting through the silence as I laugh like a hyena.

"I'm going crazy," I state between laughs. "Come save me, raccoon," I croon with my crackly voice. "Come save me with your cute tiny thumbs."

"How in the hell you became VP instead me is fucking insulting on too many levels."

Immediately my laughter shrivels and dies at the voice I know all too well.

I swallow hard to clear my desert-dry throat.

An even crazier thought than the raccoons saving me pops up. Maybe if I stay still, he won't notice me lying here, in the middle of the room, tied to a table.

Clearly I'm cracking under the pressure.

"But," he continues, his voice drawing closer, "now you'll pay for that infraction, along with many others."

Sweat slicks my forehead and dampens the back of my neck. Unlike the other two men, Shawn doesn't hide from me. He strolls the length of the table, stopping at the end by my feet. I strain to look down my body and immediately wish I hadn't. A sinister smile splits his cheeks as he surveys my restrained ankles.

"Ready for payback, Trailer?"

My heart skips, pausing entirely before thundering against my chest once again. "Not really, but thank you for asking." I grimace.

His smile falters slightly before returning to its Joker-esqe expression. "That was a rhetorical question, you fucking idiot."

"Then you should've said that," I snap. "And seriously, you want to do all this, to kill me, because Kyle chose me over you? Be pissed at him, not me. I'm innocent against that charge."

"Ah, see, you were until you lied to me. That's why you're here today, what tipped my hand to this extreme."

"You poisoned me before that," I retort.

"What can I say? Birmingham was a bore, and games are my weakness," he says, brushing off some lint from the sleeve of his dark blue jacket. "And you're too tempting to play with. That and toying with your rent-a-cop of a boyfriend. But then you went and played me, convinced me not to put the understanding of me being selected as your VP when you became president in writing. *That* is why you'll pay with your life. However," he says, tilting his chin up in a haughty move, "I can be persuaded to let you live if you do what I want."

Indignation boils inside my gut. "I won't get anywhere near your pencil dick, dick." Fuck, I need some caffeine. That insult was lame. Or water. Could be dehydration playing at my loss of unique name-calling.

A sneer curls the corner of his upper lip. "You won't get anywhere near me. I'm not willing to catch whatever shit you caught while growing up in fucking poverty to get my fat dick sucked."

I snort. "Embellish much? You've always been right about one thing, you would make a better politician than me with those kind of exaggeration skills."

Between blinks, he shifts along the table, pausing at my side. Fury burns behind those near black eyes that are intently focused on my neck. Then a steady manicured hand lashes out and wraps around my throat.

The constricting grip unleashes a floodgate of hysteria into my veins. I arch my back off the table, thrash my head, doing anything I can while restrained to dislodge his hold. Shawn laughs as he applies more pressure, slowly strangling the life from my already exhausted and bruised body.

A rasp of a cry pushes past my lips. Stars twinkle before my eyes as darkness seeps from the corners of my vision. My struggles weaken, my body going limp.

This is it. This is the end.

Unable to grasp even a single puff of needed oxygen to stay conscious, I give in to the peaceful oblivion that waits for me on the other side.

I'm sorry, Trey. I'm so, so sorry.

3

TREY

The shouts of agents and the murmuring of the crowd fall away as I continue to scour the alley for any sign this was the route they used to extract Randi. They didn't just up and disappear; they had to escape undetected and quickly before the backup arrived. These assholes had two, maybe three minutes tops before half of the American army reserves and another half-dozen agents were swarming the area.

It took a hell of a lot of planning to pull this off. And experience. This wasn't their first time handling a high-profile job like this.

But even professionals make mistakes. And I'll find it. The one rogue hair, one tear of clothing or footprint. I'll find it, and then I'll find her.

Fuck, if it were only that simple.

Tiny fur-covered bodies scurry along the alley to my right, their thin nails scratching the slime-crusted asphalt as they weave between dumpsters. Unbothered by the rats, I continue a slow prowl, going farther away from the crash.

At the cross of another back alley intersecting with the one I've been following, I pause. Going right would've been their wisest choice in order to avoid those pursuing from seeing them. Staying straight would leave them vulnerable to those following.

Right it is, then.

At two more intersections, I do the same, analyzing which way would provide the least amount of exposure before changing routes. After one turn, I pause and retreat a step, backtracking to whatever snagged my attention.

The urgency in my gut tells me there's something here... there.

Balancing on the balls of my feet, I squat and inspect the object. Not bothering to secure the glove over my sweaty hand, I use it to pick up what looks to be a fire-engine red piece of something.

Not just something—a nail.

Randi's fake nail.

It's a long shot, sure, but at this point, even a long shot is better than nothing.

Encasing the evidence in the glove, I shove it deep within a front pocket. Even with the sun rising there's not enough light to check for additional signs of a struggle. Phone out, I use the flashlight function to help me scour every nook and crevice within a ten-foot radius from where I found the nail.

On my hands and knees checking under a rank dumpster is how Tank and Champ find me.

"I think I found a bit of her nail on the ground just there," I say, gesturing behind me. Satisfied I haven't missed anything obscured under the green metal bin, I push myself up. Staying on my knees, I dig both clenched fists against the top of my thighs in frustration. "But nothing else."

"Let's keep moving," Tank says, offering a hand to help me off the ground. A clap pulses down the alley as our hands connect. With his inhuman strength, he yanks me to a standing position with ease. "Now that we know this is the way they came, we can get more agents down this way to help look." A few sharp commands into his radio and it's done, a team of various agency agents en route to our location. With an incline of his head in the direction I was headed before I stopped, Tank says, "Let's find where they loaded her. There could be evidence there as well."

On reflex, I nod at the issued command from my team lead.

With renewed adrenaline flowing at finding the minuscule piece of evidence that proves there was a struggle, it's better that I let him do all the thinking. Murder and annihilation are the most prevalent thoughts at the moment. Partly because of the uncontrollable rage pumping through my system, but also if I concentrate on the unknown person's death, then images of her scared, alone, and hurt can't consume me.

I can't function with those debilitating images. Murder and causing excruciating pain are a much better option for a fully functioning Agent Trey Benson.

Using the hem of my T-shirt, I swipe away the beading sweat from my brow and follow Tank and Champ. Their heads move on a swivel, scouring around each dumpster, every nearly disintegrated cardboard box, piles of discarded trash, and a random pile of ratty blankets.

Again something in my gut draws me up short. I skid to a halt, bits of rock shifting beneath my boots. Tank and Champ pause several steps ahead and turn to where I stand staring at the pile of blankets.

Tanks brows furrow. "What is it?"

Not wanting to spook the man or woman, I press a single finger to my lips and point at the lump on the ground.

Please don't be dead.

On quiet steps, I inch closer. A foul cloud of body odor, fluids, and who the hell knows what else engulfs me. I gag on reflex before switching to breathing through my mouth to keep from smelling the growing stench. If this guy helps us locate Randi, I'll not only offer him a shower and clean clothes but buy him a damn house with as many showers as he wants.

I still when the mountain of shredded blankets and old newspapers shifts.

"I'm not here to hurt you or make you leave," I say as calmly and sincerely as I can muster with my emotions raging like a damn hurricane inside. "I just wanted to ask if you saw something earlier. A man, and maybe a woman, come down this way."

Nothing. In fact, the person beneath the mound of debris seems to shrink further in on themselves. I hold back my growl of frustration. We don't fucking have time for this shit.

Time to step up my game. "I've got a bottle of whiskey with your name on it if you help me," I state.

A full head of slick, greasy gray hair pops from under the blanket mountain. His cloudy eyes level my way, a scowl forming beneath a white wiry beard. "I'm a vodka man."

"A handle of vodka it is, then." I breathe a sigh of relief. Finally something we might be able to use. "If you'd just answer a few questions for—"

"I'm homeless, not deaf, boy," he chastises while leveraging off the ground to sit upright. Back against the brick wall, he drapes a blanket over his crossed legs. "I heard ya the first time. Yeah, I saw people."

"People?"

"Two fellas, one hellcat." I choke on a half laugh, half sob. He points down the alley where we just came from. "Her tumblin' out that one's hold is what woke me. Fought like hell to get away."

"What happened next?" I somehow get out over the growing lump of dread lodged in my throat.

"He hauled 'er up and ran, followin' the other one in a suit."

"A suit?" all three of us question in unison. I watch Tank out of the corner of my eye. His attention is now torn between the old guy and whatever he's furiously typing on his phone.

"That's what I said. A suit and intense as anything I ever seen. I know those types and stay the hell away. I don't think he saw me. Didn't want to get on his radar, that's for damn sure."

"Those types?" I ask.

"The ones who enjoy it. Saw enough in the service." His eyes seem to grow distant, like he's chasing a memory. "The ones you were glad were on your side after you saw what they did to the enemy."

"And he was one of those guys?" I ask, trying like hell to understand what the old man is referring to.

"Where is my vodka?" he demands, crossing thin, bare arms across his chest.

"At my place. I'll give you the address and call someone to let you in."

"You one of them freaks who collect body parts?"

I almost snort, but the seriousness of the situation keeps it reined in. "No, just someone who can help and wants to." I bite at my lower lip as I decide what else to divulge. "She's my girlfriend, the woman. The hellcat."

"And thems?" He casts a suspicious glare at Champ and Tank. "What's with the light show down there anyhow? To damn hot to be time for Christmas lights, ain't it?"

"They're with me, helping me find her. So are all the cops, which are the lights you see." I rattle off my address while shooting a quick text to Gerard, letting him know a smelly visitor will be stopping by. "Someone will meet you at the front door. A hot shower, some vodka, and the best damn cookies you'll ever eat are waiting."

Not sure why I'm tempting him to leave now, but a feeling in my gut tells me whoever took Randi might double back after we're all gone and dispatch this old man just for camping along his escape route. If one of the men who took Randi is as unstable as the old man believes him to be, I sure as hell don't want my new informant waiting here like a sitting fucking duck.

I help him off the pavement, keeping a firm grasp on his hand until he's steady on his feet. The three of us watch as he hobbles down the alley before disappearing around a corner.

"Are you two thinking what I'm thinking?" Champ questions as he steps to my side, his shoulder brushing mine. "A suit. Why in the hell would someone wear a suit to an extraction?"

"Maybe to fit in with the other agents," I offer. "Maybe that's how he got close enough to trigger the explosion."

"A suit doesn't make an agent, Benson, you know that. If some random guy walked up in a suit, we would notice. We know our teams." I wait for Tank to continue as he scrubs at the top of his sweaty bald head. "No, I think it's deeper than that. Way fucking deeper."

"You think it was an actual agent." Tank's dark eyes meet mine. Suspicion and worry flash in his before he checks his phone, almost like he's avoiding telling me something. "You have an idea of who it is, don't you?" I take a menacing step closer to my best friend. "Tell me now, Davis. Tell me what the fuck you know."

"Stand down, Trey. You know who I suspect, because you've suspected the fucker since day one."

"Smith," I growl. "Where is he?"

Head shaking, he says, "I don't know. I called and texted the entire alpha team, telling them to get their asses up here and help with the investigation. Every single agent has responded to me except one."

"I'll fucking murder him," I hiss through gritted teeth. At the sudden wave of new rage, I turn with a roar and slam a fist against an already dented-to-hell dumpster. The burst of pain overtakes the urgency to find and kill Smith. Chest heaving, I massage my split and bleeding knuckles. "I knew it. I fucking knew there was a reason not to trust him."

"Calm the hell down, you fool. We need to be smart about this." Tank slaps the back of my head—hard. "If it is Smith, he can't know we suspect him. We let him lead us to her, and then we act. First we have to find him."

I rake a hand through my sweat-damp hair. "If he's not picking up, we need to start where it all began, where we first met him. She'll have his home address and background information."

"The director. Great idea. Let's go." Rocks and broken shards of glass crunch under his shoes as he twists to face Champ. "You follow this alley and find where they loaded her into the escape vehicle. There's no way in hell they're keeping her close by."

Champ nods once to Tank, then to me before turning and methodically walking down the alley the way we were headed before I spotted the homeless man.

Jogging in the opposite direction, I dodge boxes and dumpsters, all while running through the details we know over and over, hoping to make a connection that will aid in our search.

A dull ring comes from my phone shoved in my back pocket. Not bothering to slow, I slide it from my jeans and check the screen.

UNKNOWN

Ice encrusts my veins. I slow until I'm standing as still as a statue, staring at the still ringing phone in my hand.

"Who is it?" Tank asks, towering over my shoulder for a look. "That normal?"

I shake my head.

"Answer it. What if it's someone who knows something?" He shoves my shoulder, urging me into action. "Or her?"

At that, I immediately slide a finger across the screen and hold it to my ear.

"Who is this?" I demand. My girl is missing and in danger. No time for damn pleasantries.

"Vlad." A bolt of shock wakes up every strained brain cell. "I heard about your president. Have you found her?" The concern in his voice is clear, easing the tight ball of tension that's taken root in my chest. This is her friend, the Russian president, and he's worried about her. At least we have him and his unrestricted access to data on our side.

"No. We're gathering evidence now and looking into a few leads."

"I have a suggestion."

"Suggestion?"

"An inkling, if you will."

"We're on our way to investigate a suspect. I don't have time for this vague bullshit. Spit it out."

"Your secretary of state, he knows more than he tells."

"What?" Pulling the phone form my ear, I tap the Speaker button and hold the small device between me and Tank. "Why do you say Rosen?"

"I said an inkling. And I do not trust him. He works for the higher bidder, not the best of your country."

Tank nods, his thumbs already flying over the screen of his own cell, no doubt looking into the exact location of Todd now.

"We'll look into him, but, Vlad, I need more. I need to know where to find her." I clear my throat. "Can you help me?"

"I heard nothing of this. No talk. I will search as you search."

The screen flashes before going dark, signaling the call was ended.

"Todd Rosen," I muse. "I don't see it. The fucker is just a weak-ass idiot. But Vlad has never steered Randi wrong."

"Agreed. I have his location. He's at home, forty minutes away. Let's start with the director, then go see what Rosen knows."

Together we sprint down the alley, the pounding of our boots reverberating off the walls and sending the curious rats scattering.

"I won't make it if we don't find her," I admit, hoping the growing noise of the scene drowns out my fear.

"You won't have to find out, Trey. We'll find her."

When we turn the corner, we fight through the crowd, working our way toward the other side of the sea of people to Tank's SUV.

"Let's stop by my place," I tell him. "I need to change, grab my badge and papers. Maybe grab a few more weapons too."

"And whatever Beth made for breakfast," Tank adds in. "What?" His brow rises at my huff. "We have to eat to keep our energy up. We won't be sleeping until she's safe in the White House once again."

He's right. I won't sleep until she's safe in my arms.

And once she is, I'll never fucking let her go.

4

RANDI

Holy fuck, hell hurts. At least I assume I'm dead and in hell with the near suffocating dry heat. Dribbles of sweat slide along my spine and between my small boobs. And the hurting part, well, it feels like someone took a sledgehammer to my head a few hundred times. Its battering pulse feels like my brain might ooze out through my ears under the pressure.

One thousand percent positive I ended up in hell.

Cracking one eye open, ready to face the flicking flames and little red people with pointy tails, I peel the other eye open in disbelief.

"The fuck?" I rasp, my throat so parched the words feel like broken slivers of glass. "I'm not dead."

"Your low IQ is rather astounding, Trailer."

"Or maybe this is hell and you're Satan himself," I huff, licking my dry lips to ease the sting of them splitting open. Another long line of sweat slips down my spine, the sensation alerting me to the fact that I'm not only sitting up but in a different area of the warehouse I was held in before—or a different location altogether. Zero windows line the upper walls; hell, there isn't even an upper wall to speak of. In the middle of the low ceiling, a single cage-looking fixture houses a sole yellowed bulb, the only source of light.

Small, windowless, and fucking hot as hell.

My stomach rolls with unease. This new location is not a good sign for my life expectancy.

In a smooth fluid motion, Shawn stands from the small chair he was perched on and leans a shoulder against the cinder block wall, dressed in a pair of light gray slacks and an untucked white dress shirt. It's as casual as he gets, I guess. If I ever saw him in shorts and a T-shirt, I'd probably die of shock.

I snort. Little did he know all he had to do was buy the entire Banana Republic summer section to kill me.

"And what is funny about your situation, Trailer?" he asks, a small frown dipping his full lips.

His question sobers me. "Nothing, but do you even own a pair of shorts? It's a thousand degrees in here."

Disgust slips over his features. "And you're the one leading this fucking country."

I attempt to shrug but can't move my shoulders with the way my hands are tied behind me. Rotating one wrist and then the other, I determine he's used damn zip ties again. I try to test my feet but find their restraints too tight to move.

I wiggle to sit up straighter in the metal chair, causing the hard plastic ties to slice into the delicate skin of both wrists. I wince.

"What do you want, Shawn?" Between the pounding of my head and the pain in my wrists, coupled with the heat, I'm done playing games. Exhaustion has swept in, draining what little fight I had left and slowing my thoughts. "Just get it over with so I can move on and you can find a new person to torment."

"But it's been so fun."

"Not the word I would choose." I cough, though it's more of a wheeze, shoving dry air up my already scratchy throat. "Just tell me what the hell is going on."

Peering up through my lashes, I find him studying me. Brows dipped, he seems to be considering my words.

"Might as well," he says, shoving off the wall and returning to his seat. "We can't start until that sociopath gets here."

"Pot, kettle," I huff.

A small smile spreads up his thin lips. Ever so casually—not like he's holding the president captive waiting for the right moment to kill her—he withdraws a white handkerchief from his pocket and blots his forehead.

"From the start, this was about you. All of it. Making you realize you're nothing in this town and don't belong here. That VP spot should've been mine. Then the president's seat when Birmingham died unexpectedly—"

"He was your friend," I snap. "You were plotting your friend's death so you could do what... sit at the big desk?"

"Power is a motivator it seems you haven't the character or drive to appreciate. That's what was mine. That's what you took from me. For years I put up with that shithead Birmingham and his family, always staying a step back so they didn't know I was a threat to their little dynasty."

"You're sick," I whisper.

Fuck, I have to get out of here.

Twisting my wrists again, I attempt to slide a hand through the tight noose, resulting in slashing my wrists even further. Warm, thick liquid slips into my curled hands, pooling in my palm.

"It was a damn perfect plan until those dumbass advisors told him we couldn't win the election without gaining sympathy votes. Fucking Americans, basing the future of this country on their damn hearts and social agendas rather than their heads. We were the best match for the ticket, not you and Birmingham." Shawn's face flushes a deeper red than it already was from the heat. "After you won, he had a plan to get rid of you, and I would step in after you were gone. I wanted to put a bullet through your head, but unfortunately, I was overruled."

"Ah, yes, unfortunately." Each word burns in my throat, drying my already parched mouth and tongue further. "Was it you? Were you behind the attacks in Saudi Arabia and Egypt?" I have to know, even if I'm about to die and can't do anything with the information.

"You're jumping ahead," he snaps, like he's relishing the retelling of his story.

"You're boring," I huff back.

Fuck me. Why can't I keep my damn mouth shut?

No instigating the sociopath into killing you sooner than later, Randi. There is no unicorn army on their way to save you.

"The poisoning was highly entertaining."

"Fuck me, you're still going."

"You think you'd appreciate me prolonging what's to come by allowing me to divulge what was going on in the background."

"And what's to come again?" I ask, trying and failing to arch my brows.

Did I get hit in the face at some point, or is it just swelling due to the heat and whatever the hell they've given me?

"Torture, drawing it out by making sure your fuckstick of a boyfriend knows what you're going through, more torture, then you calling your VP and telling him you're stepping down."

"Fuck. No."

"To what part there, Trailer?"

"Um, all of it." I shake my head, immediately regretting it as my brain seems to slosh with the movement. "You know, growing up the way I did, where I did, I met a lot of disturbed people in my childhood. But you take the fucking cake, Shawn. The whole damn cake. Meth addicts, drug dealers, slimy-ass men, and yet you... you're the worst of them all. Parading around in your expensive suits and plastic face. You're the picture-perfect person on the outside and fucking nasty on the inside. You can't even consider for a second that I might be a better fit in this role and the VP's *because* of my background. You never considered how I could help millions because of how I grew up and finally had a platform and position to do something about it all."

He scoffs. "Of course I didn't. Because they don't matter, just like you don't. What you've failed to see this entire time your poor ass has been in DC is that no one matters but those with the money and power. I have the money. I just needed the power."

"Then thank the unicorn gods that I took it from you."

"What the hell did you say?"

"Wait, are you referring to the unicorn comment or that I took it from you?" I swear steam comes from his ears and nose. Seems I'm not doing so great on heeding my own advice of not pissing off the killer in the room. Whoops. "Even through your constant attempts on my life, and whatever sicko plan you have for today, I'll die knowing I protected the American people from you. I gave them three and a half years of someone actually caring about them and keeping them from your grasp."

Shawn scrubs at his chin, his dark eyes sliding over my restrained body. The full-body shiver that rakes down my spine causes me to tug on the stiff plastic around my wrist and ankles.

"I didn't realize your ignorance and stupidity would be this strong, keeping you from seeing the truth about your inconsequence."

"That's what you don't see. It hasn't been about me. It's never been about me. My whole damn life hasn't been about me. That's where your ignorance and stupidity are keeping *you* from seeing the truth."

His chair topples backward, crashing to the ground as he leaps from the seat. In two long strides, Shawn is in front of me, his hand pulled back with a look of pure rage on his face. Leaning as far left as I can, I attempt to shield myself from the brunt of the blow I know is coming.

The impact of the backhand across my cheek sparks stars in my vision. Pain explodes at the twist of my neck as it snaps to the side. I scream as the half second of shock gives way to a new type of pain I've never felt before.

Before I can even try to stop, what's left in my stomach erupts from my mouth and splatters onto the cracked and chipped concrete floor. A shouted curse blasts through the small space as Shawn leaps backward to keep the spray from soiling his slacks.

"You're fucking pathetic."

"Feeling's mutual," I rasp before gathering what's lingering in my mouth and spitting it in his direction.

An icy calm mask slides over his features, concealing the inferno I know is boiling beneath with hate. Only someone as sinister as Shawn can be mentally plotting how to remove your organs as painfully as possible while sporting a pleasing yet blank face.

"You will do as I say or your entire family will meet the same agonizing fate as you. Do you hear me, Trailer? At the end of this, you will call Pierce, and you will demand I take his spot as VP when he slides into the president spot after you step down. Then, only then, will the pain stop. Once you do that, I will leave you and everyone you love alone, forever. Give me what's mine and I walk away."

My lips part but no sound comes out. I'm torn. Do what he asks and all this stops and I'll never have to live in fear again. But do what he asks and put not only Sam at risk but the American people too. It would only be for half a year, six insignificant months. Or would it? No doubt Shawn has thought this through and has a plan for fixing himself into the next term too if I give in.

Live or die.

Live for my family, or die for millions I don't know and half who already hate me.

"I'll give you time to think it over. I have to go change." With a smug grin, like he knows the turmoil his options have caused, he marches to a side door I hadn't noticed and yanks it open, leaving without a single glance back.

The moment the door clicks closed, I slump in the chair, my shoulders rounding as my chin drops to my chest.

What in the hell am I supposed to do?

Live or die.

At least there's a 50/50 chance of making the right choice.

A LOUD NOISE somewhere nearby snaps me from the heat exhaustion state I slipped into after Shawn left. Jerking my head up, I blink to ease what feels like dirt coating my eyes and survey the still empty cell. The quick tug to both hands and feet signals I'm still restrained and what might be worse, I can't really feel my fingers anymore.

"If I lose my fingers, I'll be pissed," I hiss. Focusing on my fingers first, I urge them to wiggle, getting some blood flowing to them even though it hurts almost as bad as the bitch slap Shawn delivered earlier.

Time has stood still since I woke in this enclosed room. There's no way to tell how much time has passed without the sun as a somewhat guide. Hell, at this point it could've been days ago that I was abducted, but that doesn't feel right. No, days would be too long. I'm the president. There's half an army out there looking for me, as well as my guys. And probably Sarah at this point.

I smirk at the thought of what she'll do to Shawn if she gets her hands on him. It will be a glorious sight to see him cower to her. Just the image of her kicking his pompous ass has my heart beating faster and a wide smile emerging.

The fantasy vanishes at a squeaking creak as the only door swings open. I squint to ward off the bright sunlight that shines behind the man, dousing his face in a dark shadow preventing me from seeing his features. No, wait. I squint further. It's not just the shadowing but something covering his face, everything but his eyes hidden behind a black wrap of some kind. It reminds me of the covering the man who broke into my suite in Saudi Arabia wore to keep his identity hidden.

The man steps deeper into my little cinder block cell, slamming the door behind him. My eyes narrow the closer he gets. There's something familiar in his stance, something that suggests I've seen him before.

"Do I know you?" I ask as he checks the dark corners of the room.

Silence stretches as he sidesteps to move out of my line of vision. My sides ache as I twist to gain another look, but he's stopped directly at my back, preventing me from seeing him.

"Who are you?"

Silence.

I huff, letting out the frustration, exhaustion, and discomfort in one tight breath.

"Fine. I'll tell you something. They will find me. He will find me. And when he does, you'll have the full force of Trey's wrath on your head. Not to mention I have a button that could launch a nuke up your ass. Or hell, I could just call in a favor to the SEALs. We're friends." I roll my eyes at my own embellishment. "Okay, fine, maybe 'friends' is a little exaggerative, but they know me. I'm kind of a big deal."

I don't hide my snort.

"You did drag me out of a bulletproof town car among a caravan of dark SUVs, so I'm guessing you already know who I am."

"More than you know" comes a muffled voice behind me.

Stretching my neck from one side to the other, I steel my spine, readying to ask the hard questions. "Tell me, were you behind the attacks in Egypt and Saudi Arabia?"

"Yes and no."

"Okay," I say on a pushed breath. "Was it you who said I was responsible for your two friends? One of which you shot because he was assaulting me, I'd like to add." No one will miss that fucker. Who humps a scalp? I shiver in revulsion. "You did the world a favor with that one."

I scream as my head is yanked back by a fist gripping my hair.

"I'm worse." Immediately he drops his hold, and I sense rather than see him retreat a step.

"Your fingers aren't fucking my throat, and your tiny penis isn't dry humping my head, so I have to disagree with you on that one." Maybe I can get to him, make him see I'm a human being, not just a hostage and Shawn's plaything. That's what they always say on those crime shows, right? "Do you like unicorns?"

Direct tactic to building a connection. I like it.

"That fucking unicorn obsession of yours is strange."

My ears perk up at that. So he knows I'm oddly fascinated by the mystical, beautiful creatures. Interesting. Only my inner circle and friends know that. Well, them and my....

Realization washes over me like a bucket of ice water.

My agents, the ones by me every day and night. They'd all know about my unicorn-loving heart.

So that means this man, one of the two who abducted me, is not only someone I know but someone who was on my protection detail.

Trey and T were right all along.

But it's worse than a mole.

Way worse.

This agent wasn't just leaking information.

He's a damn traitor who wants me dead.

5

TREY

"Come on, hurry the fuck up," I demand as the elevator slowly descends toward the lobby. Worry-filled glances are exchanged among the few business-dressed men and women. My impatience and combat attire, plus exposed guns, warrant their unease.

Before the elevator can level off at our destination, I wedge my fingers between two doors and pry them open. An alarm goes off, but I ignore it and the whispers as I rush through the busy lobby and shove through the revolving door. The morning sun's heat is already brutal in its assault as I step from the shade of the drive-through canopy and onto the sidewalk. Spotting Tank's idling SUV parallel parked up ahead, I increase my pace, eager to hunt for Smith.

"The hell you wearing, Benson?" Tank asks as I slide into the passenger seat. I slam the door shut behind me with one hand and adjust the cold air flow toward my face with the other.

Before I respond, I shift along the leather until I'm comfortable and secure the seat belt behind my back in case I need to make a quick exit. "They brought the war to me, to my turf. Don't expect me to get dressed up for their fucking funeral."

He purses his lips like he wants to make another comment. I dare him with a sharp gaze to question the black cargo pants, black T-shirt, and combat boots. Sure, it's not standard uniform, but neither are all the exposed weapons. But fuck protocol. Fuck uniforms. Fuck the Secret Service right now. I'm getting my girl back come hell or high water, in one piece, safe, and I'll burn the world down to do it if that's what it takes.

"No fucking way I could do what needs to be done in a suit."

"Are you talking to me or yourself like your crazy girlfriend?"

Turning to the window, I smirk because honestly, I don't know.

"What did you bring me for breakfast?" Tank asks, eyeing my empty hands as he weaves through traffic toward downtown.

Digging into a side pocket of my cargo pants, I toss one of the two granola bars onto his wide lap. Reaching to my other pant leg, I pull out two travel-size protein shakes. After setting both in the cup holder, I lean back and stare out the windshield.

"It's all I had. Beth was busy feeding that guy from earlier." I pause, thinking through the events of the morning for the thousandth time. "I think whoever took Randi would've doubled back after everyone was gone to make sure he didn't leave behind any witnesses."

"It's a possibility." Tank tosses his phone across the console. I snag it midair before it can hit me square in the chest. "Get someone to stake out the area after the scene is cleaned up to watch for any abnormalities."

With more force than necessary, he flicks the blinker, signaling as we enter the highway.

Running a hand through my hair, I observe the trees and other cars whiz past the window as Tank speeds along the shoulder of the road to miss all the early morning traffic. "We need to be a hundred different places at once right now. Fuck!" I yell, pushing all my frustration into the one word.

"It's why we have a team, Benson. A solid team. We're doing the digging while the others are at the site working the investigation with the FBI and Homeland. From there they'll peel off and search elsewhere. But we're here. This is our focus. You're no good to me, or her, scattered."

A slight vibration along my thigh signals an incoming text or call on my phone I'd shoved deep into a pocket of my cargo pants before running out of the condo earlier. To miss a stalled car, Tank jerks into the HOV lane before weaving in and around the congested four-lane highway. One hand gripping the "oh shit" bar for dear life, I rummage around the few pockets in search for the now silent phone.

Flipping it one-handed, I press the side button to see who reached out. A text box appears from a number not saved as a contact with a thumbnail-size picture attached. Loving a distraction from Tank's *Fast and Furious* style of driving, I swipe the screen and open the messaging app.

What fills my screen is so unexpected, I can only stare at it for a few seconds.

Everything shuts down. My lungs, my heart, my mind—every cell is nonfunctional as I fixate on the picture of the woman I love. Fear and shock resonate behind her hazel eyes. Blood soils her hairline and speckles her cheeks like red freckles. A blueish tint darkens the fair skin along her fore-head down to her cheekbone.

"What's going on?" I don't respond to Tank. I can't. "Trey, answer me." Eyes wide, I rip my stare from the screen to look unfocused at the driver seat. "You're scaring me. What's going on?"

It's only now I realize trembles are racking my body, the phone in my hand shaking. Pitching forward, I rest my head between my knees and gulp down air to keep me from passing out.

"Randi," I say between gasps. I hold the phone across the console for him to get a quick glimpse.

"Shit," Tank barks. The SUV's tires screech as we fishtail along the shoulder. Only when he regains control does he slam on the gas pedal, sending me flying against the seat. "It's fine. It means she's alive. Shoot it over to our guys at the FBI to get a track set up on that number and analyze the hell out of that picture."

I nod numbly as I send the picture to our FBI contact. Against my better judgment, I enlarge the picture of Randi again. "She looks fucking terrified. What the hell did they do to her?" The picture blurs as wetness gathers in my lower lids.

"You're letting your relationship and feelings for her cloud your judg-ment again, Benson. Stay focused. My guess, whatever you see on the screen is from the wreck, not them. We saw the town car, the splintered passenger window. They're not hurting her."

Yet. That's the word he leaves off for my sake. But he's right. I am letting my feelings for her and our personal relationship hamper any unbiased, unemotional thinking. Not that knowing I need to detach myself can actu-ally help me do it.

She's scared and hurt. My girl, the one I swore to protect as my job and as the love of my life. I failed her. This is proof that I don't deserve her or the love and trust she so freely offers me.

"Snap out of it, Trey, or I'll pull this fucking truck over and beat some sense into you, which will waste valuable time. Time she doesn't have."

He's right. Like always.

Fuck, I need a cigarette. The craving hits hard and fast, making my fingers tremble with need for nicotine to calm my restless nerves.

To help realign my focus, I swipe the picture, ready to delete the entire text. If it's still here, available for me to look at whenever I want, it'll keep pulling my focus. Maybe that's why whoever sent this....

Wait a fucking minute.

"My number isn't listed anywhere, and not many people have it," I muse while raking my hands through my hair over and over again like it might help me think faster.

"Only half of the women in DC."

I shoot an annoyed glare his direction. "Not the time for jokes, asshat."

"Just an observation."

"Fine. I'll rephrase that. Not many people capable of kidnapping the motherfucking president under the watchful eye of her Secret Service agents have my damn number."

"Agreed. So who does that leave us?"

My eyes shift back and forth, my sight unfocused as I mentally go through the list of names. "Well, all of our team, but they were at the crash site." My knuckles turn white from my clenched fists. "All but one." Fury builds in my gut, heating my blood and skin. "That motherfucker is a part of this. I know it. I just fucking know it."

The most logical explanation is he's been the one on the inside this whole time, leaking our information to those who wanted to harm Randi. I don't know why, and to be honest, I don't fucking care. All I want is her back safe and whoever responsible to have a bullet between their eyes.

"It all points toward him," Tank muses, jerking the wheel to the right. We take the exit that will take us straight to the agency's main office. "We'll know more in five minutes. Hold on."

With that quick warning, he slams on the gas, sending us hurtling through the streets. Other drivers honk, and a few even raise their hand out the window to flip us the bird. Not that I care. Fuck them and their need to get to work. We're on a mission to save a life—hell, maybe even save the country.

Not that I think Sam would do a poor job in the president role, it's just not his role to fill. Randi, as much as she can't see it, has done a phenomenal job as president and still has so much she wants to accomplish before the end of her term.

The SUV's tires squeal as Tank slams on the brakes, finagling the large vehicle into a compact car parking spot around the corner from our destination. I'm out before the engine is cut, racing through the packed downtown sidewalk, shouldering my way through as I zigzag toward the front door of the agency's building. Heavy footfalls and barked commands behind me to get out of our way tell me Tank is hot on my heels.

The glass door nearly shatters as I slam it open, the metal handle clipping the other side door with the impact. Not waiting for the elevator, I make a beeline for the stairwell and bound up the steps three at a time until I reach the floor where I know we'll find the director.

With everything that happened this morning, between the president being taken and so many agents dead, I doubt I'll find her holed up in her office. More than likely she'll be in the war room surrounded by other high-ranking officials and those she trusts.

That's my destination.

I grip the cool metal lever and give it a hard yank, but the door doesn't budge.

Locked.

The door rattles under the pounding of my fist. I relentlessly beat on it until the unmistakable click of a lock releasing reaches my ears. An inch of a gap appears between the door and the frame—all I need. Wedging a steel-toe boot into the small crack, I thrust a shoulder and hip against the thick wood.

It bursts open from my assault, and a pained cry comes from somewhere between the door and the wall, not that Tank nor I care as we storm into the room. A quick assessment of those in the room verifies what I assumed earlier. Ten directors and higher-ups sit or stand around the long conference table, folders, pictures, and documents scattered along the dark surface.

Ten sets of eyes blink in shock at the interruption. All except the director, who looks more resigned than surprised at our rude entrance.

"Agent Washington, Agent Benson, what is the meaning of this?" she shouts from where she leans over the table, a stack of pictures in front of her.

"We need answers," I snap, not releasing her furious yet exhausted look.

A sliver of guilt eats its way through my conscience. I'm being a dick when she just lost many good agents.

I shrug a shoulder at my internal turmoil, dispelling the thought on softening my tone.

"We're working on that now. Go back to the crash site, wait for further orders—"

"No," I state through clenched teeth. "We need answers now on that shady-ass agent you put on our team last year. He's associated with what happened this morning somehow. Now we just have to find him."

Her shoulders rise at my words as several tension-filled lines form along her forehead and between her brows.

"We can't find him... again," Tank adds from where he stands calm and collected beside me, his tone and stance the picture-perfect professional agent.

Fuck that shit. We need answers, even if I have to be an asswipe to get them. I'll apologize after I save Randi and lock her away for the rest of her life to ensure something like this never happens again.

A shake of her head sends several short blonde strands cascading forward, creating a makeshift shield to hide her emotions from us and the rest of the room.

"Give us a moment," she says with a sigh. The order hangs in the still room, everyone still standing exactly as they were when we barged inside. "That means now."

The shuffling of papers and scrape of chair legs along the worn paper-thin carpet fill the room as the ten people surrounding the table jolt into action. Everyone files out of the room, the one I nearly flattened to a pancake with the door the last to leave, casting a glare in my direction before slamming it closed behind him.

With everyone gone, I move deeper into the room and pause across the long conference table from the director. Pressing the tips of two fingers against a photograph, I slide it along the smooth surface toward me for a better look. Hopefully they know more than Tank and me. That way we can combine information and piece this puzzle together faster by working together and sharing intel.

"First of all, it's not what you think with Agent Smith," she says, staring at a picture on the table. It's one of the entire scene, three wrecked cars, the chaos and destruction palpable even on paper. "Second, I want you both to know I take full blame for this. I never should've approved the smaller convoy when she went out to visit her"—she flicks a wrist—"special friend."

Tank's cough has me peering over my shoulder, his sly smile there and gone in a flash. Good to know the boys have kept *who* Randi was visiting private. Who knows what the director would say if she found out Randi's "special friend" was actually me.

"No one expected this to happen, ma'am." Tank steps closer and folds his arms along the back of a chair left pulled away from the table. "It's no one's fault except the people who orchestrated the attack and abduction. Which brings us back to Smith and our suspicions that he's a part of this somehow."

"What makes you feel you have enough evidence to accuse a fellow agent of treason?" The bite in her tone signals we're walking on thin ice. True, it is a heavy allegation, but we do have proof.

"There was a witness who saw—"

"What witness?" Her sharp scrutiny levels me from where she sits. "No one has mentioned a witness being found in any of the reports that have come through."

"That was our intention." Shoving the picture away, I press both hot palms to the table's cool surface and lean forward, pressing most of my weight onto my hands. "Based on the information this man gave us, we suspect the men who attacked had inside information. Information only an agent would know. If no one knows there's a witness, then the agent responsible for leaking the president's route and the new surveillance we had installed won't know we're on to them."

"Who is it? And how do you know he's telling the truth?"

"On our inspection of various connecting alleyways—which is how we believe the attackers escaped without the backup convoy seeing them when they arrived—we came upon a homeless man." Now in full alpha team lead mode, Tank's words are cold, calculated as he recites what we know to the director. It doesn't pass my notice that his gaze hasn't dropped to the table where the pictures of our dead friends and agents lie haphazardly spread out. He's hurting at the loss. Hell, I am too, but that can't shift our focus from the current objective—finding the president.

"The homeless man stated he saw two men fleeing down the alley. One was carrying a woman, and the other, leading, was wearing a suit. A suit, Madam Director. Who do you think that suggests?" I narrow my eyes at her, hoping this information will help break down the wall of protection she has around the mysterious agent. "Based on his behavior on other assignments, disappearing when needed and now being unavailable, we suspect it's Smith who's the inside man. We find Smith, we find the president."

The chair creaks under her slight weight as she leans back and steeples two fingers beneath her chin. "You think it's an agent."

"Not just any agent. Smith," I correct. "He was forced onto our team without any say from our team lead, Davis. Then, during the couple times the president's life was in danger, Smith was conveniently unavailable or missing. We know nothing about him. Hell, I don't think I even know his first name." My chest heaves from the exertion of holding back the roar that my voice wants to morph into. Yelling at my boss won't win me any favors, so I keep my tone in check.

"It's not him specifically," she states all calm and collected, the very opposite of the war of emotions raging inside me. "But based on the witness statement and the execution of the incident, an agent leaking the information makes sense. I've been sitting here trying to piece together how these fuckers knew her route to and from the residence." She flashes an accusing glare my way. Okay, maybe she does know I'm Randi's special friend. Whatever, I'll deal with those consequences later. "And they knew about the smaller agent force and new surveillance. It didn't add up until now. So yes, Agent Benson, I concur that the circumstances coupled with that witness statement, even though unreliable, point to an agent assisting with this morning's attack on the president. But who is the—"

"It's fucking Smith." The table rattles under the weight of my fist slamming against the top. "Why are you covering for him?"

"It's not Agent Smith. Move on, focus on other possible suspects." Her delicate brows draw close. Tugging at a small necklace, she runs the charm along the length of the thin gold chain. "I'll gather the full beta team roster. It has to be one of them or an incident would've been reported that an unscheduled agent was on premises before the attack. They know the rules which are in place to prevent things like this from happening."

"Why the fuck are you adamant that it's not Smith? The evidence since he was forced onto the alpha team all points to him."

"I know it's not Agent Smith." Dropping the necklace, she casually folds her hands beneath the table, but not before I catch their small tremble. "Tell me what else you saw at the scene, what other evidence you found."

"No," I growl and shove away from the table, ready to stalk around to her side and shake some sense into her. A grip on my shoulder stops me from advancing on our boss.

Our female boss.

Fuck, what am I doing?

Scrubbing a hand down my face, I breathe in deep. "Tell me right now, Madam Director, right fucking now why we shouldn't issue a search and destroy for Smith. Explain why he shouldn't be hunted down and hung for being a traitor." Beads of sweat dot my forehead and slip down the back of my neck with my rising anger and restraint.

Her head dips in what seems to be either defeat or acceptance.

I dare a look to my friend, who appears as confused as I feel.

"Madam Director," Tank urges, his tone clipped. "The president is running out of time." I fight to hold back the gut-wrenching panic his words triggers. "If you know something about Agent Smith, why we shouldn't consider him as a suspect, tell us. Then we can move on to find the bastard who not only betrayed Randi and his country but this very fucking agency itself. Tell us. Now."

Whoa. The controlled anger in his deep voice and expression makes me flinch, and I'm not even the one he's talking to.

"I know it's not him," she murmurs, now massaging her temples with two fingers.

"How? How can you be certain. Do you even know his background?" I snap.

"Yes."

"Tell. Us. Now." I've never wanted to cause harm to a woman until now. Why the hell is she holding back? We need this information.

Sitting up tall, she collects herself, straightening her shoulders. "I do know his background, and yes, Agents Washington and Benson, I know for a fact he's not our traitor. And I know all this with 100 percent certainty because...." Turning the chair, she puts her back to us and faces the row of dark-tinted windows that look out over the city. "Because Agent Smith is my son."

What. The. Ever. Loving. Fuck?

6

TREY

"What?" Tank and I say in unison, the shock of her confession deflating the earlier tension from the room.

With the director's back still to us, I shift to face Tank, eyes wide, my mouth opening and closing as I search for words. But what in the hell do you say to *that*? Did *not* see that coming, because it makes zero sense.

By the narrowing of my friend's eyes and the sharp hitch of his chin toward the woman across the table, it seems Tank is on the same wavelength.

Grinding my teeth, I sort through what to say or ask to help clarify the million questions I have, but she beats me to it.

"He was with Homeland before I transferred him to Secret Service. I won't go into the long version, because as Agent Washington mentioned before, the president doesn't have much time. But I can tell you he was top of his class at MIT, recruited directly out of college. You have to know he's a good man and an even better agent with his observation talents and ability to pull apart truths and lies quickly." Her weighted pause has me inching closer to the edge of the table, waiting for more. "He's always had this... edge to see through things others can't. Homeland used his talents, put him in difficult scenarios right out of training, ones that still haunt him.

"Two years ago, he stopped by for a visit, and I noticed he was different. I couldn't put my finger on it, but there was a darkness weighing him down. I came to the conclusion that the years he'd put into Homeland and the types of ops and requirements needed to tackle the stateside terrorists were taking a heavy toll. Then he started showing up injured." I hold a breath as she rotates the chair around to face us. Dampness lingers along her lower lids. "I asked him what happened, asked what was going on, but he refused to open up. He didn't... doesn't have anyone. No wife, no girlfriend or friends. It's just him and me. So I knew it had to be me to save him, even if it was saving him from himself.

"I had him followed shortly thereafter. The first agent I assigned to tail him was ditched in less than ten minutes. The second even faster than that. It took months to figure out how he was gaining the injuries when he wasn't on assignment. And when I found out...." Her short blonde hair shifts along her jawline with a shake of her head. "He was in deep. I didn't confront him, knowing he'd deny any involvement or simply walk away from me and never come back. Nor did I ask for permission when I went above his head and called in a favor, having him transferred to my agency. With Ray unraveling on and off assignments, they willingly transferred what they assumed was a too-far-gone agent to the Secret Service."

Ray. So that's his first name. If I had a hundred guesses, I would've never gotten it correct. That asshole looks more like a Frank or Dave or Charlie than a Ray. No wonder he hasn't told us his name. Poor fuck is embarrassed it doesn't match his persona. Unlike mine that totally fits. I think.

"Unraveling?" I question, my voice deep with focus. It's a nice story and all, but what if she's too close to this, considering the relationship, and can't see the blaring signs that her son did unravel completely and abducted Randi?

"Taking greater risks than needed, almost as if he'd lost all self-preservation. Which is why he started...." She paused a moment, then looked at Tank. "You said you tried reaching out to him?"

"Correct, no answer."

She nods. "I'll keep trying him. In the meantime, what other leads can you pursue? With the suit tip, agent is one angle we can dive into. I'll look at the beta team roster, compare it to those who were killed in the attack, and go from there."

"What aren't you telling us about Smith?" Gripping the chair back beside me, I squeeze until my knuckles turn white. "Why shouldn't we suspect him? What's with the disappearing? You say you know."

"I do, but I'm not sure it's my story to tell. I found out by going behind his back, which cost me months of us not speaking."

"Madam Director, tell us, or I can't give up on the idea that Smith is behind this somehow. The disappearances are a huge indicator that he's up to something shady."

She huffs in seeming frustration as she purses her lips. "Fine. But not a word to him." I hold two fingers in the air with the universal sign of trustworthiness. Unfortunately for her, I was never a Boy Scout, but she doesn't need to be reminded of that right now. "Ray is mixed up with an illegal underground fighting circuit."

"Huh?" I tilt my head in complete and utter loss.

"I don't know all the details, more bits and pieces through my own digging. It's a gruesome, everything-goes type of fight club. Every time he steps into the makeshift ring, his life is at risk. Blades of any kind are allowed. No gloves, no tape, no padding. Anything goes until one person concedes to defeat or dies. And from my informants, the latter happens often."

"How does this tell me he's innocent in all this? Sounds like he has an anger problem and is off his fucking rocker."

Her thin lips press into a line at my disparaging comment about her son. "They're everywhere, these circuits. All he has to do is put his name in the pool. And with his record, it wouldn't surprise me that every time he's interested, they find a fight for him to enter."

I stare blankly at the director, needing a bit more than that to piece together whatever web she's weaving.

"Let me ask you this. After these disappearances, did you notice any signs of injury? A flinch, a bruise, or cuts?" she asks.

I start to shake my head until a flash of memory stops me short. That time in the Oval Office, and a few others he seemed stiff almost like he was sore or healing.

"I've never seen him with bruises on his face, anywhere visible," I muse. Tank paces behind me, no doubt trying to process all this new information on Smith while devising a plan for the next few hours. This isn't getting us anywhere closer to finding Randi and punishing those responsible.

"That's because most are unable to land a clean hit. He protects his face before everything else, which leaves other parts of him vulnerable, but from what I've gathered, he's the only undefeated opponent in the circuit."

There's no stopping my slack-jawed expression. *Well, hell. Now that's fucking impressive.*

"This doesn't change the fact that I don't fully trust him, but it does make me question if he's the one we should be focused on. You say you trust him?" I ask her.

"He has his issues, but yes, I trust him not to betray me or our country."

"Fine. There is a tip we can follow up on while we wait to hear from Smith," I state as I shove off the back of the chair. It tips forward before righting itself and slamming back to the floor. "You'll focus on the beta team and let us know if you find anything suspicious in their backgrounds or whereabouts last night. We'll circle back when we're done with this other lead."

"What's this lead?" she asks.

"A suggestion from someone we trust." Tank stalks toward the door. "Let us know immediately if you obtain any new information or leads." Hand on the door lever, he pauses and shifts to face the director. "I'm not happy that you hid valuable insight from me regarding Agent Smith which put my team in danger." Her lips part as she readies her defense, but Tank puts his back to her. "We'll discuss this after the president is found."

The door hurls open under the force of his yank, slamming against the opposite wall with a loud crack. Bits of drywall sprinkle to the ground from the divot the handle created.

Tank and I stomp down the stairs to follow through on Vlad's tip about Secretary of State Todd Rosen.

Halfway to the lobby, I realize my earlier doubt and suspicion of Smith has morphed into something resembling respect after the director's explanation. Respect and excitement. If he was Homeland's go-to agent for intelligence gathering, there's a chance he might have some suspicions on who our traitor is.

Now all we have to do is find the bastard.

"We interrogate the secretary of state together," Tank says as I slide into the passenger seat. He jams a finger against the Start button like it personally offended him.

"Interrogate or question?" I chuckle.

"Question. If anyone outside of this truck asks, that is."

A ghost of a smile pulls at my lips. "Noted. You know where you're going?"

He nods and yanks on the wheel, throwing the SUV into the heavy flow of traffic. A weighted silence settles around us as he weaves through the rush hour traffic. If he's like me, he's probably lost in his own thoughts, processing what was revealed in that office.

If what she says is true, then Smith truly is the badass fucker some have suspected him to be. I have no qualms with how he goes about managing his anger; it's his body, his life, his choice. From what little I know, the circuit is all consenting adults. The men—and who knows, maybe a few women— who put their name in the fight selection hat have to understand the rules and risks involved. It's violent as fuck and not my scene, but we all have to find our own way to process what we've done in our job to protect the millions of innocent lives in the US.

Do I judge him for the violence he dispenses to save himself?

Fuck no.

Hell, I might even respect him a little more now.

Not because of the violent way he deals with his anger but the fact that he *is* dealing with it in some way. The easy way would be to drown your conscience with alcohol and move on to the next soul-darkening operation, letting it all build until you implode. Him choosing another path shows dedication on his part, even if it seems a bit suicidal.

A sharp ring blares through the SUV's speakers, cutting my rambling internal thoughts on Smith and his life choices.

Both brows shoot up my forehead at the name listed on the display screen.

Agent Smith.

With a quick press of a button, Tank ends the near shrill ringing. Static crackles through the empty space before settling into silence.

"Smith." Tank's deep voice rumbles through the cab. "Where the fuck have you been?"

"Unavailable. I just caught the news. Where do you need me?" If he can sense the impatience from Tank's clipped words, he doesn't let on. Hell, his even tone makes me think he's bored, which pisses me right the fuck off.

"Why don't you call your mom and get caught up to speed with her side of the investigation first?" I snap.

A long pause fills the car. I watch the little time counter tick up in seconds, waiting for him to respond to my jab.

His heavy sigh blows over the mouthpiece. "What all do you know?"

"Everything. She told us everything. Now get your motherfucking shit together, Smith, and help us find her." A full-body tremor racks my body with the impatience racing through me. "We're headed to check out that fuckstick of a secretary of state."

"Good thinking. There's something off about him," Smith muses, clearly unruffled by my obvious anger.

"We have a witness who says one of the men running away from the scene was in a suit."

"You're thinking it was an agent and was in on it somehow."

"We do. Any thoughts on where we should focus after we question Rosen?" I hold in a breath, allowing a slow burn to tighten my lungs. We need another lead, something other than a damn inkling from the Russian president.

"I do," Smith responds calmly.

"Care to share?" Tank snaps, slamming the heel of his left palm against the dash, startling me. This man treats his SUV like his only child normally and never takes his anger out on it. Seems like it's not only me with emotions running unchecked. "She's running out of time."

"She is. I'll call you back."

Without another word, the bastard ends the call.

Tank shoots a dark look my way, promising retribution on Smith for hanging up on us, before turning his attention back out the windshield.

As he drives us toward Rosen's place, we use the downtime to talk over what we know and strategy for interrogating the secretary of state. By the time the large spacious estates with perfectly groomed yards and mature trees fill every window, we're forty minutes from downtown and have a solid plan in place.

We're still not moving fast enough. We need to be doing more, finding more. We're racing a doomsday clock, the time seeming to tick faster as the hours pass without her in my arms. I can't shake the feeling that we're running out of time. That *she's* running out of time.

Stay strong, Mess. Stay strong and wait for me.

UNEASE CHURNS MY GUT, twisting my insides as we speed down the pristine drive of Todd Rosen's massive home—mansion, really. There's no way this fool Rosen makes enough from his salary to afford something like this in this area. Before Birmingham pulled him out of obscurity, Todd Rosen was a nobody, so how does someone like him have all this?

"Family money?" I question, my hand hovering over the chrome door handle, readying to push it open the moment we come to a halt.

"Not that I know of. You know that tool would've mentioned coming from money when he made a try for our girl that time a couple years back when she was still VP. Remember that?"

"Don't remind me," I growl at my friend.

The SUV slows to a crawl as we round the front drive and come to a stop directly in front of the steps leading to the wide double front door. My boots slam onto the pristine white concrete drive moments after Tank shifted the SUV into Park.

I survey the entire area as I approach the steps and begin the short climb to the front door. Professionally sculpted hedges and brilliant flowers line the circular pull through. A high-tech security camera points directly at me with another two or three lining the edge of the brick home.

I squint, fighting off the late morning sun as it sears my eyes, making me regret forgetting the agency-issued sunglasses at home. "But the rest of that statement was true about him being a tool and flaunting his money if he had it. So then what's all this?" I wave toward the colonial-style home, immaculate grounds, and... fuck, is that a fountain I hear nearby?

"No idea, but something feels off about it all," Tank says over his shoulder as he marches up the steps.

A red monstrosity looms before us at the top. Well over ten feet tall and just as wide, the double doors feel like a warning of some kind. A hint that if you pass through the doors, you might not come out alive.

Shaking off the eerie feeling of being watched, probably from the security cameras and the person monitoring the feed, I forgo knocking. The large brass doorknob barely fits into my hand as I give it a twist, hoping to find it unlocked hoping to catch the bastard off guard. Legal ramifications of doing this without a warrant be dammed.

Of course I'm not that lucky.

Grumbling under my breath, I pound a fist against the door, the thick wood barely vibrating under my onslaught. The side of my hand burns as I continue to demand entry until it swings open, leaving my hand hovering midair. A man in a black suit stands in the middle of the doorframe, his glare darting from me to over my shoulder where Tank stands.

"Secret Service," I state, shoving my credentials an inch from his nose. His scrutinizing gaze rakes over my information. "We need to question Mr. Secretary on his involvement with the incident this morning involving the president's disappearance."

The guard's eyes widen a fraction, slack jaw erasing the earlier indignation.

Using his surprise to my advantage, I shove him aside with ease and step into the foyer.

"Where is he?" I question as I take a quick scan of the opulent foyer, searching for the fucker we're here to question. A deep ache pulses in the muscles along my jaw from the constant restraint from roaring and releasing all this held-back wrath.

"In his office," the guard states, shaking his head. Suspicion creeps in at how quickly he accepted the idea that his boss would be a part of the attack. Either he's setting us up or has seen enough while on duty to warrant our accusation. "He's been holed up in there all morning." He waves a hand up the curved stairwell. "Come with me. I'll show you the way."

Tank slaps a hand to the guard's chest to stop him from moving. "No need. We'll take it from here. All we need are directions."

The guard's eyes flick up the stairs and back to Tank. Rubbing a hand along his clean-shaven jaw, he hitches his chin toward the second level. "Take a left at the top of the stairs. It's the last door on your left." He slides his hand to the back of his neck and tightens his grip. "I'm not sure about his involvement with what you're here about, but I've been on this rotation for six months, and...."

"And?" Tank prods when the guard clams up.

Tension builds in the open entryway, Tank and I both on edge as we wait for him to continue. Hopefully it'll be something we can use during the interrogation. My tight chest and racing pulse tell me we're on to something here, but we need to hurry.

Eyes downcast, finding the black-and-white marble stone floor suddenly riveting, he raises his shoulders in a noncommittal shrug. "Things don't add up. But the pay is good, and he offers dental." He lets out an amused chuckle. "Should've known it was too good to be true." Like he's found his courage to give us the details, he raises his gaze from the floor and levels it my way. "The people who come and go from here, at all hours of the night, aren't the type of people you'd expect the secretary of state to be associated with. I've seen my share of shady businessmen, and these have it written all over them." He shakes his head. "I'm not sure what he's involved in, but there's something not right going on. And I suspect the others before me felt the same but were paid to keep quiet or knew if they spoke up about it, they wouldn't be living very long."

Done fucking waiting and hearing even more evidence for why I never liked this fuckstick, I storm to the stairs and take them two at a time. The dark wooden steps take the brunt of my urgency with each heavy pound of my boots. At the landing, I turn toward the hallway, but a tight grip lands on my shoulder and twists me the opposite way I was originally headed.

"Your other left, you idiot," Tank huffs with a mix of exasperation and humor. He gives me a shove in the new direction, and I stumble several feet.

Side by side, we stalk down the hall, guns drawn, ready for anything. After the guard's confession, we're not taking any chances at being ambushed. Rosen is mixed up in something, but what and who, only time will tell.

We clear two pristine bedrooms and one bathroom on our way toward Rosen's office. The dark oak door at the end of the hall is the only obstacle before I gain some answers that will hopefully bring us one step closer to finding Randi.

The metal knob bites into my hand under my tight grip.

Fucking locked.

Unease surges, clenching my gut. Something feels even more off up here than it did downstairs.

My breath catches at a hopeful thought. What if it's her? What if Randi is being held *here*?

Hand still gripped around the doorknob, I pitch back, gaining leverage. My shoulder and the door connect with a thump, and a pained grunt escapes me. A faint crack of wood sounds at the second attempt at using my body as a battering ram. Again I shove my body weight against the door, new fissures and cracks spreading with each hit.

After the fifth or sixth hit, I slump forward, catching my breath and giving my throbbing shoulder a quick break before going back at it.

"Stand back, you skinny-ass fool."

I grimace as I unmold my hand from the knob. Good shoulder against the wall, I wave a hand to the door. "Go right ahead, brute squad, if you think you can do better."

Of course he does. One hit. One fucking hit of one of his massive shoulders and the door splinters to pieces. If I didn't know it was physically impossible, I'd swear on the Bible that the area that took the direct impact disintegrated to sawdust right before my eyes.

"Show-off. I weakened it for you," I mumble, knowing full well I didn't do shit but maybe scratch the dark-stained finish.

Righting himself from where he'd fallen slightly forward toward the door, Tank turns with a cocky-as-hell smile.

Broken fragments of wood splinter, the larger intact pieces buckling under my boots as I step through the wreckage into the office that hopefully holds the man who can provide us with answers. Stuffed bookshelves line three of the four walls. A rolling ladder catches my gaze as I survey the office in search of that fucker Todd Rosen.

I find him sitting behind an industrial metal desk on the far side of the room. The distinct coppery scent of blood wafts up my nose, preparing me for what I'll find as I dare a few steps closer. The excitement and anticipation at getting answers from this motherfucker fall, sinking in my stomach like a damn lead cannonball. It won't happen unless we call a medium.

Because Todd Rosen, Secretary of State, is fucking dead.

And not just dead.

Executed.

7

RANDI

"Who. Are. You?" Each word scrapes against my raw throat, making them raspy and weak.

Hard, warm metal pushes against my temple. I freeze, even my breaths cease as it drags sensually down my cheek. Out of the corner of my eye, the light reflects off the metal, giving it a shape I recognize all too well.

A gun.

"No one of consequence," he says at my back.

"Your voice is familiar, and you're petting me with a gun. Pretty sure who you are holds some importance here."

Damn it, Randi, stop provoking the crazies.

"My voice? Interesting. How observant of you, Madam President. And here I thought you never saw me among the others. Good to know I had somewhat of a lasting impression." Leather-encased fingers caress the length of my neck. A shiver of revulsion races down my spine. "Good thing I won't be around long enough for you to identify me. I'm only the kidnapper in this plan, not the executioner, as much as I want to be."

I bite my upper lip, holding back a terrified whimper.

The leather of the glove, though soft, is like a knife slowly slicing through my skin, leaving damaged flesh in its wake as it moves lower.

My nostrils flare with each rapid breath. I fight the urge to scream and beg.

"So you *are* like your friend," I snap. The restraints slice through my already damaged skin as I shift to move away from his touch. "Taking advantage of a bound woman. That's how you get your fucking rocks off, you sick bastard?"

The scream I fought to hold back erupts up my throat, crackling and breaking as my neck snaps back. His fisted grip on my hair doesn't lessen; in fact, my pleas seem to encourage his hold rather than ease.

"Far from it, Randi. You want to know what gets my rocks off? What I envision while I fist my cock and explode in the shower night after night? This." He inhales deeply, the fabric covering his face brushing against my ear and snagging a wisp of hair. "This. The smell of fear, the terror in your wide eyes, all because of me. No, Randi, I won't touch you the way you're thinking, but your screams and soft little cries and pleas will fuel my dirty fantasies for weeks to come."

"Fear? You fuck your own hand to fear?" I almost laugh. Almost. The terror he loves so much kills the giggle before it can even attempt to escape.

"That and the memory of the pain I inflicted to cause said delicious fear." Almost to prove his point, he wraps the earlier caressing fingers around my neck and squeezes. "This, the moment when you realize your life is in my hands and there's no escape. That your existence is over. The array of emotions that will flash across your face is fucking erotic as hell." He presses the gun against my temple so hard a stifled cry escapes even with his crushing grip cutting off my air supply. "That is what I'll fuck my own hand to tonight. That and the fantasies of slicing apart that fucker Benson piece by piece."

Just like he hoped, terror rockets through my system. Rational thought vanishes, and I thrash in the chair, trying to escape.

His masked face hovers beside mine. Even through the blood pounding in my ears, his excited panting is clear.

"That's it," he coos. "Fight me. Fight back like you have a chance."

His fingers tighten, cutting off my airway. Red-hot burning engulfs my lungs, and I twist along the seat in a failed attempt to dislodge his hold. Darkness grows in my vision, my muscles loosening and trembling with the need for oxygen. A second before I give in to his strangling hold those tight fingers relax. I gasp for breath, my tears leaking down my cheeks and slipping inside my parted lips.

"Which you don't, Randi. No one will find you before it's too late. I've made sure of that."

"Please," I sob, any hope of not showing this monster how much he terrifies me gone. "Why are you doing this?"

"Why did I plan all this, take you knowing his end plans for you?" The torturous fingers tighten again. I scream before it's cut off to a gurgle. "Because he paid me. Because they paid me. Because it's fun. But ultimately it comes down to money. A shit ton of money, all for delivering you." I scream through panic engulfing my every thought, but nothing comes out until his grip relaxes once again. Too busy sucking down air, despite the sharp stabs of pain that radiate from my right side with each breath, I stay silent and let him continue without another plea or comment. "So really you only have yourself to blame for all this. At some point in your life, you made a bad choice. That decision or action put you in unfavorable light with many influential parties. Which brought me to you." I slump as his fingers slip off my skin. With little force behind it, he slaps at my already bruised cheek. I can't even muster enough energy to cringe at the pain. "And I have to tell you, Randi, for the first time in my professional career, I had two contracts for the same damn mark. You. So thank you for living, making those poor choices, and ultimately dying, because in doing so, you've made me a very rich man."

I shut my eyes and pray for a miracle. A realistic miracle like a heart attack or stroke.

When neither happens, I peel my lids back open, requiring more effort than normal.

"What are you?" I breathe. I'd like to say the "what" instead of "who" was carefully crafted to be a jab, but it wasn't. In fact, I'm not sure how my overexerted and dehydrated mind is even forming complete understandable sentences at this point in all this.

"You can think of me as an entrepreneur of sorts. I saw a niche market that needed... filling and stepped in. The skills beaten into me by a certain agency helped me become the most efficient and successful of people in my line of work."

He pauses, a heaviness lingering in the silence like he's not through with the conversation just lost in thought. "However, with this contract fulfilled, I'll have to relocate and change up my look a bit."

"Because you know they'll put two and two together. And when they do, they will hunt you down. Every agency will be looking for you. They will find you, and they will kill you for the traitor you are." The last words slur, my exhaustion overtaking my ability to speak.

"Doubtful. I've just gotten back from tying up loose ends. And you know what? I have to tell you, that felt good. The slimy bastard was always one I had to keep an eye on. Never knew when his loyalties would shift. But no, after this, I'll disappear for a while, reinvent myself somewhere new."

"Sounds lonely." My shoulders round, the muscles too fatigued to keep me sitting up straight, but the small move tugs my wrists against the restraints. I hiss at the feel of hard plastic digging deep into my skin and force myself to sit up to ease the tightness. "Any chance you can you take these off? You've watched me, traveled with me. You know I pose no threat to someone with your skills."

Just saying the small praise forces bile up my throat. But if downplaying my abilities by building up his ego helps get these fucking zip ties off, I'll do it. Hell, I'll throw him a damn parade if it gets my hands free.

"Not a chance."

Disappointment surges, but I hold back the tears and instead rack my brain for what to say next. Get him talking, or angry, or hell, anything that might disrupt the plan.

Shawn's plan.

If inflating his ego didn't get him on my side, maybe deflating it will push him to make a mistake of some kind.

Or get me killed faster.

It's worth a shot. Either I die now or later. Neither is ideal, but if dying now means I don't have to sit in this hotbox any longer, then I'll take door number one all day every day.

"Yeah, I get that," I say on a cough. Clearing my throat, I swallow a few times to help my raspy voice. Being nearly choked to death—twice—does a number to your vocal cords apparently. "Especially considering you failed twice before this to get your hands on me. I wouldn't trust your skills either with an unarmed, bound woman. Too big of a risk of you failing again, am I right?"

My eyes widen at his fast movement. One second he was across the room, and the next his cloth-covered face is so close his stank breath wafts up my nose even through the black fabric.

"Watch your motherfucking mouth, cunt." Damn, I hate that word. My hackles rise with distaste and annoyance. "Those failed attempts were not my fault."

"That's what they all say." I raise my brows in defiance. Well, I think I do. Can't really feel my forehead, or my eyebrows, for that matter. Have I ever been able to feel my eyebrows? Can anyone feel their eyebrows? "Can you feel your eyebrows?"

"I provided the intel." Okay, so clearly we're still stuck on his failures and not the eyebrow thing. Fine. If I live through this, I'll start a government-funded study on the question. "Those idiots hired the ones to execute the mission based on the accurate"—he cuts a look my way—"intel."

"Like your friend." I'm going on sheer gut instinct at this point. I have no idea what I'm digging for, but keeping him talking keeps his hands away from my throat, which I consider a win. "Go me," I whisper so silently my lips move with no sound.

"That night's failure," he hisses as he shoves off the chair, going back to pacing the short length of the cinderblock wall. Weightlessness rips out a gasp from me as the chair I'm secured to rocks backward from the force of his move. "That was that motherfucker Benson's fault. He wasn't supposed to be in your room. You should've been alone."

Those words. I've heard them before, but more formed as a question. Add in the radiating anger and it tickles a distant memory. He's said something similar to me before. But who, where? Every time I think I've wrapped my mental fingers around the memory it slips away leaving me frustrated.

"You killed the guards that night, not your friend who came through the balcony. You're the one who gave him the key." My voice rises with each accusation. That night... fuck, if Trey hadn't been there....

"They were tools anyway. No loss with their deaths."

"And you're the toolbox." I snort at my words. "I said the same thing to Kyle once." I narrow my eyes at my captor, who's clearly not laughing at the joke. "He didn't find it funny either."

"Speaking of the dead. What did you hold over him?" Something like curiosity sparks in his tone instead of being cold and emotionless. "Did you fuck him?"

"Ew, no. I'd rather die first." I wince. "Wrong choice of words considering my current situation."

A low chuckle rumbles from where he stands now leaning back against the wall, arms crossed over his black T-shirt. It's the same man as earlier;

guess he switched his suit out for this mercenary look. All black, even down to the turban-type covering wrapped around his face and head. "Believe me, that fucker Birmingham felt the same way, even at the end."

"How...?" Realization sucks the words right out of my throat. A cold chill races through my body, freezing me to the bone. Tears pool before escaping out of the corners of both eyes. I was right, Kyle didn't commit suicide. This asshole killed him. "Why?" I choke out.

"Money. Money is always the answer to the 'why' question. Don't let anyone ever tell you otherwise."

"You. It was you. All of this was you."

"Ah, see, that's where you're wrong. All of this was *you*. I'm simply the man hired to execute what was already put in motion. All those people, all the death that's happened in the last year, was all because of you. Those agents dead or injured—your fault. The death of that pompous ass Birmingham—your fault. And today, your death—your fault."

"Unless I agree to his demands."

Silence. I swear it's so silent I can hear the sweat dripping between my breasts.

"What?" he asks calmly, but the change in his stance from relaxed to defensive with my simple statement tells me otherwise. I watch in fascination as he begins to pace again.

"What the what?" I respond innocently, even though I know exactly what I've just uncovered. Shawn is a sociopath and willing to lie, steal, and kill whoever to get what he wants. Apparently this idiot in front of me took Shawn at his word that I'd be dead by morning.

A hysterical laugh tickles in my lungs, wiggling its way up until it bursts from my dry lips.

"You actually trusted him?" Another fit of giggles shakes my shoulders. "Oh, you are so fucked."

A bone-crunching backhand lands squarely on my right cheek. I scream at the impact, the force like razors up my throat.

"No one plays me," he snaps. "You don't know what you're talking about."

"He's playing you." Swiping my thick tongue back and forth, I gather the sticky liquid filling my mouth and spit the blood to the floor. "You have no idea who you're dealing with."

"Wrong, Randi. Fucking wrong."

"Right, and unicorns aren't real."

"Stop it with the fucking unicorn shit," he bellows. Lacing his fingers behind his head, he paces from one end of the room to the other. "You'll be dead by the end of the night, and I'll get to rip apart your boyfriend in the very near future. I deliver you, keep you compliant until the next stage of his plan, and then I leave and kill Benson. This is the plan."

My heart lodges in my throat at the idea of Trey being in danger—because of me. "Don't hold it against me that I hope you're wrong about the me being dead bit. Don't take it personally, but I like this thing called living and want to keep doing it."

"Fuck, you're strange."

"Thanks?" The rhythmic clip of his boot heels against the hard floor fills the quiet as I debate my next move. It's like chess. No, screw that. I don't know how to play chess. Checkers. This is like checkers. "The big-set ones like they sell at Cracker Barrel."

"If you don't stop talking to yourself, I will kill you now despite the amount of money it'll cost me if I do."

"Or you could kill Shawn," I suggest. "He told me he'd let me go if I willingly stepped down and he moves into the VP role when Sam moves up to president. Which means I'll have to step down publicly. Which means I'll have to be breathing, as in alive."

"I know the difference between dead and alive, you idiot."

"Just wanted to make sure I was clear." I roll my eyes. "What about Egypt? Was that your fuckup too?" Totally on a roll. I can't feel my fingers or toes, but damn, I'm on top of it with my psychological game.

Who knew, right?

"I. Don't. Fuck. Up." The pause between each word emphasizes his disagreement to my accusation. "They did. Not me. Those motherfucking idiots wanted me hands off, said anything else would be too obvious it was me, which would lead the FBI straight to their door. But you took care of that anyway, didn't you? Which, I must say, helped me in the long run. Got those fuckers out of my hair so I didn't have to keep playing their information game, allowing me to do what I do best."

"Monologuing?"

I flinch at his menacing step in my direction.

"Kill. Slowly."

"Why do you hate him so much?" I ask. This I'm truly curious about.

"Trey, that is? Why hold such a grudge when all he was doing was his job? And me, I guess." I wiggle in the chair to ease the numbness in my ass and immediately regret it. The shift puts pressure on my at-max-capacity bladder. "Oh shit. I've got to pee. Can I get a hall pass?"

"Then pee." He nods to the chair I'm sitting in.

"Ew. Surely there's a spare bucket or cup or tin can lying around this place that I can use? Come on, do you really want to torture me wet and stinky with my own piss?"

That makes him debate the pros and cons of allowing me this one small freedom. With an exasperated huff, he reaches an arm back, withdrawing a menacing-looking blade. With two steps, he crouches in front of me. I wince as the ties holding my ankles to the chair tighten before releasing altogether. Relief floods through me at the little bit of mobility as I flex and straighten my feet.

I stare at the covered face still kneeling in front of me. His dark eyes narrow, no doubt waiting for me to attempt an escape. Lucky for me I'm not that stupid. My hands are still fucking tied, which means I'd get nowhere fast. Plus with the exhaustion and dehydration, I'm in no condition to run or fight or even stand on my own.

A tightening followed by a rush of blood shoots to my fingers at the loss of the zip tie. Leaning forward, I shake out my hands before bringing them up to inspect the damage.

I cringe at the slices of ruined flesh marking my wrists and shy away from looking at my ankles. A tight grip under my arm hauls me upright before I'm immediately released, like he can't stand the thought of touching me longer than necessary. Each step is agony, but I rejoice in the freedom of walking free.

Bright sunlight assaults my sensitive eyes as we stumble out of the windowless room. I squint to ease the pain, using the brief opportunity to take in some of the details of where I'm being held—but there's nothing. Just the same abandoned warehouse as before. It seems I wasn't moved at all, just relocated from one open space to a more intimate one.

A finger pokes between my shoulder blades, urging me forward. I stumble, barely regaining my footing before I fall forward and slam against a wall, my shoulder taking the brunt of the impact.

"There's your bucket." He hitches his chin toward a rickety plastic construction bucket. "Piss."

"Fucking animal," I grumble. "Turn around, at least." My shaky fingers are already working the top button of my jean shorts as I survey the damage. As expected, both ankles look as sliced and raw as my wrists. Both legs have long-dried red streaks crisscrossing the skin, along with some that still weep crimson, possibly injuries from the wreck and the broken glass. The jean material of my shorts is stiff with dark red. I pause the inspection and shoot my captor, who's still facing me, a questioning look. "I asked if you'd turn around."

"I wasn't born yesterday, Madam President. Piss with me watching or don't piss at all."

"Don't watch. That's fucking creepy," I snap.

"Not a chance."

"Creep," I mutter as I place my back to him and tug the stiff shorts and underwear down to midthigh. Palm pressed against the cracked drywall, I balance myself as much as possible and squat, then focus on peeing. At this awkward angle. With someone watching. Hell, I can't perform like this. A burning sensation radiates in my bladder, an urgent demand to pee. "Can you hum or something?" I huff over my shoulder. "I can't pee when it's this quiet."

"You've got to be kidding me."

"You're the one who took me, so don't get all pissy that I ask for a little tune to help me pee."

"I could always stab you in the thigh. I've found excruciating pain triggers the release of all bodily functions."

Almost like my body understood the threat in his deep tone, the barrier holding me back vanishes. I nearly groan at the delightful sensation of my full bladder releasing. By the time I'm done, both thighs tremble from the exertion of squatting, and the pain in my side and neck have gone from ouch to debilitating.

All thumbs and no fingers, I work the top button of my shorts, failing three times to push it through the small slot before giving up. I turn, mouth open to tell this asshole to kill me or leave me be, when a groan of metal has both of us turning toward the sound.

I stagger back, my backside pressed hard against the drywall as I dart my gaze around the warehouse, desperate for an exit. A sinister smile plays on Shawn's handsome face, the promise of pain brightening his eyes as he strides to where we stand.

"Well, well, well. Look who's on her feet. So glad you're awake for this. Now the real fun begins."

My knees wobble and give out. Sliding down the wall, I sink to the floor, unable to do anything other than make myself as small as possible.

"I've waited too long for this, Trailer." Hand raised, he gestures back toward the windowless hellhole I just walked out of. "Don't keep me waiting."

I swallow hard, relishing the burn along my dry tongue and throat. This cannot be happening. I thought I'd have more time, a chance to escape.

Now, with both men and the wicked gleams in their eyes, I understand the gravity of the situation.

This is the day I die.

8

―――――――

TREY

"Fucking hell," I mumble under my breath as I methodically creep toward the slumped body of Todd Rosen, checking each small section of the floor for evidence before stepping closer. "What the hell happened here?" I rake trembling fingers through the longer part of my hair and yank the ends.

The metal desk within my reach, I pause my careful steps to stare at the dead body. It's slouched, somehow still sitting in the leather office chair, head tossed back, jaw slack, and mouth open wide, the expression resembling ecstasy, as if someone unseen was blowing him off beneath the desk. Well, it would look like ecstasy until you took in the one-inch blackened hole between his thin brows and fragments of brain and skull splattered over the back of his chair and wall.

Shaking off the disturbing scene, I shift my focus to the desk. A single black laptop sits open. Not able to see the screen from this angle, I tilt over the desk and find the screen is black. A single cell phone lies haphazardly nearby, plugged into its charger with another exact replica charger a few inches away. Odd. Why would he have two chargers for the same type of phone? Unless he had two, one conveniently missing from a room with a dead shady politician.

Nothing seems amiss, no signs of a struggle happening here or anywhere around the spacious office. Leather armchairs are upright, magazines and papers neatly stacked on top of the glass coffee table, and even here on the desk, the pen holder and other small objects sit undisturbed. In fact, the only thing in this office that looks out of place is the body, blood, and gore.

Bending at the waist, I put myself closer to the desk's surface, looking for... fuck, who knows. I'm an agent, not a detective. The surface shines, minimal dust gathered around the unused areas, but a large area around the laptop seems smeared. As if a dirty cloth was used to clean instead of one with polish or cleaner.

Standing back to full height, I glance over my shoulder and point to the desk. "Whoever did this wiped this area clean of fingerprints." A single step to the right offers a different angle. Then another and another until I've rounded the desk and am standing just outside the blood splatter congealed on the oriental rug. This close, I scour the body without touching in hopes of finding more clues to what happened here. "His fingers look to be broken, unless they always had a ninety-degree angle that I didn't notice." Swiping a pen from the desk, I lean closer to the right hand and use the pen to carefully lift a stiff finger. "I'm no coroner, but there seems to be bruising and blood around the worst breaks, meaning it was done before the bullet to the brain."

Tank's silence at my brilliant discovery draws my attention from the dead secretary to where he stands in the middle of the room. Head down, phone in hand, his thumbs fly across the screen completely absorbed, clearly not listening to my findings.

"What are you doing?" I question, annoyed at my friend for being distracted by whatever's on his phone.

"I'm calling the FBI," he snaps. Cutting those dark eyes my way, he tosses a hand toward the body. "In case you haven't noticed, a fucking political figurehead was executed in his uppity fucking office."

"No, not yet," I grunt as I step away from the desk. Marching toward Tank, I rip the phone from his hand. "Did you hear me? Don't call them yet."

"Benson." The deep rumble of his voice is laced with warning. "Give me back the phone."

"Five minutes. Give us five minutes to piece together what we can on our own before you call." Only thinking of the need to delay that damn call, I shove the phone in my hand down the front of my cargo pants and nestle it neatly into my boxer briefs right beside my balls.

"Bastard," he growls. "Get my phone away from your dick. That screen touches my face."

"I know, and I'm sorry, but it's Randi's life on the line, Davis." I angle my head toward the body. "It isn't a coincidence that Vlad said he didn't trust Rosen, believing him to be dirty somehow, and the man turns up dead the same day the president is abducted. Something isn't right here. You know it and I know it. Give us a five-minute window alone with the evidence to see what we can find, then call the FBI. You know as well as I do those bastards will swoop in, take over the scene, and give us shit for answers. We need the answers now, not later. Please, we need this to help us find her. I know it."

Dark, assessing eyes glance from me to the body and back again, each time looking more resigned to the fact that I'm right. With an exaggerated sigh, he crosses his arms over his chest. "You have your five minutes, Benson. Find something useful." Disgust crosses his face as he hitches his chin toward my crotch. "And you're disinfecting my fucking phone."

"Is it on vibrate?"

"Yes," he answers, brows tugging inward. At my growing smirk, he tosses his hands in the air, knowing full well why I asked. "Fuck you, Trey. That's disgusting."

"What? I'm just saying I hope someone calls."

"Four minutes thirty seconds. Use your time wisely, you idiot."

Smirk still stuck to my face, I stride back to the body, this time with a little more confidence, and squat low to the floor to inspect the area beneath the desk and chair.

"Benson." I pop my head over the desk's edge. "Don't leave any damn fingerprints." A pair of latex gloves comes flying at me. I snatch them midair before they can smack me in the face.

"You really need to wash that mouth of yours out with soap," I say loud enough for him to hear as I examine the worn oriental rug. "Sarah will have your ass if she hears you picked up cursing as a new bad habit."

Hands to my knees, I push up with a groan. There's nothing on the damn floor that looks abnormal. I skip over the laptop, not enough time in my small five-minute window to crack the password and to access the data inside. I move to the iPhone and quirk a brow. I don't need a password for that if I have the owner's thumbprint, which I do. Well, I actually have the whole thumb, but all I need is the print.

"First of all, I'm fucking stressed, so cut me some slack. Second, my Sarah knows how you talk. She'll blame you as the bad influence."

I scoff as I snap on the latex gloves. "Even more reason to clean up your act before you get home. You wouldn't want to be responsible for my death, now would you."

"Depends on the day, Playboy."

"Ouch." I chuckle. Phone in hand, I draw it closer to the dead body and hold it below his right hand. "Just so you know, I do feel bad about this," I say to the dead man. "But not enough to not do it. You understand, right?" The wrist bends under my slight grip; the guy hasn't been dead very long if he's still movable. It takes a few tries to maneuver the limp digit, but finally I find the right angle and apply pressure, clicking the phone unlocked.

Excited to see what the device holds inside, I release the hand. It falls to the side, clipping the armrest on it's fast descent.

"Careful, you idiot. Don't leave any bruises we can't explain."

I nod even though I have zero clue what he just said. I'm too invested in what I'm not finding on the dead man's phone.

Nothing. No texts, no emails, no calls or contacts. Everything is gone.

With a groan of frustration, I click on the Pictures app, hoping there's something in there that can tell us what the hell Todd Rosen was mixed up in that ended with him shot in the forehead.

"Fuck me," I grumble.

"What? What did you find?" Tank's by my side, ripping the phone from my gloved hand and cradles it in his own. His eyes widen on the screen. With a hiss, he slams his eyes shut and drops the phone. It clatters to the desk before falling to the floor. "Little warning, asshole."

"I feel sorry for whoever was receiving those dick pics," I grumble as I retrieve the phone to continue flipping through the photos. Holding it at arm's length in case more pictures of his tiny junk appear, I swipe through the pictures. "Hell, nothing here either."

"The text history wiped?"

"That and his call logs and search history, but I doubt this was his only phone. There's a second charger with no phone attached. This one was probably his personal one based on the pictures and the other government issued. That one seems to have been taken from the scene." I set the phone back where I found it, plug it back in, and proceed to strip off the gloves. "There's no sign of a struggle here or anywhere around the room. Based on the brain splatter along the wall behind him, this is where he was killed. So what? He was restrained while whoever put a gun barrel between his eyes and pulled the trigger?" I shake my head and move away from the desk to stare out the windows overlooking the back gardens. "Something doesn't add up here, Tank. He's dirty."

"No doubt about that, but that's not why we're here. Give me my phone so I can call the FBI. They'll do their digging and find out what this sleaze was up to. I don't think the evidence in this room will help us find Randi."

My heavy shoulders slump in defeat, knowing he's right.

"Time's running out," I say through grinding teeth. "She's been gone for hours now. What if...? I have to find her." Turning from the window, I allow the wide array of emotions to bleed through my eyes. "I have to find her."

"We will—"

I jump with a giggled curse at the tickling sensations against my balls.

"Um, you seem to be getting a call," I say with a little bit of remorse. Jamming a hand down the front of my pants, I tug it free. I cringe and wipe the screen off on my pants before extending it between us. "Sorry, it was a little sweaty."

"You're not sorry, you ass," he snaps. "Thank fuck I still have gloves on." Swiping a thumb across the screen, he answers the call and switches it to speakerphone. "What?"

"I have something." I snap my attention to the illuminated screen. My pulse races with hope at Smith's words. "Benson asked me months ago, right after the Cairo incident, if I'd help find the leak. Since then I've watched, listened, and monitored every agent on the alpha and beta teams. There were ten possible agents on my list of suspects."

"Why didn't you bring this evidence and list to me?" Tank questions, a hint of annoyance in his grumbled tone.

"It was all circumstantial and a damn Hail Mary. I couldn't tell you I suspected someone of treason because they littered one day at the park while walking their dog."

"Seriously? Litter?" I question, breaking into his speech.

"It's a lack of respect and empathy for what their actions will do on the environment."

"It's a stretch," I muse.

"Exactly why I didn't bring this list to you months ago. But now we're here and need to find the fucker who leaked information regarding the

Cairo trip. Something tells me the person behind that attack and the president being kidnapped are one and the same."

"Agreed," Tank and I say in unison.

"Give us the ten names and we can—" I start, but Smith continues, cutting me off.

"I called the director—"

"Your mother," Tank clarifies.

Cold silence pours from the phone. I smack Tank's shoulder and flip him the bird. Idiot. He needs to keep his mouth shut until we get that fucking list of names. If the director was telling the truth about Smith once being in Homeland, I trust his gut, which means one of the men on his list is our guy. The one we have to locate to find Randi.

And when we do, the fucker dies.

"We thought you were the one who betrayed us," I say to clarify why the director let their relationship slip. "It's why we went there initially, since Tank couldn't reach you."

"Me?" he says, wonder in his voice. "You think I'd betray the team, the president, my country?"

"Someone did, and your disappearing acts haven't helped you appear innocent in all this."

"Noted." Smith clears his throat. "I spoke to the director and asked for backgrounds on the ten I suspected. Five are on the alpha team and have reported since the incident this morning. I'm willing to bet the person who took the president won't leave her alone just to make appearances at work."

"Those five are out, then," Tank says.

"Agreed. Which leaves us five others, all on the beta team."

I want to strangle the phone. To slip through the damn device so I can wrap my hands around Smith's neck and demand he spit it out. Fuck this explaining, I need a name. *The* name. The name of the man I have every intention of killing with my bare hands. And enjoying it. "Two were pronounced dead this morning. One is on vacation with his family. Two are alive and have checked in but haven't been seen."

"Two," I say on an easy breath. "We can cover two suspects. One of them—"

"There's more. I asked the director to look into their files. To locate how long they'd been on the team, where they came from, test scores, hell, anything. And that's when she found an anomaly. One of the two is a recent hire. A hire that was personally vouched for by a part of the White House team—Secretary of State Todd Rosen."

Tank and I turn in silence to face the dead body. I cringe knowing what Smith is about to ask.

"We need to talk to the secretary, find out why he referenced this agent and ordered him to be put on the beta team—"

"That won't happen," I say as I massage both temples.

"Aren't you both on your way there?"

"We're here."

"Even better."

"He's dead."

Silence. A heavy breath weighs down my lungs as I wait for his response to that bomb.

"Have some of your contacts look into him," Tank suggests. "We were sent here by a tip that Rosen wasn't to be trusted. Based on his estate and finding him shot point-blank between the eyes, he was deep into some shady shit." I narrow my eyes at Tank and his cursing. He's really on edge if he keeps using language like that. Foul mouth and consistently irresponsible is my job, not his. "More than your normal politician, from what I can tell."

"Who's the agent, Smith?" I demand, ripping the phone out of Tank's hand. "Who is the final suspect on your list?"

"I have a few... associates digging through the application and profile submitted to the agency when he applied. I already found one inconsistency, which I'm on my way to check out now."

"Where?" I ask.

"The address listed on his application and the townhome I've followed him to on a few occasions for surveillance are different. I'm headed to the place where I know he lives instead of the one listed."

"Good idea." Tank nods.

Anger and frustration surge, making me tense and on edge. "Who's the agent?" I beg to the phone. "Give me anything to go off of."

"If I tell you, do not engage with him until we know more. Do not call, do not search him out. If he knows we're on to him and he has the president, he will kill her."

"I understand," I mumble. "Who is it."

"Agent Ponder."

The name booms through my brain like a giant gong being struck. I stare at the phone; Smith's voice is still pouring through, but I don't hear any of it. I'm too busy flipping through every memory I have with Ponder in it, trying to come up with anything that will help us in our hunt for him.

"After Saudi Arabia, he was openly angry at me for being in Randi's room the night of the attack. At the time, I thought it was because he had a thing for her and didn't want me around because of that. Which was why I told the beta team lead to move him to the shitty shifts and stations. I didn't want him around her." I shift my focus to the details surrounding our trip to Cairo. "There were several beta team agents sitting close when Tank and I discussed the new sniper placements outside the embassy. I don't remember Ponder specifically, but he could've been sitting close enough, making him privy to the changes." My eyes snap to Tank's. "We're missing a big piece to this puzzle. The why? Why in the hell would Rosen go to so much trouble to get him on a Secret Service detail? Why try to abduct the president knowing the risks?"

"He doesn't want a female president?" Smith offers as an option.

"That's a weak reason to finagle your way onto the Secret Service when you could take her out anytime she was out in public." Phone cradled in my hand, I pace from one end of the office to the other, carefully missing the shards of broken door still littering the ground. "It has to be more than sexist idealisms."

"Revenge."

I shake my head at Tank's suggestion only to stop short. The rug catches beneath the rubber sole of my boots as I twist back the way I came. Eyes wide, I hold a breath to quiet the thundering in my chest at the new thought.

"What if it's not *his* revenge? What if it's someone else's revenge that he's helping enact by taking the president? Someone we know would go to any lengths to see her miserable and taken out of the picture?"

The corner of Tank's lips curls in a disgusted sneer. "Whit."

I nod instead of answering out loud. Smith's gruff voice blasts through the speaker, demanding to know who we're talking about.

"This asshat who's had it out for Randi since she started campaigning with Birmingham. Shawn Whit was Kyle Birmingham's original VP choice until Randi came into the picture. He's resented her ever since and has done everything possible to destroy her, even going as far as poisoning her a while back hoping she'd be too sick to continue serving in the VP role. If he's the one behind this, then Ponder isn't doing this for himself." I shake my head as all the pieces of the puzzle fall into place. "He was hired."

"Shit," Smith grunts. "I'm pulling up to the town house now. Doesn't seem to be anyone home."

"Break in," Tank commands.

"Really?" The sarcasm in that one word makes a stiff chuckle erupt from my chest. "I was just going to knock and hope someone would let me in."

"Smith," I say with surprise, blinking at the phone. "Was that a joke?" Maybe hell has frozen over.

"I'll let you know what I find. You do your digging on this Whit fucker. Maybe we can find something that will tell us where they took her. It can't be far. That's one thing we have going for us."

"Why do you say that? That they didn't take her far?" Optimism surges at his claim. If she's close, then we'll get there in time. I can save her.

"Just a hunch. If it were me, I'd want to spend what little time I had with her—knowing an army is out there looking for her—on fulfilling my objective." And just like that, my rising optimism plummets, deflating me to the core once again. "No, he'll want to torture—"

"Call us when you have something." Tank snatches the phone from my hand and hits the Off button while Smith continues describing all the ways he'd use his time with her, making her pay. "Don't listen to him. Look, this guy here hasn't been dead long. The larger puddles of blood aren't even tacky yet. Which means *if* Ponder is our guy, he came here recently to tie up loose ends. We'll get to her in time, Trey. I swear we will get to your girl before it's too late."

I clear my throat. "Our girl."

After removing the black latex gloves, he slaps a hand on my shoulder and squeezes.

"*Your* girl. Now let's go somewhere we can do some digging on Whit while Smith checks out Ponder's place. Your place or mine?"

"Yours," I say as I follow him out of the office. "Don't forget to call the FBI. Maybe they can pull something from Rosen's laptop or get a warrant for his phone records."

"Already sent the text," Tank says, looking up from his phone with his thumbs still flying across the screen. "Come on, let's go find that fucker Whit."

A slow sinister smile pulls up my lips, bunching my cheeks. "And then kill him."

Anticipation races through my veins as the vivid images of him bloody and beaten from my pounding fists flash through my thoughts. For too long that asshat has tormented Randi. For too long he's gone unchecked.

No longer.

Today I execute justice for what he's done to her and many others.

Death.

A nice slow, tormenting, grueling death.

I should be terrified at the excitement and joy that brings me. But I'd sell my soul to the devil himself if it means getting Randi back unharmed.

With Whit in the picture, that's exactly what I might have to do to save her.

Who needs a soul anyway?

9

RANDI

My ass slams to the unforgiving seat of the chair I'm to be secured to again. Ligaments and tendons stretch awkwardly, screaming in protest as both arms are wrenched behind me. Panic surges and kicks up my fight-or-flight instinct, supplying enough to fight against his hold. Not that it does much; his grip doesn't even falter. A hard yank draws my hands farther back than my fatigued muscles can handle. I scream through clenched teeth as the discomfort turns unbearable.

"Did you send the picture?" Shawn asks, like I'm not sitting here being manhandled to the equivalent of drawn and quartered. Well, hopefully not the quartered part. That would really suck. There's no coming back from that.

"Have to have your guts to live." My head falls forward, rolling from side to side with each tug to my arms as the one wearing the head scarf secures the zip ties. Each breath hisses through my teeth as I breathe through the pain, not wanting to give them the satisfaction of hearing my cries again.

"Yes, sent the picture," says the still unknown traitor at my back before moving on to my ankles. With the last tie secured, he stands. With a minuscule nod at his work, he turns to Shawn. "Destroyed and ditched the phone a second after hitting Send. I'm not a damn amateur."

"Do you have another?" Shawn questions, a snap in his tone.

What if I can get them to fight? That way they'd ignore me for a while, giving Trey more time to find and save me. Which I know they will. Trey, T, and the rest of my loyal agents will find me. I know it deep in my gut.

The mystery man mumbles something I can't make out with the cloth still secured around his face.

"Take that shit off your face," Shawn barks. "She dies in the end anyway. Doesn't matter if she sees your face."

"Maybe it's not me he's worried about." It's a shot in the dark, thinking these two haven't met before.

"Shut the fuck—" Shawn bellows, his loud voice echoing in the small, now even more cramped room, only to be cut off.

"She's right."

"Boom." Out of instinct, I attempt to raise a hand to high-five my captor only to remember it's tied to the chair. "Imaginary high five, then."

"Shut up," both men shout in my direction.

At the taut tension and palpable anger filling the room, I seal my lips shut. I dart my somewhat blurry gaze from one man to the other, trying to judge how this will turn out.

"You paid me to bring her to you and keep her compliant until the others come. That is what I've done and will do, but there is nothing in our agreement that states you get to know who I am."

"Wait," I say more to myself than them, forgetting their demand for my silence. "If Shawn isn't the one who helped you secure a position on the Secret Service team, then who did? This isn't making a whole lot of sense. I feel like we need to back this—"

His eyes narrow on me, almost like a silent command to shut the hell up. Which I do.

Shawn adjusts in his more comfortable-looking chair a few feet from where I sit tied up. His gaze rakes the mystery man up and down before zeroing in on his face. "You were on her security team." Shawn slides his hollow gaze to me. "That's how you pulled the abduction off. Seems an elaborate ruse for taking one woman."

"The most protected woman on the planet," he adds.

"Who helped you?" Shawn demands more than asks.

"Doesn't matter," the masked man grumbles as he leans a shoulder against the far wall. The stance makes him appear to be calm, but the tension radiating off him, the tightness in his shoulders and crossed arms, tells a different story.

"It does if it leads them back to you, to here." Shawn stands, sliding both hands into the pockets of his dark-wash jeans. Guess he wasn't joking earlier about having to change out of his puke-spattered slacks.

"It won't. I tied up those loose ends earlier."

"Except me," Shawn bites out. "Am I a loose end after this?"

"That's the reason for the face wrap. This is how I've always done contracts that request the client to be on-site during the interrogation. It stays on so you can't identify me even though others can if they put two and two together. Do not tell me what to do or how to do it. This is my domain. This is where I excel and why you paid me. Command me again and I'll kill you, then her."

I shiver at the promise in his bored tone. There's no doubt this man would withdraw the nine millimeter secured in his waistband and pop a bullet between Shawn's brows without thinking twice.

"Does he know about the other client who wanted me dead? The one who paid you for intel and helped you finagle your way onto the Secret Service?"

If it's possible, the man's eyes harden more than before, that hatred zeroed in on me. Shoving off the wall, the mercenary strides to stand directly in front of my chair, the hard rubber of his boots grazing the bare tips of my toes. He pulls his fist back, readying a killing blow. I shy away, my eyes closing on instinct at the hit I know has the potential to loosen a few teeth. But instead he aims lower. That heavy fist sinks into my relaxed stomach, shoving every minuscule amount of air out of my lungs in a forceful heave.

I can't breathe.

Eyes wide with panic, I try to suck in oxygen but can't get anything down past the constriction in my throat. I gasp, cough, and squirm until my body responds to my desperate demands and eases the tight hold, allowing slivers of air to finally slip through.

The first full gulp of air cuts like splinters down my throat before embedding in my lungs. A pitiful whimper escapes as I breathe through the agony, knowing suffocating or passing out around these two would be worse than dealing with the pain each gulp of oxygen brings.

As the world and my surroundings come back into focus, gruff, demanding words reach my ears, but I can't make out what's being said through my own panting. Desperate to have a foothold on what's going on around me, I force myself to take smaller breaths, quieting the thundering in my own ears.

"That's what took you so long to fulfill the contract. You said it was timing."

"It was."

"Who was it who hired you? And how did they secure you a spot in the Secret Service?"

"Someone they hired. A mediator of sorts."

"Who?" Shawn's voice is clear now that my breathing has quieted. There's no way the man who took me doesn't hear the annoyance in his rising voice. Sounds to me like Shawn's patience is wearing thin. Maybe it won't be too hard to get these two to turn against each other after all. It'll still leave me with one psychopath to deal with, but hey, one psycho holding me captive is a hell of a lot better than two.

"Even I can do that math," I croak, then look up to find the two men have stopped talking, their annoyed faces turned to me. "He's playing you." Fuck, each word hurts. I'm in desperate need of water for more reasons than staving off dehydration. "Shawn isn't someone to trust."

A soft sarcastic chuckle rumbles through the nearly vacant room. Both corners of Shawn's lips tick upward as he shakes his head.

"No, Trailer. I didn't play him, I played you. Did you really think I'd let you out of this with your pathetic excuse for a life? I will get what I want, and then you will."

"What's that?" But I know the answer. And it's terrifying to think he might be right.

"For the pain to end."

With a whisper and nod toward me, the other man advances on me once again. A harsh cry trembles my lips as I brace myself for another hit. This time knuckles slam against my right temple. The force snaps my neck to the left, both eyes rolling to the back of my head as the dark cloud of unconsciousness engulfs me, cutting off other sensations. Yet even with the hard impact of his fist, I subconsciously know he pulled back or I'd be dead.

I work to stay awake, to push back against the demanding need to black out. I can't do that, not here; who knows what they'll do to me if I'm that vulnerable? But the sweet pain-free calmness, the oblivion of nothingness, calls to me.

Sounds, smells, even the feel of the heated air along my bare skin fade.

Two shadows hover over me, muffled deep voices barely reaching my ears. Something scrapes beneath my nose, making it twitch out of reflex. At least I think it twitches; considering I can't feel the tip of my nose, there's no way to know. Fuck, that hurt. Hurts. There's no end in sight for the relentless throb of agony that now has its own slow pulse along my cheek and jaw.

I reach deep within myself, searching for an ounce of energy or emotion that will keep me from pitching over the edge into oblivion. But there's nothing there. Even the small glimmer of hope that's been a constant companion since the wreck has almost faded into nothing as the hours have ticked by and no one has found me.

Like a Red Bull to my veins, energy rockets through me, jostling every cell awake. The world comes roaring back to life, every sound, taste, and smell more vibrant than just moments before. I blink away the dryness crusting my eyes, every muscle thrumming with the need to move as my heart races with excitement, thumping heavily against my ribs.

Nothing hurts. How in the hell does nothing hurt?

Fuck, I could do anything right now if they'd just let me loose.

"Give her more adrenaline. I need her awake."

"I didn't hit her that hard, I thought." I stare at the man whose voice seems soft with concern. Concern about me, probably not, more about getting paid. Like he so eloquently stated before, this is business, not personal. "You're not the first one who's requested a woman to be beaten. I know what I'm fucking doing."

"I'm starting to question that."

I force my focus on the man's eyes as they search my face. "She's coming to. I'll save the next dose in case we need it later." With that, he steps out of my sight, but with every nerve ending on overdrive, I can almost feel him standing close.

A heaviness settles in the long strands of hair hanging down my back before it's yanked and my face is forced to face the ceiling. That should hurt, but it doesn't. I feel fucking fantastic.

Shawn's sneering face looms above, his searching gaze sizing me up and no doubt finding me lacking like always.

Maybe it's the adrenaline speaking, but I feel his hate, loathing, and unending selfishness that bleeds through his eyes into my own. My stomach rolls with a queasy feeling. With nothing in it, only stomach acid rises up my throat, burning in its ascent.

I rip my gaze from his, breaking the connection.

"Make the call to Pierce. Tell him exactly what I tell you to say, and then this ends."

With his fingers wrapped through my long strands, I don't dare move to shake my head.

"No." The word is more of a breath than anything.

The hold in my hair tightens before my head is slammed forward. The room blurs as the tip of my chin connects with my collarbone. I grit through the screech of pain that escapes.

"Make. The damn. Call."

"How. About. No?" I spit whatever's in my mouth to the floor, a string of saliva hanging on to the edge of my snarled lips. "Go. To. Fucking. Hell."

At his rage-filled roar, I squeeze my eyes shut, not wanting to feel whatever they have planned for me next.

"Again." Shawn's voice is harsh, the single word like the crack of a whip.

The mystery man obeys. I hear his heavy exhale and brace myself for what comes next. Just like Shawn ordered, the blows come again, followed by the same demand that I call Sam. Which, of course, is followed by the same response.

Again. And again. And again. This cycle continues until all I know is pain, fear, and hopelessness.

Until all I want is for it to end.

10

TREY

e've got something.

Both feet bounce with anticipation, my knees bobbing relentlessly with the movement as we speed back across town. I rake my fingers through my disheveled hair for what might be the thousandth time today, my nerves maxed out with the news that was relayed only moments ago.

Good news.

Fucking finally.

We were just pulling out of Rosen's estate after passing off the scene to the herd of FBI agents when the call came through, disrupting our original plan of posting up at Tank's to dig into Whit's background while we waited for a new lead. But that research will have to wait.

Because we have a fucking lead.

Tires screech against the blacktop as Tank swerves through the light traffic, slamming his hand on the horn, urging people to get the hell out of our way. The call came from one of Smith's buddies at Homeland who was able to approximate a four-block radius from where the person was when they sent the photo of Randi to me.

The way this technology finds a location without the phone physically being on and with a more precise radius than ever before is new and only available to Homeland. Which means whoever took Randi didn't know about it or they wouldn't have sent the picture in the first place. It's amazing —and a bit creepy—what Big Brother is capable of these days in its ability to spy on American citizens.

The shrill of an incoming call pierces through my rambling thoughts. The ringing blares through the speakers again, cutting off halfway when Tank answers the call with a push of a button on the steering wheel.

"What did you find?" No hello or how you doing, Tank's no-nonsense wording mimics his cold tone.

"Nothing good."

"Tell us," I snap to the speakers, wishing it was Smith's face. I swipe both clammy palms along my thighs, wiping the cold sweat onto the black fabric of my cargo pants. We're close to finding her and those responsible. I can feel it.

"He wasn't planning to stick around if he is the one associated with the abduction. I found two duffel bags packed, the kitchen cleaned out, and what I assume was a makeshift armory empty."

"Prints?" It's a wonder Tank can even follow along with the conversation with his full concentration out the windshield, making sure we don't wreck or cause someone else to.

"Dusted a few doorknobs and switches. Sent the pictures over to my buddies. We'll know more about him soon, but I don't think that will help us find the president. If he's a contract assassin, it doesn't matter about his background, only where he is now. And nothing here tells me where he would've gone."

"We're headed to check out a lead now. ETA ten minutes." The front right of the SUV comes within inches of clipping a semi's trailer. Knowing he hates it when I react, I hold in my curse and death grip on the "oh shit" handle. "Make that seven," I grumble. "Get us there alive, for fuck's sake. We're no good to her dead."

Tank grumbles something I can't make out as he leans against his door with an arm propped up like he hasn't a care in the world.

"Text me the location and I'll meet you there." Static crackles down the line before the SUV is doused in quiet again. Well, except for Tank's honking and the offended cars honking back.

"Bye to you too, motherfucker," I mutter. "After everything we've learned today and seeing him in action the last year or so, I'm damn glad he's on our side."

"True. He could've ended up like the bastard we know as Ponder, taking what he learned at Homeland and using it for his own gain. I wonder if that happens more than we realize."

"Maybe." I yank a bottle of water from the side door and twist off the cap. "We need more than this lead though. I don't think it'll be enough for us to find her in the time frame we're working under. Who knows how long she has?" Just saying the words causes my throat to close up with emotion.

His bald head dips in agreement. "There's one thing we haven't considered."

"What's that?" I ask incredulously. "I've gone over this so many damn times in my head it's all I fucking know."

"Her."

"Her? Randi? What do you mean? She's all I've been considering. All I've been consumed by since you called me. She is the only thing that matters in any of this." The hand not holding on for dear life fists along my thigh.

"I'm saying we haven't considered her as the hostage and what that means to all this. What do we know about her? What have we witnessed since we were assigned to her security detail?"

Inhaling deep, I fight the irritation at my best friend's words and attempt to process what he's suggesting.

What have I noticed since that first day we met when I hauled her out of that burning limo?

Natural beauty.

Desperation to help others.

Witty sense of humor and crazy as hell.

Lips that beg for you to kiss them or have them wrapped around your cock.

A pussy that tastes like honey and feels like heaven.

I adjust along the leather seat to keep my growing hard-on from being noticed.

But the side-eye glare Tank's shoots me signals I wasn't as covert at adjusting myself as I hoped.

"Stop thinking like that, you horny ass. I'm talking about Randi being Randi. Everyone who knows her falls for her. Not in love with her, thank fuck, or you'd have a murder rap sheet a mile long, but they care for her. They see her kindness in a city and profession where there is none. People who know her gravitate to that naïveté from not being raised in politics. That's what we're not considering, what we haven't added to the equation."

Well, fuck. Here I was thinking about all the physical aspects I love about Randi and forgot about the reason I fell for her in the first place.

"You're right," I say, scrubbing a hand down my face. "So where does that leave us? If it is Whit, he knows her and still loathes her."

"But not the men who took her."

"If we're right about Ponder being the one who was behind the abduction for Whit, then yeah, he does know her. He's been with her for the past year on the beta team detail. He knows her and still took her."

Tank runs a hand over his sweaty bald head before slamming it to the steering wheel. "You're right."

"But," I say as I think through the various ways Randi being Randi could be a benefit, "he's never seen her like we do, considering I had him moved to the shit list on the beta team. He's never had one-on-one time with her, so if he stuck around after the abduction, she could influence him then. So you're right, maybe Randi can sway Ponder. But that's only if he didn't drop her at a location and leave her alone for Whit to find. Fuck." I groan. "There are too many variables and not enough solid leads. We need something to turn in our favor." I glance out the window to the early afternoon sun, its bright rays a complete opposite to the darkness consuming me. "What if we do find her and she's…? What if he's broken her by the time we get there?"

"Would that change anything for you?" Tank asks. I lurch forward, the seat belt catching against my chest with our sudden stop. I blink, realizing he's just whipped us into a parallel parking spot along a street lined with shops and business. He turns in his seat to stare me down. "Answer me."

"You think that little of me?" I snap, the hurt leaking through my harsh tone. "Of course not. I love her no matter what. I just want her back. If he's broken her mind or her spirit, I will help her heal. I'll be there for her every step of the way. I just want—" I shake my head. "I need her with me. I need her by my side for the rest of my life and me beside her for the rest of hers. This is it for me. *She's* it for me."

"Good." Without another word, he swings open the driver side door and climbs out into the afternoon heat. I follow suit, stepping onto the sidewalk and scanning the few pedestrians scurrying about. "We're in the center of the radius where the picture was sent. This is where we start our search. If we find the phone, it could have prints, maybe even enough juice left that we can use it to backtrack where it's been. We find that phone, we're one step closer to finding her."

With a determined curt nod, I split from Tank, heading straight for the trash can at the corner of an intersection while he slips back around the SUV and cuts across the street.

The stainless steel dome lid clatters to the ground with an erupting bang loud enough to be heard several streets over. A few curious and apprehensive glances come my way as people walk by, giving me a wide berth as I rummage through the full trash bag. Cold, lumpy coffee, something sticky like old yogurt—yep, I'm going with yogurt to keep my sanity—and crumbs of food slide through my searching fingers, caking beneath my short nails. Halfway through, I force myself to lean away from the stench and suck in a lungful of fresh air before continuing digging. At the bottom, I curse at not finding the cell phone, those wasted efforts and minutes. Hot metal burns a line across my palm as I shove off the rounded edge, sending the can crashing to the side of its metal protective cage.

Fat drops of thick, semi-solid liquid dribble from my dangling fingers onto the warm concrete sidewalk as I stride to the next visible trash can. Halfway through the third trash can, I hear my name bellowed from somewhere close by. My head snaps up, hands still embedded in the refuse as I search for Tank. Across the street, he stands beside a pile of trash, holding something high in the air. I squint, resting a disgusting hand above my brows to shield the glare.

A cell phone.

Hell to the fucking yeah. Finally.

The rubber soles of my boots pound on the pavement as I jog across the street, nearly getting run over twice. The yelling of the furious drivers fades in the distance as they continue on. I stop beside Tank, whose focus is on the small device.

"It's smashed," he says, defeated. Those large boulder-like shoulders slump.

"What do you want to bet Smith's friends at Homeland can still pull information from it?" I keep a cautious eye on him. If he becomes too frustrated and launches the phone, there'd be no coming back from that. Carefully pulling the broken device from his hand, I place it gently on the brick window ledge of the nearby building. Only after wiping the layers of gunk off my hands do I dig through the side pocket of my cargo pants and retrieve my phone. Thank fuck I sent Smith's contact information to my phone from Tank's earlier in case I needed it in the future. Hitting the Call button, I set it to speaker and hold it face-up between me and my pacing friend.

"I'm five minutes out" are Smith's first words.

"We have something we need your buddies at Homeland to work on. We think we found the cell phone used to send the picture of Randi, but it's smashed."

"They'll be able to pull something. Everything is traceable."

The screen flashes, signaling the call has ended.

"Now what?" I ask the universe.

"We use every available contact, every fucking favor owed, to dig up information on Whit." Before the last word is past his lips, his cell phone is gripped in a grime-covered palm. "The director sent a message stating they're in a standstill like we are," he says, his eyes scanning the screen. "FBI as well. Everyone is on standby waiting for a location."

"It's our save. My kill." My jaw works back and forth. "Ponder and Whit are mine."

"You find them first, you kill them first."

"Will there be a second killing?" An almost smirk plays at my lips.

"I won't let you have all the fun."

The smirk grows wider into a full sinister smile at his need for revenge almost matching my own.

Both our heads whip in the direction of a roaring engine. A bright red vintage Chevy Camaro barrels down the street before screeching to a halt along the curb. Dirt, clouds of smoke from the tires, and the scent of burned rubber float around the car as I bend down, leaning into the passenger side through the open window.

Without a legit evidence baggie, I finagle the cell phone down into an unused latex glove and tie the end to keep it from slipping out.

"Here." I toss our only lead onto the black leather seat. For a split second, I allow myself to appreciate the car and the care Smith's obviously put into restoring it. "Find us something."

I barely have a second to lean back out of the window before the engine revs, tires squeal, and the classic car shoots into oncoming traffic like he has zero fucks to give about the possibility of a head-on collision.

At my back, Tank's deep voice snaps and directs orders. I watch him pace at a fast clip with his phone pressed to his ear, face in a deep scowl.

I tap my own phone against my thigh in quick rhythm, matching my pulse. With a deep inhale, I tilt my face to the sky and close my eyes.

I'm coming, Randi.

Hold on, baby. I'm coming for you.

11

RANDI

Everything aches. My bones, my skin, my head and ringing ears. After that initial neck-snapping punch to the face, the man who I still haven't identified eased back—even further than he had before, if I believe what he told Shawn about not hitting me at full force. The smacks to the face and punches to the gut still hurt like hell, but they're not nearly as bone-crunching and brain-rattling as that initial hit.

What worries me the most is that after the third or fourth hit to the gut, it hurt to breathe deeply. Hell, it hurt to breathe at all because of the stomach shots, but this is different. There's a pinch or a stabbing sensation every time my lungs fully fill with air, almost like a rib or something else is jabbing into it.

I've lost count of how many times they've revived me either with smelling salts—which should be renamed as smelly salts because they're nasty—or a quick adrenaline shot. Those I'm growing to like with the way they amp up my body enough to forget the pain for a few short minutes.

After multiple punches, backhands, taunting, and threats, I still haven't given in to Shawn's request. And I won't. Why does it matter at this point? I'm not getting out of this alive unless Trey finds me. And there's a piece of me that's taking sick pleasure in watching Shawn's anger rise with my resistance to his demands.

Does that make me a masochist? I'm not getting wet on the pain, just finding a sliver of joy in this fucked-up situation. So maybe that makes me an opportunist?

"Opportunist masochist?" A sharp stinging sensation bites across my lower lip as I mouth the words, deepening a split along the edge.

Thank goodness there's no one to respond to my ramblings or give me hell for talking to myself. I'm finally alone after what felt like hours of being a human punching bag and thinking up creative ways to tell Shawn to fuck off before the two men stormed from the room.

The moment the door slammed shut, I sagged in relief. In the movies, now is the time I'd figure out a way to escape the bindings holding me to the chair and bust out of here, rescuing myself.

But that's in the movies, and I'm no heroine.

I'm trailer trash Barbie playing dress-up in DC. I've had a lot of time to think about the choices I made to bring me to this point. The two biggest life-changing decisions were going to Harvard and convincing Kyle to put me on the presidential ballot as his VP. Both are what set all this in motion. Or maybe it was dreaming of having a better life away from the trailer park I grew up in that started all of this.

Whatever it was, put me here.

Fate? Destiny? The plotting of a sociopath?

Call it whatever, but it doesn't change the outcome. Or the good I've done since arriving in DC or the good that will continue to be done once I'm gone from office—either dead or replaced during the next election. Not going to lie, my hope is on the latter.

Plus, on top of all the good I've done while in DC, I met him.

Trey Benson.

Mischievous, fun-loving, hot-as-hell Trey Benson. He's mine, and I'm his. Even if I die today knowing my past choices could've kept me from all this pain, I'll never regret a single one because they all led me to him.

A single warm tear slips down my cheek, leaving a stinging burn in its wake as the salt aggravates the slices across my skin. I should've known someone like me wouldn't be allowed a happily ever after.

All I want is one more kiss, one more smirk, the feel of his protective arms wrapped around me. Just once. Half a second is all I'm praying for. It's all I'll need to say goodbye.

Hot dry air wafts across me with the opening of the door, moving the few strands of hair that aren't stuck to my sticky skin, but I don't look up. Lids drooping, I continue to stare unseeing at the cracked floor now dotted with drops of crimson.

Soft murmurs reach my ears along with the stomp of feet. Something gentle yet firm slides beneath my chin, raising it off my chest until I'm staring into a set of searching eyes.

My breaths rattle in my lungs. "Don't do this," I rasp. "You see it. See he's crazy. Let me go, please."

The corners of his eyes wrinkle. He breaks the intense gaze to scan my beaten face, no doubt appraising the work he's done so far.

"I'll kill you, end it now before I leave." The words are low, muffled through the fabric wrapped around his face.

"No thank you?" In my attempt to shake my head, it lolls to the side, my chin slipping off the two leather glove-covered fingers holding me steady. His grip tightens, keeping me upright. "He can't win."

"Protect yourself. Give the fuck in." There's an urgency in his voice, one that hasn't been there before now.

"I have to protect them."

"Who?" I swear his head angles in a curious tilt.

"Everyone." Exhaustion makes my words slur, or maybe it's the swollen lips and blood clotting in my mouth. "I swore to protect."

"You're a fool," he hisses.

Looking him dead in the eye, I summon what courage and defiance I have left. "No. I'm the president, and I don't negotiate with assholes."

The door swings open, banging against the wall before slamming shut. With zero energy left, I can't physically turn to identify who's entered. Instead I cut my eyes to the left and search my periphery to find the asshole himself stomping back into the room.

"I've misjudged your tolerance for pain, Trailer. We've discussed, and it's time to change tactics." I stop tracking Shawn's calculated steps to search the gaze of the man still crouched in front of me. Eyes narrowed, he stays silent. "We've decided to... *force you.*" Shawn's Joker-like smile spreads up his cheeks, crinkling the corners of his eyes.

A chill races down my spine at Shawn's ominous choice of words and the almost desperation emanating from the mystery man.

"No," I whisper. In my gut, I know what Shawn's referring to, and I'm not sure I'll stay strong if one of them forces themselves on me. The pain in my face will fade, my ribs will mend, but the mental damage from being raped by my abductor and captor might never heal—if I live long enough, that is.

"Please," I beg the man in front of me. Saliva drips off my trembling split lips. Something in the way he's holding back, not as overly excited like Shawn, makes me wonder if he's not as keen on this new turn of events. Tears leak down my cheeks as I tug at the restraints, this new horror giving me a shock of desperation-laced panic and making me thrash, cutting the plastic farther into my skin. "You said you weren't like your friend. Please don't do this. Kill me, hit me, but not that." My cries turn into sobs, strangling the words to nearly unintelligible.

The man stands from his crouched position and faces Shawn. "I told you I'm a mercenary for hire," he states. "I will torture, kill, hunt, and threaten, dishing out whatever the client paying wants, but not that—not what you're asking. I draw the line at lowering myself to a rapist."

"You are who I pay you to be." I flinch at the vehemence in Shawn's bellow.

"Just let me kill her, get this over with, and we're done here."

"You're the employee, you fool. I hired you. I pay you. You do not tell me what to do." Nose to nose, Shawn's yelled words echo off the cinder block walls. "Fall in line or you won't get the last of the payment. I have more planned for her after this." His dark eyes find mine from across the room. "Others who will be more than happy to have their fun with our little president."

I'm a blubbering mess, begging for the man not to do it, to hit me instead or just leave. But one thing I won't allow to cross my lips is the surrender to Shawn's demands.

The arguing voices fade into the background as I mentally curl within myself, frightened of what's to come. The door opens, a waft of hot air drying my tearstained cheeks. A bolt of hope stutters my heart at the thought that it's Trey breaking down the door, finally here to save me. But it's not. The man with his face still covered stands with his hand on the door, back to the room, pausing half in and half out when Shawn calls out to him.

"Where the fuck do you think you're going?"

"Keep your damn money. My final payment of this contract will be seeing that bastard Benson dead at my hands. Do what you want with her. I did my part, and now I'm out." Without turning the man continues into the larger part of the abandoned warehouse disappearing as the door falls shut with its own weight.

Shawn's dark chuckle at the man's response chills my blood and churns my stomach. "Sounds like your boyfriend has made a bloodthirsty enemy." He sighs and dusts off his hands. "That bastard leaving saved me a million dollars. Too bad for you it didn't save you from shit. The others will be here soon. Then we'll start the real fun."

My heart races, thundering in my chest as he steps closer. The vileness in his eyes, malice in his smile, and genuine hate in his dark aura have me flinching back, doing anything to put distance between me and the sinister man, but there's nowhere to go.

With far too much enjoyment, Shawn slips on one blue latex glove before tugging one on the opposite hand. The legs of the chair he once occupied scrape along the rough floor as he drags it close. His gaze never leaves mine as he folds into his seat, our knees brushing.

"All you have to do is make the call to Pierce," he mutters. Those dark eyes dip to my lips before tracing lower, leaving a dirty feel in their wake. "I can't say I wasn't hoping it would come to this. I'll find my own enjoyment watching them break you."

I sink my teeth into my bottom lip in an attempt to keep my terror-filled tears at bay.

A barely there touch ghosts across my road-rashed knee, eliciting a pathetic whimper even with my jaw locked and lips sealed. The countless scrapes along both legs, from the wreck, fighting my captors, and rolling around like a rag doll in a trunk, snag the soft latex glove as the tip of a single finger tracks higher. At the edge of my bloodied jean shorts, two fingers dance along the hem, dipping beneath before retreating just as quickly.

A scream builds in my chest, desperate to be let loose, making my revulsion known. But I clamp it down, sealing my lips even tighter and breathing hard through the one nostril that's not clogged with tacky blood. I will not give him the satisfaction of hearing me scream, of hearing exactly what his touch does to me.

Those same two fucking fingers fiddle with the top button of my shorts where it still hangs open from my earlier bathroom break.

"Convenient," he mutters. "Did you two start the fun before I got here, hmm?"

The tendons and muscles along my neck protest as I twitch my head left and right.

"Good. That's good." The hem of my shirt rises just enough for him to dip beneath. "I want to hear all your screams," Shawn whispers in my ear. Nothing in the world could hold back the desperate cry of agony that erupts from my soul and pours past my parted lips. "Make. The fucking. Call."

Make the call.

Make the call.

It could all end. Right here, right now. I wouldn't have to endure another second with him too close. Wouldn't have to temper the revulsion rolling in my stomach or the dark thoughts that are racing through my mind. All I have to do is make a simple call. A difficult decision, a simple act.

But ... then what?

It doesn't feel right. Something is keeping me from folding, from giving in despite my body begging me. Maybe not something. Maybe a someone. Trey. I know he's out there searching for me, and he will come. He will always come for me. I just have to stay strong a little longer to give him time.

I have to believe in him.

"No." The word is a hiss as it passes through my clenched teeth.

With a rage-filled yell, he wraps a gloved hand around my throat and squeezes. The pressure triggers my instinct to fight back, both arms twitching in earnest, desperate for release. But still I don't scream, don't make a sound as I glare right back at Shawn, pouring as much hate and loathing and disgust into our stare-down as I can muster.

"You fucking cunt," he screams in my face. Spit sprinkles across my cheek, but still I don't look away. "You're nothing—*nothing*—compared to me. You do not deserve the role that was handed to you by that fucker Birmingham."

I'm sorry. What?

Okay, so now I know my line.

Call me a cunt, talk about raping me, beat me to shit. But tell me something was *handed* to me? To Randi fucking trailer trash Sawyer?

Hell. To. The. No.

"You listen and you listen good, you pompous piece of shit." My voice is strong, my words like a damn whip. "I've worked my ass off my entire life. Scraping by, doing whatever I could to make a better life for myself and my daughter. Nothing, and I mean *nothing*, has been handed to me. So get your pink panties out of your ass and realize you fucking lost your shot to a hell of a woman who is twice the man you are and will ever be."

My nostrils flare as heated blood pumps through my veins, warming my skin and causing sweat to build along my neck and forehead once again.

Two seconds. That's what it takes for him to process my declaration.

Three seconds. That's what it takes for him to shove against my neck so hard that my windpipe almost snaps from the pressure and the chair rocks backward on the two back legs.

My eyes widen as the sensation of falling flips my stomach and steals the little air left in my lungs. Shoulders tucked in tight, I lean forward as far as I can with my hands tied behind me to prepare for the impact I know is coming. The chair slams to the floor, my back smacking the metal immediately after. The force snaps my neck, whacking the back of my head against the unforgiving dusty floor. All the air whooshes from my lungs and stars spark behind my open eyes even as the darkness of unconsciousness creeps in.

My head lolls to the side in time to see a tan loafer sailing toward my side. A scream crackles through the stale air, scratching and tearing out of my throat at the impact of his kick against my already battered ribs.

"You think you're fucking tough, do you? Have this all figured out how you're the one with power?" A roaring evil laugh bounces off the walls. The toe of his loafer nudges my cheek until I'm facing the ceiling where his sneering face looms over me. "I'll have him fuck you in the ass dry, how about that? Make him bleed you from the inside out, shoving in deep until you're hoarse from the screams." The slight movement of him adjusting his hardening dick catches my eye. Bile slides up my throat, burning as it settles just behind my tongue before I can swallow it back.

"I'll even record it for that rent-a-cop boyfriend of yours. Let him relive this over and over again, knowing he couldn't do shit to stop it. Because I'm the one with power here, Trailer. Not you, not him, not Birmingham. Me. And I will get my way even if I have to fuck it out of you myself."

The way his tongue swirls around his cheek, I know what's coming before his lips purse and the thick wad of saliva and mucus splatters against my cheek and neck. Without the use of my hands, I can't wipe the disgusting glob from my face; instead I'm forced to feel every centimeter it slides down my skin until it drips to the surface.

Chest heaving, he continues to lord over me, contempt burning behind his dark eyes. His lips part, no doubt ready to let loose another stream of hatred my way, when his attention slides to the door. His brows furrow. "Where the hell are the others?" With a quick check down to me, he turns on his heels and makes for the single door.

Only once he's gone do I give over to the agony pulsing through every part of my battered body and tattered mind. He'll be back with other men, which means the worst is yet to come.

I swallow back the tears clogging my throat. If I'm to live through this, come out whole on the other side, I have to prepare for the horrors I'll face under their ministrations.

Focusing on a dark corner of my mind, I feed all the good, happy memories into the tiny corner, shoving them deep and preparing a happy cavern to escape to when the torture begins again. It's not much, but it's all I have.

My tiny corner filled with Trey memories will have to work until the real one comes to save me.

12

———————

TREY

Nowhere. We're wasting valuable time and getting fucking nowhere. After an hour of calling in every favor to gather information on Whit, all I've found is validation that he's a shady-ass politician who's used his power and money to escape multiple accusations of assault, extortion, and one battery charge. All those cases were dropped; none of the accusations stuck or saw the inside of the courtroom.

Fucking rich bastards thinking they own the damn world because of what they're worth.

Sure, I was a rich bastard too, but I never used my family name or money to cover my mistakes. No, I spent it all on clothes, shoes, and fast bikes and cars. But it seems I'm an anomaly.

Midafternoon sun blazes high in the cloudless blue sky, its unrelenting rays scorching the exposed skin of my neck. Even with the material of my T-shirt wicking the sweat from my back as soon as it forms, I've sweated through the entire shirt from the intense summer heat. I've stood here, feet from where we found the cell phone, calling and digging for information on Whit while waiting for Smith's Homeland buddies to give us another lead to track.

Tank's deep voice rumbles from across the street, where he chose to post up in the shade. But me, I couldn't move from this spot. For some reason, the thought of crossing the street to be more comfortable made me angry. Why in the hell should I be comfortable, not sweating like a pig and dying of thirst, when Randi is out there probably feeling the same way without any option of escaping the heat?

That's why I can't bring myself to move. It makes no sense, but in the back of my mind, it feels like I'm betraying her if I search for relief from my discomfort.

The thin, solid metal of the phone slides beneath my tight grip with the sweat slicking my hands. I tuck the device into the back pocket of my cargo pants and wipe both soaked palms down the front of my shirt, which only wicks up the sweat from my chest, dampening the shirt further. I could wring the thing out at this point.

"Fuck," I mutter under my breath. Drops of sweat sprinkle from the tips of my hair as I rake a hand through the damp locks. "Where are you, Mess? Where the fuck are you?"

A tickle against my ass draws me out of my discomfort. I retrieve the vibrating cell phone, flip it around, and check the screen.

My eyes narrow at the call coming through.

UNKNOWN

A line of smeared sweat is left along the bottom part of the screen as I hastily swipe to answer Vlad's call.

"Please tell me you have something." I hold my breath, tugging at my hair as I pace from the brick building to the curb and back again.

"Do not expect me to ever tell you how this information was found."

"Yes, yes, of course. I don't give a fuck if you have damn spies lurking around DC and that's how you got it. Just give me what you have."

"Coordinates will be sent to this number now. You make him pay for this, yes?"

"Without a doubt." I growl.

"Good luck, then."

The glass peels from my ear as I pull the phone forward, eyes glued to the screen. A text flashes, the coordinates Vlad promised. But coordinates to what, he didn't say. All that matters is this could be the location where I'll find her.

Gripping the phone so tight the frame bends, I shake out of the stunned stupor I'd frozen into and race across the street toward the SUV. I shout at Tank, yelling at him to hurry the hell up. At the first tug, the chrome door handle slips from my hand, rocking me back on my heels. Narrowing my eyes at the door like it personally offended me, I yank it open with more force than necessary and slide into the passenger seat before slamming the door closed behind me.

The driver side door slams shut immediately after. "Where are we headed?" The engine roars to life. Warm dry air pumps from the vents before changing to lifesaving air-conditioned cold gusts.

"Here." I plug the coordinates into my phone and link the screen to the navigation system on the dash. "It's a lead from the Russian. He told me not to ask how or where he got it."

"Probably has spies everywhere." Without checking the mirrors, Tank slams on the gas, shooting us onto the street. The tires squeal as he makes a tight U-turn, unconcerned about the cars coming straight for us. Their brakes lock up as they come to a screeching halt to not T-bone us.

"That's what I said, but I don't give a fuck right now. All that matters is her."

"It could be nothing, or hell, a trap."

I nod in agreement, but the feeling in my gut tells me the information is solid. "Vlad likes Randi, as strange as that relationship is. I think he's actually concerned with her well-being and probably called in a few favors of his own to gain this information. I doubt he'd send us into a trap."

Tank shoots a cautious glance my way. "We need to let everyone know what's going on. We have to call in backup." The navigation voice tells us we're ten minutes away. "We're so far from the crash site they probably won't have enough men over to us in time. We should wait—"

"We're not waiting," I growl. "I agree on the backup. I'm texting the director now to send whatever air and land power they can drum up to this area. But we're not waiting." After messaging the director, I shoot a quick text to Smith with the same coordinates. A response comes almost immediately with his ETA. "Smith is twenty out. He'll go in with us."

"Make sure they send an ambulance with her blood type—"

"I fucking know what she might need," I snap as my thumbs fly across the screen, texting back and forth with the director. "I'm not a fool. I know what I might be walking into and what I might find. But I'm not going there right now, Davis. Right now I'm focusing on the fact that we have a lead, and that puts us one step closer to her and me murdering those fucksticks."

"I get where your head needs to be now, but if we're going in without backup, you cannot turn into a possessive, protective boyfriend when you see her in rough shape. I need Agent Benson with me covering my ass."

"It's a big one to cover," I slide in, trying like hell to laugh through the panic inside me.

"Seriously. We clear the area, get the president somewhere safe, and then you can freak the fuck out."

"I know what I'm doing," I say as I will a cool calm to wash through me. It's the same focused calm I learned to settle into during the few battles I engaged in during my stint in the army. It covered all emotions with a blanket, readying me to do whatever it took to save my own life and those of my brothers fighting alongside me. And I'll do whatever it takes now to save her. "Just remember what we agreed."

"I remember."

"I don't care if the place is crawling with cops and agents. I get my alone time with them."

Outside the windshield, well-kept buildings and businesses fade from this part of town, replaced with warehouses. The farther we drive the more deserted the area becomes. Litter collects along the curb, spilling over onto the sidewalk in some areas. Twenty minutes from where we found the phone, we've gone from trendy business district to the forgotten side of the city.

Vacant warehouses with missing windows and doors line the street. Tall dried weeds sprout between the numerous cracks along the street and pieces of sidewalk that remain. A few buildings that are clearly abandoned are protected by hole-riddled chain-link fences that have failed at their job of keeping looters and vandals at bay.

Gravel crunches beneath the SUV's tires as it slows to a rolling stop. Tense silence swells, only broken by the grind of metal as I engage the slide on one of my nine millimeters. In the driver seat, Tank checks a clip before slamming it into place and doing the same with another three handguns. Tension rises to a near snapping point as we finish the last of our checks.

"Ready?" His tone is gruff with worry. "Trey, if this—"

"Ready." There's no need to voice both our fears. His is that this could be a trap, mine that this is a false lead. Neither fear will help the situation; we have to suck it up, shove it back, and do what we came here to do.

Save the president.

The specific warehouse smack in the middle of the coordinates Vlad sent is still a block away from where Tank parked the SUV, carefully hidden between two buildings. Even with the distance between us and the warehouse, we soundlessly ease the doors open, careful to not break the desolate quiet that's engulfed this place. Remnants of asphalt, litter, and shards of glass crunch beneath our quick steps as we creep closer, using forgotten dumpsters, stairwells, and sides of other buildings as cover.

At the corner of a tall brick wall, Tank's dark fist bolts into the air. I skid to a stop, nearly slamming my nose against his back. Chest ballooned out with a fortifying inhale, he peers around the building for a visual on our goal. Gun held tight between my hands, I seal myself to the crumbling brick while he debates our next move.

Tank taps my shoulder moments later, pointing forward and then right, indicating which way we'll zigzag heading for the new cover. Without hesitation, I follow behind him as he slips around the corner and dashes across the crumbling blacktop. The glare blinds me momentarily as I shift from the cool comfort of the shadows to race across the empty parking lot, dodging panes of glass and empty bottles to keep our approach silent.

Breathing hard from the anticipation thrumming through my veins, I crouch beside Tank, who's pressed against the building. Just steps away, around the corner, we're concealed behind a set of steps leading up to a closed army green dented and rusted door. Elbows resting on my bent knees, bouncing on the balls of both feet, I wait for him to detail our game plan. Because that's what he does. I'm the jokester who everyone loves, and Tank's the planner. It works for us.

"Let's assume there are at least five armed men in that building plus the president. There's no way Ponder took out all those agents, detonated the blast, and took out the surveillance system on his own. That team plus Whit." With a quick glance around the corner of the building to the front door, he ducks back. "We need another point of entry," he mutters low enough for me to hear but keeps his voice from traveling. "If this is a trap, they'll be expecting us to come through the front door."

"There's a low window around back." Both our guns whip to the right at the first muffled word, our sights zeroed in between Smith's brows. "Don't shoot." You'd think a man would be terrified with two guns pointed at his head while he stands unmoving, no gun drawn, but not Smith. No, that dumbass just stares us down with a hint of a smile tugging at his lips.

"Tempting," I mutter while lowering the gun. How the hell we didn't hear him approach is either a testament to our focus on saving Randi or his training. "Did you see anything else?"

Crouching low next to me, he shakes his head and leans back against the building. "Just that one point of entry besides the massive loading dock doors, but those look rusted and would make a hell of a lot of noise. I peeked through the window before finding you two, didn't see any movement."

"My gut tells me we're at the right place." I incline my head back toward the warehouse.

"It could just be the two inside and that's why we don't hear anything. Maybe they killed off those who helped them this morning already. If I were them, that's what I would do." I raise both brows at Smith in surprise at his statement. "What? The fewer people involved, the less likely for things to leak or go sideways. If it were me, I'd only want me and the client to be breathing after this."

"Fucking hell," I mumble. "Ten, five, two—who the fuck cares how many are in there? We need to get inside now."

"True. She might already be dead." I lunge toward Smith, ready to snap his neck, but two strong hands grip my shoulders and hold me back. "Is the backup on its way?" Angling his head one way and then the other, he cracks his neck, the picture of casualness in this tense-as-hell situation.

"Ten minutes out. I asked them to hold back until we give the signal." A worried look crosses Tank's sweaty dark features. "I don't want to risk them feeling cornered. Shit will go sideways real quick if they do. If it is Whit behind that door with Randi, he's liable to kill her and then himself before surrendering."

"Good pep talk," I hiss. Moving the gun to my opposite hand, I flex my fingers in an effort to get the blood flowing from my white-knuckled grip. "Let's be realistic here. If Whit sees me, he'll immediately know Tank isn't far behind." The various potential scenarios shuffle through my thoughts. "But he doesn't know about you." I incline my head to Smith. "You take the window you spotted and lie low until absolutely necessary. The longer he doesn't know you're around, the better." Turning on the balls of my feet, I face him square on. "Whit and the fucker who took her are mine. If you have to intervene, wound them, but do not take the kill shot. Understand?"

His light eyes search mine before he nods and slips back the way he came.

I wait until he's out of sight before turning back to Tank.

"I'm going through the front door. You can come with me or find another way in. I agree about not making Whit feel cornered, and if it's several of his hired guys against one, he won't. There's no way that fucker is in there alone, which means all their attention will be turned to me. That will give you a chance to slip in and get Randi somewhere safe."

"You're a fool."

"You love me."

He shakes his head. "For some fucked-up reason."

"Again with the language. I really don't want to get on your wife's shit list."

"How about I make you a deal, Playboy?"

Despite what we're about to walk into, I smirk. "I'm listening."

"I won't tell my Sarah about you teaching me such foul language if you make it out of here alive today."

The smirk turns into a full-on smile. "And if I don't?"

"Then I'll let them bring you back to life just so she can kill you herself."

I cringe. "Deal. No dying or I'll die twice. Now there's a motivational speech for you. You should cross-stitch that shit on a pillow."

Not waiting for his response, I stand, suppressing a groan as my knees crack, then switch the gun back to my dominant shooting hand.

"I've got your back, Benson. But please, for everything that is holy, don't do anything stupid."

Glancing over my shoulder, I offer him a smile. "Same, bestie."

"Gotta go and make it all weird." He shakes his head, but a hint of a smile pulls at his lips.

This is what we needed. A beat to relax, forget about the potential death we're walking into, to ease the pressure the task of saving the president has resting on our shoulders.

Brown weeds drape over the crumbling sidewalk and fill the thick cracks running along the cement as I walk along. I take the three steps in one leap, putting me directly in front of the door. On a burst of hot, dry wind, it swings open half an inch before squeaking closed once again.

I pause, trepidation filling my gut and turning it sour as I stare at the unlocked door. No one would be that careless unless it's part of the trap, allowing easy access to the inside of the building so they can ambush whoever is dumb enough to walk through that door.

The heated metal burns my palm as I place a steady hand on the rough surface, but I hold it there despite the pain while I give myself a final inhale to focus every thought and muscle on what's about to happen.

Thoughts clear, I step forward, inching the door open, when a loud curse from the other side has every muscle locking in place.

I know that voice.

Hatred and loathing infiltrate my earlier calm at the sound of Whit's string of curses.

A slow, cruel smile spreads across my cheeks as his voice filters through.

He's here, which means she's here.

I've found her.

Time to play, motherfucker.

13

RANDI

A shout, or maybe a string of shouted words, breaks through the peaceful darkness I'd slipped into. Nothing hurts here. No fear, no pain, no... anything. Just the calmness only the deepest shadows of my mind can offer, protecting me from what waits for me out in reality. I should remember this dark corner for the next deficit budget meeting.

Reality creeps closer as the shouting intensifies, shattering my little unconscious haven. Shawn's raised voice and quick curses assault my ears, almost like he's yelling directly beside my head. I cringe as he continues, demanding me to get up. A whimper escapes at a hard jostle of my shoulder, shaking my entire broken and bruised body and sending agony shooting along every bone, joint, and muscle.

"Get up," Shawn demands with a swift kick to my hip. I roll with the impact only to flop back to the floor.

I can't move. From the fact that every inch of my body is in pain, I know I'm awake and able to feel, but for some reason, my attempts to lift myself off this floor fail. Maybe I'm broken, too far gone inside my own mind, or perhaps my broken body has finally given up completely, leaving me defenseless to what's to come.

The conversation from earlier blares to the forefront of my mind, reminding me of what my unresponsive body has left me vulnerable to. A trickle of fear slithers through my veins and weighs in my gut like a lead ball, but still all I can do is stare unseeing at the far wall, my body limp.

A shudder racks through my weak body at another incentivizing nudge against my side. My body moves with the motion, rolling halfway only to flop back to the floor like a limp rag doll.

A distant part of my mind screams at me to wake the hell up and fight, to not give in this easily. I've put up a good fight; would it be that terrible to give in to the pain and fear, let it suck me under, never to breach the surface again?

But the sadness of the truth holds back that fight. The truth that my whole life, everything I've done and worked for, no longer matters. I'll never see Trey again. Never hold my grandbaby or hug my beautiful daughter again.

Even with the end looming, I focus on the good memories. I've lived a good life with lots of love, struggles, and successes. The best part of my life started with that positive pregnancy test all those years ago and ended with Trey asking me to marry him.

Grief's claws shred my heart knowing we'll never get our happily ever after. Never have lazy Sundays on the couch binge-watching Netflix or consecutive mornings waking up next to one another. Grieving the life I'll never have but always wanted hurts and offers more physical pain than the injuries I've sustained so far. I have to accept the end of Randi Sawyer is near. No one will find me in time and save me from this terrible fate. Because even though it hurts to accept that we won't be together until we're old and gray, it hurts worse clinging to a false hope that all this will be over soon.

If they get their way and take my body against my will, I won't recover. Not from that. I'm not strong enough like other women who've been assaulted and come back from the dark wells of despair and self-loathing as a survivor instead of a victim. I'm strong in a lot of ways, or I was, but that... that will wreck me beyond recovery.

A blurred face appears above me.

"Get up now, you worthless cunt." The words are hollow, like they've traveled through an empty barrel from far away to reach me. More words are spoken, a few shouted, but they're too fast, too loud to understand in this state of teetering oblivion.

The blurry form shifts closer, now hovering mere inches away.

The inflexible plastic bindings tighten around my wrists before loosening, the sharp edges peeling away from my damaged skin until I can't feel the zip tie at all. The brief feel of freedom breathes renewed strength into my soul, encouraging me to not give up, not yet. The back of my head rolls along the concrete as I shift to get a better view of the man now bending toward my ankles still secured to the chair.

Several fast blinks clear the lingering glaze from my eyes. Shawn slices through the zip tie around my left ankle before moving to the next. Both legs immediately slip, falling to the floor and leaving me somewhat spread eagle around the chair's legs.

My frantic gaze flicks from the clearly tense Shawn to where my legs lie spread open. I still have shorts on, but I sure as hell don't want to be in this position, even with clothes covering my lady bits. Hissing through the pain, I wiggle back enough to seal my thighs and knees together.

His perfectly plump lips press together in a thin line.

"Good, you're not comatose. Now get the fuck up. It's time to leave."

The quiet crunch of leaves or debris beneath my hair sounds as I shake my head along the cement floor.

"That wasn't a question," he bites out. "The others will be here soon, and we need to be ready to haul out of here."

"I won't break, Shawn." Speaking burns, each word torture. "Leave me. And if I were you—" Connecting our gaze, I wait a moment, ensuring I have his full attention. "—I'd run. Run, because he will find you, and he will kill you for what you've done."

"I'm not afraid of that clown you call an agent."

"You should be." Love and conviction strengthen my voice. "You really fucking should be. And maybe this makes me a bad person, but I hope he takes his time, like you've done with me. Reenacts exactly what you've done, what you're planning to do, on you. But it will be worse for you, because you'll know."

"Know what?" he huffs, crossing both arms across his chest, careful to keep the knife he used to cut my restraints away from his skin.

"You'll know no one cares enough about you to even attempt to find you. No one will care when you're lying broken and rotting somewhere. Because your whole life has been about manipulating those around you and lying to get your way, leaving you unremembered and forever forgotten."

It could be the light playing tricks on my tired eyes, but I swear a hint of color leaches from his unnaturally tanned skin. His throat bobs with a hard swallow.

Well, shit, that even left a chill slithering along my spine. Guess my hate for the man runs deeper than I ever knew. The last few hours have really driven those feelings home, though it's not like I've carried this hate and loathing baggage with me since day one of meeting Shawn. "I've got enough baggage on my own without adding that asshole."

"Not if he kills Benson first. " Rolling his shoulders, Shawn looks down his nose with an evil gleam. "Or maybe he'll do me the favor and kill himself after he sees what I did. How you begged for me to stop, to kill you and end the pain." Heat singes my lungs as my breaths turn to short gasps. "I wish I could be there when he sees the recording you and I will do together. What he'll think when he sees his trailer trash girlfriend fucked in every hole until only a sliver of life remains."

"Why?" The word leaves my lips before I can stop myself.

Shawn rolls his eyes. "Because I can't deal with this heat. And I never planned for this to end here, Trailer. We're going somewhere far away, where they will never think to look."

"He'll find me no matter where you take me."

"Maybe, but it'll be too late to save you." He bends closer, fingers delving into the thick of my hair and tightening into a fist. There's zero warning before he yanks hard enough for several chunks to rip from my scalp. I scurry along after him, attempting to alleviate some of the pressure as Shawn drags me toward the door.

A cracked shriek erupts from my throat. Wrenching my arms up, muscles screaming in protest, I clumsily smack at his forearm and wrist before wrapping it in a tight hold to help support my dragging weight. Bright sunlight sears into my overly sensitive eyes as I'm hauled from the small dim room into the main warehouse. Bare heels scrambling to gain traction on the dust-slick warehouse floor, I thrash from side to side, struggling to dislodge his grip.

Each of his steps is slow with my added weight and the fight I'm putting up. Shawn yells over his shoulder for me to stop, but that only reinforces my efforts, knowing it's causing him more work.

My cracking voice is barely a whisper as I try to call out for help while also cursing Shawn and his pencil dick.

Between shallow inhales is when I hear it. It's faint, but I'd know that sound anywhere after riding in Marine One so many times.

Helicopters.

I hold in my loud breathing, straining to hear the sound again, hoping like hell I didn't imagine it. This time the distinct rhythmic thump of the blades sounds closer, like they're flying as fast as they can in this direction.

Shawn's hurried steps halt as if he also heard the sound.

Releasing my held breath, I pant, joy and relief now flowing through my veins.

They found me.

Despite the pain I know the movement will cause on my scalp, I twist to watch an army of soldiers and agents bust through the door and high windows. Frantic, I flick my gaze around the empty warehouse, but no one crashes through armed and ready.

"You won't get away with this. They're here." I fight Shawn's grip, this time digging jagged nails into his skin, ripping and shredding as I scratch like a deranged kitten. "Get off me, you psychotic freak," I snap at the top of my lungs, which comes out more like a rasp.

Instead of releasing me—let's be honest, that was a false hope anyway—Shawn raises the fist wrapped in my hair, hauling me upright. The concrete slides beneath the soles of my feet as my noodle-like legs scramble to find footing.

The deep groan of heavy metal scraping against stone halts my frenzied attempts to break free. A furious curse vibrates in my ear as my back seals against Shawn's chest and hard, warm metal digs into my temple.

Scanning the desolate warehouse for whatever made him tense, my eyes land on a man dressed in all black, an angel of death, standing in front of a closed metal door, gun raised, the barrel pointing slightly above my head.

"I suggest you drop my girl."

14

TREY

The fact that I haven't pulled the trigger and splattered the bastard's brains against the dingy warehouse wall is a testament to my willpower. Before Randi, I would've fired without thinking of the consequences. But now, my life literally stands between me and the man I want to slowly torture to death.

The gun grip digs into my palms, my fingers aching at the firm hold.

I could take the shot. I would *make* the shot. But that slim chance Whit could move, putting Randi in the direct path of my bullet, keeps me from pulling the trigger. The odds of that happening are slim, but *if* it happened, then the next bullet fired from my gun would be lodged in my own skull.

I wasn't prepared for the first thing I saw after slipping through the door being fucking Whit himself dragging her behind him by her hair. I almost lost it then, almost went apeshit like Tank was adamant I *not* do. Since that one glimpse, I haven't dared look at her again. That was enough to recognize the treatment she's received up to this point in her captivity.

"I won't ask again." My voice is cold, calm, deadly. "Release the president."

"The president or your girlfriend, Benson?"

"They're one and the same. Drop her."

"Not a chance." For emphasis, he tightens his hold, adjusting her limp body tighter against his. A whisper of a pain-laced whimper reaches me. I grind my teeth, tightening my jaw from the force to keep my eyes on Whit. "How does it feel, rent-a-cop? Knowing there's nothing you can do to stop the inevitable?"

"Half the military is on standby just a couple miles away, waiting for my command. Three helicopters, a few fighter jets, and more guns than in all of Russia are ready to blow you into dust, yet you think you're the one holding the cards."

"Ah, but they won't attack, just like you, with her in the crosshairs." Her grip on his arm tenses at his demanding shake to my girl. Breaking our stare-down, he surveys the abandoned building. "Now where's your friend?"

"Didn't come." He knows it's a lie, but I have to give Tank and Smith time to get into position. Even if that means having to keep hearing this fucker's annoying-ass voice.

A harsh laugh rattles in the emptiness. "Lie. You two fuckbuddies never go anywhere alone." An evil glint flashes in his eyes as he leans forward, putting his lips beside her ear. Fury builds, fighting for escape as his lips move, his malicious gaze locked on me. "Call out for him."

Randi shakes her head, then winces as Whit jams the barrel of the gun harder against her temple. "No."

Whit tsks. "Wrong answer."

A broken scream erupts from her parted lips. Unable to fight it any longer, I steal a glance down at Randi's battered face. Eyes sealed, a pain-filled grimace scrunches her features.

What the hell is he doing to her?

"Stop," I shout, the word out before I can hold it back. "Stop whatever the hell you're doing." Sighing in defeat, I call out to Tank. "Davis, come out where he can see you."

Randi pitches forward with a relieved gasp only to be snapped against his chest once again. Her head lolls to the side, but still that gun stays firmly held to her head.

To the left, several feet from where I stand, a shadow shifts. Davis moves into the light, his own gun raised and trained on Whit.

A commotion in the back of the warehouse catches my attention. The way Tank inclines his head in the direction of the new voices suggests he hears it too.

"Ah, perfect timing." From somewhere in the back, coming out of nowhere, a group of men dressed similarly to me swaggers closer. "Now. You two will put your guns on the floor and kneel."

"Fuck you," I seethe, but my confidence is waning as more men pour into the room—none of them ours. "Let her go, Whit, and take the last few minutes of your life like a man not hiding behind a woman."

"Hmm." The sound and sight of him running his nose through her hair makes every muscle twitch in eagerness to wrap my hands around his throat. "For a trailer park whore, she's a damn good fuck. I don't mind being behind her."

No. I don't dare search Randi's face to see if his words are true.

"Get on the floor and remove all your weapons. She and I have some... unfinished business."

A pitiful whimper and string of begging pleas snap my full attention to Randi. Pain laces her features, and tears streak her dirty, bloody face.

Desperate to find the cause of whatever excruciating pain he's causing, I scan the two. The gun barrel hasn't moved from her temple, still digging into the tender flesh. The other arm is wrapped around her ribs, Whit's forearm and bicep flexed.

"You don't have long," Whit says, snapping my attention away from his hold. "I'm assuming it's a broken rib that's on the verge of puncturing a lung based on her excruciating pain and short breaths. It hurts, doesn't it, Trailer?"

Those split, bloody lips press into a thin line in defiance before parting for another pain-filled scream.

"Stop. Fucking stop," I shout. "Fine." This is a mistake. He'll have me shot the second I put my gun on the floor. But maybe that's the opening we need. If he moves the gun to shoot me, Tank can take his own shot. Then there's also Smith out there somewhere who can pick off the group of men watching, waiting.

If I die for her to live, that's fine. She's the one who matters. She's all that matters. No one will miss a disinherited playboy like me. But millions would miss her. Taeler would be devastated, and that sweet baby needs to know her grandmother.

Me, no one will miss.

Her, the world would tip on its axis with the loss. Not because she's the president but because she's Randi Sawyer. Crazy, beautiful, foul-mouthed, and heart of gold. The impact of her death would be a ripple spanning out from this warehouse to the world.

"Don't," Randi pleads. "Trey, don't." The last word is more of a sob.

Bits of crumbled cement and a thick layer of dust brush against my fingertips as I place the gun on the floor. Glancing up through my lashes, I lock onto those wet hazel eyes and wink. Straightening, I give her a confident smirk.

"Don't worry, Mess. We'll get you out of this." A hard mask slips over my features as I shift to Whit. "You won't get away. Even an arrogant ass like you can see that. You'll be dead before you even step a fucking foot out that door. There are at least a dozen snipers out there itching to take out the fool who took her. And when they see her, see what you did?" I click my tongue and shake my head. "Not only did you hurt the president, but you hit a woman. A bastard like that doesn't deserve a quick death. No, that bullet will hit where it hurts, to incapacitate. The killing will come later."

"Good thing I don't plan on walking out of here. On your knees," Whit growls, the confidence in his tone and choice of words confusing me. "Hands behind your head since I know you have more weapons on you than that one."

Slowly lowering to the ground, I don't look away from Randi. Dust wafts up in the wake of my knees crashing to the floor.

"Baby, you're okay. Maybe need a shower and a couple ice packs, but you're okay." Something blooms in my chest at the sight of her lips twitching upward in an attempt at a smile.

"That's what you're going with?" she wheezes. "Get off the floor, Trouble. Kill him. Don't let him take me." The tremble in her usually strong voice shreds my heart. "Don't let him take me. I can't—" A scream vibrates through the still air. "Fuck you," she pants like each breath is more difficult to take in than the last.

"Later." He laughs into her hair while raising a single brow in my direction. "Your turn, Davis, or Trailer here will have a perfect bullet-sized hole in her ignorant little head."

"T, kill him."

"Can't do that, Randi," Tank's deep voice rumbles.

"Think of your wife. You can't leave her. He'll kill you and then rape me," she cries.

My shoulders stiffen at that word. Sweat slips down my spine and temples from the need to kill burning through my veins and the stifling heat inside this shithole. Eyes narrowed, I shoot a glare across the room to my friend, begging him to do what that fuckstick asked.

A minuscule nod eases the grasp fear had around my chest. Smith is out there, watching, waiting. I know that, Tank knows that, but Whit does not. He thinks he has us trapped, but we might still have the element of surprise on our side.

The moment he swings that gun to me, thinking both Tank and I are unarmed and the threat's only outside these doors, Smith will take the shot.

In my periphery, Tank sets his gun on the ground, then sends it skittering across the floor with a hard shove.

Deep breath. This is it. We're both disarmed, prime targets for Whit to take the kill shot.

But the shot doesn't come.

Shifting my focus from Randi, I narrow my brows at Whit, who's still focused on me, a wide smile on his face.

"Don't look so surprised. You're worth more to me alive than dead. Plus, taking you will make that coward livid that I took your life instead of him. Serves him right for leaving before the contract was fulfilled."

Come on, move the gun. Move the motherfucking gun from her head.

All Smith needs is one clear shot and all this will be over. Once Whit is dead, the merry band of idiots along the wall will run back the way they came.

"Trailer here wasn't as... forthcoming as I hoped. Yes, you just might break what little resolve she has left."

"No." Randi's cry is a bullet to the heart as she jerks in Shawn's hold. "I'll do it, whatever you want."

"We'll see about that," he says as a new guy, walking with an air of importance, strides from an office-looking room. Whit chuckles at Tank and me on our knees. "If either of you make a move, I'll paint the walls with her blood." The new man, dressed in all black like the others, stops beside Whit and whispers something in his ear. "Good. We'll need it after all. Search those two, leave cell phones and any guns you find, and then tie them up. They're coming with us."

The man beside Whit calls out to the others. They shove off the wall, eager to do his bidding. Five march in my direction while eight or ten head for Tank.

Where did these fuckers come from? There's no way they got through the secured perimeter the military and agency have set up by now, and their laughter and sick jokes tossed back and forth would've been audible if they were here earlier, even with the thick walls of the warehouse.

Two of them scan Randi with a blatant lust-filled once-over as they pass Whit. My jaw muscle pulses from clenching to keep me from bolting off the floor and cutting their eyes out of their heads. But that wouldn't do me or her any good. I'd be dead before I stood from the floor. No, to help her, I play it safe and stay alive. I fought all morning to find my girl; I won't risk dying, leaving her alone once again.

A stolen look across the room to Tank tells me he agrees.

The five stop directly in front of me. One toes my discarded gun.

"Ten dollars." One eye squinted to block out the blinding light, I smile up at the bastard. "It's the government's, so really I'd be making money. Not like I bought it."

Brown stains coat his crooked teeth, his rank breath pungent even from a couple feet away. Stale body odor floats on the air as another one of Whit's hired hands steps closer. Features scrunched with disgust, one spits, the brown sludge splattering on the floor near my knees.

"Keep yer mouth shut, pig."

I fight the urge to roll my eyes. At least these fuckers will be easier to dispatch than trained men. With the sounds, smells, and looks of these stragglers, Whit picked them up at the local Bad-Guys-R-Us store and went for the cheapest option available.

A grunt rumbles in my chest as I'm shoved and stretched every which direction with their search for my many weapons. Four guns, two knives, and my cell phone clatter to the ground as they pat and dig down my body. When the last of the guns is tossed to the floor, both wrists are secured behind my back. Thin bindings dig into my wrists.

"Clean," one shouts before shoving a boot heel to my shoulder, sending me toppling forward. Concrete approaching fast, I twist to keep my face from slamming into the unforgiving floor.

"We leave now. The whole fucking army will be here soon."

Fragments of rock and other debris dig and scrape along my arm as I search for Randi and Whit. Hauled upright by hands beneath both armpits, I attempt to throw their loose hold. Something hard slams against my back. Grunting, I stumble forward, barely keeping myself upright.

"Move."

I barely hear the command over my harsh inhales and exhales as I breathe through the pain.

One hand firmly grips my elbow and another shoves my back, forcing me forward. I shoot an annoyed glare to Methhead Fucksticks One and Two as they drag me toward a small alcove Whit and Randi slipped into disappearing from sight.

I take the opportunity to scan for any sign of Smith. He has to be in here witnessing all this. A shift in a shadow, so minute I almost miss it myself, makes me pause. Examining the dark corner, I crane my neck to see any additional signs of our only hope.

Gray eyes reflect the light, the rest of his face remaining concealed. "Wait." My lips move without sound, a silent plea to Smith before I'm dragged between two walls. The stench intensifies a thousand percent as we cram into the tight space. Sweat slicks every inch of skin sandwiched between these two assholes.

At an opening in the floor, I'm forced to descend the wooden steps. At the bottom, loose dirt shifts beneath my boots, and a musty, stale air engulfs me. It's pitch black except for the few flashlights up ahead.

The prick at my back slams against me for the hundredth time since we squeezed down this tight tunnel. "Is that a gun, or are you just happy to see me?" I snap over my shoulder.

"Nah, pig. Just thinking about how that cunt up there will feel once we get where we're goin'."

Nope.

With a feral growl, I dip my chin before knocking back right into Fuckstick One's face. Bone cracks beneath my skull, the impact sending a vibration through my brain all the way to the tip of my nose. A howl of pain pulses down the gouged-out dirt walls. Thick tacky liquid snakes along the back of my neck, mixing with the rivers of sweat before gliding beneath the crew neck of my shirt.

Shouts erupt ahead of us, asking what's going on in the back.

"Motherfucker." A damp, coarse hair-covered arm wraps around my neck, the crook of his elbow tightening around my windpipe, cutting off my air supply. "Just for that, I'll make you watch." Spit sprinkles my ear and neck with his rage-filled words.

Stars spark in my vision as his choke hold tightens.

With both wrists secured, I'm at his mercy. Digging my heels into the shifting dirt, I lean back and twist to dislodge his hold. Pins and needles explode along my legs and fingertips.

"Enough," someone up ahead shouts. Dirt rains down from above, sprinkling my face. His sweaty-as-fuck arm loosens, sneaking in an elbow to the jaw before slipping away entirely. Not giving him the satisfaction of seeing me struggle, I inhale short gulps through my nose and release through tight lips.

A heavy hand slams between my shoulder blades, forcing me forward. A few inches separate me from the man ahead, the same with the motherfucker behind me. Blinking away the blur near asphyxiation causes, I try to focus on anything that could help us if we manage to escape these bastards.

Dirt. Below me, along the walls, above me.

We're underground.

A tunnel of some kind. A tunnel leading us far from the military force surrounding the warehouse, waiting to swoop in and save us and the president at Tank's command.

A command that will never come.

Oh hell, this is bad. Really, really fucking bad. We barely found Randi in time before they moved her to the new location. What are the odds the director and Smith can find us if Whit smuggles us out from under their noses?

At the thought of Smith, optimism flares within me, cutting through my thoughts.

There is some hope. Smith is still out there and probably saw us leave. He could be following us now, or better yet radioing to tell the others we're on the move so they can follow. It won't take them long to find the escape hatch and—

An eardrum-shattering boom blasts down the tunnel. My knees buckle at the ground trembling beneath my feet. With a curse, I lean to the right, my shoulder taking the brunt of the impact as I fall to my knees. The men in front of me all stumble and fall, some leaning against the shaking walls, others flat on their asses in the dirt. Chunks of dirt fall from the ceiling.

Ears ringing, body still vibrating, I shift along the tunnel to look the way we came only to whip back around and shield my face as best I can from the approaching cloud of dust.

Shouts of confusion cut through the ringing in my ears. I shake my head, trying to clear away the fog, coughing and sneezing from the dust tickling my nose and throat.

What the hell was that? As I lean against the tunnel wall, more vibrations travel along the dirt, but they're much weaker than before.

"Could've fucking warned us," the asshole at my back shouts, probably thinking he's whispering. "We were too close to the explosion, the fucker. I won't be able to hear for a damn week."

Explosives?

There's no way. I think back to what the one guy said to Whit, and a knowing feeling sinks my gut. He blew the warehouse. That bastard Whit never planned to leave any evidence of where he escaped to. And we—no, *I* played right into his hands.

He blew the warehouse with Smith, our only hope, presumably inside.

Now what the fuck are we going to do?

15

RANDI

Cool air chills my bare, sweaty arms and legs, goose bumps sprouting in its wake. The same steady throbbing beat that's been a constant pain drums against my skull. My lips part on a soundless cry at a simple move of my head.

But it's not just my head, or my neck, or even the sliced-up skin of my wrists and ankles. Everything fucking hurts. There isn't a single muscle, bone, or patch of skin that doesn't hurt like hell. I should come to terms with the fact that this will be my state of existence for the rest of my short life. However long that will be. Damn, that's a depressing thought. A very clear depressing thought. Of course, nothing else makes sense around me except that little ticking clock in the back of my mind reminding me my life is in danger and I might die soon.

"Thanks for the encouraging thoughts, brain." My voice is hoarse and raspy, barely above a whisper.

Each shallow breath is a hiss through clenched teeth. A quick tug of my wrists and ankles confirms both are still bound. Thin material—sheets, maybe—slides beneath my sticky cheek, the smoothness an unexpected sensation. Where am I? This is obviously different than the hotbox warehouse.

Continuing to breathe through the pain, I struggle to remember the last thing I saw or heard.

The ground trembling beneath my feet, dust and dirt pelting my face.

Someone carrying me, the stench of weed and body odor a distinct contrast to the musty scent that surrounded us.

Blinding light, welcomed fresh air. Trees. Lots of trees and men.

Shouting. A familiar voice yet filled with a rage and fear I'd never heard it hold before.

Then... nothing.

Not a single memory, just darkness and peace only oblivion can offer.

Compelling one lid open, then the other, I blink to clear the blur and focus on my new unfamiliar surroundings. Soft rays of dusky sunlight stream through a single rectangular window along the far wall, the only one on this side of the room that I can see. Unfinished walls, wires, insulation exposed, a simple concrete floor, wooden stairs leading up to a single door, and a low ceiling above. A basement, maybe? I have zero clue where I am, but at least this place has air conditioning. Even the stabbing pain radiating from my side is manageable without the suffocating heat.

"Mess."

My frantic gaze bounces around the room, searching for the owner of the hollow voice. A squeak of a mattress spring and the rattle of a flimsy metal bed frame sound as I shift to roll to my back. With a grunt, I flip, the bindings biting into my wrists with my slight weight lying on my secured hands. The white sheet slides beneath my heels as I struggle to gain leverage to flip again. Pushing and rolling my shoulders, I finally rotate to rest on my side, facing the opposite direction from before.

That's when I see him.

My eyes widen in shock at his disheveled state, but it's the sheer devastation behind his dull honey eyes that catches my breath.

"It's okay. We'll get you out of here." His tone is dull and lifeless, lacking its normal cocky arrogance.

"What's wrong?" I rasp. The sadness radiating off his slack features fuels my panic. "Trey," I beg. *Fuck, what if it's him? What if he's hurt beyond repair?* I skim his dark T-shirt and pants in search of an injury.

"Randi, I need you to focus on me." Reluctantly, I do as he asks. "Don't be scared, baby. The others will find you, but—" He swallows hard, his Adam's apple bobbing with the effort. "—I don't know when. I need you to listen to me, okay?" I nod, too transfixed on his words to utter a response. "They're going to use us against each other to get what he wants. And I need you to be strong for me, strong for you."

"I'll give it to him." My voice is as panicked as I feel. "I can't—"

"You have to, Mess. Whit is...." His eyes flick to something behind me and stare unfocused. "This is beyond what I ever imagined him capable of. I knew he was an evil son of a bitch, but this is... different. His need for revenge on you, on us.... All he can focus on is making us pay for what happened four years ago."

"I know what he wants, and I'll give it to him. He wants me to call Sam. For me to step down and have Sam select Shawn as the VP. I'll give it to him. I'll give him whatever he wants. I can't watch—"

"It's not as simple as the VP spot anymore, you know that. It might have started as that, and you getting that spot instead of him might have been the catalyst, but this is more than that. Now it's personal to him. He won't stop this until we're both...." He shakes his head. "Shawn's been planning this for a while, and it's carefully thought out and well-funded. We wondered where he's been the last year. Well, now we know. Planning all this."

"How do you know all this?"

His slight sad smile tugs at my already bleeding heart. "You were drugged during the drive here, baby. I wasn't. I heard it all, I know what he has planned for you and me. The longer they're focused on me, the better. I'll be the distraction to keep their filthy fucking hands off you and give Smith and the others time to find you."

What he's asking me to do clicks into place. Despite the sharp stab of pain in my neck, I shake my head. Locks of stiff hair fall into my line of vision. "No. I won't watch them hurt you." I can't do what he's suggesting, can't let them torture him for as long as possible, with me watching, to give the others time to find me again.

"It's not a suggestion, Randi." A sliver of my Trey, that commanding, dominant tone, hardens his voice. "I can't—" His voice cracks. "I'll do whatever it takes to keep their focus off you. I can't watch them hurt you" His shoulders slump. "I'm not strong enough for that."

"Trouble—"

"You're the one who matters, Mess. Not me. You have to live. Because if you don't, I'll be dead anyway. I don't want a life without you in it."

"Where is T?" I whisper, unsure where Shawn and the others are at the moment. T was with us earlier, that I do remember. He'll talk Trey out of this ridiculous idea. "T, where are you? Talk some sense into him."

A grief-filled sob swings my attention back to Trey. Head bowed, shoulders trembling, he doesn't look up when I whisper his name.

"What's going on, Trey?" I say louder. "Tell me what the hell is going on." I yank at the restraints preventing me from comforting him, hating them more in this moment than ever before.

"He's gone." I narrow my brows, not understanding. "Tank... Davis is gone."

"Where do they have him?" Deep down, I know what he means by "gone," but I can't go there. No, there has to be another explanation. Maybe they let him go. That's a possibility, right? Maybe Shawn realized he didn't need T for me to talk and let him walk away.

Yes, T is out there free somewhere, putting together a plan on how to save us. That's who Davis Washington is, the badass sweetheart who always has a plan.

He has to be okay.

He has to be. I won't accept any other outcome. That's how it works, right? If I don't accept that something terrible happened to Trey's best friend and Sarah's husband, then it never occurred.

"Trey?" I beg but seal my lips at the shake of his head.

The faded memory from earlier comes flooding back, this time brighter, clearer, allowing me to remember every horrid detail.

A sob shakes my chest and shoulders.

I had one part right. Shawn didn't need T for his plans for me.

Shawn's bored voice after we emerged from the tunnel slowly becomes clearer in my memory.

"Take that one and dispose of him... No, I don't care how you fucking do it...."

Then a distant gunshot.

A single shot. The kind where there's no question that the bullet killed its intended victim.

"No." My voice cracks with the surge of grief. Trey nods, still not meeting my imploring stare that's begging him to tell me it's not true. "Did you see it?" My words come fast, spilling from my lips as my mind grasps on to this one sliver of hope. "Did you see them kill him?"

"No." Trey's gruff voice is filled with the same soul-aching emotions rolling through myself. "I tried to fight them, tried to.... I couldn't do shit as they carried you in one direction and dragged him in another. I had to choose. And I chose you, Randi. Every day, I choose you. I didn't want them to take me out too, leaving you alone again with that fuckstick, so I stopped fighting back to make them think I gave up, but really I was going all in."

"For me."

"Always, Mess. It's you or nothing."

"But he's... your best friend. How could you—"

"If you're asking if it was a difficult choice, no. If you're asking if it feels like my fucking heart is ripped in two right now, yes. We all know what we're risking when we sign on with the agency. Davis knew, Grem knew, I knew. I just never expected the choice between them and you to be so easy."

A roar of voices and laughter sounds above us. Both our gazes lift to the ceiling.

"It won't be long now, Mess. We've been down here a while. I need you to stay strong. Stay strong for me, for Tae, for—" He clears his throat. "For Tank. Don't let his sacrifice be for nothing. You live."

"Live for what if you're not with me?" The jabbing pain in my side turns to more of a burn as my breaths quicken. "You think you're the only one who can't picture a life without us together? Without you? No." I shake my head with the same conviction I put in the short word.

"Did you not hear me, Randi? I'm not strong enough to watch them hurt you. Don't make me see that. Don't let that be the last thing I see."

"Same, Trouble."

"Mess." He groans. "Please. Let me do this for you. For Taeler. For our country. Let my sacrifice mean something."

Hot streams of tears track down my cheeks before dripping to the sheet.

"I don't want to do this alone," I whisper.

"Do what, baby?"

"Any of it. I finally have you, finally have someone I can depend on and who sees me. The real me and still loves me despite it—"

"Because of it, Mess. I love you *because* of the mess that you're so aptly nicknamed for."

"I love you, Trey, and I don't want to live another minute without you in it. You're it for me. Us, you and me. You promised me a future," I cry. "You promised me forever."

"I know. I know I did, and I wish I could keep that promise, Randi, but it's just not in the cards. We knew Whit was a malicious bastard after the poisonings, but I never thought—*we* never thought—he'd go to this extent. That was my mistake in underestimating how deep his hate and need for revenge ran for you." A smirk tugs at his lips. "You couldn't have chosen a less diabolical nemesis?"

"What can I say? I've always had lofty goals." I sink my teeth into my lower lip to calm the trembling. A fresh trickle of blood seeps over my tongue from the reopened split. "All this, today, the poisoning, the attacks during the campaign... all of it is because of him, wasn't it? All because I didn't want to be Kyle's wife and chose the option that helped better me, better our country."

"Oh, Trailer." I twist, a bolt of stabbing pain shooting down my spine as I crane my neck in the direction of Shawn's voice. "This is about much more than that."

The creak of wood draws my attention to the set of stairs I noticed when I first woke up. Dressed in a different pair of dark jeans and a pristine white dress shirt with the sleeves rolled to his forearms, he descends the stairs.

"This is a little overboard even for you." Rolling back to my side, I face Trey, whose whole focus is zeroed in on Shawn, the vulnerability I witnessed earlier completely gone, leaving a hard stone face in its place. "You've taken pouting because you didn't get your way to a whole new level."

"I'm not pouting," Shawn says, his voice now directly behind me. "It's called restitution, and I plan to use you two to fully recover what I've lost."

"Your mind?" I snap. "This is crazy, Shawn."

"Ah, see, that's where you're wrong. I'm focused, driven. I wouldn't expect someone like you to understand the need to recover what was taken from me."

"It was never yours to begin with. I was the reason we won. You wouldn't have made it onto the final ticket. I did that, my background and compassion for the American people. They would've seen through your fake exterior to your psycho soul and run the other way. Don't talk like winning the non-incumbent ticket was a done deal."

"We would've found a way. It was Birmingham's advisors who suspected we would lose if we didn't have someone more...."

"Trustworthy?" I pipe up.

"Common."

"I'll testify to the fact that there is nothing common about Randi Sawyer."

"Thank you." I shoot a small smile at Trey, who doesn't even notice as he tracks Shawn's movements.

"You stole the power from me, and power is everything in DC. After Birmingham chose you for a running mate, I was nothing in that damn city. Connections, business relations, everything went to shit the moment he announced you as his VP candidate. You cost me millions." The bite in his harsh voice makes me cringe.

"Sorry?" I squeak.

"Sorry?" The chuckle he gives as he rounds the bed makes me shudder. "Sorry doesn't even begin to cover what I've lost because of you. My family name means nothing now. All they see is the man who was passed over for a trailer trash whore. You made me look like a fool. Everything I've worked for my entire life crumbled at my feet that day, then again when you and Birmingham somehow won the election. Which is why you're here, to ease the suffering you caused me, my family name. Rent-a-cop here is a bonus I wasn't expecting. Two birds, one stone today or whenever we finish this. I won't lie, the idea of this extended for a few days sounds perfect to me."

"If we last that long, you arrogant fuck. She won't last another hour or two unless she gets some water. Or did you miss class that day where they taught us humans need water and food to survive?" A devious smile spreads across Trey's face. "Let me guess, your boyfriend had you bent over the bleachers that day they covered survival in science."

"Oh snap." The giggle dies on my lips at the look of fury on Shawn's flushed face, his narrowed eyes fixed on me. Terrible idea. Really the worst decision I've made in a really long time. "What? It was funny."

"You two don't get it, do you? You two won't just die down here. You will suffer—"

"Trembling in my boots," Trey says on a yawn. "About that water. Do you put an order in with room service? I'd like sparkling, flavored if you have it. Randi?"

"Plain is fine for me."

Brows raised, we turn our expectant faces to Shawn, who looks like he's about to blow a damn gasket.

"Now if you don't mind, we were having a private conversation." In dismissal, Trey turns, putting his full focus back on me. A slight twinkle in his gaze tells me he's having way too much fun pushing Shawn's buttons. We're idiots, of course, taunting a lunatic, but this is us, and I wouldn't want my last few hours of life to be without a few smiles and giggles. Trey's wink tells me he feels the same. "So back to that text I sent. What do you say? Yes or no?"

Ah, wondered when he'd bring that up. Thought maybe he'd let it slide considering our circumstances but apparently not. Such a guy, not letting the hope of anal fade just because we might die a horrible death.

"Think that's allowed in heaven?"

"Probably not. In hell, no doubt."

"Then why does anyone want to go up when down seems to be where the eternal party is held?"

"Fake news fed to us by the churches to keep us from having fun."

"Figured. Plus I'm always cold, so hell might be pleasant for someone like me."

"You mean cold-blooded."

I roll my eyes. "You've always thought that joke was funny."

"It is."

"Enough," Shawn shouts. I swear he almost stomps his foot like a petulant toddler. Someone needs to spank him, teach him not to pout and get all murder-y because he didn't get his way.

"Or what?" Trey's snort sounds as forced as the supposed calm his body radiates. "We both know you won't get your hands dirty now that you've changed. Wouldn't want to ruin that Kmart clearance rack dress shirt. Lord knows it'll disintegrate after one wash."

"It's Armani," Shawn barks.

"Darmani maybe," I quip, earning me a smirk from Trey.

"Now about that water—"

Shawn's roar drowns out whatever Trey was going to say next as he lunges, fist swinging through the air. Flesh smacks flesh, and Trey's head snaps to the right with the force of the hit. For a moment, my own heavy wheezing breaths—*note to self: that doesn't sound or feel good; Shawn could've been right about the punctured lung assessment earlier*—are all I can hear.

The spite-filled glare Trey shoots Shawn as he spits a mouthful of crimson liquid to the floor causes a blast of heat to burn in my lower belly. That promise of death in Trey's bright honey brown eyes should not turn me on, but it does. I've always said there was something terribly wrong with me.

Eh, I'm hours from an excruciating death. Not going to change anything now. Might as well revel in my messed-up fetishes.

"And look, I'm already tied up," I mutter.

"I like where your head's at, Mess." Peeking through my lashes, I find Trey's bloody lips stretched in a full smile. "Later."

"You two think this is funny?" Shawn cradles his hand against his chest, massaging the knuckles he smashed across Trey's face.

"You know what I don't get," Trey says after spitting another mouthful of blood to the floor. "The tunnel. Fuck knows you didn't dig it."

"Ah." Shawn drops his hand and sits in a chair I failed to see earlier. "You are correct there. I did not build it. I've had a very long time to plan out every detail. From hiring the best mercenary to abduct Trailer, to securing a private location with an escape route, to here. Where you'll never be seen again after I'm through with you."

"How did you get the asshole we know as Ponder on the beta team?" Trey asks.

"Ponder?" I mouth. "It was Ponder?"

Trey nods, pressing his lips into a thin line, telling me he has more to say on that topic.

"Ah, see, that was a surprise to me too. I didn't place him on her security detail, someone else did. Someone else wants her dead, whereas I wanted her... vulnerable. He was to abduct Trailer, help me ensure her compliance during our escape—"

"Is that what you call beating the shit out of me? Making me compliant?"

A shoulder rises and falls with Shawn's unconcerned shrug. "It worked, didn't it? I will admit they found you sooner than I expected, but that was why I had a plan C in place on the off chance our location was discovered before we could escape."

"That's why you blew the entrance to the tunnel—"

"The warehouse, not just the tunnel entrance. I didn't want to lead the Secret Service and FBI to investigate why I chose that warehouse in the first place, or then they'd know where the tunnel ended. See, the FBI raided that warehouse years ago. A known human trafficking ring utilized it to receive their shipments, then the tunnel to export them without anyone knowing. Not that it matters now, because even if they do discover the tunnel's exit, we're far from there now. Far from anything, actually." That icy stare narrows in my direction. "No one to hear you beg except me."

"All this for what?" I croak. "For revenge."

"No, Trailer. Like I said earlier, for restitution. Which I will bleed from your boyfriend first, then you. But don't worry, I'll make sure to take my time so you have a chance to say goodbye."

I swallow down the tears clogging my throat. "I'll do it. I'll call Sam, make him take you on as the VP. Just give me a phone. I'll make the call."

In three slow, calculated steps, he pauses in front of my face. Twisting to lean against my bound hands, I stare up at him. A wide smile splits his face —a knowing smile.

"Oh, Trailer. It's too late for that. There is nothing left, no bargaining chip you hold to stop what's to come. Not that it ever would have."

I feel my face pale. He never expected me to make that call. It was a distraction. A reason to beat me into submission and taunt me with what's to come. Fuck, I should've known that wasn't his endgame after all. There's no way it ever could've happened.

This right here, right now, was his plan all along. Me, alone and vulnerable. Trey and Tank finding me so fast just offered up a little bonus for Shawn and his evil plot. They played into his hands without even knowing it.

Now for the final stage of his diabolical plan.

Trey's death.

Then mine.

16

RANDI

Shawn's humorless chuckle seems to echo long after he climbed the stairs and slipped back through the unseen door. The entire conversation runs on repeat as I stare with glassy eyes up at the unfinished ceiling.

My hair slides along the sheets as I shift my angle for a different view of the exposed floor joists and wiring. It's that exposed wiring that holds my rapt attention.

"You know, one time when I was still living with my mom, our trailer almost caught on fire." Shifting again, I study the various rubber-coated colors differentiating the wire's purpose. "It was the burning rubber that I smelled first. Thank the unicorn gods the side window was open or I wouldn't have noticed something was off before it was too late. Two frayed wires near the electrical output we were hooked up to had caught fire, the flames slowly working their way along the rubber coating toward the trailer." Laying my cheek along the bed, I catch Trey's obvious confusion as to why the hell I'm bringing this up. "Did you know you can't put an electrical fire out with water? It has to be some kind of flame suppressant like... flour. It's only by sheer luck we'd learned about it the week before in science class."

"Ah, so you were in science class that day, not bent over the bleachers like that fuckstick upstairs." A mischievous gleam flickers in his gaze.

"No, Ben was not fucking me on the bleachers." Trey's responding possessive growl somehow eases the fear strangling my lungs. "Hey, you said it, not me."

"Don't say his name again."

"Yeah, yeah. Anyway, I bring this up because that wiring above us is exposed and runs along the wall behind you. None of the walls are finished, so everything down here is exposed."

"You're suggesting we catch the place on fire."

I attempt a shrug only to grimace as the motion tugs at my bindings. "If we had a way to cut out of these zip ties and fray the wiring without electrocuting ourselves... yeah. But we're not that lucky." If we were, we wouldn't be sitting down here waiting for our deaths.

"I might have something that would work."

"Okay...."

Trey quickly scans the room, zeroing in on the spot we last saw Shawn.

"My boot." The words are so mumbled and low, I barely make them out.

"Yes, you're wearing boots."

For half a second, that focus shifts from the top of the stairs to me. He rolls his eyes and goes back to watching for the evil incarnate.

"There's a Swiss Army knife in my boot. But I can't reach it." I eye the restraints on his wrists and ankles holding him to the chair, very similar to how they had me tied up back at the warehouse. "You'd have to roll off the bed without a sound, somehow make it across the floor to me, swing around so your hands can reach inside my boot...." Not a single dark, wet lock of hair shifts as he shakes his head.

"I'll do it." It might not work, but it's better than lying here waiting to watch my fiancé get beaten to death and then me raped to death. Yeah... I'll choose zero fucking chances of escape but will die trying than the other option any day.

Pride radiates off him. "That's my girl. Now roll off the bed—"

"I don't need a play-by-play," I hiss. "Let me concentrate."

"Sorry."

With a huff, I shuffle to the edge of the bed. Okay, so this is like playing mermaid in the community pool. I can't separate my feet. Except in that scenario, I was able to use my arms.

"Hey, Mess."

"What?" I don't hide the exasperation in my tone. "What's so important that you need to tell me now right before I smack my already beaten body to the hard floor without hands or feet to ease the impact?"

"Right, poor timing, but I just wanted to tell you how fucking hot you look."

It takes a bit of finagling, but I meet his wide, clear eyes and raise both brows in question. "Seriously?"

"Hell. Yes. You have this determined look on your face that's sexy as hell. It's the same one you get when you put those pompous assholes in the House and Senate in their place after a rude or derogatory comment."

"You notice that?"

"Have you not noticed them not coming within twenty feet of you again?"

"Yeah, I just thought they didn't like having their bigot asses handed to them by a woman."

"That and they didn't like having their bigot assess handed to them later by me and Tank to teach them a lesson on how to properly speak to our girl." A wash of sadness shifts over his features. "Right, carry on."

"He's not dead. I know it, Trey. I just know it. Have some faith in, T." I suck in as big a breath as I can stand before it causes pain. "Okay, here I go. One. Two." Before saying "Three," I roll off the bed, hoping I can somehow rotate in the three feet to land on my back and not my—

Oomph.

"Fuck," I hiss as all the air whooshes from my lungs at the impact between the floor and my chest. "That did not go like I planned."

"Are you okay?" Worry and concern fill his whispered words, keeping me from making a quip about being fucking golden despite the shard of rib that seems to be stabbing through my lung into my kidney.

"Yep," I grunt. "All good."

"You're lying," he hisses. "Fuck, I can't make you do this. You're already hurt—"

Lifting my head, I rest the opposite cheek on the ground to see in Trey's direction. The cool cement feels nice against my swollen cheek. "In case you haven't noticed, you didn't make me do anything. I'm doing this on my own because, quite frankly, I don't want to die down here and... setting this house on fire would really piss Shawn off." My lips sting as they pull into a smile. "Okay, on the count of three, I'm caterpillar-crawling over to you. One. Two. Three."

I don't move. Can't move.

"Randi?"

"Yep."

"You didn't move."

"Yeah, about that... I just needed another second."

"Baby, we don't have many to waste. I know you're hurt, and this fucking sucks since you're the one doing all the work, but if we want this to happen, you need to move."

He's right. At any point Shawn could open that door and stop our attempt to break out of this insane asylum. But everything still aches. Breathing really fucking hurts. Blinking... blinking doesn't hurt, so that's a positive to focus on.

"Flip to your back. That way you can dig your heels into the floor and use the leverage to slide your body instead of... what did you call it?"

"Caterpillar crawling. Wait, too long. Caterpillaring."

"Whatever the hell that is, it doesn't sound pleasant. On the count of three, Randi, flip. One." I bite my lip, readying to hold back a pain-filled yell. "Two." Quickening my breaths, I prepare my mind to do this, even though I know it'll hurt like a bitch. "Three."

With a muffled grunt, I rock side to side until I build enough momentum to roll onto my back. My arms and hands dig into my back and the plastic bites into my skin, but I don't dwell on any of it. Breathing fast, I bend both knees, dig my bare heels into the ground, and shove.

A soft cry escapes as the rough floor scrapes my raw skin.

"Randi, you're almost there. Just a little farther." Over and over, his soft voice and encouraging words console and inspire. Tears and sweat mix, disappearing into my hairline as I continue forcing my way across the floor.

Eyes sealed shut—concentrating on not screaming in pain takes all my focus, it seems—I don't notice that I've reached Trey until my head bumps against his leg. Slowly cracking one eye open and then the other, I stifle a joyful sob at the sight of Trey smiling down right above where I lie.

"You're doing great, Mess. Now the knife in my right boot." He taps a black boot on the floor, indicating the one I should aim for. His smiling eyes never leave mine as I rock and wiggle to place my bound hands along his shin. "It's down near the sole. You'll have to dig to find it."

It only takes a few tries to realize I'll never find it like this. Fiddling with the laces, I concentrate on slowly loosening them little by little.

"Can you wiggle the boot off?" The back of my head hits his knee as I turn to search his face.

"If you can hold on to the heel, yeah, I think I can."

My slick fingers lose the grip on the boot twice before Trey's able to work his foot free.

"Shit, I think it was the other boot."

"What?" I start to shout but quickly remember our situation. "You've got to be fucking kidding me."

"I am." That damn smirk. Oh, how I love that damn smirk and the man currently wearing it.

Grumbling a string of curses, I dip both hands into the wet boot. "Ew, it's wet. Why is it wet?"

"I'm a guy. Our feet sweat. I'm a little stressed, if you haven't noticed."

"Sweaty feet might be a deal killer, Trouble. I didn't know you had swamp feet." My fingers fumble with the loose hard plastic of the knife before scooping it up into my palm. "Got it. Now what?"

"Oh, so now you want a play-by-play?"

"Trey, I fucking swear I will sentence you to be killed by an assassin unicorn."

"You and your unicorns," he grumbles, but the lightness in his tone belays any annoyance. "Can you get it to me? Put it in one of my hands? I can open it and cut through the tie on my wrist."

"Yeah, I think so."

"I know from experience how flexible you are, Randi. I believe in you."

"Oh hell." I shouldn't be smiling, not at a time like this, but I can't help it. It's him. I should be a bumbling mess right now, terrified of the fate Shawn so clearly laid out for us, but I'm not. Instead I'm fighting, smiling, and, most importantly, hoping. And that's all Trey Benson's doing. Knowing him, he knows exactly what his words, jokes, and innuendos are doing.

And I fucking love him a little more for it.

Because we're in this together. A team.

Forever.

A warm, comforting sensation tingles up my arm as our fingers touch. The small hard plastic case falls into his palm. Before I can pull away, he closes his fist, sealing our hands together with a quick firm hold. It's over as fast as it happened, allowing me to shuffle back away from the sharp knife his dexterous fingers just flicked open.

From the knife sawing through the zip tie, to his cringing face, to the stairwell, and back again, I shift my nervous gaze as my heart races with the anticipation. *Will we get out of this in time? Will Shawn open the door now and ruin everything I just painstakingly fought for?*

A faint tap draws my attention to a long string of plastic sliced in half lying close to my bent knees.

The zip tie. The *cut* zip tie. I stare at it, amazed that it fucking worked. That hard ring of plastic with the slice through it no longer holds Trey's wrist. Or confines our freedom.

Damp palms press to my cheeks, tilting my gaze up from off the floor.

"Randi, you with me?" Trey searches my face as he kneels in front of me.

Kneels.

"You're free," I rasp.

"And so are you. Now come on, we need to fray those wires. I liked your plan of setting the place on fire. Seems a worthy exit, don't you think?"

17

TREY

This has to be the craziest thing I've ever done—setting a house on fire with me and my girl trapped in the basement. That's a bold statement considering all the shit I got into during those international trips prior to Randi. Hell, there are several countries I'm banned from ever entering again because of those... creative antics.

What can I say? I was a rich dipshit with short-term goals focused solely on women, booze, and having fun pre-Randi.

With a cautious glance to the sole door leading to the main part of the house, I say a silent prayer that this works. It has to. We don't have any other options, not with Tank....

My heart seizes just thinking his name.

My best friend, the one who's saved me more times than I can count. Gone.

Breathing becomes difficult as the weight of what happened earlier engulfs me, drowning me in waves of grief.

"Hey. Look at me, Trey." Reluctantly, I tilt my face to hers. I don't want her to see me this broken. Because that's how my soul feels. Broken. Shattered. Unrepairable. All that and more must reflect on my face as she presses a palm to my swollen cheek.

"He would've known what to do."

"We're doing okay, aren't we? We're free. Plus we don't know if he's actually gone. Have some faith in your friend. If anyone could get out of that situation, it was T."

I swallow hard. "Okay." Fingertips to the ground, I push off the cool floor to stand. Careful of her injuries, I scoop Randi into my arms and gently rest her on the chair I was tied to just moments ago. "You stay here. I'll figure out what we do next."

Not waiting for a reply, I turn on the one boot heel and wet sock toward the sheet-covered mattress. A shiver of revulsion races down my spine at the sight, keenly aware why there's a bed and she was lying on it instead of me. My fingers tighten into fists at the thought.

Nails digging into the white sheet, I rip it from the bed and wrap it around my forearm. I tilt my face to the ceiling, surveying the beams and exposed wires. Placing the igniting point far from Randi is a given, but I also need to consider that we'll need the smoke close to the door; that way when they realize what we've done and come storming in, the smoke will conceal us to a certain point. The last thing we want is for them to have a clear shot. If I start the fire and keep the smoke near the door, it could offer the split-second opportunity to disarm the first one through the door before they know what's happening.

But the smoke....

The sheet will have multiple uses today, it seems. Uncoiling it from my forearm, I use the handy-dandy Swiss Army knife to slice two wide strips. Bunching them together, I toss the small bundle to Randi's lap.

"Hold on to those. We'll use them as face coverings for the smoke."

A somewhat plan in place, I stride across the room, my one boot heel clicking with every other step, to inspect the rectangular window. A frown tugs my lips downward. It's too small for Randi to wiggle through and too high. Our only way out of here is up the stairs. Through the dozen or so armed men waiting beyond the door. Through a house I'm about to set fire to.

Not great, but it's too late to turn back now, not that I want to. As sketchy of a plan as this might be, it's still a better alternative to dying without even trying to fight.

With the remaining section of sheet, I dip beneath the wooden stairs' supports, shimmying along until I'm directly beneath the landing above. I glance from the wires to my one boot and back again. The sole is rubber, so hopefully it'll prevent me from electrocuting myself and leaving a roasted corpse for Whit to laugh over later. I just have to do all this while standing on one foot.

Fuck me.

Wire held between two fingers, I begin methodically stripping a red cord, careful to not scrape the copper wiring beneath. A spark and zap pops, jolting a bolt of electricity all the way up my arm. The wooden support beam for the stair slams into my spine as I'm shot backward, cursing. Eyeing the wire like it's a coiled snake, I sluggishly push to a crouch and start on the next wire. Again a bolt of electric current lashes through my fingers and up my arm, though this time I stay upright on my one foot like a badass, indicating I've hit the mark.

The thin sheet molds beneath my hands as I bunch it into a tight ball and cram it between two studs, situating it behind the exposed wires. Pinching the two wires between my fingers, I carefully guide the exposed sides until they're only a hairbreadth away from one another.

"Fuck, I hope this works." Grimacing and leaning my face as far away as possible, I offer up one final prayer to anyone who's listening and press the two exposed live wires together.

Blue sparks crackle and brighten. Powerful electrical currents surge up my arm and through my body. The force propels me back a couple of feet, my back once again colliding with the wooden stud with a crack. Tingles scurry along my skin while literal shimmering stars dance in my vision.

"Whoa." I cough, gripping my chest and digging the heel of my palm into my sternum. "I think my heart stopped for a second."

"Don't worry, I know mouth-to-mouth," Randi's quiet voice says, sounding closer than it should. Chin to my shoulder, I find her standing just a foot behind me, arm cradling her waist.

"You know what I've heard works better?" I cough again. Each breath feels singed and too warm to be normal.

"Do I even want to know?"

Lips numb my attempt at a smirk fails. "Mouth to dick works even better."

"Are you suggesting blow jobs save lives?"

I nod. "We should make that a slogan."

The faint scent of burning fabric turns me back to the wires that almost killed me. Finger slightly shaking, I point at the small tendril of smoke swirling upward. "Look at that. It worked."

Maneuvering around the beams Randi squats in front of the smoldering embers. Her back rises and falls as she blows a steady stream of air. Over and over she fans the small flame until a soft glow brightens the shadows cast by the ascending wooden stairs above us.

Sitting back on her heels, she glances over her shoulder. "Now what?"

A commotion above us has us both freezing. Heavy feet stop, and shouts and the sounds of a scuffle vibrate down the wall. I hold a tight breath, waiting for the door to open.

"It's not working fast enough." Fingertips to the ground, I shove to stand. "We need to give it time to really catch and a flame to build, but if they look down here and find us gone, all of this work was a waste."

"You're suggesting we go back to where they left us?" A deep line forms between her brows, her focus on the bed they dumped her on.

"But this time we won't be tied up. I can fight back when they come at me, catch them off guard."

"*We* can fight back," she corrects.

"You're hurt. I fight back. I've trained for this. I've done this. Let me do what I do best, Mess."

"And what's that?"

"Neutralize the threat by any means possible." That lust-filled fire once again flares in her hazel eyes. "I love that violence turns you on, baby. We're perfect for each other, you and me."

"Despite your sweaty feet," she adds with a smirk.

I glance down to the offending foot. "Unless you want to bat for the other team, you'll always be with someone with sweaty feet. Now come on, we need to hurry."

At the bed, I ease her down to the bare floral print mattress. The grimace of pain that flashes across her face before she can control her reaction stokes the rage already burning bright. Before, I tempered that need for violence, the need for revenge, because I couldn't do a fucking thing about it tied up.

But now I'm not.

Now I'm free and able to protect my soul's other half.

The spot under the stairs has a thin trail of smoke coming from the burnt sheet, but it's still not enough to offer the concealment we need to even the odds. I scan the room for what feels like the hundredth time in search of any accelerant that will turn the small flame into a roaring inferno.

No fluid containers, no cleaning supplies.

The only thing in this room is the bed frame, mattress, and chair.

Looks like I'll have to fight without any smoke for cover after all.

The voices upstairs grow louder, strengthening my sense of urgency.

Bending forward, I seal my lips to her hot forehead for a quick encouraging kiss.

"We've got this, Mess. Don't worry, and please, please do not interfere when shit goes down. When you see me fight back, I want you to get as far away as possible. Hell, hide under the bed if you can't get away. Don't let them grab you and use you."

"Trouble?"

"Yeah, Mess?"

"We're going to get out of this, right?"

"Yeah, Randi. We're getting out of this. The promise of anal is a hell of an incentive." I shoot her a wink as I step backward toward the chair. Settling down into the seat, I shake out both hands and roll my neck, mentally and physically preparing myself for what's to come.

"When did I agree to that?" The smile in her tone eases a part of me that thrives on her being happy and protected.

I open my mouth to respond, but the door swings open, slamming against the banister. Three members of Shawn's cheap muscle descends the stairs. A held-in snort tickles my nose. Three against one is never ideal for a fight, but these three are untrained fools, helping my odds.

The one with a pug nose sniffs the air, a line forming between his bushy eyebrows. Fuck. I need a distraction to keep their focus on this side of the room.

"Took you long enough," I shout, drawing all three men's attention. "Did you bring my sparkling water? I'm feeling a bit parched."

"He told us you'd be mouthy," one snaps. At the bottom of the stairs, he creeps closer to where Randi lies, eyes sealed shut. "Sent us down here to shut you up so he didn't have to hear it later. But don't worry, he'll be back before we break you both completely."

That sinister leer he grazes along Randi's trembling form snaps something inside me.

"So you're his bitch, is that it? Here to rough me up but not able to finish the job until your master gives the command?" Tongue to my cheek, I click it in an obvious taunt. "Fucking pathetic."

All three puff out their chests, shoulders squaring, ready for a fight. They stomp closer, the scent of something burning and the vulnerable woman both forgotten. Two flank the sides of the chair while one widens his stance directly in front of where I sit, still pretending to be tied up. His combat boots come toe to toe with....

Oh fuck.

I'm an idiot.

My motherfucking boot.

I know the moment he sees it. The boot lying haphazardly to the side of the chair leg, beside my foot. His brows narrow like its taking all his fucking brain matter to think through how my boot could be off. Behind me, I slowly flick open the knife blade and tighten a death grip on the handle until it becomes one with my skin.

Our eyes lock. Understanding finally smacks him, his features going from confusion to shock in a blink.

I'm out of my chair, the blade swinging through the air toward the bulging vein running down his thick neck before he can utter a word of caution to the other two idiots. The blade slams into his neck, slicing through his jugular, the exact target I intended. Hot red blood bubbles between my fingers, coating my hand and sliding down my wrist and forearm. With zero remorse, I jerk the small blade from his neck with a pop of suction as the metal slides free. Meaty fingers wrapped around his neck, he shoots pleading frantic glances to his two friends. Gurgling, blood spilling from his lips, he falls to his knees.

The other two are just as slow as the idiot clutching the gaping hole in his neck. With brutal efficiency, I lunge for the one on my right, aiming for his neck, while I kick out with the boot-covered foot toward the other man, connecting with his stomach. He stumbles back but stays on his feet. The other sways back, dodging the knife, the sharp blade barely skimming over his neck as he bats my hand away.

Shit.

The stiff red casing digs into my blood-slick hand as I tighten and loosen my grip to work some feeling back into my cramping fingers. I don't dare take my eyes off these two asshats to see if Randi obeyed the earlier order. My sole focus is on these two and taking them out before they're able to alert others of what's going on down here.

In my periphery, a hairy-knuckled fist flies toward my face from the side. I stoop to miss the blow but can't dodge the other man's shoulder from ramming into my stomach. I grunt from the impact and the shove of air forced out of my lungs. Wrapping him in a bear hug, I stumble backward, slamming into the other guy. A cheap shot comes to my kidney. Gritting my teeth, I keep my curses as quiet as possible. Fisting the small blade still secured in my grip, I slam it into his lower back and drag it up his spine.

His screams rattle around the room as I slice through skin and muscle, keeping the blade deep to do as much damage as possible. Something hard slams to the back of both knees, dropping me to the floor. Slick blood and sweat loosens my hold, and the knife slips from my hand, remaining embedded in his shoulder.

My knees crack against the concrete. I use the new angle to my advantage and wrap both arms around the legs of the man I stabbed and yank hard, forcing him off balance so he falls to the floor beside me. A shriek beats around the room as he falls to his back, shoving the knife deeper. The blade is too small to do too much damage, but being stabbed hurts like a bitch. Not only that but it was probably just deep enough to slice through tendons and keep him immobile with pain for a while.

A shadow descends with a warrior's battle cry. Shifting right, I roll and pop back to my feet, fists ready to defend and strike. Chest heaving, sweat streaming down my face and neck, I take several short breaths and charge the last man standing. My first punch connects with his jaw, cracking his bone and a few of my knuckles. But I push past the discomfort as I pull back to smash into his face again and again. Blood sprays everywhere and bones audibly crack and snap beneath my never-ending blows.

He drops to his knees, cries of pain and pleas to stop slipping from his blood-swollen lips, but I don't listen or care. Gripping his greasy blond hair, I hold his face toward the floor and swing a knee with as much force as I can leverage. A spray of red shoots around me like an arc.

A thrill rushes through my veins, both loving and hating the violence. I hate doing this, taking a life, but it's either mine and Randi's or theirs, and that's not even a choice.

Eyes puffy and swollen shut, nose gushing blood and cheeks split, he slumps to the floor, landing in the puddle of his own blood.

A deep groan has me turning to the last man breathing. My one boot stomps against the floor as I approach the bleeding idiot who's attempting to crawl away using one arm, the other limp by his side. With zero hesitation, I jerk the small knife from his upper back. His scream of pain is cut short on a gurgle as I slide the sharp blade across his neck.

Shoving his face to the floor, I slowly stand, wiping the blood from the knife onto my black cargo pants before flicking it back into the casing. The silence sits heavy on my conscience as the weight of taking three lives in less than five minutes settles. I press both hands to my knees, bending forward to catch my breath.

"Forgot how exhausting fighting for your life can be," I mutter, hoping it will relieve some the guilt. There was no choice but to kill them, but it doesn't make the aftermath any easier to process. "We need to get out of here. Now."

"I like that plan," says a soft voice at my side. Turning just my face toward Randi, I search her hazel eyes, looking for signs of disgust or accusations, but I only find understanding. "Come on, Trouble. Take me home."

Sliding her fingers through mine, I study our entwined hands, allowing the connection to center me. Bring me back to what's important and what I'm fighting for. And that's what will get me through the next step of escape.

Her.

Us.

Forever.

18

RANDI

Whoa. That was... intense? Not sure if that's the right word or not. A little scary, attractive in a badass way, and awesome. So is that intense? I'll have to look up the actual definition when we get back to the White House.

"Wonder if the library has a Webster's dictionary on hand."

At his hard tug, I stumble against Trey's rapidly rising and falling solid chest. From exertion or the thrill of it all, I'm not sure, but my quick pulse is definitely from the latter. Dry lips seal to my forehead, the arm around my hips holding our lower halves snuggly together.

"I love you, Randi. Even the crazy-ass shit you think."

With a smile, I steal a chaste kiss and then step back, putting some space between us before I give in to the need urging me to rip off his pants and straddle his waist.

"Come on, let's go." I nod to the door that remained closed during the fight. "Surprised no one came down to investigate the yelling."

"Those idiots were sent to rough me up before Whit does whatever he has planned. I bet they were expecting to hear some screams and yells."

"Good point." Hands on my hips, I slowly turn 360 degrees, my bare heels swiveling easily on the concrete floor. "That door is the only way out, and our fire isn't anything to write home about. So what're our options now?"

At his silence, I check over my shoulder and find him considering the mattress.

"*If* this is an older mattress, then it will be extremely flammable. We could use it to help with the smoke cover."

One hand in the air, I offer it up for a high five. When he simply laughs instead of returning it, I slap my other hand against the raised palm, high-fiving myself.

"You know that's seven years bad luck to leave someone hanging like that."

"I think that's breaking a mirror," he replies on a chuckle as he tugs on and laces up his black boot.

How in the hell we can have this conversation in this moment is beyond me, but it's distracting. And I desperately need it before I implode from the pain and stress. I know the odds of us making it out of here alive, and they aren't good. There are more of them than there are of us, and right now it would be like shooting fish in a barrel.

"Let's do this, MacGyver." I barely have a chance to grip the other side of the thin mattress when his hand connects with mine, batting me away. With a grunt, Trey hauls it over his shoulder, carrying it on his own. I gnaw on a chipped nail, the sharp edges poking into my tongue and gums as I watch his fine ass flex with each step he takes. "You should wear cargo more often."

"Focus, Mess."

"I am focused." I offer a smile when he glances over his shoulder. "On your cute ass."

The mattress thumps against the wall, covering the area that's still slightly smoking. Ignoring my comment, he crouches between the wall and mattress.

"Want some help blowing?" I shuffle from foot to foot, my anxious gaze darting from above the door to directly below it, where Trey attempts to stoke our measly fire.

"Sure. You are a good blower. I know this from experience." He tilts his head up, a wide mischievous smile on his blood-splattered face.

"Thanks?" On tiptoes, I maneuver around the stairs' supports and squat beside Trey. The T-shirt's damp fabric slides beneath my chin as I rest it on his shoulder. I inhale deeply, pushing past the tightness in my lungs and the ache in my ribs before letting out a steady stream of breath directly toward the glowing, charred sheet.

We alternate stoking the growing flicker until it's bright orange end dances close to the dingy floral cover of the mattress. Crossing my fingers and toes, I watch with hope and fascination as the fabric melts with the heat. Foul-smelling black smoke rises from the burn marks, floating up and over the edge of the mattress.

Additional smoke billows upward as the mattress finally catches and burns without our assistance.

Trey turns with a proud smile, the tips of our noses brushing.

"Well done," I whisper. Reaching out, I wipe a few speckles of blood from his cheek. "I knew you'd save me."

"I'll always come for you, Randi. Always." A frown dips his lips. Unable to stop myself, I place a soft kiss to each corner. "I tried to get to you sooner. It was actually Vlad who gave us the coordinates to the warehouse. Ponder covered—"

"Ponder," I huff. "I knew I recognized that voice."

A profound line forms between Trey's dark brows. "How did you not know it was him? Was he not at the warehouse with Whit?"

I nod, the small movement rolling my brain around my skull. "He kept his face covered the entire time. But I knew I recognized the voice and figured out he was an agent at some point. I haven't seen him since Shawn had him smack me around to make me compliant or whatever the hell he was trying to achieve."

Trey's face hardens. Placing a palm to his cheek, I shake my head, wanting to chase away the self-accusing thoughts I know are rolling through his mind because he didn't get there sooner. "Besides a few bruises, I'm fine. You came for me, Trouble. I didn't let them break me because I knew, I *knew* without a doubt you'd find me. And look, here we are about to turn the tables on the asshole." Sitting back on my heels, I give him a smile that probably looks like a grimace. "We really need to get out of here though. I need to get back to work."

"Everyone is looking for you. It's the first time I've seen all the different agencies work together for a sole focus."

"What about Sam?"

"They moved him to a bunker the moment we realized you were taken."

"Taeler?"

"What do you think?"

"Hysterical." My laugh turns into a groan. Wrapping a protective arm around my waist, I offer a small smile. "Think this is enough cover for you to do your Rambo act?"

"Rambo act?" Bones and joints crack as he stands. Hands on his hips, he towers over where I still kneel. Heat flares behind those honey eyes as he reaches forward to run a hand over my matted hair. "Fuck, Mess. Even with your face bruised and swollen, you're beautiful."

The sound of stomping boots and shouts snaps his attention above us.

The hand cupping the back of my head glides forward, dangling in the air between us. Slipping my hand into his, I allow him to pull me up. He wraps both arms around my shoulders, tugging me into a gentle hug.

"I need you to find cover wherever you can find it and make a break for it the moment you get a chance. Once you're out of this fucking house, do not stop running—"

"What about you?" His sweat-slick shirt sticks to my chest and cheek.

"I have unfinished business with that psycho upstairs."

"That sounds ominous," I say as I pull back to see him staring straight up, almost like he can see through the landing, past the door, and into the rest of the house.

"I'll enjoy killing him."

That should not be a turn-on.

"Something is really wrong with me," I mutter as I step out of his hold.

"That makes two of us, because I'm so fucking hard it hurts." I track the movement as he grips his cock over those sexy pants. "If I thought we had time, I would've kept you on your knees for a little longer. Now repeat what I said."

"You're so hard it hurts." My voice is deeper than usual, husky with the need pumping through my veins and tightening my gut.

At his chuckle, I rip my stare from his crotch to find a wide smile splitting his face. "Not that, Mess. The part about you running and not looking back."

"Oh, right. Take cover, run, don't look back. Got it."

I open my mouth to tell him not to damage anything important only to have a billow of smoke fill my nose. I inhale on instinct, and the poisonous smoke burns through my nostrils and down my throat. Immediately my lungs revolt, sending me into a full-fledged coughing fit. Each flex of my abs attempting to force the smoke from my lungs sends stabbing pain blasting through every muscle.

Eyes watering, I blindly follow where Trey directs me with a firm hand pressed to my lower back. Soft material wraps around my face twice, covering my nose, mouth, and neck. Using the edge of the clean material, I wipe at my eyes and blink to clear my vision.

The sight of Trey with the white sheet wrapped around his face, only exposing his eyes, startles me. I know it's not Ponder, I know that, but my subconscious apparently now freaks out at any face covering.

I step back, and my calves slam against something hard, knocking me off balance. I whirl my arms through the air as I tilt backward. In a flash, Trey is there. An arm locks behind my back, steadying me on my feet. Something like concern flashes in his narrowed eyes as he moves back, giving me space.

"I'm sorry—"

The words disappear as a rain of gunfire and male voices sounds upstairs. The distinct crack of rapid-fire shots booms through the empty room as a war seems to have broken out in the upper part of the house. A ground-trembling blast rattles my bones and has me seeking out Trey for answers. Without a word, he grips my hand and gently tugs me toward the base of the stairs.

"Sounds like our friends are here." The words are distant, muffled through the layers of sheet around his mouth. "Thank fuck. Keep your back to the wall."

The wooden studs dig into my back every few feet as I follow Trey up the stairs. He pauses at the landing. At his concerned glance over his shoulder, I shoot him a thumbs-up with my free hand. Fine lines crinkle at the edges of his eyes as he shakes his head.

"I'm going through first. You stay back until the firefight dies down, and then you make a break for it. We didn't go through all this for you to get shot."

"Good talk," I mutter.

"I love you."

Those long finger slip from my grip as he positions himself in front of the door, hand white-knuckling the metal knob. After several deep inhales, Trey yanks the door open.

The ear-rattling noise amps to a deafening level. Without glancing back, Trey slips through. A second later, a body sails through the doorframe, his back slamming to the wooden railing with a thud. The entire staircase shudders with the impact. Blood gushes from his nose, and thin rivers cover his arms and neck, but still he struggles to stand, a gun dangling from a limp hand.

Time freezes as his gaze lands on me. The earlier fear vanishes, turning calculating. With more strength than just a few moments ago, he grips the railing and hauls himself to a somewhat standing position.

A fury-filled roar snaps both our heads to whatever's happening outside the door.

My hero in black storms through, boots stomping toward the man. Without hesitating, Trey slams the heel of his palm against the other man's chest, sending him toppling over the railing into the puffs of dark smoke still rising from below. His bellow of protest cuts short with a hollow-sounding thump. I don't dare look over the railing to see if he's dead.

"Come on." Trey extends a crimson-covered hand, the other now gripping a black handgun. "Time to bust out of this joint."

My knees tremble, leg muscles feeling more like noodles than something that can actually support my weight. I cringe as another round of shots sounds behind my back, where the firefight is still going strong.

"I can't," I whisper. The words are nearly silent with the covering over my mouth, so I shake my head so he knows. I'm weak—mentally and physically. The strain from the last twenty-four hours is finally coming to a head. I've held on as long as I can, but all my fight is gone.

Tugging off the sheet from around his face, he nods. "Okay, baby. I'll help you."

Careful to keep his movements slow, Trey steps closer. Blood-coated fingers pull at the sheet, causing it to lower and then pool around my neck. Mindful of my injuries, he scoops me in his arms and holds me tight to his chest. "I've got you, Mess."

I slide my forearms over his sweaty neck, interlacing my fingers at his nape to help me hold on. Not wanting to see the chaos we're walking into, I press my nose to his chest and seal both eyes shut.

Then we're moving. Each of his heavy steps jostles me in his arms, but I stay silent despite the agony it causes. The shouted commands, cries of pain, and blasts of large guns assault my ears. I press one ear to Trey's collarbone and attempt to cover the other with a raised shoulder.

A muffled curse has me peeling my eyes open to see what's happening.

Bleeding bodies litter the floor. The heavy scent of gunpowder and blood fills my nose. My stomach rolls, but I swallow back the nausea. We're in what looks to be an unfurnished dining room when Trey turns, taking us into another section of the house.

One of Shawn's douchebag guys tucks into the room at the same time, his focus out the window. He catches our movement, doing a double take.

I watch in horror as the gun between his extended hands swings our way. It only makes it halfway before an ear-shattering boom rings out. He folds to the floor, the gun clattering beside him. Eyes wide, ears ringing, I search the room and beyond for the shooter who saved us when I find the hand beside my shoulder gripping a smoking gun.

"Wow," I say. Or I think I say. Hard to tell when one of your eardrums is busted.

Keeping the gun raised, Trey restarts our trek through the house. Every so often he hides us around a corner, keeping us out of the direct path of the firefight or from others' view. He does all this, fighting our way to freedom, while mumbling all the dirty-ass things he wants us to try once we're out of here and back at the White House.

The frequency of shots slows, creating a bubble of hope in my chest that the terrifying day is almost done. A long hall looms ahead of us, a door at the end with the top glass shattered. Trey takes a step down the hall, then another. The door busts open, the wood splintering at the hinges before falling to the floor with a loud crash. I shout in terror, curling closer into Trey as men dressed in all black and armed to the teeth pour through the door like ants at a picnic.

I knew this was too good to be true. We're not making it out of here alive. I'll die in this hellhole. Panic rising, I barely hear Trey's shouted words over my own thundering heart.

"Was wondering when you special boys would join the party," Trey says above me. His arms relax a fraction, the gun barrel dipping to the floor.

No one responds to his quip as they continue streaming past us, marching through the house and rounding each corner gun first in a uniform precision only military training can perfect.

Ten feet from the door, I relax my near choking grip on Trey's neck. Half-moon indentions and a few slices from broken nails mark his skin.

Five feet from the door, I breathe easy, accepting that it's all over and we're safe.

Three feet from the door, a massive shadow lengthens down the parquet hall floor as a mountain of a man blocks our exit.

Trey trembles behind me, a silent sob catching in his throat.

Me? My smile is so wide all the cuts along my lips reopen, but I don't give a damn. Happy tears leak from my eyes.

"I told him you weren't dead."

19

RANDI

T smiles wide as he holsters the gun into his shoulder harness. Trey's heart thunders against my side, his grip tightening a fraction, putting pressure on my hurt ribs. A pushed breath hisses through my clenched teeth as I fight through the pain; Trey's too focused on his best friend being alive to notice he's nearly squeezing me to death.

"Why don't you pass her over to me," T murmurs, keeping his attention on Trey. "I'll get her to the ambulance that's waiting."

"You're here." Tipping my chin up, I try to read Trey's expression. "The fuck?" He barks a laugh. "I saw them—"

"It's a long story, but yeah, I know what you saw, Benson. Now hand me the president, because Smith and I have a present waiting for you."

At the mention of the other agent, I turn back to the door. Smith now stands beside T, leaning against the doorframe dressed in similar tactical clothing as the small army still sweeping the house.

The house that smells like death and smoke.

Smith's nose twitches as those all-seeing eyes scan the house like he can see through the walls. "Did you set the house on fire?"

I attempt a shrug, but Trey's tight hold prevents the movement. "That was my idea."

"Of course it was." T sighs.

"What's my present?" Trey asks above me, curiosity in his tone.

"Hand over the president and I'll show you." When Trey doesn't make a move to pass me off, T sighs. "You've protected her, got her out alive, but we need to get her checked out by a doctor. I'm sure some of that dried blood is hers, right, Madam President?"

His pointed tone urges me to respond. "Uh, yeah?"

"And you need to see a doctor, right?"

"Yes?"

"And you'll be safe and protected if Benson here puts you in the ambulance and lets them look you over."

"Well, yeah. T, just spit it out. What are you getting at?"

"Look at him, Randi. Really look at him." With a sigh, I do as he asks. Scanning Trey's blood-streaked face I don't see anything off—well, besides the blood—until I reach his honey brown eyes. There's a wildness swirling, one I haven't seen before. "He's not himself, not after seeing... hell, I don't want imagine what he saw or did to keep you alive."

"Thanks. And yeah, it was rough, but he was fine until now. Trey?" Leaning closer, I place a hand on his chest, allowing his natural heat to soak through to my palm. "I'm good now. You got us through it all, but now I need to get my ribs checked out." For the first time since we left the basement, his entire focus shifts to me. "Remember my ribs? They hurt like hell, and I'm pretty sure I have a concussion. My thoughts are way more random than normal, even for me." I offer him a small smile. "I'll be fine. Just let me down, okay?"

Earlier I needed him to be strong for me. To carry me when I couldn't fathom going another step, feeling too weak to carry on, even if that meant safety. Freedom. Now I need to be the strong one and help him let me go. I don't want to—I want to stay in these safe arms forever—but I know that's what he needs.

"Mess." His voice is ragged. "I can't let you go just yet. I'll take you."

"Okay, Trouble." Turning to T and Smith, I dip my chin. "Lead the way, boys."

Against my better judgment, I take a deep inhale the moment we clear the threshold and step out onto the small wooden porch. Enormous trees surround us, a thin gravel driveway the only break between them. Above us, the thump of several helicopter blades fills the early evening air. Pale pinks and blues highlight the sky in a peaceful feel that contradicts the twenty or so SWAT vehicles and SUVs surrounding the cabin.

Trey clomps down the few stairs, his hold tight to keep me from jostling around. We stay close to T as he leads us through the crowd of people now staring. In true Randi fashion, I hold up both thumbs like the idiot I am.

The small gesture cracks the ice surrounding Trey. The deep lines along his forehead lessen; the concern and focus surrounding his narrowed eyes lifts. His footsteps smooth, his strides slow to a less urgent pace. Against my shoulder, I feel his chest balloon out with a deep inhale.

T directs us to the red ambulance, its lights still flashing, where two familiar faces wait.

"Oh goodie it's Bert and Ernie," I grumble.

The back doors are already open when Trey pauses in front of the doctors. Inside, another team of medical personnel stares, eyes wide. Based on their expressions and those we just passed, I must look way worse than I realize.

Bert... or maybe Ernie... whoever steps forward, gesturing inside the ambulance. Trey's hold tightens a fraction.

"Why don't you sit with me?" I offer as I tug on Trey's shirt to gain his full attention. "And then you can find out what present T and Agent Smith have for you. I bet it's a unicorn."

"That would be a present for you, not me. Come on, up you go." A heavy breath pushes over my matted hair as he steps into the ambulance and squats low, maneuvering past the awaiting medical staff and stretcher.

Sighing in relief, I close my eyes, anticipating him lowering me to the stretcher.

But he doesn't. Those arms cradling me to his lean chest don't loosen a fraction as he sits down on a bench. Shifting, he leans against the shelves of supplies, his hold never wavering.

"Sir, we need—" Ernie says as he wrings his thin fingers, glancing from me to Trey.

"Do what you need to do, but she's staying right here." A *thunk* reverberates around the ambulance as Trey slams the stolen gun to the bench. "Do we have a problem?"

"No, no problem, Agent... Agent—"

"Benson," I chime in. "Agent Benson."

"Right, okay. Well, let's see what we have here," Bert says as he steps into the ambulance and shuffles toward us.

He stills at Trey's inhuman growl.

"Agent Benson, we need to—"

"Her," he grunts and nods toward the quivering female medic in the back. "Not you, not him. Her."

"Okay, big boy," I say, softly patting his chest. I shoot T a panic-filled glance, which only earns me a shoulder shrug. "Seriously, T. Help me out here."

"I would, but I'd be doing the same thing with my Sarah. Let him have this, Randi. Once he feels comfortable, he'll be back to the same old idiot we know and love."

"If I weren't in so much pain and at the point of near exhaustion, I'd balk at this behavior, Trey Benson." I jab a finger to his sternum to let him know I mean business. But the answering smirk tells me he sees through my bravado. "Okay, fine, I love it." Shifting to face the still terrified female medic, I extend both arms, palms up. "Do your worst."

"Or best."

"Right." I tilt my head toward Trey. "What he said."

Her hands shake as she takes mine. "Madam President—"

"Randi, please. I'm covered in blood. I think we're past the formalities."

"Um, right, Randi. Let's start with what hurts the most, and then we'll do a full-body scan and workup when we get to the hospital."

"Um, okay, so let's see here. It hurts to breathe. Seriously, every breath feels like someone is stabbing an ice pick into my lungs. Not fun. Oh, and my ears are ringing from Rambo behind me shooting his gun too close to my ear."

"Saving our lives, I'd like to add."

"Noted. What else? Oh, I think a few teeth are loose, my head feels like there's a high school marching band tryout bashing and clashing in my skull, and there's something going on with my pinkie toe."

Everyone in the ambulance glances at my feet. I wiggle the sore toe.

"Yep, that one. Other than a few cuts, bruises, and maybe a busted kidney or two, I'm good."

Her long dark lashes slowly lower in an exaggerated blink.

Awesome. This should be fun. And quick.

After what feels like fourteen and a half hours later, my ribs are wrapped and not broken—yay, me—most of the blood is cleaned off my arms, legs, and face, and all the cuts have been cleaned and bandaged. My pinkie toe is broken. Sadly there's nothing they can do about that; it just has to heal on its own.

Sitting on the bumper of the ambulance, I stare at the tiny swollen appendage, feeling sorry for the little guy. During the exam and treatment, Trey loosened his death hold and slipped out of the ambulance. Well, after he put approximately forty heavily armed men around the mobile hospital and a few snipers sprinkled about for good measure.

Men.

Overprotective men.

But let's be honest: I fucking love it. His firm yet gentle hold keeping me safe while they worked on my bruised and broken body had me hot and ready for him to take me on the stretcher even with people watching.

A few happy tears might have slipped out as I watched him and T hug. It was beautiful. Not that I'd ever tell them that. At least not today. No, I'll use that later when they're not expecting it or still riding the emotional high the last day has brought.

Even now, with the last of dusk slipping into the night, those two talk, Smith awkwardly the third wheel but adding in a few jabs and comments when he can.

Maybe it's because of today, everything I went through and stayed strong. Or seeing these three talking and laughing despite it all. But right here, with the warm metal digging into the backs of my thighs and my body covered in bandages, I know two things.

Trey is it for me.

And I want to run for another term.

It'll take its toll on us. He'll have to step down from the Secret Service and become a full-fledged First Husband—the first one ever. But today proved to me that we can handle it. That with the help of our friends, and the US military, FBI, and Homeland Security, we can make it through anything.

"I don't want to quit just yet."

Trey turns, his hand gripping T's shoulder. "Was wondering when you'd figure that out." A loud *smack* bounces through the trees as Trey slaps T's back. "Okay, I'm good. She's... taken care of for now. What's this present or surprise or whatever you said you had for me?" Trey rubs his hands together, brows raised and excitement radiating off him.

"Should they look you over first?" I toss out, knowing full well what the response will be.

"Nah, I'm fine. Just a few bruises. Nothing that won't heal on their own."

I roll my eyes to the pink and blue sky.

"We have Whit," T states as calmly as discussing the weather.

That gets my attention and overrules any annoyance at Trey's macho behavior.

"What?" he and I say at the same time.

That name. Just hearing it has my heart racing. My hands tighten on the ambulance bumper, the metal digging into my palms and fingers. I shoot Trey a panic-filled glance. Seeing my distress, he strides over to where I sit and drapes a protective arm over my shoulder.

"You're okay, baby," he murmurs into my hair. "He won't hurt you again." Standing tall, he faces T and Smith, who are grinning ear to ear. Yes, even Smith is wearing a smile. There's something off about both though, almost evil or vindictive in a way.

I lean against Trey's hard thigh. "What do you mean, you have that son of a bitch?"

Smith clears his throat directing our focus to him. "He means we caught the pussy trying to escape out the back when we attacked that shithole behind you. And we... kept him just over there for you to handle."

"Handle?" Trey's bicep tightens, curling me to his side. "Any way I like?"

"Any way you like. As long as I get a few... words in too." T sneers. "That bastard ordered my execution, and I'd like him to know how much I didn't appreciate that."

My shoulder vibrates with Trey's chuckle. "I can do that. Where?"

"Why not in the house that's on the verge of burning? Less evidence to clean up." I gape at Smith. He offers a half shrug. "Just trying to be practical. Cleaning up evidence is a bitch, and I'm too tired to deal with that today."

I bark a laugh that turns into a groan. "I don't know if I've ever heard you this talkative. What happened while I was... detained?"

"A lot," Trey says above me. "A whole fucking lot. But we can talk about that and how in the hell Tank cheated certain death later. Right now, I want to go have that chat with Whit."

He starts to pull away only to hesitate.

"I'm fine. The doctors are right. I need to get to the hospital." I go to chew on a nail only to taste dirt, ash, and blood. "Fuck. I need to set up a press conference, have my press secretary alert the media that I'm okay, talk to Sam, call Todd to reach out—"

"Benson didn't tell you?" T questions, running a hand over his bald head and giving me a reluctant look.

"Tell me what?"

"Didn't really have time while we were devising an escape plan and I was dying a bit inside at the thought of my best friend being shot in the fucking head."

"Damn, you're dramatic." T sighs, but a small smile tugs at his lips. "Your secretary of state is dead."

"What?" I shout. Things still around us, all eyes focused on me as I shove off the bumper. "What are you talking about? Why? I mean…." I sway from the jolt of pain that shoots through me at the sudden movement. "I need more painkillers to handle this."

Like magic, two white pills appear in a small outstretched hand. Without even looking to see who that hand belongs to, I swipe them from the open, slightly sweaty palm, pop both into my mouth, and swallow. The pills irritate my raw throat, but at least the four bottles of water I drank in the ambulance while they fixed me up soothed some of the scratchiness.

"I'll tell you everything after we're done," Trey says, rubbing a hand down my back.

"Agent Benson, we really need to get her to the hospital for a full-body scan in case of internal injuries," Ernie says nervously no doubt worried about Trey's reaction.

Patting Trey's chest, I sigh. "Trouble, you and the other two go do what you need to do. I'll be safe. We'll even take a helicopter instead of the ambulance if that makes you feel better."

And me too. Not really excited about the idea of being in an automobile again anytime soon.

Trey smiles before sealing a hard kiss to my forehead. "Love you, baby. I'll tell everyone to follow you out. With ten special forces teams surrounding you, I feel good about letting you go on ahead. I'll meet you at the hospital."

With a nod to the other two, he turns and follows their lead into the woods, T already shouting the orders for the units to follow the ambulance to the hospital.

The first dose of painkillers kicks in, making my thoughts fuzzy as I watch the three disappear.

At least that's what I'm blaming my wayward thoughts on.

Because there's no other reason for me to think about his hot ass and how badly I need him inside me all while he marches off to kill a man.

Yep, totally the painkillers.

Maybe.

20

TREY

Last fall's dried and decaying leaves crunch beneath my feet as I trail behind Smith and my best friend. I'm not looking at where I'm going. No, my focus is on that brilliant bald head. I thought... I really thought I lost him. Thought Tank was a casualty of this job and I'd have to beg Witness Protection to take me in order to avoid Sarah's wrath.

But now I don't because he's here—alive. How the fuck that happened, I still don't know.

"You stashed him in the woods?" I duck under a low-hanging evergreen limb, the stiff needles scraping across my bare forearm.

"If no one knows he's missing, then no one will have anything to report."

I scoff at Smith's remark, making him pause. "Guessing that was your idea? No way in hell the big guy would ever break rules. Believe me, I've tried to get him to loosen up, but it never happens."

"Things change when a man looks you straight in the face and, without giving two shits, tells his skunk-ass boys to kill you." The growing shadows from the dipping sun and tree cover keep me from reading Tank's face. "But still." He turns with a smile. "You're right, it was his idea."

"Fucking knew it. You owe me a drink." Swiping a twig from the ground, I launch it at Tank's head. "In all seriousness, I'm glad you're not dead. Thanks for living."

"You have this bastard to thank for that." He hooks a thumb in Smith's direction. "I was good as dead being tied up and surrounded. Then he showed up, taking them all out before they even knew what was going on."

"How—"

"I saw you go through the escape tunnel and figured if the man orchestrated the abduction of the president and held her hostage without a single slipup, then he had an escape scenario in place in case we found him before he was ready," Smith says like it's no big deal.

"You knew he would blow the warehouse." As we step into a small clearing, I quicken my steps to walk beside Tank. "Hey, bestie."

"Don't make this awkward," Tank says on a sigh.

"I figured he would blow the warehouse or the tunnel, leaving me shit out of luck or dead. And considering neither was a scenario I was good with, I followed the last guy through the tunnel." Smith swings the assault rifle over his shoulder, allowing it to hang from the strap. "The dumbasses didn't even think to turn and look to see if they were followed."

"That must have put you near the explosion itself."

He nods. "I've had worse. Can't hear out of my right ear, but I'm guessing that will come back eventually."

Lifting the hem of my T-shirt, I wipe my forehead and upper lip. "Where the fuck did you guys leave Whit? North Carolina?"

"Just past the clearing. Stop whining. We did something nice for you." Tank shoves my bicep hard, sending me staggering a few feet to stay upright.

"You're the best gift giver, Tank. My fiancée's nemesis in chains—"

"Rope. We were fresh out of chains." I smirk at Smith's response. Maybe he'll fit in with us after all. Now that I know what I know, he's not half bad. I didn't realize how my suspicions had dampened how I acted around him.

"Either way, you caught him and tied him up for me to dispose of." I clap a hand on Tank's wide shoulder. "It's better than a blow job on Christmas morning."

"You're sick." Tank shakes his head but can't hide his growing grin.

"You love me." Letting go of his shoulder, I begin to crack the knuckles on one hand before moving to the other. "So you followed us through the tunnel, popped out—""

"Snuck out," Smith cuts in. "I'm not a damn bunny."

"Right, snuck out, saw what was about to go down with Tank, and killed everyone before freeing him and following us." I run through the events in my mind, but the details don't match up with my memory. "I only heard one shot. Do you have a silencer?"

Smith holds up his agency-issued nine millimeter in one hand and the silencer in another. "Standard issue from Homeland."

"Fuck, I knew those bastards get all the good toys." I reach across Tank to grab it from Smith's hand only for him to jerk it out of my reach just as my fingers graze the smooth metal. "Can you get me one?"

"Maybe."

"Maybe? Come on, help your fellow amigo out."

At the edge of the clearing, we pause. Tank raises his hand, finger pointed into a thick cluster of trees. I follow his line of sight to a man slumped forward, upper body tied to a tree. Two special forces boys stand guard, their guns pointed at Whit's head.

"Amigo?" Smith's question sounds distant as the anger and fury from the last twenty-four hours come roaring back, demanding an outlet.

"Three amigos, that's us. Now if you'll excuse me." I shove past Tank only to be yanked to a stop. I glare at his hold on my wrist. "Let go."

"We do this back at the house, remember?"

"Right. The house. I want him to pay, Tank. Pay for every second he had her, for every cut and bruise. Every foul word he said and every damn fear he implanted in her mind. Is there a punishment that will get back the last twenty-four hours?" I rake a shaky hand through my hair. "He took her. Hurt her. He hurt what's mine."

"I have a few ideas," Smith tosses out. His words hang on the air.

My tight lips curl in a sinister smile. "I knew I always liked you." Swiveling back around, I slow my long strides toward the man I'm desperate to kill.

No, not kill.

Torture.

Even that might not be enough for him to pay for what he did to Randi.

But I've never been a quitter.

One way or another, I'll extract my pound of flesh from this bastard and savor the knowledge that his last hours of life were terrible. Just like he had planned for Randi and me.

Fair's fair, after all.

THE RETURN TREK takes longer than the initial hike through the woods due to the dead weight I'm dragging. Already exhausted thigh and calf muscles scream and burn with each grueling step, almost giving out completely as I take the last back porch stair. Pausing, I swipe at the rivers of sweat pouring down my forehead and neck, scanning the now empty and quiet clearing.

Fuck, even with the sun down it's hot as Hades. Guess I should get used to it considering I'll be spending eternity in hell after what I'm about to do. Well, I guess you could say this is my final nail in the coffin, so to speak, on which direction I'll go when I kick the bucket. I'm no angel by any means, but murdering a man in cold blood because he hurt the one you love... well, I'm pretty sure that's a big no-no for the holy one upstairs.

The gagged Whit twists at the end of the rope, trying to break free, the end clutched in my hand swinging back and forth with the movement. A hard flick turns the loose part of the rope into a makeshift whip. It slaps across his scratched and dirty face.

None of us wanted to carry shit-for-brains here. That left us with the only way to get him back to the small cabin being to drag him. Through the woods. Over every rock, stump, and a few piles of animal shit if the smells wafting off him tell me anything.

"Need help?" I shake my head at Smith's question but immediately turn it into a nod. "Thought so. Beating a man to death takes a lot of energy. You need to conserve."

"Thanks?" It's an odd way to show support, but this whole situation is fucked, so I'll go with it.

Tugging Whit's leash from my now raw and rope-burned palm, he hauls Whit through the remains of the splintered back door.

Both arms stretched high, I tip my head back and take in the star-filled sky.

"You don't have to do this," Tank says behind me.

I stare at the brightest star I can find and think over his words. Swallowing, I nod. "Yeah I do. I'm just fucking terrified by how much I'm looking forward to it." Dipping my chin, I level a concerned look at my best friend, who wears the same expression. "Does that make me the same man as him? Or Ponder?"

"You already know the answer to that, Benson. You know you're not, just like I'm not. This fucker deserves everything he's about to get. It's not just about tonight, or this past year, or the year before that. The torment and constant targeting of Randi makes him dangerous. If he leaves here today, she's not safe, and neither are you. We do this tonight to protect her. To protect all of us."

As the words sink in, I slowly nod. "You're right." His wide stance blocks my entry into the house. "But if I get carried away, I want you to stop me. Pull me back."

Tank dips his chin in agreement, then turns and marches over the pieces of broken wood and shattered glass. I follow hot on his heels.

In the living room area, I pause, taking in the lack of bodies littering the floor. Large dark red blood lakes mark the floor but no dead assholes.

"What did they do with all the dead pricks?" I ask absentmindedly as Smith secures Whit to the decorative column dividing this space from the dining room

"The basement," Smith responds. "We get to light this place up and ensure it burns to the ground when we're done with him."

Stepping back, he slams a fist into Whit's face. Whit's knees buckle with the force, leaving him hanging limp from the rope around his chest and shins. He hisses and glares at the man who dared hurt him.

Smith nods at the bindings and steps back. "Sorry, wanted to test the knots and make sure they held."

"Maybe I should try too," Tank offers, stepping forward without waiting for our approval. I cringe away from the sound of crunching bones under Tank's fist colliding with Whit's ribs.

"How does it feel?" I ask. Each step is calm, calculated as I move closer to the now wheezing Whit. "Broken ribs, that is?" When he doesn't respond, I nod toward the gag that keeps his words muffled. Tank yanks it away the cloth tearing from Whit's teeth. "Randi lived with it for hours. Wonder how long you'd last with the pain."

"You'll never be able to save her," Whit says, his voice high-pitched, borderline hysterical. "I wasn't the only one who put a hit out on her. She'll be dead before the end of the year."

"And you'll be dead before the end of the hour." My words are confident, but worry churns in my gut. He could be lying, but something tells me he's not. "What do you know about the other hit?"

A dark chuckle rattles from his throat before turning to a cough and wheeze. "Like I'd tell you. Trey fucking Benson. You never could cut it in our world, which is why you did this." A sneer pulls at his lips as he glares at me with the one eye not swollen shut. "You fucking losers deserve each other."

"Tell me how you did it all. How you managed to coordinate the abduction of the president of the United States." My voice is steady, calm. Too calm. It sounds eerie to my own ears.

Whit only sneers back instead of responding.

"Fine. Any question that goes unanswered will come with a penalty." I nod at Tank, who's massaging his knuckles like he's warming them up for the next hit. The big guy has to be careful or he'll kill Whit with one blow.

Whit smiles. Blood coats his normally perfect white teeth. The various cuts from the forest floor have dried, leaving flaking crimson streaks all along his face. "Fuck you and that cunt you fuck. You both deserved everything you got today. Only thing better could've been you watching some of those dirty bastards fuck every single one of her holes before slitting your throat."

"Wow," I mouth as I angle my neck to the right and left in an effort to relieve the knotting tension. "Here's the thing, Whit." Shoving off the wall, I pause a foot away from where he's wheezing and bleeding all over the floor from the split cheek Smith gifted him. "I know what you're trying to do. You're trying to get under my skin so I'll snap that weak little neck of yours, to make your death faster than what I have planned for you. But here's the thing." Blood, sweat, and hell, maybe some tears slick my palm as I grip his face in a single hand. "If you mention raping my fiancée one more time tonight, I'll cut your tongue out, then continue to kill you slowly. Nothing will rush me. Tonight is a night I'll savor for years to come as the night I fucking killed Shawn Whit."

Stepping back, I grimace at the blood on my hand and wipe it down the stiff material of my pants.

"Now, tell me everything you know about that fucker we know as Agent Ponder."

21

TREY

"Well, that didn't last long." Tank sighs.

"That's what she said," I toss over my shoulder as I press two fingers to the blood- and sweat-slick neck. Nothing. "He's dead."

"That's usually what happens when you snap someone's neck," Smith says to Tank.

Frustrated, Tank starts to run a hand over his head but pauses with a grimace when blood glazes over his scalp. "I didn't hit him that hard," he grumbles.

I hold up a hand to pause their bickering. "It's fine. We got what we needed out of him."

Knuckles split and bleeding, Tank rests his mitt of a hand on my shoulder. "I'm sorry I took that from you." He squeezes, the strength in his grip lacking the usual power.

Still crouched by the dead body, I stare into the lifeless eyes, processing the fact that Whit is dead. "If it wasn't me, then I'm good with it being you." The crack and pop of my joints fills the quiet room as I stand with a groan. "Besides, I got to have my fun."

Fun. Fuck yeah, it was fun. Each hit lifted a sliver of the heavy dark cloud that's fogged my brain since Tank called saying Randi was missing. After several bone-rattling punches, exhaustion from the day made it nearly impossible to continue with my torture plan. That's when Tank and Smith stepped in.

It was clear Smith has experience holding back killing blows. It was like some disturbing form of art as he moved his attacks around Whit's restrained body to keep from hitting the same spot twice.

Then there's Tank. Love him, but the big guy is all brawn and no tact when it comes to pulling punches.

Hence why Whit is dead, and not by my hand.

There was honesty in my words. I am good with not being the one who delivered the final blow. Whit is dead, and that's what matters most. Even though the information he had on who we know as Ponder was little, we still know more about the hired assassin than when we started. This way, if he doesn't return to his townhome to collect the things he'd clearly set aside for a quick escape, we have a few bread crumbs for Smith's friends at Homeland to follow. Hopefully it'll be enough for us to catch the bastard who devised the plan to kidnap my girl.

"Now what?" The wall rattles under my weight as my back slams against it, supporting me from collapsing to the blood-splattered floor.

Without a word, Smith moves through the room and disappears down the hall but in the opposite direction of the back door. The creak of hinges has me leaning along the wall to see if it was him leaving or someone else coming inside the cabin via the surprisingly still fully intact front door.

Two red plastic fuel containers dangle from Smith's fingers as he shuffles back down the hall and into the living room. Liquid sloshes inside as they thump to the floor.

"Where the hell were you keeping those?" I sniff the air. "Diesel or gas?"

"Diesel. I'm not an idiot. One of the special forces guys left them on the porch for cleanup. Plus these." He holds up a thin matchbook between two fingers. "We're to make all the evidence of tonight disappear. Everybody, the entire house. This never happened. I'll pour one canister over the bodies in the basement. You"—he hitches his chin to Tank—"start spilling the other all along this floor. Make sure you leave a trail out the back."

Tank nods and reaches for the accelerant-filled canister. Smith grabs the other container and leaves the room. Heavy feet against the wooden stairs followed by a few curses about the stench of death grow distant as he descends to the basement.

I meet Tank's worried dark eyes from where I'm still posted up against the wall. There's a strong possibility that if I move, I'll fall to the floor and never get back up.

"You look like shit."

"I look better than Whit."

Tank's lips twitch. "Not sure that's much of a positive, Playboy. You're comparing yourself to a dead man."

"It's been a hell of a day."

He nods. "One for the books, that's for sure. You worried?"

"Because that fucker who planned and executed the kidnapping of the president for money is still out there and wants me dead? Yeah, yeah I am."

"Me too. But we'll find him."

"And we'll kill him too."

"Bloodthirsty?"

A cruel smile pulls at my lips, the skin along my cheeks stretching under the dried blood. "Only for those who deserve it."

Smith stomps into the room and eyes the still full can. "You two are worse than any woman I've ever known."

"You should see our pillow fights." The words are more of a moan as I push off the wall to stand on my own. The room sways, darkness encroaching in the corners of my vision.

"Come on." Without invitation, Smith ducks under my arm and lodges himself beneath my shoulder, supporting my weight. Halfway down the hall, I part my lips, readying to thank him, when he shoots me a sharp look. "Don't make this fucking weird or I'll drop your ass."

Stepping out of the death, blood, and fuel stench in the house, the fresh air smacks my face, revitalizing some of my depleted energy stores. Behind us, the smell of diesel grows stronger, even out in the open. Smith leans my weak ass against a support beam of the small porch before releasing his hold to go help Tank.

At the threshold, Tank upturns the fuel container, using every last drop before tossing the empty canister back into the house. Both men turn to face me, Smith with the matchbook between his outstretched fingers.

The edge of the two-by-four beam digs between my shoulder blades as I use it for leverage and shove off. The first step toward Smith brings a hiss of pain from between my clenched teeth. *Fucking hell, I need a good fuck and an ice bath.* My thigh muscles tremble under my weight. *Okay, maybe ice bath first, a nap, and then a fuck.* Wouldn't want to smother Randi because I physically can't push myself off her.

I snatch the thin flexible cardboard from Smith's outstretched fingers and hold it toward the light to read the writing and brand on the front. Even this exhausted, I somehow bark out a laugh. I arch a brow at Smith. "Seriously, Tails and Twats?"

His eyes roll to the night sky. "Not mine, remember? Sounds classy though."

"Randi will never believe you've said two jokes in one day."

A tiny smile tugs at his lips.

Turning back to the still open door, I toe the threshold and stare down the hall. An emotion I can't pinpoint swirls within me, tightening my chest. Once I light this match, it's over. Today, tonight, all of it done.

The cardboard flap bends back under my trembling fingers. I rip three matches from the booklet and pinch the flap to the back with the flimsy matches against the flint strip. With a quick tug, sparks flare and a minor bright flame bursts to life.

I stare into the flickering flame, watching it creep closer to where my fingers pinch the ends. Heat bites at my skin as the flame draws nearer. With a deep inhale, I flick the three nearly spent matches toward the shiny liquid puddled a foot from where I stand.

Two flicker out before hitting the accelerant, but the final match hits the mark.

The sudden flash of blistering heat has me stumbling backward square into a solid chest. A rolling roar grows, chasing away the quiet night as flames race down the line of diesel, igniting the rest of the house. Within seconds, the heat from the intense flames forces all of us off the porch.

"Benson."

I don't turn, mesmerized by the red-and-orange glow lighting up the surrounding area.

"Benson." I reluctantly turn to my friend, who looks just as mesmerized as I am by the destruction we've left in our wake. "Randi is at the hospital and asking for you." I blink, tilting my head to understand what he's talking about. It's only now that I notice the heavily armed man standing beside Tank. "They're concerned about her mental stability."

"Apparently she won't stop rambling about unicorns to anyone who will listen in between demanding they not sedate her until you're there," the guy states absentmindedly as he too becomes enraptured by the fire now billowing out the windows and crawling up the exterior walls.

"The unicorn stuff is normal for her," I say on a huff. Turning back to the flames now swallowing the entirety of the cabin, I suck in a breath and raise both middle fingers. "She won, motherfucker. See you in hell," I whisper.

Turning on my heels, I push through the stiffness in my muscles and stride in the direction of the single black SUV that will take me to the only thing that matters in this world.

Her.

MY LIDS FEEL like they're glued shut as I attempt to open my eyes. Finally forcing them open, I blink past the haze covering my vision.

A rhythmic beeping close by reaches my ears first. A sharp antiseptic scent floods my nose, and the white walls and various machines come into view as my vision sharpens. Soft material cushions my cheek. A steady heartbeat beneath my ear soothes the unexpected rush of adrenaline that flashed through my system upon waking up in an unfamiliar room.

"Go back to sleep, Benson," a familiar voice whispers from somewhere in the dark room. "You're both safe."

The grogginess of too little sleep tugs at my lids, making them too heavy to keep open.

I tighten my hold, molding my body even tighter around the soft one in my arms, and give in to sleep once again.

LIPS PARTED, chest rising and falling in a smooth and steady cadence, Randi sleeps peacefully. Unable to stop myself, I draw closer to her bed, needing a simple touch, skin to skin, to remind me she's safe—alive.

With a featherlight touch, I trace along her healing lips and purple-and-blue bruised jaw. For two days, they've kept her under observation. Mostly sedated due to her constant arguing about being fine and needing to get back to work. But not today. No, today she gets to go home. She'll return to the White House and finally see Taeler and that sweet grandbaby.

Which means I get to leave too, even though I could've gone home anytime I wanted. No doctor was holding me back from leaving. But she was. No way could I leave her here alone. I might never leave her alone again. If she thought I was overbearing before, she's in for a rude awakening starting the moment we get back to the White House.

Now I know what it's like to nearly lose your soul mate. The very person who encourages and challenges you. The very reason your heart continues to beat and who pushes the encroaching darkness away. I'll never allow harm to come to her again.

A twitch of movement behind her closed lids snags my attention. Beside the bed, the heart rate monitor beeps increase, the rapid pace ramping up my own pulse. A sharp, scared whimper whispers past her dry lips.

Another nightmare.

This isn't the first she's had, and I suspect it won't be the last with all she went through in those horrible hours we searched for her while she was alone with those fuckers. I made Shawn detail every bit of pain they inflicted. What he and Ponder did before Tank and I arrived. Then I delivered it all right back to him. It won't stop the fear from slipping into her dreams or keep her from future panic attacks, but it might help ease the anger and resentment I know will brew within her over the next few months.

Leaning forward, I press a kiss to her forehead and tighten the hold on her hand.

Helpless. This is what I feel as she struggles in her dreamscape. The only place I can't help her. I could wake her up, but for the first time since she was admitted, the sleep she's experiencing now is on her own, not drug induced, and I'm not sure if I should interrupt even if every instinct screams at me to shake her awake.

A breathy plea moves through my hair, brushing against my ear.

Dipping lower, I place my lips over hers. "I'm here, Mess. I'm here."

The twitching settles, and her rapid breaths ease. I watch as those long dark lashes flutter open. She doesn't flinch at finding me hovering so close, our noses almost touching. Instead she does the unexpected.

Her cold fingers slip up the exposed portion of my bicep, over my shoulder, and gently clasp the back of my neck, sealing our lips together with a desperation that scours my soul and rips through my heart.

Elbow braced on the bed, I lean into the kiss, giving her everything I've held back the past couple of days. Pouring my sorrow and anger into this one binding kiss. Her tongue slides against my own, lips parted, opening herself to me. Those chipped and broken nails scrape along my scalp.

It's a desperate kiss, displaying how badly we need each other. I can't touch enough of her, and the way her other hand plays along my taut back muscles tells me she feels the same. We need this. A reminder of our physical connection. A release of the pent-up emotions and frustrations that sit brimming at the surface, ready to erupt.

My breath shudders with the flood of need, making me edgy and harder than a damn rock. I tear my hungry lips from hers, shifting to kiss down the column of her neck, each fading fingerprint bruise. My tongue trails lower, savoring every inch of her I get to taste. From one side to the other, I run the tip along her collarbone, nibbling and sucking the delicate skin.

Her fingers tighten in my hair, tugging at my scalp. With a yank, she rips my face up to meet hers. Breaths labored, dick straining against the zipper of my jeans, I press against the mattress, hovering above her and meeting those lust-filled hazel eyes.

"Remind me," she breathes.

"Remind you of what, Mess?"

"Of what I have waiting for me on the other side of all this. Of the normalcy. That you still want this broken person they turned me into." A single tear drips, slipping along her temple before disappearing into her hairline. "Remind me I'm still me. Remind me of who I am, Trouble. Remind me of what it feels like to feel good."

Even though her words fracture my heart into a thousand pieces, I smile.

I smile for her.

I smile for me.

I smile for us.

And I give her exactly what she needs in this moment.

Me.

22

RANDI

I'm broken. Not just parts of my body but my entire being. The fear Shawn beat into me during those hours in the warehouse seeped into my muscles with each hit, every taunt. My bones ache, but that's nothing compared to the soul-rattling despair and terror that's now dug it's claws into me.

I've never been scared. Always dove into an issue head on, not worrying about the consequences.

But now? Now I know what can happen and how much it will hurt. I know the fear of death staring you in the face and accepting you won't live to see another day. That did something to me. Between the beatings, talk of rape, and knowing I would die, a part of me is frozen in fear.

I'm scared. Terrified that one day Shawn or the other man will come back and make good on their promises of me dying a slow death. At least that's how it plays out in the recurring nightmare that seems to be imprinted in my brain, ready to replay anytime I dare to sleep.

The doctors thought I didn't want to rest because I had work to do, which is what I told them, but that was a front of truth-laced lies. I just didn't want to close my eyes without the sedation. With the sedation, everything was black, nothing. But when I sleep on my own, I'm back in that warehouse and Trey is gone.

I need him close by. Need his warmth, protection, and understanding.

He's my salvation.

My savior.

My everything.

Staring into those honey brown eyes hovering just inches above me, I move a lock of dark hair from in front of them. He might think I'm crazy for asking for this, asking for him, but I need us. Need that connection. Like I told him, I need the reminder that we're good. That something in my life is still stable.

My heart is cracked wide open, 100 percent vulnerable with the request, offering him a side of me I never allow myself to show. I don't need anyone, never have. I've done everything to this point on my own. Undergrad. Law school. Campaign. Politics. But this I can't get through alone. And maybe I don't want to.

It's more terrifying than anything Shawn said, opening myself up to Trey like this. Letting him see just how much I need him. All it would take is one word, a hesitation even, or a flat-out refusal. I wouldn't recover from his rejection, even if it did come from a loving place of not wanting to hurt me while my body is still healing. Recover from the abduction and torture? Sure. With enough therapy, I'll be okay. But being turned away when I'm desperate for help, begging for someone to ground me and them refusing— there aren't enough prescription drugs in the world to make that kind of rejection go away.

I hold my breath, waiting for his response. My heart races, fingers trembling as I run them through his clean hair.

A smirk. That playful smirk tugs at his lips, and I know I have my answer.

Trey Benson, my soul mate, won't back away when I need him most. No, he leans in, knowing exactly what I need.

I don't need to be perfect for Trey.

I never have been. And that's why he loves me.

"What hurts, Mess?" he asks, that all-seeing gaze raking over my face and lower, hunger growing with each inch he covers.

I take a quick stock of my injuries. "My ribs when I take a deep breath. That's it. Trey—" I start, ready to beg again, when he seals those soft lips against my own.

"One second," he whispers against my mouth.

With a grunt, he pulls away. Using the bedside rail as leverage, he stands, adjusting the sizable bulge in his jeans before awkwardly walking to the door and pulling it open. With most of his body remaining inside the room, he talks in a low tone to someone outside the door before closing it once again and flipping the lock. "There. Now we won't be disturbed."

His mischievous smirk causes heat to bloom in my lower belly and dampness to slick the inside of my thighs.

A predatory glint shines in his eyes as they sweep me from head to toe. Each step is steady, calculated from the door to where I lie trembling with excitement. Long fingers fist the mound of blankets covering my bare legs and slowly drag the heavy material to the floor, leaving me exposed in the ugly-as-sin hospital gown I've been forced to wear.

I nibble at my upper lip to keep my grimace from showing as I take in the state of my legs. Bruises and lacerations litter my upper thighs, and layers of gauze wrap from shin to ankle. I don't let myself think about the damage that lies beneath. Not now. Not when the heat from Trey's sweeping gaze could light the sheets beneath me on fire.

The bottom sheet snags on jagged nails as I ball it into a tight fist. Something about this triggers anxiety and sends my pulse racing. The bed, the basic sheet, bare legs exposed.

"Randi."

I hear him call my name, but I just can't look away from the sheet gripped between my fingers. The sight has me locked in a trance that transports me back to that basement.

"Randi, look at me."

Shame and fear clash as I shift to stare at the hospital gown, grounding myself to the present. I really am broken. What if he doesn't want to deal with this mess I've become?

"I'm a mess," I whisper.

"You've always been my mess, Mess."

"But now... now I'm more like some hoarder's trailer than a mess. I'm unsalvageable. Not even a TLC special could clear out the baggage and trash that's been shoved in here." I tap the side of my head.

"Mess, baby, I hate to be the one to tell you this, but you've always been a bit of a work in progress."

My eyes widen, challenge flaring in my chest. "I'm sorry."

"Don't give me that look. All I'm saying is... fuck, I'm saying this wrong."

"You think?" Indignation swirls within me.

"You've climbed an uphill battle your entire life and survived. Not only made it through but bettered your life. You clawed your way out of that trailer park, away from the life you were destined for. I know you can do the same now. It won't be easy, you know that from experience, but this time you have me, and you have Tank and Sarah. We won't let you go through this alone. Don't ever think you're too damaged or too much work to save. If that was the case, Tank would've walked away from me years ago. We don't give up on family. We don't give up on the ones we love."

My lower lip trembles. "Promise?"

"Promise." His eyes twinkle, completely at odds with the solemn conversation. "How about we seal it with a kiss?"

That desire-filled heat from earlier sparks in my lower gut again. I lick my chapped, healing lower lip.

"Full disclosure. I don't know when I last brushed my teeth," I admit, sinking into the pillow at my back as he prowls closer. I've showered several times in the en-suite bathroom, giving me confidence that I don't reek of body odor or still have crusted blood covering me, at least.

"Madam President, I don't give a flying fuck as long as I get to kiss you."

I have a smart reply ready only for it to be swallowed up by his lips sealing to mine and his tongue pushing past to tangle with my own. He consumes me, each swipe of his tongue and moan of pleasure from the simple kiss burning away the fear and doubt of his desire for this broken version of myself.

It's not enough. The kiss is perfection, but I'm desperate for all of him. Grasping on to his shoulders I urge him onto the bed with me.

If it were any other hospital bed, we might not fit. But it's not. This king-size hospital bed really is fit for a king... or president. Finally the perks of the job are paying off, so I can fuck my fiancé in the hospital and still be comfortable.

The small tug is all it takes for him to toe off his shoes and climb onto the bed. Careful of my IV and other wires, Trey hovers over me, bracing himself on both elbows digging into the mattress on either side of my head. I run a finger down his hard chest over the soft material of his dark gray T-shirt.

Hooking the collar, I give it a quick yank. "Off."

Trey smirks, hooking his own finger into the collar of the hospital gown. "Ditto, baby. I need a good look at what's mine."

I watch in awe, a bit of drool collecting and slipping out of the corner of my gaping mouth, as he rips the shirt over his head, those defined muscles rippling and stretching with the movement. Kneeling between my parted legs, he grins, hooking both thumbs into the waistband of his dark jeans. That deep V and those washboard abs have me licking my lips, itching for a taste. I bend, readying to sit up and lick his stomach and lower, only for a pinch of pain to stop me cold.

"What level of hell is this?" I hiss, gently cupping my ribs. "All I wanted was to lick your stomach."

A dark chuckle scatters the remaining ache in my side, reminding me of the slow, steady throb between my thighs. "As much as I'd love that, baby, any licking will have to wait. Right now, I focus on you. Reminding you that no matter what you've been through, no matter the aches"—three of his fingers caress from one side of my ribs to the other, dragging the gown's thin material with it—"or the bruises." He trails those same fingers up, and I hiss through clenched teeth at the barely there touch over one nipple. Trey cups my jaw, swiping his thumb over my cheekbone. "I'll remind you that no matter what, you're still mine and so fucking beautiful it physically hurts."

His free hand grips the bulge in his jeans and squeezes. Those dark lashes flutter shut on a groan. "Especially right now. I think I need this more than you. To feel you from the inside. I need to be reminded that you're here, with me. Something in me snapped when Tank called about you being missing. And I don't think...." He shakes his head. "I don't know when I'll be able to close my eyes or leave you alone without the fear that you'll be taken again engulfing and paralyzing me."

Love, concern, and a touch of fear splay across his pinched features. I grip the wrist near my face and give it a gentle reassuring squeeze.

"We'll get through this together, Trouble. You and me." Tightening my hold, I use his arms as leverage to carefully roll onto my side. I hitch my chin over my shoulder toward the ties securing my gown. "I'll need a little help. Can't take this off on my own."

A bright smile tugs at his lips, chasing away the cloud that settled over him at the thought of losing me again. His hot palm sizzles against the bare skin of my ass cheek with a hard pat to each side. Teeth digging into my lower lip, I muffle the groan of pleasure that wants to escape, knowing there are guards just outside the door. One tie slackens, the ends dancing along my spine as he slips the strips of cotton free. He makes quick work of untying the one secured at the nape of my neck before helping me lie back against the conforming mattress.

His hungry gaze eats up each bare inch of skin he exposes as he slips the gown over my shoulders. The stiffer material of the neckline snags on both peaked nipples, causing them to bounce as he drags the gown lower. The movement stills only for the material to drag back up over my nipples before applying more pressure and dragging the taunting cloth back down.

My eyes flutter closed at the teasing swipes of the fabric against the sensitive buds. "Trouble," I groan, moving my hands up to cup both breasts.

"Do it, baby. Let me see you play with yourself. Pinch those rosy nipples like I would."

"I want you to do it," I beg, but my fingers are already obeying his order, pinching and flicking the hard peaks to the point of pain before easing off.

He hums in disagreement, the small sound causing increased desire to flow through my veins. The increasing beeps of the heart rate monitor offer Trey an inside look at how much his words and my own hands affect me.

Another hum, this one laced with need, rumbles in his chest. "This could be a fun little game. Let's see what gets that heart of yours racing, baby."

Done with playing, Trey rips the gown away and drops it to the floor. Goose bumps sprout along my stomach and down my legs at the sudden exposure to the chilled air.

"Don't stop," he commands. The force behind those words makes my lower stomach clench with want. "Harder, like this." Cupping my hands, Trey's fingers manipulate my own, placing each peak between my thumbs and index fingers. His light brown eyes flash as he applies pressure. My gasp turns to a groan at the spike of pain as he twists. My pulse skyrockets, the rapid beeping filling the room. A mischievous smile pulls up his scruff-dusted cheeks.

"Like that. Don't stop until I tell you to."

"Or what?" I breathe, my back arching off the bed as I tug my own nipples toward the ceiling.

A *smack* cracks through the room as his palm connects with the side of my ass.

"That might be incentive." I groan as the sting left behind fades.

"Fuck, you're perfect, you know that?"

"Because I like foreplay a little dark and dangerous?"

"Because *I'm* a little dark and dangerous."

"We're perfect for each other, then." My fingers still, all my focus going to where he's softly caressing the inside of both thighs. "We should get married."

The bed trembles with his laugh. "No more talking unless it's you moaning or screaming my name." I seal my lips shut and nod. "Good girl." A single finger easily glides between my slick center. "Even without that damn machine I'd know how much you like this, Mess. Look how wet you are for me." His gaze darkens as he stares between my legs. "Let's see what this does."

Cupping my pussy, he grinds the heel of his hand against my swollen nub and shoves three fingers inside me. I gasp at the force of his fast entry. Eager for more, I widen my legs, both knees bent and lying along the bed, giving him all the access he needs to do his worst.

Fuck, I hope he does his worst.

In and out he pistons those fingers, curling and scissoring with each thrust as he pounds the heel of his palm against my clit. Higher and higher I climb, every muscle taut with the building release. The monitor beeps at an erratic pace, offering an unexpectedly erotic background noise.

Just as I hit the top, my body primed to fall into ecstasy, Trey withdraws his fingers completely. I whimper as I pinch my nipples harder, desperate to do whatever it takes to find my release. My lids flick open at a faint sucking sound.

Smiling around those three fingers, Trey wraps his lips around the lowest knuckle and sighs. His own eyes flutter closed. The hand not at his mouth flicks the top button of his jeans, allowing the band to gape enough that the purple head of his engorged cock peeks out. A bead of precum glistens at the top. I lick my lips, eager for a taste.

"You want this?" His voice is low and raspy with the need that's clearly written across his tight features. He swipes a thumb over the head, wiping the tempting drop away. Leaning forward, Trey shoves his thumb into my awaiting mouth. "Suck it clean, baby."

"Fuck," I mutter around his thumb as I lick it. He yanks it away before I'm ready, causing it to pop from my lips.

"Your turn." Gripping my forearm, careful of the IV and gauze covering my wrists, he yanks my hand from my breasts. Like a puppet arm, he guides my hand lower, the dangling fingers barely ghosting over my sensitive skin.

Interlacing his fingers over mine, he forces my own palm to cup my drenched pussy. "Feel what drives me absolutely insane. Feel yourself from the inside with me."

The machine goes wild, the beeping turning to an ear-piercing alarm. With a growl of frustration Trey leans over the bed and yanks the plug from the wall. Chest heaving, he looms over me, a small smile spreading over his face.

"It was fun while it lasted, but I think I know exactly how you feel about all this." For emphasis, he forces two of my fingers into my channel. My eyes roll into the back of my head, my hips lurching off the mattress. Sitting back on his heels, Trey unzips his jeans.

Two of his thicker fingers slip between my own, the combination tight and fucking awesome. I clench around our combined fingers, loving the fullness.

"Your tit, Randi. Pinch that nipple hard like my teeth would feel."

Don't have to tell me twice. I'm quick to do as I'm told.

"Look at me. Look at what you do to me." I force my eyes open. His free hand is wrapped around his thick cock, knuckles white as he pumps up and down. "Every time you're in the room. Every time you cross my mind, I get hard enough to club someone with my damn dick. But this, watching you fingerfuck yourself, playing with your tits, it fucking hurts so damn good." He increases our pace, shoving our combined fingers in and out. "Come around our fingers, baby. Come for me."

Pressing the heel of my hand down, he grinds it against my clit.

I almost bolt off the bed as the intensity of the orgasm crashes over me, but Trey keeps me pinned with our hands pressed to my mound. My head lolls to the side, the release of built-up emotions draining all my thoughts and energy. Every muscle trembles with exhaustion. Relieved tears build behind my sealed lids before slipping out and dripping down my temples.

With a curse, Trey withdraws our hands. I whimper at the loss. It turns to a cry of shock as he falls forward, catching himself with an elbow to the mattress as he slams in deep in the same movement. On a hot puff of air, his mumbled curse brushes against my ear.

"Fuck yes," Trey grunts as he flexes and rotates his hips to seat himself deeper.

I dig both heels into his flexing ass, urging him to take everything. Fingers wrapped around my hip bone, he tilts my pelvis. With shallow thrusts at the new angle, he hits a spot that has stars sparking behind my eyes.

"There," I breathe. "Fuck, right there. More," I beg.

"Yes, Madam President," he whispers against my neck.

The bed creaks, the legs grinding against the floor as it shifts with each of Trey's powerful thrusts.

I tighten around him, eager to find the release that's building once again.

"You're squeezing the life out of my cock," he grunts. "Don't fucking stop." His thrusts slow as he works against me. "Fuck," he curses. "Come with me, baby. Come around my dick like you did your dirty little fingers." Teeth sink into my neck, hard but without breaking the skin.

That pinch of pain does it. I shatter. Everything floats away. Nothing matters but this out-of-body feeling only a soul-shattering orgasm can offer. I forget to breathe as I chase the last trembles and waves of pleasure.

"Breathe, baby," Trey pants. His hot breath brushes my sweat-slick neck.

I gasp, sucking in a lungful of air.

"An orgasm so good you forgot to breathe. That's a new one." He chuckles. We both moan at the vibration it causes where our bodies are still connected.

"I don't ever want to move," I admit. Leaning up, I press a kiss to his damp shoulder.

"Pretty sure you can't run the free world with my cock buried in your pussy."

I smile, blinking away the tears still clinging to my lashes. "I could always try, but it might make press conferences a bit porn-ish."

"We need to get you ready to go home. They're releasing you today."

With a few protests that are said more like curses, Trey pushes off the bed. He rests his hands beside my ears, his love-filled gaze chasing away the remaining fears of what's to come.

"One more time?" I ask, biting my lower lip.

A wide smile breaks across his face, those straight white teeth on full display.

"You're the boss," he mutters as his lips dip to my straining nipple.

My lids flutter closed as I rake a hand through his soft strands.

Later, reality will need to be addressed. Work will be overwhelming once again.

Tomorrow, I'll have to address the world and explain what happened along with other news they've been impatiently waiting for.

But right now?

Right now it's just him and me.

And that's all that really matters in the end.

23

RANDI

Out of all I've done in my life, this has to be the most nervous I've ever been. Of all the debates, challenging powerful men, and living through unnerving situations, why am I afraid now?

I hate this. The worry, anxiety, the voices in the back of my head telling me I can't do it. Is that Shawn taunting me from the grave, still whispering in my ear about how I'm not good enough, nor will I ever be good enough, strong enough? I don't know, maybe. Or has it always been there but my drive and self-built confidence have been enough to always drive it away?

The firm cushion of the buttercream sitting chair shifts as I lean forward. Elbows on my knees, I wring my fingers and attempt a deep breath to settle my nerves.

A twinge of discomfort causes a grimace, but it's not as painful as it was. My body is healing quickly thanks to the days my doctors required me to rest. I hated every second.

I smile to myself despite the turmoil of thoughts running through my head. *Well, I hated every second except that last hour with Trey in my bed before I was discharged.*

I stare at my nude pumps. The shoes that cost more than three months' mortgage on my trailer back in Boone. I don't even want to think about the comparative cost to the tailor-fit pantsuit I'm wearing. Or the expensive toiletries and makeup stocked in my bathroom.

I shake my head, long silky dark locks slipping over my shoulder to frame my face.

"It's just a press conference," I mutter to myself. "It's fine. I'm fine." Releasing my fingers, I shake them out, allowing the cool air to wick away the clamminess. A quick glance at my watch tells me I have thirty minutes before I'm expected.

Fuck, I hate the waiting. I could've scheduled it earlier—I am the president, after all, and it's me they want to hear from—but under the guise of needing more time, I forced them to wait until today. Two days after my release. Four days from when Trey found me. Five days from when I was abducted and beaten.

I swallow hard. There's a slight tremble in my hand as I raise a red-tipped finger to my teeth. Really I needed the past few days to get my shit together. Not that I have it all together now, but each day is better. Plus it gave me time to reconnect with Tae and that sweet little baby. We didn't leave each other's side for twenty-four hours after she nearly tackled me the moment I stepped foot into the resident side of the White House.

There was also something else I needed to do. Something personal I've been meaning to take care of for Trey. Between taking calls from the bed, the physical training exercises, and Tae popping in every hour to make sure I was still here, I was able to accomplish what I'd set my mind to. He doesn't know yet. Well, at least I don't think he does, unless his attorney called him the minute the funds were released.

Some might call it an abuse of power, but screw them. It wasn't that at all. Yeah, it made reaching the attorney general way easier, since I have his number programed into my favorites list, but that's not why he authorized the release of Trey's trust fund.

No, that was all me and my Harvard education mixed with my debate experience. Once he saw the evidence and traced the funds back to the original source—Trey's grandfather—the attorney general realized the oversight and corrected it.

Boom.

"That might be better than a boob punch to Celia," I mutter.

"Who are you boob punching?"

I jump an inch from the seat, the hand at my lips coming to press against my racing heart. Breathing hard, I shoot Sam an accusing glare. "Don't scare me like that."

"I knocked." Those dark brows furrow as concern flashes across his features. "Randi, no one expects you to be fine after what you went through."

"I know," I say on a sigh and lean back against the chair, angling my body to face where he stands by the door. "It's just... I'm constantly on edge now, you know? Like every sound, every move might be the one that happens right before I'm taken again."

"Are you seeing someone?" He steps deeper into the room and sits on the footboard of my bed.

"Yeah, and a friend." Said friend, Sarah, has been a lifeline. Taking my calls at all times of the night, letting me ramble on and on. Helping me feel strong again by taking me through simple self-defense lessons until my body is fully healed and we can get back to our old workout routine—i.e. her kicking my ass. That first day back in the White House, she stopped by with T. I'll never forget her look of absolute fury when she saw my bruised face. If Shawn wasn't burned to a crisp and nothing more than ash and a bad memory, I think Sarah would've dug up his remains and killed him all over again.

I smile at the thought. I love my protective friend. Everyone needs a Sarah in their life. And a T. And a Trey.

"You'll get through it. I have no doubt Benson will make sure of it."

My smile widens. "Yeah." Shaking my head, I disperse the memories that are trying to force their way forward. "What's up? Why are you here?"

Sam's bright green eyes burn through me. "We're friends, Randi. I'm here to check on you."

Him and Vlad, it seems. Vlad has called every day to check on my recovery progress and sent over enough Russian vodka to keep me drunk for decades. He says it's a cure-all, though I haven't had the time to test out his theory just yet.

"And stopping by to make sure I still plan to announce we're running for a second term." Amusement lightens my tone.

"You *are* known for making surprising statements to the media, so yeah, I want to make sure you're still on board."

I grin around the nail between my teeth. "No need to worry. I'm in this, and I'm ready to let the world know."

Shoulder against the bedpost, Sam surveys the room. "I can't believe Rosen was dirty."

"I can." Shock registers on Sam's face. "It was little things here and there." I shrug. Little did I know the extent of the dirt on Todd's hands, of course. That fool had his hooks in just about every dirty transaction in this city, wheeling and dealing to keep the money coming his way. Vlad was right about him, he did sell his loyalty to the highest bidder—and paid the price for it with his life.

"I'll have to find his replacement," I grumble. Massaging my temples, I focus on calming breaths.

"Let me work on that for you, Randi. Let me take something off your plate for a little while."

I shoot him a grateful tight-lipped smile that doesn't reach my eyes. "Thank you. Oh, and you're not too far off on typical Randi announcing shocking things to the media."

That puts his full attention on me. "I'm scared to ask what bomb you're planning to drop on them today."

I cringe at his choice of words. "Let's not say it like that when I actually hold the authority to drop real bombs on people, okay?"

"Touché. What will you—" He waves a hand like he's searching for the perfect word. "—expose to the media today, Madam President?"

A soft snort escapes me. I don't know why, but when he says it, I always laugh. Maybe because he knew me back in law school, or because we plotted Kyle's demise together. Or maybe it's because his own eyes hold a bit of humor when he says my title. We're a good team, Sam and me. And we will be again for another four years if the voters agree.

"I'm announcing today about—"

"You should be resting."

Sam and I turn to the owner of that deep, commanding voice. My heart does a little skip at the sight of Trey in a form-accentuating suit. Arms crossed over his chest, he shifts his displeased expression from me to Sam and back again. The two guns holstered near his chest peek out, drawing my gaze. "Give us a few, would you, Pierce?"

Sam dips his chin and shoves off the bedpost. "It's nothing crazy, right?" he asks, alluding to what I was about to reveal before Trey slipped into the room.

I shake my head, more of my dark hair falling over my shoulders and tickling my cheeks. "Nothing crazy. At least now you'll be as surprised as the rest of the world," I say with a wide grin. I'm sure it's eating him up not knowing.

He huffs, tossing his hands in the air, making his dress shirt sleeves slip up his arms and expose the bright inked skin beneath. Grumbling about something, Sam exits the bedroom, leaving Trey and me alone.

"You okay?" he asks, coming to where I sit and crouching low to put us at eye level.

I force a reassuring smile. "Yeah, just nervous."

He blinks, confusion clear in his eyes. "Why? You've done this a hundred times before." Something dark flashes over his face, making his features harden. "You don't have to tell them shit about what happened, Mess. Tell them there was an incident and it's over, handled by your very capable Secret Service team." He winks at the end, but it lacks the lightness he's attempting to create.

I chew on the tip of my pinkie nail. "It's that and...." Trey's gentle fingers grip my tender wrist and lower the hand from my lips. "Everything is about to change, Trey. Are you ready for that? Are you really ready to stop being an agent, to be the first First Husband? What if you resent me for making you give it all up? What if—"

He cuts me off with a hard kiss, making me swallow the next words. Callused palms cup my cheeks. I give in to the kiss, relaxing into him until it's only his hands holding me upright. All the stress, worry, and fear slip to the background. He hasn't taken them, just moved them aside to remind me of the only thing that matters.

Him.

He pulls back an inch, leaving me panting for more. I lean forward to seal our lips together again.

"Breathe, Randi."

Closing my eyes, I do what I'm told, inhaling as deeply as my still healing ribs will allow before becoming unbearable and then releasing it slowly.

"I was going to do this after the press conference, but, well, I think we both need this now. Just know I had a whole thing planned." His words go in one ear and out the other as I continue my deep breathing. "Open your eyes, Mess."

After one more exhale, I lift my lids. The smile that was pulling at my lips freezes on my face. I blink once, twice, expecting the image to change.

But it doesn't. Nope Trey, my Trey, is still on his knees with a small red velvet box held out between us.

I swallow, my breaths short and shallow.

You'd have to be an idiot to not know what's about to happen. I know. He knows I know. And I know he knows I know. Yet I still can't bring myself to shift my eyes away from the box to the man holding it.

Then he goes and makes it worse. He opens the damn box. I thought it held my undivided attention before, but now I want to disappear into the brilliant glittering diamond blinking beneath the few sun rays that have slipped past the blinds and curtains.

"I...." That's all I got. Yep. A Harvard graduate, president of the United States of America, and that one little word, which was more like a gurgle than a word, is all I can think to say.

"My world starts and stops with you, Randi Sawyer. I didn't understand what living was until I pulled you from that burning limo and met you. Every moment we share is one I savor. When we're apart, it's like a part of me is missing until you're back in my arms. I want you for the rest of my life. I need to be by your side every day and to hold you in my arms every night." The emotion is clear in his shaky voice and damp eyes. "I never want to wake up without you beside me again. Please say yes. Say yes to me worshiping you, loving you, and protecting you for the rest of our lives. Marry me, Mess. Please fucking marry me."

Streams of tears drip from my cheeks. Forgetting about the layers of makeup that were applied for the upcoming press conference, I swipe the dampness away with the back of a hand.

"Trouble." I swallow back a sob. Apprehension flashes across his face. "There's no coming back from you, from us. You're all I want. You're all I need. None of this matters if we're not together, if I'm not facing this shit show called life with you by my side. Yes, I'll fucking marry you."

Pitching forward, I forget about the enormous diamond between us and lunge out of the seat. A quick flash of shock crosses his face and the red box falls as I crash against him, my arms going around his neck as we tumble to the floor. Holding me close, Trey takes the brunt of our fall, twisting so his back slams against the thin carpet with me pressed to his chest.

I swipe at the trail of wetness streaking his cheek before leaning forward and kissing away the remaining tears. His fingers delve into my hair, fisting at the base and dragging my lips down to smash against his.

I nearly sob with happiness into his mouth. The hand along my back tightens, sealing us even closer together. A bold, joyful laugh bursts from his lips. Hand to the floor, I push up and gaze down at the man I love. A breath catches in my throat at the pure happiness radiating from his wide smile.

"You made me drop the ring," he whispers as he rakes both hands through my hair.

"I don't care about the ring. All I want is you."

"Good thing you get both." He drops one of his hands and pats along the ground. "Ah." Lifting the box overhead, he withdraws the ring before tossing the box across the room. Slowly he lowers the glittering engagement ring to eye level. "They released my funds from my trust."

"Did they now?" I say, mesmerized by the way the diamond sparkles even in the shadows.

"You don't sound surprised." I raise a noncommittal shoulder. "Hmm, I thought so. Either way, this was the ring I wanted for you. What I've wanted for you for the past several months. Ask Tank." A soft chuckle from his chest tickles my own. "I dragged him to that jewelry store at least once a week to look at it. I made them keep it in the back until I was able to buy it." A spark of mischief dances in his honey brown eyes. "I've been a good customer for years."

I smack his shoulder only for him to snatch my hand and flip us so I'm pinned beneath him. He takes the hand he's captured and brings it to his lips, kissing the ring finger before slipping the ring down. For half a second, I worry it won't fit as it catches on my knuckle, making Trey use a little more effort for it to slide over.

I let out a held breath when he releases my hand, leaving the sparkling jewel secured around my finger.

"Wow," I whisper. "I never thought this would happen to me."

"The big rock?" Trey waggles his eyebrows.

"No," I say, sticking my tongue out at him. "This feeling of sheer happiness. For so long I've done this all on my own, always an uphill battle, and now... now I know I won't have to do it by myself. That no matter how hard it gets, I know you'll be there by my side."

"Always, Mess." Leaning forward, he brushes his nose against mine. "I will always be by your side."

"Ditto, Trouble. We're in this together."

"Forever."

"Forever."
Forever might not be long enough.

24

RANDI

The murmurings of the press corps quiet the moment I appear through the side door. Careful to not snag a heel, I step up to the podium and grip both sides for support. Flashes momentarily blind me as a few dozen pictures are snapped. I hear more than one gasp when I face them full on, allowing them to see the healing damage still apparent on my face.

Most of the swelling has gone down, but there's no hiding the black-and-green bruises across my jaw, cheekbones, and circling one eye.

It's fine. I'm fine. It was a shock the first time I saw my reflection, of course. And I might have overreacted slightly by shattering the mirror that exposed the horror that was my face. But I'm better now. I'm fine.

I scan the somewhat familiar faces and smile.

"First off, I'd like to thank every single person who prayed for my safe return during those long hours I was missing. I have no doubt that me standing here today is a direct result of those prayers. There are a few things I'd like to discuss with you today, but I know the main point of interest is where the hell I was those missing hours." The reporters chuckle, and a few smile and nod, shrugging like I caught them red-handed on something. "On June 15 at 3:30 a.m., my convoy was attacked as I left a residence deep in the city. The entire team that was escorting me back to the White House was killed in the direct attack."

"Why were you in the city at that time of night?" one reporter shouts out.

"What do you think I was doing in the city at that time of night?" I leave off the string of names I want to call the fool. "I'm the president, but I'm still a single woman."

Well, not really single anymore, but I'll get to that in a minute.

"After the motorcade was eliminated, I was abducted from the wreckage, drugged, and then held hostage at a warehouse across town. As you can see from my face, it was not a pleasant experience—"

"Was it terrorism?" someone shouts.

"In a way, yes it was. The technical definition of terrorism is 'unlawful use of violence in the pursuit of political aims,' which was exactly what he was after. He wasn't a new threat but someone who's been after me since the day I stepped into Washington. This man was threatened by me. Threatened by my background and how it is directly influencing the policies I'm determined to put in place while in office. He was a weak, selfish man who, thankfully, is no longer a threat to me or the people of this country.

"That's all the detail I'm willing to give at his moment in time. The funerals for the brave men and women who died trying to protect me will be held over the next week. I would appreciate you respecting the families' wishes and staying away from the family-only services and burials. With that behind us, we can now look toward the future. The next four years."

Chairs creak and a hum of low voices reaches my ears as I take a second to let those words sink in.

"I've been asked many times if Sam Pierce and I intend to run for office again. Until now, I wasn't ready to make that decision. As I said earlier, I'm a single woman with a daughter who now has a beautiful baby of her own. Taking on another four years would be challenging and put additional strain on my family. That was not a decision I wanted to take lightly. However, after the incident and many, many hours of internal debate and talking with family, I've decided to run for office in this next election cycle with Sam Pierce once again as my running mate."

The room erupts to life. A few even leap from their chairs, shouting their questions.

Holding up both hands, I shake my head, not saying another word until they've calmed down.

"There are a few things I'd like for everyone to know about me now that I've decided to run for president. I normally keep my personal life private, but I know with campaigns, anything is fair game to the other party. First—"

Shrugging off my jacket, I carefully lay it over the edge of the podium and place my hands on my hips. "—I have tattoos." Raising my arms, I roll my shoulder and bicep so everyone can get a good look at my half sleeve. "Hope this doesn't offend anyone, but I needed to put this out there because I'm tired of hiding the art on my skin."

Crickets.

"Okay," I whisper to myself. I glance to Trey, who gives me two thumbs up. "On to the next topic. Earlier you asked why I was in the city at that hour. Well, to be completely honest, I was there seeing my boyfriend."

There's a sharp gasp and... Oh hell, did that lady faint?

"Well, not really boyfriend anymore. Now my fiancé." I hold up my hand, allowing the light to catch the diamond, shooting rays of sparkling light around the room.

"Who is he?" one of the reporters in the front row asks. In her excitement, she's shifted to the very edge of the cheap chair in an effort to catch every word of my response.

Smiling, I point to where Trey leans along the side wall wearing a shit-eating grin.

"Trey Benson, ladies and gentlemen."

The man doesn't miss a beat. As every eye in the room turns toward him, he simply waves and gives the crowd a dynamic smile.

Shaking my head at his showmanship, I clear my throat, directing their attention back to me. "He's currently a member of my alpha Secret Service detail, but that might change with the engagement. And before any of you ask, no, I will not go into detail about how all his happened... yet. One day, sure, but I'll be honest, I'm exhausted." The crowd chuckles. "This job eats up every second of every day, and it's still not enough to get it all done. It's beautiful, terrifying, exhausting, and thrilling all in the same moment. And I wouldn't want it any other way. I'm thrilled to run for the incumbent president seat in the next election cycle, and I hope you'll vote for me once again so I can continue making the changes this pompous-ass government needs."

The speech is perfect... until I pull a fucking Randi.

One hand tosses up a peace sign while the other gives the room a thumbs-up as I step to the side. I examine the riveting floral carpet, grumbling about my traitorous hands and how they always fuck things up for me when someone grips my biceps. Trey smirks. The air grows heavy with anticipation as everyone focuses on our simple interaction.

"That was perfect, Madam President. Especially that last bit about the 'pompous-ass government.' You surely sealed a few votes with that closing line." His smile grows at an obnoxious catcall that cracks through the room, coming from...

I glance over his shoulder to find a grinning Sam.

Cameras flash as Trey cups my cheek, turning my attention back to him. "So it's official."

"Official," I whisper, my eyes darting to the crowd of reporters that seems closer than just moments ago.

Their shouted questions finally reach my ears.

"When's the wedding?"

"Where will it be?'

"Will you invite the Russians?"

What is their deal with the Russians? I roll my eyes at the last question and wave a hand, dismissing them all without a single reply.

"They're all yours," I say to Sam, patting his shoulder with the hand that's not interlaced with Trey's. "Go win us some votes."

"Should I show my tats too?"

I look him up and down, considering the idea. "Couldn't hurt, but I'd be worried about most of the women in America showing up on your doorstep." He laughs, humor alight in his green eyes. "Let's talk strategy for the campaign tomorrow. See ya."

Stepping through the side door, I wait until it's closed and the noise diminished before leaning against the wall to catch my breath.

Varying emotions battle within me as the gravity of what I just revealed to the world settles.

"Oh shit," I curse under my breath. Slipping out of my shoes, I step forward to race down the hall.

"What?" Trey's hand tightens around mine, holding me back. "What's wrong?"

The four agents around me draw their guns. Keeping the barrels pointed to the ground, they form a brick wall around me.

Leveraging one of my thin shoulders between two agents, I force them apart and take off down the hall, this time without Trey's restraint.

"I just told the whole world about our engagement and totally forgot to tell Tae!" I shout over my shoulder.

Trey's boisterous laugh chases me down the hall. "Good luck with that."

As I jog through the maze of hallways, I say a prayer to the unicorn gods that she wasn't watching the press conference. At her door, I slump forward, slamming the heel of my hand against it, making it rattle under my weight to keep me upright. Breathing ragged, I curl an arm around my sore ribs, hoping cradling my waist will relieve the ache.

But then the door swings open.

"Shit." Unable to catch myself, I stumble forward, crashing into Taeler. Her own curse slips out as we tumble to the ground. The lamp beside the bed shakes and the picture frames along the wall shift with the impact of both our bodies slamming to the ground.

Groaning, I roll to my back and stare at the ceiling.

"Fuck, Mom," she cries.

"Language," I hiss back.

"You just tackled me for no good reason and you're—"

"I said yes." Now my racing heart is from trepidation, not exertion or free-falling to the floor. The carpet flattens under my head as I roll it to the side. "He asked, and I said yes."

"You told me that. You said the night you were kidnapped he asked you and you said yes, so why the hell did you assault me?"

"I didn't assault you. You opened the door—"

"My bedroom door when someone knocked."

"The door I was using as support because I raced over here from the press room because I forgot to tell you before the press conference."

"Tell me what?"

I raise my left hand into the air and hold it between us. Tae's eyes go wide when they latch on to the sparkling diamond decorating my finger.

"He asked, and I said yes."

I wince at her high-pitched scream. Before I know what's happened, she's on top of me, arms wrapped around my neck, crying, laughing, and still screaming.

That's how he finds us.

Leaning against the doorframe, Trey smirks down at us. "I don't even want to know how you two ended up on the floor. By the amount of tears and happy screaming that can be heard through the entire White House, I'm guessing you told her."

My cheeks hurt with my wide smile. Her soft blonde hair tickles my nose as I lean forward and take a deep inhale.

"Mom, you're so weird." Her tone lacks the bite it used to. Gone is the snarky teen who thinks she has to help her mom through life because she can't catch a break. Gone is my little girl; she now has a little babe of her own.

Gone is my loneliness.

Gone is the need to fight this thing called life alone.

Whole is how I feel.

Whole and happy.

"Where are we going?" My breath fogs the tinted window of the Beast. The busy sidewalks and crowded businesses of downtown DC flicker past. The leather cools my overheated skin as I lean back and rest my head against the headrest.

"You okay?" Trey's fingers tighten around my own.

I nod only for it to turn into a shake, then a half shrug. "My stomach is in knots, and my palms are as sweaty as a teen boy's on his first date. But is that because this is my first time really out and about since... since the abduction or because I don't know where we're going and what you have waiting for the surprise you're clearly giddy over?"

"I'm a badass. I don't get fucking giddy."

"You're giddy."

I shoot a grin at T, who sits as far away as possible. Holding out a hand toward Trey's best friend and future best man, I say, "See? He sees it too."

"It's a surprise. A good one. You already got the best part I had planned." Lifting my left hand, he holds the engagement ring close to my nose. My eyes cross staring at it so close. "Now I get to enjoy the night too, since I'm not nervous about messing it all up."

The limo slows. Turning toward the door, I press my cheek to the window to see to the top of the building we've parked in front of. My skin slowly peels away from the glass as I sit back after a moment, allowing the agent outside the door to swing it open without me falling face-first to the sidewalk.

I only get a hairbreadth across the leather seat before I'm tugged back to make way for T's massive frame to squeeze past as he exits the limo first. His all-seeing dark eyes scan the area, a finger pressed to his ear while he listens to the rest of the team. Seeing his earpiece triggers me to lean back against Trey's chest.

"Where's your radio?" I ask, leaning back farther to check both ears. I was right, no earpiece.

"I took the day off. This is about us, not work."

"But you're carrying."

"Baby, I'll never not carry around you. These guns go wherever you go. Call it paranoia, but I'd rather be prepared even if I'm not on duty."

"What about when you're the First Husband?" I wait, holding a breath.

"Let's figure that out later, Mess. Tonight, let's just be a regular couple celebrating the fact that they found the person they want to spend the rest of their lives with."

"Okay." How could I not agree with that love-filled gaze, pouting full lower lip, and tender tone?

Careful to not crush me, Trey climbs over my lap and steps out the open door. After adjusting his suit jacket, he turns and extends a hand into the limo. Without hesitation, I place my hand in his, allowing him to guide me out into the evening air.

Several agents block off a clear path, keeping the spectators at bay as we walk hand in hand toward the nondescript revolving door. The glass door slowly whooshes past. Trey urges me into the next compartment and follows me in, keeping a tight hold on my hand.

The moment we step from the revolving door, a blast of cold air-conditioned air brushes my face, cooling the sheer layer of sweat building along my hairline. Even though we were only outside for a short time, I feel overheated, like fire flickers in my veins. It's strange considering I've always been cold even in the heat of summer, but something triggered in my body those hours Shawn held me hostage. Now I can't get cool enough; I'm always just a tinge too warm wherever I go.

Following where Trey leads, I take in the small nondescript lobby area before we're led up a circular staircase. My heels fall silent as I step from the marble floors to the spotless red carpet runner along the steps. We pause at the second-floor landing. Soft movement above us has me looking up to a four-foot-wide chandelier. The crystals sway slightly with the heavy blast of air pouring from the air vents above.

Trey speaks with a man briefly before urging me to follow him once again. Up another level. Then another. On the fourth floor, my breaths become labored from the climb in heels. Sensing my need for help, Trey snakes an arm around my waist with a gentle tug until I'm leaning against him, allowing him to support some of my weight as we're led down a dark hall.

The gun digging into my side offers some reassurance that we're safe. That and the two agents ahead of us and at least four taking up the rear of our little train.

"Toot toot. We're all on the Randi train."

Trey snorts, the vibration going from his chest to mine. "Please don't say that. People will start to think you're collecting agents for your harem."

Scrunching my face like I'm contemplating the idea, I can only hold it for a few seconds before bursting out laughing at his scowl.

Turning a corner, we step into a private room. My laugh dries up immediately, catching in my chest at the sight of the single table covered in a brilliant white tablecloth with two chairs halfway tucked beneath.

But that's not what has me speechless.

Releasing his hand, I move across the room, unable to take my eyes off the glittering lights of the city. In the distance the Washington Monument stands tall and proud with the dome of the Capitol Building barely visible just beyond.

It's beautiful. I press a hand to the cool glass. A body pauses behind mine.

"You like it?" There's an uncertainty in his voice that grips my heart.

"It's perfect. I love seeing the city like this. Like I'm just a bystander. Able to watch everyone go on with their lives without my presence interrupting their day."

He sweeps my hair from my neck, warm lips pressing where it meets my shoulder. I'm too caught up in watching the streets below to notice when he steps away. When I can finally rip my gaze from the life happening just below us, I find him at the door, whispering with T. The conversation stops when they notice my attention.

Trey shoots T a look I don't understand before pushing him out the door and flipping a lock. With all the confidence in the world, he leans back against the closed door and shoves his hands into the pocket of his slacks.

"It's just you and me now, baby. Ready to celebrate our engagement properly?"

25

TREY

Even from across the room, the flush that smears over her cheekbones at my words is clear. Shoving off the door, I pound my fist against it to ensure the lock holds even though I know it will. The guys checked the entire building out earlier today, even left a few agents behind to make sure no one messed with the locks or surveillance equipment or placed anything in the room I had reserved for the night.

Because I wanted this room specifically for one reason.

Absolute privacy. I'd expected to be pouring my heart out and asking the beautiful woman in front of me to marry me, none of which I wanted to be seen by anyone else, even my fellow alpha team brothers. This moment is for us.

We've cut the video and audio feeds in this room and ensured the windows are completely blacked out, meaning a reporter—or sniper—can't see anything when looking in.

Reaching out, I tuck a lock of dark silky hair behind her ear. The skin beneath my fingers pebbles with tiny goose bumps as I trace along her jaw and down her neck.

"Are you hungry?" I know she is, and I'm an ass for even hoping she'll say no so I can eat my fill of the only meal I've wanted for days. My roaming fingers follow the deep V of her sleeveless silk top, shifting to move along the swells of her breast.

"Are you?" Her reply is filled with want. Even with a bra, the stiff peaks of her tight nipples are visible, calling for me to take a quick nibble.

"I think you know what I'm hungry for, Mess. What I'm always hungry for with you." I overtake the small gap between us, sliding a hand down her spine and pushing her hips flush with my own. A sharp breath of air pushes past my tight lips at the heat pouring from between her thighs and straight into my stiffening cock. I grind against her, enjoying how her body immediately responds, flexing against my own.

"Trey," she breathes. Her hands rest on my shoulders, short blunt nails dig into my jacket.

Too many clothes.

Way too many damn clothes between us for what I have in mind.

Releasing her, I retreat a step and shrug out of the suit jacket and shoulder harness, keeping the latter close in case of an emergency. Her perky tits rise and fall in rapid succession. Those hazel eyes are glazed over with her rising lust as she tracks every move I make. After removing both cufflinks, I shove the platinum studs into the silk lining of my slacks pocket.

That dirty, sweet tongue I want lapping my dick flicks out, wetting her lips.

A dark chuckle rumbles in my chest. Using one hand, I tug at the black tie still secured around my neck until it hangs loosely enough to slip over my head. I lay it atop the jacket I slung over the back of a dining chair. One by one, I thumb open the top three buttons of my dress shirt. Her rapt attention on my fingers as I roll both sleeves up my forearms does something dangerous inside me.

It's in her drooped lids, those delicious thighs she keeps pressing together, that damn fingernail in her mouth. All of it combined with the way she can't rip her gaze away makes me feel invincible, dominant, and fucking horny as hell.

I flick a hand toward the table. "I think I'll have my dessert first tonight." On the way to my seat, I snag her hand and bring her with me. The chair flexes under my weight as I sit back, maneuvering her with a hand on each hip to stand between me and the table.

Thank fuck she changed into a skirt for tonight. I have no patience for pants or any other hindrances.

Her legs tremble under my touch as I cup just above each knee and glide my hands up, bunching the black pleated skirt around my wrists as I go.

I slide my fingers inward to snag the front of her panties, where only neatly trimmed curls scrape against the pads instead of lace. I snap my gaze to hers. A shy, almost mischievous smile plays at her red-painted lips.

"Thought I'd take a play out of your handbook and go commando."

"Get on the table," I grunt.

Standing quickly, she teeters backward, a hand smacking onto the table to keep her upright. Not waiting for her to catch her balance, I grip her thin waist and haul her onto the tabletop, ass barely hanging on the edge. "Lean back, elbows on the table so you don't fall."

To my utter surprise, she does exactly as she's told. She doesn't look away as she gets comfortable, her head still raised, watching to see what I have planned. With little flair, I flip her skirt up, bunching it around her hips, and unceremoniously shove her knees apart.

I swipe the tip of my tongue along my lower lip as I stare at her slick pussy. Along the inside of one thigh, I plant soft grazing kisses. At the apex, I blow a gentle steady stream of air over her slit before kissing down the opposite leg to her knee. Leaning back, I admire the spread in front of me.

The chair's legs thump on the floor as I scoot forward, close enough for her to plant a foot on each armrest. Glancing up from between her thighs, I make sure she's watching, then slowly lean in and kiss the sweetest pussy I've ever tasted.

My own groan of pleasure slips out as I suck her swollen nub between my lips. Her sharp exhale and moan drive me crazy. Slipping a hand beneath each cheek, I lift her off the table and devour her whole.

Tiny gasps, my name whispered and then shouted fill the room as I lick every drip off her until she's coming around my tongue buried deep inside her.

I could eat her all day every day and never have enough. Even now I can't stop kissing, sucking, and nibbling. Only when her nails scrape across my scalp and dig in, yanking my face away, do I stop. Smile wide and satisfied, I lick my upper lip as our gazes clash over her heaving chest.

Finger at my belt, I deftly unfasten it with one hand as I stand and extend the other to help Randi off the table. Her legs wobble, making her cling to me for stability. I wrap an arm around her waist, and we walk side by side to the floor-to-ceiling windows. With a little push, I propel her forward, her palms smacking the glass to keep her from falling.

"Turn around and get on your knees."

She turns, lips parted and chest flushed. Reaching out, she grips my forearm and slowly drops to her knees at my feet. Tilting her face up, she licks those red lips eager for everything I'm about to feed her.

"You're so beautiful kneeling in front of me, baby," I say as I make quick work of unfastening my slacks and tugging the zipper down. Her hazel eyes flare with desire as I tug my pants low, my stiff cock pointing directly to her mouth like it knows where it belongs.

Soft dark strands flatten beneath my palm as I run my hand from the crown of her head down to cup her jaw. My dress shoes slide on the floor, widening my stance as I guide her lips to the already slick head. Being the vixen she is, she darts that pink tongue out, lapping up the beads of precum. Her lashes flutter closed with a soft hum of approval.

Fuck, this was a bad idea. I should've just pinned her to the window like I planned. If she keeps this up, I won't last long enough to fuck her the way she likes.

"Take it all, Madam President. Swallow me whole in front of all of DC." Holding a tight grip on her jaw, I draw her forward, smacking the other hand against the window for support as her lips wrap around my cock. My eyes roll in the back of my head as she takes me to the base and swallows, her throat constricting around the tender head.

Up and down I guide her, making her take every inch, the groans and moans of approval and nails digging into my bare ass a sign she's loving this as much as I am.

Head drooped forward, I watch as my dick slides between her lips. Loosening my hold on her chin, I slide my fingers back through her hair and grip a handful at the base of her neck. At my gentle tug, those hazel eyes meet mine.

Locked in place, I take control, thrusting into her mouth. Saliva spills down her chin, dripping to the floor and making the scene even more erotic. I curse, fingers scratching at the window when she cups my balls and gently rolls them between her fingers.

Enough playing.

Grip firm, I hold her steady and take a step back, withdrawing my entire length. Her whimper of displeasure turns into a gasp as I haul her upright and twist her around to face the window.

"Keep your hands on the glass, baby. I can't wait to be inside of that sweet-tasting pussy of yours."

Her rapid warm breaths fog the window, those long nails scratching at the glass as she curls her hands into fists. Dipping beneath the skirt, I haul the bottom hem up to her waist. Foot to each ankle, I kick her feet wider and bend her forward so that sweet ass of hers is jutted out, vulnerable and at my mercy.

Her dark hole holds my attention. "Tell me when it's too much," I mutter into Randi's ear as I slide a hand down her ass cheek to her slit and dip two fingers into her drenched channel. Her head lolls backward onto my shoulder as I slam my fingers in and out, taking her hard like she likes. Which is why I know she'll fucking love what's coming next.

Leaving a trail of her wetness in my wake, I position those two slick fingers against that tight rim. Beneath my chest, her back rises and falls with exaggerated breaths, but she hasn't asked me to stop. Pressing forward, I breach through her virgin hole to the first knuckle.

Her back arches, a soft cry leaving her lips. Kissing along her neck, I suck at a tender spot and push deeper in to the base knuckle.

"How does that feel?" I whisper against her ear before nipping at the lobe. Between us, my rock-hard cock bobs with excitement, tapping the crease of her ass.

"Strange," she breathes. Chin to her shoulder, she sighs. "Strange good. Dirty."

"There's my dirty girl," I coo. "Now for the fun part."

Hard grip around myself, I line up with her pussy and slam forward, burying myself to the hilt in one hard thrust. Seated fully inside her, I pump those two fingers, pressing hard at the base for her to feel the fullness and pressure that makes ass play fucking awesome. Even I can feel how much tighter she is with just two fingers in the opposite hole. I don't let myself imagine what it will be like with a fuller toy or how tight it will be around my dick once she's comfortable.

"More," she cries, slamming her hips back into mine.

I groan, smacking the glass to stay upright and not put my full weight on top of her. Pulling out all the way, I tease her with the head against her clit before thrusting inside. Over and over I push and tease until we're both slick with sweat.

"Hold on," I grunt and bite her neck, not releasing as I fuck her hard. Balls tight, I increase my pace even more, chasing my own release. Beneath me, Randi screams, her forehead falling forward and hitting the glass, her hands squeaking down as her hold slips. Arm around her upper waist, I help hold her weight.

With a roar I come undone, burying myself deep inside her. Knees wobbling and legs weak, I guide us both to the floor, hissing a breath from between my teeth as I pull out so she can nestle on my lap. Wayward strands of hair tickle my nose, but exhaustion makes it impossible to swipe them away.

"Okay, now I see what you mean," she says, still breathing hard.

"Told you. Wait until we get more in there." She whips her face to mine, eyes wide. "Don't worry, baby, we won't until you're ready. But I have a feeling my dirty little president will want more sooner than later."

A wide shy smile splits her face. Nodding, she dips to lean a cheek against my chest.

"I love you, Trey," she whispers. "I had no idea utter happiness felt this good."

I wrap both arms around her and hold her tighter. "I love you too, Randi. This is just the beginning of our happily ever after. There are many, many more years and experiences to come. Now let's get cleaned up. I'm hungry for your sweet dessert again."

26

TREY

The Filson duffel, stuffed to max capacity with dress shoes, slaps to the cement floor beside the other equally as stuffed duffel of non-work shoes. I would say I have a shoe problem based on the fact that there are two more bags already shoved into the SUV, but the number of shoes I've collected over the years doesn't compare to the sheer number of suits I already had sent to the White House earlier.

It's been a week since I officially proposed, but today is the first day neither of us is drowning in work, offering a small window to officially move my residence from the condo I shared with Gerard and Beth to the White House. Sure, there were a few tears just now as I walked out that condo door with Beth still tightly clinking around my neck. It's not that they're sad to see me go, especially since I gifted them the condo the moment the funds from my trust were released. No, they're so fucking happy for me they can't even stand it.

Maybe it's because they know my childhood, saw me desperate for even a sliver of my parents' love or attention but never receiving it until I did their bidding. Now I have that love I craved in spades from Randi, and they see it. Everyone sees it.

The hard leather handle of the navy Filson duffel digs into my palm as I heft it up into the open trunk. I haul the other in next and stare in dismay at the already full trunk of my Bentley SUV.

Damn, I might have to make two trips. Knew I should've made Tank help me. Not that he could right now, because the bastard's too busy working. The only time I've seen my best friend the past week has been on shift. All his spare time is spent with Smith. That should irk me, and it would've in the past, but it doesn't now because I know what they're working on.

Ponder, or whatever the hell his real name is, is still out there. That's what they've researched, tracked, and obsessed over since Whit and his hooligans were barbecued. We all know Ponder is biding his time, waiting in the shadows like the damn coward he is until he has a chance to take out Randi or me. Too bad for him, we've laid our own trap to ensure he's the one six feet under and not me or my girl.

Not sure what I ever did to the fucker to warrant a bullet in the head, but he sure does hate me. That was one thing Whit was very clear about during our... conversation his last night of living. Maybe it was because I confronted him on his personal questions to Randi, or that I had him moved to the shitty shifts or stations because of said questions to Randi.

I smirk at the memory. Even though it put me in that asshole's crosshairs, seeing him stationed outside in the damn heat sweating his balls off or in the winter freezing to death was 100 percent worth it. I knew there was something off about him, the arrogance too... violent with him. I couldn't pinpoint then what it was that urged me to push him away from Randi, but now I can. Good to know my gut instincts still work.

A bang rattles through the packed garage as I slam the trunk closed.

This is the last of my clothes, the rest already at the White House. By the end of the day, I'll be an official resident of the most iconic house in the world.

Who would have ever fucking thought?

My parents dreamed this day would happen, me in the White House. Too bad for them it's not the way they hoped. And I'm good with that. More than good with that. I never wanted the politician route—they did.

I swing the key fob around my middle finger, my unseeing stare focused on the shiny black finish of the SUV's bumper, then pull out the phone vibrating in my pocket.

"You ready?" Tank's gruff voice is barely audible with the whistling wind in the background.

"Hi, baby. I miss you too." Warm metal presses into my spine as I relax against the SUV like I don't have a care in the world. For this plan to work no one can know I have eyes tracking my every breath from blocks away.

"Laying it on thick, aren't you?" he grumbles. Using my shoulder, I hold the phone to my ear as I dig into the front pocket of my jeans and slide the half-gone cigarette pack and lighter out. "Thought you were quitting?"

My lips spread around the butt between them as I light the end. Only after a couple deep inhales do I respond. "Soon." Closing my eyes, I rest my head back against the rear window.

The hairs on the back of my neck stand tall as a sensation of foreboding washes over me.

"Don't do anything stupid." The line goes dead in my ear, but I don't drop the phone. Instead I continue to talk into it like there's still someone on the line.

"Yes, of course, we can do that position again tonight, baby. Yeah, you screaming my name was music to my ears too." Okay, maybe this is a little thick, but Tank and Smith didn't tell me I couldn't exaggerate a little while playing prey. "In fact, later I want you to recite the oath while I—"

The distinct click of a slide engaging catches my ear, cutting off my next words. I peek one eye open, the late morning sun bright as it pours through the open gaps of the parking garage. A shadow moves to my right. Peeling the other eye open, I flick the spent cigarette to the cement and extinguish the glowing ember with the heel of my shoe.

I shove the phone into my back pocket and frantically scan the row of luxury cars. Somewhere in the distance, the clink of a bottle rolling down the slope of the ramp cuts through the stiff silence.

"Hello?" I say to no one as I scan the parking garage again. My face drops as my hands connect with the soft cotton of the T-shirt instead of the hard grip of my gun. The gun that's in the center console four feet away. "Fuck," I mutter.

A familiar figure steps from the recessed shadows cast by a thick support column.

My eyes narrow at the gun casually hanging at his side.

"What are you doing here?" I snag another cigarette, hands slightly shaking, taking three attempts to light the end before I'm successful. Little does this fucker know it's adrenaline and not fear that's causing the tremor. Adrenaline, blood lust, the need to murder... yeah, we're going with adrenaline.

"Cut the damn act," Ponder chides. "You know I was behind it all. You and those dumbasses have been tracking me—unsuccessfully, I might add."

"What's your plan now? Kill me, then go after her again?"

He leans his head one way and then the other like he's considering the options. "She was a job. Which I completed by delivering her unharmed and helping keep her... compliant."

"Until Whit changed tactics on you." I release a billow of smoke and cock my head to the side. At least that's what Randi thinks. She clearly remembers him being against forcing himself on her, and that's why he left without finishing the job. "Who would've thought someone like you has standards."

He purses his lips. "I'm a killer, not a rapist. Then the fucker went and crossed me by taking you. You did me a favor killing him that night, saved me the trouble."

"You kill all your clients?"

"Just ones who have the potential to double-cross me or who actually do. The latter don't live long."

"And Rosen?"

The man huffs, using the barrel of the gun to scratch an itch along his scalp. "He was as weak as they come. That wasn't the first time he ordered a hit for someone else. I fucking hate middlemen." The loathing in his hard tone lays truth to the statement.

"So what now? You plan to kill me, then her, and then escape to...." I wave a hand in front of me, indicating for him to finish the statement.

"Just you."

Both my brows rise up my forehead. "The other client with a hit on the president won't be happy about that, will they? I didn't figure you as the type of sociopath who'd go back on his commitments."

The roar of a car engine fills the garage. We both tense as a white compact car from the level above rounds the corner, its tires squealing as it takes the tight turn. Ponder slips the hand with the gun behind his back and nods to the driver as he passes. If anyone were to see us, they'd think we were simply neighbors having a nice chat in the garage.

"You're personal. All the contracts on that bitch are voided considering most are incarcerated or dead. So now it's just you and me." He frowns at my empty hands. "I was hoping for more of a fight, but I have a plane to catch."

My pulse races as he slides the hand with the gun forward and raises it, pointing the end of the barrel right between my eyes. Sweat beads and drips along my forehead, catching in the dark scruff I was too lazy to shave off this morning.

A sharp whizzing noise zaps through the air milliseconds before Ponder's head explodes. Blood, brain matter, and bits of skull spray along the cement and splatter the windows and trunks of nearby cars. I watch as his body crumples in slow motion.

A warm breeze wafts through the wide open-air gap between the cement barrier and the next level. I let out a sharp whistle and stroll toward the dead assassin. Stopping just outside the growing puddle of blood, I toss the spent cigarette into it, watching as the sticky liquid quickly douses the ember and the filter absorbs all it can until it's as red as the ground.

My ass vibrates. I smirk around the new cigarette between my teeth, waiting until I've taken a few hits before slipping the phone free. Swiping the screen, I immediately hit the speaker button and hold it close to my lips.

"Cleanup on level 3."

"Funny."

I huff and take another deep inhale, allowing the repetitive motions to calm my nerves.

"That was closer than I expected. What took you so long?"

"Took me so long?" Smith's voice drips with indignation. "We're four buildings over, the wind is gusting outside, and I had a four-foot break between levels to shoot through. All in all, I consider what I did fucking quick."

I snort and take another drag. "Fine, color me impressed. Where's Tank?"

"On his way to you."

"Thanks for making the shot."

"Told you I could."

Shaking my head, I end the call. Even with the man who was out for my blood dead at my feet, anxiety rushes through my veins. One down, how many more to go?

Lost in thought, I roll the filter along my lower lip.

One question keeps going through my mind.

Now what?

27

RANDI

August

The grainy sand seeps between my toes as I race down the beach like I'm being chased.

Because I am.

Adrenaline races through my veins and blood thunders in my ears as I push harder, urging my legs to move faster. Sand flies behind me in my wake, hopefully giving my pursuer a mouthful of it and hindering their ability to get close enough to snatch me.

My skin tingles with the awareness that someone is close. Too close. The muscles of my thighs protest, my legs feeling like noodles, but the flickering light of my destination urges me past the pain. Huffing, I pump my arms harder and fight the need to sneak a glance over my shoulder.

Dark shadows move along the beach. Massive shadows. I smile despite the air wheezing from my chest.

Twenty feet.

Almost there. I can make it.

Fifteen feet.

The pounding of another set of feet slapping the sand seems much closer than before.

Ten feet.

An arm snakes around my waist, hauling me backward. I scream in frustration as my back collides with the still warm sand and a massive body straddles my hips.

Wet dark hair glistens in the moonlight. The house security lights cast a shadow over the body, making it impossible to see the expression on the man's face.

"You're going to pay for that, Mess."

Somehow even with my labored breaths and zero energy to even blink, I laugh. Trey's thighs tighten around my hips when I try to buck him off. Half-heartedly, I slap at his chest and shove at his shoulder in an attempt to get him off me.

His large hand snags one of mine before it can smack his bare chest a third time, then the other just as easily. Leaning at the waist, he holds both my wrists in one hand and digs them into the sand above my head.

Desire warms my lower belly, making me squirm beneath him, this time with zero hopes of dislodging the delicious weight settled over me.

"Is that any way to treat your husband?" he chides, but there's a hint of laughter in his voice. He twists to talk to the four agents behind us, dousing his face in the light. Just as I expected, a smile graces his face, those fine laugh lines crinkled at the edges of his eyes.

"You'd already jumped off the cliff once and said it was fun."

"You pushed me." He laughs, turning his full attention back to me. "Then ran."

"You said you wanted to race home."

"Together. Race home together."

"How's that fair?" I grumble.

"We have twenty-four hours to celebrate our honeymoon, baby. Is this really how you want to spend it?"

Yes, I want to scream. Don't get me wrong, I love us making love, the sweet and gentle stuff. But I love our frustrated, angry, punishing fucks just as much. Hell, maybe even more. And with us being on the campaign trail and me still running a country, that hasn't been on the menu as of late.

And I really, really, really want it to be.

I bite my lower lip and nod.

Understanding washes over his face as he sits up, bringing my wrists up with him. Looping them around his neck, Trey dips his head, pressing those wet lips against my ear. I shiver as his breath sends goose bumps flaring down my neck.

"If you wanted a good hard fuck, all you had to do was ask, baby."

"Trey," I gasp as his teeth sink into my earlobe.

Before I can beg, we're off the sand and I'm cradled against his chest. Bits of sand dig into my exposed thigh and stomach where our bare skin rubs together as he strides toward the infinity pool. As he leaps up the steps like he's not carrying a grown woman in his arms, I take in our surroundings.

For twenty-four hours, this place is ours. Only ours. A private beach, far away from the media or any watching eyes. It's not much of a honeymoon, but let's be honest, it wasn't much of a wedding, much to every woman in America's disappointment. A simple white dress—yeah, yeah, I know it was silly to wear white. I obviously wasn't a virgin considering I had living proof running around with her own tiny human to care for. Trey was in one of his sexiest suits, and the justice of the peace. Of course he came to us at the house instead of us having to go through the downtown area of Honolulu, which was nice. Plus with T and the rest of the secret service team by our side we had plenty of witnesses as we signed the marriage certificate.

The moon's reflection shimmers on top of the pool water. Trey stops just at the edge, his toes hanging over the tile. This close to the house, the lights offer a clear view of his face. The face that now wears a mischievous grin and highlights the sparkle in his honey brown eyes.

"Oh no you—"

The bastard does exactly what I suspect. My sharp squeal is immediately cut off as we plunge into the cool pool. Trey's grasp tightens around me as he shoves off the bottom, rocketing us back to the surface. I gasp in a deep breath and turn, swiping the soaking hair from my eyes to glare at my gorgeous husband.

Gorgeous doesn't do him justice. There's a playfulness about him always, but then there's this glimmer of intense badassery.

Badassery. That's a word, right?

"The art of being badass?"

Trey's laugh brushes over my shoulder as he swims us to the edge. "I like where your head's at, Mess."

At the edge, he walks us down to the shallow end of the pool. I sink a bit when he releases his hold before finding my footing and standing so my upper half is exposed to the night air. The sound of rushing water snaps my attention back to Trey, who's pushed himself out of the pool and is now sitting on the deck, legs spread.

Nail between my teeth, I move to stand between his spread thighs and rest my hands on either side of his hips.

Without breaking eye contact, Trey calls out to Tank, "I've got her covered. You guys make yourself scarce. And turn off all the motherfucking lights, would you?"

Tank grumbles something in return, but I don't pay him any attention.

One by one, the overbearing spotlights the guys had set up for security around the property wink out. The last one to flicker off is the one by the pool. The last thing I see before we're doused in complete darkness is Trey's smirking face.

The sudden darkness takes my breath away. Within seconds my eyes adjust to the low light coming from the house and the soft blue illumination of the pool from the underwater light.

Callused hands grip my biceps. When Trey's lips brush over the shell of my ear, a soft chuckle tightens my lower belly.

"Come on, wife. Let's play your dirty games out here." Teeth sink into my earlobe, and I jerk in surprise, then lean harder into him. "Then we'll go upstairs and play mine. I think you'll enjoy the... additions I purchased for our twenty-four-hour honeymoon."

I swallow, my throat suddenly dry.

Additions.

Fuck, I hope they hurt so good.

Damnit. There really is something wrong with me.

A CONTENT SIGH pushes past my lips. Shifting around, I plant a soft kiss on his shoulder and relax against him. For the first time in months, I'm... content. The worries of the world—not exaggerating—aren't swarming my thoughts and spiking my ever-present anxiety. No thoughts of the campaign, of upcoming debates, the election this fall. Nothing as I stare up at the beautiful star-filled sky while curled against the man I love. Well, nothing except for the "additions" Trey mentioned earlier. Those sound fun. But that will come later. Right now, this is exactly where I want to be.

"I wish we could do this every day," I whisper.

"We can. Just say the word. Neither of us has to work another day, but I know you'd hate it." His breath pushes over my damp shoulder. A quick nip of his teeth to my neck causes a giggle to tickle my chest.

I pause, debating if his words hold any truth.

He's right. I'd hate it. After working my entire life, fighting for more, I'd hate a leisurely lifestyle of doing nothing. But for twenty-four hours? Hell yes.

For several minutes we stay like this, his fingers finding my wet hair and playing with the ends as we let the moment envelop us in peace.

"Will it ever be easy?" I ask the night, not expecting Trey to respond to my deep thought.

"No. It won't." Unease curls in my gut. "But we knew that going into this, Mess." He grips my chin to turn my face toward his. "I didn't ask you to marry me because I thought it would be easy. I didn't say 'I do' because I had false ideas of how the next four years will go when you win." I smile at the "when" instead of "if." "It will be tough. We'll have to fight for us every fucking day. I'll remind you when you're taking too much on and need to lean on those around you. In return, you'll let me know when I'm being an arrogant ass."

"So daily. You're saying I'll remind you daily."

A burst of giggles and snorts escapes when he digs his fingers into my side, wiggling them between my ribs and tickling the hell out of me.

"We'll have to fight for time together. But I promise you this, Randi, I won't ever stop fighting for you. Fighting for us. Every day I'll wake up ready to battle for what we have, and I know, I *know* you will too. We've been through shit together and made it through. What's forever compared to all that?"

His tentative smile and those honest words chase away all fears that have been my ever-present company since he slid that rock on my finger. Leaning close, I seal my lips to his and pour every ounce of love that's gushing in my heart and soul into him.

Sealing our battle plan for us with a kiss.

We will make it through this shit show called life.

He's right. We will fight for each other—for us—every day.

Because I've never failed in my life, and I sure as hell don't plan to start with him.

My name's Randi Benson, and I will fight for him with all I have, no matter the cost.

Forever.

EPILOGUE
TREY

March the following year

My whistling tune is off pitch and rhythm, sounding nothing like the "Jeremiah was a Bullfrog" song I was aiming for. Not that it matters. There's no one around to hear my awful rendition. It's been seven months since I married the unlikeliest president and the love of my life, four months since we won the election, and almost two and a half since she was officially sworn in for her second term as president.

I round a corner. A younger agent I recognize catches sight of me and stands a little straighter.

With a smile, I stride past the kid and continue toward the Oval Office.

The sounds of a bustling office grow louder the farther I stray from the resident side. Men and women discuss world events loudly on one side of the hall while the other side is too focused on their zillion-line spreadsheets to even notice anyone else is around.

Blake, Randi's chief of staff, offers a sharp nod as I pass and then continues railing on whoever he's on the phone with. I take a sharp corner, colliding with someone, their iPad jabbing into my sternum.

"Oomph," I grunt. On reflex I reach out and grab hold of the person I nearly flattened to keep them from tumbling to the ground like their iPad.

A string of creative murmured curses reaches my ear. I chuckle as the woman rips her thin arms from my hold and narrows her eyes up at me. Holding up both hands in surrender, I take a step back, giving her some space. The mix of fear and loathing at my proximity has me curious. Obviously she doesn't recognize me or she'd know I'm no threat to her.

Or any woman, for that matter. Not that I ever was. Well, if they were single, hot, and willing, then okay, maybe I was a threat to be wary of. But since Randi, I haven't looked at another woman with interest. Mostly because Randi is all I need, but also because Sarah threatened to, and I quote, "Slice off my balls and dick, place them on a skewer with light seasoning, grill them over an open flame, and then force-feed them to me" if I ever looked at another woman or hurt Randi.

I rather like my balls and dick attached, as does Randi most nights—and sometimes during a long lunch—so yeah, I don't look at women.

"Sorry, didn't see you there." I readjust my jacket to make sure both nine millimeters are concealed. Keeping my features neutral but friendly, I move to step around the unfamiliar woman.

She grumbles something in return about being lost and late as she bends to retrieve the iPad from the ground. She dashes off in the direction she was originally heading before I have a chance to offer any help with the lost part. I know this place like the back of my hand from years of working as an agent and living here personally; I could've helped her get wherever she needed if she would've waited.

As I approach the office, my smile widens. Both hands tucked into my slacks, the picture of nonchalance and ease, I stroll toward the duo.

"Howdy, amigos," I say in greeting, leaning against the opposite wall and crossing a foot over the other ankle.

"You know I hate that," Smith states, his annoyed glare flicking to me before scanning the halls once again. "But I assume that's why you keep saying it."

"Bingo, amigo." I chuckle at his attempt to flip me off discreetly. "You guys see a little blonde woman, about yea high"—I hold my hand to midbicep—"holding an iPad, looked flustered and a little pissy?"

Tank growls. "That's Sam's new secretary. Why?"

"She ran into me, literally, in the hall. Never seen her before, so I wanted to vet her out, make sure she had clearance to be here."

"She does for now." I arch a brow. "She's not doing so great. I overheard a conversation between the two, and the poor girl just couldn't keep up with everything he was throwing at her."

"He's a hard-ass, for sure," I admit. "It'll take someone with a backbone and brains to handle Sam. And someone who won't throw themselves at him." A chunk of dark hair slides across my forehead as I shake my head. "Last I heard, he's debating hiring an all-male staff."

"Did you hear the one last month, the Yale grad?" I nod even though I can't picture who Tank's talking about. "Sam walked into his own office, and she was sitting on his desk butt-ass naked. He lost his shit and fired her on the spot."

"I'm sure that's not the reaction she was hoping for." I shake my head.

"I've got a ten on the new one not lasting a week."

"I'll toss in twenty for her lasting two weeks but getting fired for accidentally emailing a confidential document to Sam's entire contact list."

"You don't even know how long she's been in the role." Smith cross his arms across his chest. "Besides, the pool is an alpha team bet."

Faking shock, I stand and press a hand to my heart. "Tank, bestie, are you going to let him talk to me that way?"

"For fuck's sake, you two," he grumbles in return, running a hand over his fluffy dark and gray hair. He says Sarah wants him to grow it out. I think he's feeling old and trying to look young again. Either way, it's not a good look for him. "Where are your agents, by the way?"

A grin pulls up my lips as I shrug.

"Oh hell, what did you do to them?" Tank's exasperation is palpable and hilarious. The latter more for me than him.

"Nothing. I'm doing what you asked me to do—training them."

When I officially resigned from the alpha team to become the First Husband, it was... difficult at first, to say the least. The days were boring while Randi was working, changing the world one community at a time, and even most of the nights, considering she worked almost eighteen hours a day. Me doing nothing but sitting around and pestering the agents assigned to shadow me lasted only a few days before everyone was over my complaining and sour attitude—their words, not mine.

That's when Randi, the director, and Tank came up with their brilliant plan. And I'll admit it is a great plan. It gives me purpose again and the opportunity to have a little mischievous fun at another's expense. Like today.

Since I can clearly handle myself and have demanded I stay armed at all times even without being an agent, they've assigned the greener agents to my detail.

The First Husband detail.

It's not a title I'm a huge fan of, but I am a fucking fan of being her husband, so I'm going with it.

I've agreed to train the agents as we go, help them know what to look for while we're traveling, how to spot weaknesses in a plan or protection detail. We work out together as well, sparring at times too to help with reflexes and hand-to-hand fighting skills.

To be honest, it's been fun as well as rewarding. After losing Grem, I realized there was a lot I didn't teach him. If I had maybe, he'd still be here today and holding his sweet little baby instead of six feet under.

I shake off those dark thoughts and turn to look down the hall as the sound of running feet rumbles closer.

"I wanted to see how long it would take them to realize I'd snuck past them." I steal a look at my watch. "Seven minutes." The four twentysomething-year-old kids skid to a stop, looking between me, Smith, Tank, and back to me, barely winded after the short sprint across the White House.

"How'd you get by us?" the lead of the four asks, ire gleaming in his gaze as his nostrils flare with annoyance. "We were at all the doors."

"Were you?" I arch a brow to add a drop of doubt to their self-assured conclusion. I hitch my chin to the youngest one in the back. "Never get distracted. You took a call, leaving me the chance to slip past."

"You were the caller," he snaps. "You're the one who distracted me."

"Still, you were distracted." There's no hiding the amusement in my tone. Yeah, I tricked him, but one, he should've known better, and two, it was fun. "We'll head to the gym after I see what Randi wants to talk to me about."

Without knocking, I twist the brass doorknob and push the door leading to the Oval Office open. "See ya, amigos."

Smith whispers something about killing me slowly, but I shut the door, cutting off whatever creative torture he was concocting.

The moment the door closes, I freeze. Something's off. The air is too cold; normally the heat is blasting in the office, making it feel like summer instead of the tail end of winter. There's something else too, like there's a live wire ready to spark and burn the place to flames.

Muscles tense, ready for anything, I take in the room but only find Randi behind the desk, no one else. Each step is tentative as I approach her.

Face in her hands, elbows on the shiny oak surface, she looks unhappy. I pause beside her, only now able to hear her faint whispering, talking to herself about who knows what.

My chest tightens with worry as I gaze down at her. Something is wrong.

Reaching out, I stroke down her long silky dark hair over and over, giving her a moment before I force her to tell me what the fuck is going on.

"Who do I need to kill, Mess?" I say it like a joke, but we both know it's not. I'd kill anyone who hurt her. Been there, done that twice already.

Her shoulders shake.

Fuck, is she crying?

Not giving two shits about personal space or giving her time to tell me what's wrong, I grip both her shoulders and swivel the chair around until she's facing me. Hand beneath her jaw, I tilt her face up to mine.

Eyes rimmed in red. Damp cheeks. Rosy nose and cheeks.

Fuck.

"I'll kill them. I just need a name, baby. Tell me." It takes work to soften my tone and not unleash the worry and frustration that's swirling in me. The last thing I want to do is upset her more.

"Trey." She half laughs, half cries. "Stop with the murder talk." I swipe a tissue from the box on her desk and pass it to her. "You do know that if you ever do, you can't tell me or I won't be able to defend you."

"I'd only be in court if they find a body."

Her snort and small smile ease some of the growing tension between us.

"Seriously, Randi. Tell me what's wrong. We can fix it. We always do."

Watery eyes search my face. "We do, don't we?"

"And we always will. But whatever this is, you can't do it on your own. I'm here. Lean into me. Then I'll lean into whoever made you cry and possibly crush them to death." I flash her my trademark smirk, hoping that will ease some of her sadness.

Boom. Nailed it.

"It's you."

My smirk falls and my heart sinks into my stomach as nausea spikes.

"What?"

"It's you—" Her face pales as she shoves both palms against my shoulders, sending her chair wheeling backward two feet. Twisting faster than I knew she was capable of moving, Randi falls to floor, her knees slamming to the carpet in front of a white plastic trash can.

I tilt my head at the new random and cheap addition to her office.

Shaking off the curiosity, I move the chair out of the way, the wheels squeaking in protest as I shoot it across the room, and gather her hair into a low ponytail as she vomits into the can.

Her moans of pain and annoyance eat at my soul. I feel helpless standing here, unable to do anything but hold her hair and pray to her unicorn gods that all this will be over soon so she can tell me what the fuck she meant by me being the problem.

Me.

I know I'm not perfect, but things have been great. Stressful, sure, but she is running America, and her best friend is Russian, so yeah, things can get tense at times.

Her left hand smacks at my leg to get my attention. "Tissue, please."

I pass her the box, not really knowing exactly how many she'll need to clean up... that.

When she leans back onto her heels, she smiles up at me. Even after puking and crying, she's still beautiful. How the hell I got so lucky, I'll never know.

"Randi, I don't know what I did, but—"

"Oh, you know." She laughs.

I take her extended hand and help her off the floor. Placing a steady hand on the desk, she leans a hip against it and bites her lip.

"I really don't."

"Last night." She raises her brows like that should give me some kind of clue.

Last night. Last night. Fuck, what did we do last night?

Oh, right, we fucked.

Oh shit.

I compile everything and only come to one conclusion, but then my head goes blank. I blink down at Randi, not sure if I want to ask the question or just keep staring, hoping I'm reading the signs right.

Because fuck, I want to be right. We've never talked about a family because we're both older and she already has Taeler, and I didn't want to press the issue. But now....

Please, unicorn gods, let my beautiful wife be pregnant.

"Trey?" she asks, furrowing her brow. "You okay?"

"Randi, tell me what's going on."

Nibbling on a nail, she glances all around the room, her chest ballooning out with a deep inhale. Like she's finally made the decision to tell me the big news, she locks her hazel eyes on mine and smiles.

"I'm pregnant."

And just like that, when I thought my life couldn't get any better, it absolutely fucking does.

ALSO BY KENNEDY L. MITCHELL

In Clear Sight: A Small Town, WITSEC Interconnected Standalone Series

Safe Haven - FREE Prequel

Guarded by the Marshal

Cherished by the Agent

Saved by the Officers

Hidden by the Doctor

Protection Series: A Dark Romantic Thriller Interconnected Standalone Series

Mine to Protect *

Mine to Save *

Mine to Guard *

Mine to Keep *

Mine to Hold *

Mine to Love *

Mine to Share

*Now available in audio!

SEALs and CIA Series: A Navy SEAL Interconnected Standalone Series

Covert Affair

Covert Vengeance

More Than a Threat Series: A Connected Bodyguard Romantic Suspense Series

More Than a Threat

More Than a Risk

More Than a Hope

More Than a Threat Series Boxset: Complete Series

Power Play Series: A Protector Romantic Suspense Connected Series

Power Games (FREE!)

Power Twist

Power Switch

Power Surge

Power Term

Standalones:

Finding Fate - Dark, Captive Romantic Suspense

Memories of Us - Contemporary, Small Town Romance

ABOUT THE AUTHOR

Kennedy L. Mitchell lives outside Dallas with her husband, son and two very large goldendoodles. She began writing in 2016 after a fight with her husband (You can read the fight almost verbatim in Falling for the Chance) and has no plans of stopping.

She would love to hear from you via any of the platforms below or her website www.kennedylmitchell.com You can also stay up to date on future releases through her newsletter or by joining her Facebook readers group - Kennedy's Book Boyfriend Support Group.

Thank you for reading.

ACKNOWLEDGMENTS

This book wouldn't have happened without my three alpha readers. Chris, Em, and Kristin. You three encourage me daily and I will never, ever be able to thank you for all your calls, texts and hours spent reading my first drafts.

And of course the support of my hubs. He really does try to understand this industry LOL. Love him for it too. Mostly he supports me by being so proud of my writing career. Good or bad his focus is always on the fact I wrote a book. And you know, I did and that's pretty awesome.

Okay so all the people who helped make this series the best it could be. Of course my editor Kristin with Hot Tree Editing (who's probably cringing at all the grammatical mistakes and misspellings in this acknowledgements - sorry) who takes my words and makes them readable. I love her comments and suggestions.

And my amazing ARC team. Thank you. For fucking real you ladies are amazing. I never would've thought I'd get to the point to be surrounded by so many book influencers like you guys. I see every comment, like and share and sit in awe at the fact you're doing all that to help support me and my writing career. Thank you.

And of course the readers. Thank you for sticking with the series! Hopefully you love my writing style and will go check out my other books! Hope Trey and Randi were able to provide you with the brief escape from this terrible year we all desperately need.

Thank you.
Happy reading
KLM